Hamlet

哈姆雷特

（英汉对照）

［英］威廉·莎士比亚 著

李其金 译

ZHEJIANG UNIVERSITY PRESS

浙江大学出版社

浙大版《哈姆雷特》译本序

又一个《哈姆雷特》译本问世了，很值得祝贺。

中国出版界究竟出了多少版本的《哈姆雷特》，现在真的无法统计，因为就在作者写这篇序言的时候，便闻讯还有另外三个《哈姆雷特》译本正在审订之中。而我自己翻译《哈姆雷特》译本也在两年前就已经交付出版社，只是因为需要和别的作品整体推出，所以尚未付梓。

但目前这个译本可谓捷足先登。漂亮的清样，考究的版式，显示出出版社对译本的认真态度。

当然，必定有读者会问：有必要出版这么多的重译本吗？

我的回答是肯定的。

同一名作的日益增多的译本不仅仅标示着原作的巨大影响力，还标示着中国在翻译方面，至少在文学翻译方面，已经成了不折不扣的翻译大国。

《圣经》《老子》的译本，都达到数百种之多，相比之下，《哈姆雷特》目前还只有十来种，因此，新的《哈姆雷特》译本应该说仍然有拓展的空间。其实，这本来不是一个问题，因为在市场经济发展模式下，只要存在着读者、购买者方面的需要，市场就必定会满足这种需要而不断推出新的译本。

但是新译本并非只是为了读者市场而存在，它还是中国翻译者不断探索新的翻译对策与技巧的试验场。正如西方的各种新的文学理论往往把莎士比亚的作品作为其理论应用的试验场一样，不断产生的新的翻译对策也往往把莎士比亚的作品作为其翻译对策是否有效的试金石。

那么，目前这个译本有些什么新的翻译对策呢？

简而言之，将《哈姆雷特》的翻译诗体化。

《哈姆雷特》本来就是一部诗剧。其实何止《哈姆雷特》？莎士比亚的全部剧本都是诗剧。

何谓诗剧？ 分行、节奏（音步），甚至还有韵律。 这就够了？不，还有更重要的因素。 那就是：诗剧的用语几乎全部都应该是诗化的语言。 所谓诗化的语言，意即在修辞造句、音韵格律方面有一整套规则的语言。 诗化语言是与白话迥然不同的语言。

人们忘记一个关键的因素：话不是诗。 诗是话的改进、锤炼、升华。

一百年前，中国人说："太阳下山了。"这是话。 没人认为它是诗。 但是同样的意思写成"白日依山尽"，就是诗，没人认为它是话。

何以前者是话，后者是诗？ 因为前者是人人说得出来的口语句子，后者却是只有少数专门写诗的人才折腾得出来的句子。

前者的每个字不讲究音韵平仄。 后者的每个字都必须符合格律诗的平仄规定，并且有韵脚，语序也可以因为格律的需要而有所变动。

当然，清末以来至今的一百年间也有人认为"太阳下山了"这种句子是诗，叫白话诗。 早年白话运动中的一些年轻人，例如年仅 25 岁的胡适等人，混淆诗与话的艺术性区别，强行把话与诗同格，结果就诌出自相矛盾的白话诗这种概念，让经历了一千多年的进化才从白话中升华出来的诗歌重新退化为白话，谓之白话诗。 当然，在文学艺术尤其是诗歌之外的领域，如哲学、政治学、经济学、伦理学、科学等诸如此类的领域推行白话文运动，是对的，是伟大的进步。 但是，在诗歌语言领域将口语类白话奉为唯一的正宗、排斥诗词曲的伟大传统，却是一种文化大倒退。 口语类白话抒情作品完全可以作为传统诗词曲的一个不同类别与传统文学艺术共同存在，如果武断地将它分离出来、无限地拔高它的地位，并用以取代传统诗词曲，就是一种荒唐的行为。

问题不仅如此。 这种艺术性大大退化的所谓白话诗不仅阻碍了中国诗歌的正常发展，也大大地阻碍了外国诗歌的翻译。 惠特曼之类的白话诗固然可以译为白话汉语诗。 可是，荷马、但丁、莎士比亚、歌德、雨果等大量外国诗人的作品都是用高度格律化的非白话语言写成的，而它们全部被翻译成了白话口语中文诗。 想想，三千年前的荷马怎么会写出民国时期才出现的白话自由诗？ 四百年前的莎士比亚怎么会写出在他死后三百多年才出现的白话汉诗？

当然，我不是主张要将荷马的史诗翻译成《诗经》的风格，但是，我们完全可以让它们的语言风格有某种稍稍古雅的风格或稍带文言的风格，至少不能将它们翻译得与现代白话汉语一样。 须知这些作者是古人，不是当代人啊！把他们的作品翻译成完全的当代白话文，就等于把李白、杜甫的诗翻译成了当代白话文一样。 这两种文体差别有如糖浆和白开水的滋味差别一样。 可是，糟糕的是，当年胡适、陈独秀这类年轻人却居然认为白开水滋味才是正宗，而糖浆滋味居然是应该完全抛弃的腐朽的滋味。

说到文言的风格，许多人误以为文言就是难懂的语言。 其实文言有佶屈聱牙的文言，也有浅近易懂的文言。 而宋词、元曲就具有浅近易懂的文言风格。 当然，如果我们使用这种文言风格，我们还可以写得比宋词、元曲所使用的文言更浅近一些，但是没有必要写得和现代口语白话一样。

基于这样的思路，我在二十八年前，就力主将西方诗歌中的一些作品以传统诗词曲风味的方式加以迻译。① 当然，"我所谓的词曲体，并不是指严格意义上字字讲究平仄音韵的词曲体，而主要是指词曲体那种长短句式、词汇风味等，使人一读，觉得像词曲，仔细辨别，却又不是，恰在似与不似之间，凡所措词，总以达志传情摹形追韵为宗旨"②。 换句话说，我们应该尽量以诗歌独有的方式（例如具有诗化语言和高度格律特点的方式）来处理外国诗歌翻译问题。

正是这个原因，当李其金先生邀请我为他的《哈姆雷特》译本写篇序言的时候，我答应了，因为我发现他的努力方向，与我提倡的理论在某个方向上是一致的。 至于他究竟在用诗体翻译诗体这种努力中取得了多大

---

① 参见辜正坤，"西诗汉译词曲体略论"，《四川师大学报》，1986 年第 5 期。 又见辜正坤，《中西诗比较鉴赏与翻译理论》（第 2 版），清华大学出版社，2010 年。

② 同上。

的成就，我想读者会有自己的判断。 他的译本显然并没有采用词曲风味体或较多的文言用语，但是他的译本语言流畅自然，他也确实是在努力将汉译本《哈姆雷特》尽可能诗化，就这个基本的努力方向而言，他无疑是正确的。

所以，我在前文中认为他的译本是某种新的翻译对策的结果。 抛开别的不谈，只从这一点出发，这个重译本的必要性和价值就是理所当然的了。

是为序。

辜正坤

2012 年秋于北京大学世界文学研究所

跨越时空的《哈姆雷特》

——阿登第二版《哈姆雷特》前言

莎士比亚最著名的剧本《哈姆雷特》，"作为世上最有魅力和最富争议的作品，剧中几乎没有哪一行对白未曾引起人们的关注并为此发表过一两篇述评"（Harold Jenkins）。《哈姆雷特》令多少观众心驰神往，令多少读者念念不忘！难怪英国诗人兼文学评论家艾略特（T. S. Eliot）先生将其称为"文学界的蒙娜丽莎"。

美国莎学专家科勒姆（Richard Corum）先生在论及《哈姆雷特》跨越时空的魅力时也曾高度赞誉道："如果我们将莎士比亚的作品看成文学界的喜马拉雅，那么《哈姆雷特》则可谓他的珠穆朗玛：'世界上最著名的作家所写就的最著名的剧本'，何况又是世界上最长、最复杂、要求最高、讨论最多、影响最大的文学作品——'该杰作依然占据着西方文学中心的中心'（Newsweek，1997）。有谁不熟悉这部作品……有谁不曾吟诵其中的一两句名言？又有谁不觉得该剧难懂？"

好了，亲爱的读者朋友，译者的任何话语在《哈姆雷特》面前都未免多余或不合时宜。现在请允许他选取詹金斯先生所编《哈姆雷特》前言中的部分内容代为译文的序言或导读吧。

创作日期
（Date）

有关《哈姆雷特》的具体创作日期，尽管缺乏确凿的证据，但大致的创作时间却相当清晰，即 1599 年年中至 1601 年年底。

故事来源
（Principal Source）

人们当然有理由认为《哈姆雷特》源自一部同类题材的早期剧本，学者们将其称为"《哈姆雷特》原本（*Ur-Hamlet*）"。该剧本已经佚失，显然也从未刊印，但同时代的资料显示，大家都知道确有这么一部戏剧。

既然该剧已经佚失，有关该剧的详情和内容便很难加以确认。……至于莎氏从该故事中所继承下来的要素和情节，我们可追溯至更早的相关记述。

1. 萨克索（Saxo）

萨克索·格莱默提克斯（Saxo Grammaticus）在其《丹麦史》（*Historiae Danicae*）中首先讲述了这么一位英雄，即人们后来所熟知的哈姆雷特。该书写于 12 世纪末，出版于 1514 年。

萨克索在书中讲述了阿姆莱斯（Amleth = Hamlet）的父亲——霍文迪尔（Horwendil = King Hamlet）和叔父——芬高（Fengo = Claudius），在丹麦国王罗里克（Rorick）的统领下如何治理日德兰半岛（Jutland）。霍文迪尔的英勇事迹激起了挪威王的敌意，在一次单打独斗中，霍文迪尔将他杀死。他赢得了罗里克国王的赏识，娶了他的女儿——葛露莎（Gerutha = Gertrude），然后生了一个儿子——阿姆莱斯。芬高出于嫉妒将哥哥杀害，并在凶杀之外加上乱伦——与葛露莎结婚。年轻的阿姆莱斯因担心自身的安全而装疯卖傻，经常脾气乖戾、满身泥污。他开始制作带有弯钩的棍棒，并用火炙烤顶端以使其坚硬，若有人提问，他会说那是替父亲报仇用的标枪。他的这种举动引起了（叔父）私下的怀疑并设法使他中计，因为相信装疯难过美人关，便派一位美女（= Ophelia）前去诱他；不过，阿姆莱斯通过一位结义兄弟（= Horatio）的警告以及该女子的配合避免了落入圈套，该女子曾是他儿时的玩伴。她答应否认他曾与她同房，因此，当阿姆莱斯对外据实以告时，人们倒觉得那是疯话。然而，芬高的一位朋友（= Polonius）对此表示怀疑，设计了另一种试探——派人偷听阿姆莱斯跟母亲的会谈，相信他不会隐瞒。 芬高的这位朋友便藏在她房间的被褥下面，但阿姆莱斯在疯狂的举动（啼叫、振臂，在被褥上面上蹿下跳）中发现了他并把他杀死，把他的尸体肢解后扔进了阴沟、让猪吞食。 他慷慨激昂地斥责了母亲乱伦的婚姻——嫁给了弑兄的弟弟，让她忏悔，并向她透露了装疯的真相和复仇的意图。 他讲述了偷听者消失的真相，可人们再次表示怀疑，对他的发疯好像已深信不疑，但这却加深了芬高的疑心并促使芬高谋划将他除掉。芬高把他派遣到英国，由两位随从（= Rosencrantz 和 Guildenstern）陪伴，他们携带一封信函，信中指使国王将他处死；不过，阿姆莱斯趁同伴熟睡时更换了信件，转而告诉国王将两位随从处死，并请求他将女儿许配给他；他完全如愿以偿。 阿姆莱斯离开英国之前吩咐母亲在大厅里挂起帷幕，并在一年之后为他举行葬礼；他如期回到家里，葬礼正在进行，他的出现使大臣们大吃一惊，他设宴款待，直到他们大醉。 然后他拉下母亲挂起的帷幕罩住他们，并用自己早已备好的、带有弯钩的棍棒将帷幕固牢。 然后放火焚烧大厅，接着前往已入睡的芬高的卧室。 阿姆莱斯因不断被自己的剑刺伤，他便用钉子把它固定在鞘里，用它更换了芬高的利剑，以便等他醒来时，告诉他复仇的时刻已到，他手中的那把剑无法拔出，于是便毙命于自己的那把利剑。 第二天，阿姆莱斯在向人们的演说中为自己正名，并被人们欢呼为国王。

2．贝尔佛莱（Belleforest）

当然，这并不意味着莎士比亚曾读过萨克索的原著，直接的从中受惠可能性不大。 该故事之所以能在伊丽莎白时代的读者之间流行，还要归功于当时的法国人——贝尔佛莱，因为是他（用法语）将该故事重讲一遍。 他对萨克索原著中的情节也相对忠实，只是他的故事比原著长了一倍。

评论性导读

（Critical Introduction）

1. 王子与国王兄弟（The Prince and the Brother Kings）

我们不妨顺着莎士比亚本人最初下笔时的线索开始。 一个人被他的弟弟杀害，要由儿子替父亲报仇：这就是《哈姆雷特》一剧的故事梗概。替父报仇的情节，作为剧本的基本框架，从头至尾贯穿其中。 故事以一位亡父的显灵拉开序幕，随后展示他的继任者，并向儿子揭露凶杀的真相，儿子承担起复仇的使命，从而把剧情推向高潮。

在场面宏大的中场，凶杀的场景在舞台上两次再现，让凶手面对自己的罪恶。 但这也让凶手警觉到了复仇的威胁，并促使他将计就计，结果导致了灾难性的结局——主人公在复仇成功的同时，也献出了自己的生命。 在故事的开头、中间以及结尾处的三次宫廷礼仪中，儿子与叔父以一种秘而不宣的敌意相互对立，形成了一种戏剧性的对称。

其中的第一次对立，是在鬼魂显灵的场景之间，展现了父亲、叔父与儿子之间的三角关系。 广受赞誉的开场，以最令人惊恐的方式向我们展示了一个"很像已故国王"的身影，由这个沉默的幽灵所带来的期待，现已聚集到了必须被告知此事的"小哈姆雷特"身上，因为：

> 对我们沉默的幽灵,会对他讲话。(1.1.176)

在我们尚未见到剧中的主人公之前，已经知道他是已故国王的儿子，将要接受鬼魂的指令。 当我们看到他在宫廷出现时，他却与众不同、身穿丧服，正为死去的父亲感到悲痛。 他对新任国王的愤恨之情在他们首次对话时便暴露无遗：

> 好啦,我的侄儿哈姆雷特,我的儿——
>
> 　　血缘有余,但是亲情不足。
>
> 您这人怎么依然阴云笼罩？
>
> 　　不,陛下,我倒受不了太阳的热乎儿。(1.2.64-7)

哈姆雷特在其首次使用的双关语中，反驳并拒绝了新任国王将其称为儿子的企图，声明了自己对父亲的效忠。 莎士比亚在此所强调的是：父子之间的紧密关系。 当儿子最后面对父亲的亡灵，不得不进行复仇时，又再三强调了这一点：

> 假如你曾爱过你亲爱的父亲……(1.5.23)
>
> 假如你还有孝心……(1.5.81)

国王兄弟二人之间的对照，是剧本有关道德和戏剧结构的重要组成部分之一。 在我们看到新任国王之前，英勇威武的已故国王，已通过自身的幽灵展示在我们面前；而且，新任国王刚离开舞台，哈姆雷特的第一次独白就对他们两人进行了鲜明的对比。 哈姆雷特的独白既将本场一分为二，又将它们紧密相连，我们的注意力此刻又随着前来向"小哈姆雷特"汇报鬼魂显灵的哨兵转向了已故国王。 就这样，当剧情朝向哈姆雷特与鬼魂相遇的时刻发展的同时，哈姆雷特对亡父的态度已让我们牢记在心。 这位"好国王"，人类完美的典范，在他的心眼里显现：

> 他是男子的典范,尽善尽美:
>
> 我再也见不到他那样的完人。(1.2.187-8)

哈姆雷特对那位想取代其父亲地位的新任国王表示怀疑之后，接着就表达了对父亲的崇敬之情，将父亲誉为：

> 一位多好的君王,与这位相比,
>
> 真是天神之与怪兽。(1.2.139-140)

此处的天神指的是，以人的形体出现的太阳神，怪兽则指的是一种半人半羊的畜生；因此，这种意象生动地向我们暗示了人类身上的双重性格，哈姆雷特对此将一再反思。 我们千万不要忘记他们两人是同胞兄弟。 当其中的一位残害了另一位的时候，他们的亲密关系就会让这种凶杀变得"邪恶至极，最为无情和稀奇"。 但是，这种"无情"又在情理之中：人类天性中的神性与兽性本属同一棵生命之树。 在他们兄弟两人身上我们意识到了人类自身所具有的邪恶与善良，以及剧中人物及其行动所体现出的高尚与淫荡。 哈姆雷特对凶杀一事毫无所知之前，就已清楚自己的处境：天神般的男人已经死去，取而代之的则是一只怪兽。 更糟糕的是，自己的亲生母亲已经停止对这位天神的哀悼，转而去委身于这只怪兽，从而使自己变得禽兽不如，因为：

> 缺乏理性的畜生都会
>
> 哀悼得更久（1.2.150-1）

哈姆雷特之所以想摆脱这副"肮脏透顶的躯壳"，是因为王后和王国都被一个无赖据为己有，他的困境涉及整个"丹麦王国"。可以说，丹麦王国那种"糟糕"的事情，也就是天神般的男人已被一只禽兽取代。那种为丹麦王国赢得了"蠢猪"绰号的通宵滥饮，也能说明这一点；而此时，哈姆雷特他们正在等候鬼魂的显现。鬼魂最终讲述的那种可怕的经历也进一步发展了这种兽性般的意象：

> 对，是那个乱伦、通奸的禽兽，
>
> ……使他的兽欲如愿以偿，
>
> 俘获了我那最貌似忠贞的王后。

因为：

> 淫荡，纵有光明的天使相伴，
>
> 也会对神圣的恩爱感到腻烦，
>
> 转而猎取破烂。（1.5.42-57）

此处交替使用的词汇，如"天使"与"神圣"，以及带有动物含义的词汇，如"腻烦"与"猎取"，旨在表明一种堕落——从天使般的恩爱跌落到畜生似的兽欲。这正是哈姆雷特要去挽救的局面。鬼魂在给哈姆雷特的命令中也说道：

> 不要让丹麦王国的皇床变成
>
> 一种供人淫荡与乱伦的卧榻。（1.5.82-3）

哈姆雷特的使命，若从最广泛的道义而论，不是杀死残害父亲的凶手，而是要通过这一举动将世上的怪兽除掉，从而把这个世界归还给天神。亲生父亲给人残害至死，作为儿子，也许还作为人类的后裔，哈姆雷特在第一幕结尾时说道：

> 时代杂乱无章，噢，糟糕透顶，
>
> 竟让我负起拨乱反正的使命！（1.5.196-7）

有关兄弟两人在道德方面的对照，随着剧情的自然发展也不断重现。哈姆雷特在与母亲单独会面期间，再次对她的第二个丈夫进行了谴责，并以此开始了"天神之与怪兽"的对照。 哈姆雷特在描绘自己的父亲时说道：

> 看看这位是何等的眉清目秀，
>
> 太阳神的卷发，朱庇特的前额，
>
> 战神一般的眼睛威风凛然，
>
> 他的身姿就像信使墨丘利
>
> 刚刚落到高吻苍穹的山巅……(3.4.55-9)

其中的每一种相貌特征都显示出一位天神的崇高之美。 这些特征汇聚一起，便造就了这样一副完美无缺的形象：

> 好像每位天神都盖上封印，
>
> 以给世界一个男人的榜样。(3.4.61-2)

这是对一位至高无上的男子的描绘，哈姆雷特称这位男子"尽善尽美"。但不幸的是，这位完人的皇冠却被一个"一钱不值的国王"窃取。

2．三位儿子(The Sons)

莎士比亚戏剧艺术的一条准则就是，让次要情节重复出现，或让它们与主要情节进行对照，比如：他在剧中展示了另外两位儿子，与哈姆雷特进行对比。 在首次出现的宫廷场景中，新任国王所应对的三位年轻人当中，哈姆雷特是最后一位。 这样安排可以让我们心中充满悬念，以便增强国王对哈姆雷特所说的第一句话的作用，也就是用弗廷布拉和雷厄提斯作为铺垫，逐渐将人们的注意力引向哈姆雷特，因为他们两人的情况就是用来反衬哈姆雷特的处境。 弗廷布拉，作为已故国王的儿子，现任国王的侄儿，积极地采取措施为死去的父亲报仇，与哈姆雷特形成了鲜明的对比。 在我们尚未听到有关"小哈姆雷特"的任何消息之前，该剧一开场就向我们介绍了"小弗廷布拉"，作为一帮亡命之徒的首领，对丹麦的和平构成了威胁。 他为父亲复仇的热情一开始就展现在我们的面前。

至于雷厄提斯，他目前倒没什么故事可言，他的父亲尚未死去；但是，就他得到准许可以返回法国这件事情而言，却与被人劝阻而未能返回威登堡的哈姆雷特形成了巧妙的对比。 因为雷厄提斯随后还要出场，我们必须对他的身份有所了解。 显然正是由于他的特殊身份，国王才会在九行诗句中连续四次呼唤他的名字（1.2.42-50）。 如果这一点表明国王对他恩爱有加，也可以为他们后来的结盟埋下伏笔。 但是，此刻的关键在于，我们的注意力已被集中到他的身上，即：他跟哈姆雷特一样，与父亲紧密相连。 国王恩准雷厄提斯的请求，是因为他的父亲为丹麦王国立下了功劳。 国王在询问雷厄提斯是否得到了父亲的准许时，波洛纽斯在剧中的第一次发言就是陈述他已经答应了儿子的请求。 莎士比亚在此展示了高超的伏笔艺术，但又不惹人注目。 在雷厄提斯启程之前，将有一场亲人告别的场景，其间，不仅引出了他的妹妹以及她与哈姆雷特之间的爱情这一次要情节，而且还表明雷厄提斯得到了父亲的两次祝福。 随后他又得到了慈父一番善意的劝告。 正当我们不禁要想象雷厄提斯会在巴黎如何寻花问柳的时候，很快却看到哈姆雷特，肩负着鬼魂指令的重大压力，步履蹒跚。 波洛纽斯的仆人雷纳尔多受命前往法国打探雷厄提斯的行踪，刚刚离开，剧情的焦点便转向了波洛纽斯那位惊慌失措的女儿身上。 但是，我们怎么也不会忘记，波洛纽斯也有一位儿子。 当自己的父亲遇害时，即便没有鬼魂的召唤，这位儿子也会返回。 显而易见，剧作家在自己的构思中早已设计好了这第二桩复仇。

同样显而易见的是，弗廷布拉，一位热衷于采取行动的儿子，最初被设想成了另一位复仇者，与哈姆雷特形成对比。 但奇怪的是，弗廷布拉入场时那种作为儿子的身份很快即被抛弃。 当第一幕早些时候派出的大使，在第二幕开始不久便返回的时候，他想收回父亲所失领地的努力已告结束，他的士兵转而去攻打"波兰国王"，对丹麦王国不再有任何威胁。但是，目前的弗廷布拉跟雷厄提斯一样正在等待，当剧情发展到第四幕时，又需要他们二人重新登场。

3．奥菲丽娅（Ophelia）

人们所说的"修道院"场景，以及奥菲丽娅在剧中的整个角色经常遭到误解：可以毫不夸张地说，对奥菲丽娅的误解阻碍了对全剧的理解。

实际上，奥菲丽娅在剧中的作用在于：她是一位哈姆雷特有可能迎娶却并未迎娶的女人。 我们从故事的开场就了解到，哈姆雷特曾用"山盟海誓"向她求爱，但她随后却遵照父命予以拒绝。 然而，批评家们却将伊丽莎白时代的戏剧与现实生活，或至少与浪漫小说，混为一谈；他们认为哈姆雷特定会对此作出反应，从而将他们自身的怨恨之情转嫁给了哈姆雷特。 他们指责奥菲丽娅拒绝了哈姆雷特，以为他遭到了抛弃或背叛，定会与情人之间发生口角或制造麻烦。 谁若认为哈姆雷特对奥菲丽娅的态度是因为她拒绝了他的求爱信件，那就跟波罗纽斯所犯的错误没什么区别，而该剧却明显地否定了他的这种观点。 波罗纽斯的这种错误观念自然有其重要意义，因为正是他这种想对自己的观点予以验证的念头才导致了"修道院"场景的出现；然而，当我们看到"修道院"那一场景时，若能理解他们所说的话语而不是期望他们该说些什么，我们便会发现：是哈姆雷特拒绝了奥菲丽娅的爱情，而不是恰恰相反。 他只字未提奥菲丽娅对自己的拒绝；然而，使奥菲丽娅颇感惊讶的是，哈姆雷特竟然问她是否贞洁，认为贞洁与美丽无法兼得，并暗示她也不会例外。 他随后要对母亲予以谴责的脆弱，现已在奥菲丽娅身上得以预见。他抨击了女人的涂脂抹粉、背叛夫君，以及她们所惯犯的所有罪过，并把矛头指向了奥菲丽娅。 然而，很容易被人忽略的是，他最初所提及的那些罪过就属于自身：

> 仙女，在你的祷告里可要记住
>
> 我的所有罪行。(3.1.89-90)

他很快又接着说道：

> 我有许多罪过应该自责，竟企望我的母亲
>
> 不曾将我生下。(3.1.123-4)

至于是什么罪过，我们不得而知；因为他的罪过跟奥菲丽娅的一样，与其说是真实，不如说是可能。 哈姆雷特承认自己曾爱过奥菲丽娅，但随即便予以否认；爱之所以不是爱的悖论，我认为，在于哈姆雷特的本性：在他那神圣的盟誓之中潜伏着怪兽的身影。 若以他的母亲为例，因为她已让"婚姻誓言变得跟赌徒的咒语一样虚张"，那就不难理解他为何会对奥菲丽娅说"咱们是不会结婚的"。 但是，除此之外，他还担心奥菲丽娅不会忠诚，令他更为担心的是，奥菲丽娅很看重他的爱情，甚至还给予了

到自身的这种双重性格：

<blockquote>
不过这是天意，

惩罚我杀死他，惩罚他被我杀，（3.4.175-6）
</blockquote>

　　大家可能会想，如此博学多才、能言善辩的哈姆雷特竟然未对自己的双重角色予以阐释，似乎有些奇怪。　但是，戏剧除了用言辞表达自己的宗旨外，还有其他的方式，行动已清晰展示的东西无须再加以明说。　此时，在戏剧的中场，复仇者在台上犯下的罪行以及野蛮地将尸体从我们眼前拖过的场景，显而易见怎么也不会亚于所再现的国王的杀兄之罪。　我们若意识不到哈姆雷特为了给自己的父亲复仇而杀害了别人的父亲这种罪行的重要意义，那就很难真正地理解该剧的结局。

　　可以说，正是由于哈姆雷特身上的双重角色，才造就了他的双重性格。　因为，在《哈姆雷特》剧本的创作过程中，当然是角色决定性格，而不是性格决定他的言行。　在萨克索和贝尔佛莱的故事中，那位遭到杀戮和碎尸万段的密探大臣，让几头猪给吞下之后即告完结。　而莎士比亚笔下的这位大臣，身后却留下了一位儿子，那么，杀死这位大臣的凶手所面临的处境就会有所不同。　萨克索和贝尔弗莱所描绘的主人公均有隐秘而坚定的目标，都是以勇气和美德而著称的英雄。　而我们的英雄却在寻求伸张正义的过程中犯下了罪行，他的志向和成就与他的失败和罪行相当，善与恶的潜在性在他身上萦绕并存。　正是这一点，才让一位纯粹的复仇者变成了代表我们大家的复杂人物。

　　我们是否也可以在此找到哈姆雷特之所以拖延的理由？　一位悲剧式的英雄，就是惩罚与被惩罚，在行善的同时犯下罪行。　当然，这并不是说哈姆雷特当初为父亲的去世、母亲的再婚深感痛心时，早已料到自己在戏剧收场之前注定会杀死波洛纽斯，并被雷厄提斯刺杀。　但是剧本本身却很清楚哈姆雷特的这种命运，并为此作了精心的安排。　剧作家根据自己的想象塑造了这种结局，可以表达出主人公内心的一种无奈，或者是，不情愿——不是真想杀死波洛纽斯，尽管哈姆雷特对此并未予以表露。但是，他不得不根据自身的处境生活在一个好像由邪恶主宰着的世界，对此他一开始就表露无遗。　从这一点上讲，如果说哈姆雷特故事的拖延是必然的，也许不无道理：不仅仅是因为故事要求将复仇的行为拖延到最后，而且是因为它要将主人公引向一种一位渴望正义的人士所不愿接受的命运。

6. 哈姆雷特的处境 (Hamlet in His World)

这并不是说，人们可据此解释文学界最富有争议的人物——哈姆雷特的性格在莎士比亚心中的成长过程。 剧作家最初的构思肯定是按照剧情的要求进行的；但剧情的发展却无疑超越了这些要求，即：哈姆雷特所逃避的不再是复仇的行为，而是整个人生的负担。 我们发现哈姆雷特所提出的问题，更多的是涉及人的本性，而不是复仇本身，莎士比亚以此将我们引入哈姆雷特的内心世界，并借此将他本人的好奇之心通过哈姆雷特之口表达出来。 但是，由于哈姆雷特具有复仇者的双重角色，他能够，而且是不得不对这些问题进行发问。

哈姆雷特为丹麦的现状感到痛心，父亲的王位由叔父继承，善变的公众随即表达了他们的效忠，王后也随之投入他的怀抱。 哈姆雷特想离开丹麦前往威登堡，却听从了母亲的劝告留在宫中。 他对丹麦王宫的传统深表反感，但同时又不得不承认自己"在此生长，对这种风尚习以为常"。 他清楚自己身上拥有他所厌恶的某些品质，对此他无法避免。 哈姆雷特的天性在他的父母身上得到了体现：因为他既属于一位天神般完美的父亲，又属于一位将天神换成了怪兽的母亲。 在戏剧中场母子会面的那一重要场合，当母亲问他是否忘了她是谁时，哈姆雷特清楚地表明了母亲乱伦的事实：

　　　　您是王后,您丈夫的弟弟的妻子, (3.4.14)

随后又意味深长地补充道：

　　　　但愿并非如此! 您是我的母亲。(3.4.15)

然而，并非仅仅因为母亲的所作所为才将他玷污。 他觉得自己属于一种病态的血统。 在他看来，"世上的一切多么可厌"，只有"杂草"在"肆意繁衍"。 他为世上的所有邪恶和不公感到苦恼，只有死亡才能带来解脱。

当他发誓只有鬼魂的命令才能留在自己的脑海，并"与下贱的东西分离"时，那种无法消融的"肉体"所肩负的重担他早已背起，尽管他本人可能会暂时忘记。 他在第一次独白中，将叔父与父亲对照时说道：

> 可他不像我父亲，
>
> 我也不像赫克勒斯。(1.2.152-3)

这表明，甚至在鬼魂的命令下达之前，他已经感到了自身的软弱和不足。

他的"性情失调"可在第二幕第二场与两位校友的闲谈中清晰见到。他失去了所有的欢乐；丹麦是一座监狱；世界也是一座监狱；就连他大加褒扬的整个宇宙，对他来说，好像也是另一番景象：

> 　　　　　　　　大地——这一
>
> 座优美的框架，对我来说只不过是一片
>
> 荒芜的海岬；这顶最杰出的华盖——天空，
>
> 你们注意，这座壮丽高悬的苍穹，这片
>
> 金碧辉煌、庄严雄伟的屋顶，唉，对我
>
> 来说，不过是一团恶臭和致命的瘴气。 (2.2.297-302)

人，这一件"多么精巧的杰作"，对他来说，不过是"一尊源于泥土的精英"。 他以装疯卖傻作为一种心理掩护，针对一些引人注目的话题，道出了不少让"理智与常情"都"望尘莫及"的妙语。 他的冷嘲热讽涉及诚信的缺失、个人的应得、命运的不公以及老年的衰朽等等。

波洛纽斯曾率真地问他："您愿意进去避避风吗，殿下？"此刻他那种去死的愿望突然再现，便不假思索地答道："到我的坟里？"许多零散的思想最终汇成了那场有关生死存亡的独白，在这场独白中，他那种去死的愿望，在对那死后的惧怕中找到了答案。 尽管这场独白的内容超越了哈姆雷特个人的苦难，但目前看来，也许正是由于他所遭受的苦难才引发了这场独白。 因为这场独白在该剧的中场，围绕哈姆雷特这一戏剧性的角色，展开了一场半正式的辩论：面对"尘世的羁绊"，是选择"活着"，还是选择"死去"？ 面对这种两难的境地，在接受与拒绝人类的命运之间进行选择，那就是折中，或者是，没有选择。

7. 终场(The Final Act)

然而，等到最后一幕，情况却发生了变化。 我们发现哈姆雷特在教堂墓地对死亡进行沉思。 而此刻所涉及的死亡，已不再是为解脱肉体痛苦而令人向往的某种手段，也不再是因为对那死后的惧怕而加以躲避的阴影。 在掘墓者开始挖坟生涯当天出生的哈姆雷特，在死亡的阴影中度过了自己的整个人生。 针对掘墓者扔出的头骨，他看清了人类所共有的命运，一种他现在好像要予以接受的命运。 在最后一场，就在致命的比剑开始之前，他说道：

> 若是现在，就不是将来；……
>
> ……若不是现在，那就是将来。（5.2.216-8）

随后又补充道："做好准备是关键。"因此，他此刻已经做好了准备去迎接死亡——终结生命的普遍方式。 因为此刻他在欣然接受世间善恶的同时，已经看到其间存在着一种至高无上或神秘的力量。 他已不再痛击"世间的一切"，不再将大地这座"优美的框架"看成"一片荒芜的海岬"，也不再哀叹自己生来居然要肩负起"拨乱反正"的使命，而是坚定了自己的信念：

> 有一种神灵主宰我们的结局，
>
> 不管我们怎样砍劈。（5.2.10-11）

他从自身前往英国的途中所发生的事情看到了这种神灵的主宰。 他谈到自己将罗森克兰和盖登斯顿所带的国书更换之后如何封印时，说道：

> 唉，甚至连这一点都是天意。（5.2.48）

以罗森克兰和盖登斯顿的下场为鉴，复仇的结果依然是那么残酷无情，但他现在已经意识到并顺从了这种神圣的力量，他原有的那种不情愿的心情已经消失。 "活着"还是"死去"的难题，已经得到了解答。 他现在已能接受自己在世间的处境，已不再回避人生所牵连的负担，而是愿意负起应有的使命，这方面的例证不止一个。 在奥菲丽娅的葬礼期间，他突然出现，声称自己是"丹麦君王，哈姆雷特！"这表明他不仅接受了自己"在此生长"的事实，而且还领取了迄今只适合于克劳狄斯的国王封号；曾称为一座监狱的丹麦，现在却称之为自己的王国。 而且，他在中场断然否认的爱情，现在却毅然予以肯定：

> 我爱奥菲丽娅，四万个兄弟的

　　　　爱加在一起，也赶不上我的

　　　　分量。(5. 1. 264-6)

令人可悲的是，爱情与婚姻现在已无法实现。 他也很快意识到自己对雷厄提斯发出的豪言壮语不免有些可笑。 但这却表明他一直爱着奥菲丽娅，虽然他压抑着自己的这份感情。

　　哈姆雷特与雷厄提斯在墓地的打斗，以及随后的和解，以另一种方式预示着很快就会发生的事情。 雷厄提斯，作为克劳狄斯的工具和帮凶，他本身也是一位下毒者；但他却是哈姆雷特伤害过的"弟兄"，哈姆雷特从自身的境况出发，也能理解他的情形。 在最终的比赛中，两位儿子为各自的父亲复仇；然而，他们每个人身上都拥有自己想要消灭的邪恶，互相惩罚，但临终却能相互原谅。 而国王身上的邪恶当然是无法通过调解得以消除的。 复仇者在将他杀死的同时，自己也受到了致命的创伤，并最终承当了自己所担负的双重角色。

　　许多人都知道，约翰逊①曾经说过："莎士比亚的创作好像没有任何的道义目的。"然而，《哈姆雷特》是一部含有明显道义的作品，这种道义既简明又深刻。 因为他所颂扬的主人公，在对人生的意义进行了积极的探索之后，开始接受自己的命运；因此，当他经历过世间的各种丑恶，深表厌恶而试图加以回避之后，尽管此刻死亡已经临近，最终还是甘愿面对人生、身体力行，而且还从言行两方面回应了"做好准备是关键"。

---

　　① 塞缪尔·约翰逊（Samuel Johnson，1709—1784）：英国作家，评论家。 编有《莎士比亚集》。

译者序[*]

一、版本说明

本译文所采用的英文版本系詹金斯（Harold Jenkins）先生所编著的阿登版第二版《哈姆雷特》（The Arden Shakespeare，*Hamlet*，Second Series，1982）。之所以要采用这一版本，主要是因为译者认为：该书附有权威的版本考证、准确的文字注释、详尽的背景分析，以及精辟的剧本导读等诸多优点。这些优点对译者正确理解原文的思想内涵及文体风格等均可提供巨大的便利与帮助。现谨选取詹金斯先生有关《哈姆雷特》版本考证方面的部分内容以资说明："在莎氏的全部作品中，唯有《哈姆雷特》拥有三个独立的版本，即：第一版四开本（The First Quarto），第二版四开本（The Second Quarto），和第一版对开本（The First Folio）。它们之间的关系错综复杂，在某些方面实在令人费解。我们可根据各个剧本对人物的具体描述情况作出如下推论：第一版四开本为盗印本；第二版四开本为真善本，根据莎士比亚的手稿印制而成。种种迹象表明，第一版对开本是源于某一剧场的抄本，其中有一些为了适应舞台演出所作的改写，但在很大程度上还是根据第二版四开本印制而成。""自从多佛尔·威尔逊①于 1934 年将第二版四开本确认为最可信的版本以来，

＊ 再版说明：值此《莎士比亚四大悲剧合集》（英汉对照）出版之际，译者又对 2012 年出版的《哈姆雷特》译文作了一些修改，其中包括：针对"译者序"里所提及的"三美"原则分别增添了相应的译例予以说明；删节和改动；补上了第一版所遗漏的人物表，并选译了有关剧中人物的史料说明；在序言中增加了《哈姆雷特》的创作日期和故事来源；对译文中的错字、别字和欠通顺词句等进行了改正，同时又增加了一些脚注。

① 多佛尔·威尔逊（John Dover Wilson）：英国莎士比亚作品编撰家（1881—1969）。

所刊印的绝大多数版本都是采用这一版本。 本书所采用的版本主要是依据第二版四开本，同时也参照对开本增补了第二版四开本所遗漏的部分内容。”

二、标准与宗旨

作为一种探索与尝试，本译文主要以许渊冲教授在诗歌翻译方面所倡导的“三美”原则为标准。 其宗旨是：“要在传达原文意美的前提下，尽可能传达原文的音美；还要在传达原文意美和音美的前提下，尽可能传达原文的形美；努力做到三美齐备。”（许渊冲，1984）具体做法大致如下：

1．意美：按照“三美”原则，“意美”就是译文要忠实地传达原文的内容，不能错译、漏译、多译。 另外，考虑到莎士比亚所处的伊丽莎白时代已与我们相距甚远，除了语言变化之外，文化背景也时过境迁。莎氏又爱玩弄文字游戏，善于利用各种意象或意象连缀来表达复杂的意念甚至主题，所以我们在阅读与理解莎剧的过程中会面临许多语言及文化方面的障碍。 因此，为了能够尽量帮助读者架设一座跨越语言及文化障碍的桥梁，同时也为了能够充分传达原文的意美，译文也根据原文的注解增加了详细的脚注，并附有各自的出处，以便于查阅。 现谨以克劳狄斯在第三幕第三场里的一段祷文为例予以说明：

故事发展到此刻，“哈姆雷特所设计的戏中戏又一次刺痛了克劳狄斯悔恨的心灵。 ……随之，一段最为优美的祷文便从他那遭受折磨的心中脱口而出”（Cyrus Hoy：187）：①

O, my offence is rank, it smells to heaven;	噢，我的罪恶已经臭气熏天；
It hath the primal eldest curse upon't—	它要遭受最为远古的诅咒——
A brother's murder. Pray can I not,	那就是杀兄之罪。 我无法祈祷，
Though inclination be as sharp as will,	尽管我的意愿和决心一样热切，

---

① Cyrus Hoy，*Hamlet*，New York：W. W. Norton & Company，1992.

40　My stronger guilt defeats my strong intent,	更强的内疚却击溃了强烈的意愿，　　40
And, like a man to double business bound,	犹如一人同时想做两件事情，
I stand in pause where I shall first begin,	不知该从何入手而犹豫不决，
And both neglect. What if this cursed hand	结果全都忽略。　这只黑手若因
Were thicker than itself with brother's blood,	兄弟的鲜血更加肮脏又会怎样，
45　Is there not rain enough in the sweet heavens	难道上天就没有充足的甘霖　　45
To wash it white as snow? Whereto serves mercy	将它洗得雪白？　怜悯的目的
But to confront the visage of offence?	不就是让人正视罪恶面孔？
And what's in prayer but this twofold force,	祈祷不就是拥有两种作用：
To be forestalled ere we come to fall	在我们失足之前加以预防，
50　Or pardon'd being down? Then I'll look up.	堕落之后得到宽恕？　那我要抬头。　50
My fault is past—but O, what form of prayer	我的罪已犯下——可是噢，哪种祈祷
Can serve my turn? 'Forgive me my foul murder?'	能对我有用？　"饶恕我邪恶的凶杀？"
That cannot be, since I am still possess'd	那不可能，因为我还占有着
Of those effects for which I did the murder—	我从谋杀之中所获得的好处——
55　My crown, mine own ambition, and my queen.	我的王冠、我的野心、我的王后。　　55
May one be pardon'd and retain th'offence?	能否既保留赃物又得到宽恕？
In the corrupted currents of this world	在当今这个腐败盛行的世界
Offence's gilded hand may shove by justice,	镀金的凶手可将正义推开，
And oft 'tis seen the wicked prize itself	邪恶的赃物常被人们用来
60　Buys out the law. But 'tis not so above:	将法律收买。　天上可不是这样：　60
There is no shuffling, there the action lies	那里无法抵赖，所有的罪行
In his true nature, and we ourselves compell'd	在那里原形毕露，我们本人
Even to the teeth and forehead of our faults	不得不直接面对自己的罪过
To give in evidence. What then? What rests?	——招供。　怎么办？　怎么办？
65　Try what repentance can. What can it not?	试一试忏悔吧。　它有啥不能做？　65
Yet what can it, when one cannot repent?	可它有啥用，我连忏悔都不能？
O wretched state! O bosom black as death!	噢，可怜的处境！　噢，污黑的心胸！
O limed soul, that struggling to be free	噢，沉沦的灵魂，越想挣脱羁绊
Art more engag'd! Help, angels! Make assay.	越是纠缠不清！　救命，天使！　尽力。
70　Bow, stubborn knees; and heart with strings of steel,	弯下，顽固的双膝；铁石的心肠　　70
Be soft as sinews of the new-born babe.	要像婴儿的筋肉一样柔软。
All may be well. [*He kneels.*]	一切还会好转。　［国王跪下。］

毫无疑问，克劳狄斯的罪大恶极是导致该剧所有不幸的根源。 然而，作为哈姆雷特的主要对手，克劳狄斯却"很少能从读者那里得到应有的注意。但是，无论在心理上还是在戏剧效果上他都引人注目。 一方面，他并不缺乏令人尊敬的品质。 作为国王，他谦恭有礼，也从未失尊；他对自己的职责行之有效；他对国家的利益也考虑周到。 ……他对自己来路不正的妻子好像也是情真意切，人们没有理由怀疑他只是把她当作一种获取王位的工具。 他的良心，尽管不起作用，但远非泯灭"（Bradley：143）。①

也许就像人们常说的那样，若想判断一个人的高度，要看他的对手是谁。 因此，我们若想判断哈姆雷特的高度，就应该看看他的对手——克劳狄斯。 因为"国王的高度越低，哈姆雷特的高度就会越低"，正如英国著名莎学家哈利迪所说的那样："克劳狄斯是个奸夫及杀人凶手，这是该剧的本质，也是其他剧情赖以存在的前提。 ……但他也有自己的美德：聪明、机敏、果断、勇敢。 如果我们要想公平地对待哈姆雷特，我们就必须公平地对待克劳狄斯。 莎士比亚做到了这一点，……他将克劳狄斯塑造成了与哈姆雷特更为匹配的对手。"（Halliday：139）②

就本段台词的"意美"而言，应该说译文忠实地传达了原文的内容，即没有出现错译、漏译或多译现象。 同时，为了能帮助读者朋友更好地理解和欣赏原文的意美，译者还根据三种原文的注解选取并翻译了下列四处脚注（见正文，209 页）。

2．音美：作为原文精华及主要内容的无韵诗，是一种没有韵脚但富有节奏的诗体：每行五个音步，每个音步又有一轻一重两个音节，读起来抑扬顿挫、节律鲜明。 因此，为了能够充分传达原文这种明快的"音美"效果，译文也采用我国译莎前辈所倡导的"以顿代步"的原则，让每行大都以五顿、十二字与原文予以对应，并尽力使译文富有节律，顺口、好听。

在韵式方面也尽力做到与原文完全一致，剧中的歌谣、偶韵体、打油

---

① A. C. Bradley, *Shakespearean Tragedy*, New York：Macmillan Press Ltd. 1992.

② F. E. Halliday, *The Poetry of Shakespeare's Plays*, London：Gerald Duckworth & Co. Ltd., 1964.

诗等均按原文的韵律悉数再现。 至于剧中的双关语，因为它们大都只能依据具体的语境意会，不可言传，译者只能将部分双关语尽量迻译，或者附加脚注予以说明。

如果说形式是诗歌的外表，韵律则可谓诗歌的灵魂。 因此，尽管原文为无韵诗，但在不影响原文"意美"的前提下，也适当译出了一些脚韵或句中韵，希望以此传达原文的"音美"效果，但原则是"可遇"而不"苛求"。 现以哈姆雷特在第一幕第四场里的一段台词为例予以说明：

哈姆雷特如约在晚上十一二点之间前来与哨兵们见面。 就在他们一起等候鬼魂显灵的期间，哈姆雷特对丹麦王国和国王的酗酒成风及其恶劣影响进行了无情的嘲讽；随后他又进一步论及了个人的情况。 本段台词对"理解哈姆雷特所面临的两难境地至关重要。 ……它揭示了剧中的根本性问题以及哈姆雷特本人所面临的难题：邪恶只是一种表象——人性从"动物界的典范"身上偏离，还是"与生俱来"？ （Mahood：116-7）①：

But to my mind, though I am native here	但以我所见，尽管我在此生长，	
15 And to the manner born, it is a custom	对这种风尚习以为常，与其	15
More honour'd in the breach than the observance.	加以遵守还不如打破它体面。	
This heavy-headed revel east and west	这种狂欢滥饮让我们遭到	
Makes us traduc'd and tax'd of other nations—	东西方各国的指责与诽谤——	
They clepe us drunkards, and with swinish phrase	他们叫我们酒鬼，而且还污蔑	
20 Soil our addition; and indeed it takes	我们是蠢猪；这的确会让	20
From our achievements, though perform'd at height,	我们的成就，尽管非常宏伟，	
The pith and marrow of our attribute.	失去其应有的精华与光辉。	
So, oft it chances in particular men	就个人而言，情况也往往如此，	
That for some vicious mole of nature in them,	某些人由于生来就带有恶痣，	
25 As in their birth, wherein they are not guilty	与生俱来，并非个人的过失	25
（Since nature cannot choose his origin）,	（因为天生无法选择起源），	
By their o'ergrowth of some complexion,	由于某种性情的过度发展，	

---

① M. M. Mahood, *Shakespeare's Wordplay*, London：Methuen & Co. Ltd., 1968.

Oft breaking down the pales and forts of reason,	往往就会冲破理智的防线，
Or by some habit, that too much o'erleavens	或是由于某种陋习对得体的
30 The form of plausive manners—that these men,	举止造成太多的冲击——这些人，　30
Carrying, I say, the stamp of one defect,	我敢说，带着某种缺陷的烙印，
Being Nature's livery or Fortune's star,	无论与生俱来还是不幸酿成，
His virtues else, be they as pure as grace,	他的其他美德，无论多么纯洁，
As infinite as man may undergo,	多么高贵，多么无尽无穷，
35 Shall in the general censure take corruption	他都会因为这一具体的缺陷　35
From that particular fault. The dram of evil	而遭受人们非议。　这点瑕疵
Doth all the noble substance often dout	将会抹杀他所有的高尚品格，
To his own scandal.	而让他声名狼藉。

不难看出，译者在尽力传达原文"意美"的前提下，也适当译出了一些脚韵或句中韵，比如 14 行的"生长"与 15 行的"风尚""为常"，以及 18 行的"诽谤"等，希望以此传达原文的"音美"效果。

3．形美：译文在应对原文无韵诗方面，每行大都采用五顿、十二字予以对应，全文只有几行为十四字。　译文在尽力做到与原文等值的前提下，也力求与原文等行。　每一幕、每一场、每一位演员的台词行数，以及全剧的所有诗文、散文、歌谣、舞台指示的行数，均与原文一致。　在散文方面，译文也采用相应的散文形式予以对应。　原文每行大都在十四个音节左右，译文则试图将每行的字数控制在十六个左右；并尽力让每位演员的台词排列整齐、长短统一，从而比较醒目地体现散文与诗体的区别，希望以此来传达原文应有的"形美"效果。　现以哈姆雷特在第五幕第一场里的一段散文台词为例予以说明。

哈姆雷特在被送往英格兰的途中遭遇海盗，他将计就计得以脱险，返回丹麦。　他与何瑞修如约会面之后，巧遇正为奥菲丽娅挖坟的掘墓者。　此刻，他针对掘墓者扔出的头骨浮想联翩、诘问不断，从而对当时臭名昭著、损人利己的律师进行了辛辣的嘲讽：

There's another. Why, may not that be the skull of a lawyer? Where be his quiddities now, his quillities, his cases, his tenures, and his tricks? Why does he suffer this mad knave now to knock him about the	又有一个！咳，难道那不可能是一位律师的头骨？他的狡辩如今何在，他的遁词呢，他的案子呢，他的保有呢，和他的伎俩呢？现在为什么要忍受这个狂徒用一把肮脏的

100 sconce with a dirty shovel, and will not tell him of his action of battery? Hum, this fellow might be in's time a great buyer of land, with his statutes, his recognizances, his fines, his double vouchers, his recoveries . Is this the fine of his fines and the

105 recovery of his recoveries, to have his fine pate full of fine dirt? Will his vouchers vouch him no more of his purchases, and double ones too, than the length and breadth of a pair of indentures? The very conveyances of his lands will scarcely lie in this box, and

110 must th'inheritor himself have no more, ha?

铁锨将自己的头颅敲来敲去，而不去告他 100
犯下了伤害之罪。嗯，这个家伙生前也许
是个很大的土地买主，他利用法规，使用
具结，他谈判协商，寻求双重保人，追讨
应得的地产。难道这就是他协商出的结果，
讨回来的一切，让他那精明的脑袋充满了 105
精细的尘土？难道他的保人，甚至是双重
保人，不再担保他的置地，只为他留下了
契约这么一片大小的土地？这个匣子很难
将他置地的契约全部装下，而匣子的主人
难道就不能再多拥有一丁点土地，哈？ 110

三、感想与希望

通过对《哈姆雷特》十几年的翻译实践与探索，译者现有许多体会与感想：首先，假如译者的译文在某些方面比现有的译本能有所改进，那么，这些改进也都是站在巨人的肩膀上取得的。 这些巨人便是我们所熟悉并景仰的朱生豪先生、梁实秋先生、卞之琳先生等译莎专家及前辈，因为他们准确而流畅的译文为译者正确理解原文打下了坚实的基础。

其次，译者在修改译文的过程中，深刻体会到了学无止境与美中不足的古训是多么真切！ 因为，每当译者对自己的译文改完一遍，都会感到心满意足，甚至沾沾自喜；然而没过多久，当再次对译文进行查看时，又会发现仍有许多地方冗长拗口、辞不达意，只能老实地对译文重新加以修改。

所幸的是，译者的翻译及修改过程大都是伴随着动听的古典音乐进行的，这也算是苦中有乐吧。 同时，也多么希望音乐里的某些音符能够变成译文中的字符啊！ 总之，由于译者水平所限，文中一定仍有不少谬误与不足，还请读者朋友批评指正。

译　者

2019 年 10 月于宁波大学

史料说明

1. 哈姆雷特（Hamlet）：源于古斯堪的纳维亚语，表明某人愚笨（dim-witted），或假装愚笨。在《哈姆雷特》的故事来源中称为"Amleth"。

2. 克劳狄斯（Claudius）：国王的这一名字仅在 1.2 入场时的舞台指示中出现过，此后未再用过。在故事来源中被称为"Fengo"或"Fengon"，莎氏为一位丹麦国王取用这种名字不免令人意外；不过，该名字显然与罗马皇帝克劳狄斯一世有关，他曾娶了自己的侄女——阿格丽派娜（Agrippina），即尼禄的母亲，后被妻子毒死，妻子后来又被儿子——尼禄杀死。剧中曾在 3.2.384-5 予以提及。

4. 葛楚德（Gertrude）：在故事来源中分别被称为"Gerutha"和"Geruthe"，莎氏将其英语化了。

5. 波罗纽斯（Polonius）：编辑们通常依照 1676 年的四开本将其称为"Lord Chamberlain（宫务大臣）"。威尔逊（Dover Wilson）认为莎氏将其视为国务大臣（a Secretary of State），波罗纽斯本人显然也认同这种观点（2.2.166）。

6. 雷厄提斯（Laertes）：该名字可令人想起一种著名的父子关系，不过令人奇怪的是，莎氏明知雷厄提斯为荷马史诗《奥德赛》中的主人公——奥德修斯（Odysseus）的父亲，却把它给了一位儿子（见《泰特斯·安德洛尼克斯》1.1.380）。

7. 奥菲利亚（Ophelia）：该名字源于希腊语，意为"救助（succour）"，常被视为欠妥，尽管剧中曾将她称为"救护的天使"。不过，该名字的选用也许是把"Opheleia"跟"Apheleia"混淆了，后者意为"单纯，天真（simplicity, innocence）"。

8. 何瑞修（Horatio）：该名字可令人想起《西班牙之悲剧》中那位被害的儿子——一位忠诚的朋友。

9-10. 罗森克兰、盖登斯顿（Rosencrantz, Guildenstern）：这种铿锵有力的名字具有明显的丹麦色彩。他们两人好像从未单独出场。

11. 弗廷布拉（Fortinbras）：源于法语，意为"臂力强劲（strong-in-arm）"，可令人想起传奇故事中的武士形象。像哈姆雷特一样，他也跟父亲同名。故事来源中称其为"Coller"。

12. 福提曼德（Voltemand）：系"Valdemar"的讹误，后者为多位丹麦国王的名字。

13. 科尼留斯（Cornelius）：实为波兰人的名字，可能取自在丹麦定居的波兰人。

14-16. 马塞勒斯、巴纳多、弗兰斯科（Marcellus, Barnardo, Francisco）：可能是莎氏从自己看过的各种读物中捡取的名字。

17. 奥斯瑞克（Osric）：尽管有时会被当成丹麦人的名字，实为盎格鲁·撒克逊人的常用名。

18. 雷纳尔多（Reynaldo）：系"Reynard"的变体，该名字适合于那些品性狡诈的男士。

LIST OF ROLES

Hamlet, *Prince of Denmark.*

Claudius, *King of Denmark, Hamlet's uncle.*

The Ghost *of the late king, Hamlet's father.*

Gertrude, *the Queen, Hamlet's mother, now wife of Claudius.*

Polonius, *councillor of State.*

Laertes, *Polonius's son.*

Ophelia, *Polonius's daughter.*

Horatio, *friend and confidant of Hamlet.*

Rosencrantz,
Guildenstern, } *courtiers, former schoolfellows of Hamlet.*

Fortinbras, *Prince of Norway.*

Voltemand,
Cornelius, } *Danish councillors, ambassadors to Norway.*

Marcellus,
Barnardo, } *members of the King's Guard.*
Francisco,

Osric, *a foppish courtier.*

Reynaldo, *a servant of Polonius.*

Players.

A Gentleman *of the court.*

A Priest.

A Grave-digger.

The Grave-digger's *Companion.*

A Captain *in Fortinbras's army.*

English Ambassadors.

Lords, Ladies, Soldiers, Sailors, Messengers, and Attendants.

Scene. *Elsinore: the Court and its environs.*

剧中人物

哈姆雷特 　　丹麦王子
克劳狄斯 　　丹麦国王，哈姆雷特的叔父
鬼魂 　　　　已故国王，哈姆雷特的父亲
葛楚德 　　　王后，哈姆雷特的母亲，现为克劳狄斯之妻
波洛纽斯 　　国务大臣
雷厄提斯 　　波洛纽斯的儿子
奥菲丽娅 　　波洛纽斯的女儿
何瑞修 　　　哈姆雷特王子的知心朋友
罗森克兰 ⎫
盖登斯顿 ⎭　侍臣，哈姆雷特王子的校友
弗廷布拉 　　挪威王子
福提曼德 ⎫
科尼留斯 ⎭　丹麦王国的顾问，派往挪威的使臣
马塞勒斯 ⎫
巴纳多 　　⎬　国王的警卫人员
弗兰斯科 ⎭
奥斯瑞克 　　矫揉造作的侍臣
雷纳尔多 　　波洛纽斯的仆人
演员
宫廷一绅士
牧师
掘墓者
掘墓者的伙伴
弗廷布拉的陆军上尉
英国大使
贵族、女士、士兵、水手、信差与侍从

地点：埃尔西诺：王宫及其近郊。

第一幕
ACT I

SCENE   I

Enter Barnardo and Francisco, two Sentinels.

	Barnardo	Who's there?
	Francisco	Nay, answer me. Stand and unfold yourself.
	Barnardo	Long live the King!
	Francisco	Barnardo?
5	**Barnardo**	He.
	Francisco	You come most carefully upon your hour.
	Barnardo	'Tis now struck twelve. Get thee to bed, Francisco.
	Francisco	For this relief much thanks. 'Tis bitter cold,
		And I am sick at heart.
10	**Barnardo**	Have you had quiet guard?
	Francisco	Not a mouse stirring.
	Barnardo	Well, good night.
		If you do meet Horatio and Marcellus,
		The rivals of my watch, bid them make haste.
15	**Francisco**	I think I hear them.

第一场

巴纳多与弗兰斯科——两位哨兵上。

巴纳多	那是谁？	
弗兰斯科	您先回答！站住并通报姓名！	
巴纳多	国王万岁！	
弗兰斯科	巴纳多？	
巴纳多	正是。	5
弗兰斯科	您来得不早不晚，非常准时。	
巴纳多	十二点了。 你去睡吧，弗兰斯科。	
弗兰斯科	多谢您来替我！天气真冷，	
	我心里非常难受。	
巴纳多	放哨期间平静吗？	10
弗兰斯科	一只老鼠都没见。	
巴纳多	好吧，晚安。	
	若遇到何瑞修和马塞勒斯——	
	我的放哨伙伴，让他们快点。	
弗兰斯科	好像是他们到啦！	15

---

1. 1. 2. 您先回答：因为弗兰斯科此刻正在站岗，所以有权对前来换岗的巴纳多进行盘问，从而营造出一种紧张的气氛（Thompson）。 3. 国王万岁：可能是接头的暗号（尽管显得有些可笑）（Thompson）。

Enter Horatio and Marcellus.

Stand, ho! Who is there?

Horatio Friends to this ground.

Marcellus And liegemen to the Dane.

Francisco Give you good night.

Marcellus O, farewell honest soldier, who hath reliev'd you?

Francisco Barnardo hath my place. Give you good night. *Exit.*

20 **Marcellus** Holla, Barnardo!

Barnardo Say, what, is Horatio there?

Horatio A piece of him.

Barnardo Welcome, Horatio. Welcome, good Marcellus.

Horatio What, has this thing appear'd again tonight?

25 **Barnardo** I have seen nothing.

Marcellus Horatio says 'tis but our fantasy,

And will not let belief take hold of him,

Touching this dreaded sight twice seen of us.

Therefore I have entreated him along

30 With us to watch the minutes of this night,

That if again this apparition come,

He may approve our eyes and speak to it.

Horatio Tush, tush, 'twill not appear.

Barnardo Sit down awhile,

何瑞修与马塞勒斯上。

站住！那是谁？

何瑞修	本地的朋友。
马塞勒斯	丹麦国王的臣民。
弗兰斯科	祝你们晚安！
马塞勒斯	噢，诚实的军士再见，谁接的班？

弗兰斯科　巴纳多接了我的班。　祝你们晚安！　　　　　　　下。

马塞勒斯　你好啊，巴纳多！　　　　　　　　　　　　　　　20

巴纳多　　喂，怎么，那是何瑞修吗？

何瑞修　　他的手臂一只！

巴纳多　　欢迎，何瑞修！欢迎，好马塞勒斯！

何瑞修　　哎，那个东西今晚又出现了吗？

巴纳多　　我啥也没见。　　　　　　　　　　　　　　　　　25

马塞勒斯　何瑞修说咱们两次目睹的

　　　　　奇怪现象不过是一种虚幻，

　　　　　他无论如何也不愿意相信。

　　　　　所以今晚我请他亲自前来，

　　　　　以便与我们一起仔细守望，　　　　　　　　　　　30

　　　　　假如那个幽灵再一次出现，

　　　　　他就会相信我们并对它发话。

何瑞修　　瞎说，瞎说，它不会出现。

巴纳多　　　　　　　　　　　　　　请稍坐，

---

　　22. 手臂一只：何瑞修此时可能举起一只手臂，以此来证明自己的身份；但因为此时正是黑夜，其身体的其他部位尚无法显露。　有关何瑞修诙谐风趣的谈吐，请参看：1.2.169（其中阿拉伯数字"1"代表每一幕的序号，"2"代表每一场的序号，"169"则表示具体的行数。　——译者附注）。同时，还请参看：1.5.131-2、3.2.273、279、5.1.199（Jenkins）。　24. 那个东西：鬼魂。　莎士比亚通过这种泛指的方式可使我们心生悬念。　直到鬼魂确实显现时，他才告诉我们：那个身影"跟已故国王一样"（Jenkins）。　27. 奇怪现象：鬼魂显灵。　——译者附注。

And let us once again assail your ears,

35   That are so fortified against our story,

What we have two nights seen.

Horatio   Well, sit we down.

And let us hear Barnardo speak of this.

Barnardo   Last night of all,

When yond same star that's westward from the pole,

40   Had made his course t'illume that part of heaven

Where now it burns, Marcellus and myself,

The bell then beating one—

Enter Ghost.

Marcellus   Peace, break thee off. Look where it comes again.

Barnardo   In the same figure like the King that's dead.

45 **Marcellus**   Thou art a scholar, speak to it, Horatio.

Barnardo   Looks a not like the King? Mark it, Horatio.

Horatio   Most like. It harrows me with fear and wonder.

Barnardo   It would be spoke to.

Marcellus   Question it, Horatio.

Horatio   What art thou that usurp'st this time of night,

50   Together with that fair and warlike form

In which the majesty of buried Denmark

Did sometimes march? By heaven, I charge thee speak.

Marcellus   It is offended.

Barnardo   See, it stalks away.

Horatio   Stay, speak, speak, I charge thee speak.   *Exit Ghost.*

55 **Marcellus**   'Tis gone and will not answer.

	尽管您对我们的讲述充耳不闻，	
	我们还是想把两夜来的所见	35
	再向您灌输一番。	
何瑞修	好，咱们坐下。	
	就让巴纳多给我们讲一讲吧。	
巴纳多	就在昨天夜里，	
	正当北斗星西端的那颗星星，	
	运行到其目前正在闪耀的	40
	那片星空时，时钟刚敲过一点，	
	马塞勒斯和我——	

鬼魂上。

马塞勒斯	安静，别说了！快看它又来了！	
巴纳多	他的身影跟已故国王一样。	
马塞勒斯	你是位学者，何瑞修，对他说话。	45
巴那多	难道他不像先王？ 看好，何瑞修。	
何瑞修	很像。 它让我感到惊讶和恐慌。	
巴那多	它想让人问话。	
马塞勒斯	快问它，何瑞修。	
何瑞修	你是何物，居然装扮成已故	
	丹麦王行军时的飒爽英姿，	50
	在这深更半夜里出来侵扰？	
	我以上天的名义，命你快说！	
马塞勒斯	它生气了。	
巴那多	看，它昂着头走了。	
何瑞修	站住！快说，快说！我命你快说！ 鬼魂下。	
马塞勒斯	它走了，不愿意回答。	55

48. 快问它：人们普遍相信，鬼魂在听到人们的招呼之前不会首先开口（Jenkins）。 53. 生气：可能是由于何瑞修的用词不当，或是由于他的语气过于强硬（一个臣民竟敢命令国王？）（Thompson）。

Barnardo   How now, Horatio? You tremble and look pale.

Is not this something more than fantasy?

What think you on't?

Horatio   Before my God, I might not this believe

60   Without the sensible and true avouch

Of mine own eyes.

Marcellus   Is it not like the King?

Horatio   As thou art to thyself.

Such was the very armour he had on

When he th'ambitious Norway combated.

65   So frown'd he once, when in an angry parle

He smote the sledded Polacks on the ice.

'Tis strange.

Marcellus   Thus twice before, and jump at this dead hour,

With martial stalk hath he gone by our watch.

70   **Horatio**   In what particular thought to work I know not,

But in the gross and scope of my opinion,

This bodes some strange eruption to our state.

Marcellus   Good now, sit down, and tell me, he that knows,

Why this same strict and most observant watch

75   So nightly toils the subject of the land,

And why such daily cast of brazen cannon

And foreign mart for implements of war,

Why such impress of shipwrights, whose sore task

Does not divide the Sunday from the week.

80   What might be toward that this sweaty haste

Doth make the night joint-labourer with the day,

Who is't that can inform me?

巴那多	怎么样,何瑞修? 您苍白又发抖。	
	难道这还仅仅是一种虚幻?	
	您有何感想?	
何瑞修	向上帝发誓,若不是我本人	
	亲眼所见,我怎么也不会相信	60
	这种现象。	
马塞勒斯	难道它不像先王?	
何瑞修	正像你跟你一样。	
	当他与野心勃勃的挪威国王	
	搏斗时,穿的正是这身盔甲。	
	当他与波兰雪橇兵在冰凌上	65
	搏杀时,也曾这样愁容满面。	
	真是奇怪。	
马塞勒斯	前两次,也是在这寂静的时刻,	
	他昂首挺胸从我们面前跨过。	
何瑞修	对此我也不知该从何说起,	70
	但是总而言之,我个人认为,	
	这预示着我国会有一番突变。	
马塞勒斯	好吧,坐下,告诉我,有谁知道:	
	为何要如此这般戒备森严,	
	让全体臣民夜间遭受煎熬?	75
	为何整天都在铸造铜炮,	
	整天都在从国外进口弹药?	
	为何征募这么多造船工人,	
	他们连礼拜天都不能清闲?	
	如此夜以继日地慌张与流汗,	80
	这究竟意味着要发生什么,	
	有谁能告诉我?	

Horatio   That can I.

At least the whisper goes so: our last King,

Whose image even but now appear'd to us,

85   Was as you know by Fortinbras of Norway,

Thereto prick'd on by a most emulate pride,

Dar'd to the combat; in which our valiant Hamlet

(For so this side of our known world esteem'd him)

Did slay this Fortinbras, who by a seal'd compact

90   Well ratified by law and heraldry

Did forfeit, with his life, all those his lands

Which he stood seiz'd of to the conqueror;

Against the which a moiety competent

Was gaged by our King, which had return'd

95   To the inheritance of Fortinbras,

Had he been vanquisher; as, by the same cov'nant

And carriage of the article design'd,

His fell to Hamlet. Now, sir, young Fortinbras,

Of unimproved mettle, hot and full,

100   Hath in the skirts of Norway here and there

Shark'd up a list of lawless resolutes

For food and diet to some enterprise

That hath a stomach in't, which is no other,

As it doth well appear unto our state,

105   But to recover of us by strong hand

And terms compulsatory those foresaid lands

So by his father lost. And this, I take it,

何瑞修　　　　　　　我能告诉你。

至少是大家都在这么议论：

刚向我们显形的已故国王，

你们知道，曾被高傲好胜的　　　　　　　　　　85

挪威国王弗廷布拉所激怒，

奋勇应战；英勇的哈姆雷特

（因为我们西方都这样尊称）

杀死了这位弗廷布拉，按照

法律和骑士制度签订的协议，　　　　　　　　　90

他不仅丢掉了性命，而且还将

自己的所有领地划给了胜者；

就这一赌注而言，我们先王

赌上一份领土即可等量齐观；

假如弗廷布拉能够获胜，　　　　　　　　　　95

先王的那份领土将归他所有；

于是，按照双方事先的约定，

他的归哈姆雷特。 可小弗廷布拉，

现在羽翼未丰、跃跃欲试，

他在挪威边区的某些地方　　　　　　　　　　100

笼络起来一帮亡命之徒，

正像人的肚皮离不开食粮，

他的勾当需要一些乌合之众。

他的企图，我国早已看清，

那就是企图通过强硬手段　　　　　　　　　　105

强行收回他父亲所失去的

上述领土。 我认为，这就是

92. 划给了胜者：相互敌对的国王常用自己占有的领地（而不是自己的王国）作为双方战争的赌注，直至战死（Gill）。 94. 一份领土：哈姆雷特国王只要将自己的部分国土押上，即可与弗廷布拉的赌注等量（Gill）。

Is the main motive of our preparations,

The source of this our watch, and the chief head

110 Of this post-haste and rummage in the land.

Barnardo I think it be no other but e'en so.

Well may it sort that this portentous figure

Comes armed through our watch so like the King

That was and is the question of these wars.

115 **Horatio** A mote it is to trouble the mind's eye.

In the most high and palmy state of Rome,

A little ere the mightiest Julius fell,

The graves stood tenantless and the sheeted dead

Did squeak and gibber in the Roman streets;

120 As stars with trains of fire and dews of blood,

Disasters in the sun; and the moist star,

Upon whose influence Neptune's empire stands,

Was sick almost to doomsday with eclipse.

And even the like precurse of fear'd events,

125 As harbingers preceding still the fates

And prologue to the omen coming on,

Have heaven and earth together demonstrated

Unto our climatures and countrymen.

Enter Ghost.

But soft, behold. Lo, where it comes again.

I'll cross it though it blast me.   *Ghost spreads its arms.*

130   Stay, illusion!

If thou hast any sound or use of voice,

	我们进行备战的主要动机，	
	我们在此放哨的原因，以及	
	举国上下慌乱与骚动的根源。	110
巴那多	我认为正是由于这一缘故。	
	难怪那恰似先王的不祥身影，	
	身着盔甲，穿行于我们的岗哨，	
	历来的战争原来都与他有关。	
何瑞修	这只不过是一点心腹之患。	115
	就在罗马帝国的鼎盛时期，	
	强大无比的尤利乌斯遇害前，	
	坟墓空虚，裹着尸布的僵尸	
	都在罗马的街上吱吱乱叫；	
	星星拖着火焰、露水血红、	120
	太阳显出凶象；就连那颗	
	能够左右潮汐起落的月亮，	
	犹如世界的末日即将来临，	
	也变得黯然无光。 正如大难	
	临头之前总会伴有先兆，	125
	天灾降临之日少不了序言，	
	天上人间已将类似的凶兆	
	展现给了这一地区和同胞。	

鬼魂上。

安静，快看！看，它又过来了！

哪怕中邪我也拦截。 鬼魂张开双臂。

站住，幽灵！ 130

假如你能够发声或者说话，

---

117. 尤利乌斯：尤利乌斯·恺撒大帝（Bevington）。 123. 世界的末日：即耶稣的第二次降临之际，天空漆黑一片，"月亮也将黯然无光"（《圣经》"马太福音" 24 章 29 节）（Jenkins）。 130. 拦截：人们普遍相信，面对鬼魂易受伤害（Jenkins）。

Speak to me.

If there be any good thing to be done

That may to thee do ease, and grace to me,

135   Speak to me;

If thou art privy to thy country's fate,

Which, happily, foreknowing may avoid,

O speak;

Or if thou hast uphoarded in thy life

140   Extorted treasure in the womb of earth,

For which they say your spirits oft walk in death,

Speak of it, stay and speak.   *The cock crows.*

    Stop it, Marcellus.

Marcellus Shall I strike at it with my partisan?

Horatio Do if it will not stand.

145 **Barnardo** 'Tis here.

Horatio 'Tis here.   *Exit Ghost.*

Marcellus 'Tis gone.

We do it wrong, being so majestical,

To offer it the show of violence,

150   For it is as the air, invulnerable,

And our vain blows malicious mockery.

Barnardo It was about to speak when the cock crew.

Horatio And then it started like a guilty thing

Upon a fearful summons. I have heard

155   The cock, that is the trumpet to the morn,

Doth with his lofty and shrill-sounding throat

Awake the god of day, and at his warning,

快对我说!

若有什么善举能让你得到

安慰,也能使我感到体面,

快对我说!　　　　　　　　　　　　　　　　　　135

假如你知道祖国将面临危难,

那么,借助预知,也许能幸免,

噢,快说!

也许你将自己生前积聚的

不义之财深深地藏入地下,　　　　　　　　　　　140

听说你们鬼魂常因此出没。

快说,站住,快说!　　　　　　　　　　　　鸡叫。

截住它,马塞勒斯!

马塞勒斯	是否要用我的长戟刺它?	
何瑞修	它若不站住就刺。	
巴那多	在这儿!	145
何瑞修	在这儿!	鬼魂下。
马塞勒斯	它走了。	

对于这个如此尊贵的亡灵,

我们不该有任何冒犯举动,

因为它就像不会受伤的空气,　　　　　　　　　150

我们的徒劳打击只是虚张恶意。

巴那多	它刚要开口说话鸡就叫了。
何瑞修	它就像一位罪人听到骇人的

传唤为之一惊。　我曾经听说,

报晓的雄鸡,就是清晨的号角,　　　　　　　　155

用那高亢嘹亮的歌喉将白昼

之神唤醒,一听到它的警告,

Whether in sea or fire, in earth or air,

Th'extravagant and erring spirit hies

160 To his confine; and of the truth herein

This present object made probation.

Marcellus It faded on the crowing of the cock.

Some say that ever 'gainst that season comes

Wherein our Saviour's birth is celebrated,

165 This bird of dawning singeth all night long;

And then, they say, no spirit dare stir abroad,

The nights are wholesome, then no planets strike,

No fairy takes, nor witch hath power to charm,

So hallow'd and so gracious is that time.

170 **Horatio** So have I heard and do in part believe it.

But look, the morn in russet mantle clad

Walks o'er the dew of yon high eastward hill.

Break we our watch up, and by my advice

Let us impart what we have seen tonight

175 Unto young Hamlet; for upon my life

This spirit, dumb to us, will speak to him.

Do you consent we shall acquaint him with it

As needful in our loves, fitting our duty?

Marcellus Let's do't, I pray, and I this morning know

180 Where we shall find him most convenient.   *Exeunt.*

那些在海上、在火里、在地面，

或者在空中依然游荡的幽灵，

便会迅速返回各自的穴巢； 160

其中的真情已让这幽灵验证。

马塞勒斯 鬼魂在雄鸡啼鸣时隐退而去。

有人说就在我们庆贺救主

降临尘世的那个季节之前，

这只报晓的雄鸡整夜啼鸣； 165

他们说，当时，亡灵不敢骚动、

夜晚平安宁静、天体祥和运行、

精灵停止布咒、妖巫无力施魔，

此刻是如此圣洁，如此神圣。

何瑞修 我听人说过，现在也有些相信。 170

快看，那身披褐色斗篷的清晨，

正踏着高山的露珠从东方走来。

现在我们解散，我的建议是，

让我们把昨晚的所见透露给

小哈姆雷特；我以性命担保， 175

对我们沉默的幽灵，会对他讲话。

你们是否赞同将此事转告于他，

无论出于爱心，还是应尽义务？

马塞勒斯 我们告诉他吧，务请，我知道

今天上午最易在哪里见到他。 同下。 180

SCENE II

Flourish. Enter Claudius, King of Denmark,
Gertrude the Queen, Council, including Voltemand,
Cornelius, Polonius and his son Laertes,
Hamlet [dressed in black], with Others.

King
Though yet of Hamlet our dear brother's death
The memory be green, and that it us befitted
To bear our hearts in grief, and our whole kingdom
To be contracted in one brow of woe,

5
Yet so far hath discretion fought with nature
That we with wisest sorrow think on him
Together with remembrance of ourselves.
Therefore our sometime sister, now our queen,
Th'imperial jointress to this warlike state,

10
Have we, as 'twere with a defeated joy,
With an auspicious and a dropping eye,
With mirth in funeral and with dirge in marriage,
In equal scale weighing delight and dole,
Taken to wife. Nor have we herein barr'd

第二场

　　　　号角齐鸣。丹麦国王——克劳狄斯、
　　　　葛楚德王后、群臣，包括福提曼德、
　　　　科尼留斯、波洛纽斯及其儿子雷厄提斯、
　　　　*[身着黑衣的]*哈姆雷特，与众人上。

国王	尽管我对哈姆雷特兄长的	
	辞世记忆犹新，我们本该	
	心怀悲痛，我们全国上下	
	应该连成一体而满面愁容，	
	但理智与感情进行了交锋：	5
	对他表示适度哀悼的同时，	
	我也不应忘记自己的处境。	
	因此以前的长嫂，如今的王后，	
	这个尚武之邦的王室承继者，	
	就像是带着一种忧伤的喜悦，	10
	一只眼睛喜笑，一只眼睛哭泣，	
	葬礼上有欢颜，婚礼中伴挽歌，	
	喜悦与悲伤可谓旗鼓相当，	
	已结为夫妻。　就此我也未曾	

---

1. 2.　1-2. 兄长的辞世：在诸如丹麦这种君主制国家，克劳狄斯本可通过选举合法加冕，但他自身的处境，就像他的言辞一样，模棱两可、含糊不清——其油腔滑调的风格不能完全掩饰其对自身地位的不安（Gill）。　8. 以前的长嫂，如今的王后：王后原本为克劳狄斯的兄嫂；英格兰教会禁止类似的婚姻，认为这是乱伦（Gill）。

15   Your better wisdoms, which have freely gone

With this affair along. For all, our thanks.

Now follows that you know young Fortinbras,

Holding a weak supposal of our worth,

Or thinking by our late dear brother's death

20   Our state to be disjoint and out of frame,

Colleagued with this dream of his advantage,

He hath not fail'd to pester us with message

Importing the surrender of those lands

Lost by his father, with all bonds of law,

25   To our most valiant brother. So much for him.

Now for ourself, and for this time of meeting,

Thus much the business is: we have here writ

To Norway, uncle of young Fortinbras—

Who, impotent and bedrid, scarcely hears

30   Of this his nephew's purpose—to suppress

His further gait herein, in that the levies,

The lists, and full proportions are all made

Out of his subject; and we here dispatch

You, good Cornelius, and you, Voltemand,

35   For bearers of this greeting to old Norway,

Giving to you no further personal power

To business with the King more than the scope

Of these dilated articles allow.

Farewell, and let your haste commend your duty.

40 **Cor.**
    Volt. }   In that, and all things, will we show our duty.

King   We doubt it nothing. Heartily farewell.

忽略各位的高见,你们都欣然　　　　　　　　　　　15
接受这门亲事。　我谢谢大家。
下面要说的是小弗廷布拉,
他对我国的实力不屑一顾,
或以为因我兄长的新近过世,
我国会骚动不安,离析分崩,　　　　　　　　　　20
加上他可以居高临下的美梦,
便不断致函与我进行纠缠,
索要他父亲依据法律条文
划给我英勇王兄的那些领土。
关于小弗廷布拉,先讲这些。　　　　　　　　　　25
下面谈谈自己,和聚会的目的,
目前的情况是:我已给挪威王
写好国书,小弗廷布拉的叔父——
虚弱无力、卧床不起,很少听说
侄子的这一动机——让他阻止　　　　　　　　　　30
他的行动,因为他的税赋、
士兵以及军需全部出自于
他的臣民。　因此我现在派您,
好科尼留斯,还有您,福提曼德,
前去将此函送与挪威老王,　　　　　　　　　　　35
不许你们在这些详细规定的
许可范围以外,擅自与挪威
国王再进行任何别的摊牌。
再见,让你们的速度证明效忠。

| 科尼留斯
福提曼德 | 对此,及一切,我们都会尽职。 | 40 |
| 国王 | 我深信不疑。　祝你们一路平安! | |

21

Exeunt Voltemand and Cornelius.

And now, Laertes, what's the news with you?

You told us of some suit: what is't, Laertes?

You cannot speak of reason to the Dane

45   And loose your voice. What wouldst thou beg, Laertes,

That shall not be my offer, not thy asking?

The head is not more native to the heart,

The hand more instrumental to the mouth,

Than is the throne of Denmark to thy father.

What wouldst thou have, Laertes?

50 **Laertes**   My dread lord,

Your leave and favour to return to France,

From whence though willingly I came to Denmark

To show my duty in your coronation,

Yet now I must confess, that duty done,

55   My thoughts and wishes bend again toward France

And bow them to your gracious leave and pardon.

 King   Have you your father's leave? What says Polonius?

 Polonius He hath, my lord, wrung from me my slow leave

By laboursome petition, and at last

60   Upon his will I seal'd my hard consent.

I do beseech you give him leave to go.

 King   Take thy fair hour, Laertes, time be thine,

And thy best graces spend it at thy will.

　　　　　　　　　　　　　　　　　科尼留斯与福提曼德同下。

　　该您了,雷厄提斯,您有什么事?

　　您说过要求我:是什么,雷厄提斯?

　　您对丹麦王讲明理由不会

　　白费口舌。　什么请求,雷厄提斯,　　　　　　　　45

　　你若不请求,叫我如何准许?

　　丹麦国与你父亲之间的关系,

　　胜过头脑之与心脏休戚相关,

　　超越双手之与嘴巴乐此不疲。

　　你要什么,雷厄提斯?

雷厄提斯　　　　　　　　敬畏的陛下,　　　　　　　　50

　　请您开恩准许我返回法国,

　　尽管我情愿从那里赶回丹麦,

　　参加陛下的加冕以示效忠,

　　可现在必须明说,该职已尽,

　　我的心思和意愿又飞向法国,　　　　　　　　55

　　现恭请陛下能够宽恕与恩准。

国王　　您父亲答应吗?　波洛纽斯您说?

波洛纽斯　陛下,他费尽周折向我央求,

　　最终我才勉强在他的心愿

　　之上加封了艰难的"同意"二字。　　　　　　　　60

　　我请求陛下能够给他放行。

国王　　享受年华吧,雷厄提斯,时间归你,

　　你的才华可以任意发挥。

---

　　48. 头脑……心脏:克劳狄斯在用身体与政体之间的相似之处进行比喻,旨在强调丹麦王国与波洛纽斯之间的紧密关系。　在中世纪的譬喻中,国王通常被比作"首脑",大臣则为"心脏"。在下一句中,国王就是"双手",养活自己的臣民　("嘴巴")　(Jenkins)。

But now, my cousin Hamlet, and my son—

65 **Hamlet** A little more than kin, and less than kind.

King How is it that the clouds still hang on you?

Hamlet Not so, my lord, I am too much in the sun.

Queen Good Hamlet, cast thy nighted colour off,

And let thine eye look like a friend on Denmark.

70 Do not for ever with thy vailed lids

Seek for thy noble father in the dust.

Thou know'st 'tis common: all that lives must die,

Passing through nature to eternity.

Hamlet Ay, madam, it is common.

Queen If it be,

75 Why seems it so particular with thee?

Hamlet Seems, madam? Nay, it is. I know not 'seems'.

'Tis not alone my inky cloak, good mother,

Nor customary suits of solemn black,

Nor windy suspiration of forc'd breath,

80 No, nor the fruitful river in the eye,

Nor the dejected haviour of the visage,

Together with all forms, moods, shapes of grief,

That can denote me truly. These indeed seem,

For they are actions that a man might play;

85 But I have that within which passes show,

These but the trappings and the suits of woe.

好啦,我的侄儿哈姆雷特,我的儿——

哈姆雷特	血缘有余,但是亲情不足。	65
国王	您这人怎么依然阴云笼罩?	
哈姆雷特	不,陛下,我倒受不了太阳的热乎儿。	
王后	好哈姆雷特,快脱掉你的黑衣,	
	你要把丹麦国王看成朋友。	
	不要总是用你那沮丧的目光	70
	去追寻你已经入土的慈父。	
	你知道这很普通:活着的必死,	
	都要通过世间进入永恒。	
哈姆雷特	是的,夫人,是很普通。	
王后	若这样,	
	那为啥对你又好像如此不同?	75
哈姆雷特	是"好像"吗,夫人?　不,是的确。	
	既不是我漆黑的外套,好母亲,	
	也不是庄严肃穆的传统丧服,	
	也不是迫不得已的唉声叹气,	
	不,也不是将泪水汇成江河,	80
	也不是面部沮丧消沉的表情,	
	纵有悲痛的千形万状,也不能	
	表达我的真情。　它们才是"好像",	
	因为这些行为人们可以表演,	
	它们只是悲伤的外衣和装扮,	85
	而我内心的悲痛却无法外显。	

67. 我倒受不了太阳的热乎儿:原文"sun (太阳)"与64行的"son (儿子)"为谐音双关。哈姆雷特此刻心情忧郁,更愿隐藏起来,讨厌被带到大庭广众之下,或宫廷的欢乐之中,或是更为明确地讨厌国王的恩宠。"太阳"传统上可象征"王室、国王"。哈姆雷特觉得他与克劳狄斯之间的关系有些"过亲",而克劳狄斯对他的称呼则有些"过分"(因为他们并非真正意义上的父子)。哈姆雷特以此强烈地驳斥了国王将其称为"儿子"的主张(Jenkins)。"热乎儿",可指国王的恩宠、亲热,译文中的"乎"同"呼"字谐音,希望能以此对原文的双关之义有所传达。　——译者附注。

King	'Tis sweet and commendable in your nature, Hamlet,
	To give these mourning duties to your father,
	But you must know your father lost a father,
90	That father lost, lost his—and the survivor bound
	In filial obligation for some term
	To do obsequious sorrow. But to persever
	In obstinate condolement is a course
	Of impious stubbornness, 'tis unmanly grief,
95	It shows a will most incorrect to heaven,
	A heart unfortified, a mind impatient,
	An understanding simple and unschool'd;
	For what we know must be, and is as common
	As any the most vulgar thing to sense—
100	Why should we in our peevish opposition
	Take it to heart? Fie, 'tis a fault to heaven,
	A fault against the dead, a fault to nature,
	To reason most absurd, whose common theme
	Is death of fathers, and who still hath cried
105	From the first corse till he that died today,
	'This must be so'. We pray you throw to earth
	This unprevailing woe, and think of us
	As of a father; for let the world take note
	You are the most immediate to our throne,
110	And with no less nobility of love
	Than that which dearest father bears his son
	Do I impart toward you. For your intent

国王　　　　您向亡父致哀尽孝的品性，

哈姆雷特，令人高兴、值得颂扬，

但要知道，您父亲失去过父亲，

那位失去的父亲也失去过父亲——　　　　　　　90

孩子出于孝道理应对亡父

表示一段时间的哀悼。　然而，

顽固地沉溺于哀伤只是一种

不敬的偏执、一种懦弱的悲伤，

表明那是对上天的公然违抗，　　　　　　　　95

表明他信念不足、缺乏忍耐，

表明他理解简单和缺乏教养；

既然我们知道此事难以避免，

跟其他显见的事情一样普通——

那为何还要对此耿耿于怀？　　　　　　　　　100

呸，这是违背天理的罪行，

对死者的亵渎、对自然的违抗，

荒谬绝伦、缺乏理性，因为

自然的普遍主题便是丧父，

从第一具尸体到今天的死者，　　　　　　　　105

它总在呼喊"此事不可避免"。

求您埋葬徒劳的悲伤，把我

当成亲父；我要让世界知道，

您是我最直接的王位继承人，

我要像最为慈祥的父亲疼爱　　　　　　　　　110

自己的儿子，向您奉献我的

崇高爱心。　至于您想返回

---

105. 第一具尸体：亚当与夏娃之子亚伯（Abel），为其胞兄该隐（Gain）所害（见《圣经》"创世纪"4章8节）（Gill）。

In going back to school in Wittenberg,

It is most retrograde to our desire,

115   And we beseech you bend you to remain

Here in the cheer and comfort of our eye,

Our chiefest courtier, cousin, and our son.

Queen   Let not thy mother lose her prayers, Hamlet.

I pray thee stay with us, go not to Wittenberg.

120 **Hamlet**   I shall in all my best obey you, madam.

King   Why, 'tis a loving and a fair reply.

Be as ourself in Denmark. Madam, come.

This gentle and unforc'd accord of Hamlet

Sits smiling to my heart; in grace whereof

125   No jocund health that Denmark drinks today

But the great cannon to the clouds shall tell,

And the King's rouse the heaven shall bruit again,

Re-speaking earthly thunder. Come away.

Flourish. Exeunt all but Hamlet.

Hamlet   O that this too too sullied flesh would melt,

130   Thaw and resolve itself into a dew,

Or that the Everlasting had not fix'd

	威登堡大学继续求学的意愿，	
	这可与我的心愿完全相反，	
	我求您能够屈身留在这里，	115
	看到您我会感到赏心悦目，	
	我的首席大臣、侄儿和儿子。	
王后	别让妈妈的祈祷白费，哈姆雷特。	
	我求你留下来吧，别去威登堡。	
哈姆雷特	我会尽力听您的吩咐，夫人。	120
国王	哎，这是个可爱和动听的回答。	
	在丹麦您跟我一样。　来，夫人。	
	哈姆雷特的这种温和与顺从	
	令我心旷神怡；为了表示谢意，	
	丹麦王今天的每一次举杯，	125
	都要让礼炮之声昭告云端，	
	响彻天空的炮声荡回大地，	
	再次宣告国王的畅饮。　走吧。	

号角齐鸣。除哈姆雷特以外全下。

哈姆雷特	但愿这肮脏透顶的肉体能消融，	
	将自身融化消解成一滴雨露，	130
	或者是上帝不曾下达禁止	

113. 威登堡大学：德国的一所大学，创建于 1502 年（Jenkins）。 120. 听您的吩咐：哈姆雷特有意对克劳狄斯的劝告不屑一顾（Jenkins）。 122. 跟我一样：犹如国王（Thompson）。 125. 每一次举杯：国王的纵酒引人注目；与其相关的每件事情均可成为喝酒的良机。 参见：1.4.8-20, 2.2.84, 3.2.294, 3.3.89, 5.2.264，与最终的报应——5.2.330-1（Jenkins）。 126. 礼炮……云端：这种庆贺方式属于丹麦的风俗，表明莎士比亚有意在剧中展示一些地方色彩。 类似的庆贺方式另见：1.4.6, 5.2.267-75（Jenkins）。 129. 肮脏透顶的肉体：之所以肮脏是因为他是人——易于犯罪；同时也因为他是其母亲肉体中的一部分（Gill）。 131-2. 禁止自杀的律令：基督教教义十诫中的第六条规定："不准杀生"， 一般理解为禁止自杀。 请参见《圣经》"出埃及记"20 章 13 节（Gill）。

His canon 'gainst self-slaughter. O God! God!

How weary, stale, flat, and unprofitable

Seem to me all the uses of this world!

135 Fie on't, ah fie, 'tis an unweeded garden

That grows to seed; things rank and gross in nature

Possess it merely. That it should come to this!

But two months dead—nay, not so much, not two—

So excellent a king, that was to this

140 Hyperion to a satyr, so loving to my mother

That he might not beteem the winds of heaven

Visit her face too roughly. Heaven and earth,

Must I remember? Why, she would hang on him

As if increase of appetite had grown

145 By what it fed on; and yet within a month—

Let me not think on't—Frailty, thy name is woman—

A little month, or ere those shoes were old

With which she follow'd my poor father's body,

Like Niobe, all tears—why, she—

150 O God, a beast that wants discourse of reason

Would have mourn'd longer—married with my uncle,

My father's brother—but no more like my father

Than I to Hercules. Within a month,

自杀的律令！噢，上帝啊！上帝！

这个世界的一切对我来说

是多么可厌、陈腐、乏味和无用！

呸，啊呸，这是一片荒芜的花园，   135

让茂密污秽的杂草遍地丛生、

肆意繁衍。 结果竟然会这样！

去世才俩月——不，还不到，不到——

一位多好的君王，与这位相比，

真是天神之与怪兽。 他是如此   140

疼爱我的母亲，竟不许天风

将她的脸庞吹疼。 天啊，地呀！

我怎能忘记？ 唉，犹如享用了

佳肴会使胃口大增，她对父亲

曾是不离形影；却在一月之内——   145

不想他了——脆弱啊，你的名字是女人——

仅仅一个月，就在她为可怜的

父亲奔丧所穿的鞋子破旧之前，

简直像个泪人——唉，她——

噢，上帝，缺乏理性的畜生都会   150

哀悼得更久——她就嫁给我的叔父，

我父亲的弟弟——可他不像我父亲，

我也不像赫克勒斯。 一月之内，

---

140. 天神（Hyperion，许珀里翁）：希腊神话中光荣的太阳神（Gill）。 140. 怪兽（Satyr，萨梯）：希腊神话中一种半人半羊的怪物；另外，该词也可指酒鬼或好色之徒（Thompson）。 141-2. 不许……吹疼：相比之下，王后的爱则更像是肉欲 （见下文 143-4）（Jenkins）。 149. 泪人（Niobe，尼俄伯）：希腊神话中悲伤女性的代表，为自己被杀的子女悲痛欲绝、哭泣不止，最终化成石头继续流泪（Jenkins）。 153. 赫克勒斯 （Hercules）：希腊神话中的超人。 哈姆雷特在尚未知晓自己的使命之前，已经意识到自身的不足（Jenkins）。

Ere yet the salt of most unrighteous tears

155 Had left the flushing in her galled eyes,

She married—O most wicked speed! To post

With such dexterity to incestuous sheets!

It is not, nor it cannot come to good.

But break, my heart, for I must hold my tongue.

Enter Horatio, Marcellus, and Barnardo.

Horatio Hail to your lordship.

160 **Hamlet**   I am glad to see you well.

Horatio, or I do forget myself.

Horatio The same, my lord, and your poor servant ever.

Hamlet Sir, my good friend, I'll change that name with you.

And what make you from Wittenberg, Horatio? —

165 Marcellus.

Marcellus My good lord.

Hamlet I am very glad to see you. —[*to Barnardo*] Good even,

sir. —

But what in faith make you from Wittenberg?

Horatio A truant disposition, good my lord.

170 **Hamlet** I would not hear your enemy say so,

Nor shall you do mine ear that violence

To make it truster of your own report

Against yourself. I know you are no truant.

But what is your affair in Elsinore?

175 We'll teach you to drink deep ere you depart.

她那虚伪的眼泪还没擦干，

她那双眼的红肿尚未消退，　　　　　　　　　　　155

就改嫁与人——噢，最可恶的迅速！

竟如此娴熟地钻进乱伦的被褥！

这很不光彩，也不会得到好报。

碎了，我的心，因为我必须闭嘴。

何瑞修、马塞勒斯与巴那多上。

何瑞修	向殿下致意。
哈姆雷特	见您安好我很高兴。　　　　160

是何瑞修，假如我没有认错。

何瑞修	正是，殿下，您一如既往的奴仆。
哈姆雷特	先生，是好友，我愿意这样称呼。

您为何离开了威登堡，何瑞修？　——

马塞勒斯！　　　　　　　　　　　165

马塞勒斯	我的好殿下。
哈姆雷特	见到您我非常高兴。　——〔向巴那多〕下午好，

先生！　——

可您究竟为何要离开威登堡？

何瑞修	我是想要逃学，我的好殿下。
哈姆雷特	您的仇敌这么说我都不接受，　　　　170

即使您能将我的耳朵刺破，

也无法让它相信您对自己的

恶意中伤。　我知道您不会闲逛。

但是您到埃尔西诺来做什么？

离开前我们会教您如何酗酒。　　　　　　175

---

154. 虚伪的眼泪：因为她的行为出卖了她的眼泪（Jenkins）。　159. 必须闭嘴：据说未吐露的痛苦会令人心碎（Jenkins）。　175. 如何酗酒：哈姆雷特在嘲笑丹麦人的饮酒习惯（Gill）。

	Horatio	My lord, I came to see your father's funeral.
	Hamlet	I prithee do not mock me, fellow-student.
		I think it was to see my mother's wedding.
	Horatio	Indeed, my lord, it follow'd hard upon.
180	**Hamlet**	Thrift, thrift, Horatio. The funeral bak'd meats
		Did coldly furnish forth the marriage tables.
		Would I had met my dearest foe in heaven
		Or ever I had seen that day, Horatio.
		My father—methinks I see my father—
	Horatio	Where, my lord?
185	**Hamlet**	In my mind's eye, Horatio.
	Horatio	I saw him once; a was a goodly king.
	Hamlet	A was a man, take him for all in all:
		I shall not look upon his like again.
	Horatio	My lord, I think I saw him yesternight.
	Hamlet	Saw? Who?
190	**Horatio**	My lord, the king your father.
	Hamlet	The king my father?
	Horatio	Season your admiration for a while
		With an attent ear till I may deliver
		Upon the witness of these gentlemen
		This marvel to you.
195	**Hamlet**	For God's love let me hear!
	Horatio	Two nights together had these gentlemen,
		Marcellus and Barnardo, on their watch
		In the dead waste and middle of the night
		Been thus encounter'd: a figure like your father

何瑞修	殿下,我是来看您父亲的葬礼。	
哈姆雷特	求您别嘲笑我了,我的校友。	
	我想您是来看我母亲的婚礼。	
何瑞修	不错,殿下,婚礼紧随其后。	
哈姆雷特	真节俭啊,何瑞修! 葬礼的残羹	180
	冷炙正好摆向婚宴的餐桌。	
	宁愿在天上遇见我的仇敌,	
	也不愿见到那一天,何瑞修!	
	我的父亲——我仿佛看到了父亲——	
何瑞修	在哪里,殿下?	
哈姆雷特	在我心眼里,何瑞修。	185
何瑞修	我见过他一次,他是位好国王。	
哈姆雷特	他是男子的典范,尽善尽美:	
	我再也见不到他那样的完人。	
何瑞修	殿下,我昨晚好像看见他了。	
哈姆雷特	看见? 谁?	
何瑞修	是您的父王,殿下。	190
哈姆雷特	我的父王?	
何瑞修	请您对自己的惊讶稍加克制,	
	仔细听我将那段奇遇禀报,	
	现有这两位先生在此作为	
	见证。	
哈姆雷特	看在上帝的份上,快说!	195
何瑞修	连续两个夜晚,这两位先生,	
	马塞勒斯和巴那多,他们在	
	万籁俱静的午夜放哨时意外	
	碰见了:一个像您父亲的身影,	

---

182. 在天上遇见我的仇敌:死去,旨在加强语气(Thompson)。

200   Armed at point exactly, cap-à-pie,

       Appears before them, and with solemn march

       Goes slow and stately by them; thrice he walk'd

       By their oppress'd and fear-surprised eyes

       Within his truncheon's length, whilst they, distill'd

205   Almost to jelly with the act of fear,

       Stand dumb and speak not to him. This to me

       In dreadful secrecy impart they did,

       And I with them the third night kept the watch,

       Where, as they had deliver'd, both in time,

210   Form of the thing, each word made true and good,

       The apparition comes. I knew your father;

       These hands are not more like.

Hamlet   But where was this?

Marcellus My lord, upon the platform where we watch.

Hamlet   Did you not speak to it?

Horatio   My lord, I did,

215   But answer made it none. Yet once methought

       It lifted up it head and did address

       Itself to motion like as it would speak.

       But even then the morning cock crew loud,

       And at the sound it shrunk in haste away

       And vanish'd from our sight.

220 **Hamlet**   'Tis very strange.

Horatio   As I do live, my honour'd lord, 'tis true;

       And we did think it writ down in our duty

       To let you know of it.

Hamlet   Indeed, sirs; but this troubles me.

那身影全副武装，从头到脚，　　　　　　　　　200

在他们面前出现，以庄严的步伐

从他们身旁舒缓走过；他三次

从他们困惑与惊恐的眼前穿过，

相距不过他的权杖之遥，而他们，

因为害怕几乎被吓成肉冻，　　　　　　　　　205

目瞪口呆地站着，没对他说话。

他们悄悄地将此事告知于我，

第三夜我去跟他们一起守望。

那个东西出没的时间和形状，

与他们描绘的情况一模一样，　　　　　　　　210

鬼魂再现。　我熟悉您的父亲；

他与鬼魂就像双手一样。

哈姆雷特　　　　　　　　　　　　在哪里？

马塞勒斯　殿下，在我们放哨的瞭望台上。

哈姆雷特　您没对它说话？

何瑞修　　　　　　　我说了，殿下，

但它并没回答。　但我想有一次，　　　　　　215

它曾经抬起了头部并且动了

一下，好像它要开口说话。

但就在此刻雄鸡开始鸣叫，

一听到鸡叫，它便匆忙隐身，

从我们眼前消失。

哈姆雷特　　　　　　　真是奇怪。　　　　　220

何瑞修　正像我还活着，尊敬的殿下，真的；

我们认为让您知道此事

应是我们的职责。

哈姆雷特　没错，先生们；可这让我不安。

Hold you the watch tonight?

225 **All**   We do, my lord.

Hamlet Arm'd, say you?

All   Arm'd, my lord.

Hamlet From top to toe?

All   My lord, from head to foot.

Hamlet Then saw you not his face?

Horatio O yes, my lord, he wore his beaver up.

230 **Hamlet** What look'd he, frowningly?

Horatio A countenance more in sorrow than in anger.

Hamlet Pale, or red?

Horatio Nay, very pale.

Hamlet   And fix'd his eyes upon you?

Horatio Most constantly.

Hamlet   I would I had been there.

Horatio It would have much amaz'd you.

235 **Hamlet**   Very like.

Stay'd it long?

Horatio While one with moderate haste might tell a hundred.

Mar.
Bar. } Longer, longer.

Horatio Not when I saw't.

240 **Hamlet** His beard was grizzled, no?

Horatio It was as I have seen it in his life,

A sable silver'd.

Hamlet   I will watch tonight.

Perchance 'twill walk again.

	你们今晚还放哨吗？	
众人	放哨，殿下。	225
哈姆雷特	身穿盔甲，是吗？	
众人	是的，殿下。	
哈姆雷特	从头到脚？	
众人	从头到脚，殿下。	
哈姆雷特	没看见他的脸吗？	
何瑞修	噢，看见了，殿下，他掀起了面甲。	
哈姆雷特	他表情怎样，严肃吗？	230
何瑞修	与其说愤怒，倒不如说忧伤。	
哈姆雷特	脸白，还是红？	
何瑞修	不红，煞白。	
哈姆雷特	他的眼睛盯着你们？	
何瑞修	目不转睛。	
哈姆雷特	但愿我当时在场。	
何瑞修	那定会让您惊恐万状。	
哈姆雷特	很可能。	235
	它待得久吗？	
何瑞修	若用一般的速度可数到一百。	
马塞勒斯 和巴那多	更长，更长！	
何瑞修	当时就那么长。	
哈姆雷特	他胡子花白，对吗？	240
何瑞修	就像我在他生前所见的一样， 黑白相间。	
哈姆雷特	我今夜要去站岗。 也许它会再现。	

---

229. 面甲：头盔上的护脸面罩，可上下移动（Jenkins）。

Horatio		I war'nt it will.
Hamlet	If it assume my noble father's person,	
245	I'll speak to it though hell itself should gape	
	And bid me hold my peace. I pray you all,	
	If you have hitherto conceal'd this sight,	
	Let it be tenable in your silence still;	
	And whatsomever else shall hap tonight,	
250	Give it an understanding but no tongue.	
	I will requite your loves. So fare you well.	
	Upon the platform 'twixt eleven and twelve	
	I'll visit you.	
All	Our duty to your honour.	
Hamlet	Your loves, as mine to you. Farewell.	

Exeunt Horatio, Marcellus, and Barnardo.

255　My father's spirit—in arms! All is not well.

I doubt some foul play. Would the night were come.

Till then sit still, my soul. Foul deeds will rise,

Though all the earth o'erwhelm them, to men's eyes.

Exit.

何瑞修	我保证它会的。
哈姆雷特	假如它以我父亲的身影出现，

哈姆雷特　假如它以我父亲的身影出现，
　　　　　哪怕地狱张开大口让我闭嘴，　　　　　　　　　　245
　　　　　我也要对它说话。　我求你们，
　　　　　如尚未把这种现象透露出去，
　　　　　那就请你们继续保持沉默；
　　　　　无论今晚还会发生些什么，
　　　　　你们只能意会不可言传。　　　　　　　　　　　　250
　　　　　我会报答你们的爱心。　再见。
　　　　　晚上十一二点之间，到瞭望台
　　　　　见面。

众人　　　　　　　为您效劳是我们的职责。
哈姆雷特　是爱心，正如我对你们一样，再见。

　　　　　　　　　　　　何瑞修、马塞勒斯与巴那多同下。

　　　　　父亲的亡魂——身穿盔甲！事情不妙；　　　　255
　　　　　我怀疑有诈。　愿夜幕赶快降临。
　　　　　要安静，我的心。　恶行终将败露，
　　　　　哪怕用所有泥土也无法盖住。

　　　　　　　　　　　　　　　　　　　　　　　　下。

---

256. 怀疑有诈：哈姆雷特马上意识到鬼魂显灵的另一理由（何瑞修在第一场中并未提及），即：它有意向人们揭露世间的罪恶（Gill）。

SCENE III

Enter Laertes and Ophelia, his sister.

Laertes		My necessaries are embark'd. Farewell.
		And sister, as the winds give benefit
		And convoy is assistant, do not sleep,
		But let me hear from you.
	Ophelia	Do you doubt that?
5	**Laertes**	For Hamlet, and the trifling of his favour,
		Hold it a fashion and a toy in blood,
		A violet in the youth of primy nature,
		Forward, not permanent, sweet, not lasting,
		The perfume and suppliance of a minute,
		No more.
	Ophelia	No more but so?
10	**Laertes**	Think it no more.
		For nature crescent does not grow alone
		In thews and bulk, but as this temple waxes,
		The inward service of the mind and soul
		Grows wide withal. Perhaps he loves you now,
15		And now no soil nor cautel doth besmirch

第三场

雷厄提斯与妹妹——奥菲丽娅上。

雷厄提斯 我的行李已经上船。 再见。

妹妹啊,如果是风向帮忙儿,

交通也很方便,可不要贪睡,

要给我写信。

奥菲丽娅 这还用您怀疑?

雷厄提斯 至于哈姆雷特,及其感情的玩弄, 5

要视为一时的冲动、青年的本性,

一朵初春时节绽放的紫罗兰,

早开而短暂,芬芳却不长久,

不过是一分钟的芳香与悦目,

而已。

奥菲丽娅 仅此而已?

雷厄提斯 别想它了。 10

因为成长不只是筋骨与体格的

增强,而是随着躯壳的增大,

内心深处的责任也会相应

拓宽。 也许他现在真的爱您,

目前还没有什么恶劣行径 15

---

1. 3. 5.感情的玩弄:雷厄提斯与波洛纽斯均认为哈姆雷特是在玩弄奥菲丽娅的感情
(Gill)。 8.芬芳却不长久:富有讥讽意味的是,好像的确如此。 参见 3.1.99(Jenkins)。
13-4.责任……拓宽:雷厄提斯暗示哈姆雷特不仅要考虑对奥菲丽娅的爱情,还要考虑其他更多的
事情(Gill)。

The virtue of his will; but you must fear,

His greatness weigh'd, his will is not his own.

For he himself is subject to his birth:

He may not, as unvalu'd persons do,

20 Carve for himself, for on his choice depends

The sanity and health of this whole state;

And therefore must his choice be circumscrib'd

Unto the voice and yielding of that body

Whereof he is the head. Then if he says he loves you,

25 It fits your wisdom so far to believe it

As he in his particular act and place

May give his saying deed; which is no further

Than the main voice of Denmark goes withal.

Then weigh what loss your honour may sustain

30 If with too credent ear you list his songs,

Or lose your heart, or your chaste treasure open

To his unmaster'd importunity.

Fear it, Ophelia, fear it, my dear sister,

And keep you in the rear of your affection

35 Out of the shot and danger of desire.

The chariest maid is prodigal enough

If she unmask her beauty to the moon.

Virtue itself scapes not calumnious strokes.

The canker galls the infants of the spring

40 Too oft before their buttons be disclos'd,

And in the morn and liquid dew of youth

玷污他的纯情；但您要注意，

考虑到他的显贵，他身不由己。

因为他本人要受身份支配：

他也许不能像平民那样可以

自作主张，因为他的选择 20

涉及整个国家的康健与富强；

因此他的选择必须得到

他在其中作为首脑的那个

政体的同意。 如果他说他爱您，

您要明白，您只能就其 25

特殊身份能够说到做到的

地步予以相信；他的行动

不能超越丹麦人的许可范围。

要考虑您会遭受多大的毁誉，

假如您轻信他的甜言蜜语， 30

或者对他倾心相爱，或者对

他那失控的强求以身相许。

当心啊，奥菲丽娅，亲爱的妹妹，

您要把自己藏在感情的后方，

以免欲望的利箭将您射中。 35

纯洁的姑娘已属相当放浪，

如果她面向月亮展露娇容。

贞节本身难逃诽谤和中伤。

春天的蓓蕾在花瓣展开之前，

常会遭受尺蠖的骚扰与叮咬。 40

因此晶莹剔透的青春年华

23. 作为首脑：雷厄提斯认为哈姆雷特迟早要继承王位（Gill）。 34-5. 藏在……后方……以免射中：在这一则富有军事意味的比喻中，奥菲丽娅的感情被喻为先遣部队，去面对危险；而她本身则应留在后方，以免被敌军击中（Jenkins）。

Contagious blastments are most imminent.

Be wary then: best safety lies in fear.

Youth to itself rebels, though none else near.

45 **Ophelia** I shall th'effect of this good lesson keep

As watchman to my heart. But good my brother,

Do not as some ungracious pastors do,

Show me the steep and thorny way to heaven,

Whiles like a puff'd and reckless libertine

50 Himself the primrose path of dalliance treads,

And recks not his own rede.

Laertes O fear me not.

I stay too long.

Enter Polonius.

But here my father comes.

A double blessing is a double grace:

Occasion smiles upon a second leave.

55 **Polonius** Yet here, Laertes? Aboard, aboard for shame.

The wind sits in the shoulder of your sail,

And you are stay'd for. There, my blessing with thee.

And these few precepts in thy memory

Look thou characteR. Give thy thoughts no tongue,

60 Nor any unproportion'd thought his act.

Be thou familiar, but by no means vulgar;

Those friends thou hast, and their adoption tried,

Grapple them unto thy soul with hoops of steel,

But do not dull thy palm with entertainment

易遭受迫在眉睫的侵害和摧残。

要当心：最好的安全在于警惕。

青春自会骚动，无须别的刺激。

奥菲丽娅　　我会把此番劝诫当成警卫　　　　　　　　45

把守我的心。　可是我的好哥哥，

不要像某些虚伪的牧师那样，

为我指明通向天堂的艰辛路，

而他自己却像一位浮夸

放荡的浪子穿梭于花街柳巷，　　　　　　　　50

把自己的劝告遗忘。

雷厄提斯　　　　　　　　噢，别担心！

我该走了。

波洛纽斯上。

可父亲已经来临。

两度的祝福就是双重恩赐：

再次的告别确实令人庆幸。

波洛纽斯　　还没走，雷厄提斯？　快上船，不像话！　　55

现在正好顺风，大家都在等你。

好吧，现在我来为你祝福。

下面这些劝诫你定要牢记：

不要让自己的思想脱口而出，

不要把鲁莽的念头付诸行动。　　　　　　　　60

平易近人，但不能自我贬低；

那些早已经过考验的朋友，

要用钢箍将他们牢系在心，

但是不要对那些新交的年轻

65	Of each new-hatch'd, unfledg'd courage. Beware
	Of entrance to a quarrel, but being in,
	Bear't that th'opposed may beware of thee.
	Give every man thy ear, but few thy voice;
	Take each man's censure, but reserve thy judgment.
70	Costly thy habit as thy purse can buy,
	But not express'd in fancy; rich, not gaudy;
	For the apparel oft proclaims the man,
	And they in France of the best rank and station
	Are of a most select and generous chief in that.
75	Neither a borrower nor a lender be,
	For loan oft loses both itself and friend,
	And borrowing dulls the edge of husbandry.
	This above all: to thine own self be true,
	And it must follow as the night the day
80	Thou canst not then be false to any man.
	Farewell, my blessing season this in thee.

Laertes Most humbly do I take my leave, my lord.

Polonius The time invests you; go, your servants tend.

Laertes Farewell, Ophelia, and remember well
What I have said to you.

85 **Ophelia**   'Tis in my memory lock'd,
And you yourself shall keep the key of it.

Laertes Farewell.   *Exit.*

Polonius What is't, Ophelia, he hath said to you?

Ophelia So please you, something touching the Lord Hamlet.

90 **Polonius** Marry, well bethought.

	侠客热情洋溢。 注意不要跟	65
	别人争吵,可一旦争吵起来,	
	就要让对手知道你并非好惹。	
	倾听别人谈话,不要轻易发言;	
	接纳他人意见,但要进行判断。	
	要尽财力所能购买高档衣服,	70
	但别赶时髦;华丽而不浮艳;	
	因为服饰往往会体现人品,	
	法国的那些名流要人都以	
	服饰品位的高雅而出类拔萃。	
	不要向人借钱,也别借钱给人,	75
	因为借钱给人往往人财两空,	
	向人借钱则削弱节俭的利锋。	
	尤其是:你自己要表里如一,	
	犹如白天过后定是黑夜,	
	你就不会背信于任何别人。	80
	再见,愿我的祝福让劝告对你生效。	
雷厄提斯	我最恭敬地向您告辞,父亲。	
波洛纽斯	时间在催你;走吧,仆人在等。	
雷厄提斯	再见了,奥菲丽娅,您要好好	
	记住我的话。	
奥菲丽娅	已经锁进我的心,	85
	然而开启的钥匙由您来保存。	
雷厄提斯	再见了。	下。
波洛纽斯	他对你说了些什么,奥菲丽娅?	
奥菲丽娅	禀报父亲,与哈姆雷特殿下有关。	
波洛纽斯	天哪,想得很周到!	90

81. 愿……生效:原文中 Season = ripen, mature; this = my advice(Thompson)。

'Tis told me he hath very oft of late

Given private time to you, and you yourself

Have of your audience been most free and bounteous.

If it be so—as so 'tis put on me,

95 And that in way of caution—I must tell you

You do not understand yourself so clearly

As it behoves my daughter and your honour.

What is between you? Give me up the truth.

Ophelia   He hath, my lord, of late made many tenders

100 Of his affection to me.

Polonius   Affection? Pooh, you speak like a green girl,

Unsifted in such perilous circumstance.

Do you believe his tenders, as you call them?

Ophelia   I do not know, my lord, what I should think.

105 **Polonius**   Marry, I will teach you. Think yourself a baby

That you have ta'en these tenders for true pay

Which are not sterling. Tender yourself more dearly

Or—not to crack the wind of the poor phrase,

Running it thus—you'll tender me a fool.

110 **Ophelia**   My lord, he hath importun'd me with love

In honourable fashion.

Polonius   Ay, fashion you may call it. Go to, go to.

Ophelia   And hath given countenance to his speech, my lord,

With almost all the holy vows of heaven.

115 **Polonius**   Ay, springes to catch woodcocks. I do know,

When the blood burns, how prodigal the soul

Lends the tongue vows. These blazes, daughter,

人们告诉我他近来频繁地

和你幽会,而你自己对他

也是非常大方、有求必应。

果真如此——人们如此告诫,

为了保持警惕——我得告诉你,　　　　　　　　　　95

你对什么举止才适合我的

女儿和你的名声还了解不清。

你们都做了什么?　快如实讲明。

奥菲丽娅　　他近来,父亲,经常向我表白

他的爱慕之情。　　　　　　　　　　　　　100

波洛纽斯　　爱慕之情?　噗,真是个稚嫩的女孩,

从来还未经历过类似的险境。

难道你就相信他的所谓表白?

奥菲丽娅　　我不知道,父亲,该如何思想?

波洛纽斯　　天哪,我教你:要把你想成婴孩儿,　　105

你将他的虚情假意当成了

肺腑之言。　你可要多加自重,

否则——弯子不能绕得太远,

这样绕下去——会把你绕成傻瓜。

奥菲丽娅　　父亲,他向我求爱的方式可是　　　　110

光明正大。

波洛纽斯　　对,方式,你可以这么说。　得啦,得啦!

奥菲丽娅　　为了证明他的真心,父亲,

他的话几乎都是山盟海誓。

波洛纽斯　　对,捕捉丘鹬的圈套。　我知道,　　　　115

欲火燃烧时脑袋会让嘴巴

信誓旦旦。　这些火焰,女儿啊,

---

115. 捕捉丘鹬的圈套:谚语。　丘鹬被认为是一种"笨鸟",易中圈套（Gill）。　另见 5.2.312（Jenkins）。

Giving more light than heat, extinct in both

Even in their promise as it is a-making,

120   You must not take for fire. From this time

Be something scanter of your maiden presence,

Set your entreatments at a higher rate

Than a command to parley. For Lord Hamlet,

Believe so much in him that he is young,

125   And with a larger tether may he walk

Than may be given you. In few, Ophelia,

Do not believe his vows; for they are brokers

Not of that dye which their investments show,

But mere implorators of unholy suits,

130   Breathing like sanctified and pious bawds

The better to beguile. This is for all.

I would not, in plain terms, from this time forth

Have you so slander any moment leisure

As to give words or talk with the Lord Hamlet.

135   Look to't, I charge you. Come your ways.

Ophelia   I shall obey, my lord.   *Exeunt.*

发出来的更多是光而非热，

誓言发出时都会光消热散，

千万不要把它们当成真情。　　　　　　　　　　120

今后你可要减少抛头露面，

你要抬高身价，别一听招呼

就出面相谈。　至于哈姆雷特殿下，

你应该相信的是，他还年轻，

而且他的活动空间要比　　　　　　　　　　　125

你的更大。　总之，奥菲丽娅，

别信他的誓言；因为那只是

表里不一、口是心非的掮客，

不过是罪恶勾当的诉求者，

犹如貌似正经而真诚的老鸨，　　　　　　　　130

更容易让人上当。　到此为止。

说白了，那就是从现在开始，

不许你再糟蹋自己的闲暇，

给哈姆雷特殿下捎信或谈话。

要当心，我命令你！快跟我来！　　　　　　　135

奥菲丽娅　　我听您的，父亲。　　　　　　　　　同下。

---

123. 出面洽谈：利用军事术语来形容求爱是一种传统。　奥菲丽娅在此被喻为城堡的守卫者，不能因为围攻者提出了谈判的请求就轻易接待或与之洽谈（Jenkins）。

SCENE IV

Enter Hamlet, Horatio, and Marcellus.

Hamlet   The air bites shrewdly, it is very cold.

Horatio   It is a nipping and an eager air.

Hamlet   What hour now?

Horatio   I think it lacks of twelve.

Marcellus   No, it is struck.

Horatio   Indeed? I heard it not.

5   It then draws near the season

Wherein the spirit held his wont to walk.

A flourish of trumpets, and two pieces [of ordnance] go off.

What does this mean, my lord?

Hamlet   The King doth wake tonight and takes his rouse,

Keeps wassail, and the swagg'ring upspring reels;

10   And as he drains his draughts of Rhenish down,

The kettle-drum and trumpet thus bray out

The triumph of his pledge.

第四场

哈姆雷特、何瑞修与马塞勒斯上。

哈姆雷特	现在寒风刺骨，天气真冷。	
何瑞修	真是寒风凛冽、冷气逼人。	
哈姆雷特	现在几点？	
何瑞修	我想还不到十二点。	
马塞勒斯	到了，钟已敲过。	
何瑞修	真的？　我没听见。	

那么此刻已经接近　　　　　　　　　　　　　　　　5

那个幽灵惯于出没的时刻。

　　　　　　　　　　　　　　　号角齐鸣，火炮两声。

这是什么意思，殿下？

哈姆雷特	今天夜里国王要举杯畅饮，	

他要纵酒欢闹、手舞足蹈；

每当他喝干一杯莱茵美酒，　　　　　　　　　　　10

都会这样锣鼓喧天、号角齐鸣，

以此宣告他的欢庆。

　　1.4.　　6.（舞台指示）火炮两声，为1.2.126所指的礼炮。 具有讽刺效果的是——也许读者或观众不一定意识到——克劳狄斯用来庆贺哈姆雷特答应留在丹麦的礼炮，却让哈姆雷特在等待亡父显灵的时刻听到。 当国王的狂欢滥饮（下文8行始）之声依然回荡在我们的耳畔时，先王的鬼魂突然出现，讲述克劳狄斯是如何将自己的兄长残害，并窃取了王位（Jenkins）。 12-3. 这是风俗……是的：令人感到奇怪的是，何瑞修作为丹麦人（1.1.128，5.2.346），居然不知道这种风俗。 该剧表明，在莎士比亚的心目中，何瑞修的身份并无确切的界定。 在第一幕第一场中，何瑞修好像属于丹麦本土，并且对丹麦的情况见多识广。 可在第一幕第二场164行以后，哈姆雷特在埃尔西诺见到他却感到吃惊，说起来好像何瑞修并非丹麦人似的（Jenkins）。

| | Horatio | | Is it a custom? |
| | **Hamlet** | Ay marry is't, |

                     But to my mind, though I am native here

15   And to the manner born, it is a custom

                     More honour'd in the breach than the observance.

                     This heavy-headed revel east and west

                     Makes us traduc'd and tax'd of other nations—

                     They clepe us drunkards, and with swinish phrase

20   Soil our addition; and indeed it takes

                     From our achievements, though perform'd at height,

                     The pith and marrow of our attribute.

                     So, oft it chances in particular men

                     That for some vicious mole of nature in them,

25   As in their birth, wherein they are not guilty

                     (Since nature cannot choose his origin),

                     By their o'ergrowth of some complexion,

                     Oft breaking down the pales and forts of reason,

                     Or by some habit, that too much o'erleavens

30   The form of plausive manners—that these men,

                     Carrying, I say, the stamp of one defect,

                     Being Nature's livery or Fortune's star,

                     His virtues else, be they as pure as grace,

                     As infinite as man may undergo,

35   Shall in the general censure take corruption

                     From that particular fault. The dram of evil

                     Doth all the noble substance often dout

                     To his own scandal.

何瑞修　　　　　　　　　　这是风俗？

哈姆雷特　　　是的，没错，
　　　　　　　但以我所见，尽管我在此生长，
　　　　　　　对这种风尚习以为常，与其　　　　　　　　　　15
　　　　　　　加以遵守还不如打破它体面。
　　　　　　　这种狂欢滥饮让我们遭到
　　　　　　　东西方各国的指责与诽谤——
　　　　　　　他们叫我们酒鬼，而且还污蔑
　　　　　　　我们是蠢猪；这的确会让　　　　　　　　　　　20
　　　　　　　我们的成就，尽管非常宏伟，
　　　　　　　失去其应有的精华与光辉。
　　　　　　　就个人而言，情况也往往如此，
　　　　　　　某些人由于生来就带有恶痣，
　　　　　　　与生俱来，并非个人的过失，　　　　　　　　　25
　　　　　　　（因为天生无法选择起源），
　　　　　　　由于某种性情的过度发展，
　　　　　　　往往就会冲破理智的防线，
　　　　　　　或是由于某种陋习对得体的
　　　　　　　举止造成太多的冲击——这些人，　　　　　　　30
　　　　　　　我敢说，带着某种缺陷的烙印，
　　　　　　　无论与生俱来还是不幸酿成，
　　　　　　　他的其他美德，无论多么纯洁，
　　　　　　　多么高贵，多么无尽无穷，
　　　　　　　他都会因为这一具体的缺陷　　　　　　　　　　35
　　　　　　　而遭受人们非议。　这点瑕疵
　　　　　　　将会抹杀他所有的高尚品格，
　　　　　　　而让他声名狼藉。

Enter Ghost.

Horatio	Look, my lord, it comes.
Hamlet	Angels and ministers of grace defend us!

40   Be thou a spirit of health or goblin damn'd,

Bring with thee airs from heaven or blasts from hell,

Be thy intents wicked or charitable,

Thou com'st in such a questionable shape

That I will speak to thee. I'll call thee Hamlet,

45   King, father, royal Dane. O answer me.

Let me not burst in ignorance, but tell

Why thy canoniz'd bones, hearsed in death,

Have burst their cerements, why the sepulchre

Wherein we saw thee quietly inurn'd

50   Hath op'd his ponderous and marble jaws

To cast thee up again. What may this mean,

That thou, dead corse, again in complete steel

Revisits thus the glimpses of the moon,

Making night hideous and we fools of nature

55   So horridly to shake our disposition

With thoughts beyond the reaches of our souls?

Say why is this? Wherefore? What should we do?

Ghost beckons.

Horatio	It beckons you to go away with it,

As if it some impartment did desire

To you alone.

60 **Marcellus**   Look with what courteous action

鬼魂上。

何瑞修	看,殿下,它来了!
哈姆雷特	天使和守护之神,快保佑我们!

你是善良天使还是邪恶妖魔?   40

引来天堂和风还是地狱狂飙?

你是慈悲为怀还是居心叵测?

你的这副形状是如此可疑,

我要对你发话。 我叫你哈姆雷特、

国王、父亲、丹麦王? 噢,回答我!   45

别让我蒙在鼓里,你要告诉我

为什么你那按教规入殓的躯体,

从裹尸布里冲出? 为什么我们

亲眼见你已平安入住的坟茔,

又张开它那笨重的大理石嘴巴   50

将你吐出? 这究竟意味着什么,

而你,一具僵尸、全身铠甲,

趁着闪现的月光再次来访,

使黑夜阴森可怖,让我们这些

自然的玩偶变得如此惊慌,   55

就连自己的思想都无法名状?

这是为啥? 为啥? 我们该做什么?

鬼魂招手。

何瑞修	它在向您招手,想让您过去,

好像有些事情要单独向您

透露。

马塞勒斯	您看它招手的姿势多么 60

It waves you to a more removed ground.

But do not go with it.

Horatio   No, by no means.

Hamlet   It will not speak. Then I will follow it.

Horatio   Do not, my lord.

Hamlet   Why, what should be the fear?

65   I do not set my life in a pin's fee,

And for my soul, what can it do to that,

Being a thing immortal as itself?

It waves me forth again. I'll follow it.

Horatio   What if it tempt you toward the flood, my lord,

70   Or to the dreadful summit of the cliff

That beetles o'er his base into the sea,

And there assume some other horrible form

Which might deprive your sovereignty of reason

And draw you into madness? Think of it.

75   The very place puts toys of desperation,

Without more motive, into every brain

That looks so many fathoms to the sea

And hears it roar beneath.

Hamlet   It waves me still.

Go on, I'll follow thee.

Marcellus You shall not go, my lord.

80 **Hamlet**   Hold off your hands.

Horatio   Be rul'd; you shall not go.

Hamlet   My fate cries out

礼貌,让您去更为偏僻之地。

可不要跟它去!

何瑞修　　　　　　　　不去,绝对不去!

哈姆雷特　它不会开口的。　我要跟上它。

何瑞修　别去,殿下!

哈姆雷特　　　　　　为啥,有啥可怕?

我把我的生命看得一钱不值,　　　　　　　　　65

至于我的灵魂,它能将它怎样,

因为它与鬼魂一样永垂不朽?

它又在向我招手。　我要跟上去。

何瑞修　如果他把您引向大海,殿下,

或把您骗到可怖的悬崖之巅,　　　　　　　　70

那里挂着它朝向大海的据点,

然后再扮成某种狰狞面目,

从而剥夺您至高无上的理智,

使您发疯怎么办?　您想一想:

如果伫立于千丈悬崖的顶端,　　　　　　　　75

闻听海水在下面咆哮,即便

毫无其他动因,也会使人突发

轻生之念。

哈姆雷特　　　　　　它还在向我招手。

走吧,我跟着你!

马塞勒斯　您不能去,殿下!

哈姆雷特　　　　　　把手拿开!　　　　　　80

何瑞修　听话;您别去!

哈姆雷特　　　　　　我的命运在呼唤,

61

And makes each petty artire in this body

As hardy as the Nemean lion's nerve.

Still am I call'd. Unhand me, gentlemen.

85   By heaven, I'll make a ghost of him that lets me.

I say away. —Go on, I'll follow thee.

Exeunt Ghost and Hamlet.

Horatio He waxes desperate with imagination.

Marcellus Let's follow. 'Tis not fit thus to obey him.

Horatio Have after. To what issue will this come?

90 **Marcellus** Something is rotten in the state of Denmark.

Horatio Heaven will direct it.

Marcellus   Nay, let's follow him. *Exeunt.*

　　　　让我周身的每根血脉都变得

　　　　跟尼米亚猛狮的神经一样硬坚！

　　　　它还在召唤！放开我，先生们！

　　　　我发誓，谁再阻拦，就让他去死！　　　　　　　　　　85

　　　　给我躲开！——走吧，我跟着你去！

　　　　　　　　　　　　　　　鬼魂与哈姆雷特同下。

何瑞修　　幻觉已使他变得孤注一掷。

马塞勒斯　快跟上，不能这样听之任之。

何瑞修　　跟上。　这究竟会有什么结局？

马塞勒斯　丹麦王国定有糟糕的事情。　　　　　　　　　　90

何瑞修　　听天由命吧。

马塞勒斯　　　　　　不行，咱们得跟上。　　　同下。

---

　　82. 血脉：原文中的 artire = artery（动脉）（Jenkins）。　83. 尼米亚猛狮：希腊神话中一种被认为不可战胜的猛兽。　大力神赫克勒斯（Hercules）将它杀死，此举成为他所立十二大功绩中的第一功（Gill）。　91. 不行：不能听天由命，我们自己要采取行动（Jenkins）。

SCENE V

Enter Ghost and Hamlet.

Hamlet	Whither wilt thou lead me? Speak, I'll go no further.	
Ghost	Mark me.	
Hamlet	I will.	
Ghost	My hour is almost come	

Ghost: My hour is almost come
When I to sulph'rous and tormenting flames
Must render up myself.

Hamlet   Alas, poor ghost.

5 **Ghost** Pity me not, but lend thy serious hearing
To what I shall unfold.

Hamlet   Speak, I am bound to hear.

Ghost So art thou to revenge when thou shalt hear.

Hamlet What?

Ghost I am thy father's spirit,

10 Doom'd for a certain term to walk the night,
And for the day confin'd to fast in fires,
Till the foul crimes done in my days of nature
Are burnt and purg'd away. But that I am forbid
To tell the secrets of my prison-house,

15 I could a tale unfold whose lightest word
Would harrow up thy soul, freeze thy young blood,

第五场

鬼魂与哈姆雷特上。

哈姆雷特	你把我带向何方？　说，我不走了。
鬼魂	听我说。
哈姆雷特	我会的。
鬼魂	我的时刻快到，
	那时我得返回炼狱继续遭受
	烈火的灼烧。
哈姆雷特	唉，可怜的鬼魂！
鬼魂	别可怜我，要仔细听我会向你　　　　　　5
	披露些什么。
哈姆雷特	说吧，我会听的。
鬼魂	那么你听完之后要替我报仇。
哈姆雷特	报仇？
鬼魂	我是你父亲的魂灵，
	注定在一定期限内夜游人间，　　　　　　10
	白天要忍饥遭受烈火烧燃，
	直到我生前所犯下的罪过
	能够烧干化净。　若不是禁止我
	将牢狱中的秘密泄露出去，
	我会透露些内情，即使轻描淡写，　　　　15
	都会让你魂不附体、热血顿凝，

Make thy two eyes like stars start from their spheres,

Thy knotted and combined locks to part,

And each particular hair to stand on end

20 Like quills upon the fretful porpentine.

But this eternal blazon must not be

To ears of flesh and blood. List, list, O list!

If thou didst ever thy dear father love—

Hamlet O God!

25 **Ghost** Revenge his foul and most unnatural murder.

Hamlet Murder!

Ghost Murder most foul, as in the best it is,

But this most foul, strange and unnatural.

Hamlet Haste me to know't, that I with wings as swift

30 As meditation or the thoughts of love

May sweep to my revenge.

Ghost   I find thee apt.

And duller shouldst thou be than the fat weed

That roots itself in ease on Lethe wharf,

Wouldst thou not stir in this. Now, Hamlet, hear.

35 'Tis given out that, sleeping in my orchard,

A serpent stung me—so the whole ear of Denmark

Is by a forged process of my death

Rankly abus'd—but know, thou noble youth,

The serpent that did sting thy father's life

40 Now wears his crown.

Hamlet O my prophetic soul! My uncle!

Ghost Ay, that incestuous, that adulterate beast,

让你的双眼犹如星球脱轨，

让你蓬乱的华发各自分离，

让你每根头发犹如狂怒的

豪猪身上的刺毛根根竖起。　　　　　　　　　　20

但这对永恒的描绘不能告诉

血肉之躯。　听着，听着，噢，听着！

假如你曾爱过你亲爱的父亲——

哈姆雷特　　噢，上帝！

鬼魂　　报复他残忍和灭绝人性的凶杀。　　　　　　25

哈姆雷特　　凶杀！

鬼魂　　最为残忍的凶杀，无与伦比、

邪恶至极，最为无情和稀奇。

哈姆雷特　　快告诉我，好让我插上犹如

冥想与情思一样迅速的翅膀　　　　　　　　30

飞向我的仇敌！

鬼魂　　　　　　　我看你会的。

你若是对此无动于衷，说明你

比那植根于忘河之畔的肥草

还要迟钝。　好了，哈姆雷特，听着：

人们传说，我在花园午睡时，　　　　　　　35

让毒蛇咬伤——因此丹麦臣民

全被公然编造的谎言蒙骗——

但是你要知道，高贵的青年，

将你父亲咬死的那条毒蛇，

正戴着他的皇冠。　　　　　　　　　　　40

哈姆雷特　　噢，我已料到！我的叔父！

鬼魂　　对，是那个乱伦、通奸的禽兽，

1.5.　33.忘河：在希腊神话里面，人们死后的魂灵在被引往冥府之前，都要聚集到忘河岸边饮水（从而忘却世间的一切）（Gill）。

With witchcraft of his wit, with traitorous gifts—

O wicked wit, and gifts that have the power

45 So to seduce! —won to his shameful lust

The will of my most seeming-virtuous queen.

O Hamlet, what a falling off was there,

From me, whose love was of that dignity

That it went hand in hand even with the vow

50 I made to her in marriage, and to decline

Upon a wretch whose natural gifts were poor

To those of mine.

But virtue, as it never will be mov'd,

Though lewdness court it in a shape of heaven,

55 So lust, though to a radiant angel link'd,

Will sate itself in a celestial bed

And prey on garbage.

But soft, methinks I scent the morning air:

Brief let me be. Sleeping within my orchard,

60 My custom always of the afternoon,

Upon my secure hour thy uncle stole

With juice of cursed hebenon in a vial,

And in the porches of my ears did pour

The leperous distilment, whose effect

65 Holds such an enmity with blood of man

That swift as quicksilver it courses through

The natural gates and alleys of the body,

And with a sudden vigour it doth posset

And curd, like eager droppings into milk,

70 The thin and wholesome blood. So did it mine,

他用机智的巫术、背信的礼物——

噢，邪恶的机智和如此诱人的

礼物！——使他的兽欲如愿以偿， 45

俘获了我那最貌似忠贞的王后。

噢，哈姆雷特，这是何等的堕落！

我对她的爱情是那样高贵，

我对她发出的婚礼誓言始终

如一、完全信守，而她竟然 50

委身于一位天赋与我相差

甚远的恶棍。

正如贞操，永远都不会动摇，

哪怕魔鬼扮成天使予以引诱；

而淫荡，纵有光明的天使相伴， 55

也会对神圣的恩爱感到腻烦，

转而猎取破烂。

且慢，我好像闻到了清晨气息：

我必须简明扼要。　当天下午

一如既往我正在花园午睡， 60

你的叔父趁我毫无戒备时，

拿着装满毒药的小瓶溜进，

然后便将一种致命的药汁

灌入我的耳孔，这种药汁的

毒性与人的血液势不两立， 65

它就像水银一样迅速流过

我全身的各条门径与血脉；

就像硫酸被人滴进了牛奶，

这种药汁顿时将我那清纯

与康健的血液凝固。　就这样， 70

And a most instant tetter bark'd about,

Most lazar-like, with vile and loathsome crust

All my smooth body.

Thus was I, sleeping, by a brother's hand

75   Of life, of crown, of queen at once dispatch'd,

Cut off even in the blossoms of my sin,

Unhousel'd, disappointed, unanel'd,

No reck'ning made, but sent to my account

With all my imperfections on my head.

80   O horrible! O horrible! most horrible!

If thou has nature in thee, bear it not,

Let not the royal bed of Denmark be

A couch for luxury and damned incest.

But howsomever thou pursuest this act,

85   Taint not thy mind nor let thy soul contrive

Against thy mother aught. Leave her to heaven,

And to those thorns that in her bosom lodge

To prick and sting her. Fare thee well at once:

The glow-worm shows the matin to be near

90   And gins to pale his uneffectual fire.

Adieu, adieu, adieu. Remember me.   *Exit.*

Hamlet   O all you host of heaven! O earth! What else?

And shall I couple hell? O fie! Hold, hold, my heart,

And you, my sinews, grow not instant old,

95   But bear me stiffly up. Remember thee?

我那光滑的周身,犹如染上

麻风,顿时便布满了可憎的

疮痂和疱疹。

就这样,我在睡梦之中,让兄弟

顷刻间夺去了性命、皇冠、王后,　　　　　　　　　　75

带着满身的罪过一命归阴,

未领圣餐、未做准备、未能涂膏、

没有机会忏悔,不得不带着

所有罪过去面对上帝的审判。

噢,可怕呀! 可怕! 最最可怕!　　　　　　　　　　80

假如你还有孝心,就不要容忍,

不要让丹麦王国的皇床变成

一种供人淫荡与乱伦的卧榻。

但是不管你怎样进行复仇,

都不能对你母亲存有任何的　　　　　　　　　　85

恶意和图谋。 把她留给上帝,

让她遭受自己内心愧疚的

刺痛与折磨。 马上与你告别:

萤火虫的微光已开始暗淡,

这一点表明清晨就在眼前。　　　　　　　　　　90

再见,再见,再见! 要记住我!　　　　　　　　（下。）

哈姆雷特　　天上的神明啊! 大地呀! 还有吗?

还要呼唤地狱? 呸! 挺住啊,我的心,

还有你,肌腱,可不要立刻衰朽,

你要将我的躯壳撑起。 记住你?　　　　　　　　95

---

　　77. 圣餐:一种基督教圣礼,将 (经过祝圣的) 圣餐面饼或酒分食给在场人员,以此来纪念耶稣的受难。 ——译者附注。 77. 未做准备:没有忏悔自己的罪过从而得到赦免（Gill）。 77. 涂膏:敷擦圣油的仪式。 哈姆雷特的父亲 （鬼魂） 在临终前被剥夺了一位基督教教徒应享有的所有仪式（Thompson）。

Ay, thou poor ghost, whiles memory holds a seat

In this distracted globe. Remember thee?

Yea, from the table of my memory

I'll wipe away all trivial fond records,

100   All saws of books, all forms, all pressures past

That youth and observation copied there,

And thy commandment all alone shall live

Within the book and volume of my brain,

Unmix'd with baser matter. Yes, by heaven!

105   O most pernicious woman!

O villain, villain, smiling damned villain!

My tables. Meet it is I set it down

That one may smile, and smile, and be a villain—

At least I am sure it may be so in Denmark. [*Writes.*]

110   So, uncle, there you are. Now to my word.

It is 'Adieu, adieu, remember me.'

I have sworn't.

Enter Horatio and Marcellus [calling].

Horatio   My lord, my lord.

Marcellus   Lord Hamlet.

115 **Horatio** Heaven secure him.

Hamlet   [*aside*] So be it.

是的,可怜的亡魂,只要这只

困惑的脑袋尚有记忆。　记住你?

是的,我要从脑海里抹去所有

琐碎和愚蠢的记录、所有警句、

所有形象,以及年轻时通过　　　　　　　　　　　　100

观察所留下来的所有印记,

唯有你的命令才能保留在

我身上这本记忆的书卷里,

与下贱的东西分离。　对,向天发誓!

噢,最为恶毒的女人!　　　　　　　　　　　　　　105

噢,恶棍,恶棍,喜笑可憎的恶棍!

我的本子。　我该把这一点记下:

人可以喜笑、喜笑,却是个恶棍——

我肯定至少在丹麦大概如此。〔写下。〕

好了,叔父,记下您了!我的箴言呢?　　　　　　110

那就是,“再见,再见,记住我啊!”

我已发过誓了。

何瑞修与马塞勒斯上〔呼喊〕。

何瑞修　　　殿下,殿下!

马塞勒斯　　哈姆雷特殿下!

何瑞修　　　上天保佑他吧!　　　　　　　　　　　115

哈姆雷特　　〔旁白〕但愿如此!

---

97. 困惑的脑袋:因为哈姆雷特不知道该如何看待鬼魂刚才所说的言辞(Gill)。　104. 与下贱的东西分离:然而正是由于某些“下贱的东西”才造成了哈姆雷特的困境。　因为他既不能将那些“下贱”的东西从自己的人性中根除,又不能将那些“下贱”的东西从自己的意识中抹去(Jenkins)。　105. 最为恶毒的女人:哈姆雷特此时已忘记85-6的告诫;而且,这种感情的迸发正是他刚刚发誓要摈弃的“下贱的东西”(Gill)。

	Marcellus	Hillo, ho, ho, my lord.
	Hamlet	Hillo, ho, ho, boy, come, bird, come.
	Marcellus	How is't, my noble lord?
120	**Horatio**	What news, my lord?
	Hamlet	O, wonderful!
	Horatio	Good my lord, tell it.
	Hamlet	No, you will reveal it.
	Horatio	Not I, my lord, by heaven.
125	**Marcellus**	Nor I, my lord.
	Hamlet	How say you then, would heart of man once think it—
		But you'll be secret?
	Hor. ⎫ **Mar.** ⎭	Ay, by heaven.
	Hamlet	There's never a villain dwelling in all Denmark
130		But he's an arrant knave.
	Horatio	There needs no ghost, my lord, come from the grave
		To tell us this.
	Hamlet	Why, right, you are in the right.
		And so without more circumstance at all
		I hold it fit that we shake hands and part,
135		You as your business and desire shall point you—
		For every man hath business and desire,
		Such as it is—and for my own poor part,
		I will go pray.
	Horatio	These are but wild and whirling words, my lord.
140	**Hamlet**	I am sorry they offend you, heartily—

马塞勒斯	嘿,嗬,嗬,我的殿下!	
哈姆雷特	嘿,嗬,嗬,伙计! 快来,鸟儿,快来!	
马塞勒斯	怎么样,我尊贵的殿下?	
何瑞修	什么消息,殿下?	120
哈姆雷特	噢,棒极了!	
何瑞修	我的好殿下,快讲。	
哈姆雷特	不讲,你们会泄露的。	
何瑞修	我不会,殿下,我发誓。	
马塞勒斯	我也不会,殿下。	125
哈姆雷特	那你们说说,谁会想到这事儿——	
	可你们能保密吗?	
何瑞修 马塞勒斯	能,向天发誓。	
哈姆雷特	全丹麦从来没有哪个恶棍——	
	不是十足的无赖。	130
何瑞修	这可用不着鬼魂从坟里出来	
	告诉我们,殿下。	
哈姆雷特	哎,对,说得对!	
	因此,咱们无须再多费口舌,	
	我想大家该就此握手道别,	
	你们去做该做和想做的事情,	135
	因为每人都有事情和心愿——	
	就是这样——至于可怜的我呢,	
	我要去祈祷。	
何瑞修	这些不过是胡言乱语,殿下。	
哈姆雷特	我的话冒犯了你们,很抱歉,真的——	140

117. 嘿,嗬:马塞勒斯喊话的口气就像是驯鹰员在呼喊自己的猎鹰。 哈姆雷特以同样的方式作答(Gill)。 129-30. 没有……无赖:哈姆雷特显然正要将秘密透露出去,却突然改变话题,转而吐出一句俏皮话(Jenkins)。

Yes faith, heartily.

Horatio   There's no offence, my lord.

Hamlet   Yes by Saint Patrick but there is, Horatio,

And much offence too. Touching this vision here,

It is an honest ghost, that let me tell you.

145   For your desire to know what is between us,

O'ermaster't as you may. And now, good friends,

As you are friends, scholars, and soldiers,

Give me one poor request.

Horatio   What is't, my lord? We will.

Hamlet   Never make known what you have seen tonight.

150   **Hor.**
       Mar.   }   My lord, we will not.

Hamlet   Nay, but swear't.

Horatio   In faith, my lord, not I.

Marcellus   Nor I, my lord, in faith.

Hamlet   Upon my sword.

155   **Marcellus**   We have sworn, my lord, already.

Hamlet   Indeed, upon my sword, indeed.

Ghost   [*Cries under the stage*] Swear.

Hamlet   Ah ha, boy, say'st thou so? Art thou there, truepenny?

Come on, you hear this fellow in the cellarage.

Consent to swear.

是真的,真的。

何瑞修　　　　　　　没有冒犯,殿下。

哈姆雷特　向圣巴特里克起誓,冒犯了,何瑞修,

是严重的冒犯。 至于这个幽灵,

它是个正直的鬼魂,我告诉你们。

至于想了解我俩交谈的意愿,　　　　　　　　　145

请你们尽量克制。 现在,好朋友,

既然你们是朋友、学者、和军人,

请答应我。

何瑞修　　　　　　　答应啥,殿下? 我们会的。

哈姆雷特　决不把今晚看见的事情泄露。

何瑞修
马塞勒斯　}　我们不泄露,殿下。　　　　　　　　　　　150

哈姆雷特　不行,要起誓。

何瑞修　真的,殿下,我不会。

马塞勒斯　我也不会,殿下,真的。

哈姆雷特　按着剑起誓。

马塞勒斯　我们已发过誓了,殿下。　　　　　　　　　　155

哈姆雷特　一定,按着剑起誓,一定。

鬼　魂　〔在舞台下面喊叫〕起誓!

哈姆雷特　啊哈,伙计,你说的? 你在吗,老实人?

快来,听到地下的伙计怎么说的。

赶快发誓吧。

---

142. 圣巴特里克:爱尔兰圣徒,早期的基督教传统将其与炼狱的幽灵连在一起,哈姆雷特将其用以发誓(Gill)。　154. 按着剑起誓:剑柄形似十字架,手按剑柄发誓,更为庄严、神圣(Gill)。　157. 在舞台下面喊叫:在演出过程中,舞台下面通常被当作地狱,供“鬼魂”躲藏(Jenkins)。　158. 伙计:哈姆雷特此刻在同伴面前对鬼魂的滑稽昵称,是在延续其在本场118行开始所采用的轻佻语气(Jenkins)。

160	**Horatio**	Propose the oath, my lord.
	Hamlet	Never to speak of this that you have seen.
		Swear by my sword.
	Ghost	Swear. *[They swear.]*
	Hamlet	*Hic et ubique?* Then we'll shift our ground.
165		Come hither, gentlemen,
		And lay your hands again upon my sword.
		Swear by my sword
		Never to speak of this that you have heard.
	Ghost	Swear by his sword. *[They swear.]*
170	**Hamlet**	Well said, old mole. Canst work i'th' earth so fast?
		A worthy pioner! Once more remove, good friends.
	Horatio	O day and night, but this is wondrous strange.
	Hamlet	And therefore as a stranger give it welcome.
		There are more things in heaven and earth, Horatio,
175		Than are dreamt of in your philosophy.
		But come,
		Here, as before, never, so help you mercy,
		How strange or odd some'er I bear myself—
		As I perchance hereafter shall think meet
180		To put an antic disposition on—
		That you, at such time seeing me, never shall,
		With arms encumber'd thus, or this head-shake,
		Or by pronouncing of some doubtful phrase,
		As 'Well, we know', or 'We could and if we would',
185		Or 'If we list to speak', or 'There be and if they might',
		Or such ambiguous giving out, to note

何瑞修	准备好誓言,殿下。	160
哈姆雷特	决不把你们看见的事情提起。	
	按着我的剑起誓。	
鬼魂	起誓!	[二人发誓。]
哈姆雷特	你无处不在?　那我们再换个地方。	
	快过来,先生们,	165
	你们要再一次按住我的剑柄,	
	按住我的剑发誓:	
	你们听见的内容决不提起。	
鬼魂	按着他的剑起誓!	[二人发誓。]
哈姆雷特	说得好,老鼹鼠!在地下干得这么快?	170
	多棒的矿工!再换个地方,好朋友。	
何瑞修	噢,我的天哪,真是稀奇古怪!	
哈姆雷特	那就像对外人一样欢迎它吧。	
	天地之间发生的事情,何瑞修,	
	任何科学也都无法想象。	175
	注意听,	
	现在,就像刚才,若想得到宽恕,	
	无论我的行为是多么古怪——	
	因为今后我也许会在自己	
	认为适当的时候行为乖张——	180
	你们,见我此时的情景,决不,	
	这样双手叉腰,或这样摇头晃脑,	
	或者发出一些含糊的言辞,	
	如"哟,我们懂",或"若愿意,我们会",	
	或"若我们想说",或"若允许,他们会",	185
	或类似的模棱两可,好像你们	

160. 誓言:共有三个,首先,他们不得将当晚的所见告诉别人（161）;其次,他们不得将当晚的所闻告诉别人（168）;最后,他们决不能暗示好像了解他的底细似的（186-7）（Jenkins）。

79

That you know aught of me—this do swear,

So grace and mercy at your most need help you.

Ghost   Swear.   [*They swear.*]

190 **Hamlet**   Rest, rest, perturbed spirit. So, gentlemen,

With all my love I do commend me to you;

And what so poor a man as Hamlet is

May do t'express his love and friending to you,

God willing, shall not lack. Let us go in together.

195   And still your fingers on your lips, I pray.

The time is out of joint. O cursed spite,

That ever I was born to set it right.

Nay, come, let's go together.   *Exeunt.*

了解我的底细似的——就此发誓，

好在最需要时得到怜悯与宽恕。

鬼魂　　　起誓！　　　　　　　　　　　　　　　　　［二人发誓。］

哈姆雷特　安息吧，忧心的亡灵！好吧，先生们，　　　　　　190

我用全部的情怀向你们致意；

尽管哈姆雷特是如此可怜，

但是他对你们的爱心和友情，

若上帝允许，不会缺乏。　一块走吧。

要继续保持沉默，我求你们。　　　　　　　　　　　195

时代杂乱无章，噢，糟糕透顶，

竟让我负起拨乱反正的使命！

不，快来，咱们一起走。　　　　　　　　　　　同下。

---

188. 最需要时：接受上帝审判的时刻（Gill）。　190. 安息吧：人们发出复仇的誓言 （或业已复仇） 之后，鬼魂才会安息（Thompson）。

第二幕
ACT 2

SCENE I

Enter old Polonius, with his man Reynaldo.

Polonius	Give him this money and these notes, Reynaldo.
Reynaldo	I will, my lord.
Polonius	You shall do marvellous wisely, good Reynaldo,
	Before you visit him, to make inquire
	Of his behaviour.

5 **Reynaldo**   My lord, I did intend it.

Polonius   Marry, well said, very well said. Look you, sir,

Inquire me first what Danskers are in Paris,

And how, and who, what means, and where they keep,

What company, at what expense; and finding

10   By this encompassment and drift of question

That they do know my son, come you more nearer

Than your particular demands will touch it.

Take you as 'twere some distant knowledge of him,

As thus, 'I know his father, and his friends,

15   And in part him'—do you mark this, Reynaldo?

Reynaldo   Ay, very well, my lord.

Polonius   'And in part him. But', you may say, 'not well;

But if't be he I mean, he's very wild,

Addicted so and so'—and there put on him

第一场

年迈的波洛纽斯及其仆人雷纳尔多上。

波洛纽斯	把这些钱和信给他,雷纳尔多。
雷纳尔多	遵命,大人。
波洛纽斯	见他之前您若能,好雷纳尔多,
	打探一下他的表现,那将会
	再好不过。

雷纳尔多　　　大人,我是这样打算。　　　　　　　　　　5

波洛纽斯　哎呀,说得好,说得很好。　要注意,

先打听哪些丹麦人待在巴黎,

他们的条件、姓名、财源和住处,

与谁来往、花费大小;以拐弯

抹角的方式弄清他们确实　　　　　　　　　　　10

认识我的儿子,这要比直接的

发问更容易达到您的目标。

要装出对他恍惚认识的样子,

诸如"我认识他父亲、他的朋友,

对他略知一二"——懂了吗,雷纳尔多?　　　　　　15

雷纳尔多　懂了,很好,大人。

波洛纽斯　"对他略知一二。　但",可以说,"不熟;

但若真的是他,他可非常放荡,

有如此这般的嗜好"——随意给他

85

20   What forgeries you please—marry, none so rank

As may dishonour him—take heed of that—

But, sir, such wanton, wild, and usual slips

As are companions noted and most known

To youth and liberty.

Reynaldo   As gaming, my lord.

25 **Polonius**   Ay, or drinking, fencing, swearing,

Quarrelling, drabbing—you may go so far.

Reynaldo   My lord, that would dishonour him.

Polonius   'Faith no, as you may season it in the charge.

You must not put another scandal on him,

30   That he is open to incontinency—

That's not my meaning; but breathe his faults so quaintly

That they may seem the taints of liberty,

The flash and outbreak of a fiery mind,

A savageness in unreclaimed blood,

35   Of general assault.

Reynaldo   But my good lord—

Polonius   Wherefore should you do this?

Reynaldo   Ay, my lord, I would know that.

Polonius   Marry, sir, here's my drift,

And I believe it is a fetch of warrant.

40   You laying these slight sullies on my son,

As 'twere a thing a little soil'd i'th' working,

Mark you,

Your party in converse, him you would sound,

Having ever seen in the prenominate crimes

45   The youth you breathe of guilty, be assur'd

	捏造一些陋习——哎,不能太不像话,	20
	以至伤及声誉——要注意这一点——	
	但是,老兄,不过是一些青年	
	和浪子经常犯的过失而已,	
	诸如轻率、放荡等。	
雷纳尔多	如赌博,大人?	
波洛纽斯	对,或酗酒、击剑、诅咒、	25
	吵架、嫖娼——这些您都可以说。	
雷纳尔多	大人,那会败坏他的名声。	
波洛纽斯	不会的,因为您可以轻描淡写。	
	但千万不要对他另加中伤,	
	竟说他荒淫无度、毫无节制——	30
	那不是我的意思;要说得如此婉转,	
	听起来好像就是浪子的瑕疵,	
	火热的大脑一时冲动和发泄,	
	血气方刚的青年大都难免的	
	野性而已。	35
雷纳尔多	可是,大人您——	
波洛纽斯	为何要您这么做?	
雷纳尔多	是的,大人,我想知道。	
波洛纽斯	哎,老兄,我的用意是,	
	我相信这是一种正当的花招。	
	您对我儿子的缺点稍加罗列	40
	好像那是成长时难免的污点,	
	注意听,	
	您的谈话伙伴——要打探的对方,	
	若是看见过您所责备的那位	
	青年曾经犯下上述罪过,你放心,	45

He closes with you in this consequence:

'Good sir', or so, or 'friend', or 'gentleman',

According to the phrase or the addition

Of man and country.

Reynaldo   Very good, my lord.

50 **Polonius**   And then, sir, does a this—a does—what was I about

to say? By the mass, I was about to say something.

Where did I leave?

Reynaldo   At 'closes in the consequence'.

Polonius   At 'closes in the consequence', ay, marry.

55   He closes thus: 'I know the gentleman,

I saw him yesterday', or 'th'other day',

Or then, or then, with such or such, 'and as you say,

There was a gaming', 'there o'ertook in's rouse',

'There falling out at tennis', or perchance

60   'I saw him enter such a house of sale'—

Videlicet a brothel, or so forth.

See you now,

Your bait of falsehood takes this carp of truth;

And thus do we of wisdom and of reach,

65   With windlasses and with assays of bias,

By indirections find directions out.

So by my former lecture and advice

Shall you my son. You have me, have you not?

Reynaldo   My lord, I have.

Polonius   God buy ye, fare ye well.

70 **Reynaldo**   Good my lord.

Polonius   Observe his inclination in yourself.

他就会表示赞同，并这样说道：

"好先生"，或者"朋友"，或者"先生"，

具体用什么称呼要根据个人

或各国的习惯而定。

雷纳尔多　　　　　　　　　很好，大人。

波洛纽斯　然后，老兄，他就会——他就会——我要　　　50

说什么来着？ 天哪，我是要说点啥的。

我说到哪里了？

雷纳尔多　说到"他就会表示赞同"。

波洛纽斯　说到"他就会表示赞同"。 对，没错。

他会这样说："我认识这位先生，　　　　　55

昨天还见过他呢"，或"前几天"，

或某时、某日、与某某、某某一起，

"像您所说的赌博"、"喝得烂醉"、

"在网球场上与人闹翻"，或许是，

"我见他进了这么一家售卖店"——　　　60

也就是妓院，或类似的地点。

现在懂了吧？

用虚情假意套出肺腑之言；

我们这些精明老道的家伙，

通过拐弯抹角、旁敲侧击，　　　　　　65

以迂回方式查明真实情况。

您打探我的儿子，就按上述

劝诫和忠告。 您听懂了没有？

雷纳尔多　听懂了，大人。

波洛纽斯　　　　　　　　上帝保佑你，再见。

雷纳尔多　再见，大人。　　　　　　　　　　　70

波洛纽斯　您自己也要观察他的习性。

Reynaldo	I shall, my lord.	
Polonius	And let him ply his music.	
Reynaldo	Well, my lord.	*Exit.*

Enter Ophelia.

Polonius	Farewell. How now, Ophelia, what's the matter?
75 **Ophelia**	O my lord, my lord, I have been so affrighted.
Polonius	With what, i'th' name of God?
Ophelia	My lord, as I was sewing in my closet,
	Lord Hamlet, with his doublet all unbrac'd,
	No hat upon his head, his stockings foul'd,
80	Ungarter'd and down-gyved to his ankle,
	Pale as his shirt, his knees knocking each other,
	And with a look so piteous in purport
	As if he had been loosed out of hell
	To speak of horrors, he comes before me.
Polonius	Mad for thy love?
85 **Ophelia**	My lord, I do not know,
	But truly I do fear it.
Polonius	What said he?
Ophelia	He took me by the wrist and held me hard.
	Then goes he to the length of all his arm,
	And with his other hand thus o'er his brow
90	He falls to such perusal of my face
	As a would draw it. Long stay'd he so.
	At last, a little shaking of mine arm,
	And thrice his head thus waving up and down,

雷纳尔多	我会的,大人。
波洛纽斯	要让他学习音乐。
雷纳尔多	好的,大人。　　　　　　　　　　　　　　　　下。

　　　　　　　奥菲丽娅上。

波洛纽斯　再见。　怎么了,奥菲丽娅,什么事?

奥菲丽娅　噢,父亲啊,父亲,我非常害怕! 　　　　　　75

波洛纽斯　看在上帝的份上,怕啥?

奥菲丽娅　父亲,当我正在屋里缝纫时,
　　　　　　哈姆雷特殿下,他穿的上衣
　　　　　　大敞四开,帽子没戴,袜子污浊,
　　　　　　袜带松脱,犹如镣铐裹住脚脖, 　　　　　　80
　　　　　　脸色跟他的衬衫一样煞白,
　　　　　　双膝相互碰撞,表情如此可怜,
　　　　　　好像从地狱返还,向人间诉说
　　　　　　其中的恐怖,他来到我的面前。

波洛纽斯　因为爱你而发疯?

奥菲丽娅　　　　　　我不知道,父亲, 　　　　　　85
　　　　　　可我有些担心。

波洛纽斯　　　　　　他说些什么?

奥菲丽娅　他抓住我的手腕紧紧不放。
　　　　　　然后他拉直手臂向后退去,
　　　　　　用另一只手就这样遮住额头,
　　　　　　对我的面容观察得如此细致, 　　　　　　90
　　　　　　好像他要画下。这样停留许久。
　　　　　　最后,轻轻地摇了摇我的手臂,
　　　　　　他的头就这样上下摆动三次,

He rais'd a sigh so piteous and profound

95 As it did seem to shatter all his bulk

And end his being. That done, he lets me go,

And with his head over his shoulder turn'd

He seem'd to find his way without his eyes,

For out o' doors he went without their helps,

100 And to the last bended their light on me.

Polonius Come, go with me, I will go seek the King.

This is the very ecstasy of love,

Whose violent property fordoes itself

And leads the will to desperate undertakings

105 As oft as any passion under heaven

That does afflict our natures. I am sorry—

What, have you given him any hard words of late?

Ophelia No, my good lord, but as you did command,

I did repel his letters and denied

His access to me.

110 **Polonius**   That hath made him mad.

I am sorry that with better heed and judgment

I had not quoted him. I fear'd he did but trifle

And meant to wrack thee. But beshrew my jealousy!

By heaven, it is as proper to our age

115 To cast beyond ourselves in our opinions

As it is common for the younger sort

To lack discretion. Come, go we to the King.

	他发出一声长叹如此可怜，	
	好像他要粉碎自己的躯干，	95
	结束生命。 之后，他把我松开，	
	然后他就将头部转了过来，	
	他好像不用眼睛也能前行，	
	因为他走出门时没有看路，	
	他一直盯着我，目不转睛。	100
波洛纽斯	来，跟我来，我要去面见国王。	
	这些现象正是爱的疯狂，	
	它的狂热本性会毁灭自身，	
	而且会引导人们孤注一掷，	
	跟天下折磨我们本能的任何	105
	激情一模一样。 我很抱歉——	
	怎么，你最近对他措辞强硬？	
奥菲丽娅	没有，父亲，我只是按您的指示，	
	已将他的信件退还，并拒绝他	
	与我会面。	
波洛纽斯	这是他发疯的根源。	110
	很抱歉我未能对他进行更细的	
	观察和判断。 我担心他只是想	
	戏弄你、糟蹋你。 我的疑心该死！	
	我的天哪，正如年轻的人们	
	往往都会缺乏慎重，而我们	115
	这些上了年纪的家伙就爱	
	捕风捉影。 走，咱们去见国王。	

2.1. 106. 我很抱歉——：波罗纽斯突然住口，然后又在 111 行接上话题（Jenkins）。
113. 疑心：波洛纽斯在责备自己的疑心。 他认为是这种"疑心"阻止了他真正了解哈姆雷特的行为（Gill）。

This must be known, which, being kept close, might move

More grief to hide than hate to utter love.

120　　Come.   *Exeunt.*

这事要挑明，尽管会生怨恨之情，

而隐瞒，可能会导致更大不幸。

快来。　　　　　　　　　　　　　　　　同下。　　120

SCENE II

*Flourish. Enter King and Queen, Rosencrantz and
Guildenstern, with Attendants.*

King   Welcome, dear Rosencrantz and Guildenstern.

Moreover that we much did long to see you,

The need we have to use you did provoke

Our hasty sending. Something have you heard

5   Of Hamlet's transformation—so I call it,

Sith nor th'exterior nor the inward man

Resembles that it was. What it should be,

More than his father's death, that thus hath put him

So much from th'understanding of himself

10   I cannot dream of. I entreat you both

That, being of so young days brought up with him,

And sith so neighbour'd to his youth and haviour,

That you vouchsafe your rest here in our court

Some little time, so by your companies

15   To draw him on to pleasures and to gather,

So much as from occasion you may glean,

Whether aught to us unknown afflicts him thus

That, open'd, lies within our remedy.

Queen   Good gentlemen, he hath much talk'd of you,

第二场

号角齐鸣。国王、王后、罗森克兰、
盖登斯顿、与侍从上。

国王　　欢迎，亲爱的罗森克兰和盖登斯顿。
除了我们非常想念二位之外，
还因为需要你们帮忙，所以
才匆匆将你们召来。　你们已听说
哈姆雷特的变态——我这样称谓，　　　　　　　5
是因为无论他的外表还是内心，
都与从前判若两人。　除了他
父亲的去世，究竟还有什么
别的原因让他变得如此疯狂，
我实在无法想象。　我请求二位，　　　　　　10
因为你们与他一起长大成人，
你们对他的脾性如此熟悉，
因此我请求你们能够答应
在宫中稍住。　通过你们的相伴，
鼓励他参加一些娱乐，说不定，　　　　　　　15
你们还能趁机搜集一些我们
尚不了解，却在折磨他的原因，
病因一旦摸清，即可对症下药。

王后　　二位好先生，他经常说起你们，

20   And sure I am, two men there is not living

To whom he more adheres. If it will please you

To show us so much gentry and good will

As to expend your time with us awhile

For the supply and profit of our hope,

25   Your visitation shall receive such thanks

As fits a king's remembrance.

Ros.   Both your Majesties

Might, by the sovereign power you have of us,

Put your dread pleasures more into command

Than to entreaty.

Guild.   But we both obey,

30   And here give up ourselves in the full bent

To lay our service freely at your feet

To be commanded.

King   Thanks, Rosencrantz and gentle Guildenstern.

Queen   Thanks, Guildenstern and gentle Rosencrantz.

35   And I beseech you instantly to visit

My too much changed son. Go, some of you,

And bring these gentlemen where Hamlet is.

Guild.   Heavens make our presence and our practices

Pleasant and helpful to him.

Queen   Ay, amen.

Exeunt Rosencrantz and Guildenstern [and an Attendant].

而且我确信,当今没有谁能比　　　　　　　　　　20
你们俩让他感到更加亲近。
你们能否出于礼貌和善意,
与我们一起在此稍作停留,
让我们如愿以偿并从中受益,
你们的光临,将会得到一位　　　　　　　　　　25
国王应赐的谢意。

罗森克兰　　　　　　　　二位陛下,
您可凭借自己对我们的权威,
将您尊贵的意愿直接吩咐,
而不是请求。

盖登斯顿　　　　　　我们全都服从,
我们心甘情愿地留在此处,　　　　　　　　　　30
时刻恭候您的随意吩咐
以效犬马之劳。

国王　　　谢谢,罗森克兰和好盖登斯顿。

王后　　　谢谢,盖登斯顿和好罗森克兰。
求你们立刻去探望我那变化　　　　　　　　　　35
异常的儿子。　去,你们中的一个,
带这两位先生去见哈姆雷特。

盖登斯顿　愿上帝保佑我们的出面和行动
能让他愉快并受益。

王后　　　　　　　　是的,阿门。

　　　　　　　　罗森克兰与盖登斯顿〔与一侍从〕同下。

Enter Polonius.

40	**Polonius**	Th'ambassadors from Norway, my good lord,
		Are joyfully return'd.
	King	Thou still hast been the father of good news.
	Polonius	Have I, my lord? I assure my good liege
		I hold my duty as I hold my soul,
45		Both to my God and to my gracious King;
		And I do think—or else this brain of mine
		Hunts not the trail of policy so sure
		As it hath us'd to do—that I have found
		The very cause of Hamlet's lunacy.
50	**King**	O speak of that: that do I long to hear.
	Polonius	Give first admittance to th'ambassadors.
		My news shall be the fruit to that great feast.
	King	Thyself do grace to them and bring them in. *Exit Polonius.*
		He tells me, my dear Gertrude, he hath found
55		The head and source of all your son's distemper.
	Queen	I doubt it is no other but the main,
		His father's death and our o'er-hasty marriage.
	King	Well, we shall sift him.

Enter Polonius, Voltemand, and Cornelius.

Welcome, my good friends.

Say, Voltemand, what from our brother Norway?

波洛纽斯上。

波洛纽斯	尊贵的陛下,派往挪威的大使,	40
	兴高采烈地回来了。	
国王	你依然是我们的喜讯之父。	
波洛纽斯	真的吗,陛下？ 我向陛下保证,	
	我把我对上帝和陛下的义务	
	看得就像我自己的灵魂一般;	45
	我认为——否则就是这颗脑袋	
	已不像往常那样嗅觉灵敏、	
	百发百中——我已经发现了	
	哈姆雷特发疯的真正原因。	
国王	噢,快说说:我倒很想听一听。	50
波洛纽斯	请陛下首先召见回国的使臣。	
	我的消息可作盛宴后的甜点。	
国王	你向他们致意并带他们进来。	波洛纽斯下。
	他告诉我,亲爱的葛楚德,他已	
	发现您儿子精神失常的原因。	55
王后	我想不是别的,主要是他父亲的	
	去世与我们过于仓促的成婚。	
国王	好吧,我要盘问他。	

波洛纽斯、福提曼德与科尼留斯上。

欢迎,好朋友。

喂,福提曼德,挪威王兄怎么说？

60 **Voltemand**   Most fair return of greetings and desires.

Upon our first, he sent out to suppress

His nephew's levies, which to him appear'd

To be a preparation 'gainst the Polack;

But better look'd into, he truly found

65 It was against your Highness; whereat griev'd

That so his sickness, age, and impotence

Was falsely borne in hand, sends out arrests

On Fortinbras; which he, in brief, obeys,

Receives rebuke from Norway, and, in fine,

70 Makes vow before his uncle never more

To give th'assay of arms against your Majesty:

Whereon old Norway, overcome with joy,

Gives him three thousand crowns in annual fee

And his commission to employ those soldiers

75 So levied, as before, against the Polack,

With an entreaty, herein further shown, [*Gives a paper.*]

That it might please you to give quiet pass

Through your dominions for this enterprise

On such regards of safety and allowance

As therein are set down.

80 **King**   It likes us well;

And at our more consider'd time we'll read,

Answer, and think upon this business.

Meantime, we thank you for your well-took labour.

Go to your rest, at night we'll feast together.

Most welcome home.

福提曼德	他回敬最诚挚的问候和祝愿。	60
	一了解我们的来意,他就下令	
	制止侄儿的征兵,他原以为	
	那些士兵准备征战波兰国王;	
	可是经过仔细的盘问以后,	
	他才发现矛头所向实为陛下;	65
	他为自己因疾病、年迈、体衰	
	而遭蒙骗深感痛心,向弗廷布拉	
	发出禁令;简言之,他唯命是从,	
	接受了挪威王的训斥,最后,	
	他还当面向叔父立下誓言,	70
	永远不再兴兵向陛下挑衅:	
	挪威老王对此不胜欢喜,	
	当即奖赏他三千克朗年金,	
	并且委派他继续统帅原先	
	募集的士兵去攻打波兰国王。	75
	他还在这封信中恳请陛下,[呈上信函。]	
	是否能按这封信中所说的	
	安全以及许可条款,准许	
	他的远征军队从丹麦境内	
	予以通过。	
国王	对此我非常满意;	80
	有空时我将仔细阅读信函,	
	认真考虑此事,并予以答复。	
	同时,感谢你们的辛苦和功劳。	
	请稍事休息,晚上再一起赴宴。	
	欢迎归来。	

 2.2. 78.安全以及许可条款:丹麦允许弗廷布拉从国内路过,但弗廷布拉必须保证丹麦的安全(Jenkins)。

Exeunt Voltemand and Cornelius.

85 **Polonius**   This business is well ended.

My liege and madam, to expostulate

What majesty should be, what duty is,

Why day is day, night night, and time is time,

Were nothing but to waste night, day, and time.

90   Therefore, since brevity is the soul of wit,

And tediousness the limbs and outward flourishes,

I will be brief. Your noble son is mad.

Mad call I it, for to define true madness,

What is't but to be nothing else but mad?

But let that go.

95 **Queen**   More matter with less art.

Polonius   Madam, I swear I use no art at all.

That he is mad 'tis true; 'tis true 'tis pity;

And pity 'tis 'tis true. A foolish figure—

But farewell it, for I will use no art.

100   Mad let us grant him then. And now remains

That we find out the cause of this effect,

Or rather say the cause of this defect,

For this effect defective comes by cause.

Thus it remains; and the remainder thus:

105   Perpend,

I have a daughter—have while she is mine—

　　　　　　　　　　　　　　　福提曼德与科尼留斯同下。

波洛纽斯　　　　　　此事已圆满结束。　　　　　　　　　　　　85

　　　　　　　陛下和夫人,若要探询什么

　　　　　　　应是帝王的尊严、臣民的本分,

　　　　　　　为何日是日、夜是夜、时间是时间,

　　　　　　　那只是浪费日夜、浪费时间。

　　　　　　　因此,既然简洁是智慧的灵魂,　　　　　　　　90

　　　　　　　冗长为外部的花饰与枝叶,

　　　　　　　长话短说:您的贵子已发疯。

　　　　　　　我称为发疯,是因为要解释真疯,

　　　　　　　除非自己疯了,还能有别的情形?

　　　　　　　不提它了。

王后　　　　　　　　多谈实际,少弄玄虚!　　　　　　　　95

波洛纽斯　　夫人,向您发誓我未弄玄虚。

　　　　　　　他疯了是真的;是真的很遗憾;

　　　　　　　很遗憾是真的。　愚蠢的花言——

　　　　　　　再见。　因为我不想故弄玄虚。

　　　　　　　让我们暂定他已发疯。　剩下的　　　　　　　100

　　　　　　　就是要找出这种后果的前因,

　　　　　　　或者说是这种病态的根本,

　　　　　　　因为病态的结果事出有因。

　　　　　　　这就是现状;现状就是这样:

　　　　　　　请注意,　　　　　　　　　　　　　　　　　105

　　　　　　　我有个女儿——当她依然归我时——

---

　　93. 要解释真疯:此处可能是仿效古罗马诗人赫拉斯《讽刺诗集》中的观念。　该诗集的主题是:我们所公认的疯子并不比他人更疯。　因此,真正的疯狂是整个世界。　难怪波洛纽斯也明智地以"不提它了"结束话题(Jenkins)。

Who in her duty and obedience, mark,

Hath given me this. Now gather and surmise.

[*Reads*] *To the celestial and my soul's idol, the most*

110   *beautified Ophelia* — That's an ill phrase, a vile phrase,

'beautified' is a vile phrase. But you shall hear —

these; in her excellent white bosom, these, etc.

Queen   Came this from Hamlet to her?

Polonius   Good madam, stay awhile, I will be faithful.

115   *Doubt thou the stars are fire,*

Doubt that the sun doth move,

Doubt truth to be a liar,

But never doubt I love.

O dear Ophelia, I am ill at these numbers. I have not art to

120   *reckon my groans. But that I love thee best, O most best,*

believe it. Adieu.

Thine evermore, most dear lady, whilst this

machine is to him,   *Hamlet.*

This in obedience hath my daughter shown me,

125   And, more above, hath his solicitings,

As they fell out by time, by means, and place,

All given to mine ear.

King   But how hath she receiv'd his love?

Polonius   What do you think of me?

130 **King**   As of a man faithful and honourable.

Polonius   I would fain prove so. But what might you think,

When I had seen this hot love on the wing—

As I perceiv'd it, I must tell you that,

Before my daughter told me—what might you

我女儿出于顺从与本分，注意，
她把这个给了我。　你们来猜一猜。
［读信］致天仙及我心灵的偶像，最艳美的
奥菲丽娅——那是个糟糕的字眼，可恶用语，　　　　110
'艳美'是个可恶的用语。　你们听下去——
这信；要放在她雪白的酥胸，这信，等等。

王后　　　这是哈姆雷特写给她的？

波洛纽斯　夫人您，请稍等，我会如实禀报。

你怀疑星星是火焰，　　　　115

你怀疑太阳会转动，

你怀疑真理是谎言，

决不要怀疑我的情。

噢，亲爱的奥菲丽娅，我不善格律。我无法
用诗歌表达痛苦。但我最爱你，最最爱你，　　　　120
相信我。再见。

永远属于你，最亲爱的姑娘，只要

他躯体能动，　哈姆雷特。

我女儿乖乖地把这展示给我，
除此之外，还有他求爱的时间、　　　　125
求爱的手段以及求爱的地点，
全都传入我的耳朵。

国王　　　她对他的爱情反应如何？

波洛纽斯　陛下以为我怎样？

国王　　　你这人不仅忠诚而且体面。　　　　130

波洛纽斯　但愿我能验证。　可您会怎么想，
当我看到这场恋爱热火朝天——
我这样认为，我必须告诉您，
在我女儿告诉我以前——陛下您

135   Or my dear Majesty your queen here think,

If I had play'd the desk or table-book,

Or given my heart a winking mute and dumb,

Or look'd upon this love with idle sight—

What might you think? No, I went round to work,

140   And my young mistress thus I did bespeak:

' Lord Hamlet is a prince out of thy star.

This must not be. ' And then I prescripts gave her,

That she should lock herself from his resort,

Admit no messengers, receive no tokens;

145   Which done, she took the fruits of my advice,

And he, repelled—a short tale to make—

Fell into a sadness, then into a fast,

Thence to a watch, thence into a weakness,

Thence to a lightness, and, by this declension,

150   Into the madness wherein now he raves

And all we mourn for.

King   Do you think 'tis this?

Queen   It may be; very like.

Polonius Hath there been such a time—I would fain know that—

That I have positively said ' 'Tis so',

When it prov'd otherwise?

155 **King**   Not that I know.

Polonius Take this from this if this be otherwise.

[*Points to his head and shoulder.*]

If circumstances lead me, I will find

Where truth is hid, though it were hid indeed

Within the centre.

或亲爱的王后陛下会怎么想，　　　　　　　　135

假如我要为他们穿针引线，

或者对这种爱情装聋作哑，

或者熟视无睹、袖手旁观——

您会怎么想？　不，我立即行动，

对我那年轻的小姐这样说道：　　　　　　　140

"哈姆雷特身为王子，高不可攀。

这绝对不行。"然后我发出指令，

要她闭门不出、拒绝他来访，

不许她接待使者、收受信物；

她采纳了我的忠告，且行之有效，　　　　　　145

而他，遭到了拒绝——长话短说——

首先忧郁寡欢，然后不思茶饭，

然后夜不能寐，然后虚弱憔悴，

然后头晕目眩，就这样每况愈下，

最后疯癫，他因此语无伦次，　　　　　　　　150

我们都为之痛心。

国王　　　　　　　　　您想是这样吗？

王后　也许是吧；很可能。

波洛纽斯　是否有过哪一次——我很想知道——

我肯定地说过"情况就是这样"，

而证明却是那样？

国王　　　　　　　　　我尚未见过。　　　　155

波洛纽斯　否则，就把这个从这上面拿下。

　　　　［指向自己的头和肩。］

假如条件许可，我将会查明

其中的真相，哪怕它被藏在

地球的中央。

King	How may we try it further?
160 **Polonius**	You know sometimes he walks four hours together
	Here in the lobby.
Queen	So he does indeed.
Polonius	At such a time I'll loose my daughter to him.
	Be you and I behind an arras then,
	Mark the encounter. If he love her not,
165	And be not from his reason fall'n thereon,
	Let me be no assistant for a state,
	But keep a farm and carters.
King	We will try it.

Enter Hamlet, reading on a book.

Queen	But look where sadly the poor wretch comes reading.
Polonius	Away, I do beseech you both, away.
170	I'll board him presently. O give me leave.

Exeunt King and Queen [and Attendants].

	How does my good Lord Hamlet?
Hamlet	Well, God-a-mercy.
Polonius	Do you know me, my lord?
Hamlet	Excellent well. You are a fishmonger.
175 **Polonius**	Not I, my lord.
Hamlet	Then I would you were so honest a man.
Polonius	Honest, my lord?
Hamlet	Ay sir. To be honest, as this world goes, is to be one

国王	下一步如何试探？	
波洛纽斯	您知道他有时在大厅里走动	160

长达几个小时。

王后	他的确这样。
波洛纽斯	此时就把我女儿放出去诱他。

然后，咱们两个就躲在幕后，

观察他们相遇。　假如他不爱她，

假如他没有为之神魂颠倒，　　　　　　　　　　165

那就别让我担任国务大臣，

让我去种田、去赶车。

国王	我们试试吧。

哈姆雷特上，读着一本书。

王后	快看，这可怜的孩子念着书走来。	
波洛纽斯	避开，我请求你们二位，避开。	
	我立即上前搭讪。　噢，快离开。	170

国王与王后［及侍从］同下。

哈姆雷特殿下还好吗？

哈姆雷特	还好，上帝保佑您。	
波洛纽斯	您认识我吗，殿下？	
哈姆雷特	一清二楚。　您是一个鱼贩。	
波洛纽斯	我不是，殿下。	175
哈姆雷特	我但愿您是一位诚实之人。	
波洛纽斯	诚实吗，殿下？	
哈姆雷特	是 的，先 生。　在 当 今 这 个 世 界，诚实	

---

174. 鱼贩：若按常识，这种荒唐的称呼很不适合波洛纽斯的身份。　不过，若按其另一种意思却很贴切，即：人们常认为鱼贩子的女儿具有非凡的生育习性，正如下文 181-5 行所指（Jenkins）。

man picked out of ten thousand.

180 **Polonius** That's very true, my lord.

Hamlet For if the sun breed maggots in a dead dog, being a good kissing carrion—Have you a daughter?

Polonius I have, my lord.

Hamlet
185 Let her not walk i'th' sun. Conception is a blessing, but as your daughter may conceive—friend, look to't.

Polonius [*aside*] How say you by that? Still harping on my daughter. Yet he knew me not at first; a said I was a fishmonger. A is far gone. And truly in my youth I
190 suffered much extremity for love, very near this. I'll speak to him again—What do you read, my lord?

Hamlet Words, words, words.

Polonius What is the matter, my lord?

Hamlet Between who?

195 **Polonius** I mean the matter that you read, my lord.

Hamlet Slanders, sir. For the satirical rogue says here that old men have gray beards, that their faces are wrinkled, their eyes purging thick amber and plum—, tree gum, and that they have a plentiful lack of wit
200 together with most weak hams—all which, sir, though I most powerfully and potently believe, yet I hold it not honesty to have it thus set down. For yourself, sir, shall grow old as I am—if like a crab you could go backward.

	的人可是万里挑一。	
波洛纽斯	一点不假,殿下。	180
哈姆雷特	因为假如太阳能在死狗身上孵育蛆虫, 因为那是可口的腐肉——您有个女儿吗?	
波洛纽斯	我有,殿下。	
哈姆雷特	别让她露面。怀有东西本是一种赐福, 但因为您的女儿也会怀上东西——朋友, 要注意。	185
波洛纽斯	[*旁白*]我说得没错吧?依然念着我的女儿! 可他最初并没认出我来;他说我是个鱼贩。 他已神志不清。我年轻的时候也确实为了 爱情疯疯癫癫,跟这非常接近。我要继续 和他攀谈。 ——您在读什么,殿下?	190
哈姆雷特	胡言,胡言,胡言。	
波洛纽斯	是什么事情,殿下?	
哈姆雷特	谁跟谁?	
波洛纽斯	我是指您书里的事情,殿下。	195
哈姆雷特	是诽谤,先生。因为这位爱挖苦人的无赖 在这里说道,老年人胡子花白、皱纹满面, 他们都满目眼屎、泪水不断;他还进一步 说道,他们大都缺乏理智,并且大腿发软 ——所有这些,先生,尽管我对此深信不疑, 可是我认为要是如此记录下来却有些不妥。 因为,就您本人而言,先生,您完全可以 变得与我年龄相当——假如您能像螃蟹那样 可以倒行。	200

181-2. 太阳……腐肉:太阳能在尸体上面孕育新生是一种古老的观念,哈姆雷特此刻从书本上朗读,或假装朗读类似内容恰如其分(Jenkins)。

205	**Polonius**	[*aside*] Though this be madness, yet there is method in't. —Will you walk out of the air, my lord?
	Hamlet	Into my grave?
	Polonius	Indeed, that's out of the air. —[*aside*] How pregnant sometimes his replies are—a happiness that often
210		madness hits on, which reason and sanity could not so prosperously be delivered of. I will leave him and suddenly contrive the means of meeting between him and my daughter. —My lord, I will take my leave of you.
215	**Hamlet**	You cannot, sir, take from me anything that I will not more willingly part withal—except my life, except my life, except my life.
	Polonius	Fare you well, my lord.
	Hamlet	These tedious old fools.

Enter Rosencrantz and Guildenstern.

220	**Polonius**	You go to seek the Lord Hamlet. There he is.
	Ros.	God save you, sir. *Exit Polonius.*
	Guild.	My honoured lord.
	Ros.	My most dear lord.
	Hamlet	My excellent good friends. How dost thou,
225		Guildenstern? Ah, Rosencrantz. Good lads, how do you both?
	Ros.	As the indifferent children of the earth.

| 波洛纽斯 | ［旁白］尽管这是疯话，但却很有见地。 | 205 |

波洛纽斯　［旁白］尽管这是疯话，但却很有见地。　　　205
　　　　　您愿意进去避避风吗，殿下？

哈姆雷特　到我的坟里？

波洛纽斯　不错，那是个避风之处。——［旁白］他
　　　　　的回答，有时竟是那么一针见血——
　　　　　只有疯狂往往才会道出的妙语，然而　210
　　　　　理智与常情却只能望尘莫及。我现在
　　　　　离开他一会儿，我要设法让他跟我的
　　　　　女儿不期而遇。——我的殿下，我要辞别
　　　　　于您。

哈姆雷特　凡是我不愿意舍弃的东西，先生，您　215
　　　　　都无法从我这里带去——除了我的生命，
　　　　　除了我的生命，除了我的生命。

波洛纽斯　再见了，殿下。

哈姆雷特　这些讨厌的老傻瓜！

　　　　　　　罗森克兰与盖登斯顿上。

波洛纽斯　你们去找哈姆雷特殿下？　他就在那里。　220

罗森克兰　上帝保佑您，先生。　　　　　　　　波洛纽斯下。

盖登斯顿　我尊贵的殿下！

罗森克兰　我最亲爱的殿下！

哈姆雷特　我亲爱的好友！你好吗，盖登斯顿？
　　　　　啊，罗森克兰！好伙计，你们两个　225
　　　　　还好吗？

罗森克兰　就像世上的平庸之辈一样。

---

206. 进去避避风：波洛纽斯把哈姆雷特当成病人，让他进到屋里避开冷风（Gill）。

207. 到我的坟里：哈姆雷特继续按字面意义对波罗纽斯予以反驳——假如要想真正地"避风"，还有什么地方能比坟墓更加安全？　（Jenkins）

Guild.	Happy in that we are not over-happy; on Fortune's cap we are not the very button.
230 **Hamlet**	Nor the soles of her shoe?
Ros.	Neither, my lord.
Hamlet	Then you live about her waist, or in the middle of her favours?
Guild.	Faith, her privates we.
235 **Hamlet**	In the secret parts of Fortune? O most true , she is a strumpet. What news?
Ros.	None, my lord, but the world's grown honest.
Hamlet	Then is doomsday near. But your news is not true. Let me question more in particular. What have you,
240	my good friends, deserved at the hands of Fortune that she sends you to prison hither?
Guild.	Prison, my lord?
Hamlet	Denmark's a prison.
Ros.	Then is the world one.
245 **Hamlet**	A goodly one, in which there are many confines, wards, and dungeons, Denmark being one o'th' worst.
Ros.	We think not so, my lord.
Hamlet	Why, then 'tis none to you; for there is nothing
250	either good or bad but thinking makes it so . To me it is a prison.
Ros.	Why, then your ambition makes it one; 'tis too narrow for your mind.

盖登斯顿	幸福的是我们并非过分幸福：我们不是	
	幸运女神帽顶上的那颗纽扣！	
哈姆雷特	也不是她的鞋底？	230
盖登斯顿	也不是，殿下。	
哈姆雷特	那么你们就在她的腰部，或是她宠幸的	
	正中？	
盖登斯顿	没错，就是她的私处！	
哈姆雷特	在命运女神的私处？噢，太对了，她是	235
	一个婊子！什么消息？	
罗森克兰	没有，殿下，只是这世界变得诚实起来。	
哈姆雷特	那么世界的末日已经来临。可您的消息	
	并不可靠。让我好好盘问盘问。你们都	
	干了些什么，我的好友，竟让命运女神	240
	送入这座监狱？	
盖登斯顿	什么监狱，殿下？	
哈姆雷特	丹麦是一座监狱。	
罗森克兰	这个世界也是一座。	
哈姆雷特	是一座很好的监狱，里面有许多牢房、	245
	囚室、和地牢，丹麦属于其中最糟的	
	一座。	
罗森克兰	我们不这样认为，殿下。	
哈姆雷特	唉，那么对你们来说不是；因为世上	
	的事情本无好坏，只是人们思想各异。	250
	对我来说就是监狱。	
罗森克兰	咳，那是因为您野心太大：丹麦太小，	
	您无法施展。	

236. 婊子：因为命运本身反复无常、变幻莫测，所以才这样称谓（Jenkins）。 238. 世界的末日已经来临：因为诚实与这个世界格格不入 （见本场178-9），所以这个世界行将毁灭（Jenkins）。

	Hamlet	O God, I could be bounded in a nut shell and count
255		myself a king of infinite space—were it not that I
		have bad dreams.
	Guild.	Which dreams indeed are ambition; for the very
		substance of the ambitious is merely the shadow of a
		dream.
260	**Hamlet**	A dream itself is but a shadow.
	Ros.	Truly, and I hold ambition of so airy and light a
		quality that it is but a shadow's shadow.
	Hamlet	Then are our beggars bodies, and our monarchs
		And outstretched heroes the beggars' shadows. Shall
265		We to th' court? For by my fay, I cannot reason.
	Ros. ⎫ **Guild.** ⎭	We'll wait upon you.
	Hamlet	No such matter. I will not sort you with the rest of
		my servants; for, to speak to you like an honest man,
		I am most dreadfully attended. But in the beaten
270		way of friendship, what make you at Elsinore?
	Ros.	To visit you, my lord, no other occasion.
	Hamlet	Beggar that I am, I am even poor in thanks, but I
		thank you. And sure, dear friends, my thanks are too
		dear a halfpenny. Were you not sent for? Is it your
275		own inclining? Is it a free visitation? Come, come,

哈姆雷特	上帝啊，我可以把自己装进一个果壳	
	而自认为是一个拥有无限空间的国王——	255
	若不是我常做噩梦。	
盖登斯顿	噩梦其实就是野心；因为野心家所	
	获取的一切，也不过是一种梦想的	
	影子。	
哈姆雷特	梦想本身不过是一种影子。	260
罗森克兰	不错，野心的本质如此虚无、如此缥缈，	
	我认为它不过是一种影子的影子。	
哈姆雷特	那么，我们的乞丐就是原型，而我们的	
	帝王和出人头地的英雄则是乞丐的影子。	
	我们要上法庭吗？因为我确实无法辩明。	265
罗森克兰 } 盖登斯顿 }	我们愿伺候殿下。	
哈姆雷特	没这回事儿。我不愿把你们与我的仆人	
	混为一谈；因为，说实在的，我受到的	
	服侍糟糕透顶。看在朋友的份上，别再	
	拐弯抹角，你们为何来到埃尔西诺？	270
罗森克兰	来看看您，殿下，没什么别的。	
哈姆雷特	我身为乞丐，我的谢意同样可怜，但我要	
	感谢你们。当然，亲爱的朋友，我的谢意	
	半分钱都会太贵。难道你们不是奉命而来？	
	是你们自己的意愿吗？是自愿来访吗？来，	275

257-9. 野心家……影子：对一位有野心的人来说，他首先会梦想自己将要力争获取什么东西，当他得到这些东西之后，又会去效仿梦想中的情景（影子）。因为是他的梦想创造了这些"东西"，所以说这些"东西"就是他那种梦想的"影子"，也可以说是一种影子的影子（因为梦想本身就是一种影子）（Jenkins）。 263-4. 乞丐……影子：哈姆雷特在继续争论刚才的话题：假如野心就像刚才所说的那样虚无缥缈，那么真实的人必定是那些毫无野心的人（"乞丐"）；而那些有野心的人（"帝王"和"英雄"）一定是这些乞丐的影子。这些"出人头地"的英雄就像是伸长的影子，看上去比自身更为高大（Jenkins）。

deal justly with me. Come, come. Nay, speak.

Guild. What should we say, my lord?

Hamlet Anything but to th' purpose. You were sent for, and there is a kind of confession in your looks, which your
280 modesties have not craft enough to colour. I know the good King and Queen have sent for you.

Ros. To what end, my lord?

Hamlet That, you must teach me. But let me conjure you, by the rights of our fellowship, by the consonancy of
285 our youth, by the obligation of our ever-preserved love, and by what more dear a better proposer can charge you withal, be even and direct with me whether you were sent for or no.

Ros. [aside to Guildenstern] What say you?

290 **Hamlet** Nay, then I have an eye of you. If you love me, hold not off.

Guild. My lord, we were sent for.

Hamlet I will tell you why; so shall my anticipation prevent your discovery, and your secrecy to the King and
295 Queen moult no feather. I have of late, but wherefore I know not, lost all my mirth, forgone all custom of exercises; and indeed it goes so heavily with my disposition that this goodly frame, the earth seems to me a sterile promontory, this most excellent canopy
300 the air, look you, this brave o'erhanging firmament, this majestical roof fretted with golden fire, why, it

	来，如实告诉我。　来，来。　不行，快说！	
盖登斯顿	我们该说些啥呢，殿下？	
哈姆雷特	凡是离题的东西都行。你们是奉命而来，	
	你们的表情早已供认，因为你们的朴实	
	尚未老练得能加以掩盖。我知道是好心	280
	的国王和王后派你们前来。	
罗森克兰	为了什么，殿下？	
哈姆雷特	这一点，你们必须赐教。但我恳求你们，	
	本着我们牢固的友情，本着我们年轻时	
	的和睦，本着我们长期的关爱，本着某	285
	位更会提供誓言者所能提供的任何理由，	
	请直截了当地告诉我，你们是奉命而来	
	还是自愿。	
罗森克兰	［向盖登斯顿］您怎么说？	
哈姆雷特	不行，我看着你们呢。假如你们爱我，	290
	就不要推托。	
盖登斯顿	殿下，我们是派来的。	
哈姆雷特	我来告诉你们为啥；好让我的预见防止	
	你们的露馅，好让你们跟国王和王后的	
	秘密毫毛未损。我近来，但不知为什么，	295
	失去了所有的欢乐，忽略了所有的正常	
	活动；心情变得如此沉重，大地——这一	
	座优美的框架，对我来说只不过是一片	
	荒芜的海岬；这顶最杰出的华盖——天空，	
	你们注意，这座壮丽高悬的苍穹，这片	300
	金碧辉煌、庄严雄伟的屋顶，唉，对我	

---

278. 凡是离题的东西都行：哈姆雷特已经怀疑罗森克兰与盖登斯顿的诚意，因此他断定他们不会给他任何坦率的回答（Gill）。　300. 壮丽高悬的苍穹：装饰华丽的屋顶。　批评家认为，哈姆雷特此刻所描述的是伊丽莎白时代的剧院——也许正是莎士比亚自己的环球剧院（Gill）。

appeareth nothing to me but a foul and pestilent con-
gregation of vapours. What piece of work is a man,
how noble in reason, how infinite in faculties, in form
305 and moving how express and admirable, in action
how like an angel, in apprehension how like a god:
the beauty of the world, the paragon of animals—
and yet, to me, what is this quintessence of dust?
Man delights not me—nor woman neither, though
310 by your smiling you seem to say so.

Ros. My lord, there was no such stuff in my thoughts.

Hamlet Why did ye laugh then, when I said man delights
not me?

Ros. To think, my lord, if you delight not in man, what
315 Lenten entertainment the players shall receive from
you. We coted them on the way, and hither are they
coming to offer you service.

Hamlet He that plays the king shall be welcome—his Majesty shall have tribute on me, the adventurous knight
320 shall use his foil and target, the lover shall not sigh
gratis, the humourous man shall end his part in peace,
the clown shall make those laugh whose lungs are
tickle a th' sear, and the lady shall say her mind
freely—or the blank verse shall halt for't. What
325 players are they?

Ros. Even those you were wont to take such delight in,
the tragedians of the city.

Hamlet How chances it they travel? Their residence, both

来说,只不过是一团恶臭和致命的瘴气。
人是一件多么精巧的杰作,他拥有多么
高贵的理性、多么无限的技能,他仪表
多么端庄,举止多么美妙,他行动多像 305
天使,他理解多像上帝:人世间的秀美,
动物界的典范——然而,对我来说,这一
尊源于泥土的精英又算得了什么?男人
无法令我高兴——女人也不能,尽管你们
的微笑暗示好像并非如此。 310

罗森克兰 我心里并没有这种意思,殿下。

哈姆雷特 那么当我说到男人无法令我高兴时,你
为何发笑?

罗森克兰 我是想,殿下,假如您不喜欢男人的话,
那么,那帮演员将会得到您何等的冷遇。 315
我们在路上追上了他们,他们正要来此
向您献艺。

哈姆雷特 扮演国王者会受到欢迎——他这位陛下
将会得到我应有的谢意,那爱冒险的
骑士自然要挥盾舞剑,情人的哀叹将 320
不会白费,性情乖张的男子将会随意
叫嚣,小丑自会让那一触即发的观众
捧腹大笑,女士将会畅所欲言——否则
素体诗听起来就会蹩脚。他们都是些
什么演员? 325

罗森克兰 就是那些您向来都很喜欢的——本市的
悲剧演员。

哈姆雷特 他们怎么走起了江湖?他们在自己的

320-23. 骑士……舞剑……畅所欲言:哈姆雷特在列举专业剧团里某些演员的行为特征(Gill)。

in reputation and profit, was better both ways.

330 **Ros.**   I think their inhibition comes by the means of the late innovation.

Hamlet   Do they hold the same estimation they did when I was in the city? Are they so followed?

Ros.   No, indeed are they not.

335 **Hamlet**   How comes it? Do they grow rusty?

Ros.   Nay, their endeavour keeps in the wonted pace; but there is, sir, an eyrie of children, little eyases, that cry out on the top of question, and are most tyran- nically clapped for't. These are now the fashion, and
340   so berattle the common stages—so they call them— that many wearing rapiers are afraid of goose-quills and dare scarce come thither.

Hamlet   What, are they children? Who maintains 'em? How are they escotted? Will they pursue the quality
345   no longer than they can sing? Will they not say afterwards, if they should grow themselves to com- mon players—as it is most like, if their means are no better—their writers do them wrong to make them exclaim against their own succession?

350 **Ros.**   Faith, there has been much to do on both sides; and the nation holds it no sin to tar them to controversy. There was for a while no money bid for argument

剧院里坐地演出,本是名利双收。

罗森克兰　我认为他们的停演是因为最近的时局　　　330
　　　　　动乱。

哈姆雷特　他们的演出是不是跟我在城里时一样
　　　　　受人喜欢？　他们的观众还多吗？

罗森克兰　不多,确实不多了。

哈姆雷特　怎么会呢？　演技已经荒疏？　　　　　335

罗森克兰　不是,他们的努力跟往常一样；只是,
　　　　　殿下,有一群娃娃——小小的雏鹰,在
　　　　　台上放开嗓门大喊大叫,反而博得了
　　　　　观众的疯狂喝彩。这已成为一种时髦,
　　　　　将公共剧院——人们都这样称谓——已经　　340
　　　　　糟蹋到这等地步,好多身佩长剑的人士
　　　　　因害怕鹅毛笔管而不敢前往剧院。

哈姆雷特　什么,一群娃娃？谁保护他们？他们
　　　　　如何生活？难道他们的嗓子喊破之后
　　　　　就不再演戏？假如他们一旦成为普通　　　345
　　　　　演员——因为情况多半如此,如果他们
　　　　　找不到更好的谋生之路,难道他们那
　　　　　时就不会埋怨——是害人的编剧让他们
　　　　　砸了自己的饭碗？

罗森克兰　的确,双方为此纷争不断；而且观众也　　350
　　　　　唆使他们相互漫骂,反而感到心安理得。
　　　　　曾经有一段时间,只有那些涉及编剧和

---

342. 害怕鹅毛笔管：雄辩胜于利剑的例证。 身佩利剑的勇士因害怕受到讥讽而对公共剧院望而却步（Jenkins）。 350. 双方为此纷争不断：莎士比亚此处所影射的是,在私人剧院里演出的儿童演员与在公共剧院里演出的专业演员之间的冲突,该冲突分别由当时的英国剧作家本·琼森与托马斯·德克领导（Gill）。 352-3. 编剧和演员之间：为儿童演员撰写剧本的剧作家与专业演员之间相互漫骂（Jenkins）。

unless the poet and the player went to cuffs in the
question.

355 **Hamlet**   Is't possible?

Guild.   O, there has been much throwing about of brains.

Hamlet   Do the boys carry it away?

Ros.   Ay, that they do, my lord, Hercules and his load too.

Hamlet   It is not very strange; for my uncle is King of Den-
360   mark, and those that would make mouths at him
while my father lived give twenty, forty, fifty, a
hundred ducats apiece for his picture in little.
'Sblood, there is something in this more than
natural, if philosophy could find it out.

A flourish of trumpets.

365 **Guild.**   There are the players.

Hamlet   Gentlemen, you are welcome to Elsinore. Your
hands, come then. Th'appurtenance of welcome is
fashion and ceremony. Let me comply with you in
this garb—lest my extent to the players, which I tell
370   you must show fairly outwards, should more appear
like entertainment than yours. You are welcome.
But my uncle-father and aunt-mother are deceived.

Guild.   In what, my dear lord?

Hamlet   I am but mad north-north-west. When the wind is

演员之间就此相互攻击的剧本，才会有

人出钱。

哈姆雷特　　这可能吗？　　　　　　　　　　　　　　　　355

盖登斯顿　　噢，双方为此绞尽脑汁、唇枪舌剑。

哈姆雷特　　是不是娃娃们占了上风？

罗森克兰　　是的，殿下，赫克勒斯及其地球也被卷走。

哈姆雷特　　这并不很稀奇；因为我的叔父一旦当上

丹麦国王，那些当我父亲在世时，常常　　　　360

对他做鬼脸的人们，现在竟愿拿出二十、

四十、五十、一百块金币换取他的一张

小像。上帝作证，其中的情理有些反常，

假如科学能将其探明。

号角齐鸣。

盖登斯顿　　演员们要来了。　　　　　　　　　　　　　　365

哈姆雷特　　先生们，欢迎你们来到埃尔西诺。快来，

咱们握握手。握手表示欢迎是一种礼节

和时尚。我也按照这种方式对你们表示

欢迎——恐怕我对演员们的招呼，超过了

对二位朋友的欢迎程度，因为我对他们　　　370

一定会显得热情洋溢。欢迎你们。不过

我的叔父和婶娘上了当。

盖登斯顿　　在哪方面，亲爱的殿下？

哈姆雷特　　西北风吹来时我才有点失常。南风

---

358. 赫克勒斯及其地球也被卷走：赫克勒斯为传说中的超人，曾一度身背地球，莎士比亚将其用作自己剧院的标志。　莎士比亚的好多剧本，包括《哈姆雷特》在内都在此上演。　此处好像是说，娃娃们的成功甚至影响到了莎士比亚的环球剧院（Gill）。　364. 舞台指示："号角齐鸣"，演员们通常用这种方式宣告自己的到来（Jenkins）。　372. 叔父和婶娘：国王本是哈姆雷特的叔叔（uncle），现已通过婚姻成了他的继父（stepfather），所以称为"叔父（uncle-father）"；哈姆雷特的母亲——王后，也是通过该婚姻现已成为他的"婶子（aunt）"，所以称为"婶娘（aunt-mother）"（Thompson）。　374. 西北风……失常：人们认为疯子的情绪会因天气变化而波动（Jenkins）。

375   southerly, I know a hawk from a handsaw.

Enter Polonius.

Polonius   Well be with you, gentlemen.

Hamlet   Hark you, Guildenstern, and you too—at each ear a hearer. That great baby you see there is not yet out of his swaddling-clouts.

380 **Ros.**   Happily he is the second time come to them, for they say an old man is twice a child.

Hamlet   I will prophesy he comes to tell me of the players. Mark it. —You say right, sir, a Monday morning, 'twas then indeed.

385 **Polonius**   My lord, I have news to tell you.

Hamlet   My lord, I have news to tell you. When Roscius was an actor in Rome—

Polonius   The actors are come hither, my lord.

Hamlet   Buzz, buzz.

390 **Polonius**   Upon my honour—

Hamlet   Then came each actor on his ass—

Polonius   The best actors in the world, either for tragedy, comedy, history, pastoral, pastoral-comical, his-torical-pastoral, tragical-historical, tragical-comical-

395   historical-pastoral, scene individable, or poem un-

吹来时,我可不会把老鹰当成白鹭。　　　　　　　　　375

波洛纽斯上。

波洛纽斯	祝你们好运,先生们。
哈姆雷特	注意,盖登斯顿,还有您——你们都过来 仔细听着。你们看那边那个老小孩尚未 脱去襁褓。
罗森克兰	也许他是二次入襁,因为人们都说老人　　380 就是再生的儿童。
哈姆雷特	我敢断言他是来向我通报演员们的事情。 听着。——你说得对,先生,星期一上午, 正是那个时候。
波洛纽斯	殿下,我有消息向您汇报。　　　　　　　385
哈姆雷特	阁下,我有消息向您汇报。当罗西乌斯 在罗马当演员时——
波洛纽斯	演员们已经到了,殿下。
哈姆雷特	罢了,罢了!
波洛纽斯	以我的名誉担保——　　　　　　　　　390
哈姆雷特	演员都骑着蠢驴到来——
波洛纽斯	他们是天下最棒的演员,无论悲剧、喜剧、 历史剧、田园剧、田园喜剧、历史田园剧、 悲剧历史剧、悲喜历史田园剧、无法分类 的,还是包罗万象的。不怕塞内加的悲剧　　395

---

375. 不会把老鹰当成白鹭:哈姆雷特在警告自己的校友:他并未完全丧失理智,因此也能识破伪装(Jenkins)。　386. 罗西乌斯:古罗马著名演员。　哈姆雷特在波罗纽斯宣布演员到来之前首先提及演出事宜,旨在让他有窘迫之感(Thompson)。　391. 演员……到来:可能源自一首歌谣;原文中的"ass"也可指屁股(arse)(Thompson)。　395-6. 塞内加……普劳图斯:普劳图斯和塞内加被誉为古罗马最好的喜剧作家和悲剧作家。　他们两人均对莎士比亚的剧本创作产生了很大影响(Thompson)。

limited. Seneca cannot be too heavy, nor Plautus too light. For the law of writ, and the liberty, these are the only men.

Hamlet   O Jephthah, judge of Israel, what a treasure hadst
400   thou!

Polonius   What a treasure had he, my lord?

Hamlet   Why,

   One fair daughter and no more,

   The which he loved passing well.

405 **Polonius** [*aside*] Still on my daughter.

Hamlet   Am I not i'th' right, old Jephthah?

Polonius   If you call me Jephthah, my lord, I have a daughter that I love passing well.

Hamlet   Nay, that follows not.

410 **Polonius** What follows then, my lord?

Hamlet   Why,

   As by lot God wot,

and then, you know,

   It came to pass, as most like it was.

415   The first row of the pious chanson will show you more, for look where my abridgement comes.

太深沉,不嫌普劳图斯的喜剧太轻快。无
论剧本的创作是循规蹈矩,还是自由发挥,
他们都是无与伦比。

哈姆雷特　噢,耶弗他,以色列的士师,你有件多棒的
宝贝! 　　　　　　　　　　　　　　　　　　400

波洛纽斯　他有一件什么宝贝,殿下?

哈姆雷特　哎,

　　　只有一位美丽的女儿,

　　　对她的疼爱无微不至。

波洛纽斯　[旁白]还在念叨我的女儿! 　　　　　　405

哈姆雷特　我说得不对吗,老耶弗他?

波洛纽斯　您若叫我耶弗他,殿下,我是有个女儿,

　　　对她的疼爱无微不至。

哈姆雷特　不对,并非如此。

波洛纽斯　那究竟如何,殿下? 　　　　　　　　　410

哈姆雷特　唉,

　　　命中注定,上帝有灵,

　　然后,您知道,

　　　当时的局势,大致已定。

这首圣经歌谣的第一节会告诉您更多, 　　　415

快看,我的谈话让谁给打断!

---

399. 耶弗他,以色列的士师:源于一首歌谣,讲述耶弗他的故事（见《圣经》"士师记"
11 章 30-40 节）,他为了政治目的而牺牲了自己的女儿——波洛纽斯正要步其后尘。哈姆雷特在
吟诵其中的诗句（Gill）。 403-4. 只有……不至:哈姆雷特在引述该歌谣中有关耶弗他的两行诗
句（Thompson）。 409. 并非如此:波洛纽斯跟耶弗他一样也有一位女儿,但他并不像耶弗他那
样疼爱自己的女儿（Jenkins）。 411-4. 哈姆雷特假装误解了波洛纽斯的意思,并未按照逻辑回答
波洛纽斯的"究竟如何",而是说出了上述歌谣的下文如何（Jenkins）。

Enter the Players.

You are welcome, masters. Welcome, all. —I am glad to see thee well. —Welcome, good friends. —O, old friend, why, thy face is valanced since I saw thee

420   last. Com'st thou to beard me in Denmark? —What, my young lady and mistress! By'r lady, your ladyship is nearer to heaven than when I saw you last by the altitude of a chopine. Pray God your voice, like a piece of uncurrent gold, be not cracked within the

425   ring. —Masters, you are all welcome. We'll e'en to't like French falconers, fly at anything we see. We'll have a speech straight. Come, give us a taste of your quality. Come, a passionate speech.

1st Player   What speech, my good lord?

430 **Hamlet**   I heard thee speak me a speech once, but it was never acted, or if it was, not above once—for the play, I remember, pleased not the million, 'twas caviare to the general. But it was, as I received it— and others, whose judgments in such matters cried in

435   the top of mine—an excellent play, well digested in the scenes, set down with as much modesty as cunning. I remember one said there were no sallets in the lines to make the matter savoury, nor no matter in the phrase that might indict the author of affection,

440   but called it an honest method, as wholesome as

众演员上。

欢迎，大师们。欢迎各位。——看到大家
很好我很高兴。——欢迎，好朋友。——噢，
老朋友，咳，自从上次见面以后，你脸上
多了一层饰物！你是来向我吹胡子的吗？ 420
嗬，我的妙龄女郎和情人！我的圣母呀，
小姐您比我们上次见面时离天又接近了
一鞋底！上帝保佑，您那金子般圆润的
嗓子可不要变成不管用的破锣！大师们，
欢迎你们各位！我们要像法国猎人那样， 425
对所见的一切都要进行搜索。我们这就
来一段台词。快，让我们领略一下你们
的演技。 快，来一段激昂的台词！

演员甲　什么台词，我的好殿下？

哈姆雷特　我曾听你朗诵过一段台词，但这个剧本 430
从未演过，即使演过，也不过一次——因
为该剧，我记得，并未赢得大众的喜爱。
它简直是阳春白雪。不过，我倒是认为——
还有一些在这方面比我更有发言权的人
也认为——该剧是一部杰作，场景安排得 435
井井有条，创作手法朴实无华，又娴熟
巧妙。我记得有一个人说过，字里行间
既没有庸俗的插科打诨，也没有任何的
遣词造句能表明作者具有哗众取宠之嫌，
而是把它称为一种率真的写法，健康而 440

419-20. 脸上多了一层饰物：长出了胡子（Gill）。　422-3. 离天又接近一鞋底：长高了。 这
位男扮女装的演员可能穿着一双当时颇为流行的软木底高跟鞋（Jenkins）。

sweet, and by very much more handsome than fine.
One speech in't I chiefly loved— 'twas Aeneas' tale
to Dido—and thereabout of it especially when he
speaks of Priam's slaughter. If it live in your memory,

445 begin at this line—let me see, let me see—
The rugged Pyrrhus, like th'Hyrcanian beast—
'Tis not so. It begins with Pyrrhus—
The rugged Pyrrhus, he whose sable arms,
Black as his purpose, did the night resemble

450 *When he lay couched in the ominous horse,*
Hath now this dread and black complexion smear'd
With heraldry more dismal. Head to foot
Now is he total gules, horridly trick'd
With blood of fathers, mothers, daughters, sons,

455 *Bak'd and impasted with the parching streets,*
That lend a tyrannous and damned light
To their lord's murder. Roasted in wrath and fire,
And thus o'ersized with coagulate gore,

又甜美,更注重自然得体而非刻意雕琢。

其中有段台词我很喜爱——就是埃涅阿斯

对狄多诉说——尤其是当他讲到普里阿姆

遇害时候的那一节。如果您还能够记得,

就从这里开始——让我想想,让我想想—— 445

野蛮的皮洛斯,如赫凯尼亚猛虎——

不是这样。 是以皮洛斯开头的——

野蛮的皮洛斯,穿着漆黑的盔甲,

正如他的企图,黑夜般阴森可怖,

伏身藏入那预示凶险的木马, 450

这个可怕的阴影已糊上一层

红色更显杀气腾腾。从头到脚,

浑身血红,令人恐怖地沾满了

父亲、母亲、女儿、儿子的鲜血,

已被灼热的街道烘干焙硬, 455

发出一丝凶残和该死的亮光,

导致主人丧命。经过怒火的烧烤,

周身已裹上一层凝固的血污,

442-3. 埃涅阿斯对狄多诉说:《希神》埃涅阿斯是特洛伊战争中的英雄。 特洛伊沦陷后,他背父携子逃出火城,经长期流浪到达意大利。 据说他的后代就在那里建立了罗马。 狄多,是迦太基(Carthage)的建国者及女王。 拉丁史诗说她坠入埃涅阿斯的情网,后因埃涅阿斯与她分手感到失望而自杀(陆谷孙《英汉大词典》)。 文中的"诉说",是指埃涅阿斯为女王叙述遇难时的情景。 具体故事,请参见维吉尔的史诗《埃涅伊特》(Aeneid) 第二卷(Jenkins)。 443. 普里阿姆:《希神》特洛伊最后一位国王。 统治期间发生了特洛伊战争。 (陆谷孙:英汉大词典)。 446. 皮洛斯:希腊英雄阿基里斯(Achilles)之子,率军攻打特洛伊城,为死去的父亲报仇,并杀死了特洛伊国王普里阿姆及其家人(Thompson)。 446. 赫凯尼亚:为里海南岸的一个地区,曾以盛产猛虎而出名(Thompson)。 450. 凶险的木马:就是希腊人借以进入特洛伊城的木马(Jenkins)。 455. 灼热的街道:街道之所以灼热,该是由于宫殿起火所致(Thompson)。

With eyes like carbuncles, the hellish Pyrrhus

460 Old grandsire Priam seeks.

So proceed you.

Polonius 'Fore God, my lord, well spoken, with good accent
and good discretion.

1st Player Anon he finds him,

465 Striking too short at Greeks. His antique sword,

Rebellious to his arm, lies where it falls,

Repugnant to command. Unequal match'd,

Pyrrhus at Priam drives, in rage strikes wide;

But with the whiff and wind of his fell sword

470 Th'unnerved father falls. Then senseless Ilium,

Seeming to feel this blow, with flaming top

Stoops to his base, and with a hideous crash

Takes prisoner Pyrrhus' ear. For lo, his sword,

Which was declining on the milky head

475 Of reverend Priam, seem'd i'th' air to stick;

So, as a painted tyrant, Pyrrhus stood,

And like a neutral to his will and matter,

Did nothing.

But as we often see against some storm

480 A silence in the heavens, the rack stand still,

The bold winds speechless, and the orb below

As hush as death, anon the dreadful thunder

Doth rend the region; so after Pyrrhus' pause

Aroused vengeance sets him new awork,

瞪着火红双眼,阴险的皮洛斯

搜寻老祖宗普里阿姆。 460

您接着说。

波洛纽斯 天哪,您朗诵得真好,殿下,抑扬顿挫、

非常得体!

演员甲 　　　　　　　很快发现他,

对希腊兵鞭长莫及。他的旧宝剑, 465

蔑视他的手臂,在原地躺着,

不听使唤。双方的力量悬殊,

皮洛斯追赶普里阿姆,乱砍一气;

惊慌的老人竟被他那挥舞的

利剑一下扇倒。无知的伊利昂, 470

似乎也感到这一击,楼顶冒着

火光一坍到底,一声可怕的巨响

让皮洛斯戛然而止。请看,他那

劈向可敬的普里阿姆银白色

头顶的利剑,好像粘在了空中; 475

犹如画中的暴君,皮洛斯站着,

好像要在意愿与行为之间中立,

一动不动。

可正如我们常常看到暴风雨

来临之前,天空宁静,乌云压顶, 480

急风沉默,大地死一般沉寂;

顷刻间可怕的雷鸣响彻云端;

皮洛斯如此稍事停顿之后,

他的复仇之心又重新点燃,

---

460. 老祖宗:普里阿姆因生有50个儿子而出名(Gill)。 470. 伊利昂:特洛伊城堡(Gill)。

485   *And never did the Cyclops' hammers fall*

On Mars's armour, forg'd for proof eterne,

With less remorse than Pyrrhus' bleeding sword

Now falls on Priam.

Out, out, thou strumpet Fortune! All you gods

490   *In general synod take away her power,*

Break all the spokes and fellies from her wheel,

And bowl the round nave down the hill of heaven

As low as to the fiends.

Polonius   This is too long.

495 **Hamlet**   It shall to the barber's with your beard. —Prithee say on. He's for a jig or a tale of bawdry, or he sleeps. Say on, come to Hecuba.

1st Player   *But who—ah, woe! —had seen the mobbled queen—*

Hamlet   'The mobbled queen'.

500 **Polonius**   That's good.

1st Player   *Run barefoot up and down, threat'ning the flames*

With bisson rheum, a clout upon that head

Where late the diadem stood, and, for a robe,

About her lank and all o'erteemed loins

505   *A blanket, in th'alarm of fear caught up—*

Who this had seen, with tongue in venom steep'd,

'Gainst Fortune's state would treason have pronounc'd.

But if the gods themselves did see her then,

就连赛克罗普为战神铸造　　　　　　　　485

永固的铠甲而猛打的铁锤，

也不如皮洛斯用滴血的利剑

劈向普里阿姆时凶狠。

滚，滚，娼妓般的命运女神！

全体天神一起剥夺她的权力，　　　　　　490

将其轮盘的辐条和轮辋砸烂，

让那圆圆的轮毂从天堂的山顶

滚向地狱的深渊！

波洛纽斯　这太长了。

哈姆雷特　该跟您的胡子一起去理发店了。——请您　　495

说下去。他想来点闹剧或刺激，否则他会

瞌睡。继续，说说赫卡柏。

演员甲　要是谁——啊，哎哟！——看到蒙头的王后——

哈姆雷特　"蒙头的王后"。

波洛纽斯　很好！　　　　　　　　　　　　　　　　500

演员甲　光着双脚上下奔跑，用满眼的

瞎泪威胁烈火，用一块破布

替代以前的皇冠裹在头上，

恐慌中抓起毛毯当作礼袍，

裹住她那过于多产的细腰——　　　　　　505

谁见这种惨状都会唇枪舌剑，

唾骂命运之神的主宰与背叛。

假如众神目睹她当时的情形，

---

485. 赛克罗普：为锻冶之神伍尔坎（Vulcan）工作的三位独眼巨人。据说他们锻造了阿基里斯（Achilles）和埃涅阿斯（Aeneas）所穿的铠甲（Thompson）。491. 轮盘：人们习惯用车轮象征命运之神，因为她总是在不停地运转，而且反复无常（Jenkins）。497. 赫卡柏：特洛伊国王普里阿姆的妻子，目睹自己的丈夫与孩子在特洛伊战争中惨遭杀戮，从而成为忍受痛苦的女性典范（Gill）。505. 过于多产：据说她为普里阿姆国王生育了20个儿子（Thompson）。

When she saw Pyrrhus make malicious sport

510   *In mincing with his sword her husband's limbs,*

The instant burst of clamour that she made,

Unless things mortal move them not at all,

Would have made milch the burning eyes of heaven

And passion in the gods.

515 **Polonius**   Look whe'er he has not turned his colour and has tears in's eyes. Prithee no more.

Hamlet   'Tis well. I'll have thee speak out the rest of this soon. —Good my lord, will you see the players well bestowed? Do you hear, let them be well used, for

520   they are the abstract and brief chronicles of the time. After your death you were better have a bad epitaph than their ill report while you live.

Polonius   My lord, I will use them according to their desert.

Hamlet   God's bodkin, man, much better. Use every man

525   after his desert, and who shall scape whipping? Use them after your own honour and dignity: the less they deserve, the more merit is in your bounty. Take them in.

Polonius   Come, sirs.

530 **Hamlet**   Follow him, friends. We'll hear a play tomorrow. [*to First Player*] Dost thou hear me, old friend? Can you play *The Murder of Gonzago*?

1st Player   Ay, my lord.

Hamlet   We'll ha't tomorrow night. You could for a need

	当她看到皮洛斯恶毒地用剑	
	切剁丈夫肢体时发出的哀号，	510
	定让天上的群星泪水涟涟，	
	让那不朽的众神深表同情，	
	除非凡人的事情一点都不能	
	将他们感动。	
波洛纽斯	请看他的脸色是否已改变，是否已经	515
	热泪盈眶。　请别再说了。	
哈姆雷特	那好吧。我很快就会让你吟诵剩下的	
	台词。——好阁下，您愿意好好地招待	
	这些演员吗？听见了吧，要善待他们，	
	因为他们就是这个时代的简史和摘要。	520
	宁可死后有一篇糟糕的墓志，也不要	
	生前让他们说您的坏话。	
波洛纽斯	殿下，我会按照他们的应得对待他们。	
哈姆雷特	看在上帝的份上，更好一些！若按每人	
	的应得予以对待，谁能逃得脱一顿鞭子？	525
	要按照您的荣誉和尊严对待他们：他们	
	应得的越少，您的功德就越高。领他们	
	进去。	
波洛纽斯	来吧，各位。	
哈姆雷特	跟他走，朋友们。我们明天要演一场戏	530
	［向演员甲］你听我说句话好吗，老朋友？	
	你是否能演《贡扎古之死》？	
演员甲	我能，殿下。	
哈姆雷特	我们明天晚上就演。您将根据需要背诵	

535	study a speech of some dozen or sixteen lines, which
	I would set down and insert in't, could you not?
1st Player	Ay, my lord.
Hamlet	Very well. [*To all the Players*] Follow that lord, and
	look you mock him not. *Exeunt Polonius and Players.*
540	[*To Rosencrantz and Guildenstern*] My good friends,
	I'll leave you till night. You are welcome to Elsinore.
Ros.	Good my lord. *Exeunt Rosencrantz and Guildenstern.*
Hamlet	Ay, so, God buy to you. Now I am alone.
	O what a rogue and peasant slave am I!
545	Is it not monstrous that this player here,
	But in a fiction, in a dream of passion,
	Could force his soul so to his own conceit
	That from her working all his visage wann'd,
	Tears in his eyes, distraction in his aspect,
550	A broken voice, and his whole function suiting
	With forms to his conceit? And all for nothing!
	For Hecuba!
	What's Hecuba to him, or he to her,
	That he should weep for her? What would he do
555	Had he the motive and the cue for passion
	That I have? He would drown the stage with tears,
	And cleave the general ear with horrid speech,
	Make mad the guilty and appal the free,
	Confound the ignorant, and amaze indeed

	一段大约十二或十六行的台词，它们由	535
	我写出插入剧中，您行不行？	
演员甲	行，殿下。	
哈姆雷特	很好。［向众演员］跟上那位大人，可	
	不要嘲笑他！　　　　　波罗纽斯及众演员同下。	
	［向罗森克兰与盖登斯顿］我的好朋友，	540
	咱们晚上再见。　欢迎来到埃尔西诺。	
罗森克兰	再见，殿下。　　　　　罗森克兰与盖登斯顿同下。	
哈姆雷特	好吧，再见。　现在就剩下我了。	
	噢，我是一个多么卑鄙的贱货！	
	看看这位演员，他仅仅凭借	545
	虚构，利用梦幻一般的情感，	
	就能迫使他的心灵符合虚幻，	
	在心灵的作用下他脸色苍白、	
	眼含泪水，看上去心烦意乱、	
	声音颤抖，所有举止符合想象，	550
	难道这不奇怪？　全是无中生有！	
	为了赫卡柏！	
	赫卡柏与他何干，他与她何连，	
	他竟然为她泪流满面？　他若有	
	我那样的动情理由，他又会如何	555
	展现？　他会用泪水将舞台淹没，	
	用骇人的言词把众人耳膜刺破，	
	使罪人发疯，让无辜者惊恐，	
	使无知者困惑，而且也一定	

---

535. 十二或十六行的台词：至于此处所提及的台词，目前尚无人能在第三幕第二场的戏中戏里予以确认。　对此有两种普遍的选择：（1）国王扮演者的台词（183-208）；（2）卢西安纳的台词（249-54）。　然而，前者未免太长（26行），而后者又未免太短（6行）。　哈姆雷特所插入的这段台词可能根本就没在戏剧《贡扎古之死》中出现，演员们尚未来得及表演，演出即被叫停（Thompson）。　559. 无知者：不了解凶杀真相的人（Thompson）。

560   The very faculties of eyes and ears.

            Yet I,

            A dull and muddy-mettled rascal, peak

            Like John-a-dreams, unpregnant of my cause,

            And can say nothing—no, not for a king,

565   Upon whose property and most dear life

            A damn'd defeat was made. Am I a coward?

            Who calls me villain, breaks my pate across,

            Plucks off my beard and blows it in my face,

            Tweaks me by the nose, gives me the lie i'th' throat

570   As deep as to the lungs—who does me this?

            Ha!

            'Swounds, I should take it: for it cannot be

            But I am pigeon-liver'd and lack gall

            To make oppression bitter, or ere this

575   I should ha' fatted all the region kites

            With this slave's offal. Bloody, bawdy villain!

            Remorseless, treacherous, lecherous, kindless villain!

            Why, what an ass am I! This is most brave,

            That I, the son of a dear father murder'd,

580   Prompted to my revenge by heaven and hell,

            Must like a whore unpack my heart with words

            And fall a-cursing like a very drab,

            A scullion! Fie upon't! Foh!

            About, my brains. Hum—I have heard

585   That guilty creatures sitting at a play

            Have, by the very cunning of the scene,

会让人们的耳目感到惊愕。　　　　　　　　560

而我，

一个迟钝和麻木的无赖，如入

梦幻，无精打采，对自己的使命

无动于衷，哪怕父王最宝贵的

生命被人葬送，也都一言不发——　　　　565

默不作声。　我是不是一个懦夫？

谁叫我孬种，把我的脑袋劈开，

拔掉我的胡子吹向我的面孔，

拧着我的鼻子，骂我是一个

彻头彻尾的骗子——谁来这么做？　　　　570

哈！

看在上帝的份上，我应该接受：

因为这表明我是鸽子肝，没胆汁，

受人欺压也不会怨恨；否则，

我早该用这个贱货的五脏养肥　　　　　　575

空中的老鹰。　残忍、下流的恶棍！

冷酷、奸诈、淫荡、无情的恶棍！

咳，我真是蠢驴！真是棒极了，

而我，亲爱的父亲被人杀害，

天堂和地狱都在督促我报仇，　　　　　　580

我却像娼妓那样口诛笔伐，

像一个荡妇那样漫骂诅咒，

贱货！丢人啊！丢人！

动起来，我的脑筋。　呣——我听说

有一些罪人在看戏的时候，　　　　　　　585

因为场景再现得非常逼真，

第三幕
ACT 3

SCENE I

Enter King, Queen, Polonius, Ophelia,
Rosencrantz, Guildenstern.

King And can you by no drift of conference
Get from him why he puts on this confusion,
Grating so harshly all his days of quiet
With turbulent and dangerous lunacy?

5 **Ros.** He does confess he feels himself distracted,
But from what cause a will by no means speak.

Guild. Nor do we find him forward to be sounded,
But with a crafty madness keeps aloof
When we would bring him on to some confession
Of his true state.

10 **Queen** Did he receive you well?

Ros. Most like a gentleman.

Guild. But with much forcing of his disposition.

Ros. Niggard of question, but of our demands
Most free in his reply.

Queen Did you assay him
15 To any pastime?

Ros. Madam, it so fell out that certain players

第一场

国王、王后、波洛纽斯、奥菲丽娅、
罗森克兰、盖登斯顿上。

国王	你们能否用迂回婉转的方式	
	探出他为什么这样神志不清,	
	甘愿让他那安宁的日子变得	
	如此狂乱、如此危险和疯癫?	
罗森克兰	他倒是承认自己有些心烦,	5
	至于什么原因却闭口不谈。	
盖登斯顿	对我们的问话也不乐意回答,	
	当我们让他吐露一些真情时,	
	他却装出一副疯癫的样子,	
	神情冷淡。	
王后	他对你们还好吗?	10
罗森克兰	简直像位绅士。	
盖登斯顿	但是对我们好像很不情愿。	
罗森克兰	尽管有些勉强,对我们的问话	
	还是乐意回答。	
王后	你们是否劝他	
	找些消遣?	15
罗森克兰	夫人,我们在路上碰到了一群	

3.1. 2. 探出他……神志不清:国王好像已开始怀疑哈姆雷特的"行为乖张"（Gill）。

We o'erraught on the way. Of these we told him,

And there did seem in him a kind of joy

To hear of it. They are here about the court,

20 And, as I think, they have already order

This night to play before him.

Polonius   'Tis most true,

And he beseech'd me to entreat your Majesties

To hear and see the matter.

King   With all my heart; and it doth much content me

25 To hear him so inclin'd.

Good gentlemen, give him a further edge,

And drive his purpose into these delights.

Ros.   We shall, my lord. *Exeunt Rosencrantz and Guildenstern.*

King   Sweet Gertrude, leave us too,

For we have closely sent for Hamlet hither

30 That he, as 'twere by accident, may here

Affront Ophelia.

Her father and myself, lawful espials,

We'll so bestow ourselves that, seeing unseen,

We may of their encounter frankly judge,

35 And gather by him, as he is behav'd,

If't be th'affliction of his love or no

That thus he suffers for.

Queen   I shall obey you.

And for your part, Ophelia, I do wish

That your good beauties be the happy cause

演员。　我们已经把这条消息

转告于他,听到之后他好像

露出了笑脸。　演员们已经入宫,

而且,我想,他们已接受命令　　　　　　　　　　20

今晚就为他表演。

波洛纽斯　　　　　　　　　千真万确,

而且,他还求我恳请二位陛下

前去观看演出。

国王　　　我非常乐意;他对演出如此喜欢,

令我心满意足。　　　　　　　　　　　　　　25

可爱的先生们,要对他多加鼓励,

督促他的兴趣转向这些娱乐。

罗森克兰　遵命,陛下。　　　　　　　　　罗森克兰与盖登斯顿同下。

国王　　　　　　　亲爱的葛楚德,您也离开,

我已暗中派人去叫哈姆雷特,

就像是出于巧合,让他在此　　　　　　　　　30

与奥菲丽娅碰面。

他的父亲和我,合法的密探,

我们要躲藏起来,偷偷察看,

以便客观评判他们的会面,

并根据他的行为方式,看看他　　　　　　　　35

到底是不是因为失恋的痛苦

才变得如此疯癫。

王后　　　　　　　　我听您的。

至于您的角色,奥菲丽娅,

但愿您的美貌就是哈姆雷特

---

32. 合法的密探:因为他们的目的光明正大(Gill)。　39-40. 但愿……根源:王后担心哈姆雷特的疯狂是由于她本人的行为所致　(2.2.56-7),若能证明这种担心是错误的,她定会非常高兴;另一方面,王后也不断表明自己赞同儿子与奥菲丽娅之间的爱情　(5.1.236-8)(Jenkins)。

60 And by opposing end them. To die—to sleep,

No more; and by a sleep to say we end

The heart-ache and the thousand natural shocks

That flesh is heir to: 'tis a consummation

Devoutly to be wish'd. To die, to sleep;

65 To sleep, perchance to dream—ay, there's the rub:

For in that sleep of death what dreams may come,

When we have shuffled off this mortal coil,

Must give us pause—there's the respect

That makes calamity of so long life.

70 For who would bear the whips and scorns of time,

Th'oppressor's wrong, the proud man's contumely,

The pangs of despriz'd love, the law's delay,

The insolence of office, and the spurns

That patient merit of th'unworthy takes,

75 When he himself might his quietus make

With a bare bodkin? Who would fardels bear,

To grunt and sweat under a weary life,

But that the dread of something after death,

The undiscover'd country, from whose bourn

80 No traveller returns, puzzles the will,

And makes us rather bear those ills we have

Than fly to others that we know not of?

Thus conscience does make cowards of us all,

And thus the native hue of resolution

85 Is sicklied o'er with the pale cast of thought,

通过反抗了却一切？　死去——睡去，　　　　　　　　60
仅此而已；如果说睡去能了结
肉体注定要承受的伤心以及
千百次的打击：那可是一种
朝思暮念的结局。　死去，睡去；
睡去，也许还做梦——啊，障碍在这里：　　　　　　65
因为当我们摆脱了尘世的羁绊，
进入死亡的长眠还会做啥梦，
定让人犹豫——正是这一点
才使不幸变得竟如此长命。
谁愿意忍受时世的鞭打和讥讽，　　　　　　　　　70
压迫者的冤屈，傲慢者的无礼，
爱被轻蔑的剧痛，法律的拖延，
官僚的怠慢，德才兼备者遭受
小人的欺凌，而他本人仅用
一把短刀即可将自己的债务　　　　　　　　　　　75
全部清算？　谁愿意身负重担，
拖着疲惫的身躯呻吟流汗，
不过是因为对那死后的惧怕，
那个神秘的国度，所有行者
有去无还，让我们神迷意乱，　　　　　　　　　　80
从而宁愿忍受现有的痛苦，
而不愿飞向我们未知的磨难？
因此意识让我们全成了懦夫，
原本赤诚的决心就这样因为
思虑而蒙上一层苍白的病容，　　　　　　　　　　85

69.　不幸……长命：正是人们的"犹豫"才使得自己的苦难如此漫长（Gill）。　但是，除了其中的字面意义之外，人们也很难排除的另一种感受则是："长命"本身也被认为是一种不幸（Jenkins）。

And enterprises of great pitch and moment

With this regard their currents turn awry

And lose the name of action. Soft you now,

The fair Ophelia! Nymph, in thy orisons

Be all my sins remember'd.

90 **Ophelia**   Good my lord,

How does your honour for this many a day?

Hamlet   I humbly thank you, well.

Ophelia   My lord, I have remembrances of yours

That I have longed long to redeliver.

I pray you now receive them.

95 **Hamlet**   No, not I.

I never gave you aught.

Ophelia   My honour'd lord, you know right well you did,

And with them words of so sweet breath compos'd

As made the things more rich. Their perfume lost,

100   Take these again; for to the noble mind

Rich gifts wax poor when givers prove unkind.

There, my lord.

Hamlet   Ha, ha! Are you honest?

Ophelia   My lord?

105 **Hamlet**   Are you fair?

Ophelia   What means your lordship?

伟大而崇高的事业就此逆流
转向,从而失去了行动之名。
安静一下,美丽的奥菲丽娅!
仙女,在你的祷告里可要记住
我的所有罪行。

奥菲丽娅	我的好殿下,	90

您最近这一段时间还好吗?

哈姆雷特　我不胜感激,还好。

奥菲丽娅　殿下,您送给我的几件礼物,
很久以来我很想予以归还。
现在求您收下吧。

哈姆雷特	不,我不收。	95

我从未送过您什么。

奥菲丽娅　尊贵的殿下,您知道自己送过,
您当时还说了一些甜言蜜语,
让礼物更重。 它们的芳香已散,

	请收回吧;因为对自尊者而言,	100

重礼也变轻,假如赠送者心变。
收下吧,殿下。

哈姆雷特　哈,哈! 您贞洁吗?

奥菲丽娅　殿下?

哈姆雷特	您漂亮吗?	105

奥菲丽娅　殿下是什么意思?

---

　　96. 从未送过您什么:哈姆雷特之所以撒谎,可能是因为自己的自尊受到了伤害:奥菲丽娅已经拒绝与他会面,现在又试图将他赠送的礼物予以归还。 因此他才假装自己从未送过她什么(Thompson)。 99. 芳香已散:具有讥讽意味的是,此处可以让人想起 1.3.7-9 雷厄提斯的论断(Jenkins)。 103-51. 哈姆雷特在回答奥菲丽娅的对偶句时由诗体变为散文,这样可让他们两人之间进行一种节奏更快的问答式的对话(Thompson)。

Hamlet   That if you be honest and fair, your honesty should admit no discourse to your beauty.

Ophelia   Could beauty, my lord, have better commerce than
110   with honesty?

Hamlet   Ay, truly, for the power of beauty will sooner transform honesty from what it is to a bawd than the force of honesty can translate beauty into his likeness. This was sometime a paradox, but now the
115   time gives it proof. I did love you once.

Ophelia   Indeed, my lord, you made me believe so.

Hamlet   You should not have believed me; for virtue cannot so inoculate our old stock but we shall relish of it. I loved you not.

120 **Ophelia**   I was the more deceived.

Hamlet   Get thee to a nunnery. Why, wouldst thou be a breeder of sinners? I am myself indifferent honest, but yet I could accuse me of such things that it were better my mother had not borne me. I am very
125   proud, revengeful, ambitious, with more offences at my beck than I have thoughts to put them in, imagination to give them shape, or time to act them in. What should such fellows as I do crawling between

哈姆雷特	假如您既贞洁又漂亮，您的贞洁就该拒绝与您的美丽交结。
奥菲丽娅	难道美丽，殿下，除了跟贞洁以外还会有更好的交结？

110

哈姆雷特	没有，真的没有。因为相比之下，美丽的力量更容易把贞洁化为淫荡，而贞洁的力量却很难将美丽同化，这曾是一种荒谬之谈，可是现在它已经得到了验证。我以前确实爱过您。

115

奥菲丽娅	是的，殿下，您让我信以为真。
哈姆雷特	您不该相信我；因为美德即便能嫁接到我们腐朽的躯壳，我们也会保留罪恶的本色。我没爱过您。
奥菲丽娅	我可真的受骗了。

120

哈姆雷特	去修道院吧！为什么，难道你想繁殖一群罪人？我这个人还算正派，可我仍然拥有许多罪过应该自责，竟至于企望我的母亲不曾将我生下。我这个人娇气横生、复仇心切、野心勃勃，还有那么多的恶意等待执行，我的思想竟然不能完全将它们容下，想象都无法将它们加工成型，也没有时间将它们付诸行动。像我这样的家伙，为何

125

107-8. 你的贞洁……交结：为了保持自己的贞洁，奥菲丽娅不应让任何人与她的美丽接触（Jenkins）。 109-10. 难道美丽……交结：不少人认为奥菲丽娅的回答误解了哈姆雷特的意思，其实不然。 尽管奥菲丽娅对哈姆雷特的本意未予理会，但她很可能明白其中的含义，即：如果贞洁与美丽结合，遭受损失的将是她的贞洁。 一位女人常会因为她的美丽而受到伤害，而贞洁的职责就是保护她的美丽。 哈姆雷特与奥菲丽娅对此并无异议；而且哈姆雷特还为她考虑好了一种保护措施——进修道院去（Jenkins）。 114. 得到了验证：哈姆雷特好像是在影射自己的母亲（Jenkins）。 117. 不该相信我：具有讽刺意味的是，哈姆雷特此处应验了波罗纽斯对奥菲丽娅的忠告："别信他的誓言。"（1.3.127）（Thompson）

130 earth and heaven? We are arrant knaves all, believe none of us. Go thy ways to a nunnery. Where's your father?

Ophelia At home, my lord.

Hamlet Let the doors be shut upon him, that he may play the fool nowhere but in's own house. Farewell.

135 **Ophelia** O help him, you sweet heavens.

Hamlet If thou dost marry, I'll give thee this plague for thy dowry: be thou as chaste as ice, as pure as snow, thou shalt not escape calumny. Get thee to a nun-nery, farewell. Or if thou wilt needs marry, marry a

140 fool; for wise men know well enough what monsters you make of them. To a nunnery, go—and quickly too. Farewell.

Ophelia Heavenly powers, restore him.

Hamlet I have heard of your paintings well enough. God

145 hath given you one face and you make yourselves another. You jig and amble, and you lisp, you nick-name God's creatures, and make your wantonness your ignorance. Go to, I'll no more on't, it hath made me mad. I say we will have no more marriage. Those

150 that are married already—all but one—shall live; the rest shall keep as they are. To a nunnery, go. *Exit.*

Ophelia O, what a noble mind is here o'erthrown!

The courtier's, soldier's, scholar's, eye, tongue, sword,

Th'expectancy and rose of the fair state,

	还要在天地之间匍匐？我们全都是十足的	
	恶棍，你一个也不要相信。进修道院去吧。	130
	你父亲现在何处？	
奥菲丽娅	在家里，殿下。	
哈姆雷特	那就别让他出来，也好让他只是在自己	
	的家里卖傻。　再见。	
奥菲丽娅	噢，救救他，可爱的天神！	135
哈姆雷特	如果你要嫁人，我就送你这句咒语作为	
	陪嫁：即使你像冰一样坚贞，像雪一样	
	纯洁，也逃不脱谗言的中伤。去修道院，	
	再见。假如你定要嫁人，那就嫁给一个	
	傻瓜；因为聪明的男人都清楚，你们会	140
	把他们变成怎样的怪物。进修道院，去——	
	赶快去。　再见。	
奥菲丽娅	天上的神灵啊，让他康复！	
哈姆雷特	我知道你们都在涂脂抹粉。上帝给了	
	你们一副面孔，而你们自己却要另造	145
	一副。你们拿腔捏调、举止轻浮，给	
	上帝的造物乱起诨名，把你们的淫荡	
	当成无知。得啦，我受够了，都把我	
	气疯了。我说咱们不会结婚的。那些	
	已结过婚的——除一人之外——可以存活；	150
	其余的要维持现状。　进修道院，去。　　下。	
奥菲丽娅	噢，何等高贵的心灵已经毁掉！	
	廷臣的眼神、军人的剑术、学者的	
	舌辩、芬芳的玫瑰、全国的瞩望、	

135，143：奥菲丽娅以为哈姆雷特是真的疯了（Jenkins）。　141. 怪物：头上长角（戴绿帽子），暗示所有妻子迟早都会背叛自己的丈夫（Gill）。　150. 除一人之外——可以存活：躲在幕后的克劳狄斯定能听见，并且明白其中的威胁，但哈姆雷特对此并不知情（Gill）。

155   The glass of fashion and the mould of form,

Th'observ'd of all observers, quite, quite down!

And I, of ladies most deject and wretched,

That suck'd the honey of his music vows,

Now see that noble and most sovereign reason

160   Like sweet bells jangled out of tune and harsh,

That unmatch'd form and feature of blown youth

Blasted with ecstasy. O woe is me

To have seen what I have seen, see what I see.

Enter King and Polonius.

King   Love? His affections do not that way tend,

165   Nor what he spake, though it lack'd form a little,

Was not like madness. There's something in his soul

O'er which his melancholy sits on brood,

And I do doubt the hatch and the disclose

Will be some danger; which for to prevent,

170   I have in quick determination

Thus set it down: he shall with speed to England

For the demand of our neglected tribute.

Haply the seas and countries different,

With variable objects, shall expel

175   This something settled matter in his heart,

Whereon his brains still beating puts him thus

From fashion of himself. What think you on't?

Polonius   It shall do well. But yet do I believe

时尚的明镜以及行为的典范、 155

全体臣民的景仰,毁了,全毁了!

而我,这位最最凄惨的女子,

曾从他悦耳的盟誓中汲取蜜意,

现在却要目睹那崇高的理智,

犹如银铃失声变得嘈杂刺耳, 160

他那无比的身姿,秀美的相貌,

被疯狂摧折。 噢,我真是不幸,

目睹往日荣光,面对今朝处境!

国 王 与 波 洛 纽 斯 上 。

国王 爱情? 他的情感并未转向那方,

他的话,尽管有些语无伦次, 165

但也不像疯话。 他有某种心事,

正由他的忧郁盘绕孵化,

我担心雏儿一旦破壳而出,

将意味着某种险情;为了预防,

我已经当机立断做出决定, 170

那就是:他将迅速前往英国,

去追讨他们所拖欠的贡赋。

也许大海以及异域的风光,

能够排遣他胸中盘踞的心事,

因为正是由于他那种恍惚 175

不定的神志,才让他的言行

变得如此失常。 您以为怎样?

波洛纽斯 那样很好。 不过我还是相信,

---

172. 追讨……贡赋:从公元 10 世纪起,英国国王为了保护本土的安全,每年都向丹麦进贡。伊丽莎白一世期间,丹麦重新向英国提出这一要求(Gill)。

The origin and commencement of his grief

180 Sprung from neglected love. How now, Ophelia?

You need not tell us what Lord Hamlet said,

We heard it all. My lord, do as you please,

But if you hold it fit, after the play

Let his queen-mother all alone entreat him

185 To show his grief, let her be round with him,

And I'll be plac'd, so please you, in the ear

Of all their conference. If she find him not,

To England send him; or confine him where

Your wisdom best shall think.

King   It shall be so.

190 Madness in great ones must not unwatch'd go.   *Exeunt.*

让他痛苦的源头就是失恋。

怎么样，奥菲丽娅？　你不用告诉　　　　　　　　　　　　180

我们哈姆雷特殿下说了什么，

我们全都听见。　陛下，您看着办，

不过您若认为合适，演出之后，

让他的母后单独求他表露

痛苦的根源，让她开门见山，　　　　　　　　　　　　　185

我躲在暗处，如您准许，偷听

他们的会谈。　假如探不出真相，

就派他去英国；或把他禁闭到

您认为最好的地方。

国王　　　　　　　　　　就这么办。

大人物的疯狂决不能袖手旁观。　　　　　　　同下。　190

SCENE II

Enter Hamlet and three of the Players.

Hamlet   Speak the speech, I pray you, as I pronounced it to
you, trippingly on the tongue; but if you mouth it as
many of your players do, I had as lief the town-crier
spoke my lines. Nor do not saw the air too much with
5   your hand, thus, but use all gently; for in the very
torrent, tempest, and, as I may say, whirlwind of
your passion, you must acquire and beget a temperance that may give it smoothness. O, it offends me
to the soul to hear a robustious periwig-pated fellow
10   tear a passion to tatters, to very rags, to split the ears
of the groundlings, who for the most part are capable
of nothing but inexplicable dumb-shows and noise.
I would have such a fellow whipped for o'erdoing
Termagant. It out-Herods Herod. Pray you avoid it.
15   **1st Player**   I warrant your honour.
Hamlet   Be not too tame neither, but let your own discretion be your tutor. Suit the action to the word,

第二场

哈姆雷特与三位演员上。

哈姆雷特 请按我刚才给您朗诵的那种样子朗诵这段
台词,节奏要明快;要是您朗诵得跟其他
演员并无两样,那我宁愿让大街上的公告
宣传员过来帮助我喊叫。您也不要像这样
过分振臂挥拳,动作要温和适度;因为在 5
感情的激流、暴雨、也可以说是旋风之中,
您要学会节制才能化险为夷。噢,要是我
听到一个头戴假发的汉子将一段深情撕成
碎片,将站场观众的耳鼓震破,我一定会
恨之入骨,因为他们除了会欣赏一些莫名 10
其妙的哑剧以及喧闹之外,大多都是一窍
不通。要是有谁做得比喧嚣之神还要喧嚣,
我定要抽他一顿鞭子。它比暴君希律还要
暴君。 求您加以避免!

演员甲 我向殿下保证。 15

哈姆雷特 但也不要过分温顺,要让您自己的判断
充当您的导演。让动作适应言辞,言辞

3.2. 9.站场观众:站在戏院里看戏的观众,票价最低(Gill)。 12.喧嚣之神(Termagant):一种异教徒所信奉的喧嚣之神,常在中世纪的剧作中出现(Gill)。 13.希律(Herod):《圣经》中的暴君,常以暴怒的形象出现于中世纪的剧本中(参见"马太福音"2章16
节)(Gill)。

the word to the action, with this special observance, that you o'erstep not the modesty of nature. For any-

20 thing so o'erdone is from the purpose of playing, whose end, both at the first and now, was and is to hold as 'twere the mirror up to nature; to show virtue her feature, scorn her own image, and the very age and body of the time his form and pressure. Now

25 this overdone or come tardy off, though it makes the unskilful laugh, cannot but make the judicious grieve, the censure of the which one must in your allowance o'erweigh a whole theatre of others. O, there be players that I have seen play—and heard

30 others praise, and that highly—not to speak it pro-fanely, that neither having th'accent of Christians, nor the gait of Christian, pagan, nor man, have so strutted and bellowed that I have thought some of Nature's journeymen had made men, and not made

35 them well, they imitated humanity so abominably.

1st Player   I hope we have reformed that indifferently with us.

Hamlet   O reform it altogether. And let those that play your clowns speak no more than is set down for them—

40 for there be of them that will themselves laugh, to set on some quantity of barren spectators to laugh too, though in the meantime some necessary ques-tion of the play be then to be considered. That's villainous, and shows a most pitiful ambition in the

45 fool that uses it. Go make you ready.   *Exeunt Players.*

适应动作。要特别注意的是,不要超越
自然的中和。因为任何过火的言行都会
违背戏剧初衷。戏剧的目的,古往今来,　　　　　　20
就是要充当自然的一面明镜;要让美德
得以彰显,使丑恶原形毕露,再现时代
的烙印,反映历史的真实。您要是演得
过火,或者火候不够,尽管会博得外行
的大笑,然而却难免会让行家为之心痛,　　　　　25
您必须把这些行家的评判看得要比全场
观众的感受还要贵重。噢,我曾观看过
演员的演出——也听到过别人的赞颂——
还是很高的赞颂——说句无意亵渎神灵的
话,他们既没有正派人的腔调,也没有　　　　　　30
正派人、异教徒或者是人的姿态。他们
竟是如此趾高气扬、声嘶力竭,反倒会
让我觉得不是大自然本身,而是她雇佣
的短工创造了人,而且还没把他们造好,
他们将人类模仿得竟然如此糟糕。　　　　　　　35

演员甲　　我希望我们已经对这一点作出了适度的
改变。

哈姆雷特　　噢,要彻底改变。还要让那些丑角演员
除了脚本为他们规定的台词以外,不要
多说——因为有一些小丑会私自发出笑声,　　　40
从而将某些无知的观众逗笑,然而,就
在此刻,剧中却有严肃的问题正好需要
思考。他们的这种行经非常恶劣,同时
也表明这一类丑角最为可鄙,以及痴心
妄想。　你们去准备吧。　　　　　　　演员同下。　45

Enter Polonius, Rosencrantz, and Guildenstern.

	How now, my lord? Will the King hear this piece of work?
Polonius	And the Queen too, and that presently.
Hamlet	Bid the players make haste. *Exit Polonius.*
50	Will you two help to hasten them?
Ros.	Ay, my lord. *Exeunt Rosencrantz and Guildenstern.*
Hamlet	What ho, Horatio!

Enter Horatio.

Horatio	Here, sweet lord, at your service.
Hamlet	Horatio, thou art e'en as just a man
55	As e'er my conversation cop'd withal.
Horatio	O my dear lord.
Hamlet	Nay, do not think I flatter,
	For what advancement may I hope from thee
	That no revenue hast but thy good spirits
	To feed and clothe thee? Why should the poor be flatter'd?
60	No, let the candied tongue lick absurd pomp,
	And crook the pregnant hinges of the knee
	Where thrift may follow fawning. Dost thou hear?
	Since my dear soul was mistress of her choice,
	And could of men distinguish her election,
65	Sh'ath seal'd thee for herself; for thou hast been

　　　　　　　波洛纽斯、罗森克兰与盖登斯顿上。

　　　　　　　怎么样，我的阁下？国王他愿意来看
　　　　　　　戏吗？

波洛纽斯　　还有王后呢，而且马上就到。

哈姆雷特　　叫演员们快一些。　　　　　　　波洛纽斯下。
　　　　　　　你们俩也去催一催好吧？　　　　　　　　　　50

罗森克兰　　好的，殿下。　　　　罗森克兰与盖登斯顿同下。

哈姆雷特　　哎呀，何瑞修！

　　　　　　　　　　何瑞修上。

何瑞修　　到，亲爱的殿下，为您效劳。

哈姆雷特　　何瑞修，在我平生结交的人中，
　　　　　　　只有你才算得上真正的稳重。　　　　　　　55

何瑞修　　噢，亲爱的殿下！

哈姆雷特　　　　　　　别以为我在奉承，
　　　　　　　我能从你那里得到什么好处，
　　　　　　　你除了自食其力的良好精神
　　　　　　　别无长物？　为什么要奉承穷人？
　　　　　　　不，让甜嘴儿去舔舐乏味的虚荣，　　　　　60
　　　　　　　让灵活的膝盖到摇尾乞怜可得
　　　　　　　奖赏的地方下跪。　你听见没有？
　　　　　　　自从我亲爱的灵魂能够驾驭
　　　　　　　自己的选择，分辨所选的男士，
　　　　　　　她便一眼将你看中；因为你　　　　　　　65

---

　　63. 灵魂：在伊丽莎白时代，人们把友情看得很重，甚至胜过异性之爱。　人的灵魂传统上为阴性（Gill）。

Enter Trumpets and Kettle-drums and sound a flourish.

90	**Hamlet**	They are coming to the play. I must be idle.
		Get you a place.

Enter King, Queen, Polonius, Ophelia, Rosencrantz,
Guildenstern, and other Lords attendant,
with the King's Guard carrying torches.

	King	How fares our cousin Hamlet?
	Hamlet	Excellent, i'faith, of the chameleon's dish. I eat the
		air, promise-crammed. You cannot feed capons so.
95	**King**	I have nothing with this answer, Hamlet. These
		words are not mine.
	Hamlet	No, nor mine now. —[*To Polonius*] My lord, you
		played once i'th' university, you say?
	Polonius	That did I, my lord, and was accounted a good
100		actor.
	Hamlet	What did you enact?
	Polonius	I did enact Julius Caesar. I was killed i'th' Capitol.
		Brutus killed me.
	Hamlet	It was a brute part of him to kill so capital a calf
105		there. Be the players ready?
	Ros.	Ay, my lord, they stay upon your patience.
	Queen	Come hither, my dear Hamlet, sit by me.
	Hamlet	No, good mother, here's metal more attractive.
		[*Turns to Ophelia.*]

号角与锣鼓上,随之齐鸣。

哈姆雷特	他们来了。　我必须若无其事。	90
	您快找个地方。	

国王、王后、波洛纽斯、奥菲丽娅、罗森克兰、
盖登斯顿、其他贵族侍从及国王的卫兵
手持火把上。

国王	我的哈姆雷特侄儿可好?	
哈姆雷特	好极了,真的,我吃的是变色龙。喝的是 空气,前途无量。　您喂食阉鸡可无法这样。	
国王	我不明白您的意思,哈姆雷特。这与我的 问话无关。	95
哈姆雷特	也与我无关了。——[对波洛纽斯]阁下,您 说自己曾在大学里演过戏,是吗?	
波洛纽斯	我演过,殿下,而且人们还都以为我演得 不错。	100
哈姆雷特	您演什么角色?	
波洛纽斯	尤利乌斯·恺撒。我是在朱比特神庙遇害的。 布鲁图杀了我。	
哈姆雷特	他真是太残忍了,竟在那里残杀一头这么 棒的牛犊! 演员准备好了吗?	105
罗森克兰	好了,殿下,他们在等您的吩咐。	
王后	过来,亲爱的哈姆雷特,挨着我坐。	
哈姆雷特	不,好母亲,这块宝贝儿引力更大。	
	[转向奥菲丽娅。]	

---

97. 也与我无关了: 一句格言说道,"一个人的话语一旦出口,就不再属于本人。"(Jenkins)。　104-5. 杀死……牛犊:戏杀一头牛犊是化装哑剧中的部分娱乐内容;同时,"牛犊"一词还有"傻瓜"之义,此处为一语双关(Gill)。

Polonius		[*aside to the King*] O ho! do you mark that?
110	**Hamlet**	[*lying down at Ophelia's feet*] Lady, shall I lie in your lap?
	Ophelia	No, my lord.
	Hamlet	I mean, my head upon your lap.
	Ophelia	Ay, my lord.
115	**Hamlet**	Do you think I meant country matters?
	Ophelia	I think nothing, my lord.
	Hamlet	That's a fair thought to lie between maids' legs.
	Ophelia	What is, my lord?
	Hamlet	Nothing.
120	**Ophelia**	You are merry, my lord.
	Hamlet	Who, I?
	Ophelia	Ay, my lord.
	Hamlet	O God, your only jig-maker. What should a man do but be merry? For look you how cheerfully my
125		mother looks and my father died within's two hours.
	Ophelia	Nay, 'tis twice two months, my lord.
	Hamlet	So long? Nay then, let the devil wear black, for I'll have a suit of sables. O heavens, die two months ago and not forgotten yet! Then there's hope a great
130		man's memory may outlive his life half a year. But by'r lady a must build churches then, or else shall

波洛纽斯	［转向国王］啊哈！您看见了没有？	
哈姆雷特	［在奥菲丽娅的脚旁躺下］小姐，我能躺在 您的大腿上吗？	110
奥菲丽娅	不能，殿下。	
哈姆雷特	我是说，把头枕在您的腿上。	
奥菲丽娅	可以，殿下。	
哈姆雷特	您以为我有下流之意吗？	115
奥菲丽娅	我没以为，殿下。	
哈姆雷特	躺在小姐的两腿之间真是惬意。	
奥菲丽娅	什么惬意，殿下？	
哈姆雷特	空洞。	
奥菲丽娅	您很高兴，殿下。	120
哈姆雷特	谁，我吗？	
奥菲丽娅	是的，殿下。	
哈姆雷特	噢，上帝，您最棒的笑星！一个人除了 高兴还要干啥？您看我母亲现在是多么 高兴，而我父亲两小时之内就会死去。	125
奥菲丽娅	不对，已经四个月了，殿下。	
哈姆雷特	这么久了？那就让魔鬼去穿丧服，因为 我要换上貂皮盛装。噢，天哪，去世已 两个月了，还没被人遗忘！那么对一位 伟人的记忆就有望在他死后再延续半年。 但向圣母起誓，他必须修建教堂，否则	130

---

119. 空洞：原文 nothing，既可明指内容的空洞，亦可暗喻女性的生殖器官或童贞（Jen-kins）。　125. 两小时：戏剧的演出时间（Thompson）。　126. 四个月：假如奥菲丽娅所说的时间准确，那么自从哈姆雷特悼念亡父"去世才俩月"（1.2.138）到目前已过去了两个月的时间；也可以说，自从哈姆雷特与鬼魂相遇之后已过去了两个月的时间（Thompson）。

a suffer not thinking on, with the hobby-horse, whose epitaph is 'For O, for O, the hobby-horse is forgot'.

The trumpets sound. A dumb-show follows.

Enter a King and a Queen, the Queen embracing him and he her.

She kneels, and makes show of protestation unto him. He takes her up, and declines his head upon her neck. He lies him down upon a bank of flowers. She, seeing him asleep, leaves him. Anon comes in another Man, takes off his crown, kisses it, pours poison in the sleeper's ears, and leaves him. The Queen returns, finds the King dead, makes passionate action. The Poisoner with some Three or Four comes in again. They seem to condole with her. The dead body is carried away. The Poisoner woos the Queen with gifts. She seems harsh awhile, but in the end accepts his love.   *Exeunt.*

	Ophelia	What means this, my lord?
135	**Hamlet**	Marry, this is miching malicho. It means mischief.
	Ophelia	Belike this show imports the argument of the play.

Enter Prologue.

	Hamlet	We shall know by this fellow. The players cannot keep counsel: they'll tell all.
	Ophelia	Will a tell us what this show meant?
140	**Hamlet**	Ay, or any show that you will show him. Be not you ashamed to show, he'll not shame to tell you what it

就会像柳条马一样被人遗忘,它的挽歌
是'不幸噢,不幸噢,柳条马被忘了'。

号角响起。哑剧随后。

国王和王后入场,王后拥抱国王,国王拥抱王后。
王后跪在地上,向国王表白心声。国王将她扶起,
低头依偎王后的脖颈。国王在花丛中躺下。王后
发现国王已入睡之后便起身离去。很快又进来了
另一男子,摘去国王头上的皇冠,亲了亲,然后
将毒药灌入睡眠者的耳中,然后离去。王后返回,
发现国王死去,捶胸顿足。下毒者又带领三、四
人返回。他们像是对她表示安慰。尸体被人抬下。
下毒者呈上礼物,向王后求爱。最初她显得表情
冷淡,但最后还是接受了他的爱意。　　　　　　　　同下。

奥菲丽娅	这是什么意思,殿下?	
哈姆雷特	天哪,这是阴谋诡计!就是恶作剧。	135
奥菲丽娅	这场哑剧大概就是剧情的体现吧。	

致开场白者上。

哈姆雷特	这个小伙会告诉我们。演员们不会	
	保密:他们会道破一切。	
奥菲丽娅	他会告诉我们这是何意?	
哈姆雷特	对,无论您想向他展现什么。只要您	140
	好意思展现出来,他都会大言不惭地	

---

132. 柳条马:莫利斯舞蹈者在化装舞会上经常使用的一种马形道具;"柳条马被忘了"好像
成了一句流行语。 此处可能是指,这种令人喜爱的柳条马因为清教徒的反对而不得不在五朔节
(May Games)及其他节日的欢庆中消失(Thompson)。

means.

Ophelia   You are naught, you are naught. I'll mark the play.

Prologue   *For us and for our tragedy,*

145   *Here stooping to your clemency,*

                     We beg your hearing patiently.   *Exit.*

Hamlet   Is this a prologue, or the posy of a ring?

Ophelia   'Tis brief, my lord.

Hamlet   As woman's love.

Enter [the Player] King and Queen.

150 **P. King**   *Full thirty times hath Phoebus' cart gone round*

                   Neptune's salt wash and Tellus' orbed ground,

                   And thirty dozen moons with borrow'd sheen

                   About the world have times twelve thirties been

                   Since love our hearts and Hymen did our hands

155   *Unite commutual in most sacred bands.*

   P. Queen   *So many journeys may the sun and moon*

                   Make us again count o'er ere love be done.

                   But woe is me, you are so sick of late,

                   So far from cheer and from your former state,

160   *That I distrust you. Yet though I distrust,*

                   Discomfort you, my lord, it nothing must;

                   For women's fear and love hold quantity,

                   In neither aught, or in extremity.

                   Now what my love is, proof hath made you know,

予以阐明。

奥菲丽娅　您不像话,您不像话。　我要看戏了。

致开场白者　　　悲剧马上就要亮相,

　　　　　　　　恭请大家宽宏大量, 145

　　　　　　　　恳求各位耐心观赏。 下。

哈姆雷特　这是开场白,还是戒指上的座右铭?

奥菲丽娅　很简短,殿下。

哈姆雷特　就像女人的爱情。

[扮演]国王与王后者上。

演国王者　日神的马车已飞转三十春秋, 150

　　　　　环绕着茫茫大海及圆形地球,

　　　　　三十打明月借来一片光辉,

　　　　　绕行地球已经三百六十回,

　　　　　自从许门把我们两个双手牵,

　　　　　神圣爱情让咱们二人心相连。 155

演王后者　愿日月继续环饶地球周游,

　　　　　让我们再相爱三十个春秋。

　　　　　可是您近日多病,令我忧伤,

　　　　　您如此郁郁寡欢,不如往常,

　　　　　尽管我在为您的健康担忧, 160

　　　　　陛下可千万不要为此忧愁;

　　　　　因为女人的担忧与爱情相当,

　　　　　不是二者全无,就是彼此过量。

　　　　　我是如何爱您,已经不言而喻,

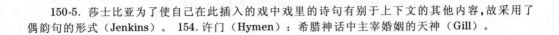

150-5. 莎士比亚为了使自己在此插入的戏中戏里的诗句有别于上下文的其他内容,故采用了偶韵句的形式(Jenkins)。　154. 许门(Hymen):希腊神话中主宰婚姻的天神(Gill)。

165   *And as my love is siz'd, my fear is so.*

                         Where love is great, the littlest doubts are fear;

                         Where little fears grow great, great love grows there.

P. King   *Faith, I must leave thee, love, and shortly too:*

                         My operant powers their functions leave to do;

170   *And thou shalt live in this fair world behind,*

                         Honour'd, belov'd; and haply one as kind

                         For husband shalt thou—

P. Queen   *O confound the rest.*

                         Such love must needs be treason in my breast.

                         In second husband let me be accurst;

175   *None wed the second but who kill'd the first.*

Hamlet   [*aside*] That's wormwood.

P. Queen   *The instances that second marriage move*

                         Are base respects of thrift, but none of love.

                         A second time I kill my husband dead,

180   *When second husband kisses me in bed.*

P. King   *I do believe you think what now you speak;*

                         But what we do determine, oft we break.

                         Purpose is but the slave to memory,

                         Of violent birth but poor validity,

185   *Which now, the fruit unripe, sticks on the tree,*

                         But fall unshaken when they mellow be.

                         Most necessary 'tis that we forget

                         To pay ourselves what to ourselves is debt.

                         What to ourselves in passion we propose,

190   *The passion ending, doth the purpose lose.*

	因为爱的痴迷，才会如此忧虑。	165
	爱情若是伟大，疑虑便成惧怕；	
	疑虑若成惧怕，大爱由此生发。	

演国王者　亲爱的，我很快就要与你永别：

因为我的身心已精疲力竭；

你将独自活在这美丽世界，　　　　　　　　　170

享受世间荣华及人们爱戴；

也许会另有所爱——

演王后者　　　　　　　　噢，诅咒下文！

若另有所爱，我定是负心之人！

如果再嫁，就让我遭受诅咒；

再嫁的定是杀害前夫的毒手。　　　　　　　175

哈姆雷特　［旁白］可真苦啊！

演王后者　促使我再次结婚的真正动因，

定是出于私欲，而非出于爱心。

第二个丈夫上床吻我之时，

就等于再一次将前夫杀死。　　　　　　　　180

演国王者　相信您现在说的是肺腑之言；

自己的决定我们却经常背叛。

决心只是记忆的奴隶而已，

来势凶猛，但是效力很低，

犹如果子，成熟前紧挂枝头，　　　　　　　185

熟透后自会跌落，无须摇抖。

难以避免的是，我们会忘怀

支付我们对自己所欠的债。

因为一时冲动我们许下宏愿，

激情一旦结束，决心即刻消散。　　　　　　190

---

176. 可真苦啊：哈姆雷特的评论好像是在暗示：他母亲的再婚与第一个丈夫的死亡有关（Gill）。

The violence of either grief or joy

Their own enactures with themselves destroy.

Where joy most revels grief doth most lament;

Grief joys, joy grieves, on slender accident.

195 *This world is not for aye, nor 'tis not strange*

That even our loves should with our fortunes change,

For 'tis a question left us yet to prove,

Whether love lead fortune or else fortune love.

The great man down, you mark his favourite flies;

200 *The poor advanc'd makes friends of enemies;*

And hitherto doth love on fortune tend:

For who not needs shall never lack a friend,

And who in want a hollow friend doth try

Directly seasons him his enemy.

205 *But orderly to end where I begun,*

Our wills and fates do so contrary run

That our devices still are overthrown:

Our thoughts are ours, their ends none of our own.

So think thou wilt no second husband wed,

210 *But die thy thoughts when thy first lord is dead.*

P. Queen *Nor earth to me give food, nor heaven light,*

Sport and repose lock from me day and night,

To desperation turn my trust and hope,

An anchor's cheer in prison be my scope,

215 *Each opposite, that blanks the face of joy,*

Meet what I would have well and it destroy,

Both here and hence pursue me lasting strife,

If, once a widow, ever I be a wife.

无论痛不欲生，还是欣喜若狂，
感情一旦迸发，行动随即消亡。
欢天喜地意味着痛哭流涕，
稍有变故，喜变悲，悲变喜。
这世界并非永恒，也不足为奇，　　　　　　　195
就连爱也会随着境遇而迁移，
因为这一点仍需我们去检验，
是爱引领境遇，还是恰恰相反。
伟人失势，往日的亲朋全躲开；
小人得志，原来的仇敌友相待；　　　　　　200
这表明爱是围着境遇而徘徊：
因为顺境中决不会缺乏友爱，
身处逆境向虚假朋友去求援，
他定会直截了当跟你把脸翻。
还是按条理回到我最初论点，　　　　　　　205
我们的意愿和命运适得其反。
我们的神机妙算总归于枉然：
思想属于我们，结局毫不相干。
所以尽管你自以为不会改嫁，
恐怕我一旦死去你就要变卦。　　　　　　　210

演王后者　愿地不供我食粮，天不给光明，
白天没有娱乐，夜晚不得安宁，
将我的信心和希望化为泡影，
隐士般的生活就是我的情形。
愿我欢快的容颜化为伤悲，　　　　　　　　215
愿我向往的一切事与愿违，
生前死后都让我永远受苦，
假如，我一旦寡居，再为新妇。

	Hamlet	If she should break it now.
220	**P. King**	*'Tis deeply sworn. Sweet, leave me here awhile.*
		My spirits grow dull, and fain I would beguile
		The tedious day with sleep.
	P. Queen	*Sleep rock thy brain,*
		And never come mischance between us twain. *Exit. He sleeps.*
	Hamlet	Madam, how like you this play?
225	**Queen**	The lady doth protest too much, methinks.
	Hamlet	O, but she'll keep her word.
	King	Have you heard the argument? Is there no offence in't?
230	**Hamlet**	No, no, they do but jest—poison in jest. No offence i'th' world.
	King	What do you call the play?
235	**Hamlet**	*The Mousetrap*—marry, how tropically! This play is the image of a murder done in Vienna—Gonzago is the Duke's name, his wife Baptista—you shall see anon. 'Tis a knavish piece of work, but what o' that? Your Majesty, and we that have free souls, it touches us not. Let the galled jade wince, our withers are unwrung.

Enter Lucianus.

		This is one Lucianus, nephew to the King.
240	**Ophelia**	You are as good as a chorus, my lord.

哈姆雷特	说不定她马上食言！	
演国王者	真是信誓旦旦。亲爱的，请先回。	220
	我现在无精打采，想在此小睡，	
	消磨乏味光阴。	
演王后者	但愿你能安眠，	
	厄运永远降不到我们俩中间。	下。国王入睡。
哈姆雷特	夫人，您觉得这出戏怎样？	
王后	我认为，那个女的誓言太多。	225
哈姆雷特	噢，可她却会信守。	
国王	您了解剧情吗？里面就没有令人讨厌的	
	东西？	
哈姆雷特	没有，没有，他们在开玩笑——下毒玩笑。	
	世上没有罪恶。	230
国王	这出戏叫什么名字？	
哈姆雷特	《捕鼠器》——天哪，多好的比喻！这出戏	
	反映的是维也纳的一起凶杀——公爵的名字	
	叫贡扎古，他的妻子叫巴普蒂斯塔——很快	
	您就会看到。是一出恶作剧，但那有什么	235
	关系？陛下您和我们这些问心无愧的人们，	
	不会受到影响。让擦伤肩的驽马畏缩不前，	
	我们的肩膀可是完好无损。	

卢西安纳上。

	这就是卢西安纳，国王的侄儿。	
奥菲丽娅	您简直就像解说员，殿下。	240

---

234. 贡扎古：据信该剧是根据 1538 年发生在意大利的一起凶杀案编写而成。 该凶杀情节与本剧的凶杀情节大致相同。 不同之处在于：凶手与受害者之间为叔侄关系（即侄子杀害叔父），而本剧却为兄弟关系（即弟弟杀害兄长）。 但根据侄子杀害叔父的情节，也可暗示哈姆雷特对克劳狄斯所构成的威胁（Jenkins）。

Hamlet		I could interpret between you and your love if I could see the puppets dallying.
Ophelia		You are keen, my lord, you are keen.
Hamlet		It would cost you a groaning to take off my edge.
245	**Ophelia**	Still better, and worse.
	Hamlet	So you mis-take your husbands. —Begin, murderer. Leave thy damnable faces and begin. Come, the croaking raven doth bellow for revenge.

Lucianus   *Thoughts black, hands apt, drugs fit, and time agreeing,*

250   *Confederate season, else no creature seeing,*

Thou mixture rank, of midnight weeds collected,

With Hecate's ban thrice blasted, thrice infected,

Thy natural magic and dire property

On wholesome life usurps immediately.

[Pours the poison into the sleeper's ears.]

255   **Hamlet**   A poisons him i'th' garden for his estate. His name's Gonzago. The story is extant, and written in very choice Italian. You shall see anon how the murderer gets the love of Gonzago's wife.

	Ophelia	The King rises.
260	**Hamlet**	What, frighted with false fire?
	Queen	How fares my lord?
	Polonius	Give o'er the play.
	King	Give me some light. Away.
	Polonius	Lights, lights, lights. *Exeunt all but Hamlet and Horatio.*

哈姆雷特	假如我能看见您和情人之间进行调戏，	
	我也能加以解说。	
奥菲丽娅	您很尖刻，殿下，您很尖刻。	
哈姆雷特	您必须呻吟才能把我的锐气消磨！	
奥菲丽娅	越发尖刻，更加糟糕！	245
哈姆雷特	那么您要背叛自己的丈夫。——动手吧，	
	凶手！露出你的狰狞面目动手吧！快，	
	呱呱叫的乌鸦马上要复仇！	
卢西安纳	心狠、手辣、药毒、时辰正好，	
	真是天赐良机，无人看得到，	250
	你这半夜采集的毒草熬的汤，	
	巫神咒语念三遍，毒性强又强，	
	快用你那可怕的魔力和毒性，	
	立刻将这健康的生命来吞并！	
	［向睡眠者的耳内灌药。］	
哈姆雷特	他是为了谋财在花园里对他下毒。他的	255
	名字叫贡扎古。确有其事，是用优美的	
	意大利语写成。您很快就会看到凶手是	
	如何赢得了贡扎古夫人的爱情。	
奥菲丽娅	国王起身了。	
哈姆雷特	怎么，给空枪吓着了？	260
王后	陛下还好吗？	
波洛纽斯	停止演出！	
国王	快给我掌灯。　回去！	
波洛纽斯	火把，火把，火把！ 　　　　　　除哈姆雷特与何瑞修以外全下。

---

248. 呱呱叫的乌鸦马上要复仇：哈姆雷特因为对自己设计好的下一个场景迫不及待，便顺口从匿名的《理查三世的悲剧》中误引出本句（Gill）。

265	**Hamlet**	*Why, let the strucken deer go weep,*
		The hart ungalled play;
		For some must watch while some must sleep,
		Thus runs the world away.

Would not this, sir, and a forest of feathers, if the rest

270 of my fortunes turn Turk with me, with Provincial roses on my razed shoes, get me a fellowship in a cry of players?

Horatio   Half a share.

Hamlet   A whole one, I.

275 *For thou dost know, O Damon dear,*

This realm dismantled was

Of Jove himself, and now reigns here

A very, very—pajock.

Horatio   You might have rhymed.

280 **Hamlet**   O good Horatio, I'll take the ghost's word for a thousand pound. Didst perceive?

Horatio   Very well, my lord.

Hamlet   Upon the talk of the poisoning?

Horatio   I did very well note him.

285 **Hamlet**   Ah ha! Come, some music; come, the recorders.

For if the King like not the comedy,

Why then, belike he likes it not, perdie.

Come, some music.

哈姆雷特	嗨,让受伤的驯鹿去流泪,	265
	让无恙的公鹿来嬉戏;	
	有人要失眠,有人会酣睡,	
	世界就这样物换星移。	

先生,假如日后的命运将我背叛,我这点
花招,在帽子上系一束羽毛,开口的鞋上　　　270
再插上几朵玫瑰,难道还不能在演艺圈里
混碗饭吃?

何瑞修　半个股份!

哈姆雷特　一整股,我要!

因为你知道,噢,亲爱的达蒙,　　　275

这被篡夺的国度原属

朱庇特天神,而现在的王公

是个非常、非常的——贱货!

何瑞修　你还可以押韵呢!

哈姆雷特　噢,好何瑞修,我敢打赌鬼魂的话可是　　　280
千真万确。　你看清了吗?

何瑞修　很清楚,殿下。

哈姆雷特　当谈到下毒的时候?

何瑞修　我看得一清二楚。

哈姆雷特　啊哈! 快来,奏乐! 快来,笛子!　　　285

因为假如国王不爱滑稽戏,

天作证,大概他就是不爱戏!

快来,奏乐!

265-8. 好像引自一首无名的歌谣。　哈姆雷特将"受伤的驯鹿"与"无恙的公鹿"予以对照,
接续 237 行的暗喻（擦伤肩的驽马）,旨在将有罪的国王与无辜的王子进行对比（Thompson）。
275-8. 哈姆雷特又在吟诵另一首歌谣。　"达蒙"是田园诗中一个为人所熟知的牧者（Gill）。
277. 朱庇特（Jove）:统治众神的主神,此处显然比作哈姆雷特的父亲,因为他的国度已被篡夺;
克劳狄斯被比作"贱货"（pajock）（Gill）。　279. 押韵:歌谣第四行末尾的"pajock"若换成
"ass（蠢驴）"之类的词,即可与第二行末尾的"was"押韵（Gill）。　286-7. 因为……滑稽
戏:哈姆雷特是在模仿基德所著《西班牙悲剧》里的台词（Gill）。

Enter Rosencrantz and Guildenstern.

Guild.	Good my lord, vouchsafe me a word with you.
290 **Hamlet**	Sir, a whole history.
Guild.	The King, sir—
Hamlet	Ay, sir, what of him?
Guild.	Is in his retirement marvellous distempered.
Hamlet	With drink, sir?
295 **Guild.**	No, my lord, with choler.
Hamlet	Your wisdom should show itself more richer to signify this to the doctor, for for me to put him to his purgation would perhaps plunge him into more choler.
300 **Guild.**	Good my lord, put your discourse into some frame, and start not so wildly from my affair.
Hamlet	I am tame, sir. Pronounce.
Guild.	The Queen your mother, in most great affliction of spirit, hath sent me to you.
305 **Hamlet**	You are welcome.
Guild.	Nay, good my lord, this courtesy is not of the right breed. If it shall please you to make me a wholesome answer, I will do your mother's commandment; if not, your pardon and my return shall be the end of
310	my business.

罗森克兰与盖登斯顿上。

盖登斯顿	好殿下,请允许我跟您说句话。	
哈姆雷特	先生,您只管陈说!	290
盖登斯顿	先生,国王他——	
哈姆雷特	是的,先生,他怎么了?	
盖登斯顿	他回去以后感到心烦意乱。	
哈姆雷特	因为酒吗,先生?	
盖登斯顿	不是,殿下,因为脾气。	295
哈姆雷特	凭借您的聪明才智,您本该把这种 症状告诉他的医生才是,因为要是 让我给他下药,恐怕会使他的脾气 更大。	
盖登斯顿	我的殿下,请您把话说得条理一些, 不要离题太远。	300
哈姆雷特	我洗耳恭听,先生,说吧。	
盖登斯顿	您的母后,感到万分苦恼,她委派我 前来见您。	
哈姆雷特	欢迎您。	305
盖登斯顿	别这样,我的好殿下,您的这种客气 有些不大适宜。如果您愿意给我一个 合理的回答,我就转达您母亲的旨意; 不然,那就只好请您原谅,恕我回去 交差了。	310

---

298. 下药:（1）就是让他服用泻药或放血,以便治疗其生理上的失调;（2）督促他坦白自己的罪行,以便解脱其精神上的负担（Gill）。

Hamlet		Sir, I cannot.
Guild.		What, my lord?
Hamlet		Make you a wholesome answer. My wit's diseased.
		But sir, such answer as I can make, you shall com-
	315	mand—or rather, as you say, my mother. Therefore
		no more, but to the matter. My mother, you say—
Ros.		Then thus she says: your behavior hath struck her
		into amazement and admiration.
Hamlet		O wonderful son, that can so astonish a mother! But
	320	is there no sequel at the heels of this mother's admir-
		ation? Impart.
Ros.		She desires to speak with you in her closet ere you go
		to bed.
Hamlet		We shall obey, were she ten times our mother.
	325	Have you any further trade with us?
Ros.		My lord, you once did love me.
Hamlet		And do still, by these pickers and stealers.
Ros.		Good my lord, what is your cause of distemper? You
		do surely bar the door upon your own liberty if you
	330	deny your griefs to your friend.
Hamlet		Sir, I lack advancement.
Ros.		How can that be, when you have the voice of the King
		himself for your succession in Denmark?
Hamlet		Ay, sir, but while the grass grows—the proverb is
	335	something musty.

哈姆雷特	先生,我不能。	
罗森克兰	不能什么?	
哈姆雷特	不能给您一个合理的回答。我神志不清。	
	可是先生,至于我能作的回答,您可以	
	吩咐——或者如您所说,我母亲可以吩咐。	315
	因此少废话,直说吧。　您说我母亲——	
罗森克兰	她是这样说的:您的行为已经让她感到	
	惊恐万分。	
哈姆雷特	噢,多么棒的儿子,竟让母亲如此惊恐!	
	可是,这位母亲惊恐之后,难道就没了	320
	下文?　快说!	
罗森克兰	她想让您在睡觉之前到她的房间里跟她	
	谈话。	
哈姆雷特	哪怕她做十次我的母亲,我也都会听从。	
	您还有什么别的贵干?	325
罗森克兰	殿下,您曾经是爱我的。	
哈姆雷特	我依然爱您,凭这双扒手起誓!	
罗森克兰	我的好殿下,是什么原因让您性情失调?	
	如果您拒不将自己悲伤的缘由告诉朋友,	
	您定会自讨苦吃。	330
哈姆雷特	先生,我缺乏晋升。	
罗森克兰	那怎么可能,国王不是已亲口推举殿下	
	继承丹麦王位?	
哈姆雷特	对,先生,可是等到草长出——这则谚语	
	有些陈腐。	335

---

327. 这双扒手:出自基督教的《教理问答》,其中有一条教义教导人们"不要偷窃"
(Jenkins)。 334. 等到草长出:这则谚语的后半句为,"马儿早饿死(the horse starves)"
(Jenkins)。

Enter the Players with recorders.

O, the recorders. Let me see one. —To withdraw
with you , why do you go about to recover the wind
of me, as if you would drive me into a toil?

Guild.   O my lord, if my duty be too bold, my love is too
340   unmannerly.

Hamlet   I do not well understand that. Will you play upon
this pipe?

Guild.   My lord, I cannot.

Hamlet   I pray you.

345 **Guild.**   Believe me, I cannot.

Hamlet   I do beseech you.

Guild.   I know no touch of it, my lord.

Hamlet   It is as easy as lying. Govern these ventages with
your fingers and thumb, give it breath with your
350   mouth, and it will discourse most eloquent music.
Look you, these are the stops.

Guild.   But these cannot I command to any utterance of
harmony. I have not the skill.

Hamlet   Why, look you now, how unworthy a thing you
355   make of me. You would play upon me, you would
seem to know my stops, you would pluck out the
heart of my mystery, you would sound me from my
lowest note to the top of my compass; and there is
much music, excellent voice, in this little organ, yet

演员们携笛子上。

噢,笛子来了,让我看看。——我私下里
问问你们,你们为何拐弯抹角总想占我
上风,好像要把我赶入你们设下的陷阱?

盖登斯顿　　噢,殿下,我的言行若太过放肆,那是
因为我的爱已不拘小节。　　　　　　　　　340

哈姆雷特　　我不太明白您的意思。　您想吹一吹这只
笛子吗?

盖登斯顿　　殿下,我不会。

哈姆雷特　　我求您。

盖登斯顿　　相信我,真不会。　　　　　　　　　　345

哈姆雷特　　我恳求您了。

盖登斯顿　　我不知道怎么吹,殿下。

哈姆雷特　　这跟撒谎一样轻松。您先用手指和拇指
堵住这些小孔,然后再用您的嘴巴吹气,
随后它就会发出最为流畅的乐音。您看,　　350
这些就是音孔。

盖登斯顿　　可我却不能让它们发出任何悦耳的声音。
我没那种本事。

哈姆雷特　　哎,您看看,您把我当成一件多么不值
钱的东西。您想玩弄我,您以为对我的
心窍了如指掌,您想拨弄出我内心深处　　355
的秘密,您想从我的最低音探听到我的
最高音;在这只小小的乐器里是隐藏着
不少悦耳的音乐、动听的声音,而您却

360   cannot you make it speak. 'Sblood, do you think I
am easier to be played on than a pipe? Call me what
instrument you will, though you fret me, you cannot
play upon me.

Enter Polonius.

God bless you, sir.

365 **Polonius**   My lord, the Queen would speak with you, and
presently.

Hamlet   Do you see yonder cloud that's almost in shape of
a camel?

Polonius   By th' mass and 'tis—like a camel indeed.

370 **Hamlet**   Methinks it is like a weasel.

Polonius   It is backed like a weasel.

Hamlet   Or like a whale.

Polonius   Very like a whale.

Hamlet   Then I will come to my mother by and by. —

375   [*aside*] They fool me to the top of my bent. — I will
come by and by.

Polonius   I will say so.   *Exit.*

Hamlet   ' By and by' is easily said. —Leave me, friends.

Exeunt all but Hamlet.

'Tis now the very witching time of night,

380   When churchyards yawn and hell itself breathes out
Contagion to this world. Now could I drink hot blood,
And do such bitter business as the day

无法让它出声。该死的,您以为我会比　　　　　　　　360
一只笛子还容易玩弄?随便您把我叫作
什么乐器,尽管您拨弄我,可是您无法
玩弄我。

　　　　　　　　波洛纽斯上。

上帝保佑您,先生!

波洛纽斯　　殿下,王后她想跟你谈一谈,而且是　　　　365
　　　　　　马上。

哈姆雷特　　您看天边那朵云彩,是不是很像骆驼
　　　　　　的形状?

波洛纽斯　　天哪,就是——真的很像一头骆驼。

哈姆雷特　　我认为它像一只鼬鼠。　　　　　　　　370

波洛纽斯　　它的背部倒像鼬鼠。

哈姆雷特　　或像一条鲸鱼。

波洛纽斯　　很像一条鲸鱼。

哈姆雷特　　过一会儿我就去见我的母亲。——
　　　　　　[旁白]他们把我愚弄到了极点。——我　　　　375
　　　　　　过一会儿就来。

波洛纽斯　　我会如实禀报。　　　　　　　　　　　　　　　　下。

哈姆雷特　　"过一会儿"已脱口而出。——去吧,朋友

　　　　　　　　　　　　　　除哈姆雷特以外全下。

此刻正是妖巫猖獗的黑夜,
坟墓张开大口,地狱向人间　　　　　　　　　　　　380
喷吐瘴气。　现在我能喝饮热血,
干出白天所惨不忍睹的勾当。

---

360. 该死的('Sblood = by God's blood):诅咒语(an oath)。　此刻,有的演员会在盛怒之下将笛子折断(Thompson)。　另见2.2.363。　362. 尽管您拨弄我:哈姆雷特本来把自身比作一件吹奏乐器(pipe),可现在出于"拨弄(fret)"字意的双关需要,将比喻的意象换成了一件弹拨乐器:因为"拨弄"除了有"弹拨"意义之外,还有"挑拨,激怒(irritate)"之意(Jenkins)。

Would quake to look on. Soft, now to my mother.

O heart, lose not thy nature. Let not ever

385   The soul of Nero enter this firm bosom;

Let me be cruel, not unnatural.

I will speak daggers to her, but use none.

My tongue and soul in this be hypocrites:

How in my words somever she be shent,

390   To give them seals never my soul consent.   *Exit.*

等一等,现在要去面见母亲。

噢,心啊,可别失去天良! 别让

尼禄的灵魂进入这健壮的胸膛; 　　　　　　　　385

我可以残忍,不能没有孝心。

我要口出利剑,手下留情。

我要矫揉造作,口是心非:

不管用怎样的言辞将她指控,

我的心决不许它们付诸行动。　　　　　　　下。　390

---

385. 尼禄:古罗马帝王,将自己的母亲杀害,因为她毒死了自己的丈夫——尼禄的父亲(Gill)。

SCENE Ⅲ

Enter King, Rosencrantz, and Guildenstern.

King   I like him not, nor stands it safe with us

To let his madness range. Therefore prepare you.

I your commission will forthwith dispatch,

And he to England shall along with you.

5   The terms of our estate may not endure

Hazard so near us as doth hourly grow

Out of his brows.

Guild.   We will ourselves provide.

Most holy and religious fear it is

To keep those many many bodies safe

10   That live and feed upon your Majesty.

Ros.   The single and peculiar life is bound

With all the strength and armour of the mind

To keep itself from noyance; but much more

That spirit upon whose weal depends and rests

15   The lives of many. The cess of majesty

Dies not alone, but like a gulf doth draw

What's near it with it. Or it is a massy wheel

Fix'd on the summit of the highest mount,

第三场

国王、罗森克兰与盖登斯顿上。

国王　　　我不喜欢他，放任他的疯癫

也不安全。　因此你们赶快准备。

你们的委任状我马上就办，

要让他跟你们一起前往英国。

就我的职责而言，也不能容忍　　　　　　　　5

他的横眉显露出如此日益

临近的危险。

盖登斯顿　　　　　　　我们将做好准备。

这真是一种神圣而虔诚的担心，

因为有那么那么多臣民的生死

存亡全都仰赖于陛下一人。　　　　　　　　10

罗森克兰　　既然每个人都会竭尽全力

让自己远离祸殃；更何况一位

自身的康健关乎万民的君王。

帝王的去世可不是一死了之，

而是像旋涡将附近的一切卷入。　　　　　　15

或者像是一个庞大的车轮，

安在一座最高山峰的顶端，

在这一个巨大的轮辐之上，

3.3.　16. 庞大的车轮：绘画作品常显示君王占据着命运车轮的顶端，下面有许多"附庸"紧紧地抱住车轮的边缘（Jenkins）。

To whose huge spokes ten thousand lesser things

20   Are mortis'd and adjoin'd, which when it falls,

Each small annexment, petty consequence,

Attends the boist'rous ruin. Never alone

Did the King sigh, but with a general groan.

King   Arm you, I pray you, to this speedy voyage,

25   For we will fetters put upon this fear

Which now goes too free-footed.

Ros.   We will haste us.

                       Exeunt Rosencrantz and Guildenstern.

Enter Polonius.

Polonius   My lord, he's going to his mother's closet.

Behind the arras I'll convey myself

To hear the process. I'll warrant she'll tax him home,

30   And as you said—and wisely was it said—

'Tis meet that some more audience than a mother,

Since nature makes them partial, should o'erhear

The speech of vantage. Fare you well, my liege.

I'll call upon you ere you go to bed,

And tell you what I know.

35 **King**   Thanks, dear my lord.

                              Exit Polonius.

O, my offence is rank, it smells to heaven;

It hath the primal eldest curse upon't—

	紧紧牵连着数以万计的附庸,	
	车轮一旦跌落,每一个小小的	20
	附件和无足轻重之物,都会	
	随之倾覆。　国王的一声哀叹,	
	总会有万民的呻吟与之相伴。	

国王　快准备,我求你们立即出发,
因为我要把这种恐怖铸住, 25
它的自由已经过分。

罗森克兰　　　　　　　　我们抓紧。

罗森克兰与盖登斯顿同下。

波洛纽斯上。

波洛纽斯　殿下,他正前往他母亲的房间。
我要躲在幕后偷听他们的谈话。
我保证她定会对他义正词严,
正如您所说的——真是英明论断—— 30
应另外派人监听他们的密谈,
因为天性会让母亲们有所
偏心。　请多保重,我的陛下。
我会在您就寝之前再来拜望,
并禀报情况。

国王　　　　　　谢谢,亲爱的阁下。 35

波洛纽斯下。

噢,我的罪恶已经臭气熏天;
它要遭受最为远古的诅咒——

---

30. 正如您所说的:其实为波洛纽斯本人的主意。　参见 3.1.186-7(Jenkins)。　37. 最为远古的诅咒:出自《圣经》"创世纪"4 章 11-12 节。　亚当和夏娃的长子(该隐)杀死了自己的弟弟(亚伯)之后所受到的上帝的诅咒:"¹¹现在你要遭受世上的诅咒,大地已张开嘴巴要从你手上吸取你兄弟的鲜血。¹²你所耕种的土地将是不毛之地。　你将在世上颠沛流离。"另外,具有讽刺意味的是,此处对该隐杀兄之罪的提及已在 1.2.105 埋下伏笔,并在 5.1.75-6 得以回应(Jenkins)。

A brother's murder. Pray can I not,

Though inclination be as sharp as will,

40 My stronger guilt defeats my strong intent,

And, like a man to double business bound,

I stand in pause where I shall first begin,

And both neglect. What if this cursed hand

Were thicker than itself with brother's blood,

45 Is there not rain enough in the sweet heavens

To wash it white as snow? Whereto serves mercy

But to confront the visage of offence?

And what's in prayer but this twofold force,

To be forestalled ere we come to fall

50 Or pardon'd being down? Then I'll look up.

My fault is past—but O, what form of prayer

Can serve my turn? 'Forgive me my foul murder?'

That cannot be, since I am still possess'd

Of those effects for which I did the murder—

55 My crown, mine own ambition, and my queen.

May one be pardon'd and retain th'offence?

In the corrupted currents of this world

Offence's gilded hand may shove by justice,

And oft 'tis seen the wicked prize itself

那就是杀兄之罪！我无法祈祷，

尽管我的意愿和决心一样热切，

更强的内疚却击溃了强烈意愿，　　　　　　　40

犹如一人同时想做两件事情，

不知该从何入手而犹豫不决，

结果全都忽略。　这只黑手若因

兄弟的鲜血更加肮脏又会怎样，

难道上天就没有充足的甘霖　　　　　　　　45

将它洗得雪白？　怜悯的目的

不就是让人正视罪恶面孔？

祈祷不就是拥有两种作用：

在我们失足之前加以预防，

堕落之后得到宽恕？　那我要抬头。　　　　50

我的罪已犯下——可是噢，哪种祈祷

能对我有用？　"饶恕我邪恶的凶杀？"

那不可能，因为我还占有着

我从谋杀之中所获得的好处——

我的王冠、我的野心、我的王后。　　　　　55

能不能既保留赃物又得到宽恕？

在当今这个腐败盛行的世界，

镀金的凶手可将正义推开，

邪恶的赃物经常被人用来

43-6. 这只……雪白：类似的意象也出现在了其他的莎剧之中，如《麦克白》里的血手（the bloody hand），《威尼斯商人》里的怜悯之甘霖（the raining mercy）。 它们都与《圣经》里的经文相关："你们的罪虽像朱红，必变成雪白"（"以赛亚书"1章18节）。 "求你洗涤我，我就比雪更白"（"诗篇"51篇7节）（Gill）。 48. 两种作用：克劳狄斯记住了主祷文里的祈求："不叫我们遇见试探"以及"救我们脱离凶恶"——既要'使我们避免犯罪（prevent us from sinning）'，又要"赦免我们已经犯下的罪（forgive us for the wrong we have already done）"（Gill）。 55. 我的野心：即"野心的得逞（the achievement of my ambition）"（Thompson）。

60   Buys out the law. But 'tis not so above:

There is no shuffling, there the action lies

In his true nature, and we ourselves compell'd

Even to the teeth and forehead of our faults

To give in evidence. What then? What rests?

65   Try what repentance can. What can it not?

Yet what can it, when one cannot repent?

O wretched state! O bosom black as death!

O limed soul, that struggling to be free

Art more engag'd! Help, angels! Make assay.

70   Bow, stubborn knees; and heart with strings of steel,

Be soft as sinews of the new-born babe.

All may be well. [*He kneels.*]

Enter Hamlet.

Hamlet   Now might I do it pat, now a is a-praying.

And now I'll do't. [*Draws his sword.*]

And so a goes to heaven;

75   And so am I reveng'd. That would be scann'd:

A villain kills my father, and for that

I, his sole son, do this same villain send

To heaven.

Why, this is hire and salary, not revenge.

80   A took my father grossly, full of bread,

With all his crimes broad blown, as flush as May;

And how his audit stands who knows save heaven?

将法律收买。　天上可不是这样：　　　　　　　　60
那里无法抵赖，所有的行为
在那里原形毕露，我们本人
不得不直接面对自己的罪过
——招供。　怎么办？　怎么办？
试一试忏悔吧。　它有啥不能做？　　　　　　　65
可它有啥用，我连忏悔都不能？
噢，可怜的处境！噢，污黑的心胸！
噢，沉沦的灵魂，越想挣脱羁绊，
越是纠缠不清！救命，天使！尽力。
弯下，顽固的双膝，和铁石心肠，　　　　　　　70
要像婴儿的筋肉一样柔软。
一切还会好转。　［国王跪下。］

哈姆雷特上。

哈姆雷特　我现在动手正好，他在祈祷。
我这就动手。　［拔剑。］
他可以就此升天；
我因此报了仇！这可需要思量：　　　　　　　75
一个恶棍杀死了我父亲，为此，
我，他的独生子，却把这个恶棍
送入天堂。
这哪是复仇，而是回报和酬劳！
父亲遇害的时候满腹俗念、　　　　　　　　　80
罪恶昭彰，犹如五月鲜花怒放；
他如何受审，除了上帝谁能知道？

74. 就此升天：哈姆雷特认为他的叔父因为能够祈祷，可以接受天恩，因而不会像他父亲那样，死后要遭受炼狱的折磨（Gill）。

But in our circumstance and course of thought
'Tis heavy with him. And am I then reveng'd,

85 To take him in the purging of his soul,
When he is fit and season'd for his passage?
No.
Up, sword, and know thou a more horrid hent:
When he is drunk asleep, or in his rage,

90 Or in th'incestuous pleasure of his bed,
At game a-swearing, or about some act
That has no relish of salvation in't,
Then trip him, that his heels may kick at heaven
And that his soul may be as damn'd and black

95 As hell, whereto it goes. My mother stays.
This physic but prolongs thy sickly days.   *Exit.*

King   My words fly up, my thoughts remain below.
Words without thoughts never to heaven go.   *Exit.*

可是按照我们目前的想法，
却是相当糟糕。 在他净化心灵，
准备好上路之时，我却结果了   85
他的性命，难道这就是报仇？
不行。
入鞘吧，剑，要找个更好的时机：
当他喝醉入睡，或大发雷霆，
或在床上发泄乱伦的情欲，   90
或在赌博时诅咒，或者从事
一些毫无希望得救的勾当时
再送他上路，让他双脚蹬天，
灵魂就像其行将坠入的地狱
一样可恶与黑暗。 母亲在等待。   95
这服药剂只是延长你的病态。   下。

国王　言辞已经飞起，思想还在下面，
没思想的言辞永远到不了上天。   下。

---

93. 双脚蹬天：该隐喻一方面表明克劳狄斯蔑视上天；另一方面也表明他将头朝下方（跌入地狱）（Jenkins）。 96. 这服药剂：即国王的祷告（Jenkins）。

SCENE IV

Enter Queen and Polonius.

Polonius   A will come straight. Look you lay home to him,

Tell him his pranks have been too broad to bear with

And that your Grace hath screen'd and stood between

Much heat and him. I'll silence me even here.

Pray you be round.

5 **Queen**   I'll war'nt you, fear me not.

Withdraw, I hear him coming.

[*Polonius hides behind the arras.*]

Enter Hamlet.

Hamlet   Now, mother, what's the matter?

Queen   Hamlet, thou hast thy father much offended.

Hamlet   Mother, you have my father much offended.

10 **Queen**   Come, come, you answer with an idle tongue.

Hamlet   Go, go, you question with a wicked tongue.

Queen   Why, how now, Hamlet?

Hamlet   What's the matter now?

Queen   Have you forgot me?

第四场

王后与波洛纽斯上。

波洛纽斯	他马上就到。您对他不要客气,
	让他知道他的胡闹已无法容忍,
	夫人您已经替他遮挡了许多
	愤怒。我躲在这里保持沉默,
	求您直截了当!
王后	我保证,别担心。　　　　5
	快躲开,我听见他来了。

[波洛纽斯藏在帷幕之后。]

哈姆雷特上。

哈姆雷特	哎,母亲,有什么事儿?
王后	哈姆雷特,你大大冒犯了你父亲。
哈姆雷特	母亲,您大大冒犯了我父亲。
王后	得啦,得啦,你的回答净是胡扯。　　10
哈姆雷特	算啦,算啦,您的问话纯属恶言。
王后	哎,怎么了,哈姆雷特?
哈姆雷特	什么怎么了?
王后	你忘了我是谁?

3.4.　4.保持沉默:富有讥讽意味的是,他并未做到这一点（22行）,从而断送了自己的性命——永远保持沉默（Jenkins）。

	Hamlet	No, by the rood, not so.
		You are the Queen, your husband's brother's wife,
15		And, would it were not so, you are my mother.
	Queen	Nay, then I'll set those to you that can speak.
	Hamlet	Come, come, and sit you down, you shall not budge.
		You go not till I set you up a glass
		Where you may see the inmost part of you.
20	**Queen**	What wilt thou do? Thou wilt not murder me?
		Help, ho!
	Polonius	[*behind the arras*] What ho! Help!
	Hamlet	How now? A rat! Dead for a ducat, dead.
		[*Thrusts his rapier through the arras.*]
	Polonius	[*behind*] O, I am slain.
	Queen	O me, what hast thou done?
25	**Hamlet**	Nay, I know not.
		Is it the King?
		[*Lifts up the arras and discovers Polonius, dead.*]
	Queen	O what a rash and bloody deed is this!
	Hamlet	A bloody deed. Almost as bad, good mother,
		As kill a king and marry with his brother.
	Queen	As kill a king?
30	**Hamlet**	Ay, lady, it was my word. —
		Thou wretched, rash, intruding fool, farewell.
		I took thee for thy better. Take thy fortune:
		Thou find'st to be too busy is some danger. —
		Leave wringing of your hands. Peace, sit you down,

哈姆雷特	没有,天作证,没忘。	
	您是王后,您丈夫的弟弟的妻子,	
	但愿并非如此,您是我的母亲!	15
王后	要不,我去叫别人过来跟你谈。	
哈姆雷特	得啦,得啦,您给我坐下,不要动。	
	我要把一面镜子放在您面前,	
	也许您能看到自己的内心。	
王后	你要干啥? 你不会杀了我吧?	20
	救命啦!	
波洛纽斯	〔在幕后〕怎么啦! 救命!	
哈姆雷特	怎么? 有老鼠! 贱货死去,死去!	
	〔拔剑刺穿帷幕。〕	
波洛纽斯	〔在幕后〕噢,我遇害了!	
王后	天哪,你干了什么?	
哈姆雷特	我不知道。	25
	是国王吗?	
	〔掀开帷幕,发现波洛纽斯已经死去。〕	
王后	噢,这是多么鲁莽、残忍的行为!	
哈姆雷特	是残忍的行为! 好母亲,就像杀死	
	国王又嫁给他弟弟一样糟糕。	
王后	杀死国王?	
哈姆雷特	对,夫人,是我说的。——	30
	你这可怜、莽撞、多事的傻瓜,再会。	
	我以为是你的上司。 自认倒霉吧:	
	你明白了爱管闲事有多危险。——	
	别再拧搓您的手。 别动,您坐下,	

---

16. 意为:"你不尊重我,我就让更有说服力的人来对付你。"可能是指国王(Thompson)。 30. 杀死国王:葛楚德的反应可表明她对国王的遇害清白无辜(Gill)。 32. 上司:即国王(Thompson)。

A station like the herald Mercury

New-lighted on a heaven-kissing hill,

60   A combination and a form indeed

Where every god did seem to set his seal

To give the world assurance of a man.

This was your husband. Look you now what follows.

Here is your husband, like a mildew'd ear

65   Blasting his wholesome brother. Have you eyes?

Could you on this fair mountain leave to feed

And batten on this moor? Ha, have you eyes?

You cannot call it love; for at your age

The heyday in the blood is tame, it's humble,

70   And waits upon the judgment, and what judgment

Would step from this to this? Sense sure you have,

Else could you not have motion; but sure that sense

Is apoplex'd, for madness would not err

Nor sense to ecstasy was ne'er so thrall'd

75   But it reserv'd some quantity of choice

To serve in such a difference. What devil was't

That thus hath cozen'd you at hoodman-blind?

Eyes without feeling, feeling without sight,

Ears without hands or eyes, smelling sans all,

他的身姿就像信使墨丘利

刚刚落到高吻苍穹的山巅，

真是一副完美无缺的形象，　　　　　　　　60

就像每位天神都盖上封印，

以给世界一个男人的榜样。

这是您的夫君。　再看另一个。

这是您丈夫,就像霉烂的谷穗

将健康兄弟侵害。　您长眼了吗?　　　　65

您能舍弃这座青山去吞食

这种污淖?　哈,您长眼了吗?

您不能称之为爱吧;因为到了

您这把年纪情欲早已平淡,

应受理智支配,是什么理智　　　　　　　70

居然就此而舍彼?　您肯定有知觉,

否则不会有行动;可那种知觉

已经麻木,因为疯狂和幻觉

都不至于差错到这种地步,

而会保留一定的选择能力　　　　　　　75

来区分如此悬殊。　是什么恶魔

趁捉迷藏之际竟这样骗您?

让您有眼无珠,熟视无睹,

耳聪但手眼不灵,或只嗅觉管用,

58.墨丘利(Mercury):众神的信使,以其身姿优美而著称(Jenkins)。　71.就此而舍彼:
参见1.5.47-52(Jenkins)。　71-2.您肯定有知觉,否则不会有行动:古罗马哲学家亚里士多德认
为,所有能够运动的生物（包括动物和植物,但不包括石头）都有知觉(Gill)。　76-7.恶魔……
这样骗你:葛楚德的知觉失灵,不像是自身生理的因素所致,而是因为魔鬼作祟。　人们普遍认为,
魔鬼不仅可以骗人,还会削弱人们的判断能力,从而让他们欺骗自己（参见2.2.597）(Jenkins)。　哈姆雷特此处是说,在这种捉迷藏的游戏中,魔鬼肯定是趁葛楚德蒙住眼睛时将克劳狄斯
推到了她的身旁(Bevington)。　78-9.有眼无珠……嗅觉管用:就71-5行提及的知觉进行具体
描述(Jenkins)。

80   Or but a sickly part of one true sense

          Could not so mope. O shame, where is thy blush?

          Rebellious hell,

          If thou canst mutine in a matron's bones,

          To flaming youth let virtue be as wax

85   And melt in her own fire; proclaim no shame

          When the compulsive ardour gives the charge,

          Since frost itself as actively doth burn

          And reason panders will.

Queen   O Hamlet, speak no more.

          Thou turn'st my eyes into my very soul,

90   And there I see such black and grained spots

          As will not leave their tinct.

Hamlet   Nay, but to live

          In the rank sweat of an enseamed bed,

          Stew'd in corruption, honeying and making love

          Over the nasty sty!

Queen   O speak to me no more.

95   These words like daggers enter in my ears.

          No more, sweet Hamlet.

Hamlet   A murderer and a villain,

          A slave that is not twentieth part the tithe

          Of your precedent lord, a vice of kings,

          A cutpurse of the empire and the rule,

有一点正常知觉,也不会如此　　　　　　　　　　　80
呆滞！噢,丢人,你的廉耻何在？
骚动的妖魔,
既然你能在婆娘的骨子里作祟,
就让贞操像烛蜡一样在青春的
火焰中熔化吧；当强烈的情欲　　　　　　　　　　85
进犯时,也不再有羞耻可言,
因为冰霜本身都主动燃烧,
理智迎合激情。

王后　　　　　　　　　噢,哈姆雷特,别说了！
你让我看到了自己的灵魂深处,
让我看到了自己难以洗清的　　　　　　　　　　　90
许多污点和羞耻。

哈姆雷特　　　　　　　得啦,您只管
在满是臭汗、油渍斑斑的床上
自甘堕落,躺在肮脏的猪圈里
谈情做爱去吧！

王后　　　　　　　　　噢,别再说了！
这番话就像利剑刺进我双耳。　　　　　　　　　　95
别说了,好哈姆雷特！

哈姆雷特　　　　　　　　　　一个凶手
和恶棍,一个不及您的先君
二百分之一的小人,一个魔王,
一个篡国夺权的奸臣贼子,

---

82. 骚动的妖魔：与理智作对的情欲（Gill）。　84-5. 就让……熔化吧：对激情四溢的青年来说,就让贞操像烛蜡一样在自己的火焰中熔化吧（既然一位中年妇女做出了如此糟糕的表率,还能指望年轻人自我克制吗？）（Bevington）。　87. 冰霜：中年妇女（婆娘）身上较为冷淡的性欲（Jenkins）。　88. 理智迎合激情：理智的作用本来是控制激情,而不是予以逢迎（Jenkins）。　94. 谈情（honeying）：彼此以"宝贝"相称（calling each other *honey*）（Thompson）。　95. 就像利剑：应验了哈姆雷特在 3.2.387 的言辞（Jenkins）。

100		That from a shelf the precious diadem stole
		And put it in his pocket—
	Queen	No more.
	Hamlet	A king of shreds and patches—

Enter Ghost.

		Save me and hover o'er me with your wings,
105		You heavenly guards! What would your gracious figure?
	Queen	Alas, he's mad.
	Hamlet	Do you not come your tardy son to chide,
		That, laps'd in time and passion, lets go by
		Th'important acting of your dread command?
		O say.
110	**Ghost**	Do not forget. This visitation
		Is but to whet thy almost blunted purpose.
		But look, amazement on thy mother sits.
		O step between her and her fighting soul.
		Conceit in weakest bodies strongest works.
115		Speak to her, Hamlet.
	Hamlet	How is it with you, lady?
	Queen	Alas, how is't with you,
		That you do bend your eye on vacancy,
		And with th'incorporal air do hold discourse?
		Forth at your eyes your spirits wildly peep,
120		And, as the sleeping soldiers in th'alarm,
		Your bedded hair, like life in excrements,

	从架子上将珍贵的王冠窃取，	100
	装进了自己的口袋——	
王后	别说了！	
哈姆雷特	一个下贱丑陋的国王——	

鬼魂上。

	天上的卫士，救救我，用你们的	
	翅膀护卫我！陛下您想要什么？	105
王后	哎呀，他疯了！	
哈姆雷特	难道您不是来责备迟缓的儿子，	
	因为他耽误了时间，冷淡了热情，	
	错过了您可怕命令的及时执行？	
	噢，快说！	
鬼魂	不要忘记。此次来访	110
	只想磨砺你几乎已迟钝的决心。	
	快看，你母亲现在惊恐万分。	
	噢，快去安慰她挣扎中的灵魂。	
	身体最弱的人最易产生幻觉。	
	对她说话，哈姆雷特。	115
哈姆雷特	你怎么样，夫人？	
王后	哎呀，你怎么样，	
	居然将你的眼睛凝视着虚空，	
	对着虚无的空气喃喃自语？	
	竟神经错乱地向四处张望，	
	犹如睡梦中的士兵听到报警，	120
	你平展的头发，仿佛有了生命，	

---

107. 责备：据信，假如鬼魂最初的要求未被及时执行，他们就会反复出现（Gill）。121-2. 头发……竖立：哈姆雷特的头发被比喻成睡梦中的士兵，被警报惊醒之后立刻下床，立正待命（Jenkins）。

	Start up and stand an end. O gentle son,
	Upon the heat and flame of thy distemper
	Sprinkle cool patience. Whereon do you look?
125 **Hamlet**	On him, on him. Look you how pale he glares.
	His form and cause conjoin'd, preaching to stones,
	Would make them capable. —Do not look upon me,
	Lest with this piteous action you convert
	My stern effects. Then what I have to do
130	Will want true colour—tears perchance for blood.
Queen	To whom do you speak this?
Hamlet	Do you see nothing there?
Queen	Nothing at all; yet all that is I see.
Hamlet	Nor did you nothing hear?
135 **Queen**	No, nothing but ourselves.
Hamlet	Why, look you there, look how it steals away.
	My father, in his habit as he liv'd!
	Look where he goes even now out at the portal. *Exit Ghost.*
Queen	This is the very coinage of your brain.
140	This bodiless creation ecstasy
	Is very cunning in.
Hamlet	My pulse as yours doth temperately keep time,
	And makes as healthful music. It is not madness
	That I have utter'd. Bring me to the test,
145	And I the matter will re-word, which madness
	Would gambol from. Mother, for love of grace,
	Lay not that flattering unction to your soul,

	突然惊起,根根竖立。 好孩子,	
	快在你那神志混乱的火焰上	
	喷撒冷静的耐性。 你在看什么?	
哈姆雷特	看他,看他! 您看他脸色多白!	125
	他的情形及缘由,向顽石述说,	
	也会让它们感动。 ——别看着我,	
	否则您那可怜的举止会动摇	
	我的意志。 我要做的事情也许	
	会失去本色——以挥泪替代流血!	130
王后	你在跟谁说话?	
哈姆雷特	看不见那边有啥?	
王后	看不见;尽管我能看到一切。	
哈姆雷特	什么也没听见?	
王后	没有,除了我们的谈话。	135
哈姆雷特	咳,您看那边,他正悄悄地离去!	
	我的父亲,穿着他生前的便衣!	
	您看他现在就要走出大门!	鬼魂下。
王后	这不过是你脑海里的虚构。	
	因为疯狂就是擅长这样的	140
	无中生有。	
哈姆雷特	我的脉搏跟您的一样正常,	
	节律明快而健康。 我刚才说的,	
	并非疯话。 不信您让我试试,	
	我可以复述,然而疯狂却只能	145
	含糊其辞。 母亲,看在上帝的份上,	
	别向您的灵魂涂抹自慰的油膏,	

---

133. 看不见:按照伊丽莎白时代的信仰,鬼魂出现时,有些人能看见;而在场的另一些人可能什么也看不见。 因此,葛楚德看不到鬼魂的身影;也听不见它与哈姆雷特之间的对话(Jenkins)。

That not your trespass but my madness speaks.

It will but skin and film the ulcerous place,

150   Whiles rank corruption, mining all within,

Infects unseen. Confess yourself to heaven,

Repent what's past, avoid what is to come;

And do not spread the compost on the weeds

To make them ranker. Forgive me this my virtue;

155   For in the fatness of these pursy times

Virtue itself of vice must pardon beg,

Yea, curb and woo for leave to do him good.

Queen   O Hamlet, thou hast cleft my heart in twain.

Hamlet   O throw away the worser part of it

160   And live the purer with the other half.

Good night. But go not to my uncle's bed.

Assume a virtue if you have it not.

That monster, custom, who all sense doth eat

Of habits evil, is angel yet in this,

165   That to the use of actions fair and good

He likewise gives a frock or livery

That aptly is put on. Refrain tonight,

And that shall lend a kind of easiness

To the next abstinence, the next more easy;

170   For use almost can change the stamp of nature,

And either (lodge) the devil or throw him out

With wondrous potency. Once more, good night,

And when you are desirous to be blest,

只说我的疯狂,不提您的罪过。

那只能在溃烂之处覆盖皮毛,

让恶臭的腐烂暗中蔓延,其间的　　　　　　　　　　150

感染不得而见。　要向上帝坦白,

您要忏悔过去,预防未来;

别给杂草施肥从而让它们

更加繁茂。　原谅我这种善意;　　　　　　　　　　155

因为在这个浮夸放荡的时代,

美德必须向邪恶乞求宽恕,

为他做好事,还得屈膝央求。

王后　　　　　噢,哈姆雷特,你把我的心劈成两半!

哈姆雷特　　　噢,就把那更糟的一半丢弃,

用另一半较为清白地活着。　　　　　　　　　　160

晚安。　但不要跟我叔父同床。

如果您没有贞操,就开始培养。

习惯,这个怪物,既可通过

陋习吞噬我们的善恶之感,

而它又是天使,可以仰赖　　　　　　　　　　165

我们的善举帮助我们养成

良好的风范。　今晚忍耐一下,

会让下一次的节制容易一些,

再下一次的节制就更加容易;

因为习惯几乎能改变天性,　　　　　　　　　　170

它有奇妙的潜能,既可受到款待,

也可遭到驱除。　再道一声,晚安,

等您有意祈求上帝的恩赐时,

---

158. 把我的心劈成两半:一半对自己的行为表示悔恨,一半对现在的丈夫保持忠诚（Jenkins）。　173-4. 等您……祝福:当您准备忏悔并祈求上帝的宽恕时,我才会像一位孝子应该做的那样——请求您的祝福（Bevington）。

I'll blessing beg of you. For this same lord

175 I do repent; but heaven hath pleas'd it so,

To punish me with this and this with me,

That I must be their scourge and minister.

I will bestow him, and will answer well

The death I gave him. So, again, good night.

180 I must be cruel only to be kind.

This bad begins, and worse remains behind.

One word more, good lady.

Queen   What shall I do?

Hamlet Not this, by no means, that I bid you do:

Let the bloat King tempt you again to bed,

185 Pinch wanton on your cheek, call you his mouse,

And let him, for a pair of reechy kisses,

Or paddling in your neck with his damn'd fingers,

Make you to ravel all this matter out

That I essentially am not in madness,

190 But mad in craft. 'Twere good you let him know,

For who that's but a queen, fair, sober, wise,

Would from a paddock, from a bat, a gib,

Such dear concernings hide? Who would do so?

No, in despite of sense and secrecy,

195 Unpeg the basket on the house's top,

	我再请您祝福。　至于这位老臣，	
	我后悔莫及；不过这是天意，	175
	惩罚我杀死他,惩罚他被我杀,	
	我必须充当天意的干将和刑具。	
	我先把他藏好,然后再来担当	
	杀害他的罪过。　再道一声,晚安。	
	只是出于善意我才必须凶残。	180
	灾殃已经开始,大祸还在后面。	
	再说一句,好夫人。	

王后　　　　　　　　我该怎么办？

哈姆雷特　决不做,我让您做的下列事情：
让那位臃肿的国王诱您上床，
搔弄您的脸蛋儿,把您称为耗子，　　　　185
并让他,通过几口恶臭的亲吻，
或用该死的指头抓挠您的脖子，
让您将所有的秘密和盘托出，
告诉他我实际上并非真疯，
而是假装。　您让他知道也好，　　　　190
因为哪位美丽、从容、明智的王后，
会将如此重要情报隐瞒于一只
蛤蟆、蝙蝠或雄猫？　谁会这么做？
不会的,任凭常识与谨慎，
您也会打开房顶上的笼子，　　　　195

---

176. 惩罚我……被我杀：正如哈姆雷特（通过刺杀波罗纽斯）对他进行了惩罚,而他本人也将会（因为刺杀波罗纽斯）而受到（国王,或良心的）惩罚（Thompson）。　188. 将……和盘托出：王后并未将哈姆雷特告诉她的秘密（142-8）泄露给克劳狄斯以消除其心中的疑惑（Jenkins）。　190. 您让他知道也好：哈姆雷特对葛楚德的讥讽在逐步升级（Gill）。　193. 蛤蟆、蝙蝠或雄猫：哈姆雷特在辱骂克劳狄斯,将巫术中常用的上述妖精与其相提并论（Gill）。

Let the birds fly, and like the famous ape,

To try conclusions, in the basket creep,

And break your own neck down.

Queen   Be thou assur'd, if words be made of breath,

200   And breath of life, I have no life to breathe

What thou hast said to me.

Hamlet   I must to England, you know that?

Queen   Alack,

I had forgot. 'Tis so concluded on.

Hamlet   There's letters seal'd, and my two schoolfellows,

205   Whom I will trust as I will adders fang'd—

They bear the mandate, they must sweep my way

And marshal me to knavery. Let it work;

For 'tis the sport to have the enginer

Hoist with his own petard, and't shall go hard

210   But I will delve one yard below their mines

And blow them at the moon. O, 'tis most sweet

When in one line two crafts directly meet.

This man shall set me packing.

I'll lug the guts into the neighbour room.

215   Mother, good night indeed. This counsellor

Is now most still, most secret, and most grave,

Who was in life a foolish prating knave.

Come, sir, to draw toward an end with you.

Good night, mother.

Exit lugging in Polonius. [*The Queen remains.*]

把鸟儿放出，就像那出名的猿猴，

也想试验一番，爬进笼子，

将自己的脖子摔断！

王后　　　你放心吧，假如话语来自气息，

气息来自生命，我已没有生命　　　　　　　　　200

吐出你的话语。

哈姆雷特　我要去英国，您知道这事？

王后　　　　　　　　　　　　哎呀，

我都给忘了。　就是这么定的。

哈姆雷特　信已封好，那两位校友将承担

送信使命——我要像信任毒蛇　　　　　　　　205

那样信任他们；他们会伴我同行

并把我引入陷阱。　随它的便吧；

让他们搬起石头砸自己的脚

倒很有趣，除非我时运不及，

我要在他们的雷下深挖三尺，　　　　　　　　210

把他们崩向月球！噢，两种计谋

若狭路相逢，那真是妙趣横生。

这位老兄将会督促我上路。

我先把这具尸体拖进隔壁。

母亲，最后道声晚安。　该大臣　　　　　　　215

生前是一位愚蠢、啰嗦之小人，

此刻倒是最安静、最嘴紧、最深沉。

来吧，先生，我和您就此了结。

晚安，母亲。

　　　　　　　　　　　拖着波洛纽斯的尸体下。[王后未动。]

196. 出名的猿猴：该寓言说的是，一只猴子看到鸟儿从笼子里出来时可以飞翔，自己也想试试，结果将自己的性命断送。　哈姆雷特是在警告母亲不要将他的秘密泄露（把鸟儿从笼中放出），以免招来杀身之祸（Jenkins）。　215-7. 该大臣……最深沉：该对偶句可当作波洛纽斯的墓志铭（Gill）。

第四幕
ACT 4

SCENE   I

[To the] Queen, Enter King, with Rosencrantz and
Guildenstern.

King   There's matter in these sighs, these profound heaves,

You must translate. 'Tis fit we understand them.

Where is your son?

Queen   Bestow this place on us a little while.

Exeunt Rosencrantz and Guildenstern.

5   Ah, mine own lord, what have I seen tonight!

King   What, Gertrude, how does Hamlet?

Queen   Mad as the sea and wind when both contend

Which is the mightier. In his lawless fit,

Behind the arras hearing something stir,

10   Whips out his rapier, cries 'A rat, a rat',

And in this brainish apprehension kills

The unseen good old man.

King   O heavy deed!

It had been so with us had we been there.

His liberty is full of threats to all—

15   To you yourself, to us, to everyone.

Alas, how shall this bloody deed be answer'd?

It will be laid to us, whose providence

第一场

国王、罗森克兰与盖登斯顿，

[面向]王后上。

国王　　这些叹息定有原因,这些唉声,

您必须解释。　应该让我知道。

您儿子呢?

王后　　请你们二位暂时回避一下。

　　　　　　　　　　　　罗森克兰与盖登斯顿同下。

啊,陛下,今晚的事情真是可怕!　　　　　　　5

国王　　怎么了,葛楚德,哈姆雷特怎样?

王后　　疯癫得犹如狂风欲与大浪

试比高下。　在神迷意乱之中,

他听见幕后传出了一点动静,

便拔出利剑,喊道,"老鼠,老鼠",　　　　10

在这种狂乱之中刺死了那位

藏在幕后的善良老人。

国王　　　　　　　噢,暴行!

要是我躲在那里,也照死不误。

他的自由对大家充满了威胁——

对您本人,对我,对每一个人。　　　　　　15

唉,这种血腥的行为如何交代?

人们要责备我,我本该对这个

Should have kept short, restrain'd and out of haunt

This mad young man. But so much was our love,

20   We would not understand what was most fit,

But like the owner of a foul disease,

To keep it from divulging, let it feed

Even on the pith of life. Where is he gone?

Queen   To draw apart the body he hath kill'd,

25   O'er whom—his very madness, like some ore

Among a mineral of metals base,

Shows itself pure—a weeps for what is done.

King   O Gertrude, come away.

The sun no sooner shall the mountains touch

30   But we will ship him hence; and this vile deed

We must with all our majesty and skill

Both countenance and excuse. —Ho, Guildenstern!

Enter Rosencrantz and Guildenstern.

Friends both, go join you with some further aid.

Hamlet in madness hath Polonius slain,

35   And from his mother's closet hath he dragg'd him.

Go seek him out—speak fair—and bring the body

Into the chapel. I pray you haste in this.

                  Exeunt Rosencrantz and Guildenstern.

Come, Gertrude, we'll call up our wisest friends,

And let them know both what we mean to do

疯狂的青年严加看管，不让他

到处乱串。　但我是如此爱他，

结果竟不知道该如何是好， 20

就像一位顽疾缠身的患者，

把疾病遮掩，而让它将生命的

精髓吞噬。　他到哪里去了？

王后　拖着遇害者的尸体出去了，

他的疯狂，犹如矿渣里的金子， 25

显露无遗——他正趴在那一具

尸体上面——为自己的行为哭泣。

国王　噢，葛楚德，快来。

太阳出山之前就得让他离岸；

至于这桩凶杀，我必须用尽 30

我的权威和技巧，既承担责任

又找一些借口。　——喂，盖登斯顿！

　　　　　罗森克兰与盖登斯顿上。

二位朋友，你们再找些人手。

哈姆雷特疯狂中杀了波洛纽斯，

已从他母亲屋里把尸体拖走。 35

去找找他——说话要委婉——然后

把尸体抬进教堂。　求你们赶快。

　　　　　罗森克兰与盖登斯顿同下。

来，葛楚德，我们要召集最明智的

朋友，让他们知道我们的意图

---

4. 1.　29. 太阳……离岸（The sun…hence）：意为"天一亮我们就让他上船（We will make him take ship as soon as dawn breaks）"。　这些话语可提醒我们此刻仍是夜色（Thompson）。

40 And what's untimely done. (So envious slander),

Whose whisper o'er the worlds' diameter,

As level as the cannon to his blank,

Transports his poison'd shot, may miss our name

And hit the woundless air. O come away,

45 My soul is full of discord and dismay. *Exeunt.*

及最终结果。（因此流言蜚语），　　　　　　　　　　　　40
尽管它像百发百中的大炮，
能将毒箭射向世界的每一个
角落,也许会错过我的名声,
击中刀枪不入的空气。　噢,快走,
我真是忐忑不安、充满忧愁。　　　　　　　　同下。　45

40.（因此流言蜚语）:原文此处为空白,该台词系后人根据上下文完整的语义要求所加
(Gill)。

SCENE II

Enter Hamlet.

Hamlet   Safely stowed.   [*Calling within.*]

But soft, what noise? Who calls on Hamlet? O, here
they come.

Enter Rosencrantz, Guildenstern, and others.

Ros.   What have you done, my lord, with the dead body?

5 **Hamlet**   Compounded it with dust, whereto 'tis kin.

Ros.   Tell us where 'tis, that we may take it thence and
bear it to the chapel.

Hamlet   Do not believe it.

Ros.   Believe what?

10 **Hamlet**   That I can keep your counsel and not mine own.
Besides, to be demanded of a sponge—what replica-
tion should be made by the son of a king?

Ros.   Take you me for a sponge, my lord?

Hamlet   Ay, sir, that soaks up the King's countenance, his
15   rewards, his authorities. But such officers do the

第二场

哈姆雷特上。

哈姆雷特　　已经藏好。　　　　　　　　　　　　　　［内有叫喊声。］

等一等,啥声音? 谁在叫哈姆雷特? 噢,

他们来了!

　　　　　　　罗森克兰、盖登斯顿与众人上。

罗森克兰　　您把尸体给怎么了,我的殿下?

哈姆雷特　　用土埋了,让它物归原处。　　　　　　　　　　　　5

罗森克兰　　告诉我们尸体在哪里,我们好把它抬进

教堂。

哈姆雷特　　我不相信。

罗森克兰　　不信什么?

哈姆雷特　　我连自己的秘密都保不住,还能为你们　　　　10

保密。再说,被一块海绵问来问去——

作为王子又该如何回答?

罗森克兰　　您把我当成一块海绵吗,殿下?

哈姆雷特　　是的,先生,浸满了国王的宠爱、他的

奖赏、他的权威。可是这样的官员最后　　　　　15

4.2. 5.物归原处:出自《圣经》"创世纪"3章19节:"你需要汗流满面才能糊口,直到你归于尘土,因为你是由尘土而来;你本是尘土,终要归于尘土。"(Jenkins)10-11. 还能为你们保密:此处采用了一句格言:一个人如果将自己的秘密泄露出去,那么他就很难为别人保密(Jenkins)。

King best service in the end: he keeps them, like an ape, in the corner of his jaw—first mouthed, to be last swallowed. When he needs what you have gleaned, it is but squeezing you and, sponge, you shall be dry again.

20

Ros.   I understand you not, my lord.

Hamlet   I am glad of it. A knavish speech sleeps in a foolish ear.

Ros.   My lord, you must tell us where the body is and go with us to the King.

25

Hamlet   The body is with the King, but the King is not with the body. The King is a thing—

Guild.   A thing, my lord?

Hamlet   Of nothing. Bring me to him.   *Exeunt.*

对国王最为有用：就像猿猴那样，他把
他们存在嘴角——首先入口，最后吞下。
他需要你们的囊中之物时，只消把你们
挤压一下。然后，作为海绵，你们又会
干干巴巴。　　　　　　　　　　　　　　　20

罗森克兰　　我不懂您的话，殿下。

哈姆雷特　　听不懂我很高兴。一个傻瓜听不懂风凉
话。

罗森克兰　　殿下，您要告诉我们尸体在哪里，然后
跟我们去见国王。　　　　　　　　　　　25

哈姆雷特　　尸体与国王同在，可是国王并非与尸体
共存。　国王是个东西——

盖登斯顿　　是个东西，殿下？

哈姆雷特　　无谓的东西。　带我去见他。　　　　同下。

26-7. 尸体……共存：哈姆雷特令人费猜的回答可作如下解释：波洛纽斯的尸体与国王都在
宫里（同在），但因克劳狄斯依然活着，所以他不可能与波洛纽斯共存。　人们也可据此得到一种
暗示：假如哈姆雷特没有误杀波洛纽斯，后果又将如何（Jenkins）。

SCENE III

Enter King and two or three [Lords].

KING   I have sent to seek him and to find the body.

How dangerous is it that this man goes loose!

Yet must not we put the strong law on him:

He's lov'd of the distracted multitude,

5   Who like not in their judgment but their eyes,

And where 'tis so, th'offender's scourge is weigh'd,

But never the offence. To bear all smooth and even,

This sudden sending him away must seem

Deliberate pause. Diseases desperate grown

10   By desperate appliance are reliev'd,

Or not at all.

Enter Rosencrantz, [Guildenstern,] and others.

How now, what hath befall'n?

Ros.   Where the dead body is bestow'd, my lord,

We cannot get from him.

King   But where is he?

Hamlet Without, my lord, guarded, to know your pleasure.

King   Bring him before us.

第三场

国王与两三位［大臣］上。

国王　　　　我已派人找他，也去找找尸体。
　　　　　　这个人放任自流是多么危险！
　　　　　　可我们又不能对他绳之以法：
　　　　　　因为冲动的民众都很爱他，
　　　　　　他们从表象出发，而非理智，　　　　　　　　　5
　　　　　　因此，对罪人的惩罚会遭非议，
　　　　　　而对罪行本身却置之不理。
　　　　　　为了息事宁人，立即送他出境
　　　　　　定是深思熟虑。　严重的疾病
　　　　　　要用猛烈的药物进行治疗，　　　　　　　　　10
　　　　　　否则毫无功效。

罗森克兰、［盖登斯顿］与众人上。

怎么样，结果如何？

罗森克兰　至于尸体藏在哪里，陛下，
　　　　　　我们无法问出。

国王　　　　　　　　　　可他在哪里？

罗森克兰　外面，陛下，看守着，等候您发落。

国王　　　　把他带进来。

| 15 | **Ros.** | Ho! Bring in the lord. |

Enter Hamlet with Guards.

	King	Now, Hamlet, where's Polonius?
	Hamlet	At supper.
	King	At supper? Where?
	Hamlet	Not where he eats, but where a is eaten. A cer-
20		tain convocation of politic worms are e'en at him.
		Your worm is your only emperor for diet: we fat all
		creatures else to fat us, and we fat ourselves for
		maggots. Your fat king and your lean beggar is but
		variable service—two dishes, but to one table.
25		That's the end.
	King	Alas, alas.
	Hamlet	A man may fish with the worm that hath eat of a
		king, and eat of the fish that hath fed of that worm.
	King	What dost thou mean by this?
30	**Hamlet**	Nothing but to show you how a king may go a
		progress through the guts of a beggar.
	King	Where is Polonius?
	Hamlet	In heaven. Send thither to see. If your messenger
		find him not there, seek him i'th'other place your-
35		self. But if indeed you find him not within this
		month, you shall nose him as you go up the stairs into
		the lobby.
	King	[*To some Attendants*] Go seek him there.

| 罗森克兰 | 喂！带殿下进来！ | 15 |

哈姆雷特与卫兵上。

国王　　哎，哈姆雷特，波洛纽斯在哪里？

哈姆雷特　在吃晚饭。

国王　　吃晚饭？　在哪里？

哈姆雷特　不是在吃饭的地方，而是在被吃的地方。
　　　　　一群狡猾的蛆虫正在他身上美餐。国王　　20
　　　　　也不过是蛆虫的小菜一碟：我们将其他
　　　　　所有动物养肥供我们享用，我们再把自
　　　　　己养肥去喂蛆虫。肥胖的国王与消瘦的
　　　　　乞丐只是不同的菜肴——两道菜，一张桌。
　　　　　就这么回事。　　　　　　　　　　　　　25

国王　　哎呀，哎呀！

哈姆雷特　人们可用吃过国王的蛆虫去钓鱼，然后
　　　　　再吃掉那条吞下蛆虫的鱼。

国王　　你这话是什么意思？

哈姆雷特　没什么，只想让您明白一位国王将如何　　30
　　　　　到乞丐肚里巡游一圈。

国王　　波洛纽斯在哪里？

哈姆雷特　在天上。派人到那里去找吧。如果您的
　　　　　使者在那里找不到他，您亲自到另一处
　　　　　去找吧。但是，假如你们在本月之内还　　35
　　　　　找不到他，您上楼入室的时候就会闻到
　　　　　他了。

国王　　［向若干侍从］去那里找吧。

4.3. 34. 另一处：地狱（Gill）。

| | **Hamlet** | A will stay till you come. | *Exeunt Attendants.* |

40 **King**   Hamlet, this deed, for thine especial safety—

Which we do tender, as we dearly grieve

For that which thou hast done—must send thee hence

With fiery quickness. Therefore prepare thyself.

The bark is ready, and the wind at help,

45   Th'associates tend, and everything is bent

For England.

Hamlet   For England?

King   Ay, Hamlet.

Hamlet   Good.

50 **King**   So is it, if thou knew'st our purposes.

Hamlet   I see a cherub that sees them. But come, for

England. Farewell, dear mother.

King   Thy loving father, Hamlet.

Hamlet   My mother. Father and mother is man and wife,

55   man and wife is one flesh; so my mother. Come, for

England.   *Exit.*

King   Follow him at foot. Tempt him with speed aboard,

Delay it not—I'll have him hence tonight.

Away, for everything is seal'd and done

60   That else leans on th'affair. Pray you make haste.

Exeunt all but the King.

And England, if my love thou hold'st at aught—

As my great power thereof may give thee sense,

Since yet thy cicatrice looks raw and red

哈姆雷特	他会等着你们的。	侍从同下。

国王　　　哈姆雷特,你干的这种事情,　　　　　　　　　40

不仅让我忧虑,也让我痛心。

特别是为了你的安全——我们

要火速让你离开。　你收拾一下。

帆船已经备好,风向也顺,

你的同伴在等候,准备就绪　　　　　　　　　45

驶往英国。

哈姆雷特　　驶往英国?

国王　　　是的,哈姆雷特。

哈姆雷特　　很好。

国王　　　是很好,假如你了解我的苦心。　　　　　　　50

哈姆雷特　　我看见一只天使看透了它们。　走吧,

去英国!再见了,亲爱的母亲。

国王　　　是你亲爱的父亲,哈姆雷特。

哈姆雷特　　是我的母亲。父亲和母亲是夫妻,夫妻

原本为一体;因此,是我的母亲,走吧,　　　55

去英国。　　　　　　　　　　　　　　下。

国王　　　快跟上他。　要快速诱他上船,

不要耽搁——我今晚就要他离开。

快去,因为与此事相关的一切

已经办妥。　求你们赶快一点。　　　　　　60

　　　　　　　　　　　　　除国王以外全下。

英格兰王,你若珍重我的情谊——

既然丹麦的刀剑给你的疤痕

尚未痊愈,你就该对我的威力

54-5.夫妻原本为一体:出自《圣经》"创世纪"2章23-24节:"^23那个男的说:这是我骨中的骨、肉中的肉;她将被称为'女人',因为她是出自男人之身。^24因此,男人要离开自己的父母与妻子相聚,从而成为一体。"(**Jenkins**)

After the Danish sword, and thy free awe

65   Pays homage to us—thou mayst not coldly set

Our sovereign process, which imports at full,

By letters congruing to that effect,

The present death of Hamlet. Do it, England;

For like the hectic in my blood he rages,

70   And thou must cure me. Till I know 'tis done,

Howe'er my haps, my joys were ne'er begun.   *Exit.*

有所领悟,你也甘心对我们

俯首称臣——你大概不会冷落   65

本王的旨意,其中的具体详情,

已在信中阐明,那就是立即将

哈姆雷特处死。 执行吧,英格兰王;

因为他像高烧在我血液里肆虐,

你必须治好我。 获悉事成之前,   70

无论发生什么,我都露不出笑脸。   下。

SCENE IV

Enter Fortinbras with his Army [*marching*]
over the stage.

Fort.   Go, captain, from me greet the Danish king.

Tell him that by his licence Fortinbras

Craves the conveyance of a promis'd march

Over his kingdom. You know the rendezvous.

5   If that his Majesty would aught with us,

We shall express our duty in his eye;

And let him know so.

Captain   I will do't, my lord.

Fort.   Go softly on.   *Exeunt all but the Captain.*

Enter Hamlet, Rosencrantz, [*Guildenstern,*]
and Others.

Hamlet   Good sir, whose powers are these?

10 **Captain**   They are of Norway, sir.

Hamlet   How purpos'd, sir, I pray you?

Captain   Against some part of Poland.

Hamlet   Who commands them, sir?

Captain   The nephew to old Norway, Fortinbras.

15 **Hamlet**   Goes it against the main of Poland, sir,

Or for some frontier?

第四场

弗廷布拉及其部下［行军］

入场。

弗廷布拉　　去，上尉，代我向丹麦王致意。

告诉他弗廷布拉按照他的

许诺，现在请求从他的国内

安全通过。　您知道会合地点。

假如国王陛下有什么事情，　　　　　　　　　　　　　　5

我可以亲自前去予以拜见；

要让他知道这一点。

上　尉　　　　　　　　　　　　遵命，殿下。

弗廷布拉　　行进要轻缓。　　　　　　　　除上尉之外全下。

哈姆雷特、罗森克兰、［盖登斯顿］

与众人上。

哈姆雷特　　请问，这是谁的军队？

上　尉　　　是挪威王的，先生。　　　　　　　　　　　　10

哈姆雷特　　请问先生，为何发兵？

上　尉　　　攻打波兰的某部。

哈姆雷特　　谁统帅他们，先生？

上　尉　　　挪威老王的侄儿，弗廷布拉。

哈姆雷特　　是去攻打波兰的本部，先生，　　　　　　　　15

还是某一边塞？

Captain	Truly to speak, and with no addition,
	We go to gain a little patch of ground
	That hath in it no profit but the name.

20   To pay five ducats—five—I would not farm it;

Nor will it yield to Norway or the Pole

A ranker rate should it be sold in fee.

Hamlet   Why, then the Polack never will defend it.

Captain   Yes, it is already garrison'd.

25 **Hamlet**   Two thousand souls and twenty thousand ducats

Will not debate the question of this straw!

This is th'impostume of much wealth and peace,

That inward breaks, and shows no cause without

Why the man dies. I humbly thank you, sir.

Captain   God buy you, sir.   *Exit.*

30 **Ros.**   Will't please you go, my lord?

Hamlet   I'll be with you straight. Go a little before.

                         Exeunt all but Hamlet.

How all occasions do inform against me,

And spur my dull revenge. What is a man

If his chief good and market of his time

35   Be but to sleep and feed? A beast, no more.

Sure he that made us with such large discourse,

Looking before and after, gave us not

That capability and godlike reason

To fust in us unus'd. Now whether it be

40   Bestial oblivion, or some craven scruple

Of thinking too precisely on th'event—

上尉	说真的,毫无添枝加叶之意,	
	我们只是想攻取一小块土地,	
	毫无利益可言,只是名誉而已。	
	五块钱——五块——我都不会租用;	20
	若全部出售,也不会为挪威王	
	或者波兰王带来更多的利益。	
哈姆雷特	咳,那么波兰王决不会设防了?	
上尉	不,他们已派兵把守。	
哈姆雷特	两千条性命以及两万块军费,	25
	竟解决不了这一桩区区小事!	
	这是富足和太平滋生的脓肿,	
	里面腐烂,却看不出行将死亡的	
	踪影。　多谢您的赐教,先生。	
上尉	上帝保佑您,先生。　　　　　下。	
罗森克兰	咱走吧,殿下?	30
哈姆雷特	我很快就跟上,你们先走一步。	

除哈姆雷特以外全下。

遇见的情景怎么都在责备我,	
鞭策我迟钝的复仇之心。　若把	
自己的大好时光只用以睡和吃,	
那他还算个人吗?　畜生而已。	35
上帝给我们如此精湛的推理,	
让我们瞻前顾后,肯定不是	
让这种能力和神圣的理智	
在我们身上白白浪费。　究竟是	
因为畜生般的健忘,还是因为	40
对后果的过虑而产生的顾忌——	

4.4.　32. 遇见的情景:与演员的意外相见,现在又与弗廷布拉的部队不期而遇,这些场景好像都在责备哈姆雷特的优柔寡断（Gill）。

A thought which, quarter'd, hath but one part wisdom

And ever three parts coward—I do not know

Why yet I live to say this thing's to do,

45 Sith I have cause, and will, and strength, and means

To do't. Examples gross as earth exhort me,

Witness this army of such mass and charge,

Led by a delicate and tender prince,

Whose spirit, with divine ambition puff'd,

50 Makes mouths at the invisible event,

Exposing what is mortal and unsure

To all that fortune, death, and danger dare,

Even for an eggshell. Rightly to be great

Is not to stir without great argument,

55 But greatly to find quarrel in a straw

When honour's at the stake. How stand I then,

That have a father kill'd, a mother stain'd,

Excitements of my reason and my blood,

And let all sleep, while to my shame I see

The imminent death of twenty thousand men

That, for a fantasy and trick of fame,

Go to their graves like beds, fight for a plot

Whereon the numbers cannot try the cause,

Which is not tomb enough and continent

65 To hide the slain? O, from this time forth

My thoughts be bloody or be nothing worth.   *Exit.*

若把思虑四分,仅有一份智慧,

其余三份全是懦弱——我不明白

我为何要活着呼喊这事要办,

因为我有理由、有意愿、有能力、　　　　　　　　45

有办法。 天大的榜样都在激我:

看看这一支气势浩荡的军队,

由一位敏锐温情的王子统领,

你看他意气风发、雄心勃勃,

公然蔑视无法预见的后果,　　　　　　　　50

胆敢让血肉之躯与命运抗争、

面对危险、迎接死亡,哪怕为了

一个蛋壳。 真正的伟大不在于

没有剧烈的冲突就不妄动,

而在于当荣誉受到威胁时,　　　　　　　　55

为一根稻草也要力争。 而我呢,

父亲给人杀害,母亲被人玷污,

我的思想、感情都应为之激怒,

我却无动于衷。 令我蒙羞的是,

现在却要目睹这两万名士兵,　　　　　　　　60

他们为了一种缥缈的虚荣,

即将送命,将坟墓视为床铺,

所争夺的地盘都无法容下

所有的参战士兵,不够阵亡

将士葬身之用? 噢,从此刻开始,　　　　　　65

让思想充满血腥,否则一钱不值!　　　　　　下。

53-6. 真正的……力争（Rightly…the stake）：本句的结构为：真正的伟大不是这样而是那样；需将原文中的单一否定视为双重否定（the single negative requires to be taken in a double sense），即"Is not to stir = Is not not to stir"（Jenkins）。 60. 两万名士兵：作者（而非哈姆雷特）将人数与钱数混淆了（见25行）（Jenkins）。

SCENE   V

Enter Queen, Horatio, and a Gentleman.

Queen   I will not speak with her.

Gent.   She is importunate,
Indeed distract. Her mood will needs be pitied.

Queen   What would she have?

Gent.   She speaks much of her father, says she hears
5   There's tricks i'th' world, and hems, and beats her heart,
Spurns enviously at straws, speaks things in doubt
That carry but half sense. Her speech is nothing,
Yet the unshaped use of it doth move
The hearers to collection. They aim at it,
10   And botch the words up fit to their own thoughts,
Which, as her winks and nods and gestures yield them,
Indeed would make one think there might be thought,
Though nothing sure, yet much unhappily.

Horatio   'Twere good she were spoken with, for she may strew
15   Dangerous conjectures in ill-breeding minds.

Queen   Let her come in.   *Exit Gentleman.*
[*Aside*] To my sick soul, as sin's true nature is,
Each toy seems prologue to some great amiss.

第五场

王后、何瑞修与一绅士上。

王后	我不想理她。
绅士	她非见您不可，

真的疯了。　她的神情令人可怜。

王后	她想要什么？
绅士	她不断提及自己的父亲，说她

听说世上有诈，她哼唧、捶胸，　　　　　　　　　　　　　　5
区区小事大动肝火，说起话来
模棱两可。　她说的都是废话，
只是她那语无伦次的方式
让听众臆测。　他们都在尽力，
将她的眼色、点头以及示意　　　　　　　　　　　　　　10
拼凑起来去附会各自的揣测，
尽管无法肯定是什么事情，
确实会让人以为存有险恶。

何瑞修	和她谈谈也好，因为她会让

心怀鬼胎的人们捕风捉影。　　　　　　　　　　　　　　15

王后	让她进来。　　　　　　　　　　　　　绅士下。

　　　　［旁白］沉重的心灵，就像罪恶的本性，
每一件琐事预示着巨大不幸。

---

　　4. 5.　17. 沉重的心灵：哈姆雷特在第三幕第四场对她的责备已经收到了预期的效果
（Jenkins）。

So full of artless jealousy is guilt,

20   It spills itself in fearing to be spilt.

Enter Ophelia.

Ophelia	Where is the beauteous Majesty of Denmark?
Queen	How now, Ophelia?
Ophelia	[*Sings*] *How should I your true love know*

From another one?

25   *By his cockle hat and staff*

And his sandal shoon.

Queen	Alas, sweet lady, what imports this song?
Ophelia	Say you? Nay, pray you mark.

[*Sings*] *He is dead and gone, lady,*

30   *He is dead and gone,*

At his head a grass-green turf,

At his heels a stone.

O ho!

Queen	Nay, but Ophelia—
35 **Ophelia**	Pray you mark.

[*Sings*] *White his shroud as the mountain snow—*

Enter King.

Queen	Alas, look here, my lord.

愧疚之心充满了拙劣的猜忌，

越是害怕泄露，越是泄露无遗。　　　　　　　　　　　20

奥菲丽娅上。

奥菲丽娅　美丽的丹麦王后陛下在哪里？

王后　怎么了，奥菲丽娅？

奥菲丽娅　［唱］叫我如何来区分，

　　　　谁是您的真情人？

　　　　他头戴扇帽手握杖，　　　　　　　　　　　　　25

　　　　一双草鞋穿脚上。

王后　哎呀，可爱的姑娘，这歌什么意思？

奥菲丽娅　您不懂？　别吭，请您听好：

　　　［唱］他已死去归大地，姑娘，

　　　　他已死去归大地，　　　　　　　　　　　　　　30

　　　　头顶一片青草皮，

　　　　脚边一块墓碑石。

　　　　噢嗬！

王后　别唱了，奥菲丽娅——

奥菲丽娅　求您听好：　　　　　　　　　　　　　　　35

　　　［唱］寿衣白似山上雪——

国王上。

王后　哎呀，您看看，陛下！

23-40. 叫我……如雨下：这是奥菲丽娅所唱五首歌谣中的第一首。　这是口头吟唱的歌谣，以问答的方式叙事。　歌中所指的情人头戴海扇帽（上面嵌着贝壳），手持拐杖，脚穿草鞋，是一位朝圣者的标志。　这首歌谣可根据上下文的意思有几种影射：（1）波洛纽斯的死亡及其悄悄的埋葬（本歌谣39行）；（2）奥菲丽娅被哈姆雷特遗弃的爱情，因为该歌谣的主题就是关于一位女士在寻找离去的情人。　另外还有一种富有讥讽意味的影射是：（3）这首歌谣指向王后（28，35行），她未能区分谁是"她的真情人"，也没有"情泪如雨下"（Jenkins）。

Ophelia	[*Sings*]	*Larded with sweet flowers*
		Which bewept to the grave did not go
40		*With true-love showers.*

King   How do you, pretty lady?

Ophelia   Well, good dild you. They say the owl was a baker's daughter. Lord, we know what we are, but know not what we may be. God be at your table.

45 **King**   Conceit upon her father.

Ophelia   Pray let's have no words of this, but when they ask you what it means, say you this.

[*Sings*] *Tomorrow is Saint Valentine's day,*

All in the morning betime,

50   *And I a maid at your window,*

To be your Valentine.

Then up he rose, and donn'd his clo'es,

And dupp'd the chamber door,

Let in the maid that out a maid

55   *Never departed more.*

奥菲丽娅	〔唱〕　　芬芳的鲜花上面撒，	
	未哭到坟前去永别，	
	也没有情泪如雨下。	40
国王	您好吗，美丽的小姐？	
奥菲丽娅	好，上帝报答您。　人们说猫头鹰是面包师	
	的女儿变的。　陛下，我们知道自己现在是	
	啥，可不知将来会是什么。　上帝与您同在！	
国王	心疼她的父亲。	45
奥菲丽娅	请别再提及此事了，但是假如有人问您它是	
	何意，就这样说吧：	
	〔唱〕明天就是情人节，	
	我要早早就出门，	
	到您窗前去停歇，	50
	去做您的意中人。	
	他坐起身，穿上衣，	
	走向前去打开门，	
	将一个姑娘迎到里，	
	姑娘出来已失身。	55

42-3. 猫头鹰是面包师的女儿变的：一则民间传说讲的是，耶稣曾到一家面包店乞求面包，店主的女儿吩咐不要给得太多，当场就变成了一只猫头鹰。　有些专家认为猫头鹰是悲哀的象征（Jenkins）。　另一则民间故事里讲道，面包店主的女儿由于对顾客缺斤短两而变成了一只猫头鹰（Gill）。　48. 情人节：传说在情人节这一天（2月14日），青年男女会爱上自己第一眼看见的异性（Gill）。　48-66. 明天……我的床：这是奥菲丽娅所唱歌谣的第二首。　正如她的第一首和最后一首一样，这一首歌谣也是关于令人失望的爱情，尽管风格有所不同。　奥菲丽娅这种不雅观的辞令让批评家们感到迷惑不解；不过，至于她如何以及何时学到的这些辞令则与主题无关。　该歌谣的主题是：一个情人占有了一位姑娘的童贞之后又将她抛弃——我们知道这种印象是由她的哥哥和父亲分别在 1.3.5-44 和 91-131 灌输到她的脑海里。　然而，这首歌谣所展现的情形与波洛纽斯及雷厄提斯所担心并警告奥菲丽娅要加以提防的情形却有所不同。　富有讥讽意味的是，奥菲丽娅并未遭受该歌谣中的主人所遭受的那种经历；哈姆雷特并未占有她的童贞，而是拒绝了她的爱情（3.1）。　这首歌谣应是唱给克劳狄斯的，影射他对葛楚德的勾引（1.5.45-6）（Jenkins）。

King	Pretty Ophelia—
Ophelia	Indeed, without an oath, I'll make an end on't.

> *By Gis and by Saint Charity,*
>
> *Alack and fie for shame,*
>
> 60 *Young men will do't if they come to't—*
>
> *By Cock, they are to blame.*
>
> *Quoth she, 'Before you tumbled me,*
>
> *You promis'd me to wed.'*

He answers,

> 65 *'So would I a done, by yonder sun,*
>
> *And thou hadst not come to my bed.'*

King	How long hath she been thus?
Ophelia	I hope all will be well. We must be patient. But I

cannot choose but weep to think they would lay

70 him i'th' cold ground. My brother shall know of it.

And so I thank you for your good counsel. Come,

my coach. Good night, ladies, good night. Sweet

ladies, good night, good night.   *Exit.*

King   Follow her close; give her good watch, I pray you.

Exit Horatio.

75 O, this is the poison of deep grief: it springs

All from her father's death. And now behold—

O Gertrude, Gertrude,

When sorrows come, they come not single spies,

But in battalions. First, her father slain;

80 Next, your son gone, and he most violent author

Of his own just remove; the people muddied,

Thick and unwholesome in their thoughts and whispers

国王	美丽的奥菲丽娅——
奥菲丽娅	真的,不用发誓,我也会把它唱完:

凭借耶稣与神圣之爱,

　　竟没有廉耻和羞愧,

小伙子若是有机总会来——　　　　　　　　　60

　　发誓他们要受责备。

她说道,"在您占有我之前,

　　已答应让我做新娘。"

他答道,

　　"发誓我将会守诺言,　　　　　　　　　65

　　假如你没上我的床。"

国王	她这个样子已有多久?
奥菲丽娅	我希望一切安好。我们必须耐心。但是,

一想到人们要把他放入冰冷的地下,我

就禁不住要哭。我的哥哥也会知道此事。　　70

因此我感谢你们的好意。来,我的马车!

晚安,女士们,晚安了。可爱的女士们,

晚安,晚安。　　　　　　　　　　　　　下。

国王	快跟上她;要好好照看,求您了。

　　　　　　　　　　　　　　　　　何瑞修下。

噢,这真是令人沉痛的毒药:　　　　　　　75

都源于她父亲的死亡。　看看吧——

噢,葛楚德,葛楚德,

不幸降临时,不会是单枪匹马,

而是成群结队。　首先,她父亲遇害;

然后,您儿子走了,他遭到流放　　　　　　80

是罪有应得;但民众迷惑不解,

满心猜疑,对好波洛纽斯的死亡

For good Polonius' death—and we have done but
  greenly
In hugger-mugger to inter him; poor Ophelia
85 Divided from herself and her fair judgment,
Without the which we are pictures, or mere beasts;
Last, and as much containing as all these,
Her brother is in secret come from France,
Feeds on this wonder, keeps himself in clouds,
90 And wants not buzzers to infect his ear
With pestilent speeches of his father's death,
Wherein necessity, of matter beggar'd,
Will nothing stick our person to arraign
In ear and ear. O my dear Gertrude, this,
95 Like to a murd'ring-piece, in many places
Gives me superfluous death.   *A noise within.*

                        Attend!
Where are my Switzers? Let them guard the door.

Enter a Messenger.

What is the matter?

Mess.   Save yourself, my lord.
The ocean, overpeering of his list,
100 Eats not the flats with more impetuous haste
Than young Laertes, in a riotous head,
O'erbears your officers. The rabble call him lord,
And, as the world were now but to begin,
Antiquity forgot, custom not known—

窃窃私语——我的做法也非常

　愚蠢，

悄悄将他埋葬；可怜的奥菲丽娅

已神志失常，没有正常的理智， 85

我们只是图画，或者就是禽兽；

最后，与这一切同样糟糕的是，

她哥哥已从法国秘密返回，

他对此耿耿于怀，行踪诡秘，

少不了长舌之徒向他耳朵里 90

灌输他父亲死亡的流言蜚语，

他们需要借口，但又缺乏证据，

自然会交头接耳地对我非议。

噢，我亲爱的葛楚德，这件事情，

就像一枚榴弹炮，四处开花， 95

让我对死亡应接不暇！ 内有喧嚷声。

来人！

我的保镖呢？　让他们把门把好！

一报信者上。

出什么事了？

报信者　　　　　快躲一躲吧，陛下。

那波涛汹涌、吞没平地的大海，

也赶不上小雷厄提斯的叛军 100

向您的士兵扑来的势头那样

迅猛。　这群暴徒称他为陛下，

仿佛一个新的世界刚刚开始，

传统抛在脑后，习惯一概不知——

---

100. 雷厄提斯的叛军：本来为弗廷布拉设想的叛乱行为（1.1.98及以下），现在却由雷厄提斯顶替（Jenkins）。

105   The ratifiers and props of every word—

          They cry, 'Choose we! Laertes shall be king.'

          Caps, hands, and tongues applaud it to the clouds,

          'Laertes shall be king, Laertes king.'

Queen   How cheerfully on the false trail they cry.

110   O, this is counter, you false Danish dogs.   *A noise within.*

King   The doors are broke.

Enter Laertes with Followers.

Laertes   Where is this king? —Sirs, stand you all without.

Followers   No, let's come in.

Laertes   I pray you give me leave.

Followers   We will, we will.

115 **Laertes**   I thank you. Keep the door.   *Exeunt Followers.*

                        O thou vile king,

          Give me my father.

Queen   [*Holding him*]   Calmly, good Laertes.

Laertes   That drop of blood that's calm proclaims me bastard,

          Cries cuckold to my father, brands the harlot

          Even here between the chaste unsmirched brow

          Of my true mother.

120 **King**   What is the cause, Laertes,

          That thy rebellion looks so giant-like? —

这些支撑文明的规范与准则—— 105

喊道，"要选举！雷厄提斯当国王！"

扔帽子、鼓掌、欢呼声响彻云霄，

"雷厄提斯当国王，雷厄提斯国王！"

| 王后 | 嗅错了踪迹，还叫得这么高兴。 | | |

噢，方向反了，背信的丹麦狗！ 　　　　　　内有喧嚷声。 110

| 国王 | 门给冲破了！ |

雷厄提斯及其追随者上。

雷厄提斯	国王呢？ ——弟兄们，你们都站外面。
追随者	不行，让我们进去。
雷厄提斯	请你们离开。
追随者	遵命，遵命。
雷厄提斯	谢谢！把住门。 　　　　　　追随者同下。 115

噢，你这可恶的国王，

还我父亲！

| 王后 | ［抓住他］冷静些，好雷厄提斯！ |
| 雷厄提斯 | 有一滴血液能够冷静，就表明 |

我是杂种，管我的父亲叫乌龟，

在我母亲洁白的额头上打满

娼妓的烙印！

| 国王 | 　　　　　　是啥原因，雷厄提斯， | 120 |

让你的反叛显得如此凶猛？——

106."要选举"：丹麦属于实行选举制的君主政体，尽管国王要由前任提名，但他却需要通过选举而得到广大民众的认可（Gill）。

Let him go, Gertrude. Do not fear our person.

There's such divinity doth hedge a king

That treason can but peep to what it would,

125   Acts little of his will. —Tell me, Laertes,

Why thou art thus incens'd. —Let him go, Gertrude. —

Speak, man.

Laertes   Where is my father?

King   Dead.

Queen   But not by him.

King   Let him demand his fill.

130 **Laertes**   How came he dead? I'll not be juggled with.

To hell, allegiance! Vows to the blackest devil!

Conscience and grace, to the profoundest pit!

I dare damnation. To this point I stand,

That both the worlds I give to negligence,

135   Let come what comes; only I'll be reveng'd

Most throughly for my father.

King   Who shall stay you?

Laertes   My will, not all the world's.

And for my means, I'll husband them so well,

They shall go far with little.

King   Good Laertes,

140   If you desire to know the certainty

Of your dear father, is't writ in your revenge

That, swoopstake, you will draw both friend and foe,

　　　　　放开他,葛楚德。　别为我担心。
　　　　　因为国王有神圣的力量护佑,
　　　　　叛逆只能窥视其非分之想,
　　　　　却难以如愿。　——告诉我,雷厄提斯, 　　　　　125
　　　　　你为何如此大怒?　——放开他,葛楚德。　——
　　　　　说吧,小子!

雷厄提斯　　我父亲呢?

国王　　　　　　　死了。

王后　　　　　　　　　可不是他干的!

国王　　　只管让他问吧。

雷厄提斯　　他是怎么死的?　别给我耍花招。 　　　　　130
　　　　　忠诚,下地狱吧!誓言,见鬼去吧!
　　　　　良心与天恩,滚向无底的深渊!
　　　　　我不怕罚入地狱。我立场坚定,
　　　　　今生来世我都不在乎,无论
　　　　　发生什么,只要我能够彻底地 　　　　　135
　　　　　为父亲报仇。

国王　　　　　　　谁会阻拦您呢?

雷厄提斯　　除了我的意愿,谁也不能。
　　　　　至于手段吗,我可以得心应手,
　　　　　定让它们一蹴而就。

国王　　　　　　　好雷厄提斯,
　　　　　您若想了解心爱父亲的真正 　　　　　140
　　　　　死因,难道您的复仇行为,
　　　　　要像赛场的赌金,统吃统赢,

---

123. 神圣的力量护佑:在伊丽莎白时代,人们认为国王就是上帝在人间的代表 (皇权神授)。 因此,他在执政期间就会得到上帝的保佑。 克劳狄斯从未像目前这样显现出帝王般的威严 (Gill)。 132-6. 良心……报仇:雷厄提斯与哈姆雷特形成了鲜明的对比,见 3.1.78-83 (Jenkins)。

It sends some precious instance of itself

After the thing it loves.

Ophelia [*Sings*] *They bore him bare-fac'd on the bier,*

165   *And in his grave rain'd many a tear—*

Fare you well, my dove.

Laertes Hadst thou thy wits and didst persuade revenge,

It could not move thus.

Ophelia You must sing *A-down a-down*, and you *Call him*

170 *a-down-a*. O, how the wheel becomes it! It is the

false steward that stole his master's daughter.

Laertes This nothing's more than matter.

Ophelia There's rosemary, that's for remembrance—pray

you, love, remember. And there is pansies, that's for

175 thoughts.

Laertes A document in madness: thoughts and remembrance

fitted.

Ophelia There's fennel for you, and columbines. There's

rue for you. And here's some for me. We may call it

180 herb of grace a Sundays. You must wear your rue

with a difference. There's a daisy. I would give you

some violets, but they withered all when my father

所爱的人一旦离去,那种深情的
部分标志便随之消散。

奥菲丽娅　　[唱]他躺进棺材面无遮护,

　　　　　　　雨似的泪水打湿坟墓——　　　　　　　　165

　　　　　　再见了,我的宝贝!

雷厄提斯　　假如你神志正常,劝我报仇,

　　　　　　也不会这样感动。

奥菲丽娅　　您得唱啊当啊当,您要叫他啊当啊。噢,

　　　　　　歌谣的叠句是多么和谐!是背信弃义的　　　　170

　　　　　　管家将主人的女儿拐走。

雷厄提斯　　这种疯话意味更强。

奥菲丽娅　　这是迷迭香,它们表示追忆——我求您,

　　　　　　亲爱的,要记住。这是三色堇,代表

　　　　　　思念。　　　　　　　　　　　　　　　　　175

雷厄提斯　　疯话里面有教诲:思念和追忆,恰如

　　　　　　其分。

奥菲丽娅　　这是给您的茴香,和楼斗花。这是给

　　　　　　您的芸香。这些留给我。礼拜天我们

　　　　　　还可以叫它宽恕草。您佩带芸香定会　　　　180

　　　　　　不同。这是雏菊。我本想送给您几朵

　　　　　　紫罗兰,可当我父亲去世以后,它们

　　164-5.棺材……坟墓:这是奥菲丽娅所唱五首歌谣中的第三首——葬礼的挽歌(Jenkins)。
169.您得唱"啊当啊当":奥菲丽娅吩咐在场的人们一起演唱该歌谣的叠句(即,歌谣中重复演唱
的歌词,通常在每一段的尾部)(Jenkins)。　170-1.是背信弃义的管家:奥菲丽娅的心中依然想
着不幸的少女和被欺骗的爱情(Jenkins)。　173-83.花草具有象征意义,奥菲丽娅将不同的花草
分送给在场的人员。把代表追忆的迷迭香与表示思念的三色堇送给哥哥雷厄提斯。将代表献媚
的茴香与表示对婚姻不忠的楼斗花送给王后。芸香既可表示悲伤,又可表示悔罪。奥菲丽娅留
给自己的芸香应代表悲伤,而送给国王的芸香则应表示悔罪,正像奥菲丽娅对国王所说的那样.
"您佩带芸香定会不同。"表示愚蠢和具有欺骗性的雏菊送给国王。代表忠诚的紫罗兰也送给国
王;因为波洛纽斯应被视为忠诚的表率(1.2.47-9);又因为他一旦离去,紫罗兰就凋谢了(Jenkins)。

died. They say a made a good end.

[*Sings*] *For bonny sweet Robin is all my joy.*

185 **Laertes**   Thought and affliction, passion, hell itself

She turns to favour and to prettiness.

Ophelia   [*Sings*] *And will a not come again?*

And will a not come again?

No, no, he is dead,

190   *Go to thy death-bed,*

He never will come again.

His beard was as white as snow,

All flaxen was his poll.

He is gone, he is gone,

And we cast away moan.

God a mercy on his soul.

And of all Christian souls. God buy you.   *Exit.*

Laertes   Do you see this, O God?

King   Laertes, I must commune with your grief,

200   Or you deny me right. Go but apart,

Make choice of whom your wisest friends you will,

And they shall hear and judge 'twixt you and me.

If by direct or by collateral hand

They find us touch'd, we will our kingdom give,

205   Our crown, our life, and all that we call ours

To you in satisfaction; but if not,

Be you content to lend your patience to us,

都凋谢了。　人们说他的下场很好。

　　　　　［唱］健美的罗宾是我全部欢欣。

雷厄提斯　　她将悲伤、磨难、痛苦,和地狱　　　　　　　　　185

　　　　　本身化为了妩媚,变成了美丽。

奥菲丽娅　　［唱］难道他不会再回来?

　　　　　　难道他不会再回来?

　　　　　　　不会的,已死亡,

　　　　　　　等到你上灵床,　　　　　　　　　　　　190

　　　　　　他也不会再回来。

　　　　　　他的胡须白似雪,

　　　　　　他的头发灰如麻。

　　　　　　　他走啦,他走啦,

　　　　　　　我们的泪水已白洒。　　　　　　　　　195

　　　　　　上帝怜悯他的灵魂吧!

　　　　　和所有基督徒的灵魂。　上帝保佑。　　　　　　　　下。

雷厄提斯　　您看见了吗,上帝啊?

国王　　　雷厄提斯,我要分担您的不幸,

　　　　　除非您予以拒绝。　稍停片刻,　　　　　　　　　200

　　　　　您去挑选几个最明智的朋友,

　　　　　请他们评判您我之间的纠纷。

　　　　　他们若是发现我罪责难逃,

　　　　　不管直接间接,我愿将我的

　　　　　王国、王冠、性命,和我的一切,　　　　　　　　205

　　　　　全都送给您作为赔偿。　若没有,

　　　　　那您就应该对我心平气和,

---

184. 健美……欢欣:奥菲丽娅所唱五首歌谣中的第四首,选自一首歌谣。　好像是在表达一种令人欢欣鼓舞的爱情;但是,在接下来的另一首歌谣里又突然回到了绝望之中,不免令人感到更加痛心(Jenkins)。　187-96. 难道他……灵魂吧:奥菲丽娅所唱五首歌谣中的最后一首,尽管这首抒情诗是对一位老人的挽歌(192-3),但同时也会让我们想起这也是对所失去的恋人的哀悼(Jenkins)。

And we shall jointly labour with your soul

To give it due content.

Laertes   Let this be so.

210   His means of death, his obscure funeral—

No trophy, sword, nor hatchment o'er his bones,

No noble rite, nor formal ostentation—

Cry to be heard, as 'twere from heaven to earth,

That I must call't in question.

King   So you shall.

215   And where th'offence is, let the great axe fall.

I pray you go with me.   *Exeunt.*

我将与您一起设法而让您
得到应有的满足。

雷厄提斯　　　　　　　　就这样定了。

他的暴死身亡,他的悄然埋葬——　　　　　　　　　　　210
尸骨上面既没宝剑,也没徽章,
缺乏像样葬礼,没有正规礼仪——
哭喊之声,如从天上传到人间,
因此我要问个究竟。

国王　　　　　　　　　我想您会。

谁是罪魁,就把大斧劈向谁。　　　　　　　　　　　215
我求您跟我来。　　　　　　　　　　　　　　　　同下。

---

211. 既没宝剑:按照传统,一位爵士下葬时,应将他生前的头盔、刀剑挂在他的坟墓之上以示追悼,有些遗物依然可在教堂里见到（Jenkins）。　211. 也没徽章:按照传统,应先将象征家族标志的盾形徽章挂在死者的灵堂外面,等死者入葬之后,再把它挂在死者的坟墓上面以表纪念（Jenkins）。

SCENE   VI

Enter Horatio and a Servant.

Horatio   What are they that would speak with me?

Servant   Seafaring men, sir. They say they have letters for you.

Horatio   Let them come in.   *Exit Servant.*

I do not know from what part of the world

5   I should be greeted, if not from Lord Hamlet.

Enter Sailors.

1st Sailor   God bless you, sir.

Horatio   Let him bless thee too.

1st Sailor   A shall, sir, and please him. There's a letter for

you, sir. It came from th'ambassador that was bound

10   for England—if your name be Horatio, as I am let

to know it is.

Hor.   [*Reads the letter*] *Horatio, when thou shalt have overlooked*

this, give these fellows some means to the King. They have

letters for him. Ere we were two days old at sea, a pirate of

15   *very warlike appointment gave us chase. Finding ourselves*

too slow of sail, we put on a compelled valour, and in the

第六场

何瑞修与一仆人上。

何瑞修　　是什么人想跟我说话？

仆人　　　是几个水手，先生。他们说有封信给您。

何瑞修　　让他们进来。　　　　　　　　　　　　　　仆人下。

不知世上会有谁给我写信，

若不是来自哈姆雷特殿下。　　　　　　　　　　　　　5

水手上。

水手甲　　上帝保佑您，先生。

何瑞修　　让他也保佑你。

水手甲　　他会的，先生，如果他愿意。这儿有您的
一封信，先生。它是那位前往英国的大使
写的——假如您就是何瑞修的话，正如我被　　　　10
告知的那样。

何瑞修　　［读信］何瑞修，读完信后，设法让来人
去见国王。他们有封信给他。我们航行还
不到两天，一伙全副武装的海盗开始追逐
我们。我们发现自己速度太慢，只好应战。　　　　15
就在两船靠近期间，我登上了他们的帆船。

4.6.　16. 在两船靠近期间：海盗可能向哈姆雷特他们所乘坐的船只抛出了抓钩，以便与其
靠拢——哈姆雷特因此便可轻而易举地跳向对方的船只（实为躲避罗森克兰和盖登斯顿）
（Gill）。

grapple I boarded them. On the instant they got clear of our
ship, so I alone became their prisoner. They have dealt
with me like thieves of mercy. But they knew what they did:
20 *I am to do a turn for them. Let the King have the letters I*
have sent, and repair thou to me with as much speed as thou
wouldest fly death. I have words to speak in thine ear will
make thee dumb; yet are they much too light for the bore of
the matter. These good fellows will bring thee where I am.
25 *Rosencrantz and Guildenstern hold their course for England;*
of them I have much to tell thee. Farewell.

He that thou knowest thine,

Hamlet.

Come, I will make you way for these your letters,
30 And do't the speedier that you may direct me
To him from whom you brought them.   *Exeunt.*

他们驶离我们船只的刹那,我本人就成了
他们的俘虏。他们倒像是一帮仁慈的盗贼,
对我还好。但他们也明白自己为何要这样
待我:因为我能为他们服务。让国王接到　　　　　　　20
我送去的信后,你要用逃命似的速度快来
见我。我有话要对你说,会让你目瞪口呆;
但它们还远不能揭示事情的险恶本性。这
几位好伙计将会带你前来见我。罗森克兰
与盖登斯顿继续驶往英国;关于他们两个　　　　　　25
我还有许多要说。再会。

　　　　　　　　　　你所熟知的好友,

　　　　　　　　　　　　哈姆雷特。

快来,我现在就领你们去送信,
你们要速去速回,以便领我　　　　　　　　　　　　30
去见那个让你们送信的先生。　　　　　　　同下。

SCENE VII

Enter King and Laertes.

King   Now must your conscience my acquittance seal,

And you must put me in your heart for friend,

Sith you have heard, and with a knowing ear,

That he which hath your noble father slain

Pursu'd my life.

5   **Laertes**   It well appears. But tell me

Why you proceeded not against these feats,

So crimeful and so capital in nature,

As by your safety, wisdom, all things else

You mainly were stirr'd up.

King   O, for two special reasons,

10   Which may to you perhaps seem much unsinew'd,

But yet to me th'are strong. The Queen his mother

Lives almost by his looks, and for myself—

My virtue or my plague, be it either which—

She is so conjunctive to my life and soul

15   That, as the star moves not but in his sphere,

I could not but by her. The other motive

Why to a public count I might not go

第七场

国王与雷厄提斯上。

国王　　　现在您必须承认我的无辜，

您还要把我当成您的心腹，

因为您已用聪敏的双耳获悉，

杀害您父亲的凶手企图断送

我的性命。

雷厄提斯　　　　　很像如此。但告诉我　　　　　　　5

您为何对这些暴行无动于衷，

它们是如此凶恶和死有余辜，

您的安全、智慧和一切都遭到

强烈挑衅。

国王　　　　　　　噢，有两个特殊理由，

对您来说也许显得软弱无力，　　　　　　　10

对我而言却强劲无比。　他的母后，

对他百依百顺，至于我本人——

无论这是我的美德还是祸根——

她与我的身心是如此相连，

犹如星星离不开自己的轨道，　　　　　　　15

我只能围着她转。　我之所以

不能公开起诉他的另一个

4.7.　12-6.　我本人……围着她转：有人认为国王此处所表白的对王后的依恋正是其杀害哈姆雷特父亲的动因；然而，他的此番话语却很难令人相信（Thompson）。

Is the great love the general gender bear him,

Who, dipping all his faults in their affection,

20   Work like the spring that turneth wood to stone,

Convert his gyves to graces; so that my arrows,

Too slightly timber'd for so loud a wind,

Would have reverted to my bow again,

And not where I had aim'd them.

25 **Laertes** And so have I a noble father lost,

A sister driven into desp'rate terms,

Whose worth, if praises may go back again,

Stood challenger on mount of all the age

For her perfections. But my revenge will come.

30 **King** Break not your sleeps for that. You must not think

That we are made of stuff so flat and dull

That we can let our beard be shook with danger

And think it pastime. You shortly shall hear more.

I lov'd your father, and we love ourself,

35   And that, I hope, will teach you to imagine—

Enter a Messenger with letters.

Mess. These to your Majesty, this to the Queen.

King From Hamlet! Who brought them?

Mess. Sailors, my lord, they say. I saw them not.

They were given me by Claudio. He receiv'd them

Of him that brought them.

理由是,广大民众都很爱他,

他们对他的缺点也深表喜爱,

就像那能把木材石化的泉水,　　　　　　　　20

将他的羞辱化为体面;我的箭,

面对如此大风会箭杆太轻,

不仅射不中我所瞄准的目标,

反而还会返回弓中。

雷厄提斯　　我就这样失去了尊贵的父亲,　　　　25

让自己的妹妹给人逼进绝境,

她的才貌,假如能恢复如前,

那真是完美无缺、盖世无双。

可是我的仇恨迟早要报。

国王　　您不要为此失去睡眠。　别以为　　　　30

我生来就是如此愚钝,让人家

凶恶地揪着胡子,自己还以为

那是消遣。　您很快会得到音信。

我爱您的父亲,也爱我自身,

这一点,我希望,能够教您想到——　　　　35

　　　　　　　一信差带信上。

信差　　这是给陛下的,这是给王后的。

国王　　哈姆雷特写的! 谁送来的?

信差　　听说是水手,陛下。　我没有见到。

是克劳狄奥给我的。　他是从送信人

那里接到的。

---

20. 把木材石化的泉水:英格兰确有几处类似的泉水,水中丰富的矿物质可将浸入的物体变成化石(Gill)。　33. 得到音信:克劳狄斯可能期望得到英国王室传来的消息——但富有讥讽意味的是,想不到此刻却送来了哈姆雷特的信函(Jenkins)。

40 **King**   Laertes, you shall hear them. —

Leave us.   *Exit Messenger.*

[*Reads*] *High and mighty, You shall know I am set naked on*

your kingdom. Tomorrow shall I beg leave to see your kingly

eyes, when I shall, first asking your pardon, thereunto recount

45   *the occasion of my sudden and more strange return.*

                                                        Hamlet.

What should this mean? Are all the rest come back?

Or is it some abuse, and no such thing?

Laertes Know you the hand?

King   'Tis Hamlet's character.

50   'Naked'—

And in a postscript here he says 'Alone'.

Can you advise me?

Laertes I am lost in it, my lord. But let him come.

It warms the very sickness in my heart

55   That I shall live and tell him to his teeth,

'Thus diest thou'.

King   If it be so, Laertes—

As how should it be so, how otherwise? —

Will you be rul'd by me?

Laertes   Ay, my lord,

So you will not o'errule me to a peace.

60 **King** To thine own peace. If he be now return'd,

As checking at his voyage, and that he means

No more to undertake it, I will work him

国王	雷厄提斯,您来听听。——　　　　　　　　　　40
	请退下。　　　　　　　　　　　　　　　　信差下。
	[读信]至高无上,您要知道我已赤身踏上
	您的国土。请准许我明天前去拜见陛下的
	尊容,如能成行,我将首先请求您的宽恕,
	然后再禀报我此次突然和更为奇特的返还。　　45
	哈姆雷特。
	什么意思？ 其他人也回来了吗？
	莫非其中有诈,并无此事？
雷厄提斯	您认识笔迹吗？
国王	是哈姆雷特写的。
	"赤身"——　　　　　　　　　　　　　　　　　50
	他又在附言中写上了"独身"。
	您能解释一下吗？
雷厄提斯	我也不懂,陛下。 不过让他来吧。
	一想到我能活着当面告诉他,
	"你见鬼去吧",我那冰凉的心里　　　　　　　55
	就热乎起来。
国王	若是这样,雷厄提斯——
	怎么会这样,不这样又能怎样？ ——
	您愿意听我吩咐吗？
雷厄提斯	愿意,陛下,
	只要您不让我跟他讲和就行。
国王	为了你的平和。 如果他已回来,　　　　　　60
	因为半途而废,肯定不想再去,
	我要激发他去干一件事情,

56-7. 若是这样……不这样又能怎样: (1) 人们通常认为,克劳狄斯此刻正在考虑哈姆雷特不可能回来,又不可能没有回来,这让他颇感困惑 (见47行)。 (2) 这可能与雷厄提斯的上述言论有关:克劳狄斯以为雷厄提斯不可能下决心将哈姆雷特置于死地,但他又没有别的选择,国王并为此想出了一条新的计策(Jenkins)。

To an exploit, now ripe in my device,

Under the which he shall not choose but fall;

65   And for his death no wind of blame shall breathe,

But even his mother shall uncharge the practice

And call it accident.

Laertes   My lord, I will be rul'd,

The rather if you could devise it so

That I might be the organ.

King   It falls right.

70   You have been talk'd of since your travel much,

And that in Hamlet's hearing, for a quality

Wherein they say you shine. Your sum of parts

Did not together pluck such envy from him

As did that one, and that, in my regard,

Of the unworthiest siege.

75 **Laertes**   What part is that, my lord?

King A very ribbon in the cap of youth—

Yet needful too, for youth no less becomes

The light and careless livery that it wears

Than settled age his sables and his weeds

80   Importing health and graveness. Two months since

Here was a gentleman of Normandy—

I have seen myself, and serv'd against, the French,

And they can well on horseback, but this gallant

Had witchcraft in't. He grew unto his seat,

85   And to such wondrous doing brought his horse

As had he been incorps'd and demi-natur'd

With the brave beast. So far he topp'd my thought

我的计策刚刚成熟，一旦中计，

他必死无疑；他的死亡也不会

引起任何非议，就连他的母亲　　　　　　　　65

都不会追究，而只会把它当成

意外事故。

雷厄提斯　　　　　　陛下，我愿意服从，

不过您最好能够想方设法

让他死在我的手中。

国王　　　　　　　　　　不约而同。

您出国之后，人们不断议论，　　　　　　　　70

在哈姆雷特面前，说您有一种

耀眼的本领。　您的成就加起来

还不如那种本领更让他妒嫉，

而那种本领，在我看来，倒是

不值一提。

雷厄提斯　　　　　是什么本领，陛下？　　　　75

国王　不过是青年帽子上的一根彩带——

但是也需要，因为正如上了

年纪的人们适合于安康持重

的深色服装，年轻人就应该

装扮得轻快洒脱。　两个月以前，　　　　　80

曾有这么一位诺曼底绅士——

我亲眼目睹，也曾与法国人交手，

他们的马术精湛，但这位勇士

简直会施魔法。　他坐在马背上，

随心所欲，仿佛与自己的骏马　　　　　　　　85

融为一体，从而变成了半人

半马。　他的动作竟然如此地

That I in forgery of shapes and tricks

Come short of what he did.

Laertes   A Norman was't?

90 **King**   A Norman.

Laertes   Upon my life, Lamord.

King   The very same.

Laertes   I know him well. He is the brooch indeed

And gem of all the nation.

King   He made confession of you,

95   And gave you such a masterly report

For art and exercise in your defence,

And for your rapier most especial,

That he cried out, 'twould be a sight indeed

If one could match you. The scrimers of their nation

100   He swore had neither motion, guard, nor eye,

If you oppos'd them. Sir, this report of his

Did Hamlet so envenom with his envy

That he could nothing do but wish and beg

Your sudden coming o'er to play with you.

Now out of this—

105 **Laertes**   What out of this, my lord?

King   Laertes, was your father dear to you?

Or are you like the painting of a sorrow,

A face without a heart?

Laertes   Why ask you this?

King   Not that I think you did not love your father,

110   But that I know love is begun by time,

出神入化，我就是绞尽脑汁

都无法想象。

雷厄提斯　　　　　　他是诺曼人吧？

国王　　　是的。　　　　　　　　　　　　　　　　　　　　90

雷厄提斯　我以性命担保，定是拉莫！

国王　　　　　　　　　　　　正是。

雷厄提斯　我了解他。　他的确是全国的

胸章与珍宝。

国王　　　他提到过您的本领，

对您在防御方面表现出的　　　　　　　　　　95

敏捷和剑法，尤其是对您的

轻剑，给予了如此非凡的褒扬，

并喊道，谁能与您匹敌那定是

一种奇观。　他发誓，本国的剑手

若与您对阵，也定会动作僵硬、　　　　　　　100

防不胜防、眼花缭乱。　先生，

这番话让哈姆雷特如此嫉妒，

他竟然希望并乞求您能够

立即返回以便与他决斗。

可以由此——

雷厄提斯　　　　　由此什么，陛下？　　　　　　　　105

国王　　　雷厄提斯，您真爱您的父亲？

还是只像一幅忧伤的图画，

有面无心？

雷厄提斯　　　　您为何要问这个？

国王　　　不是我以为您不爱您的父亲，

而是我知道爱是由时间促成，　　　　　　　110

110-22. 国王这一段有关时间的论述，进一步拓展了本剧的主题　（参见 3.2.182-194）
（Gill）。

And that I see, in passages of proof,

Time qualifies the spark and fire of it.

There lives within the very flame of love

A kind of wick or snuff that will abate it;

115   And nothing is at a like goodness still,

For goodness, growing to a pleurisy,

Dies in his own too-much. That we would do,

We should do when we would: for this 'would' changes

And hath abatements and delays as many

120   As there are tongues, are hands, are accidents,

And then this 'should' is like a spendthrift sigh

That hurts by easing. But to the quick of th'ulcer:

Hamlet comes back; what would you undertake

To show yourself in deed your father's son

More than in words?

125 **Laertes**   To cut his throat i'th' church.

    King   No place indeed should murder sanctuarize;

Revenge should have no bounds. But good Laertes,

Will you do this, keep close within your chamber;

Hamlet, return'd, shall know you are come home;

130   We'll put on those shall praise your excellence,

And set a double varnish on the fame

The Frenchman gave you, bring you, in fine, together,

And wager o'er your heads. He, being remiss,

Most generous, and free from all contriving,

135   Will not peruse the foils, so that with ease—

通过充分的例证,我已看清,

时间可以将爱的火花削弱。

在爱的火焰里面存在一种

能将其熄灭的灯芯或烛花;

什么都不能保持良好如初,　　　　　　　　115

因为良好,一旦变得过分,

自会消亡。　我们想做的事情,

想做时就该做:因为"想"字会变,

有许多因素会让它削弱和耽搁,

如有人劝阻、插手,或意外事故,　　　　　120

而这个"该"字犹如枉然的叹息,

看似舒心而受害。　问题的要害是:

哈姆雷特已经回来;除了言辞

您用啥行动证明您这位儿子

是亲生?

雷厄提斯　　　　　　教堂里面割破他的喉!　　　　125

国王　本不该有啥地方让凶手庇护;

复仇不应限定场所。　好雷厄提斯,

假如您愿意,您可以闭门不出;

哈姆雷特已回,会听说您已返还;

我将派人对您的本领大加赞扬,　　　　　130

对法国人给您的名声添枝加叶,

最终,把你们二人带到一起,

再为你们打赌。　他,粗心大意,

又宽宏大量,一点也不会算计,

是不会检查备好的轻剑,因此　　　　　　135

----

122. 看似舒心而受害:假如我们只是对某种责任的意识 (我们应该做的事情) 感到心满意足,而并不采取行动,这是有害的 (因为通过让我们的良心感到轻松,却削弱了我们的道德观念)。　叹息在减轻人们心灵痛苦的同时,也浪费了生命赖以生存的血液 (因为人们认为,叹息需要从心里往外抽血) (Jenkins)。

Or with a little shuffling—you may choose

A sword unbated, and in a pass of practice

Requite him for your father.

Laertes   I will do't.

And for that purpose, I'll anoint my sword.

140 I bought an unction of a mountebank

So mortal that but dip a knife in it,

Where it draws blood, no cataplasm so rare,

Collected from all simples that have virtue

Under the moon, can save the thing from death

145 That is but scratch'd withal. I'll touch my point

With this contagion, that if I gall him slightly,

It may be death.

King   Let's further think of this,

Weigh what convenience both of time and means

May fit us to our shape. If this should fail,

150 And that our drift look through our bad performance,

'Twere better not essay'd. Therefore this project

Should have a back or second that might hold

If this did blast in proof. Soft, let me see.

We'll make a solemn wager on your cunnings—

155 I ha't!

When in your motion you are hot and dry—

As make your bouts more violent to that end—

And that he calls for drink, I'll have prepar'd him

A chalice for the nonce, whereon but sipping,

160 If he by chance escape your venom'd stuck,

Our purpose may hold there. But stay, what noise?

就轻而易举——或者设下骗局——
您可选一把开刃的利剑,刺他
一下便报了杀父之仇。

雷厄提斯　　　　　　　　　我会的。
为达目标,我还要在剑上涂药。
我从江湖医生那里买了种油膏,　　　　　　　　140
毒性如此剧烈,只要拿剑一蘸,
皮肤一旦擦破,任何灵丹妙药,
哪怕是月夜采集的药草熬成,
也无法让受害者起死回生。
我要把这种毒药涂在我的　　　　　　　　145
剑头之上,只要擦他一下,
即可毙命。

国王　　　　　　　让我们再考虑考虑,
掂量掂量什么时间与手段
对我们方便,万一这一招失灵,
我们笨拙的行动露出了破绽,　　　　　　　　150
还不如不干。　因此本次行动,
为了预防万一该有个后援
或第二方案。　等等,让我看看。
我要为您的剑术押上大注——
有了!　　　　　　　　155
你们交起手来定会又热又渴——
为此您要让比赛更加激烈——
他肯定要喝水,我将为他备上
毒酒一杯,只要他抿上一口,
假如他能侥幸逃过您的毒剑,　　　　　　　　160
我们也能如愿。　等等,什么声音?

143.　月夜采集的药草:人们认为,在月光下采集的药草药性更强(Gill)。

Enter Queen.

Queen	One woe doth tread upon another's heel,
	So fast they follow. Your sister's drown'd, Laertes.
Laertes	Drown'd? O, where?
165 **Queen**	There is a willow grows askant the brook
	That shows his hoary leaves in the glassy stream.
	Therewith fantastic garlands did she make
	Of crow-flowers, nettles, daisies, and long purples,
	That liberal shepherds give a grosser name,
170	But our cold maids do dead men's fingers call them.
	There on the pendent boughs her crownet weeds
	Clamb'ring to hang, an envious sliver broke,
	When down her weedy trophies and herself
	Fell in the weeping brook. Her clothes spread wide,
175	And mermaid-like awhile they bore her up,
	Which time she chanted snatches of old lauds,
	As one incapable of her own distress,
	Or like a creature native and indued
	Unto that element. But long it could not be
180	Till that her garments, heavy with their drink,
	Pull'd the poor wretch from her melodious lay
	To muddy death.

Laertes	Alas, then she is drown'd.
Queen	Drown'd, drown'd.
Laertes	Too much of water hast thou, poor Ophelia,

王后上。

王后	不幸的事件真是接踵而至。
	您的妹妹淹死了，雷厄提斯。
雷厄提斯	淹死了？　在哪里？
王后	在小河旁边斜长着一棵柳树，　　　　　165

银白的树叶倒映在清澈水面。

她用柳枝、剪秋罗、荨麻、雏菊

和红门兰编成了漂亮的花环，

放肆的牧者给起的名字更俗，

我们纯洁的姑娘称其为"死人指"。　　　170

她爬到一根下垂的树枝去挂

花环，一根恶毒的枝条折断，

花环掉落的同时，她自己也跌入

呜咽的河中。　她的环裙四散，

让她美人鱼般片刻漂浮水面，　　　　175

此刻她却唱起了古老的赞歌，

好像对自己的险境毫无知觉，

或者好像她原本就在水中

生活。　但这种状况不能长久，

直到她的衣服，全被水浸透，　　　　180

把可怜的姑娘从优美的歌中

拖向河底。

雷厄提斯	唉，那么她已淹死？
王后	淹死，淹死。
雷厄提斯	你喝的水太多，可怜的奥菲丽娅，

---

165. 柳树：象征被抛弃或被遗忘的情人。　王后此时的言辞具有一种超然的口气，好像信使与
信息毫不相干（Gill）。

185   And therefore I forbid my tears. But yet
      It is our trick; nature her custom holds,
      Let shame say what it will. [*Weeps.*] When these are gone,
      The woman will be out. Adieu, my lord,
      I have a speech o' fire that fain would blaze
      But that this folly douts it.   *Exit.*

190 **King**   Let's follow, Gertrude.
      How much I had to do to calm his rage.
      Now fear I this will give it start again.
      Therefore let's follow.   *Exeunt.*

因此我要忍住自己的泪水。　　　　　　　　　　185

不过这是常情；天性支配习惯，

不管会多么丢人。［哭泣。］眼泪一旦掉下，

女人气就会消失。　再见了,陛下。

我行将燃烧的言辞,却被这种

愚行一下扑灭。　　　　　　　　　　　　　　下。

国王　　　　　　　　　咱们跟上,葛楚德。　　　190

为让他息怒我费了多少心机。

我担心他的怒火会重新燃起。

因此咱们要跟上。　　　　　　　　　　　同下。

第五幕
ACT 5

SCENE I

Enter two Clowns [*the Grave-digger and Another*].

Grave.　Is she to be buried in Christian burial, when she
　　　　wilfully seeks her own salvation?

Other　I tell thee she is, therefore make her grave straight.
　　　　The crowner hath sat on her and finds it Christian
5　　　burial.

Grave.　How can that be, unless she drowned herself in her
　　　　own defence?

Other　Why, 'tis found so.

Grave.　It must be *se offendendo*, it cannot be else. For here
10　　　lies the point: if I drown myself wittingly, it argues
　　　　an act, and an act hath three branches — it is to act,
　　　　to do, to perform; argal, she drowned herself
　　　　wittingly.

Other　Nay, but hear you, Goodman Delver—

15 **Grave.**　Give me leave. Here lies the water—good. Here
　　　　stands the man—good. If the man go to this water
　　　　and drown himself, it is, will he nill he, he goes,

第一场

两位小丑 [掘墓者与另一位] 上。

掘墓者 难道这位自愿寻死的姑娘还要按照
基督教的仪式下葬吗？

另一位 我告诉你是的，所以你就赶紧挖吧。
验尸官已验过并裁定要按基督教的
仪式下葬。   5

掘墓者 那怎么可能，除非她是出于自卫才将
自己淹死？

另一位 咳，已经证实。

掘墓者 肯定是正当防卫，不可能是别的。因为
关键在于：假如我故意淹死自己，这就   10
意味着一种行为，而一种行为包含三个
部分——就是想做、要做和真做；所以说，
她是投河自尽。

另一位 不，您听我说，掘墓者老兄——

掘墓者 听我说。这儿是水——好吧。这儿站着一个   15
人——好吧。假如这个人下到水里淹死自己，
那是他自己下去的，无论他想不想。注意

5.1. 1-2. 按照基督教的仪式下葬：一直延续到 19 世纪的基督教教规规定：不得为自杀身亡者举行正式的葬礼，自杀者的尸体也不能葬入神圣的场所（见 222 行），通常只能埋在路口，堆上石头（见 224 行），并用一根木桩穿透（Jenkins）。 9. 正当防卫：原文 *se offendendo* 意为"自残"；但掘墓者的本意为"se defendendo（自卫）"，属于是非混淆、黑白颠倒（Jenkins）。

mark you that. But if the water come to him and drown him, he drowns not himself. Argal, he that is

20 not guilty of his own death shortens not his own life.

Other But is this law?

Grave. Ay, marry is't, crowner's quest law.

Other Will you ha' the truth an't? If this had not been a gentlewoman, she should have been buried out o'

25 Christian burial.

Grave. Why, there thou say'st. And the more pity that great folk should have countenance in this world to drown or hang themselves more than their even-Christen. Come, my spade. There is no ancient

30 gentlemen but gardeners, ditchers, and grave-makers—they hold up Adam's profession.   [*He digs.*]

Other Was he a gentleman?

Grave. A was the first that ever bore arms.

Other Why, he had none.

35 **Grave.** What, art a heathen? How dost thou understand The Scripture? The Scripture says Adam digged. Could he dig without arms? I'll put another question to thee. If thou answerest me not to the purpose, confess thyself—

40 **Other** Go to.

Grave. What is he that builds stronger than either the mason, the shipwright, or the carpenter?

Other The gallows-maker, for that frame outlives a

	这一点。但假如是水朝他袭来并把他淹死， 那就不是他淹死自己。因此凡是不想自寻 短见的人，对自己的死亡便是无辜。	20
另一位	难道这是律法？	
掘墓者	是的，没错，验尸官的验尸法。	
另一位	您想知道实情吗？假如死者不是一位高贵 的女士，那就不会按照基督教的仪式为她 下葬了。	25
掘墓者	咳，你真说对了！令人感到更遗憾的是， 在这个世界上，大人物居然可以比他们 的基督教教友享有更多的特权去投河或 上吊。快，拿锹来。远古时代没有绅士， 只有种花的、挖沟的、和掘墓的——他们 维持着亚当的职业。　　　　　〔开始挖掘。〕	30
另一位	他是一位绅士吗？	
掘墓者	他是第一个戴徽章的人。	
另一位	咳，他啥都没戴！	
掘墓者	什么，你是异教徒吗？你的圣经是怎么 读的？圣经里面说亚当是挖地的。如果 他没带手臂，他怎么挖地？我再来问你 一个问题。如果你回答得文不对题，你 就得认输——	35
另一位	说吧。	40
掘墓者	哪位工匠能比石匠、船匠，或者是木匠 建造的东西更加坚固？	
另一位	造绞刑架的。因为架子的寿命可以超过	

　31. 亚当的职业：亚当要为上帝照管伊甸园（"创世纪"3章23节）（Gill）。　33. 徽章：盾形徽章，作为绅士出身的标志（Gill）。　37. 手臂：原文"arms"为双关语，既可指"手臂"；也可指"徽章"（如上述33行）。掘墓者在用该词的双关语义取笑对方（Gill）。

thousand tenants.

45	**Grave.**	I like thy wit well in good faith, the gallows does well. But how does it well? It does well to those that do ill. Now, thou dost ill to say the gallows is built stronger than the church; argal, the gallows may do well to thee. To't again, come.
50	**Other**	Who builds stronger than a mason, a shipwright, or a carpenter?
	Grave.	Ay, tell me that and unyoke.
	Other	Marry, now I can tell.
	Grave.	To't.
55	**Other**	Mass, I cannot tell.
	Grave.	Cudgel thy brains no more about it, for your dull ass will not mend his pace with beating. And when you are asked this question next, say 'A grave-maker'. The houses he makes lasts till doomsday.
60		Go, get thee to Yaughan; fetch me a stoup of liquor.

    Exit the Other Clown. [*The Grave-digger continues digging.*]

 [*Sings*] *In youth when I did love, did love,*

    Methought it was very sweet:

   To contract—O—the time for—a—my behove,

   O methought there—a—was nothing—a—meet.

[*While he is singing,*] enter Hamlet and Horatio.

65	**Hamlet**	Has this fellow no feeling of his business a sings in

成千的用户。

掘墓者	我确实喜欢你的妙语,绞刑架是个很好	45
	的回答。可它好在哪里?好在它适合于	
	那些作恶的人。你说绞刑架比教堂还要	
	坚固,表明你心术不正;所以,绞刑架	
	对你来说倒很合适。 快,再猜。	

| 另一位 | 谁比石匠、船匠,或者木匠建造的东西 | 50 |
| | 更加坚固? | |

掘墓者 是的,告诉我就收工。

另一位 哎呀,我知道了!

掘墓者 快说。

另一位 天哪,我还是不知道。 55

掘墓者	别再绞你的脑汁了,因为对一头笨驴来说,	
	打死它,它也快不到哪里去的。要是下次	
	再有人问你这个问题,就说:"是挖坟的"。	
	因为他建造的房子要住到世界的末日!快,	
	到约翰那里,给我打一壶酒来。	60

　　　　　　　　　　　　　　另一小丑下。[掘墓者继续挖掘。]

[唱] 　年轻时我曾经爱过、爱过,

　　　　想起来真是非常甜蜜:

　　　要想缩短——啊——那种美妙时刻,

　　　在我看来——啊——已经不合时宜。

　　　　[他哼唱期间,]哈姆雷特与何瑞修上。

哈姆雷特 　难道这家伙对自己的工作已经麻木,掘墓　　65

----

61. 年轻时我曾经爱过: 掘墓者所唱的三节歌谣 (包括随后两节) 选自一首名为"老情人
摈弃爱情"的诗歌,经过篡改、剪贴而成。 原诗共十四节,为英国诗人托马斯·福克斯(Thomas
Lord Vaux)所作。 该歌谣从掘墓者的口中唱出可谓恰如其分,此处用以承接并表达奥菲丽娅在
第四幕第五场所唱歌谣的主题——爱情的死亡——进入他正在挖掘的坟墓。 令人痛心的是,那种
适合于老年的伤感之情,此处却转嫁到了青年 (奥菲丽娅) 身上(Jenkins)。

grave-making?

Horatio Custom hath made it in him a property of easiness.

Hamlet 'Tis e'en so, the hand of little employment hath the daintier sense.

70 **Grave.** [*Sings*] *But age with his stealing steps*

Hath claw'd me in his clutch,

And hath shipp'd me intil the land,

As if I had never been such.

[*He throws up a skull.*]

Hamlet That skull had a tongue in it, and could sing once.

75 How the knave jowls it to th' ground, as if 't were Cain's jawbone, that did the first murder. This might be the pate of a politician which this ass now o'er-offices, one that would circumvent God, might it not?

80 **Horatio** It might, my lord.

Hamlet Or of a courtier, which could say, 'Good morrow, sweet lord. How dost thou, sweet lord?' This might be my Lord Such-a-one, that praised my Lord Such-a-one's horse when a meant to beg it, might it

85 not?

Horatio Ay, my lord.

Hamlet Why, e'en so, and now my Lady Worm's, chopless, and knocked about the mazard with a sexton's spade. Here's fine revolution and we had the trick to see't.

90 Did these bones cost no more the breeding but to play

	时还在唱歌？	
何瑞修	习惯已经让他养成了一种坦然。	
哈姆雷特	一点不错，游手好闲的巴掌摸起来会更加 敏感。	
掘墓者	［唱］年龄的脚步却悄悄逼近， 　　　一下使我老态龙钟， 　　把我送入地下安寝， 　　　好像我从来没有年轻。	70

[扔出一块头骨。]

哈姆雷特	那块头骨原先有一根舌头，曾经也能哼唱。 那个家伙怎么把它扔到地上，好像它就是 该隐的下巴——犯下世上的首例凶杀。这头 蠢驴现在所摆弄的那块头骨，也许属于一 位连上帝都敢欺骗的政客，难道这不可能 吗？	75
何瑞修	可能，殿下。	80
哈姆雷特	或者是属于一位侍臣，他会说，"早上好， 亲爱的陛下。您好吗，亲爱的陛下？"这 也许是某某大人，他对某某大人的马大加 赞扬，实际上却想将马乞为己有，不可能 吗？	85
何瑞修	可能，殿下。	
哈姆雷特	咳，没错，现在属于我的蛆虫夫人，下巴 脱落，让掘墓者用铁锹敲来敲去。这真是 奇妙的轮回，我们有能力将它看破。这些 骨头养育成型，难道只是为了用作投掷的	90

76. 该隐的下巴：该隐的罪行不仅是凶杀，而且还是杀兄，也就是克劳狄斯的原型（见 3.3.37）（Jenkins）。 90-1. 投掷的木块：游戏中用以投向目标的木块（Gill）。

at loggets with 'em? Mine ache to think on't.

Grave.   [*Sings*] *A pickaxe and a spade, a spade,*

For and a shrouding-sheet,

O a pit of clay for to be made

95   *For such a guest is meet.*

[*Throws up another skull.*]

Hamlet   There's another. Why, may not that be the skull of a lawyer? Where be his quiddities now, his quillities, his cases, his tenures, and his tricks? Why does he suffer this mad knave now to knock him about the

100   sconce with a dirty shovel, and will not tell him of his action of battery? Hum, this fellow might be in's time a great buyer of land, with his statutes, his recognizances, his fines, his double vouchers, his recoveries. Is this the fine of his fines and the

105   recovery of his recoveries, to have his fine pate full of fine dirt? Will his vouchers vouch him no more of his purchases, and double ones too, than the length and breadth of a pair of indentures? The very conveyances of his lands will scarcely lie in this box, and

110   must th'inheritor himself have no more, ha?

Horatio   Not a jot more, my lord.

Hamlet   Is not parchment made of sheepskins?

Horatio   Ay, my lord, and of calveskins too.

Hamlet   They are sheep and calves which seek out assurance

木块？　想起来就让我头疼。

掘墓者　　　［唱］一把镐来、一把锹、一把锹，

再加上一块裹尸布，

噢，一个土坑要挖刨，

好让这宾客来居住。　　　　　　　　　　　　　95

［又扔出一块头骨。］

哈姆雷特　　又有一个。咳，难道那不可能是一位律师
的头骨？他的狡辩如今何在，他的遁词呢，
他的案子呢，他的保有呢，和他的伎俩呢？
现在为什么要忍受这个狂徒用一把肮脏的
铁锹将自己的头颅敲来敲去，而不去告他　　100
犯下了伤害之罪？呣，这个家伙生前也许
是个很大的土地买主，他利用法规，使用
具结，他谈判协商，寻求双重保人，追讨
应得的地产。难道这就是他协商出的结果，
讨回来的一切，让他那精明的脑袋充满了　　105
精细的尘土？难道他的保人，甚至是双重
保人，不再担保他的置地，只为他留下了
契约这么一片大小的土地？这个匣子很难
将他置地的契约全部装下，而匣子的主人
难道就不能再多拥有一丁点土地？　哈？　　110

何瑞修　　　一点也不能，殿下。

哈姆雷特　　皮纸不是用羊皮做的吗？

何瑞修　　　是的，殿下，也有用牛皮做的。

哈姆雷特　　只有蠢驴才会在皮纸里寻求担保。我

---

102. 土地买主：像其他许多渴望通过拥有大量土地而跻身于上流社会的人们一样，这种行为在律师之间早已臭名昭著，他们常被指控利用自己的法律专长谋取私利（Jenkins）。　108. 匣子：（1）契约保险箱；（2）棺材（Jenkins）；（3）也有学者认为是指颅骨（Thompson）。

115		in that. I will speak to this fellow. —Whose grave's this, sirrah?
	Grave.	Mine, sir.
		[*Sings*] *O a pit of clay for to be made—*
	Hamlet	I think it be thine indeed, for thou liest in't.
120	**Grave.**	You lie out on't, sir, and therefore 'tis not yours. For my part, I do not lie in't, yet it is mine.
	Hamlet	Thou dost lie in't, to be in't and say 'tis thine. 'Tis for the dead, not for the quick: therefore thou liest.
125	**Grave.**	'Tis a quick lie, sir, 'twill away again from me to you.
	Hamlet	What man dost thou dig it for?
	Grave.	For no man, sir.
	Hamlet	What woman then?
	Grave.	For none neither.
130	**Hamlet**	Who is to be buried in't?
	Grave.	One that was a woman, sir; but rest her soul, she's dead.
135	**Hamlet**	How absolute the knave is. We must speak by the card or equivocation will undo us. By the Lord, Horatio, this three years I have took note of it, the age is grown so picked that the toe of the peasant comes so near the heel of the courtier he galls his kibe. —How long hast thou been grave-maker?

	要跟这个家伙谈一谈。——这是谁的墓， 老兄？	115
掘墓者	我的，先生。	
	〔唱〕　噢，一个土坑要挖刨——	
哈姆雷特	我想它一定是你的，因为你在里面瞎捣。	
掘墓者	您在外面胡诌，先生，所以它不是您的。 至于我，我并未捣在里面，可它是我的。	120
哈姆雷特	你撒谎，你在里面就说是你的。它是给 死人的，不是给活人的：所以你在撒谎。	
掘墓者	它是个活的谎言，先生，它会从我这里 跳到您的身上。	125
哈姆雷特	这是给哪个人挖的？	
掘墓者	不是给男人，先生。	
哈姆雷特	是给哪个女人？	
掘墓者	也不是给女人。	
哈姆雷特	那要把谁埋在里面？	130
掘墓者	她曾经是女人，先生；愿她的灵魂安息， 她死了。	
哈姆雷特	这家伙是多么严谨！我们说话必须循规 蹈矩，含糊其辞就会遭到非议。我发誓， 何瑞修，近三年我注意到，如今的人们 已变得如此考究，农民的脚趾那么接近 廷臣的脚跟，他竟然会把他的冻疮踩伤。 ——你干挖坟这一行已经多久？	135

119-20. ……瞎捣……胡诌：原文“lie”为双关语（Jenkins），有“卧躺”与“撒谎”之意；此处分别译成“瞎捣”与“胡诌”，以期能利用其间的谐音模仿一二，即：“捣——倒”和“诌——走”。 ——译者附注。

	Grave.	Of all the days i'th' year I came to't that day that
140		our last King Hamlet o'ercame Fortinbras.
	Hamlet	How long is that since?
	Grave.	Cannot you tell that? Every fool can tell that. It was that very day that young Hamlet was born—he that is mad and sent into England.
145	**Hamlet**	Ay, marry. Why was he sent into England?
	Grave.	Why, because a was mad. A shall recover his wits there. Or if a do not, 'tis no great matter there.
	Hamlet	Why?
150	**Grave.**	'Twill not be seen in him there. There the men are as mad as he.
	Hamlet	How came he mad?
	Grave.	Very strangely, they say.
	Hamlet	How ' strangely'?
	Grave.	Faith, e'en with losing his wits.
155	**Hamlet**	Upon what ground?
	Grave.	Why, here in Denmark. I have been sexton here, man and boy, thirty years.
	Hamlet	How long will a man lie i'th' earth ere he rot?
160	**Grave.**	Faith, if a be not rotten before a die—as we have many pocky corses nowadays that will scarce hold the laying in—a will last you some eight year or nine year. A tanner will last you nine year.
	Hamlet	Why he more than another?
	Grave.	Why , sir , his hide is so tanned with his trade that

掘墓者	一年三百多天里,我是从先王哈姆雷特战胜弗廷布拉的那一天开始的。

140

哈姆雷特	到现在已有多久?
掘墓者	连这都不知道?一个傻瓜都清楚。就是小哈姆雷特出生的那一天——他现在疯了,人们已把他送往英国。
哈姆雷特	唉,真是的。为啥要把他送往英国?

145

掘墓者	为啥,因为他疯了呗。他会在那里得到康复。即使不能,在那里也没多大关系。
哈姆雷特	为啥?
掘墓者	在那里看不出他是疯子,因为那里的人都跟他一样。

150

哈姆雷特	他是怎么疯的?
掘墓者	非常奇怪,人们说。
哈姆雷特	怎么"奇怪"?
掘墓者	真的,神志都失常了。
哈姆雷特	根源何在?

155

掘墓者	咳,就在丹麦。我从小到大从事这一行已有三十年了。
哈姆雷特	一个人躺在地下需要多久才会腐烂?
掘墓者	实际上,假如他死去之前还没腐烂——因为近来有许多患梅毒的尸体在下葬之前已经腐烂——他可以支撑八年或者九年。硝皮匠可以支撑九年。

160

哈姆雷特	为什么他比别人更长?
掘墓者	咳,先生,他的肉皮已在工作中硝得如此

139-57:许多莎剧评论家都试图根据本场的时间去推算哈姆雷特的年龄,但不一定准确。(Gill)我认为,剧作家之所以安排掘墓者开始掘墓生涯的第一天不仅与哈姆雷特的生日巧合,而且也与哈姆雷特国王战胜弗廷布拉的那一天巧合,旨在做到首尾呼应——使掘墓者的活动横跨全剧,同时也可展示哈姆雷特本人自从降生于这个多事之秋之日起,所跨越的整个人生历程。至于哈姆雷特的确切年龄,相对来说并不重要(Jenkins)。

165   a will keep out water a great while, and your water is a sore decayer of your whoreson dead body. Here's a skull now hath lien you i'th' earth three and twenty years.

Hamlet   Whose was it?

170 **Grave.**   A whoreson mad fellow's it was. Whose do you think it was?

Hamlet   Nay, I know not.

Grave.   A pestilence on him for a mad rogue! A poured a flagon of Rhenish on my head once. This same

175   skull, sir, was Yorick's skull, the King's jester.

Hamlet   This? [*Takes the skull.*]

Grave.   E'en that.

Hamlet   Alas, poor Yorick. I knew him, Horatio, a fellow of infinite jest, of most excellent fancy. He hath bore

180   me on his back a thousand times, and now—how abhorred in my imagination it is. My gorge rises at it. Here hung those lips that I have kissed I know not how oft. Where be your gibes now, your gambols, your songs, your flashes of merriment, that were

185   wont to set the table on a roar? Not one now to mock your own grinning? Quite chop-fallen? Now get you to my lady's chamber and tell her, let her paint an inch thick, to this favour she must come. Make her laugh at that. —Prithee, Horatio, tell me one thing.

190 **Horatio**   What's that, my lord?

柔软,要过好长时间水才能渗入他的体内, 165
对狗屁尸体来说,水是一种剧烈的腐蚀剂。
这儿又是一块头骨,他已在地下呆了二十又
三年。

哈姆雷特　是谁的?

掘墓者　是一个无赖疯子的。　您以为这块头骨会是 170
谁的?

哈姆雷特　我不知道。

掘墓者　一个下流的疯子无赖!他曾将一壶葡萄酒
浇到了我的头上。这块头骨,先生,就是
国王的弄臣,尤里克的头颅! 175

哈姆雷特　是他?〔拾起头骨。〕

掘墓者　正是。

哈姆雷特　哎呀,可怜的尤里克!我认识他,何瑞修,
他是一个滑稽百出、异想天开的家伙。他
把我驮在背上有一千次之多,可现在——想 180
起来是多么令人厌恶!让我作呕。这里
曾经挂着两片嘴唇,我不知道自己当初是
如何频繁地亲吻。您的嘲讽呢,您的蹦蹦
跳跳呢,您的歌声呢,您让满座捧腹大笑
的才干呢?难道就没留下一句妙语来嘲笑 185
您自己的龇牙咧嘴?您垂头丧气了?快到
我那小姐的闺房去告诉她,让她抹上一寸
脂粉,最后也要变成这副模样。让她就此
一笑。——求您,何瑞修,告诉我一件事情。

何瑞修　啥事情,殿下? 190

	Hamlet	Dost thou think Alexander looked o' this fashion i'th' earth?
	Horatio	E'en so.
	Hamlet	And smelt so? Pah! [*Puts down the skull.*]
195	**Horatio**	E'en so, my lord.
	Hamlet	To what base uses we may return, Horatio! Why, may not imagination trace the noble dust of Alexander till a find it stopping a bung-hole?
	Horatio	'Twere to consider too curiously to consider so.
200	**Hamlet**	No, faith, not a jot, but to follow him thither with modesty enough, and likelihood to lead it. Alexander died, Alexander was buried, Alexander returneth to dust, the dust is earth, of earth we make loam, and why of that loam whereto he was converted might
205		they not stop a beer-barrel?
		Imperious Caesar, dead and turn'd to clay,
		Might stop a hole to keep the wind away.
		O that that earth which kept the world in awe
		Should patch a wall t'expel the winter's flaw.
210		But soft, but soft awhile. Here comes the King,
		The Queen, the courtiers.

哈姆雷特	你是否认为亚历山大在地下也是这副
	模样？
何瑞修	是的。
哈姆雷特	也这么臭吗？　呸！〔扔下头骨。〕
何瑞修	是的，殿下。　　　　　　　　　　195
哈姆雷特	我们会沦落到何等下贱的用途，何瑞修！
	咳，难道我们的想象无法追索亚历山大
	那尊贵的尘土去堵桶口？
何瑞修	要想想到这一点太需要奇思妙想了。
哈姆雷特	不需要，真的，一点都不需要，只要能　200
	稍加思索，就可以想象得到。亚历山大
	死了，亚历山大埋了，亚历山大化成了
	尘土，尘土就是土，我们用土和成了泥，
	那为什么由他和成的那一团泥，就不会
	去堵啤酒桶？　　　　　　　　　　205
	威武的恺撒死去之后化为土，
	也许会为了挡风去把洞口堵。
	噢，那曾威震四海的一团泥，
	居然会为了抵御寒风补破壁。
	等一等，要等一等。　国王来了，　210
	还有王后、大臣。

---

191. 亚历山大：人们所熟知的最伟大的征服者，同时也以其长相英俊而出名（Gill）。　亚历山大生前体味芳香、皮肤白皙。　很久以来人们通常把他用作对死亡进行沉思的对象，即：死亡是一个均衡器——亚历山大死后跟他的仆人并无两样（Jenkins）。　206. 恺撒：尤利乌斯·恺撒，罗马帝国的君王，人们常把他与亚历山大相提并论（Gill）。　206-9. 这四句诗好像是哈姆雷特即兴所作（Jenkins）。

Enter [Bearers with] a Coffin, a Priest,

King, Queen, Laertes, Lords Attendant.

	Who is this they follow?
	And with such maimed rites? This doth betoken
	The corse they follow did with desp'rate hand
	Fordo it own life. 'Twas of some estate.
215	Couch we awhile and mark.
Laertes	What ceremony else?
Hamlet	That is Laertes, a very noble youth. Mark.
Laertes	What ceremony else?
Priest	Her obsequies have been as far enlarg'd
220	As we have warranty. Her death was doubtful;
	And but that great command o'ersways the order,
	She should in ground unsanctified been lodg'd
	Till the last trumpet: for charitable prayers
	Shards, flints, and pebbles should be thrown on her.
225	Yet here she is allow'd her virgin crants,
	Her maiden strewments, and the bringing home
	Of bell and burial.
Laertes	Must there no more be done?
Priest	No more be done.
	We should profane the service of the dead
230	To sing sage requiem and such rest to her

[数人抬着] 棺材、一位神父、
国王、王后、雷厄提斯及侍臣上。

这是给谁送葬？

仪式竟这么简单？　这表明他们

送葬的死者是在绝望中结束了

自己的生命。　死者还有些地位。

我们先躲起来看看。　　　　　　　　　　215

雷厄提斯　还有什么别的仪式？

哈姆雷特　那是雷厄提斯,很高尚的青年。　注意。

雷厄提斯　还有什么别的仪式？

神父　我们已在许可的范围内对她的

葬礼给予宽待。　她的死因不明;　　　　　220

若不是上面下令更改了常规,

就该把她埋到荒郊野外,直到

审判日到来:不是慈悲的祷告,

而是向她扔瓷片、瓦砾和卵石。

现在却让她覆盖象征贞洁的　　　　　　　　225

花环与鲜花,还要敲响丧钟

为她安葬。

雷厄提斯　一定就这些了吗？

神父　　　　　　就这些了。

若像对待寿终正寝的灵魂,

为她伴唱庄重的弥撒或圣歌,　　　　　　　230

---

220. 给予宽待:如果某人的死因受到怀疑,除了验尸官可根据验尸情况提出惩罚之外,正如神父随后所解释的那样,教堂还可以施加额外的惩罚(Gill)。　223. 审判日:(世界的末日来临之际) 号角将会响起,死者复活 (在上帝面前接受审判)(Thompson)。

As to peace-parted souls.

Laertes   Lay her i'th' earth,

And from her fair and unpolluted flesh

May violets spring. I tell thee, churlish priest,

A minist'ring angel shall my sister be

When thou liest howling.

235 **Hamlet**   What, the fair Ophelia!

Queen   [*scattering flowers*] Sweets to the sweet. Farewell.

I hop'd thou shouldst have been my Hamlet's wife:

I thought thy bride-bed to have deck'd, sweet maid,

And not have strew'd thy grave.

Laertes   O, treble woe

240   Fall ten times treble on that cursed head

Whose wicked deed thy most ingenious sense

Depriv'd thee of. —Hold off the earth awhile,

Till I have caught her once more in mine arms.

[*Leaps into the grave.*]

Now pile your dust upon the quick and dead,

245   Till of this flat a mountain you have made

T'o'ertop old Pelion or the skyish head

Of blue Olympus.

Hamlet   What is he whose grief

Bears such an emphasis, whose phrase of sorrow

Conjures the wand'ring stars and makes them stand

250   Like wonder-wounded hearers? This is I,

便是对葬礼的亵渎。

雷厄提斯　　　　　　　放她入土，
愿她那美丽纯洁的肉体长出
紫罗兰。　我告诉你，咨詈的神父，
你躺在地狱哀号时，我妹妹将是
救护天使！

哈姆雷特　　　　　什么？　美丽的奥菲丽娅？　　　　　　235

王后　［散花］香花送美人。　永别了！
本想你嫁给我的哈姆雷特：
我想装点你的婚床，好姑娘，
而不是你的坟墓。

雷厄提斯　　　　　　　噢，愿千灾
万祸降临到那个该死的头上，　　　　　　240
是他那邪恶的行为剥夺了你
最机敏的心智！——先不要埋土，
直到我再拥抱她最后一次。
［跳入坟墓。］
现在把活的与死的一起埋葬，
直到一座高山拔地而起，超越　　　　　　245
古老的佩里昂或高耸云端的
奥林帕斯。

哈姆雷特　　　　　　谁的悲恸竟如此
动情，谁的哀伤可召唤行星，
使它们听了之后目瞪口呆、
一动不动？　那就是我，丹麦君王，　　　250

---

233. 紫罗兰：象征忠贞爱情的紫罗兰与象征爱情被遗弃的杨柳一起，暗示了奥菲丽娅悲剧的
性质（Jenkins）。　246. 佩里昂：希腊神话中的一座名山。　与天神作战的巨人把佩里昂山堆积到
附近的另一座高山——奥萨山之上，以便到达天神所居住的奥林帕斯山的山顶（Jenkins）。
250. 丹麦君王：哈姆雷特此时以丹麦君王自称，应是他本人内心变化的一种迹象（Jenkins）。

Hamlet the Dane.

Laertes *[grappling with him]* The devil take thy soul!

Hamlet Thou pray'st not well.

I prithee take thy fingers from my throat,

For though I am not splenative and rash,

255 Yet have I in me something dangerous,

Which let thy wiseness fear. Hold off thy hand.

King Pluck them asunder.

Queen Hamlet! Hamlet!

All Gentlemen!

260 **Horatio** Good my lord, be quiet.

Hamlet Why, I will fight with him upon this theme

Until my eyelids will no longer wag.

Queen O my son, what theme?

Hamlet I lov'd Ophelia. Forty thousand brothers

265 Could not with all their quantity of love

Make up my sum. What wilt thou do for her?

King O, he is mad, Laertes.

Queen For love of God forbear him.

Hamlet 'Swounds, show me what thou't do.

270 Woo't weep, woo't fight, woo't fast, woo't tear thyself,

Woo't drink up eisel, eat a crocodile?

I'll do't. Dost come here to whine,

To outface me with leaping in her grave?

Be buried quick with her, and so will I.

275 And if thou prate of mountains, let them throw

哈 姆 雷 特！

雷厄提斯	［揪住哈姆雷特］你给我见鬼去吧！	
哈姆雷特	你不怀好意。	
	我求你不要掐住我的喉咙，	
	因为尽管我并非暴躁鲁莽，	
	但我也有一些危险的个性，	255
	你应该惧怕才是。 把手放开！	
国王	把他们拉开。	
王后	哈姆雷特！哈姆雷特！	
众人	先生们！	
何瑞修	冷静点，好殿下！	260
哈姆雷特	咳，我要为这个主题与他搏斗，	
	直到我的眼皮不再眨动！	
王后	噢，好孩子，什么主题？	
哈姆雷特	我爱奥菲丽娅。 四万个兄弟的	
	爱加在一起也赶不上我的	265
	分量。 你要为她做些什么？	
国王	噢，他疯了，雷厄提斯！	
王后	看在上帝的份上让着他吧！	
哈姆雷特	该死的，让我看看你要干啥！	
	你要哭、要打、要绝食、要撕碎自己？	270
	你要喝醋，你要吞食鳄鱼？	
	我都会干的。 难道你到此哀号，	
	跳进她的墓穴想把我吓倒？	
	和她一起活埋，我心甘情愿！	
	如果你吹嘘高山，就让百万顷	275

---

270. 你要：原文中的 Woo't = wouldst thou（系口语体用法）（Thompson）。

Millions of acres on us, till our ground,

Singeing his pate against the burning zone,

Make Ossa like a wart. Nay, and thou'lt mouth,

I'll rant as well as thou.

Queen   This is mere madness,

280   And thus awhile the fit will work on him.

Anon, as patient as the female dove

When that her golden couplets are disclos'd,

His silence will sit drooping.

Hamlet   Hear you, sir,

What is the reason that you use me thus?

285   I lov'd you ever. But it is no matter.

Let Hercules himself do what he may,

The cat will mew, and dog will have his day.   *Exit.*

King   I pray thee, good Horatio, wait upon him.   *Exit Horatio.*

[*To Laertes*] Strengthen your patience in our last night's

speech:

290   We'll put the matter to the present push. —

Good Gertrude, set some watch over your son.

This grave shall have a living monument.

An hour of quiet shortly shall we see;

Till then in patience our proceeding be.   *Exeunt.*

泥土抛向我们，直到头顶的

地面耸立云端被烈日烤焦，

让奥萨山像颗肉瘤。　不，你叫吧，

我决不会示弱。

王后　　　　　　　　　　这只是疯话。

过一会儿他就会好起来的。　　　　　　　　　　　　280

很快，就会像一只温顺的母鸽，

孵出一对金黄色的乳鸽之后，

变得心平气和。

哈姆雷特　　　　　　　听我说，先生，

是什么理由竟让您这样待我？

我一直爱您。　可这并不重要。　　　　　　　　　285

尽管赫克勒斯他能力无限，

猫总要咪叫，狗总会时来运转。　　　　　　　下。

国王　我求你，好何瑞修，快跟上他。　　　何瑞修下。

［对雷厄提斯］我们昨晚的谈话会让您

　　耐心：

我们马上就把计划付诸行动。　——　　　　　290

好葛楚德，要看好您的儿子。

该坟墓将有一块不朽的墓碑。

安静一小时即可见到分晓；

此前我们还需要耐心周到。　　　　　　　　同下。

286-7. 尽管……运转：哈姆雷特可能是说，尽管大力神赫克勒斯能够为所欲为、能力无边（见 1.2.153 与 1.4.83 注），却无法阻止猫的咪叫，因此我也无法阻止雷厄提斯那令人厌倦的夸夸其谈；我自己的时运终将到来，即使赫克勒斯（或叫嚣的雷厄提斯）也无法阻拦，即"狗总会时来运转"（Thompson；Bate）。　292. 不朽的墓碑：克劳狄斯可能在暗示——雷厄提斯也明白——其中的险恶用心（Gill）。

SCENE II

Enter Hamlet and Horatio.

Hamlet   So much for this, sir. Now shall you see the other.

You do remember all the circumstance?

Horatio   Remember it, my lord!

Hamlet   Sir, in my heart there was a kind of fighting

5   That would not let me sleep. Methought I lay

Worse than the mutines in the bilboes. Rashly—

And prais'd be rashness for it: let us know

Our indiscretion sometime serves us well

When our deep plots do pall; and that should learn us

10   There's a divinity that shapes our ends,

Rough-hew them how we will—

Horatio   That is most certain.

Hamlet   Up from my cabin,

My sea-gown scarf'd about me, in the dark

Grop'd I to find out them, had my desire,

15   Finger'd their packet, and in fine withdrew

To mine own room again, making so bold,

My fears forgetting manners, to unseal

Their grand commission; where I found, Horatio—

第二场

哈姆雷特与何瑞修上。

哈姆雷特	这件事到此为止。　现在谈另一件。
	您是否依然记得当时的情景？
何瑞修	我记得，殿下！
哈姆雷特	先生，我当时真是忐忑不安、
	无法入眠。　我觉得自己比戴
	镣铐的叛徒还要糟糕。　冲动地——
	还真多亏了冲动：我们要记住，
	当深谋远虑无用时，冲动倒会
	行之有效；这应该教我们明白：
	有一种神灵主宰我们的结局，
	不管我们怎样砍劈——
何瑞修	千真万确。
哈姆雷特	我从房舱里爬起，
	裹上一件航海罩衣，黑暗之中
	找寻他们的踪迹，我如愿以偿，
	摸到了他们的公文，最后我又
	回到了自己的房舱，如此胆大，
	忧虑使我忘了礼仪，打开了
	他们的国书；我发现，何瑞修——

其中行号标注：5（第5行）、10（第10行）、15（第15行）

---

5. 2.　1. 谈另一件：正如他在 4. 6. 22 所许诺的那样（Jenkins）。

Ah, royal knavery! —an exact command,

20 Larded with many several sorts of reasons

Importing Denmark's health, and England's too,

With ho! such bugs and goblins in my life,

That on the supervise, no leisure bated,

No, not to stay the grinding of the axe,

My head should be struck off.

25 **Horatio**   Is't possible?

Hamlet Here's the commission, read it at more leisure.

But wilt thou hear now how I did proceed?

Horatio I beseech you.

Hamlet Being thus benetted round with villainies—

30 Or I could make a prologue to my brains,

They had begun the play—I sat me down,

Devis'd a new commission, wrote it fair—

I once did hold it, as our statists do,

A baseness to write fair, and labour'd much

35 How to forget that learning, but, sir, now

It did me yeoman's service. Wilt thou know

Th'effect of what I wrote?

Horatio   Ay, good my lord.

Hamlet An earnest conjuration from the King,

As England was his faithful tributary,

40 As love between them like the palm might flourish,

As peace should still her wheaten garland wear

And stand a comma 'tween their amities,

啊,阴险的国王!——有一道训令,

矫饰着许多这样那样的理由:　　　　　　　　　　　　　20

涉及丹麦王与英格兰王的安康,

还有,嗬! 我简直成了魑魅魍魉,

读完信后,他们会毫不迟疑,

连磨砺斧头的时间都等待不及,

我的头颅便被砍去!

何瑞修　　　　　　　　　　　　这可能吗?　　　　　　　　　25

哈姆雷特　国书就在这里,空闲时去看吧。

是否想听我随后是怎么做的?

何瑞修　　求您快讲。

哈姆雷特　被困在恶棍编织的罗网之中——

我尚未想好该如何开场之前,　　　　　　　　　　　　30

脑袋已抛头露面——我坐了下来,

写了一封新的信函,字体工整——

我一度认为,正如政客们一样,

字体工整有失身份,我曾努力

忘掉那种本领,可现在,先生　　　　　　　　　　　　35

它为我立下了汗马之功。 是否

想知道我写了什么?

何瑞修　　　　　　　　　　　是的,好殿下。

哈姆雷特　我以国王的名义发出恳求,

因为英国是他的忠诚藩属,

以便其友爱能像棕榈昌盛,　　　　　　　　　　　　40

以便和平能常戴小麦花环,

以便能和睦相处、紧密相连,

40.像棕榈昌盛: 出自《圣经》"诗篇"92篇12节,即:"正直的人们会像棕榈那样繁荣昌盛。"(Jenkins)。 41. 小麦花环:用小麦编织的花环象征繁荣、富足与和平(Jenkins)。

And many such-like 'as'es of great charge,

That on the view and knowing of these contents,

45   Without debatement further more or less,

He should those bearers put to sudden death,

Not shriving-time allow'd.

Horatio   How was this seal'd?

Hamlet   Why, even in that was heaven ordinant.

I had my father's signet in my purse,

50   Which was the model of that Danish seal,

Folded the writ up in the form of th'other,

Subscrib'd it, gave't th'impression, plac'd it safely,

The changeling never known. Now the next day

Was our sea-fight, and what to this was sequent

55   Thou knowest already.

Horatio   So Guildenstern and Rosencrantz go to't.

Hamlet   Why, man, they did make love to this employment.

They are not near my conscience, their defeat

Does by their own insinuation grow.

60   'Tis dangerous when the baser nature comes

Between the pass and fell incensed points

Of mighty opposites.

Horatio   Why, what a king is this!

Hamlet   Does it not, think thee, stand me now upon—

He that hath kill'd my king and whor'd my mother,

65   Popp'd in between th'election and my hopes,

Thrown out his angle for my proper life

和许多如此举足轻重的"以便"，

看完并领会了这些内容之后，

他应该毫不迟疑、决不含糊地　　　　　　　　　　　　45

将送信人处死，连忏悔的时间

都不会准许。

何瑞修　　　　　　　您是如何封的印？

哈姆雷特　哎，甚至连这一点都是天意。

我兜里装着父亲的戒指图章，

跟丹麦的那枚玉玺一模一样，　　　　　　　　　　　　50

我按照原来的样子把信叠好，

又签上字，封好印、放回原处，

这种调包没人会知晓。　第二天

我们遭遇了海盗，随后的事情

你已经知道。　　　　　　　　　　　　　　　　　　　55

何瑞修　盖登斯顿与罗森克兰去送死了？

哈姆雷特　咳，伙计，他们热衷于这门差使。

我并不为他们感到什么愧疚，

他们爱管闲事，这是自作自受。

无名小卒穿梭于强劲对手的　　　　　　　　　　　　60

刀光剑影之间，那可要危及

自身安全。

何瑞修　　　　　　　唉，这是什么国王！

哈姆雷特　难道你，不认为我已义不容辞——

他杀了我父亲，玷污了我母亲。

阻断我通过大选继位的希望，　　　　　　　　　　　　65

用如此狡诈的伎俩，抛出鱼钩

---

65. 阻断……希望：在第一幕第二场里并没有暗示任何类似的"希望"，或是克劳狄斯就此要了什么可耻的花招。　但现在好像是说，他阻止了正常的"选举"程序，因此阻断了哈姆雷特即位的希望（Jenkins）。

And with such coz'nage—is't not perfect conscience

To quit him with this arm? And is't not to be damn'd

To let this canker of our nature come

70   In further evil?

Horatio   It must be shortly known to him from England

What is the issue of the business there.

Hamlet   It will be short. The interim is mine.

And a man's life's no more than to say ' one'.

75   But I am very sorry, good Horatio,

That to Laertes I forgot myself;

For by the image of my cause I see

The portraiture of his. I'll court his favours.

But sure the bravery of his grief did put me

Into a tow'ring passion.

80   **Horatio**   Peace, who comes here?

Enter Osric, a Courtier.

Osric   Your Lordship is right welcome back to Denmark.

Hamlet   I humbly thank you sir. —Dost know this water-
fly?

Horatio   No, my good lord.

85   **Hamlet**   Thy state is the more gracious, for 'tis a vice to
know him. He hath much land and fertile. Let a
beast be lord of beasts and his crib shall stand at the
king's mess. 'Tis a chuff, but, as I say, spacious in the

诱杀我的性命——我用这把利剑

回报给他,难道不是问心无愧?

让体内这种溃疡继续恶化,

难道天理能容? 　　　　　　　　　　　　　70

何瑞修　　他很快就会从英国那里获悉

有关这件事情的处理结果。

哈姆雷特　是会很快。　这段时间还是我的。

人的生命说声"一"字即可了结。

但是我非常懊悔,好何瑞修, 　　　　　　75

我不该对雷厄提斯忘乎所以;

因为从我的境况出发,我能

理解他的情形。　我要求他宽恕。

可他那虚张声势的悲恸确实

令我火冒三丈。

何瑞修　　　　　　安静,是谁来了? 　　　　80

　　　　　　侍臣奥斯瑞克上。

奥斯瑞克　热烈欢迎殿下返回了丹麦!

哈姆雷特　我不胜感激,先生。　——是否认识这一只

水蝇?

何瑞修　　不认识,好殿下。

哈姆雷特　你比我幸运多了,因为认识他是一种堕落。 　　85

他拥有大片沃土。只要一头畜生拥有大批

畜生,那么他的食槽即可摆向国王的餐桌。

他是个乡巴佬,不过,如我所说,他可是

77-8. 从我的境况……他的情形:富有讥讽意味的是,哈姆雷特能够明白雷厄提斯跟他本人一样,一定会为死去的父亲报仇;但哈姆雷特却只字未提雷厄提斯所要报仇的对象就是他本人,而我们对这一点却不会忽略(Jenkins)。

possession of dirt.

90	**Osric**	Sweet lord, if your lordship were at leisure, I should impart a thing to you from his Majesty.
	Hamlet	I will receive it, sir, with all diligence of spirit. Your bonnet to his right use: 'tis for the head.
	Osric	I thank your lordship, it is very hot.
95	**Hamlet**	No, believe me, 'tis very cold, the wind is northerly.
	Osric	It is indifferent cold, my lord, indeed.
	Hamlet	But yet methinks it is very sultry and hot for my complexion.
100	**Osric**	Exceedingly, my lord, it is very sultry—as 'twere—I cannot tell how. My lord, his Majesty bade me signify to you that a has laid a great wager on your head. Sir, this is the matter—
	Hamlet	[*Signing to him to put on his hat*] I beseech you remember—
105	**Osric**	Nay, good my lord, for my ease, in good faith. Sir, here is newly come to court Laertes—believe me, an absolute gentleman, full of most excellent differences, of very soft society and great showing. Indeed, to speak feelingly of him, he is the card or calendar of gentry; for you shall find in him the continent of what part a gentleman would see.
110		
	Hamlet	Sir, his definement suffers no perdition in you, though I know to divide him inventorially would dozy th'arithmetic of memory, and yet but yaw

　　　　　　　　　地产广阔。

奥斯瑞克　　亲爱的殿下，如果殿下有空，我想把陛下　　　　90
　　　　　　　　　托付的一件事情向您转达。

哈姆雷特　　您说吧，先生，我会全神贯注、洗耳恭听。
　　　　　　　　　您的帽子该物归原主：它是为脑袋而做。

奥斯瑞克　　我谢谢殿下，天气很热。

哈姆雷特　　不热，相信我，天气很冷，吹的是北风。　　　　95

奥斯瑞克　　是相当冷，殿下，不错。

哈姆雷特　　不过我觉得对我这样的体质来说，倒是
　　　　　　　　　又闷又热。

奥斯瑞克　　太对了，殿下，是非常的闷热——就像是
　　　　　　　　　——我无法形容。殿下，陛下他让我告诉　　　　100
　　　　　　　　　您，他已经在您身上押下了大注。先生，
　　　　　　　　　事情是这样的——

哈姆雷特　　［示意奥斯瑞克把帽子戴上］我求您不要
　　　　　　　　　忘了——

奥斯瑞克　　不戴，我的好殿下，为了我的舒服，真的。　　　　105
　　　　　　　　　先生，雷厄提斯最近来到宫中——相信我，
　　　　　　　　　他是一位完美无缺的绅士，他的个性出类
　　　　　　　　　拔萃，他的举止温文尔雅，他的外表雍容
　　　　　　　　　华贵。真的，说句公道话，他是绅士风度
　　　　　　　　　的向导或楷模；因为在他身上您可以找到　　　　110
　　　　　　　　　一位绅士应包含的所有优点。

哈姆雷特　　先生，您对他的褒扬真可谓是滴水不漏，
　　　　　　　　　尽管我知道自己要将他的品质一一列出，
　　　　　　　　　将会让我原有的算术知识变得模糊不清，

---

　　93. 物归原主：在伊丽莎白时代，人们在室内常戴着帽子，与人打招呼时摘下；当遇到比自己地位高的人时，只有等到对方准许之后方可戴上，但奥斯瑞克好像并不太乐意接受哈姆雷特对他的恩赐态度（Gill）。

115		neither, in respect of his quick sail. But, in the verity of extolment, I take him to be a soul of great article and his infusion of such dearth and rareness as, to make true diction of him, his semblable is his mirror and who else would trace him his umbrage, nothing
120		more.
	Osric	Your lordship speaks most infallibly of him.
	Hamlet	The concernancy, sir? Why do we wrap the gentle-man in our more rawer breath?
	Osric	Sir?
125	**Horatio**	Is't not possible to understand in another tongue? You will to't, sir, really.
	Hamlet	What imports the nomination of this gentleman?
	Osric	Of Laertes?
	Horatio	His purse is empty already, all's golden words are
130		spent.
	Hamlet	Of him, sir.
	Osric	I know you are not ignorant—
	Hamlet	I would you did, sir. Yet in faith if you did, it would not much approve me. Well, sir?
135	**Osric**	You are not ignorant of what excellence Laertes is —
	Hamlet	I dare not confess that, lest I should compare with him in excellence; but to know a man well were to know himself.
	Osric	I mean, sir, for his weapon; but in the imputation
140		laid on him, by them in his meed, he's unfellowed.

与他的快速航行相比，我只能绕远前行。　　　　　115
不过，出于真诚的赞美，我认为他这个
人物非同小可，他的品性如此罕见稀有，
说句实在的，只有镜子中的他才会像他，
任何想步其后尘之辈只能是尾随的影子，
仅此而已。　　　　　　　　　　　　　　　120

奥斯瑞克　殿下您对他的评价真是恰如其分。

哈姆雷特　与我们何干，先生？我们为何挖空心思
对这位绅士评头论足？

奥斯瑞克　什么？

何瑞修　别人说出来难道您就不懂了？您能行的，　　125
先生，真的。

哈姆雷特　为什么要专门提及这位绅士？

奥斯瑞克　指雷厄提斯？

何瑞修　他的皮囊早已空虚，他的花言巧语已经
用光。　　　　　　　　　　　　　　　　130

哈姆雷特　是他，先生。

奥斯瑞克　我知道您并非无知——

哈姆雷特　但愿您知道，先生。可实际上，您若知道，
也不会让我光彩多少。　然后呢？

奥斯瑞克　您不会不明白雷厄提斯有什么特长——　　135

哈姆雷特　这我可不敢表态，以免我会与他相提并论；
因为一个人在了解别人之前，他必须首先
了解自己。

奥斯瑞克　我是说，先生，他的武艺；了解他长处的
人们对他的评价是，盖世无双。　　　　　140

---

125. 别人……不懂了："尽管您自己能够夸夸其谈，而别人以同样的方式说出来的话您就不懂了？"（Gill）；何瑞修可能是针对奥斯瑞克说的，或是让两人采用更为简单的语言进行交流（Thompson）。

Hamlet		What's his weapon?
Osric		Rapier and dagger.
Hamlet		That's two of his weapons. But well.
Osric	145	The King, sir, hath wagered with him six Barbary horses, against the which he has impawned, as I take it, six French rapiers and poniards, with their assigns, as girdle, hanger, and so. Three of the carriages, in faith, are very dear to fancy, very responsive to the hilts, most delicate carriages, and of
	150	very liberal conceit.
Hamlet		What call you the carriages?
Horatio		I knew you must be edified by the margin ere you had done.
Osric		The carriages, sir, are the hangers.
155 **Hamlet**		The phrase would be more german to the matter if we could carry a cannon by our sides—I would it might be hangers till then. But on. Six Barbary horses against six French swords, their assigns, and three liberal-conceited carriages—that's the French
	160	bet against the Danish. Why is this—impawned, as you call it?
Osric		The King, sir, hath laid, sir, that in a dozen passes between yourself and him he shall not exceed you three hits; he hath laid on twelve for nine. And it
	165	would come to immediate trial if your lordship would vouchsafe the answer.
Hamlet		How if I answer no?

哈姆雷特	他使用什么武器？	
奥斯瑞克	长剑和短刀。	
哈姆雷特	那是他用的两件武器。　又怎样？	
奥斯瑞克	先生，国王已与他赌下了六匹巴巴里骏马，	
	而他对此所下的赌注，据我所知，则是六	145
	把法国长剑与短刀，而且上面还配有一些	
	附件，比如腰带、吊带之类的东西。其中	
	有三条拖带，说真的，简直令人浮想联翩，	
	与剑柄珠联璧合，拖带也精美绝伦、绚丽	
	多彩。	150
哈姆雷特	您所说的拖带是何物？	
何瑞修	我就知道您必须借助页边的注释才能够	
	明白。	
奥斯瑞克	拖带吗，先生，就是吊带。	
哈姆雷特	要是我们腰间能挂上一门大炮，这种用词	155
	倒可能更为贴切——我想还是暂且把它称为	
	吊带吧。说下去。六匹巴巴里骏马对六把	
	法国宝剑，连同它们的附件，和三条别具	
	匠心的拖带——就是拿法国货与丹麦货打赌。	
	为什么将要进行这么一番——正如您所说的	160
	打赌？	
奥斯瑞克	国王他，先生，赌的是，在您与雷厄提斯	
	交手的十二个回合当中，他领先您的回数	
	不会超过三个；他打赌要在十二个回合中	
	获得九胜。如果殿下愿意答应下来，马上	165
	就可以比试。	
哈姆雷特	要是我回答个"不"呢？	

142. 长剑和短刀：当时颇为时髦的武器。　短刀握在左手用以抵挡对手的长剑（Gill）。
144. 巴巴里骏马：一种阿拉伯骏马，以其快速和品种优良而著称（Jenkins）。

Osric		I mean, my lord, the opposition of your person in trial.
170	**Hamlet**	Sir, I will walk here in the hall. If it please his Majesty, it is the breathing time of day with me. Let the foils be brought, the gentleman willing, and the King hold his purpose, I will win for him and I can; if not, I will gain nothing but my shame and the odd hits.
175		
	Osric	Shall I deliver you so?
	Hamlet	To this effect, sir, after what flourish your nature will.
	Osric	I commend my duty to your lordship.
180	**Hamlet**	Yours. *Exit Osric.*
		A does well to commend it himself, there are no tongues else for's turn.
	Horatio	This lapwing runs away with the shell on his head.
	Hamlet	A did comply with his dug before a sucked it. Thus has he—and many more of the same bevy that I know the drossy age dotes on—only got the tune of the time and, out of an habit of encounter, a kind of yeasty collection, which carries them through and through the most fanned and winnowed opinions; and do but blow them to their trial, the bubbles are out.
185		
190		

奥斯瑞克	我是说，殿下，假如您愿意亲自接受挑战。	
哈姆雷特	先生，我就在这大厅里走动。如果国王陛下高兴，现在倒正是我一天当中进行活动的时刻。若把花剑拿来，那位绅士乐意，国王也信守诺言，我会为他取胜，我能够取胜；假若不能，只有丢人现眼，多挨几下。	180 175
奥斯瑞克	就按您这样回复吗？	
哈姆雷特	就是这个意思，先生，随便您怎么添枝加叶。	
奥斯瑞克	为殿下效劳我心甘情愿。	
哈姆雷特	请吧。　　　　　　　　　　奥斯瑞克下。	180
	他自我夸耀倒是很好，因为没有别人会为他美言。	
何瑞修	这只乌头麦鸡顶着蛋壳逃走了！	
哈姆雷特	他在吃奶之前对奶妈的乳房倒彬彬有礼。他这个人——以及我所了解的这个堕落时代所钟爱的许多一路货色——通过习惯性的交际，只不过是学会了一套时髦的滥调、一堆空洞的陈词，便使自己穿梭于名流之间高谈阔论；然而只要把他们拿来一试，他们就会像泡沫一样，一吹即破。	185 190

---

183. 乌头麦鸡：一种水鸟。幼鸟出壳几个小时之后便离开巢穴——被称为幼稚的傻瓜。可能是奥斯瑞克出门时戴上了帽子，让何瑞修联想到了蛋壳（Gill）。

Enter a Lord.

Lord	My lord, his Majesty commended him to you by young Osric, who brings back to him that you attend him in the hall. He sends to know if your

195

pleasure hold to play with Laertes or that you will take longer time.

Hamlet   I am constant to my purposes, they follow the King's pleasure. If his fitness speaks, mine is ready. Now or whensoever, provided I be so able as now.

200 **Lord**   The King and Queen and all are coming down.

Hamlet   In happy time.

Lord   The Queen desires you to use some gentle entertainment to Laertes before you fall to play.

Hamlet   She well instructs me.   *Exit Lord.*

205 **Horatio**   You will lose, my lord.

Hamlet   I do not think so. Since he went into France, I have been in continual practice. I shall win at the odds. Thou wouldst not think how ill all's here about my heart; but it is no matter.

210 **Horatio**   Nay, good my lord.

Hamlet   It is but foolery, but it is such a kind of gaingiving as would perhaps trouble a woman.

Horatio   If your mind dislike anything, obey it. I will forestall their repair hither and say you are not fit.

215 **Hamlet**   Not a whit. We defy augury. There is a special provi-

一侍臣上。

侍臣	殿下,陛下他指派年轻的奥斯瑞克前来向您问好,他回去向国王禀报说,您就在大厅里等他。他派我来问问您是愿意现在就跟雷厄提斯进行比赛,还是等等再说。

185

哈姆雷特	我说话算数,就看国王是否高兴。要是他觉得方便,我随时都行。现在或任何时候,假如我能像目前这样状态良好。

侍臣	国王和王后以及众人就要到了。

200

哈姆雷特	来得正好。

侍臣	王后希望进行比赛之前您能对雷厄提斯以礼相待。

哈姆雷特	她指教得很好。 侍臣下。

何瑞修	您会输的,殿下。

205

哈姆雷特	我看未必。自从他去了法国以后,我一直都在不停地操练。那几个回合我能够取胜。你不知道此刻我是多么心神不安;不过这无关紧要。

何瑞修	不行,我的好殿下。

210

哈姆雷特	这只是愚蠢的表现,不过是一种也许会让女人感到烦恼的担忧。

何瑞修	如果您心里不喜欢做某件事情,那就别做。我可以不让他们前来,就说您身体不适。

哈姆雷特	千万不要。我们蔑视预兆。就连一只麻雀

215

215-6. 一只麻雀的跌落都是天意:哈姆雷特是在证实《圣经》"马太福音"10章29节中的教义:"两只麻雀不是能卖一个铜板? 若圣父不许,一只也不会跌落。"(Gill)

dence in the fall of a sparrow. If it be now, 'tis not to
come; if it be not to come, it will be now; if it be not
now, yet it will come. The readiness is all. Since no
man, of aught he leaves, knows aught, what is't to
220   leave betimes? Let be.

*A table prepared. Trumpets, Drums, and Officers with
cushions. Enter King, Queen, Laertes, [Osric,] and all the State,
and Attendants with foils and daggers.*

King   Come, Hamlet, come, and take this hand from me.
         [*Puts Laertes's hand into Hamlet's.*]

Hamlet   Give me your pardon, sir. I have done you wrong;
         But pardon't as you are a gentleman.
         This presence knows, and you must needs have heard,
225   How I am punish'd with a sore distraction.
         What I have done
         That might your nature, honour, and exception
         Roughly awake, I here proclaim was madness.
         Was't Hamlet wrong'd Laertes? Never Hamlet.
230   If Hamlet from himself be ta'en away,
         And when he's not himself does wrong Laertes,
         Then Hamlet does it not, Hamlet denies it.
         Who does it then? His madness. If't be so,
         Hamlet is of the faction that is wrong'd;
235   His madness is poor Hamlet's enemy.
         Sir, in this audience,
         Let my disclaiming from a purpos'd evil

的跌落都是天意。若是现在，就不是将来；

若不是将来，就是现在；若不是现在，那

就是将来。做好准备是关键。既然没有人

知道自己身后会留下什么，那么早点离去

又有何妨？ 不说啦！ 220

桌子准备就绪。号角齐鸣、锣鼓喧天，军官

携坐垫。国王、王后、雷厄提斯、[奥斯瑞克]

以及众侍臣、侍从携花剑与短刀上。

国王 过来，哈姆雷特，来，握握这只手。

[将雷厄提斯的手放入哈姆雷特手中。]

哈姆雷特 请您原谅我，先生。 我伤害了您；

您是位有教养的绅士，原谅我吧。

在场的人知道，您肯定也曾听说，

严重的神经错乱把我害得多苦。 225

我的所作所为，

若激怒了您的感情、荣誉和愤慨，

我在此声明那都是疯狂所致。

是哈姆雷特伤害了雷厄提斯？

绝对不是。 若哈姆雷特失去理智， 230

身不由己时伤害了雷厄提斯，

就不是哈姆雷特干的，他要否认。

祸首是谁？ 他的疯狂。 若如此，

那么哈姆雷特也是受害一方；

哈姆雷特的仇敌就是他的疯狂。 235

先生，当着众人在场

我否认自己的行为心怀恶意，

Free me so far in your most generous thoughts

That I have shot my arrow o'er the house

And hurt my brother.

240 **Laertes**   I am satisfied in nature,

Whose motive in this case should stir me most

To my revenge; but in my terms of honour

I stand aloof, and will no reconcilement

Till by some elder masters of known honour

245   I have a voice and precedent of peace

To keep my name ungor'd. But till that time

I do receive your offer'd love like love

And will not wrong it.

Hamlet   I embrace it freely,

And will this brothers' wager frankly play. —

250   Give us the foils.

Laertes   Come, one for me.

Hamlet   I'll be your foil, Laertes. In mine ignorance

Your skill shall like a star i'th' darkest night

Stick fiery off indeed.

Laertes   You mock me, sir.

250 **Hamlet**   No, by this hand.

King   Give them the foils, young Osric. Cousin Hamlet,

You know the wager?

Hamlet   Very well, my lord.

Your Grace has laid the odds o'th' weaker side.

King   I do not fear it. I have seen you both,

260   But since he is better'd, we have therefore odds.

希望您的大度能对我宽恕，
只当我是箭力过猛误伤了
隔壁弟兄。

雷厄提斯　　　　　　要论感情我已满足，　　　　　　　240
它本应激起我最强的复仇之心；
但就荣誉而言我却无法接受，
我要等待某些德高望重的
长辈宣布类似的和解先例，
确保我的荣誉未受损失，　　　　　　　　　245
才愿意跟您和解。　可在此之前，
我把您给我的友爱当作友爱，
且不会予以慢待。

哈姆雷特　　　　　　　　我欣然接受，
也愿和这位兄弟真诚地比赛。　——
把剑拿来。　　　　　　　　　　　　　250

雷厄提斯　来，给我一把。

哈姆雷特　我是您的陪衬，雷厄提斯。我的
剑术浅陋，您的技艺会像黑夜的
星辰光彩夺目！

雷厄提斯　　　　　　您嘲笑我，先生。

哈姆雷特　没有，举手发誓。　　　　　　　255

国王　给他们剑，小奥斯瑞克。　哈姆雷特侄儿，
您了解赌注吧？

哈姆雷特　　　　　　非常清楚，陛下。
陛下把赌注押到了弱者一方。

国王　我不怕。　我见过你们俩的剑法，
可人们说他更好，才让几个回合。　　　　　260

Laertes		This is too heavy. Let me see another.
Hamlet		This likes me well. These foils have all a length?
Osric		Ay, my good lord. [*They prepare to play.*]

[*Enter Servants with*] *flagons of wine.*

	King	Set me the stoops of wine upon that table.
265		If Hamlet give the first or second hit,
		Or quit in answer of the third exchange,
		Let all the battlements their ordnance fire:
		The King shall drink to Hamlet's better breath,
		And in the cup an union shall he throw
270		Richer than that which four successive kings
		In Denmark's crown have worn—Give me the cups—
		And let the kettle to the trumpet speak,
		The trumpet to the cannoneer without,
		The cannons to the heavens, the heaven to earth,
275		' Now the King drinks to Hamlet. ' Come, begin.
		And you, the judges, bear a wary eye.
	Hamlet	Come on, sir.
	Laertes	Come, my lord. [*They play.*]
	Hamlet	One.
280	**Laertes**	No.
	Hamlet	Judgment.
	Osric	A hit, a very palpable hit.
	Laertes	Well, again.
	King	Stay, give me drink. Hamlet this pearl is thine.

雷厄提斯	这一把太重。 让我看看另一把。
哈姆雷特	我喜欢这把。 这些剑一样长吗？
奥斯瑞克	是的,好殿下。 ［二人准备比赛。］

［侍从端着］酒壶上。

国王	给我端几杯酒来放到桌上。	
	若哈姆雷特在前两回合击中,	265
	或在第三回合与对手持平,	
	就让所有的城墙将大炮点燃:	
	国王要为哈姆雷特的气势干杯,	
	他要向酒杯里投放一颗珍珠,	
	它要让丹麦四代世袭国王	270
	皇冠上镶嵌的珍珠相形见绌——	
	给我酒杯——让锣鼓对喇叭发话,	
	再让喇叭将外面的炮手召唤,	
	炮声告知于天,天再告知于地,	
	"国王现在要为哈姆雷特干杯。"	275
	快,开始! 你们裁判,可要看好。	
哈姆雷特	来吧,先生。	
雷厄提斯	来吧,殿下。 ［二人比剑。］	
哈姆雷特	一下!	
雷厄提斯	没有!	280
哈姆雷特	裁判!	
奥斯瑞克	击中了,这显而易见。	
雷厄提斯	好吧,再来。	
国王	等等,给我酒。 哈姆雷特,珍珠归你啦!	

---

261. 太重:雷厄提斯可趁机挑选一把开了刃的利剑,并涂上毒药(Gill)。

		Here's to thy health. *Drums; trumpets; and shot goes off.*
285		Give him the cup.
	Hamlet	I'll play this bout first. Set it by awhile.
		Come. [*They play again.*]
		Another hit. What say you?
	Laertes	I do confess't.
	King	Our son shall win.
290	**Queen**	He's fat, and scant of breath.
		Here, Hamlet, take my napkin, rub thy brows.
		The Queen carouses to thy fortune, Hamlet.
	Hamlet	Good madam.
	King	Gertrude, do not drink.
295	**Queen**	I will, my lord, I pray you pardon me.
		[*She drinks, and offers the cup to Hamlet.*]
	King	[*aside*] It is the poison'd cup. It is too late.
	Hamlet	I dare not drink yet, madam—by and by.
	Queen	Come, let me wipe thy face.
	Laertes	My lord, I'll hit him now.
	King	I do not think't.
300	**Laertes**	[*aside*] And yet it is almost against my conscience.
	Hamlet	Come for the third, Laertes. You do but dally.
		I pray you pass with your best violence.
		I am afeard you make a wanton of me.
	Laertes	Say you so? Come on. [*They play.*]
305	**Osric**	Nothing neither way.
	Laertes	Have at you now. [*Laertes wounds Hamlet; then,*]
		in scuffling, they change rapiers.

	为你的健康干杯！	锣鼓、号角响起；炮声隆隆。

　　　　　　把酒杯给他。　　　　　　　　　　　　　　　285

哈姆雷特　我先赛完这一回合。　放一会儿吧。

来吧。　［二人再次比剑。］

又击中了。　您说呢？

雷厄提斯　我承认击中。

国王　我儿要赢了！

王后　　　　　　　　他体力不支，还气喘。　　　　　290

过来，哈姆雷特，给你手帕，擦擦汗。

王后为你的成功干杯，哈姆雷特！

哈姆雷特　谢谢母亲！

国王　葛楚德，您别喝！

王后　我要喝，陛下，我请求您原谅。　　　　　　295

［饮酒，并把酒杯递向哈姆雷特。］

国王　［旁白］正是下毒的那一杯。　太晚了！

哈姆雷特　我现在还不敢喝，夫人——再等等。

王后　过来，让我给你擦擦脸。

雷厄提斯　陛下，我可要刺他了。

国王　　　　　　　　我不相信。

雷厄提斯　［旁白］可是我依然有些于心不忍。　　　300

哈姆雷特　第三回合，雷厄提斯。　您只是敷衍。

我求您使出自己的浑身解数。

可别把我当成小孩耍来耍去。

雷厄提斯　此话当真？　来吧！［二人交手。］

奥斯瑞克　两边都没中。　　　　　　　　　　　　305

雷厄提斯　您吃我一剑！　　　　［雷厄提斯刺伤哈姆雷特；然后，］

　　　　　　　　　撕打之中，二人交换了长剑。

	King	Part them; they are incensed.
	Hamlet	Nay, come again. [*He wounds Laertes.*] [*The Queen falls.*]
	Osric	Look to the Queen there, ho!
310	Horatio	They bleed on both sides. How is it, my lord?
	Osric	How is't, Laertes?
	Laertes	Why, as a woodcock to mine own springe, Osric.
		I am justly kill'd with mine own treachery.
	Hamlet	How does the Queen?
	King	She swoons to see them bleed.
315	Queen	No, no, the drink, the drink! O my dear Hamlet!
		The drink, the drink! I am poison'd. [*Dies.*]
	Hamlet	O villainy! Ho! Let the door be lock'd.
		Treachery! Seek it out. *Exit Osric.*
	Laertes	It is here, Hamlet. Hamlet, thou art slain.
320		No medicine in the world can do thee good;
		In thee there is not half an hour's life.
		The treacherous instrument is in thy hand,
		Unbated and envenom'd. The foul practice
		Hath turn'd itself on me. Lo, here I lie,
325		Never to rise again. Thy mother's poison'd.
		I can no more. The King—the King's to blame.
	Hamlet	The point envenom'd too! Then, venom, to thy work.
		[*Wounds the King.*]
	All	Treason! treason!
	King	O yet defend me, friends. I am but hurt.
330	Hamlet	Here, thou incestuous, murd'rous, damned Dane,
		Drink off this potion. Is thy union here?

国王	快拉开；他们发火儿了！	
哈姆雷特	不行,再来！［刺伤雷厄提斯。］［王后倒地。］	
奥斯瑞克	快照看一下王后,停！	
何瑞修	双方都在流血。　怎么回事,殿下？	310
奥斯瑞克	怎么回事,雷厄提斯？	
雷厄提斯	唉,像一只丘鹬落入自己的圈套,	
	奥斯瑞克。　我自作自受、罪有应得。	
哈姆雷特	王后怎么了？	
国王	见他们流血晕倒了。	
王后	不,不,是酒,是酒！　噢,我亲爱的	315
	哈姆雷特！是酒,是酒！我中毒了！［死去。］	
哈姆雷特	噢,罪恶呀！嗝！快把门锁上！	
	奸贼！把他搜出来！　　　　　　　奥斯瑞克下。	
雷厄提斯	是我,哈姆雷特。　你已经遇害。	
	世上没有药物能对你有用；	320
	你顶多还能活上半个钟头。	
	奸诈的凶器就在你的手中,	
	既锋利又有毒。　奸计落到了	
	我自己头上。　看,我已经倒下,	
	再也不能起来。你母亲中了毒。	325
	我说不下去了。　国王——都怪国王！	
哈姆雷特	剑头还有毒！那好,毒药,发威去吧！	
	［刺伤国王。］	
众人	反了！反了！	
国王	噢,保护我,朋友！我只是受了伤。	
哈姆雷特	你这个乱伦、残暴、该死的丹麦王,	330
	把这些酒喝了！你的珍珠在吗？	

Horatio   What is it you would see?

If aught of woe or wonder, cease your search.

Fort.   This quarry cries on havoc. O proud Death,

370   What feast is toward in thine eternal cell,

That thou so many princes at a shot

So bloodily hast struck?

1st Ambass.   The sight is dismal;

And our affairs from England come too late.

The ears are senseless that should give us hearing

375   To tell him his commandment is fulfill'd,

That Rosencrantz and Guildenstern are dead.

Where should we have our thanks?

Horatio   Not from his mouth,

Had it th'ability of life to thank you.

He never gave commandment for their death.

380   But since, so jump upon this bloody question,

You from the Polack wars and you from England

Are here arriv'd, give order that these bodies

High on a stage be placed to the view,

And let me speak to th'yet unknowing world

385   How these things came about. So shall you hear

Of carnal, bloody, and unnatural acts,

Of accidental judgments, casual slaughters,

Of deaths put on by cunning and forc'd cause,

何瑞修　　　　　　　您想看什么场景？

若是灾难与不幸,就不用再找。

弗廷布拉　这堆尸体意味着屠杀。　傲慢的

死神,你那永恒的幽窟要举办　　　　　　　　　370

什么酒宴,竟一下子残杀了

这么多贵人？

使臣甲　　　　　　　真是目不忍睹;

我们从英国带回的消息太迟。

本想告诉他的命令已经执行,

罗森克兰与盖登斯顿已被处死,　　　　　　　375

要听取汇报的耳朵却已失灵。

我们该向谁领取酬谢？

何瑞修　　　　　　　即使他

能够复活,也不会感谢你们。

因为他从未下令将他们处死。

既然您从波兰收兵,你们从　　　　　　　　　380

英国赶来,碰上这种残状,

请下令将这些尸体抬到高台

之上以便能让众人们瞻仰,

然后让我向莫名的世人讲述

事情的经过。　你们就可以了解　　　　　　　385

乱伦、血腥,以及无情的勾当,

有关上天的报应、意外伤亡,

阴谋和弄虚作假导致的死伤,

386-8. 乱伦……死伤:“乱伦”是指克劳狄斯与王后的婚姻;“无情”(见 1.5.25) 是指克劳狄斯的残害兄长。　波洛纽斯、哈姆雷特、雷厄提斯、克劳狄斯的死亡均属“血腥”。　“上天的报应、意外伤亡”是指波洛纽斯 (见 3.4.175-6)、雷厄提斯与王后的伤亡;“阴谋和弄虚作假导致的死伤”是指罗森克兰与盖登斯顿、以及哈姆雷特本人的伤亡 (Jenkins)。

And, in this upshot, purposes mistook

390 Fall'n on th'inventors' heads. All this can I

Truly deliver.

Fort.   Let us haste to hear it,

And call the noblest to the audience.

For me, with sorrow I embrace my fortune.

I have some rights of memory in this kingdom,

395 Which now to claim my vantage doth invite me.

Horatio Of that I shall have also cause to speak,

And from his mouth whose voice will draw on more.

But let this same be presently perform'd

Even while men's minds are wild, lest more mischance

On plots and errors happen.

400 **Fort.**   Let four captains

Bear Hamlet like a soldier to the stage,

For he was likely, had he been put on,

To have prov'd most royal; and for his passage,

The soldier's music and the rite of war

405 Speak loudly for him.

Take up the bodies. Such a sight as this

Becomes the field, but here shows much amiss.

Go, bid the soldiers shoot.

Exeunt marching, [*bearing off the bodies,*]

after which a peal of ordnance is shot off.

FINIS

以及最后是如何事与愿违，
策划者自食其果。　这些我都能　　　　　　　　390
如实宣讲。

弗廷布拉　　　　　　　赶快让我们听听，
也将大臣们召来充当听众。
我要忧伤地接受自己的幸运。
记得我在这个王国还有些权利，
此刻倒是我予以索取的良机。　　　　　　　　395

何瑞修　　关于这一点我也有话要说，
他的表态会激励更多人响应。
不过先让我澄清事情的真相，
因为此刻人们焦虑不安，以免
节外生枝又起祸殃。

弗廷布拉　　　　　　　让四名上尉　　　　　400
把哈姆雷特当成军人抬到台上，
因为假如他，能够加冕登基，
定会是一位贤明盖世的君王；
我们要奏军乐行军礼，对他的
去世深表哀悼。　　　　　　　　　　　　　405
快把尸体抬起。　这样的景况
适合于战场，可在此却不恰当。
去，让士兵们鸣炮！

　　　　　　　　　　　行军齐下，［尸体抬出，］
　　　　　　　　　　　　随之炮声隆隆。

剧　终

389-390. 事与愿违……自食其果：参见本场 312-3，323-4，332-3。 尽管此处特指克劳秋斯与雷厄提斯两人最终的阴谋诡计，但这自然也是该剧的首要主题；具体而言，可体现在罗森克兰与盖登斯顿两人的命运方面（3.4.208-9），一般而言，可体现在全剧有关凶杀与复仇的情节方面（3.2.206-7）（Jenkins）。

参考文献

1. Harold Jenkins, *Hamlet*, The Arden Shakespeare, London：Methuen & Co. Ltd，1982.

2. Alan Durband, *Hamlet*, Shakespeare Made Easy, Barron's，1986.

3. A. C. Bradley, *Shakespearean Tragedy*, New York：Macmillan Press Ltd.，1992.

4. Cyrus Hoy, *Hamlet*, William Shakespeare, Norton Critical Edition，1992.

5. Roma Gill, *Hamlet*, Oxford School Shakespeare, 外语教学与研究出版社，1997.

6. Carla Lynn Stockton, *Hamlet*, Cliffsnotes, New York：Wiley Publishing Inc.，2000.

7. Lamb Sidney, *Shakespeare's Hamlet*，Cliffs Complete. New York：Hungry Minds Inc.，2000.

8. Sparknotes, *Hamlet*, New York：Sparknotes Publishing，2002.

9. David Bevington, *Four Tragedies*, *Shakespeare*, Bantam Classic，2005.

10. Jonathan Bate, *William Shakespeare*, Complete Works, RSC，外语教学与研究出版社，2008.

11. Corum Richard, *Understanding Hamlet*（《哈姆雷特解读》），中国人民大学出版社，2008.

12. Ann Thompson, *Hamlet*, The Arden Shakespeare，中国人民大学出版社，2008.

13. 周兆祥，《汉译〈哈姆雷特〉研究》，（中国香港）中文大学出版社， 1981。

14. 许渊冲，《翻译的艺术》（论文集）， 中国对外翻译出版公司，1984。

15. 卞之琳，《哈姆雷特》（莎士比亚悲剧四种）， 人民文学出版社， 1988。

16. 陆谷孙，《英汉大词典》，上海译文出版社，1993。

17. 裘克安，《哈姆雷特》， 商务印书馆， 1998。

18. 彭镜禧，《哈姆雷》，（中国台湾）台北经联出版社， 2001。

19. 方平，《哈姆雷特》（新莎士比亚集）， 河北教育出版社，2001。

20. 梁实秋，《哈姆雷特》（莎士比亚四大悲剧）， 中国广播电视出版社， 2002。

21. 朱生豪，《哈姆雷特》（莎士比亚喜剧悲剧集）， 译林出版社，2002。

22. 辜正坤，《中西诗比较鉴赏与翻译理论》，清华大学出版社，2003。

后 记

翻译《哈姆雷特》的起因，可以说在很大程度上是出于偶然。 2002年春，译者去北京出差期间，在外文书店买回几本由外研社与牛津大学出版社联合出版、页边附有详细注解的莎士比亚原著，其中包括《哈姆雷特》（Roma Gill，1997）。 将该剧读了几遍之后，于当年秋天，作为西气东输郑州监理分部的英文翻译，去安徽利辛出差期间又有幸在书店看到了朱生豪先生的译本。 当时只是凭印象觉得译文在形式及内容方面都与原文存有一定的差异，便情不自禁地产生了能否将该剧重新翻译的念头。随后又将该剧重读几遍，然后便于 2003 年 3 月初，参照朱生豪先生的译文，开始了翻译尝试。

在翻译过程中，又有幸发现了梁实秋、卞之琳与方平先生的汉语译本。 同样有幸的是，2003 年 4 月调入宁波大学后，又在图书馆发现了由Harold Jenkins 先生编著的 《哈姆雷特》 （The Arden Shakespeare，*Hamlet*，1982）；随后便将该版本定为译文的首要蓝本。 2008 年暑假去北京出差期间，又从中国人民大学出版社发现了由 Ann Thompson 女士主编的阿登版的最新版本（The Arden Shakespeare， *Hamlet*， 2008）。同年，译者的好学生何才玲同学又将其研读用的贝文顿版《四大悲剧》赠予译者（David Bevington， 2005）。 2010 年夏，译者又发现了由 Jonathan Bate 先生主编、英国皇家莎士比亚剧团所推出的《莎士比亚全集》（*William Shakespeare Complete Works*， 2008）。 可以说，每增添一种新的原文版本，译者都会依照其中的注释对自己的译文修改一遍。

回想起来，自从 2003 年初自己决定重译《哈姆雷特》至今，已有十个年头了。 由于自己才疏学浅，又不自量力，其间所面临的困难与挑战可想而知！但值得庆幸的是，他非常荣幸地得到了众多专家、教授及师友们的殷切指教与热情相助。 首先，非常感谢我国莎学前辈裘克安教授。

裘教授通过信函与当面教诲就国内外莎学研究、翻译现状以及译者自己的译文等方面均给予了许多指教与关爱。　其间，译者也非常荣幸地得到了我国莎学专家辜正坤教授的深切指教与鼓励。　辜教授还在百忙之中应邀为本书撰写了序言，就莎剧的汉译及本译文的特点等从宏观的高度给予了具体的指教与褒扬，令译者不胜荣幸与感激。　译者也非常感谢中国台湾大学外文系的彭镜禧教授所给予的关爱与帮助，彭教授将自己亲自翻译的《哈姆雷》一书赠予译者，译者在拜读之后获益匪浅。

　　非常感谢河南人民出版社译文处的刘玉军先生为该剧的翻译提供了许多富有建设性的意见、信息、关心与帮助。　同时，译者还要衷心感谢香港中文大学的刘宓庆教授，河南大学的王宝童教授，安阳师范学院中文系的刘根源恩师，宁波大学外语学院的许希明教授、杨成虎教授、卢植教授、于善志教授、王松林教授、于应机教授等众多朋友与同事。　非常感谢浙江大学宁波理工学院的吴会芹好友与魏健师友。　魏健老师从头至尾将译文检阅一遍，不仅指出了译者自以为是的许多错字、别字，而且还在译文的改进与编排等方面均给予了真诚而具体的指教与帮助。　当然，译者也不应忘了感谢吴秀琼女士，因为她不仅为译文提出了许多批评性的意见，而且还为译者的整个翻译过程提供了可靠的后勤保障。

　　另外，译者还要衷心感谢美国亲友——Mrs. Gladys Fancher 女士，她专门为译者选取并寄来多种有关《哈姆雷特》剧作的原文读本。　美国明尼苏达大学的莎剧专家兼演员——Michael Kissin 教授帮助译者解答了许多有关该剧的疑难问题，并捎来许多有关莎氏语言、文体及舞台演出等方面的论著。　最后，译者还要感谢美国芝加哥大学的著名莎学专家 David Bevington 教授，因为他也非常及时并热情地帮助译者解答了一些困扰其多年的疑难问题，令译者感到非常荣幸和庆幸。　上述各位专家、教授、亲友与同事均在译文的翻译、修改、编排与出版等方面给予了极大的关心、支持与帮助，译者谨在此深表感激与谢意！谢谢！谢谢！！

李其金

2012 年 4 月

图书在版编目(CIP)数据

哈姆雷特：英汉对照／（英）威廉·莎士比亚著；
李其金译. —杭州：浙江大学出版社，2020.4
（莎士比亚四大悲剧合集）
ISBN 978-7-308-19749-6

Ⅰ.①哈… Ⅱ.①威… ②李… Ⅲ.①悲剧—剧本—
英国—中世纪—英、汉 Ⅳ.①I561.33

中国版本图书馆 CIP 数据核字(2019)第 271131 号

李 尔 王

（英汉对照）

［英］威廉·莎士比亚　著

李其金　译

ZHEJIANG UNIVERSITY PRESS

浙江大学出版社

译 者 序

一、版本说明

本译文所采用的原文版本为最新的阿登版第三版《李尔王》[①]。 该版本的优点不仅在于它具有公认的准确性和权威性，还在于它附有详尽的脚注和精辟的导读，这些优点对译者和读者准确理解并欣赏该剧均可提供很大的帮助。 此外，译者在翻译过程中还参阅了另外四种原文版本和两种现代英语译本（见参考文献），并从原文中选取和翻译了大量的脚注。同时，译者在翻译过程中还参阅了我国译莎前辈梁实秋、朱生豪、卞之琳、孙大雨和彭镜禧先生的译文，并借鉴了他们的不少妙笔佳译。

二、翻译标准与原则

译文主要依照刘宓庆先生在其《翻译美学导论》中所倡导的翻译标准——翻译再现主要是借助于"内模仿"，即："'模仿'相当于'对应'，是审美再现的基本手段，翻译尤然。"（刘宓庆，2012：255）[②]译者在翻译过程中始终遵循了这一原则，并尽力使译文在形、音、意三方面能与原文一一对应。 具体做法请看下文三至五节中的详细说明。

---

① R. A. Foakes，《李尔王》，The Arden Shakespeare， Third Series，中国人民大学出版社，2008。

② 刘宓庆，《翻译美学导论》，第二版，中国出版集团公司，2012。

三、对原文无韵诗的模仿

就莎剧的行文形式而言，其中以无韵诗（blank verse）为主，这是一种没有韵脚却富有节奏感的诗体：一般是每行有五个音步，一个音步又有一轻一重的两个音节，即抑扬格，读起来抑扬顿挫、朗朗上口。据统计，《李尔王》剧中的韵文部分约占 75%。

"也许没有哪一部戏剧能像《李尔王》那样能令人聚精会神、心潮澎湃并充满好奇。"英国作家兼评论家约翰逊[①]在论及《李尔王》悲剧时曾说，"对各种利害关系的巧妙糅合，明显对立的正反面人物，命运的突遭变故，以及接二连三的事件，始终令人忐忑不安、充满义愤、深表同情和满怀希望。每一场都在促使人们痛苦加重或者采取行动，每一行又对本场的情节发展起到了引领作用。"（Ioppolo：170）[②]

下面就让我们以李尔在第一幕第四场里的两段无韵诗台词为例，请读者朋友先对原文的诗意美欣赏一番。

我们知道，李尔在开场时当众宣布了私下的计划：将国土分为三份赠送给三个女儿，以便"使老身摆脱所有牵挂和责任，/将它们交托给年轻一代，我好/轻松地爬向死亡"。然而，令他始料未及的是，他最为疼爱的小女儿考迪丽娅，却未像两位姐姐那样信誓旦旦地当众表达对父亲的孝心，这让李尔颜面尽失，一怒之下竟剥夺了她的继承权利，并与她断绝了父女关系。随后，李尔与他的随从便按计划先搬到长女贡纳丽家里居住。也许像贡纳丽所说的那样，李尔这个"没用的老头儿，/他依然想要行使自己的权力，/尽管已经放弃"（1.3. 17-9），因此他跟贡纳丽及其家人之间的矛盾与冲突逐渐加剧，最后竟使李尔恼羞成怒、忍无可忍。下面选取的两段台词就是李尔在遭到贡纳丽的慢待和责备之后所进行的回击：

---

① 约翰逊（Samuel Johnson）：英国作家、评论家、辞书编撰者（1709—1784），编有《英语词典》《莎士比亚集》等。

② Grace Ioppolo，*King Lear*，New York：A Norton Critical Edition，2008.

[*to Goneril*]　　Detested kite, thou liest.	[向贡纳丽]可憎的老鹰,你胡说!
255 My train are men of choice and rarest parts	我的随从都是难得的精英,　　255
That all particulars of duty know,	他们知道自己的具体职责,
And in the most exact regard support	并且都在一丝不苟地维护着
The worships of their name.	自己的尊荣。
…………	…………
Hear, Nature, hear, dear goddess, ᶠhearᶠ:	听着,造化,亲爱的女神,听着:
Suspend thy purpose if thou didst intend	假如你曾有意让这个东西
To make this creature fruitful.	生儿育女,请你改变主意!
270 Into her womb convey sterility,	你要使她的子宫无法孕育,　　270
Dry up in her the organs of increase,	使她的生育器官完全枯干,
And from her derogate body never spring	使她堕落的躯体永远生不出
A babe to honour her. If she must teem,	可荣耀她的婴儿! 若定要生产,
Create her child of spleen, that it may live	就让她孩子暴戾,好让它活着
275 And be a thwart disnatured torment to her.	并变得固执无情把她折磨。　　275
Let it stamp wrinkles in her brow of youth,	让她那年轻的额头布满皱纹,
With cadent tears fret channels in her cheeks,	让她的面颊被落泪冲出沟槽,
Turn all her mother's pains and benefits	将她母亲的全部疼爱和欢欣
To laughter and contempt, that she may feel	化为轻蔑和嘲笑,好让她感受
280 How sharper than a serpent's tooth it is	忘恩负义的孩子造成的伤痛　　280
To have a thankless child. Away, away! (1. 4)	比遭蛇咬还糟! 快走,快走!

英国文学评论家布拉德利(A. C. Bradley,1851—1935)在论及《李尔王》的一大显著特点时曾说,"剧中不断地提及低级动物以及它们与人类之间的相似之处;这种特点只有《雅典的泰门》可与之相提并论。 这种情况在剧中随处可见,好像莎士比亚对该主题念念不忘:要是有哪一页未对此加以提及,他就无法写下去似的。 诸如狗、马、牛、羊、猪、狮子、熊、狼、狐狸、猴子、鸡貂、灵猫、鹈鹕、猫头鹰、乌鸦、寒鸦、鹪鹩、苍蝇、老鼠、青蛙、蝌蚪、壁虎、蝾螈、虫子等等。 ……剧中有时会或明或暗地将某人与其中的某一动物相比。"①(Bradley:227-8)

---

① A. C. Bradley, *Shakespearean Tragedy*, New York:Macmillan Press Ltd., 1992.

从上述引文中可以看出，对李尔来说，贡纳丽现已成了一只"可憎的老鹰"，她的忘恩负义所造成的伤痛比蛇咬还糟。她还有"狼一般的嘴脸，她像一只秃鹰，把无情的利喙拴在父亲的胸膛；对她的丈夫来说，她是一条花蛇；在格洛斯特看来，她的无情就像獠牙。她和李根都是狼心狗肺，她们是猛虎，不是女儿；她们相互警惕，好像对方就是毒蛇；她们两人都披上了一层兽皮。奥斯华德是个狗杂种，趋炎附势，一只蠢鹅。对李根来说，格洛斯特是一只忘恩负义的狐狸。……对我们来说，好像所有畜生的灵魂都进入了这些人的体内；他们的恶毒、野蛮、淫念、欺骗、懈怠、残酷、肮脏令人可怕；而他们的软弱、赤裸、无助、盲目又令人可怜"（同上：228）。

另外，至于是什么力量在主宰着这个世界，竟造成了《李尔王》中这么巨大的痛苦和损失，布拉德利在谈及这一点时曾说："至于这种问题，不用我们来问，因为剧中的角色也都在问。而且，该剧对宗教信仰的提及也超过了莎士比亚的其他悲剧，其中所提及的频率也许能跟他最后所创作的剧本相提并论。他还让不同的角色在提及命运、星辰或神灵时的用语各具特色，表明他们心里都不禁在问'是什么力量主宰着这个世界'。比如，他们对该问题的回答分别是：

肯特 这是星辰(the stars)，/天上的星辰决定了我们的人品。 （4. 3. 33-4）

埃德蒙 自然啊(nature)，你是我女神；你的法则/我有义务遵循。 （2. 1. 1-2）

格洛斯特 神明(the gods)待我们就像顽童待苍蝇，/以杀死我们为乐。 （4. 1. 38-9）

埃德加 想必是最公正的神灵（the clearest gods）救了你，/ 他们能制造奇迹受人敬重。 （4. 6. 73-4）

从上述四行台词中我们不难看出，就主宰世界的力量而言，他们四人各有自己的看法。"（同上：232-3）另外，值得注意的是，李尔在上述台词中所祈求的神明跟埃德蒙所祈求的神明竟毫无二致，即"造化（nature）"和"女神（goddess）"；其间的区别仅在于"李尔是把'自然'祈求为一种创造性的力量（creative force），但他那种可怕的诅咒却会使自然变得违反自然，因此几乎让自己与埃德蒙同流"（Foakes：208）。

同时，我们也不难看出："大多数比较善良的角色，在贯穿于该剧的后半部里，都会对主宰世界的终极力量这一问题非常专注，并急于用它去解释各种反常的现象，不然他们就会感到绝望。 他们对该问题的专注及其心理需要，连同其他方面的影响，会令人产生的一种印象是，该剧跟《神曲》和《奥赛罗》多少有些相似。"（Bradley：235）

然而，"对但丁来说，《神曲》所记录的却是上帝的正义和爱。 那么《李尔王》又为莎士比亚记录下了什么呢？ 两者之间仿佛截然相反。 莎士比亚在该剧中向人们展示了最为可怕的画面。 在其他任何一部悲剧中，人类好像都没有脆弱得这么可怜，或者是坏得这么无可救药。 与格洛斯特的儿子和李尔的女儿们的无情相比，伊阿古对一位令他嫉妒的外人所怀有的恶意又算得了什么？ 奥赛罗作为一条硬汉所遭受的痛苦能与无助的老人所遭受的痛苦同日而语吗？"（同上：235）

自此，我们通过几位莎学专家的相关评述已对本段台词进行了一番观赏和领悟，并对原文的某些显著特征有了一个比较清晰的了解和认识。 下面再让我们看看译文针对原文的"形美、音美和意美"所作的模仿。

针对原文无韵诗的模仿而言，应该说，译文尽力做到了"在双语可译性限度内，充分保留了原语的行文形式体式（stylistic format）。 例如，诗歌中的格律和韵律、韵式和分节式……以及其他的行文形式特征，例如不能将分行诗译成不分行的散文，等等"（刘宓庆：186）。

因此，译者根据莎剧原文的特点，遵照我国译莎前辈所倡导的"以顿代步"的翻译原则，在尽量忠实地再现原文"意美"的前提下，采用"三控"原则，也尽力对原文的行文形式与内在韵律进行了模仿。 具体措施为：

（1）严格控制全剧译文的行数，以使译文的行数与原文的行数完全相等。

（2）严格控制每行译文的字数，以此做到与原文的音节数量尽量相等：每行译文大都为十一字或十二字。

（3）尽量控制每行译文的顿数，以此模仿原文的行文形式与内在格律，从而再现原文应有的"形美"与"音美"效果：每行译文大都为五顿。

另外，译文除了在行文形式与内在格律方面尽量对原文进行了模仿以外，还尽力发挥了汉语诗歌的谐韵优势，使译文押了一些散韵或句中韵，因为"谐韵除了使诗句平添音乐性之外，还使读者产生期待、产生共鸣、产生满足。 韵律使读者的审美意识处于积极的活跃状态，是使作者与读者达至审美体验'融合'的一种催化剂。 从翻译美学上分析，这是不少人主张译诗必须押韵的原因"（刘宓庆：80）。

四、对原文押韵诗的模仿

《李尔王》剧中除了无韵诗之外，还有傻子以及装扮成疯乞丐的埃德加所哼唱或吟诵的歌谣等。 就此而言，译者也力求对原文中的韵式做到一一对应。

我们知道，剧中的傻子是一位职业弄臣，"尤其是在第一幕里，其作用主要是以概括性的韵文和歌谣为李尔'捧场'；有时也会直接对观众讲话，因为老国王这位巨人如此独断专行、动辄暴怒，傻子因此可在观众与国王之间成为一种纽带。 傻子可被视为是闪电的导体，将君王的威力接地，使李尔变得富有人性。 起初，李尔主要是充当傻子的配角，因为相比之下，傻子在智力方面要略胜一筹，能看出李尔的分封王国会带来什么样的后果，以及由此显现出的愚蠢：'如今你成了前面没数字的零蛋；我现在都比你强。 我是个傻子，你啥都不是'（1. 4. 183-5）"（Foakes：57-8）。 但等到李尔在第二幕第二场末尾发疯以后，直到第三幕第六场结束之前，"傻子的评论主要是针对诸如肯特和观众的，其韵文和歌谣主要表达了一种民间的智慧"（同上：58）。 例如，在第二幕第二场里，受国王委派去见李根的信差——肯特竟被锁进了足枷，国王认为这种奇耻大辱"比凶杀还糟"；当时在场的傻子针对肯特的这种遭遇顺口吟诵了下面一段韵文：

Fathers that wear rags	父亲若破衣烂衫，
Do make their children blind,	子女会不管不问，
But fathers that bear bags	父亲若腰缠万贯，
Shall see their children kind:	子女会格外孝顺：
Fortune, that arrant whore,	命运，臭名的娼妇，
Ne'er turns the key to the poor.	从不把穷人眷顾。（2. 2. 238-43）

其中，原文里的前四行为隔行押韵，后两行为对句。 译文也就此进行了相应的模仿。

另外，布拉德利在谈及《李尔王》中为数众多的人物时曾说："若抛开李尔、格洛斯特和阿班尼不论，其他人物可分为截然不同的两类：考迪丽娅、肯特、埃德加、傻子属于一类，贡纳丽、李根、埃德蒙、康瓦尔、奥斯华德属于另一类。……这边是无私和忠诚的爱，那边是无情的自私自利。而且，这两类人身上所共有的品性都达到了登峰造极的程度：爱不会因为受到伤害而变得冷淡，自私不会因为怜悯而有所收敛。"（Bradley：225）就此而言，一个颇有说服力的例证便是：贡纳丽、李根和康沃尔合伙将父王拒之门外，把他逼向了"方圆几英里以内难见树丛"的荒郊野外；正是肯特和傻子他们在狂风暴雨肆虐的黑夜陪伴着可怜的国王，始终不离不弃，从而"在他们身上体现出了一种'忠诚和奉献的完美典范'"（同上：275）。

五、对原文散文的模仿

我们都知道，除了无韵诗、歌谣、偶韵体、打油诗等文体之外，莎剧还有另外一种重要的组成部分——没有韵律的散文。剧中的不同角色或者同一角色之所以采用不同的文体，都与他们的身份、说话的对象、当时的心境或语境等因素密切相关。比如，埃德蒙在第一幕第二场里共有三段独白，其中的第二段独白便采用了散文形式，因为采用这种形式不仅可使他更加自如地对父亲的迷信思想加以嘲讽，也可使他为自己的玩世不恭进行辩解，从而"通过直接向观众表白而得到他们的同情"（Foakes：179）。

This is the excellent foppery of the world, that when we are sick in fortune, often the surfeit of our
120 own behavior, we make guilty of our disasters the sun, the moon and ᵠtheᵠ stars, as if we were villains on necessity, fools by heavenly compulsion, knaves, thieves and treachers by spherical predominance; drunkards, liars and adulterers by an enforced obedience of
125 planetary influence; and all that we are evil in by a divine thrusting on. An admirable evasion of

这可真是世界上最棒的愚蠢，当我们命运不济时，往往是因为自己的行为过分放纵，反而把我们的灾难归咎于 120 日月星辰，好像我们成为恶棍是迫不得已，犯傻是因为天意，无赖、盗贼、和叛徒是因某个星球左右；我们酗酒、撒谎和通奸是因为不得不顺从天体的支配；我们的一切罪恶行径都是上天 125 强加给的。这是好色之徒一种绝妙的

whoremaster man, to lay his goatish disposition on the charge of a star. My father compounded with my mother under the dragon's tail and my nativity was 130 under Ursa Major, so that it follows I am rough and lecherous. ᑫFut!ᑫ I should have been that I am had the maidenliest star in the firmament twinkled on my bastardizing. (1. 2. 118-33)

借口，要把他自己的好色性情怪罪于星星负责。我父亲在天龙座的降交点与我母亲交媾，我就是在那大熊星座下面降生，因此我自然就是既粗野又 130 好色。狗屁！播下我这野种时，哪怕空中最为贞洁的星星在闪烁，我依然会是现在的我。

　　布拉德利在谈到埃德蒙的这一段独白时曾说："尽管埃德蒙与伊阿古明显不同，却常会令人想起他们之间的相似之处；他的那段独白'这可真是世界上最棒的愚蠢'，跟伊阿古论及'意志的权威'时所采用的腔调一模一样。"（Bradley：209）此外，埃德蒙与伊阿古的相似之处还在于："他在勇气、意志力、谈吐、利己主义、异常的无情、有幽默感方面也会令人想起他的老前辈。……但埃德蒙显然要比伊阿古年轻许多。他的性情也更为轻快、更为肤浅。……而且，他也更为直率。他之所以能令人称奇并感到恐怖只是因为他这么年轻，品质却如此恶劣，实在令人费解。埃德蒙是一位纯粹的和单纯的冒险家。他的行动都带有目标，而且他若有什么喜爱或者厌恶，也都会置之不理。他下决心要飞黄腾达，首先要占据兄长的土地，然后——随着机会的拓展——戴上王冠；在他看来，男男女女，无论高尚还是卑鄙，连同亲情、友情、或者忠诚，对他的目标来说只不过是一种障碍或者帮手。……当然，埃德蒙的私生子身份并不能成为他作恶多端的借口，但这一点或多或少地会影响我们的感情。那不是他的过错，他却因此被视为另类。他是大自然的产儿——自然会为了自身的权益跟社会秩序抗争；他在这种秩序中被拒绝赋予一席之地。因此他便转向大自然表示忠心，因为自然的法则是强者生存；他也不承认那些社会道义，因为它们只是一种'恶俗'或者'过分挑剔'而已。"（同上：262-3）

　　我们已借助布拉德利先生的相关评述，对埃德蒙所处的社会背景及其性格特征有了一个比较清晰的了解和认识。下面再让我们回顾一下原文中的诗文和散文的编排形式。

　　不难看出，莎剧中的无韵诗与散文之间除了内在的韵律存在着区别，在编排格式上也有明显的不同，即每行无韵诗的第一个单词的首字母均为大写，而且右边也没有顶格或分散对齐。 然而，每行散文的第一个单词的首字母（除特殊情况外）均无须大写；而且，若某个角色的台词长度在两行以上，自第一行起至倒数第二行为止均为左右分散对齐，以此来区分诗文与散文之间的外在差异。

在这一点上，译文也试图与原文予以对应：以每行十六个汉字对应原文十二个左右的音节。 另外，若某个角色的台词在两行以上，自第一行起至倒数第二行为止均为字数相等、整齐划一（不包括行末的标点符号），以使诗文与散文之间的差别一目了然。

另外，考虑到"翻译是一种时空跨度很大的语际转换活动。 历史的演变和社会文化的发展可使原语成为很难为当代人透彻和准确理解的'化石'"（刘宓庆：192），因此，"时空差产生艺术鉴赏的不等效，古今同理。 ……地缘之隔也必然会产生审美体验上的差异"（同上：137）。由此我们不难想象，中国的莎剧读者和观众与伊丽莎白时代的莎剧读者和观众之间会有多大的时空差异。 不过，鉴于"审美主体与客体之间的关系是能动的、交互的、实践的关系"（同上：138），为了帮助读者对原文进行更好的审美体验，也为了能够充分再现原文的蕴涵之美，审美主体（译者）可尽力发挥其主观能动性，即为读者架设一座跨越时空、跨越文化、跨越语言障碍的桥梁——为译文增加详尽的脚注。

据此，译者依照五种原文版本的相关评注甄选并翻译了大量的注解，并附上各自的出处以便于查阅。 就本段台词而言，译者从三种原文注解中至少选取并翻译了下列四处脚注：

118. 最棒的（excellent）：此处意为"讥讽"（Foakes）。 120-1. 把我们的……星辰（make…stars）：埃德蒙此处将父亲有关预兆的言论扩展到了人们对占星术的信仰——人的一生是由他们出生时日月星辰所处的位置掌控（Mowat）。 128. 天龙座的降交点（dragon's tail）：即月球向南移动时，其轨道与黄道相交的节点（此时易出现日食）（Bevington）。 129. 大熊星座（Ursa Major）：即"Great Bear"，因此"粗野和好色（rough and lecherous）"；该星座也可代指北斗七星（Foakes）。

好了，亲爱的读者朋友，译者已对自己的译文详细地标榜了一番。

但同时他也非常清楚，由于学识所限，文中的缺点和谬误在所难免。 敬请读者朋友批评指正！

写到这里，本该自然收笔才是；但译者却有一项夙愿：希望这个译本能够帮助读者朋友更好地学习和欣赏原文！ 因此，译者很想在此节外生枝：在最后译完的四大悲剧中的《李尔王》里，跟读者朋友分享一下如何更好地阅读和朗诵莎剧。 译者于 2015 年秋在莎士比亚故乡访学期间，曾有幸看过一本《读莎教程》（*Teaching Reading Shakespeare*）①，也做了一些笔记。 现请允许译者根据自己的笔记和体会，结合四大悲剧中的实例，看一看该如何阅读莎剧。

六、阅读莎剧

我们必须承认，阅读莎剧原文确实会存在着某些困难；因为与现代英语相比，莎剧中的句式结构相对复杂，其中的某些词汇现已变成了废词。 也许，这就是为什么同学们常会以单数第二人称代词"thou ［ðaʊ］"和"thee ［ði:］"为例，来证明莎剧的阅读是多么困难。 其实，我们也大都知道"thou"意为"你"，是主格形式，而"thee"是"thou"的宾格形式，这一点并不难掌握；困难主要在于它后面所跟的动词形式会有所变化，比如：现代英语中的第二人称单数"you are"，在莎剧中则为"thou art"；现代英语中的第二人称单数"you have"，在莎剧中则为"thou hast"。 实际上，这种动词形式的变化也很有规律可循，熟悉了就好了。 有关第二人称单数（thou）后面所跟的动词形式将在下文第 2 节中列出，以供读者朋友参考。

另外，之所以有不少读者和同学觉得阅读莎剧高不可攀，部分原因可能是误以为莎剧是用古英语写的。 其实，剧中所使用的语言是属于 15 世纪中叶至 18 世纪中叶的近现代英语（**Early Modern English**），而不是流行

---

① John Haddon, *Teaching Reading Shakespeare*, London & New York：Routledge, 2009.

于公元 5 世纪至 11 世纪中叶的古英语（Old English），也不是流行于 14 世纪中叶至 15 世纪中叶的中古英语（Middle English）。 现以《圣经》"马太福音"第 6 章中的前几节主祷文（the Lord's Prayer）为例，分别以古英语、中古英语和近现代英语将其排列如下，以供读者朋友对照：

Fæder ure þu þe eart on heofonum；	Oure fadir that are in heuenes,	Our Father which art in heaven,
Si þin nama gehalgod	halewid be thi name；	Hallowed be thy name.
to becume þin rice	thi kyngdoom come to；	Thy kingdom come.
gewurþe ðin willa	be thi wille don,	Thy will be done,
on eorð an swa swa on heofonum.	in eathe as in heuene.	In earth as it is in heaven.

从上述三种文体中不难看出，古英语和中古英语跟现代英语之间差异巨大，而莎剧所采用的近现代英语已跟现代英语几乎毫无差异。 当然，剧中的语言与现代英语还是存在着一些差异。 下面就让我们具体看一看莎剧的语言特色及其与现代英语之间的主要差异。

1. 第二人称代词（you，thou，thee，thy，thine）

在近现代英语里，"you（您）"被语言学家称为"无标记体（un-marked form）"，属于寻常的称谓，不会引人注意，适用于地位相同的人士之间；而"thou（你）"则被称为"标记体（marked form）"，表明该称谓与众有所不同，因为它既可表示诸如朋友或情人之间的亲密，也可表示跟地位低下的人谈话时感到有所屈尊等。 比如，在《哈姆雷特》第一幕第二场里主要人物首次亮相时，克劳狄斯国王对哈姆雷特采用了比较正式的称谓"you（您）"，而他的母亲则采用了更为亲切的"thou（你）"：

King	How is it that the clouds still hang on **you**？	您这人怎么依然阴云笼罩？
Hamlet	Not so， my lord， I am too much in the sun.	不，陛下，我倒受不了太阳的热乎儿。
Queen	Good Hamlet， cast **thy** nighted colour off，	好哈姆雷特，快脱掉你的黑衣，
	And let **thine** eye look like a friend on Denmark.	你要把丹麦国王看成朋友。
	Do not for ever with **thy** vailed lids	不要总是用你那沮丧的目光
	Seek for **thy** noble father in the dust.	去追寻你已经入土的慈父。
	Thou know'st 'tis common：all that lives must die，	你知道这很普通：活着的必死，
	Passing through nature to eternity.	都要通过世间进入永恒。

我们可从王后的上述台词中看出："thou（你）"的所有格形式分别为："thy（你的）"用于辅音开头的词前；"thine（你的）"用于元音开头的词前。

再如，《哈姆雷特》第五幕第一场里，当雷厄提斯发现妹妹奥菲丽娅的葬礼过分简单时，便采用了表示轻蔑的称谓——"thou"和"thee"，以此向主持仪式的神父表达了不满之情：

Laertes	I tell **thee**, churlish priest,	我告诉你，吝啬的神父，
	A minist'ring angel shall my sister be	你躺在地狱哀号时，我妹妹将是
	When **thou** liest howling.	救护的天使！

值得注意的是，you 和 thou 之间的上述区别在现代英语中已不复存在，尽管这种区别在其他语言里还依然活跃。关于 you 和 thou 之间的更多区别，请参见《李尔王》序言4～5页中所列的其他例证。

2. 词形之间的区别（Morphological Differences）

创作于四百多年以前的莎剧，其中的某些词语的形式与现代英语有所不同也属自然。掌握这一点对读懂原文和欣赏原文都会有所帮助。这种变化或不同主要体现在动词的词尾方面，而且这种不同也仅限于第三人称单数（he, she, it）跟第二人称单数（thou）之间。用于第三人称单数的动词形式多以"-eth"结尾，用于第二人称单数"thou"的动词形式多以"-est"结尾。比如：

动词（verbs）	第三人称单数（he, she, it）	第二人称单数（thou）
To be	He is	Thou art
	He was	Thou wast
To do	He doth	Thou dost
	He did	Thou didst
To have	He hath	Thou hast
	He had	Thou hadst
To say	He says	Thou say'st / sayst
	He said	Thou said'st
To give	He gives	Thou giv'st
	He gave	Thou gav'st

续表

动词（verbs）	第三人称单数（he，she，it）	第二人称单数（thou）
Will	He will	Thou wilt
	He would	Thou wouldst
Shall	He shall	Thou shalt
	He should	Thou shouldest
Can	He can	Thou canst
	He could	Thou couldst
Might	He might	Thou might'st
	To rain	It raineth

除了上述列出的系动词、助动词、情态动词和部分常用动词的词尾有所不同之外，还有极少数单词的形式与现在的词形不同，如：whither = where， thither = there， hither = here， ere（读作"air"）= before 等。

另外，莎剧中还有一些常见的感叹词（语），尽管现已很少使用，如：

fie = an expression of disgust or reproach（表示厌恶或责备）

marry = a mild oath（委婉的咒语）

Alack！= desperation，regret（绝望，懊悔）

Ay me = sorrow，pity（哀伤，遗憾）

Ha！= triumph，surprise（得意，惊讶）

Out！= reproach，indignation（责备，义愤）

Pish！= impatience，contempt（厌烦，轻蔑）

3. 缩约形式（Contraction）

其实，缩约形式的使用在现代英语中也相当普遍，比如：it's，don't， won't， can't， aren't， weren't 等。 人们之所以采用缩约形式也许是出于偷懒、不拘礼节、节奏变化或强调等。 这种缩约形式在莎士比亚时代也很普遍，理由相同。 莎剧里常见的缩约形式有：'tis = it's， i' = in， 't = it， o' = of／on， th' = the， o'er = over， ne'er = never 等。 例如《麦克白》中的：

Ross	In viewing **o'er** the rest **o' th'** self-same day, (1. 3)	查看当天的其他平叛战况时，
Macbeth	If it were done, when **'tis** done, then **'twere** well	行动若能干净利落，那最好
	It were done quickly. If **th'** assassination (1. 7)	还是速战速决。 若这次暗杀

此外，采用缩约形式的另一个原因是需要向五步抑扬格诗行里填充意义或思想，比如：麦克白在第五幕第五场里，听到信差报告说伯南树林好像在移动——巫婆预言麦克白行将灭亡的预兆之一，他"有些丧失信心，并且开始怀疑恶魔那模棱两可的鬼话，以假乱真"，随后的四行台词便是：

Macbeth	I' gin to be aweary of the sun,	我已开始对人生感到厌倦
	And wish **th'** estate **o' th'** world were now undone.	并希望整个宇宙混乱不堪。
	Ring the alarum bell! Blow wind, come wrack,	敲响警钟！ 风吹吧，毁灭来吧，
	At least we'**ll** die with harness on our back. (5. 5)	死去时我身上至少要穿着铠甲。

从上述诗行中可以看出，若不采用缩约形式而将"'gin"还原为"begin"，结果则会由原来的一个音节变为两个音节；同理，若将随后的诗行还原为"And wish **the** estate **of the** world were now undone"，则会由原来的十个音节扩展为十二个音节，由此将固有的节律打乱。

4. 否定式和疑问式(Forms of Negative and Interrogative)

现代英语的否定式需要借助系动词一起构成，而莎剧里的否定式常把"not"直接放在动词的后面，如：

Horatio	In what particular thought to work I **know not**,	对此我也不知该从何说起，
	(*Hamlet*, 1. 1)	
Edgar	Leave, gentle wax; and manners, **blame** us not.	对不起，尊贵的封蜡；恕我无礼。
	(*King Lear*, 4. 6)	
Othello	I **found not** Cassio's kisses on her lips;	看不出凯西奥曾吻过她的嘴唇；
	(*Othello*, 3. 3)	
Banquo	To me you **speak not**. (*Macbeth*, 1. 3)	对我却沉默。

下面再看一看莎剧中疑问式的构成方式：常以动词的直接前置，或以疑问词直接加上主谓语的倒装构成，不需要借助于助动词"do"。 如：

Lady	**Know you not**, he has?	叫了，您不知道？
	(*Macbeth*，1.7)	
Brabantio	Why? **Wherefore ask you** this?	为啥？ 您为啥问这？
	(*Othello*，1.1)	
King	**Have you** your father's leave?	您父亲答应吗？
	What says Polonius?　(*Hamlet*，1.2)	波洛纽斯怎么说？
Edmund	Himself. **What sayst** thou to him?	他本人。 对他有啥可说？
	(*King Lear*，5.3)	

5. 倒装 (Inversion)

在读莎过程中，我们还常会遇到的另一种语法现象就是倒装（Inversion）；要是让我们排列句中的语序，往往会有所不同。 在下列两种情况下常会出现语序倒装的形式：

（1）当一个句子以副词、副词短语或介词短语开头时，往往会采用倒装：

Lady	When Duncan is asleep,	邓肯入睡后，
	Whereto the rather shall his day's hard **journey**	白天的路途劳顿会使他更快
	Soundly **invite** him,　(*Macbeth*，1.7)	酣然入眠，
Macbeth	If't be so,	若是这样，
	For Banquo's issue have I filed my mind;	为班柯的子孙我玷污了灵魂；
	For them, the gracious Duncan have I	为了他们，杀害了慈祥的邓肯；
	murdered;　(*Macbeth*，3.1)	
Edmund	And **hardly shall I** carry out my side,	我对她许下的诺言很难兑现，
	(*King Lear*，5.1)	

其中,第一例以副词短语"Whereto the rather"开头,所以采用了倒装;正常的语序应为:his day's hard journey shall the rather (= the sooner) invite him soundly (to be asleep)。第二例中的两句均以介词短语"For"开头,所以也采用了倒装。第三例以副词"hardly"开头,故采用了倒装。正

常的语序应为：and I shall hardly carry out my side。就此而言，莎剧中的倒装形式跟现代英语之间并无区别。

（2）当句中的宾语被放在句首时也会采用倒装。这种倒装可能是为了强调：

Lady	**his two chamberlains**	他的两名侍卫，
	Will I with wine and wassail so convince,	我会用酒宴把他们完全制伏，
	（*Macbeth*，1. 7）	

有时也可能是为了与上文所说的内容保持一种联系而将宾语前置，采用倒装。 比如，奥赛罗终于明白了自己上当受骗的真相之后自杀身亡，就像副官凯西奥所担心的那样：

| Cassio | **This did I fear**，but thought he had no | 我就怕这样，本想他没有武器， |
| | weapon，（*Othello*，5. 2） | |

6. 意象（Metaphor）

若想细致深入地阅读莎剧，还应该了解的一点就是剧中经常出现的明喻和暗喻。 前者显而易见，因为它们常以介词 like 和 as 表示；但后者却不然，因为它们在莎剧中通常并不是用来装点门面的，而是思想和感情中所固有的，是言语的组成部分，与上下文密不可分。 比如，麦克白在第五幕第五场里听到夫人的死讯后所说的下列台词：

She should have died hereafter;	她早晚都会死的；
There would have been a time for such a word.	这样的消息到时总会传来。
Tomorrow，and tomorrow，and tomorrow,	明天，接着明天，接着明天，
Creeps in this petty pace from day to day,	就这样一天一天地匍匐向前，
To the last syllable of recorded time;	直到最后一个音节记录在案；
And all our yesterdays have lighted fools	所有的昨天都为傻瓜照亮了
The way to dusty death. Out，out，brief candle,	入土的归途。 熄灭吧，短暂的烛光！
Life's but a walking shadow，a poor player,	人生只是个走影，可怜的演员，
That struts and frets his hour upon the stage,	在台上怒气冲冲，趾高气扬，

And then is heard no more. It is a tale　　　然后销声匿迹。　白痴讲述的
Told by an idiot, full of sound and fury,　　故事而已，充满了喧嚣与狂暴，
Signifying nothing. (*Macbeth*, 5. 5. 16-27)　没有任何意义。

就句法和喻义而言，本段台词都相当复杂难懂，因为隐喻里面又有隐喻：他首先感到人生就像一次旅程（a journey），然后又将意象发展为一部手稿（a manuscript）、一台戏剧（a stage play）、一篇故事（a narration）；其中，又采用呼语法将人生称为一根蜡烛（a candle）。

麦克白在闻听心爱的夫人死去之后，也是在该剧即将结束的时刻发出了上述感慨，他所采用的意象大都非常直观，犹如一幅幅图画，对全剧所要表达的意义十分重要。

另外，《奥赛罗》里有许多关于孕育的丑陋意象（monstrous conception and birth），《哈姆雷特》里充满了有关疾病的意象（metaphors of disease），《李尔王》里则有许多关于畜生的意象（images of beasts），这些意象都值得我们多加注意和深入研究。

7. 典故 (Allusion)

每个人都会用典，只是我们对此并未留心而已。　莎剧里的典故大都出自古希腊或古罗马的经典作品，以及基督教信仰。　这些知识可从阅读荷马史诗和《圣经》中积累或了解。　出自《圣经》中的引文有时会带有某种特殊的教义。　这种引文的指向也许会相当明确，比如《麦克白》第一幕第二场里，那位"满身血污的"上尉向邓肯国王描述麦克白和班柯的英勇顽强时所说的那样：

Captain　Except they meant to bathe in reeking wounds,　　除非他们想在血泊中沐浴，
　　　　Or memorize another **Golgotha**, (1. 2)　　　或让人铭记另外一处各各他

其中，"Golgotha（各各他）是指"骷髅地（place of a skull）"，基督在此被钉死在十字架上，为救赎人类的罪过而献身。　具体经文请见"马可福音"15 章 22 节。

　　有时，引文的指向并不明确，如《李尔王》第一幕第一场里，考迪丽娅并未像两位姐姐那样当面向父王表达孝敬的心声，从而遭到了李尔的厌弃和勃艮第公爵的嫌弃。 此刻，同样是前来向考迪丽娅求婚的法兰西国王却从中看到了她的价值和美德：

France　　Fairest Cordelia, that art **most rich being poor**, 最美的考迪丽娅，贫穷却最富，

　　　　　　Most choice forsaken and most loved despised, 被抛弃但最精美，受鄙视最可爱，

　　　　　　（1. 1）

　　其中，"most rich being poor（贫穷却最富）"可令人想起《圣经》中有关基督的论述，即"哥林多后书"6 章 10 节："poor, yet making many rich; having nothing, and yet possessing everything（似乎贫穷，却叫许多人富有；似乎一无所有，却样样都有）"。 由此可见，上述两例都或明或暗地指向了耶稣基督。

　　又如，精通古典文学和希腊神话的哈姆雷特，"使用意象的方式在莎剧中可谓独一无二。 他一旦开始讲话，各种意象宛如溪流一般从他的脑海自然涌现。 ……同时，哈姆雷特所使用的意象也表明他的教育背景非常广泛"①。 比如他在第三幕第四场里为赞美天神般的父亲顺口所引用的四种典故：

Hamlet　　See what a grace was seated on this brow, 看看这位是何等的眉清目秀，

　　　　　　Hyperion's curls, the front of **Jove** himself, 太阳神的卷发，朱庇特的前额，

　　　　　　An eye like **Mars** to threaten and command 战神一般的眼睛威风凛然，

　　　　　　A station like the herald **Mercury** 他的身姿就像信使墨丘利

　　　　　　New-lighted on a heaven-kissing hill, （3. 4） 刚刚落到高吻苍穹的山巅，

　　其中，"Hyperion"是指希腊神话中的太阳神，他大概拥有一头金色的卷发，故如此比喻。 "Jove"即朱庇特（Jupiter），罗马神话中统治众神的主神。 "Mars"即罗马神话中主管战争之神，可能怒目而视，威风

---

① Wolfgang Clemen, *Shakespearean Criticism*, Detroit：Gale Research Company, p. 189，1984.

凛然。 "Mercury"即众神的信使墨丘利，以其身姿优美而著称，源自罗马神话。 若将文中所引用的这些典故删去，定会影响它的分量；但若能借助于简短的脚注对这些典故加以了解，其意义或寓意则并不难懂。

七、剧本朗诵

提起剧本朗诵（Play Reading），译者首先想与读者朋友分享一段个人的经历：译者在莎士比亚学院访学期间，曾有幸参加过学院组织的剧本朗诵活动。 该活动于周四晚上 7 点钟开始，由教师预先指定一部或两部较短的剧本，大都是莎士比亚同时代的剧作家的作品，如：韦伯斯特①的《马尔菲公爵夫人》（*The Duchess of Malfi*），格林②的《修士培根与修士邦吉》（*Friar Bacon and Friar Bungay*）等。 参加人员 20 名左右，有学院的老师、在校学生和当地的退休人员等；剧中的角色由老师或某个学生负责分派，若遇剧中人物较多时，有人可能会同时担任几个角色。颇感惭愧的是，译者一开始竟没有勇气承担任何角色，只是旁听而已。等后来开始担任某个配角时，又由于紧张和读得可能比较卖力，读完一段台词后额头不禁冒出汗来。

当大家读到约半个剧本时，就会停下来休息 20 分钟左右；其间还会品尝参加人员自愿带去的红酒。 大约需要 3 个小时将一部剧本读完。 令译者印象深刻的是，他们朗诵得抑扬顿挫、声情并茂，仿佛是在进行演出前的彩排，听起来真是一种享受。

现在回到我们的主题——剧本朗诵。 至于如何才能做到抑扬顿挫、声情并茂地朗诵莎剧，说实在的，译者对此困惑已久，因为他仅仅知道剧中的台词大都是由五步抑扬格组成的无韵诗行，但并不清楚具体该怎么朗诵。 因此，译者便给曾有幸认识的英国皇家戏剧艺术学院前院长兼导演

① 韦伯斯特（John Webster）：英国剧作家（1580？—1625？），以其悲剧《白魔》和《马尔菲伯爵夫人》著称。

② 格林（Robert Greene）：英国剧作家（1558—1592）、诗人和散文家，以对莎士比亚的攻击而闻名；其作品对同时代的剧作家，如马洛和莎士比亚，都产生了不小的影响。

巴特（Nicholas Barter）先生写信请教。 译者根据自己的理解，将麦克白在上述第"3"节里的四句诗文（I'gin to be…our back.），按照规范的五步抑扬格的方式将格律标出，请求指教。 现将巴特先生回信的主要内容翻译如下：

"等到莎士比亚创作《麦克白》时，他对五步抑扬格中的扬音（stresses）的处理已更为自由。 因此，您对第一行诗文的标示是对的（因为它符合规范），但另外三行需要根据意义加以重读。 演员不必按照严格的抑扬格式，他们需要重读关键词语。 莎士比亚的创作风格越到后期越发自由。 若按您所标示的那种方式加以重读，意义不通（To stress as you have written the line would not make sense）！"

另外，为了让笔者更好地了解应如何正确地朗诵莎剧，巴特先生还特意推荐了英国莎剧著名导演巴顿先生的一本专著——《莎剧表演》（*Playing Shakespeare*），尤其是其中的第二章：诗行的运用（Using the Verse）。① 现在就允许笔者摘译书中的部分内容，以期能对读者朋友更好地朗诵莎剧有所帮助或启迪：

"莎剧中的绝大多数台词都是诗文（verse），或是激昂华丽的散文（heightened rhetorical prose）。 无韵诗（blank verse）可能是伊丽莎白时代文化传统中的中心，也许是莎剧演员需要接受的最大挑战。 ……

莎士比亚的诗行有时会被称为五步抑扬格（iambic pentameter），这是个可怕的用语，我尽量避而不用。 不过，它只是指这种无韵诗主要是轻音和重音之间的转换，其基本节律是：'de dum de dum de dum de dum de dum（嘚嗒 嘚嗒 嘚嗒 嘚嗒 嘚嗒）'，共十个音节，轻重音交替，五个轻音，五个重音。 这就是无韵诗的规范，其节奏最接近我们自然的日常会话（natural everyday speech）。 实际上，这种无韵诗在我们的日常会话中，在书刊里或者电视里可谓俯拾即是。 比如，18世纪的女

———————————

① John Barton, *Playing Shakespeare*, Anchor Books, A Division of Random House, Inc. New York, 2001.

演员西登斯夫人①对她所点的饮料而发表的评论：

'I asked for porter and you gave me beer. '　　　　'我点了麦酒您却给我啤酒。'

又如狄更斯的小说，《大卫·科波菲尔》的结尾：

'O Agnes， o my soul， so may thy face　　　'噢，艾格尼丝，我的心肝，愿你
Be by me when I close my life indeed. '　　　在我临终时能够与我相伴！'

为什么无韵诗这种诗形（verse-form）这么适合于戏剧台词呢？ 证明这一点的最好方式也许是看两处莎士比亚之前的戏剧所采用的诗形。 下面是节选自神迹剧②中的几行诗文：

'All hail! All hail! Both blithe and glad!　　　'恭喜！恭喜！高兴又快乐！
For here come I， a merry lad!　　　　　　　　我已来到，欢乐的小伙儿！
Pray cease your din my master bade　　　　　　主人吩咐您别再吵闹，
Or else the devil will you speed. '　　　　　　否则您快到地狱报到。'

　　　　　　　　　　（*The Killing of Abel*）　　　　　　　　　　（《亚伯之死》）

这是打油诗，不是台词。 每行有八个音节、四个重音，比我们日常的谈话节奏稍短。 再让我们听听另外一种节奏：

'O doleful day， unhappy hour that loving　　'噢，悲伤的日子，不幸时刻，可爱的孩子
　　child should see　　　　　　　　　　　　　竟目睹
His father dear before his face thus put to　　他那亲爱的父亲在他面前惨遭杀戮！
　　death should be!
Yet father， give me blessing thine， and　　可是父亲唉，你给我祝福，让我再次拥抱
　　let me once embrace

①　西登斯夫人（Sarah Siddons）：英国悲剧女演员（1755—1831），尤以扮演麦克白夫人而出名。
②　神迹剧（miracle play）：中世纪时期的一种戏剧，以《圣经》中的圣母及圣徒们的事迹为题材。

| Thy comely corpse in folded arms, and | 你那健美的尸体，亲吻你饱经沧桑的 |
| kiss thy ancient face!' (*King Cambises*) | 面孔！'　　　（《冈比西斯国王》）① |

这也不算是台词，不过是嬉耍的歌谣而已（rollicking jingle）。 每行有十四个音节和七个重音，对我们通常的会话节奏来说，显得太长和呆板。 相比之下，每行有十个音节的无韵诗，则更接近我们真实的会话方式。 实际上，莎士比亚常把它用作自然会话的载体，比如安东尼奥的 'In sooth I know not why I am so sad（真不知道我为何这么难过）'。（《威尼斯商人》，1. 1）

我说过无韵诗的规范格律是：

dĕ dum dĕ dum dĕ dum dĕ dum dĕ dum

但事实上往往并非如此，有时候它会符合规范，但更多的时候却不合规范。 比如《亨利五世》中的下面一行就不符合规范：

HENRY V: Once more, unto the breach, dear friends, once more (*Henry V*，3.1)

若将该诗行的格律标示为规范的五步抑扬格，即：

Once more, unto the breach, dear friends, once more 再次冲向豁口，亲爱的朋友，再次，

这样读起来一点都不自然。 显然这不是剧作家的本意。 那么，如何朗诵才算自然呢？

Once more, unto the breach, dear friends, once more 共有七个重音。

莎士比亚为啥会这么做呢？ 那好，我们可扪心自问亨利五世为啥会这么做呢？ 他是何意？ 那就是想说服他的士兵向城墙的豁口再次发起冲锋。 一位疲倦、气喘吁吁的将领竭力想使其士兵重整旗鼓。 这一点可在其超乎寻常的重读音节中得以加强。 该例证也很好地体现了莎士比亚对演员的潜在指示（hidden direction）——如何运用无韵诗行。

我想以此说明的是，类似无韵诗的格律是不确定的（neutral）。 莎

---

① 选自英国剧作家普雷斯顿（Thomas Preston：1537—1598）的作品：《冈比西斯国王之悲剧》（*Lamentable Tragedy*：*Cambises*）（1569）。 主要讲述了古波斯帝国国王——冈比西斯二世的生平。

士比亚是靠诗行的格律变化达到他的戏剧效果。 他首先确立一种规范（de dum de dum de dum de dum de dum），需要增加重音时再将规范打破。 **'Once more** unto the **breach， dear friends， once more'** 是一种非常有力的诗行，因为它有额外的重音。 其中有七个重音，而不是五个。 额外的重音强化了亨利对士兵们的恳求和敦促。 我们再看看接下来的几行诗文（其中，上标的 '˘' 为轻音， '—' 为重音；而且上标的横线越长，表明该音节的音值越重——译者附注）：

Once more unto the breach, dear friends, once more, 　　再次冲向豁口，亲爱的朋友，再次，

Or close the wall up with our English dead ! 　　否则用我们英军的尸体封堵！

注意本行里对 'wall up' 的连续重读。

In peace there's nothing so becomes a man 　　和平时期最适合一个男人的

本行是符合规范的诗行。

As modest stillness and humility; 　　莫过于适当的节制和谦卑；

本行也相当规范，只是有四个重音，而不是通常的五个。 另外，由于其中有分量的词语较少，重读的音节便会引起格外的注意。

But when the blast of war blows in our ears, 　　然而当军号在我们耳畔响起，

本行也是规范的诗行，只是 'blow' 被放在了非常规的位置（offbeat position），即本该为弱拍的位置，因此需要特别重读。

Then imitate the action of the tiger: 　　我们就该像虎狼那样行动：

本行也相当规范，只是由一个弱音节结尾，关于这一点我们随后再谈。

Stiffen the sinews, conjure up the blood, 　　就要让肌肉绷紧，热血沸腾，

其中， 'Stiffen' 和 'conjure' 被放在了非常规的位置，需要重读。这种做法增强了亨利恳求的急迫性。

Disguise fair nature with hard-favoured rage.　　凶恶的狂怒掩盖善良的天性。

其中，'fair'与'hard-favoured'之间的对照通过重读予以显现，两词都被放在了非常规的位置。

你们是否已明白了无韵诗如何发挥作用（how blank verse works）？所谓的五步抑扬格不过是莎士比亚大致遵循的一种规范，然而当某个重要的词语被放在弱拍的位置（offbeat）而不是常规的位置时，就会有额外的重音不断出现。　这种情况下，我们所遇到的节奏就会是'dum de'，而不是'de dum'。　因此我们可以说莎士比亚对无韵诗的使用方式是，先确立一种规范，然后再不断打破。

David Suchet（参加座谈的一位演员。　因本书的主要内容及编排方式是导演和演员之间的对话，旨在探讨如何表演莎剧——译者附注）：如此说来，若想正确地应对无韵诗，我们需要知道在一行诗里哪该重读，哪不该重读。　但我们怎么才能确信这一点呢？

我想可从两方面做到这一点。　首先，常识十之八九会告诉您答案。不妨问问自己的日常会话是怎么根据意义加以重读的，而实际上您并未考虑轻重音的辨析问题。　再看一看这一行：

Disguise fair nature with hard-favoured rage

其中的重读无疑都比较自然。　第二，您若心存疑虑，还有一种比较保险的准则：寻找长元音，寻找复合元音。　您若慢慢地发出这些声音，就会听到它其实是两个音，而不是一个：'fair,' 'hard,' 'rage.'。　所有的长元音通常都会重读，很少会有例外。

我们再看看另外一例：

To be, or not to be, that is the question;　　活着，还是死去，这是个难题；

Whether 'tis nobler in the mind to suffer　　哪种选择更为高贵：是甘心忍受

The slings and arrows of outrageous fortune　　残暴命运的那些飞石流箭，

Or to take arms against a sea of troubles　　还是奋起搏击无边的苦海

ˇ — ˇ — ˇ — ˇ —
And by opposing end them. (*Hamlet*：3. 1)　　通过反抗了却一切？

在第二和第三行里，只有四个重音，而不是五个。 请注意前四行的每行结尾处都有额外的第十一个音节。 这种音节被称为双音韵（或阴韵）（feminine ending）。 这种额外的音节总是弱读，而不是重读，这也是给每位无韵诗作者的一种特许。"（Barton：27-34）

好了，亲爱的读者朋友，以上是译者所列出的有关莎剧的语言特色及其与现代英语之间的主要区别，以及如何才能比较准确地朗诵莎剧里的无韵诗台词。 希望它们能对您更好地理解和学习原文有所帮助！ 同时也衷心希望读者朋友都能爱上莎剧，并由此受益终身！

谢谢！

李其金

2018 年 12 月

序　言
（节选）

　　作为莎士比亚的竭力想象而结出的硕果，《李尔王》就像巨人一般矗立在他创作成就的中央。　就其涉及的社会阶层而言，它涵盖了从国王到乞丐的整个社会，我们的想象需要穿梭于皇家的宫殿和荒野的茅屋之间。情绪变化的幅度则从极端的暴怒到李尔与考迪丽娅重归于好时的柔肠寸断。　通过李尔的被迫面对狂风暴雨，以及格洛斯特的眼睛在舞台上被挖出的场景，该剧明确地记录了由于人的惨无人性而给人带来的极度痛苦。该剧在毫不吝惜地讲述了人类的无情和悲惨的同时，也意味深长地描绘了人类的善良、奉献、忠诚和自我牺牲。　通过傻子的评论、可怜的汤姆之"疯"话，以及李尔和格洛斯特在患难中获取的洞察，该剧生动地揭示了人类的愚蠢、贪婪和堕落。　它具有田园诗和传奇般的色彩，令人想起道德剧，其主人公达到了"史诗般的"高度，这些特点及其丰富的想象，还有它的语言和意象，促使许多人按照普世的价值观念将该剧视为患难者的精神之旅。

　　很久以来，人们认为该剧不适合演出，要么因为它所展示的残酷和痛苦令人难以接受，要么因为它所涉猎的范围过于宏大。　内厄姆·泰特（Nahum Tate）曾对该剧进行改写从而赋予它一种皆大欢喜的结局，致使 1681 年至 1834 年之间的所有舞台演出均以此为准。　将该剧视为莎士比亚"最伟大的杰作"但"过于宏大而不宜演出"——这种观点一直持续到 20 世纪。　第二次世界大战结束后的数十年里，人们才逐渐认可《李尔王》是一部伟大的舞台戏剧；近来演出不断，也拍摄了几部影片以供影院和电视台放映。　在集中营、凝固汽油弹、杀伤性地雷以及人们均已耳熟的恐怖主义行动的背景下，剧中所揭露的那种令人可怕的折磨和痛苦已不再显得惨不忍睹。　它对权威、正义和生存需要的质问可在当今社会的关注中找到共鸣；李尔、格洛斯特和埃德加被社会抛弃并变得穷困潦倒的情况也可令人联想到现今的人们对老龄和贫穷的焦虑。……有些人好像认为该剧表现了一种虚无主义，觉得它并未表现出人生是一种潜在的英雄般的旅程或朝圣，而是逐步走向绝望或虚无而已。《李尔王》能够引起如此相互冲突的解读，可表明该剧既有很强的生命力，又可提供各种各样的可能性。

<h2 style="text-align:center">创作日期
（Date）</h2>

该剧很可能创作于1605—1606年之间，尽管没有直接的证据表明何时创作，或何时首演。

<h2 style="text-align:center">故事来源
（Principal Source）</h2>

在莎氏借鉴有关李尔的故事之前，该故事已以多种版本存在。莎氏有可能，但我觉得并不一定，曾查阅过该故事最为古老的版本——（威尔士编年史家）杰弗里（Geoffrey of Monmouth）所编撰的《不列颠帝王史》（*Historia regium Britanniae*）（1135），因为他必须阅读该书的拉丁语手稿。书中记述了已显老迈的李尔（Leir）对女儿的爱心测验，决定为她们寻找配偶。Gonorilla 和 Regan 分别嫁给了亨纽纳斯（Henuinus）——康瓦尔公爵，和马格劳纳斯（Maglaunus）——阿班尼公爵，他们每人分得了半个王国，而高卢（法兰西）国王——阿格尼帕斯（Aganippus）追求并娶了没有嫁妆的考黛拉（Cordeilla）。后来等李尔身体虚弱时，两位公爵谋反并剥夺了李尔的王权；最初允许他拥有六十名侍卫，但 Gonorilla 和 Regan 将他们削减得只剩一名，李尔便在这名侍卫的陪护下去了法国，得到了伤心的考黛拉的安慰。阿格尼帕斯集结了一支军队，跟李尔一起回到了英国，击败了那两位女婿，李尔恢复王位并统

治了三年，随后由考黛拉继位。 她统治了五年，后被 Gonorilla 和 Regan 的儿子们推翻，投入监狱，最后自杀。

尽管该故事后经各种各样的改写，但故事的梗概基本相同，均以李尔恢复王位，考黛拉继位、后被推翻并自杀而告终。 莎氏很可能读过霍林西德的《编年史》中的相关记述（1. 446-8），该书出版于 1587 年，是莎氏创作历史剧的依据。

其他来源还应包括希金斯（John Higgins）的《治理通鉴》（*The Mirror for Magistrates*）（1574），斯宾塞（Edmund Spenser）的《仙后》（*Faerie Queene*）（1596）。

《李尔王》的阅读与演出
(*Reading and Staging King Lear*)

你(莎士比亚)走得如此匆匆令人吃惊，

从世界舞台,走向寂静的后庭。

以为你已离去,可你这些墨宝

却告诉观众,你又迈起了双脚,

入场于喝彩之中。演员的技能

会荒疏,演好角色则可以长生。

（J. M.，"纪念威廉·莎士比亚先生"，第一版对开本,1623）

我们的职责只是为你们收集他的作品,而不是将他称颂。你们的责任就是读他。因此我们希望,你们会根据各自的能力,从中发现足够的内容能够吸引你们、留住你们;因为他的才智不会丢失,也无法遮掩。因此,要读他,一遍,又一遍。

（约翰·海明吉与亨利·康德尔，"前言"，第一版对开本,1623）

戏剧拥有双重的生命:头脑里可以阅读,舞台上可以演出;阅读一部戏剧和观看它的演出是两种不同的经历,但同样有效和有用。 莎士比亚的演员同仁将其作品收集在第一版对开本里以供读者阅读，而且后来的编辑也都把读者记挂在心；即便是供演出用的脚本也需要先进行阅读。 曾有一种评论思潮认为，"真正的戏剧是演出，而不是文本（real play is the performance, not the text）"。 在我看来，我们所阅读的文本同样也是"真正的戏剧"，或许就像我们观看舞台演出那样，在自己的脑海里表演出来；剧本就是导演和演员从编者为他们提供的阅读文本中为演出而编写的东西。 《李尔王》可谓是一个特例，因为出现在第一版对开本（1623）里的剧本跟出现在第一版四开本（1608）里的剧本在许多细节方面均有不同，两个文本里都有一些台词并未出现在另一个文本里面；因此我们才会就同一部戏剧拥有不同的文本。 此版本包含了两个文本中出现的所有段落，若该内容只出现在四开本里（Quarto），便在该内容的前后用上标的"Q"标示；若该内容只出现在对开本里（Folio），则在该内容的前后用上标的"F"标示。 该版本的宗旨有三：首先，让文本的编辑方式能使读者明白两个文本之间的关系并意识到因为文本的差异而导致的问题；其次，帮助读者想象剧中的某些行动该如何表演；再者，就该剧的如何表现和阐释提供各种各样的可能。

　　一部戏剧在人们头脑里的生命可能与它在舞台上的生命有很大区别。《李尔王》的篇幅很长，也比较复杂，将该剧完整地演出的情况相当少见，通常会通过删减、重新编排或者改写后再搬上舞台。 1608 年出版的四开本的扉页上声称该剧的文本"曾在白厅献演于国王陛下面前"，上演时间为 1608 年 12 月 26 日晚；但是四开本里所刊印的这一版本很可能源于一部从未用于演出的手稿。 1623 年出版的第一版对开本里有不少变化和修改，好像是莎士比亚剧团从 1608 年以后为了重演所作的修改。 然而，除了有证据表明该剧曾于 1610 在约克郡上演过以外，直到查理二世复辟后又于 1664 年重演，在此期间没有别的演出记录。

　　尽管该剧篇幅较长且较为复杂，但它的排演要求却相对简单。 它只需要一些普通的道具如：信件、钱包、兵器、火把和椅子，还有一些不太常用的如：一张地图、一顶小型冠冕和供肯特使用的足枷，这都是一些普通的器物。 对暴风雨的某些展现也是需要的，在英王詹姆斯一世时期的舞台上，雷鸣可通过擂鼓或在金属板上滚动铁球予以模仿，而闪电则会通过燃放小鞭炮予以仿效。 埃德蒙曾在 2.1.20 呼喊哥哥"下来吧"；这是剧中唯一一处表明需要有个阳台或高于舞台的某个地方。 至于可怜的汤姆在 3.4.37 从中出现的"茅屋"，只要用舞台上的一扇门即可表示。该剧也很好地利用了直观的动作和视觉效果：队伍、打斗、化装、火把、兵器、死亡、酷刑（弄瞎格洛斯特的眼睛），甚至是想象中的悬崖坠落等，全是为了像环球剧院那种露天舞台而设计的，以此为观众提供不同且往往是激动人心的情节和场景，而无须舞台布景或现代化的照明。

　　观众站在或坐在舞台的三边（左、右、前），跟舞台非常接近，也跟演员使用同一种照明，因此演员和观众之间的关系相当亲密。 莎剧的创作目的是为了让观众通过耳朵获取消息，接受教育（比如讲道），以及娱乐；许多观众都是文盲，当时也没有报纸。 在视觉文化越来越盛行的当下，我们很难想象凭借倾听舞台对白中那些雄辩的韵文和散文即可令人激动不已，这种娱乐吸引着数以千计的伦敦市民前往剧院。 《李尔王》的情节扣人心弦，容易听懂，然而现代技术手段的缺乏意味着剧中的气氛，观众对地点、时间、外景的感知，以及人物的意念和情绪，大都需要通过对白加以领会。 莎士比亚对语言的运用表明他期望自己的观众里面能包括许多有文化的听众，他们能够明白剧中的双关语、悖论和语义的细微差别。 他也期望观众能注意到复杂的隐喻和意象，还有一些新造的词语等。

　　针对文本的评注主要涉及此类内容。 莎士比亚使用语言的其他方面若在此考虑一下也许会更为有益，因为这些方面不易被人注意。 我们对人人平等这种观念已习以为常，而且都是以"您（you）"相称；莎士比亚会在剧中利用某些差异来反映他的世界。 最明显的做法就是，他会通过在人物之间分配韵文和散文的方式来区分他们的社会地位和情绪状态。他还会通过语言的运用表达人与人之间的关系亲疏，就本剧而言，他充分利用了"你（thou）"和"您（you）"之间的微妙差别："你（thou）"既可暗示对亲朋的喜爱，也可表示上级对下级的好感，又可表示说话者对级别相同的人心怀敌意；而"您（you）"却是一个普通和更为折中的称谓。 比如，李尔于2.2见到李根时，最初对她使用了表示慈爱和恳求的"你（thou）"，希望能得到她的善待，但当他意识到李根与贡纳丽一样对他心怀敌意时，便改用表示疏远的"您（you）"（见2.2. 383）。 肯特与奥斯华德在2.2开场争吵时彼此之间以"你（thou）"相称，以此表达了他们的敌意；埃德蒙和埃德加在5.3相互挑战时彼此之间也是这样称谓。 贡纳丽对埃德蒙的感情不能自已时送上了一吻；此前她对他都是以"您（you）"相称，此后便以表示亲爱的"你（thou）"相称，"你才配得上女人的献身"（见4.2.22和27）。 本场的晚些时候，当阿班尼与贡纳丽争吵时，他们便从日常的"您（general 'you'）"改称为"你（thou）"，以此表示夫妻之间的怨恨之情。

莎士比亚的语言与当代的普通用语之间的最大差异也许在于它的丰富多彩、信息密集和灵活多变（richness, density and flexibility）；这种叠加的结果就是对其含意的阐释似有无限的可能。 ……剧中与看见、瞎眼和洞察（seeing, blindness and insight）有关的意象具有突出的意义，它们都与主题相关，……剧中多次提及了动物并把人贬低成畜牲，象征着如果将人们的衣服扒光，"人就会贱如牲畜"（2.2.456）。 另外，剧中还有两种语言特色也与主题相关。 其中之一可见于平铺直叙（plain speech）和辞藻华丽（rhetoric）之间的对比；该剧总体上偏向于坦率直言和朴素无华，然而，将平铺直叙视为得体，把辞藻华丽当作奉承或虚伪这种想法却应加以避免，因为肯特在2.2的直言不讳为他"赢得"了足枷刑罚，可以说为李尔帮了倒忙；然而李尔在第三幕暴风雨里的激情却只有通过慷慨陈词般的呼号才能予以表达。 第二种语言特色，与第一种特色相关，涉及言辞与意图，或言辞与行动之间也许存在着差距。 肯特最初曾提醒人们注意贡纳丽和李根的雄辩有可能华而不实——

> 愿你们华丽的言辞付诸实施，
> 好让甜言蜜语结出甜蜜果子。

（1.1.185-6）

——但李尔只是在经历了磨难之后才明白了言辞与行动之间存在着很大差

异（见1.1.55及注，和4.6.96-104）。

"让众神……搜出他们的仇敌"
(*Let the great gods…find out their enemies now*)

若强调李尔是一位国王，那么该剧所涉及的重点也许就是他本人的所作所为；若强调李尔是一位老人，那么该剧所涉及的重点也许就是人们对他的所作所为。

许多批评家将李尔视为人类的代表（representative of Man），从普通人群中提取并加以大写，遭受了读者和观众难以承受的苦难。……基督教阐释者则倾向于将该剧视为李尔个人的"朝圣"——探寻受难的人类，以圣洁的考迪丽娅为中介得以救赎的人生旅程。

诸如"朝圣（pilgrimage）""救赎（salvation）"之类的术语表明，该剧可令人想起基督教的某些教义，比如逆境中需要容忍和耐心这样的观念（见2.2.458-60和3.4.28-36及注），或者与绝望有关的念头（见4.6.33-4及注）。

同时，即使考迪丽娅在四开本里被赋予一种圣洁的光环，《李尔王》所明指的神灵却属于异教神明（pagan gods）。有人认为《李尔王》最初上演时所面对的观众大都是基督教教徒，他们可能会把该剧视为"关于异教徒世界的基督教戏剧（Christian play about a pagan world）"。……剧中的神灵可谓不可思议，好像对凡人的事情漠不关心，也许根本就不存在。

"你是我的血肉，我的女儿"
(*Thou art my flesh, my blood, my daughter*)

如果李尔这一人物在剧中占据着支配地位，无论他作为国王，作为可怜的老人，还是作为人类的代表，剧中还充满了其他形形色色的人物。尽管考迪丽娅出场不多且台词较少，她却占有重要的分量。若按主宰20世纪上半叶文艺批评的救赎主义学派（redemptionist）的阐释，考迪丽娅主要被视为李尔获得救赎的使然力（agent），并把她理想化为圣洁的人物，或是爱的化身。 若认为考迪丽娅代表着"纯洁的救赎热情"（a pure redeeming ardour），或是变成了"真理、公义、博爱的典范（perfection of truth， justice， charity）"，那就有可能在李尔终场时俯身死去的考迪丽娅的场景里找到"现世的圣母怜子图（secular Pietà）"——圣母玛利亚悲痛地抱着耶稣遗体的画面。

19 世纪的考迪丽娅扮演者们在其首次亮相中常因为可爱、天真和羞怯而受到赞许。 以这种方式扮演考迪丽娅倒是比较容易，假如她是一位灰姑娘式的人物，由两位邪恶的姐姐相伴左右。 20 世纪的导演和批评家们开始意识到剧中的开场意味深长：其中并未提供有关贡纳丽和李根年龄的任何线索，没有提及她们的母亲，也没有暗示一位 80 岁的君王为何或者如何会有一个才到适婚年龄的女儿，年轻得完全可做他的孙女，也没有解释李尔为何明显想让考迪丽娅嫁给勃艮第公爵。 他们也注意到了那种国家礼仪的正式性质，导致考迪丽娅拒绝向李尔公开表达自己的爱心。……父女之间应有的亲密关系被这种国家礼仪的正式性打断，因为那种场合要求国王与臣民之间保持距离。

至于贡纳丽和李根，也不必把她们演成纯粹的阿谀奉承者，而要把她们当成已婚妇女，嫁给了贵族丈夫，已经熟悉了宫廷生活及惯例。 剧中的开场越是显得正式，考迪丽娅对父王的回答就越有可能显得刚愎自用。

大家好像都知道考迪丽娅是李尔的宠儿，但她对国王的回答"没有，父亲"所体现出的对立姿态很可能令詹姆斯一世时期的观众感到吃惊。 ……如果人们期望国王的女儿首先应该顺从，并像贡纳丽和李根那样予以表达，那么考迪丽娅在开场时的言行就会显得肆无忌惮。

从一开始我们也许就能感觉到李尔的女儿们多么像他：考迪丽娅出乎意料地与他对抗，贡纳丽和李根一旦大权在握就对他横眉冷对。 对开本里有更多的诗行描述了李尔的一百名侍卫在贡纳丽家里的暴乱行为，这使得她对父亲的抱怨显得更为有理。 当然，即使她的言行有些道理，也不能成为她慢待父亲的理由；但李尔逐渐意识到，他从贡纳丽行使职权时的恣意妄为中看到了自己的身影：

> 但你是我的血肉，我的女儿，
>
> 也可以说是我体内的顽疾，
>
> 我要承认是我的。

（2.2.410-12）

这种"顽疾（disease）"被李尔称为"癔病（mother）"（2.2.246），它折磨女人，尤其是少女和寡妇，从子宫往上涌到心头，可令人窒息而死。……如果她们姊妹两人在具有男性品质方面像他，可以说，李尔"若能意识到女儿们是他身体的一部分，自然就该意识到他不仅有赖于自身以外的女性力量，而且他的体内同样也存在着那种可怕的女性气质"。

这也许能解释李尔发疯时为何会产生如此严重的厌女心态：

> ……她们从腰部以下都是
>
> 禽兽，尽管上半身是女人。腰部以上
>
> 属于神，以下属于魔鬼。

（4.6.121-3）

李尔这种恶毒的言论曾被误以为是该剧或莎士比亚本人的厌女心态，但这种心态源于老王自身的经历。贡纳丽和李根对他的虐待导致他拒绝"女人们的武器——水滴"（2.2.466）而选择了盛怒，只是当他恢复理智之后跟考迪丽娅和好时才屈服于泪水的治愈能力（4.7.47，71）。李尔的厌女心态也可理解为与代沟有关。李尔由一百名侍卫服侍左右，沉溺于狩猎并醉心于与男子汉气概有关的价值观念；他在1.4之所以雇用化了装的肯特是因为他的"服侍"——痛打了奥斯华德。他的女儿们也许可被视为新一代的代表：她们的世界更为精致，就像李根所穿的"光鲜"衣服并不保暖（2.2.456-9），还有奥斯华德的外表对肯特来说好像花花公子一般（2.2.32，53-4）。

贡纳丽与李根是莎士比亚所创作的最强大的两位女性人物，却很少得到应有的评论。她们常被视为邪恶的姐妹，在考迪丽娅的美德面前她们象征着淫念；但这种评判对她们来说却有失公平。……贡纳丽作为长女，若按长嗣继承权规定，可能会期望自己成为女王，但王国却被李尔随意分割；而且她（就像考迪丽娅，按照父亲的意愿？）嫁给了一个令她鄙视的丈夫，以至于她也许有很好的理由对李尔心怀敌意。 李根与贡纳丽的区别在于她有一位跟她同样粗暴的丈夫，因此，她作为王室出身，不得不通过抢丈夫的镜头来维护自己的权威。 姊妹两个，就像她们的父亲，喜欢行使职权：贡纳丽威吓阿班尼，李根则在康瓦尔试图发号施令时将他打断，以此占据上风（2.2.132，146-8）。 假如她们两人都被李尔嫁给了年纪较大的丈夫（康瓦尔在3.5.25曾提出要当埃德蒙的"慈父"），她们对年轻活泼的埃德蒙颇感兴趣便顺理成章。 但颇具反讽的是，并非她们的野心，而是她们对于一个男人——埃德蒙的爱——一种她们拒绝给予父亲的爱，最终使她们弄巧成拙。 如果说她们两人最终以中毒和自杀身亡收场有些夸张，那么莎士比亚必须找到某种方式让她们死去，以便最后的场景能够展示李尔与三位女儿的尸体相聚一起——自从他分封王国以来逐渐酿成的毁灭性结局。

"我有个儿子"

(*I had a son*)

《李尔王》可谓莎氏主要悲剧中唯一一部拥有从属情节（subplot）的悲剧。 格洛斯特及其两个儿子的故事与李尔三位女儿的故事类似，但又明显不同。 该剧的开场突显了考迪丽娅对父亲的反抗，接下来的主要场景便是埃德蒙对父亲及李尔所祈求的神明的反叛。 由于将该剧看成主要是李尔的救赎旅程这种观念占据上风，评论家们大都认为我们会赞同剧中所呈现的基本社会秩序，看到两个家庭里的一位好女儿和一个坏儿子之间在道义上的鲜明对比。 考迪丽娅受到了人们的热爱和敬重，而埃德蒙却被布拉德利（Bradley，302）描绘成一个普通的小偷：

> 实际上，他的心态就是职业罪犯的心态。"你说我不属于你，"他好像对社会说，"那好吧：我会设法进入你的宝库。假如我这样做会伤及人命，那是你的事情。"

这种观点将埃德蒙妖魔化为一个纯粹的恶棍，从而忽略了他最初所起的作用。 可在人物与观众之间建立一种紧密联系的独白在剧中颇为少见，但埃德蒙在他的首场里就有三段，他的活力、他的脾性和自控立刻引起了我们的兴趣。 正如柯勒律治①所说的那样："勇气、才华和性格魅力这三种力量最令人钦佩；……若抛开道义方面不论，这种力量定会令人赞赏和满足。"柯勒律治也注意到莎士比亚提供了各种各样的场合让我们对埃德蒙予以赞赏，比如他的私生（不是他的过错），以及他被送到生人家里养育（"他外出已经有九年，而且他很快还要出门"[1.1.31-2]）。若格洛斯特被视为是在羞辱埃德蒙（"他这个野种我是不认不行"），并且就像李尔那样代表着一种旧的家长制和暴君似的权力结构，那么埃德蒙也许会因为他的"革命性的怀疑态度"而受到赞许。

人们常认为该剧反映了旧秩序向新秩序的过渡。 当然，这在很大程度上有赖于人们如何看待这种过渡。 既可将这种过渡视为一种从有益的旧秩序向以利己主义为中心的新秩序的过渡，其中旧的秩序可以埃德加为代表，天性善良（如李尔所呼吁的"孝敬父母、子女应尽义务"，（2.2.367），新的秩序可以埃德蒙为代表，生性邪恶，崇尚丛林法则（"因为是偷情所生"，1.2.11），也可将这种过渡视为专制的旧秩序让位于资产阶级价值观的新秩序。 ……对埃德蒙的评价也许有赖于阐释者是更喜欢旧秩序还是更喜欢新秩序而定。 无论如何，埃德蒙是一个不安分的人物，他生气勃勃、精力充沛，正如对女演员来说，扮演贡纳丽和李根会比扮演考迪丽娅受益更大一样，对一位现代的男演员来说，扮演埃德蒙会比扮演埃德加更令人满足。

埃德蒙通常被装扮成文雅灵动，而不是横冲直撞的角色，或是哗众取宠的"虚张声势者"。 相比之下，埃德加倒会显得笨手笨脚，甚至愚蠢，因为他那么轻易地就受到了弟弟的欺骗；他也试图为自己的行为寻找理由。 与埃德蒙不同的是，埃德加在开场时并没有什么个性，只是在经过一系列的伪装之后他才逐渐获得了自己的高度，并在终场时以自己的真实身份重现。 如果在道义上把他理想化为善良的代表，可与考迪丽娅相

---

① 柯勒律治（Samuel Coleridge）：英国诗人、评论家（1772—1834）。

提并论，那就有些过分简单化了。 若只把埃德加视为一名凡夫俗子，经历过一系列的伪装——可怜的汤姆、村夫、信差、骑士，最终成了一位统治者，分享王国，这未免又降低了他的分量。 有些人认为詹姆斯一世时期的观众可能会意识到历史上的埃德加——英格兰国王（959—975），他的统治曾被视为黄金时期，因为他为英格兰制定了法规、修建了寺院并关心宗教，这些事迹为他赢得了圣徒的称号。

"然后杀，杀，杀，杀，杀，杀！"

(*Then kill，kill，kill，kill，kill，kill！*)

《李尔王》所描绘的是一个专制社会，认为暴力是理所当然。 这种暴力在该剧的前半部分主要跟李尔和他的随从有关。 李尔在开场时就试图袭击肯特，他们的对白表明他曾拔出剑来好像要刺他（1. 1. 161-3）。贡纳丽在1. 3里说过李尔打了她的"侍从"，我们在下一场里又看到李尔击打奥斯华德，并因为肯特踹了他而加以奖赏。 贡纳丽与李根抱怨李尔一百名侍卫的暴乱行为，对开本里就此增添了一些台词从而强调了李尔的肆无忌惮，因为他要求女儿为他以及那么多的随从安排住宿：

> 让他保留一百名武装的侍卫，
> 真是精明和安全！对，哪怕是梦、
> 流言蜚语、虚幻、抱怨、不满，
> 即可利用他们保护他的昏聩，
> 咱的性命由他支配。

（1. 4. 316-20）

李尔的随从中最显而易见的放纵者当属肯特，他因为击打奥斯华德而被锁进足枷。 埃德蒙曾拔出剑来"假装"刺向埃德加，随后将自己刺伤以便在除掉哥哥的计谋上博得人们的信任，此刻又拔出剑来阻止肯特对奥斯华德的袭击。

效劳（service）这种观念在剧中相当重要，肯特常被视为"好仆人的典范"。 肯特可与自私自利的埃德蒙形成对照，因为后者为了达到个人目的甘愿向任何一位主人表示效忠。 或许，肯特也可跟奥斯华德进行对比，后者与埃德蒙不同，他对贡纳丽的忠诚可谓死心塌地，比如他曾拒绝让李根看其女主人的信件（4.5.19-20）。 奥斯华德有时会被轻蔑地跟《哈姆雷特》里那位别具一格的侍臣——奥斯瑞克相比，因为肯特曾在2.2把他作为花花公子进行过虐待；或者，就该剧的道义而言，假如在善良与邪恶之间存在着清晰的两极分化，他也许就像埃德加在他死后所形容的那样——一个"殷勤的恶棍"（4.6.247）。 然而，若从另一角度来看，奥斯华德倒可被视为一个"可靠的仆人"（4.2.18），因为他满足了詹姆斯一世对臣民的主要要求——顺从为先；人们应该将国王视为"上帝在人间的代理，对他的命令百依百顺"。 ……肯特在情绪失控时袭击了奥斯华德，假如他就此向李尔显示了同样死心塌地的效忠，那么他跟奥斯华德的不同之处在于：他的悖逆和冒死是为了给李尔提供一种无私的效劳，这种效劳超出了纯粹的忠诚。

有趣的是，在詹姆斯一世国王面前上演的这部戏剧中竟有四人明显地抗命：开场时的肯特，不顾贡纳丽与李根"残酷命令"而帮助李尔的格洛斯特（3.4.145），以及试图提供"最好服务"而阻止康瓦尔挖掉格洛斯特眼睛的仆人（3.7.73）。 此外，还必须加上考迪丽娅，因为她"缺乏孝顺"（1.1.280），拒绝向李尔表达爱心。 有人认为《李尔王》针对高尚的违抗和愚蠢的效忠（virtuous disobedience and improper loyalty）之间的区别进行了仔细的审查，以此标志着莎士比亚政治见解的重要阶段。 假如詹姆斯一世于1606年观看该剧演出时注意到了这种现象，他也不必为此担心，因为他们通过被流放、挖掉眼睛或者死亡都受到了惩罚；然而，正如该剧就有关效忠的理念提出了令人不安的问题，它也搅乱了人们有关顺从的观念。

李尔最初的行动在很大程度上要为公认的价值观念的错位负责。 宣布亲生儿子埃德加为叛徒的格洛斯特，因为帮助了李尔，对掌权的李根和康瓦尔来说却成了"邪恶的叛徒"（3.7.32），因此奥斯华德可以合法地将他杀死。 埃德加杀死了奥斯华德，并指责陷害阿班尼"这位杰出国君"的埃德蒙为叛徒。 在第五幕第三场里，化装和匿名的埃德加与代表阿班尼迎战法军并刚刚获胜的弟弟进行了搏斗，这场搏斗标志着剧中的暴力和价值观的混乱达到了高潮。 这种搏斗也算是部分的收场，在这场象征性的单打独斗中善良战胜了邪恶，亚伯胜过了该隐①。 然而，埃德蒙却是为了"正义的（right）"一方而战——不是吗？ 希望挽救李尔和考迪丽娅性命的阿班尼却把他们当成入侵之敌予以抗击。 由李尔和格洛斯特挑起的冲突只能以暴力告终：摧毁家庭，导致兄弟反目、姐妹成仇。 这两位老人也造成了国家之间的不和与战争，为此李尔变成了敌人，考迪丽娅变成了侵略者。 假如说，这两位老人遭受得最多，那么根本原因在于他们的行为助长了暴力以及剧中的杀戮冲动。

R. A. 福克斯（R. A. Foakes）

---

① 亚伯（Abel）：《圣经》中的人物，亚当和夏娃的次子，被其兄长该隐（Cain）所杀。 见"创世纪"第4章。 ——译者附注。

史料说明

1. 李尔(Lear)：莎氏之所以选用该拼写，也许是想有别于其故事来源中的称谓——King Leir。

2. 贡纳丽(Goneril)：在该剧的故事来源——霍林西德的《英格兰编年史》(King Leir)中称为"Gonorilla"。

3. 李根(Regan)：在《英格兰编年史》中称为"Ragan"。

4. 考迪丽娅(Cordelia)：在《英格兰编年史》中称为"Cordella"，莎氏采纳了斯宾塞所著《仙后》中的拼法，也许是考虑到该名称中的"cor"源于拉丁语，意为"心(heart)"，采用回文构词法也可将其中的"delia"拼写为"ideal(典范)"。

5. 阿班尼(Albany)：不列颠的首位国王——布鲁图——将自己的王国分封给了儿子，其中的第三子名为"Albanact"，分得了苏格兰。

6. 康瓦尔(Cornwall)：布鲁图将威尔士分给了次子——康瓦尔。

7. 法兰西国王(King of France)：通常被称为"France(法兰西)"，仅出现于开场。

8. 勃艮第(Burgundy)：莎氏所杜撰的人物——考迪丽娅的求婚者，仅出现于开场。

9. 格洛斯特(Gloucester)：在四开本里拼写为"Gloster"，在对开本里也常如此拼写，旨在表明该名字的读音。从属情节(格洛斯特一家)中的名字均为莎氏所编造。

10. 埃德加(Edgar)：撒克逊人的名字，可令人想起历史上的埃德加——英格兰国王(959-75)，一位著名的英雄，以其残忍而著称。

11. 埃德蒙(Edmund)：好几位撒克逊国王以此命名。

12. 肯特(Kent)：系莎氏所编造。

13. 傻子(Fool)：莎氏对该剧所添加的最富独创性的人物。

LIST OF ROLES

Lear *King of Britain*

Goneril *his eldest daughter*

Regan *his second daughter*

Cordelia *his youngest daughter*

Duke of Albany *married to Goneril*

Duke of Cornwall *married to Regan*

King of France

Duke of Burgundy

Earl of Gloucester

Edgar *his elder son*

Edmund *his younger bastard son*

Earl of Kent

Fool *attendant on Lear*

Oswald *Goneril's steward*

Curan *a follower of Gloucester*

Old Man *Gloucester's tenant*

[A Herald, a Captain, an Officer,
A Doctor (Q only), Knights, Gentlemen,
Attendants, Servants and Messengers]

剧中人物

李尔　不列颠国王

贡纳丽　李尔的长女

李根　李尔的次女

考迪丽娅　李尔的幼女

阿班尼公爵　贡纳丽的丈夫

康瓦尔公爵　李根的丈夫

法兰西国王

勃艮第公爵

格洛斯特伯爵

埃德加　格洛斯特的长子

埃德蒙　格洛斯特的私生子

肯特伯爵

傻子　李尔的弄臣

奥斯华德　贡纳丽的管家

柯伦　格洛斯特的随从

老人　格洛斯特的佃户

[传令官、队长、军官、
医生（限四开本）、侍卫、绅士、
侍从、仆人及信差]

第一幕
ACT I

SCENE I

Enter Kent, Gloucester, and Edmund.

Kent I thought the King had more affected the Duke of Albany than Cornwall.

Gloucester It did always seem so to us: but now, in the division of the kingdom, it appears not which of the dukes he values most, for equalities are so weighed that curiosity in neither can make choice of either's moiety.

Kent Is not this your son, my lord?

Gloucester His breeding, sir, hath been at my charge. I have so often blushed to acknowledge him that now I am

第一场

肯特、格洛斯特与埃德蒙上。

肯特 我原以为国王喜爱阿班尼公爵要胜过
康瓦尔公爵。

格洛斯特 我们好像总是这样认为：可现在，就
国土的分封而言，却看不出他更偏重
哪一位公爵，因为他分配得如此均匀，   5
即使再斤斤计较也不会选择另外一份。

肯特 这不是您公子吗，大人？

格洛斯特 他的养育，先生，是由我负责。过去
我一旦认他就会脸红，现在我的脸皮

1.1. 原文有些内容如单词、词组或段落等，若只出现在四开本里（Quarto），便在该内容的前后用上标的"Q"标示；若该内容只出现在对开本里（Folio），则在该内容的前后用上标的"F"标示。 尤其是本场，四开本里的一些单词或短语并未出现在对开本里，这些词语均属格外音节（extra-metrical），即：*do*, 55；*Sir*, 69；*But*, 82；*How*, 90；*Well*, 109。 （R. A. Foakes, Arden Shakespeare, Third Series, 2008；即本译文所采用的蓝本，下称"Foakes"。 文中的所有脚注，若未标明出处，均出自该书。 ——译者附注。）0（1）舞台上面可能会放有一把宝座或御座，表明这是一种正式场合，也为国王的入场做好准备；可能还会插上带有徽章或标志的旗帜，以表明这是英国的宫廷。 1-32. 本场以熟人之间非正式的散文对话开头和收尾，以此为李尔宣布退休以及考迪丽娅的婚事安排营造一种庄重的气氛。 4. 分封（division）：肯特和格洛斯特都了解李尔想分封王国的意图，也未就此表示反对。 5-6. 因为……一份（for…moiety）：原文结构复杂、难懂，现引原注以助理解："shares are so balanced, one against the other, that the most careful scrutiny of either share could not induce either of the dukes to prefer his fellow's portion to his own." （Kennith Muir, Arden Shakespeare, Second Series, 1967；下称"Muir"。 ——译者附注）。

10		brazed to't.
	Kent	I cannot conceive you.
	Gloucester	Sir, this young fellow's mother could; whereupon she grew round-wombed, and had, indeed, sir, a son for her cradle ere she had a husband for her bed.
15		Do you smell a fault?
	Kent	I cannot wish the fault undone, the issue of it being so proper.
	Gloucester	But I have a son, sir, by order of law, some year elder than this, who yet is no dearer in my account.
20		Though this knave came something saucily into the world before he was sent for, yet was his mother fair, there was good sport at his making, and the whoreson must be acknowledged. Do you know this noble gentleman, Edmund?
25	**Edmund**	No, my lord.
	Gloucester	[*to Edmund*] My lord of Kent: remember him hereafter, as my honourable friend.
	Edmund	My services to your lordship.
	Kent	I must love you, and sue to know you better.

	已经厚了。	10
肯特	我不懂您的意思。	
格洛斯特	先生,可这位小青年的母亲却能;她 把肚皮搞得滚圆,而且,的确,先生, 她床上还没丈夫,摇篮里便有了儿子。 您是否觉得有错?	15
肯特	我不希望这错没有犯过,它结的果子 如此出色。	
格洛斯特	但我有个儿子,先生,合法生的,比 这个大一岁左右,可我对他并不更亲。 尽管这个无赖莽莽撞撞地来到了世上, 不请自到,可他的妈妈很美,在制造 他时其乐融融,因此他这个野种我是 不认不行。您认识这位高贵的绅士吗, 埃德蒙?	20
埃德蒙	不认识,父亲。	25
格洛斯特	[向埃德蒙]他是肯特大人:今后可要 记住,他是我的尊贵朋友。	
埃德蒙	我向大人您致敬。	
肯特	我定会爱您,也很想和您更熟。	

---

11. 懂(conceive):意为"理解(understand)"。 格洛斯特在下文则采用了该词的另一意义,即"怀孕(become pregnant)"。 12-24. 埃德蒙若听见父亲这种粗俗的玩笑和吹嘘,便会有助于解释其后来的行为。 另外,值得注意的是,格洛斯特在此将埃德蒙说成是他母亲的儿子,而把埃德加宣称为自己的儿子(18)。 15. 觉得有错(smell a fault):可指"觉察到一种罪过或恶行(smell a sin or wrongdoing)";也可暗指"女性生殖器(with a punning allusion to the female genitals)"。 本行开启了一系列的相关意象(如 1.4.110-1 与 1.5.22-3),直到李尔在 4.6.120-7对女人的谴责达到高潮。 16. 果子(issue):一语双关,可指"结果(outcome)";也可指"子孙(offspring)"。 20-2. 无赖(knave)……野种(whoreson):分别为"boy(家伙)"和"fellow(小伙子)"的戏称,但它们都有轻蔑之义,会让埃德蒙想起自己的私生子身份,低人一等。

30	**Edmund**	[*to Kent*] Sir, I shall study deserving.
	Gloucester	He hath been out nine years, and away he shall again. The king is coming.

Sennet.

^Q*Enter one bearing a coronet, then*^Q *Lear, Cornwall,*
Albany, Goneril, Regan, Cordelia and Attendants.

	Lear	Attend the lords of France and Burgundy, Gloucester.
	Gloucester	I shall, my lord. ^F*Exit.*^F
35	**Lear**	Meantime we shall express our darker purpose.
		^FGive me^F the map there. Know ^Fthat^F we have divided
		In three our kingdom; and 'tis our fast intent
		To shake all cares and business from our age,
		Conferring them on younger strengths, ^Fwhile we
40		Unburdened crawl toward death. Our son of Cornwall,
		And you, our no less loving son of Albany,
		We have this hour a constant will to publish
		Our daughters' several dowers, that future strife
		May be prevented now.^F
45		The ^Qtwo great^Q princes, France and Burgundy,
		Great rivals in our youngest daughter's love,
		Long in our court have made their amorous sojourn,

6

埃德蒙	［向肯特］先生,我尽力赢得您的厚爱。	30
格洛斯特	他外出已经有九年,而且他很快还要 出门。　国王来了。	

喇叭鸣奏。

一人捧小冠冕,李尔、康瓦尔、阿班尼、

贡纳丽、李根、考迪丽娅与侍从随之入场。

李尔	去陪同法兰西王和勃艮第公爵,格洛斯特。	
格洛斯特	遵命,陛下。	下。
李尔	同时我要宣布私下的计划。	35
	把地图给我。　我宣布已将国土	
	分为三份;我已经下定决心	
	使老身摆脱所有牵挂和责任,	
	将它们交托给年轻一代,我好	
	轻松地爬向死亡。　贤婿康瓦尔,	40
	还有您,我同样喜爱的贤婿阿班尼,	
	此时此刻我决意宣布女儿们	
	各自的嫁妆,以便将来的纷争	
	可从此预防。	
	两位王公,法兰西以及勃艮第,	45
	争着向我幼女求爱的情敌,	
	已在我们的宫中流连了多日,	

---

31. 外出(out):离家(away from home)。　贵族家的子弟通常会在国内其他贵族家中或到国外接受教育。　如当时的英国国王詹姆斯一世的长子,就被安排在马尔伯爵的家中。　然而,格洛斯特也可能是有意与埃德蒙保持距离。　35. 我(we):李尔使用了表示国王身份的复数形式(the royal plural),很适合此时的庄重场合。　39-44. 我好……预防(while…now):这几行台词只出现在对开本里,为李尔提供了行动的缘由,引入了死亡的念头,并增加了一种讽刺意味,因为李尔的行为实际上确保了将来的纷争,而不是预防纷争。

And here are to be answered. Tell me, my daughters—

^FSince now we will divest us both of rule,

50 Interest of territory, cares of state—^F

Which of you shall we say doth love us most,

That we our largest bounty may extend

Where nature doth with merit challenge. —Goneril,

Our eldest born, speak first.

55 **Goneril** Sir, I ^Qdo^Q love you more than words can wield the matter,

Dearer than eyesight, space and liberty,

Beyond what can be valued, rich or rare,

No less than life, with grace, health, beauty, honour.

As much as child e'er loved, or father found,

60 A love that makes breath poor and speech unable,

Beyond all manner of so much I love you.

Cordelia [*aside*] What shall Cordelia speak? Love, and be silent.

Lear Of all these bounds, even from this line to this,

With shadowy forests^F and with champaigns riched,

65 With plenteous rivers^F and wide-skirted meads,

We make thee lady. To thine and Albany's issues

Be this perpetual. —What says our second daughter,

Our dearest Regan, wife of Cornwall? ^QSpeak.^Q

Regan Sir, I am made of that self mettle as my sister,

70 And prize me at her worth. In my true heart

	此刻需要答复。　告诉我,女儿——	
	因为现在我就要摘下王冠,	
	放弃领土的拥有、王国的操劳——	50
	告诉我你们中间谁最爱我,	
	以便我可把最大的奖赏赐给	
	孝顺和贤德般配的那位。　——贡纳丽,	
	我的长女,你先说。	
贡纳丽	父亲,我爱您超过了言语表达,	55
	胜过眼睛、拥有土地和自由,	
	简直无法估量,珍贵或稀有,	
	不亚于尊贵、健康、美丽人生,	
	子女献过、父亲见过的爱心,	
	这种爱使表达徒劳,言语乏力,	60
	我爱您的分量无与伦比。	
考迪丽娅	[旁白]考迪丽娅该说啥呢?　爱,和沉默。	
李尔	所有这些区域,从这里到这里,	
	内有茂密的森林,肥沃的原野,	
	其中河流遍布,草原广阔,	65
	由你管辖。　你和阿班尼的子孙	
	可世代相传。　——我的二女儿呢,	
	我最亲的李根,康瓦尔夫人?　你说。	
李根	我跟姐姐的气质一模一样,	
	我的爱可与她相当。　我从心里	70

49. 摘下（divest）：由此开始了一系列有关衣服的意象（clothing images），直到李尔在 3.4. 106-7 要扒掉身上的衣服达到高潮。　53. 孝顺……那位（where…challenge）：意为"孝心和贤德都有权要求得到我丰厚馈赠的那一位（where both natural affection and merit claim our bounty as its due）"（David Bevington; The New Bantam Shakespeare, 2005; 下称"Bevington"。——译者附注）。　55-76. 贡纳丽和李根此处的话语可谓非常虚伪,但考虑到她们的处境倒可以理解,因为李尔是在怂恿奉承,无论他有意与否。　姐妹俩好像是在发表专门为此刻排练过的演讲。　63. 从这里到这里（from…this）：地图在此成了重要的道具,李尔会在上面指指划划,或从上面撕下一块当作礼物递给贡纳丽。

I find she names my very deed of love:

Only she comes ᶠtooᶠ short, that I profess

Myself an enemy to all other joys

Which the most precious square of sense possesses,

75 And find I am alone felicitate

In your dear highness' love.

Cordelia *[aside]*   Then poor Cordelia,

And yet not so, since I am sure my love's

More ponderous than my tongue.

Lear To thee and thine hereditary ever

80 Remain this ample third of our fair kingdom,

No less in space, validity and pleasure

Than that conferred on Goneril. —�QButQ now our joy,

Although the last and least, to whose young love

ᶠThe vines of France and milk of Burgundy

85 Strive to be interested,ᶠ what can you say to draw

A third more opulent than your sisters? ᶠSpeak.ᶠ

Cordelia Nothing, my lord.ᶠ

Lear Nothing?

Cordelia Nothing.ᶠ

90 **Lear** �QHow,Q nothing will come of nothing. Speak again.

Cordelia Unhappy that I am, I cannot heave

My heart into my mouth. I love your majesty

According to my bond, nor more nor less.

Lear How, how, ᶠCordelia?ᶠ Mend your speech a little,

Lest you may mar your fortunes.

感到她说出了我真实的爱心：

只是她说得不够，因为我声明

我要弃绝身体最敏感的部位

所能感受到的所有欢娱，

唯有陛下您的慈爱才能   75

使我高兴。

考迪丽娅   [*旁白*]   可怜的考迪丽娅，

又不可怜，因为我确信我的爱

比言辞更有分量。

李尔   你和你的子孙后代永远

继承这三分之一的美丽国土，   80

无论面积、价值和乐趣，不亚于

赐给贡纳丽的那份。 ——我的宝贝，

尽管你娇小年幼，花蕾初开，

法兰西的葡萄和勃艮第的牛奶

在争相索取，为了领取比您   85

姐姐更好的一份，你有啥可说？

考迪丽娅   没有，父亲。

李尔   没有？

考迪丽娅   没有。

李尔   没有那只能没有。 再说一遍。   90

考迪丽娅   我是多么不幸，我没有办法

把心提到嘴里。 我按照我的

本分敬爱陛下，既不多也不少。

李尔   怎么了，考迪丽娅？ 快修正一下

以免毁了您的良机。

---

84. 牛奶（milk）：即牧场，属于因果换位（the effect for the cause）（Muir）。 86. 更好的（more opulent）：李尔可能把最为富饶的三分之一国土留给了考迪丽娅（可能是其余的英格兰国土，如果贡纳丽分得了苏格兰，李根分得了威尔士和康瓦尔郡）。

95	**Cordelia**	Good my lord,
		You have begot me, bred me, loved me. I
		Return those duties back as are right fit,
		Obey you, love you and most honour you.
		Why have my sisters husbands, if they say
100		They love you all? Haply when I shall wed,
		That lord whose hand must take my plight shall carry
		Half my love with him, half my care and duty.
		Sure I shall never marry like my sisters
		^QTo love my father all.^Q
105	**Lear**	But goes thy heart with this?
	Cordelia	Ay, my good lord.
	Lear	So young and so untender?
	Cordelia	So young, my lord, and true.
	Lear	^QWell,^Q let it be so. Thy truth then be thy dower,
110		For by the sacred radiance of the sun,
		The mysteries of Hecate and the night,
		By all the operation of the orbs
		From whom we do exist and cease to be,
		Here I disclaim all my paternal care,
115		Propinquity and property of blood,
		And as a stranger to my heart and me
		Hold thee from this for ever. The barbarous Scythian,
		Or he that makes his generation messes
		To gorge his appetite, shall ^Fto my bosom^F
120		Be as well neighboured, pitied, and relieved,
		As thou my sometime daughter.

12

考迪丽娅	好父亲,	95

您生了我,养育我,爱我。 我
对这些加以回报恰如其分,
顺从您,爱您并且尽力孝敬您。
我的姐姐为何要嫁人,若声称
唯独爱您? 也许我出嫁的那天,   100
接受我婚约的夫君将带走我
一半爱心、一半关怀和责任。
我决不会像我姐姐那样结婚
是为爱我父亲一人。

李尔　这是你心里话吗?   105

考迪丽娅　是的,好父亲。

李尔　这么年轻却这么无情。

考迪丽娅　这么年轻,父亲,却真诚。

李尔　那好吧。 你的真诚作你的嫁妆,
因为凭着太阳的神圣光辉,   110
凭着巫神和黑夜的神秘礼仪,
凭着所有那些主宰着我们
生死存亡和运行中的天体,
我在此放弃对于你的父爱,
断绝亲属以及骨肉关系,   115
从今以后我将会永远与你
形同陌路。 野蛮的锡西亚人,
或者那些将后代当作食物
吞吃的人,他们得到我内心的
亲近、同情和救助,也不会   120
少于你——我曾经的女儿。

---

111. 巫神（Hecate）：赫卡忒,冥府的女神,掌管巫术和魔法,也曾在《麦克白》里出现（Muir）。 117. 锡西亚人（Scythian）：传说居住在黑海和小亚细亚周围的野人。

Kent   Good my liege—

Lear   Peace, Kent,

Come not between the dragon and his wrath!

I loved her most, and thought to set my rest

125   On her kind nursery. [*to Cordelia*] Hence and avoid my
            sight.

So be my grave my peace, as here I give

Her father's heart from her. Call France. Who stirs?

Call Burgundy.   [*Attendants rush off.*]

                    Cornwall and Albany,

With my two daughters' dowers, digest this third.

130   Let pride, which she calls plainness, marry her.

I do invest you jointly with my power,

Pre-eminence and all the large effects

That troop with majesty. Ourself by monthly course,

With reservation of an hundred knights

135   By you to be sustained, shall our abode

Make with you by due turn; only we still retain

The name, and all th'addition to a king: the sway,

Revenue, execution of the rest,

Beloved sons, be yours; which to confirm,

This coronet part betwixt you.

140 **Kent**   Royal Lear,

Whom I have ever honoured as my king,

Loved as my father, as my master followed,

As my great patron thought on in my prayers—

肯特	好陛下——	
李尔	闭嘴,肯特,	
	别闯入巨龙和它的泄愤物之间!	
	我最爱她,本打算我的晚年	
	靠她亲切照看。〔向考迪丽娅〕滚,别让我	125
	看见!	
	既然我想死后安息,就要取消	
	对她的父爱。 去叫法兰西。 快去!	
	去叫勃艮第。　　　　　　　　　〔侍从急下。〕	
	康瓦尔和阿班尼,	
	你们和妻子再分这三分之一。	
	让高傲——她所谓的坦率,帮她嫁人。	130
	我要把我的权力以及跟帝王	
	相伴的优越地位和各种排场	
	授予你们共享。 我自己按月,	
	保留一百名由你们供养的	
	随从人员,将会轮流到你们	135
	家里居住;只是我将会保留	
	国王的称号和头衔:至于政权、	
	税收、其他各种事务的执行,	
	两位贤婿,交给你们;作为证明,	
	这项王冠你们分。	
肯特	高贵的李尔,	140
	我一向把您敬重为我的君王,	
	爱您如父,当成主人跟随,	
	在我的祷告里把您视为恩人——	

---

126. 既然……安息(So…as):既然我希望能在坟墓里得到安息(As I hope to rest peacefully in my grave)(Bevington)。 127. 快去(Who stirs?):即"Be quick!"在场的侍臣均被吓呆(Muir)。 133-9. 我自己……你们(Ourself…yours):李尔使用了表示国王身份的复数形式;他希望保留与国王称号相符的荣誉和仪式,也许会戴着王冠,尽管他表面上己放弃了自己的权力(131)。

	Lear	The bow is bent and drawn; make from the shaft.
145	**Kent**	Let it fall rather, though the fork invade
		The region of my heart: be Kent unmannerly
		When Lear is mad. What wouldst thou do, old man?
		Think'st thou that duty shall have dread to speak,
		When power to flattery bows? To plainness honour's bound
150		When majesty stoops to folly. Reverse thy state,
		And in thy best consideration check
		This hideous rashness. Answer my life my judgment,
		Thy youngest daughter does not love thee least,
		Nor are those empty-hearted, whose low sounds
		Reverb no hollowness.
155	**Lear**	Kent, on thy life, no more.
	Kent	My life I never held but as ^{Q}a^Q pawn
		To wage against thy enemies, ne'er fear to lose it,
		Thy safety being ^{Q}the^Q motive.
	Lear	Out of my sight!
	Kent	See better, Lear, and let me still remain
160		The true blank of thine eye.
	Lear	Now, by Apollo—
	Kent	Now by Apollo, King,
		Thou swear'st thy gods in vain.
	Lear	^{F}O^F vassal! Miscreant!

李尔	弓弦已经拉满；你避开利箭。	
肯特	就让它射吧,哪怕箭头射进	145
	我的心间：李尔发疯的时候,	
	肯特只好失礼。 你想干啥,老头子?	
	你以为当权者向谄媚屈服时,	
	忠臣不敢诤谏? 君王疯狂时,	
	忠臣就需要直言。 要保留王权,	150
	你要好好考虑一下,要制止	
	这可怕的鲁莽。 我以生命断言,	
	你的小女儿并非最不爱你,	
	没有空洞回音的低声细语	
	并非没有爱心。	
李尔	肯特,若想活,就住口。	155
肯特	我向来把我的生命视为赌注,	
	供你向仇敌抛掷,为你安全	
	起见,决不怕丢失。	
李尔	给我滚开!	
肯特	看准些,李尔,让我永远做你	
	眼中的可靠靶心。	160
李尔	我凭阿波罗——	
肯特	我凭阿波罗,国王,	
	你祈求的神灵没用。	
李尔	奴才! 恶棍!	

147. 你……老头子（thou…man）：在正式场合对依然在位的李尔这样称谓显然有些非礼, 但肯特却让李尔和我们注意到国王最终所不得不承认的事实："我承认我已老了" （2. 2. 343）。 154. 空洞（hollowness）：即 1. 2. 113 行所说的虚伪（insincerity）和轻浮 （emptiness）,令人想起谚语"空洞的器皿声音最响（Empty vessels make most sound）"。 160. 靶心（blank）：即位于靶中央的白点。 肯特在邀请李尔向他寻求忠告。 随着剧情的展开, 李尔和格洛斯特两人均将学会"看准一些（see better）"。 161. 阿波罗（Apollo）：（古希腊 和古罗马神话中的）太阳神。

| Albany } | Dear sir, forbear. |
| Dornwall } | |

Kent   ^QDo,^Q kill thy physician, and the fee bestow

165   Upon thy foul disease. Revoke thy gift,

Or whilst I can vent clamour from my throat

I'll tell thee thou dost evil.

Lear   Hear me, ^Frecreant,^F on thine allegiance, hear me:

That thou hast sought to make us break our vows,

170   Which we durst never yet, and with strained pride

To come between our sentences and our power,

Which nor our nature, nor our place can bear,

Our potency made good, take thy reward.

Five days we do allot thee for provision,

175   To shield thee from disasters of the world,

And on the sixth to turn thy hated back

Upon our kingdom. If on the next day following,

Thy banished trunk be found in our dominions,

The moment is thy death. Away! By Jupiter,

180   This shall not be revoked.

Kent   ^QWhy,^Q fare thee well, King, since thus thou wilt appear,

Freedom lives hence and banishment is here.

[*to Cordelia*] The gods to their dear shelter take thee, maid,

That justly think'st and hast most rightly said;

[*to Regan and Goneril*] And your large speeches

185   may your deeds approve,

That good effects may spring from words of love.

Thus Kent, O princes, bids you all adieu;

阿班尼 康瓦尔	好先生,请息怒!	
肯特	杀吧,杀掉医生,把酬金送给	
	恶臭的疾病。 收回你的礼物,	165
	否则只要我能够发出抗议,	
	我就会说你在作恶。	
李尔	听着,叛贼,凭你臣服的义务,听着:	
	鉴于你企图让我违背誓言,	
	对此我从来不敢,你狂妄自大	170
	竟然干扰我的决定和权威,	
	我的性情和地位都不能容忍,	
	我要行使权力,你赶快领赏。	
	我给你五天时间去做准备,	
	以便使你免遭世间的厄运,	175
	在第六天里你要离开这个	
	恨你的王国。 若从当天之后	
	发现你被流放的躯体没走,	
	就立即处死。 滚吧!凭朱庇特起誓,	
	本处罚不可撤回。	180
肯特	再会了,国王,既然你是这样,	
	远离才能自由,留下只有流放。	
	[向考迪丽娅]愿神明给你提供庇护,姑娘,	
	因为你心地正直,言语恰当;	
	[向李根和贡纳丽]愿你们华丽的言辞	
	付诸实施,	185
	好让甜言蜜语结出甜蜜果子。	
	王公们,肯特这就告别故土;	

181-8. 肯特的对句表明他经过与李尔的激烈交锋之后现已回归平静。 182. 远离……流放（Freedom…here）:首次表明了因为李尔的行动而导致的本末倒置、是非颠倒（the inversion of order and values）,随后傻子将对该主题一再重申,如他在 3. 2. 79-96 的预言。

He'll shape his old course in a country new.   ^F*Exit.*^F

^F*Flourish.*^F

Enter Gloucester with France, and Burgundy

and ^F*attendants*^F.

	Cornwall	Here's France and Burgundy, my noble lord.
190	**Lear**	My lord of Burgundy.

We first address toward you, who with this king

Hath rivalled for our daughter. What in the least

Will you require in present dower with her,

Or cease your quest of love?

Burgundy   ^FMost^F royal majesty,

195   I crave no more than hath your highness offered—

Nor will you tender less?

Lear   Right noble Burgundy,

When she was dear to us, we did hold her so,

But now her price is fallen. Sir, there she stands:

If aught within that little-seeming substance,

200   Or all of it, with our displeasure pieced,

And nothing more, may fitly like your grace,

She's there, and she is yours.

Burgundy   I know no answer.

Lear   ^QSir,^Q will you, with those infirmities she owes,

Unfriended, new adopted to our hate,

205   Dowered with our curse and strangered with our oath,

Take her or leave her?

在新的国度里他将我行我素。   下。

号角齐鸣。

格洛斯特与法兰西国王,和勃艮第公爵,

及侍从上。

康瓦尔	法兰西和勃艮第到,尊贵的陛下。
李尔	我的勃艮第阁下, 190
	我先对您说吧,您和这位国王
	争着向我女儿求婚。 您至少
	需要她有多少随身的嫁妆,
	否则便不再追求?
勃艮第	至尊的陛下,
	我的要求不会超过您的许诺—— 195
	您也不会少给?
李尔	高贵的勃艮第,
	我喜爱她时,把她视为珍宝,
	可她现已跌价。 她就在那里:
	自以为是的东西若有价值,
	或者全部,再加上我的讨厌, 200
	别无他物,阁下若真正喜欢,
	她就在那里,归您。
勃艮第	我无法回答。
李尔	先生,她拥有上述那些缺陷,
	没有亲朋,我又刚开始恨她,
	发誓与她疏远,诅咒作为陪嫁, 205
	您是否愿意娶她?

---

188. 在……我素(shape…new):肯特是指他将在一个新的国度里继续坦率直言(he will, in a foreign land, pursue his old ways of speaking plainly)(Muir)。 189. 舞台指示:在四开本里,是由格洛斯特宣布法兰西和勃艮第的到来;对开本里的这一更改旨在使李尔在看到格洛斯特从另一扇门里入场之前目睹肯特退场。

Burgundy   Pardon me, royal sir;

Election makes not up in such conditions.

Lear   Then leave her, sir, for, by the power that made me,

I tell you all her wealth. [*to France*] For you, great king,

210   I would not from your love make such a stray

To match you where I hate, therefore beseech you

T'avert your liking a more worthier way

Than on a wretch whom nature is ashamed

Almost t'acknowledge hers.

France   This is most strange,

215   That she who even but now was your ᵠbestᵠ object,

The argument of your praise, balm of your age,

The best, the dearest, should in this trice of time

Commit a thing so monstrous, to dismantle

So many folds of favour. Sure her offence

220   Must be of such unnatural degree

That monsters it, or your fore-vouched affection

Fallen into taint, which to believe of her

Must be a faith that reason without miracle

Should never plant in me.

225 **Cordelia**   I yet beseech your majesty,

If for I want that glib and oily art

To speak and purpose not—since what I well intend,

I'll do't before I speak—that you make known

It is no vicious blot, murder, or foulness,

230   No unchaste action or dishonoured step,

That hath deprived me of your grace and favour,

But even for want of that for which I am richer,

勃艮第	请原谅,陛下;
	这种情况下不可能会有选择。
李尔	那就放弃吧,因为由神明作证,
	我已说出她全价。　[向法兰西]至于您,大王,
	我可不愿意违背您的厚爱
	让您娶我的仇人,因此我请您
	把爱慕转向更为值得的地方,
	而不是这个连造化都羞于
	认可的东西。
法兰西	这真是奇怪至极,
	刚才她还是您最好的宝贝,
	您所赞美的主题,老年的安慰,
	最棒的亲人,竟在转眼之间
	犯下可怕的罪过,千恩万宠
	竟被剥夺。　她的罪行肯定
	达到了一种违反常情的地步,
	如此丑恶;否则您声称的恩爱
	必遭贬损,相信她犯那种恶行,
	若不出现奇迹,想让我信以
	为真绝不可能。
考迪丽娅	不过我要恳请陛下,
	若因我缺乏那种油腔滑调,
	口是心非——因为我若真想做,
	就会先做后说——求您声明
	不是因我有污点、凶杀,或不忠,
	不是因下流行为或可耻举动,
	才失去了您对我的喜爱和恩宠,
	只因我缺乏,缺乏倒使我更富,

210

215

220

225

230

A still soliciting eye and such a tongue

That I am glad I have not—though not to have it

Hath lost me in your liking.

235 **Lear**   ^QGo to, go to,^Q better thou

Hadst not been born than not to have pleased me better.

France   Is it ^Qno more^Q but this? —a tardiness in nature,

Which often leaves the history unspoke

That it intends to do? My lord of Burgundy,

240   What say you to the lady? Love's not love

When it is mingled with regards that stands

Aloof from th'entire point. Will you have her?

She is herself a dowry.

Burgundy   Royal King,

Give but that portion which yourself proposed,

245   And here I take Cordelia by the hand,

Duchess of Burgundy.

Lear   Nothing: I have sworn, ^FI am firm.^F

Burgundy   [*to Cordelia*] I am sorry then you have so lost a father

That you must lose a husband.

Cordelia   Peace be with Burgundy.

250   Since that respects of fortunes are his love,

I shall not be his wife.

France   Fairest Cordelia, that art most rich being poor,

Most choice forsaken and most loved despised,

一贯邀宠的眼睛以及我庆幸

自己没有的巧舌——尽管没有它

让我失去了您的喜爱。

李尔　　　　　　　　　　　你这么 235

令我生气,还不如未曾生你。

法兰西　就因为这吗？ ——一种天生的迟缓,

经常是心中想做的事情口头

并未表达出来？ 勃艮第阁下,

您以为小姐如何？ 爱不是真爱, 240

假如它与爱情毫不相干的

顾虑牵扯起来。 您是否娶她?

她的嫁妆是自身。

勃艮第　　　　　　　尊贵的陛下,

只要把您许诺的那一份给我,

在此我就和考迪丽娅牵手, 245

让她做公爵夫人。

李尔　不给。 我已发誓,我很坚决。

勃艮第　[向考迪丽娅]我很抱歉,您这样失去了父亲,

也必须失去夫君。

考迪丽娅　　　　　　再见吧,勃艮第。

既然他爱的是名声和财富, 250

我不会做他夫人。

法兰西　最美的考迪丽娅,贫穷却最富,

被抛弃但最精美,受鄙视最可爱,

240-2. 爱……起来（Love…point）：十四行诗 116 首阐发了类似的论点。 245. 和考迪丽娅牵手（take…hand）：象征着喜结连理。 勃艮第此时握住了考迪丽娅的手,但当他听到李尔的言论之后随即松开,接着便由法兰西在 254 行占据（seize）。 252. 贫穷却最富（most…poor）：可令人想起《圣经》中有关基督的论述,即"哥林多后书"6 章 10 节："似乎贫穷,却叫许多人富足；似乎一无所有,却是样样都有"（Muir）。

Thee and thy virtues here I seize upon,

255 Be it lawful I take up what's cast away.

Gods, gods! 'Tis strange that from their cold'st neglect

My love should kindle to inflamed respect.

Thy dowerless daughter, King, thrown to my chance,

Is queen of us, of ours and our fair France.

260 Not all the dukes of waterish Burgundy

Can buy this unprized, precious maid of me.

Bid them farewell, Cordelia, though unkind;

Thou losest here a better where to find.

Lear Thou hast her, France; let her be thine, for we

265 Have no such daughter, nor shall ever see

That face of hers again. Therefore, be gone,

Without our grace, our love, our benison.

Come, noble Burgundy.

^F*Flourish.*^F *Exeunt* ^Q*Lear and Burgundy*^Q [*,Conrwall, Albany,*
Gloucester, Edmund and attendants].

France Bid farewell to your sisters.

270 **Cordelia** The jewels of our father, with washed eyes

Cordelia leaves you. I know you what you are,

And like a sister am most loath to call

Your faults as they are named. Love well our father.

To your professed bosoms I commit him,

275 But yet, alas, stood I within his grace

I would prefer him to a better place.

你和你的美德我就此占据，

若是合法，别人丢的我捡起。 255

神明啊，神明！ 想不到他们的冷淡，

会将我炽热的敬重和爱情点燃。

你这没嫁妆的女儿，正好归我，

做我的王后，拥有美丽的法国。

水乡勃艮第的所有王公都别想 260

从我这里买走这位无价的姑娘。

向他们告辞，考迪丽娅，尽管无情；

你舍弃此地，到别处寻觅佳境。

李尔　　她归你，法兰西，让她归你，因为我

没有这样的女儿，我再也不想 265

看见她的面孔。 因此，快走吧，

我不会给她恩宠、慈爱和祝福。

来，高贵的勃艮第。

号角齐鸣。李尔与勃艮第［、康瓦尔、阿班尼、

格洛斯特、埃德蒙及侍从］下。

法兰西　　向您姐姐告辞。

考迪丽娅　父亲的宝贝，考迪丽娅含泪 270

向你们告别。 我了解你们的本性，

作为妹妹我不愿将你们的

过错直接挑明。 照顾好父亲。

我把他托给你们宣称的爱心，

可是，唉，我若依然蒙他爱怜， 275

会为他推荐一个更好的地点。

---

260. 水乡（waterish）：（指地点）水汪汪的（abounding in water）；（指人）乏味的（vapid）。 274. 宣称的爱心（professed bosoms）：原注为" = the love you have professed"；其中"professed"读作"professèd"，三个音节。

So farewell to you both.

Regan Prescribe not us our duty.

Goneril Let your study

Be to content your lord, who hath received you

280 At fortune's alms. You have obedience scanted,

And well are worth the want that you have wanted.

Cordelia Time shall unfold what plighted cunning hides,

Who cover faults at last with shame derides.

Well may you prosper.

France Come, ^{F}my^F fair Cordelia.

Exeunt France and Cordelia.

285 **Goneril** Sister, it is not ^{Q}a^Q little I have to say of what most nearly appertains to us both. I think our father will hence tonight.

Regan That's most certain, and with you. Next month with us.

290 **Goneril** You see how full of changes his age is. The observation we have made of it hath ^{Q}not^Q been little. He always loved our sister most, and with what poor judgment he hath now cast her off appears too grossly.

Regan 'Tis the infirmity of his age, yet he hath ever but

295 slenderly known himself.

就此与你们告别。

李根　　我们不用您来吩咐。

贡纳丽　　　　　　　您只管

讨好您夫君去吧，他收留您，

那是命运的施舍。　您缺乏孝顺，　　　　　　　280

您想要却得不到活该受损。

考迪丽娅　时间会把隐藏的诡计揭穿，

遮掩过错终将会丢人现眼。

愿你们亨通。

法兰西　　　　　走吧，美丽的考迪丽娅。

　　　　　　　　　　　　　　　法兰西与考迪丽娅同下。

贡纳丽　　妹妹，我有很多话要说，它们与咱们　　　　285

两个密切相关。　我想我们的父亲今晚

就要离开这里。

李根　　那是肯定的，先跟您住，下一个月再

跟我。

贡纳丽　　您看他年老了是多么变化无常，我们　　　　290

已经观察到的类似例证可谓比比皆是。

他向来最爱我们的妹妹，现在却把她

抛弃，他的糊涂就此可显而易见。

李根　　这是他年老昏庸，可是他向来就很少

会有自知之明。　　　　　　　　　　　　　　　　295

---

280. 命运的施舍（At fortune's alms）：命运施舍的慈善礼物（以使她摆脱贫困）（as a charitable gift of fortune [relieving her poverty]）。　281. 您……受损（are…wanted）：您活该遭受求之而不得的损失（即陪送的嫁妆和父爱）（deserve the loss of what you have both lacked and desired [i. e. a dowry, and parental love]）。　284. 愿你们亨通（Well…prosper）：考迪丽娅以间接提及《圣经》中一节诗文的方式圆满结束了对姐姐的挖苦，即"箴言"28 章 13 节："遮掩自己罪过的，必不亨通（He that hideth his sins, shall not prosper）"。　288. 先跟您住（with you）：李尔先跟长女住在一起合情合理。　289. 我（us）：她是在使用表示王后身份的复数形式，还是指她和康瓦尔两人？

Goneril	The best and soundest of his time hath been but rash; then must we look from his age to receive not alone the imperfections of long-engrafted condition, but therewithal ᶠtheᶠ unruly waywardness that infirm
300	and choleric years bring with them.
Regan	Such unconstant starts are we like to have from him as this of Kent's banishment.
Goneril	There is further compliment of leave-taking between France and him. Pray ᶠyouᶠ let us hit
305	together. If our father carry authority with such dispositions as he bears, this last surrender of his will but offend us.
Regan	We shall further think of it.
Goneril	We must do something, and i'the heat. *Exeunt.*

贡纳丽	即使他在风华正茂的时候,也是急躁 鲁莽;那我们不仅要做好准备去应对 他根深蒂固以及习惯成性的心理缺陷, 而且还有遭受他因年迈和古怪而导致 的刚愎自用。
李根	就像他一时感情冲动把肯特流放那样, 我们也会面临类似的乖张。
贡纳丽	他和法兰西王之间还要举行一种正式 的告别仪式。 求您要让咱们两个通力 合作。 假如我们的父亲继续以这样的 脾性行使职权,他最近的退位只会给 我们带来祸患。
李根	我们可要考虑一下。
贡纳丽	我们必须行动,要趁热打铁。 同下。

300

305

---

304. 仪式(compliment):贡纳丽的消息好像是误报;参考 1. 2. 23。

SCENE II

Enter [Edmund, the] Bastard [, holding a letter].

Edmund   Thou, Nature, art my goddess; to thy law

My services are bound. Wherefore should I

Stand in the plague of custom, and permit

The curiosity of nations to deprive me?

5   For that I am some twelve or fourteen moonshines

Lag of a brother? Why bastard? Wherefore base?

When my dimensions are as well compact,

My mind as generous and my shape as true

As honest madam's issue? Why brand they us

10   With base? With baseness, bastardy? ᶠBase, base?ᶠ

Who in the lusty stealth of nature take

More composition and fierce quality

Than doth within a dull stale tired bed

第二场

私生子[埃德蒙,手持信函]上。

埃德蒙　　自然啊,你是我女神;你的法则

我有义务遵循。　为何我要让

自己遭受恶俗的折磨,允许

世间的过分挑剔剥夺我权益?

只因为我比一位哥哥小了　　　　　　　　　　　　5

一岁稍多? 为啥私生? 为啥低等?

与正派女人的子孙相比,我的

身材不是同样的匀称,心胸

不是同样的高尚? 为啥把我们

标为低等? 杂种? 低等,低等?　　　　　　　　　10

我们,因为是偷情所生,相较于

那些在陈旧而乏味的床上,

于睡意蒙眬之间制造出来的

1.2. 第一场以诗文为主,辅之以两段散文作为框架;本场的安排与之相反,即以散文为主,辅之以埃德蒙的两段独白作为框架。 他在这一场里实有三段独白,包括118-33行的散文独白,通过直接向观众表白以便得到他们的同情。 0(1)本场的背景为格洛斯特伯爵的家中,正如李根在2.2.447行所说的那样,地方很小,不足以容纳李尔及其随从。 1-2. 自然啊……遵循(Thou…bound):"nature(自然)"一词在剧中具有多种含义,其中包括"自然的约束力(the bonds of nature)","父子之间的人之常情(the ties of natural affection between parent and child)"等。 埃德蒙实际上是在拒绝这些束缚(ties),转而求助于丛林法则,与野兽结为联盟,对抗习俗、道义和秩序,以此为自己辩护。 3. 遭受恶俗的折磨(Stand…custom):忍受习俗或法律的邪恶,因为它们拒绝私生子的继承权利(remain subject to the evil of customary usage or laws, which denied a bastard any share by inheritance in his father's property);参考2.1.84-5。

| | | Go to the creating ^Qof^Q a whole tribe of fops |

Go to the creating ᵠofᵠ a whole tribe of fops

15   Got 'tween a sleep and wake. Well, then,

Legitimate Edgar, I must have your land.

Our father's love is to the bastard Edmund

As to the legitimate. ᶠFine word, 'legitimate'!ᶠ

Well, my legitimate, if this letter speed

20   And my invention thrive, Edmund the base

Shall top the legitimate. I grow, I prosper:

Now gods, stand up for bastards!

Enter Gloucester.

Gloucester   Kent banished thus? And France in choler parted?

And the King gone tonight? Prescribed his power,

25   Confined to exhibition? All this done

Upon the gad? —Edmund, how now, what news?

Edmund   [*Pockets the letter.*] So please your lordship, none.

Gloucester   Why so earnestly seek you to put up that

letter?

30   **Edmund**   I know no news, my lord.

Gloucester   What paper were you reading?

Edmund   Nothing, my lord.

Gloucester   No? What needed then that terrible dispatch

of it into your pocket? The quality of nothing

35   hath not such need to hide itself. Let's see. —Come, if

it be nothing, I shall not need spectacles.

成群傻瓜,体格会更加健壮,

精力更加旺盛。 那么,好吧, 15

婚生的埃德加,您的土地要归我。

我们父亲喜爱婚生的,也喜爱

私生的埃德蒙。 动听的字眼,"婚生"!

那好,我的婚生,若这封信奏效,

我的计谋得逞,低等的埃德蒙 20

将胜过那位婚生。 我发展,我成功:

神明啊,保佑我们杂种!

格洛斯特上。

格洛斯特 肯特这样流放? 法兰西一怒而去?

国王昨晚已走? 保留部分权利,

仅靠赡养费为生? 这些都是 25

一时冲动? ——埃德蒙,怎么了,啥消息?

埃德蒙 [把信装进口袋。]禀告大人,没有。

格洛斯特 你为啥这么急切地把那封信

藏起来?

埃德蒙 我没啥消息,父亲。 30

格洛斯特 你刚才看的是啥?

埃德蒙 没啥,父亲。

格洛斯特 没啥? 那你何必还要那么惊慌失措地

把它藏进口袋? 要是没啥重要,那就

用不着藏起来了。 叫我看看。——快, 35

若真的没啥,我就不用戴眼镜了。

23-6. 肯特……冲动(Kent…gad):格洛斯特好像并未注意到埃德蒙的出现;他好像刚刚听到了惊人的消息,并用数行台词告诉观众法兰西王一怒之下突然离去,李尔前往贡纳丽的宫殿,但他的权利受到限制。

	Edmund	I beseech you, sir, pardon me. It is a letter from my brother that I have not all o'er-read; ^{F}and^F for so much as I have perused, I find it not fit for your o'er-looking.
40	**Gloucester**	Give me the letter, sir.
	Edmund	I shall offend, either to detain or give it. The contents, as in part I understand them, are too blame.
	Gloucester	Let's see, let's see.
	Edmund	I hope, for my brother's justification, he wrote
45		this but as an essay, or taste of my virtue.
	Gloucester	[^{F}*Reads*^{F}] 'This policy, ^{F}and reverence^F of age. makes the world bitter to the best of our times, keeps our fortunes from us till our oldness cannot relish them. I begin to find an idle and fond bondage in the
50		oppression of aged tyranny, who sways not as it hath power, but as it is suffered. Come to me, that of this I may speak more. If our father would sleep till I waked him, you should enjoy half his revenue for ever and live the beloved of your brother. Edgar.' Hum! Conspiracy!
55		'Sleep till I wake him, —you should enjoy half his revenue,' — My son Edgar, had he a hand to write this? A heart and brain to breed it in? When came this to you? Who brought it?
	Edmund	It was not brought me, my lord, there's the
60		cunning of it; I found it thrown in at the casement of my closet.
	Gloucester	You know the character to be your brother's?
	Edmund	If the matter were good, my lord, I durst swear it were his; but, in respect of that, I would fain think it

埃德蒙	我求您,先生,原谅我。信是我哥哥写的,还没看完;而且就我所看过的内容而言,我觉得不适合您看。	
格洛斯特	把信给我,小子。	40
埃德蒙	无论给您还是不给,我都会冒犯您的。信的内容,据我所理解,太不像话。	
格洛斯特	我看看,我看看。	
埃德蒙	我希望,为哥哥说句公道话,他写信不过是想试探试探我的品性。	45
格洛斯特	[读信]"这种习俗,必须尊敬老人,使我们的风华正茂变成一种苦恼,使我们的财产无法继承,直到老了无法享用。我开始感到老暴君的压迫真是徒劳愚蠢的奴役,他能摆布不是因为有力,而是我们能忍。过来吧,就此我会详谈。假如我们的父亲能够一睡方休,您就会永远享受他的一半税收,哥哥也会爱您。埃德加。"哼!阴谋!	50
	"一睡方休,您就会享受他的一半税收"——我的儿埃德加,这是他写的?他心里会有这种想法?你是何时收到它的? 谁送来的?	55
埃德蒙	不是谁送来的,父亲,这就是其中的狡猾所在。是从我卧室的窗户缝里塞进来的。	60
格洛斯特	确认这是你哥哥的笔迹?	
埃德蒙	假如内容是好的,父亲,我敢发誓是他的笔迹;但因为内容,我宁愿相信	

65		were not.
	Gloucester	It is his?
	Edmund	It is his hand, my lord; but I hope his heart is not in the contents.
70	**Gloucester**	Has he never before sounded you in this business?
	Edmund	Never, my lord. But I have heard him oft maintain it to be fit that, sons at perfect age and fathers declined, the father should be as ward to the son and the son manage his revenue.
75	**Gloucester**	O villain, villain! His very opinion in the letter. Abhorred villain! Unnatural, detested, brutish villain—worse than brutish! Go, sirrah, seek him. I'll apprehend him. Abominable villain, Where is he?
80	**Edmund**	I do not well know, my lord. If it shall please you to suspend your indignation against my brother till you can derive from him better testimony of his intent, you should run a certain course; where, if you violently proceed against him, mistaking his purpose, it would make a great gap in your own honour and shake in
85		pieces the heart of his obedience. I dare pawn down my life for him, ᶠthatᶠ he hath writ this to feel my affection to your honour and to no other pretence of danger.
	Gloucester	Think you so?
90	**Edmund**	If your honour judge it meet, I will place you where you shall hear us confer of this and by an

	不是。	65
格洛斯特	是他的吗？	
埃德蒙	是他的笔迹，父亲；可我希望这并非出自他的内心。	
格洛斯特	难道他从来没有在这件事情上试探过你吗？	70
埃德蒙	从来没有，父亲。不过我倒是常听他念叨：儿子一旦成年，父亲已经衰老，父亲就该由儿子监护，并由儿子掌管他的财产。	
格洛斯特	噢恶棍，恶棍！跟他信里的观点一样。可恶的恶棍！无情、可憎、畜生般的恶棍——畜生不如！去，小子，找他。我要逮捕他。可恶的恶棍，他在哪里？	75
埃德蒙	我不太清楚，父亲。假如您能够暂且控制一下对我哥哥的怒气，直到您能搜集到有关其意图的更为确切的证据，您就会万无一失；然而，如果您这就对他采取强制措施，误解了他的意图，那将会使您的荣誉严重受损，并伤透他的一片孝心。我敢拿我的性命打赌，他写这封信的目的是想试探我对大人您的爱心，不会有任何其他的危险的用意。	80 85
格洛斯特	你这样认为？	
埃德蒙	如果大人您觉得合适，我会把您安排到某个地方，您可听到我们商谈此事，	90

---

77. 小子（sirrah）：这种称呼可表明格洛斯特的权威。

auricular assurance have your satisfaction, and that
without any further delay than this very evening.

Gloucester   He cannot be such a monster.

95 ᵠ**Edmund**   Nor is not, sure.

Gloucester   To his father, that so tenderly and entirely loves
him. Heaven and earth!ᵠ Edmund, seek him out.
Wind me into him, I pray you: frame the business after
your own wisdom. I would unstate myself to be in a

100   due resolution.

Edmund   I will seek him, sir, presently, convey the business
as I shall find means and acquaint you withal.

Gloucester   These late eclipses in the sun and moon portend
no good to us. Though the wisdom of Nature

105   can reason ᶠitᶠ thus and thus, yet nature finds itself
scourged by the sequent effects. Love cools, friendship
falls off, brothers divide: in cities, mutinies; in
countries, discord; ᶠinᶠ palaces, treason; ᶠandᶠ the bond
cracked 'twixt son and father. ᶠThis villain of mine

110   comes under the prediction—there's son against father.
The King falls from bias of nature—there's father
against child. We have seen the best of our time.
Machinations, hollowness, treachery and all ruinous
disorders follow us disquietly to our graves. ᶠFind out

115   this villain, Edmund; it shall lose thee nothing . Do it
carefully. —And the noble and true-hearted Kent
banished, his offence honesty! ᶠ'Tisᶠ strange, ᵠstrange!ᵠ

Exit.

通过亲耳所闻,您就会消除您的疑心,

这件事情也无须拖延,今晚就办。

格洛斯特　他不可能是这样的畜生。

埃德蒙　他不是,肯定。　　　　　　　　　　　　　95

格洛斯特　对他的父亲,我这么深情和全心地爱

他。苍天和大地啊!埃德蒙,去找他。

求你为我取得他的信任:这一件事情

你看着办吧。我愿放弃一切,只要能

确信无疑。　　　　　　　　　　　　　100

埃德蒙　我去找他,父亲,立刻,我会设法把

这件事情办好,并就此向您汇报。

格洛斯特　最近的这些日食以及月食对我们来说

可不是好的兆头。尽管自然科学可以

提供这样或那样的解释,随后的灾难　　105

却令世间痛苦不堪。爱成冷漠,朋友

翻脸,兄弟失和:城市里,有暴乱;

乡间,有争端;宫里,有叛贼;父子

之间的亲情了断。我的这个逆子正好

应了这种预言——就是儿子对抗父亲。　　110

国王他违背了天性——就是父亲对抗

孩子。我们最好的时光已经成为过去。

阴谋诡计、虚伪、背叛以及各种毁灭

性的混乱将烦扰我们直到埋葬。搜出

这个逆子,埃德蒙;你不会有啥损失。　　115

要谨慎行事。——高贵和真诚的肯特

竟被流放,他的罪过是诚实!奇怪!

下。

Edmund   This is the excellent foppery of the world, that when we are sick in fortune, often the surfeit of our

120   own behavior, we make guilty of our disasters the sun, the moon and ^Qthe^Q stars, as if we were villains on necessity, fools by heavenly compulsion, knaves, thieves and treachers by spherical predominance; drunkards, liars and adulterers by an enforced obedience of

125   planetary influence; and all that we are evil in by a divine thrusting on. An admirable evasion of whoremaster man, to lay his goatish disposition on the charge of a star. My father compounded with my mother under the dragon's tail and my nativity was

130   under Ursa Major, so that it follows I am rough and lecherous. ^QFut!^Q I should have been that I am had the maidenliest star in the firmament twinkled on my bastardizing.

Enter Edgar.

Pat he comes like the catastrophe of the old comedy.

135   My cue is villainous melancholy, with a sigh like Tom o'Bedlam. —O, these eclipses do portend these divisions. ^FFa, sol, la, mi.^F

Edgar   How now, brother Edmund, what serious contemplation are you in?

埃德蒙	这可真是世界上最棒的愚蠢,当我们
	命运不济时,往往是因为自己的行为
	过分放纵,反而把我们的灾难归咎于

这可真是世界上最棒的愚蠢,当我们
命运不济时,往往是因为自己的行为
过分放纵,反而把我们的灾难归咎于
日月星辰,好像我们成为恶棍是迫不
得已,犯傻是因为天意,无赖、盗贼、
和叛徒是因某个星球左右;我们酗酒、
撒谎和通奸是因为不得不顺从天体的
支配;我们的一切罪恶行径都是上天
强加给的。这是好色之徒一种绝妙的
借口,要把他自己的好色性情怪罪于
星星负责。我父亲在天龙座的降交点
与我母亲交媾,我就是在那大熊星座
下面降生,因此我自然就是既粗野又
好色。狗屁!播下我这野种时,哪怕
空中最为贞洁的星星在闪烁,我依然
会是现在的我。

　　　　埃德加上。

来得正好,就像老派喜剧编造的结局。
我的角色要求郁郁寡欢,像精神病院
的疯子哀叹。——噢,这些日食月食
预示着纷争!法、骚、拉、米。

| 埃德加 | 怎么了,埃德蒙兄弟,您在沉思默想 |
| | 啥呀? |

120

125

130

135

---

118. 最棒的（excellent）：此处意为"讥讽"。　120-1. 把我们的……星辰（make…stars）：埃德蒙此处将父亲有关预兆的言论扩展到了人们对占星术的信仰——人的一生是由他们出生时日月星辰所处的位置掌控（Mowat）。　128. 天龙座的降交点（dragon's tail）：即月球向南移动时,其轨道与黄道相交的节点（此时出现日食）（Bevington）。　129. 大熊星座（Ursa Major）：即"Great Bear",因此有"粗野和好色（rough and lecherous）"；该星座也可代指北斗七星。　135-6. 精神病院的疯子（Tom o'Bedlam）：来自疯人院或伦敦伯利恒精神病院的乞丐常以此自谓。　137. 法、骚、拉、米（Fa, sol, la, mi）：埃德蒙在哼唱,以便假装自己并未觉察到埃德加的到来（Muir）。

140 **Edmund**   I am thinking, brother, of a prediction I read this
other day, what should follow these eclipses.

Edgar   Do you busy yourself with that?

Edmund   I promise you, the effects he writes of succeed
unhappily, ^Qas of unnaturalness between the child and
145   the parent, death, dearth, dissolutions of ancient
amities, divisions in state, menaces and maledictions
against King and nobles, needless diffidences,
banishment of friends, dissipation of cohorts , nuptial
breaches and I know not what.

150 **Edgar**   How long have you been a sectary astronomical?

Edmund   Come, come,^Q when saw you my father last?

Edgar   ^QWhy,^Q the night gone by.

Edmund   Spake you with him?

Edgar   ^FAy,^F two hours together.

155 **Edmund**   Parted you in good terms? Found you no displeasure
in him, by word nor countenance?

Edgar   None at all.

Edmund   Bethink yourself wherein you may have offended
him, and at my entreaty forbear his presence till some
160   little time hath qualified the heat of his displeasure;
which at this instant so rageth in him that with the
mischief of your person it would scarcely allay.

Edgar   Some villain hath done me wrong.

Edmund   That's my fear. ^FI pray you have a continent
165   forbearance till the speed of his rage goes slower; and,

埃德蒙	我在想，哥哥，前两天我看过的一则	140
	预言，最近的日食月食意味着什么。	
埃德加	您在关心这种事情？	
埃德蒙	我向您保证，作者所提及的后果非常	
	地不幸，例如子女与父母之间的违反	
	常情，死亡，饥荒，久经考验的友情	145
	破裂，国家之间纷争，国王和贵族们	
	遭到威胁与诽谤，满心猜疑毫无根据，	
	朋友遭到流放，士兵逃离，婚姻破裂，	
	我不知道还有哪些。	
埃德加	您从何时做起了占星家的信徒？	150
埃德蒙	罢了，罢了，上次您见父亲是在何时？	
埃德加	昨天晚上。	
埃德蒙	和他说话了？	
埃德加	说了，有两个钟头。	
埃德蒙	在友好的气氛中告别？没发现他有所	155
	不满，无论言辞还是表情？	
埃德加	没有啊。	
埃德蒙	好好想一想您是否在什么地方得罪了	
	他，我求您要避免与他见面，过一段	
	时间之后，等他的怒气变得有所缓和；	160
	此时此刻他是如此怒不可遏，就是把	
	您打死他的怒气也难平息。	
埃德加	我遭到了恶人的陷害。	
埃德蒙	我怕也是。我求您先克制一下，暂且	
	避开，直到他的怒气舒缓下来；同时，	165

---

148. 士兵逃离（dissipation of cohorts）：莎士比亚是否在指李尔的 100 名侍卫？

	as I say, retire with me to my lodging, from whence I
	will fitly bring you to hear my lord speak. Pray ye, go:
	there's my key. If you do stir abroad, go armed.
Edgar	Armed, brother?[F]
170 **Edmund**	Brother, I advise you to the best, [Q]go armed.[Q] I

Edgar Armed, brother?[F]

170 **Edmund** Brother, I advise you to the best, [Q]go armed.[Q] I
am no honest man if there be any good meaning towards
you. I have told you what I have seen and heard — but
faintly , nothing like the image and horror of it. Pray
you, away!

175 **Edgar** Shall I hear from you anon?

Edmund I do serve you in this business.   *Exit Edgar.*
A credulous father and a brother noble,
Whose nature is so far from doing harms
That he suspects none—on whose foolish honesty

180 My practices ride easy. I see the business.
Let me, if not by birth, have lands by wit;
All with me's meet that I can fashion fit.   *Exit.*

依我说,您跟我回到住处,我会趁机
安排您听见父亲的谈话。求您,快走:
给您钥匙。　您若外出,要带武器。

埃德加　　带武器,兄弟?

埃德蒙　　兄弟,我这都是为了您好,带上武器。　　　　　　　170
要是有人对您怀有好意,那我就是个
骗子。已告诉您我的见闻——我说得
很委婉;与可怕的实情相去甚远。求
您,快走!

埃德加　　您很快就传来消息?　　　　　　　　　　　　　175

埃德蒙　　在这件事上我会帮您。　　　　　　　*埃德加下。*
轻信的父亲加上厚道的哥哥,
他如此天真无邪从不害人,
因此不会疑心——他的愚忠
容易被我操纵。　我知道该咋办了。　　　　　　180
靠出身得不到土地,就靠智力;
一切都很正当,只要能达目的。　　　　　　　　*下。*

SCENE Ⅲ

Enter Goneril, and [Oswald, her] steward.

Goneril	Did my father strike my gentleman for chiding
	of his fool?
Oswald	Ay, madam.
Goneril	By day and night he wrongs me. Every hour

5 He flashes into one gross crime or other

That sets us all at odds. I'll not endure it.

His knights grow riotous and himself upbraids us

On every trifle. When he returns from hunting,

I will not speak with him; say I am sick.

10 If you come slack of former services

You shall do well; the fault of it I'll answer.

[Horns within.]

Oswald   He's coming, madam, I hear him.

Goneril   Put on what weary negligence you please,

You and your fellows; I'd have it come to question.

15 If he distaste it, let him to my sister,

Whose mind and mine I know in that are one,

第三场

贡纳丽与［奥斯华德，她的］管家上。

贡纳丽	我父亲打了我的侍从，因为责怪他的 傻子？
奥斯华德	是的，夫人。
贡纳丽	他始终都在害我。　每时每刻 他都会犯下这样那样的罪行，　　　　　　　　　5 使我们大家不和。　我不再容忍。 他的侍卫已很猖狂，而他自己 也动辄骂人。　当他打猎回来时， 我不想和他说话；就说我病了。 您服侍他若不如以前周到，　　　　　　　　　10 那会很好；出了事由我负责。

　　　　　　　　　　　　　　　　　　　　［幕后鸣号。］

奥斯华德	他来了，夫人，我听见了。
贡纳丽	您只管随心所欲地表示轻慢， 您和您的伙伴；我想和他争辩。 他要是反感，让他去我妹妹家里，　　　　　15 我知道我们的心思就此一致，

1.3.　自1.1到现在已经过去一段时间，因为李尔及其随从现已在贡纳丽和阿班尼的家里安顿下来，也就是本场的背景所在。　1-2. 我……傻子（Did…fool）：剧中是由李尔首先动手打人，如他试图袭击肯特（1.1.162），以及现在击打贡纳丽的侍从。　这也是剧中首次提及傻子这一角色。

^QNot to be overruled. Idle old man,

That still would manage those authorities

That he hath given away. Now by my life,

20   Old fools are babes again and must be used

With checks as flatteries, when they are seen abused.^Q

Remember what I have said.

Oswald   ^QVery^Q well, madam.

Goneril   And let his knights have colder looks among you,

What grows of it no matter; advise your fellows so.

25   ^QI would breed from hence occasions, and I shall,

That I may speak. ^QI'll write straight to my sister

To hold my ^Qvery^Q course. ^QGo^Q, prepare for dinner.

Exeunt.

不会对他让步。　没用的老头儿，

他依然想要行使自己的权力，

尽管已经放弃。　我以性命担保，

老傻瓜就是婴儿，因此当他们　　　　　　　　　20

被引入歧途时，就要恩威并用。

我的话您要记住。

奥斯华德　　　　　　　好的，夫人。

贡纳丽　　对他的侍卫也要更加冷淡，

别担心后果；也告诉您的伙伴。

我想以此创造机会，我就会　　　　　　　　　25

有话可说。　我这就向妹妹致函

告诉她我的计划。　去准备午餐。

　　　　　　　　　　　　　　　　　　　　同下。

17-21．不会……并用（Not…abused）：上述诗行，以及下文25-6行的"我想……可说（I…speak）"，未出现在对折本里，以此可使贡纳丽的性格得以缓和（softens the character of Goneril），即删除了她对父亲的侮辱性语言，以及有意对父亲的暗算（conscious plotting against him）。　26-7．我这就……计划（I'll…course）：参见1.1.308-9，姐妹俩提及如何一起谋划；但事实表明她们并没有备好的行动计划。

SCENE IV

Enter Kent [disguised].

Kent   If but as well I other accents borrow

That can my speech defuse, my good intent

May carry through itself to that full issue

For which I razed my likeness. Now, banished Kent,

5   If thou canst serve where thou dost stand condemned,

^FSo may it come^F thy master, whom thou lov'st

Shall find thee full of labours.

^F*Horns within.*^F

Enter Lear,^F*and*^F*[four or more Knights as]* ^F*attendants.*^F

Lear   Let me not stay a jot for dinner; go, get it ready.

[Exit 1 Knight.]

[to Kent] How now, what art thou?

10 **Kent**   A man, sir.

Lear   What dost thou profess? What wouldst thou with

us?

第四场

肯特［化装］上。

肯特　　如果我也能改变自己的口音，
　　　　使语调难以辨认，我的善意
　　　　也许就能取得圆满的结局，
　　　　为此我已毁容。　流放的肯特啊，
　　　　你若能在惩罚你的地方效忠，　　　　　　　　　　　5
　　　　但愿能成功，你所喜爱的主人
　　　　会发现你不遗余力。

　　　　　　　　幕后号角声。
　　　　李尔与［四五位身为侍卫的］侍从上。

李尔　　别让我等着用餐；去，快给我备好！

　　　　　　　　　　　　　　　　　　　　　　　［侍卫甲下。］

　　　　［向肯特］哎吆，你是谁呀？

肯特　　是人，先生。　　　　　　　　　　　　　　　　　　　10

李尔　　你是做什么的？你来找我有什么事情
　　　　吗？

　　1．4．　0（1）自称被流放的肯特经过乔装打扮之后又在第四场出现，这种伪装可使他充分表达自己对李尔的耿耿忠心。　本场的背景依然是贡纳丽和阿班尼的家中。　7（1-2）．这是李尔首次与他的部分侍卫一起入场，他曾在1.1.134要求保留一百名侍卫。　正如1.3.7-8所暗示的那样，这些侍卫在舞台上通常会带有武器、不守纪律、吵吵闹闹，有时还会带着猎狗。　这些侍卫的行为越是粗暴，贡纳丽在191-4行以及随后的抱怨也就越有道理，因此他们此时的行为举止相当重要。　8．别让我等着用餐（Let…dinner）：李尔此处的散文与其开场时的正式诗文形成了鲜明的对比，不过他依然盛气凌人。　另外，餐（dinner），即正餐（the main meal），通常在中午享用。

Kent	I do profess to be no less than I seem; to serve him truly that will put me in trust, to love him that is
15	honest, to converse with him that is wise and says little, to fear judgment, to fight when I cannot choose—and to eat no fish.
Lear	What art thou?
Kent	A very honest-hearted fellow, and as poor as the
20	King.
Lear	If thou be'st as poor for a subject as he's for a king, thou art poor enough. What wouldst thou?
Kent	Service.
Lear	Who wouldst thou serve?
25 **Kent**	You.
Lear	Dost thou know me, fellow?
Kent	No, sir; but you have that in your countenance which I would fain call master.
Lear	What's that?
30 **Kent**	Authority.
Lear	What services canst ᶠthouᶠ do?
Kent	I can keep honest counsel, ride, run, mar a curious tale in telling it and deliver a plain message bluntly, That which ordinary men are fit for I am qualified in,
35	and the best of me is diligence.

肯特	我声称不亚于我的外表；会忠心服侍	
	那些信任我的人，会爱那些诚实的人，	
	会与那些聪明并且少言寡语的人交往，	15
	不会作恶，我会动武若别无选择——	
	也不吃鱼。	
李尔	你是谁？	
肯特	一个诚心诚意的家伙，他与国王一样	
	贫穷。	20
李尔	作为臣民，你要是与国王他一样贫穷，	
	那可是真穷。　你想要啥？	
肯特	工作。	
李尔	为谁工作？	
肯特	您。	25
李尔	你认识我吗，伙计？	
肯特	不认识；不过您的仪表里有某种东西，	
	让我愿意叫您主人。	
李尔	什么东西？	
肯特	权威。	30
李尔	你会做什么工作？	
肯特	能保守正当的秘密，能骑，能跑，把	
	好故事讲糟，呆板地传递简单的口信。	
	只要是常人能做到的事情我都很在行，	
	我的最大优点就是勤奋。	35

16. 不会作恶（fear judgement）：原注为"do no evil"。　观众也许会联想到上帝对"恶人（the wicked）"的审判（"诗篇"1篇6节）；或指审判日（day of judgement）（"马太福音"10章15节）。　17. 不吃鱼（eat no fish）：可有两种解释：（1）我是一个虔诚的新教徒（Protestant），不会像罗马天主教徒（Roman Catholic）那样在星期五吃鱼；（2）我身体并不瘦弱（I am no weakling）。　肯特此处也可能含有淫秽之义，即"不会嫖娼（not to have sex with prostitutes）"（Muir）；（Jonathan Bate, Royal Shakespeare Company, 2007；下称"Bate"）。——译者附注。）

	Lear	How old art thou?
	Kent	Not so young, ^Fsir,^F to love a woman for singing, nor so old to dote on her for anything. I have years on my back forty-eight.
40	**Lear**	Follow me, thou shalt serve me; if I like thee no worse after dinner, I will not part from thee yet. Dinner, ho, dinner! Where's my knave, my fool? Go you, and call my fool hither. [*Exit 2 Knight.*]

Enter Oswald.

You, ^Fyou,^F sirrah, where's my daughter?

45	**Oswald**	So please you—	^F*Exit.*^F
	Lear	What says the fellow there? Call the clotpoll back.	

[*Exit 3 Knight.*]

Where's my fool? Ho, I think the world's asleep.

Enter 3 Knight.

How now, where's that mongrel?

	3 Knight	He says, my lord, your daughter is not well.
50	**Lear**	Why came not the slave back to me when I called him.
	3 Knight	Sir, he answered me in the roundest manner, he would not.
	Lear	He would not?
55	**3 Knight**	My lord, I know not what the matter is, but to my judgment your highness is not entertained with that ceremonious affection as you were wont. There's a

56

李尔	你多大年纪？	
肯特	已不年轻，不至于因女人会唱就爱她， 但也不老，不至于随便就溺爱她。我 已经四十八了。	
李尔	跟着我吧，可做我的仆人；若午饭后 我还喜欢你的话，那就不会把你赶走。 午饭，喂，午饭！我仆人呢，傻子呢？ 您去，把我的傻子叫来。	40 　　　〔侍卫乙下。〕

奥斯华德上。

您，您，先生，我女儿在哪里？

| 奥斯华德 | 对不起—— | 下。 45 |
| 李尔 | 那家伙在说啥？　叫那个蠢货回来。 | |

　　　〔侍卫丙下。〕

我的傻子呢？　嗨，看来都在沉睡。

侍卫丙上。

怎么回事，那个杂种呢？

侍卫丙	他说，您的女儿不舒服，陛下。	
李尔	我叫那个奴才的时候，他怎么不回来 呢？	50
侍卫丙	先生，他直截了当地回答我，他不想 回来。	
李尔	不想回来？	
侍卫丙	陛下，我不知道是怎么回事，但以我 看来，陛下您现在所受到的待遇不如 往常那样礼貌亲近。　他们的爱心已经	55

---

45. 对不起（So please you）：请原谅，我很忙（Excuse me, I'm busy）。　即贡纳丽在1. 3. 13所劝告的那种轻慢（weary negligence）。　奥斯华德，跟其他仆人一样，是在遵循贡纳丽的指示，因为李尔从未吃上他所呼喊的那顿午饭。

great abatement ^{F}of kindness^F appears as well in the
general dependants as in the Duke himself also, and
60 your daughter.

Lear   Ha? Sayst thou so?

3 Knight   I beseech you pardon me, my lord, if I be mistaken,
for my duty cannot be silent when I think your
highness wronged.

65 **Lear**   Thou   but   rememberest   me   of   mine   own
conception. I have perceived a most faint neglect of
late, which I have rather blamed as mine own jealous
curiosity than as a very pretence and purpose of
unkindness. I will look further into't. But where's my
70 fool? I have not seen him this two days.

3 Knight   Since   my   young   lady's   going   into   France,   sir,
the fool hath much pined away.

Lear   No more of that , I have noted it ^{F}well^F. Go you and
tell my daughter I would speak with her.   [*Exit 3 Knight.*]
75 Go you; call hither my fool.   [*Exit 4 Knight.*]

^{F}*Enter Oswald.*^{F}

O you, sir, you, come you hither, sir: who am I, sir?

Oswald   My lady's father.

Lear   My lady's father? My lord's knave, you whoreson
dog, you slave, you cur!

80 **Oswald**   I am none of these, my lord, I beseech your
pardon.

Lear   Do you bandy looks with me, you rascal?   [*Striks him.*]

大打折扣,不只是这里的仆人看上去

如此,就连公爵本人,以及您的女儿

都不例外。　　　　　　　　　　　　　　60

李尔　　哈？　此话当真？

侍卫丙　　我请求您原谅,陛下,假如我说错了,

我的职责也不许我沉默,如果我觉得

您受了冤屈。

李尔　　你倒是提醒了我自己所注意到的某些　　65

现象。我最近觉察到一种最为懈怠的

轻慢,对此我宁愿归咎于自己的神经

过敏,而不愿怪罪他们是在存心不仁。

我会对此多加留意。可是我的傻子在

哪里？　我有两天没见他了。　　　　70

侍卫丙　　自从我的小公主去了法国以后,先生,

傻子他已日渐憔悴。

李尔　　别提这件事了,我也注意到了。您去

告诉我女儿我要跟她说话。　　　　　[侍卫丙下。]

您去;把我的傻子叫来。　　　　　　[侍卫丁下。]　75

奥斯华德上。

是您呀,先生,您过来:我是谁呀,先生？

奥斯华德　　夫人的父亲。

李尔　　夫人的父亲？主人的恶棍,你这狗娘

养的,奴才,恶狗!

奥斯华德　　您说的这些我都不是,大人,我求您　　80

原谅。

李尔　　你敢跟我瞪眼儿,你这无赖？　　　　　[打他。]

Oswald	I'll not be strucken, my lord.
Kent	[*Trips him.*] Nor tripped neither, you base football
85	player.
Lear	I thank thee, fellow. Thou serv'st me and I'll love thee.
Kent	Come, sir, ^Farise, away, ^F I'll teach you differences.

Oswald I'll not be strucken, my lord.

Kent [*Trips him.*] Nor tripped neither, you base football
85 player.

Lear I thank thee, fellow. Thou serv'st me and I'll love
thee.

Kent Come, sir, ᶠarise, away, ᶠ I'll teach you differences.
Away, away; if you will measure your lubber's length
90 again, tarry; but away, ᶠgo to,ᶠ have you wisdom? ᶠSo!ᶠ
[*Pushes him out.*]

Lear Now, ᶠmyᶠ friendly knave, I thank thee. There's
earnest of thy service. [*Gives him money.*]

Enter Fool.

Fool Let me hire him too; [*to Kent, holding out his cap*]
here's my coxcomb.

95 **Lear** How now, my pretty knave, how dost thou?

Fool [*to Kent*] Sirrah, you were best take my coxcomb.

Kent Why, fool?

Fool Why? For taking one's part that's out of favour.
Nay, an thou canst not smile as the wind sits, thou'lt
100 catch cold shortly. There, take my coxcomb. Why, this
fellow has banished two on's daughters, and did the

奥斯华德	您不能打我，大人，
肯特	［踹倒他。］还不能踹呢，你这踢足球
	的贱货。　85
李尔	谢谢你，伙计。你帮了大忙，我会爱
	你的。
肯特	快，起来，滚吧，我教给你啥叫区别。
	滚吧，滚吧；如果你还想被踹趴在地，
	那就留下；滚吧，得了，你识好歹吗？　90
	［将他推出。］
李尔	喂，你是个好仆人，我谢谢你。这是
	雇你的定金。　［递钱给他。］

傻子上。

傻子	我也要雇他；［把他的帽子递向肯特］
	这是我的鸡冠帽。
李尔	你好，我的好伙伴，你好吗？　95
傻子	［向肯特］老兄，您最好收下我的帽子。
肯特	为啥，傻子？
傻子	为啥？因为跟一个失宠的人站在一边。
	不，假如你不会趋炎附势，很快就会
	吃尽苦头。好吧，收下我的帽子，嗨，　100
	这伙计流放了他的两个女儿，却违心

84-5. 踢足球的贱货（base football player）：足球属于下等人玩的游戏，因为它"野蛮和狂暴"（was a lower-class game of 'beastly fury and extreme violence'）；相比之下，网球对年轻人来说则是一种很好的运动。　88. 我……区别（I'll…differences）：我要教你明白自己的身份——你与国王之间的差别（I'll teach you your position, the differences between yourself and the king）（Muir）。　94. 鸡冠帽（coxcomb）：职业小丑的帽子，顶部有一种鸡冠状饰物。　99-100. 假如……苦头（an…shortly）：隐秘的表达方式，意为"如果你不能取悦于当权者，你很快就会为此受苦（if you cannot please those in power, you'll soon suffer for it）"。　101. 流放了……女儿（banish'd…daughters）：逆说法（paradoxically），李尔将自己的王国分给了贡纳丽和李根，把自己交由她们支配，结果却失去了她们两个（by giving Goneril and Regan his kingdom, Lear has lost them, given them power over him）（Bevington）；不过，傻子故意使用"流放（banish'd）"一词，旨在影射李尔对考迪丽娅的待遇，其中，原文 on's = of his（他的）（Muir）。

third a blessing against his will — if thou follow him,
thou must needs wear my coxcomb. [*to Lear*] How now,
nuncle? Would I had two coxcombs and two daughters.

105 **Lear**   Why, my boy?

Fool   If I gave them all my living, I'd keep my coxcombs
myself. There's mine; beg another of thy daughters.

Lear   Take heed, sirrah, the whip.

Fool   Truth's a dog ᵠthatᵠ must to kennel; he must be
110   whipped out, when the Lady Brach may stand by the
fire and stink.

Lear   A pestilent gall to me.

Fool   Sirrah, I'll teach thee a speech.

Lear   Do.

115 **Fool**   Mark it, nuncle:

> *Have more than thou showest,*
> *Speak less than thou knowest,*
> *Lend less than thou owest,*
> *Ride more than thou goest,*

赐福给了那第三个——你要是跟随他，

必须戴上我的帽子。〔向李尔〕你好吗，

老伯？　但愿我有两顶帽子和两个女儿。

李尔	为啥，孩子？	105
傻子	我若把财产全给她们，我就会有两顶	
	帽子。　这顶给你；你向女儿再借一顶。	
李尔	当心，小子，挨抽。	
傻子	真理是一条狗，要被关进窝里；会被	
	抽打出去，而猎狗夫人却会站在炉旁	110
	散发臭气。	
李尔	真使我烦恼不已！	
傻子	老兄，我给你讲段话吧。	
李尔	讲吧。	
傻子	听好了，老伯：	115

多积财产少露富，

莫将知识全说出，

有钱不可全借净，

尽量骑马少步行，

101-2. 违心……第三个（a blessing…will）：通过诅咒和流放考迪丽娅，李尔却使她成了法国王后，并救她避免嫁给勃艮第公爵（Muir）。　104. 老伯（nuncle）：系"mine uncle"的缩约词。　职业弄臣（a licensed fool）通常这样称谓自己的主子（Muir）。　105. 孩子（boy）：一种亲切的称呼，尤对仆人，不一定与年龄有关。　剧中的傻子扮演者有少年也有老者；许多人认为他的智慧应该源自成年（spring from maturity）。　106-7. 我若……帽子（If…myself）：可令人想起谚语"傻瓜去世之前会将财产散完（He that gives all before he dies is a fool）"（Foakes）。我就会有两顶帽子（keep my coxcombs）：作为愚蠢的证据（as proof of my folly）（Bevington）。　107. 这顶……一顶（There's…daughters）：就此将李尔称为十足的傻子（Thus he calls Lear a double-dyed fool）（Muir）。　108. 挨抽（whip）：傻子如果越界可能就会遭到鞭打（Fools were liable to be whipped if they overstepped the mark）。　109-10. 真理……出去（Truth…out）：被赶出去的真理也许暗指考迪丽娅、肯特或傻子。　110. 猎狗（Brach）：母猎狗（bitch hound）（此处被比作贡纳丽和李根，尽管她们满口尽是虚伪的奉承，却受到了优待〔here likened to Goneril and Regan, who have been given favored places despite their reeking of dishonest flattery〕）（Bevington）。　118. 有钱（owest）= own（拥有）。

120
> *Learn more than thou trowest,*
>
> *Set less than thou throwest;*
>
> *Leave thy drink and thy whore,*
>
> *And keep in-a-door,*
>
> *And thou shalt have more*

125
> *Than two tens to a score.*

Kent This is nothing, fool.

Fool Then ᶠ'tisᶠ like the breath of an unfee'd lawyer, you gave me nothing for't. [*to Lear*] Can you make no use of nothing, nuncle?

130 **Lear** Why no, boy; nothing can be made out of nothing.

Fool [*to Kent*] Prithee tell him, so much the rent of his land comes to; he will not believe a fool.

Lear A bitter fool.

Fool Dost ᶠthouᶠ know the difference, my boy, between a
135 bitter fool and a sweet fool?

Lear No, lad, teach me.

ᵠ**Fool** That lord that counselled thee to give away thy land, Come place him here by me; do thou for him stand. The sweet and bitter fool will presently appear,

> 耳听八方别全信，　　　　　　　　　　　　　　120
>
> 一注不可掷千金，
>
> 放弃酗酒和嫖娼，
>
> 不要游荡出门房，
>
> 结果你会更富裕，
>
> 利上加利有盈余。　　　　　　　　　　　　　125

肯特　　这没啥新意，傻子。

傻子　　那这就像未拿报酬的律师所给的忠告，

您没给我什么。 ［向李尔］难道您不能

无中生有，老伯？

李尔　　当然不能了，孩子；没有那只能没有。　　130

傻子　　［向肯特］请你告诉他，他把国土给人，

却没有租金；他不会相信傻子。

李尔　　尖酸的傻子。

傻子　　你知道他们的区别吗，孩子，什么是

苦涩的傻子和可爱的傻子？　　　　　　135

李尔　　不知道，告诉我。

傻子　　要是谁曾经劝你把国土全分完，

他来和我站一起，那种人你扮演。

可爱的傻子与苦涩傻子即刻显现，

---

120. 全信（trowest）= believe（相信）。　121. 原注为"don't stake all on a single throw （of the dice）（不可将全部赌注一下掷完）"。　124-5. 结果……盈余（And…score）：存钱并赢利（save money and make a profit）（Foakes）。 另一原注为"And you'll end up with more / Than two tens to a twenty"（Sparknotes, no fear Shakespeare：*King Lear*；下称"Sparknotes"——译者附注）。　127-8. 就像……什么（like…for't）：律师以贪财出名："律师只为酬金辩护（A lawyer will not plead but for a fee）"。　137-48. 要是……抢夺（That…snatching）：傻子的这段台词只出现在了四开本里。 对折本之所以将其省略，也许是因为审查制度（见下文146行注），或因为它只是在让傻子继续抨击李尔：（1）将自己的国土赠送出去，（2）表明他是傻瓜。 而且，唯有此处明确提及了傻子身穿彩衣——专职的宫廷弄臣标志。　137-40. 该四句韵诗可"证明（proves）"李尔确实是个苦涩的傻子。

140	The one in motley here, the other found out there.
Lear	Dost thou call me fool, boy?
Fool	All thy other titles thou hast given away; that thou wast born with.
Kent	This is not altogether fool, my lord.
145 **Fool**	No, faith, lords and great men will not let me; if I had a monopoly out, they would have part on't; and ladies too, they will not let me have all the fool to myself, they'll be snatching.^Q Nuncle, give me an egg and I'll give thee two crowns.

150 **Lear**	What two crowns shall they be?
Fool	Why, after I have cut the egg i' the middle and eat up the meat, the two crowns of the egg. When thou clovest thy crown i'the middle, and gav'st away both parts, thou bor'st thine ass on thy back o'er the dirt.
155	Thou hadst little wit in thy bald crown when thou gav'st thy golden one away. If I speak like myself in this, let him be whipped that first finds it so.

	这一个身穿彩衣，另一个站在那边。	140
李尔	你叫我傻子吗，孩子？	
傻子	别的头衔你都给了他人；这一个是你生来自带。	
肯特	这并非全是傻话，陛下。	
傻子	不，真的，贵族大人们不会准许；我要是有犯傻的专利，他们也都想有份；还有女士们，她们也不让我独自扮演傻子角色，她们会抢夺。老伯，给我个鸡蛋，我给你两顶皇冠。	145
李尔	那会是怎样的皇冠？	150
傻子	嗨，我把鸡蛋从中间一刀两断，把肉吃完，不就成了两顶蛋壳皇冠！当你把你的皇冠从中间一劈两半，将它们送人时，你就像是在土路上背着驴走。你把金冠给人之后，你那光秃的脑壳便没多少智慧可言。傻子这话是心直口快，谁先觉得是在犯傻，谁该挨打。	155

140. 那边（there）：指向李尔，或把他的笨伯杖（bauble）递向李尔。　146. 专利（monopoly）：经营某一商品，或与某一特定国家进行贸易的特权。　詹姆斯国王一世，跟他之前的伊丽莎白女王一样，将这种专利（垄断）作为一种奖赏授予大臣，但在其后期的统治期间，这种专利的数量变得如此众多，竟导致国会于1620-1621年就此发起了抵制运动。　也许是因为此时的审查制度（censorship），或者自查导致了这些台词的删除。　153. 皇冠（crown）：王国（kingdom）。154. 你……走（thou…dirt）：傻子是指《伊索寓言》中的那位老人，他骑着毛驴想取悦每一个人，当有人说他快把那头可怜的牲口压垮了时，他便把自己的毛驴背到了市场；大家都在笑他，一气之下他竟把毛驴扔进了河里。　其中的教义在于：谁若想使人人高兴，结果会没人高兴（in trying to please all he pleases no one）。　另外，该寓言也可提供另一种意象——本末倒置（the inversion of order）。　150. 傻子上文的谜底显而易见，但李尔是在有意扮演滑稽戏中的配角——作为主角打趣的对象（Muir）　156-7. 傻子……挨打（If…so）：原注为"If I speak（truth）like a fool in saying this, let him（Lear）be whipped who first finds it to be foolish（如果我这是傻子一般道出了真相，就让那首先发现这是犯傻的［李尔］挨抽鞭子）"。

[*Sing*]   *Fools had ne'er less wit in a year,*

For wise men are grown foppish,

160   *And know not how their wits to wear,*

Their manners are so apish.

Lear   When were you wont to be so full of songs, sirrah?

Fool   I have used it, nuncle, e'er since thou mad'st thy
daughters thy mothers; for when thou gav'st them the

165   rod and putt'st down thine own breeches,

[*Sing*]   *Then they for sudden joy did weep,*

And I for sorrow sung,

That such a king should play bo-peep,

And go the fools among.

170   Prithee, nuncle, keep a schoolmaster that can teach thy
fool to lie; I would fain learn to lie.

Lear   An you lie, ^Fsirrah,^F we'll have you whipped.

Fool   I marvel what kin thou and thy daughters are.
They'll have me whipped for speaking true, thou'lt

175   have me whipped for lying, and sometimes I am whipped
for holding my peace. I had rather be any kind o'thing
than a fool, and yet I would not be thee, nuncle. Thou
hast pared thy wit o'both sides and left nothing i'the
middle. Here comes one o'the parings.

〔唱〕　傻子现如今最为失宠，

　　　　因为智者已不再聪明，

　　　　不知道如何展示才智，　　　　　　　　　　　160

　　　　举止竟如此装腔作势。

李尔　　您啥时候爱上了唱歌，先生？

傻子　　自从你把女儿当作了母亲之后，我就
　　　　惯于哼唱，老伯；因为你把棍棒交给
　　　　她们，自己脱下裤子时，　　　　　　　　165

　　　　〔唱〕　她们顿时高兴得哭泣，

　　　　　　悲伤之中我开始歌唱，

　　　　　　这样的国王竟然儿戏，

　　　　　　在傻子之间来来往往。

　　　　我求你，老伯，雇一位老师来教你的　　　　170
　　　　傻子撒谎；我很想学会撒谎。

李尔　　你若撒谎，小子，我用鞭子抽你。

傻子　　我纳闷你和你的女儿之间是什么关系。
　　　　要是我说实话她们就会打我，要是我
　　　　说假话你就会打我，有时我要是啥都　　　175
　　　　不说也会挨打。只要不当傻子，当啥
　　　　我都愿意，可我不想当你，老伯。你
　　　　把脑瓜儿劈成了两半，那中间啥都没
　　　　剩。　其中的那一半来啦。

158-61. 傻子……装腔作势（Fools…apish）：原注为 "There was never a time when fools were less in favour than now, and the reason is they were never so little wanted, for wise men now supply their place（傻子从未像现在这样不讨人喜欢，原因在于他们已不再稀缺，因为聪明人已取而代之）"（Muir）。　162. 您……唱歌（When…songs）：是否表明傻子很少歌唱？ 也许他的韵文大都是说出来的，比如他在 116-25 所讲的那段话 "speech"。　见 2.2.238-43 及注。　168. 儿戏（bo-peep）：儿童玩的游戏，他们轮番躲藏起来并出其不意地发出叫声，以便吓唬对方或以此逗乐（Foakes）。　这种游戏更像是捉迷藏，而不像现代的躲猫猫（bo-peep）。　傻子此处旨在暗示李尔蒙住了眼睛，躲藏起来（即退位），或者是在胡闹（has blinded himself [i.e. abdicated], or played silly pranks）（Muir）。

Enter Goneril.

180 **Lear** How now, daughter! What makes that frontlet on?

^QMethinks^Q you are too much of late i'the frown.

Fool Thou wast a pretty fellow when thou hadst no need

to care for her frowning. Now thou art an O without a

figure; I am better than thou art now. I am a fool, thou

185 art nothing. [*to Goneril*] Yes, forsooth, I will hold my

tongue; so your face bids me, though you say nothing.

Mum, mum!

He that keeps nor crust nor crumb,

Weary of all, shall want some.

190 [*Points to Lear*] That's a shelled peascod.

Goneril Not only, sir, this your all-licensed fool,

But other of your insolent retinue

Do hourly carp and quarrel, breaking forth

In rank and not to be endured riots. Sir,

195 I had thought by making this well known unto you

To have found a safe redress, but now grow fearful

By what yourself too late have spoke and done,

That you protect this course and put ^Fit^F on

贡纳丽上。

| 李尔 | 怎么了，女儿？　为何愁眉苦脸？ | 180 |

我看您近来的皱眉过于频繁。

| 傻子 | 当你不用在乎她是否皱眉时，你这人 |

倒很幸运。如今你成了前面没数字的

零蛋；我现在都比你强。我是个傻子，

你啥都不是。[向贡纳丽] 对，我这就 185

闭嘴；您的脸色告诉了我，尽管没说。

嘘，嘘！

谁把面包全给人，

厌弃一切，困自身。

[指向李尔] 那是一个豌豆壳。 190

| 贡纳丽 | 不只是您这位随心所欲的傻子， |

还有您那些傲慢无礼的随从

时刻都在找碴儿吵闹，放荡

不羁以及暴行难容。　父亲，

我本想通过将此事告知与您， 195

以便得到补救，可现在您本人

最近的言行开始令人担忧，

您是在袒护这种行为，并通过

---

180. 愁眉苦脸（frontlet）：即"愁眉不展（frown）"；严格说来，该词本指戴在额头上的一种饰带（an ornamental band worn on the forehead）。　贡纳丽此刻也许会系着一根绷带，因为她在 1. 3. 9 及本场 49 行都转告李尔说她病了。　188-9. 将李尔喻为一位厌弃负责的人物（见 1.1. 37-40），把自己拥有的一切都给了出去（他的整个面包：面包皮、面包屑），将来会缺衣少食。194. 不羁（rank）：excessive, uncontrolled（过分，失控）（Bate）。

		By your allowance; which if you should, the fault
200		Would not scape censure, nor the redresses sleep,
		Which in the tender of a wholesome weal
		Might in their working do you that offence
		Which else were shame, that then necessity
		Will call discreet proceeding.
205	**Fool**	For you know, nuncle,

> *The hedge-sparrow fed the cuckoo so long*
> *That it's had it head bit off by it young.*

So out went the candle and we were left darkling.

Lear   Are you our daughter?

210 **ONERIL**   ^QCome, sir,^Q

I would you would make use of that good wisdom,
Whereof I know you are fraught, and put away
These dispositions, that of late transform you
From what you rightly are.

215 **Fool**   May not an ass know when the cart draws the horse? Whoop, Jug, I love thee.

Lear   Doth any here know me? ^QWhy^Q, this is not Lear. Doth Lear walk thus, speak thus? Where are his eyes?

　　　　　默许予以纵容；若果真如此，

　　　　　追究不可避免，纠正也不会延缓，　　　　　　200

　　　　　基于我想让社会井井有条，

　　　　　惩戒措施也许会将您冒犯，

　　　　　在平时会丢人，可现因迫不得已

　　　　　而被视为审慎明断。

傻子　　　您可知道，老伯，　　　　　　　　　　　205

　　　　　　　麻雀喂养了布谷鸟这么久，

　　　　　　　结果被它的小鸟咬掉了头。

　　　　　蜡烛已灭，我们陷入黑暗之中。

李尔　　　您是我女儿吗？

贡纳丽　　得啦，父亲，　　　　　　　　　　　　210

　　　　　我希望您能运用自己的智慧，

　　　　　这一点我知道您是有的，放弃

　　　　　您这种脾性，它们近来已让您

　　　　　变得情绪失常。

傻子　　　难道一头蠢驴不知道什么时候是车子　　　215

　　　　　拉马？　吆嗬，宝贝儿，我爱你。

李尔　　　这里有谁认识我吗？这不是李尔。

　　　　　李尔这样走，这样说？他的眼睛呢？

　　199-204. 若果真……明断（which…proceeding）：原注为："If you should do this, I will censure you for it, and take steps to check the riotous behaviour of your knights. My disciplinary measures, due to my desire to have a healthy state, may well offend you; which would in other circumstances be disgraceful, but now, because such actions are necessary, they will be seen as judicious."（Muir；Foakes）　贡纳丽故意使自己的台词拐弯抹角（tortuous），但其中的意义还是相当清晰（Muir）。　206. 布谷鸟（cuckoo）：这种鸟将蛋下到其他鸟的窝里（Bevington）。　207. 它的小鸟（it young）= its young，即小布谷鸟儿。　源于一则警世寓言——忘恩负义的子女（Bevington）。　208. 黑暗（darkling）= in the dark（处在黑暗之中）。　傻子此处是否预见到了即将来临的苦难？　（见243-6）215-216. 难道……拉马（May…horse）：原注为"May not a Fool see that there is something obviously wrong, when a daughter gives instructions to her royal father?"（Muir）216. 宝贝儿（Jug）：即"琼（Joan）"的昵称。　贡纳丽也许对傻子做出了怪相，或有威胁似的举动，这是傻子躲避性的回应。

	Either his notion weakens, ^Qor^Q his discerning are
220	lethargied—Ha! ^QSleeping or^Q waking? ^QSure^Q 'tis not
	so. Who is it that can tell me who I am?

^FFool^F Lear's shadow.

^QLear I would learn that, for by the marks of sovereignty,
knowledge and reason, I should be false persuaded I

225 had daughters.

Fool Which they will make an obedient father.^Q

Lear Your name, fair gentlewoman?

Goneril This admiration, sir, is much o'the savour
Of other your new pranks. I do beseech you

230 ^FTo^F understand my purposes aright:
As you are old and reverend, should be wise.
Here do you keep a hundred knights and squires,
Men so disordered, so debauched and bold,
That this our court, infected with their manners,

235 Shows like a riotous inn. Epicurism and lust
Makes ^Fit^F more like a tavern or a brothel
Than a graced palace. The shame itself doth speak
For instant remedy. Be then desired,
By her that else will take the thing she begs,

240 A little to disquantity your train,
And the remainders that shall still depend
To be such men as may besort your age,

	不是他的智力衰退，就是他的识别力	
	迟钝——哈！睡着了还是醒着？肯定	220
	不是。 有人能说出我是谁吗？	
傻子	李尔的影子。	
李尔	我想知道这一点，因为我威严的标示、	
	知识和理智，都会使我误以为自己曾	
	有过女儿。	225
傻子	她们可使你成为听话的父亲。	
李尔	您的大名，亲爱的女士？	
贡纳丽	这种惊讶的样子，父亲，跟您	
	最近的胡闹性质一样。 我求您	
	可要正确地理解我的用心：	230
	既然您年高德劭，也应该聪明。	
	您在此养着一百名侍卫和乡绅，	
	他们是如此骚乱、放荡和鲁莽，	
	致使我这宫廷，受其行为污染，	
	像是喧闹的客栈。 贪吃和纵欲	235
	使它倒更像一家酒馆或妓院，	
	不像庄严的王宫。 这种耻辱	
	需要立即纠正。 因此请求您，	
	否则她求的事情自己会执行：	
	请稍微减少您的随从人员，	240
	而且您所留下来的那些随从	
	也要和您的年龄相互匹配，	

220-1. 哈……不是（Ha…so）：也许"李尔此时会拧一下自己或晃动一下身子，以确保自己没有入睡或做梦"，以此确信自己的感觉正常（参照4.7.55-7）。 223. 这一点（that）：我是谁（who I am）（Bevington）。 223. 威严的标示（marks of sovereignty）：只在四开本里出现的该短语表明李尔会展示某些王权的标志，好像他仍是国王。 234. 我这宫廷（our court）：贡纳丽已将自己视为女王，采用了表示国王身份的复数形式。

Which know themselves, and you.

Lear   Darkness and devils!

Saddle my horses; call my train together.

245 Degenerate bastard, I'll not trouble thee:

Yet have I left a daughter.

Goneril You strike my people, and your disordered rabble

Make servants of their betters.

Enter Albany.

Lear Woe that too late repents! —^QO sir, are you come?^Q

250 Is it your will? Speak, sir. —Prepare my horses.

[*Exit a Knight.*]

Ingratitude, thou marble-hearted fiend,

More hideous when thou show'st thee in a child

Than the sea-monster.

^F**Albany**^F Pray, sir, be patient.

^F**Lear**^F [*to Goneril*]   Detested kite, thou liest.

255 My train are men of choice and rarest parts

That all particulars of duty know,

And in the most exact regard support

The worships of their name. O most small fault,

How ugly didst thou in Cordelia show,

明白约束自己,和您。

李尔　　　　　　　　　　　　地狱和魔鬼!

给我套马;把我的随从们召来。

堕落的杂种,我不会麻烦你的: 　　　　　　　　　　　　　　　245

可我还有个女儿。

贡纳丽　　您打我的人,您那放肆的暴徒

将其上级当作奴仆。

　　　　　　　　　　　阿班尼上。

李尔　　　追悔莫及真可悲! ——噢,先生,您来啦?

是您的意思吗? 说呀,先生。 ——给我备马。 　　　　　250

　　　　　　　　　　　　　　　　　[一侍卫下。]

忘恩负义,铁石心肠的恶魔,

当你在孩子身上显现时比那

海怪还可怕。

阿班尼　　先生,请息怒。

李尔　　　[向贡纳丽] 可憎的老鹰,你胡说!

我的随从都是难得的精英, 　　　　　　　　　　　　　　255

他们知道自己的具体职责,

并且都在一丝不苟地维护着

自己的尊荣。 噢,多么小的瑕疵,

你在考迪丽娅身上显得多丑,

---

243. 明白……您(Which…you):知道他们和您该如何检点自己(who knows how they and you should behave)(参见 1.1.295)。 243-5. 地狱……你的(Darkness…thee):李尔此时的勃然大怒跟他在开场时对待考迪丽娅的情形一样。 245. 杂种(bastard):将她与埃德蒙相提并论。 李尔一怒之下将贡纳丽以及随后的李根(2.2.319-20)想象为私生;相比之下,考迪丽娅纯粹像是她父亲的孩子,与一位好妇母亲无关。 253. 海怪(sea-monster):海怪经常出现在传说中或神话里面;《圣经》"诗篇"中也有提及(见 74 章 13-4 节)。 254. 先生,请息怒(Pray…patient):明显属于对开本里所增添的内容,跟下文 321 行一样,旨在加强阿班尼这一角色的分量。

260

Which like an engine wrenched my frame of nature

From the fixed place, drew from my heart all love

And added to the gall. O Lear, Lear^F, Lear^F!

[*striking his head*] Beat at this gate that let thy folly in

And thy dear judgment out. Go, go, my people.

                [*Exeunt Kent, Knights and attendants.*]

265 **Albany**   My lord, I am guiltless as I am ignorant

          ^FOf what hath moved you.^F

Lear   It may be so, my lord.

          Hear, Nature, hear, dear goddess, ^Fhear^F:

Suspend thy purpose if thou didst intend

To make this creature fruitful.

270

Into her womb convey sterility,

Dry up in her the organs of increase,

And from her derogate body never spring

A babe to honour her. If she must teem,

Create her child of spleen, that it may live

275

And be a thwart disnatured torment to her.

Let it stamp wrinkles in her brow of youth,

With cadent tears fret channels in her cheeks,

Turn all her mother's pains and benefits

To laughter and contempt, that she may feel

280

How sharper than a serpent's tooth it is

你就像一根撬棒将我的天性　　　　　　　　　260

原地翘起,把我的爱心抽干,

填充上苦胆。　李尔啊,李尔,李尔!

[击打头部]敲打这脑门,是它将愚蠢放进,

把明智放出。　走,走,我的人员。

　　　　　　　　　　　　　　[肯特、侍卫及随从下。]

阿班尼　　陛下,我是无辜的,我不清楚　　　　　265

是什么让您动情。

李尔　　　　　　　　　也许吧,阁下。

听着,造化,亲爱的女神,听着:

假如你曾有意让这个东西

生儿育女,请你改变主意!

你要使她的子宫无法孕育,　　　　　　　　270

使她的生育器官完全枯干,

使她堕落的躯体永远生不出

可荣耀她的婴儿! 若定要生产,

就让她孩子暴戾,好让它活着

并变得固执无情把她折磨。　　　　　　　　275

让她那年轻的额头布满皱纹,

让她的面颊被落泪冲出沟槽,

将她母亲的全部疼爱和欢欣

化为轻蔑和嘲笑,好让她感受

忘恩负义的孩子造成的伤痛　　　　　　　　280

260-1. 就像……翘起(like…place):就像一根杠杆或工具将我的慈爱拧走,使它脱离自己的根基(like a lever or implement wrenched my natural affection away from where it should be centred)。　263. 愚蠢(folly):最终承认了傻子曾向他指出的事实(见 98-107,137-40)。267. 造化(Nature):令人想起埃德蒙在 1. 2. 1 对自然(Nature)的呼求,只是意义有所区别;李尔是把"自然"祈求为一种创造性的力量(creative force),但他这种可怕的诅咒却会使"自然"变得违反自然(make nature unnatural [disnatured,275]),因此几乎让自己与埃德蒙同流(aligns him with Edmund)。

To have a thankless child. Away, away!

^F*Exeunt*^F [*Lear and Fool*].

Albany   Now gods that we adore, whereof comes this?

Goneril   Never afflict yourself to know more of it,

But let his disposition have that scope

285   As dotage gives it.

^F*Enter Lear*^F [*followed by the Fool*].

Lear   What, fifty of my followers at a clap?

Within a fortnight?

Albany   What's the matter, sir?

Lear   I'll tell thee. [*to Goneril*] Life and death, I am ashamed

That thou hast power to shake my manhood thus,

290   That these hot tears, which break from me perforce,

Should make thee worth them. Blasts and fogs upon ^Fthee^F!

Th'untented woundings of a father's curse

Pierce every sense about thee. Old fond eyes,

Beweep this cause again, I'll pluck ye out,

295   And cast you with the waters that you loose

To temper clay. ^QYea, is't come to this?^Q

^FHa? Let it be so.^F I have another daughter,

Who I am sure is kind and comfortable:

When she shall hear this of thee, with her nails

300   She'll flay thy wolvish visage. Thou shalt find

That I'll resume the shape which thou dost think

I have cast off for ever: ^Qthou shalt, I warrant thee.^Q ^F*Exit.*^F

比遭蛇咬还糟！快走，快走！

[李尔与傻子]同下。

阿班尼	可爱的众神啊，这是怎么回事？
贡纳丽	千万别打听缘由而自寻烦恼，
	只管让他尽情地使性子去吧，
	他已昏聩年老。 285

[傻子跟着]李尔上。

李尔	怎么，一下减去了五十个随从？
	在两周之内？
阿班尼	怎么回事，陛下？
李尔	我告诉你。 [向贡纳丽]我发誓，我感到羞耻，
	你能这样动摇我的男子气概，
	我这些禁不住流出的热泪， 290
	好像你配！愿邪风瘴气侵袭你！
	愿父亲诅咒的无法医治的创伤
	刺穿你每个感官！愚蠢的老眼，
	若再为此哭泣，就把你们挖出，
	跟你们流出的眼泪丢在一起 295
	去湿润大地。　结果竟会这样？
	哈？　由它去吧。　我还有个女儿，
	我肯定她会既和蔼又体贴：
	她若知道你这种行径，会用指甲
	撕破你狼一般的嘴脸。　你会发现 300
	我将恢复王权，尽管你以为
	我已永久放弃。　我说话算数。　　　　下。

---

283. 原注为"Never try to find out what will pain you"。　284-5. 尽情……年老（that…it）:（行使）老态龙钟所允许的行动自由（that freedom of action senility allows），即"雷声大，雨点稀（violent talk and little action）"（Foakes）。　其中，原文中的 As = that（Bevington）。

	Goneril	Do you mark that, ^Qmy lord^Q?
	Albany	I cannot be so partial, Goneril,
		To the great love I bear you—
305	**Goneril**	^FPray you, content.^F

Goneril (305):

^QCome, sir, no more.^Q ^FWhat, Oswald, ho?^F

[*to the Fool*] You, ^Fsir,^F more knave than fool, after
    your master.

Fool Nuncle Lear, nuncle Lear, tarry, ^Qand^Q take the
fool with ^Fthee:^F

310

A fox when one has caught her,

And such a daughter,

Should sure to the slaughter,

If my cap would buy a halter;

So the fool follows after.   ^F*Exit.*^F

315 **Goneril** ^FThis man hath had good counsel—a hundred knights!

'Tis politic, and safe, to let him keep

At point a hundred knights! Yes, that on every dream,

Each buzz, each fancy, each complaint, dislike,

He may enguard his dotage with their powers

320

And hold our lives in mercy. Oswald, I say!

Albany Well, you may fear too far.

Goneril Safer than trust too far.

Let me still take away the harms I fear,

Not fear still to be taken. I know his heart;

325

What he hath uttered I have writ my sister.

If she sustain him and his hundred knights

When I have showed the unfitness—^F

贡纳丽	您看到了吧,夫君?
阿班尼	可是我却不能偏心,贡纳丽,
	尽管我非常爱您——

贡纳丽　　　　　　　　　　　　　求您,住口吧。　　　　　　　305
　　快,先生,别说了。　奥斯华德呢,嗬?
　　[向傻子]您这傻子更像恶棍,跟
　　　　主子去吧。

傻子　　李尔老伯,李尔老伯,等一等,要把
　　傻子带上。

　　　　　狐狸谁若捉到她,　　　　　　　310
　　　　　还有这个女儿家,
　　　　　定会送去被宰杀,
　　　　　傻帽若能当绳扎;
　　　　　傻子这就去追他。　　　　　　　　下。

贡纳丽　这个人想得真棒——一百名侍卫!　　　315
　　让他保留一百名武装的侍卫,
　　真是精明和安全! 对,哪怕是梦、
　　流言蜚语、虚幻、抱怨、不满,
　　即可利用他们保护他的昏聩,
　　咱的性命由他支配。　奥斯华德,喂!　　320

阿班尼　哎,您也许担心过分。
贡纳丽　要胜过过分信任。
　　我宁愿消除我所担心的祸患,
　　不愿总提心吊胆。　他的品性我懂;
　　我已写信把他说的通知妹妹。　　　　　325
　　我已指出其中的不妥,她若
　　供养他和那一百侍卫——

　　315-27. 这……侍卫(This…unfitness):对开本里所增加的这些台词像是要与贡纳丽这一角色的其他变化保持一致,以使她对父亲的慢待好像更有道理。 其中的一行加给了谨慎的阿班尼公爵。 317. 精明(politic):跟315行的"真棒(good = bad)"一样,贡纳丽当然是在讥讽。

^F*Enter Oswald.*^F

^Q**Oswald**	Here, madam.^Q
Goneril	^FHow now, Oswald?^F What, have you writ
330	that letter to my sister?
Oswald	Ay, madam.
Goneril	Take you some company and away to horse.

Inform her full of my particular fear,

And thereto add such reasons of your own

335   As may compact it more. Get you gone,

And hasten your return.   [*Exit Oswald.*]

No, no, my lord,

This milky gentleness and course of yours,

Though I condemn not, yet, under pardon,

You are much more attasked for want of wisdom

340   Than praised for harmful mildness.

Albany   How far your eyes may pierce I cannot tell;

Striving to better, oft we mar what's well.

Goneril   Nay then—

Albany   Well, well, th'event.   *Exeunt.*

奥斯华德上。

奥斯华德　来了,夫人。

贡纳丽　怎么样,奥斯华德? 您给我妹妹
　　　　　写信了没有?　　　　　　　　　　　　　330

奥斯华德　写了,夫人。

贡纳丽　您叫几个同伴快上马出发。
　　　　　把我个人的担心全告诉给她,
　　　　　您自己也可添加一些理由
　　　　　以便更加可信。 您快去吧,　　　　　335
　　　　　您要尽快返回。　　　　　　［奥斯华德下。］

　　　　　　　　　不,不,夫君,
　　　　　您这种奶油小生似的习性,
　　　　　尽管我不谴责,但恕我直说,
　　　　　您因缺乏智慧而应受到责备,
　　　　　不是因有害的厚道而受赞美。　　　　340

阿班尼　您的目光能看多远我不知道;
　　　　　力求更好,往往把好的弄糟。

贡纳丽　不对——

阿班尼　那好,咱等着瞧。　　　　　　　　同下。

---

342. 像是对一句谚语的改动,即 "Let well alone（别画蛇添足）"。

SCENE V

Enter Lear, [F]*Kent, and Fool.*[F]

Lear	[*to Kent*] Go you before to Gloucester with these letters . Acquaint my daughter no further with anything you know than comes from her demand out of the letter. If your diligence be not speedy, I shall be there afore you.
Kent	I will not sleep, my lord, till I have delivered your letter. *Exit.*
Fool	If a man's brains were in's heels, were't not in danger of kibes?
Lear	Ay, boy.
Fool	Then I prithee be merry; thy wit shall not go slipshod.
Lear	Ha, ha, ha!
Fool	Shalt see thy other daughter will use thee kindly, for though she's as like this as a crab's like an apple, yet I can tell what I can tell.

5

10

15

第五场

李尔、肯特[化装]与傻子上。

李尔	[向肯特]您带这些信件先到格洛斯特 去吧。您可以就信里面的内容回答我 女儿的各种提问,除此之外,您不要 多说。您要是不尽力赶路,我会比您 先到。
肯特	我把您的信送到之前,陛下,我不会 睡觉。
傻子	一个人的脑子若长在脚跟,难道不会 生出冻疮?
李尔	会,孩子。
傻子	那我求你尽管开心;你的脑筋不需要 拖鞋。
李尔	哈,哈,哈!
傻子	你将看到你的另一位女儿会对你很好, 因为尽管她与这个相似,就像酸苹果 跟苹果一样,我心中有数。

5

下。

10

15

1.5. 　1. 格洛斯特(Gloucester):此处应为地名,位于贡纳丽的宫殿与康瓦尔公爵的府邸之间。　11-2. 你的……拖鞋(thy…slipshod):傻子是在暗示李尔出发去见李根是缺乏脑筋(brainless)(Foakes)。 现代译文为:Your brains won't need slippers to protect them from frostbite, since your brains aren't in your feet—if they were, you wouldn't take this useless journey to see Regan(你的脑子不用穿拖鞋以防冻伤,因为你的脑子没长在脚上——它们若长在脚上,你就不会徒劳无益地去见李根)(Sparknotes)。 14. 很好(kindly):在玩弄该词的两种意义:"亲切的(with affection)";和"天生的(according to her kind or nature)",即"无情地(cruelly)"。 16. 我心中有数(I…can tell):对一句谚语的改动,"I know what I know = I am in on a secret(我了解内情)"。

	Lear	^QWhy,^Q what canst ^Qthou^Q tell, ^Qmy^Q boy?
	Fool	She will taste as like this as a crab does to a crab.
20		Thou canst ^Qnot^Q tell why one's nose stands i'the middle on's face?
	Lear	No.
	Fool	Why, to keep one's eyes of either side's nose, that what a man cannot smell out he may spy into.
	Lear	I did her wrong.
25	**Fool**	Canst tell how an oyster makes his shell?
	Lear	No.
	Fool	Nor I neither; but I can tell why a snail has a house.
	Lear	Why?
30	**Fool**	Why, to put's head in, not to give it away to his daughters and leave his horns without a case.
	Lear	I will forget my nature: so kind a father! Be my horses ready?
	Fool	Thy asses are gone about 'em. The reason why the seven stars are no more than seven is a pretty reason.
35	**Lear**	Because they are not eight.
	Fool	Yes, ^Findeed,^F thou wouldst make a good fool.
	Lear	To take't again perforce—monster ingratitude!
	Fool	If thou wert my fool, nuncle, I'd have thee beaten

李尔	哎,你有啥数,孩子?	
傻子	她也会是这个味道,酸苹果对酸苹果。	
	难道你不懂人们的鼻子为什么会长在	
	脸的中间?	20
李尔	不懂。	
傻子	嗨,是为了把人的眼睛放在鼻子两边,	
	人们闻不出来时,可以看得出来。	
李尔	我冤枉了她。	
傻子	你知道牡蛎是怎样造壳的吗?	25
李尔	不知道。	
傻子	我也不知道;可我知道蜗牛为啥有窝。	
李尔	为啥?	
傻子	嗨,好把头放进去呀,不会把它送给	
	女儿,结果使他的双角无处可藏。	30
李尔	我要忘记父爱:多仁慈的父亲!我的	
	马备好了吗?	
傻子	你的蠢驴已去准备。北斗七星之所以	
	只有七颗自有它的道理。	
李尔	因为它没有八颗。	35
傻子	没错,你可做个很好的傻子。	
李尔	要用武力收回——丑恶的忘恩负义!	
傻子	你要是我的傻子,老伯,我会打你,	

---

24. 我冤枉了她(I…wrong):通常被认为是指考迪丽娅,作为1.4.258-64的后续;但也可能是指贡纳丽。李尔此刻思绪混乱,对傻子的话语并未完全在意。　30. 双角(horns):傻子无意把李尔称为了乌龟(即头上长角):他只是相信头戴绿帽是已婚男人不可避免的装饰(Muir)。31. 忘记父爱(forget my nature):不再当慈父(cease to be a kind father)(Muir)。其中,"nature"是指"natural affection or kindness(父爱或仁慈)"(Foakes)。　33. 蠢驴(asses):臣仆(servants)(是否暗示侍奉李尔的都是傻子?)。　37. 要用武力收回(To…perforce):可指"贡纳丽竟将许诺给我的特权强行收回(Goneril would forcibly take back again the privileges guaranteed to me!)";也可指"李尔是在沉思用武力恢复自己的王权(meditating an armed restoration of his monarchy)"(Bevington)。

for being old before thy time.

40 **Lear** How's that?

Fool Thou shouldst not have been old till thou hadst been wise.

Lear O let me not be mad, ^Fnot mad,^F sweet heaven! ^QI would not be mad.^Q

45 Keep me in temper, I would not be mad.

[Enter a Gentleman.]

^FHow now,^F are the horses ready?

Gentleman Ready, my lord.

Lear Come, boy. ^Q*Exeunt*^Q [*Lear and Gentleman*].

Fool She that's a maid now, and laughs at my departure,

50 Shall not be a maid long, unless things be cut shorter.

Exit.

因为你未老先衰。

李尔　　此话怎讲？ 40

傻子　　你应该等到变得聪明一些之后再变
　　　　老啊。

李尔　　噢，别让我发疯，可爱的苍天！我
　　　　不想发疯。
　　　　让我神志正常，我不想发疯。 45

[一绅士上。]

怎么样，马套好了吗？

绅士　　好了，陛下。

李尔　　快，孩子。　　　　　　[李尔与侍从]同下。

傻子　　若有哪个姑娘嘲笑我退场，
　　　　除非阴茎被截短，很快会遭殃。

下。 50

---

43. 发疯（mad）：首次预感（Muir）。 49-50. 若有……遭殃（She…shorter）：该对句是针对观众讲的，有些编者认为并非出自莎氏本人。 傻子是在说：若有哪位少女只是觉得傻子的嘲弄好笑，意识不到李尔行将踏上悲惨的旅途，就是傻瓜，因为她不懂如何保护童贞（The maid who sees only the funny side of the Fool's gibes, and does not realize that Lear is going on a tragic journey is such a simpleton that she won't know how to preserve her virginity）（Muir）。

第二幕
ACT 2

SCENE I

Enter Edmund and Curan severally.

Edmund   Save thee, Curan.

Curan   And you, sir. I have been with your father and
given him notice that the Duke of Cornwall and
^FRegan^F his Duchess will be here with him this
5   night.

Edmund   How comes that?

Curan   Nay, I know not. You have heard of the news
abroad? — I mean the whispered ones, for they are
yet but ear-bussing arguments.

10   **Edmund**   Not I; pray you, what are they?

Curan   Have you heard of no likely wars toward 'twixt the
^Qtwo^Q dukes of Cornwall and Albany?

Edmund   Not a word.

Curan   You may ^Fdo^F then in time. Fare you well, sir.   ^F*Exit.*^F

15   **Edmund**   The Duke be here tonight? The better—best!
This weaves itself perforce into my business.
My father hath set guard to take my brother,
And I have one thing of a queasy question

第一场

埃德蒙与柯伦分头上。

埃德蒙	保佑你,柯伦。
柯伦	也保佑您,先生。我刚见过您的父亲,
	并且我已经通知他康瓦尔公爵和他的
	公爵夫人李根今天晚上要赶到他这里
	过夜。
埃德蒙	那是为啥?
柯伦	我不知道。您是否已听到外面在传的
	消息?——我是说私下的谣传,因为
	它们只是道听途说而已。
埃德蒙	没听到;求您,是啥消息?
柯伦	难道您没听说康瓦尔和阿班尼这两位
	公爵之间有可能发生内战?
埃德蒙	没听说过。
柯伦	也许您很快会听说。再会了,先生。　下。
埃德蒙	公爵今晚要到?　好上——加好!
	这可与我的计谋完全吻合。
	父亲已派人准备逮捕我哥哥,
	我还有一件令人不安的事情

5

10

15

---

2. 1.　0（1）分头（*severally*）: separately（分别地）。　柯伦与埃德蒙从格洛斯特家的不同方位出来,好像偶然相遇;此刻埃德加正躲在埃德蒙的房间里面。　1. 保佑你（Save thee）:即"上帝保佑你（God save thee）"——一种常见的招呼（Muir）。　柯伦（Curan）:只在本场出现,像是格洛斯特家的一员。　也许莎氏最初曾想进一步发展这一角色,因为,通常是不会给这么微不足道的角色取名的。

Which I must act. Briefness and fortune work!

20 Brother, a word; descend, brother, I say.

Enter Edgar.

My father watches; O ^Fsir^F, fly this place!

Intelligence is given where you are hid:

You have now the good advantage of the night.

Have you not spoken 'gainst the Duke of Cornwall ^Qaught^Q? —

25 He's coming hither, now, i'the night, i'the haste,

And Regan with him. Have you nothing said

Upon his party 'gainst the Duke of Albany?

Advise yourself.

Edgar   I am sure on't, not a word.

Edmund I hear my father coming—pardon me;

30 In cunning I must draw my sword upon you.

^FDraw,^F seem to defend yourself; now quit you well.

[*loudly*] Yield, come before my father! Light, ho, here!

[*to Edgar*] Fly, brother, ^Qfly^Q! [*loudly*] Torches,

torches! —[*to Edgar*] So farewell.   ^F*Exit Edgar.*^F

Some blood drawn on me would beget opinion

Of my more fierce endeavour.   [*Cuts his arm.*]

35   I have seen drunkards

Do more than this in sport. Father, father!

Stop, stop, no help?

需要执行。　敏捷和运气帮我！

哥哥，我有话要说；下来吧，哥哥！　　　　　　　　　　　20

埃德加上。

父亲在监视；噢，哥哥，赶紧逃吧！

您的藏身之处已经被发现：

现在的夜幕对您非常有利。

您没说过康瓦尔公爵的坏话吧？　——

他正在连夜匆忙赶往这里，　　　　　　　　　　　　　　25

李根与他一起。　您没有站在

他这边反对过阿班尼公爵吧？

好好想想。

埃德加　　　　　　　　　我肯定，从未说过。

埃德蒙　　我听见父亲来了——请您原谅；

我必须拔出剑来假装刺您。　　　　　　　　　　　　　　30

拔剑，好像是自卫；要奋力还击。

[大声地]投降吧，去见父亲！掌灯，来人哪！

[向埃德加]快逃，哥哥！[大声地]火把，

　火把！——[向埃德加]再见吧。　　　　　　埃德加下。

身上如果流血会让人以为

我在奋力搏杀。[刺伤手臂。]

　　　　　　　　　我见过醉汉　　　　　　　　　　　35

为取乐比这还狠。　父亲，父亲！

站住，站住，没人吗？

---

30. 假装（In cunning）：作为一种策略（as a device）（Foakes）。　以避免他们好像是在串通一气（to avoid the appearance of collusion）（Muir）。　32. 投降吧，去见父亲（Yield…father!）：故意想让格洛斯特听见，旨在表明他是在保护父亲。　35-6. 我……还狠（I…sport）：年轻的豪侠在借助酒力的情况下，常会为了向情人祝酒而刺伤自身，然后把血混入酒内（Muir）。

Enter Gloucester,^F and Servants, with torches.^F

Gloucester	Now, Edmund, where's the villain?
Edmund	Here stood he in the dark, his sharp sword out,
	Mumbling of wicked charms, conjuring the moon
	To stand ^Q's^Q auspicious mistress.

40   **Gloucester**   But where is he?

       Edmund   Look, sir, I bleed.

       Gloucester   Where is the villain, Edmund?

       Edmund   Fled this way, sir, when by no means he could—

       Gloucester   [*to Secvants*] Pursue him, ^Fho!^F Go after! [*Servants rush off.*]

                                              — 'By no means' what?

       Edmund   Persuade me to the murder of your lordship,

45   But that I told him the revenging gods

               'Gainst parricides did all their thunders bend,

               Spoke with how manifold and strong a bond

               The child was bound to the father. Sir, in fine,

               Seeing how loathly opposite I stood

50   To his unnatural purpose, in fell motion,

               With his prepared sword, he charges home

               My unprovided body, latched mine arm;

               But when he saw my best alarumed spirits,

               Bold in the quarrel's right, roused to th'encounter,

55   Or whether ghasted by the noise I made,

               Full suddenly he fled.

       Gloucester   Let him fly far:

格洛斯特、与仆人，持火把上。

格洛斯特	埃德蒙,恶棍呢?
埃德蒙	他就站在这暗处,拔出利剑,
	口中念着邪咒,召唤月亮
	做他的保护女神。

格洛斯特　　　　　可他在哪里?　　　　　　　　　　40

埃德蒙　您看,我在流血。

格洛斯特　　　那个恶棍呢,埃德蒙?

埃德蒙　朝这边跑了,父亲,当他无法——

格洛斯特　[向仆人]去追他,嗬! 快去追! [众仆人下。]
　　　　　　　　　　——"无法"什么?

埃德蒙　无法说服我杀害父亲大人,
　　　当我告诉他复仇心切的神明　　　　　45
　　　早把全部霹雳瞄准了弑父者,
　　　告诉他父子之间的亲情曾是
　　　多么坚固和紧密;总之,父亲,
　　　看到我是多么强烈地反对
　　　他那种残忍的用心,便用拔出的　　　50
　　　利剑拼命一击,直接刺向我
　　　毫无防备的身体,刺伤我手臂;
　　　但是当他看到我精神抖擞,
　　　义无反顾,奋起与他交战时,
　　　或是被我的喊叫声音吓住,　　　　55
　　　他突然逃走。

格洛斯特　　　　不管他走多远,

---

42. 朝这边（this way）:可能会指向相反的方向,因为埃德加若被捉住,有可能会揭示真相。

Not in this land shall he remain uncaught,

And found—dispatch! The noble Duke, my master,

My worthy arch and patron, comes tonight;

60   By his authority I will proclaim it,

That he which finds him shall deserve our thanks,

Bringing the murderous coward to the stake:

He that conceals him, death!

Edmund   When I dissuaded him from his intent,

65   And found him pight to do it, with curst speech

I threatened to discover him. He replied,

'Thou unpossessing bastard, dost thou think,

If I would stand against thee, would the reposal

Of any trust, virtue or worth in thee

70   Make thy words faithed? No, what I should deny,

As this I would, ^Qay,^Q though thou didst produce

My very character, I'd turn it all

To thy suggestion, plot and damned practice;

And thou must make a dullard of the world,

75   If they not thought the profits of my death

Were very pregnant and potential spurs

To make thee seek it.'   ^F*Tucket within.*^F

Gloucester   ^FO^F strange and fastened villain,

Would he deny his letter, ^Fsaid he?^F ^QI never got him.^Q

在这个国度里他都无法逃脱，

发现了——就处决！我的主人，公爵，

尊贵的主要庇护者，今晚就到；

经过他的准许我将会宣布，　　　　　　　　　　60

谁若发现这个残忍的懦夫

并把他带到刑场，会得到酬谢：

谁要是藏匿，处死！

埃德蒙　我劝他不要对您图谋不轨，

发现他决心已定，我怒气冲冲，　　　　　　　65

威胁要把他揭发。　他回答我说，

你这无继承权的野种，你以为，

我若反驳你，别人对你的信赖，

或你自身的美德、价值能让人

相信你说的是真？　不，我会否认，　　　　70

我一定会的，哪怕你出具我的

笔迹作证，我也会将这一切

归咎于你的邪念、阴谋和诡计；

你一定会把世人当成了傻子，

他们若看不出你想把我置于　　　　　　　　　75

死地的明显而强烈动机是为了

一己私利。　　　　　　　　　　　　　　幕后鸣号。

格洛斯特　　　　　　　无情而顽固的恶棍，

他说会否认写信？　我不是他父亲。

---

58. 发现了——就处决（found…dispatch）：格洛斯特也许会做出将他斩首的手势或其他表示处决的举动。　不经审判，他就鲁莽地给埃德加判了死刑。　70-7. 不……私利（No…it）：颇富讥讽的是，尽管格洛斯特对此并未察觉，埃德蒙强加在埃德加身上的这些话语却道出了他自己的本相。　74-7. 你……私利（thou…seek it）：原注为 "you must think the world is stupid if you think people would not be aware that the benefits for you, should I die, are powerful incitements to you to seek my death"（Barbara A. Mowat, Folger Shakespeare Library, 2009；下称 "Mowat"。　——译者附注）。

Hark, the Duke's trumpets; I know not why he comes.

80 All ports I'll bar, the villain shall not scape;

The Duke must grant me that. Besides, his picture

I will send far and near, that all the kingdom

May have ᶠdueᶠ note of him; and of my land,

Loyal and natural boy, I'll work the means

85 To make thee capable.

Enter Cornwall, ᶠRegan, and attendants.ᶠ

Cornwall   How now, my noble friend? Since I came hither,

Which I can call but now, I have heard strange news.

Regan   If it be true, all vengeance comes too short

Which can pursue th'offender. How dost, my lord?

90 **Gloucester**   ᶠOᶠ madam, my old heart is cracked, it's cracked.

Regan   What, did my father's godson seek your life?

He whom my father named, your Edgar?

Gloucester   O lady, lady, shame would have it hid.

Regan   Was he not companion with the riotous knights

95 That tended upon my father?

Gloucester   I know not, madam; 'tis too bad, too bad.

Edmund   Yes, madam, he was ᶠof that consortᶠ.

Regan   No marvel, then, though he were ill affected.

'Tis they have put him on the old man's death,

100 To have th'expense and waste of his revenues.

I have this present evening from my sister

听,公爵的号声;不知他为何来了。

要封锁所有通道,那恶棍逃不了; 　　　　　　　　　80

公爵会允许我的,此外,我要把

他的情形通知各地,以便全国

都能注意到他;至于我的封地,

忠诚和孝顺的孩子,我会想法

让你能继承。　　　　　　　　　　　　　　　85

康瓦尔、李根与侍从上。

康瓦尔　　怎么了,我的好友?　我来了之后,

就是刚才,听到了奇怪的消息。

李根　　若消息属实,对那罪犯的所有

报复都会太轻。　您好吗,阁下?

格洛斯特　噢,夫人,我的心都碎了,碎了! 　　　　90

李根　　怎么,我父亲的教子想要您性命?

我父亲给起过名的,您的埃德加?

格洛斯特　噢,夫人,夫人,我羞于启齿!

李根　　他是否常跟伺候我父亲的那帮

喧闹的侍卫们厮混? 　　　　　　　　　　　95

格洛斯特　我不知道,夫人,太可怕了,太可怕。

埃德蒙　是的,夫人,他跟他们同伙。

李根　　那就难怪他会有险恶用心。

是他们煽动他谋害这位老人,

以便能将他的财产挥霍殆尽。 　　　　　　100

就在今晚我才从姐姐那里

91-2. 我……埃德加(my…Edgar):李尔在1.1所祈求的只是异教徒的神明(pagan gods),而此处却把他称为埃德加的教父,由此将他们二人与基督教术语连在一起;同时也可暗示埃德加也许就是李尔心目中的儿子。　95. 喧闹的(riotous):在重复贡纳丽所用过的词语(1.4.325)。

Been well informed of them, and with such cautions

That if they come to sojourn at my house,

I'll not be there.

Cornwall   Nor I, assure thee, Regan.

105 Edmund, I hear that you have shown your father

A child-like office.

Edmund   It was my duty, sir.

Gloucester [*to Cornwall*] He did bewray his practice, and received

This hurt you see, striving to apprehend him.

Cornwall Is he pursued?

110 **Gloucester** Ay, my good lord.

Cornwall If he be taken, he shall never more

Be feared of doing harm, make your own purpose

How in my strength you please. For you, Edmund,

Whose virtue and obedience doth this instant

115 So much commend itself, you shall be ours.

Natures of such deep trust we shall much need;

You we first seize on.

Edmund I shall serve you, ᶠsir,ᶠ truly, however else.

Gloucester For him I thank your grace.

120 **Cornwall** You know not why we came to visit you?

Regan Thus out of season, threading dark-eyed night?

Occasions, noble Gloucester, of some poise

了解到那些侍卫,她还告诫,

如果他们要到我家里逗留,

我不要在家。

康瓦尔 我也不会的,李根。 105

埃德蒙,我听说您对父亲尽了

应尽的孝心。

埃德蒙 那是我本分,先生。

格洛斯特 ［向康瓦尔］他揭发了他的阴谋,在试图

逮捕他时,便受了这一刀伤。

康瓦尔 有人去追他吗?

格洛斯特 有,我的好殿下。 110

康瓦尔 他若被捉住,人们再也不用

担心他会害人,您只管用我的

资源满足心愿。 至于您,埃德蒙,

您这种高尚的忠心此时此刻

多么值得称颂,您跟着我吧。 115

我很需要这种可靠的品性;

您要先归我了。

埃德蒙 我愿为您效劳,先生,永不变心。

格洛斯特 我替他谢谢殿下。

康瓦尔 您是否知道我为何前来见您? 120

李根 这么突然,穿过漆黑的夜晚?

有一些重要事情,好格洛斯特,

---

103. 我家里（my house）：李根在本场宣称了她的个人权威（asserts her personal authority），比如此处,以及她从 121 行接住康瓦尔的话茬之后,尽管他们两人从 115 行开始都在使用表示君王身份的复数形式。 112-3. 您只管……心愿（make…please）：原注为“achieve your aim（to seize Edgar）using my authority and resources as you please（您可任意使用我的权威和资源达到目的［逮捕埃德加］）”。 121. 这么（Thus）：李根从丈夫嘴里抢过话茬,以此表明他处于次要地位（he is subordinate）（Muir）。

Wherein we must have use of your advice.

Our father he hath writ, so hath our sister,

125   Of differences, which I least thought it fit

To answer from our home. The several messengers

From hence attend dispatch. Our good old friend,

Lay comforts to your bosom, and bestow

Your needful counsel to our business,

Which craves the instant use.

130 **Gloucester**   I serve you, madam:

Your graces are right welcome.   *Exeunt.* ^F*Flourish.*^F

我有必要让您给我以忠告。
我父亲和姐姐都写来了信件，
谈及争吵，我想我最好不在　　　　　　　　　　　125
家里给他们回信。　那几个信差
正在此等候派遣。　我的老朋友，
您要感到心安理得，并就此
向我提供一些必要的建议，
这需要立刻就办。

格洛斯特　　　　　　　　　为夫人效劳。　　　　　　　　　130
欢迎你们大驾光临。　　　　　　　同下。号声响亮。

　　125-6. 不在家里（from our home）：如果李根不在家里，李尔就不可能逗留。　正如布拉德利和其他评论家所注意到的那样，莎士比亚有意让剧中除考迪丽娅以外的所有主角都集中到格洛斯特家里，由此可在第二幕达到一种高潮——贡纳丽与李根将李尔拒之门外。

SCENE II

Enter Kent [disguised] and Oswald, ᶠ*severally.*ᶠ

Oswald Good dawning to thee, friend. Art of this house?

Kent Ay.

Oswald Where may we set our horses?

5 **Kent** I'the mire.

Oswald Prithee, if thou lov'st me, tell me.

Kent I love thee not.

Oswald Why then, I care not for thee.

Kent If I had thee in Lipsbury pinfold, I would make
10 thee care for me.

Oswald Why dost thou use me thus? I know thee not.

Kent Fellow, I know thee.

Oswald What dost thou know me for?

Kent A knave; a rascal, an eater of broken meats; a base,

第二场

肯特［化装］与奥斯华德，分头上。

奥斯华德	黎明好，朋友。你是这家里面的仆人
	吗？
肯特	唉。
奥斯华德	我们该把马拴在哪里？
肯特	泥潭。

5

奥斯华德	求你，如果你爱我，告诉我。
肯特	我不爱你。
奥斯华德	那好，我不用理你了。
肯特	要是我能让你陷入我的牙关，我就会
	让你理我。

10

奥斯华德	你为何这样待我？我又不认识你。
肯特	伙计，我认识你。
奥斯华德	那我是谁呀？
肯特	一个恶棍、无赖、吃人剩饭的；卑劣、

2.2.　0（1）分头（*severally*）：好像是在格洛斯特家的外面偶然相遇似的。　3.唉（Ay）：不屑与他攀谈？因为肯特不是格洛斯特家的仆人。　9.陷入我的牙关（in Lipsbury pinfold）：通常被认为是指"陷入我的牙齿之间（trapped between my teeth）"。其中，"Lipsbury = lips-town（牙关镇）"（其实并无此地名）；"pinfold"是指圈住走失家畜的畜栏（a pound for stray animals）。　14-38.肯特此处对奥斯华德的怒斥，将他骂为卑贱的奴仆（他作为管家，其实职位很高），以及他对奥斯华德的人身攻击（1.4.84），很难说有什么正当的理由。他在217-33就此的解释是：他受到了李根和贡纳丽的冷待，怒不可遏。不管怎样，观众的感受可通过肯特的怒骂得以戏剧性地表达。

15   proud, shallow, beggarly, three-suited-hundred-pound,

filthy, worsted-stocking knave; a lily-livered, action-

taking ^{Q}knave, a^Q whoreson, glass-gazing, super-

serviceable finical rogue; one trunk-inheriting slave,

one that wouldst be a bawd in way of good service and

20   art nothing but the composition of a knave, beggar,

coward, pander and the son and heir of a mongrel

bitch; ^{F}one^F whom I will beat into clamorous whining if

thou deniest the least syllable of thy addition.

Oswald ^{F}Why,^{F} what a monstrous fellow art thou, thus to

25   rail on one that is neither known of thee, nor knows

thee!

Kent   What a brazen-faced varlet art thou to deny thou

knowest me? Is it two days ^{Q}ago^Q since I tripped up thy

heels, and beat thee before the King? Draw, you rogue,

30   for though it be night, ^{F}yet^F the moon shines. [*Draws

his sword.*] I'll make a sop o'the moonshine of you.

^{Q}Draw^Q you whoreson cullionly barber-monger! Draw!

Oswald   Away, I have nothing to do with thee.

Kent   Draw, you rascal! You come with letters against the

傲慢、肤浅、乞丐般、年薪百镑三套　　　　　　15

服装、污秽、穿毛袜的贱货；胆怯的、

好告状的小人，杂种，爱虚荣、过分

殷勤、做作的恶棍；一箱家产的奴才，

为了能提供好服务甘愿为人拉皮条的、

只不过是个恶棍、乞丐、懦夫、老鸨、　　　　　20

狗娘养的狗崽子以及兼而有之的狗杂

种；我会把你打得嗷嗷乱叫，如果你

否认我所给你的任何一种称号。

奥斯华德　嗨，你是个多么可恶的东西，竟这样

责骂我，你既不认识我，我也不认识　　　　　25

你！

肯特　多么厚颜无耻的无赖，你竟然否认你

认识我？不是两天前我才在国王面前

端了你的脚跟？拔剑吧，你这个恶棍，

即便现在是夜晚，可是月亮很亮。［拔　　　　　30

剑］我要让你千疮百孔，可以浸透月光。

你这个卑鄙的花花公子！拔剑！

奥斯华德　滚开，我跟你没有来往。

肯特　拔剑，恶棍！你带来了对国王不利的

15-6. 年薪百镑三套服装（three…pound）：奥斯华德作为管家，或贡纳丽家的总管，衣着考究。 三套服装像是此类仆人的一种津贴；参考3. 4. 131-2。 年薪百镑在当时是很高的收入。 有些人认为此处可能暗示詹姆斯国王售卖爵士头衔的价码。 16. 穿毛袜的（worsted-stocking）：毛袜不如丝袜，适合仆人。 17. 好告状的（action-taking）：好打官司的（litigious）；采取法律行动（taking legal action），而不是搏斗（rather than fighting）。 19. 拉皮条的（bawd）：奥斯华德后来倒是为贡纳丽与埃德蒙之间传递过信件，对贡纳丽却很忠诚。 31. 我要……月光（I…you）：肯特打算用剑刺他，好让月光或水塘里反射的月光浸透他的躯体，就像漂浮在液体里的面包片一样（Muir）。 32. 卑鄙的花花公子（cullionly barber-monger）：总是光顾理发店的、卑劣的花花公子。

35   King, and take Vanity the puppet's part against the
        royalty of her father. Draw, you rogue, or I'll so
        carbonado your shanks! —draw, you rascal, come your
        ways!

Oswald   Help, ho! Murder, help!

40 **Kent**   Strike, you slave. Stand, rogue, stand you neat slave,
        strike!   [*Beats him.*]

Oswald   Help, ho! Murder, murder!

Enter Edmund, ᵠ*with his rapier drawn,*ᵠ *Cornwall, Regan,*
        Gloucester [*and*] ᶠ*Servants.*ᶠ

Edmund   How now, what's the matter? ᶠPart!ᶠ

Kent   [*to Edmund*] With you, goodman boy, if you please.

45   Come, I'll flesh ye; come on, young master.

Gloucester   Weapons? Arms? What's the matter here?

Cornwall   Keep peace, upon your lives: he dies that
        strikes again. What is the matter?

Regan   The messengers from our sister and the King.

50 **Cornwall**   [*to Kent*] What is your difference? Speak.

Oswald   I am scarce in breath, my lord.

	信件,站在虚荣傀儡的一边,反对她	35
	的父王。 拔剑,你这无赖,否则我把	
	你的小腿划开!——拔剑,恶棍,赶	
	快!	
奥斯华德	救命啊! 杀人啦,救命!	
肯特	来呀,奴才。 站住,恶棍,你这干净	40
	的奴才,来呀![打他。]	
奥斯华德	救命啊! 杀人啦,杀人啦!	

埃德蒙,拔出剑来,康瓦尔、李根、

格洛斯特[与]仆人上。

埃德蒙	怎么了,怎么回事? 住手!	
肯特	[向埃德蒙]跟你斗,傲慢的好小子,你	
	若喜欢。来,我让你尝尝血腥;小主子。	45
格洛斯特	刀剑? 搏斗? 这是怎么回事?	
康瓦尔	住手,否则拿命来见:谁再动手,谁就	
	死去。 怎么回事?	
李根	是我姐姐和国王派来的信差。	
康瓦尔	[向肯特]你们为何争吵? 快说。	50
奥斯华德	我现在气喘吁吁,殿下。	

---

35. 虚荣傀儡（Vanity the puppet）：即贡纳丽。 被想象成傀儡（或浓妆艳抹的女人），即虚荣的化身（the personification of vanity）（Bate）。 37-8. 赶快（come your ways）：奥斯华德佩有利剑,但拒绝拔出,并向后退去而不是站住（40）并搏斗。 40. 干净（neat）：跟32行一样,再次影射奥斯华德雅致的外表或花花公子般的装束。 42（1）埃德蒙,拔出剑来（Edmund…drawn）：埃德蒙听到喊声,拔出剑来,在他的上级之前冲了出来,打破了常规,以此显示他对康瓦尔是多么效忠。 44. 跟你斗……小子（With…boy）：我要跟你搏斗,傲慢的年轻人（I'll fight with you, whipper-snapper）；其中"goodman"一词略带侮辱,用以称谓一位自耕农或客栈掌柜;地位低于一位绅士（gentleman）（Foakes; Mowat）。 45. 让你尝尝血腥（flesh thee）：原为一狩猎术语,"就像我们把野兽的鲜肉喂给猎狗,以便刺激他奋力奔跑一样"（Muir）；同时这也是对埃德蒙的一种侮辱,好像他从未经历过战斗似的（Foakes）。

	Kent	No marvel, you have so bestirred your valour, you cowardly rascal; nature disclaims in thee—a tailor made thee.
55	**Cornwall**	Thou art a strange fellow—a tailor make a man?
	Kent	^QAy,^Q a tailor, sir; a stone-cutter or painter could not have made him so ill, though he had been but two years o'the trade.
	Cornwall	[*to Oswald*] Speak yet: how grew your quarrel?
60	**Oswald**	This ancient ruffian, sir, whose life I have spared at suit of his gray beard—
	Kent	Thou whoreson zed, thou unnecessary letter! My lord, if you will give me leave, I will tread this unbolted villain into mortar and daub the wall of a jakes with
65		him. [*to Oswald*] Spare my grey beard, you wagtail?
	Cornwall	Peace, sirrah. You beastly knave, know you no reverence?
	Kent	Yes, sir, but anger hath a privilege.
	Cornwall	Why art thou angry?
70	**Kent**	That such a slave as this should wear a sword,
		Who wears no honesty. Such smiling rogues as these
		Like rats oft bite the ^Fholy^F cords atwain
		Which are too intrince t'unloose; smooth every passion

肯特	怪不得，你刚才是如此胆大气粗，你这	
	胆小的恶棍；造化都拒绝认你——你是	
	裁缝造的。	
康瓦尔	你可真是个怪人——裁缝能够造人？	55
肯特	对，裁缝造人，先生；一位石匠或画匠	
	都不会把他造得这么糟糕，哪怕他们只	
	学徒两年。	
康瓦尔	［向奥斯华德］快说：是怎么吵起来的？	
奥斯华德	这个老流氓，先生，因为他的花白胡子	60
	求情，我才饶了他性命——	
肯特	你这个狗杂种，你这多余的东西！我的	
	殿下，您若允许，我会把这个没筛过的	
	恶棍踩成泥浆，用他去涂抹厕所的墙壁。	
	［向奥斯华德］饶了我的命，你这马屁精？	65
康瓦尔	安静，老兄。您这野蛮的无赖，难道您	
	不懂尊敬？	
肯特	懂，先生，但是发怒优先。	
康瓦尔	你为何发怒？	
肯特	像他这样的奴才竟身佩利剑，	70
	却无诚实可言。 这样的笑面虎	
	像耗子一样，常把圣洁和难分	
	难解的亲情纽带咬断；迎合	

53-4. 你是裁缝造的（a…thee）：源于谚语"人靠衣装（The tailor makes the man）"。 肯特再次暗示奥斯华德是金玉其外，败絮其中。 58. 学徒两年（two years）：学徒期总共七年。 61. 求情（at the suit of）：意为"在…请求之下（at the petition of）"，好像肯特曾求他饶命。 62. 杂种（zed）："z"字母之所以多余，是因为它的大部分功能可由"s"表示；而且拉丁语里也没有这个字母。 63. 没筛过的（unbolted）：既可指（因为块头大）"没有被筛下去的（unsifted）"；也可指"未上拴的（unbolted）"，意为"女人气的/阳痿的（unmanly / impotent）"。 原文"bolt"也可指"阴茎"（Bate）。 68. 发怒优先（anger…privilege）：有权表达，可以不顾礼貌（the right to speak out in defiance of propriety）；源于谚语。

That in the natures of their lords rebel,

75 Bring oil to fire, snow to their colder moods,

Renege, affirm and turn their halcyon beaks

With every gale and vary of their masters,

Knowing naught, like dogs, but following.

[*to Oswald*] A plague upon your epileptic visage.

80 Smile you my speeches as I were a fool?

Goose, if I had you upon Sarum plain,

I'd drive ye cackling home to Camelot.

Cornwall What, art thou mad, old fellow?

Gloucester How fell you out, say that.

85 **Kent** No contraries hold more antipathy

Than I and such a knave.

Cornwall Why dost thou call him knave? What's his fault?

Kent His countenance likes me not.

Cornwall No more, perchance, does mine, nor his, nor hers.

90 **Kent** Sir, 'tis my occupation to be plain:

I have seen better faces in my time

Than stands on any shoulder that I see

Before me at this instant.

Cornwall This is some fellow

	其主子难以抑制的叛逆情绪，	
	火上浇油，或者雪上加霜，	75
	摇头，点头，根据主人的风向	
	变化转动他们翠鸟般的嘴尖，	
	一无所知，狗似的，只知道跟随。	
	［向奥斯华德］诅咒你那皮笑肉不笑的面孔！	
	你在笑我，好像我是傻子？	80
	蠢鹅，我若在塞勒姆平原碰见你，	
	定让你咯咯叫着回到卡米洛。	
康瓦尔	什么，你疯了，老家伙？	
格洛斯特	说说是怎么吵起来的。	
肯特	没有谁会像我跟这个恶棍	85
	这样不共戴天。	
康瓦尔	你为何叫他恶棍？　他哪里错了？	
肯特	他的长相我不喜欢。	
康瓦尔	你也许不喜欢我的，他的，或她的。	
肯特	先生，我向来喜欢坦率直言：	90
	我曾经见识过俊美的面容，	
	比我此刻眼前所见的任何	
	嘴脸都要好看。	
康瓦尔	这种家伙，	

---

77. 翠鸟般的嘴尖（halcyon beaks）：据信，将风干后的翠鸟挂起，其嘴尖可随风向转动；因此，爱奉承的奴仆也总会附和其主人的情绪变化。　79. 皮笑肉不笑（epileptic）：奥斯华德脸色苍白，吓得发抖，可他却在微笑并试图做出一副若无其事的样子（Muir）。　81-2. 我……卡米洛（If…Camelot）：意义不清。　但大意却比较明显："你要是由我支配，我会让你逃命似的滚开"。　奥斯华德的笑声，就像鹅的咯咯叫声，象征着愚蠢，激怒了肯特；但不知为何会与塞勒姆（Sarum）联在一起。　塞勒姆位于英格兰南部城市索尔茨伯里（Salisbury）或卡米洛附近，后者为传说中的亚瑟王宫廷所在地，并与温切斯特接壤。　温切斯特鹅（Winchester goose）可指一种性病或一位妓女；因此，此处也许存在着某些隐含的关联。

		Who, having been praised for bluntness, doth affect
95		A saucy roughness and constrains the garb
		Quite from his nature. He cannot flatter, he;

Who, having been praised for bluntness, doth affect

95   A saucy roughness and constrains the garb

Quite from his nature. He cannot flatter, he;

An honest mind and plain, he must speak truth;

An they will take it, so; if not, he's plain.

These kind of knaves I know, which in this plainness

100   Harbour more craft and more corrupter ends

Than twenty silly-ducking observants

That stretch their duties nicely.

Kent   Sir, in good faith, ᵠorᵠ in sincere verity,

Under th'allowance of your great aspect,

105   Whose influence, like the wreath of radiant fire

On flickering Phoebus' front—

Cornwall   What mean'st ᵠthouᵠ by this?

Kent   To go out of my dialect, which you discommend so
much. I know, sir, I am no flatterer. He that beguiled
you in a plain accent was a plain knave, which for my

110   part I will not be, though I should win your displeasure
to entreat me to't.

Cornwall   [*to Oswald*] What was th'offence you gave him?

Oswald   I never gave him any.

It pleased the King his master very late

115   To strike at me upon his misconstruction,

素以耿直见称，假装自己

直言不讳，因此将原本简明的　　　　　　　　　　　95

言语扭曲。　他声称不会奉承，他；

心地诚实坦率，要实话实说；

人们若认可，很好；若不，他很坦率。

我懂这种无赖，坦率的背后

藏着更多的奸诈和险恶用心，　　　　　　　　　　100

超过二十位卑躬屈膝、兢兢

业业的愚蠢仆人。

肯特　　先生，千真万确，或实事求是，

有鉴于您这位伟人的准许，

您的星力，犹如闪烁在太阳神　　　　　　　　　　105

前额的耀眼光环——

康瓦尔　　　　　　　　　　　　你这是何意？

肯特　　想换一种说法，因为您这么不喜欢直言。

我知道，先生，我这人不会奉承。凡是

用坦率骗您的就是坦率的恶棍，至于我，

我可不做，哪怕您求我，我也会冒着让　　　　　　110

您生气的危险将您拒绝。

康瓦尔　　[向奥斯华德]您是怎么得罪他的？

奥斯华德　　我从未得罪过他。

最近他的国王加主人由于

某种误解随意扇了我耳光，　　　　　　　　　　　115

94-6. 假装……扭曲（doth…nature）：原注为 "pretends to be plain-spoken, and thus twists plain speech away from its own nature（that is, truth）"（Mowat）。 96. 他声称不会奉承（He…he）：冷嘲热讽（said sardonically）（Bevington）。 110-11. 哪怕……拒绝（though…to't）：本句也许是说，即使您求我坦率，我也会予以拒绝，尽管那会惹您生气（even though I may displease you [by refusing to be plain] when you ask me to be）（Mowat）。 肯特宁愿使康瓦尔不快，因为他康瓦尔只喜欢阿谀奉承者；直到目前肯特好像才发现坦率直言最容易冒犯，然而此刻他又带着嘲弄的口气争辩说，他再也不能坦率直言了，因为他的坦率直言会被视为欺骗（Bevington）。

When he, compact and flattering his displeasure,

Tripped me behind, being down, insulted, railed,

And put upon him such a deal of man

That worthied him, got praises of the King

120   For him attempting who was self-subdued;

And in the fleshment of this dread exploit,

Drew on me here again.

Kent   None of these rogues and cowards

But Ajax is their fool.

Cornwall   Fetch forth the stocks, ᵠho ᵠ!

[*Exeunt one or two servants.*]

You stubborn, ancient knave, you reverend braggart,

We'll teach you.

125 **Kent**   ᶠSir, ᶠ I am too old to learn.

Call not your stocks for me; I serve the King,

On whose employment I was sent to you.

You shall do small respect, show too bold malice

Against the grace and person of my master,

Stocking his messenger.

130 **Cornwall**   Fetch forth the stocks!

As I have life and honour, there shall he sit till noon.

Regan   Till noon? Till night, my lord, and all night too.

Kent   Why, madam, if I were your father's dog

　　　　　　　而他，与他串通，恶意奉承，

　　　　　　　从后面把我绊倒；他又骂又笑，

　　　　　　　好像这种举动使他成了英雄，

　　　　　　　为他赢得荣耀，因为袭击一个

　　　　　　　不想抵抗者而受到国王称颂；　　　　　　　　　　　　120

　　　　　　　因为初试得逞而感到鼓舞，

　　　　　　　现又拔剑逼我。

肯特　　　　　　　　　　　这些恶棍和懦夫

　　　　　　　比埃阿斯还会吹嘘。

康瓦尔　　　　　　　　　　拿足枷来！

　　　　　　　　　　　　　　　　　　［一二个仆人下。］

　　　　　　　你这顽固的老恶棍，吹牛大王，

　　　　　　　我要教训你。

肯特　　　　　　　　　先生，我老了，学不会。　　　　　　　125

　　　　　　　别对我用刑；我在服侍国王，

　　　　　　　我是奉他的差遣前来见您。

　　　　　　　您会显得过分放肆，心怀恶意，

　　　　　　　侮辱我主人的尊严和人格，

　　　　　　　将他的使者枷起。

康瓦尔　　　　　　　　把足枷拿来！　　　　　　　　　　130

　　　　　　　以生命和荣誉打赌，让他坐到中午。

李根　　　　　到中午？　到夜里，夫君，坐一整夜。

肯特　　　　　嗨，夫人，我若是您父亲的狗，

　　122-3. 这些……吹嘘（None…fool）：你总会发现这种恶棍和懦夫在夸口方面要超过爱吹嘘的埃阿斯（You never find any rouges and cowards of this sort who do not outdo the blustering Ajax in their boasting）（Bevington）。　埃阿斯（Ajax）：希腊神话及莎剧《特洛伊罗斯与克瑞西达》中的人物，特洛伊战争中的希腊英雄，以愚蠢和夸口著称（Mowat）。　126. 我在服侍国王（I…King）：李尔已经放弃王权，因此"国王"这种称号现在只是礼节性的，肯特的诉求也就没有多少分量；但重要的是，李尔依然被人们视为国王，如奥斯华德（114 行）和格洛斯特（143 行）。132. 李根就爱插话，以此维护自己的权威；见 2.1.103 注。

You should not use me so.

Regan   Sir, being his knave, I will.

^FStocks brought out.^F

135 **Cornwall**   This is a fellow of the selfsame colour

Our sister speaks of. Come, bring away the stocks.

Gloucester   Let me beseech your grace not to do so.

^QHis fault is much, and the good King, his master,

Will check him for't. Your purposed low correction

140   Is such as basest and contemnedst wretches

For pilferings and most common trespasses

Are punished with.^Q

The King, ^Fhis master, needs^F must take it ill

That he, so slightly valued in his messenger,

Should have him thus restrained.

145 **Cornwall**   I'll answer that.

Regan   My sister may receive it much more worse

To have her gentleman abused, assaulted,

^QFor following her affairs. Put in his legs.^Q

[*Kent is put in the stocks.*]

Cornwall   Come, my ^Qgood^Q lord, away.

^FExeunt^F[*all but Gloucester and Kent.*]

150 **Gloucester**   I am sorry for thee, friend; 'tis the Duke's pleasure,

Whose disposition all the world well knows

Will not be rubbed nor stopped. I'll entreat for thee.

Kent   Pray ^Qyou^Q do not, sir. I have watched and travelled hard.

Some time I shall sleep out, the rest I'll whistle.

也不会这样对待。

李根　　　　　　　　　　　　是他的无赖,我就会。

　　　　　　　　　　　　　　　　　　　　　　足枷抬出。

康瓦尔　　　这正是我们姐姐所提及的　　　　　　　　　135
　　　　　那种家伙。　快,把足枷拿来。

格洛斯特　　我要请求殿下您不要这样。
　　　　　他过失不小,他的主人——国王,
　　　　　会就此训他。　您打算采用的这种
　　　　　有失体面的惩戒措施适用于　　　　　　　　140
　　　　　那些最为卑贱的无耻之徒,
　　　　　因为小偷小摸。
　　　　　国王——他的主人,定会怨恨,
　　　　　他派来的信差受到如此轻慢,
　　　　　竟把他这样拘禁。

康瓦尔　　　　　　　我来负责。　　　　　　　　　　145

李根　　　　我的姐姐也许会更加生气,
　　　　　让他的绅士遭受伤害和袭击,
　　　　　因为给她办事。　把他的腿放进去。

　　　　　　　　　　　　　　[肯特被锁进足枷。]

康瓦尔　　　快,好阁下,走吧。

　　　　　　　　　　　[除格洛斯特与肯特外]全下。

格洛斯特　　很抱歉,朋友,这是公爵的意愿,　　　　　150
　　　　　他的秉性全世界都一清二楚,
　　　　　会一意孤行。　我将为你求情。

肯特　　　　请不要,先生。　我连夜赶路辛苦。
　　　　　我会睡几个时辰,醒了吹吹口哨。

155	A good man's fortune may grow out at heels.
	Give you good morrow.
Gloucester	The Duke's too blame in this; 'twill be ill taken. ^F*Exit.*^F
Kent	Good King, that must approve the common saw,
	Thou out of heaven's benediction com'st
160	To the warm sun.
	Approach, thou beacon to this under globe,
	That by thy comfortable beams I may
	Peruse this letter. Nothing almost sees miracles
	But misery. I know 'tis from Cordelia,
165	Who hath most fortunately been informed
	Of my obscured course, [*reading the letter*] 'and
	shall find time
	From this enormous state, seeking to give
	Losses their remedies'. All weary and o'erwatched,
	Take vantage, heavy eyes, not to behold
170	This shameful lodging.
	Fortune, good night: smile once more; turn thy wheel.
	^Q[*Sleeps.*]^Q

	好人有时候也会衣不蔽体。	155
	祝您早安！	
格洛斯特	公爵太不像话；会令人怨恨。	下。
肯特	好国王啊,验证了那句民谚,	
	你离开上帝的庇护来到这个	
	无情的世间。	160
	升起来吧,你这颗大地的灯塔,	
	好让我借用你那舒适的光线	
	把信看完。　患难之中见奇迹。	
	我知道这是考迪丽娅来的,	
	所幸她已知道我隐姓埋名的	165
	生活状况,［读信］"将会	
	寻找时机	
	从这种混乱的局面之中,设法	
	将损失补偿"。　我现已困倦不堪,	
	趁机睡吧,沉重的双眼,别看	
	这种丢人的寓所。	170
	晚安,命运女神：笑一笑；让车轮旋转。	
	［入睡］。	

---

155. 好人……蔽体（A…heels）：好人有时也会遭受厄运（Even good men suffer decline in fortune at times）（Bevington）。 原文"grow out at heels"意为"就像袜子在脚跟处磨破（like stockings worn through at the heel）",也许指肯特此刻被锁进足枷,脚跟外露（Mowat）。 158. 常言（saw）：即"turn out of God's blessing into the warm sun",意为"由好变糟",从天堂之乐到无情的世间（from a state of bliss into the pitiless world）（Bevington）。 161. 灯塔（beacon）：太阳（sun）。 依然是凌晨。 163. 患难之中见奇迹（Nothing…misery）：因为我们绝望时,任何救助都像是奇迹（Muir）。 166. 原文 obscured = obscurèd（三音节）。 170. 该短行表明肯特在尽力使自己舒服一些以便入睡,随后便恳求命运女神。 171. 让车轮旋转（turn thy wheel）：让我时来运转（命运女神常被描绘为旋转着一个车轮,众生在上面升降沉浮［rise and fall］）（Mowat）。 171（1）埃德加上（Enter Edgar）：四开本和对折本此处均未标明另起一场,但多数编者和导演都会这样做,将埃德加的独白作为第二幕的第三场。 埃德加此时并未看见肯特,像是在乡间,不在格洛斯特的家附近；但对观众而言,这种安排可将遭受羞辱、流放并伪装的两个人物带到一起（尽管肯特的羞辱咎由自取）,从而提供一种直观而强烈的标志——李尔的愚蠢及埃德蒙的阴谋所造成的反常局面（enormous state）。

Enter Edgar.

Edgar   I heard myself proclaimed,

And by the happy hollow of a tree

Escaped the hunt. No port is free, no place

175   That guard and most unusual vigilance

Does not attend my taking. While I may scape

I will preserve myself, and am bethought

To take the basest and most poorest shape

That ever penury in contempt of man

180   Brought near to beast. My face I'll grime with filth,

Blanket my loins, elf all my hair in knots,

And with presented nakedness outface

The winds and persecutions of the sky.

The country gives me proof and precedent

185   Of Bedlam beggars, who, with roaring voices,

Strike in their numbed ᶠandᶠ mortified �\^Qbare\^Q arms

Pins, wooden pricks, nails, sprigs of rosemary;

And with this horrible object, from low farms,

Poor pelting villages, sheepcotes and mills,

190   Sometime with lunatic bans, sometime with prayers,

Enforce their charity. Poor Turlygod, poor Tom,

That's something yet: Edgar I nothing am.   *Exit.*

埃德加上。

埃德加　　听说我已经被宣布为逃犯，

幸好我藏进一棵树洞里头

才躲过追捕。　无路可以通行，

没有哪里不是戒备森严，　　　　　　　　　　　　　175

等着拿我归案。　只要我能逃脱，

就该保护自己，已打定主意

让我的形状最为卑贱和可怜，

竟叫那表明人们卑贱的贫穷

贬到禽兽一般。　我用污泥涂脸，　　　　　　　　180

用毛毯围腰，并让头发打结，

用我裸露的躯体勇敢地面对

天空之下的各种风吹和雨打。

来自疯人院的乡间乞丐可做

榜样和先例,他们又喊又叫，　　　　　　　　　　185

将别针、木扦、铁钉、迷迭香枝条

刺进他们那麻木僵死的手臂；

以这种可怕情形,向穷苦的农场、

贫贱的乡村、羊圈或者磨坊，

有时用疯狂咒语,有时用祷告，　　　　　　　　　190

索要施舍。　可怜的图里格,穷汤姆，

那还有身份：而埃德加已经蒸发。　　　　　　下。

---

179. 表明人们卑贱的（in…man）：表明人这种动物是多么卑贱（to show how contemptible a creature man is）（Muir）。　嘲笑人们自称优于牲畜的（scorning man's claim to be superior to beasts）（Foakes）。　180-92. 我用……蒸发（My face…am）：演出时埃德加通常会一边独白,一边撕掉自己的衣服,在观众面前将自己变成可怜的、几乎赤身的疯乞丐。　184. 疯人院……乞丐（Bedlam beggars）：其中，"Bedlam" 是指15世纪建造于伦敦的伯利恒医院（Bethlehem Hospital）,旨在收留疯子或装疯的人。　另见1. 2. 135-6注。　191. 图里格（Turlygod）：无解；也许是在假装说起了疯话。　192. 还有……蒸发（something…nothing）：作为穷汤姆,他还有一种身份，而作为埃德加,他已经不存在了（As Poor Tom he has an identity, as Edgar he is non-existent）。

Enter Lear, ^F*Fool and a Knight.*^F

Lear	'Tis strange that they should so depart from home
	And not send back my messenger.
Knight	As I learned,
195	The night before there was no purpose ^Fin them^F
	Of this remove.
Kent	[*Wakes.*] Hail to thee, noble master.
Lear	Ha? Mak'st thou this shame thy pastime?
^F**Kent**	No, my lord.^F
Fool	Ha, ha, ^Qlook,^Q he wears cruel garters. Horses are
	tied by the heads, dogs and bears by the neck, monkeys
200	by the loins and men by the legs. When a man's
	overlusty at legs, then he wears wooden nether-stocks.
Lear	[*to Kent*] What's he that hath so much thy place mistook
	To set thee here?
Kent	It is both he and she,
	Your son and daughter.
205 **Lear**	No.
Kent	Yes.
Lear	No, I say.
Kent	I say, yea.
^Q**Lear**	No, no, they would not.
210 **Kent**	Yes, they have.^Q

李尔、傻子与一侍卫上。

李尔　奇怪,他们竟这样离家而去,
　　　　不派我的信差回来。

侍卫　　　　　　　　我听人说,
　　　　昨晚以前他们还没有打算　　　　　　　　195
　　　　更换住处。

肯特　[醒来。]向你致意,高贵的主人!

李尔　哈?　你拿羞耻当消遣?

肯特　　　　　　　　　不是,陛下。

傻子　哈,哈,你看,他穿着一双酷袜带!马
　　　　被拴着头,狗和熊被拴着脖子,猴子被
　　　　拴着腰,而人被拴着腿。人的腿要是太　　　200
　　　　活跃了,那他就得穿上木短袜。

李尔　[向肯特]是谁如此误解了你的职务,
　　　　把你锁在这里?

肯特　　　　　　　就是他和她,
　　　　您的女婿和女儿。

李尔　不是。　　　　　　　　　　　　　　　　　205

肯特　是的。

李尔　不是,我说!

肯特　我说,是的。

李尔　不,不,他们不会的!

肯特　是的,他们做了。　　　　　　　　　　　　210

---

　193. 他们(they):李根与康瓦尔。　198. 酷袜带(cruel garters):即足枷;原文"cruel
(残酷的)"与"crewel(织袜用的精纺纱线)"为谐音双关。　200-1. 腿要是太活跃了(over-
lusty at legs):倾向于逃跑的,或性欲旺盛的(given either to running away, or to sexual activity)。　201. 短袜(nether-stocks):裹住小腿的袜子(stockings for the lower legs);裹住大腿
的袜子则较为宽松,叫作"(过膝)长袜(upper-stocks)"。

Lear By Jupiter, I swear no.

ᶠ**Kent** By Juno, I swear ay.

Learᶠ   They durst not do't:

They could not, would not do't—'tis worse than murder

To do upon respect such violent outrage.

215 Resolve me with all modest haste which way

Thou might'st deserve or they impose this usage,

Coming from us.

Kent   My lord, when at their home

I did commend your highness' letters to them,

Ere I was risen from the place that showed

220 My duty kneeling, came there a reeking post,

Stewed in his haste, half breathless, panting forth

From Goneril his mistress, salutations;

Delivered letters, spite of intermission,

Which presently they read; on those contents

225 They summoned up their meiny, straight took horse,

Commanded me to follow and attend

The leisure of their answer, gave me cold looks;

And meeting here the other messenger,

Whose welcome I perceived had poisoned mine,

230 Being the very fellow that of late

Displayed so saucily against your highness,

Having more man than wit about me, drew.

He raised the house with loud and coward cries.

李尔	我凭朱庇特起誓,不会的!
肯特	我凭朱诺起誓,是的!
李尔	他们不敢:

他们不能,不会——这比凶杀还糟,

竟有意对你这样侮辱和粗暴。

赶快跟我说明你究竟为何　　　　　　　　　　215

该受这种礼遇,还是他们逼迫,

我的使者。

肯特	陛下,当我把您的

信件送到他们家里的时候,

还没来得及从跪着尽职的

地方站起,一个急切的信差,　　　　　　　　220

满头是汗,气喘吁吁地到来,

替他女主人,贡纳丽,表达致意;

递交了信函,尽管把我给打断,

他们立即读信;了解内容后,

他们召集好随从,上马就走,　　　　　　　　225

命令我紧随其后并等待他们

有空时再给以回复,给我冷眼;

来到这里又遇见那位信差,

我发现因为欢迎他才对我慢待,

就是那同一个家伙,他最近　　　　　　　　230

对待陛下您是如此傲慢无礼,

我一时血气,欠缺考虑,拔剑。

他那胆怯的呼喊将众人唤起,

---

　　217. 我的(from us):李尔又习惯性地使用了表示国王身份的复数形式;康瓦尔与李根早已采用了这种具有支配地位的称谓。 另见2. 1. 103注。 231. 如此傲慢无礼(Displayed so saucily):见1. 4. 76-90。 肯特此处的言论也许会令人想起他本人在康瓦尔面前的"直言不讳"(90-3);尽管肯特此处并未完全承认自己的过错,但他被锁进足枷还是罪有应得。

		Your son and daughter found this trespass worth
235		The shame which here it suffers.
	^F**Fool**	Winter's not gone yet, if the wild geese fly that
		way.

> *Fathers that wear rags*
> > *Do make their children blind,*

240
> *But fathers that bear bags*
> > *Shall see their children kind:*
> *Fortune, that arrant whore,*
> > *Ne'er turns the key to the poor.*

		But for all this thou shalt have as many dolours for thy
245		daughters as thou canst tell in a year.^F
	Lear	O, how this mother swells up toward my heart!
		Hysterica passio, down, thou climbing sorrow,
		Thy element's below. Where is this daughter?
	Kent	With the Earl, sir, ^Fhere^F within.
250	**Lear**	Follow me not; Stay here. ^F*Exit.*^F
	Knight	Made you no more offence but what you speak of?
	Kent	None. How chance the King comes with so small a
		number?
	Fool	An thou hadst been set i'the stocks for that question,
255		thou hadst well deserved it.

您的女婿女儿觉得这种过失

应该受这种羞耻。 235

傻子 如果大雁朝南方飞去,表明严冬尚未

过去。

父亲若破衣烂衫,

子女会不管不问,

父亲若腰缠万贯, 240

子女会格外孝顺:

命运,臭名的娼妇,

从不把穷人眷顾。

尽管如此,你会因为女儿的缘故有很多

悲伤,一年之内都难以数清。 245

李尔 噢,这种癔病快要涌上心头!

癔病啊,下去,你这上涌的悲痛,

你本该在下面。 我这位女儿呢?

肯特 跟伯爵一起,陛下,就在里面。

李尔 不要跟我,这里待着。 下。 250

侍卫 除了您所说的,没再犯别的过错?

肯特 没有。国王怎么只带来这么一小部分

人员?

傻子 假如你为了这个问题而坐进足枷,那

可是罪有应得。 255

238-43. 李尔在 1.4.162 曾问傻子"啥时候爱上了唱歌";但四开本和对开本均未在本场标明他是否需要歌唱,因此不太清楚他的歌谣部分有多少是哼唱出来的。 245. 悲伤(dolours):傻子带着挖苦的意味在玩弄文字游戏,即原文的"dolours(忧伤)"与"dollars(银币)"为双关语。 246-8. 噢……下面(O…below):女人多患的一种疾病;英语里称为"the mother, or the suffocation of the mother(窒息)",学名为"癔病(*hysterica passio*)";症状之一就是李尔此刻因为悲愤交加而感到即将窒息。 据信,该病是由错乱的子宫引起,其位置本在下面(belonged below),而不是在心口(not up near the heart)(Mowat;Foakes)。

	Kent	Why, fool?
	Fool	We'll set thee to school to an ant, to teach thee there's no labouring i'the winter. All that follow their noses are led by their eyes but blind men, and there's
260		not a nose among twenty but can smell him that's stinking. Let go thy hold when a great wheel runs down a hill lest it break thy neck with following ^Qit^Q; but the great one that goes upward, let him draw thee after. When a wise man gives thee better counsel, give me
265		mine again; I would have none but knaves follow it, since a fool gives it.

> *That sir which serves ^Fand seeks^F for gain,*
> > *And follows but for form,*
>
> *Will pack when it begins to rain,*
> > *And leave thee in the storm;*
>
> *But I will tarry, the fool will stay,*
> > *And let the wise man fly:*
>
> *The knave turns fool that runs away,*
> > *The fool no knave perdy.*

275	**Kent**	Where learned you this, fool?
	Fool	Not i'the stocks, ^Ffool.^F

肯特	为啥,傻子?	
傻子	我们要叫你好好向蚂蚁学习,要教你	
	不要在冬天里劳作。只要是向前走的,	
	除了瞎子,都必须靠眼睛看路,而且,	
	二十个瞎子中没有一个闻不出他身上	260
	的霉味。一副大车轮滚下山时,你要	
	松手,免得因为紧跟将脖子折断;但	
	某个大人物向上爬时,让他把你带上。	
	要有聪明人给了你更好的忠告,就把	
	我的还我;我只想让恶棍采纳,因为	265
	这是傻子给的。	

> 仆人若把利指望,
>
> 　就会装模又作样,
>
> 风雨欲来收行囊,
>
> 　让你独自受灾殃; 270
>
> 傻子不走要留下,
>
> 　让聪明人高飞远行:
>
> 恶棍逃走是犯傻,
>
> 　我不当恶棍天作证。

肯特	您从哪里学的,傻子?	275
傻子	不是从足枷里,傻子。	

257-63. 我们……带上(We'll…after):傻子从三方面阐述了侍卫对李尔的抛弃,它们都强调了李尔正走向困境:李尔已迎来寒冬(Lear is in his winter)(对蚂蚁来说,这是一个徒劳的季节,现在跟随李尔也同样徒劳无益);李尔因处逆境而发臭(Lear stinks with misfortune)(就连瞎子都能闻出他的腐臭〔decay〕);李尔就像一副巨大的车轮(great wheel)滚下山去,将附在上面的一切毁灭(Mowat)。 重复《圣经》中教导人们要向蚂蚁学习的教义:"你去察看蚂蚁的动作,就可得智慧……尚且在夏天预备食物("箴言"6 章 6-8 节)"(Foakes)。 267. 仆人(sir):指李尔的侍卫。 273-4. 傻子在此摈弃他刚提及的世俗的智慧,赞同内心的忠诚:"抛弃其主人的恶棍(仆人)最终定会被视为傻瓜;但我这个傻子将会留下,因此,上帝作证(perdy = by God, from French par Dieu),我不是恶棍"。 傻子似在暗示李尔的许多侍卫已将他抛弃。

Enter Lear and Gloucester.

Lear Deny to speak with me? They are sick, they are weary,

They ^Fhave^F travelled all the night? —mere fetches ^Qay^Q,

The images of revolt and flying off.

Fetch me a better answer.

280 **Gloucester** My dear lord,

You know the fiery quality of the Duke,

How unremoveable and fixed he is

In his own course.

Lear Vengeance, plague, death, confusion!

285 Fiery? What quality? Why, Gloucester, Gloucester,

I'd speak with the Duke of Cornwall and his wife.

^F**Gloucester** Well, my good lord, I have informed them so.

Lear 'Informed them'? Dost thou understand me, man?^F

Gloucester Ay, my good lord.

290 **Lear** The King would speak with Cornwall, the dear father

Would with his daughter speak, commands—tends—service.

^FAre they informed of this? My breath and blood!

'Fiery'?^F The fiery Duke, tell the hot Duke that ^QLear^Q—

No, but not yet, maybe he is not well;

295 Infirmity doth still neglect all office

Whereto our health is bound. We are not ourselves

When nature, being oppressed, commands the mind

To suffer with the body. I'll forbear,

李尔与格洛斯特上。

李尔 不跟我说话？ 他们病了,累了,

他们赶了一夜路？ ——借口而已,

这可是明显的背叛和抛弃。

去要个更好的回复。

格洛斯特 我的好陛下, 280

您知道公爵那种火爆的脾性,

他做起事来是多么固执己见

和刚愎自用。

李尔 该死,天灾,死亡,毁灭!

火爆？ 脾性？ 嗨,格洛斯特,格洛斯特, 285

我要跟康瓦尔公爵和他夫人说话。

格洛斯特 嗳,好陛下,我已通知他们了。

李尔 "通知他们了"？ 你懂我意思吗,老兄?

格洛斯特 懂,好陛下。

李尔 国王要跟康瓦尔说话,亲爱的父亲 290

要跟女儿说话,命令——等候——服侍。

他们知道此事吗？ 我以性命起誓!

火爆？ 火爆公爵,告诉那爆公爵——

不,先不要,也许他身体不好;

我们生病时总会忽略健康时 295

必须履行的职责。 我们身不由己,

生理失常时,就会导致心理

与身体一起难受。 我要克制,

---

291. 命令——等候（commands—tends）：李尔的身份从"国王（King）"降到了"父亲（father）",口气也相应地从命令降到了"等候（tends = attends, or waits for）"。 295-6. 我们……职责（Infirmity…bound）：原注为"When ill we always neglect the performance of duties we are bound to carry out when in health"。

And am fallen out with my more headier will

300 To take the indisposed and sickly fit

For the sound man. [*Notices Kent.*]

Death on my state! Wherefore

Should he sit here? This act persuades me

That this remotion of the Duke and her

Is practice only. Give me my servant forth.

305 ^FGo^F tell the Duke and's wife I'd speak with them,

Now, presently: bid them come forth and hear me,

Or at their chamber door I'll beat the drum

Till it cry sleep to death.

Gloucester   I would have all well betwixt you.   ^F*Exit.*^F

310 **Lear**   O ^Fme,^F my heart! My ^Frising^F heart! ^FBut down!^F

Fool   Cry to it, nuncle, as the cockney did to the eels

when she put 'em i'the paste alive: she knapped 'em

o'the coxcombs with a stick, and cried ' Down, wantons,

down!' 'Twas her brother that in pure kindness to his

315 horse buttered his hay.

Enter Cornwall, Regan, ^F*Gloucester,* [*and*] *servants.*^F

Lear   Good morrow to you both.

并对我的急不可耐感到生气，

错把身体欠安和疾病发作者　　　　　　　　　　　　　300

视为康健。［看见肯特。］

　　　　　　我的王权该死！他为何

坐在这里？ 该行为使我相信

公爵和她的这种避而不见

只是策略。 把我的仆人放开！

去告诉公爵和夫人我有话要说，　　　　　　　　　　305

现在,立刻：叫他们前来听着，

否则我会在他们寝室门前敲鼓，

直到把睡眠聒死。

格洛斯特　　希望你们之间相安无事。　　　　　　　　　　　下。

李尔　　我的心啊！上涌的心！下去！　　　　　　　　　310

傻子　　对它喊吧，老伯，就像那娇小姐把活着

的鳗鱼放进面糊后所做的那样：用棍棒

敲打它们的头部,大喊,"下去,调皮鬼,

下去!"也正是她的弟弟出于纯粹地爱马,

给草料伴上黄油。　　　　　　　　　　　　　　　315

康瓦尔、李根、格洛斯特［与］仆人上。

李尔　　你们二位早安。

---

301. 我的王权该死（Death…state）：这种普通的诅咒在此却具有特殊的意义,因为"state"既可指李尔的老态龙钟（his condition as an old man）,也可指他的王权（his power as King）,尽管已名存实亡。 然而,他一看到肯特便又发号施令起来,好像他依然大权在握。 303. 避而不见（remotion）：可指他们离家来到格洛斯特的住处,或指疏远（remoteness）,或指不露面（failure to present themselves）。 311-4. 对它……下去（Cry…down）：这则笑话说的是,有位娇小姐（一位可爱或做作的女人 [a nice or affected woman]）不懂应该先把鳗鱼杀好后再和到面里进行烘烤,于是她便措手不及地用棍棒击打它们的头部（coxcombs）,并对这些活蹦乱跳的小东西高喊"下去!",正像李尔此刻对他那颗难以驾驭的心所做的那样。 314-5. 出于……黄油（in…hay）：愚蠢的另一例证;行为是善意的,但马并不吃拌过黄油的草料。 就李尔而言,只有良好的意愿是不够的（Bevington）。

Cornwall   Hail to your grace.

^F[*Kent is set at liberty.*]^F

Regan   I am glad to see your highness.

Lear   Regan, I think you are. I know what reason

I have to think so. If thou shouldst not be glad,

320   I would divorce me from thy mother's tomb,

Sepulchring an adultress. [*to Kent*] O, are you free?

Some other time for that. —Beloved Regan,

Thy sister's naught. O, Regan, she hath tied

Sharp-toothed unkindness, like a vulture, here.

[*Lays his hand on his heart.*]

325   I can scarce speak to thee; thou'lt not believe

With how depraved a quality—O, Regan!

Regan   I pray ^Fyou^F, sir, take patience. I have hope

You less know how to value her desert

Than she to scant her duty.

^F**Lear**   Say? How is that?

330 **Regan**   I cannot think my sister in the least

Would fail her obligation. If, sir, perchance

She have restrained the riots of your followers,

'Tis on such ground and to such wholesome end

As clears her from all blame.^F

Lear   My curses on her.

康瓦尔　　　　　　　　　　　向陛下致意！

　　　　　　［肯特获释。］

李根　　　　我很高兴见到陛下。

李尔　　　　李根，我想您会的。　我知道这样想

　　　　　　自有道理。　假如你不高兴，

　　　　　　我会拒绝与你死去的母亲合葬，　　　　　　　　320

　　　　　　因为墓里是奸妇。　［向肯特］噢，您自由了？

　　　　　　此事以后再说。　——亲爱的李根，

　　　　　　你姐姐恶毒。　噢，李根，她像一只

　　　　　　秃鹰，把无情的利喙拴在，这里！

　　　　　　［手抚心口。］

　　　　　　我真是难以启齿；你不会相信　　　　　　　　325

　　　　　　她的品性是多么败坏——噢，李根！

李根　　　　我求您，父亲，要耐心。　我倒希望

　　　　　　是您对她的长处评价过低，

　　　　　　并非她有所失职。

李尔　　　　　　　　　　啊？　此话怎讲？

李根　　　　我简直无法想象我的姐姐　　　　　　　　　　330

　　　　　　会对您失职。　假如，父亲，也许

　　　　　　她阻止了您那些随从的放纵，

　　　　　　那也是有理有据，目的正当，

　　　　　　她就此毫无过错。

李尔　　　　我诅咒她！

---

　　318. 李根，我想您会的（Regan…are）：李尔温和地呼喊李根。　李尔在319 行使用了表示亲
切的"你（thou）"，表明他期望得到李根的善待。　321. 奸妇（adulteress）：李尔此刻产生了一
种虚幻，将女儿们视为私生女（如 1.4.245 将贡纳丽称为"堕落的杂种"），跟埃德蒙的私生子身
份相提并论，由此将邪恶的根源归于女人，并为他在 4.6.116-25 厌女情绪的爆发埋下了伏笔。
322. 亲爱的（beloved）：原文 beloved = belovèd（三个音节）。　324. 秃鹰（vulture）：暗指
普罗米修斯，因盗取天火而受惩罚，被锁于一块岩石，由一只秃鹰不停地啄食其肝脏。

335	**Regan**	O, sir, you are old:
		Nature in you stands on the very verge
		Of her confine. You should be ruled and led
		By some discretion that discerns your state
		Better than you yourself. Therefore I pray ᶠyouᶠ
340		That to our sister you do make return;
		Say you have wronged her, ᵠsir.ᵠ
	Lear	Ask her forgiveness?
		Do you ᶠbutᶠ mark how this becomes the house?
		[*Kneels.*] Dear daughter, I confess that I am old;
		Age is unnecessary. On my knees I beg
345		That you'll vouchsafe me raiment, bed and food.
	Regan	Good sir, no more. These are unsightly tricks.
		Return you to my sister.
	Lear	[*Rises.*] Never, Regan:
		She hath abated me of half my train,
		Looked black upon me, struck me with her tongue
350		Most serpent-like, upon the very heart.
		All the stored vengeances of heaven fall
		On her ingrateful top! Strike her young bones,
		You taking airs, with lameness!
	Cornwall	Fie, sir, fie!
	ᶠ**Lear**ᶠ	You nimble lightnings, dart your blinding flames

李根	噢,父亲,您老了:	335
	您的天年已经非常接近了	
	她的边缘。 您该由一位明辨	
	是非的人统领,他比您自己	
	更了解您的状况。 因此我求您,	
	您还是回到我姐姐那里去吧;	340
	就说您错怪她了。	

李尔　　　　　　　　　请她原谅?
　　　　您觉得这很适合皇家的尊严?
　　　　[下跪。]亲爱的女儿,我承认我已老了;
　　　　人老了无用。 我现在跪下乞求
　　　　您能赐给我衣服、床铺和食物。　　　　345

李根　　好父亲,别说了。 这是丑陋的把戏。
　　　　回我姐姐家去吧。

李尔　　[起身。]　　　　绝不,李根:
　　　　她把我的随从减去了一半,
　　　　对我怒目而视,并用毒蛇
　　　　一般的舌头刺向我的内心。　　　　350
　　　　愿上天储备的所有报复降到她
　　　　忘恩负义的头上! 致病的空气,
　　　　让她的胎儿成瘸子!

康瓦尔　　　　　　　呸,陛下,呸!

李尔　　迅疾的闪电,把你炫目的火焰

---

343. 舞台指示(SD):李尔此处向女儿的下跪提供了一种次序颠倒的视觉标志(visual emblem of the inversion of order in the play);考迪丽娅在 4.7.57-9 向李尔的下跪则标志着次序的恢复,当时她阻止李尔向她下跪。 344-5. 人……食物(Age…food):李尔这些讽刺性的话语道出了一种令人不快的事实:因为已把王国分光,他现在要靠她的施舍。 353. 胎儿(young bones):在原先的故事中(In the old play),李尔称贡纳丽因“养育子女(breeds young bones)”,或有孕在身而暴躁易怒,因此不太清楚李尔此处的诅咒是针对贡纳丽本人,还是针对她有可能怀有的孩子。

355   Into her scornful eyes! Infect her beauty,

You fen-sucked fogs, drawn by the powerful sun

To fall and blast her pride!

Regan   O the blest gods!

So will you wish on me when the rash mood ᶠis on.ᶠ

Lear   No, Regan, thou shalt never have my curse.

360   Thy tender-hefted nature shall not give

Thee o'er to harshness. Her eyes are fierce, but thine

Do comfort and not burn. 'Tis not in thee

To grudge my pleasures, to cut off my train,

To bandy hasty words, to scant my sizes

365   And, in conclusion, to oppose the bolt

Against my coming in. Thou better knowst

The offices of nature, bond of childhood,

Effects of courtesy, dues of gratitude.

Thy half o'the kingdom hast thou not forgot,

Wherein I thee endowed.

370 **Regan**   Good sir, to the purpose.

ᶠ[*Tucket within.*]ᶠ

Lear   Who put my man i'the stocks?

Enter Oswald.

Cornwall   What trumpet's that?

Regan   I know't, my sister's. This approves her letter

That she would soon be here. [*to Oswald*] Is your lady

     come?

Lear   This is a slave, whose easy borrowed pride

375   Dwells in the fickle grace of her he follows.

Out, varlet, from my sight!

射进她傲慢的双眼！腐蚀她美貌，　　　　　　　355
你这由烈日从沼泽蒸腾的瘴气，
使她满身疱疹！

李根　　　　　　　　　　　　噢，圣洁的众神！
您暴躁起来也会这样咒我。

李尔　　不，李根，我绝不会诅咒你的。
你的温柔的脾性不会使你　　　　　　　　　360
残酷无情。　她满眼凶光，可你
目光柔和不带怒火。　你天生
不会吝惜我快乐，削减我随从，
跟我顶嘴，减少我的赡养费，
总而言之，你不会大门紧闭　　　　　　　　365
不让我入住。　你也更加懂得
孝敬父母、子女应尽义务，
礼貌待人，知道应该感恩。
你那半个王国你不会忘记，
我已把它给你。

李根　　　　　　　　　好父亲，言归正传。　　　　370

　　［内鸣喇叭。］

李尔　　谁把我的人锁进足枷？

　　　　　　　　　　奥斯华德上。

康瓦尔　　　　　　　　　谁的喇叭？

李根　　我知道，是姐姐的。　如她信上所说，
她很快就到。［向奥斯华德］您的女主人
　　到了？

李尔　　这个奴才，仰仗他的女主人
所施舍的无常恩宠趾高气扬。　　　　　　　375
滚，贱货，滚开！

| Cornwall | What means your grace? |

Enter Goneril.

	Lear	Who stocked my servant? Regan, I have good hope
		Thou didst not know on't. Who comes here? O heavens!
		If you do love old men, if your sweet sway
380		Allow obedience, if ^Fyou^F yourselves are old,

Allow obedience, if ᶠyouᶠ yourselves are old,

Make it your cause. Send down, and take my part!

[*to Goneril*] Art not ashamed to look upon this beard?

O, Regan, wilt thou take her by the hand?

Goneril   Why not by the hand, sir? How have I offended?

385   All's not offence that indiscretion finds

And dotage terms so.

Lear   O sides, you are too tough!

Will you yet hold? How came my man i'the stocks?

Cornwall   I set him there, sir; but his own disorders

Deserved much less advancement.

Lear   You? Did you?

390 **Regan**   I pray you, father, being weak, seem so.

If till the expiration of your month

You will return and sojourn with my sister,

Dismissing half your train, come then to me.

I am now from home and out of that provision

395   Which shall be needful for your entertainment.

Lear   Return to her? And fifty men dismissed?

No! Rather I abjure all roofs and choose

To wage against the enmity o'the air—

To be a comrade with the wolf and owl—

400   Necessity's sharp pinch! Return with her?

康瓦尔　　　　　　　　　陛下这是何意？

　　　　　　　　　　贡纳丽上。

李尔　　谁对我仆人用了足枷？　希望你

　　　　不知道此事。　是谁来啦，噢，上天！

　　　　假如你爱老人，假如你的权威

　　　　赞许孝顺，假如你自己也年老，　　　　　　　380

　　　　就不要旁观。　给我派下来支援！

　　　　［向贡纳丽］你看见这把胡子不觉得脸红？

　　　　噢，李根，您竟愿意跟她牵手？

贡纳丽　为啥不牵手，先生？　我哪里错了？

　　　　年老昏聩的人所谓的冒犯　　　　　　　　　385

　　　　不一定就是冒犯。

李尔　　　　　　　胸膛啊，你太硬了！

　　　　你能撑住？　我的人怎么锁上足枷？

康瓦尔　是我锁的，陛下；可他的胡闹

　　　　还不配这种殊荣。

李尔　　　　　　　你？　你干的？

李根　　我求您，父亲，人老了，就该服老。　　　390

　　　　假如您愿意回到我姐姐那里

　　　　住到您的月份期满为止，

　　　　削减一半的随从，再来我家。

　　　　此刻我又不在家里，因此

　　　　无法给您提供适当的照顾。　　　　　　　　395

李尔　　回她那里？　削减五十个随从？

　　　　不！我宁愿弃绝所有的房屋，

　　　　宁愿与那野外的敌意抗争——

　　　　宁愿与豺狼和猫头鹰为伴——

　　　　忍受贫苦交加！跟她回去？　　　　　　　　400

Why, the hot-blooded France, that dowerless took

Our youngest born, I could as well be brought

To knee his throne and squire-like pension beg,

To keep base life afoot. Return with her?

405 Persuade me rather to be slave and sumpter

To this detested groom. [*Points at Oswald.*]

Goneril   At your choice, sir.

Lear   ᵠNowᵠ I prithee, daughter, do not make me mad:

I will not trouble thee, my child. Farewell:

We'll no more meet, no more see one another.

410 But yet thou art my flesh, my blood, my daughter,

Or rather a disease that's in my flesh,

Which I must needs call mine. Thou art a boil,

A plague sore, or embossed carbuncle

In my corrupted blood. But I'll not chide thee:

415 Let shame come when it will; I do not call it,

I do not bid the thunder-bearer shoot,

Nor tell tales of thee to high-judging Jove.

Mend when thou canst; be better at thy leisure:

I can be patient, I can stay with Regan,

I and my hundred knights.

420 **Regan**   Not altogether so, ᵠsirᵠ.

I looked not for you yet, nor am provided

For your fit welcome. Give ear, sir, to my sister;

For those that mingle reason with your passion

　　　　　　嗨,我宁愿去见易怒的法兰西王,

　　　　　　他没要嫁妆就娶了我的幼女,

　　　　　　在他面前跪求家臣般的奉养,

　　　　　　奴颜婢膝地生活。 跟她回去?

　　　　　　我宁愿给这个可恶的奴才　　　　　　　　　　405

　　　　　　当牛做马。〔指向奥斯华德〕

贡纳丽　　　　　　　　　先生,随您的便吧。

李尔　　　我求你,女儿,不要让我发疯:

　　　　　　我不会麻烦你的,孩子,别了:

　　　　　　我们不再见面,不再相见。

　　　　　　但你是我的血肉,我的女儿,　　　　　　　　410

　　　　　　也可以说是我体内的顽疾,

　　　　　　我要承认是我的。 你是个脓疱,

　　　　　　一个毒疮,或是红肿的毒瘤,

　　　　　　病根在我这里。 我并不怪你:

　　　　　　到时你自会害臊;不用我祈求,　　　　　　　415

　　　　　　我不会叫那位雷神降下霹雳,

　　　　　　也不向天上的朱庇特判官申冤。

　　　　　　你能改就改,你可慢慢改进:

　　　　　　我有耐心,可以住李根家里,

　　　　　　我和我一百名侍卫。

李根　　　　　　　　　　那可不行,　　　　　　　420

　　　　　　我还没盼您前来,也没备好

　　　　　　适当的招待。 要听大姐的,父亲;

　　　　　　只要能对您的冲动施以理性,

---

　　407. 不要让我发疯(do…mad):为 475 行埋下了伏笔。 410-14. 但……这里(But…blood):李尔在女儿身上发现了自己邪恶的根源,因此他不能不认她们。 咒她们就等于咒自己。416. 雷神(thunder-bearer):他在 211 行曾召唤过的朱庇特。 423. 只要……理性(mingle…passion):该剧在探问莎士比亚时代所公认的一种观点:人们被赋予理性旨在让他们控制激情。理性与激情之间的关系在该剧中显得更为复杂;鉴于李尔的冲动,李根与贡纳丽此刻有理由呼吁理性,但李尔在 453 行对理性的呼唤却更为有力。

Must be content to think you ^Qare^Q old, and so—

But she knows what she does.

425 **Lear**   Is this well spoken ^Qnow^Q?

Regan   I dare avouch it, sir. What, fifty followers?

Is it not well? What should you need of more?

Yea, or so many, sith that both charge and danger

Speak 'gainst so great a number? How in one house

430   Should many people, under two commands,

Hold amity? 'Tis hard, almost impossible.

Goneril   Why might not you, my lord, receive attendance

From those that she calls servants or from mine?

Regan   Why not, my lord? If then they chanced to slack ye

435   We could control them. If you will come to me—

For now I spy a danger—I entreat you

To bring but five and twenty: to no more

Will I give place or notice.

Lear   I gave you all—

Regan   And in good time you gave it.

440 **Lear**   —Made you my guardians, my depositaries,

But kept a reservation to be followed

With such a number. What, must I come to you

With five and twenty? Regan, said you so?

Regan   And speak't again, my lord: no more with me.

445 **Lear**   Those wicked creatures yet do look well favoured

When others are more wicked; not being the worst

Stands in some rank of praise. [*to Goneril*] I'll go with thee;

定会看出您已经老了,因此——

她可知道她的行动。

李尔　　　　　　　　　　此话当真?　　　　　　　　　　425

李根　　我敢保证,父亲。　五十个随从?

还不行吗?　您何必需要更多?

甚至五十,因为费用和危险

都声讨如此之众?　一个屋里

这么多成员,两人发号施令,　　　　　　　　430

怎能和睦?　很难,简直不可能。

贡纳丽　您为何不能,大人,用她的仆人

或者我的仆人来侍奉您呢?

李根　　何不呢,大人?　他们若偶尔慢待,

我们也好惩戒。　您若前来我家——　　　　435

因为我现在觉察到危险——我求您

只带二十五名:多了我不给

住处,也不会认可。

李尔　　我全给了你们——

李根　　　　　　　　　给得非常及时。

李尔　　——把你们当作我的管家、受托者,　　　　440

只保留一项权力:拥有这么多

随行人员。　怎么,我到您家里

只能带二十五位?　李根,是您说的?

李根　　再说一遍,大人:我不许再多。

李尔　　与更为邪恶的人相比,恶人　　　　　　445

倒会显得面善;不是最坏的

就该得到些赞许。　［向贡纳丽］我跟你去;

---

424. 因此(and so):李根突然住口,好像要重复她在 335-9 曾说过的话语。　428. 危险(danger):可令人想起李根在(对开本中)331-4 的相关言论。

Thy fifty yet doth double five and twenty,

And thou art twice her love.

Goneril   Hear me, my lord:

450   What need you five and twenty? Ten? Or five?

To follow in a house where twice so many

Have a command to tend you?

Regan   What need one?

Lear   O, reason not the need! Our basest beggars

Are in the poorest thing superfluous;

455   Allow not nature more than nature needs,

Man's life's as cheap as beast's. Thou art a lady;

If only to go warm were gorgeous,

Why, nature needs not what thou gorgeous wear'st,

Which scarcely keeps thee warm. But for true need—

460   You heavens, give me that patience, patience I need!

You see me here, you gods, a poor old man,

As full of grief as age, wretched in both:

If it be you that stir these daughters' hearts

Against their father, fool me not so much

465   To bear it tamely; touch me with noble anger,

你的五十可是二十五的两倍，

比她的爱翻了一番。

贡纳丽　　　　　　　　　听我说，大人：

何必要二十五个？　十个？　或五个？　　　　　　　　450

因为屋里已有加倍的侍从

可以听您使唤？

李根　　　　　　　　　　需要一个吗？

李尔　　　噢，请别论需要！最穷的乞丐

都会拥有一些多余的破烂；

若不许人们拥有身外之物，　　　　　　　　　　　　455

人就会贱如牲畜。　你是位夫人；

如果穿得暖和就算是体面，

你就不需要这么衣着光鲜，

因为它并不保暖。　而真正的需要——

上天啊，给我忍耐，我需要忍耐！　　　　　　　　　460

你们看，众神，我这可怜的老人，

充满悲伤和年迈，困苦不堪：

若是你们鼓动这些女儿的内心

反对她们父亲，别把我愚弄得

这么温顺：给我些高贵的愤怒，　　　　　　　　　　465

---

449. 比她的爱翻了一番（twice her love）：李尔尚未意识到爱无法量化，正如他在 459 所谈及的 "真正的需要" 也无法量化一样。　455-6. 若不许……牲畜（Allow…beast's）：原注为 "If you do not allow （human） nature more than （animal） nature needs, man's life is as worthless as that of a beast." 458-60. 需要……忍耐（needs…need）：李尔从李根或贡纳丽所穿华服难以满足的身体需要（bodily need），过度到忍受痛苦的能力——这种无法衡量的精神需要（spiritual need）。　尽管李尔在继续呼唤众神（gods），他对忍耐（patience）的哀求却不乏基督教色彩：患难生忍耐，忍耐生老练，老练生盼望（"罗马书" 3 章 3-4 节）。　465-75. 给我……疯了（touch…mad）：李尔在呼唤适合男人伟大胸怀的愤怒，但他随后那种空洞可笑且难以想象的誓言报复却使它烟消云散。　尽管李尔声称自己会拒绝象征女人气的泪水，一些著名的演员如加里克（Garrick）和欧文（Irving）此刻离开舞台时都会哭泣或啜泣，由此令人想起贡纳丽首次动摇了他的男子汉气概时，使他禁不住流出了热泪（1. 4. 290）。　李尔后来与考迪丽娅言归于好时，终于向象征着爱与同情并具有治愈能力的女人泪水屈服（见 4. 7. 47 和 71）。

And let not women's weapons, water—drops,

Stain my man's cheeks. No, you unnatural hags,

I will have such revenges on you both

That all the world shall—I will do such things

470   What they are yet I know not, but they shall be

The terrors of the earth! You think I'll weep,

No, I'll not weep. ^{F}[*Storm and tempest.*]^F

I have full cause of weeping, but this heart

Shall break into a hundred thousand flaws

475   Or e're I'll weep. O fool, I shall go mad!

     Exeunt ^{Q}*Lear, Gloucester, Kent, Fool*^{Q}[*and Knights*].

Cornwall Let us withdraw; 'twill be a storm.

Regan This house is little; the old man and's people

Cannot be well bestowed.

Goneril 'Tis his own blame; hath put himself from rest

480   And must needs taste his folly.

Regan For his particular, I'll receive him gladly,

But not one follower.

Goneril   So am I purposed.

Where is my lord of Gloucester?

Enter Gloucester.

Cornwall Followed the old man forth—he is returned.

485 **Gloucester** The King is in high rage.

別让女人们的武器——水滴，

玷污我的面颊。　无情的妖婆，

我要对你们两人进行报复，

好让世界——我要做这样的事情——

具体还不清楚,但它们将会　　　　　　　　　　　470

让世界震惊！你们以为我会哭，

不,我不哭。　[狂风暴雨。]

我有理由哭泣,然而只有当

这颗心破裂为千万碎片时,

我才会哭泣。　傻子啊,我要疯了！　　　　　　475

　　　　　　李尔、格洛斯特、肯特、傻瓜[及侍卫]下。

| 康瓦尔 | 咱们进屋吧；暴风雨来了。 |
| 李根 | 房子很小；老头子和他的随从
很难全部住下。 |

贡纳丽　　是他的过错；他不安分守己，

　　　　　就必须自食其果。　　　　　　　　　　　　　480

李根　　　至于他本人,我倒高兴接纳，

　　　　　但随从绝对不行。

贡纳丽　　　　　　　　我也会这样。

我的格洛斯特大人呢？

　　　　　　　　格 洛 斯 特 上。

康瓦尔　　跟着老头子去了——他回来了。

格洛斯特　国王在大发雷霆。　　　　　　　　　　　　485

---

　　475. 傻子啊,我要疯了（O…mad）：对傻子的亲切呼唤,自从康瓦尔和李根于315（1）入场之后,他一直在默默地支持着李尔。　479. 不安分守己（put…rest）：离开了自己的住处,且变得心神不宁（removed or turned himself away from both a place to sleep and peace of mind）。

^F**Cornwall**	Whither is he going?
Gloucester	He calls to horse,^F but will I know not whither.
Cornwall	'Tis best to give him way; he leads himself.
Goneril	[*to Gloucester*] My lord, entreat him by no means to stay.

490 **Gloucester**   Alack, the night comes on, and the high winds

Do sorely ruffle; for many miles about

There's scarce a bush.

Regan   O sir, to wilful men

The injuries that they themselves procure

Must be their schoolmasters. Shut up your doors.

495   He is attended with a desperate train,

And what they may incense him to, being apt

To have his ear abused, wisdom bids fear.

Cornwall   Shut up your doors, my lord; 'tis a wild night.

My Regan counsels well; come out o'the storm.   *Exeunt.*

康瓦尔	他要去哪里啊？
格洛斯特	他叫人备马，但我不知去何处。
康瓦尔	最好由他去吧；他自以为是。
贡纳丽	［向格洛斯特］大人，千万不要求他留下。

格洛斯特　哎呀，天快黑了，而且大风　　　　　　　　　　490
　　　　　在疯狂怒号；方圆几英里以内
　　　　　难见树丛。

李根　　　　　　　　　先生，对固执者来说，
　　　　　必须让他们从自找的伤害中
　　　　　去接受教训。　您把门关上吧。
　　　　　他有一帮亡命之徒服侍，　　　　　　　　　495
　　　　　易被他们误导，他们会鼓动他
　　　　　做些什么，理智会吩咐你惧怕。

康瓦尔　　关上门吧，大人；今晚狂风暴雨。
　　　　　我的李根说得好；快进屋躲避。　　　　　　同下。

---

498. 关上门吧（Shut…doors）：格洛斯特尽管很不情愿，还是服从了命令（Muir）。

第三幕
ACT 3

SCENE I

^F*Storm still.*^F *Enter Kent* [*disguised*] *and a Knight severally.*

Kent   Who's there, besides foul weather?

Knight   One minded like the weather, most unquietly.

Kent   I know you. Where's the King?

Knight   Contending with the fretful element;

5   Bids the winds blow the earth into the sea,

             Or swell the curled waters 'bove the main,

             That things might change, or cease; ^Qtears his white hair,

             Which the impetuous blasts with eyeless rage

             Catch in their fury and make nothing of,

10   Strives in his little world of man to outscorn

             The to and fro conflicting wind and rain;

             This night wherein the cub-drawn bear would couch,

             The lion and the belly-pinched wolf

             Keep their fur dry, unbonneted he runs,

             And bids what will take all.^Q

第一场

暴风雨依旧。肯特〔化装〕与一侍卫分头上。

肯特	这坏天气,是谁在哪里?
侍卫	他像这天气一般,心烦意乱。
肯特	我认识您。 国王呢?

侍卫　正在搏击发怒的风雨雷电;

恳求狂风把大地吹向海里,　　　　　　　　　5

或让翻腾的海浪席卷大地,

让万物混乱毁灭;他撕扯银发,

盲目肆虐的狂风盛怒之下

一把将它抓住,任意摆布,

他这个渺小的世人奋力蔑视　　　　　　　　10

冲突中来回打旋的狂风暴雨;

饥饿的母熊今晚都会躲在窝里,

狮子和饥肠辘辘的豺狼都会

保持皮毛干燥,他却光着头跑,

拼命地喊叫。

　　3.1. 0(1)暴风雨依旧(*Storm still*):在环球剧院里,导演常会通过在钢板上滚动铁球予以模仿;在这种风雨交加的背景下,李尔的扮演者必须提高嗓门。 0(1)分头(*severally*):正如2.1.0(1)一样,或从不同的门里分别出场。 2. 他像……意乱(minded…unquietly):外界的暴风骤雨与内心的骚动不安紧密相连,这种现象贯穿于整个暴风雨场景之中。 5-7. 恳求……毁灭(Bids…cease):李尔在呼唤世界复归混沌,或末日到来(Lear cries out for the return of chaos, or the end of the world),如5.3. 261-2中的景象。 6. 翻腾的(curled):其中,curled = curlèd(双音节)。 12. 饥饿的(cub-drawn):奶水已被熊仔吸干,因此会饿极而贪吃(sucked dry by her cubs, and so ravenous)。

15　**Kent**　　　　　　　　　　　　　　But who is with him?

　　Knight　　　None but the fool, who labours to outjest

　　　　　　　His heart-struck injuries.

　　Kent　　　　　　　　　　　　Sir, I do know you

　　　　　　　And dare upon the warrant of my note

　　　　　　　Commend a dear thing to you. There is division,

20　　　　　　Although as yet the face of it be covered

　　　　　　　With mutual cunning, 'twixt Albany and Cornwall,

　　　　　　　^FWho have, as who have not that their great stars

　　　　　　　Throned and set high, servants, who seem no less,

　　　　　　　Which are to France the spies and speculations

25　　　　　　Intelligent of our state—what hath been seen,

　　　　　　　Either in snuffs and packings of the dukes,

　　　　　　　Or the hard rein which both of them have borne

　　　　　　　Against the old kind King, or something deeper,

　　　　　　　Whereof, perchance, these are but furnishings. —^F

30　　　　　　^QNow to you:

　　　　　　　If on my credit you dare build so far

　　　　　　　To make your speed to Dover, you shall find

　　　　　　　Some that will thank you, making just report

　　　　　　　Of how unnatural and bemadding sorrow

| 肯特 | 有谁跟他一起？ | 15 |

侍卫　只有傻子,为抚慰他的伤心
尽力开些玩笑。

肯特　　　　　先生,我认识您,
凭借我对您的观察,我敢把
一件大事向您托付。　阿班尼
与康瓦尔之间出现了裂痕,　　　　　20
尽管双方都设法掩盖真相,
他们都有——官运亨通者有谁
没有——一些貌似正宗的仆人,
其实却是法王的间谍和密探,
向他通风报信——他们已发现,　　　　25
无论是公爵之间的怨恨和阴谋,
还是他们两人对仁慈老王的
苛刻和压迫,或是某些隐情,
上述问题也许是一种表象。　——
至于您:　　　　　　　　　　　30
假如您已经对我足够信任
敢迅速赶往多佛,您将发现
会有人感激,因为如实报告
国王无端遭受了多么反常

---

15. 拼命地喊叫（bids … all）:赌徒最后孤注一掷时会喊叫"赢家全拿（Winner takes all）"。　原文的 what = whoever。李尔是说:谁想要世界,就把它拿去,即让世界毁灭,可令人想起5-7行的话语。　16. 伤心（heart-struck injuries）:参见 2.4.349-50。　22-9. 他们……表象（Who…furnishings）:就肯特此处的消息而言,四开本与对开本有所不同。　四开本里明确提及法军已在英格兰秘密登陆,并准备张开大旗,暗示他们已抵达多佛。　对开本里的相关内容则更为含糊,只是暗示英国的间谍在向法国国王提供情报。　我省去了四开本里的四行台词,但收录了只在四开本里出现的30-8行台词,因为这些台词向侍卫提出了指示,也是首次提及了多佛,因此看似必要。　对开本此处之所以会有所改变,也许是想把英军的入侵推迟到第三幕第六场和第七场里。　27-8. 他们……压迫（hard…King）:源于骑马时把缰绳勒紧的意象（riding a horse on a tight rein）。　1.4.57-60 曾提及阿班尼慢待李尔,但后来他声称对贡纳丽的行为一无所知,并未参与折磨李尔（1.4.265-6）。　值得注意的是,他在 2.2 缺席;此时贡纳丽、李根与康瓦尔一起将李尔驱逐到暴风雨里。　32. 多佛（Dover）:首次暗示李尔在前往此地,并为他备好某些帮助。

35	The King hath cause to plain.
	I am a gentleman of blood and breeding,
	And from some knowledge and assurance
	Offer this office to you.[Q]
Knight	I will talk further with you.
Kent	No, do not.
40	For confirmation that I [F]am[F] much more
	Than my out-wall, open this purse and take
	What it contains. If you shall see Cordelia,
	As fear not but you shall, show her this ring,
	And she will tell you who your fellow is
45	That yet you do not know. Fie on this storm!
	I will go seek the King.
Knight	Give me your hand.
	Have you no more to say?
Kent	Few words, but to effect
	More than all yet: that, when we have found the King,
	In which your pain that way, I'll this,
50	He that first lights on him holla the other. *Exeunt.*

和令人发疯的伤痛。 35

我是个有身份有教养的绅士，

因为了解的信息确实可靠，

才把此任交付给您。

侍卫 咱们要进一步商讨。

肯特 不，不要。

为了证明我确实远远胜过了 40

本人的外表，打开这个钱包

把东西取走。 若见到考迪丽娅，

您一定会的，给她看这枚戒指，

她会告诉您谁是您目前尚不

认识的这位伙伴。 该死的风暴； 45

我去寻找国王。

侍卫 咱握握手吧。

没有别的可说？

肯特 话虽少，但比

其他重要：您找到国王的时候，

劳驾您请走那边，我走这边，

谁先见到他，向对方呼喊一下。 同下。 50

SCENE II

^F*Storm still.*^F *Enter Lear and Fool.*

Lear   Blow winds and crack your cheeks! Rage, blow!
You cataracts and hurricanoes, spout
Till you have drenched our steeples, drowned the cocks!
You sulphurous and thought-executing fires,
5   Vaunt-couriers of oak-cleaving thunderbolts,
Singe my white head! And thou, all-shaking thunder,
Strike flat the thick rotundity o'the world,
Crack nature's moulds, all germens spill at once
That make ingrateful man!

10 **Fool**   O, nuncle, court holy-water in a dry house is better
than this rain-water out o' door. Good nuncle, in, ^Qand^Q
ask thy daughters blessing. Here's a night pities neither
wise man nor fools.

Lear   Rumble thy bellyful! Spit fire, spout rain!

第二场

暴风雨依旧。李尔与傻子上。

李尔　　吹吧,狂风,吹破你的面颊! 怒吼!
　　　　天降的瀑布和龙卷的激流,喷注
　　　　直到将塔尖浸泡,风信鸡淹死!
　　　　你这硫黄般窒息思想的闪电,
　　　　可将橡树劈开的霹雳之先驱,　　　　　　　　　5
　　　　烧焦我白头! 震天动地的雷公,
　　　　将这个圆滚的世界夷为平地,
　　　　粉碎造化的模型,将孕育忘恩
　　　　者的种子一起摧毁!

傻子　　噢,老伯,宫里的恭维话要比这野外　　　　　10
　　　　的雨水好受得多了。好老伯,进去吧,
　　　　求你女儿祝福。这样的夜晚既不怜悯
　　　　贤哲也不怜悯傻子。

李尔　　你尽管轰隆吧! 吐火舌,喷雨水!

3.2. 1. 吹破你的面颊（crack your cheeks）：在当时的地图上,风常被绘制为从其面颊中吹出（the winds are pictured as puffing out their cheeks as they blow）（Mowat）。 6. 震天动地的雷公（And…thunder）：李尔在呼喊朱庇特天神（thou）。 该诗行也许会令观众想起上帝,因为他对约伯讲话时"雷声轰轰,大发威严"。 见《圣经》"约伯记"37章4-5节。 8. 粉碎造化的模型（Crack…moulds）：将大自然使生灵成型的模子打烂——毁灭世界的系列隐喻之一（借鉴孙大雨先生译文。 ——译者附注）。 12. 求你女儿祝福（ask…blessing）：此举将意味着李尔承认了她们的权威（Bevington）。

15   Nor rain, wind, thunder, fire are my daughters;

I tax not you, you elements, with unkindness.

I never gave you kingdom, called you children;

You owe me no subscription. ᵠWhyᵠ then, let fall

Your horrible pleasure. Here I stand your slave,

20   A poor, infirm, weak and despised old man.

But yet I call you servile ministers

That have with two pernicious daughters join

Your high-engendered battles 'gainst a head

So old and white as this. O, ꜰho!ꜰ 'tis foul.

25 **Fool**   He that has a house to put's head in has a good

headpiece:

     The codpiece that will house

       Before the head has any,

     The head and he shall louse:

30   *So beggars marry many.*

     The man that makes his toe

       What he his heart should make,

     Shall of a corn cry woe,

       And turn his sleep to wake.

风雨雷电都不是我的女儿； 　　　　　　　　　　15

我不指控你们这些天象无情。

我从未给你们国土,叫你们孩子；

你们无须对我孝顺。　你们就

尽情肆虐。　你们的奴仆站在这里,

我这可怜、虚弱、遭鄙视的老人。 　　　　　　20

可我要指责你们是卑贱的帮凶,

竟用你们在天庭募集的兵力

与两位恶毒的女儿一起攻击

这位白头老翁。　噢,嗬,可恶!

傻子　　谁有屋子可住在里头,谁就有个好的 　　　　25

罩头:

脑袋还没有住房,

鸡巴便找了鸡窝,

他会把虱子喂养:

乞丐讨好多小婆。 　　　　　　30

谁若是亲疏颠倒,

把脚趾当作心肝,

就会因鸡眼哭叫,

夜晚也不得安眠。

---

26. 罩头（headpiece）:双关语,可指头盔、头罩（a helmet, a covering for the head）；也可指脑袋,即头脑（a head, i. e. brain）（Muir）。　27-30. 脑袋……小婆（The…many）:若一位男人尚无安身之处便满足自己的性欲,最终他会娶一位妻子,并分享她的虱子。29 行是指乞丐与好多妓女有染。　（The man who satisfies his sexual appetites before he has a house to live in will end up by marrying a wife, and share her lice. L. 29 refers to the beggar's long train of doxies）（Muir）。　28. 鸡巴（codpiece）:阴茎。　本指男子马裤前裆的袋状附属物,用以遮盖生殖器并使其突显（Bate）。　31-4. 谁若……安眠（The…wake）:谁若鄙视或摈弃自己本应亲爱之人（考迪丽娅?）,或错误地喜爱卑劣之物,就会陷入痛苦与失眠。　在身体各部位的等级制中,脚趾属于"最低,最劣,最差的级别（lowest, basest, poorest'）"（Foakes）。　弄臣是在嘲弄李尔抛弃考迪丽娅,却厚待其恶毒女儿的愚行（Muir）。

35   For there was never yet fair woman but she made
mouths in a glass.

Enter Kent [disguised].

Lear   No, I will be the pattern of all patience,
I will say nothing.

Kent   Who's there?

40   **Fool**   Marry, here's grace and a codpiece—that's a wise
man and a fool.

Kent   [*to Lear*] Alas, sir, are you here? Things that love night
Love not such nights as these. The wrathful skies
Gallow the very wanderers of the dark,

45   And make them keep their caves. Since I was man
Such sheets of fire, such bursts of horrid thunder,
Such groans of roaring wind and rain I never
Remember to have heard. Man's nature cannot carry
Th'affliction, nor the fear.

Lear   Let the great gods

50   That keep this dreadful pudder o'er our heads
Find out their enemies now. Tremble, thou wretch,
That hast within thee undivulged crimes,
Unwhipped of justice. Hide thee, thou bloody hand,
Thou perjured, and thou simular man of virtue

55   That art incestuous. Caitiff, to pieces shake,
That under covert and convenient seeming

因为从没有哪位美女不会在镜子前面　　　　　　　　35

挤眉弄眼。

肯特［化装］上。

李尔	不,我要做个能忍耐的楷模,
	我啥都不说。
肯特	那是谁?
傻子	天哪,我们是陛下和屌袋儿——一个　　40
	聪明一个傻。
肯特	［向李尔］唉,先生,您在这里?　爱黑夜的东西
	也不会爱这种黑夜。　愤怒的天空
	会使那夜间漫游的野兽惧怕,
	使他们待在洞里。　我成年以来,　　45
	这样的电闪,这样可怕的雷鸣,
	这样咆哮的狂风骤雨,我好像
	还从未听说。　人是无法忍受
	这种折磨或恐惧。
李尔	让那在我们
	头顶制造这可怕喧嚣的众神　　50
	搜出他们的仇敌。　颤抖吧,小人,
	你们犯下了尚未泄露的罪行,
	仍在逍遥法外。　躲避吧,凶手,
	你们作伪证者,实为乱伦的
	道貌岸然者。　身体粉碎吧,恶棍,　　55
	你们包藏祸心、假冒伪善、

35-6. 镜子……弄眼（made…glass）：暗指贡纳丽的虚荣（见 2.2.35 与脚注）,或暗指她和李根的虚伪。　55. 道貌岸然者（simular of virtue）：原文"simular = simulator（假装者）"（Muir）。　参考李尔在 4.6.116-19 所用的意象——皮笑肉不笑的夫人（simp'ring dame）（Foakes）。

Hast practised on man's life. Close pent-up guilts,

Rive your concealing continents and cry

These dreadful summoners grace. I am a man

More sinned against than sinning.

60 **Kent**   Alack, bareheaded?

Gracious my lord, hard by here is a hovel:

Some friendship will it lend you 'gainst the tempest.

Repose you there, while I to this hard house—

More harder than the stones whereof 'tis raised,

65   Which even but now, demanding after you,

Denied me to come in—return and force

Their scanted courtesy.

Lear   My wits begin to turn.

[*to the Fool*] Come on, my boy. How dost my boy? Art cold?

I am cold myself. [*to Kent*] Where is this straw, my fellow?

70   The art of our necessities is strange,

That can make vile things precious. Come; your hovel.

[*to the Fool*] Poor fool and knave, I have one part in my heart

That's sorry yet for thee.

Fool   *He that has* ᶠ*and*ᶠ *a little tiny wit,*

75   *With heigh-ho, the wind and the rain,*

Must make content with his fortunes fit,

Though the rain it raineth every day.

暗中害人。　让隐秘的愧疚之心

从藏匿之处冲出来,并向这些

可怕的传讯官求饶。　我这个人

受害多于害人。

肯特　　　　　　　　　唉,还光着头?　　　　　　　　　60

我的陛下,附近有一间茅屋:

可以帮您躲避这狂风暴雨。

去休息一下,我去那心硬的人家——

他们的心比那房屋的石头还硬,

就在刚才,我去找您的时候,　　　　　　　65

拒绝让我进去——我回去强求

他们克扣的礼仪。

李尔　　　　　　　　　　　我开始发昏。

[向傻子]来吧,孩子。　你好吗,孩子?　冷吗?

我很冷。　[向肯特]茅屋在哪里,我的伙计?

我们所受的艰难有一种神力,　　　　　　70

可将草芥化为珍稀。　快,去茅屋。

[向傻子]可怜的傻子,我的心里倒是

有些为你难过。

傻子　　　　　谁若还有点真知灼见,

嘿,嗬,真是风雨交加,　　　　　　　　75

他定会做到随遇而安,

尽管大雨它天天在下。

---

60. 还光着头(bareheaded):李尔入场时应该戴着一顶皇冠,见1.1.33(1);在1.4与侍卫(打猎?)回家时也该戴着帽子;于1.5终场动身前往李根家里时,无疑也像其他绅士那样戴着帽子。　肯特此处的担心表明出门在外的国王竟然没戴帽子是多么反常,更何况是在暴风雨中。　65. 他们(which):房屋的主人;或屋里的人们(the owners of which; or the people in it)。　见2.2.1(Muir)。　68-9. 孩子……伙计(my boy…fellow):李尔在对傻子和肯特说话,他在暴风雨中首次"意识到了别人的痛苦"。　70-1. 我们……珍稀(The…precious):原注为"The power of the hardships we suffer is strange, and can make us value wretched stuff (like straw) as precious."也可以说李尔是在重新解释"真正的需要(true need)";见2.2.459。74. 谁……灼见(He…wit):傻子也许是在指李尔,或他自己(Muir)。

Lear   True, ^Qmy good^Q boy. [*to Kent*] Come, bring us to this
          hovel.   [*Exeunt Lear and Kent.*]

^F**Fool**   This is a brave night to cool a courtesan. I'll speak
80   a prophecy ere I go:

> *When priests are more in word than matter,*
>
> *When brewers mar their malt with water,*
>
> *When nobles are their tailors' tutors,*
>
> *No heretics burned but wenches' suitors;*
>
> 85   *When every case in law is right;*
>
> *No squire in debt, nor no poor knight;*
>
> *When slanders do not live in tongues,*
>
> *Nor cut-purses come not to throngs;*
>
> *When usurers tell their gold i'the field,*
>
> 90   *And bawds and whores do churches build,*
>
> *Then shall the realm of Albion*
>
> *Come to great confusion:*
>
> *Then comes the time, who lives to see't,*
>
> *That going shall be used with feet.*

95   This prophecy Merlin shall make, for I live before
          his time.   *Exit.*^F

李尔　　　　对,好孩子。　［向肯特］快,带我们去

　　　　　　茅屋。　　　　　　　　　　　　　［李尔与肯特同下。］

傻子　　　　这么棒的夜晚可平息妓女的淫念。我

　　　　　　离开前要说个预言:　　　　　　　　　　　　　　　80

　　　　　　　　等到牧师们言行不一,

　　　　　　　　酿造者用水把麦酒释稀,

　　　　　　　　等到贵族们教裁缝缝补,

　　　　　　　　被烧的是嫖客,不是异教徒;

　　　　　　　　等到全都能秉公办案,　　　　　　　　　　85

　　　　　　　　乡绅不负债,骑士不可怜;

　　　　　　　　等到诽谤者不再开口,

　　　　　　　　扒手不到人群里游走,

　　　　　　　　等到放债人公开数钱,

　　　　　　　　老鸨妓女把教堂修建,　　　　　　　　　　90

　　　　　　　　到那时这个阿尔比恩,

　　　　　　　　那就会变得死气沉沉:

　　　　　　　　等到那时,人们会发现,

　　　　　　　　他需要用脚迈步向前。

　　　　　　先知莫林会作这种预言,因为我生在　　　　　95

　　　　　　他的前面。　　　　　　　　　　　　　　　下。

---

　　79. 棒的……淫念（brave…courtesan）：原注为“great night to cool the lust of a courtier's mistress”。 这些话语好像与前面的台词无关,但与90行的“妓女（whores）”,以及3.4.83-8,4.2,4.5,4.6场所强调的淫欲相关。 79-96. 上述台词并未出现在四开本里。 傻子前半部分的预言在暗讽时弊：牧师更关心言辞而不是实际,酿造者向啤酒里兑水,贵族们追赶时髦,情人染上梅毒（priests concerned with words not substance, brewers diluting their beer with water, nobles devoting themselves to the latest fashion, lovers burned by syphilis）；预言的第二部分描绘的是一种虚无缥缈的理想,英格兰每天所发生的事情实际上与之恰恰相反。 84. 烧（burned）：双关语,也可指梅毒的烧灼（Muir）。 91. 阿尔比恩（Albion）：不列颠的古称（源自古罗马对该地的称呼）。 94. 戏剧性突降法：不会有任何变化;别指望这种乌托邦似的梦想能够实现（Bevington）。 95. 莫林（Merlin）：亚瑟王统治时期传说中的预言家。 据史料记载,李尔王的统治时期为公元前8世纪,亚瑟王的统治时期为公元6世纪。 从某种意义上讲,傻子确实生在莫林之前。

SCENE III

Enter Gloucester and Edmund, ^Qwith lights^Q.

Gloucester   Alack,   alack,   Edmund,   I   like   not   this
unnatural   dealing.   When   I   desire   their   leave   that   I
might pity him, they took from me the use of mine own
house; charged me on pain of their perpetual displeasure
5   neither   to   speak   of   him,   entreat   for   him,   or   any   way
sustain him.

Edmund   Most savage and unnatural.

Gloucester   Go to; say you nothing. There's a division between
the dukes, and a worse matter than that: I have
10   received a letter this night— 'tis dangerous to be spoken
— I have locked the letter in my closet. These injuries
the King now bears will be revenged home. There is
part of a power already footed; we must incline to the
King. I will seek him and privily relieve him. Go you
15   and maintain talk with the Duke, that my charity be not
of him perceived. If he ask for me, I am ill, and gone to
bed. If I die for it—as no less is threatened me—the
King my old master must be relieved. There is strange
things toward, Edmund; pray you, be careful.   *Exit.*

20 **Edmund**   This courtesy, forbid thee, shall the Duke
Instantly know and of that letter too.

第三场

格洛斯特与埃德蒙上。手持火把。

格洛斯特　哎呀,哎呀,埃德蒙,我不喜欢这种
违反常情的行为。当我求他们准许我
怜悯他时,他们便将我的房屋使用权
夺去;命令我——否则对我终生不满
——不要提他,为他求情,或者给他　　　　5
任何资助。

埃德蒙　多么凶恶和无情无义!

格洛斯特　罢了,你别多嘴。两位公爵之间出现
了裂痕,还有件更糟的事情:我今晚
收到了一封信函——说出来都很危险　　　10
——我已把信锁进了密室。国王所受
的这些屈辱会得到彻底的报复。有一
部分法军已经登陆;我们要站在国王
这边。我去找他并且暗中救济。你去
和公爵谈谈话,好让他发现不了我的　　　15
善举。他要问我,就说我病了已休息。
哪怕我为此死去——他们是这样威胁
——也要救助我的国王老主人。怪事
即将来临,埃德蒙;求你,要小心。　　　　下。

埃德蒙　这种殷勤,明令禁止,要立即　　　　　20
向公爵报告,还有那封信件。

This seems a fair deserving and must draw me

That which my father loses, no less than all.

The younger rises when the old doth fall.   *Exit*.

奖赏会相当可观,父亲丧失的
一定会由我获取,应有尽有。
老的跌落时小的才能出头。　　　　　　　　　下。

SCENE Ⅳ

Enter Lear, Kent [in disguise] and Fool.

Kent   Here is the place, my lord; good my lord, enter;

The tyranny of the open night's too rough

For nature to endure.   [F]*Storm still.*[F]

Lear   Let me alone.

Kent   Good my lord, enter [F]here[F].

Lear   Wilt break my heart?

5 **Kent**   I had rather break mine own. Good my lord, enter.

Lear   Thou think'st 'tis much that this contentious storm

Invades us to the skin: so 'tis to thee,

But where the greater malady is fixed,

The lesser is scarce felt. Thou'dst shun a bear,

10 But if thy flight lay toward the raging sea,

Thou'dst meet the bear i'the mouth. When the mind's free,

The body's delicate: the tempest in my mind

Doth from my senses take all feeling else,

Save what beats there, filial ingratitude!

15 Is it not as this mouth should tear this hand

For lifting food to't? But I will punish home;

第四场

国王、肯特[化装]与傻子上。

肯特 就是这里,陛下:好陛下,进去吧;

外面的这种夜晚太过残酷,

血肉之躯无法忍受。 　　暴风雨依旧

李尔 　　　　　别管我。

肯特 好陛下,进去吧。

李尔 　　　　你想让我心碎?

肯特 我宁愿自己心碎。 好陛下,进去吧。　　　　　　　5

李尔 你以为这种肆虐的狂风暴雨

可渗透我们的肌肤:那是对你,

可当你心情沉重时,轻微的伤痛

就难以察觉。 你会躲避大熊,

但你要面向汹涌的大海逃生,　　　　　　10

就会直面那头大熊。 心静时,

身体就会敏感:我心中的风暴

已让其他的感觉消失殆尽,

只剩内心的折磨——儿女的忘恩!

难道不像这只嘴巴撕咬这手,　　　　　　15

因为给它喂食? 我会彻底惩罚;

3.4. 1. 这里（the place）：3.2.61 所提及的茅屋。 4. 你想让我心碎（Wilt…heart）：暴风雨可以让李尔分心,暂且忘记女儿的忘恩负义（14）,否则会使他心碎。 8. 沉重（fixed）：（正如 12-4 行所解释的那样,已在他心中）根深蒂固（rooted in his mind）。

No, I will weep no more. ^FIn such a night

To shut me out? Pour on, I will endure.^F

In such a night as this? O, Regan, Goneril,

20   Your old, kind father, whose frank heart gave ^Qyou^Q all—

O, that way madness lies, let me shun that;

No more of that.

Kent   Good my lord, enter ^Fhere^F.

Lear   Prithee go in thyself, seek thine own ease.

This tempest will not give me leave to ponder

25   On things would hurt me more. But I'll go in;

[*to the Fool*] ^FIn boy, go first. You houseless poverty—

Nay, get thee in. I'll pray, and then I'll sleep. *Exit*^F[*Fool*].

[*Kneels.*] Poor naked wretches, wheresoe'er you are,

That bide the pelting of this pitiless storm,

30   How shall your houseless heads and unfed sides,

Your looped and windowed raggedness, defend you

From seasons such as these? O, I have ta'en

Too little care of this. Take physic, pomp,

Expose thyself to feel what wretches feel,

35   That thou mayst shake the superflux to them

And show the heavens more just.

[*Enter Fool, as from the hovel.*]

^F**Edgar**   [*Within*] Fathom and half, fathom and half: Poor

不,我不会再哭。 在这种夜晚

关我外面? 你下吧,我能忍受。

在这种夜晚? 噢,李根,贡纳丽,

你们慈祥的老父,全给了你们——   20

噢,这么想会发疯的,我要避免;

别想它了。

肯特   好陛下,快进去吧。

李尔   你请进吧,让自己舒服一点。

这种风暴可以阻止我思考

更伤心的事情。 可我会进去;   25

[向傻子]你先进,孩子。 无家可归的穷人——

不,你进。 我要祈祷,然后再睡。   [傻子]下。

[跪下.]可怜的穷人,无论你们在哪里,

忍受这种无情的滂沱大雨,

你们光着的脑袋,空空的肚皮,   30

你们的破衣烂衫,如何让你们

躲避这种狂风暴雨? 噢,我对此

关心太少! 吃点苦吧,贵人,

让自己感受一下穷人的感受,

你好把多余的东西分给他们,   35

好让上天显得公平。

[傻子上,似出自茅屋。]

埃德加   [在内]一英寻半,一英寻半:可怜的

---

28. 跪下(*Kneels*):对开本和四开本里本无此舞台指示,但演员们发现此刻跪下会颇为合适。 自从他在2.2.343下跪讽刺李根,到4.7.58跪下向考迪丽娅表示悔罪,这无疑可表明李尔朝谦卑迈进了一步。 28-36.上述诗行列举了基督教新教徒有关苦难的教义:"同情受苦受难的人们,对基督徒来说是一种必要的美德。 但谁若从未经历过试探、苦难,或折磨,就很难同情他人";因此"受苦和忍耐是一种智慧的象征"。 33. 苦(physic):通常指一种泻药(a purge)。 37-8.埃德加……汤姆(F Edgar…Tom F):只出现在对开本里。 埃德加的喊叫好像是在从船上或茅屋里面探测水深。

		Tom!^F

Tom!^F

Fool Come not in here , nuncle , here's a spirit . Help me,
40   help me!

Kent Give me thy hand. Who's there?

Fool A spirit, ^Fa spirit.^F He says his name's poor Tom.

Kent What art thou that dost grumble there i'the straw?
      Come forth.

Enter Edgar [,disguised as Poor Tom.]

45 **Edgar** Away, the foul fiend follows me. Through the sharp
      hawthorn blows the ^Qcold^Q wind. ^FHumh,^F go to
      thy ^Qcold^Q bed and warm thee.

   Lear Didst thou give all to thy ^Qtwo^Q daughters? And art
      thou come to this?

50 **Edgar** Who gives anything to poor Tom? Whom the foul
      fiend hath led through fire and ^Fthrough flame,^F
      through ford and whirlpool, o'er bog and quagmire;
      that hath laid knives under his pillow and halters in his
      pew; set ratsbane by his porridge, made him proud of
55   heart, to ride on a bay trotting horse over four-inched
      bridges, to course his own shadow for a traitor. Bless

汤姆！

傻子	你别进去，老伯，里面有鬼。 救命啊，	
	救命啊！	40
肯特	抓住我的手。 那是谁？	
傻子	是鬼，是鬼。 他说他名叫可怜的汤姆。	
肯特	你是谁，竟然在那稻草堆里嘀嘀咕咕？	
	快出来。	

埃德加［扮成可怜的汤姆］上。

埃德加	走开，有个魔鬼在跟我。 穿过尖利的	45
	山楂树有冷风吹过。哼，快去你冰冷	
	的床上暖和暖和。	
李尔	难道你已把你的一切都给了女儿？你	
	竟然至此？	
埃德加	谁会给可怜的汤姆什么？邪恶的魔鬼	50
	已经引领他穿过了大火，穿过了火焰，	
	穿过了浅滩和漩涡，跨过沼泽和泥潭；	
	在他的枕头下放了尖刀，在教堂放了	
	绞索；在他的粥里下了毒，使他心高	
	气傲，骑着枣红马跨过四吋宽的小桥，	55
	把自己的影子当叛徒追逐。保佑你的	

---

48. 难道……女儿（Didst…daughters）：一个可怜和赤裸的乞丐突然出现，使李尔想起了自己的苦难。 可怜的汤姆或多或少地取代了傻子的位置，成了李尔关注的中心。 对许多评注者和演员来说，李尔从此开始发疯。 50-8. 邪恶的……侵袭（foul…taking）：从本段台词开始，莎士比亚开始从同时代的英国作家及大主教——哈斯尼特（Samuel Harsnett）的《宣言》（*Declaration*）中借用词语、短语、形象等。 53-4. 尖刀……绞索（knives…halters）：据信魔鬼会向绝望者提供此类用具，鼓励他们自杀，让其灵魂永受诅咒。 55. 骑着……小桥（ride…bridges）：需要有鬼神的相助才能做到。

thy five wits, Tom's a-cold. ^FO do, de, do, de, do de:^F

bless thee from whirlwinds, star-blasting and taking!

Do poor Tom some charity, whom the foul fiend vexes.

60 There could I have him now, and there, and there

again, ^Fand there.^F   ^F*Storm still.*^F

Lear   Have his daughters brought him to this pass?

Couldst thou save nothing? Wouldst thou give'em all?

Fool   Nay, he reserved a blanket, else we had been all

65 shamed.

Lear   [*to Edgar*] Now all the plagues that in the pendulous air

Hang fated o'er men's faults light on thy daughters!

Kent   He hath no daughters, sir.

Lear   Death, traitor! Nothing could have subdued nature

70 To such a lowness but his unkind daughters.

Is it the fashion that discarded fathers

Should have thus little mercy on their flesh?

Judicious punishment, 'twas this flesh begot

Those pelican daughters.

75 **Edgar**   *Pillicock sat on Pillicock hill,*

Alow, alow, loo, loo!

	五能，汤姆很冷。嘟嘚，嘟嘚，嘟嘚：	
	保佑你免遭旋风、灾星和疾病的侵袭！	
	救救可怜的汤姆，他在遭受魔鬼折磨。	
	我现在能逮住他了，他在那里，就在	60
	那里，在那里！ 暴风雨依旧。	
李尔	是他的女儿害他到这种地步？	
	你身无分文？一切都给了她们？	
傻子	没有，他还有条毛毯，否则我们都会	
	害羞。	65
李尔	［向埃德加］悬在空中定要惩罚恶人的	
	所有瘟疫降到你女儿身上！	
肯特	他没有女儿，陛下。	
李尔	该死，叛徒！啥都不能把常人	
	贬到这种程度，除了他的女儿。	70
	被遗弃的父亲竟遭受这样的	
	摧残，难道这是一种时髦？	
	公正的惩罚，正是这副躯体	
	生了那些吸血女。	
埃德加	鸡公坐上了鸡公山，	75
	啊噜，啊噜，噜，噜！	

---

57. 五能（five wits）：大脑的五种能力（five faculties of the mind），与身体的五官平行，即常识、想象、幻想、估算和记忆（common wit, imagination, fantasy, estimation and memory）。 嘟嘚（do…de）：牙齿打颤的声音。 60-1. 他在……那里（There…there）：埃德加是想把自己体内的魔鬼赶走，或是从身上寻找虱子或魔鬼？ 66-7. 悬在……瘟疫（in…faults）：疾病被想象为悬在空中（pendulous），受星辰的影响从天而降，对人们的罪过进行惩罚。 71-2. 遭受……摧残（little…flesh）：可指埃德加的可怜，或指他身上扎进去的尖刺（Muir）。 74. 吸血女（pelican daughters）：暗指一则古老的寓言，说是鹈鹕（pelican）用自己的血液哺育雏鸟。 75-6. 埃德加，作为可怜的汤姆，现已吸引了李尔的注意，并取代了傻子的某些作用；其标志是现由他说出一些韵诗或歌谣，而非傻子。 75. 鸡公（Pillicock）：俚语，指阴茎；鸡公山（Pillicock hill）可指维纳斯山（the mount of Venus）或女性生殖器。 76. 啊噜……噜（Alow…loo）：可有多种解释：呼唤狗去追逐猎物，疯子吹出的号角声，或一首歌谣的副歌（Muir）。

Fool	This cold night will turn us all to fools and madmen.
Edgar	Take heed o'the foul fiend; obey thy parents, keep thy word justly, swear not, commit not with man's sworn spouse, set not thy sweet-heart on proud array. Tom's a-cold.
Lear	What hast thou been?
Edgar	A serving-man, proud in heart and mind, that curled my hair, wore gloves in my cap, served the lust of my mistress' heart and did the act of darkness with her; swore as many oaths as I spake words and broke them in the sweet face of heaven. One that slept in the contriving of lust and waked to do it. Wine loved I deeply, dice dearly; and, in woman, out-paramoured the Turk: false of heart, light of ear, bloody of hand; hog in sloth, fox in stealth, wolf in greediness, dog in madness, lion in prey. Let not the creaking of shoes, nor the rustling of silks, betray thy poor heart to woman. Keep thy foot out of brothels, thy hand out of plackets, thy pen from lenders' books, and defy the foul fiend. Still through the hawthorn blows the cold wind,

80

85

90

95

傻子	这种寒夜会把我们都变成傻瓜或疯子。	
埃德加	注意这个恶魔；顺从你的父母，你要 言语公正，不要起誓，也不要跟有夫 之妇通奸，不要渴慕那些华丽的衣服。	80
	汤姆很冷。	
李尔	你原来干啥？	
埃德加	当过仆人，心高气傲、得意忘形，我 头发卷曲，帽子上挂着手套，满足我 情人心中的欲望，跟她做过见不得人	85
	的勾当；我张嘴就起誓，然后在仁慈 的上天面前一一违背。我在睡眠之中 孕育着淫念，醒来后付诸行动。我爱 喝酒，喜欢赌博；我的女人比苏丹王 还多：内心狡诈，爱听谗言，手残忍；	90
	猪一般懒散，狐狸般狡猾，像狼贪婪， 疯得像狗，狮子一般凶狠。别让女人 咯噔的鞋声或绫罗的沙沙声使你神不 守舍。你不要踏进妓院，别把手伸进 裙衩里面，债主薄上别签名，要挑战	95
	恶魔。依然有股冷风从山楂树中吹过，	

78-80. 顺从……衣服（obey…array）：对《圣经》里"十诫"的模仿（"出埃及记"20章3-17节）：当孝敬父母，不可作假证（换言之，要按照经义使自己言辞公正），不可妄称耶和华你神的名（或起誓；另见"马太福音"5章34节），不可奸淫，要避免贪欲。　83-96. 这些台词跟当时的其他讽刺内容一样（如《复仇者的悲剧》［*The Revenger's Tragedy*］），旨在抨击宫廷的狂欢、淫欲和腐败。　其中，"仆人（serving-man）"可指奥斯华德似的侍从（attendant），他作为管家地位很高，打扮得也像个臣子；也可指"情人（lover）"，就像埃德蒙那样，想与贡纳丽保持暧昧关系（4. 2. 18-28）。　84. 头发卷曲（curled my hair）：人们将烫发与自高自大相连。　84. 帽子上挂着手套（gloves…cap）：作为情人的信物或青睐。　89. 苏丹王（the Turk）：即土耳其君主苏丹王（the Grand Turk or Sultan），以妻妾成群而著称。　91-2. 猪……凶狠（hog…prey）：可让灵魂死亡的七大罪行常以不同的动物为象征（Muir）。

says suum, mun, nonny, Dauphin my boy, ^Qmy^Q boy, *cessez*! Let him trot by.   ^F*Storm still.*^F

Lear

100

^QWhy,^Q thou wert better in thy grave than to answer with thy uncovered body this extremity of the skies, Is man no more than this? Consider him well. Thou ow'st the worm no silk, the beast no hide, the sheep no wool, the cat no perfume. ^FHa?^F Here's three on's are sophisticated; thou art the thing itself.

105

Unaccommodated man is no more but such a poor, bare, forked animal as thou art. Off, off, you lendings! come, unbutton ^Fhere^F.

[*Tearing at his clothes, he is restrained by Kent and the Fool.*]

^F*Enter Gloucester, with a torch.*^F

Fool

110

Prithee, nuncle, be contented; 'tis a naughty night to swim in. Now a little fire in a wild field were like an old lecher's heart, a small spark, all the rest on's body cold: look, here comes a walking fire.

Edgar

115

This is the foul ^Qfiend^Q Flibbertigibbet: he begins at curfew and walks till the first cock; he gives the web and the pin, squinies the eye and makes the harelip; mildews the white wheat and hurts the poor creature of earth.

飕飕,曼,喃呢,多芬好孩子,孩子,
好了! 让他过去。 暴风雨依旧。

李尔 嗨,你这赤裸的身体遭受空中的这种
极端天气,还不如进入你的坟墓好些。 100
难道一个人不过如此? 看看他吧。你
不欠蚕茧一根丝,野兽一张皮,绵羊
一根毛,灵猫一滴香。哈? 我们三个
都是掺了假的;而你却是本来的面目。
剥去文明的装饰,人就是你这样可怜、 105
赤裸的两条腿动物。脱去,身外之物!
快,解开扣子。
[撕扯衣服,被肯特和傻子制止。]

格洛斯特上,手持火把。

傻子 求你,老伯,冷静些;这么糟的夜晚
不适合游泳。野地里的一丝亮光就像
老色鬼的心脏,一处火热,全身发凉: 110
瞧,有团火走了过来!

埃德加 这是恶魔弗里伯提伯特:他在傍晚时
出现,漫游到开始鸡叫;他让人眼生
白内障,使人成斜眼,让人唇上长豁;
使成熟的麦子发霉,将世上可怜生灵
伤害。 115

97-8. 飕飕……过去(suum…by):莫名其妙;可能是故意说的疯话:"飕飕,曼(suum, mun)"也许是在模仿风声;"喃呢(nonny)"像一首歌谣的副歌。 埃德加随后好像是在告诉想象中的、名叫多芬的马停止某种行动,然后又让大家给马让道。 其中,"cessez"为法语,意为"cease, stop(停住)"。 103. 灵猫(cat = civet cat):一种香料(灵猫香),从雌灵猫尾部的腺体分泌物中提炼而成。 112. 弗里伯提伯特(Flibbertigibbet):魔鬼的名字。 112-3. 傍晚……鸡叫(at curfew…cock):从黄昏至黎明(幽灵可外出游荡的时段)。

Swithold footed thrice the wold;

He met the nightmare and her nine foal,

Bid her alight and her troth plight,

120   *And aroint thee, witch, aroint thee.*

Kent   How fares your grace?

Lear   What's he?

Kent   [*to Gloucester*] Who's there? What is't you seek?

Gloucester   What are you there? Your names?

125 **Edgar**   Poor Tom, that eats the swimming frog, the toad, the tadpole, the wall-newt and the water—; that in the fury of his heart, when the foul fiend rages, eats cow-dung for s alads; swallows the old rat and the ditch-dog; drinks the green mantle of the standing pool; who is

130   whipped from tithing to tithing and stocked, punished and imprisoned—who hath ᵠhadᵠ three suits to his back, six shirts to his body,

Horse to ride, and weapon to wear.

But mice and rats and such small deer

135   *Have been Tom's food for seven long year.*

Beware my follower. Peace, Smulkin, peace, thou fiend!

Gloucester   What, hath your grace no better company?

圣维特霍三次来到野外；

遇见恶魔和她九个幼崽，

令她站住并誓不再来，

你快滚开,巫婆,你滚开！　　　　　　　　　　　　120

肯特　　　您好吗,陛下？

李尔　　　他是谁？

肯特　　　〔向格洛斯特〕那是谁？ 您想找谁？

格洛斯特　你们是谁？ 叫啥名字？

埃德加　　可怜的汤姆,吃游泳的青蛙、癞蛤蟆、　　　125

　　　　　　小蝌蚪、壁虎和蝾螈——；他在满腔

　　　　　　怒火之下,恶魔肆虐的时候,曾经把

　　　　　　牛粪当色拉；吞下死老鼠和沟里的狗；

　　　　　　喝下死水池里的绿水藻；从一个教区

　　　　　　被赶到另一个教区,也坐过柳,受过　　　　130

　　　　　　惩罚和监禁——他这人曾经有过三套

　　　　　　服装,六件衬衫,

　　　　　　　　他有马骑也佩带武器。

　　　　　　　　小鼠大鼠这样的东西

　　　　　　　　七年来汤姆靠它们充饥。　　　　　　135

　　　　　　当心我的鬼。安静,斯毛金,安静,你这

　　　　　　魔鬼！

格洛斯特　怎么,陛下您没有更好的伙伴？

---

　　117. 圣维特霍（Swithold = Saint Withold）：盎格鲁—撒克逊人的魔法师,此处像是在用符咒驱逐据信可以折磨睡眠者的"梦魇（nightmare）"或"魔鬼（demon）"（Bevington；Mowat）。　125-180. 埃德加此间也许会显得非常紧张,怕被父亲认出；他的装疯会更加卖力,他会待在李尔身旁,也许会把李尔当成挡箭牌,因此埃德加此刻的言辞会更令人心酸。　129-30. 从……教区（from…tithing）：1598 年颁布的一项法令规定,"教区（parish）或十户区（tithing）"逮捕的流浪汉将被"鞭打示众,直到身上血红,再被从一个教区送到另一个教区,直到返回他/她原来的属地"。　131-2. 三套服装（three suits）：重复肯特在 2. 2. 15 对奥斯华德的评判。　埃德加在83-6 称自己曾当过仆人。　136. 斯毛金（Smulkin）：魔鬼的名字。

Edgar		The prince of darkness is a gentleman. Modo
140		he's called, and Mahu.
Gloucester		Our flesh and blood, my lord, is grown so vile
		That it doth hate what gets it.
Edgar		Poor Tom's a-cold.
Gloucester		[*to Lear*] Go in with me. My duty cannot suffer
145		T'obey in all your daughters' hard commands.
		Though their injunction be to bar my doors
		And let this tyrannous night take hold upon you,
		Yet have I ventured to come seek you out,
		And bring you where both fire and food is ready.
150	**Lear**	First let me talk with this philosopher.
		[*to Edgar*] What is the cause of thunder?
	Kent	Good my lord,
		Take his offer, go into the house.
	Lear	I'll talk a word with this same learned Theban:
		What is your study?
155	**Edgar**	How to prevent the fiend and to kill vermin.
	Lear	Let me ask you one word in private.
	Kent	[*to Gloucester*] Importune him ^Fonce more^F to go, my lord;
		His wits begin t'unsettle.
	Gloucester	Canst thou blame him? ^F*Storm still.*^F
		His daughters seek his death. Ah, that good Kent,

埃德加	幽暗世界的王子是一位绅士。 他名叫
	摩多,和麻胡。 140
格洛斯特	我们的骨肉,陛下,变得如此可恶,
	竟仇恨他们的父母。
埃德加	可怜的汤姆很冷。
格洛斯特	[向李尔]跟我走吧。 我的责任感不容我
	完全听从您女儿的残酷指令。 145
	尽管她们命令我大门紧闭,
	听任这狂暴之夜将您摆布,
	可我还是冒险到外面找您,
	并把炉火饭菜备好,带您回去。
李尔	先让我和这位哲学家说句话吧: 150
	[向埃德加]天为啥会打雷呀?
肯特	我的好陛下,
	接受他的提议,进屋去吧。
李尔	我要和这位大学者说句话:
	你是研究啥的?
埃德加	如何抵御魔鬼和杀死害虫。 155
李尔	让我私下里问您件事情。
肯特	[向格洛斯特]您再次督促他回去吧,阁下;
	他开始神志不清。
格洛斯特	你能怪他吗? 暴风雨依旧。
	他女儿想害他。 啊,那位好肯特,

139-40. 幽暗……麻胡（The prince…Mahu）：即在阴间集结力量的冥王,参考《圣经》“以弗所书”6 章 12 节。 其中,摩多和麻胡为他的两位将军。 141. 骨肉（flesh and blood）：孩子。格洛斯特可能从（疯乞丐的）音调里想起了自己的儿子,便将埃德加的所谓的邪恶与贡纳丽和李根的邪恶连在一起（Gloucester, reminded perhaps by some tone or inflection in his son's voice, links Edgar's supposed villainy with that of Goneril and Regan）（Muir）。 153. 大学者（learned Theban）：来自古希腊城邦——底比斯（Thebes）的贤哲（Bate）。 156. 让我……事情（Let…private）：实际上是一种舞台指示,旨在让李尔和埃德加暂时离开。

160   He said it would be thus, poor banished man.

Thou sayest the King grows mad; I'll tell thee, friend,

I am almost mad myself. I had a son,

Now outlawed from my blood; he sought my life,

But lately, very late. I loved him, friend,

165   No father his son dearer. True to tell thee,

The grief hath crazed my wits. What a night's this!

[*to Lear*] I do beseech your grace.

Lear   O, cry your mercy, ^Fsir.^F

[*to Edgar*] Noble philosopher, your company.

Edgar   Tom's a-cold.

170 **Gloucester**   In, fellow, there, into the hovel; keep thee warm.

Lear   Come let's in all.

Kent   This way, my lord.

Lear   With him;

I will keep still with my philosopher.

Kent   Good my lord, soothe him; let him take the fellow.

Gloucester   Take you him on.

175 **Kent**   Sirrah, come on; go along with us.

Lear   Come, good Athenian.

Gloucester   No words, no words; hush.

Edgar   *Childe Rowland to the dark tower came,*

                    His word was still ' Fie, foh and fum,

180   *I smell the blood of a British man'.*   ^F*Exeunt.*^F

他说过会这样的,可怜的流放者!　　　　　　　　　　160

你说国王快疯了;告诉你吧,朋友,

我也差一点发疯。　我有个儿子,

已断绝关系被通缉;想要我性命,

就在最近,最近。　我爱他,朋友,

我对他的父爱无人能比。　说真的,　　　　　　　165

我难受得快发疯了。　多糟的夜晚!

[向李尔]我求您了,陛下。

李尔　　　　　　　　　　　　　　　噢,请原谅,先生。

[向埃德加]高贵的哲学家,咱们一起。

埃德加　汤姆很冷。

格洛斯特　进去,伙计,去茅屋里面;暖和一下。　　　　170

李尔　来,咱都进去。

肯特　　　　　　　　　　这边,陛下。

李尔　　　　　　　　　　　　和他一起;

我想一直和我的哲学家一起。

肯特　好阁下,迁就他吧;让他带上他。

格洛斯特　您带上他吧。

肯特　老兄,走吧;跟我们走吧。　　　　　　　　　　175

李尔　来,雅典学者。

格洛斯特　别说了,别说了;嘘!

埃德加　　　骑士罗兰来到幽暗的高塔,

　　　　　他的暗语总是"伐,弗,法,

　　　　　我闻到不列颠人的血腥啦"。　　　　同下。　180

178-80. 骑士……血腥啦(Childe…man):无实际意义(nonsense verses)。　可能出自已遗失的一首歌谣,关于法国传奇英雄罗兰的故事。

SCENE   V

Enter Cornwall and Edmund.

Cornwall I will have my revenge, ere I depart his house.

Edmund How, my lord, I may be censured that nature thus gives way to loyalty, something fears me to think of.

5 **Cornwall** I now perceive it was not altogether your brother's evil disposition made him seek his death, but a provoking merit set a-work by a reprovable badness in himself.

Edmund How malicious is my fortune, that I must repent to
10 be just? This is the letter ^Fwhich^F he spoke of, which approves him an intelligent party to the advantages of France. O heavens! That this treason were ^Fnot^F, or not I the detector!

Cornwall Go with me to the Duchess.

15 **Edmund** If the matter of this paper be certain, you have mighty business in hand.

Cornwall True   or   false,   it   hath   made   thee   Earl   of

第五场

康瓦尔与埃德蒙上。

康瓦尔　　　我离开他家之前就会报复他的。

埃德蒙　　　人们会怎么看我，殿下，我竟然为了
尽忠而不顾孝心，想起来就让我有些
害怕。

康瓦尔　　　我现在发现不全是因为您的哥哥生性　　　　5
邪恶才使他想谋害他的父亲，还因为
他的自尊心被他父亲那种应受谴责的
邪恶激起。

埃德蒙　　　我的命运多么不幸，我必须感到内疚
因为做对了事情？这是他所说的信函，　　　10
这可以证明他为了法国的利益充当了
一名间谍。噢，天哪！但愿这种叛国
并未发生，或者未被我发现！

康瓦尔　　　跟我去见公爵夫人。

埃德蒙　　　假如这封信的内容属实，您会有重要　　　　15
事情需要处理。

康瓦尔　　　无论真假，这已经使你成了格洛斯特

3.5.　1. 他家（his house）：表明本场的场景应为格洛斯特的家中。　5-8. 不全是……激起（it…himself）：原注为：probably "it was not simply Edgar's evil disposition that made him seek Gloucester's death, but a sense of his own worth inciting him (*provoking merit*), stimulated by a reprehensible wickedness in Gloucester"。　10. 做对了（just）：正义的（righteous），即揭露了他父亲的叛国（Muir）。

Gloucester. Seek out where thy father is, that he may be
ready for our apprehension.

20 **Edmund**   [*aside*] If I find him comforting the King, it
will stuff his suspicion more fully. [*to Cornwall*] I will
persevere in my course of loyalty, though the conflict be
sore between that and my blood.

Cornwall   I will lay trust upon thee and thou shalt find a
25   dearer father in my love.   *Exeunt.*

伯爵。去找一找你父亲在哪里，我们
好把他缉拿归案。

埃德蒙　　[旁白]假如我能发现他正在帮助国王，　　　　　　20
　　　　　　那会使他更加疑心：[向康瓦尔]我会
　　　　　　在效忠的道路上继续前进，尽管忠孝
　　　　　　之间的冲突令人痛苦。

康瓦尔　　我对你完全信任，而且你将发现我会
　　　　　　像慈父那样爱你。　　　　　　　　　　　同下。　25

22-3. 埃德蒙此间对康瓦尔表示恭顺时的圆滑和虚伪表明他最为卑鄙。　他在 1.2 和 2.1 中那种吸引人的轻松、活泼已经荡然无存；参考肯特在 2.2.70-8 对"笑面虎"（smiling rogues）的描述。

SCENE VI

Enter Kent [disguised] and Gloucester.

Gloucester   Here   is   better   than   the   open   air;   take   it
thankfully. I will piece out the comfort with what
addition I can. I will not be long from you.

Kent   All the power of his wits have given way to ^Fhis^F

5   impatience. The gods reward your kindness!

Exit [Gloucester].

Enter Lear, Edgar [disguised as Poor Tom] and Fool.

Edgar   Frateretto calls me, and tells me Nero is an angler
in the lake of darkness. Pray, innocent, ^Fand^F beware the
foul fiend.

Fool   Prithee, nuncle, tell me whether a madman be a

10   gentleman or a yeoman?

Lear   A king, a king!

^F**Fool**   No, he's a yeoman that has a gentleman to his son;
for he's a mad yeoman that sees his son a gentleman
before him.

第六场

肯特[化装]与格洛斯特上。

格洛斯特 这里要比露天地里好得多了；要为此
感到高兴。我会增补别的物品以便让
你们更舒服一些。 我去去就来。

肯特 他的心智因为不胜悲痛现在已经完全
丧失。 上帝报答您的好意！   5

[格洛斯特]下。

李尔、埃德加[扮成可怜的汤姆]与傻子上。

埃德加 弗莱特雷托在叫我,告诉我说尼禄是
冥湖里的钓客。祈祷吧,傻瓜,当心
魔鬼。

傻子 求你,老伯,告诉我疯子是一位绅士
还是一位农民？   10

李尔 是国王,国王！

傻子 不对,他是个农民,但有个绅士儿子；
因为他这个农民若看到儿子先成绅士
会气疯的。

    3.6.   1. 这里（Here）：本场的场景并不明确,好像是格洛斯特带领李尔与他的同伴离开
了茅屋,回到了他住处外面的房间里面。 6. 弗莱特雷托（Frateretto）：哈斯尼特《宣言》中的
另一位魔鬼的名称；尼禄（Nero）：公元 1 世纪古罗马时期的暴君（在此被罚入地狱垂钓）
（Mowat）。 10. 农民（yeoman）：拥有财产的自耕农,地位低于绅士（Bevington）。 12-4. 不
对……气疯的（No…him）：傻子此刻可能会扫视一下李尔,因为他已把更高的地位给了他的"儿
子（1.1.40-1）"和女儿。

15	**Lear**[F]	To have a thousand with red burning spits
		Come hissing in upon 'em!
	[Q]**Edgar**	The foul fiend bites my back.
	Fool	He's mad that trusts in the tameness of a wolf, a
		horse's health, a boy's love or a whore's oath.
20	**Lear**	It shall be done, I will arraign them straight.
		[*to Edgar*] Come, sit thou here, most learned justicer;
		[*to the Fool*] Thou sapient sir, sit here. No, you she-foxes—
	Edgar	Look where he stands and glares! Want'st thou
		eyes at trial, madam?
25		*Come o'er the bourn, Bessy, to me.*
	Fool	*Her boat hath a leak,*
		And she must not speak
		Why she dares not come over to thee.
	Edgar	The foul fiend haunts Poor Tom in the voice of a
30		nightingale. Hopdance cries in Tom's belly for two
		white herring. Croak not, black angel, I have no food
		for thee.
	Kent	How do you, sir? Stand you not so amazed.
		Will you lie down and rest upon the cushions?
35	**Lear**	I'll see their trial first. Bring in the evidence.
		[*to Edgar*] Thou robed man of justice, take thy place.

李尔	愿成千的魔鬼用烧红的铁扦	15
	嘶嘶作响地挥向她们！	
埃德加	魔鬼在咬我的背。	
傻子	只有疯子才会相信狼的温顺，马的	
	康健，小伙子的爱情，妓女的诺言。	
李尔	我会做的，我这就控告她们。	20
	［向埃德加］来，你坐这里，最博学的法官；	
	［向傻子］你这位贤哲，坐这里。 不，母狐狸——	
埃德加	你看她已就位并且瞪眼！难道你想要	
	观众吗，夫人？	
	过河来，贝茜，来我这里。	25
傻子	她的船有缝隙，	
	她不能提及	
	为何她不敢到这里见你。	
埃德加	这个恶魔在用夜莺的声音缠扰可怜的	
	汤姆。赫波旦斯在汤姆肚里呼叫两条	30
	鲜鲱鱼。别叫了，恶魔，我没有食物	
	给你。	
肯特	怎么了，先生？ 别这样站着发呆。	
	您躺在垫子上休息一下好吗？	
李尔	我先看她们受审。 带上来证人。	35
	［向埃德加］你这穿长袍的法官，快就位吧。	

15-6. 烧红的……她们（red…upon 'em）：李尔想象贡纳丽和李根已下到地狱。 哈斯尼特的作品中有许多有关燃烧、烘烤和地狱之火的形象。 18-9. 狼的……康健（tameness…health）：狼无法驯服，马容易得病（Bevington）。 25-8. 过河来……见你（Come…thee）：首句源自一首古老的歌谣；傻子即兴完成了该四行诗的另外三句。 他的诗行也许有淫秽的暗示，即原文中的"leak（缝隙）"可指月经或淋病。 29-30. 夜莺……汤姆（voice…nightingale）：是否在指傻子的歌喉？ 30. 赫波旦斯（Hoppedance）：源自哈斯尼特的作品，该魔鬼与音乐有关。

[*to the Fool*] And thou, his yoke-fellow of equity,

Bench by his side. [*to Kent*] You are o'the commission;

Sit you too.

40   **Edgar**   Let us deal justly.

> *Sleepest or wakest thou, jolly shepherd?*
>
> > *Thy sheep be in the corn;*
>
> *And for one blast of thy minikin mouth,*
>
> > *Thy sheep shall take no harm.*

45   Purr, the cat is grey.

Lear   Arraign her first, 'tis Goneril — I here take my oath

before this honourable assembly — kicked the poor King

her father.

Fool   Come hither, mistress: is your name Goneril?

50   **Lear**   She cannot deny it.

Fool   Cry you mercy, I took you for a joint-stool.

Lear   And here's another whose warped looks proclaim

What store her heart is made on. Stop her there!

Arms, arms, sword, fire, corruption in the place!

55   False justicer, why hast thou let her 'scape?[Q]

Edgar   Bless thy five wits!

Kent   O pity! Sir, where is the patience now

That thou so oft have boasted to retain?

　　　　　　　［向傻子］还有你,他的公正的陪审员,

　　　　　　　坐在他旁边。 ［向肯特］您这委任的法官;

　　　　　　　也就坐吧。

埃德加　　咱们要秉公断案。　　　　　　　　　　　　　40

　　　　　　　　睡着了还是醒着,快活的牧者?

　　　　　　　　　羊群进了庄稼地;

　　　　　　　　但是你若用嘴巴尖声一喊,

　　　　　　　　　羊群便没了危险。

　　　　　　　噗儿,这只猫是灰的。　　　　　　　　　　45

李尔　　　先审她,这是贡纳丽——我现在宣誓,

　　　　　　　在诸公面前——她曾踢过可怜的国王

　　　　　　　她父亲。

傻子　　　过来,夫人:您叫贡纳丽吗?

李尔　　　她无法否认。　　　　　　　　　　　　　　50

傻子　　　请原谅,我以为您是细木凳子。

李尔　　　还有一个,她狰狞的面孔表明

　　　　　　　她的心肠是用啥做成。 拦住她!

　　　　　　　武器,刀剑,点灯,这法庭太黑!

　　　　　　　徇私的法官,为何让她逃走?　　　　　　55

埃德加　　保佑你的五能!

肯特　　　噢,可怜! 先生,您时常夸口的

　　　　　　　那种自控如今到哪里去了?

　　41-4. 睡着了……危险(Sleepest…harm):无实际意义。 可能指瞌睡中的牧者准许其羊群擅自进入麦田,羊群会在里面吃得过饱而胀气并因此死去,但他只要用力一喊即可把羊群召回。可怜的汤姆此刻也许会瞥一眼李尔这位管理者(牧者),因为他的臣民走向了歧路。 45. 噗儿(Purr):哈斯尼特作品中另一魔鬼的名字,但此处很可能是指以灰猫显形的魔鬼所发出的声音(Muir)。 51. 请……细木凳子(Cry…joint-stool):通常作为一种忽略了对方的借口。 其中,“细木凳子”是指由细木工人而非粗糙的木匠制作而成的矮凳。 也许是指舞台上确实存在的凳子。 (Foakes;Bevington)。 54. 点灯……太黑(fire…place):在李尔的想象中法庭突然变成了地狱;参照4.6.123-5。 56. 五能(five wits):见3.4.57注。

Edgar [*aside*] My tears begin to take his part so much

They mar my counterfeiting.

60 **Lear**   The little dogs and all,

Trey, Blanch and Sweetheart, see, they bark at me.

Edgar Tom will throw his head at them: avaunt, you curs!

> *Be thy mouth or black or white,*
>
> *Tooth that poisons if it bite;*
>
65 > *Mastiff, greyhound, mongrel grim,*
>
> *Hound or spaniel, brach or him,*
>
> ^{*F*} *Or* ^{*F*} *bobtail tyke or trundle-tail,*
>
> *Tom will make him weep and wail;*
>
> *For, with throwing thus my head,*
>
70 > *Dogs leap the hatch and all are fled.*

Do, de, de, de. ^F*Cessez!*^F Come, march to wakes and

fairs and market towns. Poor Tom, thy horn is dry.

Lear Then let them anatomize Regan; see what breeds

about her heart. Is there any cause in nature that make

75 these hard hearts? [*to Edgar*] You, sir, I entertain ^Qyou^Q

for one of my hundred; only I do not like the fashion of

your garments. You will say they are Persian ^Qattire^Q,

but let them be changed.

Kent Now, good my lord, lie here ^Fand rest^F awhile.

埃德加	[旁白]我对他如此同情,眼泪开始	
	毁了我的伪装。	
李尔	甚至小狗们,	60
	特雷、布兰、和甜心,瞧,她们咬我!	
埃德加	汤姆会用头撞她们:滚开,你们恶狗!	
	无论你嘴巴黑与白,	
	带毒的牙齿把人害;	
	獒犬、灰狗、杂种狗,	65
	猎狗、长毛狗,母猎狗,	
	尾巴短还是尾巴卷,	
	汤姆让他摇尾乞怜;	
	因为我这样头一撞,	
	狗就会夺门全逃亡。	70
	嘟,喎,喎。停住!快去庙会逛市场。	
	可怜的汤姆,你的牛角是空的。	
李尔	就让他们解剖李根吧;看看她的心是	
	怎么长的。看看造化为什么竟会使她	
	这么心硬?[向埃德加]先生,我雇您	75
	进我的百名侍卫团;只是不喜欢您的	
	衣服样式。您可以说它们是波斯华服,	
	但还是换一换吧。	
肯特	嗳,好陛下,躺下休息一会儿吧。	

61. 特雷……甜心(Trey…Sweetheart):暗示贡纳丽、李根和考迪丽娅。 特雷(Trey)可能意味着"痛苦(pain)"或"背叛(betray)";布兰(Blanch)可指使人因害怕而脸色苍白;考迪丽娅将成为李尔的宝贝儿。 62. 用头撞她们(throw…them):无解;但他会做出某种举动,下文69行将予以重复,也许会低头怒视。 19世纪的舞台演出常让汤姆把一顶草帽向想象中的狗投去。 71. 嘟,喎,喎(Do…de):见3.4.57;汤姆可能再次冻得发抖。 72. 牛角(horn):用来喝水的牛角,乞丐随身携带,还可用来收集人们的施舍。

80 **Lear**   Make no noise, make no noise, draw the curtains.

So, so, ^Qso^Q; we'll go to supper i'the morning ^Qso, so, so.^Q

[*He sleeps.*]

^F**Fool**   And I'll go to bed at noon.^F

Enter Gloucester.

Gloucester   Come hither, friend; where is the King my master?

Kent   Here, sir, but trouble him not; his wits are gone.

85 **Glouester**   Good friend, I prithee take him in thy arms.

I have o'erheard a plot of death upon him.

There is a litter ready; lay him in't

And drive toward Dover, friend, where thou shalt meet

Both welcome and protection. Take up thy master:

90   If thou shouldst dally half an hour, his life,

With thine and all that offer to defend him,

Stand in assured loss. Take up, take up,

And follow me, that will to some provision

Give thee quick conduct.

^Q**Kent**   Oppressed nature sleeps.

95   This rest might yet have balmed thy broken sinews,

Which if convenience will not allow,

Stand in hard cure. [*to the Fool*] Come, help to bear thy master;

Thou must not stay behind.^Q

Gloucester   Come, come away!

Exeunt [*all but Edgar; Kent and the Fool supporting Lear*].

^Q**Edgar**   When we our betters see bearing our woes,

李尔	别出声了,别出声了,把床帷拉下吧。　　　　80
	对,对,咱明天早上再晚餐,对,对。
	［入睡。］
傻子	我要到中午再睡眠。

格洛斯特上。

格洛斯特	快过来,朋友;我的主人国王呢?
肯特	这里,先生,别打扰他吧;他疯了。
格洛斯特	好朋友,我求你把他抱起来吧。　　　　　85
	我偶然听到有人密谋害他。
	有辆马车已备好;把他放进去
	并驶往多佛,朋友,那里会有人
	欢迎并保护你们。　把主人抱起:
	若耽搁半个小时,他的性命,　　　　　90
	你的,以及他的支持者的性命,
	肯定都会失去。　抱起来,抱起来,
	跟我来吧,我这就带你们取些
	必要的用品。
肯特	磨难使他入眠。
	熟睡可抚慰你的神经错乱,　　　　　95
	如果环境不允许这种休息,
	便难以治愈。　［向傻子]快,帮我抬你主人;
	你不能待在这里。
格洛斯特	快,快走吧!
	［埃德加除外;肯特与傻子抬李尔]全下。
埃德加	看到我们的上级同样受难,

---

82. 我……睡眠（I…noon）:谚语,意为"我也会犯傻（I'll play the fool too）"。　92:原文中的 assured = assurèd（三音节）。

100   We scarcely think our miseries our foes.

Who alone suffers, suffers most i'the mind,

Leaving free things and happy shows behind.

But then the mind much sufferance doth o'er skip,

When grief hath mates and bearing fellowship.

105   How light and portable my pain seems now,

When that which makes me bend makes the King bow,

He childed as I fathered. Tom, away;

Mark the high noises, and thyself bewray

When false opinion, whose wrong thought defiles thee,

110   In thy just proof, repeals and reconciles thee.

What will hap more tonight, safe 'scape the King.

Lurk, lurk!^Q   [*Exit.*]

我们便很难想到自身的可怜。　　　　　　　　　　100

谁若独自忍受,谁心中最苦,

忘记自己的无忧无虑和幸福。

心中的痛苦却会得以减缓,

假如痛苦能有忍受的同伴。

我的痛苦已显得多容易忍受,　　　　　　　　　105

使我弯腰的负担让国王低头,

他孩子无情我父无义,汤姆,走;

关注高层的动静,真相别显露,

除非能证明你遭到了恶意中伤,

自证清白后,父亲会召回流放。　　　　　　　　110

无论今晚发生什么,愿国王脱险!

躲开,躲开!　　　　　　　　　　　　　　　[下。]

101-4. 谁……同伴 (Who…fellowship):原注为:Anyone who has no companionship in suffering undergoes the mental anguish of forgetting entirely the carefree ways and happy scenes that were once enjoyed, whereas fellowship in grief enables the mind to rise above such suffering (i. e. Misery loves company [见同病得慰藉]) (Bevington)。 108-10. 关注……流放 (Mark …thee):原注为:Observe what is being said about those in high places or about great events, and reveal your identity only when the general opinion that now slanders you, at length establishing your innocence, recalls you from banishment and restores you to favor (Bevington)。

SCENE VII

Enter Cornwall, Regan, Goneril, Edmund ^F*and Servants.*^F

Cornwall [*to Goneril*] Post speedily to my lord your husband.

Show him this letter: the army of France is landed.

[*to Servants*] Seek out the traitor, Gloucester.

Regan Hang him instantly!   [*Some Servants rush off.*]

5 **Goneril** Pluck out his eyes!

Cornwall Leave him to my displeasure. Edmund, keep you

our sister company; the revenges we are bound to

take upon your traitorous father are not fit for your

beholding. Advise the Duke where you are going to a

10 most festinate preparation; we are bound to the like.

Our posts shall be swift and intelligent betwixt us.

Farewell, dear sister; farewell, my lord of Gloucester.

Enter Oswald.

How now, where's the King?

Oswald My lord of Gloucester hath conveyed him hence.

15 Some five- or six-and-thirty of his knights,

第七场

康瓦尔、李根、贡纳丽、埃德蒙与仆人上。

康瓦尔　　　［向贡纳丽］赶快去见我的殿下您夫君。

让他看看这封信：法军现在已经登陆。

［向侍从］搜出叛徒，格洛斯特！

李根　　　　立即绞死他！　　　　　　　　　　　　　［几位仆人速下。］

贡纳丽　　　挖掉他的眼睛！　　　　　　　　　　　　　　　　　　　　　5

康瓦尔　　　把他交给我来处置。埃德蒙，您去陪

我们的姐姐；我们必须对您那位叛国

的父亲进行惩处，这种刑罚不适合您

观看。您现在去见那位公爵，告诉他

要立即备战；我们也会立即做好准备。　　　　　　　　　　　10

我们的信差会快速地为我们通风报信。

再会，好姐姐；再会，格洛斯特伯爵。

奥斯华德上。

怎么样，国王呢？

奥斯华德　　格洛斯特伯爵已把他送走。

约有三十五六名他的侍卫，　　　　　　　　　　　　　　　　15

3.7. 考虑到康瓦尔与李根是格洛斯特家中的客人，他们对他的残忍就更为恐怖；另见 30 行及注。　**3.** 叛徒（traitor）：对新统治者康瓦尔和李根来说，格洛斯特变成了叛徒，由此强调了剧中价值观念的混乱；对李尔表示忠诚，对他的女儿来说却是叛徒。　**7.** 姐姐（sister）：贡纳丽（sister-in-law）。　**12.** 格洛斯特（Gloucester）：埃德蒙，由康瓦尔于 3.5.17-8 任命；但易混淆，因为在 3 和 14 行里埃德蒙的父亲仍被称为格洛斯特。

Hot questrists after him, met him at gate,

Who with some other of the lord's dependants

Are gone with him toward Dover, where they boast

To have well-armed friends.

20 **Cornwall**   Get horses for your mistress.   [*Exit Oswald.*]

Goneril   Farewell, sweet lord and sister.

Cornwall   Edmund, farewell.   *Exeunt* ^Q*Goneril and Edmund*^Q.

[*to Servants*]   Go seek the traitor Gloucester;

Pinion him like a thief, bring him before us. [*Servants leave.*]

Though ^Fwell^F we may not pass upon his life

25   Without the form of justice, yet our power

Shall do a courtesy to our wrath, which men

May blame but not control. Who's there? The traitor?

Enter Gloucester, ^Q*brought in by two or three*^Q ^F*Servants.*^F

Regan   Ingrateful fox, 'tis he.

Cornwall   Bind fast his corky arms.

Gloucester   What mean your graces?

30   Good my friends, consider; you are my guests.

Do me no foul play, friends.

Cornwall   Bind him, I say—

[*Servants bind his arms.*]

Regan   Hard, hard. O, filthy traitor!

Gloucester   Unmerciful lady as you are, I'm none.

Cornwall   To this chair bind him. [*to Gloucester*] Villain, thou

shalt find—   [*Regan plucks his beard.*]

急切地找他,在门口与他相遇,
还有伯爵的其他几位侍从
已跟他前往多佛,声称那里有
武装精良的朋友。

康瓦尔	快给您家夫人备马。	［奥斯华德下。］　20
贡纳丽	再会,亲爱的殿下和妹妹。	
康瓦尔	埃德蒙,再会。	贡纳丽与埃德蒙同下。

［向仆人］　去搜叛徒格洛斯特;
把他当盗贼绑起,带他来见我。　　　　　　　　　［仆人下。］
尽管我们不经正式的审判
无法判他死刑,但我们有权　　　　　　　　　　　　　　　25
顺从我们的愤怒,人们也许会
谴责但无法制止。　是谁?　叛徒吗?

　　　　　　两三位仆人带格洛斯特上。

李根	忘恩负义的狐狸!　是他。	
康瓦尔	把他干瘪的手臂绑紧!	
格洛斯特	殿下何意?	
	好朋友,别忘了,您是我的客人。	30
	可别胡来,朋友。	
康瓦尔	绑起来,我说——	
	［仆人捆住其手臂。］	
李根	绑紧,绑紧。　噢,邪恶的叛徒!	
格洛斯特	你这无情的夫人,我不是叛徒。	
康瓦尔	把他绑到椅子上。　恶棍,你会	
	明白——［李根拔掉他的胡须。］	

---

23. 绑起（Pinion him）：捆住双臂；以这种方式对待一位贵族令人震惊。　30. 客人（guests）：作为朋友,在主人的家里袭击主人,是对殷勤好客的极大冒犯。

35	**Gloucester**	By the kind gods, 'tis most ignobly done
		To pluck me by the beard.
	Regan	So white, and such a traitor?
	Gloucester	Naughty lady,
		These hairs which thou dost ravish from my chin
		Will quicken and accuse thee. I am your host;
40		With robber's hands my hospitable favours
		You should not ruffle thus. What will you do?
	Cornwall	Come, sir, what letters had you late from France?
	Regan	Be simple answerer, for we know the truth.
	Cornwall	And what confederacy have you with the traitors,
		Late footed in the kingdom?
45	**Regan**	To whose hands
		Have you sent the lunatic King. Speak.
	Gloucester	I have a letter guessingly set down
		Which came from one that's of a neutral heart,
		And not from one opposed.
	Cornwall	Cunning.
	Regan	And false.
	Cornwall	Where hast thou sent the King?
50	**Gloucester**	To Dover.
	Regan	Wherefore to Dover? Wast thou not charged at peril—
	Cornwall	Wherefore to Dover? Let him ᵠfirstᵠ answer that.
	Gloucester	I am tied to the stake and I must stand the course.
	Regan	Wherefore to Dover, ᵠsirᵠ?

格洛斯特	仁慈的上天作证,你这样拔掉	35
	我的胡子极其可耻!	
李根	白发苍苍,还在卖国?	
格洛斯特	你这泼妇,	
	你从我脸上拔走的胡子将会	
	复活并告你。 我是您的主人;	
	您不该用盗贼似的双手这样	40
	亵渎我的殷勤。 您想干啥?	
康瓦尔	你最近从法国收到什么信件?	
李根	要直截了当,我们知道真相。	
康瓦尔	你和最近登陆我国的叛军	
	都有哪些勾结?	
李根	你把发疯的	45
	国王送到了他们手里。 快说!	
格洛斯特	我收到过一封猜测性的信函,	
	来自于一位保持中立的人士,	
	不是来自于对手。	
康瓦尔	狡辩!	
李根	骗人!	
康瓦尔	你把国王送到了何处?	
格洛斯特	多佛	50
李根	为何到多佛? 没令你别去冒死——	
康瓦尔	为何到多佛? 先让他回答这个。	
格洛斯特	我被拴到了桩上,要遭受狗咬。	
李根	为何到多佛?	

---

51. 冒死(at peril):冒生命危险(on peril of your life)(Bevington);指李根于3. 4. 146-7 对格洛斯特的指令;另见3. 3. 2-6。 53. 我……狗咬(I…course):格洛斯特将自己视为一头熊被拴到了木桩上面,不得不经受猎狗的轮番攻击。 当时流行的一种观赏性游戏;参考《麦克白》5. 7. 1-2。

55	**Gloucester**	Because I would not see thy cruel nails
		Pluck out his poor old eyes; nor thy fierce sister
		In his anointed flesh stick boarish fangs.
		The sea, with such a storm as his bare head
		In hell-black night endured, would have buoyed up
60		And quenched the stelled fires.
		Yet, poor old heart, he holp the heavens to rain.
		If wolves had at thy gate howled that stern time,
		Thou shouldst have said, 'Good porter, turn the key,
		All cruels else subscribed'; but I shall see
65		The winged vengeance overtake such children.
	Cornwall	See't shalt thou never. Fellows, hold the chair;
		Upon these eyes of thine I'll set my foot.
	Gloucester	He that will think to live till he be old,
		Give me some help! —O cruel! O you gods!
70	**Regan**	One side will mock another—the other too.
	Cornwall	If you see vengeance—
	1 Servant	Hold your hand, my lord.
		I have served ᶠyouᶠ ever since I was a child,
		But better service have I never done you
		Than now to bid you hold.
	Regan	How now, you dog?

格洛斯特	因为我不愿看你残忍的指甲	55
	挖出他可怜的老眼；也不愿看你	
	凶狠的姐姐用獠牙刺进他圣体。	
	在地狱般的黑夜，他光着头顶	
	忍受这种狂风暴雨，大海都会	
	腾空浇灭那闪耀的繁星。	60
	可怜的老人，却帮上天降雨。	
	在那可怕的时刻若豺狼叫门，	
	你都会说，"好门卫，开门吧，残暴的	
	生灵都会动情"；可我会看到	
	上天的报复临到这样的子女。	65
康瓦尔	你休想看到。　伙计们，按住椅子；	
	我要用脚踩你这两只眼睛。	
格洛斯特	你们有谁若想要长命百岁，	
	就帮帮我吧！——噢，残忍！噢，天哪！	
李根	两边很不对称——另一只也挖！	70
康瓦尔	你若能看到报复——	
仆人甲	住手，大人！	
	我从孩子起就开始为您服务，	
	但我对您的最好服务莫过于	
	现在叫您住手。	
李根	什么，狗东西？	

---

57. 圣体（anointed flesh）：国王受过涂膏仪式的肉身（Muir）。　61. 帮上天降雨（holp…rain）：用泪水——可怜的象征。　其中，"holp"为"helped"的古语形式。　63-4. 你……动情（Thou…subscribed）：本句的意义颇富争议。　现引两处原注以助理解："Good porter, unlock the door and let the wolves in. All other cruel creatures yield to compassion, on such a night as this; and so will I too"（Muir）。　"All other cruel creatures would show forgiveness except you; this cruelty is unparalleled（除你之外，所有其他凶残的生灵都会表示宽恕；这种残忍无与伦比）"（Bevtington）。　67-9. 用脚……残忍（set…cruel）：表明康瓦尔挖掉了格洛斯特的一只眼睛，把它丢到地上并用脚猛踩。

75	**1 Servant**	If you did wear a beard upon your chin,
		I'd shake it on this quarrel. What do you mean?
	Cornwall	My villain? [*They*] *draw and fight.*
	1 Servant	Nay, then, come on, and take the chance of anger.
		[*He wounds Cornwall.*]
	Regan	Give me thy sword. A peasant stand up thus?
		She takes a sword and runs at him behind. *Kills him.*
80	**1 Servant**	O, I am slain! My lord, you have one eye left
		To see some mischief on him. O! [*He dies.*]
	Cornwall	Lest it see more, prevent it. Out, vile jelly,
		Where is thy lustre now?
	Gloucester	All dark and comfortless? Where's my son Edmund?
85		Edmund, enkindle all the sparks of nature
		To quit this horrid act.
	Regan	Out, treacherous villain,
		Thou call'st on him that hates thee. It was he
		That made the overture of thy treasons to us,
		Who is too good to pity thee.
90	**Gloucester**	O my follies! Then Edgar was abused?
		Kind gods, forgive me that and prosper him.
	Regan	[*to a Servant*] Go, thrust him out at gates and let him smell
		His way to Dover. How is't, my lord? How look you?
	Cornwall	I have received a hurt. Follow me, lady.
95		[*to Servants*] Turn out that eyeless villain. Throw this slave
		Upon the dunghill.

仆人甲	假如您的面颊上面长有胡须，	75
	我会就此向您挑战。　您想干啥？	
康瓦尔	你这奴才？［他们］拔剑并搏斗。	
仆人甲	那好，来吧：冒一冒恶战的风险。	
	［刺伤康瓦尔。］	
李根	把剑给我。　奴才竟如此放肆？	
	拿剑从他背后猛刺。	
仆人甲	噢，我遇害了！大人，您还有只眼睛	80
	能看见他遭受报应。　噢！［死去。］	
康瓦尔	我要防止它看见。　出来，臭肉冻！	
	你还会闪光吗？	
格洛斯特	一片漆黑和痛苦？　儿子埃德蒙呢？	
	埃德蒙，点燃孝心的全部火花	85
	报复这恐怖行径！	
李根	呸，奸诈的恶棍！	
	你喊叫的那个人恨你。　是他	
	向我们告发了你的叛国之罪，	
	他太好了，不会同情你的。	
格洛斯特	噢，我真傻！那我冤枉了埃德加？	90
	仁慈的神明，宽恕我，祝福他吧！	
李根	［向一仆人］去，把他扔到门外，让他凭嗅觉	
	赶到多佛。　怎么了，夫君？　您还好吧？	
康瓦尔	有一处被剑刺伤。　跟我来，夫人。	
	［向仆人］把那个瞎奸贼赶走。　把这个奴才	95
	扔到粪坑。	

78. 恶战的风险（the chance of anger）：冒险进行愤怒的决战（the risks of an angry encounter）（Bevington）。 81. 噢（O）：也许表明李根又刺他一剑。 86. 呸（Out）：感叹词，表示愤怒或不耐烦（an exclamation of anger or impatience）（Bevington）。

> *Exeunt* [*Servants*] ᶠ*with Gloucester*ᶠ [*and the body*].

Regan, I bleed apace;

Untimely comes this hurt. Give me your arm.

> *Exeunt* [*Cornwall and Regan*].

ᵠ**2 Servant**   I'll never care what wickedness I do

If this man come to good.

3 Servant   If she live long

100   And in the end meet the old course of death,

Women will all turn monsters.

2 Servant   Let's follow the old Earl and get the Bedlam

To lead him where he would. His roguish madness

Allows itself to anything.

105 **3 Servant**   Go thou: I'll fetch some flax and whites of eggs

To apply to his bleeding face. Now heaven help him!

> *Exeunt.*ᵠ

　　　　　　　　　　　　[仆人]携格洛斯特[与死尸]下。

　　　　李根,我流血不止;

　　我伤得真不是时候。　扶我一把。

　　　　　　　　　　　　　　[康瓦尔与李根]同下。

仆人乙　　　无论我怎样作恶都不会顾忌,

　　　　　　若这人能有好报。

仆人丙　　　　　　　　她若能长寿

　　　　　　而且到头来能够寿终正寝,　　　　　　　　　100

　　　　　　女人都会变成怪物。

仆人甲　　　咱们跟上老伯爵,让那个疯子

　　　　　　去给他带路。　作为发疯的乞丐,

　　　　　　叫他做什么都行。

仆人丙　　　你先走:我去拿些麻布和蛋清　　　　　　　105

　　　　　　膏抹他流血的面孔。　上天保佑他!

　　　　　　　　　　　　　　　　　　同下。

───────────────────────────────

　　101. 女人……怪物(women…monsters):因为她们看到李根作恶多端却兴旺发达。　104. 叫他做什么都行(Allow…anything):我们叫他做啥他都会答应(will take on anything we ask him to do),(因为他是疯子,不用为此担责)。　105. 麻布和蛋清(flax…eggs):可用以治疗和保护受伤的眼睛。

第四幕
ACT 4

SCENE   I

Enter Edgar [, disguised as Poor Tom].

Edgar Yet better thus, and known to be contemned
Than still contemned and flattered. To be worst,
The lowest and most dejected thing of fortune,
Stands still in esperance, lives not in fear.
5 The lamentable change is from the best,
The worst returns to laughter. ^FWelcome then,
Thou unsubstantial air that I embrace;
The wretch that thou hast blown unto the worst
Owes nothing to thy blasts.^F

Enter Gloucester, led by an Old Man.

10 ^FBut^F who comes here? My father, poorly led?
World, world, O world!

第一场

埃德加［扮成可怜的汤姆］上。

埃德加　　但这样更好，公开被人唾弃，

胜过被人当面奉承背地唾弃。

最糟、最贱和最为可怜的东西，

总会有些希望，不至于恐惧。

令人痛苦的变化是乐极生悲，　　　　　　　　　　　5

苦尽就会甘来。　那就欢迎，

我拥抱你这无影无踪的空气；

你已把他推到绝境的可怜人

什么都不欠你。

　　　　　　　一老人引格洛斯特上。

是谁来了？　我的父亲，如此寒碜？　　　　　　　10

人世，人世，噢人世！

4.1.　　0（1）埃德加上（*Enter Edgar*）：李尔在3.6收场时动身前往多佛；此刻为暴风雨过后的次日（见34行），地点离格格洛斯特的住处不远；埃德加因为已被通缉，因此会与他人保持距离。　1-2. 但……唾弃（Yet…flattered）：原注为 "It is better to be openly despised as a beggar than continually despised behind one's back and flattered to one's face"（Bevington）。　6. 苦尽就会甘来（The…laughter）：源于谚语："When things are at their worst they will mend"。　9. 什么都不欠你（Owes…Blasts）：原注为 "Being at the worst, Edgar can welcome (embrace) the air freely, because he has nothing to thank the winds for"（Foakes）。　"and therefore has nothing to fear from（因此没有什么可惧怕的）"（Mowat）。　9（1）老人（*Old Man*）：正如《麦克白》剧中的那位老人一样（2.4），属于宫廷以外的唯一平民，比较清楚过去的时间；他甚至比李尔还大；正如《皆大欢喜》中的老亚当那样，可谓仆人的典范，充满爱心，但这种品德在贡纳丽与李根的治下不再被人重视。　10. 如此寒碜（poorly led）：与他的地位不符，并且由一位穷人领着。

But that thy strange mutations make us hate thee,

Life would not yield to age.

Old Man   O my good lord, I have been your tenant and

15   your father's tenant these fourscore ^Fyears^F—

Gloucester   Away, get thee away; good friend, be gone.

Thy comforts can do me no good at all,

Thee they may hurt.

Old Man   ^QAlack, sir,^Q you cannot see your way.

20   **Gloucester**   I have no way, and therefore want no eyes:

I stumbled when I saw. Full oft 'tis seen

Our means secure us and our mere defects

Prove our commodities. O dear son Edgar,

The food of thy abused father's wrath,

25   Might I but live to see thee in my touch,

I'd say I had eyes again.

Old Man   How now? Who's there?

Edgar   [*aside*] O gods! Who is't can say 'I am at the worst'?

I am worse than e'er I was.

Old Man   [*to Gloucester*]   'Tis poor mad Tom.

Edgar   [*aside*] And worse I may be yet; the worst is not

30   So long as we can say 'This is the worst.'

要不是你那可恨的变化无常，

谁会甘心地老去。

老人　　　噢，我的好大人，我做您的佃户还有

您父亲的佃户已经八十年了——　　　　　　　　　　15

格洛斯特　走开，你快走开；好朋友，走吧。

你的安慰对我毫无益处，

他们会伤害你的。

老人　　　哎，主人，您看不见路呀！

格洛斯特　我无路可走，因此不需要看见：　　　　　20

我有眼睛时却被绊倒。　往往是

富有会令人骄傲自满，而苦难

倒证明有益。　亲爱的儿啊埃德加，

受骗的父亲发泄怒气的对象，

假如我有生之年能摸你一下，　　　　　　　　　　25

可以说又有了眼睛。

老人　　　　　　　怎么？　那是谁？

埃德加　　［旁白］噢天哪！谁能说"我现在已经最糟"？

我比以前更糟。

老人　　　［向格洛斯特］是可怜的汤姆。

埃德加　　［旁白］还可能更糟；只要我们能说

"现在最糟"，最糟的尚未来到。　　　　　　　　　30

12-3. 要不是……老去（But…age）：原注为"If it were not for your hateful inconstancy, we would never be reconciled to old age and death"（Bevington）。 18. 会伤害（may hurt）：若被人发现帮助一个已定罪的叛徒。 21. 我……绊倒（I…saw）：格洛斯特承认了自己的罪过及愚昧，他的话语是在重复《圣经》中的一个主题，即"以赛亚书"59章9-10节："我们指望光明，却行幽暗。 我们摸索墙壁，好像瞎子；我们摸索，如同无目之人。 我们晌午绊脚，如在黄昏一般。" 22-3. 富有……有益（Our…commodities）：原注为"Our prosperity makes us proudly overconfident, whereas the sheer affliction we suffer prove beneficial （by teaching us humility）"（Bevington）。 24. 受骗（abused）：该词为三个音节，即abusèd；意为"误导（misled）"。 27-30. 噢……来到（O…worst）：摈弃了1-9行的盲目乐观。

Old Man	[*to Edgar*] Fellow, where goest?	
Gloucester		Is it a beggar-man?
Old Man	Madman, and beggar too.	
Gloucester	He has some reason, else he could not beg.	

I'the last night's storm I such a fellow saw,

35 Which made me think a man a worm. My son

Came then into my mind, and yet my mind

Was then scarce friends with him. I have heard more
  since:

As flies to wanton boys are we to the gods.

They kill us for their sport.

Edgar [*aside*]   How should this be?

40 Bad is the trade that must play fool to sorrow,

Angering itself and others. [*to Gloucester*] Bless thee, master.

Gloucester Is that the naked fellow?

Old Man   Ay, my lord.

Gloucester ᑫThen pritheeᑫ get thee away. If for my sake

Thou wilt o'ertake us hence a mile or twain

45 I'the way toward Dover, do it for ancient love,

And bring some covering for this naked soul,

Who I'll entreat to lead me.

Old Man Alack, sir, he is mad.

Gloucester 'Tis the times' plague when madmen lead the blind.

50 Do as I bid thee, or rather do thy pleasure;

Above the rest, be gone.

老人	［向埃德加］小伙子,去哪里?	
格洛斯特	是不是一个乞丐?	
老人	是个疯子,和乞丐。	
格洛斯特	他没有全疯,否则不会要饭。	
	昨晚暴风雨里我见过这种小伙,	
	他让我觉得人就像虫子。　当时	35
	我想起我的儿子,尽管我那时	
	还有些恨他。　后来明白了	
	一些:	
	神明待我们就像顽童待苍蝇,	
	以杀死我们为乐。	
埃德加	［旁白］　　怎么会这样?	
	面对伤心人必须装傻是苦差,	40
	折磨自己和他人。［向格洛斯特]保佑你,大人!	
格洛斯特	是那个裸体的小伙子?	
老人	是的,大人。	
格洛斯特	请你离开吧。　若看在我的分上,	
	你可在前面一两哩处追上我们,	
	往多佛的路上,为了深情厚谊,	45
	给这个赤裸的人儿拿件衣服,	
	我会请他给我带路。	
老人	唉,先生,他是疯子。	
格洛斯特	疯子引领瞎子表明时代邪恶。	
	按我说的做吧,要么你就随意;	50
	最重要的是,走开。	

35. 觉得……虫子(think…worm):感觉到人的渺小和无助,在重复《圣经》中的另一主题,即"诗篇"22篇6节:"但我是虫,不是人,被众人羞辱,被百姓藐视。"另见"约伯记"25章6节。　40-1. 必须……他人(must…others):此刻埃德加必须扮成汤姆装疯卖傻,尽管父亲已遭遇不幸,致使自己和别人都感到苦恼(因为他不得不隐瞒真实身份?)。　50. 你就随意(do thy pleasure = do what you will):格洛斯特意识到自己现已无权吩咐。

	Old Man	I'll bring him the best 'pparel that I have,
		Come on't what will. ᶠ*Exit.*ᶠ
	Gloucester	Sirrah, naked fellow.
55	**Edgar**	Poor Tom's a-cold. [*aside*] I cannot daub it further—
	Gloucester	Come hither, fellow.
	Edgar	[*aside*] ᶠAnd yet I must.ᶠ [*to Gloucester*] Bless thy

Old Man I'll bring him the best 'pparel that I have,
Come on't what will. ᶠ*Exit.*ᶠ

Gloucester Sirrah, naked fellow.

55 **Edgar** Poor Tom's a-cold. [*aside*] I cannot daub it further—

Gloucester Come hither, fellow.

Edgar [*aside*] ᶠAnd yet I must.ᶠ [*to Gloucester*] Bless thy
sweet eyes, they bleed.

Gloucester Knowst thou the way to Dover?

Edgar Both stile and gate, horseway and footpath. Poor
60 Tom hath been scared out of his good wits. Bless thee,
goodman's son, from the foul fiend. ᑫFive fiends have
been in poor Tom at once, of lust, as Obidicut;
Hobbididence, prince of darkness; Mahu, of stealing;
Modo, of murder; Flibbertigibbet, of mopping and
65 mowing, who since possesses chambermaids and
waiting-women. So, bless thee, master.ᑫ

Gloucester Here, take this purse, thou whom the heavens' plagues
Have humbled to all strokes. That I am wretched
Makes thee the happier. Heavens deal so still!
70 Let the superfluous and lust-dieted man
That slaves your ordinance, that will not see
Because he doth not feel, feel your power quickly:

老人	我会给他拿我最好的衣服，	
	无论有啥后果。	下。
格洛斯特	喂，赤裸的小伙。	
埃德加	可怜的汤姆很冷。〔旁白〕我无法再装——	55
格洛斯特	过来，小伙子。	
埃德加	〔旁白〕可我必须。 〔向格洛斯特〕保佑你	
	流血的慧眼。	
格洛斯特	你知道去多佛的路吗？	
埃德加	我知道步行道的台阶以及马道的大门。	
	可怜的汤姆曾吓得失去理智。保佑你，	60
	自耕农的儿子，远离恶魔！有五个鬼	
	附在可怜的汤姆身上，色鬼俄毕迪卡；	
	管冥府的霍比迪登斯；管偷窃的麻胡；	
	管凶杀的摩多；管做鬼脸和做怪相的	
	弗里伯提伯特，他缠住了屋里的女仆	65
	和侍女。 因此，保佑你，大人！	
格洛斯特	来，这钱包拿去，上天的各种打击	
	你都逆来顺受。 我的不幸	
	使你幸运一些。 愿上天总这样！	
	让那过分富有和荒淫无度者，	70
	他妄用你的诫命，视而不见	
	因为没有同感，快感受你的权威：	

57. 可我必须（And…must）：埃德加在第 40 行中的"必须（must）"尚有道理，因为他不想让老人（Old Man）知道他的身份；但人们很难理解他对父亲为何也必须隐瞒身份，除非出于情节的需要。 61. 自耕农的儿子（goodman's son）：将父亲称为自耕农（yeoman）或旅店老板的儿子；但"goodman"也可指"好人（good man）"。 61-6. 五个鬼……大人（Five fiends…master）：五个鬼的名字来自哈斯尼特的作品。 67-74. 来……有饭吃（Here…enough）：格洛斯特在重复李尔有关"可怜的穷人"的台词（见 3. 4. 28-36），但重点已从"可怜的人如何感受"转移到权贵对穷人的麻木。 71. 妄用你的诫命（slaves your ordnance）：让你的指令（人们该相互关爱和帮助）服从于他自己的意愿。 该台词可令人想起《圣经》中的类似话语，即"马可福音" 10 章 21 节："去变卖你所有的分给穷人，就必有财宝在天上。"

So distribution should undo excess

And each man have enough. Dost thou know Dover?

75 **Edgar**   Ay, master.

Gloucester   There is a cliff whose high and bending head

Looks fearfully in the confined deep:

Bring me but to the very brim of it,

And I'll repair the misery thou dost bear

80   With something rich about me. From that place

I shall no leading need.

Edgar   Give me thy arm,

Poor Tom shall lead thee.   ^F*Exeunt.*^F

分发财富以消除富裕过度，

让人都有饭吃。　你熟悉多佛吗？

埃德加　　熟悉，大人。　　　　　　　　　　　　　　　　　75

格洛斯特　那里有一座峭壁，高悬的头顶

胆怯地俯视着下面的大海：

把我带到那座峭壁的边缘，

我会用携带的贵重物品补救

你所遭受的不幸。到那里以后　　　　　　　　　　80

不再需要人带路。

埃德加　　　　　　　　　　伸过手来，

可怜的汤姆领你。　　　　　　　　　　　　　　　　　同下。

SCENE II

Enter Goneril, Edmund [followed by] Oswald.

Goneril   Welcome, my lord. I marvel our mild husband

Not met us on the way. [*to Oswald*] Now, where's your master?

Oswald   Madam, within; but never man so changed.

I told him of the army that was landed;

5   He smiled at it. I told him you were coming;

His answer was ' The worse. ' Of Gloucester's treachery

And of the loyal service of his son,

When I informed him, then he called me sot,

And told me I had turned the wrong side out.

10   What most he should dislike seems pleasant to him,

What like, offensive.

Goneril   [*to Edmund*]   Then shall you go no further.

It is the cowish terror of his spirit,

That dares not undertake. He'll not feel wrongs

Which tie him to an answer. Our wishes on the way

15   May prove effects. Back, Edmund, to my brother;

第二场

贡纳丽、埃德蒙、奥斯华德［随后］上。

贡纳丽　　欢迎，阁下。　我温顺的丈夫没出来

迎接令人惊讶。　［向奥斯华德］哎，你主人呢？

奥斯华德　在里面，夫人；可他完全变了。

我曾告诉他法军已经登陆；

他对此一笑。　我告诉他您来了，　　　　　　　　　5

他回答说"更糟"。　当我告诉他

格洛斯特的叛国和他的儿子

如何忠诚，然后他叫我蠢货，

告诉我说，我这人本末倒置。

他最该厌烦的，反而显得喜欢，　　　　　　　　　10

该喜欢的，厌烦。

贡纳丽　　［向埃德蒙］　　那您别再前行。

是他那懦夫般的心惊胆战

使他不敢冒险。　他会忽视羞辱，

若需要报复。　路上提及的心愿

也许能实现。　埃德蒙，回我妹夫家吧；　　　　　15

4.2.　0（1）贡纳丽、埃德蒙和奥斯华德于3.7出发，前去跟阿班尼会合，因此本场场景应被想象为他的住处或宫殿外面。　3-11. 夫人……厌烦（Madam…offensive）：阿班尼自1.4后未再上场，当时他对贡纳丽对待李尔的行为有些疑虑；传说他与康瓦尔之间出现了裂痕（2.1.11-12和3.1.19-21），因此有关他已完全改变的说法并不奇怪（正如考迪丽娅在1.1与4.4返回期间的变化一样）。　他在道义上对贡纳丽的厌弃，使得她对埃德蒙的追求看似更为有理。　9. 本末倒置（turned…out）：就像把衣服穿反（as if the lining of a garment were placed on the outside）。14. 心愿（wishes）：既可指加深他们之间的情爱，也可指将阿班尼除掉。

Hasten his musters and conduct his powers.

I must change names at home and give the distaff

Into my husband's hands. This trusty servant

Shall pass between us. Ere long you are like to hear—

20   If you dare venture in your own behalf—

A mistress's command. Wear this.

[*She places a chain about his neck.*] Spare speech,

Decline your head. This kiss, if it durst speak,

Would stretch thy spirits up into the air.

Conceive, and fare thee well—

Edmund   Yours in the ranks of death.   ᶠ*Exit.*ᶠ

25 **Goneril**   —My most dear Gloucester!

ᶠO, the difference of man and man!ᶠ

To thee a woman's services are due;

A fool usurps my bed.

Oswald   Madam, here comes my lord.   ᴼ*Exit.*ᴼ

ᶠ*Enter Albany.*ᶠ

Goneril   I have been worth the whistling.

30 **Albany**   O Goneril,

You are not worth the dust which the rude wind

催他集合军队并由您指挥。

我得变换家庭角色，把纺纱杆

交给我丈夫。　这位可靠的仆人

为咱报信。　不久您可能会听到——

您若胆敢为自己的利益冒险——　　　　　　　　　　　　　20

情人的吩咐。　戴上这个。

［给他戴上一条项链。］别说话，

低下头来。　这一吻，它若敢发言，

会使你雄风大振直冲霄汉。

怀想吧，再会了——

埃德蒙　　为您入生出死。　　　　　　　　　　　　　　　　下。

贡纳丽　　　　　　　　——最亲的格洛斯特。　　　　　　25

噢，男人之间有多大区别！

你才配得上女人的献身；

傻瓜占着我的床铺。

奥斯华德　　夫人，殿下他来了。　　　　　　　　　　　　下。

阿班尼上。

贡纳丽　　我向来值得一顾。

阿班尼　　　　　　　噢，贡纳丽，　　　　　　　　　　　30

您连那狂风吹到您脸上的

---

21. 情人的吩咐（A…command）：原文中的"mistress"系双关语，既可指"情人（lover）"，也可指"女主人（her power as a ruler）"。　贡纳丽可能会叫埃德蒙暗杀阿班尼。（Foakes；Muir）。　23，27. 你……你（thy…thee）：接吻之后，贡纳丽对埃德蒙的称呼已从正式的"您（you）"改为表示亲密的"你"。　23. 雄风（spirits）：生命力（vital powers），暗示性能力。　暗示性欲的词语还包括下文的"conceive（想象，怀孕）""death（死亡，性高潮）""services（服务，性交）""bed（床铺，房事）"（Foakes；Bate）。　30. 值得一顾（worth the whistling）：值得关注（worth watching out for），源于格言：It's a poor dog that is not worth the whistling（只有可怜狗才不配哨声），贡纳丽注意到了阿班尼不愿出来迎她。

Blows in your face. ^QI fear your disposition;

That nature which contemns its origin

Cannot be bordered certain in itself.

35 She that herself will sliver and disbranch

From her material sap perforce must wither,

And come to deadly use.

Goneril No more, the text is foolish.

Albany Wisdom and goodness to the vile seem vile;

40 Filths savour but themselves. What have you done?

Tigers, not daughters, what have you performed?

A father, and a gracious aged man,

Whose reverence even the head-lugged bear would lick,

Most barbarous, most degenerate, have you madded.

45 Could my good brother suffer you to do it?

A man, a prince, by him so benefited?

If that the heavens do not their visible spirits

Send quickly down to tame these vile offences,

It will come:

50 Humanity must perforce prey on itself,

Like monsters of the deep.^Q

尘土都不值！我担心您的性情；

竟敢唾弃生身之本的女人，

无法指望她能够守己安分。

正像一根从树干折断的枝条　　　　　　　　　35

切断了滋养，您必定会枯干，

不会有好的下场。

贡纳丽　　好了，这种说教愚蠢。

阿班尼　　智慧和良善对恶者会显得邪恶；

污秽者只爱污秽。你们做了什么？　　　　　40

猛虎，不是女儿，你们干了什么？

一位父亲，慈祥年迈的老人，

被拽着头的野熊都会表示恭敬，

你们却野蛮下流地将他逼疯。

我的好兄弟能容忍你们如此？　　　　　　45

一条汉子、王子，这么受他恩宠？

假如上天不迅速派下具体的

使者惩罚这些邪恶的罪人，

早晚会派：

人类一定就会相互吞食，　　　　　　　　50

就像海里的怪物。

32-51. 我……怪物（I…deep）：本场共有三段台词只出现在四开本里，这是第一段，另外两段是 54-60 和 63-70；对开本缩短了阿班尼与贡纳丽之间的争吵，并删除了阿班尼有关道义的概述。以此加快了剧情的推进，却牺牲了一些优美的诗行。　37. 不会有好的下场（come…use）：遭到毁灭或导致死亡（come to a bad end, or end up causing death），正像贡纳丽的结局那样：毒死李根，自杀身亡（见 5. 289-90）。　39-40. 智慧……污秽（Wisdom…themselves）：可参考《圣经》"提多书"1 章 15 节："在洁净的人，凡物都洁净；在污秽不信的人，什么都不洁净，连心地和天良也都污秽了。"42. 年迈（aged）：aged = agèd（两音节）。　43. 被拽着头的（head-lugged = pulled by the head）：因此会被激怒。　45. 兄弟（brother）：襟弟（brother-in-law）。　49. 早晚会派（It will come）：在阿班尼本段台词的高潮到来之前，这一有力的短行可为其提供一种戏剧性的停顿（Muir）　50-1. 人类……怪物（Humanity…deep）："大鱼吃小鱼"这种观念属于老生常谈，但莎士比亚将它变成了一种可怕的同类相食。

Goneril		Milk-livered man,
	That bear'st a cheek for blows, a head for wrongs,	
	Who hast not in thy brows an eye discerning	
	Thine honour from thy suffering; ^Qthat not knowst	
55	Fools do those villains pity who are punished	

Goneril   Milk-livered man,
That bear'st a cheek for blows, a head for wrongs,
Who hast not in thy brows an eye discerning
Thine honour from thy suffering; ᵠthat not knowst
55   Fools do those villains pity who are punished
Ere they have done their mischief. Where's thy drum?
France spreads his banners in our noiseless land;
With plumed helm thy state begins to threat,
Whiles thou, a moral fool, sits still and cries,
'Alack, why does he so?' ᵠ

60 **Albany**   See thyself, devil:
Proper deformity seems not in the fiend
So horrid as in woman.

Goneril   O vain fool!

Albany   ᵠThou changed and self-covered thing, for shame,
Be-monster not thy feature. Were't my fitness
65   To let these hands obey my blood,
They are apt enough to dislocate and tear
Thy flesh and bones. Howe'er thou art a fiend,
A woman's shape doth shield thee.

Goneril   Marry, your manhood, mew! —ᵠ

贡纳丽	胆小的懦夫，	
	长的是挨揍的脸，受辱的头，	
	你的额头上没有长眼，分不清	
	哪该容忍哪该怨恨。　不知道	
	只有傻瓜才同情恶棍，不会	55
	对他们先发制人。　你的战鼓呢？	
	法王已在我平静的国土上举旗；	
	头戴羽饰开始威胁你的国家，	
	而你，论道的傻瓜，稳坐着呼喊，	
	"唉，他怎么这样？"	
阿班尼	看看你，魔鬼：	60
	适合于恶魔的丑陋在女人身上	
	显得更为可怕。	
贡纳丽	噢，无用的傻瓜！	
阿班尼	变态和掩盖本相的东西，丢人！	
	不要变成妖怪。　假如我可以	
	使这一双手顺服我的血气，	65
	它们早就会让你骨头散架、	
	血肉横飞。　尽管你是个魔鬼，	
	披着女人的外衣。	
贡纳丽	嗨，真像条汉子，呸！——	

---

51. 胆小的（Milk-livered = chicken-hearted）：胆怯（cowardice）与肝内缺血有关，乳汁（milk）与女人气相连。　52. 挨揍的脸（cheek for blows）：见《圣经》"路加福音"6 章 29节："有人打你这边的脸，连那边的脸也由他打。"53-4. 分不清……怨恨（discerning…suffering）：分不清哪些应该表示怨恨（比如对你的地位和尊严的冒犯）与哪些可以体面地容忍（what should be resented [as offensive to your rank or dignity] from what may be honourably tolerated）。　58. 羽饰（plumed = plumèd）。　61-2. 适合于……可怕（Proper…woman）：原注为"The deformity of the devil is less horrible（because it is proper, or characteristic of him）than that of a woman"。　鉴于贡纳丽此刻所表现出的恶毒和怒气，阿班尼认为她的形体和心理已经变态。　63. 变态（changed = changèd）。　63. 掩盖本相的东西（self-covered thing）：贡纳丽变成魔鬼后，掩盖了自己原本的女人容貌，从而变成了一件"东西（thing）"。

Enter a Messenger.

70 ᵠ**Albany**	What news?ᵠ
Messenger	O my good lord, the Duke of Cornwall's dead,
	Slain by his servant, going to put out
	The other eye of Gloucester.
Albany	Gloucester's eye?
Messenger	A servant that he bred, thrilled with remorse,
75	Opposed against the act, bending his sword
	To his great master, who, thereat enraged,
	Flew on him and amongst them felled him dead;
	But not without that harmful stroke which since
	Hath plucked him after.
Albany	This shows you are above,
80	You justicers, that these our nether crimes
	So speedily can venge. But, O, poor Gloucester,
	Lost he his other eye?
Messenger	Both, both, my lord.
	[*to Goneril*] This letter, madam, craves a speedy answer;
	'Tis from your sister.
Goneril	[*aside*] One way I like this well;
85	But being widow, and my Gloucester with her,
	May all the building in my fancy pluck
	Upon my hateful life. Another way

一信差上。

| 阿班尼 | 有啥消息？ | 70 |

信差　　　噢，好殿下，康瓦尔公爵死了，

要挖格洛斯特的另一只眼睛时，

被仆人杀死。

阿班尼　　　　　　　格洛斯特的眼睛？

信差　　　他培养的一个仆人，激于怜悯，

反对这一行为，将利剑对准了　　　　　　　　　　75

他的主人，公爵他勃然大怒，

向他扑去，混战中将他刺死；

但他却受到了致命的一击，

导致他随后死去。

阿班尼　　　　　　　　表明上有苍天，

你们判官，让地上的罪恶这么快　　　　　　　　　80

就遭到报应！噢，可怜的格洛斯特，

另一只眼睛也瞎了？

信差　　　　　　　　　全瞎了，殿下。

　　　　　［向贡纳丽］这封信，夫人，需要赶快回答；

是您妹妹来的。

贡纳丽　　　［旁白］　　　一方面我很喜欢；

但她已成寡妇，我的格洛斯特相伴，　　　　　　　85

这也许会摧毁我的空中楼阁，

使我的余生可憎。　另一方面

78-9. 但……死去（But…after）：原注为 "but not before Cornwall suffered the wound that has since killed him"（Mowat）。　84. 一方面我很喜欢（One…well）：她想占有埃德蒙（my Gloucester）并独揽大权，因此该消息既坏又好，坏是因为她怕李根也有野心，好是因为康瓦尔已被除掉，削弱了李根的力量。　86. 空中楼阁（building in my fancy）："空中的城堡（castle in the air）"（Muir）；即"我想占有埃德蒙的美梦（my dream of possessing Edmund）"（Foakes）。　87. 可憎（hateful）：因为毁了她对未来的计划（Muir）。

The news is not so tart.

[*to the Messenger*]   I'll read, and answer.   ᵠ*Exit.* ᵠ

Albany   Where was his son when they did take his eyes?

Messenger   Come with my lady hither.

90 **Albany**   He is not here.

Messenger   No, my good lord; I met him back again.

Albany   Knows he the wickedness?

Messenger   Ay, my good lord; 'twas he informed against him

And quit the house on purpose that their punishment

Might have the freer course.

95 **Albany**   Gloucester, I live

To thank thee for the love thou showd'st the King

And to revenge thine eyes. Come hither, friend,

Tell me what more thou knowst.   *Exeunt.*

这种消息不坏。

　　[向信差]　　　我会阅读并回复。　　　　　　　　　　下。

阿班尼　他们挖他眼睛时,他儿子何在?

信差　跟着夫人来了这里。

阿班尼　　　　　　　他没来这里。　　　　　　　　　90

信差　来了,好殿下;我遇见他返回去了。

阿班尼　他知道这种暴行吗?

信差　知道,殿下,是他告发了他
　　　并离开家里,好让他们更为
　　　随意地处罚。

阿班尼　　　　　　格洛斯特,我会　　　　　　　　　95
　　　永远感谢你对国王的厚爱,
　　　为你的眼睛报仇! 过来,朋友,
　　　告诉我还知道些什么。　　　　　　　　　　　　同下。

SCENE III

ᑫEnter Kent and a Gentleman.

Kent   Why the King of France is so suddenly gone back,
know you no reason?

Gentleman Something he left imperfect in the state which
since his coming forth is thought of, which
5   imports to the kingdom so much fear and danger that
his personal return was most required and necessary.

Kent   Who hath he left behind him general?

Gentleman The Marshal of France, Monsieur La Far.

Kent   Did your letters pierce the queen to any demonst-
10   ration of grief?

Gentleman Ay, sir. She took them, read them in my presence,
And now and then an ample tear trilled down
Her delicate cheek. It seemed she was a queen
Over her passion, who, most rebel-like,
Sought to be king o'er her.

15 **Kent**   O, then, it moved her?

第三场

肯特[化装]与一绅士上。

肯特　　　法兰西国王为何如此突然地返回去了，
　　　　　　您知道原因吗？

绅士　　　他在国内有件事情还没有办完，只是
　　　　　　等他到达这里以后才忽然想起，这件
　　　　　　事情非同小可，它关系着王国的安危，　　　　　　　　　5
　　　　　　因此他亲自回去非常必要。

肯特　　　他留下了谁来担任将军？

绅士　　　法兰西元帅，拉法先生。

肯特　　　您的信件可曾感动王后有任何悲痛的
　　　　　　表示？　　　　　　　　　　　　　　　　　　　　　10

绅士　　　有，先生。　她接信后当场就读，
　　　　　　硕大的泪珠时而从她细嫩的
　　　　　　面颊上流下。　她像王后似地
　　　　　　控制感情，而感情像个叛贼，
　　　　　　试图对她称王。

肯特　　　　　　　　噢，她受到感动？　　　　　　　　　15

　　4.3. 本场只出现在四开本里。　具有三种功能，一是解释于4.2.57已登陆英国的法王为何返回；二是为考迪丽娅确立一种圣洁的形象；三是让我们知道李尔已到达多佛。　这三种功能都与剧情的进展无关。　另外，第8行提及的"法兰西元帅"此后销声匿迹；考迪丽娅好像独自一人与法军为伴（对开本的4.4和四开本与对开本的5.2）。　0（1）绅士（*Gentleman*）：可能是肯特于3.1谈过话的同一位人士（侍卫）。　9. 信件（letters）：肯特曾委派该绅士向考迪丽娅传递口信，并以戒指作为信物（3.1.40-5），但观众对这种前后不一却不大可能觉察。

Gentleman   Not to a rage; patience and sorrow strove

Who should express her goodliest. You have seen

Sunshine and rain at once, her smiles and tears

Were like a better way. Those happy smilets

20   That played on her ripe lip seemed not to know

What guests were in her eyes, which parted thence

As pearls from diamonds dropped. In brief,

Sorrow would be a rarity most beloved

If all could so become it.

25 **Kent**   Made she no verbal question?

Gentleman   Faith, once or twice she heaved the name of 'father'

Pantingly forth, as if it pressed her heart;

Cried 'Sisters, sisters, shame of ladies, sisters!

Kent, father, sisters! What, i'the storm, i'the night?

30   Let pity not be believed!' There she shook

The holy water from her heavenly eyes,

And clamour mastered her; then away she started,

To deal with grief alone.

Kent   It is the stars,

The stars above us govern our conditions,

绅士	但没爆发；忍耐与哀伤竞争，
	看谁把她表现得最好。　您见过
	阳光下的雨露,她的微笑和泪水
	与此相似但更美。　甜甜的微笑
	挂在红红的唇边,好像不知道	20
	眼里住着什么客人,客人离去,
	好像珍珠从钻石上坠落。　总之,
	哀伤会弥足珍贵,若大家哀伤时
	能像她那样优美。

肯特	她没有向您问话？	25

绅士	问了,她曾一两次叹了声"父亲",
	气喘吁吁,好像非常揪心;
	喊道"姐姐呀,姐姐,不像话,姐姐呀!
	肯特,父亲,姐姐呀! 暴雨中,黑夜里?
	别再相信怜悯!"然后她便将	30
	圣水从她天使般的眼睛里摇落,
	她情不自禁;随后迈步离开,
	去独自面对哀伤。

肯特	这是星辰,
	天上的星辰决定了我们的人品,

---

17. 看谁……最好（Who…goodliest）：原注为"which might portray her best"；"忍耐（patience）"与"哀伤（sorrow）"在此作为女人的化身。　18-22. 阳光……坠落（Sunshine…dropped）：一只眼睛哭泣,另一只眼睛微笑往往跟虚情假意相关；但考迪丽娅甜甜的微笑（smilets = little smiles）和眼泪却像阳光和雨露一样；她的微笑和眼泪彼此毫无察觉,因此都很美好；甜甜的微笑就像挂在朱唇的果实,她的泪水和眼睛就像珍贵的宝石。　该绅士的华丽辞藻将考迪丽娅理想化为"温情"的象征（an emblem of compassion）。　23-4. 若……优美（If…it）：原注为"if all persons were as attractive in sorrow as she"（Bevington）。　31. 圣水（The holy water）：圣洁的泪水（her holy tears）（Alan Durban, Shakespeare Made Easy, 1986；——译者附注）。　真情实感（the genuine thing）,与"奉承（courtly holy-water）"相对（3. 2. 10）（Foakes）。

35		Else one self mate and make could not beget
		Such different issues. You spoke not with her since?
	Gentleman	No.
	Kent	Was this before the King returned?
	Gentleman	No, since.
	Kent	Well, sir, the poor distressed Lear's i'the town,
40		Who sometime in his better tune remembers
		What we are come about, and by no means
		Will yield to see his daughter.
	Gentleman	Why, good sir?
	Kent	A sovereign shame so elbows him. His own unkindness
		That stripped her from his benediction, turned her
45		To foreign casualties, gave her dear rights
		To his dog-hearted daughters, these things sting
		His mind so venomously that burning shame
		Detains him from Cordelia.
	Gentleman	Alack, poor gentleman!
	Kent	Of Albany's and Cornwall's powers you heard not?
50	**Gentleman**	'Tis so; they are afoot.
	Kent	Well, sir, I'll bring you to our master, Lear,
		And leave you to attend him. Some dear cause
		Will in concealment wrap me up awhile.
		When I am known aright, you shall not grieve,
55		Lending me this acquaintance.
		I pray you, go along with me. *Exeunt.*^Q

	否则,同一对父母怎么会生出	35
	这么不同的孩子! 没再跟她说话?	
绅士	没有。	
肯特	这发生在法王返回之前?	
绅士	不,之后。	
肯特	好吧,可怜悲伤的李尔现在镇上,	
	神志稍微清醒时他能够记起	40
	我们为何来到这里,但怎么	
	也不肯去见女儿。	
绅士	为啥,先生?	
肯特	他感到羞愧难当。 记得自己无情,	
	曾拒绝为她祝福,把她抛到	
	国外去冒险,将她的继承权给了	45
	狼心狗肺的女儿,这些事情	
	刺伤了他的内心,强烈的羞愧	
	使他避开考迪丽娅。	
绅士	唉,可怜人哪!	
肯特	阿班尼和康瓦尔的军队您没听说?	
绅士	听说了,已经出发。	50
肯特	好吧,我带您去见主人李尔,	
	并留下您看护。 某种重要理由	
	需要我再隐瞒一下真实身份,	
	您了解我是谁后,不会后悔	
	因为曾与我结识。	55
	我求您,跟我来吧。	同下。

---

52. 重要理由(dear cause):从未指明,但这意味着肯特可以继续伪装,只有考迪丽娅知道他的身份(4.7.10-11)。

SCENE IV

Enter, ^F*with drum and colours*^F *Cordelia, Gentleman,*
[*Officer*] ^F*and soldiers.* ^F

Cordelia   Alack, 'tis he. Why, he was met even now

As mad as the vexed sea, singing aloud,

Crowned with rank fumiter and furrow-weeds,

With burdocks, hemlock, nettles, cuckoo-flowers,

5   Darnel and all the idle weeds that grow

In our sustaining corn. [*to Officer*] A century send forth;

Search every acre in the high-grown field

And bring him to our eye. What can man's wisdom

In the restoring his bereaved sense,

10   He that helps him take all my outward worth.

[*Exit Officer, with soldiers.*]

Gentleman   There is means, madam.

Our foster nurse of nature is repose,

The which he lacks: that to provoke in him

Are many simples operative, whose power

Will close the eye of anguish.

15   **Cordelia**   All blest secrets,

All you unpublished virtues of the earth,

第四场

鼓手与旗手、考迪丽娅、绅士、[军官]
与士兵上。

考迪丽娅　　哎呀,是他! 唉,刚才有人见他

疯得像汹涌的大海,放声歌唱,

戴着蓝堇和垄草乱编的冠冕,

还有牛蒡、毒芹、荨麻、剪秋罗、

稗子和各种杂草,都长在我们　　　　　　　　　　　5

赖以生存的麦田。 [向军官]一百人前去;

找遍每一亩庄稼茂盛的田间,

把他带到我眼前。 医学知识

能为他的神志康复做些什么,

谁能治好,我的财富全都给他。　　　　　　　　　10

　　　　　　　　　　　　　　　　[军官与众士兵下。]

绅士　　有办法的,夫人。

大自然给人的营养就是睡眠,

他睡眠不足:要想让他入睡,

有很多灵验的药草,可以帮他

合上痛苦的双眼。

考迪丽娅　　　　　　　所有的妙药,　　　　　　　15

地上尚未发现却有益的药草,

　　4.4.　0(1)绅士(*Gentleman*),在四开本里为"医生(Doctor)"。 地点应在多佛附近的法军军营。 1.他(he):李尔。 3-7.戴着……田间(Crowned…field):李尔在4.6入场时戴着这种"冠冕(crown)";这与他在1.1所戴的金冠形成了鲜明的对比。 此处所提及的杂草和野花均生长在英国的夏天,这也是剧中唯一一次表明了故事所发生的季节。

Spring with my tears. Be aidant and remediate

In the good man's distress. Seek, seek for him,

Lest his ungoverned rage dissolve the life

That wants the means to lead it.

Enter Messenger.

20 **Messenger** News, madam:

The British powers are marching hitherward.

Cordelia 'Tis known before. Our preparation stands

In expectation of them. O dear father,

It is thy business that I go about;

25 Therefore great France

My mourning and important tears hath pitied.

No blown ambition doth our arms incite,

But love, dear love, and our aged father's right:

Soon may I hear and see him. *Exeunt.*

用我的泪水生发！帮助治疗

这位好人的痛苦。　去找，去找他，

以免他失控的疯狂了断生命，

他的神志已失常。

信差上。

信差　　　　　　　　　　有消息，夫人：　　　　　　　　　　20

英国军队正在朝这里进发。

考迪丽娅　　　已经知道。　我们的军队已经

做好了准备。　噢，亲爱的父亲，

我是在为了您的事务奔波；

因此法兰西国君　　　　　　　　　　　　　　25

怜悯了我悲伤和恳求的泪水。

我们出兵不是因膨胀的野心，

而是出于爱，和老父亲的权利：

愿我很快能与他相见！　　　　　　　　　　　　同下。

---

20. 他的神志已失常（That…it）：已无法健康地生活（that lacks the means to live sanely）（Bevington）。

SCENE V

Enter Regan and Oswald.

Regan	But are my brother's powers set forth?
Oswald	Ay, madam.
Regan	Himself in person ^Fthere^F?
Oswald	Madam, with much ado; your sister is the better
5	soldier.
Regan	Lord Edmund spake not with your lord at home?
Oswald	No, madam.
Regan	What might import my sister's letter to him?
Oswald	I know not, lady.
10 **Regan**	Faith, he is posted hence on serious matter.

It was great ignorance, Gloucester's eyes being out,

To let him live. Where he arrives he moves

All hearts against us. Edmund, I think, is gone

In pity of his misery to dispatch

15   His nighted life; moreover to descry

The strength o'the enemy.

第五场

李根与奥斯华德上。

李根	我姐夫的军队出发了吗？	
奥斯华德	出发了,夫人。	
李根	他亲自出马了？	
奥斯华德	夫人,颇费周折；您姐姐倒是更棒的	
	军人。	5
李根	埃德蒙伯爵没跟您家公爵说话？	
奥斯华德	没说,夫人。	
李根	我姐姐给他的信会说些什么？	
奥斯华德	我不知道,夫人。	
李根	真的,他已紧急出发去办大事。	10
	多么失策,格洛斯特眼睛瞎了,	
	却让他活着。 他所到之处会感动	
	人心反对我们。 埃德蒙,我想,	
	因可怜父亲的遭遇,前去结束他	
	暗淡无光的生命；同时也可以	15
	打探敌人的实力。	

---

4. 5.　0 (1) 奥斯华德 (Oswald)：信差于 4.2.83 将李根的信件交给了贡纳丽,贡纳丽随后退下,准备回信。 该回信好像现由奥斯华德带来,同时他还带来了贡纳丽写给埃德蒙的一封信函。 埃德蒙此刻已出发去寻找格洛斯特或查明敌情。 本场场景应想象为格洛斯特的住处或李根的王宫。 4. 颇费周折 (with much ado)：经过一番争论和劝说。 阿班尼不清楚自己的职守何在 (Muir)。 8. 会说些 (import)：既可指 "我姐姐会在信里传递什么信息 (What might my sister's letter convey?)",也可指 "她给他写信会有何意 (What might her writing to him signify?)"。 11. 失策 (ignorance)：忽略了政治后果 (ignorance of political consequences)。

Oswald   I must needs after him, ^Fmadam,^F with my letter.

Regan   Our troops set forth tomorrow; stay with us.

The ways are dangerous.

Oswald   I may not, madam;

20   My lady charged my duty in this business.

Regan   Why should she write to Edmund? Might not you

Transport her purposes by word? Belike—

Some things, I know not what—I'll love thee much;

Let me unseal the letter.

Oswald   Madam, I had rather—

25 **Regan**   I know your lady does not love her husband,

I am sure of that; and at her late being here

She gave strange oeillades and most speaking looks

To noble Edmund. I know you are of her bosom.

Oswald   I, madam?

30 **Regan**   I speak in understanding; y'are; I know't.

Therefore I do advise you take this note.

My lord is dead; Edmund and I have talked,

And more convenient is he for my hand

Than for your lady's. You may gather more.

35   If you do find him, pray you give him this;

And when your mistress hears thus much from you,

I pray desire her call her wisdom to her.

So, fare ^Fyou^F well.

If you do chance to hear of that blind traitor,

奥斯华德	我要带着信件去找他,夫人。
李根	我们的部队明天出发;住下吧。
	路上很危险。
奥斯华德	不能住下,夫人。
	我家夫人就此命令我服从。
李根	她为啥给埃德蒙写信? 您不能
	口述一下她的意思? 也许——
	有些事情,我不清楚——我会很爱你;
	让我把信打开吧。
奥斯华德	夫人,最好是——
李根	我知道您家夫人不爱她丈夫,
	这一点我深信;最近她来这里时,
	她对高贵的埃德蒙暗送秋波,
	含情脉脉。 我知道您是她心腹。
奥斯华德	我,夫人?
李根	我懂我在说啥,您也懂,我清楚。
	因此我劝您注意我的话语:
	我夫君已死;埃德蒙和我谈过,
	他更适合与我结为连理,
	而不是您家夫人。 您能猜出来。
	您若见到他,请把这个给他;
	您家夫人若听到我上述话语,
	请您告诉她可要理智行事。
	那就再会吧。
	您若能听说那个瞎眼的叛徒,

行号(右侧):20, 25, 30, 35

---

23. 有些事情（some things）：她显然在怀疑埃德蒙与贡纳丽已经相爱（Muir）。 35. 这个（this）：信物（a token），或信件（a letter）。 奥斯华德死去时,身上带有不止一封信件（4.6.244），尽管埃德加只读了贡纳丽的,也就是奥斯华德现在不让李根看的那一封（4.6.257-65）。

40   Preferment falls on him that cuts him off.

Oswald   Would I could meet ᵠhimᵠ, madam, I should show

What party I do follow.

Regan   Fare thee well.   *Exeunt.*

谁把他杀死谁会得到晋升。 40

奥斯华德 我要是遇见他，夫人，我会表明
我对哪一方忠诚。

李根 一路平安。 同下。

SCENE VI

Enter Gloucester and Edgar [in peasant's clothing
and with a staff].

Gloucester When shall we come to the top of that same hill?

Edgar You do climb up it now. Look how we labour.

Gloucester Methinks the ground is even.

Edgar   Horrible steep.

Hark, do you hear the sea?

Gloucester   No, truly.

5 **Edgar** Why then, your other senses grow imperfect

By your eyes' anguish.

Gloucester   So may it be indeed.

Methinks thy voice is altered and thou speak'st

In better phrase and matter than thou didst.

Edgar You're much deceived; in nothing am I changed

But in my garments.

10 **Gloucester**   Methinks you're better spoken.

Edgar Come on, sir, here's the place. Stand still: how fearful

And dizzy 'tis to cast one's eyes so low!

The crows and choughs that wing the midway air

第六场

格洛斯特与埃德加［扮作村夫，
手持拐杖］上。

格洛斯特　　什么时候才能到那座山顶？

埃德加　　　正往上爬呢。　您看多么费劲。

格洛斯特　　我觉得地是平的。

埃德加　　　　　　　　　陡得吓人。

听，听见海了没有？

格洛斯特　　　　　　　　没有，真的。

埃德加　　　那么，您的其他感官因为　　　　　　5
眼疼已经失灵。

格洛斯特　　　　　　　　也许是真的。
我觉得你的声音变了，你说话
要比原先更符合逻辑和优雅。

埃德加　　　您受骗了；我一点都没改变，
除了衣服。

格洛斯特　　　　我觉得你说话更好听了。　　　　10

埃德加　　　快来，先生，到了。　站稳：向这么
深的下方望去多么吓人和头晕！
飞翔在半空中的乌鸦和寒鸦

　　4.6.　　0（1）扮作……拐杖（*in…staff*）：埃德加现在身穿老人为他拿来的衣服（4.1.52），对奥斯华德来说，他看起来像个农夫（227）；他说起话来再也不像那个可怜的汤姆，正像格洛斯特在7-8所注意到的那样。　他们两人应被想象为现已到达多佛附近的某个地方，其中有一人手持拐杖（staff）或棍棒（bat），埃德加用来抵御奥斯华德的袭击（239）。　**7-8.** 你……优雅（*thou…didst*）：对观众来说，其中的主要变化就是他现在说的是韵文，而作为可怜的汤姆，他说的大都是散文。

Show scarce so gross as beetles. Half-way down
15   Hangs one that gathers samphire, dreadful trade;
Methinks he seems no bigger than his head.
The fishermen that walk upon the beach
Appear like mice, and yon tall anchoring barque
Diminished to her cock, her cock a buoy
20   Almost too small for sight. The murmuring surge
That on th'unnumbered idle pebbles chafes,
Cannot be heard so high. I'll look no more,
Lest my brain turn and the deficient sight
Topple down headlong.

Gloucester   Set me where you stand.

25   **Edgar**   Give me your hand: you are now within a foot
Of the extreme verge. For all beneath the moon
Would I not leap upright.

Gloucester   Let go my hand.
Here, friend, 's another purse, in it a jewel
Well worth a poor man's taking. Fairies and gods
30   Prosper it with thee. Go thou farther off;
Bid me farewell and let me hear thee going.

Edgar   Now fare ye well, good sir.

Gloucester   With all my heart.

Edgar   [*aside*] Why I do trifle thus with his despair

　　　　　　　看起来就像甲虫。　半山腰悬着

　　　　　　　一个采圣草的,可怕的营生!　　　　　　　15

　　　　　　　在我看来他就像一个小点儿。

　　　　　　　那些在海滩上行走的渔夫

　　　　　　　好像是老鼠,那艘高大的帆船

　　　　　　　小得像划艇,那划艇像个浮标,

　　　　　　　小得难以辨清。　汹涌的波涛　　　　　　　20

　　　　　　　拍击着无数和光秃的卵石,

　　　　　　　这么高无法听见。　我不再看了,

　　　　　　　以免我会变得头晕目眩,

　　　　　　　栽了下去。

格洛斯特　　　　　　　让我站您那里。

埃德加　　　把手给我:您现在离悬崖边缘　　　　　　　25

　　　　　　　仅一尺之遥。　给我地上的一切,

　　　　　　　我也不会蹦跳。

格洛斯特　　　　　　　　你松开手吧。

　　　　　　　朋友,还有个钱包,里面有颗宝石,

　　　　　　　值得穷人拿取。　愿精灵和神明

　　　　　　　因此向你祝福!你走远一点吧;　　　　　　　30

　　　　　　　跟我道别,让我听见你已离去。

埃德加　　　那就再会了,好先生。

格洛斯特　　　　　　　诚心诚意。

埃德加　　　[旁白]我之所以拿他的绝望玩笑,

---

　　15. 圣草(samphire):叶子芳香的植物,可用以腌菜。　源于法语,也叫彼得草(St. Peter's herb)。　29. 精灵(fairies):一种迷信,认为隐藏的财宝由精灵看守,谁若发现并将它占有,精灵就会使财宝奇迹般地增加(Muir)。　33-4. 我……治好(Why…it):可以说埃德加是在跟父亲游戏,但不免有些残忍,因为它让格洛斯特充满期待,然后又拒绝他所想要的东西——死亡。　该片段的情理颇富争议,常被视为“奇异、滑稽、荒唐、可悲(grotesque, comic, absurd, tragic)”,或兼而有之。

Is done to cure it.

Gloucester   [*ᴼHe kneels. ᴼ*]   O you mighty gods!

35   This world I do renounce, and in your sights

Shake patiently my great affliction off.

If I could bear it longer and not fall

To quarrel with your great opposeless wills,

My snuff and loathed part of nature should

40   Burn itself out. If Edgar live, O, bless ᶠhimᶠ!

Now, fellow, fare thee well. *ᴼHe falls. ᴼ*

Edgar   Gone, sir; farewell.

[*aside*] And yet I know not how conceit may rob

The treasury of life when life itself

Yields to the theft. Had he been where he thought,

45   By this had thought been past. [*to Gloucester*] Alive or
        dead?

Ho, you, sir! ᶠFriend,ᶠ hear you, sir? speak! —

[*aside*] Thus might he pass indeed. Yet he revives. —

What are you, sir?

Gloucester   Away and let me die.

Edgar   Hadst thou been aught but gossamer, feathers, air,

50   So many fathom down precipitating,

Thou'dst shivered like an egg; but thou dost breathe,

Hast heavy substance, bleed'st not, speak'st, art sound.

是想把它治好。

格洛斯特　　［跪下。］　　　　噢，伟大的神明，

我弃绝这个世界，在你们面前，　　　　　　　　　　35

平静地解脱我的巨大痛苦。

纵然我能继续容忍，不挑战

你们那种不可抗拒的旨意，

我这可恨的风烛残年也会

灯尽油干。　埃德加若活着，保佑他！　　　　　　40

小伙子，再会了。［跌倒。］

埃德加　　　　　　　　　　走了，先生，再会。

［旁白］但我不知道幻觉是否能将

生命的宝藏盗走，假如生命

自愿被盗。　他若到了想到的地方，

现已没了思想。［向格洛斯特］活着还是

　　死了？　　　　　　　　　　　　　　　　　　45

嗬，先生！朋友，听见没有？　快说！——

［旁白］也许他真的死了。　可他又活了。——

您是谁呀，先生？

格洛斯特　　　　　　　　　走开，让我死去。

埃德加　　你若不是游丝、羽毛、空气，

从那么高的顶端陡然跌下，　　　　　　　　　　　50

会碎得像个鸡蛋；可你还在呼吸，

躯体结实，没流血，能说话，很健康。

　　34-40. 噢……油干（O…out）：基督教禁止"自杀（self-slaughter）"（《哈姆雷特》1. 2. 132），该教义源于《圣经》的诫命"不可杀人"（"出埃及记"20 章 13 节）；但莎士比亚在这一出显然是异教主宰的戏剧里采取了一种摇摆不定的态度，此处他在援引斯多葛派学者为自杀所进行的辩护。　见 62-4 行及注。　42-4. 我……被盗（I…theft）：原注为"I'm not sure whether imagination（conceit）may bring about his death, when he is so willing to die（我不知道幻觉是否能令他死去，如果他这么愿意死去）"。　颇具反讽的是，埃德加的意象——"生命的宝藏（treasury of life）"与格洛斯特的意象——"风烛残年（his life as a burnt-out candle-end）"形成了鲜明的对比。

Ten masts at each make not the altitude

Which thou hast perpendicularly fell.

55   Thy life's a miracle. Speak yet again.

Gloucester   But have I fallen, or no?

Edgar   From the dread summit of this chalky bourn.

Look up a-height: the shrill-gorged lark so far

Cannot be seen or heard. Do but look up.

60 **Gloucester**   Alack, I have no eyes.

Is wretchedness deprived that benefit

To end itself by death? 'Twas yet some comfort

When misery could beguile the tyrant's rage

And frustrate his proud will.

Edgar   Give me your arm.

65   Up, so. How ᶠis't ᶠ? Feel you your legs? You stand.

Gloucester   Too well, too well.

Edgar   This is above all strangeness.

Upon the crown o'the cliff what thing was that

Which parted from you?

Gloucester   A poor unfortunate beggar.

Edgar   As I stood here below methought his eyes

70   Were two full moons. He had a thousand noses,

Horns whelked and waved like the enraged sea.

It was some fiend. Therefore, thou happy father,

十根桅杆连接起来也赶不上

你从上面垂直落下的高度。

你的生命是个奇迹。　再说说话吧。　　　　　　　　55

格洛斯特　我摔下来了,还是没有?

埃德加　从可怕的白崖顶端摔下来的。

向高处看看:尖声的云雀遥远得

已无法看见或听见。　往上看看!

格洛斯特　唉,我没有眼睛。　　　　　　　　　　　60

难道都不允许苦命人结束

他的苦命?　这也算某种安慰,

若自杀能够挫败暴君的狂怒,

使他的骄横一筹莫展。

埃德加　　　　　　　　　　　　　伸过手来。

起来,对。　怎么样?　腿能动吗?　能站稳!　　　　65

格洛斯特　太稳了,太稳了。

埃德加　　　　　　　　这真是太奇妙了。

在那座悬崖顶上离开您的

是啥东西?

格洛斯特　　　　　　一个可怜的乞丐。

埃德加　我站在下面,觉得他的眼睛

像两轮明月。　他有一千个鼻子,　　　　　　70

头上的双角扭曲得就像怒涛。

它是个恶魔。　所以,幸运的老爹,

62-4. 这……莫展('Twas…will):莎士比亚也许想到了斯多葛派思想家为自杀所做的辩护,比如了解罗马君王尼禄暴政的塞内加,在其书信与论道的文章中争辩说,掌控自己命运的权力是最伟大的权力,因为它可以使自身高于武断的外部权力。　蒙田也曾将自杀誉为"挫败残酷暴君的"手段(a means 'to frustrate the Tyrants cruelty')。　72. 恶魔(fiend):因为恶魔通常会引诱人们自杀,见3.4.53-4及注。　幸运的老爹(happy father):lucky old man。　埃德加此处以含混的方式表达了他们的父子关系,但格洛斯特并未注意。　另见215,281。

Think that the clearest gods, who make them honours

Of men's impossibilities, have preserved thee.

75 **Gloucester**   I do remember now. Henceforth I'll bear

Affliction till it do cry out itself

'Enough, enough' and die. That thing you speak of,

I took it for a man; often 'twould say

'The fiend, the fiend'; he led me to that place.

Edgar   Bear free and patient thoughts.

Enter Lear ᵠ*mad*ᵠ [*crowned with wild flowers*].

80   But who comes here?

The safer sense will ne'er accommodate

His master thus.

Lear   No, they cannot touch me for coining. I am the

King himself.

85 **Edgar**   O thou side-piercing sight!

Lear   Nature's above art in that respect. There's your

press-money. That fellow handles his bow like a crow-

keeper: draw me a clothier's yard. Look, look, a mouse:

想必是最公正的神灵救了你，

他们能制造奇迹受人敬重。

格洛斯特　我现已记住。　今后我要忍受　　　　　　　　　75

痛苦直到它意识到我已受够，

允许我死去。　您说的那个东西，

我以为那是一个人。　他常念叨

"恶魔,恶魔"；他把我领到了那里。

埃德加　要想开,要忍耐。

李尔上,已发疯[头戴花冠]。

你看是谁来啦?　　　　　　　　　80

没有哪个神志正常的人会是

这种打扮。

李尔　不,他们不能责备我铸币。我是国王,

享有特权。

埃德加　噢,令人心碎的场景!　　　　　　　85

李尔　就此而言自然胜过人工。这是给你的

入伍费。那个家伙拉起弓来像是一个

稻草人:给我把弓拉满。看,有老鼠:

73-4. 神灵……敬重（who…impossibilities）: 原注为 "who derive to themselves honour and reverence from man, by doing things which he reckons impossible"。参见《圣经》"路加福音" 18 章 27 节:耶和华说: "在人所不能的事,在神却能"（Muir）。 76-7. 直到……死去（till…die）:可有两种解释,即译文所采用的: "till affliction recognizes that I have borne e-nough, and allows me to die a natural death"。另一种为: "till affliction recognizes that I have been afflicted enough and itself dies（直到痛苦意识到我已受够,然后痛苦消逝）"（Muir）。 83-4. 责备……特权（touch…himself）:原注为 "censure me for making coins, which was a royal prerogative"。 86. 自然胜过人工（Nature…art）:李尔的前言不搭后语表明他已发疯,无法解释,尽管能找到一些蛛丝马迹。 此处他对埃德加的回应可能是说大自然要比人工造成的伤心场景更多（nature offers more heart-rending sights than art）。 88. 把弓拉满（draw…yard）:原注为 "draw the bow to the full extent of the arrow"。 15 世纪将箭的长度规定为 "一布码（cloth-yard）",即 36 英寸。

peace, peace, this ^Fpiece of^F toasted cheese will do't.

90 There's my gauntlet, I'll prove it on a giant. Bring up the brown bills. O well flown, bird, i'the clout, i'the clout! Hewgh! Give the word.

Edgar   Sweet marjoram.

Lear   Pass.

95 **Gloucester**   I know that voice.

Lear   Ha! Goneril, ^Fwith a white beard?^F They flattered me like a dog and told me I had ^Fthe^F white hairs in my beard ere the black ones were there. To say 'ay' and 'no' to everything ^Fthat^F I said 'ay' and 'no' to was no good

100 divinity. When the rain came to wet me once and the wind to make me chatter; when the thunder would not peace at my bidding, there I found 'em, there I smelt 'em out. Go to, they are not men o'their words: they told me I was everything; 'tis a lie, I am not ague-proof.

105 **Gloucester**   The trick of that voice I do well remember:

Is't not the King?

	安静，安静，这块烤奶酪能把它捉住。	
	这是我的铁手套，哪怕它是巨人。带	90
	长矛兵来。飞得好，小鸟，正中目标，	
	正中目标！飕！口令。	
埃德加	甜甜的墨角兰。	
李尔	通过。	
格洛斯特	我熟悉那声音。	95
李尔	哈！贡纳丽有白胡子？他们像狗一样	
	奉承我，说我长出黑胡子之前就有了	
	白色的胡子。我说"是"，他们也说	
	"是"，我说"不"，他们也说"不"，	
	不是好的神学。雨也曾把我打湿，风	100
	也曾使我发抖；雷电也曾不听我使唤	
	继续轰鸣，我已看穿了他们，嗅出了	
	他们。得啦，他们不是那种诚实之辈：	
	说我无所不能；是撒谎，我也会发抖。	
格洛斯特	我已听出来那种特别的噪音：	105
	那不是国王吗？	

90. 这是……巨人（There…giant）：李尔像是在挑战老鼠，而且说话算数，即使对方是个巨人。　90. 铁手套（gauntlet）：镶有金属片的皮手套，当着对方的面把它扔掉就意味着向他挑战（Muir）。　李尔发出了一种想象中的挑战；后来阿班尼与埃德蒙在5.3.94-8确实交换了这种手套（Foakes）。91-2. 飞得好……目标（well…clout）：李尔也许在想象自己看到了一只猎鹰，变成了飞箭将目标或靶心击中。　92. 飕（Hewgh）：飞箭所发出的飕飕声（the whizzing sound of the arrow）。　93. 墨角兰（marjoram）：可以治疗大脑疾病的草药，因此，埃德加的口令与李尔的疯癫有关，不只是凭空想象。　96. 贡纳丽有白胡子（Goneril…beard）：可有两种解释：（1）李尔以为格洛斯特由贡纳丽装扮而成；（2）李尔在对贡纳丽说话，问她对胡须斑白的父亲怎么会这么残忍（Muir）。　96-104. 李尔终于明白考迪丽娅和肯特开场时试图让他明白的事理：词与义（between words and meaning），或言与行（words and deeds）之间存在着一道鸿沟；见1.1.55及注。　97-8. 说……胡子（told…there）：说我未成年时已非常明智（told me I was wise when I was still a child）。　此话若能当真，也许表明李尔继承王位已有六十多年。　100. 不是好的神学（no good divinity）：因为这违背了圣经中的诫命，"你们说话，是就说是，不是就说不是，免得你们落在审判之下"（Muir）。　神学（divinity = theology）：表明他们将李尔当成了神（Foakes）。

Lear   Ay, every inch a king.

When I do stare, see how the subject quakes.

I pardon that man's life. What was thy cause?

Adultery?

110   Thou shalt not die—die for adultery? No!

The wren goes to't and the small gilded fly

Does lecher in my sight. Let copulation thrive,

For Gloucester's bastard son was kinder to his father

Than were my daughters got 'tween the lawful sheets.

115   To't, luxury, pell-mell, for I lack soldiers.

Behold yon simp'ring dame,

Whose face between her forks presages snow,

That minces virtue and does shake the head

^FTo^F hear of pleasure's name—

120   The fitchew, nor the soiled horse, goes to't with a more

riotous appetite. Down from the waist they are

Centaurs, though women all above. But to the girdle do

the gods inherit, beneath is all the fiend's: there's hell,

there's darkness, there's the sulphurous pit, burning,

125   scalding, stench, consumption! Fie, fie, fie! Pah, pah!

Give me an ounce of civet, good apothecary, ^Qto^Q

李尔	对，十足的国王。

我一瞪眼睛，看臣民如何颤抖。

我赦免那人死刑。　你犯了啥罪？

通奸？

你不会受死——为通奸而死？　不会！　　　　　110

鹪鹩都在做那事，金色的苍蝇

在我面前交配。　让交配兴旺吧，

因为格洛斯特的私生子比我

婚生的女儿待父亲更有善心。

放纵吧，淫荡，因为我缺士兵。　　　　　115

你看那个皮笑肉不笑的夫人，

她的面孔预示着她冰清玉洁，

她扭扭捏捏，一听到色情二字

便会摇头不已——

鸡貂，和吃饱鲜草的骡马，发起情来　　　　　120

也没那么放浪。她们从腰部以下都是

禽兽，尽管上半身是女人。腰部以上

属于神，以下属于魔鬼：那里是地狱，

那里是黑暗，那里是硫黄火坑，燃烧，

滚烫，恶臭，自焚！哎，哎，哎！呸！　　　　　125

呸！给我半两灵猫香，好药剂师，好

109-10. 通奸……而死（Adultery … adultery）：李尔将焦点对准了格洛斯特的罪过，按照《圣经》中的律法规定，通奸可处以死刑（见"利未记"20章10节），但该律法后由耶稣更改，他赦免了那个行淫时被捉住的妇人（见"约翰福音"8章3-11节）。　114. 更有善心（kinder）：格洛斯特现已明白了埃德蒙的"善心（kindness）"（Muir）。　120. 鸡貂（fitchew）：也是妓女的俗称。　120-7. 多数版本将本段台词编排为不规则的韵文。　随着李尔对女儿的厌恶上升为对所有女人的厌恶，他的韵文变得越来越不规则，直到最后支离破碎，变为散文；至于在何处由韵文变成了散文并不明确。　120. 吃饱鲜草的（soiled）：喂饱青饲料的马就会欢蹦乱跳（lively or skittish, being fed with fresh green fodder）。　122. 禽兽（centaurs）：传说中的动物，上半身为人，下半身为马；下半身象征禽兽或兽欲。　126. 灵猫香（civet）：香水。　李尔在对格洛斯特讲话，好像他是一位药剂师。

sweeten my imagination. There's money for thee.

Gloucester   O, let me kiss that hand!

Lear   Let me wipe it first; it smells of mortality.

130 **Gloucester**   O ruined piece of nature! This great world

Shall so wear out to naught. Dost thou know me?

Lear   I remember thine eyes well enough. Dost thou

squiny at me?

No, do thy worst, blind Cupid, I'll not love.

135   Read thou this challenge, mark ᶠbutᶠ the penning of it.

Gloucester   Were all the letters suns, I could not see ᵠoneᵠ.

Edgar   [*aside*] I would not take this from report: it is,

And my heart breaks at it.

Lear   Read.

140 **Gloucester**   What? With the case of eyes?

Lear   Oh, ho, are you there with me? No eyes in your

head, nor no money in your purse? Your eyes are in a

heavy case, your purse in a light, yet you see how this

world goes.

145 **Gloucester**   I see it feelingly.

Lear   What, art mad? A man may see how this world goes

with no eyes. Look with thine ears. See how yon justice

rails upon yon simple thief. Hark in thine ear: ᶠchange

places andᶠ handy-dandy, which is the justice, which is

150   the thief? Thou hast seen a farmer's dog bark at a

beggar?

让我的想象清新一些。 这些钱给你。

格洛斯特	噢,让我亲亲那只手吧!	
李尔	先让我擦擦,上面有死人气息。	
格洛斯特	噢,毁灭了的人哪! 整个宇宙	130
	也将会化为乌有。 你认识我吗?	
李尔	我对你的眼睛记得很清。 你在用斜眼	
	看着我吗?	
	放你的肆吧,瞎丘比特,我不会爱的。	
	看看这挑战书,注意它的笔迹。	135
格洛斯特	哪怕字母是太阳,我也看不见。	
埃德加	[旁白]这若是耳闻我不会相信:是真的,	
	我的心简直碎了。	
李尔	看呀!	
格洛斯特	怎么看? 用眼窝吗?	140
李尔	噢,嗬,那是你的借口? 你头上没有	
	眼睛,你的钱包里面没钱? 你的眼伤	
	很重,你的钱包很轻,可你能看清这	
	世界如何运行。	
格洛斯特	我凭感觉看。	145
李尔	什么,你疯了? 没眼睛也能看出世界	
	如何运行。 你用耳朵看。 看那位法官	
	如何斥责那个小偷。 用耳听:让他们	
	换位,你来挑选,哪个是法官,哪个	
	是小偷? 你见过农夫的狗对乞丐汪汪	150
	大叫?	

130-1. 世界末日说在剧中出现了几次,此处为其中的一次,直到 5.3.261-2 行的"末日的表象"达到高潮。 149. 你来挑选(handy-dandy = take your choice):源于一种儿童游戏,需要对方猜出东西藏在哪只手里。

Gloucester   Ay, sir.

Lear   And the creature run from the cur—there thou

might'st behold the great image of authority: a dog's

155   obeyed in office.

Thou, rascal beadle, hold thy bloody hand;

Why dost thou lash that whore? Strip thine own back,

Thou hotly lusts to use her in that kind

For which thou whipp'st her. The usurer hangs the cozener.

160   Through tattered clothes great vices do appear;

Robes and furred gowns hide all. ^FPlate sin with gold,

And the strong lance of justice hurtless breaks;

Arm it in rags, a pigmy's straw does pierce it.

None does offend, none, I say none. I'll able 'em;

165   Take that of me, my friend, who have the power

To seal th'accuser's lips.^F Get thee glass eyes,

And like a scurvy politician seem

To see the things thou dost not. Now, ^Fnow, now, now,^F

Pull off my boots; harder, harder, so.

格洛斯特	见过，先生。
李尔	还有那个人要逃避恶狗——由此你可
	看出权威的形象多么辉煌：狗若在位，
	你也得服从。 155
	你这个流氓执事，别下毒手；
	为啥鞭打那妓女？ 要抽打自己，
	你同样渴望与她行淫，却因她
	行淫打她。 放债的绞死诈骗的。
	透过破衣烂衫瑕疵格外显眼； 160
	长袍裘皮遮盖一切。 罪披金甲，
	正义的长矛便会一触即断；
	罪罩破布，稻草可将它刺穿。
	没人犯罪，我说没人。 我授权他们；
	听我的，朋友，我有权力封住 165
	原告的嘴巴。 你配上一副眼镜，
	就像卑鄙的政客，尽管看不见，
	却假装看得见。 好，好，好，好，
	把我的鞋子脱掉，用力，用力，好。

153-5. 本段台词表明李尔自第一幕以来身上所发生的巨大转变，当时他是权威的化身（image of authority），可令人想起他对肯特的雇用，后者在李尔身上看到了"权威"（1. 4. 30），以及李尔对奥斯华德的虐待，称他为"你这狗娘养的，奴才，恶狗！（1.4.78-9）"。 157-9. 为啥……她（Why…her）：以"你们不要论断人，免得你们被论断"开头的"马太福音"7 章 1-6 节，以及耶稣对那位淫妇的赦免，构成了本段台词的基础。 见上文 109-10 及注。 159. 放债的绞死诈骗的（usurer…cozener）：参考谚语"大偷绞死小偷（The great thieves hang the little ones）"。尽管高利贷已于 1571 年变为合法，但这种资本主义行为仍属新兴，足以让放高利贷者受到人们的怀疑和仇视，并与贪婪罪相连。 164. 授权他们（able 'em）：李尔最终的这种愤世嫉俗是说："没人犯罪，因为人人犯罪，因此他授权罪人和犯人可继续犯罪（none offends, because all do, and he authorizes sinners and criminals to go on sinning）"。 165. 权力（power）：身为国王；见 107。 166. 一副眼镜（glass eyes = spectacles）：玻璃眼睛（false eyes made of glass）直到 17 世纪末期才首次被提及。 168. 好……好（now…now）：李尔是在安慰哭泣的格洛斯特，还是在关注自己所穿或想象中的靴子？

170 **Edgar**   [*aside*] O matter and impertinency mixed,

Reason in madness!

Lear   If thou wilt weep my fortunes, take my eyes.

I know thee well enough, thy name is Gloucester.

Thou must be patient. We came crying hither:

175   Thou knowst the first time that we smell the air

We wawl and cry. I will preach to thee: mark ^Qme^Q.

Gloucester   Alack, alack the day!

Lear   When we are born, we cry that we are come

To this great stage of fools. This a good block:

180   It were a delicate stratagem to shoe

A troop of horse with felt. ^FI'll put it in proof^F

And when I have stolen upon these son-in-laws,

Then kill, kill, kill, kill, kill, kill!

Enter a Gentleman [and two attendants].

Gentleman   O, here he is: lay hand upon him. Sir,

185   Your most dear ^Fdaughter—^F

Lear   No rescue? What, a prisoner? I am even

The natural fool of fortune. Use me well,

You shall have ransom. Let me have surgeons,

I am cut to the brains.

Gentleman   You shall have anything.

190 **Lear**   No seconds? All myself?

Why, this would make a man ^Fa man^F of salt,

埃德加	［*旁白*］噢,道理与胡言混合一起,	170
	疯狂中有理智!	
李尔	你若为我哭泣,把我的眼睛拿去。	
	我跟你很熟,你叫格洛斯特。	
	你要耐心。　我们哭着来到世上:	
	你知道我们初次闻到空气时	175
	哇哇哭叫。　我要向你布道:听好。	
格洛斯特	唉,多么不幸!	
李尔	我们生下来就哭,是因为来到	
	满是傻瓜的舞台。　这是个上马垫:	
	为一批战马掌上毛毡,这主意	180
	可真是巧妙。　我要试验一下,	
	当我悄悄溜到女婿的身后时,	
	然后杀,杀,杀,杀,杀,杀!	

一绅士与［两侍从］上。

绅士	噢,他在这里:抓住他。　先生,	
	您最亲爱的女儿——	185
李尔	没人营救?　我成了犯人?　我生来	
	就遭受命运捉弄。　待我好一些,	
	我给你们赎金。　快找外科医生,	
	我的头都裂了。	
绅士	您要啥都有。	
李尔	没人支援?　就我自己?	190
	唉,这会使一个人变成泪人,	

---

　180. 毛毡(felt):《亨利八世之生平》里曾提及一次马上比武,"为了避免马蹄打滑或出声,给它们装上了毛毡或棉束"(Muir)。　183. 杀……杀(kill…kill):模仿作战时的呐喊。　李尔若想象自己在带领军队复仇,可能会挥舞想象中的武器,比如用稻草当剑,或只是挥舞手臂。

To use his eyes for garden water-pots.

^QAy, and laying autumn's dust.^Q

Gentleman   Good sir.

^Q**Lear**^Q   I will die bravely, like a ^Fsmug^F bridegroom.

195   What? I will be jovial. Come, come,

I am a king, ^Qmy^Q masters, know you that?

Gentleman   You are a royal one and we obey you.

Lear   Then there's life in't. Come, an you get it,

You shall get it with running. ^FSa, sa, sa, sa.^F

Exit ^Q*running*^Q [*followed by attendants*].

200 **Gentleman**   A sight most pitiful in the meanest wretch,

Past speaking of in a king. Thou hast one daughter

Who redeems nature from the general curse

Which twain have brought her to.

Edgar   Hail, gentle sir.

Gentleman   Sir, speed you. What's your will?

Edgar   Do you hear aught,

^FSir,^F of a battle toward?

205 **Gentleman**   Most sure and vulgar.

Everyone hears that, which can distinguish sound.

Edgar   But, by your favour, how near's the other army?

Gentleman   Near, and on speedy foot. The main descry

Stands on the hourly thought.

Edgar   I thank you, sir.

把他的眼睛当作浇花的水壶。

对,喷洒秋天的灰尘。

绅士　　　　　　　　　　　好先生。

李尔　　我要像整洁的新郎,潇洒地死去。

　　　　什么？ 我会高兴的。 来,来,　　　　　　　　　195

　　　　我是国王,先生们,你们可知道？

绅士　　您是王室人员,我们服从您。

李尔　　说明还有希望。 快,要想抓住,

　　　　你们需要追赶。 萨,萨,萨,萨。

　　　　　　　　　　　　　　奔跑下［侍从跟随］。

绅士　　乞丐到这种地步都令人心疼,　　　　　　　　200

　　　　何况是位国王！ 您有个女儿,

　　　　将人性从原始的诅咒中救赎,

　　　　是那两位导致的后果。

埃德加　　　　　　　　　　您好,先生。

绅士　　保佑您,先生。 有事吗？

埃德加　　　　　　　　　　您是否听说,

　　　　先生,要发生战争？

绅士　　　　　　　　当然,都在传。　　　　　　　　　205

　　　　大家都听说了,凡是能辨音的。

埃德加　不过,请问,英军离此有多近？

绅士　　很近,正快速前行。 他们的主力

　　　　随时都会被发现。

埃德加　　　　　　　　谢谢您,先生。

198. 还有希望（there's life in't）:没有必要潇洒地死去,因为我还能逃之夭夭。 199. 萨
……萨（Sa…sa）:国王在挑战他的追赶者:“赶快！赶快！你们来抓我呀！”系古代狩猎时的呼
喊,源于法语“ça, ça”＝“there, there（那里,那里）”。 202-3. 原始……后果（general…
to）:对人性的原罪之诅咒是由亚当和夏娃造成,贡纳丽与李根可谓他们的嫡系后裔。 206. 音
（sound）:可能是指4.4,以及下文279行所能听到的战鼓声。

210   That's all.

Gentleman   Though that the queen on special cause is here,

                    Her army is moved on.

Edgar   I thank you, sir. *Exit* [*Gentleman*].

Gloucester   You ever gentle gods, take my breath from me;

                    Let not my worser spirit tempt me again

                    To die before you please.

215 **Edgar**   Well pray you, father.

Gloucester   Now, good sir, what are you?

Edgar   A most poor man, made tame to fortune's blows,

                    Who, by the art of known and feeling sorrows,

                    Am pregnant to good pity. Give me your hand;

                    I'll lead you to some biding.

220 **Gloucester**   Hearty thanks.

                    The bounty and the benison of heaven

                    To boot, and boot.

                    Enter Oswald.

Oswald   A proclaimed prize; Most happy!

                    That eyeless head of thine was first framed flesh

                    To raise my fortunes! Thou old, unhappy traitor,

225   Briefly thyself remember. The sword is out

                    That must destroy thee.

Gloucester   Now let thy friendly hand

                    Put strength enough to't.

Oswald   Wherefore, bold peasant,

	够了。	210
绅士	尽管王后因故留在了这里，	
	她的军队在挺进。	
埃德加	谢谢您，先生。　　　　　[绅士]下。	
格洛斯特	仁慈的神灵，结束我的生命；	
	别让我的坏天使再次诱我	
	自寻短见。	
埃德加	祈祷得很好，老爹。	215
格洛斯特	嗳，先生，您是谁？	
埃德加	一个可怜人，习惯了命运的打击，	
	因为他对悲伤曾感同身受，	
	易产生恻隐之心。　伸过手来；	
	我带您找个住处。	
格洛斯特	衷心的感谢。	220
	此外，愿上天回报给你慷慨的	
	祝福！	

　　　　　　　奥斯华德上。

奥斯华德	悬赏的逃犯，多么幸运！	
	你那颗没眼的脑袋生来是为	
	让我走运！你这不幸的老奸贼，	
	反省一下罪过。　剑已经出鞘，	225
	必把你刺死。	
格洛斯特	让你友好的手臂	
	用足力气。	
奥斯华德	怎么了，大胆的村夫，	

---

　　211. 因故（on special cause）：照看李尔。　222. 悬赏的（prize）：见4.5.39-41。　227-30. 怎么了……手臂（Wherefore…arm）：埃德加已在牵着父亲的手（219），所以他此刻也许会用棍棒示以威胁（237），站到父亲前面，或做出某种掩护的姿势。

Dar'st thou support a publish'd traitor? Hence,

Lest ^Fthat^F th'infection of his fortune take

230   Like hold on thee. Let go his arm.

Edgar   Ch'ill not let go, zir, without ^Fvurther^F ' cagion.

Oswald   Let go, slave, or thou diest.

Edgar   Good gentleman, go your gait ^Fand^F let poor volk

pass. And 'ch'ud ha' been zwaggered out of my life,

235   'twould not ha' been zo long ^Fas 'tis^F by a vortnight.

Nay, come not near th'old man; keep out, che vor ye, or

I'se try whether your costard or my baton be the harder.

Ch'ill be plain with you.

Oswald   Out, dunghill! [*Draws his sword.*] ^Q*They fight.*^Q

240 **Edgar**   Ch'ill pick your teeth, zir. Come, no matter vor

your foins. [*Oswald falls.*]

Oswald   Slave, thou hast slain me. Villain, take my purse.

If ever thou wilt thrive, bury my body,

And give the letters which thou find'st about me

245   To Edmund, Earl of Gloucester. Seek him out

Upon the British party: O untimely death, death! ^Q*He dies.*^Q

Edgar   I know thee well; a serviceable villain,

As duteous to the vices of thy mistress

As badness would desire.

Gloucester   What, is he dead?

250 **Edgar**   Sit you down, father; rest you. —

Let's see these pockets: the letters that he speaks of

	你敢袒护通缉的叛徒？　走开，	
	以免你会遭受和他同样的	
	厄运。　放开他的手臂。	230
埃德加	俺不会放手，先生，要没更好理由。	
奥斯华德	放手，奴才，否则你死去。	
埃德加	好先生，赶你的路吧，放俺们这穷人	
	过去。俺这条小命要是能给人家吓死，	
	这么一种情况两个星期以前就会发生。	235
	别靠近老人；走开，俺警告你，不然，	
	俺要试试你的脑瓜和这棍棒哪个更硬。	
	俺实话告诉你了。	
奥斯华德	滚开，臭屎堆。〔拔剑。〕双方打斗。	
埃德加	我要把你的牙敲掉，先生。　来，不怕	240
	你刺。〔奥斯华德倒下。〕	
奥斯华德	奴才，你杀死我了。　把钱包拿去。	
	你若想发迹，就埋葬我的尸体，	
	并把我身上携带的信件交给	
	埃德蒙，格洛斯特伯爵。　要去	245
	英军那边找他。　噢，死得太早，太早！　死去。	
埃德加	我了解你；一个殷勤的恶棍，	
	对你女主人的邪恶尽心尽责，	
	简直罪大恶极。	
格洛斯特	怎么，他死了？	
埃德加	坐下吧，老爹；休息一下。——	250
	咱看看他的衣兜：他说的信件	

231. 俺不会（Ch'ill）：实为 "Ich will（I will）的缩约"。　埃德加在用另一种口音说话，假装是英格兰西部的乡巴佬。　当时舞台上的村夫大都采用这种方言。　主要标志是，以"z"代"s"，以"v"代"f"；其中"cagion = occasion, reason"（Foakes; Bate）。　244, 251. 信件（letters）：见 4.5.35 及注。　奥斯华德除了携带贡纳丽的信件之外，也许还带着李根的信件，尽管我们未听到它的下文。

May be my friends. He's dead; I am only sorry

He had no other deathsman. Let us see:

Leave, gentle wax; and manners, blame us not.

255   To know our enemies' minds we rip their hearts,

Their papers is more lawful.

[^F*Reads the letter.*^F]   'Let   our   reciprocal   vows   be

remembered. You have many opportunities to cut him

off. If   your   will   want   not, time   and   place   will   be

260   fruitfully   offered.   There   is   nothing   done   if   he   return

the conqueror; then am I the prisoner, and his bed my

gaol, from the loathed warmth whereof, deliver me and

supply the place for your labour. Your (wife, so I would

say)   affectionate   servant   ^Qand   for   you   her   own   for

265   venture.   ^QGoneril. '

O indistinguished space of woman's will!

A plot upon her virtuous husband's life,

And the exchange my brother! Here in the sands

Thee I'll rake up, the post unsanctified

270   Of murderous lechers; and in the mature time,

With this ungracious paper strike the sight

Of the death-practised duke. For him 'tis well

That of thy death and business I can tell.

[*Exit dragging the body.*]

Gloucester   The King is mad: how stiff is my vile sense,

也许对我有益。　他死了；只可惜

处死他的就我一人。　我看看：

对不起，尊贵的封蜡；恕我无礼。

为了解敌人的心思，我们剖心，　　　　　　　　　　255

拆信就更合法了。

［读信。］"请记住我们彼此之间发过

的誓言。您会有很多机会把他给除掉。

假如您不缺乏决心，时间和地点将会

俯拾即是。假如他胜利归来，我们将　　　　　　　260

一无所获；我便成了囚犯，他的床铺

我的监牢，救我脱离那种可恶的暖窝，

您取而代之作为酬劳。您（妻子，愿

我能说）亲爱的情人，为了您她甘愿

冒险。　贡纳丽。"　　　　　　　　　　　　　265

噢，女人的欲望真是无边无际！

密谋残害她那位高尚的丈夫，

换成我的弟弟。　我把你埋在

这片沙滩，你这邪恶的信差，

属于凶残的色鬼；在适当时候，　　　　　　　270

向生命遭到暗算的公爵展示

这封邪恶的信件。　他很庆幸，

我能汇报你的死亡和使命。

　　　　　　　　　　　　　　　　　　［拖着尸体下。］

格洛斯特　　国王疯了：可恶的知觉多么顽固，

---

255. 剖心（rip their hearts）：杀死他们，或拷打他们？　257-8. 彼此……誓言（reciprocal vows）：见 4. 2. 19-25。　258. 他（him）：阿班尼（Bevington）。　260. 俯拾即是（fruitfully）：充足的（plentifully）；还可暗示性欲的满足（sexual fulfilment）（借鉴孙大雨先生译文。——译者附注）。　269. 沙滩（sands）：只有格洛斯特会以为他们还呆在海滩（beach）。埃德加这样说也许是为了父亲好，或是莎士比亚的疏忽（Muir）。

275   That I stand up and have ingenious feeling

       Of my huge sorrows? Better I were distract;

       So should my thoughts be severed from my griefs,

       And woes by wrong imaginations lose

       The knowledge of themselves. *Drum afar off.*

         Enter Edgar.

  Edgar   Give me your hand.

280   Far off methinks I hear the beaten drum.

       Come, father, I'll bestow you with a friend. *Exeunt.*

它使我依然清醒并能感知　　　　　　　　　　　275

我的巨大伤痛？　最好我也发疯；

好让我的思想与痛苦分离，

以便我能在妄想之中不再

将我的悲伤记起。　遥闻鼓声。

埃德加上。

埃德加　　　　　　　　伸过手来。

我想我能听到远处的鼓声。　　　　　　　　　　280

来，老爹，我送您去朋友那里。　　　　　　同下。

SCENE VII

Enter Cordelia, Kent [disguised] and Gentleman.

Cordelia   O thou good Kent, how shall I live and work
                  To match thy goodness? My life will be too short,
                  And every measure fail me.

Kent   To be acknowledged, madam, is o'erpaid.
5   All my reports go with the modest truth,
                  Nor more, nor clipped, but so.

Cordelia   Be better suited;
                  These weeds are memories of those worser hours.
                  I prithee put them off.

Kent   Pardon, dear madam;
                  Yet to be known shortens my made intent.
10   My boon I make it, that you know me not
                  Till time and I think meet.

Cordelia   Then be't so, my good lord. [*to the Gentleman*] How
                  does the King?

Gentleman   Madam, sleeps still.

Cordelia   O you kind gods!
15   Cure this great breach in his abused nature;

第七场

考迪丽娅、肯特［化装］与绅士上。

考迪丽娅　善良的肯特啊，我今生怎样才能
　　　　　报答您的善意？　我的一生太短，
　　　　　无论如何都会辜负。

肯特　　得到认可，夫人，就是报答过分。
　　　　　我的汇报与事实完全相符，　　　　　　　　　　5
　　　　　不多，不少，正好。

考迪丽娅　　　　　　　　换身衣服吧；
　　　　　这身衣裳是遭难时的纪念。
　　　　　求您脱掉吧。

肯特　　　　　　　　请原谅，亲爱的夫人；
　　　　　现在显露身份有违我的计划。
　　　　　求您恩准，我认为合适以前，　　　　　　　　10
　　　　　您跟我并不相识。

考迪丽娅　就这样吧，好阁下。　［向绅士］国王
　　　　　怎么样？

绅士　　还在睡，夫人。

考迪丽娅　噢，仁慈的神明！
　　　　　治愈他这种饱受创伤的心灵；　　　　　　　　15

4.7.　0（1）考迪丽娅……上：正如考迪丽娅在4.4那样（对开本），也许会展示武器和彩旗、法国军旗或标志，好让李尔以为他身在那里（76），尽管她不再有士兵相伴。　另外，对开本里以"绅士（Gentleman）"替代了四开本里叫来的"医生（Doctor）"，以此减少一位角色。　该绅士也许正是在3.1照看李尔和4.4陪伴考迪丽娅的那位。　5.汇报（reports）：关于李尔和他本人扮作仆人的情况（Muir）。

Th'untuned and jarring senses, O, wind up

Of this child-changed father!

Gentleman   So please your majesty,

That we may wake the King? He hath slept long.

Cordelia   Be governed by your knowledge and proceed

20   I'the sway of your own will. Is he arrayed?

^F*Enter Lear in a chair carried by servants.*^F

Gentleman   Ay, madam. In the heaviness of his sleep

We put fresh garments on him.

Be by, good madam, when we do awake him.

I doubt ^Qnot^Q of his temperance.

^Q**Cordelia**   Very well.

25 **Gentleman**   Please you draw near; louder the music there.^Q

Cordelia   O my dear father, restoration hang

Thy medicine on my lips, and let this kiss

Repair those violent harms that my two sisters

Have in thy reverence made.

Kent   Kind and dear princess!

30 **Cordelia**   Had you not been their father, these white flakes

Had challenged pity of them. Was this a face

To be opposed against the warring winds?

^QTo stand against the deep dread-bolted thunder,

In the most terrible and nimble stroke

35   Of quick, cross lightning? To watch, poor perdu,

With this thin helm?^Q Mine enemy's dog

噢,调好这位孩子般的父亲,

他已经神经错乱!

绅士　　　　　　　　　恳请陛下,

能否把国王叫醒?　他睡了很久。

考迪丽娅　要遵照您的意见,您若觉得

合适,怎么做都行。　他换了衣服?　　　　　　　　20

李尔坐椅内,由仆人抬上。

绅士　　是的,夫人。　趁他熟睡的时候

我们给他穿上了新衣。

靠近,好夫人,我们要叫醒他了。

他的神志不用怀疑。

考迪丽娅　　　　　　　　　很好。

绅士　　请您靠近;音乐再响亮一些。　　　　　　　25

考迪丽娅　噢,亲爱的父亲,但愿我的

嘴唇能传递疗效,让这一吻

修复那两位姐姐对可敬的你

造成的剧烈伤害!

肯特　　　　　　　　　仁慈的公主!

考迪丽娅　即使您不是她们生父,这头白发　　　　　30

也会叫她们同情。　难道这张脸

可以迎击那种敌对的狂风?

承受那种低沉而可怕的雷霆,

待在最为可怕和迅速分叉的

闪电之间?　可怜的哨兵,用这么　　　　　　　35

单薄的头盔值夜?　敌人的狗,

---

16. 调好（wind up = put in tune）:好像将弦乐器上用以调节弦线松紧的弦轴拉紧。　孩子般的（child-changed）:可有两种解释:被变成孩子的（changed to a child）;被孩子的无情逼疯的（changed in mind by the cruelty of his children）（Muir）。　36. 头盔（helm）:头罩（covering）,或头发（helmet〔of hair〕）。

Though he had bit me should have stood that night

Against my fire; and wast thou fain, poor father,

To hovel thee with swine and rogues forlorn

40   In short and musty straw? Alack, alack!

'Tis wonder that thy life and wits at once

Had not concluded all. He wakes; speak to him.

Gentleman   Madam, do you; 'tis fittest.

Cordelia   How does my royal lord? How fares your majesty?

45   **Lear**   You do me wrong to take me out o'the grave.

Thou art a soul in bliss, but I am bound

Upon a wheel of fire that mine own tears

Do scald like molten lead.

Cordelia   Sir, ^Fdo you^F know me?

Lear   You are a spirit, I know; when did you die?

50   **Cordelia**   Still, still far wide.

Gentleman   He's scarce awake; let him alone awhile.

Lear   Where have I been? Where am I? Fair daylight?

I am mightily abused. I should e'en die with pity

To see another thus. I know not what to say.

55   I will not swear these are my hands: let's see—

I feel this pinprick. Would I were assured

尽管撕咬过我,那一晚也会

站在我炉边;您却要,可怜的父亲,

跟野猪和可怜的乞丐合住茅屋,

在零碎和发霉的稻草里?　唉!唉!　　　　　　40

您的生命没和神志同时终结

是一种奇迹。　他醒了,对他说话。

绅士　　　　　夫人,您说;最为合适。

考迪丽娅　　　我的父王好吗?　陛下您怎样?

李尔　　　　　您不该把我从墓里拖了出来。　　　　　45

你的灵魂在天堂,而我却被

绑在了火轮,自己的眼泪就像

熔化的铅水滚烫。

考迪丽娅　　　　　　陛下,认识我吗?

李尔　　　　　您是个精灵,我懂;您死在何处?

考迪丽娅　　　依然,依然离谱。　　　　　　　　　50

绅士　　　　　他尚未清醒;让他单独待会儿。

李尔　　　　　我去过哪里?　这是哪里?　已是白天?

我深受欺骗。　若看到别人这样,

我定会同情死的。　不知该说什么。

不敢相信这是我双手:我看看——　　　　　55

我能感受到刺疼。　愿我清楚

---

44. 在这最为动人的相认一场中,值得注意的是,考迪丽娅将父亲称为国王,因为她入侵英格兰的目的就是想恢复父亲的权利(4.4.28)。　45. 李尔,跟格洛斯特一样,也想死去;两人都经过了想象中的死亡之后得以复生,而且对随之而来的痛苦几乎难以承受。　46-7. 灵魂……火轮(soul…fire):李尔在想象考迪丽娅已进入基督教信仰中的天堂,而他却被罚入地狱,正在遭受某种折磨。　该形象令人想起希腊神话中的伊克西翁(Ixion),因为引诱天后(Juno)而遭受朱庇特惩罚,被绑在地狱里的轮子上,旋转不止。　55-6. 我……刺疼(Let's…pinprick):李尔此刻也许会用服饰上的胸针或其他饰品在身上测试一下。

Of my condition!

Cordelia   [*Kneels.*]   O look upon me, sir,

And hold your hands in benediction o'er me!

[*She restrains him as he tries to kneel.*]

ᵠNo, sir,ᵠ you must not kneel.

Lear   Pray do not mock ᶠmeᶠ.

60   I am a very foolish, fond old man,

Fourscore and upward, ᶠnot an hour more nor less;ᶠ

And to deal plainly,

I fear I am not in my perfect mind.

Methinks I should know you and know this man,

65   Yet I am doubtful; for I am mainly ignorant

What place this is and all the skill I have

Remembers not these garments; nor I know not

Where I did lodge last night. Do not laugh at me,

For, as I am a man, I think this lady

To be my child Cordelia.

70 **Cordelia**   And so I am, ᶠI amᶠ.

Lear   Be your tears wet? Yes, faith; I pray, weep not.

If you have poison for me, I will drink it.

I know you do not love me, for your sisters

Have, as I do remember, done me wrong.

You have some cause, they have not.

自己的情形!

考迪丽娅　［跪下。］噢,看看我吧,父亲,

请您用手按住我为我祝福!

［他试图下跪,她予以阻止。］

不,父亲,您别跪下。

李尔　　　　　　　　　　　请不要笑我。

我是个非常愚蠢昏聩的老人,　　　　　　　　　60

已经八十多岁,不多也不少;

坦率地说,

我担心自己的神志不是很清。

我想我该认识您以及此人,

可我不敢确信;我全然不知　　　　　　　　　65

这是哪里,无论如何我也

记不起这身衣服;也不清楚

昨晚住在了何处。　请别笑我,

因为,说真的,我想这位夫人

是我的孩子考迪丽娅。

考迪丽娅　　　　　　　　是的,是的!　　　　　　70

李尔　您的泪是湿的?　是的;求您别哭。

您要是给我毒药,我也会喝的。

我知道您不爱我,因为您姐姐,

根据我的记忆,曾虐待过我。

您有理由,她们没有。

57-8.　（舞台指示）跪下……下跪（*Kneels…kneel*）:对开本和四开本里均无该舞台指示,但此处的台词表明李尔试图从椅子上起身,导致考迪丽娅跪下并请求他的祝福,李尔随后又试图向她下跪。　可令人历历在目的是,李尔出于嘲弄曾向李根下跪（2.2.343）。　……但此处的下跪却富有意义而且感人,这不仅是他们相互宽恕的标志,而且也因为这可表明他们就像"墓碑上的肖像,相互面对,举起双手进入永恒的祈祷"。　64.　此人（this man）:可能是肯特,因为他在76行曾对李尔讲话。　70.　是的,是的（I am, I am）:第二个"是的"为对开本所添加,系格外音节,但好像是有意的扩展,以表达考迪丽娅的爱心,同时也可预示她在75行的重复。

75	**Cordelia**	No cause, no cause.
	Lear	Am I in France?
	Kent	In your own kingdom, sir.
	Lear	Do not abuse me.
	Gentleman	Be comforted, good madam, the great rage
		You see is killed in him, ᵠand yet it is danger
80		To make him even o'er the time he has lost.ᵠ
		Desire him to go in. Trouble him no more
		Till further settling.
	Cordelia	Will't please your highness walk?
	Lear	You must bear with me. Pray ᶠyouᶠ now, forget and
		forgive; I am old and foolish.

Exeunt. ᵠ*Kent and the Gentleman remain.*ᵠ

85	ᵠ**Gentleman**	Holds it true, sir, that the Duke of Cornwall was
		so slain?
	Kent	Most certain, sir.
	Gentleman	Who is conductor of his people?
	Kent	As 'tis said, the bastard son of Gloucester.
90	**Gentleman**	They say Edgar his banished son is with the
		Earl of Kent in Germany.
	Kent	Report is changeable; 'tis time to look about. The
		powers of the kingdom approach apace.
	Gentleman	The arbitrement is like to be bloody. Fare
95		you well, sir. *Exit.*
	Kent	My point and period will be throughly wrought,
		Or well or ill as this day's battle's fought. *Exit.*ᵠ

考迪丽娅	没有,没有。	75
李尔	我在法国?	
肯特	在您自己的国度,陛下。	
李尔	不要骗我。	
绅士	放心吧,好夫人,那种疯癫,您看,	
	已在他身上消失,然而要让他	
	连贯地追忆往事却很危险。	80
	请他进去吧。　他更为平静以前,	
	别再打扰他了。	
考迪丽娅	陛下进屋好吗?	
李尔	您必须容忍我。现在求您,忘记并且	
	宽恕;我老了,也傻了。	
	除肯特与绅士外,全下。	
绅士	您信吗,先生,康瓦尔公爵那样被人	85
	刺死?	
肯特	千真万确,先生。	
绅士	谁在率领他的民众?	
肯特	据说是,格洛斯特的私生子。	
绅士	人们说他遭流放的儿子埃德加与肯特	90
	现在德国。	
肯特	传言容易改变;现在该察看一下局势。	
	英国的军队很快就到。	
绅士	决定性的战斗可能会非常惨烈。再会	
	吧,先生。	下。 95
肯特	人生的高潮和结局即将来临,	
	是好是坏这一战即可区分。	下。

83-4. 求您……宽恕(Pray…forgive):在对开本里,本场由此结束,由李尔做出一种普遍的恳求,也许不只是恳求考迪丽娅,而是恳求大家忘记并宽恕过去的恐怖。　但尤其令人心酸的是,考迪丽娅却不能忘怀,而是坚持试图通过武力让他恢复王位。

第五幕
ACT 5

SCENE   I

Enter ^F*with drum and colours*^F *Edmund, Regan, gentlemen*
and soldiers.

Edmund	[*to a Gentleman*] Know of the Duke if his last purpose hold,
	Or whether since he is advised by aught
	To change the course. He's full of alteration
	And self-reproving. Bring his constant pleasure.

[*Exit gentleman.*]

5   **Regan**   Our sister's man is certainly miscarried.

Edmund   'Tis to be doubted, madam.

Regan   Now, sweet lord,

You know the goodness I intend upon you:

Tell me but truly, but then speak the truth,

Do you not love my sister?

Edmund   In honoured love.

10   **Regan**   But have you never found my brother's way

To the forfended place?

^Q**Edmund**   That thought abuses you.

Regan   I am doubtful that you have been conjunct

第一场

鼓手与旗手、埃德蒙、李根、众绅士
与士兵上。

埃德蒙	［向一绅士］去查明公爵是否还坚持原意，
	还是他最近受到什么劝诱
	改变了行程。 他这人反复无常，
	轻易自责。 把他的决定报给我。

［绅士下。］

李根　　　姐姐的仆人一定受到了伤害。　　　　　　　　　　5
埃德蒙　　恐怕是的，夫人。
李根　　　　　　　嗳，亲爱的阁下，
　　　　　您知道我对您怀有一片好意：
　　　　　告诉我真话，哪怕真话逆耳，
　　　　　您不爱我的姐姐？
埃德蒙　　　　　　　是体面之爱。
李根　　　难道您从未侵入过我姐夫的　　　　　　　　　　　10
　　　　　那块禁地？
埃德蒙　　　　　那想法让您丢脸。
李根　　　我担心您已和她连成一体，

5.1. 0（1）本场的地点应在多佛附近。 1. 公爵……原意（Duke…hold）：阿班尼在4.2
终场时像是三心二意，但到了4.3（对开本），他的军队已经出发（50），在4.4.21和4.6.205-9又
传来新的报告说英军正快速行进；因此他的"原意（last purpose）"是应战（to fight）。 5. 仆
人（man）：管家奥斯华德，于4.6.246被埃德加打死。 8. 哪怕真话逆耳（but then）：原注为
"even if the truth is unpalatable to me"（Muir）。 11. 那块禁地（forfended place）：被禁止
的床铺或（贡纳丽的）身体（forbidden bed or body of ［Goneril］）。 李根出于嫉妒，怀疑埃德
蒙通奸，但不无道理；见4.2.19-28和4.5.25-8。 12-3. 连成一体……极限（conjunct…hers）：
原注为"coupled with and intimate with her, to the fullest extent"。 李根想象埃德蒙占有了贡
纳丽自称所拥有的一切，但这并未削弱她对埃德蒙的欲望，而是加深了她对姐姐的敌意。

And bosomed with her, as far as we call hers.^Q

Edmund   No, by mine honour, madam.

15 **Regan**   I never shall endure her. Dear my lord,

Be not familiar with her.

Edmund   Fear ^Qme^Q not—

Enter ^Fwith drum and colours^F Albany, Goneril, [and] soldiers.

She and the Duke her husband.

^Q**Goneril**   [*aside*] I had rather lose the battle than that sister

Should loosen him and me.^Q

20 **Albany**   Our very loving sister, well be-met.

Sir, this I hear: the King is come to his daughter,

With others whom the rigour of our state

Forced to cry out. ^QWhere I could not be honest,

I never yet was valiant. For this business,

25   It touches us as France invades our land,

Not bolds the King, with others whom I fear

Most just and heavy causes make oppose.

Edmund   Sir, you speak nobly.^Q

Regan   Why is this reasoned?

Goneril   Combine together 'gainst the enemy,

30   For these domestic and particular broils

Are not the question here.

Albany   Let's then determine with the ancient of war on

our proceeding.

^Q**Edmund**   I shall attend you presently at your tent.^Q   *Exit.*

亲密无间,已经到了极限。

埃德蒙	没有,以名誉担保,夫人。
李根	我不会容忍她的。 亲爱的阁下,	15
	不要跟她亲近。
埃德蒙	不用担心——

鼓手与旗手、阿班尼、贡纳丽、[与]士兵上。

她和她的公爵丈夫!

贡纳丽	[旁白]我宁愿这次战败,也不愿妹妹
	把他和我分开。
阿班尼	非常可爱的妹妹,真是幸会。	20
	先生,我听说:国王,和那些被我国
	苛政逼得怨声四起的人,去了
	女儿那里。 我觉得不光彩的事情,
	决不会奋勇。 至于这件事情,
	只因法王侵犯了我们的领土,	25
	并非因为他鼓动国王和迫于
	真正的冤屈揭竿而起的人们。
埃德蒙	先生,说得在理。
李根	为何谈论这些?
贡纳丽	我们要团结一致共同对敌,
	因为这些内部和私下的争吵	30
	与此毫无关系。
阿班尼	那我们就和久经沙场的将领一起商讨
	如何行动。
埃德蒙	我马上去您的帐篷与您会面。 下。

16 (1) 旗手(*colours*):可能举着表明英国徽章的彩旗,比如狮子图案。 17. 她……丈夫 (She…husband):不太清楚埃德蒙是看到了贡纳丽和阿班尼的到来,还是正要谈论他们时 被打断。

35 **Regan**   Sister, you'll go with us?

   Goneril   No.

   Regan   'Tis most convenient; pray ^Qyou^Q go with us.

   Goneril   O ho, I know the riddle. I will go.

                  Exeunt [*Edmund, Regan, Goneril and*] ^F*both the armies.*^F

[*As Albany is leaving,*] *enter Edgar* [*in peasant's clothing*].

   Edgar   If e'er your grace had speech with man so poor,

                  Hear me one word.

   Albany   [*to his soldiers*]   I'll overtake you.

40   [*to Edgar*]   Speak.

   Edgar   Before you fight the battle, ope this letter.

                  If you have victory, let the trumpet sound

                  For him that brought it. Wretched though I seem,

                  I can produce a champion that will prove

45   What is avouched there. If you miscarry,

                  Your business of the world hath so an end

                  ^FAnd machination ceases.^F Fortune love you.

   Albany   Stay till I have read the letter.

   Edgar   I was forbid it.

                  When time shall serve, let but the herald cry

50   And I'll appear again.   *Exit.*

   Albany   Why, fare thee well. I will o'erlook thy paper.

李根	姐姐，您跟我走吧？	35
贡纳丽	不。	
李根	这样最好；请跟我一起走吧。	
贡纳丽	噢嗬，我明白其中的把戏。 我会的。	

　　　　　　　　　　　　〔埃德蒙、李根、贡纳丽与〕双方士兵下。

　　　　　〔阿班尼要离开时，〕埃德加〔扮作村夫〕上。

埃德加	若殿下愿跟我这种穷人说话，	
	请听我一言。	
阿班尼	〔向士兵〕　你们先走。	
	〔向埃德加〕　　　　　说吧。	40
埃德加	您参战以前，打开这封信件。	
	您若能获胜，那就吹响号角	
	把我召唤。 尽管我看似可怜，	
	我可以引来一位斗士证实	
	里面的断言。 您若战败身亡，	45
	您在尘世的事情就此结束，	
	阴谋自然终止。 祝您好运！	
阿班尼	等我看完信再走。	
埃德加	不许我如此。	
	等时候一到，可让传令官鸣号，	
	我会再次出现。	下。 50
阿班尼	那就再会。 我会细看你的信件。	

　　35-8. 姐姐……我会的（Sister…go）：姐妹俩此处的争斗为她们在5.3的彻底决裂做好了铺垫。 李根大概想跟埃德蒙待在一起并监视贡纳丽；而贡纳丽最初想跟埃德蒙谈话，但当她明白了李根的把戏（riddle）并意识到李根知道了她的意图之后，便改变了主意。 李根在35行与37行的"跟我走吧（go with us）"好像采用了表示君王称谓的复数形式。 41. 信件（letter）：从奥斯华德身上发现的那一封；见4.6.257-65。

Enter Edmund.

Edmund   The enemy's in view; draw up your powers.

[*Hand him a note.*] Here is the guess of their true

strength and forces,

By diligent discovery; but your haste

Is now urged on you.

55 **Albany**   We will greet the time.   *Exit.*

Edmund   To both these sisters have I sworn my love,

Each jealous of the other as the stung

Are of the adder. Which of them shall I take?

Both? One? Or neither? Neither can be enjoyed

60   If both remain alive. To take the widow

Exasperates, makes mad her sister Goneril,

And hardly shall I carry out my side,

Her husband being alive. Now then, we'll use

His countenance for the battle, which being done,

65   Let her who would be rid of him devise

His speedy taking off. As for the mercy

Which he intends to Lear and to Cordelia,

The battle done, and they within our power,

Shall never see his pardon; for my state

70   Stands on me to defend, not to debate.   *Exit.*

埃德蒙上。

埃德蒙	敌军已进入视线；快集合军队。	
	［呈上一便条］这是他们大致的	
	兵力和武器，	
	由细心的侦探获取；但您现在	
	需要抓紧。	
阿班尼	我会及时行动。	下。 55
埃德蒙	对姊妹两个我都曾海誓山盟，	
	她们彼此猜忌像被蛇咬过	
	而警惕毒蛇。 我要其中的哪个？	
	都要，要一个，都不要？ 若都活着，	
	一个也享用不到。 要那位寡妇	60
	会把她姐姐贡纳丽气疯惹恼，	
	我对她许下的诺言很难兑现，	
	假如她丈夫活着。 那好，要利用	
	他的威望获胜，等战争结束，	
	让那位想除掉他的女人设法	65
	尽快把他除掉。 至于他想对	
	李尔考迪丽娅所表达的怜悯，	
	战争一结束，他们由我们掌控，	
	别想得到他的赦免。 我的处境	
	需要我采取行动，而不是论争。	下。 70

---

55. 我会及时行动（We…time）：阿班尼在使用表示君王称谓的复数形式，如果他已看过埃德加呈上的信件，这也许是对埃德蒙的故意冷落；见 5.3.61。 56-70. 埃德蒙在剧中的最后一次独白，表明他几乎是在铤而走险（near-desperation）；见 1.2 及注。

SCENE II

Alarum ^Fwithin^F. Enter ^Fwith drum and colours^F Lear, Cordelia
and soldiers, [they pass] over the stage ^Fand exeunt.^F
Enter Edgar [in peasant's clothing] and Gloucester.

Edgar   Here, father, take the shadow of this tree

     For your good host. Pray that the right may thrive.

     If ever I return to you again,

     I'll bring you comfort.

Gloucester   Grace go with you, sir. *Exit [Edgar].*

Alarum and retreat ^Fwithin. Enter Edgar.

5 **Edgar**   Away, old man, give me thy hand, away!

     King Lear hath lost, he and his daughter ta'en.

     Give me thy hand; come on!

Gloucester No further, sir; a man may rot even here.

第二场

幕后号角。鼓手与旗手、李尔、考迪丽娅

与士兵上，[他们行进]穿过舞台，然后退场。

埃德加[扮作村夫]与格洛斯特上。

埃德加	来，老爹，在这棵好客的树荫下

躲避片刻。 祈祷正义之师获胜。

假如我能再次回到您的身边，

会有好消息相报。

格洛斯特　　　　　　祝您好运，先生！[埃德加]下。

幕后鸣进军号和退兵号。埃德加上。

埃德加　　快走，老人，伸过手来，快走！　　　　　　　5

李尔王败了，他和他女儿被俘。

伸过手来；赶快！

格洛斯特　　不用了，先生；在这里死去很好。

5.2.   0（1-2）幕后……退场（*Alarum…exeunt*）：对开本里要求展示一下法国的彩旗、军旗或徽章，以便跟5.1展示的英军军旗相称。 对开本和四开本均要求演员们从舞台上穿过，显然是以队列的方式行进；至于他们如何穿过舞台——从一扇门里入场，然后从另一扇门里退场，或沿着舞台周边行进，或以其他方式进行——并不清楚。 埃德加仍是4.6时的装扮。 3-4. 假如……相报（If…comfort）：戏剧性反讽（dramatic irony）（Muir）。 4（1）幕后……退兵号（*Alarum…within*）：吹过进军号之后接着吹退兵号；战争场面可以听得见，但看不见，且很快结束；视觉的焦点落到了双目失明的格洛斯特身上，他独自一人待在舞台。 莎士比亚避免在此展示战争的场面，将重点放在了下一场埃德加与埃德蒙之间的决斗。

Edgar   What, in ill thoughts again? Men must endure

10   Their going hence even as their coming hither.

          Ripeness is all. Come on.

^F Gloucester   And that's true too.   *Exeunt.*^F

埃德加	怎么,又意志消沉？ 人们要忍受		
	死亡正像他们要忍受降生一样。		10
	准备好就是了。 赶快。		
格洛斯特	言之有理。	同下。	

9-10. 人们……一样(a man…hither)：将生与死联系起来可令人想起《圣经》里的话语,如"提摩太前书"6章7节：因为我们没有带什么到世上来,也不能带什么去。 11. 准备好就是了(Ripeness is all)：本句是否可理解为："我们必须为死亡做好准备(we must be ready for death)"；或是"上天或神明掌管着我们的生存并决定何时才能成熟(when the time is ripe)"；或是"我们必须等待成熟的时间,即'注定要死去的时间'"。 该句在一定程度上可令人想起《圣经》"传道书"3章1-8节的内容,起句是"凡事都有定期"。 该句也许会令人意识到哈姆雷特的"做好准备是关键(The readiness is all [5.2.218])",但哈姆雷特是在面临死亡威胁时对自己说的上述话语,而埃德加此处的言论好像可以针对任何人。

SCENE III

Enter ^F*in conquest with drum and colours*^F *Edmund,* [*with*] *Lear*
and Cordelia as prisoners; ^F*soldiers* [*and a*] *Captain.*^F

Edmund Some officers take them away—good guard,

   Until their greater pleasures first be known

   That are to censure them.

Cordelia   We are not the first

   Who with best meaning have incurred the worst.

5   For thee, oppressed King, I am cast down;

   Myself could else outfrown false fortune's frown.

   Shall we not see these daughters and these sisters?

Lear No, no, ^Fno, no^F. Come, let's away to prison;

   We two alone will sing like birds i'the cage.

10   When thou dost ask me blessing, I'll kneel down

   And ask of thee forgiveness. So we'll live

   And pray, and sing, and tell old tales, and laugh

   At gilded butterflies, and hear poor rogues

   Talk of court news; and we'll talk with them too—

15   Who loses and who wins, who's in, who's out—

第三场

　　旗手与鼓手、埃德蒙凯旋上，[与]被俘的李尔
　　和考迪丽娅；士兵[与一]营长上。

埃德蒙　　来几个军官把他们带走——看好，

　　　　直到获悉上头是什么意思，

　　　　他们有权宣判。

考迪丽娅　　　　　　　我们并非首例，

　　　　最好的动机导致了最坏的结局。

　　　　为了你，受难的国王，我才会忧伤；　　　　　　　　5

　　　　否则我会蔑视厄运的狂妄。

　　　　我们不见见这些女儿和姐姐？

李尔　　不，不，不，不。　快，咱们去坐牢；

　　　　我们俩要像笼中鸟那样歌唱。

　　　　当你叫我祝福时，我就会跪下　　　　　　　　10

　　　　请求你宽恕。　我们就那样生活，

　　　　祷告，唱歌，讲些故事，嘲笑

　　　　那些浮华的侍臣，听那些可怜人

　　　　议论朝政；我们也跟他们议论——

　　　　谁输和谁赢，谁得势，谁失宠——　　　　　　　　15

　　5.3.　　2-3. 上头……宣判（greater…them）：在公开场合以及阿班尼的士兵（104）面前，埃德蒙遵从（比他更高大的［greater，该词属于移就用法，修饰］）阿班尼、贡纳丽和李根的决定，因为他们有权对犯人进行宣判。　他的个人意图出现于 27 行。　10-11. 当……宽恕（When…forgiveness）：可令人想起 4.7.57-9 时的场景。　13. 可怜人（poor rogues）：可能指他们的狱友或狱卒（Muir）。

And take upon's the mystery of things,

As if we were God's spies. And we'll wear out

In a walled prison packs and sects of great ones

That ebb and flow by the moon.

Edmund   [*to soldiers*]   Take them away.

20 **Lear**   Upon such sacrifices, my Cordelia,

The gods themselves throw incense. Have I caught thee?

[*Embraces her.*]

He that parts us shall bring a brand from heaven,

And fire us hence like foxes. Wipe thine eyes;

The good ^Fyears^F shall devour them, flesh and fell,

25   Ere they shall make us weep!

We'll see 'em starve first: Come.

^F*Exeunt*^F [*Lear and Cordelia, guarded*].

Edmund   Come hither, captain; hark:

Take thou this note. Go follow them to prison.

One step I have advanced thee. If thou dost

30   As this instructs thee, thou dost make thy way

To noble fortunes. Know thou this, that men

Are as the time is; to be tender-minded

Does not become a sword. Thy great employment

Will not bear question: either say thou'lt do't,

Or thrive by other means.

声称我们了解世间的隐秘，

好像是神的密探。　要在囚牢里

活过那些拉帮结派的大人物，

他们潮汐般沉浮。

埃德蒙　　　［向士兵］　　　　把他们带走。

李尔　　　对这样的牺牲，我的考迪丽娅，　　　　　　　　　　20

神明都会焚香。　我抱住你了？

［拥抱她。］

想把咱分开，要用天上的火把

熏狐狸一般把我们驱散。　擦擦眼；

时光会吞噬她们，连皮带肉，

在此之前我们不哭！　　　　　　　　　　　　　　　　25

咱要看她们首先饿死：快走。

［李尔与考迪丽娅，被押送］下。

埃德蒙　　　你过来，营长，听好：

拿上这纸条。　去，跟他们到监狱。

我已提拔你一级。　你若能按

纸条的指示照办，那你就会　　　　　　　　　　　　30

财运亨通。　你要知道，人们

应该随机应变；一名军人

不适合心慈手软。　这一重任

不允许争辩：要么你说会做，

要么另找出路。

---

17. 密探（spies）：被派下来的天使，负责观察和汇报人们的生存状况（Muir）。　20. 牺牲（sacrifices）：该词像是预示了考迪丽娅本身的牺牲，但更为明显地是指她试图为了拯救父亲所做出的牺牲，以及他们父女两人的失去自由。　行善作为一种献祭的观念也许可令人想起《圣经》"希伯来书"13章16节："只是不可忘记行善和捐输的事，因为这样的祭是神所喜悦的。"22-3. 想把……驱散（He…foxes）：意为"人的力量绝不会再把我们分开"。　该意象是指用烟把狐狸熏出洞来。

35	**CAPTAIN**	I'll do't, my lord.
	Edmund	About it and write 'happy' when thou'st done't.

Mark, I say, instantly; and carry it so

As I have set it down.

 ^Q**CAPTAIN**   I cannot draw a cart, nor eat dried oats.

40   If it be man's work, I'll do't.^Q   ^F*Exit.*^F

^F*Flourish.*^F *Enter Albany, Goneril, Regan* [*and*]
soldiers [*with a Trumpeter*].

Albany   Sir, you have shown today your valiant strain

And fortune led you well. You have the captives

That were the opposites of this day's strife:

I do require them of you, so to use them

45   As we shall find their merits and our safety

May equally determine.

Edmund   Sir, I thought it fit

To send the old and miserable King

To some retention ^Qand appointed guard,^Q

Whose age has charms in it, whose title more,

50   To pluck the common bosom on his side,

And turn our impressed lances in our eyes

Which do command them. With him I sent the queen,

My reason all the same; and they are ready

Tomorrow, or at further space, t'appear

| 营长 | 我会做的，大人。 | 35 |

埃德蒙　　行动吧，事成之后会感到庆幸。

注意，我说，立即；你要按照

我所说的执行。

营长　　我不是牲口，也不吃干的饲料。

要是人的活儿，我就做。　　　　　　　　　下。 40

号角齐鸣。阿班尼、贡纳丽、李根〔与〕

士兵〔及一小号手〕上。

阿班尼　　先生，您今天表现出英勇品性，

也受到命运的眷顾。　您已将今天

这场战斗中的对手俘获：

我要您交出他们，以便我能

按照他们的功过和国家安全　　　　　　　　45

做出正确的决断。

埃德蒙　　　　　　　　先生，我酌情

已把年迈可怜的国王送到

某处关押起来并派人看守，

他的年纪和头衔富有感召力，

会令普通的大众表示同情，　　　　　　　　50

促使我们强征入伍的士兵

反戈一击。　基于同样的理由，

也已把王后送去，他们会随时，

明天，或者晚些时候，出现在

---

39. 我……饲料（I…oats）：我不是马（I'm not a horse）；战后我不想因迫不得已而成为一名农夫（I don't want to be driven by necessity after the war to become an agricultural labourer）（Muir）。　51-2. 促使……一击（turn…them）：原注为 "turn the weapons of our enlisted soldiers against ourselves"。　Impressed = compelled to serve（强制服役的）。

55   Where you shall hold your session. ᵠAt this time

We sweat and bleed; the friend hath lost his friend,

And the best quarrels in the heat are cursed

By those that feel their sharpness.

The question of Cordelia and her father

Requires a fitter place.ᵠ

60 **Albany**   Sir, by your patience,

I hold you but a subject of this war,

Not as a brother.

Regan   That's as we list to grace him.

Methinks our pleasure might have been demanded

Ere you had spoke so far. He led our powers,

65   Bore the commission of my place and person,

The which immediacy may well stand up

And call itself your brother.

Goneril   Not so hot!

In his own grace he doth exalt himself

More than in your addition.

Regan   In my rights,

70   By me invested, he compeers the best.

Albany   That were the most, if he should husband you.

	您想进行审讯的地点。　此刻	55
	我们在流血流汗；亲友失散，	
	再好的理由，也会被情绪激动	
	饱受战争创伤的人诅咒。	
	考迪丽娅和她父亲的事情，	
	需要更合适的场合。	
阿班尼	请原谅，先生，	60
	我把您视为本场战争的下属，	
	并非同等。	
李根	那要看我如何待他。	
	我想您口出此言之前应该	
	询问我的意愿。　他率领我军，	
	拥有我的地位和我的权威，	65
	这样的亲密关系完全可使他	
	与您称兄道弟。	
贡纳丽	别这么着急！	
	他凭借自身的能力出类拔萃，	
	胜过你给的封号。	
李根	有我的权利，	
	我的权威，他能跟至高者匹敌。	70
阿班尼	那最好是，他能够娶你为妻。	

55-60. 此刻……场合（At…place）：埃德蒙在对阿班尼撒谎；他在本场台词中的傲慢语气表明他在剧中的成功已达到了顶峰。　57. 情绪激动（in the heat）：情绪冷静之前（before passion has cooled）。　埃德蒙在暗示李尔和考迪丽娅在这种情况下很难得到公正的审判（Muir）。　埃德蒙在拖延时间，以确保李尔和考迪丽娅遭到处决，同时假装他们可以得到一个公正的审判（Foakes）。　62，67. 同等（brother = equal）：也有"襟弟（brother-in-law）"之义，如4.2.15，4.5.1。　62. 看我如何（we list）：我的选择（I choose）。　李根在使用表示君王称谓的复数形式，以此申明自己对阿班尼的权威。

Regan   Jesters do oft prove prophets.

Goneril   Holla, holla!

That eye that told you so looked but asquint.

Regan   Lady, I am not well, else I should answer

75   From a full-flowing stomach. [*to Edmund*] General,

Take thou my soldiers, prisoners, patrimony;

ᶠDispose of them, of me, the walls is thine.ᶠ

Witness the world, that I create thee here

My lord and master.

Goneril   Mean you to enjoy him ᵠthenᵠ?

80 **Albany**   The let-alone lies not in your good will.

Edmund   Nor in thine, lord.

Albany   Half-blooded fellow, yes.

Regan   [*to Edmund*] Let the drum strike and prove my title thine.

Albany   Stay yet, hear reason: Edmund, I arrest thee

On capital treason, and in thine attaint

This gilded serpent. [*Points to Goneril.*]

85   [*to Regan*]   For your claim, fair sister,

I bar it in the interest of my wife:

'Tis she is sub-contracted to this lord,

And I, her husband, contradict your banns:

If you will marry, make your love to me;

My lady is bespoke.

90 ᶠ**Goneril**   An interlude!

李根	戏言常变成预言。	
贡纳丽	够啦，够啦！	
	您说此话时眼睛有些乜斜。	
李根	夫人，我不舒服，否则我会	
	满腔怒火予以回击。［向埃德蒙］将军，	75
	你收下我的士兵、囚犯、财产；	
	他们，我本人，全部由你掌管。	
	让世界见证，现在我使你成为	
	我的夫君和主人。	
贡纳丽	您想享用他了？	
阿班尼	准许与否你没有权力干涉。	80
埃德蒙	你也没有，大人。	
阿班尼	杂种，我有。	
李根	［向埃德蒙］让锣鼓宣告我的就是你的。	
阿班尼	等一等，你听好：埃德蒙，我以叛国	
	死罪将你逮捕，还有你的同谋	
	这条花蛇。［指向贡纳丽］	
	［向李根］至于您的要求，贤妹，	85
	为了我妻子的利益要加以中止：	
	她已把自己转包给这位爵士，	
	我作为她丈夫否决您的婚誓：	
	您若要嫁人，那就向我求爱；	
	我夫人已经订婚。	
贡纳丽	一出闹剧！	90

---

72. 戏言……预言（Jesters…prophets）：李根将两句谚语柔和到了一起："许多真话出自玩笑（There is many a true word spoken in jest）"，以及"傻子和孩子经常会预言（Fools [jesters] and children do often prophesy）"（Mowat）。 73. 乜斜（asquint）：带有偏见的眼光，或扭曲的视力。贡纳丽在此以另一句谚语作为回应，即"情妒令人眼斜（Love, being jealous, makes a good eye look asquint）"。 87. 转包（sub-contracted）：许配（already betrothed）；系莎氏新造词。

Albany^F   Thou art armed, Gloucester. ^FLet the trumpet sound.^F

If none appear to prove upon thy person

Thy heinous, manifest and many treasons,

There is my pledge. [*Throws down his gauntlet.*]

      I'll make it on thy heart,

95   Ere I taste bread, thou art in nothing less

Than I have here proclaimed thee.

Regan   Sick, O, sick!

Goneril [*aside*] If not, I'll ne'er trust medicine.

Edmund There's my exchange. [*Throws down his gauntlet.*]

      What in the world he is

That names me traitor, villain-like he lies.

100   Call by thy trumpet: he that dares approach,

On him, on you—who not? —I will maintain

My truth and honour firmly.

Albany   A herald, ho!

^F*Enter a Herald.* ^F

[*to Edmund*] Trust to thy single virtue, for thy soldiers,

All levied in my name, have in my name

Took their discharge.

105 **Regan**   My sickness grows upon me.

Albany She is not well; convey her to my tent.

       [*Exit Regan, supported.*]

Come hither, herald; let the trumpet sound

And read out this. ^F*A trumpet sounds.*^F

阿班尼	你全副武装,格洛斯特。　让号吹响。
	若没人出来通过决斗证明
	你是邪恶、显然和十足的叛贼,
	这是我的挑战。　[掷下铁手套。]

在进食以前,

我会彻底证明,对你的评判　　　　　　　　　　　95

毫无偏差可言。

李根	难受,噢,难受!
贡纳丽	[旁白]若不难受,我不再相信药物。
埃德蒙	这是我的回应。　[掷下铁手套。]

无论他是谁,

若叫我叛徒,就是撒谎的恶棍。

把号角吹响:有谁胆敢前来,　　　　　　　　　100

我会对他,对您——任何人?　——证明

我的忠诚和荣誉。

阿班尼	传令官呢,嗬!

传令官上。

[向埃德蒙]靠你个人的勇气,因为你的兵,

以我的名义招募,又以我的名义

全部解散。

李根	我越来越难受了。　　　　　　105
阿班尼	她不舒服,送她去我的帐篷。

[李根被扶下。]

快过来,传令官;你把喇叭吹响

并宣读这个。　喇叭吹响。

103-5. 靠……解散(Trust…discharge):至于开场始时跟埃德蒙一起入场的士兵何时退场以及如何退场,剧中并未表明。　可能是趁贡纳丽与李根争吵期间(62-90)一一走开。

HERALD		[^F*Reads.*^F] 'If any man of quality or degree within
110		the lists of the army will maintain upon Edmund,

HERALD [^F*Reads.*^F] 'If any man of quality or degree within
110 the lists of the army will maintain upon Edmund,
supposed Earl of Gloucester, that he is a manifold
traitor, let him appear by the third sound of the
trumpet. He is bold in his defence.'^F*First trumpet.*^F

HERALD Again! ^F*Second trumpet.*^F

115 **HERALD** Again! ^F*Third trumpet.*^F

^F*Trumpet answers within.*^F

Enter Edgar ^F*armed.*^F

Albany Ask him his purposes, why he appears
Upon this call o'the trumpet.

HERALD   What are you?
Your name, your quality, and why you answer
This present summons?

Edgar   ^QO^Q know my name is lost,
120 By treason's tooth bare-gnawn and canker-bit;
Yet am I noble as the adversary
I come to cope ^Qwithal^Q.

Albany   Which is that adversary?

Edgar What's he that speaks for Edmund, Earl of Gloucester?

Edmund Himself. What sayst thou to him?

Edgar   Draw thy sword,
125 That if my speech offend a noble heart,
Thy arm may do thee justice. Here is mine.

[*Draws his sword.*]

Behold: it is the privilege of mine honours,

传令官	［宣读。］"军中的现役人员若有谁
	官衔较高或出身高贵,断言埃德蒙, 　110
	所谓的格洛斯特伯爵,是个十足的
	叛贼,请他于第三次号角吹响之前
	出面。　他将勇敢地自卫。"喇叭首次吹响。
	传令官再吹!　喇叭再次吹响。
	传令官再吹!　喇叭第三次吹响。　115
	内有喇叭回应。

埃德加上。

阿班尼	去问问他的来意,他为何听到
	号角来到这里。
传令官	您是哪位?
	您的姓名、身份,您为何回应
	这种召唤?
埃德加	我的名字已消失,
	已被叛贼的牙齿蚕食干净;　120
	可我和那位我要进行决斗的
	对手同样高贵。
阿班尼	那对手是谁?
埃德加	谁代表埃德蒙——格洛斯特伯爵?
埃德蒙	他本人。　对他有啥可说?
埃德加	拔剑吧,
	假如我的话冒犯了高尚的心灵,　125
	你的无辜可用剑证明。　这是我的。

［拔剑。］

听着:拔剑是我荣耀的特权、

127-8. 拔剑……信念(It…profession):考虑到埃德加的高贵地位,以及他接受骑士准则时所立下的誓言,他拔剑挑战对手是他的特权。

My oath and my profession. I protest,

Maugre thy strength, youth, place and eminence,

130   Despite thy victor sword and fire-new fortune,

Thy valour and thy heart, thou art a traitor:

False to thy gods, thy brother and thy father,

Conspirant 'gainst this high illustrious prince,

And from th'extremest upward of thy head

135   To the descent and dust below thy foot

A most toad-spotted traitor. Say thou no,

This sword, this arm and my best spirits, are bent

To prove upon thy heart, whereto I speak,

Thou liest.

Edmund   In wisdom I should ask thy name,

140   But since thy outside looks so fair and warlike,

And that thy tongue some say of breeding breathes,

^FWhat safe and nicely I might well delay^F

By rule of knighthood, I disdain and spurn.

Back do I toss these treasons to thy head,

145   With the hell-hated lie o'erwhelm thy heart,

Which for they yet glance by and scarcely bruise,

This sword of mine shall give them instant way,

Where they shall rest for ever. Trumpets, speak.

^F*Alarums. Fight.*^F   [*Edmund falls.*]

Albany   [*to Edgar*] Save him, save him!

我的誓言和我的信念。　我声明，

尽管你年轻力壮，地位出众，

拥有胜利的宝剑，火红的时运，　　　　　　　　130

虽然你英勇顽强，却是个叛贼：

背叛了你的神明、兄弟和父亲，

阴谋陷害这位杰出的国君，

从你那颗头上的最高顶端，

直到你脚下的灰尘和脚底，　　　　　　　　135

令人憎恶的叛贼。　你若否认，

这剑、这手臂和我的骨气决心

证明，我所说的，你在撒弥天

大谎。

埃德蒙　　　　　　按理说我该问问你姓名，

但是因为你外表英俊威武，　　　　　　　　140

你的言辞证明你很有教养，

按照骑士规则我本可谨慎地

加以拖延，可我不屑一顾。

我把这叛国指控掷回你头上，

让这弥天大谎把你的心制伏，　　　　　　　　145

因为它们只能擦过不能挫伤，

我这把利剑将直插你的心脏，

让谎言在那里永驻。　喇叭，吹响。

号声。二人决斗。[埃德蒙倒下。]

阿班尼　　　[向埃德加]别杀他,别杀他!

---

130. 火红的时运（fire-new fortune）：（就像刚出锻铁炉的）全新的出师告捷以及将领的晋升（brand-new［as fresh from the forge］success in battle, and promotion as leader of an army）。 139-43. 按……一顾（In…spurn）：正如贡纳丽在150-1所说的那样，埃德蒙不必跟一位不知姓名的对手决斗。 可能是他因为自己的成功而得意洋洋,过分自信,对自己的获胜毫不怀疑。 145. 弥天大谎（hell-hated lie）：我恨（说我是叛贼）这种谎言就像我恨地狱一般（the lie［that I am a traitor］I hate as I do hell）（借鉴卞之琳先生译文。 ——译者附注）。 149. 别杀他（Save him）：很可能是对埃德加的呼喊,好让埃德蒙活着以便审讯。

Goneril   This is � mere Ꮪ practice, Gloucester.

150   By the law of arms thou wast not bound to answer

An unknown opposite. Thou art not vanquished,

But cozened and beguiled.

Albany   Shut your mouth, dame,

Or with this paper shall I stop it.

[*to Edmund*]   ᶠHold, sir,ᶠ

Thou worse than any name, read thine own evil.

155   [*to Goneril*] ᏚNayᏚ, no tearing, lady; I perceive you know it.

Goneril   Say if I do, the laws are mine, not thine.

Who can arraign me for't?   *Exit.*

Albany   Most monstrous! ᶠO!ᶠ

[*to Edmund*] Knowst thou this paper?

Edmund   Ask me not what I know.

Albany   [*to an officer, who follows Goneril*]

Go after her; she's desperate, govern her.

160 **Edmund**   What you have charged me with, that have I done,

And more, much more; the time will bring it out.

'Tis past and so am I. [*to Edgar*] But what art thou

That hast this fortune on me? If thou'rt noble,

I do forgive thee.

贡纳丽	这是诡计,格洛斯特。

按照决斗规则你不必回应　　　　　　　　　　　　　150

不知姓名的对手。　你不是战败,

而是上当受骗。

阿班尼　　　　　　　　你闭嘴,女人,

否则我用信把它封住。

〔向埃德蒙〕　　　　且慢,先生,

难以形容的恶棍,读读你的罪恶。

〔向贡纳丽〕不,别撕,夫人;我看您了解内容。　　　155

贡纳丽　了解又怎样,法是我的,不是你的。

谁能因此告我?　　　　　　　　　　　　　　下。

阿班尼　　　　多么丑恶! 噢!

〔向埃德蒙〕知道这信吗?

埃德蒙　　　　　　别问我知道什么?

阿班尼　〔向尾随贡纳丽的一军官〕

你跟上她,她已绝望,看好她。

埃德蒙　您所指控我的,我全都干过,　　　　　　　160

还有更多,更多;时间会揭露的。

完了,我也完了。 〔向埃德加〕可你是哪位,

所幸把我战胜?　假如你高贵,

我会宽恕你的。

---

153. 且慢,先生(Hold, sir):对此有多种解释,既可针对埃德加也可针对埃德蒙而言,意为"拿去(take, receive)",或"等一等(Just a moment!)"。　156-7. 法……告我(the…for't):贡纳丽声称自己作为王后不会受到指控,因为她高于法律。　158. 别问我知道什么(Ask…know):对照伊阿古的"别问我什么(Demand me nothing)"(5.2.300);与伊阿古不同的是,埃德蒙在临死前心肠有所改变。　159. 看好(govern):可指控制或看护(restrain or take care of)。　163-4. 假如……你的(If…thee):埃德蒙在死到临头之际,就出身和教养而言,已从1.2独白中那种革命性的思想回归到传统的观念。

Edgar		Let's exchange charity:
165		I am no less in blood than thou art, Edmund;
		If more, the more thou'st wronged me.
		My name is Edgar and thy father's son.
		The gods are just and of our pleasant vices
		Make instruments to plague us:
170		The dark and vicious place where thee he got
		Cost him his eyes.
Edmund		Thou'st spoken ^Fright, 'tis^F true;

Edgar   Let's exchange charity:

165   I am no less in blood than thou art, Edmund;

         If more, the more thou'st wronged me.

         My name is Edgar and thy father's son.

         The gods are just and of our pleasant vices

         Make instruments to plague us:

170   The dark and vicious place where thee he got

         Cost him his eyes.

Edmund   Thou'st spoken [F]right, 'tis[F] true;

         The wheel is come full circle, I am here.

Albany   [*to Edgar*] Methought thy very gait did prophesy

         A royal nobleness. I must embrace thee.

175   Let sorrow split my heart if ever I

         Did hate thee or thy father.

Edgar   Worthy prince, I know't.

Albany   Where have you hid yourself?

         How have you known the miseries of your father?

180 **Edgar**   By nursing them, my lord. List a brief tale,

         And when 'tis told, O, that my heart would burst!

         The bloody proclamation to escape

         That followed me so near—O, our lives' sweetness,

         That we the pain of death would hourly die

185   Rather than die at once! —taught me to shift

埃德加	咱们相互宽恕：
	就血统而言我不比你差，埃德蒙； 165
	要是更好，你对我的伤害更多。
	我叫埃德加，你父亲的儿子。
	神明很公正，利用我们寻欢
	所犯下的罪恶来惩罚我们：
	他在黑暗邪恶的地方生了你， 170
	导致他失去眼睛。
埃德蒙	说得对，真的；
	命运车轮转了一圈。 我回到底部。
阿班尼	［向埃德加］我觉得你的举止即可表明
	你出身高贵。 我必须和你拥抱。
	愿悲伤令我心碎，假如我曾 175
	恨过你或你父亲。
埃德加	可敬的公爵，我知道。
阿班尼	您在何处藏身？
	您怎么知道了您父亲的不幸？
埃德加	通过照料他，殿下。 我简述一下， 180
	讲完之后，噢，但愿我能心碎！
	为了躲避对我步步紧逼的
	死亡通缉，——噢，生活中的甜蜜，
	使我们宁愿时刻忍受死亡之苦，
	也不愿一下死去！——教我换成 185

---

164. 相互宽恕（Let's exchange charity）：让我宽恕你对我犯下的罪恶，你也宽恕我杀死了你（Muir）。 166. 要是更好（If more）：他是婚生子，而埃德蒙是个杂种（81）。 167. 我叫埃德加（My…Edgar）：埃德加会通过摘下面具或头盔向埃德蒙和阿班尼显示自己的身份。 170. 黑暗邪恶的地方（The…place）：通奸的床上，也可指通奸行为（Muir）。 172. 命运……一圈（The…circle）：埃德蒙是说他又回到了底部，即命运的车轮开始旋转之前他所在的地点（he is back to the bottom, where he was before Fortune's wheel began to revolve）（Muir）。

Into a madman's rags, t'assume a semblance

That very dogs disdained; and in this habit

Met I my father with his bleeding rings,

Their precious stones new lost; became his guide,

190 Led him, begged for him, saved him from despair,

Never—O fault!—revealed myself unto him

Until some half-hour past, when I was armed,

Not sure, though hoping of this good success.

I asked his blessing and from first to last

195 Told him my pilgrimage. But his flawed heart,

Alack, too weak the conflict to support,

'Twixt two extremes of passion, joy and grief,

Burst smilingly.

Edmund   This speech of yours hath moved me,

And shall perchance do good; but speak you on,

200 You look as you had something more to say.

Albany   If there be more, more woeful, hold it in,

For I am almost ready to dissolve,

Hearing of this.

ᵠ**Edgar**   This would have seemed a period

To such as love not sorrow; but another

205 To amplify too much would make much more

And top extremity.

Whilst I was big in clamour, came there in a man

Who, having seen me in my worst estate,

Shunned my abhorred society, but then finding

210 Who 'twas that so endured, with his strong arms,

疯子的衣裳,装出一副连狗

都鄙视的模样;穿着这种衣服

我遇到了父亲,他眼窝流血,

眼球刚被挖走;成了他的向导,

领着他,为他乞讨,救他脱离绝望,　　　　　　　190

从未——噢过错!——向他显明身份,

直到半小时以前,我穿上盔甲,

尽管希望这美好结局,但没把握。

我求他祝福,从头至尾讲述了

我们的经历。　他那颗破碎的心,　　　　　　　195

唉,脆弱得经不起这种冲击,

在悲喜交加的强烈感情之间,

微笑着离去。

埃德蒙　　　　　　　　这番话令我感动,

也许会有好处;您接着说吧,

您看上去好像还有话要说。　　　　　　　　　200

阿班尼　如果再说,更为悲惨,留着吧,

因为听到这些我几乎已经

情不自禁。

埃德加　　　　　　对于听不惯悲伤者,

这似乎已到了极限;可另一件,

如果加以详述,会更加悲惨,　　　　　　　　205

超出了极限。

我放声痛哭时进来一位男士,

他曾经目睹过我的极端困苦,

厌恶跟我做伴,但等他发现

遭此难者是谁之后,便用力　　　　　　　　　210

---

197. 悲喜交加(joy and grief):喜是因为知道埃德加依然活着,悲是因为他受了苦难;也可
理解为:此刻死去他感到高兴,同时又为他所造成的痛苦感到难过。

He fastened on my neck and bellowed out

As he'd burst heaven, threw him on my father,

Told the most piteous tale of Lear and him

That ever ear received, which in recounting

215 His grief grew puissant and the strings of life

Began to crack. Twice then the trumpets sounded

And there I left him tranced.

Albany   But who was this?

Edgar Kent, sir, the banished Kent, who in disguise

Followed his enemy king and did him service

220 Improper for a slave.^Q

Enter a Gentleman ^Qwith a bloody knife.^Q

Gentleman Help, help, ^FO, help!^F

Edgar   What kind of help?

^F**Albany**   Speak, man.

Edgar^F What means this bloody knife?

Gentleman   'Tis hot, it smokes,

It came even from the heart of—^FO, she's dead!^F

Albany Who ^Fdead^F? Speak, man.

225 **Gentleman** Your lady, sir, your lady; and her sister

By her is poisoned; she confesses it.

Edmund I was contracted to them both; all three

Now marry in an instant.

Edgar   Here comes Kent.

抱住我的脖子号啕大哭，

像要划破天空，扑到我父亲身上，

讲起了自己和李尔，那种可怜

人们从未听过，他讲述期间

愈发悲痛，直到他的心弦   215

开始绷断。 当时喇叭已响两遍，

我走时他神情恍惚。

阿班尼   这人是谁？

埃德加   肯特，先生，遭流放的肯特，他化装

跟随敌视他的国王，那种效劳

连奴隶都不适合。   220

一绅士手持血刃上。

绅士   救命啊，救命！

埃德加   救什么命？

阿班尼   你快说。

埃德加   你为何拿着血刃？

绅士   还热乎，还冒气！

刚刚从心脏拔出——噢，她死啦！

阿班尼   谁死啦？ 你快说！

绅士   您夫人，先生，您夫人；她的妹妹   225

已经被她毒死；她承认过了。

埃德蒙   我已经和她俩订婚；我们三人

此刻同时成亲。

埃德加   肯特来了。

---

212. 父亲身上（father）：格洛斯特的尸体上面。

Enter Kent.

Albany	Produce their bodies, be they alive or dead.

Goneril's and Regan's bodies brought out.

230   This judgment of the heavens that makes us tremble

      Touches us not with pity—O, is this he?

      The time will not allow the compliment

      Which very manners urges.

Kent   I am come

      To bid my King and master aye good night.

      Is he not here?

235 **Albany**   Great thing of us forgot!

      Speak, Edmund, where's the King? And where's Cordelia?

      Seest thou this object, Kent?

Kent   Alack, why thus?

Edmund Yet Edmund was beloved:

      The one the other poisoned for my sake,

      And after slew herself.

240 **Albany**   Even so; cover their faces.

Edmund I pant for life. Some good I mean to do,

      Despite of mine own nature. Quickly send—

      Be brief in it—to the castle, for my writ

      Is on the life of Lear and on Cordelia;

      Nay, send in time.

肯特上。

阿班尼	把尸体抬来,无论是死是活。	
	贡纳丽与李根的尸体被抬上。	
	上天的这种审判使我们战栗,	230
	并不使我们同情——噢,这是他吗?	
	此刻可不允许正式的问候,	
	尽管按礼应该如此。	
肯特	我是来	
	向我的国王和主人永别的。	
	他不在这里?	
阿班尼	我们忘了大事!	235
	快说,埃德蒙,国王呢?　还有考迪丽娅?	
	看到这景象了,肯特?	
肯特	唉,这是为啥?	
埃德蒙	埃德蒙是有人爱的:	
	为了我一个将另一个毒死,	
	然后自杀。	
阿班尼	是的。　把她们的脸盖上。	240
埃德蒙	我快断气。　我有意做件好事,	
	尽管我生性邪恶。　赶快派人——	
	要抓紧——去城堡,因为我的令状	
	是将李尔和考迪丽娅处死;	
	要及时赶到。	

229. 把尸体抬来(Produce the bodies):把尸体抬到舞台上面这种做法比较少见,通常是将它们抬离舞台,正如埃德蒙在254行被抬下去的那样。　莎士比亚想在这一终场里面将李尔三个女儿的尸体全部展现在舞台上面,以便回顾开场时的情景并与之形成对比;见254(1)及注。
234. 永别的(aye good night):永远的道别(farewell forever);肯特相信自己即将死去,因为他的心弦已开始绷断(Bevington)。　238. 埃德蒙是有人爱的(Yet…belov'd):埃德蒙的所思所想惟有他本人。　此处表露了他的罪恶生涯源于他感到没人爱他,这是一种高超的笔触(Muir)。

245 **Albany**   Run, run, O run!

   Edgar   To who, my lord? Who hath the office? [*to Edmund*] Send

              Thy token of reprieve.

   Edmund   Well thought on, take my sword; ᵠthe captain,ᵠ

              Give it the captain.

   Edgar   [*to gentleman*]   Haste thee for thy life.

                                        [*Exit gentleman.*]

250 **Edmund**   He hath commission from thy wife and me

              To hang Cordelia in the prison and

              To lay the blame upon her own despair,

              That she fordid herself.

   Albany   The gods defend her! Bear him hence awhile.

              [*Edmund is carried off.*]

              Enter Lear with Cordelia in his arms

                  [*followed by the Gentleman*].

255 **Lear**   Howl, howl, howl, ᵠhowlᵠ! O, you are men of stones!

              Had I your tongues and eyes, I'd use them so

              That heaven's vault should crack: she's gone for ever.

              I know when one is dead and when one lives;

              She's dead as earth.   [*He lays her down.*]

                         Lend me a looking-glass;

260   If that her breath will mist or stain the stone,

| 阿班尼 | 跑,跑,噢跑! | 245 |

埃德加　找谁呢,殿下？ 谁在负责？［向埃德蒙]带上

　　　　你的信物以示免刑。

埃德蒙　想得周到,拿上我的剑;找营长,

　　　　把剑给营长。

埃德加　[向绅士] 你要拼命奔跑。

　　　　　　　　　　　　　　　　　　　　　　　［绅士下。]

埃德蒙　他有你妻子以及我的授权, 　　　　　　　250

　　　　去把考迪丽娅吊死在狱中,

　　　　然后将罪责归咎于她的绝望,

　　　　说她是自缢身亡。

阿班尼　神明保佑她! 暂且把他抬走。

　　　　[埃德蒙被抬下。]

　　　　　　李尔双手拖住考迪丽娅上

　　　　　　　　［绅士随后]。

李尔　　哀号,哀号,哀号! 你们是石像! 　　　　255

　　　　我若有你们的舌头和眼睛,会用

　　　　它们使天穹裂缝:她永远走了。

　　　　我知道怎样算死,怎样算活;

　　　　她泥土般冰凉。[把她放下。]

　　　　　　　　借我一面镜子;

　　　　如果她的气息会使镜面模糊, 　　　　　　260

---

254. 暂且把他抬走(Bear…awhile):埃德蒙被人抬下,以便最后的场面能展示李尔与他全部死去的三个女儿聚集一起;见229及注。 254(1)双手……上(*with…arms*):演员们会以不同的方式处理这一艰难的入场:虚弱年迈的李尔,在濒临死亡之际不得不抱起一位有时会很重的演员,通常会把她放到舞台或担架上面,随后开始痛苦的呼唤。 255. 哀号……哀号(Howl…howl):可能是指一连串的痛苦哀号;或者,若该动词为祈使语气,可能是李尔最后一次在命令大家放声痛哭。 李尔此刻的入场结束了先前的繁忙行动,突然营造了一种最为动人的场景,将所有目光都吸引到了他和考迪丽娅身上。

	Why then she lives.
Kent	Is this the promised end?
Edgar	Or image of that horror?
Albany	Fall, and cease.
Lear	This feather stirs; she lives: if it be so,
	It is a chance which does redeem all sorrows
	That ever I have felt.

265 **Kent**   O, my good master!

Lear   Prithee, away.

Edgar   'Tis noble Kent, your friend.

Lear   A plague upon you, murderers, traitors all!

I might have saved her; now she's gone for ever.

Cordelia, Cordelia, stay a little. Ha?

270   What is't thou sayst? Her voice was ever soft,

Gentle and low, an excellent thing in woman.

I killed the slave that was a-hanging thee.

Gentleman 'Tis true, my lords, he did.

Lear   Did I not, fellow?

I have seen the day, with my good biting falchion

275   I would have made him skip. I am old now,

And these same crosses spoil me. [_to Kent_] Who are you?

Mine eyes are not o'the best, I'll tell you straight.

	那她还活着！	
肯特	这是指望的结局？	
埃德加	或是末日的表象？	
阿班尼	天塌下来吧！	
李尔	这羽毛在动,她活着！ 若是如此,	

那就有机会将我此前的所有

悲伤予以补偿。

肯特	噢,我的好主人！	265
李尔	求你,走开！	
埃德加	是高贵的肯特,您朋友。	
李尔	诅咒你们这些凶手和叛徒;	

我本可救她；可她永远地走了。

考迪丽娅,考迪丽娅,等等我！ 哈？

你在说啥？ 她的声音始终柔和, 　　　　　270

低声细语,在女人是一种美德。

我杀了那个吊死你的奴才。

绅士	是真的,殿下,真的。	
李尔	我没杀,伙计？	

曾几何时,我用自己的利剑

即可把他们赶跑。 我现在老了, 　　　　　275

这些苦恼把我毁了。 ［向肯特］您是谁？

我视力不是很好,我马上会认出。

---

261. 指望的结局（promised end）：肯特可能是指李尔所希望的"轻松地爬向死亡"（1.1.40），或指他本人预期中的死亡（234），但埃德加为我们解释了其中的含义,好像是指"世界末日的景象（great doom's image）",或末日审判（the last judgement）,就像基督所预言的那样（"马太福音"24章、"马可福音"13章和"路加福音"21章）。 263. 羽毛（feather）：演员们会从自己的服装上面找到羽毛,或从自己或他人的头上扯掉一根头发,或是想象有一根羽毛。 267. 你们这些凶手（you murderers）：李尔像是在谴责大家,好像他们都要为考迪丽娅的死去负责。 277. 马上（straight）：立刻（at once）；参照285。

Kent	If Fortune brag of two she loved and hated,
	One of them we behold.
Lear	ᶠThis is a dull sight: ᶠ Are you not Kent?
280 **Kent**	The same;
	Your servant Kent; where is your servant Caius?
Lear	He's a good fellow, I can tell ᶠyouᶠ that;
	He'll strike and quickly too. He's dead and rotten.
Kent	No, my good lord, I am the very man—
285 **Lear**	I'll see that straight.
Kent	That from your first of difference and decay
	Have followed your sad steps—
Lear	You are welcome hither.
Kent	Nor no man else. All's cheerless, dark and deadly;
	Your eldest daughters have fordone themselves,
	And desperately are dead.
290 **Lear**	Ay, so I think.
Albany	He knows not what he says and vain is it
	That we present us to him.

肯特	若命运女神夸口既爱又恨过两人，	
	其中一人就在眼前。	
李尔	我视物模糊。 您不是肯特吗？	
肯特	正是；	280
	仆人肯特；您的仆人卡尤斯呢？	
李尔	他是个好人，我能告诉你们；	
	他会打人，动作也快。 他死了烂了。	
肯特	没死，好陛下，我就是那个他——	
李尔	我这就查验。	285
肯特	自从您最初的变故和落难，	
	一直跟着您——	
李尔	欢迎您来这里。	
肯特	那不是别人。 一片黑暗，死气沉沉；	
	您的两个大女儿已自杀身亡，	
	在绝望中死去。	
李尔	我想是这样的。	290
阿班尼	他不知道自己在说什么，因此	
	向他引见我们无益。	

278-9. 若……眼前（If…behold）：本句可有不同的解释：如果命运女神夸口说她曾（最）爱或者（最）恨过两个人，那么我们会发现李尔就是后者。 就此处提及的命运而言，可参照上文163，172，以及李尔的个人形象："遭受命运捉弄（natural fool of fortune）"（4.6.187）（Foakes）。 有人认为肯特此处是指自己，也有人认为他是指李尔和他本人。 本句话也可复述为"If Fortune, in the history of the world, preeminently loved and then hated two persons, here in the miserable example of my king we have one of them（假如命运女神，有史以来，特别喜爱然后又特别痛恨过两个人，眼前这位可怜的国王就是其中之一）"（Muir）。 280. 视物模糊（dull sight）：此外，也可指考迪丽娅的尸体——这种"可悲的场景（melancholy sight）"（Foakes；Muir）。 281. 卡尤斯（Caius）：肯特化装时所采用的这一名字仅在此提及。 288. 那不是别人（Nor…else）：完成他的上一句话"我就是那个他——那不是别人"；同时也可指"我不受欢迎，别人也不受欢迎（I'm not welcome, nor is anyone else）"。 292. 我们（us）：我们自己（ourselves）；但阿班尼的下一个"我的（our）"就变成了表示君王称谓的复数形式，因为他现已成为国家的首领。

Enter a Messenger.

Edgar   Very bootless.

Messenger   [*to Albany*] Edmund is dead, my lord.

Albany   That's but a trifle here.

295   You lords and noble friends, know our intent:

                 What comfort to this ^Fgreat^F decay may come

                 Shall be applied. For us, we will resign

                 During the life of this old majesty,

                 To him our absolute power;

                 [*to Edgar and Kent*]   you to your rights,

300   With boot and such addition as your honours

                 Have more than merited. All friends shall taste

                 The wages of their virtue and all foes

                 The cup of their deservings. O, see, see!

Lear   And my poor fool is hanged. No, no, ^Fno^F life!

305   Why should a dog, a horse, a rat have life

                 And thou no breath at all? ^QO^Q Thou'lt come no more,

                 Never, never, never, ^Fnever, never!^F

                 [*to Edgar*] Pray you undo this button. Thank you, sir.

                   ^QO, o, o, o.^Q

                 ^FDo you see this? Look on her: look, her lips,

信差上。

埃德加	<div align="center">毫无益处。</div>
信差	〔向阿班尼〕埃德蒙死了,殿下。
阿班尼	那倒是一件小事。

各位大人和贵友,听我宣布意图: 295

我要尽一切可能为这位被毁的

国王带来安慰。 至于我,我会

在这位老陛下在世期间

把绝对的权威交还给他;

〔向埃德加与肯特〕 你们,恢复地位,

还有额外的利益和称号,因为 300

你们当之无愧。 所有的朋友

会因忠诚得到奖赏,每个仇敌

都要品尝应得的苦杯。 噢,看哪!

李尔 可怜的傻瓜已被绞死。 没了生命!

为什么狗、马、老鼠都有生命, 305

你却没了气息? 噢,你不会再来,

永不,永不,永不,永不,永不!

〔向埃德加〕请您解开这纽扣。 谢谢,先生。

噢,噢,噢,噢!

看见没有? 你看她;看,她的嘴唇,

---

304. 傻瓜(fool):昵称,指已被绞死的考迪丽娅;但也可令人想起李尔特别喜爱的另一个人物——傻子,他从3.6退场后下落不明。 307. 永不……永不(Never…never):也许是英国无韵诗中最为非凡的诗行;残酷无情的"没/不(no)"字在上文中出现了五次,现与"永不(never)"一词的重复前后呼应,致使下文的话语更为惊人。 本行也会令人想起开场时对"没有(nothing)"一词的重复。 308. 请您……纽扣(Pray…button):人们通常认为李尔是指自己的长袍或紧身上衣上面的扣子,重复他在3.4.107的"快,解开扣子"。 也可能是指考迪丽娅服装上面的扣子,或是想象中的扣子。

Look there, look there! *He dies.*^F

310 **Edgar**   He faints: my lord, my lord!

Kent   Break, heart, I prithee break.

Edgar   Look up, my lord.

Kent   Vex not his ghost; O, let him pass! He hates him

That would upon the rack of this tough world

Stretch him out longer.

Edgar   ^QO^Q He is gone indeed.

315 **Kent**   The wonder is he hath endured so long;

He but usurped his life.

Albany   Bear them from hence. Our present business

Is ^Qto^Q general woe. [*to Edgar and Kent*] Friends of my

soul, you twain,

Rule in this realm and the gored state sustain.

320 **Kent**   I have a journey, sir, shortly to go;

My master calls me, I must not say no.

看那里,看那里!　　死去。

埃德加　　　　　　　　　他晕了:陛下,陛下!　　　　　　　　　　310

肯特　　心,碎吧,求你碎吧!

埃德加　　　　　　　　　往上看,陛下。

肯特　　别扰他的亡灵;让他走吧。　谁若

让他在这个残酷的世界继续

受刑,他会恨他。

埃德加　　　　　　　　噢,他真的走了!

肯特　　他能忍受这么久真是奇迹;　　　　　　　　　　　315

他的生命只是硬撑。

阿班尼　　把他们抬走。　我们目前的事情

是举国哀悼。　[向埃德加与肯特]

你们二位知己,

维持重创的国家,将王国治理。

肯特　　我有一段旅程,先生,很快到头;　　　　　　　320

我的主人在叫我,我不能不走。

309-10. 看见……那里(Do…there):对开本里增加的这些诗行可能使布拉德利有理由认为李尔在喜悦中死去,因为他相信考迪丽娅尚有气息、依然活着。　假如李尔真这么认为,他便受到了欺骗,或者说他是在说胡话。　也有人认为这种结局令人难过,因为此处没有任何迹象可表明"从悲伤转向了喜悦(a transition from grief to joy)"。　311. 碎吧……碎吧(Break…break):肯特可能是指他本人(Muir)。　314. 受刑(rack):一种刑具(肢刑架),分尸架(instrument of torture on which a victim's limbs were stretched and torn apart)(Mowat)。323-5. 有感……见不了这么多(feel…see so much):感受和看见(feeling and seeing)在剧中具有强烈的共鸣,可令人想起李尔号召贵人们"让自己感受一下穷人的感受"(3.4.34),以及格洛斯特抱怨那些过分富有和荒淫无度者"视而不见/因为没有同感"(4.1.71-2)。　在1.1页纳丽和李根恭顺地说出了她们该说的话语(spoke dutifully what they ought to say),而考迪丽娅则认为她应该隐藏自己的感情(conceal her feelings)。　对埃德加和阿班尼来说,好像剧中那些势不可挡的事件已经使他们获得了自由,可以有感而发(speak feelingly),由于埃德加通过"对悲伤曾感同身受"(4.6.218),易生恻隐之心,这也给了他们洞察的能力,尽管年轻,因此他们无须遭难即可看准(see properly);也许他们早已明白格洛斯特的"我凭感觉看(I see it feelingly)"(4.6.145),而格洛斯特只有在自己双目失明之后才明白了这一点(Foakes)。　另外,在四开本里这四行台词被分给了阿班尼;批评家们争辩说,最后的台词应该留给地位最高的幸存者。　但埃德加必须答复阿班尼的邀请,而且"我们尚年幼"这种表述由埃德加说出要比由阿班尼说出更为自然(Muir)。

Albany   The weight of this sad time we must obey,

Speak what we feel, not what we ought to say.

The oldest hath borne most; we that are young

325   Shall never see so much, nor live so long.

^F*Exeunt with a dead march.*^F

FINIS

埃德加　　　这哀伤时刻的重但我们要接下，

　　　　　　要有感而发，不要该说啥就说啥。

　　　　　　最长者受的最多，我们尚年幼，

　　　　　　见不了这么多，也活不了这么久。　　　　　　　　325

　　　　　　　　　　　　　　葬礼进行曲，众下。

剧　终

参 考 文 献

1. Kenneth Muir, *King Lear*, The Arden Shakespeare, Second Series；Methuen & Co Ltd. 1967.

2. Alan Durban, *King Lear*, Shakespeare Made Easy, Modern English Version；Barron's, 1986.

3. David Bavington, *King Lear*, The New Bantam Shakespeare, 2005.

4. Jonathan Bate, *King Lear*, Royal Shakespeare Company, 2008.

5. R. A. Foakes, *King Lear*, The Arden Shakespeare, Third Series, 中国人民大学出版社, 2008.

6. Barbara A. Mowat, *King Lear*, Folger Shakespeare Library, 2009.

7. *King Lear*, http：//nfs. sparknotes. com/*king lear*/.

8. *The Holy Bible*, New International Version, Zondervan, Michigan, 1990.

9. 卞之琳,《李尔王》(莎士比亚悲剧四种),人民文学出版社,1988.

10. 梁实秋,《李尔王》(莎士比亚四大悲剧),中国广播电视出版社, 2002.

11. 朱生豪,《李尔王》(莎士比亚喜剧悲剧集),译林出版社,2002.

12. 孙大雨,《李尔王》(莎士比亚四大悲剧),上海译文出版社,2002.

13. 彭镜禧,《李尔王》,外语教学与研究出版社, 2016.

14.《圣经》,和合本,中国基督教协会,2008.

Macbeth

麦 克 白

（英汉对照）

[英] 威廉·莎士比亚　著

李其金　译

ZHEJIANG UNIVERSITY PRESS

浙江大学出版社

译者序

一、版本说明

本译文所采用的原文版本为最新的阿登版第三版《麦克白》①。 该版本的优点不仅在于它具有公认的准确性和权威性,还在于它附有详尽的注解与精辟的导读,这些优点对译者和读者准确理解并欣赏原文均可提供很大的帮助。 此外,译者在翻译过程中还参阅了另外四种原文版本和两种现代英语译文（详情请见参考文献）,并从原文中选取和翻译了大量的注解。 同时,译者在翻译过程中还参阅了我国译莎前辈梁实秋、朱生豪、卞之琳、孙大雨和辜正坤先生的译文,并借鉴了许多妙笔佳译。

二、翻译标准与原则

译文主要依照刘宓庆先生在其《翻译美学导论》一书中所倡导的翻译标准——翻译再现主要是借助于"内模仿",即: "'模仿'相当于'对应',是审美再现的基本手段,翻译尤然。"（刘宓庆,2012：255）②可以说,译者在整个翻译过程中始终遵循了这一原则,并尽力使译文在形、音、意三方面能与原文一一对应。 具体做法请看下文三至五节中的详细说明。

---

① Sandra Clark, *Macbeth*, The Arden Shakespeare, Third Series. London：Bloomsbury, 2015。

② 刘宓庆,《翻译美学导论》（第二版）,中国出版集团公司,2012。

三、对原文无韵诗的模仿

就莎剧的行文形式而言,其中以无韵诗(blank verse)为主,这是一种没有韵脚却富有节奏感的诗体:一般是每行有五个音步,一个音步又有一轻一重的两个音节,即抑扬格,读起来抑扬顿挫、朗朗上口。据统计,《麦克白》剧中的韵文部分占比达 95% 之多。

英国作家兼评论家黑兹利特①先生在论及《麦克白》一剧时曾说:"《麦克白》《李尔王》《奥赛罗》与《哈姆雷特》通常被视为莎士比亚的四大悲剧。《李尔王》的出众之处在于满怀深情;《麦克白》在于无拘无束的幻想和行动迅速;《奥赛罗》在于引人入胜和剧烈的感情变化;《哈姆雷特》在于思想和感情的升华。上述四部悲剧不仅展现出作者令人惊叹的创作天赋,而且每一部都异彩纷呈;它们彼此之间好像毫无关联。这种别具一格和独创性必然源于真实和自然。……他的戏剧能触及人们的心灵。他所描绘的场景令人刻骨铭心、如临其境,好像我们早已知道他所描绘的那些地点、人物和事件。《麦克白》就像是记录了一次异乎寻常的悲剧性的事件一般。……麦克白心里所经受过的一切,始终使我们感同身受。实际上有可能发生的一切,以及能够想象得到的一切,人们的所言所行,感情活动,魔法的施展等等,无不真实可信、栩栩如生。"(Robert S Miola:220)②

现谨以麦克白在第一幕第七场中的一段无韵诗台词为例,希望读者朋友在欣赏原文"真实可信、栩栩如生"的诗意之美的同时,也不妨对译文就此所作的模仿或对应予以检视。

此刻正值傍晚,邓肯国王已到达令他"感到神清气爽"的麦克白城堡,他跟麦克白夫人进行了一番寒暄之后,随之便和随从一起出席麦克白夫妇

① 黑兹利特(William Hazlitt):英国作家、评论家(1778—1830),著有《莎剧人物》、评论集《英国戏剧概观》等。

② Robert S Miola, *Macbeth*, A Norton Critical Edition, 2004.

所设的晚宴,并打算第二天一早离开。 麦克白此刻设法离开了筵席并来到厅外,就自己是否该暗杀邓肯进行了一番深思熟虑。 因为他"若要暗杀邓肯,那必定就在当晚",正如英国著名演员兼导演——雅可比爵士(Derek Jacobi)在谈及自己扮演麦克白的感受时所说的那样: "时间的急迫性也体现在了语言方面。 有时简直就像电报。 ……这种凝练的语言就是麦克白整个的思想过程: 他以闪电似的思想进程开始了自己的内心独白。" (同上:334)

If it were done, when 'tis done, then 'twere well	行动若能干净利落,那最好
It were done quickly. If th'assassination	还是速战速决。 若这次暗杀
Could trammel up the consequence, and catch	能把后患一网打尽,并使他
With his surcease, success: that but this blow	一命归阴,胜券在握: 这一击
5 Might be the be-all and the end-all, here,	也许能够一劳永逸,今生, 5
But here, upon this bank and shoal of time,	今世,在这时间的海岸和浅滩,
We'd jump the life to come. But in these cases,	甘愿拿来生冒险。 但这种行径,
We still have judgement here, that we but teach	今生总会遭报应,这只能传授
Bloody instructions, which being taught, return	冤冤相报,人们学会后,便会
10 To plague th'inventor. This even-handed justice	折磨创始者。 公平的正义之神 10
Commend th'ingredience of our poisoned chalice	会将我们杯中的毒药送到
To our own lips. He's here in double trust:	自己的嘴唇。 他在此加倍信任:
First, as I am his kinsman, and his subject,	首先,我是他的亲属和臣民,
Strong both against the deed. Then, as his host,	均抵制该行径。 其次,作为主人,
15 Who should against his murderer shut the door,	我本该房门紧闭以防刺客, 15
Not bear the knife myself. Besides, this Duncan	不该亲自操刀。 而且,他邓肯
Hath borne his faculties so meek, hath been	行使职权如此谦恭,他是
So clear in his great office, that his virtues	如此清正廉明,他的美德
Will plead like angels, trumpet-tongued, against	会像天使,放声呼号,控诉
20 The deep damnation of his taking off;	这一罪该万死的弑君行动; 20
And pity, like a naked new-born babe,	而怜悯,会像赤裸的新生婴儿,
Striding the blast, or heaven's cherubim, horsed	驾驭着狂风,或像小小的天使,
Upon the sightless couriers of the air,	骑着天空那些无形的使者,
Shall blow the horrid deed in every eye,	把这恐怖行径吹向每只眼睛,

25 That tears shall drown the wind. I have no spur   让泪水淹没狂风。 我没有踢马刺   25
To prick the sides of my intent, but only   可以驱使我的图谋,唯有
Vaulting ambition, which o'er-leaps itself,   攀爬的野心,常因用力过猛,
And falls on th'other.   而跌到另外一侧。

     "他相当迅速地说服自己放弃了那种念头。 究竟是什么在驱使他呢,他在思忖:唯有'攀爬的野心'(27 行)在加以怂恿,而那却常会因为'用力过猛而跌到另外一侧'。 他主意已定——然而就在此刻麦克白夫人出现。 假如她没在此刻出现,我相信他就不会做出那种暗杀行动。"(同上:335)

     另外,"本段独白也充满了非凡的意象——'怜悯,会像赤裸的新生婴儿',等等——此刻全部向他涌来。 ……善良与邪恶在他的脑海里交织在一起。 我们每人都具有的邪恶一面,对他而言,此刻占据了上风;但为了保持平衡,他调用了最美好、最纯洁、最无邪的意象——天使、新生婴儿、和天空。 ……良善从他们身上喷射而出,闪闪发光;在另外一侧却是黑暗、血腥、邪恶、阴险的念头。 最终他在这一段独白中选择了良善;美好的意象由此获胜——直到麦克白夫人出现并开始奚落他的男子汉气概。"(同上:335)

     自此,我们已对本段台词进行了一番观赏和领悟,已对原文的"声色之美(音美、形美)"和"意象之美(意美)"有了一个比较清晰的了解和认识。 笔者认为,这种对原文的观赏和领悟很有必要,也很有助益,因为,正如刘宓庆先生在论及翻译审美理想和审美再现问题时所指出的那样:"审美再现的起点,应是审美主体对审美客体的审美观照(contemplation)的终点,即'观''品''悟'。 翻译审美者在任何一个平面上的疏漏,都可能影响审美观照的整体性,从而有损于'再现'这第四个平面也是终端平面的过渡。"(刘宓庆:255)

     就原文无韵诗的模仿与再现而言,应该说,译文尽力做到了"在双语可译性限度内,充分保留了原语的行文形式体式(stylistic format)。 例如,诗歌中的格律和韵律、韵式和分节式……以及其他的行文形式特征,例如

不能将分行诗译成不分行的散文,等等。"(同上:186)

我们都知道,在伊丽莎白时代,按照惯例,作者"都应遵循规范性原则,该原则与公认的社会等级观念有关。 诸如国王、贵族、主教、上帝等高贵的人士都用韵文;诸如小丑、工人、疯子等卑贱的人物则都用散文"(Lamb:23)①,以此来体现不同人物的分野。 因此,"诗人把同样一句话用诗而不是散文表现出来,或者相反地用散文而不用诗表现出来,都是不能加以改变的,否则就会损伤或破坏了原有的美"(席勒格:67)。②

因此,考虑到莎剧的上述特点,译者遵照我国译莎前辈们所倡导的"以顿代步"的翻译原则,在尽量忠实地再现原文"意美"的前提下,采取"三控"原则,也尽力对原文的行文形式与内在韵律进行了模仿。 具体措施为:

(1)严格控制全剧译文的行数,以使译文的行数与原文的行数完全相等;

(2)严格控制每行译文的字数,以此做到与原文的音节数量尽量相等,每行译文大都为十一字或十二字。

(3)尽量控制每行译文的顿数,以此模仿原文的行文形式与内在格律,从而再现原文应有的"形美"与"音美"效果:每行译文大都为五顿,其中只有一行为六顿(24行)。

另外,译文除了在行文形式与内在格律方面尽量对原文进行模仿以外,还尽力发挥了汉语诗歌的谐韵优势,让译文押了一些散韵或句中韵,如:

第一行的"利落"与第二行的"速决",第二行的"暗杀"与第三行的"使他",第三行的"打尽"与第四行的"归阴"等。 因为"谐韵除了使诗句平添音乐性之外,还使读者产生期待、产生共鸣、产生满足。 韵律使读者的审美意识处于积极的活跃状态,是使作者与读者达至审美体验'融合'的一种催化剂。 从翻译美学上分析,这是不少人主张译诗必须押韵的原因"(刘宓庆:80)。

---

① Sidney Lamb, CliffsComplete, Shakespeare's *Hamlet*, New York:Hungry Minds Inc. 2000。

② 威廉·席勒格,《莎士比亚研究》,上海译文出版社,1982。

　　另外,考虑到"翻译是一种时空跨度很大的语际转换活动。　历史的演变和社会文化的发展可以使原语成为很难为当代人透彻和准确理解的'化石'"(同上:192)。　因此,"时空差产生艺术鉴赏的不等效,古今同理。　……地缘之隔也必然会产生审美体验上的差异"(同上:137)。由此我们不难想象,中国的莎剧读者和观众与伊丽莎白时代的莎剧读者和观众之间会有多大的时空差异。　不过,鉴于"审美主体与客体之间的关系是能动的、交互的、实践的关系"(同上:138),为了能尽量帮助读者对原文进行更好的审美体验,也为了能充分再现原文的蕴涵之美,审美主体可尽力发挥其主观能动性,即为读者架设一座跨越时空、跨越文化、跨越语言障碍的桥梁——为译文增加详尽的脚注。

　　据此,译者依照五种原文版本的相关评注甄选和翻译了大量的注解作为脚注,并附上各自的出处以便于查阅。　就本段台词而言,译者从四种原文注解中选取并翻译了包括下列六处在内的十一处脚注:

　　2-4. 若……在握(if…success):原注为,"if it could prevent any consequences and obtain success by his death"。　其中,"trammel up"意为"用网网住(entangle as in a net)"(Muir)。 6. 在这……浅滩(upon…time):即"今生(in this life)"。　麦克白将(今生的)时间想象为无穷之海洋中的一片沙洲或浅滩(imagines Time as a sandbank or shallow place ["shoal"] in the sea of eternity)(Gill)。 7. 甘愿拿来生冒险(We'd jump the life to come):即"我对死后的永生将毫不在意(尽管世间的罪过到时也许会受到惩罚)(I would take no notice of an eternal life after death [where there might be punishment for earthly sins]"(Gill);其中,"jump"意为"冒险(risk)"(Muir)。 8. 遭报应(judgment here):麦克白也许是说,他这样做只会自食其果,因为别人会以其人之道还治其人之身(Macbeth may mean that in behaving in this way he will only be calling down judgement on himself in the form of those who imitate his own actions)(Clark)。 22. 驾驭着狂风(Striding the blast):文艺复兴时期的绘画常把丘比特或天使如此描绘(Bevington)。 25-8. 我……另一侧(I…th'other):又一处有关骑马的意象。　……莎士比亚在此好像将两种意象合而为一:一是麦克白想行凶的意图,被想象为需要鞭笞的一匹马;二是他的野心——一位急不可耐的骑手,试图跃上马鞍,结果却跳得过远(Clark)。

四、对原文押韵诗的模仿

《麦克白》剧中除了无韵诗之外,还有女巫们那种"童谣和打油诗般的吟唱。 押韵随处可见。 《麦克白》每场结尾处的偶韵体比率在所有悲剧中仅次于《理查二世》。 ……麦克白通常都会在每场结束时使用对句"（Clark：47）。 所谓偶韵体（couplets）也叫对句,即两行尾韵相谐的诗句,旨在对本场的内容予以总结,或对后续的内容进行展望。 就此而言,译者也力求对原文中的韵式做到一一对应。 例如,麦克白在第一幕第七场就是否要暗杀邓肯一事,由最初的犹豫不决,到后来的"主意已定"——不采取行动,再到后来因为妻子出面对他进行了一番奚落和怂恿之后,最终促使他改变了主意：

Away, and mock the time with fairest show： 走,要欺骗世人就假装殷勤：
False face must hide what the false heart doth know. 必须用虚情假意包藏祸心。

（1.7.82-3）

"这种偶韵句可以充当剧中的标点符号,然而,它们还有其他的功能"（同上：47）。 例如,麦克白在第四幕第一场与女巫们所唤出的幽灵相遇之后,他及时"接上话茬,将第三个幽灵的诗行完成,好像完全进入了它的世界,在剧中首次使用了一连串的对句。 麦克白'因为急于接受幽灵的神谕,便以同样的韵律对接下去',由此与他所咨询的精灵融为一体"（同上：242）。

3 Apparition 第三幽灵
Macbeth shall never vanquished be until 麦克白永远不会被人战胜,
Great Birnam wood to high Dunsinane hill 直到大伯南树林向他进攻,
Shall come against him. 移到邓西嫩山顶。
Macbeth 麦克白
        That will never be. 那绝不可能。
Who can impress the forest, bid the tree 谁能征召森林,给树木下令

95 Unfix his earth-bound root？ Sweet bodements, good.　　让它连根拔起？　美好的预兆。　　95
　　Rebellious head, rise never till the Wood　　　　　　叛逆的死鬼,别再起来搅扰,
　　Of Birnam rise, and our high-placed Macbeth　　　　除非伯南林位移,麦克白大人
　　Shall live the lease of nature, pay his breath　　　　将会安度天年,寿终正寝,
　　To time, and mortal custom.　　　　　　　　　　　跟常人一样。

五、对原文散文的模仿

　　我们都知道,除了无韵诗、歌谣、偶韵体、打油诗等文体之外,莎剧还有另外一种重要的组成部分——没有韵律的散文。 剧中的不同角色或者同一角色之所以采用不同的文体,都与他们的身份、说话的对象、当时的心境或语境等因素密切相关。 比如麦克白夫人在第五幕第一场夜游时的几段台词。 "此处采用散文形式也许有些奇怪",英国著名莎学家布拉德利①先生曾说,"因为在重大的悲剧场景中,我们会期望更富有诗意的表达方式,而且此处也是最为著名的场景之一。 此外,我若没有记错,在莎氏所有的伟大悲剧中,唯有麦克白夫人最后出场时被拒绝了高贵的韵文。 然而,他在本场中也遵循了自己的创作惯例。 因为夜游是一种病态,他的原则是,如果有谁大脑失常,就会让谁使用散文。 就四大悲剧而言,哈姆雷特装疯时说的都是散文,然而他在独白时,在跟何瑞修谈话时,在恳求母亲时,他说的都是韵文。 李尔王精神错乱之后的所有台词几乎全是散文;他苏醒康复之后,又恢复韵文。 ……奥赛罗,在第四幕第一场一直在使用韵文,直到伊阿古告诉他凯西奥已承认（奸情）,其间有 10 行散文——惊慌失措中的叫嚷与喃喃自语——随后失去知觉,跌倒在地。 ……麦克白夫人夜游中所采用的意象或表达的思想前后并没有理性的联系。 ……其中的用词大都毫无纹饰,结构也非常简单。 "（Bradley：351-3）

　　① A. C. Bradley, *Shakespearean Tragedy*, New York：Macmillan Press Ltd, 1992.

Lady

35 Out, damned spot: out, I say. One; two. Why then 'tis time to do't. Hell is murky. Fie, my lord, fie, a soldier and afeard? What need we fear who knows it, when none can call our power to account? Yet who would have thought the old man to have

40 had so much blood in him?

Doctor

Do you mark that?

Lady

The Thane of Fife had a wife. Where is she now? What, will these hands ne'er be clean? No more o'that, my lord, no more o'that. You mar all with

45 this starting.

………

Lady

Here's the smell of the blood still. All the perfumes of Arabia will not sweeten this little hand. Oh, oh, oh!

夫人

去，该死的污点！去，我说！一；二。 35
嗨，该动手了。地狱漆黑。呸，夫君，
呸，一名军人，还怕？我们为啥要怕
有人知道，因为没有人敢拿我们试问？
可是谁又能想到这个老头儿身上竟会
有那么多鲜血？ 40

医生

您听见没有？

夫人

法福郡主曾有位妻子。可她现在何处？
怎么，这一双手再也洗不干净？别提
它了，夫君，别提它了。您这么一惊
毁了所有事情。 45

………

夫人

这里依然有那种血腥的气味。所有的 50
阿拉伯香水都无法让这一只小手变香。
嗷，嗷，嗷！

　　"这种语言效果格外令人难忘。 麦克白夫人当初的台词中那种昂扬和豪迈言犹在耳，而这种变化却令人屏声息气，心生敬畏。 该场景所包含的道义，即便是莎士比亚本人也无法言传，只能意会。 因为此时此刻，所有的韵文——就连麦克白的韵文——都会显得虚浮，这些简短而单调的句子可谓真正的言为心声。"（同上：353-4）

　　另外，英国 18 世纪的悲剧演员西登斯女士（Sarah Siddons）在谈及自己扮演麦克白夫人的体会时曾说："值得注意的是，麦克白在不断地向妻子倾诉自己的痛苦；因此他的内心负担可以不时地得以减轻，而她却在顽强地默默忍受一颗受伤心灵的巨痛。"因为："未予表达的伤悲／会向超载的心低语，使它破碎。"（4.3.210-1）（Miola：236）

　　现在我们再回顾一下原文中的韵文和散文的编排形式。 不难看出，莎剧中的无韵诗与散文之间除了内在的韵律存在着区别,在编排格式上也有明显的不同,即每行无韵诗的第一个单词的首字母均为大写,而且右边也没有顶格或分散对齐。 然而,每行散文的第一个单词的首字母(除特殊情况之外)均无须大写;而且,若某个角色的台词长度在两行以上,自第一行起至倒数第二行为止均为左右分散对齐,以此来区分散文与韵文之间的外在差异。

就此而言,译文也试图与原文予以对应:以每行十六个汉字对应原文十二个左右的音节。 另外,若某个角色的台词在两行以上,自第一行起至倒数第二行为止均为字数相等(不包括行末的标点符号)、整齐划一,以使散文与韵文之间的差别一目了然。

好了,亲爱的读者朋友,虽然译者王婆卖瓜似的对自己的译文夸耀了一番,但译者心里非常清楚:由于学识和水平所限,文中的缺点和谬误在所难免。 敬请读者朋友批评指正!

谢谢!

李其金

2017 年 10 月

序　言
（节选）

本序言共包括四部分：创作日期、《麦克白》及其故事来源、悲剧《麦克白》、时间与框架。

创作日期
（DATE）

就《麦克白》的创作日期而言，尽管依然无法确定具体时间，但好像也没有很好的理由怀疑大家所公认的 1606 年，即苏格兰国王詹姆斯六世就任英格兰国王（詹姆斯一世）三年之后，以及火药阴谋败露的数月之后。

《麦克白》及其故事来源
（*MACBETH* AND ITS SOURCES）

莎氏所创作的《麦克白》取材于多种来源，并以不同的方式加以利用。 该故事主要来源于霍林西德（Holinshed）的《编年史》（Chronicles）。 他相当忠实地采用了霍林西德有关麦克白生涯的记述，并辅之以其他苏格兰国王统治期间所留下的史料。

悲剧《麦克白》
（*MACBETH*：THE TRAGEDY）

　　《麦克白》是一部最吸引人的戏剧：它是莎剧中篇幅最短和进展最快的悲剧，最为惜墨如金和主题连贯的悲剧；其中的邪恶氛围在所有戏剧中最为明显，而它的"宗教语言同时又遍布其间"；它也许是"最伟大的道德剧"，曾被视为"世上最有教益的悲剧"，它一向被称为莎氏最合时宜、最为阴暗、最富诗意、对"野心"的剖析最为深刻的戏剧，"其中的奇思妙想远超其他悲剧"。 剧中的意象"比其他任何剧本都更为丰富多变，想象力更强"。 在莎氏所有伟大的悲剧中，唯有《麦克白》以一位凶手为男主人公。 此前，莎士比亚也曾在《理查三世》中就此予以尝试，人们也常就两剧相提并论。 然而，其中的很大差异就在于他将麦克白塑造成了一位为自己的恶行而遭受巨痛的人物，而且在一定程度上，也正是通过对这种痛苦的描绘而引起了观众的同情。 这种同情颇为特殊，也不免悖理，因为麦克白早已成了杀人凶犯。 他克服了道义上的顾忌而痛下杀手，一旦行凶之后却发现自己为了维护既得的权力而又不得不继续行凶。 他残暴地滥用职权，破坏了国家的安康；这种暴行将不可避免地以其死亡而告终。 悲剧效果也由此而生，因为莎士比亚怎么也不会让观众疏远了他的主角。 尽管最终马尔科姆将杀害父亲的凶手作为"丧命的屠夫"予以处置，然而这种用语却与观众的看法并不一致。 就某种奇特的意义而言，麦克白就是"你我中间的一个"，他与众不同，因为他的见识和感受比任何人都要深刻，又因为观众一开始就会倾向于跟他形成某种同谋关系。 该剧"将我们放进了麦克白的脑袋"。

　　麦克白清楚地意识到邓肯是一位好人和明君，对他表示效忠义不容辞——这种道德意识从未离他而去。 他想成为公序良俗中的一员，享受自己为报效祖国而赢得的"金贵好评"，并与自己"最最亲爱和高贵的伙伴儿"共同分享，他想"安度天年，寿终正寝，跟常人一样"（4.1.98-9），长命百岁时能伴以"尊敬、爱戴、顺从、朋友成群"（5.3.25）。 他却让自己变成了一位凶手并对自己的行径感到憎恶,曾希望它并未发生,意识到这一行径无可挽回地玷污了他圣洁的心灵:"向我平静的杯中投入了敌意/……将我不朽的灵魂/交给了人类那位共同的仇敌"(3.1.66-8)。 他知道自己应为本身的行为负责,却试图逃避这种念头,追随"无形的幻象";他的眼睛要对挥舞屠刀的手"眨眼"。 若有可能,他又会试图否认有一种使然力的存在。 他在幻觉中看见的那把沾满血污的短剑显然是出于他自己的意愿,却好像要将他引向邓肯的房间似的。 他在前往行凶的路上祈求"稳固的大地"别听见他的脚步。

不仅是观众从一开始就想了解麦克白的心态,而且他确实也是一个非常易受强烈感情左右的人物。 他的外表和动情的语言,比如他对女巫的预言所作出的反应,均展露了这种特点。 正如班柯所观察的那样,他为此一怔;随后他便对自己的反应开始分析起来:

> 这么一种不可思议的教唆
> 好像不坏;但也不好。若是坏,
> 它怎么给我一个成功的保证,
> 一开始就应验?我已是考道郡主。
> 若是好,怎么一想到那种诱惑,
> 它的恐怖情形令我毛骨悚然,
> 让我镇静的心脏怦怦直跳,
> 使我一反常态?可怕的事实
> 还不如可怕的想象更为恐怖。
> 我的凶杀之念只不过是虚幻,
> 竟使这可怜的躯体瑟瑟发抖,
> 因为臆测而使我一筹莫展,
> 全是幻觉,尚未实现。

(1.3.132-44)

麦克白对他所谓的那些人生大事所作出的心理反应都会探索一番,这显然增强了该剧的悲剧效果。 他始终都在思考自己的感受,他的身心对自己所选行为的毁灭性后果念念不忘。 他无法睡眠,夜晚"遭噩梦摧残",他的心中"充满了蝎子",他看上去"愁眉苦脸",他要犯病、突发惊慌,他的心怦怦直跳。 他这种强烈的自我意识以及他可让观众与他感同身受的能力,在很大程度上在于他不仅仅是一个恶棍,同时也是一位遭受痛苦的勇士,一直都在暴露自己脆弱的感情。 终场时他因不如从前感觉灵敏而产生的绝望之情更为明显:

> 我几乎已忘记恐惧的滋味。
> 从前,夜间听到一声尖叫
> 便会不寒而栗,吓人的故事
> 会让我的毛发像有生命一般
> 根根竖起。我已经饱尝恐惧;

(5.5.9-13)

观众之所以倾向于跟麦克白成为共谋,是因为他与我们分享的冲动与感受均属人之常情,即使它们并非总是值得称颂:担心并惧怕事情败露,感到自己得不偿失,尽可能向公众展示自己最佳的状态。 宴会上的失控导致他感到"一种剧烈而可悲的难堪";他在第二幕第三场所冒的危险,也就是邓肯的遇害被发现之后,不禁会令人担忧他是否能"化险为夷"。 直到终场时人们才看到麦克白的杀人行为,剧中也强调了他在邓肯与班柯死去之后所经受的痛苦无人能比。 他下令屠杀麦克达夫全家时的毫不犹豫,与他杀害邓肯之前那种痛苦的优柔寡断相比,表明他在情绪和道义方面已相去甚远。

麦克白一再犯罪的动机是一个中心议题。 黑兹利特①,跟其他浪漫主义作家一样,将他视为"遭受狂暴命运的驱使,犹如一艘船只在暴风雨中飘荡";然而这种观点却回避了女人,即女巫与他的夫人在其一生中所扮演的重要角色,以及某些更为重大的问题,即选择与使然力(choice and agency)可能会起的作用。 一开场女巫们就已计划与麦克白相会,她们正在等候他的首次出现。 他的第一句台词与她们的语调相当吻合。 正如他

---

① 黑兹利特(Hazlitt William):英国作家、评论家(1778—1830),著有《莎剧人物》等。

所说的那样，她们的教唆也许"不可思议"，好像与他本人的心愿产生了共鸣，但是此刻他对女巫们的真实身份却将信将疑，因而不想采取任何行动："若注定称王，命运会为我加冕，/不用我动手"（1.3.146-7）。 然而，女巫们有关其未来的预言与他最近的晋升之间的巧合对他的影响如此强烈，竟使"这可怜的躯体瑟瑟发抖"。 他在给妻子的信中说道，"她们拥有超凡的预知能力"（1.5.2-3）；能进一步证明她们具有魔力的证据出现在召唤神灵一场（conjuring scene）（4.1.49 及以下），此时她们将"幽灵"唤出，这些幽灵所发出的神谕般的指令使麦克白充满了灾难性的自信。 最后所展现的、代表未来斯图亚特之王朝的"国王表演"更显出她们高超的预知能力；面对与自己毫不相干的未来，他感到无能为力，这激起了他的暴怒并把它发泄到了麦克达夫的家人身上。 这一举动致使麦克达夫成了复仇者，转而导致了麦克白的身首异处。

尽管女巫们就像近代英格兰所指控的、会施魔法的老妪那样"形容枯干"，"衣着又这么难看"，而且她们的恶意、符咒和蹩脚的吟唱也很幼稚、古怪、吓人，但不可否认的是，她们的身上却具有神秘的力量，活动于自然界和社会以外，跟命运三女神类似。 她们能"洞察时间的种子"，但她们的预言都是模棱两可，正如导致俄狄浦斯毁灭的神谕那样，使他自以为胜过了命运。 也正是由于麦克白（有选择地）向妻子陈述了自己与女巫的相遇，才激起他的夫人召唤"到处怂恿人们犯罪的"幽灵，从而将她这位正常的女人变成了一位凶手。 麦克白倒是意识到了自己的跌落是女巫所致，但为时已晚，他将她们贬称为"骗人的恶魔……用模棱两可戏弄于我"。 他在本段台词中（5.8.17-22）暗自承认他本可以选择，承认他按照某种理解对女巫的预言进行了解读并采取了相应的行动。 然而，就其当时所采取行动的背景而言，显然并非所有的事件都可以解释，社会秩序也并非全都正常。 邓肯死去的当晚，人们"听到空中有哭声，惨死的怪叫，/用那可怕的声调进行预言"（2.3.56-7）。 黑夜替代了白天，动物也行为失常，邓肯的骏马彼此相食，"好像它们要/跟人类交战"（2.4.17-8）。 万物被恐怖的力量惊动："石头能移动，树木会说话"（3.4.121）。 尽管曾几何时"人道的律法使国家净化之前"，人们一死了之，可如今，他们"却能复活,/头上带着二十道致命的伤口,/将我的座位占据"(3.4.74,78-80)。 班柯,跟麦克白夫人一样,也意识到自己所生存的世界有邪恶的幽灵存在,他们"怂恿人们的罪恶行径",并时刻准备着参与人类的活动:

> 为使我们深受其害,
>
> 邪恶的爪牙就会讲些真话,
>
> 以小恩小惠赢得信任,关键时
>
> 将我们置于死地。

(1.3.125-8)

处在这样的一个世界里,麦克白能有多少自由去决定自己的选择? 是否一开始命运就在与他作对? 他好像比班柯更容易遭受女巫的影响;这是否因为她们的预言唤醒了他原有的"阴险意念"? 该剧发出了这样的疑问,但并未予以解答。 它向人们展示了一种可能,即"世间的平衡在不知不觉中向着邪恶倾斜";不过,这要看该剧的结尾部分在多大程度上恢复了那种平衡。

麦克白选择杀害邓肯可谓是一种可悲的举动,并由此决定了他的人生历程,这一选择在于妻子的怂恿,人们也常将随后所发生的许多事情的责任归咎于她。 因为她不仅下定决心要使麦克白成为女巫们的"应许",而且也坚持这种事情应走"捷径"。 她自信有能力驾驭他,并知道如何掌控:

> 你快回来,
>
> 好把我的激情灌入你的耳中,
>
> 我要用舌尖的锐气将阻止你
>
> 获取那顶金冠的障碍清洗,
>
> 既然命运和鬼神好像都要
>
> 就此助你一臂之力。

(1.5.25-30)

当他因为担心和顾虑而不愿继续他们所婉称的"大事"时,她知道如何通过怀疑他的男子气概将他争取过来。 她的凶杀计划,尤其是她将"屠杀的罪责"转嫁给他人的计划，令麦克白十分钦佩。 所有的动摇就此消失，他冲口说出了一句令人担忧的赞誉："愿你只生男子！／因为你的坚韧气质就应该／只生男儿"（1.7.73-5）。 他对杀害邓肯这种行为所怀有的疑虑在一段充满复杂想象力的独白中透露出来，这无疑说明他对待此事非常严肃；因此，也可以说是他的妻子成功地促使他改变了主意，从而使她在系列的悲剧事件中成为一种重要的使然力。 她对幽灵所发出的骇人祈求令人联想到女巫，她在为杀害邓肯而进行准备的场景中可谓强大无比。 她的重要性在于驱使麦克白成为一位"血腥的男人"；对于麦克白来说，这不仅是他逃避妻子嘲笑他懦弱的手段，同时也塑造了他未来的身份。 一旦接受了这种身份，他那种敢做"适合男人所做的一切"的观念便被抛之脑后。 麦克白夫人在凶杀过后的一段时间内依然扮演着重要角色，无论是在私下里还是在公开场合，她都在支持着变化无常的丈夫，可现在他已能在行凶的道路上独自前行。 他们一起讨论班柯和弗林斯造成的威胁，但麦克白并未向她透露行将处置他们的计划："最好一无所知，亲爱的宝贝儿，／到时拍手称快"（3.2.46-7）。 使命一旦完成，她便退化成一名无助的妻子，她在最后一次出场时，通过"胡话"展现出了心灵痛苦的各种症状："心灵的折磨"、失眠、内疚和恐惧，这些症状原本都体现在麦克白身上。 她那句声明"地狱漆黑"也许是一种报应，表明她过去曾与黑暗权势有染，并成为她最初的力量来源。

就在麦克白夫人崩溃的场景之前，马尔科姆断言："麦克白／已经摇摇欲坠，上天的军队／也已武装起来"（4.3.240-2），预示着戏剧的终场即将来临，并会体现出因果报应和命由天定。 在第四幕第三场，作为麦克白的最后一位受害者，血海深仇的麦克达夫以挑战者的身份出现，将为自己"可怜的祖国"和家人报复"苏格兰的这位恶魔"。 当那两句支撑麦克白自感刀枪不入的预言应验之后，他的自大便遭到了惩罚，并最终明白自己受到了毁灭性的欺骗。 麦克达夫对自己出生情况的戏剧性表露促使麦克白意识到，正如《李尔王》中的埃德蒙在类似的情景下所意识到的那样，命运的车轮"已转了一圈"；然而，作为一名坚持到底的斗士，他不会让自己像懦夫那样屈辱地死去。 在莎氏悲剧中的所有主人公里，唯有他没有临终遗言,取而代之的却是长久的生死搏斗,当然是毫无希望可言。 被称为苏格兰真正国王的马尔科姆,在第四幕第三场重新肯定了自己的权威,他评估战局,接受了麦克达夫的致意,然后便开始掌管王权。 这种结局究竟在多大程度上促进了国家的复原一直存有争议。 它对剧中前几场某些内容的效仿到底意味着什么? 其中对"万岁(Hail)"一词的重复是否会令人想起女巫对麦克白和班柯的招呼? 马尔科姆重复使用父亲的"栽培"意象,以及他对支持者予以报答和封爵的许诺,是否会令人想起他父亲在第一幕第四场中的类似言论,凶多吉少? 它在多大程度上暗示了周而复始的信任与背叛? 该剧是围绕着模棱两可创作而成,以女巫们的吟唱"美即丑来,丑即美"开场(1.1.9),通过女巫的预言促使麦克白继续向前,其结局可以有多种解读。 它也许起到了修复作用,使"有序从无序中兴起,真实从欺骗中浮现",马尔科姆与麦克达夫,作为维护上帝之完美秩序的工具,使饱受战争蹂躏的苏格兰恢复了"平安"。 然而,这也可能反映出该剧的结局可作多种解释,暗示暴乱与流血在苏格兰的政治进程中将会一再发生,而且马尔科姆的结束语也可表明"那种古老的循环又开始运转"。

　　这并不是说该剧的结构没有条理。 麦克白与邓肯、班柯、麦克达夫之间的关系依次决定了随后的诸多行动,并从而形成了该剧的三条主线,它们跟数字"3"形成了一种默契的重复(3 个女巫、对麦克白的 3 个预言、幽灵的 3 次显现)。 麦克白获得王位时未受到任何阻碍,但到了中场当他设宴想为自己的政权公开正名时,却传来了弗林斯逃脱的消息——标志着他将从此走向衰落。 随着因果报应的展开,麦克白又回到了最初的武士身份,就像原来那位臭名昭著的叛贼——考道郡主,遭受命运的惩罚。 然而,这种结局也许不乏某种悲剧性的精神净化或情感解脱:麦克白被命中注定的对手杀死,罪有应得,从而避免了让他充当"罗马傻瓜"的羞辱。 那种令他对自己走向犯罪感到痛苦不堪的道德意识却从未离他而去。

时间与框架

（TIME AND STRUCTURE）

至少从柯勒律治①开始，评论家们便已注意到时间在剧中所起的重要作用，甚至是主导原则。 柯勒律治认为"在莎氏的所有戏剧中，《麦克白》的剧情发展最快"，这种观点已由人们以不同的方式得以拓展。 不难看出，时间以及时间的过渡在《麦克白》一剧中所起到的中心作用。 从女巫甲开场时的提问，"三姐妹何时再聚集"，直到终场时马尔科姆的一再保证："其他事情，/随着新时代的到来也该开始……在适当的时间和地点一一照办"（5.9.30-1,39），有关时间的术语随处可见。 这种现象不只是在于可表达人类行为的时间术语丰富多彩——"何时（when）""现在（now）""今晚（tonight）""明天（tomorrow）""昨天（yesterday）""永远（forever）""今后（hereafter）""最近（late）""及时（timely）"——同时也在于它们可令人想起自然界的时辰和节奏。 例如，麦克白利用一系列详尽的迂回说法为杀害班柯所作的准备：

> 先于蝙蝠到回廊
>
> 飞行，先于金龟子响应乌黑的
>
> 赫卡忒召唤，用那催眠的鼓翅
>
> 敲响入夜的钟声，将有一件
>
> 可怕的大事完成。

（3.2.41-5）

凶手甲则以不同的心情表达了夜幕的降临：

> 西方依然闪烁着几缕微光。
>
> 晚归的旅客正在策马加鞭，

---

① 柯勒律治（Coleridge Samuel Taylor）：英国诗人、评论家（1772—1834），著名诗作有《忽必烈汗》和《古舟子咏》等。

想及时赶往旅店，

(3.3.5-7)

类似的段落还有多处，其功能显然是在制造一种紧张的心情和气氛；类似的表述在这部简练的戏剧中显而易见。 "就时间在全剧中的重要意义而言，或就人们的言谈举止所涉及的时间的频率而言，莎氏的其他悲剧都无法相比"。 换句话说，"该剧像是被一种对时间的迷恋所支配"。 这种迷恋也涉及主人公自己与时间的关系；麦克白在剧中的前半部分感到"急不可耐"，但后来等他听到妻子的死讯时却对"无尽无休的时间"产生了一种虚无之感。一个接一个的明天却未能让他们二人拥有自己所密谋和渴望的未来。

剧情好像从一开始就发生在一个精心勾画并迅速展开的时间框架之内。 女巫三姐妹一开场就在商议下一次的聚集，具体的时限为：日落西山之前，"一方战败，一方胜"，她们将在荒郊野外迎接麦克白的到来。 她们的再次聚集发生在第三场，随后罗斯与安格斯便以麦克白已晋升为考道郡主的喜讯前来迎接；到了第一幕第四场，他们便把他领到邓肯的面前接受封号。 等到第一幕第五场时，麦克白夫人便在朗读丈夫的信件，并从信差那里得知邓肯即将到来并住在他们家里，这将会让他们感到非常荣幸。 开始阶段的基调便是匆忙。 "演员们来回奔走，慌慌张张，行动前移，现在只不过是通向未来的台阶"。 之所以令人产生这种感受，不仅在于有一种凝聚力存在，而且还在于事情接连不断。 至此，事情已经开始凌乱。 麦克白本应亲自宣布邓肯的到来，然而这种消息却由信差传来，麦克白夫人对此感到如此意外，信差竟不得不就此解释一番：

回夫人，是真的：郡主他很快就到。
我的一位同伴跑在他前面，
他几乎喘不过气来，只能勉强地
传达这一消息。

(1.5.34-7)

但是，这种消息却传达得非常及时，因为在她眼里邓肯已然成了阻止她丈夫"获取那顶金冠的障碍"。 她对丈夫的招呼可表明她迫不及待地想让女巫的预言早日应验，甚至巴不得将时间的顺序抛弃：

> 高贵的葛莱密和考道！
>
> 根据未来的预言，比二者更高，
>
> 你的信件已经使我超越了
>
> 这种无知的现在，我此时此刻
>
> 就能感受未来。

（1.5.54-8）

　　麦克白跟妻子一样，也渴望掌管时间的运行。 他想让暗杀"速战速决"，而且最好是不留下任何后患，将时间的河流堵住以便他的行动能够"一劳永逸"，宁愿"拿来生冒险"（1.7）。 麦克白夫妇无法与时间和谐一致；在准备接待邓肯期间，麦克白夫人督促丈夫，要想"欺骗世人"，就要"随机应变"，"要欺骗世人就假装殷勤"。 麦克白夫妇的人生中所经历的这种时间紊乱，也在第二幕与第三幕里得到了进一步的体现，此间有一系列突如其来的事件围绕着活动密集的两个夜晚展开。 第一个夜晚，邓肯因为"对他紧追不舍"，便紧随麦克白之后到达了因弗内斯（1.6），随后几乎是马不停蹄地步入了晚宴。 麦克白与夫人在餐厅外面（1.7）通过低声细语的交流，制定好行动计划，同时等待着邓肯入睡，因为"白天的路途劳顿会使他更快/酣然入眠"。 第二幕显然是以班柯与弗林斯之间的对话拉开了时间的序幕；此刻已是深夜，但城堡里的人们却依然没有睡意。班柯所注意到的事实是，麦克白"还没睡"。 他的夫人也没睡，正准备着发出行动的暗号。 让事后惧怕的场景得以终止的敲门声天衣无缝地将活动带入了凌晨（2.3），此刻，"一直喝到了鸡叫两遍"的看门人被从酩酊大睡中猛然叫醒。 麦克达夫赶来，他想"一早"就把邓肯叫醒，怕误了时间。 "这狂暴的夜晚"，正如老人所言，迟迟不肯结束："按表已是白天，/而黑夜却把运行的明灯遮掩"（2.4.6-7）。 但麦克白可没浪费时间，马尔科姆与唐纳班刚已"偷偷溜走"，正像麦克达夫所挖苦的那样，"他已被提名，已经前往斯宫/加冕登基"（31-2）。

　　第三幕以麦克白为第二个血腥的夜晚做着准备开始，他和夫人正要举行"盛宴",再次展示邓肯莅临城堡时的那种殷勤好客。 这一次的贵宾将是班柯,男主人和蔼可亲地乞求他的到来。 然而,班柯却坚持宴会之前先进行一次午后的远足,好像他有第六感觉——最好不要返回。 麦克白多次问及他的行动安排——"下午要骑马走吗""你的路程远吗""弗林斯与你一起吗""等你晚上回来再见"——让人注意到这位新任国王很想填充时间过渡上的这种间歇。 他与王室随行人员在第一场正式登场之后,便将聚集的众人遣散:

> 让大家自由支配各自的时间,
> 直到晚上七点;为使聚会
> 更加怡人,我将独自待到
> 晚宴时间。

(3.1.40-3)

对时间的提及在该幕的前两场随处可见。 筵席如期举行。 麦克白利用下午的间歇跟两位凶手制定计划,甚至瞒着他们又安排了第三位凶手,可他对黑暗的降临急不可耐。 他向妻子暗示将有一件"可怕的大事"会在"乌黑的赫卡忒召唤"之前完成,他呼唤"蒙眼的黑夜"替代"怜悯的白天",由此以它那"血腥和无形的黑手"授权给他,准许他进行业已安排好的凶杀。 可是这个夜晚却未按计划运行(3.3)。 弗林斯不仅逃脱,就连遇害后安息在阴沟里的班柯也行为反常。 他那满是血污的鬼魂在筵席上的显现(3.4)让麦克白感到时间已严重脱节:

> 那时的情况是,
> 脑浆被敲出之后,人就会死去,
> 就此结束。可如今却能复活,
> 头上带着二十道致命的伤口,
> 将我的座位占据。

(3.4.76-80)

仓促地道过晚安之后,客人们便被打发走开,本场以只剩下麦克白夫妇两人而结束。"夜已多深？"麦克白向妻子问道。 她的回答"正与凌晨竞争，昼夜不分"，表明她已筋疲力尽。 她渴望那种自然的生活节奏，按时入睡自然醒来，以便振作精神。 然而，尽管麦克白答应去睡，他却在计划下一步的行动："我要在明天，／一早我就要，去见那三位女巫。／她们会道出更多"（130-2）。

这种对时间重要性的感受在接下来的事件中有增无减。 麦克白分秒必争，他一早就要起来去访问女巫。 但正是在此次的会面中（4.1）他要面对毁灭性的证据，即他想掌控时间和干预自然次序的努力徒劳无益。 由班柯祖传下来的一系列国王，在麦克白本人的一再恳求下，的确要延续到世界末日；这好像反而迫使他持续向前，他"要让思想伴以行动"，一怒之下竟孤注一掷，随之便将麦克达夫的家人杀害（4.2）。 但这种报复毫无意义；跟前两次的凶杀一样，真正的关键人物——邓肯和班柯的儿子们却得以逃脱，这一次是麦克达夫这位真正的敌手未被捕获。

可现在，随着活动焦点的转移，即从苏格兰转移到英格兰，从麦克白转移到马尔科姆与麦克达夫，仓促忙乱的节奏到了漫长的反思与复原的场景时几乎戛然而止（4.3）。 马尔科姆的自我评判以及他想沉浸在悲伤之中的意愿遭到了麦克达夫的责备，因为他感到时间在一天一天地过去，却没有积极的行动："每天清晨／都有新寡妇哀号，新孤儿哭泣，／新悲伤抽打上苍脸庞"（4-6）。 但马尔科姆意识到他需要等待"适当的时候"，这种适当的时候在本场末尾时好像已经来临：

> 军队已就绪，
> 我们啥都不缺只欠辞别。麦克白
> 已经摇摇欲坠……
> 长夜过后总会见到晨辉。

（4.6.239-41,243）

最后一幕中的场景表明马尔科姆和英国盟军已与苏格兰军队汇合并进展有序，期间穿插着显示麦克白与时间的关系愈发混乱的场景。 他对战斗迫不及待，几次催要铠甲，发出相互矛盾的指令，看上去浑身充满了蛮劲，实际上却已筋疲力尽。 他感到自己的人生已被浪费,他从未抓住过此时此刻。 尽管他匆匆忙忙,生活还是与他失之交臂;他活得不是"已经够长",而是太长,人生暮年却无望获得适当的慰藉。 因为"无休止地将砝码投向未来",他现已明白(5.5)未来只能是未来:那就是"明天,接着明天,接着明天"。 就连他夫人的死亡也超出了时序:"她应该等等再死"。 他最终败于麦克达夫手下,因为他这个人的生命属于一种意外,是从娘胎里"剖腹降生"。 该剧以马尔科姆的断言时序已经恢复而告终。 "篡位者的首级"一旦示众,麦克达夫便宣布"我们已自由"。 马尔科姆将会着手确立自己的王位,并"在适当的时间和地点"对一系列活动谨慎地一一照办。

桑德拉·克拉克(Sandra Clark)

帕梅拉·梅森(Pamela Mason)

史 料 说 明

1. 邓肯(Duncan Ⅰ):即邓肯一世,1034—1040 年在位,继承其祖父——马尔科姆二世之王位。在位期间战事不断。根据英国史学家霍林希德(Holinshed)的编年史及其他史料记载,他身体虚弱、"疾病缠身"。死亡时约为 39 岁。

2. 马尔科姆(Malcolm):父亲遇害时尚未成年,后作为马尔科姆三世于1058—1093 年在位。曾两度婚配,其长子邓肯从爱尔兰回国的途中遭叔父唐纳班杀害,但他仍有第二位夫人的子嗣为其传宗接代。

3. 唐纳班(Donalbain):曾旅居爱尔兰多年,作为唐纳班三世在位于 1093—1097 年。

4. 麦克白(Macbeth):跟邓肯一样,也是马尔科姆二世的嫡孙,于 1040—1057年在位。在 1058 年的一次战役中被杀。他有权凭借自己的王室出身问鼎王位,也有权通过夫人的王室血统加冕登基。据霍林希德的记载,他最初的统治并未遇到反抗,只是在经过了 10 年的善治之后他才逐渐变得残暴专横。其间,他曾于 1050年偕夫人前往罗马朝圣。

5. 麦克白夫人(Lady Macbeth):前苏格兰国王后裔,曾与前夫育有一子——卢拉奇(Lulach)。麦克白在世时也曾让这位继子继承过王位(1057—1058),但数月之后,可能就被马尔科姆杀害。

6. 班柯(Banquo):罗洽波郡郡主(Thane of Lochaber),其实并无其人,尽管在霍林希德的史料中也曾提及,但实为编年史家赫克特·博伊斯(Hector Boece)所杜撰,此举旨在为其保护人——詹姆斯国王五世(James Ⅴ)安插一位王朝先祖。

7. 弗林斯(Fleance):班柯之子,在麦克白雇凶将其父杀害之后逃亡威尔士。

8. 麦克达夫(Macduff):跟班柯一样,其实并无其人,只是被推定为中世纪法夫郡伯爵的后裔。

9. 罗斯(Ross):据霍林希德的《苏格兰编年史》记载,罗斯跟其他几位郡主一样,包括凯斯尼斯(Caithness)等,因煽动叛乱罪被麦克白处死。

10. 西华德(Siward):诺森伯兰郡伯爵,尽管身为丹麦人并最初与邓肯为敌,但与邓肯有着紧密的姻亲关系。死于 1055 年。

LIST OF ROLES

Duncan	*King of Scotland*
Malcolm	*Duncan's elder son*
Donalbain	*Duncan's younger son*
Macbeth	*Thane of Glamis*
Lady	*Macbeth's wife*
Banquo	
Fleance	*Banquo's son*
Macduff	*Thane of Fife*
Wife	*Macduff's wife*
Son	*Macduff's son*

Lennox
Ross
Angus — *Thanes of Scotland*
Menteith
Caithness

Siward	*Earl of Northumberland*
Young Siward	*Siward's son*

First Witch
Second Witch — *three weïrd sisters*
Third witch

Hecate

***Three other* witches**

Apparitions

剧中人物

邓肯　苏格兰国王

马尔科姆　邓肯的长子

唐纳班　邓肯的幼子

麦克白　葛莱密郡郡主

夫人　麦克白的妻子

班柯

弗林斯　班柯的儿子

麦克达夫　法夫郡郡主

妻子　麦克达夫的妻子

儿子　麦克达夫的儿子

兰诺克斯 ⎫
罗斯 ⎪
安格斯 ⎬ 苏格兰郡主
曼提斯 ⎪
凯斯尼斯 ⎭

西华德　诺森伯兰郡伯爵

小西华德　西华德的儿子

女巫甲 ⎫
女巫乙 ⎬ 女巫三姐妹
女巫丙 ⎭

赫卡忒

另三位女巫

幻影

Captain	
Seyton	*retainer in Macbeth's household*
Porter	*in Macbeth's household*
Old Man	
Three Murderers	
Other Murderers	
Doctor	*at the English court*
Doctor	*in Macbeth's household*
Waiting Gentlewoman	*in Macbeth's household*
Lords and Thanes	
Servants	
Messengers	
Soldier	

Attendants, Soldiers

上尉

西顿 麦克白的家臣

看门人 麦克白家室

老人

三刺客

其他刺客

医生 英格兰王室

医生 麦克白家室

女侍臣 麦克白家室

贵族与郡主

仆人

信差

士兵

侍从、兵士

第一幕
ACT I

SCENE I

Thunder and lightning. Enter three Witches.

1 Witch   When shall we three meet again?

In thunder, lightning, or in rain?

2 Witch   When the hurly-burly's done,

When the battle's lost, and won.

5   **3 Witch**   That will be ere the set of sun.

1 Witch   Where the place?

2 Witch   Upon the heath.

3 Witch   There to meet with Macbeth.

1 Witch   I come, Gray-Malkin.

2 Witch   Paddock calls.

3 Witch   Anon.

All   Fair is foul, and foul is fair,

10   Hover through the fog and filthy air.   *Exeunt.*

2

第一场

电闪雷鸣。三女巫上。

女巫甲	三姐妹何时再聚集？	
	电闪,雷鸣,或雨里？	
女巫乙	等这场喧嚣已消停,	
	一方战败,一方胜。	
女巫丙	将是日落西山暮色中。	5
女巫甲	地点何在？	
女巫乙	荒郊野外。	
女巫丙	在那里拦截麦克白。	
女巫甲	快过来,小灰猫。	
女巫乙	蟾蜍叫。	
女巫丙	马上到。	
三女巫	美即丑来,丑即美,	
	盘旋于乌烟瘴气内。	同下。 10

　　1.1. 莎剧中最为简短的开场之一,令人对剧情的进展浮想联翩:天昏地暗,骚动混乱,仪式邪恶,言辞模棱两可（Sandra Clark and Pamela Mason; Arden Shakespeare, Third Series, 2015;即本译文所采用的蓝本;下称"Clark"）。 文中的所有脚注,若未标明出处,均出自该书——译者附注）。 **4.** 战败……胜（lost, and won）:女巫可能是指邓肯的军队战胜了敌军,尽管麦克白随后的凯旋将会为邓肯带来灭顶之灾。 **8.** 快过来（I come）:原文中的"I"在当时可表示"aye（啊）"。 此处应是女巫甲在召唤供自己使用的妖精猫。 蟾蜍（paddock）:供女巫乙使用的蟾蜍精。 猫和蟾蜍都是女巫常用的动物。 **9.** 美……美（Fair…fair）:类似的悖论也可见于同时代的文学作品。 参考英国诗人斯宾塞（Spencer）的长篇寓言诗《仙后》（*Faerie Queene*）,4 章 8 节 32 行,他在描写堕落的人类之常态时曾说:"Then faire grew foul and foul grew faire in sight（顷刻之间美即变丑,丑即变美）"。 同时请参考谚语:"Fair without but foul within（金玉其外,败絮其中/口蜜腹剑）"（Clark）。 本行首次点名了该剧的主题之一——是非颠倒（the reversal of values）（Kenneth Muir; Arden Shakespeare, Second Series, 1984;下称"Muir"——译者附注）。

SCENE II

Alarum within. Enter King [Duncan], Malcolm, Donalbain,
Lennox, with Attendants, meeting a bleeding Captain.

King   What bloody man is that? He can report,
            As seemeth by his plight, of the revolt
            The newest state.

Malcolm   This is the sergeant,
            Who like a good and hardy soldier fought
5   'Gainst my captivity. Hail, brave friend.
            Say to the King the knowledge of the broil,
            As thou didst leave it.

Captain   Doubtful it stood,
            As two spent swimmers, that do cling together,
            And choke their art. The merciless Macdonald
10   (Worthy to be a rebel, for to that
            The multiplying villainies of nature

第二场

内鸣军号。邓肯国王、马尔科姆、唐纳班、
兰诺克斯与侍从上，遇一流血之上尉。

国王 那满身血污者是谁？ 根据他的
惨状，好像他能报告叛乱的
最新情况。

马尔科姆 这就是那位中士，
他可谓忠勇顽强，曾奋力搏杀
以免我被俘。 欢迎，勇敢的朋友！ 5
向国王讲一讲您刚才离开
战场时的战况。

上尉 胜败难分，
像两位疲惫的泳者，扭作一团，
本领无法施展。 残忍的麦克唐纳
（名副其实的叛贼，因为天生 10
和与日俱增的邪恶蜂拥而至，

　　1.2. 根据霍林希德的描述，麦克唐纳针对邓肯国王的反叛被麦克白平息，随即又遭到了挪威国王——斯韦诺（Sweno）的进犯，其军队被泛称为挪威人或丹麦人。 0（1）内鸣军号（*Alarum within*）：表明此刻的场景为军营。 （Roma Gill；Oxford School Shakespeare, 1997；下称（Gill）。 ——译者附注）。 "内鸣"表明号角由乐师在后台的化妆间里吹响，通常有鼓乐伴奏（Clark）。 1. 满身血污（bloody）：点名了行将贯穿全剧的主题（Clark）。 "血污（blood）"一词在剧中出现了上百次之多（Muir）。 2. 叛乱（revolt）：苏格兰此时处于内战状态。 7-23. 胜败……城垛（Doubtful…battlements）：本段台词的语言风格已有多人评说；上尉奇特的表达方式及其不规则的格律表明他的身体状况正逐渐恶化，或他此时所处的表演环境特殊等。本段台词是以史诗般的风格写成，旨在表明它与众不同，像《哈姆雷特》剧中皮洛斯（Pyrrhus）的台词一样（2.2）。

Do swarm upon him) from the Western Isles

Of kerns and gallowglasses is supplied,

And Fortune, on his damned quarry smiling,

15 Showed like a rebel's whore. But all's too weak:

For brave Macbeth (well he deserves that name),

Disdaining Fortune, with his brandished steel,

Which smoked with bloody execution,

Like valour's minion, carved out his passage,

20 Till he faced the slave,

Which ne'er shook hands, nor bade farewell to him,

Till he unseamed him from the navel to th' chops,

And fixed his head upon our battlements.

King O valiant cousin, worthy gentleman.

25 **Captain** As whence the sun 'gins his reflection,

Shipwrecking storms and direful thunders,

So from that spring, whence comfort seemed to come,

Discomfort swells: mark, King of Scotland, mark,

No sooner justice had, with valour armed,

云集其身）拥有西部群岛的

一批步兵和铁骑为其助阵，

命运女神，犹如叛贼的娼妓，

对他的可恶杀戮欢喜。 难以形容： 15

因为英勇的麦克白（他实至名归），

蔑视命运女神，挥舞着利剑，

血腥的劈杀使它热气蒸腾，

就像勇气的宠儿，杀出重围，

直到面对那恶棍， 20

没向他致意，也没跟他道别，

便一剑将他划开，从肚脐到下巴，

并把他的首级挂在我们城垛。

国王　　噢，勇猛的堂兄，可敬的绅士！

上尉　　正如曙光会从东方初现， 25

肆虐的风暴和可怕的雷霆，

也由此生成，看似鼓舞人心，

却危机四伏：注意，苏格兰王，注意，

以勇气为武装的正义之师，

---

12. 西部群岛（Western Isles）：赫布里底群岛（英国苏格兰西部）。 14-5. 命运……欢喜（Fortune…whore）：现引原文注释以助理解，"Fortune, in appearing to favour Macdonald by commending his feats of killing, behaved amorally, like a rebel's whore"。 另见谚语："Fortune is a strumpet（命运女神是个婊子）"。 22. 划开（unseamed）：意为"拆开……的线缝；纵向劈开"，注意其中的裁剪隐喻（tailoring metaphor）；剧中的类似隐喻颇多（Muir）。 23. 将败军或叛徒的首级示众颇为常见，麦克达夫在终场时即是如此。 25-8. 正如……四伏（As…swells）：现引两处原注以助理解："Just as terrible storms at sea arise out of the east, from the place where the sun first shows itself in the seeming comfort of the dawn, even thus did a new military threat come on the heels of the seeming good news of Macdonald's execution."（David Bevington; The New Bantam Shakespeare, 2005; 下称"Bevington"。——译者附注）。 "Macbeth is the source whence comfort seemed to come. From just that quarter danger threatens…Let the King of Scotland mark the omen! …The Sergeant…is of course unconscious of the undertone of meaning（麦克白就是那看似令人欣慰的源泉。 正是从他那里才带来了威胁……让苏格兰王注意这种预兆！ ……中士当然意识不到其中的含义）"（Muir）。 29. 勇气……正义（justice…valour）：上尉将邓肯的事业视为正义，将协助邓肯的麦克白拟人化为勇气。

30   Compelled these skipping kerns to trust their heels,

But the Norwegian lord, surveying vantage,

With furbished arms, and new supplies of men,

Began a fresh assault.

King   Dismayed not this our captains, Macbeth and Banquo?

35 **Captain**   Yes, as sparrows, eagles, or the hare, the lion.

If I say sooth, I must report they were

As cannons over-charged with double cracks,

So they doubly redoubled strokes upon the foe.

Except they meant to bathe in reeking wounds,

40   Or memorize another Golgotha,

I cannot tell. But I am faint;

My gashes cry for help.

King   So well thy words become thee as thy wounds,

They smack of honour both. Go get him surgeons.

[*Exit Captain with Attendants.*]

Enter Ross and Angus.

Who comes here?

45 **Malcolm**   The worthy thane of Ross.

Lennox   What a haste looks through his eyes.

So should he look, that seems to speak things strange.

Ross   God save the King.

King   Whence cam'st thou, worthy thane?

Ross   From Fife, great King,

	刚迫使这些轻兵逃之夭夭，	30
	可那挪威王，以为有机可乘，	
	他既补充军械，又增援新兵，	
	展开了新的进攻。	
国王	我们的将领不怕吗，麦克白和班柯？	
上尉	怕，正像老鹰怕麻雀，狮子怕野兔。	35
	说真的，我必须汇报他们二人	
	犹如装满双倍弹药的大炮，	
	他们倍加勇猛地杀向敌军。	
	除非他们想在血泊中沐浴，	
	或让人铭记另外一处各各他，	40
	我说不清楚。　可我晕了；	
	我的伤口在呼救。	
国王	你的言辞跟伤势同样得体，	
	都意味着荣誉。　给他叫医生去。	

　　　　　　　　　　　　　　　　　[上尉与侍从下。]

　　　　　　　　　　罗斯与安格斯上。

	是谁来了？	
马尔科姆	可敬的罗斯郡主。	45
兰诺克斯	你看他眼神多么急切！	
	看来他会讲些奇特的信息。	
罗斯	上帝保佑国王！	
国王	你从何而来，好郡主？	
罗斯	法夫，大王，	

---

　　30. 轻兵（skipping kerns）：其中，"skipping"可指"轻装的（lightly armed）"，也可指"无足轻重的（lightweight），不负责任的（irresponsible）"。　40. 各各他（Golgotha）：即"骷髅地（place of a skull）"，基督在此被钉死在十字架上；见"马可福音"15章22节（Bavington）。　45. 郡主（thane）：苏格兰当时的一种封号，与伯爵爵位相当。　49. 法夫（Fife）：法夫郡，位于苏格兰东部沿海地区。

50 Where the Norwegian banners flout the sky,

And fan our people cold.

Norway himself, with terrible numbers,

Assisted by that most disloyal traitor,

The thane of Cawdor, began a dismal conflict,

55 Till that Bellona's bridegroom, lapped in proof,

Confronted him with self-comparisons,

Point against point, rebellious arm 'gainst arm,

Curbing his lavish spirit; and to conclude,

The victory fell on us.

King   Great happiness.

60 **Ross** That now Sweno, the Norways' king, craves composition.

Nor would we deign him burial of his men,

Till he disbursed, at Saint Colme's Inch,

Ten thousand dollars, to our general use.

King No more that thane of Cawdor shall deceive

65 Our bosom interest. Go pronounce his present death,

And with his former title greet Macbeth.

Ross I'll see it done.

King What he hath lost, noble Macbeth hath won.   *Exeunt.*

嘲弄人的挪威旗飘摇之处,　　　　　　　　　　　　　　50
扇得我方胆寒。
挪威王本人,率领可怕的大军,
由那个最为不忠的叛贼协助,
即考道郡主,开始了一场血战,
直到战神的情郎,身披铠甲,　　　　　　　　　　　　　　55
旗鼓相当地与他直接对阵,
跟他针锋相对,以牙还牙,
将他的傲气制伏;总而言之,
胜利属于我方。

国王　　　　　　　　　大快人心!

罗斯　　挪威王——斯韦诺,现在请求议和。　　　　　　60
我们不许他埋葬阵亡将士,
直到他在圣科尔姆岛上赔款,
一万泰勒,以供我们公用。

国王　　那考道郡主再也不能骗取
我的信赖。 宣布将他立即处死,　　　　　　　　　　　65
以他原先的封号招呼麦克白。

罗斯　　我遵旨办理。

国王　　他所失去的,高贵的麦克白获取。　　　　　同下。

---

　　50. 嘲弄(flout):因为挪威国旗无权在法夫郡飘摇(Gill)。 53-4. 叛贼……考道(traitor…Cawdor):下一位考道郡主(Macbeth)将会扮演同一角色。 55. 战神的情郎(Bellona's bridegroom):通常认为指的是麦克白。 61. 不许他埋葬(Nor…burial):敌军须交付一笔赎金才会被允许埋葬其阵亡将士,表明这种做法在莎士比亚时期是一种战争惯例。 62. 圣科尔姆岛(Saint Colme's Inch):爱丁堡附近的福斯湾中的一座小岛。 其中,Colme 一词读作两个音节。 63. 泰勒(dollars):这是英国人对德国银币"thaler"的称谓(Clark)。 该币为德国 15—19 世纪期间所使用,1 泰勒值 3 马克(陆谷孙《英汉大词典》)。

SCENE III

Thunder. Enter the three Witches.

1 Witch	Where hast thou been, sister?
2 Witch	Killing swine.
3 Witch	Sister, where thou?
1 Witch	A sailor's wife had chestnuts in her lap,

5   And munched, and munched, and munched. 'Give me,' quoth I.

'Aroint thee, witch,' the rump-fed ronyon cries.

Her husband's to Aleppo gone, Master o'th' Tiger:

But in a sieve I'll thither sail,

And like a rat without a tail,

10   I'll do, I'll do, and I'll do.

2 Witch	I'll give thee a wind.
1 Witch	Th'art kind.
3 Witch	And I another.

第三场

雷声。三女巫上。

女巫甲	你到哪里去了,妹妹?
女巫乙	杀猪去了。
女巫丙	你呢,姐姐?
女巫甲	一位水手的妻子兜着板栗,

她嚼呀,嚼呀,嚼。"快给我,"我说。　　　　　　　　　　5

"滚开,巫婆,"大屁股贱妇喊道。

她丈夫,猛虎号船长,驶往阿勒颇:

我要乘坐筛子去那里,

扮成无尾老鼠作隐蔽,

我要做,我要做,我要做。　　　　　　　　　　　　　10

女巫乙	我给你一阵风。
女巫甲	你讲亲情。
女巫丙	我也给一阵。

　　1.3. 如女巫在1.1所言,本场应发生在荒野。　2. 杀猪去了（Killing swine）:女巫常被指控采用这种伎俩,这也许会使她们手沾鲜血。　6. 巫婆（witch）:带有侮辱性称谓。　值得注意的是,该词在剧中仅出现过两次,三女巫并不以此自称。　7. 猛虎号（th' Tiger）:莎士比亚时期的人们爱用这种名称命名船只（Muir）;阿勒颇（Aleppo）:叙利亚一贸易城市。　9. 无尾老鼠（rat⋯tail）:当时的人们相信,尽管女巫们可随心所欲地变成各种动物,却不会有尾巴,因为尽管她们可轻易地将自己的四肢变成动物的四只爪子,但她们身上却没有与动物的尾巴相匹配的部位（Muir）。　10. 我要做（I'll do）:她要变成一只老鼠溜到猛虎号的甲板而不被发现,然后再向小船和船长施魔（Muir）。　其中,"do"可指"行动（act）",也可指"做爱（perform sexually）"（Bevington）。　11. 给你一阵风（give⋯wind）:据信女巫可以呼风（produce wind）,并加以出售。　免费赠送表明姐妹间的相互支援。

1 Witch		I myself have all the other,
	15	And the very ports they blow,
		All the quarters that they know,
		I'th' shipman's card.
		I'll drain him dry as hay:
		Sleep shall neither night nor day
	20	Hang upon his penthouse lid:
		He shall live a man forbid.
		Weary sev'nights nine times nine
		Shall he dwindle, peak, and pine:
		Though his bark cannot be lost,
	25	Yet it shall be tempest-tossed.
		Look what I have.
2 Witch		Show me, show me.
1 Witch		Here I have a pilot's thumb,
		Wrecked as homeward he did come. *Drum within*
3 Witch	30	A drum, a drum:
		Macbeth doth come.
All		The weïrd sisters, hand in hand,
		Poster of the sea and land,
		Thus do go, about, about,

14

女巫甲	我自有其余那一份。	
	吹得他船只难进港，	15
	吹向水手的罗盘仪，	
	让他迷航向。	
	我把他耗尽如干草：	
	白天黑夜都难睡觉，	
	遮棚似的眼皮不下垂，	20
	他将会余生活受罪。	
	缠他九九八十又一周，	
	他将衰弱、憔悴和消瘦：	
	尽管他帆船不沉没，	
	也让他航程受颠簸。	25
	看看我有啥。	
女巫乙	我看看，我看看。	
女巫甲	这是一位舵手的拇指，	
	他在回家的途中失事。	内鸣鼓
女巫丙	鼓在敲，鼓在敲：	30
	麦克白已来到。	
三女巫	神秘姐妹手牵手，	
	海上陆上快速走，	
	就这样，转呀转，	

14-17. 结构较为复杂，其大意为"the Witches will so disorient the captain that he cannot steer his ship into safety（女巫们将使船长迷失方向，致使他无法安全返航）"。　14. 其余那一份（other）：其余的风力（other winds）。　18. 把他耗尽如干草（drain…hay）：使他性能力衰弱；该女巫也许可被视为（中世纪传说中与睡梦中男子交媾的）女淫妖（a succubus）。　20. 遮棚似的眼皮（penthouse lid）：将人的眼皮比作门廊或窗台上方附墙搭建的单斜顶棚或遮棚。　麦克白及其夫人之所以难眠，既与他们的罪行有关，也与这些女巫相连。　22. 九九八十又一周（sev'nights…nine）：数字9，跟3一样，常被女巫用在符咒之中。　见下文35-6。　24. 帆船不沉没（ship…lost）：这表明女巫的力量有限。　29. 舞台指示：内鸣鼓（Drum within），正如Muir先生所说，"令人奇怪的是，尽管只有麦克白和班柯两人入场，他们的到来却以鸣鼓为示"，因为这种声音可让人想到随后会有军队入场。　但莎士比亚显然是在为主人公的首次入场营造一种隆重的气氛。

35   Thrice to thine, and thrice to mine,

And thrice again, to make up nine.

Peace, the charm's wound up.

Enter Macbeth and Banquo.

Macbeth   So foul and fair a day I have not seen.

Banquo   How far is't called to Forres? What are these,

40   So withered and so wild in their attire,

That look not like th'inhabitants o'th' earth,

And yet are on't? Live you, or are you aught

That man may question? You seem to understand me,

By each at once her choppy finger laying

45   Upon her skinny lips. You should be women,

And yet your beards forbid me to interpret

That you are so.

Macbeth   Speak if you can: what are you?

1 Witch   All hail Macbeth, hail to thee, Thane of Glamis.

2 Witch   All hail Macbeth, hail to thee, Thane of Cawdor.

50 **3 Witch**   All hail Macbeth, that shalt be king hereafter.

Banquo   Good sir, why do you start, and seem to fear

Things that do sound so fair? —I'th' name of truth,

Are ye fantastical, or that indeed

Which outwardly ye show? My noble partner

绕你三圈,我三圈, 　　　　　　　　　　　　　　　35

再绕三圈,共九圈。

够了,魔法已备好。

　　　　　　麦克白与班柯上。

麦克白　　未见过如此糟糕美丽的时刻。

班柯　　弗瑞斯还有多远？　这是何物,

形容枯干,衣着又这么难看, 　　　　　　　　40

看上去不像是世间的居民,

却又在世间？　活的吗？　你们能否

回答提问？　你们好像懂我意思,

因为你们立刻将皱巴的手指

放在干瘪的唇上。　你们该是女人, 　　　　45

可是你们的胡须却使我无法

信以为真。

麦克白　　　　　　能说就说:你们是谁？

女巫甲　　恭喜麦克白,恭喜你,葛莱密郡主!

女巫乙　　恭喜麦克白,恭喜你,考道郡主!

女巫丙　　恭喜麦克白,今后你会做国王! 　　　　50

班柯　　大将军,您为何一怔？　好像害怕

闻听这大好消息？　——请说实话,

你们是幻影,还是像你们的外表

那样确有其身？　对我的伙伴,

35-6. 她们在跳圆圈舞,共跳九圈。　女巫此处的动作常与琼森(Ben Jonson)在其剧本中所描述的类似动作相提并论,参考《王后们的假面舞会》(*The Masques of Queens*)。　即:女巫们背对背、手牵手地跳舞,从右至左,逆时针方向。　39. 弗瑞斯(Forres):苏格兰东北部默里湾(Moray Firth)沿岸地区一小镇。　Muir 认为麦克白他们在 1.4 到达弗瑞斯,此处离麦克白在因弗内斯(Inverness)的城堡不远;但剧中人物的活动方位并非十分清晰。　44-5. 该手势表明女巫们拒绝与班柯说话;而是立即回应了麦克白的问话(Muir)。　48. 葛莱密(Glamis):(原苏格兰)安格斯郡(Angus)一村庄,位于苏格兰东部港市敦提(Dundee)以北,中世纪一城堡所在地。　该郡主封号属于麦克白家族。

55
You greet with present grace, and great prediction

Of noble having and of royal hope,

That he seems rapt withal. To me you speak not.

If you can look into the seeds of time,

And say which grain will grow, and which will not,

60
Speak then to me, who neither beg nor fear

Your favours, nor your hate.

1 Witch   Hail.

2 Witch   Hail.

3 Witch   Hail.

65 **1 Witch**   Lesser than Macbeth, and greater.

2 Witch   Not so happy, yet much happier.

3 Witch   Thou shalt get kings, though thou be none:

So all hail Macbeth, and Banquo.

1 Witch   Banquo, and Macbeth, all hail.

70 **Macbeth**   Stay, you imperfect speakers, tell me more.

By Finel's death, I know I am Thane of Glamis,

But how of Cawdor? The Thane of Cawdor lives,

A prosperous gentleman: and to be king

Stands not within the prospect of belief,

75
No more than to be Cawdor. Say from whence

You owe this strange intelligence, or why

Upon this blasted heath you stop our way

With such prophetic greeting? Speak, I charge you.

Witches vanish.

	致以即刻的恩惠,也预言他会	55
	享有荣华还有望登上王位,	
	使他欣喜若狂。 对我却沉默。	
	你们若能洞察时间的种子,	
	知道哪一粒会长,哪一粒不会,	
	就告诉我吧,我不求你们施恩,	60
	也不怕你们憎恨。	
女巫甲	恭喜!	
女巫乙	恭喜!	
女巫丙	恭喜!	
女巫甲	比麦克白小些,但又大些。	65
女巫乙	不如他幸运,却更加幸运。	
女巫丙	你会生国王,尽管你不是:	
	因此恭喜麦克白,与班柯!	
女巫甲	班柯,与麦克白,恭喜你们!	
麦克白	站住,你们说的不全,多说点!	70
	辛奈尔死后,我自然是葛莱密郡主,	
	但考道郡主从何说起? 他还活着,	
	一位显赫的绅士:至于做王,	
	同样不可思议,就像做考道	
	郡主一样。 快说你们从何处	75
	得到这些奇怪的信息,为何	
	在这荒郊野外以预言式的	
	招呼拦住我们? 说,我命令你们!	

三女巫消失。

58. 时间的种子(seeds of time):这是该剧诸多有关自然生长意象(images of natural growth)的首次出现,评论家们就此联想到孩子们的自然成长。 67. 生国王(get kings):其中,get 是指 beget(生;为……之生父)。 女巫丙将班柯视为詹姆斯六世和一世(James Ⅵ and Ⅰ)的先王,由其子弗林斯传承。 71. 辛奈尔(Finel):在霍林希德的原著中该词原本拼写为"Sinell",系麦克白之父。

19

Banquo	The earth hath bubbles, as the water has,
80	And these are of them. Whither are they vanished?
Macbeth	Into the air; and what seemed corporal,
	Melted, as breath into the wind.
	Would they had stayed.
Banquo	Were such things here as we do speak about?
85	Or have we eaten on the insane root,
	That takes the reason prisoner?
Macbeth	Your children shall be kings.
Banquo	You shall be king.
Macbeth	And Thane of Cawdor too: went it not so?
Banquo	To th' self-same tune and words. Who's here?

Enter Ross and Angus.

90 **Ross**	The King hath happily received, Macbeth,
	The news of thy success; and when he reads
	Thy personal venture in the rebels' fight,
	His wonders and his praises do contend
	Which should be thine, or his. Silenced with that,
95	In viewing o'er the rest o'th' self-same day,
	He finds thee in the stout Norwegian ranks,
	Nothing afeard of what thyself didst make,
	Strange images of death. As thick as tale
	Came post with post, and every one did bear

班柯	地上也有水泡,跟水上一样,	
	她们就是水泡。 她们何处去了?	80
麦克白	到空中去了,看似有形的东西,	
	化了,像呼出的气息随风而去。	
	但愿她们还在!	
班柯	我们所说的东西真出现过?	
	还是我们吃了害人的草根,	85
	导致我们失去理智?	
麦克白	您的子孙要做国王。	
班柯	您要做国王。	
麦克白	还要做考道郡主:难道不是?	
班柯	说的一点不错。 是谁来了?	

罗斯与安格斯上。

罗斯	国王已高兴地获悉,麦克白,	90
	你胜利的消息;每当他听到	
	你奋力搏杀叛贼的英勇事迹,	
	无法分清是对战功感到惊讶,	
	还是对你表示钦佩。 因此无语,	
	查看当天的其他平叛战况时,	95
	知道你又杀入强悍的挪威阵营,	
	对自己的杰作——敌军尸首的	
	奇形怪状——毫不畏惧。 无数的	
	信差接踵而至,每一位信差	

---

85. 害人的草根(insane root):据信,人们若吃了诸如毒芹属植物(hemlock)的草根,就会发疯。 93-4. 无法……钦佩(His…his):原注为"There is a conflict in Duncan's mind between his astonishment at the achievement and his admiration for Macbeth"(Muir)。 这是错综复杂之恭维话的又一例证(Clark)。 98-9. 无数……而至(As…with post):其中,"tale"是指"tally(计数用的签子)",该词常被修订为"hail(冰雹)",其实并无必要。 因为"thick"可指"快速(fast)"。 罗斯的意思是:麦克白的杀敌速度快得就像飞速而至的信差数不胜数(Macbeth killed men so rapidly that it was like posts [couriers] arriving so fast that they could not be counted)。

100   Thy praises in his kingdom's great defence,

And poured them down before him.

Angus   We are sent

To give thee from our royal master thanks,

Only to herald thee into his sight,

Not pay thee.

105 **Ross**   And for an earnest of a greater honour,

He bade me, from him, call thee Thane of Cawdor:

In which addition, hail most worthy thane.

For it is thine.

Banquo   What, can the devil speak true?

Macbeth   The Thane of Cawdor lives. Why do you dress me

In borrowed robes?

110 **Angus**   Who was the Thane lives yet,

But under heavy judgement bears that life

Which he deserves to lose.

Whether he was combined with those of Norway,

Or did line the rebel with hidden help

115   And vantage, or that with both he laboured

In his country's wreck, I know not,

But treasons capital, confessed and proved,

Have overthrown him.

Macbeth   [*aside*]   Glamis and Thane of Cawdor:

The greatest is behind. —Thanks for your pains.

120   [*to Banquo*] Do you not hope your children shall be kings

When those that gave the Thane of Cawdor to me

Promised no less to them?

	都带着对您保卫王国的赞誉,	100
	将其倒在国王面前。	
安格斯	我们奉命	
	向你传达国王大人的谢意,	
	只是将你引领到他的面前,	
	不是酬谢。	
罗斯	作为一种更高荣誉的保证,	105
	他令我,将你称为考道郡主:	
	用这种头衔,欢呼高贵的郡主,	
	它已是你的。	
班柯	啊,巫婆之言当真?	
麦克白	考道郡主还活着。 为啥把他的	
	袍子穿给我?	
安格斯	该郡主是还活着,	110
	然而他那条性命被判以极刑,	
	他将因此丧生。	
	至于他是与挪威军队为伍,	
	还是暗中对叛军给以支持	
	和帮助,或与二者协同作战	115
	想让祖国倾覆,我不清楚,	
	但叛国为死罪,已经招供并证实,	
	他因此被毁。	
麦克白	[旁白] 葛莱密和考道郡主:	
	最好的还在后头——多谢二位辛苦。	
	[向班柯]您不希望自己的子孙做王吗,	120
	因为她们称我为考道郡主时	
	对他们的许诺不差?	

---

121. 她们（those）：即巫婆。 麦克白好像不愿直呼其名。

Banquo   That, trusted home,

Might yet enkindle you unto the crown,

Besides the Thane of Cawdor. But 'tis strange:

125   And oftentimes, to win us to our harm,

The instruments of darkness tell us truths,

Win us with honest trifles, to betray's

In deepest consequence.

Cousins, a word, I pray you.

Macbeth   [*aside*]   Two truths are told

130   As happy prologues to the swelling act

Of the imperial theme. —I thank you, gentlemen. —

This supernatural soliciting

Cannot be ill; cannot be good. If ill,

Why hath it given me earnest of success,

135   Commencing in a truth? I am Thane of Cawdor.

If good, why do I yield to that suggestion

Whose horrid image doth unfix my hair,

And make my seated heart knock at my ribs,

Against the use of nature? Present fears

140   Are less than horrible imaginings.

My thought, whose murder yet is but fantastical,

Shakes so my single state of man

班柯	若是全信，	
	除了考道郡主之外，还会使您	
	燃起称王之心。　可真是奇怪：	
	往往是，为使我们深受其害，	125
	邪恶的爪牙就会讲些真话，	
	以小恩小惠赢得信任，关键时	
	将我们置于死地。	
	二位，咱说说话吧。	
麦克白	［旁白］　　　　两件事已验证，	
	欢快的开场预示着帝王的大戏	130
	即将亮相。　——谢谢二位先生。——	
	这么一种不可思议的教唆	
	好像不坏；但也不好。　若是坏，	
	它怎么给我一个成功的保证，	
	一开始就应验？　我已是考道郡主。	135
	若是好，怎么一想到那种诱惑，	
	它的恐怖情形令我毛骨悚然，	
	让我镇静的心脏怦怦直跳，	
	使我一反常态？　可怕的事实	
	还不如可怕的想象更为恐怖。	140
	我的凶杀之念只不过是虚幻，	
	竟使这可怜的躯体瑟瑟发抖，	

129. 二位（cousins）：班柯将罗斯与安格斯引向一旁。　130. 开场（prologues）：麦克白正在想象自己未来的大戏即将上演。　大戏（swelling act）：参考《亨利五世》开场白3-4行："整个王国作舞台，王子来表演，/并由国王观看这种大场面（A kingdom for a stage, princes to act, / And monarch to behold the swelling scene！）。"131. 谢谢二位先生（I···gentlemen）：麦克白好象突然意识到还有别人在场。　137. 恐怖情形（horrid image）：亲自杀害邓肯的情景。　139-40. 可怕的······恐怖（Present···imaginings）：意为"Real objects of fear are less terrible than those conjured by the imagination（因想象而产生的惧怕比可怕的事实还要可怕）"。　141-4. 意为"Macbeth's mind, which thinks of murder as merely fantastical, disturbs his whole being. He can do nothing because he is wondering what will happen（'surmise'）. Only the future（'what is not'）is real to him"（Gill）；这种复杂的表述说明麦克白心绪不宁（Clark）。

		That function is smothered in surmise,
		And nothing is, but what is not.
145	**Banquo**	Look how our partner's rapt.
	Macbeth	[*aside*] If chance will have me king, why chance may crown me,
		Without my stir.
	Banquo	New honours come upon him,
		Like our strange garments, cleave not to their mould,
		But with the aid of use.
	Macbeth	[*aside*] Come what come may,
150		Time, and the hour, runs through the roughest day.
	Banquo	Worthy Macbeth, we stay upon your leisure.
	Macbeth	Give me your favour. My dull brain was wrought
		With things forgotten. Kind gentlemen, your pains
		Are registered, where every day I turn
155		The leaf to read them. Let us toward the King.
		Think upon what hath chanced; and at more time,
		The interim having weighed it, let us speak
		Our free hearts each to other.
	Banquo	Very gladly.
	Macbeth	Till then, enough: come, friends. *Exeunt.*

因为臆测而使我一筹莫展，

全是幻觉，尚未实现。

班柯　　　看我们的伙伴已走神。　　　　　　　　　　　　　　145

麦克白　　［旁白］若注定称王，命运会为我加冕，

不用我动手。

班柯　　　　　　　　他刚得来的头衔，

就像我们的新衣，穿惯了之后，

才会合身。

麦克白　　［旁白］　该发生的尽管发生，

再艰难的时刻也会有止境。　　　　　　　　　　　150

班柯　　　尊贵的麦克白，我们在等候您。

麦克白　　请你们原谅。　我这迟钝的大脑

在回忆往事。　好先生，你们的辛劳，

已经记下，我每天都会翻开

书页加以朗诵。　咱们去见国王。　　　　　　　155

想想刚才发生的事情；空闲时，

在此期间好好掂量，我们再

彼此之间畅所欲言。

班柯　　　　　　　　　　　很乐意。

麦克白　　到时再谈：走吧，朋友。　　　　　　　　　同下。

---

147. 得来的（come）：come = which have come (Bevington)。　148-9. 就像……合身（Like…use）：意为"New clothes do not fit（'cleave to'）our bodies until we are accustomed to them"（Gill）。　150. 出自谚语"The longest day has an end（再长的日子也有尽头）"。　麦克白试图用谚语证明自己此刻不采取行动的决定合理正当。　其中，"run through（流过，穿过）"，犹如沙漏中的沙粒一般。　153-5. 你们的……朗诵（your…them）：意为"His memory is like a book, which he reads every day, and he will always remember their efforts（'pains'）"（Gill）。

SCENE IV

Flourish. Enter King [Duncan], Lennox,
Malcolm, Donalbain and Attendants.

King   Is execution done on Cawdor? Or not
Those in commission yet returned?

Malcolm   My liege,
They are not yet come back. But I have spoke
With one that saw him die, who did report,
5   That very frankly he confessed his treasons,
Implored your highness' pardon, and set forth
A deep repentance. Nothing in his life
Became him like the leaving it. He died
As one that had been studied in his death,
10   To throw away the dearest thing he owed,
As 'twere a careless trifle.

King   There's no art
To find the mind's construction in the face:
He was a gentleman on whom I built
An absolute trust.

第四场

号角齐鸣。邓肯国王、兰诺克斯、
马尔科姆、唐纳班与侍从上。

国王　　考道的死刑是否已执行？　负责
行刑的人员尚未返回？

马尔科姆　　　　　　　　陛下，
他们还没回来。　不过我曾跟
一位目睹他受刑者谈话，他说，
他坦白了自己的叛国之罪，　　　　　　　　　　5
恳求陛下给以宽恕，他感到
非常懊悔。　他平生行事从未
像他临终时那样得体。　他死得
好像自己对死亡已习以为常，
将自己最宝贵的东西抛弃，　　　　　　　　　10
好像那是无用的垃圾。

国王　　　　　　　无法
从人的面部看透他的内心：
我曾经把他视为正人君子，
绝对信任。

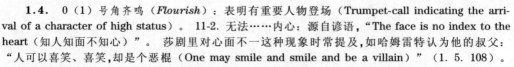

1.4.　0（1）号角齐鸣（*Flourish*）：表明有重要人物登场（Trumpet-call indicating the arrival of a character of high status）。　11-2. 无法……内心：源自谚语，"The face is no index to the heart（知人知面不知心）"。　莎剧里对心面不一这种现象时常提及，如哈姆雷特认为他的叔父："人可以喜笑、喜笑，却是个恶棍（One may smile and smile and be a villain）"（1. 5. 108）。"批评家们注意到，麦克白紧随其后的入场使该台词的讽刺意味尤为明显"（Muir）。

Enter Macbeth, Banquo, Ross and Angus.

O worthiest cousin,

15 The sin of my ingratitude even now

Was heavy on me. Thou art so far before,

That swiftest wing of recompense is slow

To overtake thee. Would thou hadst less deserved,

That the proportion both of thanks, and payment,

20 Might have been mine. Only I have left to say,

More is thy due, than more than all can pay.

Macbeth The service and the loyalty I owe,

In doing it, pays itself. Your highness' part

Is to receive our duties; and our duties

25 Are to your throne and state, children and servants,

Which do but what they should, by doing every thing

Safe toward your love and honour.

King   Welcome hither.

I have begun to plant thee, and will labour

To make thee full of growing. Noble Banquo,

30 That hast no less deserved, nor must be known

No less to have done so. Let me enfold thee

And hold thee to my heart.

麦克白、班柯、罗斯与安格斯上。

噢，我最可敬的堂兄！

此刻我为自己未能充分谢你　　　　　　　　　　　15

感到罪责沉重。　你如此遥不可及，

即使酬劳能插翅飞奔也无法

追赶上你。　但愿你应得的少些，

以便让我对你的谢意和酬劳

能成比例。　我唯一可说的是，　　　　　　　　　20

我倾尽所有也无法足以回报。

麦克白　　按本分应对陛下尽职效忠，

能做到，便是酬劳。　陛下的名分

是接受我们的效劳；我们的效劳

对您和王国而言，像子女和臣仆，　　　　　　　25

只是理应而为，当竭尽全力

保卫我们爱戴的陛下。

国王　　　　　　　　　　　　欢迎归来。

我已开始栽培你了，还会尽力

使你繁荣昌盛。　高贵的班柯，

你也劳苦功高，因此也必须　　　　　　　　　30

大加褒扬。　我来跟你拥抱，

让你和我贴心。

　　16-20.　你如此……比例（Thou…mine）：意为"Macbeth, in his deserving, is far ahead of any payment. Duncan wishes he had deserved less, so that his thanks and reward might be more in proportion"（Gill）。邓肯在剧中所采用的这种华丽文体（florid style）颇具特色，旨在表达自己的谦恭有礼（Clark）。　22-7.　按本分……陛下（The…honour）："麦克白只是在用一种表示忠诚的陈词滥调掩饰自己……是在论理而不是欢喜（*Reasoning* instead of joy）"（Muir）。27.　保卫……陛下（Safe…honour）：意为"to safeguard you whom we love and honour"（Bevington）。　28.　栽培（planted）：正直的人在《圣经》里常被比作枝繁叶茂的树木，由上帝栽培。　参考"耶利米书"12章2节："你栽培了他们，他们也扎了根，长大，而且结果。"

Banquo   There if I grow

The harvest is your own.

King   My plenteous joys,

Wanton in fullness, seek to hide themselves

35   In drops of sorrow. Sons, kinsmen, thanes,

And you whose places are the nearest, know:

We will establish our estate upon

Our eldest, Malcolm, whom we name hereafter,

The Prince of Cumberland, which honour must,

40   Not unaccompanied, invest him only.

But signs of nobleness, like stars, shall shine

On all deservers. From hence to Inverness,

And bind us further to you.

Macbeth   The rest is labour which is not used for you;

45   I'll be myself the harbinger, and make joyful

The hearing of my wife with your approach.

So humbly take my leave.

King   My worthy Cawdor!

Macbeth   [*aside*] The Prince of Cumberland: that is a step

On which I must fall down, or else o'er-leap,

50   For in my way it lies. Stars, hide your fires,

Let not light see my black and deep desires.

班柯	我若茁壮成长,	
	收获属于国王。	
国王	我丰盛的喜悦,	
	已四处洋溢,竟寻求悲伤的泪水	
	掩藏自己。 儿子、亲属、郡主、	35
	以及最最亲密的大臣,我宣布,	
	我要把我的王位继承人定为	
	长子马尔科姆,此后要称他	
	坎伯兰亲王,然而这样的荣誉,	
	并非让他独享,赋予他一人。	40
	高贵的封号,将使所有功臣	
	灿若星辰。 现在就去因弗内斯,	
	使我对您更为感激。	
麦克白	不为陛下效力,一切都无意义;	
	我要充当先行官,让我夫人	45
	知道您即将莅临,使她欣喜。	
	我就此向您告辞。	
国王	可敬的考道!	
麦克白	[旁白]坎伯兰亲王:那是一个台阶,	
	定会把我绊倒,除非将其跨越,	
	因为他当道拦阻。 星星,别闪!	50
	别让光明看见我阴险的意念。	

32-3. 我若……国王(There…own):与麦克白相比,班柯所说的恭维话要自然多了。 39. 坎伯兰亲王(Prince of Cumberland):对苏格兰王位具有当然继承权的封号。 42. 因弗内斯(Inverness):苏格兰东海岸默里湾上游一小镇,麦克白的城堡所在地。 43. 意为"(我去你家做客)将使我更加受惠于你(make me more indebted to you(as your guest))"(Jonathan Bate; Royal Shakespeare Company, 2007;下称"Bate"。 ——译者附注)。 其中,"bind us further"意为:"increase our debt(使我亏欠得更多)"(Gill)。 50. 星星(Stars):"麦克白之所以恳求星星,是因为他在思忖夜晚将是他准备行动的时间。 毫无证据表明本场是发生在夜晚"(Muir)。

The eye wink at the hand; yet let that be

Which the eye fears, when it is done, to see.   *Exit.*

King   True, worthy Banquo, he is full so valiant,

55   And in his commendations I am fed:

It is a banquet to me. Let's after him,

Whose care is gone before to bid us welcome.

It is a peerless kinsman.   *Flourish. Exeunt.*

眼睛要对手眨眼；要把它做出，

事成之后，尽管会惨不忍睹。　　　　　　　　　　　　下。

国王　　　对，可敬的班柯，他是非常勇敢，

对他的赞扬就是我的食粮：　　　　　　　　　　　　　　55

筵席般富有营养。咱们跟上他，

他先走是想好好地迎接我们。

真是盖世无双的亲人。　　　　　　　　　号角齐鸣。同下。

---

52. 眨眼（wink at）：视而不见（seem not to see）；默许，怂恿（connive）。其中，原文中的 "be = be done"（Muir）。54-5. 非常……食粮（full…fed）：邓肯的这种溢美之词，利用食物意象（food images），旨在表达：人们对麦克白的所有赞美对他来说都是一种营养（any praise for Macbeth is a sustenance to him）。

SCENE V

Enter Macbeth's wife [Lady] alone with a letter.

Lady   *They met me in the day of success, and I have*
learned by the perfectest report, they have more
in them than mortal knowledge. When I burned in
desire to question them further, they made themselves
5   *air, into which they vanished. Whiles I stood rapt*
in the ·wonder of it, came missive from the King,
who all-hailed me ' Thane of Cawdor', by which title
before these weïrd sisters saluted me, and referred
me to the coming on of time, with ' Hail King that
10   *shalt be'. This have I thought good to deliver thee,*
my dearest partner of greatness, that thou mightst
not lose the dues of rejoicing by being ignorant of
what greatness is promised thee. Lay it to thy heart,
and farewell.

15   Glamis thou art, and Cawdor, and shalt be
What thou art promised. Yet do I fear thy nature,
It is too full o'th' milk of human kindness
To catch the nearest way. Thou wouldst be great,

第五场

　　　　　麦克白的妻子[夫人]独自一人持信上。

夫人　　　就在胜利之日她们与我相遇。我现在
　　　　具有最为可靠的证据,证明她们拥有
　　　　超凡的预知能力。正当我急不可耐地
　　　　想要进一步追问她们时,她们便化为
　　　　空气,随风而去。当我站在那里为此　　　　5
　　　　感到莫名其妙时,国王派的使者赶到,
　　　　他们欢呼我为"考道郡主",三位女巫
　　　　此前曾用这种头衔向我致意。她们还
　　　　向我提及了未来,并说"恭喜,你会
　　　　做国王"。我想我该将此事告知于你,　　　　10
　　　　我最最亲爱和高贵的伙伴儿,以免你
　　　　会因为对自己的伟大应许一无所知而
　　　　失去你应得的那一份欣喜。暂且保密,
　　　　再会吧。
　　　　你已是葛莱密,和考道,然后将是　　　　15
　　　　你的应许。　可我担心你的性情,
　　　　你这人可是过分地心慈手软,
　　　　不会走捷径。　你想要大名鼎鼎,

　　1.5. 15. 将是（shalt be）：麦克白夫人在重复女巫丙的预言,本能地对"国王（King）"一词进行了回避,随之换成一个富有保留的短语（Muir）。

20

Art not without ambition, but without

The illness should attend it. What thou wouldst highly,

That wouldst thou holily; wouldst not play false,

And yet wouldst wrongly win. Thou'dst have, great Glamis,

That which cries, 'Thus thou must do', if thou have it;

And that which rather thou dost fear to do,

25

Than wishest should be undone. Hie thee hither,

That I may pour my spirits in thine ear,

And chastise with the valour of my tongue

All that impedes thee from the golden round,

Which fate and metaphysical aid doth seem

To have thee crowned withal.

Enter Messenger.

30   What is your tidings?

Messenger The King comes here tonight.

Lady   Thou'rt mad to say it.

Is not thy master with him? Who, were't so,

Would have informed for preparation.

Messenger So please you, it is true: our thane is coming.

35 One of my fellows had the speed of him,

Who, almost dead for breath, had scarcely more

Than would make up his message.

Lady   Give him tending,

He brings great news.   *Exit Messenger.*

The raven himself is hoarse

也不是没有雄心,但是缺乏

应有的恶毒。　你想要高人一等,　　　　　　　　　20

但要靠正当途径;你不想骗取,

又想暗中获胜。　你想要的,大郡主,

那王冠在喊,"你要行动",若想成功;

你只是害怕去完成那件事情,

不希望它没有完成。　你快回来,　　　　　　　　　25

好把我的激情灌入你的耳中,

我要用舌尖的锐气将那阻止你

获取那顶金冠的障碍清洗,

既然命运和鬼神好像都要

就此助你一臂之力。

　　　　　　　　　　信差上。

　　　　　　　　　有啥消息?　　　　　　　　　　　　30

信差　　国王今晚要来。

夫人　　　　　　　你胡说八道!

你主人不是跟他一起?　若这样,

他就会通知我让我做好准备。

信差　　回夫人,是真的:郡主他很快就到。

我的一位同伴跑在他前面,　　　　　　　　　　　　35

他几乎喘不过气来,只能勉强地

传达这一消息。

夫人　　　　　　去招待他吧,

他带来喜讯。　　　　　　　　　　　信差下。

　　　　乌鸦的嘶哑叫声

---

31. 国王今晚要来(The King…tonight):麦克白夫人此刻将自己的丈夫视为了国王,她以为信差指的是她的丈夫,而不是邓肯(Muir)。　31-3. 你胡说……准备(Thou'rt…preparation):麦克白夫人在回答信差的过程中泄露了自己的心思;当她看到信差为此吃惊时,便顺口说出了一种勉强的解释(Muir)。　38. 乌鸦……叫声(The raven…hoarse):乌鸦常被视为一种不祥之鸟和报丧者(a bird of ill omen and herald of death)。

That croaks the fatal entrance of Duncan

40 Under my battlements. Come, you spirits

That tend on mortal thoughts, unsex me here,

And fill me from the crown to the toe, top-full

Of direst cruelty. Make thick my blood,

Stop up th'access and passage to remorse,

45 That no compunctious visitings of nature

Shake my fell purpose, nor keep peace between

Th'effect and it. Come to my woman's breasts,

And take my milk for gall, you murdering ministers,

Wherever, in your sightless substances,

50 You wait on nature's mischief. Come, thick night,

And pall thee in the dunnest smoke of hell,

That my keen knife see not the wound it makes,

Nor heaven peep through the blanket of the dark,

To cry, 'Hold, hold!'

Enter Macbeth.

Great Glamis, worthy Cawdor,

55 Greater than both, by the all-hail hereafter,

Thy letters have transported me beyond

This ignorant present, and I feel now

The future in the instant.

已经宣告了邓肯即将到我的
城堡送命。　快来,你们这看管 40
人类杀心的幽灵,除去我的女性,
从头到脚,让我浑身都充满
最为可怕的残暴! 让血液黏稠,
堵住连接悔恨的入口和通道;
以免内疚的天良前来造访 45
将我的毒计动摇,或者阻止我
如愿以偿! 快来我女人的胸前,
把乳水变为胆汁,残忍的帮凶,
你们以无形的躯体到处怂恿
人们的罪恶行径! 快来,黑夜, 50
罩上地狱中最为黑暗的烟雾,
以免我的利刃看见它的刀口,
或上帝透过漆黑的罩毯窥见
并呼喊,"住手!"

麦克白上。

高贵的葛莱密和考道!
根据未来的预言,比二者更高, 55
你的信件已经使我超越了
这种无知的现在,我此时此刻
就能感受未来。

40, 47, 50. 快来……快来……快来(Come…come…come):跟三女巫一样,麦克白夫人也向鬼神召唤再三(makes a triple invocation)。 43. 让血液黏稠(make…blood):当时的医学理论认为人们维持生命所需的神经要通过血液传递,如果本应"清纯与康健的血液(thin and wholesome)(《哈姆雷特》1.5.70)"却变得"黏稠(thickened)",便会出现各种病态。55. 未来的预言(all-hail hereafter):future prophecy(Gill)。 女巫所预言的未来(the future prophesied by the witches)(Bate)。 57. 无知的现在(ignorant present):对未来无知的现在(this present which is ignorant of the future)(Muir)。 57-8. 我……未来(I…instant):我预感到未来的那些荣耀,但若顺其自然,目前便无法知晓(I feel by anticipation those future honours, of which, according to the process of nature, the present time would be ignorant)(Muir)。

Macbeth   My dearest love,

Duncan comes here tonight.

Lady   And when goes hence?

Macbeth   Tomorrow, as he purposes.

60 **Lady**   O never

Shall sun that morrow see.

Your face, my thane, is as a book, where men

May read strange matters; to beguile the time,

Look like the time, bear welcome in your eye,

65   Your hand, your tongue; look like the innocent flower,

But be the serpent under't. He that's coming

Must be provided for; and you shall put

This night's great business into my dispatch,

Which shall to all our nights and days to come,

70   Give solely sovereign sway and masterdom.

Macbeth   We will speak further.

Lady   Only look up clear;

To alter favour ever is to fear.

Leave all the rest to me.   *Exeunt.*

麦克白	我最亲的爱人，	
	邓肯今晚要来。	
夫人	那何时离开？	
麦克白	明天,他是这样打算。	
夫人	但愿他	60

永远见不到那个明天！

您的脸面,郡主,像书本,奇思

怪想都可以看出,想欺骗世人,

就要随机应变,您要用眼睛、

手和舌头欢迎；貌似纯洁的鲜花， 65

却是花下的毒蛇。 我们的来客

需要盛情款待；您一定要把

今晚的大事交给我来处置,

此举将会使我们一劳永逸,

让我们独揽王权主宰大地。 70

麦克白　咱要从长计议。

夫人　　　　　要若无其事；

改变脸色就是恐惧的标志。

其他都交给我了。　　　　　　　　　同下。

61. 那个明天（that morrow）：即邓肯活着离开的那一天（the day when Duncan departs alive）。 62. 脸面……书本（face…book）：将脸面比喻成书本颇为常见。 63. 欺骗世人（beguile the time）：即欺骗世界,哄骗观众（deceive the world, delude all observers）（Muir）。 64. 随机应变（Look like the time）：根据具体的场景变换表情（put on an expression suitable to the occasion）（Clark）。 （作为主人）要摆出一副恰如其分的欢迎姿态（put on the appropriate appearance［which now is that of the welcoming host］）（Gill）。 67. 盛情款待（provided for）：带有阴险的暗示。 夫妻二人对此心照不宣。 68. 大事（great business）：委婉语——麦克白夫妇本场台词中的语言特色。 我来处置（my dispatch）：这未必意味着麦克白夫人想亲自动手,只是表明她想统管这件事情（This does not necessarily mean that Lady Macbeth intended to do the actual deed, but merely that she intends to manage the whole affair）（Muir）。 其中,"dispatch"可指"处理（management）",也可指"处决（putting to death）"（Clark）。 72. "若某人的表情忐忑不安,即可暴露他有心事——这会引起怀疑（When a person shows a disturbed countenance, it is always inferred he has something in his mind—and that may rouse suspicion）"（Muir）。

SCENE VI

Hautboys and Torches. Enter King [Duncan],
Malcolm, Donalbain, Banquo, Lennox,
Macduff, Ross, Angus and Attendants.

King   This castle hath a pleasant seat, the air
Nimbly and sweetly recommends itself
Unto our gentle senses.

  Banquo   This guest of summer,
The temple-haunting martlet, does approve,
5   By his loved mansionry, that the heaven's breath
Smells wooingly here. No jutty frieze,
Buttress, nor coin of vantage, but this bird
Hath made his pendent bed, and procreant cradle:
Where they must breed and haunt, I have observed
The air is delicate.

Enter Lady.

10 **King**   See, see, our honoured hostess.
The love that follows us, sometime is our trouble,
Which still we thank as love. Herein I teach you
How you shall bid God yield us for your pains,

第六场

吹奏双簧管并掌起火把。国王〔邓肯〕、
　　马尔科姆、唐纳班、班柯、雷诺克斯、
　　麦克达夫、罗斯、安格斯与侍从上。

国王　　　这座城堡位置怡人，空气
　　　　扑面而来，流畅清新，让我
　　　　感到神清气爽。

班柯　　　　　　　　这位夏天的宾客，
　　　　时常出入庙宇的家燕，既然
　　　　在此筑巢，可表明空中的微风　　　　　　　　　　5
　　　　沁人心脾。　凡是凸出的雕带、
　　　　拥壁，以及合适的角落，这燕子
　　　　均已搭起吊床和育雏的摇篮：
　　　　它们的繁衍生息之处，我发现
　　　　总是空气新鲜。

　　　　　　　　　　　夫人上。

国王　　　　　　　　看，看，尊贵的主妇！　　　　　　10
　　　　对我的关爱，有时是一种麻烦，
　　　　因为是爱总要感激。　我就此教您
　　　　求上帝奖赏我因为叫您费力，

1.6.　　1-10. 这座……新鲜（This…delicate）：邓肯对该城堡的判断再次表明他没有能力洞
察事物的表象。　班柯此刻也未例外。

And thank us for your trouble.

Lady   All our service,

15   In every point twice done, and then done double,

Were poor and single business, to contend

Against those honours deep and broad wherewith

Your majesty loads our house. For those of old,

And the late dignities heaped up to them,

We rest your hermits.

20   **King**   Where's the Thane of Cawdor?

We coursed him at the heels, and had a purpose

To be his purveyor. But he rides well,

And his great love, sharp as his spur, hath holp him

To his home before us. Fair and noble hostess,

We are your guest tonight.

25   **Lady**   Your servants ever,

Have theirs, themselves, and what is theirs in count,

To make their audit at your highness' pleasure,

Still to return your own.

还要谢我麻烦您。

夫人　　　　　　　　　我们的效劳，

即使加倍履行，再履行加倍，　　　　　　　　　　　　15

也将会微不足道，假如要跟

陛下所赋予我们家的显赫

声誉相比。　为报答过去的恩宠，

以及最近所追加的各种封号，

我们专为您祈祷。

国王　　　　　　　　　考道郡主呢？　　　　　　　20

我对他紧追不舍，本想为他

来打前站。　可是他策马驰骋，

归心似箭，他的厚爱协助他

先一步到家。　优雅高贵的主妇，

今晚我在您家做客。

夫人　　　　　　　　　您的臣仆、　　　　　　　25

其家人、自身，以及托管之物，

陛下您无论何时都可以结算，

总会如数归还。

11-4. 对我的……麻烦您（The love…trouble）：原注为，"I am sometimes embarrassed by the love that is shown to me（'follows us'），but I am always（'still'）grateful, because it *is* love. In this I am teaching you to ask God to reward（'yield'）me for the trouble（'pains'）that *you* are having to take, and also to thank *me* for that trouble."（Gill）。 11-2. 对我的……感激（The love…love）：邓肯是在亲切地表示他的到访是一种打搅，但希望那是一种会受欢迎的打搅（Duncan is graciously suggesting that his visit is a bother, but, he hopes, a welcome one）（Bevington）。 12-4. 就此……麻烦您（Herein…trouble）："In this way I am teaching you how to pray for the good of those who cause you trouble（我就这样教您该如何为那些带给您麻烦的人祈福）"（Clark）。 19. 我们专为您祈祷（We…hermits）：其中，"hermits（隐士）"可指"beadsmen（为别人祈福者）"，他们因为誓言或受雇专为别人祷告（bound by vow or fee to say prayers for particular individuals）。 22. 来打前站（To be his purveyor）：其中"purveyor"是指一种皇室官员，专为上级的出行做好准备。 邓肯在继续使用自我贬低的格调（style of self-deprecation）。 23. 原文"holp" = helped（古体）。 25-8. 您的……归还（Your … own）：原注为："The king's servants hold everything in trust（'in compt'）for the king, and they will give an account（'make their audit'）whenever the king asks for one, and always（'still'）return everything back to him."（Gill）

King   Give me your hand.

Conduct me to mine host: we love him highly,

30   And shall continue our graces towards him.

By your leave, hostess.   *Exeunt.*

邓肯　　　　　　　　　把手给我。

领我去见主人：我非常爱他，

还将会继续对他恩爱有加。　　　　　　　　　　　30

请您允许，夫人。　　　　　　　　　　　　同下。

---

31. 请您允许（By your leave）：礼貌用语：邓肯也许会亲吻麦克白夫人的手，或挽着她的手臂一起进入城堡（Gill）。

SCENE VII

*Hautboys. Torches. Enter a Sewer, and divers
Servants with dishes and service over the stage.
Then enter Macbeth.*

Macbeth   If it were done, when 'tis done, then 'twere well
It were done quickly. If th'assassination
Could trammel up the consequence, and catch
With his surcease, success: that but this blow
Might be the be-all and the end-all, here,
But here, upon this bank and shoal of time,
We'd jump the life to come. But in these cases,
We still have judgement here, that we but teach

5

第七场

吹奏双簧管。掌起火把。司膳管家与几位
仆人手持餐具及菜肴穿梭于舞台之上。
麦克白随后上。

麦克白　　　行动若能干净利落,那最好

还是速战速决。　若这次暗杀

能把后患一网打尽,并使他

一命归阴,胜券在握:这一击

也许能够一劳永逸,今生,　　　　　　　　　　　　5

今世,在这时间的海岸和浅滩,

甘愿拿来生冒险。　但这种行径,

今生总会遭报应,这只能传授

1.7. 0（1）吹奏……火把（*Hautboys. Torches*）:表明一种礼仪式的场景正在夜间发生。1-2. 行动……速决（If…quickly）:原注为:"If the business of the murder were ended（'done'）as soon as the murder is performed（'done'）, then it would be a good thing to have it carried out（'done'）quickly."（Gill）2-4. 若……在握（if…success）:原注为,"if it could prevent any consequences and obtain success by his death"。其中,"trammel up"意为"用网网住（entangle as in a net）"（Muir）（借鉴梁译。——译者附注）。5. 一劳永逸（the…all）:意为"all that is needed to end everything（仅此一举即可了却一切）"（Gill）。6. 在这……浅滩（upon…time）:即"今生（in this life）"。麦克白将（今生的）时间想象为无穷之海洋中的一片沙洲或浅滩（imagines Time as a sandbank or shallow place["shoal"]in the sea of eternity）（Gill）。7. 甘愿拿来生冒险（We'd jump the life to come）:即"我对死后的永生将毫不在意（尽管世间的罪过到时也许会受到惩罚）（I would take no notice of an eternal life after death（where there might be punishment for earthly sins）"（Gill）。其中,"jump"意为"冒险（risk）"（Muir）。8. 遭报应（judgment here）:麦克白也许是说,他这样做只会自食其果,因为别人会以其人之道还治其人之身（Macbeth may mean that in behaving in this way he will only be calling down judgement on himself in the form of those who imitate his own actions）。

Bloody instructions, which being taught, return

10   To plague th'inventor. This even-handed justice

Commend th'ingredience of our poisoned chalice

To our own lips. He's here in double trust:

First, as I am his kinsman, and his subject,

Strong both against the deed. Then, as his host,

15   Who should against his murderer shut the door,

Not bear the knife myself. Besides, this Duncan

Hath borne his faculties so meek, hath been

So clear in his great office, that his virtues

Will plead like angels, trumpet-tongued, against

20   The deep damnation of his taking off;

And pity, like a naked new-born babe,

Striding the blast, or heaven's cherubim, horsed

Upon the sightless couriers of the air,

Shall blow the horrid deed in every eye,

25   That tears shall drown the wind. I have no spur

To prick the sides of my intent, but only

Vaulting ambition, which o'er-leaps itself,

And falls on th'other.

冤冤相报,人们学会后,便会

折磨创始者。 公平的正义之神   10

会把我们杯中的毒药送到

自己的嘴唇。 他在此加倍信任:

首先,我是他的亲属和臣民,

均抵制该行径。 其次,作为主人,   15

我本该房门紧闭以防刺客,

不该亲自操刀。 而且,他邓肯

行使职权如此谦恭,他是

如此清正廉明,他的美德

会像天使,放声呼号,控诉

这一罪该万死的弑君行动;   20

而怜悯,会像赤裸的新生婴儿,

驾驭着狂风,或像小小的天使,

骑着天空那些无形的使者,

把这恐怖行径吹向每只眼睛,

让泪水淹没狂风。 我没有踢马刺   25

可以驱使自己的图谋,唯有

攀爬的野心,常因用力过猛,

而跌到另外一侧。

8-10. 这只能······创始者(that···inventor):意为"we only teach others lessons in murder, and after the lessons have been learned, they come back to torment the man who first found them out"(Gill)。 其中,"that"可指"so that(结果)"或"in that(就此)"(Muir)。 10. 公平的(even-handed):即"不偏不倚(impartial)",拟人化用法——将正义视为手持天平者(the personification of justice as a figure holding evenly balanced scales)。 12. 加倍信任 (double trust):麦克白此刻不愿违背的实为三重的"信任关系"(three 'relations of trust'):亲属、臣民和主人。 22. 驾驭着狂风(Striding the blast):文艺复兴时期的绘画常把丘比特或天使如此描绘(Bevington)。 23. 无形的使者(sightless···air):即"风(the winds)"。 其中,"sightless"既可指"无形的(invisible)",也可指"盲目的(blind)"。 25-8. 我······一侧(I···th'other):又一处有关骑马的意象。 ······莎士比亚在此好像将两种意象合而为一:一是麦克白想行凶的意图,被想象为需要驱使的一匹马;二是他的野心——一位急不可耐的骑手,试图跃上马鞍,结果却跳得过远(anoher metaphor from horse-riding, ···Shakespeare appears to combine two images: one of Macbeth's intent to murder, imagined as a horse in need of goading on, and the other of his ambition, as an over-eager rider who tries to vault into his saddle but jumps too far)。

Enter Lady.

How now? What news?

Lady   He has almost supped. Why have you left the chamber?

Macbeth   Hath he asked for me?

30 **Lady**   Know you not, he has?

Macbeth   We will proceed no further in this business:

He hath honoured me of late, and I have bought

Golden opinions from all sorts of people,

Which would be worn now in their newest gloss,

Not cast aside so soon.

35 **Lady**   Was the hope drunk

Wherein you dressed yourself? Hath it slept since?

And wakes it now, to look so green and pale,

At what it did so freely? From this time

Such I account thy love. Art thou afeared

40   To be the same in thine own act and valour,

As thou art in desire? Wouldst thou have that

Which thou esteem'st the ornament of life,

And live a coward in thine own esteem,

Letting 'I dare not', wait upon 'I would',

Like the poor cat i'th' adage?

夫人上。

怎么了？　啥消息？

夫人　他快吃完了。　您为何离开大厅？

麦克白　他叫我了吗？

夫人　　　　　叫了,您不知道？　　　　　　　　　　　30

麦克白　这件事情我们要就此罢休:

他刚给了我尊荣,我也赢得了

各种人士们的金贵好评,

该趁现在光彩照人穿戴在身,

不该匆匆抛弃。

夫人　　　　　您用以裹身的　　　　　　　　　　　　35

热望变成了醉鬼？　它已经沉睡？

一觉醒来,竟对自己曾经的

豪迈感到恶心？　从今以后

我这样看待你的爱情。　你害怕

让自己梦寐以求的雄风大振　　　　　　　　　　　40

名副其实？　难道你想要得到

你所看重的那顶人生桂冠,

却愿做一个自以为是的懦夫,

竟让"我不敢"奉陪"我情愿",

像谚语中的可怜猫一般？

---

29. 离开大厅 (left the chamber):麦克白先于客人离席是一种失礼。　32-3. 赢得了……好评 (bought…opinions):另一处有关服饰的意象 (clothing images)。　该意象始于 1.3. 109-110。35-8. 您……恶心 (Was…freely):麦克白夫人采用了一种混合型隐喻 (mixed metaphor) 对丈夫的变化作出了回应。　其中,促使麦克白最初打算暗杀邓肯的"希望"被喻为服装;这种希望随后又被拟人化为一名醉汉,这名醉汉一觉醒来之后却对自己原先的行为感到憎恶 (The *hope* with which Macbeth formed the plan of murdering Duncan is initially an assumed attire. This is subsumed into the personification of a drunken individual, who falls asleep and wakes only to be overcome with sick nausea at his former conduct)。　39-41. 你害怕……名副其实 (Art…desire):其中,"act (做)"和"desire (欲望)"均可指性能力 (sexual potency) (Bate);这样 (Such):就像醉汉的虚张声势 (like the worthless bravado of a drunk) (Clark);参考 2.3. 29-35 (Muir)。

45 **Macbeth**   Prithee, peace.

I dare do all that may become a man,

Who dares do more, is none.

Lady   What beast was't then,

That made you break this enterprise to me?

When you durst do it, then you were a man;

50   And to be more than what you were, you would

Be so much more the man. Nor time nor place

Did then adhere, and yet you would make both:

They have made themselves, and that their fitness now

Does unmake you. I have given suck, and know

55   How tender 'tis to love the babe that milks me:

I would, while it was smiling in my face,

Have plucked my nipple from his boneless gums,

And dashed the brains out, had I so sworn

As you have done to this.

Macbeth   If we should fail?

60 **Lady**   We fail?

But screw your courage to the sticking place,

And we'll not fail. When Duncan is asleep,

Whereto the rather shall his day's hard journey

Soundly invite him, his two chamberlains

麦克白	别说了。	45

我敢做适合男人的所有事情，

谁敢越界，便无人性。

夫人	是啥畜生，	

将这种宏图大业透露给我？

您敢做时，您就是一条汉子；

若想做到超越自我，您就要　　　　　　　　　50

更像一条汉子。　时间和地点

都不合宜时，您倒想二者兼备：

天时地利现送上门来，反而

使您气馁。　我曾经哺乳，知道

疼爱吃奶的婴儿会多么温存：　　　　　　　　55

我也会，正当他朝我微笑之时，

将乳头拔出他那没牙的小嘴儿，

摔得他脑浆飞溅，我若曾像您

那样信誓旦旦。

麦克白	万一失败呢？	
夫人	失败？	60

您只管鼓足勇气蓄势待发，

我们不会失败。　邓肯入睡后，

白天的路途劳顿会使他更快

酣然入眠，他的两名侍卫，

---

45. 谚语（adage）：即"猫儿想吃鱼，却怕湿爪子（The cat wanted to eat fish but dared not get her feet wet）"。　47. 无人性（none）：即"不是人，超越了人类的范畴（not a man, outside of the bounds of humanity）"。　47. 是啥畜生（What beast）：麦克白夫人无视丈夫的顾虑，将"无人性"理解为犹如兽类一般（Ignoring her husband's scruples, Macbeth's Lady takes *none* as if it means an animal）。　50-1. 若想……汉子（And…man）：意为"In order to become greater（more）than you were, you were prepared to become even more manly"。　61. 其中，"But = only"。该意象也许源于将琴弦拉紧这种行为（this image, derived perhaps from the screwing up of the strings on a violin）（Muir）。

65   Will I with wine and wassail so convince,

That memory, the warder of the brain,

Shall be a fume, and the receipt of reason

A limbeck only. When in swinish sleep

Their drenched natures lie as in a death,

70   What cannot you and I perform upon

Th'unguarded Duncan? What not put upon

His spongy officers, who shall bear the guilt

Of our great quell?

Macbeth   Bring forth men-children only;

For thy undaunted mettle should compose

75   Nothing but males. Will it not be received,

When we have marked with blood those sleepy two

Of his own chamber, and used their very daggers,

That they have done't?

Lady   Who dares receive it other,

As we shall make our griefs and clamour roar,

Upon his death?

80   **Macbeth**   I am settled, and bend up

Each corporal agent to this terrible feat.

Away, and mock the time with fairest show:

False face must hide what the false heart doth know.

Exeunt.

我会用酒宴把他们完全制伏，　　　　　　　　65

以便使那看守大脑的记忆

变成毒气，理智的储藏之所

化为蒸馏器。　等他们猪一般沉睡，

酩酊大醉不省人事的时候，

毫无防卫的邓肯，还不能由我们　　　　　　70

任意宰割？　怎么不能嫁祸与

烂醉如泥的侍卫，让他们负起

屠杀的罪责？

麦克白　　　　　　　　　愿你只生男子！

因为你的坚韧气质就应该

只生男儿。　人们是否会不信，　　　　　　75

当我们将他房内的两名侍卫

涂满鲜血，并用他们的短剑，

表明他们是罪魁？

夫人　　　　　　　　　　谁敢不信，

因为我们将会号啕大哭，

哀悼他死去？

麦克白　　　　　　　　　我已决定，要使尽　　　　80

浑身解数履行这种可怕举动。

走，要欺骗世人就假装殷勤：

必须用虚情假意包藏祸心。

　　　　　　　　　　　　　　　　　　　　　同下。

66-8. 记忆……蒸馏器（memory…only）：用以描绘醉酒的复合型隐喻（complex meta-phor），源自炼金术：醉醺醺的大脑（the drink-sodden brain）变成了一种蒸馏器。　大脑的一部分（记忆，作为一名可提防人们重新犯错的守卫）已失去其本能（proper function），从而降为一种蒸汽；大脑的另一部分——理智的储藏所（the receptacle of reason），变成了一个蒸馏器或容器，里面烟雾缭绕（which fills with fumes）。　67. 毒气（fume）：即蒸汽，据信可从胃部上升到大脑的有毒气体（vapour, often signifying noxious vapours believed to ascend from the stomach to the brain）。　83. 参考谚语"Fair face foul heart（面善心恶）"。　麦克白是在重复夫人在 1. 5. 63-6的忠告。

第二幕
ACT 2

SCENE I

Enter Banquo, and Fleance, with a torch before him.

Banquo	How goes the night, boy?
Fleance	The moon is down; I have not heard the clock.
Banquo	And she goes down at twelve.
Fleance	I take't 'tis later, sir.
Banquo	Hold, take my sword. There's husbandry in heaven,

5   Their candles are all out; take thee that too.

A heavy summons lies like lead upon me,

And yet I would not sleep. Merciful powers,

Restrain in me the cursed thoughts that nature

Gives way to in repose.

Enter Macbeth and a Servant with a torch.

10   Give me my sword; who's there?

Macbeth	A friend.
Banquo	What, sir, not yet at rest? The King's abed.

He hath been in unusual pleasure,

And sent forth great largess to your offices.

第一场

班柯与手持火把的弗林斯上。

班柯	夜晚已过多久，孩子？
弗林斯	月亮落了；我还没听见钟声。
班柯	已经半夜了。
弗林斯	我想会晚些，父亲。
班柯	来，拿上我的剑。　上天很节俭，

　　　一根蜡烛都不点燃；也拿上这个。　　　　　　　　　5

　　　我现在昏昏欲睡疲惫不堪，

　　　可我并不想睡。　仁慈的天使，

　　　要克制我的邪念，因为歇息时

　　　它们容易浮现。

麦克白，与侍从持火把上。

　　　把剑给我；是谁？　　　　　　　　　　　　　　10

麦克白	朋友。
班柯	怎么，先生，还没睡？　国王已就寝。

　　　他今天可是异乎寻常地高兴，

　　　向您的下属赠送了大批礼物。

2.1.　5.蜡烛（candles）：即"星星（stars）"，一种常见的隐喻。　旨在强调本场的背景漆黑一片，需要观众就此想象一番。　也拿上这个（take⋯too）：不言而喻的舞台指示（implied SD），班柯就此会让弗林斯帮他从身上解下一把匕首或一件斗篷。　6-9.我现在……浮现（A heavy⋯repose）：原注为"Banquo feels heavy with sleep, as though he is called to bed, yet he wants to keep awake. He is afraid of the thoughts that come when the body is at rest"（Gill）。
8.邪念（cursed thoughts）：可能是指班柯回想起女巫对他的预言（或预言本身）时，感到内疚。

15   This diamond he greets your wife withal,

By the name of most kind hostess, and shut up

In measureless content.

Macbeth   Being unprepared,

Our will became the servant to defect,

Which else should free have wrought.

Banquo   All's well.

[Exit Fleance.]

20   I dreamt last night of the three weïrd sisters:

To you they have showed some truth.

Macbeth   I think not of them;

Yet, when we can entreat an hour to serve,

We would spend it in some words upon that business,

If you would grant the time.

Banquo   At your kind'st leisure.

25 **Macbeth**   If you shall cleave to my consent when 'tis,

It shall make honour for you.

Banquo   So I lose none

In seeking to augment it, but still keep

My bosom franchised and allegiance clear,

I shall be counselled.

Macbeth   Good repose the while.

30 **Banquo**   Thanks, sir, the like to you.   *Exit Banquo.*

Macbeth   Go bid thy mistress, when my drink is ready,

	他想把这颗钻石送给您妻子，	15
	把她称为最好的主妇,最后	
	他表示格外满足。	
麦克白	因未做准备,	
	我们很想对国王盛情款待,	
	却不能如愿以偿。	
班柯	一切都好。	

　　　　　　　　　　　　　　　〔弗林斯下。〕

	昨晚我梦见了那三个巫婆:	20
	就您而言相当准确。	
麦克白	我不想它了;	
	不过,我们若能抽出些时间,	
	如果您愿意,可就这件事情	
	进行攀谈。	
班柯	我愿悉听尊便。	
麦克白	您若听我安排在什么时间,	25
	那也会为您增光。	
班柯	假如在寻求	
	增光时不失去荣光,但我要做到	
	问心无愧,而且忠心耿耿,	
	才愿意听命。	
麦克白	祝您好好安歇!	
班柯	谢谢,先生,您也安歇。	班柯下。　30
麦克白	去告诉夫人,我的饮料备好时,	

17-9. 因未做……以偿(Being…wrought):原注为"As we were unprepared, our desire to give liberal hospitality to the king could not be fulfilled"(Muir)。 又回到1.4那种正式和晦涩的客套(Clark)。 20. 班柯的旧话重提也许表明他对女巫的念念不忘并非完全无辜。 25. 在什么时间(when 'tis):即"when the time comes"。 麦克白此处故意含混不清;他可能是指当邓肯寿终正寝时,或指加速兑现女巫的预言显得宜时,或当指他和班柯找到合适的谈话时间时。 31. 饮料(drink):用热牛奶加麦芽酒或葡萄酒调制而成(posset),以促睡眠。

She strike upon the bell. Get thee to bed.   *Exit* [*Servant*].

Is this a dagger which I see before me,

The handle toward my hand? Come, let me clutch thee.

35   I have thee not, and yet I see thee still.

Art thou not, fatal vision, sensible

To feeling as to sight? Or art thou but

A dagger of the mind, a false creation,

Proceeding from the heat-oppressed brain?

40   I see thee yet, in form as palpable

As this which now I draw.

Thou marshall'st me the way that I was going,

And such an instrument I was to use.

Mine eyes are made the fools o'th' other senses,

45   Or else worth all the rest. I see thee still,

And on thy blade, and dudgeon, gouts of blood,

Which was not so before. There's no such thing.

It is the bloody business which informs

Thus to mine eyes. Now o'er the one half-world

50   Nature seems dead, and wicked dreams abuse

The curtained sleep; witchcraft celebrates

Pale Hecate's offerings; and withered Murder,

Alarumed by his sentinel, the wolf,

叫她敲一下钟。　你去睡吧。　　　　　　　　　［仆人］下。

我的面前是否有一把短剑，

剑柄朝我？　来，让我把你抓住。

我抓不住你，却依然看得见你。　　　　　　　　　　　35

不祥的幻象，难道你只能目睹

不能感触？　或者你只不过是

一把臆造的短剑，无中生有，

从狂热的大脑中想象而出？

你还在那里，跟我拔出的这把　　　　　　　　　　　40

好像同样触手可及。

我正要前往的道路你在引领，

你这样的短剑我行将使用。

我的眼睛已被别的感官欺骗，

否则比它们管用。　你还在那里，　　　　　　　　　45

你的利刃、剑柄已沾满血污，

此前未曾出现。　其实并无短剑，

是那种血腥的使命让它在我

眼前显形。　此刻这半个世界

死一般寂静，邪恶的梦魇侵扰　　　　　　　　　　　50

床帷里的睡眠；女巫向苍白的

赫卡忒献祭；老态龙钟的凶杀，

突然被他的哨兵——豺狼——唤醒，

---

32. 敲一下钟（strike upon the bell）：可能是事先安排好的暗号，即 61 行所出现的钟声。
42. 道路你在引领（way…going）：短剑其实是在跟随麦克白的意向而移动，而不是在引导他的意向。　44-5. 眼睛……管用（eyes…rest）：麦克白对那把短剑的情形依然不敢确定。　如果它并不存在，那么他的眼睛便受到了欺骗；然而，要是没受到欺骗，那么他的眼睛就会比其他的感官更为可靠，（因为是它们告诉他那把短剑只是虚幻）。　48. 血腥的使命（bloody business）：麦克白的委婉用语，实指对邓肯的谋杀。　51-2. 苍白的赫卡忒（Pale Hecate's）：赫卡忒为月亮女神（故"苍白"），她也是巫术女神。　52. 老态龙钟的凶杀（withered Murder）：将凶杀想象成一位老人，这种拟人化的用法在莎氏其他剧中并未见到。

Whose howl's his watch, thus with his stealthy pace,

55 With Tarquin's ravishing strides, towards his design

Moves like a ghost. Thou sure and firm-set earth,

Hear not my steps, which way they walk, for fear

Thy very stones prate of my whereabout,

And take the present horror from the time,

60 Which now suits with it. Whiles I threat, he lives;

Words to the heat of deeds too cold breath gives. *A bell rings.*

I go, and it is done; the bell invites me.

Hear it not, Duncan, for it is a knell

That summons thee to heaven, or to hell.   *Exit.*

它以嚎叫为暗号,于是鬼鬼祟祟,
以塔昆式的贪婪步伐,鬼魂一般　　　　　　　　　　55
迈向目标。　你这稳固的大地,
别听见我脚步迈向何方,我怕
你会发声的石头泄露我行踪,
将此刻这可怕的沉默打破,
因为它很适合。　我恫吓,他活着;　　　　　　60
夸夸其谈让行动的热情冷漠。　　　　　　　　钟声。
我去,就等于成了;钟声在邀我。
你别听,邓肯,这是丧钟在响,
不叫你下地狱,就唤你上天堂。　　　　　　　　下。

---

55. 塔昆(Tarquin's):罗马帝国君王,奸污了朋友的妻子——贞洁的鲁克丽丝(Lucretia),导致了罗马君主政体的垮台,以及一个共和国的建立。莎士比亚曾就此写有一首长诗《鲁克丽丝受辱记》(Gill;Clark)。 58. 会发声(prate):即"喋喋不休(chatter)";"泄密(tell tales)"。 参考《圣经》"路加福音"19章40节:若是他们闭口不说,这些石头必要呼叫起来。 59. 将……打破(take…time):原注为"Macbeth seems to mean that the speaking stones would take away or remove the present horror, that is, the silence appropriate to the moment"。

SCENE II

Enter Lady.

Lady   That which hath made them drunk, hath made me bold;
What hath quenched them, hath given me fire.
Hark, peace; it was the owl that shrieked,
The fatal bellman, which gives the stern'st good night.
He is about it. The doors are open,
And the surfeited grooms do mock their charge
With snores. I have drugged their possets,
That death and nature do contend about them,
Whether they live, or die.

Enter Macbeth.

Macbeth   Who's there? What ho!
Lady   Alack, I am afraid they have awaked,
And 'tis not done. The attempt, and not the deed
Confounds us. Hark. I laid their daggers ready;
He could not miss'em. Had he not resembled

第二场

夫人上。

夫人　已让他们大醉的,却让我大胆;
　　　　已把他们浇灭的,却把我点燃。
　　　　你听,安静;是猫头鹰的叫声,
　　　　不祥的更夫,道出了致命的晚安。
　　　　他正在行动。　卧室的房门开着, 5
　　　　酩酊大醉的侍卫在用鼾声嘲笑
　　　　其职责。　我已给他们酒里掺药,
　　　　生死双方在对他们展开争夺,
　　　　不知他们是死,是活。

麦克白上。

麦克白　　　　　　　是谁?　干啥?
夫人　哎呀,我担心他们已经清醒, 10
　　　　事没办成。　企图暗杀,而未成行
　　　　倒会要命。　我已把他们的剑放好;
　　　　他定会看到。　睡梦中他若不像

2.2.　3. 猫头鹰(owl):不祥之鸟(bird of ill omen)(Clark)。　猫头鹰在此被喻为一名更夫(bellman),在(伦敦)纽盖特监狱(Newgate)的牢房外面为即将问斩的囚犯敲响丧钟(Gill)。　5. 他正在行动(He⋯it):又一处委婉用语。 8-9. 原注为"Death and Life fight over the attendants to decide whether they should live or die"(Gill)。　9. 是谁(Who's there):麦克白此处的盘问跟班柯在2.1.10的盘问一样,表明了他的格外紧张。　有些编辑会在此添加诸如"在内(within)"的舞台指示,并将麦克白的入场推迟到15行,以此解释为何麦克白夫人未回答丈夫的盘问,或直到15行时好像才注意到了他的出现。　13. 他⋯⋯他(He⋯he):她先指麦克白,后指邓肯。

My father as he slept, I had done't.

My husband?

15   **Macbeth**   I have done the deed.

Didst thou not hear a noise?

Lady   I heard the owl scream and the crickets cry.

Did not you speak?

Macbeth   When?

Lady   Now.

Macbeth   As I descended?

Lady   Ay.

Macbeth   Hark, who lies i'the second chamber?

Lady   Donalbain.

20   **Macbeth**   This is a sorry sight.

Lady   A foolish thought, to say a sorry sight.

Macbeth   There's one did laugh in's sleep,

And one cried, 'Murder', that they did wake each other.

I stood and heard them; but they did say their prayers

25   And addressed them again to sleep.

Lady   There are two lodged together.

Macbeth   One cried, 'God bless us', and 'Amen' the other,

As they had seen me with these hangman's hands.

Listening their fear, I could not say 'Amen',

30   When they did say, 'God bless us'.

　　　　　　我的父亲,我自己都会动手。

　　　　　　我的丈夫?

麦克白　　　　　　　我做了那件事情。　　　　　　　　　　　　　　15

　　　　　　你没听到噪声?

夫人　　　　我听到猫头鹰和蟋蟀的鸣叫。

　　　　　　您说话了?

麦克白　　　　　　何时?

夫人　　　　　　　　刚才。

麦克白　　　　　　　　　我下楼时?

夫人　　　是的。

麦克白　　　　　听着,谁睡在第二个房间?

夫人　　　唐纳班。

麦克白　　　　　场景真是令人可怜。　　　　　　　　　　　20

夫人　　　多么愚蠢,竟说场景可怜。

麦克白　　　有一个在梦中大笑,

　　　　　　一个呼喊,"凶杀",并彼此惊醒。

　　　　　　我站着听到;可他们祷告之后,

　　　　　　接下来又进入了梦乡。　　　　　　　　　　　　　25

夫人　　　他们俩睡在一个房间。

麦克白　　　一个喊,"上帝保佑",一个喊"阿门",

　　　　　　好像看见了我这血腥的双手。

　　　　　　听到他们惊呼"上帝保佑"时,

　　　　　　我却不能说"阿门",　　　　　　　　　　　　　30

---

　　17. 蟋蟀(crickets):多以欢快著称,如谚语"as merry as a cricket(蟋蟀般愉快)",但蟋蟀也以其叫声而出名。 另外,蟋蟀有时也被视为可供女巫传唤的妖精。 22-3. 一个……一个(one…one):关于二人的身份有些含糊不清。 有的编辑认为是指马尔科姆和唐纳班,然而指向下文51行所提的两名侍卫的可能性则更大,因为他们随后充当了麦克白的替罪羊。 28. 血腥的双手(hangman's hands):刽子手对死刑犯行刑之后还要将他们的内脏掏出,并进行分尸。 因此他们手上会沾满鲜血(Gill)。 30. 我……"阿门"(I…'Amen'):"阿门"表示对别人的祷告应声赞同。 麦克白很想参与祷告之中,却未做到。 参考犯有弑兄之罪的克劳狄斯,他同样无法祷告(《哈姆雷特》3.3. 97-8)。

Lady	Consider it not so deeply.
Macbeth	But wherefore could not I pronounce 'Amen'?
	I had most need of blessing, and 'Amen'
	Stuck in my throat.
Lady	These deeds must not be thought

35 After these ways; so, it will make us mad.

Macbeth	Methought I heard a voice cry, 'Sleep no more.
	Macbeth does murder sleep'—the innocent sleep,
	Sleep that knits up the ravelled sleeve of care,
	The death of each day's life, sore labour's bath,

40 Balm of hurt minds, great Nature's second course,

Chief nourisher in life's feast—

Lady	What do you mean?
Macbeth	Still it cried, 'Sleep no more' to all the house;
	'Glamis hath murdered sleep, and therefore Cawdor
	Shall sleep no more. Macbeth shall sleep no more.'

45 **Lady** Who was it that thus cried? Why, worthy thane,

You do unbend your noble strength, to think

So brainsickly of things. Go, get some water

And wash this filthy witness from your hand.

Why did you bring these daggers from the place?

50 They must lie there. Go, carry them, and smear

The sleepy groom with blood.

Macbeth	I'll go no more.
	I am afraid to think what I have done;
	Look on't again, I dare not.

夫人	你可不要胡思乱想。	
麦克白	可是我为什么说不出"阿门"？	
	当我最需要祝福的时候，"阿门"	
	却哽噎在喉！	
夫人	这种事情可不能	
	这样思量；不然，会使咱发疯。	35
麦克白	我仿佛听到呼喊，"别再睡眠，	
	麦克白杀了睡眠"——无辜的睡眠，	
	能够织补千愁万绪的睡眠，	
	每日活动的终结，劳工的沐浴，	
	心灵创伤的油膏，天然的主菜，	40
	人生筵席的首要营养——	
夫人	您是何意？	
麦克白	它还在对大家呼喊，"别再睡眠"；	
	"葛莱密杀了睡眠，考道因此	
	别想再睡眠。麦克白别想再睡眠。"	
夫人	是谁这样呼喊？嗨，高贵的郡主，	45
	您要是这样胡思乱想，那就	
	等于自我泄劲。去，弄些水来，	
	把这些污秽的证据从手上洗掉。	
	您为啥把这些短剑拿出了房间？	
	要放在原处。去，送回去，用血污	50
	涂抹熟睡的侍卫。	
麦克白	我不再去了。	
	我害怕想起自己所做的事情；	
	我不敢再看它一眼。	

---

40. 主菜（second course）：宴会中的第二道菜，即主要营养（chief nourisher）。时至今日，英国人依然会在进食主要的荤菜（main dish of meat）之前首先喝些汤类或吃些小鱼等（Gill）。47. 泄劲（unbend）：他的气力原本像弓一样拉得绷紧（his strength had previously been bent like a bow）（Gill）。

Lady   Infirm of purpose,

Give me the daggers. The sleeping and the dead

55 Are but as pictures; 'tis the eye of childhood

That fears a painted devil. If he do bleed,

I'll gild the faces of the grooms withal,

For it must seem their guilt.   *Exit. Knock within*

Macbeth   Whence is that knocking?

How is't with me, when every noise appals me?

60 What hands are here? Ha: they pluck out mine eyes.

Will all great Neptune's ocean wash this blood

Clean from my hand? No, this my hand will rather

The multitudinous seas incarnadine,

Making the green, one red.

Enter Lady.

65 **Lady**   My hands are of your colour, but I shame

To wear a heart so white. I hear a knocking   *Knock*

At the south entry. Retire we to our chamber;

A little water clears us of this deed.

How easy is it then. Your constancy

Hath left you unattended.   *Knock*

70   Hark, more knocking.

Get on your nightgown, lest occasion call us

夫人	意志薄弱！	
	把剑给我。　熟睡的人和死人	
	不过是画像；只有儿童的眼睛	55
	才怕看画出的魔鬼。　他若出血，	
	我就用它涂抹侍卫的面孔，	
	要显示他们有罪。	下。内有敲门声
麦克白	哪里在敲门？	
	我这是怎么了，一点响声都怕？	
	这是啥手？　哈：挖出我的眼睛！	60
	全部的海水能否将我手上的	
	鲜血洗净？　不能,我这双手	
	会把那浩瀚无垠的大海污染，	
	使碧绿的海水通红。	

夫人上。

夫人	我的手也染成红色,可我羞于	65
	您那样心灰意冷。　我听见南门	敲门声
	传来了敲门声。　咱们赶快回屋；	
	一点水就把我们洗得一干二净。	
	这是多么地容易。　您的毅力	
	已经离您而去。	敲门声
	听,又有敲门声。	70
	快穿上睡衣,万一需要咱出面	

---

55. 画像（pictures）：因为它们不会动弹。　夫人企图制止麦克白虚幻般的反应。　56. 他若出血（If…bleed）：据信,凶手现身时,遇害者的尸体会再次出血（corpses of the murdered bled afresh in the presence of the murderer）。　60. 挖出我的眼睛（pluck…eyes）：因为他的感官之间无法调和（For the idea of the senses at odds with one another）,参考 1.4. 52-3。　俄狄浦斯因不忍目睹自己（无意）所犯下的罪行,竟刺瞎了自己的眼睛。

And show us to be watchers. Be not lost

So poorly in your thoughts.

Macbeth   To know my deed, 'twere best not know myself.   *Knock*

75   Wake Duncan with thy knocking. I would thou couldst.

Exeunt.

却让人发现咱还没睡。　不要

这样自暴自弃。

麦克白　　　意识到我的为人，最好否认自身。　　　　　　　敲门声

但愿你能用敲门声唤醒邓肯！　　　　　　　　　　　　同下。　75

---

74. 意识到（know）：既可指"acknowledge（承认）"，也可指"be conscious of（意识到）"。　麦克白意识到了自己每况愈下的自我疏远（recognizes his own progressive self-aliena-tion）（Clark）。　"如果我承认自己的所作所为，那最好就不要承认我是我本人（因为那是一种该死的行为，因此他会诅咒自己）（If I recognize what I have done, it would be better that I did not recognize myself［because the deed is damnable, and he would have to condemn him-self]）（Gill）。

SCENE Ⅲ

Enter a Porter. Knocking within.

Porter　Here's a knocking indeed: if a man were porter of Hell Gate, he should have old turning the key. [*Knock*] Knock, knock, knock. Who's there, i'th' name of Belzebub? Here's a farmer that hanged

5　himself on the expectation of plenty. Come in time. Have napkins enow about you; here you'll sweat for't. [*Knock*] Knock, knock. Who's there, in th'other devil's name? Faith, here's an equivocator that could swear in both the scales against either scale, who

10　committed treason enough for God's sake, yet could not equivocate to heaven. O, come in, equivocator. [*Knock*] Knock, knock, knock. Who's there? Faith, here's an English tailor come hither, for stealing out of a French hose. Come in, tailor; here you may roast

第三场

看门人上。幕后敲门声。

看门人　　这门敲得可真急：假如一个人是为地狱
看门，他使用钥匙的次数可会相当频繁。
〔敲门声〕敲，敲，敲。那是谁，我以
魔鬼的名义来发问？这也许是一位农夫，
他因为丰收在望而自缢身亡。来得正好。　　　　5
您可要多带几条毛巾；您来这里一定会
出汗。〔敲门声〕敲，敲，那是谁，我以
另一魔鬼的名义？真的，这是一个滑头，
他这个人两面三刀、看风使舵，竟打着
上帝的旗号背信弃义，却无法模棱两可　　　　10
地混进天堂。噢，进来吧，模棱两可者！
〔敲门声〕敲，敲，敲。那是谁？真的，
这也许是个英国裁缝，做法式紧身裤时
因省料被捉。来吧，裁缝；您可在这里

2.3.　1-2. 假如……看门（if…Gate）：评论家们指出，看门人的这种条件句颇具讥讽意味。
"'假如有人在为地狱看管大门'，难道此人不就是吗？ 如若不然，何为地狱？ 它的大门又在何
处？"中世纪的神奇剧中将城堡视为地狱，莎氏从中借用。 4. 魔鬼（Belzebub）：别西卜——魔
鬼的别称。 《圣经》"马太福音"12 章 24 节将其称为"鬼王（the prince of devils）"。 看门
人此处将自己视为地狱的门卫。 4-5. 农夫……身亡（farmer…plenty）：农夫将自己的粮食囤积
起来，希望饥荒来临时能卖个好价；一听到丰收在望（粮价会跌）便上吊自尽（Gill）。 6. 毛巾
（napkins）：以便擦汗，或因地狱之火的高温，或因需要进行发汗浴以便治疗性病。 8. 另一魔鬼
的名义（th'other devil's name）：他已酩酊大醉，无法记清另一个魔鬼的名字，即撒旦（Satan）的
别称（Lucifer），但观众会明白其意。 13-4. 英国裁缝……被捉（English tailor…hose）：裁缝为
客户缝制法国紧身裤时试图偷工减料，结果因裤子做得太紧而被人逮住（Gill）。 此处之所以提
及农夫（farmer）、模棱两可者（equivocator）、裁缝（tailor），旨在暗示他们不仅为了自己的
罪过而下到地狱，也表明他们聪明反被聪明误（Muir）。

15   your goose. [*Knock*] Knock, knock. Never at quiet. What are you? But this place is too cold for hell. I'll devil-porter it no further. I had thought to have let in some of all professions that go the primrose way to the everlasting bonfire. [*Knock*] Anon, anon, I pray

20   you, remember the porter.

Enter Macduff and Lennox.

Macduff   Was it so late, friend, ere you went to bed,
That you do lie so late?

Porter   Faith, sir, we were carousing till the second cock; and drink, sir, is a great provoker of three things.

25 **Macduff**   What three things does drink especially provoke?

Porter   Marry, sir, nose-painting, sleep and urine. Lechery, sir, it provokes and unprovokes: it provokes the desire, but it takes away the performance. Therefore

30   much drink may be said to be an equivocator with lechery: it makes him , and it mars him; it sets him on, and it takes him off; it persuades him, and disheartens him; makes him stand to, and not stand to; in conclusion, equivocates him in a sleep and,

烧熨斗。［敲门声］。敲,敲,没法安宁!   15
您是谁呀? 这里太冷,做地狱不配,我
不再为地狱看门。我本想让各行各业的
人士都进来几个,他们穿过那花街柳巷
进入永恒的火海。［敲门声］就来,就来,
求你们,别忘了门卫。   20

　　　　　麦克达夫与雷诺克斯上。

麦克达夫 昨晚您是否睡得太晚,朋友,
您竟然如此拖延?

看门人 没错,先生,我们昨晚喝到了鸡叫两遍;
这酒么,先生,可挑起三件事情。

麦克达夫 那么这酒, 能够挑起尤其是哪三件事   25
情?

看门人 哎呀,先生,就是酒糟鼻、睡觉和撒尿。
性欲,先生,它既鼓劲又泄劲:它可以
挑起淫念,却阻碍人们加以兑现。因此
过量的饮酒对性欲而言,可谓口是身非。   30
它可成全你,也可毁了你;它使你充满
阳刚,又使你无力;它为你鼓气,又使
你泄气;它可使你勃起,又可使你阳痿;
最后,它用暧昧的美梦诱你入睡,然后

---

18. 花街柳巷（primrose way）:参见《哈姆雷特》类似的表述（1.3.50）。 意为"诱人的
道路会将人们引向灾难甚至地狱"。 另见《圣经》"马太福音"7章 13-14 节:"你们要进窄
门。 因为引到灭亡,那门是宽的,路是大的,进去的人也多;引到永生,那门是窄的,路是小的,找
着的人也少。"20. 别忘了门卫（remember the porter）:想让敲门的麦克达夫和雷诺克斯给点
小费,但通常是针对观众而言。 23. 鸡叫两遍（second cock）:天已破晓（full dawn）
（Clark）。 凌晨 3 点（three o'clock）（Alan Durban; *Shakespeare Made Easy*, 1984;下称
"Durban"）。 ——译者附注）。

35   giving him the lie, leaves him.

Macduff   I believe drink gave thee the lie last night.

Porter   That it did, sir, i'the very throat on me; but I requited him for his lie, and, I think, being too strong for him, though he took up my legs sometime,

40   yet I made a shift to cast him.

Enter Macbeth.

Macduff   Is thy master stirring?

               Our knocking has awaked him; here he comes.

                                [*Exit Porter.*]

Lennox   Good morrow, noble sir.

Macbeth   Good morrow, both.

Macduff   Is the King stirring, worthy thane?

Macbeth   Not yet.

45 **Macduff**   He did command me to call timely on him;

               I have almost slipped the hour.

Macbeth   I'll bring you to him.

Macduff   I know this is a joyful trouble to you;

               But yet 'tis one.

Macbeth   The labour we delight in physics pain;

50   This is the door.

Macduff   I'll make so bold to call, for 'tis my limited service.

                                [*Exit Macduff.*]

将你愚弄，一走了之。 35

麦克达夫　我相信酒昨晚确实把你给撂倒。

看门人　一点不错，先生，它让我颜面尽失；可
我并未向它示弱，而且，我想，它不是
我的对手，尽管它有时候会把我给撂倒，
而我却能设法把它掀翻。 40

麦克白上。

麦克达夫　你的主人醒了吗？
敲门声把他给惊醒；他来了。

［看门人下。］

雷诺克斯　高贵的先生，早上好。

麦克白　　　　　　　　早上好，二位。

麦克达夫　国王醒了吗，尊贵的郡主？

麦克白　　　　　　　　　还没有。

麦克达夫　他吩咐我一早就过来叫他； 45
我几乎误了时间。

麦克白　　　　　　我领您去见他。

麦克达夫　我知道您对这件事乐此不疲；
但毕竟不易。

麦克白　乐在其中的工作不觉得艰辛；
就是这一间。 50

麦克达夫　我要大胆叫门，因为事先约好。

［麦克达夫下。］

35. 将你愚弄（giving…lie）：可指"将他欺骗（tricking him）"；"（犹如摔跤时）把他摞
倒（laying him out, as in wrestling）"；"使他撒尿（making him urinate）"；"使他的勃起
消失（making him lose his erection）"。 40. 掀翻（cast）：掀翻在地，继续上文的摔跤隐喻，但
也可指"呕吐（vomit）"。 49. 我们喜欢做的工作可医治由此而产生的苦恼（Work that we do
cures ["physics"] any trouble ["pain"] that it causes us.）（Gill）。 "我们乐意做的事情
不难（What we do willingly is easy）"。 麦克白又采用了拐弯抹角的说话方式（Clark）。

Lennox   Goes the King hence today?

Macbeth   He does: he did appoint so.

Lennox   The night has been unruly: where we lay

55   Our chimneys were blown down and, as they say,

Lamentings heard i'th' air, strange screams of death,

And prophesying, with accents terrible,

Of dire combustion, and confused events

New hatched to th' woeful time. The obscure bird

60   Clamoured the livelong night. Some say the earth

Was feverous and did shake.

Macbeth   'Twas a rough night.

Lennox   My young remembrance cannot parallel

A fellow to it.

Enter Macduff.

Macduff   O horror, horror, horror.

Tongue nor heart cannot conceive nor name thee.

65   **Macbeth** ⎤

     Lennox   ⎦   What's the matter?

Macduff   Confusion now hath made his masterpiece.

Most sacrilegious murder hath broke ope

The Lord's anointed temple, and stole thence

The life o'th' building.

Macbeth   What is't you say? the life?

雷诺克斯	国王今天要走吗？	
麦克白	是的：他是这样想的。	
雷诺克斯	昨晚动荡不安：我们住处的	
	烟囱被风吹倒，人们都说，	55
	听到空中有哭声，惨死的怪叫，	
	用那可怕的声调进行预言，	
	骇人听闻的暴动，混乱的局面	
	将在这多事之秋初现。 猫头鹰	
	一夜叫个不停。 有人说大地	60
	发烧又动摇。	
麦克白	真是狂暴的夜晚。	
雷诺克斯	年轻的我尚未见过能相提	
	并论的夜晚。	

麦克达夫上。

麦克达夫	噢可怕，可怕，可怕！	
	真是难以形容，无法想象！	
麦克白 雷诺克斯	怎么回事？	65
麦克达夫	毁灭已经完成了他的杰作！	
	最为邪恶的凶手已经撬开	
	上帝膏抹的圣殿，将其中的	
	生命盗走！	
麦克白	您说什么？ 生命？	

---

59. 猫头鹰（The obscure bird = the owl）：阴暗之鸟（bird of darkness），很难见到，且只能在夜晚听到其叫声；猫头鹰也跟预言有关（associated with prophecy）。 68-9. 上帝……盗走（The Lord's…building）：邓肯的身体被想象成一座教堂，被强盗给亵渎（Duncan's body is imagined as a church which has been desecrated by a robber）（Clark）。 邓肯国王加冕登基时，（其头部或身体）会经过神圣的涂膏仪式，以此表明他是上帝在人间的代理（Gill；Bate）。

70	**Lennox**	Mean you his majesty?
	Macduff	Approach the chamber, and destroy your sight
		With a new Gorgon. Do not bid me speak—
		See, and then speak yourselves.

Exeunt Macbeth and Lennox.

Awake, awake!

Ring the alarum bell. Murder and treason.

75 Banquo and Donalbain, Malcolm, Awake,

Shake off this downy sleep, death's counterfeit,

And look on death itself. Up, up, and see

The great doom's image. Malcolm, Banquo,

As from your graves rise up, and walk like sprites

80 To countenance this horror. Ring the bell!   *Bell rings.*

Enter Lady.

	Lady	What's the business,
		That such a hideous trumpet calls to parley
		The sleepers of the house? Speak, speak.
	Macduff	O gentle lady,
85		'Tis not for you to hear what I can speak:
		The repetition in a woman's ear
		Would murder as it fell.

Enter Banquo.

O Banquo, Banquo,

| 雷诺克斯 | 您是指国王陛下？ | 70 |

麦克达夫　您进去看吧,那种场景定会
　　　　　使您呆若木鸡。　别叫我说吧——
　　　　　自己去看了再说。

麦克白与雷诺克斯下。

　　　　　　　　　醒醒,醒醒!
　　　　　有凶杀,有叛变! 快敲响警钟!
　　　　　班柯和唐纳班,马尔科姆,都醒醒,　　　　　75
　　　　　甩掉舒适的睡眠——死亡的假象,
　　　　　看看死亡本身! 起来,起来,看看
　　　　　审判日的场面! 马尔科姆,班柯,
　　　　　就像从坟里升起,幽灵一般
　　　　　前去直面这种恐怖。　快敲钟!　　　　　钟鸣。 80

夫人上。

夫人　　　是什么事情,
　　　　　竟用如此可怕的钟声将家里的
　　　　　睡客全部唤醒？　快说,快说!

麦克达夫　噢,温柔的夫人,
　　　　　我能说的话语不适合您听:　　　　　85
　　　　　向一位女人重复这种话语
　　　　　等于要她性命。

班柯上。

班柯啊,班柯,

---

72. 呆若木鸡：其中,原文中的"Gorgon（戈尔贡）"为希腊神话中的女妖,以蛇为发,只要看她一眼,立刻化为石头（mythical female monster with snakes for hair, whose look turned beholders into stone）（Clark）。　看到邓肯遇害的尸体也会导致同样的后果（The sight of Duncan's murdered body will have the same effect）（Gill）。　78. 审判日的场面（great doom's image）：世界末日来临之际,死者将会从坟墓中起来接受审判的场面（image of Judgement Day, the end of the world when the dead were supposed to rise from their graves）（Bate）。

Our royal master's murdered.

Lady   Woe, alas.

What, in our house?

Banquo   Too cruel anywhere.

90   Dear Duff, I prithee, contradict thyself

And say it is not so.

Enter Macbeth, Lennox and Ross.

Macbeth   Had I but died an hour before this chance,

I had lived a blessed time, for from this instant

There's nothing serious in mortality;

95   All is but toys; renown and grace is dead,

The wine of life is drawn, and the mere lees

Is left this vault to brag of.

Enter Malcolm and Donalbain.

Donalbain   What is amiss?

Macbeth   You are, and do not know't:

The spring, the head, the fountain of your blood

100   Is stopped, the very source of it is stopped.

Macduff   Your royal father's murdered.

Malcolm   O, by whom?

Lennox   Those of his chamber, as it seemed, had done't.

Their hands and faces were all badged with blood;

　　　　　　　我们的国王已遇害!

夫人　　　　　　　　　　哎呀,可怕!

　　　　　什么,在俺家?

班柯　　　　　　　　　在哪里都太残忍。

　　　　　亲爱的达夫,求你否认自己, 　　　　　　　　90

　　　　　别说这是真的!

　　　　　　　　麦克白、雷诺克斯与罗斯上。

麦克白　　　我若在此之前一小时死去,

　　　　　也算是美满一生,因为此后,

　　　　　人生不再有任何意义可言;

　　　　　全都是儿戏;名望和体面已去, 　　　　　　　95

　　　　　生命的美酒已被吸干,里面

　　　　　只剩渣滓可供吹嘘。

　　　　　　　　马尔科姆与唐纳班上。

唐纳班　　　什么事情?

麦克白　　　　　　您的,您尚且不知:

　　　　　你们皇族血统的源头、本源

　　　　　已被堵住,根源已被人切断。 　　　　　　　100

麦克达夫　　你们的父王已被杀害。

马尔科姆　　　　　　噢,被谁?

雷诺克斯　　好像是被他的那两个侍卫。

　　　　　他们的手上、脸上布满血污;

　　92-7. 布拉德利(A. C. Bradley)对本段台词中似是而非的矛盾说法(paradox)曾作过简练的总结:"这种言论……旨在骗人,却也是他的肺腑之言(This is…meant to deceive, but it utters at the same time his profoundest feeling)"。 这种伤感也预示了5.5.18-27行的言辞。
　　96. 里面(vault):可指"酒窖里(wine cellar)";也可指"穹苍下面的世间(world beneath the arched sky)"(Bate)。

So were their daggers, which unwiped we found

105 Upon their pillows. They stared, and were distracted;

No man's life was to be trusted with them.

Macbeth O, yet I do repent me of my fury,

That I did kill them.

Macduff   Wherefore did you so?

Macbeth Who can be wise, amazed, temperate and furious,

110 Loyal and neutral, in a moment? No man.

The expedition of my violent love

Outrun the pauser, reason. Here lay Duncan,

His silver skin laced with his golden blood,

And his gashed stabs looked like a breach in nature

115 For ruin's wasteful entrance; there, the murderers,

Steeped in the colours of their trade, their daggers

Unmannerly breeched with gore. Who could refrain,

That had a heart to love, and in that heart

Courage to make's love known?

Lady   Help me hence, ho.

120 **Macduff** Look to the lady.

Malcolm Why do we hold our tongues, that most may claim

This argument for ours?

Donalbain   What should be spoken

我们发现他们的剑,在枕头

上面血迹斑斑。 他们目瞪口呆; 105

谁的生命也不敢向他们托管。

麦克白 噢,我真后悔自己一怒之下,

竟杀了他们!

麦克达夫 您为啥杀了他们?

麦克白 谁能惊恐时明智,狂怒时平静,

忠诚时不偏不倚? 谁都不能。 110

猛烈的爱心胜过阻止者——理性,

促使我行动。 邓肯躺在那里,

银白的皮肤交织着金贵的血痕,

他的刀伤就像生命线上的豁口,

毁灭由此侵入;凶手就在旁边, 115

地道的职业杀手,他们的刀剑,

卑鄙地沾满血污。 谁能忍住,

倘若有爱心,也有勇气将他的

爱心付诸行动?

夫人 扶我离开,嗬!

麦克达夫 快照看夫人。 120

马尔科姆 为何要保持沉默,人们就此

会嫁祸给我们?

唐纳班 在此有何可言,

---

110. 忠诚时不偏不倚(Loyal and neutral):即对邓肯忠诚,对他的凶手保持客观或中立。
114-5. 他的……侵入(And his…entrance):邓肯的伤口犹如身上的洞口,毁灭由此侵入从而糟蹋他的生命(Duncan's wounds were like openings in his body where destruction ["ruins"] had forced an entrance to lay waste his life)(Gill)。 114. 生命线上的豁口(breach in nature):生命防线上的缺口(gap in the defenses of life),属于一种军事隐喻——重重包围(A metaphor of military siege)(Bevington)。

Here, where our fate, hid in an auger hole,

May rush, and seize us? Let's away,

Our tears are not yet brewed.

125 **Malcolm**   Nor our strong sorrow

Upon the foot of motion.

Banquo   Look to the lady.   [*Exit Lady.*]

And when we have our naked frailties hid,

That suffer in exposure, let us meet

And question this most bloody piece of work

130   To know it further. Fears and scruples shake us.

In the great hand of God I stand, and thence

Against the undivulged pretence I fight

Of treasonous malice.

Macduff   And so do I.

All   So all.

Macbeth   Let's briefly put on manly readiness

And meet i'the hall together.

135 **All**   Well contented.

Exeunt [*all but Malcolm and Donalbain*].

Malcolm   What will you do? Let's not consort with them.

To show an unfelt sorrow is an office

Which the false man does easy. I'll to England.

我们的死神,藏在钻孔之中,

会突然出现捉住我们?　咱走吧,

泪水尚未酿成。

马尔科姆　　　　　　　此刻也不宜　　　　　　　　　　　125

表达我们的悲恸之情。

班柯　　　　　　　　照看夫人。　　　[夫人下。]

我们暂把赤裸的恐慌隐藏,

表露会加剧恐慌,咱们集合

并追查这种最为残忍的血案,

了解背后动机。　疑虑令人不安。　　　　　　　　130

借助上帝的崇高护佑和帮助,

我要挑战这种隐秘而邪恶的

叛国图谋。

麦克达夫　　　　　我也加入。

众人　　　　　　　　全加入。

麦克白　咱们大家都赶快整装待发,

然后在大厅里聚集。

众人　　　　　　　完全同意。　　　　　　　　　　135

[除马尔科姆与唐纳班之外]全下。

马尔科姆　您怎么办呢?　咱别跟他们一起。

对一位伪君子来说,表达虚情

假意轻而易举。　我去英格兰。

---

123. 藏在钻孔之中(hid…hole):藏在一个极小的空间里面,几乎完全隐蔽。　唐纳班担心在这种秘密的叛变氛围中,他们的命运,即死亡,会毫无征兆地降临(lurking in a tiny space, almost totally concealed. Donalbain is afraid that in this atmosphere of secret treachery their own fate, i.e. their deaths, may come upon them without warning)。　127. 赤裸的恐慌(naked frailties):班柯也许是指大家此刻确实衣着不整的状态(让他们回去穿戴整齐),但更可能是指他们对这种局面的恐慌,即:若表露出来会更加恐慌(Banquo may refer literally to the state of undress of all present, but more likely he means their distress at the situation, which is exacerbated by exposure)(Clark; Bate)。

Donalbain   To Ireland, I; our separated fortune

140   Shall keep us both the safer. Where we are,

There's daggers in men's smiles; the near in blood,

The nearer bloody.

Malcolm   This murderous shaft that's shot

Hath not yet lighted, and our safest way

Is to avoid the aim. Therefore to horse;

145   And let us not be dainty of leave-taking,

But shift away. There's warrant in that theft

Which steals itself, when there's no mercy left.   *Exeunt.*

唐纳班	我,去爱尔兰;咱们分头行动	
	将会更加安全。　无论去哪里,	140
	都会有人笑里藏刀;越是近亲,	
	越接近血刃。	
马尔科姆	射出的这支毒箭	
	还没有落地,最为保险的方式	
	就是加以躲避。　因此快上马;	
	咱们不必讲究礼貌地告辞,	145
	悄悄走吧。　若没有怜悯可言,	
	偷偷摸摸,倒是情有可原。	同下。

141-2. 越是……血刃(near…bloody):那些在血缘上(与邓肯)最近的人,面临的危险最大(Those nearest in blood〔to Duncan〕are most in danger)。　142-3. 射出的……落地(This…lighted):马尔科姆的这种隐喻旨在表达的是,暗杀邓肯的图谋尚未执行完毕(the plan behind Duncan's murder is not yet fully carried out)。　146-7. 若没有……可原(there's…left):原注为"It is a justifiable theft, to steal〔oneself〕away from a place where there is no mercy(从没有怜悯之心的地方偷偷摸摸〔溜走〕,倒是无可非议)"(Gill)。

SCENE IV

Enter Ross and an Old Man.

Old Man   Threescore and ten I can remember well,

Within the volume of which time I have seen

Hours dreadful and things strange; but this sore night

Hath trifled former knowings.

Ross   Ha, good father,

5   Thou seest the heavens, as troubled with man's act,

Threatens his bloody stage. By the clock 'tis day,

And yet dark night strangles the travelling lamp.

Is't night's predominance, or the day's shame,

That darkness does the face of earth entomb

When living light should kiss it?

10 **Old Man**   'Tis unnatural,

Even like the deed that's done. On Tuesday last,

A falcon towering in her pride of place,

Was by a mousing owl hawked at and killed.

Ross   And Duncan's horses, a thing most strange and certain,

第四场

罗斯与一老人上。

老人	七十年来的事情我记忆犹新,	
	其间我曾经历过可怕的时刻、	
	奇怪的事件；这种狂暴的夜晚	
	却使它们相形见绌。	
罗斯	哈,好老爹,	
	你看上天,因对人的表现不满,	5
	威胁这血腥舞台。 按表已是白天,	
	而黑夜却把运行的明灯遮掩。	
	是黑夜的强势,还是白天的羞耻,	
	生命之光本该亲吻大地的	
	面颊时,黑暗竟将它埋藏?	
老人	是反常,	10
	跟这次凶杀一样。 上个周二,	
	一只正在制高点翱翔的猎鹰,	
	竟被一只捕鼠的猫头鹰扑杀。	
罗斯	令人难以置信的是,邓肯的	

2.4. 4. 老爹（father）：对长者的尊称（honorific term applied to an old man）。 5-6. 上天……舞台（heavens…stage）：（上天）不喜欢我们人类的凶杀场景,以日食进行威胁。 其中"上天（heavens）"也可指舞台上方装饰华丽的屋顶（the decorated roof over the stage）,以及随后的"表现（act）"与"舞台（stage）"均属戏剧意象（theatrical metaphor）（Bevington）。 7. 运行的明灯（travelling lamp）：对太阳的迂回说法。 8. 白天的羞耻（day's shame）：白天为（人们所犯下的凶杀）感到丢脸。

15   Beauteous and swift, the minions of their race,

Turned wild in nature, broke their stalls, flung out

Contending 'gainst obedience, as they would

Make war with mankind.

Old Man   'Tis said they eat each other.

Ross   They did so, to th'amazement of mine eyes

That looked upon't.

Enter Macduff.

20   Here comes the good Macduff.

How goes the world, sir, now?

Macduff   Why, see you not?

Ross   Is't known who did this more than bloody deed?

Macduff   Those that Macbeth hath slain.

Ross   Alas, the day.

What good could they pretend?

Macduff   They were suborned.

25   Malcolm and Donalbain, the King's two sons,

Are stolen away and fled, which puts upon them

Suspicion of the deed.

Ross   'Gainst nature still,

Thriftless ambition, that wilt raven up

Thine own life's means. Then 'tis most like

30   The sovereignty will fall upon Macbeth.

Macduff   He is already named, and gone to Scone

　　　几匹骏马,可谓马中的宠儿,　　　　　　　　　　　　　　　15
　　　突然变野,冲出马厩,狂踢乱跳,
　　　拒不听从使唤,好像它们要
　　　跟人类交战。

老人　　　　　　　　　　据说还彼此相食。

罗斯　　　它们的确如此,我目瞪口呆,
　　　亲眼所见。

　　　　　　　　　　　　麦克达夫上。

　　　　　　　　好麦克达夫来了。　　　　　　　　　　　　　　　20
　　　情况怎样了,先生?

麦克达夫　　　　　　　　唉,您没看见?

罗斯　　　是否已知道谁干的这种暴行?

麦克达夫　　麦克白杀死的侍卫。

罗斯　　　　　　　　　唉,天哪!
　　　他们到底图啥?

麦克达夫　　　　　　　　被人买通。
　　　马尔科姆和唐纳班,国王的二子,　　　　　　　　　　　　25
　　　已经偷偷溜走,使他们成了
　　　这一行径的嫌犯。

罗斯　　　　　　　　又违背常情,
　　　愚蠢的野心,竟然吞噬自己
　　　生命的根本。　那很有可能
　　　王位将会落到麦克白身上。　　　　　　　　　　　　　　　30

麦克达夫　　他已被提名,已经前往斯宫

　　27-9. 又违背……根本（'Gainst…means）："表面看来,这些话语跟马尔科姆和唐纳班有关……但若用以形容麦克白将会多么贴切"（Muir）。　31. 斯宫（Scone）：古老的帝王之都,离佩斯（Perth）两英里,苏格兰国王曾在此长期居住。

To be invested.

Ross   Where is Duncan's body?

Macduff   Carried to Colmekill,

The sacred storehouse of his predecessors

And guardian of their bones.

35 **Ross**   Will you to Scone?

Macduff   No, cousin, I'll to Fife.

Ross   Well, I will thither.

Macduff   Well, may you see things well done there. Adieu,

Lest our old robes sit easier than our new.

Ross   Farewell, father.

40 **Old Man**   God's benison go with you, and with those

That would make good of bad, and friends of foes. *Exeunt.*

加冕登基。

罗斯　　　　　　邓肯的遗体何在？

麦克达夫　已运往科姆基尔，

他的祖先都葬在那片圣地，

遗骸安放在那里。

罗斯　　　　　　您去斯宫吗？　　　　　　　　　　　　　35

麦克达夫　不,兄弟,我去法夫。

罗斯　　　　　　我要去那里。

麦克达夫　好吧,愿那里一切顺利! 再见,

也许我们的旧袍比新袍耐穿。

罗斯　再见吧,老爹。

老人　愿上帝赐福与您,还有那些　　　　　　　　　40

改邪归正,和化敌为友之列!　　　　　全下。

---

33. 科姆基尔（Comekill）：即艾奥纳岛（the island of Iona）,苏格兰国王大都葬于此处。
36. 法夫（Fife）：苏格兰东部沿海地区,麦克达夫的领地。 他此刻的肯定语气首次表明了他要挑战麦克白政权的决心。 我要去那里（I will thither）：我要去斯宫。 看来罗斯至少是目前已接受麦克白为王。 41. 老人也许是在暗示罗斯是一位趋炎附势者（a time-server）,也许是天真地希望将来能够和解（a future of reconciliation）。

第三幕
ACT 3

SCENE I

Enter Banquo.

Banquo   Thou hast it now, King, Cawdor, Glamis, all,

As the weïrd women promised, and I fear

Thou play'st most foully for't. Yet it was said

It should not stand in thy posterity,

5   But that myself should be the root and father

Of many kings. If there come truth from them,

As upon thee, Macbeth, their speeches shine,

Why, by the verities on thee made good,

May they not be my oracles as well,

10   And set me up in hope? But hush, no more.

Sennet sounded. Enter Macbeth as King, Lady,

Lennox, Ross, Lords and Attendants.

Macbeth   Here's our chief guest.

Lady   If he had been forgotten,

第一场

班柯上。

班柯　　　你已如愿：国王、考道、葛莱密，

跟女巫许诺的一样，可我担心

你会为此不择手段。　但按预言，

你的子孙将不会继承王位，

而我本人将会是许多国王的　　　　　　　　　　　　　　5

先祖和起源。　她们的预言若灵验，

像对你,麦克白,她们的话语吉祥，

正像已在你身上应验的那样，

那对我为啥不可能也是神谕，

使我满怀希望？　嘘,别说了。　　　　　　　　　　　　10

喇叭吹响。身为国王的麦克白、夫人、
雷诺克斯、罗斯、众贵族与侍从上。

麦克白　　这是咱的贵宾。

夫人　　　　　　　他若被忘记，

　　3.1.　1-10. 你……别说了（Thou…more）：在霍林希德的编年史中，班柯乃是麦克白谋杀邓肯的同谋；然而，由于他（邓肯）是国王詹姆斯一世的先祖,便不得不对他有所尊重。　就纯粹的戏剧效果而言，让麦克白与班柯之间形成对照,使麦克白夫妇没有同谋,这显然非常理想。　布拉德利在其《莎士比亚的悲剧》中（384-5 页），认为本段台词表明班柯实为暗杀事件的帮凶,因为他,出于野心,就女巫一事沉默不语,避免揭穿麦克白（Muir）。　10（1）喇叭吹响（*Sennet sounded*）：表明一种礼仪性的入场。　也可表明"麦克白对自己国王身份的自信和认可（Macbeth's confident assertion of his kingship）"。

It had been as a gap in our great feast

And all thing unbecoming.

Macbeth   Tonight we hold a solemn supper, sir,

And I'll request your presence.

15 **Banquo**   Let your highness

Command upon me, to the which my duties

Are with a most indissoluble tie

For ever knit.

Macbeth   Ride you this afternoon?

Banquo   Ay, my good lord.

20 **Macbeth**   We should have else desired your good advice,

Which still hath been both grave and prosperous,

In this day's council: but we'll take tomorrow.

Is't far you ride?

Banquo   As far, my lord, as will fill up the time

25 'Twixt this, and supper. Go not my horse the better,

I must become a borrower of the night

For a dark hour or twain.

Macbeth   Fail not our feast.

Banquo   My lord, I will not.

Macbeth   We hear our bloody cousins are bestowed

30 In England and in Ireland, not confessing

Their cruel parricide, filling their hearers

With strange invention. But of that tomorrow,

When therewithal we shall have cause of state,

Craving us jointly. Hie you to horse. Adieu,

	将是我们筵席中的一大缺陷，	
	完全不合礼仪。	
麦克白	先生，今晚我们要举行盛宴，	
	我想请您光临。	
班柯	请陛下对我	15
	任意指派，对此我唯命是从，	
	唯愿自己能尽臣下之责，	
	直到永远。	
麦克白	下午要骑马走吗？	
班柯	是的，好陛下。	
麦克白	不然我会在今天的会上征求	20
	您的高见，因为它们都富有	
	成效，影响深远：那明天再谈。	
	您的路程远吗？	
班柯	不远，陛下，正好占用此刻	
	至晚宴时间。　马若跑得不能更快，	25
	我将不得不向那黑夜借用	
	一两个钟头。	
麦克白	别误了我们的晚宴。	
班柯	不会的，陛下。	
麦克白	听说我那两位残忍的堂兄	
	已定居英格兰和爱尔兰，不承认	30
	自己的弑父之罪，向听众散布	
	可笑的谎言。　明天再谈此事，	
	而且我们还会有国事要谈，	
	需要咱们出席。　快上马吧。　等您	

---

16. 任意指派（Command upon me）：班柯以同样的方式回应麦克白的客气（elaborate politeness）。

35   Till you return at night. Goes Fleance with you?

Banquo   Ay, my good lord; our time does call upon's.

Macbeth   I wish your horses swift, and sure of foot;

And so I do commend you to their backs.

Farewell.   *Exit Banquo.*

40   Let every man be master of his time

Till seven at night; to make society

The sweeter welcome, we will keep ourself

Till supper time alone. While then, God be with you.

Exeunt [all but Macbeth and a Servant].

Sirrah, a word with you: attend those men our pleasure?

45 **Servant**   They are, my lord, without the palace gate.

Macbeth   Bring them before us.   *Exit Servant.*

To be thus is nothing, but to be safely thus:

Our fears in Banquo stick deep,

And in his royalty of nature reigns that

50   Which would be feared. 'Tis much he dares,

And to that dauntless temper of his mind,

He hath a wisdom that doth guide his valour

To act in safety. There is none but he,

Whose being I do fear; and under him

55   My Genius is rebuked, as it is said

Mark Antony's was by Caesar. He chid the sisters

When first they put the name of king upon me,

And bade them speak to him. Then, prophet-like,

	晚上回来再见。 弗林斯与您一起？	35
班柯	是的,好陛下；我们应该走了。	
麦克白	愿您的马疾驰如飞,马蹄稳健；	
	因此我请你们赶快上马。	
	再见。 班柯下。	
	让大家自由支配各自的时间,	40
	直到晚上七点；为使聚会	
	更加怡人,我将独自待到	
	晚宴时间。 在此之前,再见。	

[除麦克白与一仆人外]全下。

	老兄,我问您：他们在等候我吗？	
仆人	是的,陛下,就在宫门外面。	45
麦克白	带他们前来见我。 仆人下。	
	仅仅称王无用,稳坐江山才行：	
	我惧怕班柯真是心如刀割,	
	他的天性之中有一种高贵的	
	品质令我惊恐。 他非常勇敢,	50
	除了那种无所畏惧的精神,	
	他还有一种智慧引导他的	
	勇气稳健行动。 唯有他一人,	
	他的存在令我生畏；在他周围	
	我的守护神失灵,就像恺撒	55
	是安东尼的克星。 当女巫最初	
	告诉我要做王时,他责怪她们,	
	令她们对他说话。 随后,先知般,	

55-6. 就像……克星（Mark…Caesar）：参考《安东尼与克莉奥佩特拉》2.3. 18-22。 其中,占卜者曾警告安东尼要远离屋大维："因为你的精灵——你的守护之神——若远离恺撒,即可高贵、勇敢、无与伦比。 可一旦靠近,你的天使,犹如受到压制,会产生恐惧；因此你要与他保持距离。"

They hailed him father to a line of kings.

60 Upon my head they placed a fruitless crown,

And put a barren sceptre in my gripe,

Thence to be wrenched with an unlineal hand,

No son of mine succeeding. If't be so,

For Banquo's issue have I filed my mind;

65 For them, the gracious Duncan have I murdered;

Put rancours in the vessel of my peace

Only for them; and mine eternal jewel

Given to the common enemy of man,

To make them kings, the seeds of Banquo kings.

70 Rather than so, come fate into the list.

And champion me to th'utterance. Who's there?

Enter Servant and two Murderers.

Now go to the door, and stay there till we call. *Exit Servant.*

Was it not yesterday we spoke together?

Murderers It was, so please your highness.

Macbeth   Well then,

75 Now have you considered of my speeches?

Know, that it was he, in the times past,

Which held you so under fortune,

她们将他称为系列君王之父。

给我戴上了一顶绝后的皇冠，　　　　　　　　　　60

让我手握一根无益的权杖，

行将被外人之手抢夺而去，

不能传给儿子。　若是这样，

为班柯的子孙我玷污了灵魂；

为了他们，杀害了慈祥的邓肯；　　　　　　　　65

向我平静的杯中投入了敌意，

只为他们；将我不朽的灵魂

交给了人类那位共同的仇敌，

竟使班柯的子孙世代为王。

与其这样，还不如叫命运到场，　　　　　　　　70

帮助我殊死一搏。　那边是谁？

　　　　　　　　　仆人与二刺客上。

你先去门口，等我叫时再来。　　　　　　　仆人下。

我们是否在昨天已谈过话了？

刺客　　是的，尊贵的陛下。

麦克白　　　　　那好吧，

你们是否已考虑过我的话语？　　　　　　　　75

知道，是他，在过去的时间里，

使你们困苦不堪倍受压抑，

---

66. 平静的杯中（vessel of my peace）：麦克白也许是指圣餐杯受到了玷污；参考 1.7.11。敌意（rancour）：此处被视为一种毒药投到盛满健康饮品的杯中（here visualized as a poison added to a vessel full of wholesome drink）（Bevington）。　68. 共同的仇敌（common enemy）：即撒旦。麦克白已经明白自己的所作所为意味着什么。　71. 帮助我（champion me）：可指"在决斗中支持我（support me）"，或指"挑战我（challenge me, i. e. in combat）"（Bate）。尽管约翰逊认为麦克白是在挑战命运女神，但此处很可能是指麦克白想邀请命运女神与他协同作战，以便抵御班柯的子孙继任王位的可能，这样意义会更为通顺（Clark）。　76. 他（he）：即班柯。麦克白此刻避免提及班柯的名字，这可强调他与刺客之间的亲密与串通。

Which you thought had been our innocent self.

This I made good to you, in our last conference,

80 Passed in probation with you:

How you were borne in hand, how crossed;

The instruments, who wrought with them,

And all things else, that might

To half a soul, and to a notion crazed,

Say, 'Thus did Banquo'.

85 **1 Murderer**   You made it known to us.

Macbeth I did so; and went further, which is now

Our point of second meeting. Do you find

Your patience so predominant in your nature

That you can let this go? Are you so gospelled

90 To pray for this good man, and for his issue,

Whose heavy hand hath bowed you to the grave,

And beggared yours for ever?

1 Murderer   We are men, my liege.

Macbeth Ay, in the catalogue ye go for men:

As hounds and greyhounds, mongrels, spaniels, curs,

95 Shoughs, water-rugs and demi-wolves are clept

All by the name of dogs. The valued file

Distinguishes the swift, the slow, the subtle,

The housekeeper, the hunter, every one

According to the gift which bounteous nature

却以为无辜的本王是那罪魁。

上次谈话时我已就此澄清，

向你们展示了明证： 80

你们是如何受骗，如何受阻，

采用的手段，都是谁在操纵，

和其他各种情形，即使

一个半吊子，一个呆头呆脑，

都会说，"是班柯干的"。

刺客甲 您已说明。 85

麦克白 是的；我还有话要说，这也是

咱们再次会面的宗旨。 难道

你们天性中的忍耐如此强盛，

能对此予以宽容？ 如此圣洁

竟为这个好人及其子孙祈祷， 90

他的暴虐将你们逼进了坟墓，

世代沦为乞丐？

刺客甲 我们是人，陛下。

麦克白 是的，若按类分你们算人：

就像猎狗、跑狗、杂种狗、哈巴狗、

看门狗、叭儿狗、水狗和狼狗 95

统称为狗。 但是价目表却会

注明哪一条飞快、迟缓、狡猾、

擅长看家、善于狩猎，按照

慷慨的自然赋予它们各自

---

89. 圣洁（gospelled）：深受《圣经》"福音书"教义的影响（imbued with gospel teaching）（Clark）。 89-90. 圣洁……祈祷（gospelled…issue）：参考（日内瓦版）《圣经》"马太福音"5章44节："要爱你们的仇敌：祝福那些诅咒你们的人；善待那些仇恨你们的人，为那些伤害过、逼迫过你们的人祷告。"（Muir）95. 看门狗（curs）：可能指一种看门狗或牧羊犬，此处并无贬义；但莎士比亚常用它表示轻蔑。

100   Hath in him closed, whereby he does receive
           Particular addition, from the bill
           That writes them all alike: and so of men.
           Now, if you have a station in the file,
           Not i'th' worst rank of manhood, say't,
105   And I will put that business in your bosoms
           Whose execution takes your enemy off,
           Grapples you to the heart and love of us,
           Who wear our health but sickly in his life,
           Which in his death were perfect.

2 Murderer   I am one, my liege,
110   Whom the vile blows and buffets of the world
           Hath so incensed, that I am reckless what I do
           To spite the world.

1 Murderer   And I another,
           So weary with disasters, tugged with fortune,
           That I would set my life on any chance,
115   To mend it, or be rid on't.

Macbeth   Both of you know Banquo was your enemy.

Murderers True, my lord.

Macbeth   So is he mine; and in such bloody distance
           That every minute of his being thrusts
120   Against my near'st of life: and though I could
           With bare-faced power sweep him from my sight
           And bid my will avouch it, yet I must not,
           For certain friends that are both his and mine,

的禀赋,由此在一张将它们　　　　　　　　　　　　　100

统称为狗的名录之外,表明

它们的特别之处：人也是如此。

好了,你们若在男人的行列中

不属于最低一等,那就明说,

我要给你们一件秘密的差使,　　　　　　　　　　　105

一旦执行,你们既可除掉仇敌,

也可赢得我的信赖和厚爱,

只要他活着,我就没有健康,

他死去我便安然无恙。

刺客乙　　　　　　　　　　　　我这人,陛下,

饱受世人的恶意伤害和打击,　　　　　　　　　　　110

如此怒不可遏,为了报复,

对我的行为毫不介意。

刺客甲　　　　　　　　　　　　我也是,

历经磨难,遭受命运的摆布,

我会拿自己的生命孤注一掷,

要么好转,要么了断。　　　　　　　　　　　　　　115

麦克白　　你们两个知道班柯是仇敌。

刺客甲　　是的,陛下。

麦克白　　也是我的；且如此不共戴天,

他所存活的每一分钟都会

刺向我的命根：尽管我可以　　　　　　　　　　　120

公开地把他从我眼前除掉,

并心安理得,可我万万不能,

因为他和我有些共同的朋友,

---

120. 命根（near'st of life）：要害；关键部位（vital parts）（Muir）。

Whose loves I may not drop, but wail his fall

125 Who I myself struck down. And thence it is,

That I to your assistance do make love,

Masking the business from the common eye

For sundry weighty reasons.

2 Murderer   We shall, my lord,

Perform what you command us.

1 Murderer   Though our lives—

130 **Macbeth** Your spirits shine through you. Within this hour at most

I will advise you where to plant yourselves,

Acquaint you with the perfect spy o'th' time,

The moment on't—for't must be done tonight,

And something from the palace: always thought

135 That I require a clearness—and with him,

To leave no rubs nor botches in the work,

Fleance, his son, that keeps him company,

Whose absence is no less material to me

Than is his father's, must embrace the fate

140 Of that dark hour. Resolve yourselves apart:

I'll come to you anon.

Murderers   We are resolved, my lord.

Macbeth I'll call upon you straight: abide within.

[*Exeunt Murderers.*]

It is concluded: Banquo, thy soul's flight,

If it find heaven, must find it out tonight.   *Exit.*

我不想绝交,尽管我让他死去,

却要为他哀悼。　因此现在,　　　　　　　　　　125

我才会寻求你们给以帮助,

为了各种重要的理由,必须

遮掩众人耳目。

刺客乙　　　　　　　　　　俺会的,陛下,

按您的吩咐执行。

刺客甲　　　　　　　　哪怕生命——

麦克白　　你们浑身是胆。　一小时之内,　　　　130

我会告诉你们在何处就位,

以及所观察到的最佳时机,

动手时间——因为必须在今晚,

而且要远离王宫:时刻记住

我要求干净利落,不能拖泥　　　　　　　　　135

带水或漏出破绽——与他一起的,

弗林斯,他儿子,将会结伴前来,

他的缺席对我来说不比他

父亲的缺席逊色,他们两人

要同遭厄运。　你们私下决定;　　　　　　　140

我马上就来。

二刺客　　　　　　　我们决心已定,陛下。

麦克白　　我立即去见你们:在里面等着。

[二刺客同下。]

事已商定:班柯,你的灵魂飞翔,

若能找到天堂,必在今天晚上。

---

130. 你们浑身是胆(Your…you):麦克白以富有讥讽意味的恭维打断了刺客甲的誓言。

143. 灵魂飞翔(soul's flight):摆脱了肉体的灵魂被想象成一种飞鸟。

SCENE II

Enter Macbeth's Lady and a Servant.

Lady   Is Banquo gone from court?

Servant   Ay, madam, but returns again tonight.

Lady   Say to the King I would attend his leisure

For a few words.

Servant   Madam, I will.   *Exit.*

5 **Lady**   Naught's had, all's spent,

Where our desire is got without content.

'Tis safer to be that which we destroy,

Than by destruction dwell in doubtful joy.

Enter Macbeth.

How now, my lord, why do you keep alone?

10   Of sorriest fancies your companions making,

Using those thoughts which should indeed have died

With them they think on? Things without all remedy

Should be without regard: what's done, is done.

Macbeth   We have scotched the snake, not killed it:

15   She'll close, and be herself, whilst our poor malice

第二场

麦克白夫人与一仆人上。

夫人	班柯已离开了宫殿？	
仆人	是的，夫人，但晚上还会回来。	
夫人	你去告诉国王我有话等着 想对他说。	
仆人	遵命，夫人。	下。
夫人	一无所获，尽管费尽心机，	5

即使如愿以偿却不能满意。
与其害人而享受疑虑的心欢，
不如我们的受害者更为安全。

麦克白上。

怎么了，夫君，您为何独自一人？
只有凄惨的幻想与您为伴，　　　　　　　　　10
那种思想应和死者同归于尽，
你却念念不忘？　事情无法补救，
不再记挂心头：既干了，就算了。

麦克白	我们砍伤了毒蛇，并未杀死：	
	她会愈合康复，先前的毒牙	15

3.2. 3-4. 等着想对他说（attend his leisure）："麦克白夫人现在要派仆人才能与丈夫取得联系，这也许表明他们两人开始疏远"。 本场表明他们二人的伙伴关系已告结束。 7. 疑虑的心欢（doubtful joy）：矛盾修辞法，意为这种欢欣既令人恐惧，也不保险（joy which is fearful as well as uncertain）。 8. 更为安全（safer）：该词可令人想起麦克白也曾有类似的挫败之感（3.1.47-8）。

Remains in danger of her former tooth.

But let the frame of things disjoint, both the worlds suffer,

Ere we will eat our meal in fear, and sleep

In the affliction of these terrible dreams

20   That shake us nightly. Better be with the dead,

Whom we, to gain our peace, have sent to peace,

Than on the torture of the mind to lie

In restless ecstasy. Duncan is in his grave.

After life's fitful fever, he sleeps well;

25   Treason has done his worst: nor steel, nor poison,

Malice domestic, foreign levy, nothing,

Can touch him further.

Lady   Come on. Gentle my lord,

Sleek o'er your rugged looks, be bright and jovial

Among your guests tonight.

30 **Macbeth**   So shall I, love, and so I pray be you.

Let your remembrance apply to Banquo,

Present him eminence, both with eye and tongue.

Unsafe the while, that we must lave

Our honours in these flattering streams,

35   And make our faces vizards to our hearts,

Disguising what they are.

Lady   You must leave this.

依然威胁着我们虚弱的恶意。

让宇宙分崩离析,天塌地陷,

以免我们在恐惧之中进食,

以免睡眠时彻夜辗转反侧,

遭噩梦摧残。 宁愿与死人为伍,　　　　　　　　20

我们,为了心安,将其送入安眠,

也不愿忍受这种心灵的折磨,

焦躁的狂乱。 邓肯已进入坟墓,

饱经沧桑之后,他得以安息;

叛逆已登峰造极:钢刀、毒药,　　　　　　　　25

无论内忧,还是外患,都对他

鞭长莫及。

夫人　　　　　　　得了,亲爱的夫君,

别这样愁眉苦脸,要轻松愉快

迎接今晚的来宾。

麦克白　　我会,亲爱的,希望您也能如此。　　　　　　　　30

求您定要格外地关注班柯,

言谈举止要对他极为敬重。

目前还不安全,因此咱要用

滔滔不绝的奉承冲洗咱的名声,

要把咱们的面孔当着伪装,　　　　　　　　35

将咱的内心掩藏。

夫人　　　　　　　别再这样讲。

33-6. 目前……掩藏(Unsafe…are):此处的大意为,"目前我们立足未稳,因此必须通过奉承班柯,掩藏仇恨以使我们的声誉清白"。 麦克白不仅害怕自己的阴谋败露,也害怕自己被班柯暗杀(Muir)。 此处意为,"麦克白夫妇尚不安全,因此要用洪水般的奉承和持续的欺骗才能使其声誉保持清白(while the Macbeths are insecure, it is necessary for them to keep their honours clean by a deluge of flattery and continual deceit)";原文中的"Unsafe the while"也许是个独立结构(Clark)。

	Macbeth	O, full of scorpions is my mind, dear wife:
		Thou know'st that Banquo and his Fleance lives.
	Lady	But in them nature's copy's not eterne.
40	**Macbeth**	There's comfort yet: they are assailable.
		Then be thou jocund: ere the bat hath flown
		His cloistered flight, ere to black Hecate's summons
		The shard-borne beetle, with his drowsy hums,
		Hath rung night's yawning peal, there shall be done
		A deed of dreadful note.
45	**Lady**	What's to be done?
	Macbeth	Be innocent of the knowledge, dearest chuck,
		Till thou applaud the deed. Come, seeling night,
		Scarf up the tender eye of pitiful day,
		And with thy bloody and invisible hand
50		Cancel and tear to pieces that great bond
		Which keeps me pale. Light thickens,
		And the crow makes wing to th' rooky wood.
		Good things of day begin to droop and drowse,
		While night's black agents to their preys do rouse.
55		Thou marvell'st at my words: but hold thee still;
		Things bad begun, make strong themselves by ill.
		So prithee, go with me. *Exeunt.*

麦克白	噢,爱妻,我心中充满了蝎子!	
	你知道班柯弗林斯还活着没死。	
夫人	但上苍未授权他们可以永生。	
麦克白	这倒有些欣慰:他们尚可处置。	40
	你只管开心;先于蝙蝠到回廊	
	飞行,先于金龟子响应乌黑的	
	赫卡忒召唤,用那催眠的鼓翅	
	敲响入夜的钟声,将有一件	
	可怕的大事完成。	
夫人	什么大事?	45
麦克白	最好一无所知,亲爱的宝贝儿,	
	到时拍手称快。　来吧,蒙眼的黑夜,	
	将慈悲之白天的善目遮掩,	
	用你那血腥和无形的黑手	
	将那令我胆怯的道德契约	50
	废除并撕成碎片。　光线已暗,	
	成群的乌鸦正在飞回林中。	
	白天的良善之物已睡眼蒙眬,	
	夜晚的邪恶之徒正蠢蠢欲动。	
	我的话令你惊讶:但保持镇静;	55
	恶行伴以更多恶行才更强盛。	
	请你跟我来吧。　　　　　　同下。	

42-3. 乌黑的赫卡忒(black Hecate):赫卡忒起先被视为“苍白(pale)”(2.1.51),而此处却变成了“乌黑(black)”,旨在与麦克白以夜间为背景的心情保持一致(in keeping with the mood of Macbeth's night-piece)。　47. 蒙眼的(seeling):令人盲目的(blinding),驯鹰术语,即驯服猎鹰或其他鸟类的一种过程——将小鹰的眼睛缝合,此处喻为“蒙蔽,骗人(hoodwinking)”。51. 光线已暗(Light thickens):矛盾修辞法,意为“天色变暗(It grows darker)”,可令人想起女巫们在1.1所制造的那种乌烟瘴气。　56. 是对一句格言的重述,即“要想掩盖罪行需犯更大的罪行(Crimes are made secure by greater crimes)”。

SCENE III

Enter three Murderers.

1 Murderer   But who did bid thee join with us?

3 Murderer   Macbeth.

2 Murderer   He needs not our mistrust, since he delivers

Our offices, and what we have to do,

To the direction just.

1 Murderer   Then stand with us.

5   The west yet glimmers with some streaks of day.

Now spurs the lated traveller apace

To gain the timely inn, and near approaches

The subject of our watch.

2 Murderer   Hark, I hear horses.

Banquo   (*within*) Give us a light there, ho!

3 Murderer   Then 'tis he: the rest,

10   That are within the note of expectation

Already are i'th' court.

1 Murderer   His horses go about.

3 Murderer   Almost a mile; but he does usually,

第三场

三刺客上。

刺客甲	是谁让你与我们会合？	
刺客丙	麦克白。	
刺客乙	我们不用怀疑，因为他说出了	
	我们的职责，以及如何行动，	
	跟我们的指令相同。	
刺客甲	那就留下。	

几缕微光依然在西方闪现。　　　　　　　　　　　　5
晚归的旅客正在策马加鞭，
想及时赶往旅店，我们守候的
目标即将出现。

刺客丙	你听，有马蹄声。
班柯	［在内］给我们点个火把，嗨！
刺客乙	就是他：

其他在应邀之列的所有客人　　　　　　　　　　10
已经到达王宫。

刺客甲	他的马要绕行。
刺客丙	几乎一英里；但他通常如此，

3.3.　4-8.　"这些优美的的诗行……并非出自贱民之口"。　然而，"若说某些人物要比另一些人物更富有诗意，这是很危险的：因为在诗剧中每个人必然会出口成诗"（Muir）。　11. 要绕行（go about）：马经过长途奔跑之后定会出汗，所以有必要让（班柯在第9行叫来的）马夫牵着马环行一段路程，直到它们凉下来为止（Gill）。

So all men do, from hence to the palace gate

Make it their walk.

Enter Banquo and Fleance, with a torch.

2 Murderer   A light, a light.

3 Murderer   'Tis he.

1 Murderer   Stand to't.

Banquo   It will be rain tonight.

15 **1 Murderer**   Let it come down.

Banquo   O, treachery!

[*The Murderers attack. First Murderer strikes out the lights.*]

Fly, good Fleance, fly, fly, fly!

Thou mayst revenge—   [*Exit Fleance.*]

O slave!   [*Dies.*]

3 Murderer   Who did strike out the light?

1 Murderer   Was't not the way?

3 Murderer   There's but one down: the son is fled.

2 Murderer   We have lost

Best half of our affair.

20 **1 Murderer**   Well, let's away,

And say how much is done.   *Exeunt.*

大家也都这样,从这里步行

到达宫门。

班柯与弗林斯持火把上。

刺客乙	火把,火把!
刺客丙	是他。
刺客甲	就位。
班柯	今晚要下雨了。
刺客甲	就让它下吧! 15
班柯	噢,奸计!

[三刺客袭击。刺客甲扑灭火把。]

快跑,好弗林斯,跑,跑,跑!

你可以复仇——   [弗林斯逃跑。]

噢,恶棍!   [死去。]

刺客丙	是谁扑灭了火把?
刺客甲	不该扑灭吗?
刺客丙	只干掉一个:儿子跑了。
刺客乙	我们的

职责失去了大半。

刺客甲	好了,咱走吧,	20

前去汇报结果。   同下。

---

15. 就让它下吧(Let…down):可谓一种阴险的玩笑(a grim jest),因为班柯无需担心天气。 本行也传达了另一层意思:手无寸铁的受害者将会遭受阵雨般的袭击(the rain of blows)。 20. 大半(Best half):麦克白已在3.1.136-40表明了将弗林斯处死的重要性。 可以说,弗林斯的幸免于难至关重要:"弗林斯的逃生意味着麦克白的在劫难逃(The escaping Fleance carries Macbeth's doom with him)。"(Clark)弗林斯的逃跑可谓该剧的转折点(Muir)。

SCENE IV

Banquet prepared. Enter Macbeth, Lady, Ross
Lennox, Lords and Attendants

Macbeth   You know your own degrees, sit down. At first and last,

The hearty welcome.

Lords   Thanks to your majesty.

Macbeth   Ourself will mingle with society

And play the humble host. Our hostess keeps her state,

5   But in best time we will require her welcome.

Lady   Pronounce it for me, sir, to all our friends,

For my heart speaks, they are welcome.

Enter First Murderer.

Macbeth   See, they encounter thee with their hearts' thanks.

Both sides are even: here I'll sit i'th' midst.

10   Be large in mirth; anon we'll drink a measure

The table round. —There's blood on thy face.

1 Murderer   'Tis Banquo's then.

第四场

筵席备好。麦克白、夫人、罗斯、
雷诺克斯、众贵族与侍从上。

麦克白　　你们知道自己的地位,请坐。　各位,
　　　　　　衷心地欢迎你们!

众贵族　　　　　　　　谢谢陛下!

麦克白　　我本人将会与客人坐在一起,
　　　　　　好殷勤待客。　女主人留在宝座,
　　　　　　我会适时要她来欢迎大家。　　　　　　　　　5

夫人　　　请代我,先生,向朋友们致意,
　　　　　　因为我从心坎里欢迎他们。

刺客甲上。

麦克白　　你看,他们回应以诚挚的谢意。
　　　　　　两边人数相等,我在中间就座。
　　　　　　请尽情欢乐;我马上就与大家　　　　　　　10
　　　　　　一一举杯。　——你的脸上有血。

刺客甲　　那属于班柯。

3.4.　1. 地位（degrees）：即社会地位,因此大家应依次就座。　麦克白在其开场白中表明了该晚宴的正式,需遵守等级制度。　各位（At…last）：即从头至尾的每一位（to one and all）。 9. 中间（i'th midst）：一边的中间（half-way down one side）。　在当时,上座（place of hono-ur）或在餐桌的前端（either at the head of the table）,或在某一边的中间（or in the center down one side）。　然而,麦克白是在炫耀自己并未在上座就座。

	Macbeth	'Tis better thee without, than he within.
		Is he dispatched?
	1 Murderer	My lord, his throat is cut; that I did for him.
15	**Macbeth**	Thou art the best o'th' cut-throats;
		Yet he's good that did the like for Fleance.
		If thou didst it, thou art the nonpareil.
	1 Murderer	Most royal sir, Fleance is scaped.
	Macbeth	Then comes my fit again: I had else been perfect;
20		Whole as the marble, founded as the rock,
		As broad and general as the casing air:
		But now I am cabined, cribbed, confined, bound in
		To saucy doubts and fears. But Banquo's safe?
	1 Murderer	Ay, my good lord: safe in a ditch he bides,
25		With twenty trenched gashes on his head,
		The least a death to nature.
	Macbeth	Thanks for that.
		There the grown serpent lies; the worm that's fled
		Hath nature that in time will venom breed,
		No teeth for th' present. Get thee gone, tomorrow
		We'll hear ourselves again. *Exit* [*First*] *Murderer.*
30	**Lady**	My royal lord,
		You do not give the cheer: the feast is sold
		That is not often vouched, while 'tis a-making,
		'Tis given with welcome. To feed were best at home:
		From thence, the sauce to meat is ceremony,
		Meeting were bare without it.

麦克白	你在外面,胜过他在里面。
	他被处理了?
刺客甲	陛下,我已把他的喉咙割破。
麦克白	你真是一个最棒的割喉者; 15
	谁对弗林斯也那样同样很棒。
	要是你做了,就是举世无双。
刺客甲	最高贵的先生,弗林斯跑了。
麦克白	那我又要犯病,否则安然无恙;
	坚如磐石,岩石一般稳固, 20
	就像环绕的空气无拘无束:
	现在却被囚禁于斗室、牛栏,
	受傲慢的疑虑牵制。 班柯可安全?
刺客甲	是的,好陛下:安居在一条沟里,
	头上有二十道深长的切口, 25
	最轻的也能致命。
麦克白	谢谢你了。
	大蛇已躺在那里;逃走的小蛇
	到时候身上自然会生出毒液,
	目前还没长牙。 你走吧,明天
	咱们再一起交谈。 刺客[甲]下。
夫人	尊贵的陛下, 30
	您未尽主人之谊;宴会若没有
	频频祝酒就是交易,宴会期间,
	要表示欢迎。 进食最好在家里:
	离家赴宴,特殊的佐料是礼仪,
	缺了它就是寒酸。

---

12. 你在⋯⋯里面(thee⋯within):麦克白的玩笑有些牵强(Macbeth's joke is forced)。

Enter the Ghost of Banquo, and sits in Macbeth's place.

35 **Macbeth**   Sweet remembrancer.

Now good digestion wait on appetite,

And health on both.

Lennox   May't please your highness sit.

Macbeth   Here had we now our country's honour roofed,

Were the graced person of our Banquo present;

40   Who may I rather challenge for unkindness

Than pity for mischance.

Ross   His absence, sir,

Lays blame upon his promise. Please't your highness

To grace us with your royal company?

Macbeth   The table's full.

Lennox   Here is a place reserved, sir.

Macbeth   Where?

45 **Lennox**   Here, my good lord. What is't that moves your highness?

Macbeth   Which of you have done this?

Lords   What, my good lord?

Macbeth   Thou canst not say I did it: never shake

Thy gory locks at me.

Ross   Gentlemen, rise; his highness is not well.

50 **Lady**   Sit, worthy friends; my lord is often thus,

And hath been from his youth. Pray you, keep seat,

The fit is momentary; upon a thought

He will again be well. If much you note him,

班柯的鬼魂上,在麦克白的位置就座。

麦克白	可爱的提醒者。	35

祝大家食欲大振,消化力强,

二者都健康!

雷诺克斯　　　　　恳请陛下入座。

麦克白　全国的精英现在会齐聚一堂,

假如我们仁慈的班柯到场,

但愿我能责备他缺乏礼貌,　　　　　　40

不愿他出了祸殃!

罗斯　　　　　　他的缺席,先生,

表明他言而无信。　能否请陛下

与我们同坐,好让我们增光?

麦克白　全坐满了。

雷诺克斯　　　这是给您留的。

麦克白　　　　　　哪里?

雷诺克斯　这里,陛下。　陛下您这是怎么了?　　　45

麦克白　这是你们谁干的?

众贵族　　　　　啥呀,好陛下?

麦克白　你不能说这是我干的:别朝我

摇晃你血污的头发。

罗斯　先生们,请起;陛下他身体欠安。

夫人　请坐,尊贵的朋友;我丈夫常这样,　　50

从他年轻时开始。　请你们,坐下吧,

这只是暂时发作;顷刻之间

他就会康复。　你们若过分关注,

44. 全坐满了(The table's full):麦克白最初并未意识到鬼魂占据了他的座位。　47. 你不能说这是我干的(Thou…it):他有某种古怪而幼稚的念头,即:只要他的双手没有沾满班柯的鲜血,他对这第二桩凶杀就会问心无愧(would not afflict his conscience)(Muir)。

You shall offend him, and extend his passion.

55   Feed, and regard him not. [*to Macbeth*] Are you a man?

Macbeth   Ay, and a bold one, that dare look on that

Which might appal the devil.

Lady   O, proper stuff.

This is the very painting of your fear:

This is the air-drawn dagger which you said

60   Led you to Duncan. O, these flaws and starts,

Impostors to true fear, would well become

A woman's story at a winter's fire,

Authorized by her grandam. Shame itself.

Why do you make such faces? When all's done,

You look but on a stool.

65 **Macbeth**   Prithee see there.

Behold, look, lo, how say you?

[*to Ghost*] Why, what care I? If thou canst nod, speak too.

If charnel-houses and our graves must send

Those that we bury back, our monuments

70   Shall be the maws of kites.   [*Exit Ghost.*]

Lady   What? Quite unmanned in folly.

Macbeth   If I stand here, I saw him.

Lady   Fie, for shame!

Macbeth   Blood hath been shed ere now, i'th' olden time,

Ere humane statute purged the gentle weal;

反而会害他,使他的病情拖延。

吃吧,别管他了。　[对麦克白]您是男人吗?　　　　　55

麦克白　　是的,且很勇敢,令魔鬼胆寒的

场景也都敢看。

夫人　　　　　　　　　噢,一派胡言!

这真是您的恐惧绘出的画像:

像那把悬空的短剑,您说将您

引向邓肯。　噢,这种突发的惊慌,　　　　　　60

真正恐惧的幌子,更适合冬季的

炉旁听一位妇人讲述祖传的

故事时所作出的反应。　真丢人!

为何做这种鬼脸?　全都过去,

您却盯着一把凳子?

麦克白　　　　　　　你看那里!　　　　　　　　65

看哪,快看! 您怎么说?

[对鬼魂]嗨,我怕啥?　你若能点头,也说话呀!

假如坟墓必将我们埋葬的

人们送回世上,那我们只好

葬入兀鹫的胃中。　　　　　　[鬼魂消失。] 70

夫人　　怎么?　愚蠢使你懦弱。

麦克白　　正像我在此站立,看见他了。

夫人　　　　　　　　　呸,丢人!

麦克白　　古时候,在此之前也曾有流血,

人道的律法将国家净化之前;

69-70. 那我们……胃中(monuments…kites):意为"我们若想避免尸体从坟墓里返回,就必须让乌鸦将它们吞食(To prevent bodies from returning from the grave, we shall have to give them to the ravens to be devoured)"(Muir)。　74. 将国家净化(purged the gentle weal):其中,"purged"采用了预词法(即形容词的预期描写法),意为:国家经过净化之后会变得文明(*purged* is used here with proleptic force, in that the state [weal] becomes civilized [gentle] when it has been purged)。　参见 5.2. 27-9.

75 Ay, and since too, murders have been performed
Too terrible for the ear. The times have been,
That when the brains were out, the man would die,
And there an end. But now they rise again
With twenty mortal murders on their crowns,
80 And push us from our stools. This is more strange
Than such a murder is.

Lady   My worthy lord,
Your noble friends do lack you.

Macbeth   I do forget.
De not muse at me, my most worthy friends,
I have a strange infirmity, which is nothing
85 To those that know me. Come, love and health to all,
Then I'll sit down. Give me some wine, fill full.

Enter Ghost.

I drink to the general joy o'the whole table,
And to our dear friend Banquo, whom we miss—
Would he were here. To all, and him we thirst,
And all to all.

90 **Lords**   Our duties, and the pledge.
Macbeth Avaunt, and quit my sight! Let the earth hide thee.
Thy bones are marrowless, thy blood is cold;
Thou hast no speculation in those eyes
Which thou dost glare with.

Lady   Think of this, good peers,

是的,从那以后,骇人听闻的　　　　　　　　　　　75
凶杀也曾有过。　那时的情况是,
脑浆被敲出之后,人就会死去,
就此结束。　可如今却能复活,
头上带着二十道致命的伤口,
将我的座位占据。　这要比一件　　　　　　　　　80
凶杀更为惊奇。

夫人　　　　　　　　　　尊贵的陛下,
您的高贵朋友在等您。

麦克白　　　　　　　　我忘了。
别对我诧异,我最尊贵的朋友,
我有一种怪病,对了解我的人
来说不值一提。　来,为大家干杯,　　　　　　　85
我这就坐下。　给我倒酒,斟满。

　　　　　　　　　　鬼魂上。

我为在座各位的幸福干杯,
为好友班柯干杯,我很想他——
愿他在场!为大家,为渴求的他,
彼此干杯。

众贵族　　　　　　　向您致意,干杯。　　　　　　　90
麦克白　走开,别让我看见!回到地下!
你的骨头无髓,血液冰凉;
你用来凝视的那双眼睛其实
并无视力。

夫人　　　　　　　诸位,请把这视为

---

80. 将我的座位占据(push…stool):也可指承袭我的王位(take over our place in succession to the crown)。　89. 渴求的他(him we thirst):其中,"他(him)"指班柯,"渴求(thirst)"意为"思念(long for)"。

95   But as a thing of custom; 'tis no other,

                 Only it spoils the pleasure of the time.

Macbeth   What man dare, I dare.

                 Approach thou like the rugged Russian bear,

                 The armed rhinoceros, or the Hyrcan tiger,

100   Take any shape but that, and my firm nerves

                 Shall never tremble. Or be alive again,

                 And dare me to the desert with thy sword;

                 If trembling I inhabit then, protest me

                 The baby of a girl. Hence, horrible shadow,

                 Unreal mockery, hence.   [*Exit Ghost.*]

105   Why so, being gone,

                 I am a man again. [*to Lords*] Pray you, sit still.

Lady   You have displaced the mirth, broke the good meeting

                 With most admired disorder.

Macbeth   Can such things be,

                 And overcome us like a summer's cloud,

110   Without our special wonder? You make me strange

                 Even to the disposition that I owe,

                 When now I think you can behold such sights

                 And keep the natural ruby of your cheeks

                 When mine is blanched with fear.

一种慢性疾病；没有别的，　　　　　　　　　　95

只是它扫尽了今晚的兴致。

麦克白　　人敢做的，我都敢。

即使你化作一头俄罗斯大熊，

全副武装的犀牛，波斯猛虎，

只要你能有形，我坚强的气魄　　　　　　　　100

绝不会动摇。　或者你再复生，

挑战我到一块荒地进行决斗；

我若胆怯，闭门不出，就叫我

姑娘的玩偶。　滚开，可怕的幽灵！

虚假的幻象，滚开！　　　　　　　　〔鬼魂隐去。〕

怎么，它走了，　　　　　　　　　　　　　　105

我又成了男人。〔向众贵族〕你们，请坐吧。

夫　人　　您以惊人的胡闹破坏了欢聚，

搅乱了喜庆。

麦克白　　　　　　　　难道这样的事情，

能像夏天的浮云从身旁掠过，

不让人特别吃惊？　您使我觉得　　　　　　　110

我对自己的本性非常陌生，

一想到您能目睹这种场景，

竟然能够保持面颊红润，

我却被吓得苍白。

---

97. 就格律而言，本行与94行实为一行，麦克白好像并未注意到妻子的介入，而是继续对鬼魂发话。　99. 全副武装（armed）：即以它的角和硬皮（by its horn and tough skin）。　102. 荒地（desert）：即荒无人烟的地方（a deserted place）（好让决斗不受妨碍）。　103. 我若胆怯，闭门不出（If…then）：模棱两可的表述。　可指"如果我吓得发抖，待在家里（If I, trembling, stay indoors）"（Clark）；或指"到时我若害怕和发抖（if I live in fear and trembling then）"（Gill）。　110-11. 您使我……陌生（You…own）：即自我疏远（self-alienated），或是对我自己的本性感到吃惊（amazed at my own nature）。　"他本以为自己勇敢；可现在，令他自己感到丧胆的场景却使她不动声色，他的自我评价由此动摇（He had thought himself brave; now, when he sees her unmoved at sights which appal him, he is staggered in his estimate of himself）"（Muir）。

Ross	What sights, my lord?
115 **Lady**	I pray you speak not; he grows worse and worse;
	Question enrages him. At once, goodnight.
	Stand not upon the order of your going,
	But go at once.
Lennox	Goodnight, and better health
	Attend his majesty.
Lady	A kind good night to all. *Exeunt Lords.*
120 **Macbeth**	It will have blood they say: blood will have blood:
	Stones have been known to move and trees to speak;
	Augures, and understood relations, have
	By maggot-pies and choughs and rooks brought forth
	The secret'st man of blood. What is the night?
125 **Lady**	Almost at odds with morning, which is which.
Macbeth	How sayst thou that Macduff denies his person
	At our great bidding?
Lady	Did you send to him, sir?
Macbeth	I hear it by the way; but I will send.
	There's not a one of them but in his house
130	I keep a servant fee'd. I will tomorrow,
	And betimes I will, to the weïrd sisters.
	More shall they speak: for now I am bent to know
	By the worst means, the worst; for mine own good,
	All causes shall give way. I am in blood
135	Stepped in so far, that should I wade no more,

罗斯	啥场景,陛下?	
夫人	求您别说了;他现在越来越糟;	115
	会被询问激怒。 现在,就晚安。	
	大家辞别时不必依次离开,	
	立刻走吧。	
雷诺克斯	晚安,但愿陛下	
	早日康复!	
夫人	诚祝各位晚安。	众贵族下。
麦克白	人道是杀人会见血;血债要血偿:	120
	据说石头能移动,树木会说话;	
	占卜术,以及因果关系,早已	
	通过喜鹊、山鸦和乌鸦将最为	
	隐秘的凶手揭露。 夜已多深?	
夫人	正与凌晨竞争,昼夜不分。	125
麦克白	你觉得麦克达夫为何会抗命,	
	不亲自前来?	
夫人	您派人叫过他吗?	
麦克白	我听到传言;可我会派人过去。	
	我在每个贵族的家里都花钱	
	供养了一位密探。 我要在明天,	130
	一早我就去,见见那三位巫婆。	
	她们会道出更多:我要用最糟的	
	方式了解最糟的后果;为了我好,	
	其他一切都要让路。 我已涉足	
	血泊之中,即使不再前行,	135

---

117. 大家……离开（Stand……going）：麦克白夫人想尽快摆脱客人的急迫之情跟开场时的拘泥形式构成了鲜明的对比。 120. 血债要血偿（blood will have blood）：源自《圣经》"创世纪"9章16节："凡流人血的,他的血也必被人所流。"麦克白对这种名言的一再提及表明了他的消沉和退意（Macbeth's recourse to this familiar saying indicates weariness and resignation）。

Returning were as tedious as go o'er.

Strange things I have in head, that will to hand,

Which must be acted, ere they may be scanned.

Lady   You lack the season of all natures, sleep.

140 **Macbeth**   Come, we'll to sleep. My strange and self-abuse

Is the initiate fear, that wants hard use.

We are yet but young in deed.   *Exeunt.*

后退跟前进同样令人生厌。

我有些奇怪念头，要付诸行动，

在细察之前，必须将它们执行。

夫人　　您缺乏睡眠——生命所需的佐料。

麦克白　咱去睡吧。　我奇怪的自欺欺人　　　　　　　　　140

是新手恐惧，缺乏麻木不仁。

论行动我们依然稚嫩。　　　　　　　　　　同下。

---

140. 奇怪的自欺欺人（strange and self-abuse）：麦克白可能是指自己的自欺，将鬼魂视为一种幻觉（其实并不存在），或是指自己的自毁行为（Macbeth refers either to his self-deception, viewing the Ghost as a hallucination, or to his self-destructive behaviour）。　141. 新手恐惧（initiate fear）：即作为初学者或新手而产生的恐惧（the fear of a beginner or a novice）。　麻木不仁（hard use）：原注为"practice that hardens one（令人心硬的实际行动）"（Muir）。

SCENE V

Thunder. Enter the three Witches, meeting Hecate.

1 Witch   Why, how now Hecate? You look angerly.

HECATE   Have I not reason, beldams as you are,

Saucy and over-bold? How did you dare

To trade and traffic with Macbeth

5   In riddles and affairs of death;

And I, the mistress of your charms,

The close contriver of all harms,

Was never called to bear my part

Or show the glory of our art?

10   And, which is worse, all you have done

Hath been but for a wayward son,

Spiteful and wrathful, who, as others do,

Loves for his own ends, not for you.

But make amends now; get you gone,

15   And at the pit of Acheron

Meet me i'th' morning; thither he

Will come, to know his destiny.

第五场

雷声。三女巫上,与赫卡忒相遇。

女巫甲　嗨,赫卡忒好吗？　您有些生气。

赫卡忒　我没理由吗,你们这些老巫婆,

粗鲁而放肆？　你们怎敢饶舌,

竟以哑谜的方式与麦克白

做起了生死攸关的大买卖。　　　　　　　　5

而我,你们符咒的总管家,

秘密地将一切灾殃来谋划,

你们却不叫我参与其中,

以彰显我们巫术的神通？

更糟的是,所有的付出　　　　　　　　　　10

只为了一介任性的武夫,

像别人一样,恶毒易怒,

他不顾你们,唯利是图。

要赶快补救,现在就走,

你们将在那阴间的壕沟　　　　　　　　　　15

一早与我相会；他本人

会去那里打探他的命运。

3.5. 本场向来被视为（英国剧作家）托马斯·米德尔顿（Thomas Middleton）,而非莎士比亚本人所作,但近来有些学者对此提出了异议。　就其格律而言,这种四音步对偶句（tetrameter couplets）,女巫们此前尚未用过。

Your vessels and your spells provide,

Your charms, and every thing beside.

20 I am for th'air: this night I'll spend

Unto a dismal and a fatal end.

Great business must be wrought ere noon.

Upon the corner of the moon

There hangs a vaporous drop profound,

25 I'll catch it ere it come to ground;

And that, distilled by magic sleights,

Shall raise such artificial sprites

As by the strength of their illusion,

Shall draw him on to his confusion.

30 He shall spurn fate, scorn death, and bear

His hopes 'bove wisdom, grace and fear;

And you all know, security

Is mortals' chiefest enemy.   *Music, and a song*

Hark, I am called: my little spirit, see,

35 Sits in a foggy cloud, and stays for me.   [*Exit.*]

        Sing within. 'Come away, come away, etc.'

1 Witch   Come, let's make haste, she'll soon be back again. *Exeunt.*

带上你们的器皿、符咒、

魔法等等,要应有尽有。

我要升空:我要用今晚　　　　　　　　　　　　　　　20

挑起阴险而致命的事端。

一件大事午前必须做。

就在月亮的一个角落

挂着一滴奥妙的雨露,

落地之前要把它接住;　　　　　　　　　　　　　　25

然后用魔术加以提炼,

可将狡猾的精灵招揽,

凭他们魔幻般的力量,

将会导致他家破人亡。

他唾弃命运,蔑视死亡,　　　　　　　　　　　　　30

他痴心妄想,悲惨恐慌;

你们都知道,过分自信

可是凡人的最大敌人。　　　　　　　　　乐声,与歌声。

你听,有人在叫我:我的小妖魔,

坐在一片云雾里,正在等候我。　　　　　　　　[下。] 35

　　　内唱。"快离开,快离开,等等。"

女巫甲　　来,咱们赶快,她很快就回来。　　　　　　同下。

---

　　24. 雨露(vaporous drop):据信,月亮可用自己的魔力向草本植物喷施一种泡沫(It was believed that the moon shed a foam, with magical powers, on various herbs)(Gill)。 32. 过分自信(security):over-confidence(自负),参考谚语:"平安容易生变(Security gives way to conspiracy)"。

SCENE VI

Enter Lennox and another Lord.

Lennox   My former speeches have but hit your thoughts,

Which can interpret further. Only I say

Things have been strangely borne. The gracious Duncan

Was pitied of Macbeth; marry, he was dead.

5   And the right-valiant Banquo walked too late,

Whom you may say, if't please you, Fleance killed,

For Fleance fled: men must not walk too late.

Who cannot want the thought how monstrous

It was for Malcolm and for Donalbain

10   To kill their gracious father? Damned fact,

How it did grieve Macbeth! Did he not straight,

In pious rage, the two delinquents tear,

That were the slaves of drink and thralls of sleep?

Was not that nobly done? Ay, and wisely too:

15   For 'twould have angered any heart alive

To hear the men deny't. So that I say,

第六场

雷诺克斯与另一贵族上。

雷诺克斯　我刚才的话语跟您想法一致，

因此不必详述，我只是想说，

事情有些奇怪。　慈祥的邓肯

很让麦克白怜悯，可他已死去。

英勇无畏的班柯深夜赶路，　　　　　　　　　　　　5

您可以，若愿意，说是弗林斯杀害，

因为他跑了：人们可别深夜赶路。

有谁不觉得此事荒谬绝伦——

马尔科姆和唐纳班竟然

杀害了慈祥的父亲？　该死的行径，　　　　　　　10

这多让麦克白痛心！难道他没有，

义愤填膺，立刻将罪犯刺死，

那两个嗜酒和贪睡的恶棍？

该行为不高尚？　是的，也很聪明：

因为谁不会怒火中烧，若听到　　　　　　　　　　15

他们拒不承认。　所以我说，

3.6. 雷诺克斯在本场的角色可谓含混不清。　通常认为他是麦克白所犯罪行的观察者，并以迂回和讽刺性的语言风格揭露暴政的黑暗。　也有人认为，作为麦克白最为信任的郡主，"他显然是在为麦克白探秘"。　3-4. 慈祥的……死去（The gracious…dead）：雷诺克斯是在讥讽麦克白的矫揉造作，因为他是在行凶之后深表伤心（Bevington）。　10. 该死的（damned）：原文 damnèd 读作两个音节。　15-6. 因为……拒不承认（For…deny't）：他杀死了他们，免得人们因为听到他们拒不认罪而生气（He killed them so that men should not be angered by hearing them deny it）。　本句台词表明人们在暴政之下所适用的语言——模棱两可、含混不清（double-talk and equivocation）。

He has borne all things well, and I do think

That had he Duncan's sons under his key,

As, an't please heaven, he shall not, they should find

20   What 'twere to kill a father; so should Fleance.

But peace; for from broad words, and 'cause he failed

His presence at the tyrant's feast, I hear

Macduff lives in disgrace. Sir, can you tell

Where he bestows himself?

Lord   The son of Duncan,

25   From whom this tyrant holds the due of birth,

Lives in the English court, and is received

Of the most pious Edward with such grace

That the malevolence of fortune nothing

Takes from his high respect. Thither Macduff

30   Is gone, to pray the holy king, upon his aid

To wake Northumberland, and warlike Siward,

That by the help of these, with Him above

To ratify the work, we may again

Give to our tables meat, sleep to our nights,

35   Free from our feasts and banquets bloody knives;

Do faithful homage, and receive free honours,

All which we pine for now. And this report

Hath so exasperate their king, that he

他处理得恰到好处,因此我想,

邓肯的儿子若在他掌控之中——

若上帝怜悯,他不能——定会发现

弑父是什么后果;弗林斯也一样。 20

不说了;由于直言不讳,也由于

未出席这位暴君的筵席,我听说

麦克达夫遭到贬低。 能否告诉我

他现在何处安身?

贵族　　　　　　　　　邓肯的儿子,

其承袭特权被这位暴君剥夺, 25

现住英格兰王宫,受到最为

虔诚的爱德华国王格外款待,

他的尊荣并未因遭受厄运

而受到减损。 麦克达夫去了

那里,请求圣洁的国王,帮他 30

激励诺森伯兰,英勇的西华德,

通过他们的协助,还有来自

上帝的应允,我们也许能够

再次餐桌有饭,夜晚安眠,

筵席之上排除血腥的刀剑; 35

做到真诚地效忠,论功行赏,

对此我们向往已久。 这消息

使他们国王如此愤怒,竟然

---

19. 原文"an't" = if it。 在古代,"and"曾被用作连词,可与"if"同义。 27. 虔诚的爱德华(pious Edward):即(忏悔者)爱德华(Edward the Confessor)(英格兰国王,1042-1066 年在位)。 30. 帮他(upon his aid):帮助马尔科姆(Bevington)。 31. 诺森伯兰……西华德:诺森伯兰(Northumberland)为英格兰北部的一个郡,西华德(Siward)为诺森伯兰伯爵的姓氏;于 5.4 入场的"英勇的西华德"曾为诺森伯兰伯爵,实际上死于 1055 年,比麦克白早两年。 38. 他们国王(their king):常被修改为"the king(这位国王)",因为雷诺克斯的回答明显指向了麦克白。 然而,因为该贵族整段台词所谈论的对象均为爱德华国王,又因为他在第四幕中准备参战,因此,此处指他应更合原意,尽管雷诺克斯的转向麦克白有些突兀。

Prepares for some attempt of war.

40 **Lennox**   Sent he to Macduff?

Lord   He did. And with an absolute, 'Sir, not I,'

The cloudy messenger turns me his back

And hums, as who should say, 'You'll rue the time

That clogs me with this answer.'

Lennox   And that well might

45   Advise him to a caution, t'hold what distance

His wisdom can provide. Some holy angel

Fly to the court of England and unfold

His message ere he come, that a swift blessing

May soon return to this our suffering country,

Under a hand accursed.

50 **Lord**   I'll send my prayers with him. *Exeunt.*

准备诉诸武力。

雷诺克斯	他派人叫过麦克达夫？	40
贵族	是的。 回复很干脆，"先生，我不去，"	

愁容满面的信差转过身来，
哼了一声，像是说，"您会后悔
用这种答复对我搪塞。"

雷诺克斯 　　　　　　　　　这应该
提醒他小心谨慎，并竭尽全力　　　　　　　　45
保持距离。 愿某位圣洁的天使
飞往英格兰王宫，在他到来
之前披露消息，好让上天的
恩赐快回到这个在魔掌之下
受苦的国度！

贵族 　　　　　　我要为他祷告。　　　　同下。 50

---

42. 转过身来（turns me his back）：其中，"turns me = turns"，"me"在此用以强调（Bevington）。 44. 搪塞（clogs）：意为"烦扰（burdens）"，"阻碍，妨碍（obstructs）"。也许是指信差因为带回了坏消息会受惩罚。 45. 他（him）：麦克达夫。

第四幕
ACT 4

SCENE I

Thunder. Enter the three Witches.

1 Witch   Thrice the brinded cat hath mewed.

2 Witch   Thrice, and once the hedge-pig whined.

3 Witch   Harpier cries, ' 'Tis time, 'tis time. '

1 Witch   Round about the cauldron go;

5   In the poisoned entrails throw.

            Toad, that under cold stone

            Days and nights has thirty-one,

            Sweltered venom sleeping got,

            Boil thou first i'th' charmed pot.

10 **All**   Double, double, toil and trouble;

            Fire burn, and cauldron bubble.

2 Witch   Fillet of a fenny snake,

            In the cauldron boil and bake;

            Eye of newt and toe of frog,

15   Wool of bat and tongue of dog,

            Adder's fork and blind-worm's sting,

第一场

雷鸣。三女巫上。

女巫甲	灰斑猫已喵了三回。	
女巫乙	小刺猬已哼过四声。	
女巫丙	鸟怪叫,"时候到,时候到。"	
女巫甲	咱们围绕着大锅走;	
	有毒的内脏往里投。	5
	寒石底下的癞蛤蟆,	
	三十一昼夜里面趴,	
	睡眠中毒液渗出来,	
	魔锅将你们先煮开。	
三女巫	倍加努力地把火烧,	10
	火焰旺盛时锅冒泡。	
女巫乙	沼泽地里的蛇肉片,	
	大锅里煮熟再烘干;	
	蝾螈的眼睛青蛙脚,	
	狗的舌头,蝙蝠毛,	15
	蝰蛇的舌叉盲蜥刺,	

4.1. 作为该剧最为壮观的场景,本场常以"黑暗的山洞(in a dark Cave)"为背景,女巫们在其锅里调制一种符咒,并召唤用谜语进行预言的精灵。 3. 鸟怪(Harpier):供女巫丙使用的精灵。 莎士比亚也许是指希腊神话中一种半女半鸟的怪物(harpy)(Gill)。 4. 大锅(cauldron):当时的一种常用炊具。 也许会用机械手段通过舞台上的地板门把锅支起,麦克白在105行的疑问可以证明。 6-8. 癞蛤蟆……毒液(Toad…venom):人们认为癞蛤蟆有毒,也许因为它们的皮腺可分泌一种伤手的物质。 毒液(venom):伊丽莎白时代的人们认为女巫们丢进锅里的所有原料都有毒性,至少也是违反常情(unnatural)(Gill)。

Lizard's leg and owlet's wing,

For a charm of powerful trouble,

Like a hell-broth boil and bubble.

20 **All**   Double, double, toil and trouble;

Fire burn, and cauldron bubble.

3 Witch   Scale of dragon, tooth of wolf,

Witch's mummy, maw and gulf

Of the ravined salt-sea shark,

25   Root of hemlock digged i'th' dark,

Liver of blaspheming Jew,

Gall of goat and slips of yew

Silvered in the moon's eclipse,

Nose of Turk and Tartar's lips,

30   Finger of birth-strangled babe

Ditch-delivered by a drab,

Make the gruel thick and slab.

Add thereto a tiger's chaudron,

For th'ingredience of our chawdron.

35 **All**   Double, double, toil and trouble;

Fire burn, and cauldron bubble.

2 Witch   Cool it with a baboon's blood,

Then the charm is firm and good.

蜥蜴的腿肉小鹰翅，

熬成魔咒把是非搅，

迷魂汤一般煮冒泡。

三女巫　　倍加努力地把火烧；　　　　　　　　　　　　　　20

火焰旺盛时锅冒泡。

女巫丙　　龙的鳞片，狼牙齿，

巫婆使用的人干尸，

贪婪鲨鱼的喉与肚，

夜里挖出的毒芹属，　　　　　　　　　　　　　　25

渎圣犹太的黑心肝，

山羊的胆汁和紫衫，

嫩枝趁月食切成丝，

鞑靼嘴唇土耳其鼻，

降生勒死的婴儿指，　　　　　　　　　　　　　　30

由娼妓生下在阴沟，

要把粥熬得黏又稠。

里面再加上虎内脏，

合成咱们这一锅汤。

三女巫　　倍加努力地把火烧；　　　　　　　　　　　　　　35

火焰旺盛时锅冒泡。

女巫乙　　用狒狒血液来冷凝，

然后这魔咒即告成。

---

23. 人干尸（mummy）：药用物质，通常由经过防腐处理的人的干肉制成（medicinal substance, made from mummified [embalmed] flesh, usually of human beings）。 颁布于1604年的巫术法令规定，将掘出的尸首用于巫术为死罪（the use of exhumed bodies for witchcraft was a capital offence）。 25. 夜里挖出的（digged i'th dark）：据信，采集这种配料的时辰会影响其效用。 参考《哈姆雷特》3.2. 251-2。 26. 渎圣犹太（blespheming Jew）：因为，犹太人，跟土耳其人和鞑靼人一样，不承认基督的神性（denied the divinity of Christ）。 30. 降生勒死（birth-strangled）：一生下来即被处死，因此未受过洗礼。

Enter Hecate and the other three Witches.

Hecate O, well done. I commend your pains,

40   And everyone shall share i'th' gains.

     And now about the cauldron sing,

     Live elves and fairies in a ring,

     Enchanting all that you put in.

     Music and a song. ' Black spirits, etc. '

      [*Exeunt Hecate and the three other Witches.*]

2 Witch By the pricking of my thumbs,

45   Something wicked this way comes.

     Open locks, whoever knocks.

     Enter Macbeth.

Macbeth How now, you secret, black and midnight hags?

     What is't you do?

All   A deed without a name.

Macbeth I conjure you, by that which you profess,

50   Howe'er you come to know it, answer me;

     Though you untie the winds and let them fight

     Against the churches, though the yeasty waves

     Confound and swallow navigation up,

     Though bladed corn be lodged and trees blown down,

55   Though castles topple on their warders' heads,

     Though palaces and pyramids do slope

     Their heads to their foundations, though the treasure

     Of nature's germens tumble all together,

     Even till destruction sicken, answer me

赫卡忒与另三位女巫上。

赫卡忒　　噢，你们劳苦又功高！

利益每人都能分享到。　　　　　　　　　　　　40

请围着大锅一展歌喉，

精灵仙子般绕成一周，

投进的一切施展魔咒。

　　　音乐与歌声。"黑精灵，等。"

　　　　　　　　　　　　　［赫卡忒与另三女巫下。］

女巫乙　　我的拇指有些刺疼，

有恶人在向此移动。　　　　　　　　　　　　45

把锁打开，不管谁来。

麦克白上。

麦克白　　怎么了，神秘阴险的夜妖婆？

你们在干啥？

三女巫　　　　　　　一件事情无名称。

麦克白　　我祈求你们，凭你们的妖术之名，

无论它源自何处，回答我就是；　　　　　　　50

哪怕你们将风释放，让它去

袭击教堂，哪怕飞溅的波浪

将那航行的船只摧毁吞没，

哪怕庄稼倒伏，树木倒地，

哪怕城堡倒在看守的头上，　　　　　　　　55

哪怕宫殿以及尖塔的顶部

向它们的地基倾斜，哪怕

造化的种子宝库毁于一旦，

直到毁灭感到腻烦，回答

To what I ask you.

1 Witch   Speak.

2 Witch   Demand.

60 **3 Witch**   We'll answer.

1 Witch   Say, if thou'dst rather hear it from our mouths,

Or from our masters?

Macbeth   Call 'em, let me see 'em.

1 Witch   Pour in sow's blood, that hath eaten

Her nine farrow; grease that's sweaten

65   From the murderer's gibbet, throw

Into the flame.

All   Come, high or low,

Thyself and office deftly show.   *Thunder*

[*Enter*] *First Apparition: an armed head.*

Macbeth   Tell me, thou unknown power—

1 Witch   He knows thy thought:

Hear his speech, but say thou nought.

70 **1 Apparition**   Macbeth, Macbeth, Macbeth. Beware Macduff,

Beware the Thane of Fife. Dismiss me. Enough. *He descends.*

Macbeth   Whate'er thou art, for thy good caution, thanks;

Thou hast harped my fear aright. But one word more—

1 Witch   He will not be commanded. Here's another,

我的问话。

女巫甲　　　　　　　说吧。

女巫乙　　　　　　　　　　问吧。

女巫丙　　　　　　　　　　　　　我们会答。　　　　　　　　　　　60

女巫甲　说,你是想听我们亲口说出,

　　　还是让幽灵回答?

麦克白　　　　　　　　　　叫他们,让我看看。

女巫甲　吃掉九个崽的老母猪,

　　　现将她的鲜血来倒入;

　　　绞刑架上流下来的油,　　　　　　　　　　　　　65

　　　火里丢。

三女巫　　　　　　各种精灵齐来凑,

　　　现出原形,把神通展露。　　　　　　　　　　雷鸣

　　　　　　　第一幽灵显现:一戴盔的头颅。

麦克白　告诉我,神秘的幽灵——

女巫甲　　　　　　　　　　　他懂你心思:

　　　听他说吧,你别说话。

第一幽灵　麦克白,麦克白,麦克白!当心麦克达夫,　　　　70

　　　当心法福郡主。　放我走,已足够。　　　　隐入地下。

麦克白　不管你是啥,你的警告,我感谢;

　　　我的担忧你一语道破。　还有呢——

女巫甲　你不能发号施令。　又来了一个,

---

62. 幽灵(masters):显然是指幽灵(Apparitions),或是女巫们的掌管者(the powers that govern them)。　63. 母猪(及其他动物)偶尔会吃掉自己的幼崽。　67(1)一戴盔的头颅(*an armed head*):也许是指麦克白的头颅,就像终场时被麦克达夫砍下的那样;或指叛贼麦克唐纳的头颅,由麦克白在开场时砍掉,他们两人均为叛贼;或指麦克达夫的头颅——麦克白本人的行刑者。　当然,三幽灵"无疑应保持其神秘色彩(remain, as they undoubtedly should, cryptic)"。

75   More potent than the first.   *Thunder*

[Enter] Second Apparition: a bloody child.

2 Apparition   Macbeth, Macbeth, Macbeth.

Macbeth   Had I three ears, I'd hear thee.

2 Apparition   Be bloody, bold, and resolute: laugh to scorn

               The power of man, for none of woman born

80   Shall harm Macbeth.   *Descends.*

Macbeth   Then live, Macduff: what need I fear of thee?

               But yet I'll make assurance double sure,

               And take a bond of fate: thou shalt not live,

               That I may tell pale-hearted fear it lies,

               And sleep in spite of thunder.   *Thunder*

[Enter] Third Apparition: a child crowned,
with a tree in his hand.

85   What is this,

               That rises like the issue of a king

               And wears upon his baby-brow the round

               And top of sovereignty?

All   Listen, but speak not to't.

比第一个更强。　　　　　　　　　　　　　　　　　雷鸣　75

第二幽灵显现：一流血儿童。

第二幽灵　麦克白，麦克白，麦克白！

麦克白　我若有三耳，都会恭听。

第二幽灵　要残忍、勇敢、果断：人的力量

你只管嘲笑，因为女人生的休想

伤害麦克白。　　　　　　　　　　　　　　　　　隐去。　80

麦克白　活着吧，麦克达夫，我何必怕你？

但是我要做到双倍的保证，

要跟命运立约：你不能存活，

好告诉我的胆怯它在撒谎，

雷鸣之中依然梦香。　　　　　　　　　　　　　　　雷鸣

第三幽灵显现：一戴皇冠的孩童，

手执树枝。

这是什么？　　　　　　　　　　　　　　　　　　　85

看上去像是一位国王的后裔，

他那稚嫩的额头还戴着一顶

至尊的皇冠？

三女巫　　　　　　听吧，别对它说话。

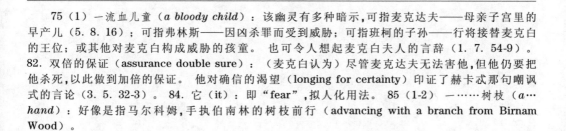

75（1）一流血儿童（*a bloody child*）：该幽灵有多种暗示,可指麦克达夫——母亲子宫里的早产儿（5.8.16）；可指弗林斯——因凶杀罪而受到威胁；可指班柯的子孙——行将接替麦克白的王位；或其他对麦克白构成威胁的孩童。 也可令人想起麦克白夫人的言辞（1.7.54-9）。 82. 双倍的保证（assurance double sure）：（麦克白认为）尽管麦克达夫无法害他,但他仍要把他杀死,以此做到加倍的保证。 他对确信的渴望（longing for certainty）印证了赫卡忒那句嘲讽式的言论（3.5.32-3）。 84. 它（it）：即"fear",拟人化用法。 85（1-2）一……树枝（*a … hand*）：好像是指马尔科姆,手执伯南林的树枝前行（advancing with a branch from Birnam Wood）。

3 Apparition   Be lion-mettled, proud, and take no care

90   Who chafes, who frets, or where conspirers are.

Macbeth shall never vanquished be until

Great Birnam wood to high Dunsinane hill

Shall come against him.   *Descend*[*s*].

Macbeth   That will never be.

Who can impress the forest, bid the tree

95   Unfix his earth-bound root? Sweet bodements, good.

Rebellious head, rise never till the Wood

Of Birnam rise, and our high-placed Macbeth

Shall live the lease of nature, pay his breath

To time, and mortal custom. Yet my heart

100   Throbs to know one thing: tell me, if your art

Can tell so much, shall Banquo's issue ever

Reign in this kingdom?

All   Seek to know no more.

Macbeth   I will be satisfied. Deny me this,

And an eternal curse fall on you. Let me know.

105   Why sinks that cauldron, and what noise is this?   *Hautboys*

1 Witch   Show.

第三幽灵	要狮子一般勇敢,高傲,别在意	
	谁发怒,谁不满,谁搞阴谋诡计。	90
	麦克白永远不会被人战胜,	
	直到大伯南树林向他进攻,	
	移到邓西嫩山顶。	隐去。
麦克白	那绝不可能。	
	谁能征召森林,给树木下令	
	让它连根拔起? 美好的预兆!	95
	叛逆的死鬼,别再起来搅扰,	
	除非伯南林位移,麦克白大人	
	将会安度天年,寿终正寝,	
	跟常人一样。 可是我的心里	
	很想知道:告诉我,你们的魔力	100
	若能够办到,班柯的子孙是否	
	会统治这个王国?	
三女巫	别再问了。	
麦克白	我定要知道。 你们若加以拒绝,	
	就要永受诅咒! 让我知道。	
	那口锅怎么下沉,这是啥声音?	双簧管鸣奏 105
女巫甲	上演!	

---

92. 伯南树林（Birnam Wood）：从 12 英里以外的邓西嫩山顶可以看到该林。 93. 邓西嫩山顶（Dunsinane Hill）：佩思东北部的一座山顶,现为一古堡遗址。 另外,Dunsinane 的重音在第二个音节,正常情况下在第一个音节。 93-100. 那……魔力（That…art）：麦克白接上话茬,将第三幽灵的诗行完成,好像完全进入了它的世界,在剧中首次使用了一连串的对偶韵句。 麦克白"因为急于接受幽灵的神谕,便以同样的韵律对接下去",由此与他所咨询的精灵融为一体（Macbeth "in eager acceptance of the oracle, continues it in the same rhymed form", thus identifying himself with the spirits he has consulted）。 96. 叛逆的死鬼（rebellious dead）：即班柯,因为他不想待在自己的坟里（Bate）。 97. 麦克白大人（our high-placed Macbeth）：奇怪的是,麦克白在此使用了第三人称,这也许表明其悲剧性的狂妄自大（imply the supreme self-confidence of tragic hubris）。 98-9. 将会……一样（Shall…custom）：原注为："will live out his full life span until it is time for him to expire (*pay his breath*) in the way of all mortals."（Bevington）

2 Witch	Show.
3 Witch	Show.
All	Show his eyes, and grieve his heart;
110	Come like shadows, so depart.

A show of eight kings, the last with a glass
in his hand; and Banquo.

Macbeth	Thou art too like the spirit of Banquo; down:
	Thy crown does sear mine eyeballs. And thy hair,
	Thou other gold-bound brow, is like the first.
	A third is like the former. Filthy hags,
115	Why do you show me this? —A fourth? Start, eyes!
	What, will the line stretch out to th' crack of doom?
	Another yet? A seventh? I'll see no more;
	And yet the eighth appears, who bears a glass
	Which shows me many more; and some I see
120	That twofold balls and treble scepters carry.
	Horrible sight. Now I see 'tis true;
	For the blood-boltered Banquo smiles upon me,
	And points at them for his. [*Exeunt kings and Banquo.*]

女巫乙	上演！
女巫丙	上演！
三女巫	让他目睹，让他心痛；

这就离开，来去无踪。　　　　　　　　　　　　　　　　110

八位国王之表演，最后一位手持
一镜；以及班柯。

麦克白　　你也太像班柯的阴魂；快滚：

你的皇冠烧我双眼。　你的头发，

也戴着皇冠，像第一个金黄。

第三个也像前者。　邪恶的妖婆，

为啥让我看这？　——第四位？　眼睛，出窍！　　　　115

怎么，这一列要延续到世界末日？

还有呢？　第七个？　我不再看了；

第八个又出现了，带着镜子，

向我展示了更多；我看见有人

拿着双重宝球和三根权杖。　　　　　　　　　　　　120

可怕的景象！看来都是真的；

因为满头血污的班柯朝我微笑，

指认他们是他的。　　　　　　　　　　［众国王与班柯同下。］

　　110（1-2）这一场景蔚为壮观，旨在表达一种次序和王权，以及麦克白所妨碍的连贯性。　该哑剧描绘了本剧创作时曾统治过苏格兰的八位国王，但不包括由伊丽莎白女王下令，于1587年处死的玛丽女王，也许因为她的出现会令人想起此事。　118. 镜子（glass）：并非詹姆斯国王用来照自己的普通镜子，而是一种可预见未来的镜子，或者魔镜（magic glass）（Muir）。　120. 双重……权杖（twofold…sceptres）：该短语颇富争议，双重宝球也许象征詹姆斯国王的两次加冕（分别于苏格兰与英格兰）；三根权杖可象征英格兰、苏格兰和威尔士三个王国的王权，但也有其他多种可能。　123. 他的（his）：即他的后裔（his descendants）。

                                        What? Is this so?

1 Witch   Ay, sir, all this is so. But why

125   Stands Macbeth thus amazedly?

                Come, sisters, cheer we up his sprites,

                And show the best of our delights.

                I'll charm the air to give a sound,

                While you perform your antic round,

130   That this great king may kindly say

                Our duties did his welcome pay.

                        Music. The Witches dance and then vanish.

Macbeth   Where are they? Gone? Let this pernicious hour

                Stand aye accursed in the calendar.

                Come in, without there.

                        Enter Lennox.

Lennox   What's your grace's will?

Macbeth   Saw you the weïrd sisters?

135 **Lennox**   No, my lord.

Macbeth   Came they not by you?

Lennox   No, indeed, my lord.

Macbeth   Infected be the air whereon they ride,

                And damned all those that trust them. I did hear

                The galloping of horse. Who was't came by?

啊？　竟然如此？

女巫甲　　　就是这样，先生，没错，

可麦克白为何如此惊愕？　　　　　　　　　　　125

快来，姊妹，使他振奋，

向他展示咱们的精品。

我要使乐音凭空产生，

你们围着他起舞助兴，

让这位大王亲切地宣称，　　　　　　　　　　130

我们的殷勤已表示欢迎。

音乐。三女巫跳舞并消失。

麦克白　　　她们呢？　走了？　让这一恶毒的时刻

在日历之中永远遭受诅咒！

进来，外面的人。

雷诺克斯上。

雷诺克斯　　　　　　陛下有何吩咐？

麦克白　　　您看见巫婆没有？

雷诺克斯　　　　　　　没有，陛下。　　　　　　135

麦克白　　　没从您身边经过？

雷诺克斯　　　　　　　真没有，陛下。

麦克白　　　愿她们乘坐的空气感染瘟疾，

谁信她们谁受诅咒！我听见

有马蹄声音。　是谁到了这里？

124-31. 可能是后来插入的台词（possible interpolation）（Muir）。　130. 这位大王（this great king）：若本段台词属于后来插入，那么本行台词也许是说给一位到场的国王，而不是麦克白（Muir）。　大王（great king）：若指麦克白，倒颇富讽刺色彩（Clark）。　134. 外面的人（without there）：雷诺克斯可能在外面守卫。　138. 谁信她们谁受诅咒（damned…them）：麦克白无意之中也包括了自己。

140 **Lennox**   'Tis two or three, my lord, that bring you word

Macduff is fled to England.

Macbeth   Fled to England?

Lennox   Ay, my good lord.

Macbeth   Time, thou anticipat'st my dread exploits.

The flighty purpose never is o'ertook

145   Unless the deed go with it. From this moment

The very firstlings of my heart shall be

The firstlings of my hand. And even now,

To crown my thoughts with acts, be it thought and done:

The castle of Macduff I will surprise,

150   Seize upon Fife, give to th'edge o'th' sword

His wife, his babes and all unfortunate souls

That trace him in his line. No boasting like a fool;

This deed I'll do before this purpose cool.

But no more sights. Where are these gentlemen?

155   Come, bring me where they are.   *Exeunt.*

雷诺克斯	有两三个人,陛下,向您报信,	140
	麦克达夫逃往英格兰。	
麦克白	逃往英格兰?	
雷诺克斯	是的,好陛下。	
麦克白	时间啊,你预先阻止了我的阴谋:	
	永远也赶不上飞逝的意图,	
	除非立即行动。　从此刻开始,	145
	我心中的念头一旦产生,	
	便会立刻执行。　甚至是此刻,	
	要让思想伴以行动,想到就做:	
	我要突袭麦克达夫的城堡,	
	占领法福,还要把他的妻子、	150
	孩子以及他家族中的所有	
	成员斩尽杀绝。　别再瞎吹;	
	心灰意冷之前要行动到位。	
	别了,幽灵! 那些信差在哪里?	
	快,带我去见他们。　　　　　同下。	155

144-5. 永远……行动（The flighty…it）：麦克白好像是说"我们的行动无法跟我们的意图保持同步,除非你立即行动"。 意图与行动之间的差距被比作两匹赛马之间的差距（The gap between intention and deed is imagined as one between a pair of racing horses）。

SCENE II

Enter Macduff's Wife, her Son and Ross.

Wife   What had he done, to make him fly the land?

Ross   You must have patience, madam.

Wife   He had none;

His flight was madness. When our actions do not,

Our fears do make us traitors.

Ross   You know not

5   Whether it was his wisdom or his fear.

Wife   Wisdom? To leave his wife, to leave his babes,

His mansion and his titles in a place

From whence himself does fly? He loves us not;

He wants the natural touch. For the poor wren,

10   The most diminutive of birds, will fight,

Her young ones in her nest, against the owl.

All is the fear and nothing is the love;

As little is the wisdom, where the flight

So runs against all reason.

Ross   My dearest coz,

第二场

麦克达夫的妻子、她的儿子及罗斯上。

妻子	他做了什么,竟使他逃离祖国?
罗斯	您要有耐心,夫人。

妻子   他却没有;

他的逃离是发疯。 尽管行为坦荡,

吓跑就是叛逃。

罗斯   您不知道

那是他的明智还是他的恐惧。   5

妻子   明智? 抛弃妻子,抛弃孩子,

抛弃他的住处和他的权利,

独自一人逃离? 他不爱我们;

他缺乏爱心。 就连可怜的鹪鹩,

这种最小的小鸟儿,都会跟   10

猫头鹰搏斗,若巢中育有雏鸟。

全因为恐惧,毫无爱心可言;

也谈不上理智,因为他这种

逃离违背情理。

罗斯   最可爱的亲人,

4.2. 这是该剧唯一一场描写家庭生活的场景。 3-4. 尽管……叛逃(When…traitors):原注为 "When we are not traitors for what we have done, we are still traitors by being afraid and running away"(Gill)。 14. 亲人(coz = cousin):该称呼在此更多的是表示友情,而非亲情(a term of friendship rather than kinship)。

15   I pray you, school yourself. But for your husband,

He is noble, wise, judicious, and best knows

The fits o'th' season. I dare not speak much further;

But cruel are the times when we are traitors

And do not know ourselves; when we hold rumour

20   From what we fear, yet know not what we fear,

But float upon a wild and violent sea

Each way and move. I take my leave of you;

Shall not be long but I'll be here again.

Things at the worst will cease, or else climb upward

25   To what they were before. My pretty cousin,

Blessing upon you.

Wife   Fathered he is, and yet he's fatherless.

Ross   I am so much a fool, should I stay longer,

It would be my disgrace and your discomfort.

30   I take my leave at once.   *Exit Ross.*

Wife   Sirrah, your father's dead; and what will you do

now? How will you live?

Son   As birds do, mother.

Wife   What, with worms and flies?

35   **Son**   With what I get, I mean; and so do they.

Wife   Poor bird. Thou'dst never fear the net nor lime,

the pitfall nor the gin.

Son   Why should I, mother? Poor birds they are not set

for. My father is not dead, for all your saying.

	我求您,要克制。　至于您的丈夫,	15
	他高尚、英明、有远见,十分清楚	
	时事的变迁。　我不敢继续多言;	
	被斥为叛徒却不知道何故,	
	说明时代残酷;我们因为恐惧	
	而听信谣言,却不知为何恐惧,	20
	只是漂流在汹涌的大海之上,	
	进退两难。　我这就向您告辞;	
	不久我就会再次回到这里。	
	事情糟到极点就会终止,否则	
	逐渐恢复如前。　我的小宝贝儿,	25
	上帝保佑您!	
妻子	他有亲爹,却跟没爹的一样。	
罗斯	要是现在不走,我定会哭泣,	
	那将会使我丢脸,让您难受。	
	我现在就走。　　　　　　　　　　　罗斯下。	30
妻子	小家伙,你爸爸死了。你现在可怎么	
	办呢?　你怎么活呀?	
儿子	像鸟那样,妈妈。	
妻子	怎么,靠虫子和苍蝇?	
儿子	捉到啥吃啥;像他们一样。	35
妻子	可怜的小鸟儿。难道你不怕天罗地网、	
	粘鸟胶或陷阱?	
儿子	为啥要怕呢,妈妈?　它们又不会捕捉	
	弱鸟儿。　我爸爸没死,不管你说什么。	

---

27. 原注为:“The child is *Fathered* in the sense of having a father who engendered him, but *fatherless* as he is without a father present to protect him(这孩子是有生身之父,却没有父亲在身旁保护)。” 28. 我定会哭泣(so…fool):莎士比亚常把哭泣与傻连在一起(connects crying with foolishness)。　如《暴风雨》3.1. 73-4. “I am a fool / To weep at what I am glad of (我可真傻／本该高兴却偏偏要哭)”。

40	**Wife**	Yes, he is dead. How wilt thou do for a father?
	Son	Nay, how will you do for a husband?
	Wife	Why, I can buy me twenty at any market.
	Son	Then you'll buy 'em to sell again.
	Wife	Thou speak'st with all thy wit, and yet, i'faith,
45		With wit enough for thee.
	Son	Was my father a traitor, mother?
	Wife	Ay, that he was.
	Son	What is a traitor?
	Wife	Why, one that swears and lies.
50	**Son**	And be all traitors, that do so?
	Wife	Every one that does so is a traitor, and must be hanged.
	Son	And must they all be hanged that swear and lie?
	Wife	Every one.
55	**Son**	Who must hang them?
	Wife	Why, the honest men.
	Son	Then the liars and swearers are fools, for there are liars and swearers enow to beat the honest men, and hang up them.
60	**Wife**	Now, God help thee, poor monkey. But how wilt thou do for a father?
	Son	If he were dead, you'd weep for him; if you would not, it were a good sign that I should quickly have a new father.
65	**Wife**	Poor prattler, how thou talk'st.

Enter a Messenger.

| | **Messenger** | Bless you, fair dame. I am not to you known, |

| 妻子 | 真的,他死了。　你没了爸爸怎么办呢? | 40 |

儿子　不,您没了丈夫怎么办呢?

妻子　嗨,我可以到集上买回来二十。

儿子　那您买来后再把他们卖掉。

妻子　尽管你说起话来稚声嫩气,但实际上,
已很有灵性。　　　　　　　　　　　　45

儿子　我爸爸是叛徒吗,妈妈?

妻子　是的,他是。

儿子　啥是叛徒?

妻子　嗨,就是背信弃义的人。

儿子　凡这样做的,都是叛徒?　　　　　　　50

妻子　谁这样做,谁就是叛徒,他必须被人
绞死。

儿子　背信弃义的人都要被绞死吗?

妻子　每个都要。

儿子　由谁来绞呢?　　　　　　　　　　　　55

妻子　嗨,诚实的人呗。

儿子　那背信弃义的人都是傻子,因为他们
的数量多得可把诚实的人打败,然后
绞死他们。

妻子　嗳,主保佑你,可怜的淘气鬼!可你　　60
没有爸爸怎么办呢?

儿子　假如他死啦,您会为他哭泣;您要是
不哭,那就是好兆头——我很快会有
一个新爸。

妻子　你真会饶舌,看你说的!　　　　　　　65

一信差上。

信差　保佑您,好夫人!您并不认识我,

Though in your state of honour I am perfect.

I doubt some danger does approach you nearly.

If you will take a homely man's advice,

70   Be not found here; hence, with your little ones.

To fright you thus, methinks I am too savage;

To do worse to you were fell cruelty,

Which is too nigh your person. Heaven preserve you!

I dare abide no longer.   *Exit Messenger.*

75   **Wife**   Whither should I fly?

I have done no harm. But I remember now

I am in this earthly world, where to do harm

Is often laudable, to do good sometime

Accounted dangerous folly. Why then, alas,

80   Do I put up that womanly defence,

To say I have done no harm?

Enter Murderers.

What are these faces?

1 Murderer   Where is your husband?

Wife   I hope in no place so unsanctified

Where such as thou mayst find him.

1 Murderer   He's a traitor.

Son   Thou liest, thou shag-haired villain.

85   **1 Murderer**   What, you egg!

Young fry of treachery!

Son   He has killed me, mother.

Run away, I pray you.   *Exit* [*Wife*] *crying* 'Murder'.

[*Exeunt Murderers.*]

但我对您的身份却非常熟悉。

我担心某种危险正向您逼近。

假如您愿意接受常人的忠告，

别待在这里；走吧，跟孩子一起。　　　　　　　　　　70

把您吓成这样，我真有些凶狠；

再继续吓您就是极其残忍，

可它已迫在眉睫。　上帝保佑您！

我不敢继续停留。　　　　　　　　　　　信差下。

妻子　　我该逃往何处？　　　　　　　　　　　　　75

我没做过坏事。　可我现在想起，

我是活在尘世，在这里作恶

常常会受到赞美，行善有时

被视为冒险的愚蠢。　唉，咋办，

是否该进行徒劳无益的抵抗，　　　　　　　80

说自己清白无辜？

众刺客上。

这是啥面孔？

刺客甲　　您丈夫在哪里？

妻子　　希望他没在那么邪恶的地方

能让你们给找到。

刺客甲　　　　　　他是叛徒。

儿子　　你撒谎，蓬头的恶棍！

刺客甲　　　　　　什么，兔崽子！　　　　　　85

叛逆的祸根！

儿子　　　　　　他杀死我啦，妈妈！

快跑，我求您！　　　　［妻子］下，呼喊"杀人啦"。

　　　　　　　　　　　　［刺客同下。］

SCENE III

Enter Malcolm and Macduff.

Malcolm   Let us seek out some desolate shade and there
Weep our sad bosoms empty.

Macduff   Let us rather
Hold fast the mortal sword, and like good men
Bestride our downfall birthdom. Each new morn
5   New widows howl, new orphans cry, new sorrows
Strike heaven on the face, that it resounds
As if it felt with Scotland and yelled out
Like syllable of dolour.

Malcolm   What I believe, I'll wail;
What know, believe; and what I can redress,
10   As I shall find the time to friend, I will.
What you have spoke, it may be so perchance.
This tyrant, whose sole name blisters our tongues,
Was once thought honest: you have loved him well;
He hath not touched you yet. I am young; but something

第三场

马尔科姆与麦克达夫上。

马尔科姆　咱们找个僻静阴凉的地方
　　　　　去哭诉一下衷肠。

麦克达夫　　　　　　咱们倒应
　　　　　紧握致命的利剑,大丈夫一般
　　　　　捍卫沦落的祖国。　每天清晨
　　　　　都有新寡妇哀号,新孤儿哭泣,　　　　　　　　　5
　　　　　新悲伤抽打上苍脸庞,竟让它
　　　　　与苏格兰感同身受,以同样的
　　　　　哀号向大地回荡。

马尔科姆　　　　　　　我信的,就哀伤;
　　　　　我清楚,才相信;我所能矫正的,
　　　　　会在适当的时候,予以矫正。　　　　　　　　　10
　　　　　您所说的,也许是真,也许。
　　　　　一提这位暴君,舌头便起疱疹,
　　　　　他曾被视为正直;您也很爱他;
　　　　　他还没碰您。　我还年轻,但您

4.3. 许多评论家认为本场单调乏味,演出时常被缩短。　然而,本场可以起到许多重要的作用,尤其是对主要人物的角色扩展,对暴政的性质及其后果的描述(especially in enlarging the roles of the main speakers and characterizing the nature and effects of tyranny)。　8-11. 我信的……也许(What…perchance):马尔科姆因不了解麦克达夫是否真心实意,说起话来颇为正式和谨慎。14-5. 但……他(but…him):您可从我身上看到他的形象(You may see something of him in me)。　马尔科姆可能是在为自己在本场接下来的自证其罪(self-incrimination)做好准备;也许是指自己在麦克白手下所遭受的苦难(his suffering under Macbeth's hands)。

| 15 | | You may discern of him through me, and wisdom |

15   You may discern of him through me, and wisdom

                         To offer up a weak, poor, innocent lamb

                         To appease an angry god.

Macduff   I am not treacherous.

Malcolm   But Macbeth is.

                         A good and virtuous nature may recoil

20   In an imperial charge. But I shall crave your pardon;

                         That which you are, my thoughts cannot transpose.

                         Angels are bright still, though the brightest fell.

                         Though all things foul would wear the brows of grace,

                         Yet grace must still look so.

Macduff   I have lost my hopes.

25 **Malcolm**   Perchance even there where I did find my doubts.

                         Why in that rawness left you wife and child—

                         Those precious motives, those strong knots of love—

                         Without leave-taking? I pray you,

                         Let not my jealousies be your dishonours,

30   But mine own safeties. You may be rightly just,

                         Whatever I shall think.

可以通过我了解他；献上一只　　　　　　　　　　15

柔弱、可怜、无辜的羔羊去平息

愤怒的神灵倒很聪明。

麦克达夫　　我可不是叛徒。

马尔科姆　　　　　　　麦克白却是。

善良的天性也许会在王命的

重压下退化。 但我要求您原谅；　　　　　　　20

我的疑心无法改变您的人品。

天使依然明亮,尽管最亮的已堕落。

虽然邪恶的东西会披上圣装,

但美善却依然故我。

麦克达夫　　　　　　　　　我已经失望。

马尔科姆　　也许这正是引起我怀疑的地方,　　　　25

为何使自己的妻儿无依无靠——

那些珍贵的动力,坚固的情结——

竟然不辞而别？ 我求您,

别以为我的疑心是想让您丢脸,

而是为自身安全。 您也许很真诚,　　　　　30

不管我怎么想。

---

16. 无辜的羔羊（innocent lamb）：在基督教传统中,羔羊象征着清白无辜（emblematic of innocence）。 19-20. 善良的……退化（A good…charge）：马尔科姆像是暗指麦克达夫在麦克白的命令之下有可能会堕落。 22. 最亮的（the brightest）：指撒旦,其代名词为"明亮之星（Lucifer）",意为"光明的使者（bearer of light）"（Clark）。 尽管撒旦这位"最明亮的（brightest）"天使已经堕落,我们可不能以为所有的天使都跟他一样,有些天使依然"明亮（bright）"（Gill）。 23-4. 虽然……故我（Though…so）：尽管邪恶的东西会披上善良的外衣,但善良定会保持其善良本色（Though evil things want to take on the appearance of good, goodness must retain its appearance of virtue）（Clark）。 "我不是说你的外表正直就证明你是叛徒；因为正直必须有其适当的表现形式,尽管恶棍会假装正直（I do not say that your virtuous appearance proves you are a traitor; for virtue must wear its proper form, though that form be counterfeited by villainy）"（Muir）。 25. 这正是（even there）：麦克达夫本希望能帮助推翻麦克白,但因为他已逃到了英格兰,便无希望可言。 而他的突然逃离则引起了马尔科姆的怀疑（Gill）。 28. 该短行所缺失的一个音步,可由"辞别（leave-taking）"后的自然停顿补齐。

Macduff	Bleed, bleed, poor country!

Great tyranny, lay thou thy basis sure,

For goodness dare not check thee. Wear thou thy wrongs;

The title is affeered. Fare thee well, lord.

35   I would not be the villain that thou think'st

For the whole space that's in the tyrant's grasp,

And the rich East to boot.

Malcolm	Be not offended;

I speak not as in absolute fear of you.

I think our country sinks beneath the yoke;

40   It weeps, it bleeds; and each new day a gash

Is added to her wounds. I think withal

There would be hands uplifted in my right;

And here from gracious England have I offer

Of goodly thousands. But for all this,

45   When I shall tread upon the tyrant's head,

Or wear it on my sword, yet my poor country

Shall have more vices than it had before,

More suffer, and more sundry ways than ever,

By him that shall succeed.

Macduff	What should he be?

50 **Malcolm**   It is myself I mean, in whom I know

All the particulars of vice so grafted

That, when they shall be opened, black Macbeth

麦克达夫	流血吧，可怜的祖国！	

十足的暴君，稳坐你的江山，

因为正义不敢阻拦。　戴好窃取王冠；

那头衔已被确认！再会了，殿下。

我可不愿做你所想象的恶棍， 35

即使将暴君攫取的王国给我，

再加上富庶的东方。

马尔科姆　　　　　您别生气；

我这样说并非对您完全疑心。

我心想祖国正在奴役下沉沦；

她在哭泣、流血，每天都会有 40

新的创伤增添。　而且我想，

会有人愿为我的事业奋战；

仁慈的英格兰王已经答应

支援精兵数千。　但尽管如此，

当我将暴君的头颅踩在脚下， 45

或挑在刀上，但我可怜的祖国

将比以往遭受更多的祸殃，

更多的苦难，方式也超从前，

假如他将继位。

麦克达夫　　　　您说的是谁？

马尔科姆　是我本人，我知道自己身上 50

已经植入各种各样的邪恶，

它们一旦怒放，阴险的麦克白

---

32. 十足的……你的（Great…thou）：麦克达夫在对麦克白使用呼语法。　33. 正义（goodness）：马尔科姆。　44-117. 但……信誉（But…honour）：马尔科姆对麦克达夫的试探。　关于本段台词有大量的评论，但多为负面。　52. 怒放（opened）：像蓓蕾一样绽放，在继续使用植物学意象（botanical metaphor），与上一行的"植入（grafted）"构成意象连缀。

Will seem as pure as snow, and the poor state

Esteem him as a lamb, being compared

With my confineless harms.

55 **Macduff**   Not in the legions

Of horrid hell can come a devil more damned

In evils to top Macbeth.

Malcolm   I grant him bloody,

Luxurious, avaricious, false, deceitful,

Sudden, malicious, smacking of every sin

60 That has a name. But there's no bottom, none,

In my voluptuousness. Your wives, your daughters,

Your matrons and your maids could not fill up

The cistern of my lust; and my desire

All continent impediments would o'erbear

65 That did oppose my will. Better Macbeth

Than such an one to reign.

Macduff   Boundless intemperance

In nature is a tyranny. It hath been

The untimely emptying of the happy throne,

And fall of many kings. But fear not yet

70 To take upon you what is yours. You may

Convey your pleasures in a spacious plenty,

And yet seem cold. The time you may so hoodwink.

We have willing dames enough; there cannot be

That vulture in you to devour so many

75 As will to greatness dedicate themselves,

将显得洁白如雪,可怜的祖国
将把他视为羔羊,假如跟我
无限的恶行相比。

麦克达夫　　　　　　就是从可怕的　　　　　　55
地狱群魔里也找不到麦克白
这样的恶棍。

马尔科姆　　　　　　我承认他很残忍、
淫荡好色、贪婪、虚伪、欺诈、
狂暴、恶毒,凡有名称的罪孽
都会品味。　而我的放荡纵欲　　　　　60
却无边无际。　你们的妻子、女儿,
你们的主妇,你们的少女都无法
满足我的淫欲;我的欲火
将会压倒一切违背我意愿的
约束和阻力。　让麦克白统治　　　　　65
要远胜这么一人。

麦克达夫　　　　　　无限的纵欲
本质上就是暴政。　它已导致
本应一帆风顺的王朝夭折,
诸多帝王跌落。　但是您别怕
继承原本属于您的。　您可以　　　　　70
私下里纵情于自己的淫欲,
但貌似正经。　您也许能蒙骗世人。
我们有的是情愿的女子;您就是
再贪得无厌,也无法吞食这么多
甘愿向一国之君献身的美餐,　　　　　75

57-60. 我……品味(I…name):显然并非所有罪过都适用于麦克白,它们只是一系列常见的罪过而已。　74. 贪得无厌(vulture):暗喻(兀鹫)贪得无厌的本性。　75. 麦克达夫此处的表述不乏厌女色彩(misogynistic)。

Finding it so inclined.

Malcolm   With this there grows

In my most ill-composed affection such

A stanchless avarice that, were I king,

I should cut off the nobles for their lands,

80   Desire his jewels and this other's house,

And my more-having would be as a sauce

To make me hunger more, that I should forge

Quarrels unjust against the good and loyal,

Destroying them for wealth.

Macduff   This avarice

85   Sticks deeper, grows with more pernicious root

Than summer-seeming lust, and it hath been

The sword of our slain kings. Yet do not fear;

Scotland hath foisons to fill up your will

Of your mere own. All these are portable,

90   With other graces weighed.

Malcolm   But I have none. The king-becoming graces,

As justice, verity, temperance, stableness,

Bounty, perseverance, mercy, lowliness,

Devotion, patience, courage, fortitude,

95   I have no relish of them, but abound

In the division of each several crime,

Acting it many ways. Nay, had I power, I should

Pour the sweet milk of concord into hell,

他的嗜好一被发现。

马尔科姆　　　　　　　　　　　除此之外，

我极其糟糕的禀性之中还有

无法满足的贪婪，我若为王，

便会处死贵族窃取其土地，　　　　　　　　　　80

渴望这个的珠宝，那个的房产，

我占有的越多，犹如佐料一样

使我更加饥饿，我竟会制造

一些无理的争端去陷害忠良，

为谋财将他们除掉。

麦克达夫　　　　　　　　　这种贪欲

若与夏天一般的淫欲相比　　　　　　　　　85

更为根深蒂固，它已经导致

众多国王死于刀剑。　可您别怕；

苏格兰有的是资源，用属于您的

满足您的欲念。　有别的美德抗衡，

这些均可忍受。　　　　　　　　　　90

马尔科姆　　我可没有。　适于帝王的美德，

诸如正义、真实、节制、稳重、

慷慨、坚持不懈、仁慈、谦恭、

虔诚、忍耐、勇敢，以及刚毅，

它们与我毫无关系，倒是浑身　　　　　　　　95

充满了分门别类的各种罪恶，

想方设法施行。　不，我若有权，

就会让甜美的和谐下到地狱，

---

85. 夏天一般的（summer-seeming）：既可指"适于夏天的（summer-beseeming）"，也可指"夏天似的（summer-like）"。　就其热切和短暂的性质而言（being hot and short-lived），性欲（lust）可能与夏天有关。

Uproar the universal peace, confound

All unity on earth.

100 **Macduff**   O Scotland, Scotland!

Malcolm   If such a one be fit to govern, speak.

I am as I have spoken.

Macduff   Fit to govern?

No, not to live. O nation miserable!

With an untitled tyrant bloody-sceptered,

105   When shalt thou see thy wholesome days again,

Since that the truest issue of thy throne

By his own interdiction stands accursed

And does blaspheme his breed? Thy royal father

Was a most sainted king; the queen that bore thee,

110   Oft'ner upon her knees than on her feet,

Died every day she lived. Fare thee well.

These evils thou repeat'st upon thyself

Hath banished me from Scotland. O my breast,

Thy hope ends here!

Malcolm   Macduff, this noble passion,

115   Child of integrity, hath from my soul

Wiped the black scruples, reconciled my thoughts

To thy good truth and honour. Devilish Macbeth

By many of these trains hath sought to win me

Into his power, and modest wisdom plucks me

120   From over-credulous haste. But God above

Deal between thee and me. For even now

I put myself to thy direction and

Unspeak mine own detraction, here abjure

将宇宙的和平搅乱,将世间的

和睦统统摧毁。

麦克达夫　　　　　　苏格兰啊,苏格兰!　　　　　　100

马尔科姆　这种人是否适于统治,你说。

我就是我说的这样。

麦克达夫　　　　　　　适于统治?

不,简直该死!噢,可怜的国家!

在窃国暴君的血腥统治之下,

你要到何时才能重见天日,　　　　　　105

因为你真正的王位继承者,

由于他自暴自弃该受诅咒,

毁谤列祖列宗?　您的父王,

是最为圣洁的国王;您的母后,

双膝跪地的时间超过了站立,　　　　　　110

在世的每天都在苦行。　再会了。

你自称所有的这些邪恶已将我

逐出苏格兰国境。　噢,我的心胸,

已毫无希望!

马尔科姆　　　　　　麦克达夫,你这种激情——

正直的明证——已将所有的猜疑　　　　　　115

从我心中抹去,使我再次信赖

你的真诚和信誉。　邪恶的麦克白

已用多种伎俩试将我骗到

他的手下,但小心谨慎阻止我

过分地轻信他人。　愿上帝在上　　　　　　120

为我们两人见证!因为此刻

我本人就要服从您的引领,

收回我的自我诋毁。　收回

The taints and blames I laid upon myself,

125   For strangers to my nature. I am yet

Unknown to woman, never was forsworn,

Scarcely have coveted what was mine own,

At no time broke my faith, would not betray

The devil to his fellow, and delight

130   No less in truth than life. My first false speaking

Was this upon myself. What I am truly

Is thine and my poor country's to command.

Whither indeed, before thy here-approach,

Old Siward, with ten thousand warlike men

135   Already at a point, was setting forth.

Now we'll together, and the chance of goodness

Be like our warranted quarrel. Why are you silent?

Macduff   Such welcome and unwelcome things at once

'Tis hard to reconcile.

Enter a Doctor.

Malcolm   Well, more anon.

140   Comes the King forth, I pray you?

Doctor   Ay, sir; there are a crew of wretched souls

That stay his cure. Their malady convinces

The great assay of art, but at his touch,

我加于自身的污点和责备，

它们与我的本性无关。　我尚未　　　　　　　　　125

近过女色，从未违背过誓言，

本属我的东西都少有贪念，

从未背弃过信仰，哪怕他是

魔鬼也不会把他出卖，喜爱

真理如同生命。　我的首次撒谎　　　　　　　　130

就是自我毁谤。　真实的我

将听从你的指挥，报效祖国。

实际上，就在你的到来之前，

年长的西华德，已与一万名

勇士准备就绪，正要出征。　　　　　　　　　　135

咱们一起走吧，但愿我们的

正义之举能获成功。　您为何沉默？

麦克达夫　这么一种悲喜交集的消息，

真是始料未及。

一医生上。

马尔科姆　　　　　　　　好吧，随后再谈。

国王来了吗，请问？　　　　　　　　　　　　　140

医生　来了，先生；有一群可怜的病人

在等他治疗。　他们的疾病已使

医术束手无策，可他一接触，

136-7. 但愿……成功（chance…quarrel）：原注为"May our good fortune be equal to the justification of our cause（但愿我们成功的机会能与我们事业的正义性相等）"。　其中，"chances of goodness ＝ possibility of success"，"goodness ＝ good fortune"。　142. 治疗（cure）：就国王通过"触摸（touching）"瘰疬病病人即可将其治愈而言，自中世纪至18世纪以来，英格兰和法国都相信国王拥有这种奇妙的治愈能力，这种能力首先归属于（忏悔者）爱德华国王（1003-1066）；詹姆斯国王（1556-1625）也曾予以实践。

Such sanctity hath heaven given his hand,

They presently amend.

145 **Malcolm** I thank you, doctor. *Exit* [*Doctor*].

Macduff What's the disease he means?

Malcolm 'Tis called the Evil:

A most miraculous work in this good King,

Which often, since my here-remain in England,

I have seen him do. How he solicits heaven,

150 Himself best knows; but strangely-visited people,

All swol'n and ulcerous, pitiful to the eye,

The mere despair of surgery, he cures,

Hanging a golden stamp about their necks

Put on with holy prayers; and 'tis spoken,

155 To the succeeding royalty he leaves

The healing benediction. With this strange virtue

He hath a heavenly gift of prophecy,

And sundry blessings hang about his throne

That speak him full of grace.

Enter Ross.

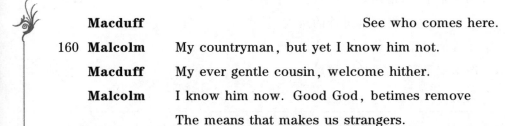

Macduff See who comes here.

160 **Malcolm** My countryman, but yet I know him not.

Macduff My ever gentle cousin, welcome hither.

Malcolm I know him now. Good God, betimes remove

The means that makes us strangers.

他手上的这种神圣来自上天，

他们立刻康复。

| 马尔科姆 | 谢谢您，医生。 | ［医生］下。 145 |

麦克达夫　　他所指的是啥病？

马尔科姆　　　　　　　　　指的是瘰疬：

这位好国王真是妙手回春，

这种奇迹，我逗留英格兰期间，

经常看见。　他如何祈求上天，

自己最清楚；但染上怪病的人们， 150

个个浮肿溃烂，惨不忍睹，

根本无法手术，他却能治好，

将一枚金币挂于他们的脖颈，

同时并伴有圣洁的祷告；据说，

他可将这种治愈疾病的恩典 155

世代相传。　除了这种独特能力，

他还有一种天赋——能够预言，

以及其他各种赐福环绕王位，

表明他充满恩惠。

　　　　　　　　罗斯上。

麦克达夫　　　　　　　看谁来了。

马尔科姆　　我的同胞，可是我并不认识。 160

麦克达夫　　我向来温和的亲人，欢迎到来。

马尔科姆　　我认出来了。　天哪，赶快除去

让咱形同陌路的障碍！

---

146. 瘰疬（the Evil = the King's Evil）：即淋巴结核（scrofula）。　154. 圣洁的祷告（holy prayers）：莎士比亚是在强调环绕爱德华国王周围的神圣光环（the aura of sanctity），以此与麦克白的穷凶极恶（diabolical qualities）形成对比。　160. 我的同胞（My countryman）：马尔科姆可通过他的衣着认出——可能头戴一顶蓝色的无边呢帽（Muir）。

| | Ross | Sir, amen. |

Macduff Stands Scotland where it did?

Ross Alas, poor country,

165 Almost afraid to know itself. It cannot

Be called our mother, but our grave. Where nothing,

But who knows nothing, is once seen to smile;

Where sighs, and groans, and shrieks that rend the air,

Are made, not marked; where violent sorrow seems

170 A modern ecstasy. The deadman's knell

Is there scarce asked for who, and good men's lives

Expire before the flowers in their caps,

Dying or ere they sicken.

Macduff O, relation too nice, and yet too true!

175 **Malcolm** What's the newest grief?

Ross That of an hour's age doth hiss the speaker;

Each minute teems a new one.

Macduff How does my wife?

Ross Why, well.

Macduff And all my children?

Ross Well too.

Macduff The tyrant has not battered at their peace?

180 **Ross** No, they were well at peace, when I did leave 'em.

Macduff Be not a niggard of your speech. How goes't?

Ross When I came hither to transport the tidings,

Which I have heavily borne, there ran a rumour

Of many worthy fellows that were out,

罗斯	先生,阿门。	
麦克达夫	苏格兰依然如故?	
罗斯	唉,可怜的国家,	
	她自己都惨不忍睹。　她不再是	165
	我们的母亲,而是坟墓。　没有人,	
	除了纯粹的无知,露出过笑容;	
	哀叹、呻吟、尖叫声划破云霄,	
	无人理会;在那里痛不欲生	
	倒像是人之常情。　死者的丧钟,	170
	无人过问为谁而鸣,好人的生命	
	比他们帽上的鲜花更先凋谢,	
	患病之前便已丧生。	
麦克达夫	噢,真是精雕细刻,可千真万确!	
马尔科姆	最近的不幸呢?	175
罗斯	一小时前的消息都让人唏嘘;	
	时刻都有新的不幸。	
麦克达夫	我妻子好吗?	
罗斯	唉,很好。	
麦克达夫	孩子们呢?	
罗斯	也都很好。	
麦克达夫	那位暴君还没有袭击他们?	
罗斯	没有,我离开时他们十分安宁。	180
麦克达夫	您说话不要吝啬,到底怎样?	
罗斯	当我来到这里要传递令人	
	沉重的消息时,有一种传言	
	——许多杰出人士已兴兵起义,	

172. 鲜花(flowers):可能是指苏格兰高地人将欧石楠别在帽子上的习俗(Muir)。　178. 很好……很好(well…well):尽管麦克达夫没有意识到,但罗斯是在利用一句谚语:"既已升天,当然很好(He is well since he is in heaven)"。

185   Which was to my belief witnessed the rather

For that I saw the tyrant's power afoot.

Now is the time of help: your eye in Scotland

Would create soldiers, make our women fight

To doff their dire distresses.

Malcolm   Be't their comfort

190   We are coming thither. Gracious England hath

Lent us good Siward, and ten thousand men;

An older and a better soldier, none

That Christendom gives out.

Ross   Would I could answer

This comfort with the like. But I have words

195   That would be howled out in the desert air,

Where hearing should not latch them.

Macduff   What concern they:

The general cause? Or is it a fee-grief

Due to some single breast?

Ross   No mind that's honest

But in it shares some woe, though the main part

Pertains to you alone.

200 **Macduff**   If it be mine,

Keep it not from me, quickly let me have it.

Ross   Let not your ears despise my tongue for ever,

Which shall possess them with the heaviest sound

That ever yet they heard.

Macduff   H'm: I guess at it.

205 **Ross**   Your castle is surprised; your wife and babes

Savagely slaughtered. To relate the manner,

Were on the quarry of these murdered deer,

这种传言倒使我更加确信， 185
因为我看见暴君的队伍在动。
现在需要您帮助：亲临苏格兰
即可兴师动众，妇女都会参战
以摆脱自身的困境。

马尔科姆 让他们放心，
我们正要前去。 仁慈的英王已将 190
西华德与万名士兵借给我们；
基督教世界里没有哪位士兵
会比他更为老成。

罗斯 但愿我能用
同样好的消息回报！可我的话语
却应在荒芜的沙漠里厉声嚎叫， 195
因为那里无人会听到。

麦克达夫 关于什么：
事关普通大众？ 还是哪一位
个人的不幸？

罗斯 凡是正派的人
都会感到痛心，尽管它主要
涉及您一人。

麦克达夫 若是与我有关， 200
那就别再隐瞒，快让我知道。

罗斯 您的耳朵会永远鄙视我的舌，
因为它要向它们灌输的沉痛
消息前所未闻。

麦克达夫 噢，我已猜到！

罗斯 您的城堡遭到突袭，妻儿老小 205
均遭到杀戮。 如果讲述惨状，
就等于使您丧命，将您追加到

		To add the death of you.
	Malcolm	Merciful heaven!
		What, man; ne'er pull your hat upon your brows:
210		Give sorrow words. The grief that does not speak
		Whispers the o'erfraught heart and bids it break.
	Macduff	My children too?
	Ross	Wife, children, servants, all that could be found.
	Macduff	And I must be from thence? My wife killed too?
215	**Ross**	I have said.
	Malcolm	Be comforted:
		Let's make us medicines of our great revenge,
		To cure this deadly grief.
	Macduff	He has no children. All my pretty ones?
220		Did you say all? O hell-kite! All?
		What, all my pretty chickens, and their dam
		At one fell swoop?
	Malcolm	Dispute it like a man.
	Macduff	I shall do so,
		But I must also feel it as a man:
225		I cannot but remember such things were
		That were most precious to me. Did heaven look on,
		And would not take their part? Sinful Macduff,
		They were all struck for thee. Naught that I am,
		Not for their own demerits, but for mine,

遇害亲人的尸堆之上。

马尔科姆	仁慈的上苍！	
	怎么了，嘿；别用帽檐遮住眼睛：	
	难过就说。　未予表达的伤悲	210
	会向超载的心低语，使它破碎。	
麦克达夫	还有孩子？	
罗斯	妻子、孩子、仆人，只要能找到。	
麦克达夫	我却要远离？　我妻子也遇害了？	
罗斯	我已说过。	215
马尔科姆	你别伤心。	
	让咱们的报仇雪恨当作良药，	
	将悲痛欲绝治疗。	
麦克达夫	他没有孩子。　我所有的宝贝儿？	
	您说全部？　噢，这个恶魔！全部？	220
	什么，所有的幼禽，和它们的妈妈	
	竟一下子残杀？	
马尔科姆	要像男子汉一般抗争。	
麦克达夫	我会的，	
	但我也必须会有人之常情：	
	我不会忘记对我来说那么	225
	珍贵的东西。　上帝竟袖手旁观，	
	不保护他们？　罪恶的麦克达夫，	
	他们都为你而死。　我真可恶，	
	不是因他们的过错，而是因我的，	

---

209. 帽檐遮住眼睛（pull…brows）：显然是一种悲伤或痛苦的表示（Clark）。 "别隐藏你的悲痛（don't keep your grief hidden）"（sparknotes）。 219. 他没有孩子（He has no children）：既可指马尔科姆（他若有孩子，说起话来就不会这么无动于衷）；也可指麦克白（Gill）。 229. 不是……我的（Not…mine）：他不是在责备自己逃离了苏格兰，而是在责备自己的罪恶本性（sinful nature）（Muir）。

230   Fell slaughter on their souls. Heaven rest them now.

Malcolm   Be this the whetstone of your sword. Let grief

Convert to anger; blunt not the heart, enrage it.

Macduff   O, I could play the woman with mine eyes,

And braggart with my tongue. But gentle heavens,

235   Cut short all intermission. Front to front

Bring thou this fiend of Scotland and myself;

Within my sword's length set him. If he scape,

Heaven forgive him too.

Malcolm   This time goes manly.

Come, go we to the King: our power is ready,

240   Our lack is nothing but our leave. Macbeth

Is ripe for shaking, and the powers above

Put on their instruments. Receive what cheer you may,

The night is long that never finds the day.   *Exeunt.*

| | 他们才遭到残害。　愿他们安息！ | 230 |

马尔科姆　您把这当成磨刀石吧。　化悲痛

为愤怒；别麻木不仁，要怒火中烧。

麦克达夫　噢，我可以女人一般哭哭啼啼，

自吹自擂。　不过，仁慈的上天，

你要打断所有的拖延。　面对面，　　　　　235

让苏格兰的这位恶魔与我之间；

让他与我一剑之隔。　他若逃脱，

上帝也对他宽恕。

马尔科姆　　　　　　　　　　　这才像条汉子。

快，咱去见国王：军队已就绪，

我们啥都不缺只欠辞别。　麦克白　　　　　240

已经摇摇欲坠，上天的军队

也已武装起来。　要感到欣慰，

长夜过后总会见到晨辉。　　　　　　　　　同下。

237-8. 他若……宽恕（If…too）：我要是让他逃脱，愿他不仅能得到我的宽恕，也愿他能得到上帝的宽恕！（麦克达夫不允许这种情况发生）（Bevington）。　241. 摇摇欲坠（ripe for shaking）：（就像成熟的果子）容易跌落（ready to fall）。

第五幕
ACT 5

SCENE I

Enter a Doctor of Physic, and a Waiting Gentlewoman.

Doctor   I have two nights watched with you, but can perceive no truth in your report. When was it she last walked?

Gentlewoman   Since his majesty went into the field, I have seen
5   her rise from her bed, throw her nightgown upon her, unlock her closet, take forth paper, fold it, write upon't, read it, afterwards seal it, and again return to bed, yet all this while in a most fast sleep.

Doctor   A great perturbation in nature, to receive at
10   once the benefit of sleep and do the effects of watching. In this slumbery agitation, besides her walking and other actual performances, what, at any time, have you heard her say?

Gentlewoman   That, sir, which I will not report after
15   her.

Doctor   You may to me, and 'tis most meet you should.

Gentlewoman   Neither to you, nor anyone, having no witness to confirm my speech.

第一场

医生与女侍臣上。

医生　我已和您一起守望了两夜，可我并未
见您所说的情况出现。她上一次梦游
是什么时间？

女侍臣　自从陛下他上了战场以后，我就见她
从床上起来，将一件睡衣披在她身上，　　5
打开保险柜子，拿出纸来，把它叠好，
在上面书写，宣读，随后封印，再次
回到床上，所有这些都在熟睡中进行。

医生　这可是严重的心神不宁，一面享受着
睡眠的好处，一面又好像做着醒时的　　10
动作。在这种沉睡的躁动之中，除了
她的漫游和其他具体行动之外，您还
听见她说过些什么？

女侍臣　这些事情，先生，我可不想背后说给
您听。　　15

医生　您可以跟我说，这也是您很应该做的。

女侍臣　没有别人证实我的话语，我不会对您，
或任何人说的。

　　5.1.　0（1）女侍臣（*Waiting Gentlewoman*）：皇后或公主的私人助理，上流社会出身（la-dy-in-waiting, personal attendant to a queen or princess, of genteel birth）。　7. 封印（seal）：用热蜡密封，表明信件真实可靠。　夫人的心思也许又回到第一幕第五场收到麦克白信件时的场景。　11. 沉睡的躁动（slumbery agitation）：矛盾修辞法，表明夫人状态异常。　17-8. 女侍臣言语谨慎，以免让自己卷入潜在的叛逆罪之中。

Enter Lady, with a taper.

		Lo you, here she comes. This is her very guise, and
20		upon my life, fast asleep. Observe her, stand close.
	Doctor	How came she by that light?
	Gentlewoman	Why, it stood by her: she has light by her continually; 'tis her command.
	Doctor	You see her eyes are open.
25	**Gentlewoman**	Ay, but their sense are shut.
	Doctor	What is it she does now? Look how she rubs her hands.
	Gentlewoman	It is an accustomed action with her, to seem thus washing her hands. I have known her continue in
30		this a quarter of an hour.
	Lady	Yet here's a spot.
	Doctor	Hark, she speaks. I will set down what comes from her, to satisfy my remembrance the more strongly.
35	**Lady**	Out, damned spot: out, I say. One; two. Why, then 'tis time to do't. Hell is murky. Fie, my lord, fie, a soldier and afeared? What need we fear who knows it, when none can call our power to account? Yet who would have thought the old man to have
40		had so much blood in him?

夫人上，手持蜡烛。

	您看，她来了！她往常就是这样，我	
	以性命打赌，正在熟睡。　看好，别动。	20
医生	她怎么端着灯呢？	
女侍臣	嗨，就在她的床边：她身旁总要有灯	
	亮着；这是她的命令。	
医生	您看她眼睛睁着。	
女侍臣	对，但它们并不管用。	25
医生	她现在正在干啥？您看，她正在搓洗	
	双手。	
女侍臣	这是她的一种习惯性的动作，她好像	
	是在洗手似的。我见她持续这么一种	
	动作一刻钟左右。	30
夫人	这里还有个污点。	
医生	您听，她说话了！我要记下她都说了	
	些什么，以便满足我的愿望，能记得	
	更牢。	
夫人	去，该死的污点！去，我说！一；二。	35
	嗨，该动手了。地狱漆黑。呸，夫君，	
	呸，一名军人，还怕？我们为啥要怕	
	有人知道，因为没有人敢拿我们试问？	
	可是谁又能想到这个老头儿身上竟会	
	有那么多鲜血？	40

22．灯（light）：因为她现在害怕黑暗（Muir）。　31．污点（spot）：参考 2.2.68-9（Muir）。　35．一；二（one；two）：她好像听到了钟表或丧钟的敲击声（如 2.1.62 时的场景）。　37．怕（afeared）：回想起自己与麦克白在 1.7 的会话。　37-8．我们……试问（What…account）：就本句的断句而言，译者采用了其他几个版本的做法，即：将原文"fear"后面的问号去掉，在"knows it"后面加上逗号，这样句义可能会更为通顺。　——译者附注。

Doctor	Do you mark that?
Lady	The Thane of Fife had a wife. Where is she now? What, will these hands ne'er be clean? No more o'that, my lord, no more o'that. You mar all with this starting.
Doctor	Go to, go to. You have known what you should not.
Gentlewoman	She has spoke what she should not, I am sure of that. Heaven knows what she has known.
Lady	Here's the smell of the blood still. All the perfumes of Arabia will not sweeten this little hand. Oh, oh, oh!
Doctor	What a sigh is there. The heart is sorely charged.
Gentlewoman	I would not have such a heart in my bosom, for the dignity of the whole body.
Doctor	Well, well, well.
Gentlewoman	Pray God it be, sir.
Doctor	This disease is beyond my practice: yet I have known those which have walked in their sleep, who have died holily in their beds.
Lady	Wash your hands, put on your nightgown, look not so pale. I tell you yet again, Banquo's buried; he cannot come out on's grave.

45
50
55
60

医生	您听见没有？	
夫人	法福郡主曾有位妻子。可她现在何处？ 怎么，这一双手再也洗不干净？别提 它了，夫君，别提它了。您这么一惊 毁了所有事情。	45
医生	得啦，得啦。您已知道您不该知道的 事情。	
女侍臣	她已说出她本不该说出的事情，对此 我敢肯定。　上帝知道她内心的秘密。	
夫人	这里依然有那种血腥的气味。所有的 阿拉伯香水都无法让这一只小手变香。 嗷，嗷，嗷！	50
医生	这是多么沉重的哀叹。她的心中苦不 堪言。	
女侍臣	哪怕让我王后加身，我也不愿自己的 胸腔拥有这样的心脏。	55
医生	好了，好了，好了。	
女侍臣	但愿如此，先生！	
医生	这种疾病我可没有办法救治：然而我 知道有些患梦游症的病人，他们都是 寿终正寝，坦然离去。	60
夫人	洗洗您的手，穿上您的睡衣，别显得 这么苍白。我再说一遍，班柯已埋葬； 他不会从坟里出来。	

---

44. 一惊（starting）：参考 3.4.60（Muir）。　46. 得啦，得啦（Go to, go to = come, come）：表示不耐烦或责备。 医生是在批评夫人的漏嘴（revelatory speech）（Clark）。　有些人认为本行是对女侍臣而言，其实不然（Muir）。　51. 阿拉伯香水（perfumes of Arabia）：自中世纪以来，阿拉伯就向西方供应香水。 夫人的夸张法令人想起麦克白就其血腥的双手而产生的类似感受（2.2.61-4）。　63. 苍白（pale）：令人想起麦克白在 2.2.59 的反应。

65	**Doctor**	Even so?
	Lady	To bed, to bed: there's knocking at the gate. Come, come, come, come, give me your hand. What's done, cannot be undone. To bed, to bed, to bed. *Exit Lady.*
	Doctor	Will she go now to bed?
70	**Gentlewoman**	Directly.
	Doctor	Foul whisperings are abroad. Unnatural deeds Do breed unnatural troubles. Infected minds To their deaf pillows will discharge their secrets. More needs she the divine than the physician.
75		God, God forgive us all! Look after her, Remove from her the means of all annoyance, And still keep eyes upon her. So, goodnight. My mind she has mated, and amazed my sight. I think, but dare not speak.
	Gentlewoman	Good night, good doctor.

Exeunt.

医生	竟然如此？		65
夫人	去睡,去睡：门口有敲门的声音。快,		
	快,快,快把您的手给我。既然干了,		
	就无法挽回。　去睡,去睡,去睡。	夫人下。	
医生	她现在会去睡吗？		
女侍臣	立刻去睡。		70
医生	谣言到处在传。　怪异的举动		
	会导致怪异的麻烦。　变态的心理		
	会对聋哑的枕头吐露秘密。		
	她更需要神职人员而非医生。		
	上帝啊,宽恕大家！照顾好她,		75
	把能伤到她的东西统统撤离,		
	要时刻对她留心。　好了,晚安。		
	她使我目瞪口呆,心烦意乱。		
	我敢想,却不敢言。		
女侍臣	好医生,晚安。		
		同下。	

---

74. 医生是在承认自己的局限,因为他意识到夫人的病态属于精神范畴而非肉体。　他这种观念的依据是一句常言：“贤哲无能为力时,由医生接管,医生无能为力,交给上天（Where the Philosopher ends, the Physician begins; and he ends［they say］where the Divine begins）。” 76. 以防她自杀。　79. 我敢想,却不敢言（I…speak）：跟女侍臣一样,医生也怕祸从口出。

SCENE II

Drum and Colours. Enter Menteith, Caithness,
Angus, Lennox, Soldiers.

Menteith	The English power is near, led on by Malcolm,
	His uncle Siward and the good Macduff.
	Revenges burn in them, for their dear causes
	Would to the bleeding and the grim alarm
	Excite the mortified man.

5   **Angus**   Near Birnam Wood

                     Shall we well meet them; that way are they coming.

Caithness   Who knows if Donalbain be with his brother?

Lennox   For certain, sir, he is not; I have a file

                     Of all the gentry. There is Siward's son,

10   And many unrough youths, that even now

                     Protest their first of manhood.

Menteith   What does the tyrant?

Caithness   Great Dunsinane he strongly fortifies.

                     Some say he's mad; others that lesser hate him,

第二场

鼓手与旗手。曼提斯、凯斯尼斯、
安格斯、兰诺克斯与众士兵上。

曼提斯　　英军已逼近,由马尔科姆、他的
　　　　　舅父西华德跟好麦克达夫率领。
　　　　　他们誓要报仇,正当的理由
　　　　　可将死者唤起浴血奋战,响应
　　　　　可怕的号令。

安格斯　　　　　　　我们将在伯南林　　　　　　　　　5
　　　　　与他们会面;他们从那里前来。

凯斯尼斯　谁知道唐纳班是否与哥哥一起?

兰诺克斯　肯定没有,先生;我有一份
　　　　　将领的名单。有西华德的儿子,
　　　　　和许多尚无胡须的小伙儿,此刻　　　　　　10
　　　　　才宣布业已成年。

曼提斯　　　　　　　　暴君正在干啥?

凯斯尼斯　加固邓西嫩城堡的防御工事。
　　　　　有人说他疯了;不太恨他的人

5.2. 0 (1) 鼓手与旗手(*Drum and Colours* = A drummer with his instrument, and a flag-bearer):当时常见的一种舞台指示,表明军事冲突由此开始。 2. 舅父西华德(his uncle Siward):据《编年史》记载,西华德本为马尔科姆的外祖父:"邓肯有两个儿子,妻子为诺森伯兰伯爵——西华德的女儿。"然而,在该剧中邓肯好像并不比西华德年轻;莎氏让他比实际年龄年长一些,并使西华德成了马尔科姆的舅父,以此与其他更改保持一致(Muir)。 3-5. 理由……号令(for …alarm):原注为"Their causes are powerful enough to rouse('Excite')a dead('morti-fied')man to come to the bloodshed and answer the call to arms('alarm')"(Gill)。

Do call it valiant fury; but for certain,

15 He cannot buckle his distempered cause

Within the belt of rule.

Angus Now does he feel

His secret murders sticking on his hands;

Now minutely revolts upbraid his faith-breach;

Those he commands move only in command,

20 Nothing in love. Now does he feel his title

Hang loose about him, like a giant's robe

Upon a dwarfish thief.

Menteith Who then shall blame

His pestered senses to recoil and start,

When all that is within him does condemn

Itself for being there.

25 **Caithness** Well, march we on,

To give obedience where 'tis truly owed.

Meet we the medicine of the sickly weal,

And with him pour we in our country's purge,

Each drop of us.

Lennox Or so much as it needs

30 To dew the sovereign flower, and drown the weeds.

Make we our march towards Birnam. *Exeunt marching.*

称之为勇敢的狂怒；但可以肯定，
他已无可救药,对众叛亲离的　　　　　　　　　　　15
王国无法掌控。

安格斯　　　　　　　　　　他现已感到
遇害者的鲜血沾满他双手；
时刻都有叛乱谴责他的背信；
他手下的士兵只是因为奉命，
不是因爱心。　现在他感到王冠　　　　　　　20
已无法戴稳,就像巨人的长袍
罩住了矮子小偷。

曼提斯　　　　　　　　　　还会有谁
责备他精神错乱、胆战心惊，
因为他的身心都在诅咒自己
竟长在那里。

凯斯尼斯　　　　　　　　那好,咱们前进，　　　　25
我们要效忠自己真正的主人。
前去迎接可医治国难的良医，
为使国家净化跟他把每一滴
鲜血抛洒。

兰诺克斯　　　　　　　　也许我们还需要
用血液滴灌王花,淹没杂草。　　　　　　　　30
咱们向伯南行进。　　　　　　　　　众下,列队行进。

　　15-6. 他已……掌控（He…rule）：其中，"cause = sickness（患病）"，本句可指：麦克白，就像因患水肿而系不上自己的腰带者（参考福斯塔夫），无法控制自己的情绪（参考"疯了（mad）"。　或指,他所统治的王国已疾病缠身并有人造反（the kingdom which he rules is sick and rebellious）（Muir）。　在短语"belt of rule"之中，"belt（皮带）"为隐喻用法,表示"控制（control）"（Clark）。　27. 良医（medicine）：可指良药（medicine）；也可指医生（physician），即马尔科姆。

SCENE III

Enter Macbeth, Doctor and Attendants.

Macbeth Bring me no more reports, let them fly all;
Till Birnam Wood remove to Dunsinane,
I cannot taint with fear. What's the boy Malcolm?
Was he not born of woman? The spirits that know

5   All mortal consequences have pronounced me thus:
'Fear not, Macbeth, no man that's born of woman
Shall e'er have power upon thee.' Then fly, false thanes,
And mingle with the English epicures;
The mind I sway by and the heart I bear,

10   Shall never sag with doubt, nor shake with fear.

Enter Servant.

The devil damn thee black, thou cream-faced loon.
Where got'st thou that goose-look?
Servant There is ten thousand.
Macbeth   Geese, villain?

第三场

麦克白、医生与侍从上。

麦克白	别再向我报告,让他们逃吧;
	在伯南林移到邓西嫩之前,
	我不会惧怕。　马尔科姆小子算啥?
	他不是女人生的?　了解所有
	人生结局的幽灵曾向我宣布: 5
	"别怕,麦克白,凡是女人生的
	都对你奈何不得。"逃吧,背信的郡主,
	跟贪图享乐的英国人厮混去吧;
	我的内在精神,和我的骨气,
	不会因疑虑而气馁,惧怕而战栗。 10

仆人上。

	愿魔鬼把你咒黑,你这白脸的贱货!
	哪来的蠢鹅面色?
仆人	有一万。
麦克白	蠢鹅,混蛋?

5.3. 麦克白远离舞台很久之后,又在本场重现,演员们有时会将他装扮得已经苍老。 麦克白也自认已经衰老(22-6)。 0(1)尽管麦克白与医生和侍从等随行人员一起入场,但直到37行当他要求医生回答问题时,他们之间才有了互动。 麦克白较长的两段台词,即1-10行,22-8行像是半独白似的(quasi-soliloquies)。 这些明显多余的旁观者的出现可强调上述台词所传递的信息——局面已经失控。 3. 马尔科姆小子(boy Malcolm):久经沙场的战将对年轻人的蔑视。 9-10. 其中的尾韵增添了一种不可改变性(finality)和沾沾自喜的色彩(a touch of complacency),然而它们却在随之而发生的事情面前不攻自破。 11-2. 麦克白好像对仆人苍白的脸色尤其反感,因为这表明他很害怕(此处,以及14行、16-7行),也许因为这是他(麦克白)所"讨厌的自怕形象(an unwelcome image of his own fear)"。 12. 蠢鹅面色(goose-look):愚蠢或笨拙的外表,因为鹅是出了名的荒唐可笑(proverbially giddy);但也可能表示苍白(pallor),因为鹅为白色。

Servant	Soldiers, sir.
Macbeth	Go prick thy face, and over-red thy fear,

15   Thou lily-livered boy. What soldiers, patch?

Death of thy soul, those linen cheeks of thine

Are counsellors to fear. What soldiers, whey-face?

Servant   The English force, so please you.

Macbeth   Take thy face hence.   *[Exit Servant.]*

                         Seyton, I am sick at heart,

20   When I behold—Seyton, I say—This push

Will cheer me ever, or disseat me now.

I have lived long enough: my way of life

Is fallen into the sear, the yellow leaf,

And that which should accompany old age,

25   As honour, love, obedience, troops of friends,

I must not look to have; but, in their stead,

Curses not loud but deep, mouth-honour, breath

Which the poor heart would fain deny, and dare not.

Seyton?

Enter Seyton.

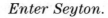

Seyton   What's your gracious pleasure?

仆人	士兵，先生。	
麦克白	去把脸刺破，将恐惧涂成红色，	
	你这胆小鬼。　什么士兵，蠢货？	15
	你真该死！你那煞白的面颊	
	会使别人害怕。　啥士兵，白脸汉？	
仆人	英国士兵，回陛下。	
麦克白	你快滚开！　　　　　　　　　　［仆人下。］	

西顿，我心烦意乱，

我看到——西顿，我说——这一攻势　　　　　　20

可使我稳坐江山，或将我推翻。

我已活得够长：我的人生历程，

就像一片黄叶，正走向凋零，

理应伴随老龄而来的东西，

如尊敬、爱戴、顺从、朋友成群，　　　　　　25

我都无法指望；取而代之的是，

低声却强烈的诅咒，口头敬重，

内心想停止的呼吸，却不敢停止。

西顿？

西顿上。

西顿	陛下您有何吩咐？

---

16. 你真该死（Death…soul）：诅咒语（an oath）。　21. 稳坐江山（cheer me ever）：其中，"cheer"可指"使感到宽慰（comfort），使振奋（encourage）"，但该词也可与"chair（王座）"，即"王位（throne）"，构成近似的谐音双关，而且意思也与下文的"推翻（disseat）"更为相符。　23. 黄叶（yellow leaf）：隐喻，表示人生的最后阶段（metaphor for the last stage of life）。　27. 口头敬重（mouth-honour = lip-service）：与真正的尊敬（true *honour*）相对（25行）。　参照《圣经》"以赛亚书"29章13节：这些人遇到麻烦时便用嘴唇尊敬我，而他们的心却远离我。　28. 内心……停止（breath…not）：现代译文为"and lingering life（'breath'），which my heart would gladly end（'fainly deny'），though I can't bring myself to do it（苟延残喘的人生，我内心会很高兴予以了结，尽管我不敢付诸行动）"（Sparknotes）。

30	**Macbeth**	What news more?
	Seyton	All is confirmed, my lord, which was reported.
	Macbeth	I'll fight, till from my bones my flesh be hacked.
		Give me my armour.
	Seyton	'Tis not needed yet.
	Macbeth	I'll put it on.
35		Send out more horses, skirr the country round,
		Hang those that talk of fear. Give me mine armour.
		How does your patient, doctor?
	Doctor	Not so sick, my lord,
		As she is troubled with thick-coming fancies
		That keep her from her rest.
	Macbeth	Cure her of that.
40		Canst thou not minister to a mind diseased,
		Pluck from the memory a rooted sorrow,
		Raze out the written troubles of the brain,
		And with some sweet oblivious antidote
		Cleanse the stuffed bosom of that perilous stuff
		Which weighs upon the heart?
45	**Doctor**	Therein the patient
		Must minister to himself.
	Macbeth	Throw physic to the dogs, I'll none of it.
		Come, put mine armour on; give me my staff;
		Seyton, send out. Doctor, the thanes fly from me—
50		Come, sir, dispatch. —If thou couldst, doctor, cast

麦克白	还有啥消息？	30
西顿	所有的传言均已证实，陛下。	
麦克白	我要一直战斗到血肉横飞。	
	把盔甲拿来。	
西顿	现在还不需要。	
麦克白	我要穿上。	
	派出更多骑兵，要踏遍全国，	35
	绞死散布恐慌者。　给我盔甲。	
	病人怎样，医生？	
医生	身体倒好，陛下，	
	主要是接连不断的幻觉困扰，	
	使她无法安眠。	
麦克白	你给她治好。	
	难道你不能医治患病的心灵，	40
	拔除记忆中根深蒂固的哀伤，	
	抹去那刻在脑海里的烦恼，	
	利用某种甜蜜的忘忧解药	
	将满腔危险和折磨心灵的	
	东西洗掉？	
医生	就此而言，病人	45
	可需要自我治疗。	
麦克白	把药喂狗去吧，我用不着它！	
	快，给我穿上盔甲，把长矛给我；	
	西顿，派兵。　医生，郡主们已逃跑——	
	快，先生，赶快。　——你若能，医生，	50

45-6.　就此……治疗（Therein…himself）：医生的回答有意模糊或中立（neutral），然而他所使用的代词"himself（本人）"，可表明麦克白所描述的症状既适用于他夫人，也适用于他本人。　49.　派兵（send out）：如35行所说，增派援军或装备。　49，50，54.　麦克白此刻的突然命令对谁而发，不太清楚。　可能像49行那样，全指向西顿，或是在场但闲着的其他侍从。

The water of my land, find her disease,

And purge it to a sound and pristine health,

I would applaud thee to the very echo,

That should applaud again. —Pull't off, I say.

55 What rhubarb, senna, or what purgative drug

Would scour these English hence? Hear'st thou of them?

Doctor Ay, my good lord: your royal preparation

Makes us hear something.

Macbeth Bring it after me.

I will not be afraid of death and bane

60 Till Birnam forest come to Dunsinane.

[*Exeunt all except Doctor.*]

Doctor Were I from Dunsinane away and clear,

Profit again should hardly draw me here. *Exit.*

化验我国的尿液,找到病因,

并能将它净化得康健如初,

我对你的赞美声将如此响亮,

它会回荡再回荡。 ——脱掉它,我说。

哪里有大黄、番泻叶,或其他泻药 55

将英国人清除? 你听说了没有?

医生 听说了,好陛下:陛下您的备战

让我们略有所闻。

麦克白 随后把它带上。

我将不会害怕死亡和祸根,

直到伯南林转移到邓西嫩。 60

　　　　　　　　　　　　　[除医生外全下。]

医生 我若能从邓西嫩溜之大吉,

金钱将很难使我再回这里。 下。

---

52. 净化(purge):参考 3.4.74(Muir)。 53-4. 我……回荡(I…again):原注为"I would praise you so loudly that my praises would echo and re-echo"(Gill)。 58. 它(it):也许是指 54 行他叫人脱掉的盔甲(Bate)。 62. 医生以贪得无厌而出名。 他结尾的偶韵句显然不是说给麦克白听的。

SCENE IV

Drum and Colours. Enter Malcolm, Siward,
Macduff, Siward's Son, Menteith, Caithness,
Angus and Soldiers marching.

Malcolm   Cousins, I hope the days are near at hand

That chambers will be safe.

Menteith   We doubt it nothing.

Siward   What wood is this before us?

Menteith   The Wood of Birnam.

Malcolm   Let every soldier hew him down a bough

5   And bear't before him; thereby shall we shadow

The numbers of our host, and make discovery

Err in report of us.

Soldier   It shall be done.

Siward   We learn no other but the confident tyrant

Keeps still in Dunsinane, and will endure

Our setting down before't.

10   **Malcolm**   'Tis his main hope.

For where there is advantage to be given,

Both more and less have given him the revolt,

And none serve with him but constrained things,

Whose hearts are absent too.

第四场

鼓手与旗手。马尔科姆、西华德、
麦克达夫、西华德的儿子、曼提斯、
凯斯尼斯、安格斯与士兵行军上。

马尔科姆　同胞们，希望我们能高枕无忧的
日子即将来临。

曼提斯　　　　　　　我们毫不怀疑。

西华德　前面是什么树林？

曼提斯　　　　　　伯南树林。

马尔科姆　让每一位战士砍下一根树枝，
举在前面；由此可以遮掩　　　　　　　　5
我军的规模，并让对方的侦探
报告我们时出错。

士兵　　　　　　　我们照办。

西华德　我们只听说那位狂妄的暴君
在邓西嫩毫无动静，将会容忍
我们包围城堡。

马尔科姆　　　　　　他别无希望。　　　　10
因为只要能够有机会脱逃，
无论高低贵贱都会反叛，
只有可怜的雇佣兵为他服役，
并非出于真心。

Macduff   Let our just censures

15   Attend the true event, and put we on

Industrious soldiership.

Siward   The time approaches,

That will with due decision make us know

What we shall say we have, and what we owe.

Thoughts speculative their unsure hopes relate,

20   But certain issue, strokes must arbitrate:

Towards which advance the war.   *Exeunt marching.*

麦克达夫　　　　　　　　要等到最终
结果再作评判,我们要像军人　　　　　　　　　　　　15
那样奋勇向前。

西华德　　　　　　　　时机已来临,
适当的结局会使我们知晓
哪是自称拥有,哪是真能得到。
沉思默想依赖于缥缈的希望,
确切的结果取决于实际战况:　　　　　　　　　　　　20
为此,我们要进军。　　　　　　　　　全体行军下。

5.4.　14-5. 要等到……评判(Let…event):原注为"Let our true judgement (of the state of Macbeth's support) await the final outcome"。　18. 意为"区别在于只是空谈,还是真正拥有(The difference between talk and true possesion)"。　西华德,跟麦克达夫一样,也是在提醒马尔科姆不要盲目乐观。　19-20. 原注为"Speculation about what will happen is based on uncertain hopes, but for a sure result (certain issue), actual fighting (strokes) must be the decider (arbitrate)"(Gill; Clark)。　21. 此(which):即"确切的结果(certain issue)"。

SCENE V

Enter Macbeth, Seyton and Soldiers,
with Drum and Colours.

Macbeth   Hang out our banners on the outward walls;

The cry is still, 'They come'. Our castle's strength

Will laugh a siege to scorn. Here let them lie,

Till famine and the ague eat them up.

5   Were they not forced with those that should be ours,

We might have met them dareful, beard to beard,

And beat them backward home.   *A cry within of women*

What is that noise?

Seyton   It is the cry of women, my good lord.

Macbeth   I have almost forgot the taste of fears.

10   The time has been, my senses would have cooled

To hear a night-shriek, and my fell of hair

Would at a dismal treatise rouse and stir

As life were in't. I have supped full with horrors;

Direness familiar to my slaughterous thoughts

15   Cannot once start me. Wherefore was that cry?

Seyton   The Queen, my lord, is dead.

第五场

麦克白、西顿与士兵，
执旗鼓上。

麦克白　　快把我们的旗帜挂到墙外；
还在喊，"他们来啦"。　城堡的坚固
可嘲笑围攻。　让他们在此安营，
直到饥荒和疟疾将他们吞没。
若非他们有我们的逃兵增援，　　　　　　　　5
我们就会迎头痛击，面对面，
把他们打回老家。　　　　　　　　　　*内有女人喊叫*
　　　　　　是什么声音？

西顿　　那是女人的叫喊，我的陛下。

麦克白　　我几乎已忘记恐惧的滋味。
从前，夜间听到一声尖叫　　　　　　　　　10
便会不寒而栗，吓人的故事
会让我的毛发像有生命一般
根根竖起。　我已经饱尝恐惧；
嗜杀的思想已对恐惧习以为常，
再不会使我惊慌。　为何有叫声？　　　　　15

西顿　　王后死了，陛下。

5.5.　8. 叫喊（cry）：麦克白夫人属于非正常死亡（Muir）。

Macbeth   She should have died hereafter;

There would have been a time for such a word.

Tomorrow, and tomorrow, and tomorrow,

Creeps in this petty pace from day to day,

20   To the last syllable of recorded time;

And all our yesterdays have lighted fools

The way to dusty death. Out, out, brief candle,

Life's but a walking shadow, a poor player,

That struts and frets his hour upon the stage,

25   And then is heard no more. It is a tale

Told by an idiot, full of sound and fury,

Signifying nothing.

Enter a Messenger.

Thou com'st to use thy tongue: thy story, quickly.

Messenger   Gracious my lord,

30   I should report that which I say I saw,

But know not how to do't.

Macbeth   Well, say, sir.

麦克白	她早晚都会死的；	
	这样的消息到时总会传来。	
	明天，接着明天，接着明天，	
	就这样一天一天地匍匐向前，	
	直到最后一个音节记录在案；	20
	所有的昨天都为傻瓜照亮了	
	入土的归途。 熄灭吧，短暂的烛光！	
	人生只是个走影，可怜的演员，	
	在台上怒气冲冲，趾高气扬，	
	然后销声匿迹。 白痴讲述的	25
	故事而已，充满了喧嚣与狂暴，	
	没有任何意义。	

一信差上。

你是来报告消息吧：那就赶快。

信差	仁慈的陛下，	
	我本该汇报我的亲眼所见，	30
	却不知如何汇报。	

麦克白	好吧，请讲。

---

16. 她早晚都会死的（She…hereafter）：可有两种解读：她迟早都会死的（she would have died at some point sooner or later）；她该等一等再死（以便能有机会为她哀悼）（she ought to have died at a future time ［when there would have been a chance to mourn her］）。 22. 入土的归途（The way…death）：参考《圣经》"创世纪"3 章 19 节：你本是尘土，仍要归于尘土。 烛光（candle）：生命（life）（Gill）。 参见《圣经》"约伯记"18 章 6 节：他寓所中的亮光将变为黑暗，他身边的烛光将随之熄灭（Muir）。 23. 走影（walking shadow）：参见《圣经》"约伯记"8 章 9 节：我们不过从昨日才有，一无所知，我们在世的日子好像影儿（For we are but of yesterday, and are ignorant: for our days upon earth are but a shadow）（Muir）。 借鉴卞之琳先生译文。 ——译者附注。 27. 没有任何意义（signifying nothing）：假象（false appearance）这一主题在此又以不同的视角重现。 不只是麦克白本人觉得人生受到了蒙骗（sees life as deceitful），该诗文如此优美，我们甚至都不得不认可剧中这种模棱两可的最终声明，好像是莎士比亚想通过这些诗行表达自己的"人生哲学"。 然而，麦克白之所以会产生这种虚无主义，是由于他自己的罪行剥夺了生命的意义：莎士比亚通过揭示这一事实从而恢复了人生的意义。 另外，本段台词被有意"放（placed）"在了最后一幕，旨在表明"有序从无序中兴起，真实从欺骗中浮现（order emerging from disorder, truth emerging from deceit）"（Muir：154, lii）。

Messenger	As I did stand my watch upon the hill,
	I look'd toward Birnam, and anon methought
	The wood began to move.
Macbeth	Liar and slave!
35 **Messenger**	Let me endure your wrath, if't be not so.
	Within this three mile may you see it coming.
	I say, a moving grove.
Macbeth	If thou speak'st false,
	Upon the next tree shalt thou hang alive
	Till famine cling thee. If thy speech be sooth,
40	I care not if thou dost for me as much.
	I pull in resolution, and begin
	To doubt th'equivocation of the fiend,
	That lies like truth: 'Fear not, till Birnam Wood
	Do come to Dunsinane', and now a wood
45	Comes toward Dunsinane. Arm, arm, and out!
	If this which he avouches does appear,
	There is nor flying hence, nor tarrying here.
	I 'gin to be aweary of the sun,
	And wish th'estate o'th' world were now undone.
50	Ring the alarum bell! Blow wind, come wrack,
	At least we'll die with harness on our back. *Exeunt.*

信差	当我在山上站岗放哨的时候， 朝伯南方向望去，忽然觉得 那树林开始移动。	
麦克白	胡说，贱货！	
信差	您只管对我发怒，要是我说错。 在三英里以内您就能看清， 我说，有森林在动。	35
麦克白	你若说错， 就把你吊在最近的一棵树上， 让你活活饿死。　你说的若真， 我毫不介意你对我同样处置。 我有些丧失信心，并且开始 怀疑恶魔那模棱两可的鬼话， 以假乱真："别怕，直到伯南林 移到邓西嫩"。　如今有座森林 正移向邓西嫩。　拿好武器，出击！ 假如他所说的确实已出现， 既不能逃跑，也不能在此拖延。 我已开始对人生感到厌倦， 并希望整个宇宙混乱不堪。 敲响警钟！风吹吧，毁灭来吧， 死去时我身上至少要穿着铠甲。	40 45 50 同下。

SCENE VI

Drum and Colours. Enter Malcolm, Siward,
Macduff and their Army, with boughs.

Malcolm   Now near enough. Your leafy screens throw down,
And show like those you are. You, worthy uncle,
Shall with my cousin, your right noble son,
Lead our first battle. Worthy Macduff and we
5   Shall take upon's what else remains to do,
According to our order.

Siward   Fare you well.
Do we but find the tyrant's power tonight,
Let us be beaten if we cannot fight.

Macduff   Make all our trumpets speak, give them all breath,
10   Those clamorous harbingers of blood and death.

Exeunt. Alarums continued.

第六场

鼓手与旗手。马尔科姆、西华德、
麦克达夫及军队,持树枝上。

马尔科姆　　已经够近了。　丢下枝叶屏障,
亮出你们的真相。　您,可敬的舅父,
将与我的表弟——您的贵子一起,
指挥首次战役。　好麦克达夫和我
会根据我们的作战部署,负责　　　　　　　　　　5
其他需要做的事宜。

西华德　　　　　　　　　　　再会。
今晚若与暴君的队伍相遇,
若不能迎战,我们宁愿捐躯。

麦克达夫　　吹响所有号角,要嘹亮高亢,
宣告即将来临的流血和死亡。　　　　　　　　　10

下。号角声不断。

5.6.　4. 我（we）：马尔科姆采用了表示国王身份的复数形式（assumes the royal plural）。　10. 舞台指示：战斗的号角首先于 5.2 吹响,然后断断续续直到终场,旨在强调军事行动的延续性。

SCENE VII

Enter Macbeth.

Macheth   They have tied me to a stake; I cannot fly,
But bear-like I must fight the course. What's he
That was not born of woman? Such a one
Am I to fear, or none.

Enter Young Siward.

Young Siward   What is thy name?
5   **Macbeth**   Thou'lt be afraid to hear it.
Young Siward   No, though thou call'st thyself a hotter name
Than any is in hell.
Macbeth   My name's Macbeth.
Young Siward   The devil himself could not pronounce a title
More hateful to mine ear.
Macbeth   No, nor more fearful.
10   **Young Siward**   Thou liest, abhorred tyrant; with my sword
I'll prove the lie thou speak'st.
                    Fight, and Young Siward slain.
Macbeth   Thou wast born of woman.

第七场

麦克白上。

麦克白　　他们已把我拴到桩上；无法逃走，
可我必须困兽犹斗。　哪一位
不是由女人所生？　只有这种人
才会使我惊恐。

小西华德上。

小西华德　你的姓名？
麦克白　　　　　听见了你会害怕。　　　　　　5
小西华德　不会,即使你比地狱的魔鬼
还要可憎。
麦克白　　　　　麦克白是我的大名。
小西华德　魔鬼本身通报的姓名也不会
令我更加憎恨。
麦克白　　　　　也不会更加吓人。
小西华德　胡说,可恶的暴君；我要用剑　　　　10
证明你所说的就是谎言。

交战,小西华德被杀。

麦克白　　你是女人生的。

5.7.　1. 拴到桩上（tied…stake）：麦克白将自己的被困（entrapment）比作被拴到桩上的一头熊,让人纵狗撕咬（a bear chained to a post and baited by dogs）——当时的一种娱乐方式和常用隐喻。

But swords I smile at, weapons laugh to scorn,

Brandished by man that's of a woman born.   *Exit.*

Alarums. Enter Macduff.

15 **Macduff**   That way the noise is. Tyrant, show thy face,

If thou be'st slain, and with no stroke of mine,

My wife and children's ghosts will haunt me still.

I cannot strike at wretched kerns, whose arms

Are hired to bear their staves. Either thou, Macbeth,

20   Or else my sword with an unbattered edge

I sheathe again undeeded. There thou shouldst be;

By this great clatter, one of greatest note

Seems bruited. Let me find him, Fortune,

And more I beg not.   *Exit.*

Alarums. Enter Malcolm and Siward.

25 **Siward**   This way, my lord, the castle's gently rendered.

The tyrant's people on both sides do fight;

The noble thanes do bravely in the war;

The day almost itself professes yours,

And little is to do.

Malcolm   We have met with foes

That strike beside us.

30 **Siward**   Enter, sir, the castle.   *Exeunt.*

武器我会蔑视,利剑我会嘲弄,
只要是由女人生的挥舞摇动。　　　　　　　　　　　下。

　　　　　　　号角齐鸣。麦克达夫上。

麦克达夫　　那边有噪音。　暴君,赶快露面,　　　　　　　15
　　　你要是死在别人的刀剑之下,
　　　我妻儿的冤魂一直会把我纠缠。
　　　不能杀可怜的步兵,他们的手臂
　　　是雇来拿木棒的。　除非你,麦克白,
　　　不然,我的剑锋会毫无毁损,　　　　　　　　　　20
　　　让它无功而返。　你会在那边;
　　　这种大的噪音,像是宣布出现了
　　　要人。　让我见到他吧,命运女神,
　　　我别无他求。　　　　　　　　　　　　　　　　下。

　　　　　　　号角齐鸣。马尔科姆与西华德上。

西华德　　这边来,殿下,城堡已轻易投降。　　　　　25
　　　暴君的士兵分成了敌我两方;
　　　高贵的郡主也都英勇奋战;
　　　胜利归属殿下几成定局,
　　　已无事可做。

马尔科姆　　　　　　　我们遭遇的敌兵
　　　竟跟我们一边。

西华德　　　　　　　进城吧,先生。　　　　　　同下。　30

　　29-30. 敌兵……一边（foes…us）：可指敌兵故意放过我们,也可指敌兵与我们并肩作战
（either enemies who deliberately miss us, or enemies who fight on our side）。

SCENE VIII

Alarum. Enter Macbeth.

Macbeth   Why should I play the Roman fool, and die

On mine own sword? Whiles I see lives, the gashes

Do better upon them.

Enter Macduff.

Macduff   Turn, hell-hound, turn.

Macbeth   Of all men else I have avoided thee.

5   But get thee back, my soul is too much charged

With blood of thine already.

Macduff   I have no words.

My voice is in my sword, thou bloodier villain

Than terms can give thee out.   *Fight. Alarum.*

Macbeth   Thou losest labour;

As easy mayst thou the intrenchant air

10   With thy keen sword impress, as make me bleed.

Let fall thy blade on vulnerable crests;

I bear a charmed life, which must not yield

To one of woman born.

Macduff   Despair thy charm,

And let the angel whom thou still hast served

第八场

号角齐鸣。麦克白上。

麦克白　　　我为何要当罗马傻瓜,死在
自己的刀下？　敌人尚在,刺向
他们岂不更好？

麦克达夫上。

麦克达夫　　　　　　　转身,地狱之狗!

麦克白　　　所有人当中唯有你我在躲避。
你回去吧,我的心灵已沾满　　　　　　　　　　　　5
你亲人太多的鲜血。

麦克达夫　　　　　　　我没啥好说。
我的剑为我发言,你这个恶棍,
残忍得无法形容。　　　　　　　　　　交战。号角齐鸣。

麦克白　　　　　　你白费气力;
你的利剑只有让刀枪不入的
空气留下印记,才能让我流血。　　　　　　　　　　10
让你的刀锋落在弱者的头上;
我有魔法护身——凡是女人生的
都不能降服。

麦克达夫　　　　　　　绝望吧,你的魔法,
让你一直信奉的魔鬼告诉你吧,

5.8. 1. 要当罗马傻瓜（play…fool）:麦克白是指罗马军人为了自己的荣誉宁愿自杀,也不愿被俘。

15   Tell thee, Macduff was from his mother's womb

           Untimely ripped.

Macbeth   Accursed be that tongue that tells me so,

           For it hath cowed my better part of man.

           And be these juggling fiends no more believed

20   That palter with us in a double sense,

           That keep the word of promise to our ear,

           And break it to our hope. I'll not fight with thee.

Macduff   Then yield thee, coward,

           And live to be the show and gaze o'th' time.

25   We'll have thee, as our rarer monsters are,

           Painted on a pole, and underwrit,

           'Here may you see the tyrant. '

Macbeth   I will not yield

           To kiss the ground before young Malcolm's feet,

           And to be baited with the rabble's curse.

30   Though Birnam Wood be come to Dunsinane,

           And thou opposed, being of no woman born,

           Yet I will try the last. Before my body

           I throw my warlike shield. Lay on, Macduff,

           And damned be him, that first cries, 'Hold, enough!'

                               Exeunt fighting. Alarums.

Enter fighting, and Macbeth slain.

                     [*Exit Macduff with Macbeth's body.*]

麦克达夫不是从娘胎里顺产，　　　　　　　　　　15
而是剖腹降生！

麦克白　　　向我说这话的舌头遭受咒诅，
它已将我的男子汉气概吓住。
不再相信这些骗人的恶魔，
她们用模棱两可戏弄于我，　　　　　　　　20
那些话听起来令人满怀期待，
然后使希望破灭。　我不跟你战。

麦克达夫　　那就投降吧，懦夫，
你就可以活着供世人参观。
我们会把你当作稀奇的怪物，　　　　　　　25
画在布上挂起，下面写上，
"此处有暴君展览。"

麦克白　　　　　　　　　　我不会投降，
去亲吻小马尔科姆脚下的泥土，
去遭受暴民们的咒骂奚落。
尽管伯南林来到了邓西嫩，　　　　　　　　30
你与我作对，并非女人所生，
可我要最后一搏。　将我威武的
盾牌举在前面。　来吧，麦克达夫，
谁先喊"住手，够了"，谁受咒诅！

　　　　　　　　　　　　　交战中同下。号角齐鸣。

　　　　二人交战之中入场，麦克白被杀。

　　　　　　　　　　[麦克达夫下，拖着麦克白的尸体。]

---

16. 剖腹降生（untimely ripped）：婴儿足月之前即被从母亲的子宫里取出。 在英格兰的近现代时期（约从15世纪中叶至18世纪中叶），这种情况通常发生在母亲临死之前或之后。 麦克达夫的声明使麦克白意识到他将女巫的预言理解为：凡是女人所生的（any man born from a woman），正如《圣经》"马太福音"11章11节所说的那样：凡妇人所生的，没有一个兴起来大过施洗约翰的。 但麦克达夫所给出的这种解释，即现在所谓的剖腹产（caesarean section），麦克白并未想到。 28. 亲吻……泥土（kiss the ground）：屈辱或彻底投降的象征。

SCENE IX

Retreat and Flourish. Enter with Drum and Colours
Malcolm, Siward, Ross, Thanes and Soldiers.

Malcolm I would the friends we miss were safe arrived.

Siward Some must go off; and yet by these I see,

So great a day as this is cheaply bought.

Malcolm Macduff is missing, and your noble son.

5 **Ross** Your son, my lord, has paid a soldier's debt:

He only lived but till he was a man,

The which no sooner had his prowess confirmed,

In the unshrinking station where he fought,

But like a man he died.

Siward   Then he is dead?

10 **Ross** Aye, and brought off the field. Your cause of sorrow

Must not be measured by his worth, for then

It hath no end.

Siward   Had he his hurts before?

Ross Aye, on the front.

Siward   Why then, God's soldier be he.

Had I as many sons as I have hairs,

第九场

鸣号收兵,号角齐鸣。鼓手与旗手上,后随
马尔科姆、西华德、罗斯、众郡主与士兵。

马尔科姆	愿下落不明的朋友安全归来。
西华德	牺牲难免;但就目前所见而言,
	这么大的胜利代价却很低廉。
马尔科姆	麦克达夫失踪,还有您的贵子。
罗斯	您儿子,将军,已尽了军人天职:

他只是活到自己刚刚成年,
他的英勇无畏刚一得到证实,
就以毫不退缩的姿势,男子汉
一般在沙场战死。

西华德	他已经死了?
罗斯	是的,已搬离战场。　您的悲痛

千万别用他的价值衡量,因为
它没有止境。

西华德	他是否前面负伤?
罗斯	是的,前面。
西华德	那好,愿他进天堂!

假如我的儿子能多如毛发,

---

15   I would not wish them to a fairer death.

And so his knell is knolled.

Malcolm   He's worth more sorrow,

And that I'll spend for him.

Siward   He's worth no more;

They say he parted well and paid his score,

And so God be with him. Here comes newer comfort.

Enter Macduff with Macbeth's head.

20 **Macduff**   Hail King, for so thou art. Behold where stands

Th'usurper's cursed head: the time is free.

I see thee compassed with thy kingdom's pearl,

That speak my salutation in their minds;

Whose voices I desire aloud with mine.

Hail, King of Scotland!

25 **All**   Hail, King of Scotland!   *Flourish*

Malcolm   We shall not spend a large expense of time

Before we reckon with your several loves

And make us even with you. My thanes and kinsmen,

Henceforth be earls, the first that ever Scotland

30   In such an honour named. What's more to do,

Which would be planted newly with the time,

As calling home our exiled friends abroad,

That fled the snares of watchful tyranny,

Producing forth the cruel ministers

	也不希望他们死得更为荣光。	15
	他的丧钟已鸣。	

马尔科姆　　　　　　　　他值得更多悲伤，

我会为他哀悼。

西华德　　　　　　　　哀悼已经够多；

都说尽了职责就是死得其所，

愿上帝与他同在！又有喜讯到来。

　　　　　　麦克达夫执麦克白首级上。

麦克达夫　国王万岁！您已是国王。　您看　　　　　20

篡位者的首级在此：我们已自由。

我看全国的人杰在围绕您四周，

他们的心里说出了我的敬意；

我希望他们与我同声欢呼。

万岁，苏格兰王！

众人　　　　　　　　万岁，苏格兰王！　　　　号角齐鸣　25

马尔科姆　用不了大量的时间我就会

对你们各位的忠心一一报答，

以免亏欠大家。　各位郡主亲族，

从此你们是伯爵，这一尊称

在苏格兰尚属首次。　其他事情，　　　　30

随着新时代的到来也该开始，

诸如召回流亡国外的朋友，

他们是为了逃避暴君的罗网；

搜出残暴的爪牙，他们受雇于

26-41.　"根据伊丽莎白时代的悲剧模式，终场的结束语应由存活下来的最高级别的人物发表，但马尔科姆远非我们最感兴趣的人物。　……也许基于这种理由，演出时本段台词常被缩短或删节"。

35   Of this dead butcher, and his fiend-like queen,

Who, as 'tis thought, by self and violent hands

Took off her life—this, and what needful else

That calls upon us, by the grace of grace,

We will perform in measure, time and place.

40   So thanks to all at once, and to each one,

Whom we invite to see us crowned at Scone.

Flourish.   Exeunt omnes.

FINIS

这位丧命屠夫和恶魔般的王后，　　　　　　　　　　　35

根据传言，她用自己的双手

将自己残害——此事，以及其他

要做的事情，凭借上帝的恩典，

在适当的时间和地点一一照办。

我对大家，对每一位深表谢意，　　　　　　　　　　40

请你们到斯宫看我加冕登基。

　　　　　　　　　　　　　　　　号角齐鸣。众下。

剧　终

参 考 文 献

1. Alan Durban, *Macbeth*, Shakespeare Made Easy, Modern English Version; Barron's, 1984.

2. Kenneth Muir, *Macbeth*, The Arden Shakespeare, Second Series, Methuen & Co Ltd. 1984.

3. Roma Gill, *Macbeth*, Oxford University Press, 外语教学与研究出版社, 1997.

4. David Bevington, *Macbeth*, The New Bantam Shakespeare, 2005.

5. Jonathan Bate, *Macbeth*, Royal Shakespeare Company, 2008.

6. Sandra Clark and Pamela Mason, *Macbeth*, The Arden Shakespeare, Third Series, Bloomsbury, 2015.

7. *Macbeth*, http://nfs.sparknotes.com/ macbeth /.

8. *The Holy Bible*, New International Version, Zondervan, Michigan, 1990.

9. 卞之琳, 莎士比亚悲剧四种《麦克白》, 人民文学出版社, 1988。

10. 梁实秋, 莎士比亚四大悲剧《麦克白》, 中国广播电视出版社, 2002。

11. 朱生豪, 莎士比亚喜剧悲剧集《麦克白》, 译林出版社, 2002。

12. 孙大雨, 莎士比亚四大悲剧《麦克白》, 上海译文出版社, 2002。

13. 辜正坤,《麦克白》, 外语教学与研究出版社, 2016。

14.《圣经》, 和合本, 中国基督教协会, 2008。

译 后 记

译者在翻译《麦克白》的整个过程中,得到了许多朋友和同事的大力帮助和殷切指教。 对此,译者感到非常荣幸,也不胜感激!

首先,要衷心感谢两位良师益友:一位是现已退休的中学语文教师——师尚亮校友,另一位是浙江大学宁波理工学院的魏健校友。 他们受托对该剧的序言、译文和脚注等都进行了非常认真细致的检查,分别对文中的错字、别字、拼写错误、拗口的句子,并对行文的编排以及不符合汉语表达习惯的标点符号等,都提出了具体而富有建设性的修改意见,译者均一一采纳。

还要感谢英国皇家戏剧艺术学院前院长巴特先生(Nicolas Batter),他通过信件或当面指教,非常详细地解答了译者在翻译该剧的过程中所遇到的各种难题,令译者感到非常荣幸和庆幸。

另外,还应感谢父母亲对译者翻译该剧的大力支持。 今年暑假期间译者又一次打着回家照看父母的旗号,把主要精力都用在了该剧的翻译上面,由此让父母在衣食住行等方面受了不少委屈。

最后,还应感谢爱人吴秀琼女士的大力支持和帮助,她为译者翻译该剧提供了可靠的后勤保障。

谢谢!

李其金

2017 年 11 月

图书在版编目(CIP)数据

麦克白：英汉对照／(英)威廉·莎士比亚著；
李其金译. —杭州：浙江大学出版社，2020.4
　(莎士比亚四大悲剧合集)
　ISBN 978-7-308-19749-6

　Ⅰ.①麦… Ⅱ.①威… ②李… Ⅲ.①悲剧—剧本—
英国—中世纪—英、汉 Ⅳ.①I561.33

中国版本图书馆 CIP 数据核字(2019)第 258307 号

Othello

奥 赛 罗

（英汉对照）

[英] 威廉·莎士比亚　著

李其金　译

ZHEJIANG UNIVERSITY PRESS

浙江大学出版社

译者序①

一、版本说明

　　本译文所采用的原文版本为最新的阿登版第三版《奥赛罗》②。该版本的优点不仅在于它具有公认的准确性和权威性，还在于它附有详尽的注解和精辟的导读，这些优点对译者和读者准确理解并欣赏该剧均可提供很大的帮助。此外，译者在翻译过程中还参阅了另外六种原文版本（详情请见参考文献），并从中选取和翻译了大量的注解作为脚注。同时，译者在翻译过程中还参阅了我国译莎前辈梁实秋、朱生豪、卞之琳与孙大雨先生的译文，并借鉴了一些妙笔佳译。

二、翻译标准

　　译文主要依照刘宓庆先生在其《翻译美学导论》③中所倡导的翻译标准——翻译再现主要是借助于"内模仿"，即："'模仿'相当于'对应'，是审美再现的基本手段，翻译尤然。"（刘宓庆：255）译者在翻译过程中始终遵循了这一原则，并尽力使译文在形、音、意三方面与原文一一对应。具体做法请看下文三至五节中的详细说明。

---

　　① 本译文系浙江省高校人文社科重点研究基地课题研究成果。项目名称为"莎士比亚悲剧的重译及美学原则研究——以《奥赛罗》为例"，项目编号为：JDW1405——译者附注。
　　② E. A. J. Honigmann, *Othello*, Arden Shakespeare, Third Series, 中国人民大学出版社，2007。
　　③ 刘宓庆，《翻译美学导论》，中国出版集团公司，2012。

三、对原文无韵诗的模仿

就莎剧的行文形式而言，其中以无韵诗（blank verse）为主，这种无韵诗是一种没有韵脚却富有节奏感的诗体：一般是每行有五个音步，一个音步又有一轻一重的两个音节，即抑扬格，读起来抑扬顿挫、朗朗上口。据统计，剧中的韵文部分占比为80%。

英国批评家兼编辑海伦·加德纳女士在论及《奥赛罗》一剧时，曾高度赞誉道："在莎士比亚的悲剧中，《奥赛罗》具有一种无与伦比的品质：美。其中的许多诗文都意象丰富，用语完美，节律稳定，昂扬而有力，令人浮想联翩、陶醉其中。《奥赛罗》剧中的这种诗意之美也可见于《罗密欧与朱丽叶》和《安东尼与克莉奥佩特拉》之中，这主要是因为它们均属同一题材。但《奥赛罗》还以另外一种美而著称，即：除了有丑角出现的那一段无关紧要的场景之外，全部剧情均与主题密切相关……最后，该剧还具有一种感人的德行之美（moral beauty）。这种美可直接唤起人们对道义的想象，即苔丝狄蒙娜身上所体现出的那种始终不渝、毫不动摇的爱情。"（Gardner：147）①

现谨以奥赛罗在第一幕第三场里的一段无韵诗台词为例，希望读者朋友在欣赏原文诗意美的同时，也不妨对译者就此所做的模仿或对应予以检视。

此刻，奥赛罗面对勃拉班修在公爵及众人面前对他的指控，即指责他使用了妖术或魔法将其女儿骗走，他一边派人去叫苔丝狄蒙娜前来作证，一边为自己的行为进行辩护，同时也向人们诉说了他们两人相爱的来龙去脉：

---

① 海伦·加德纳（Helen Gardner）：选自约翰·韦恩（John Wain）编著的《奥赛罗——论文选集》（*Othello—A Selection of Critical Essays*，Macmillan，1971）。

Her father loved me, oft invited me,	她的父亲爱我，常邀我做客，
130 Still questioned me the story of my life	不断询问我个人的生活详情，　130
From year to year the battles, sieges, fortunes	起止年月——我所经历的战斗、
That I have passed.	围攻和庆幸。
I ran it through, even from my boyish days	我讲述一遍，甚至从童年开始，
To th' very moment that he bade me tell it,	直到他让我陈说的时刻为止。
135 Wherein I spake of most disastrous chances,	其中谈到我最为不幸的遭遇，　135
Of moving accidents by flood and field,	谈到惊心动魄的海陆战争，
Of hair-breadth scapes i'th' imminent deadly breach,	千钧一发时从城墙豁口逃生；
Of being taken by the insolent foe	谈到被那傲慢的仇敌掳去
And sold to slavery; of my redemption thence	贩卖为奴；谈到随后的赎身
140 And portance in my travailous history;	以及艰辛的旅程中如何行动；　140
Wherein of antres vast and deserts idle,	历经巨大的洞窟，荒芜的沙漠，
Rough quarries, rocks and hills whose heads touch heaven,	嶙峋的巨石，高耸入云的　　峻岭，
……	…………
…My story being done,	……我的故事讲完以后，
160 She gave me for my pains a world of sighs,	她对我的苦难报以长吁短叹，　160
She swore in faith 'twas strange, 'twas passing strange,	并誓言这很奇怪，非常奇怪，
'Twas pitiful, 'twas wondrous pitiful;	真是可怜，不可思议的可怜；
She wished she had not heard it, yet she wished	她希望没听到这些，但又希望
That heaven had made her such a man. She thanked me	上帝将她造成这种男人。她感谢
165 And bade me, if I had a friend that loved her,	并吩咐我说，若有朋友爱她，　165
I should but teach him how to tell my story,	只要我教会他讲述我的经历，
And that would woo her. Upon this hint I spake:	即可赢得其芳心。我趁机说道：
She loved me for the dangers I had passed,	她因为我所经历的危难而爱我，
And I loved her that she did pity them.	我是因为她同情它们而爱她。
170 This only is the witchcraft I have used:	这就是我所用过的唯一妖术：　170
Here comes the lady, let her witness it.	小姐她来啦，让她自己见证吧。

就原文无韵诗的模仿与再现而言，应该说，译文尽力做到了"在双语可译性限度内，充分保留了原语的行文形式体式（stylistic format）。例如，诗歌中的格律和韵律、韵式和分节式……以及其他的行文形式特征；

例如不能将分行诗译成不分行的散文，等等"（刘宓庆：186）。

我们都知道，在伊丽莎白时代，按照惯例，作者"都应遵循规范性原则，该原则与公认的社会等级观念有关。 诸如国王、贵族、主教、上帝等高贵的人士都用韵文；诸如小丑、工人、疯子等卑贱的人物则都用散文"（Lamb：23）[1]，以此来体现不同人物的分野。 因此，"诗人把同样一句话用诗而不是散文表现出来，或者相反地用散文而不用诗表现出来，都是不能加以改变的，否则就会损伤或破坏了原有的美"（席勒格：67）[2]。

因此，考虑到莎剧的上述特点，译者遵照我国译莎前辈所倡导的"以顿代步"的翻译原则，在尽量忠实地再现原文"意美"的前提下，也尽力对原文的行文形式与内在韵律进行了模仿。 具体措施为：

（1）严格控制译文的行数，以使译文的行数与原文的行数完全相等；

（2）严格控制每行译文的字数，以此做到与原文的音节数量尽量相等，每行译文大都为十一字或十二字，其中只有两行为十三字，即 164 行和 168 行；

（3）尽量控制每行译文的顿数，以此模仿原文的行文形式与内在格律，从而再现原文应有的"形美"与"音美"效果：文中大都为五顿，只有两行为六顿，即 160 行和 164 行。

另外，译文除了在行文形式与内在格律方面尽量对原文进行了模仿以外，还尽力发挥了汉语诗歌的谐韵优势，让译文押了一些散韵或句中韵，如：133 行的"开始"与 134 行的"为止"，136 行的"战争"与 137 行的"逃生"，140 行的"行动"，142 行的"峻岭"，等等。 句中韵如：129 行的"爱我""做客"与 131 行的"年月"等。 因为"谐韵除了使诗句平添音乐性之外，还使读者产生期待、产生共鸣、产生满足。 韵律使读者的审美意识处于积极的活跃状态，是使作者与读者达至审美体验'融

---

① Sidney Lamb, Cliffs Complete Shakespeare's *Hamlet*, New York：Hungry Minds Inc. 2000.
② 威廉·席勒格，《莎士比亚研究》，上海译文出版社，1982。

合'的一种催化剂。 从翻译美学上分析，这是不少人主张译诗必须押韵的原因。"（刘宓庆：80）

四、对原文押韵诗的模仿

剧中除了无韵诗之外，还有歌谣、偶韵体等行文形式。 译文也试图做到与原文对应。 现以第一幕第三场的 18 行偶韵体翻译为例。 所谓偶韵体（couplets）也叫对句，即两行尾韵相谐的诗句。 上文提及奥赛罗向公爵及众人讲述了自己的恋爱经过，以此自证清白无辜；随后苔丝狄蒙娜来到现场，当众宣告自己也有权对夫君摩尔人尽责尽心。 苔丝狄蒙娜的这一举动使父亲勃拉班修感到悔恨交加、大失所望。 此时公爵出面，想用格言劝慰勃拉班修，勃拉班修则对此番劝慰作出回应：

DUKE　　　　　　　　　　　　　　　　　公爵

When remedies are past the griefs are ended　　事情无法补救便不再哀伤，

By seeing the worst which late on hopes depended.　既已目睹本想规避的灾殃。

205 To mourn a mischief that is past and gone　对已过去的不幸感到悲痛，　205

Is the next way to draw new mischief on.　那就自然会招致更多不幸。

What cannot be preserved when Fortune takes,　命运要夺走的不能够保全，

Patience her injury a mockery makes.　耐心使她的伤害丢人现眼。

The robbed that smiles steals something from the thief,　被盗者微笑可令盗贼被盗，

210 He robs himself that spends a bootless grief.　无益的悲伤等于自寻烦恼。　210

BRABANTIO　　　　　　　　　　　　　　勃拉班修

So let the Turk of Cyprus us beguile,　就让土耳其骗取塞浦路斯，

We lose it not so long as we can smile;　咱未失去它若能以笑置之；

He bears the sentence well that nothing bears　有谁只接受宣判中的抚慰，

But the free comfort which from thence he hears:　即可表明他这人善于受罪：

215 But he bears both the sentence and the sorrow　若靠可怜的耐心减轻忧伤，　215

That, to pay grief, must of poor patience borrow.　他既忍受宣判又忍受惆怅。

These sentences to sugar or to gall,　这些宣判的疗效相当显著，

Being strong on both sides, are equivocal.　适用于幸福，也适用于痛苦。

But words are words：I never yet did hear
　　　　但话总归是话：我从未听说

220　That the bruised heart was pierced through the ear.
　　破碎的心灵可通过耳朵愈合。　220

　　如上所述，原文属于每两行尾韵相谐的对句，译文也对此进行了相应的模仿或对应。

　　另外，考虑到"翻译是一种时空跨度很大的语际转换活动，历史的演变和社会文化的发展可以使原语成为很难为当代人透彻和准确理解的'化石'"（刘宓庆：192）。因此，"时空差产生艺术鉴赏的不等效，古今同理。……地缘之隔也必然会产生审美体验上的差异。"（同上：137）由此我们不难想象，中国的莎剧读者和观众与伊丽莎白时代的莎剧读者和观众之间会有多大的时空差异。不过，鉴于"审美主体与客体之间的关系是能动的、交互的、实践的关系"（同上：138），为了能尽量帮助读者对原文进行更好的审美体验，也为了能充分再现原文的蕴涵之美，审美主体（译者）可尽力发挥其主观能动性，即为读者架设一座跨越时空、跨越文化、跨越语言障碍的桥梁——为译文增加详尽的脚注。

　　据此，译者依照六种原文版本的相关评注甄选并翻译了大量的脚注，并附上各自的出处以便于查阅。就上述台词而言，译者选取并翻译了下列四处脚注：

　　203-4. 事情……灾殃（When…depended）：当事情已无可救药时，我们的忧伤就该到此为止，因为我们知道自己近期所希望不要发生的最坏事情业已发生（When all hope of remedy is past，our sorrows are ended by realizing that the worst has already happened which lately we hoped would not happen）（Bevington）。

　　207-8. 命运……现眼（What…makes）：当命运（女神）将我们无法保留的东西夺走时，耐心可使她的恶行成为笑柄（When fortune takes away what cannot be saved，patience makes a mockery of fortune's wrongdoing）（Bevington）。

　　217-8. 这些……痛苦（These…equivocal）：这些优美的格言模棱两可，既可适用于幸福，又可适用于痛苦（These fine maxims are equivocal，being equally appropriate to happiness or bitterness）（Bevington）。

　　220. 破碎……愈合（That…ear）：一颗破碎的心灵仅靠通过耳朵传入的话语即可得到宽慰（That the crushed heart was relieved by mere words that reach it

through the ear）（Honigmann）。

五、对原文散文的模仿

我们也知道，莎剧除了有无韵诗、歌谣、偶韵体、打油诗等文体之外，还有一种重要的组成部分——没有韵律的散文。 剧中的不同角色或者同一角色之所以采用不同的文体，都与他们的身份、谈话对象、当时的心境或语境等因素密切相关。 比如剧中的伊阿古与奥赛罗之间的对白就很少使用散文，而他跟被愚弄的威尼斯青年罗德利哥之间的对白，除了开场以外几乎全用散文，以便能更加自如地表达他们的淫心邪念。 现再转引第一幕第三场里伊阿古与罗德利哥之间的一段对白为例，予以说明。

RODERIGO

What should I do？ I confess it is my shame to be so fond， but it is not in my virtue to amend it.

IAGO

320 Virtue？ A fig！ 'Tis in ourselves that we are thus， or thus. Our bodies are gardens， to the which our wills are gardeners. So that if we will plant nettles or sow lettuce， set hyssop and weed up thyme， supply it with one gender of herbs or distract it with many， either to
325 have it sterile with idleness or manured with industry —why， the power and corrigible authority of this lies in our wills. If the balance of our lives had not one scale of reason to poise another of sensuality， the blood and baseness of our natures would conduct us
330 to most preposterous conclusions. But we have reason to cool our raging motions， our carnal stings， our unbitted lusts；whereof I take this， that you call love， to be a sect or scion.

罗德利哥

那我该咋办？我承认自己如此痴迷非常丢脸，但我又没有能力予以补救。

伊阿古

能力？去你的！我们之所以这样，或者 320
那样，全都在自己。我们的身体是花园，
意志是园丁。因此我们要栽荨麻或者种
莴苣，栽种海索草，拔除百里香，里面
只种植一种芳草，或分成小块多种几种，
或因游手好闲使它荒废，或者辛勤耕耘 325
——嗨，这种能施以矫正的权威就在于
我们的意志。假如我们生命的天平之上
没有一盘理智与另一盘肉欲抗衡，我们
身上的那些七情六欲会把我们引向一种
最为荒谬的结局。然而我们却拥有理智 330
使我们暴虐的情绪、冲动的性欲、放纵
的欲望得以平息；就你所谓的爱情而言，
我想只是一根插条或接穗。

此刻，罗德利哥目睹自己的心爱之人——苔丝狄蒙娜——当众宣告自己对奥赛罗的爱情忠贞不渝，这使他感到自惭形秽、无能为力，只好向伊阿古诉苦和求助。 伊阿古随后便动之以情、晓之以理地对他进行了一番"开导"。 此外，本段台词也可帮我们"更好地观察一下伊阿古的精神世界，以便更好地理解该悲剧之所以产生的根源。 首先，我们发现，正如剧中所暗示的那样，他这个人具有非凡的智力（powers of intellect）……同时，他这个人还具有非凡的意志力（strength of will）。 就伊阿古所表现出的自制力而言，就连苏格拉底，或恬淡寡欲的贤哲都难以超越。这不仅在于他从未背叛过自己的本色，还在于他好像能对会影响其意志的所有情绪都控制得得心应手。 在其阴谋付诸实施的险要关头，哪怕是稍有疏忽或出现意外，他都会必死无疑，而他却从未显露出丝毫的不安。当奥赛罗揪住他的脖子要他拿出证据时，他只是凭借自己惯用的机敏便化险为夷。 当他在最后遭到攻击并被刺伤时，他也丝毫不为所动……因此，我们不得不承认他这种对意志的掌控，既是他的信条又是他的践行，难能可贵，几乎令人崇敬。"（A. C. Bradley：187-8）①

我们不难看出，莎剧中的无韵诗与散文之间除了在韵律方面存在区别之外，在编排格式上也有明显的不同，即每行无韵诗的第一个单词的首字母均为大写，而且右边也没有顶格或分散对齐。 然而，每行散文的第一个单词的首字母（除句首或专有名词之外）均无须大写；而且，若某个角色的台词长度在两行以上，自第一行起至倒数第二行为止均为左右分散对齐，以此来区分散文与韵文之间的外在差异。

在这一点上，译文也试图做到与原文予以对应：以每行十七个汉字对应原文十二个左右的音节。 另外，若某个角色的台词在两行以上，自第一行起至倒数第二行为止均为字数相等、整齐划一（不包括行末的标点符号），以使散文与韵文之间的差别一目了然。

---

① A. C. Bradley, *Shakespearean Tragedy*, New York：Macmillan Press Ltd. 1992.

六、感想与希望

英国莎学专家布拉德利先生在谈及作为诗人的奥赛罗时曾说："（与莎士比亚其他悲剧中的主角相比），奥赛罗可谓其中最伟大的诗人。……我们觉得这种想象力定与他相伴终生。 他曾用诗人的眼光观看过富有疗效的树脂从阿拉伯树上流淌，目睹过印度人将千载难得的珍珠随意抛弃；他曾在令人着迷的梦幻中注视着黑海奔腾，一去不返；他曾经感受过高贵的韵文、壮丽的诗篇以及正义的战场；他的这种感受独一无二（因为他自己说起来好像如此）。 ……他就这样来到了我们的面前，既黑暗又伟岸，有一丝来自故乡的阳光映射在他的身上。"（Bradley：160-1）。

因此，若想把剧中这么"高贵的韵文、壮丽的诗篇"在译文中再现，实在很难。 所以译者在翻译及修改译文的整个过程中，既深刻体会到了莎剧的博大精深及魅力无穷，又深刻体会到了学无止境的古训是多么真切！因此，尽管他已尽了自己最大的努力，但因水平所限，文中谬误之处在所难免，敬请读者朋友批评指正！

李其金

2016 年 12 月

序　言
（节选）

最伟大的悲剧？
（The Greatest Tragedy）

　　1599 年至 1608 年前后，莎士比亚可能以下列顺序创作了一系列悲剧：《尤里乌斯·恺撒》《哈姆雷特》《奥赛罗》《李尔王》《麦克白》《安东尼与克莉奥佩特拉》《克里奥兰纳斯》，还有一部不易确定日期的——《雅典的泰门》。 世界公认这些悲剧作品确立了他在世界戏剧舞台上的领先地位；而且，也会有不少人希望称之为举世无双。 以《哈姆雷特》为首的四五部戏剧通常被视为其成就的巅峰。 许多批评家将《哈姆雷特》或《李尔王》誉为他的最佳悲剧。 为何不是《奥赛罗》最佳呢？ 作为莎氏第三部成熟的悲剧，《奥赛罗》可能包含最为精彩的情节，最具独创性的两个角色，最为震撼的场面，以及首屈一指的韵文。我们有理由将该剧称为最最动人——甚至令人难以忍受地动人——因此，为何它不是最伟大的悲剧呢？ 当然，人们不愿将《奥赛罗》视为莎氏的最佳悲剧自有其道理，而将该剧视为莎氏的最佳悲剧同样自有其道理。

创作日期与原文版本
（Date and Text）

　　创作日期：（1601 年下半年至）1602 年。 传统的说法为：1603 年或 1604 年。

原文版本：阿登第三版编者认为早期的两种版本，即四开本（Quarto）与对开本（Folio）均源自作者的手稿，至于两种版本中的某些差异可解释为莎士比亚最初的想法与日后的改动。 然而两种版本都存在不少差错及文本讹误：我们往往不太清楚其中的不同之处是该归因于作者的后来想法（authorial afterthoughts），还是该归因于文本的讹误（textual corruption）。

故事来源
（Principal Source）

该剧主要来源于意大利作家吉拉尔蒂·钦狄奥（Giraldi Cinthio）所创作的《百篇故事集》（*Hecatommithi*）（1565）。

莎士比亚在 1601 年或 1602 年开始考虑创作《奥赛罗》时，可能会断定伦敦的许多戏剧观众已经目睹，也许还曾跟摩尔人和威尼斯人进行过交谈。 至于剧中的情节，他便求助于钦狄奥的《百篇故事集》——一部短篇小说集，其中的一篇为该剧提供了故事的概要和大量的细节。 原作的故事梗概如下：

威尼斯有一位名叫苔丝狄蒙娜的淑女，爱上了一位英勇的摩尔人，不顾亲属（＝勃拉班修）的反对，跟他结婚。 他们在威尼斯幸福地度过了一些时日，直到威尼斯元老将摩尔人推选为塞浦路斯统帅为止。 她想与他相伴，于是他们一起航行。 摩尔人"连队里有一位长相俊美但最为卑鄙的旗官"（＝伊阿古），娶了一位漂亮而真诚的年轻女子（＝爱米利娅）。 这位旗官爱上了苔丝狄蒙娜；她对他未予理睬，于是他便猜想她爱上了一位下士（＝凯西奥），这位下士常去摩尔人家里做客；该旗官出于报复，决定指控苔丝狄蒙娜与下士私通。 此后不久，摩尔人因该下士在执勤期间刺伤一位士兵（＝蒙塔诺）将其官职免除。 苔丝狄蒙娜试图使摩尔人与下士和好；旗官向摩尔人暗示她这样做有其充分理由，却不愿进一步阐明，这使摩尔人痛苦万分，他开始威胁自己的妻子；但妻子的回应非常谦卑。 然后旗官对摩尔人说他妻子与下士相爱。 摩尔人勃然大怒，要求证据。 旗官有一个三岁的女儿；苔丝狄蒙娜去拜访他妻子时，旗官将孩子递给苔丝狄蒙娜，并顺手将她珍贵的手帕偷走。 他将该手帕丢进下士的房间；然后，他将摩尔人安排在能旁听他和下士谈话的地方，谈话期间下士开怀大笑；随后旗官告诉摩尔人下士已供认了自己的奸情，苔丝狄蒙娜还将那块手帕赠送给他。 某天晚饭后，摩尔人向她索要那块手帕。 她假装寻找，之后便说无法找到。 摩尔人便产生了杀妻之念。她注意到丈夫变化很大，便向她的朋友——旗官的妻子——请求忠告；而她，尽管"知道一切"（因为旗官曾企图使她成为同谋），却不敢明说，因为她怕她丈夫。 下士让手下的一位女人（＝比安卡）为他描摹那块手帕中的绣花图案；因为她是在窗前进行描摹，旗官便使摩尔人目睹了这一场景。 摩尔人便请求旗官将下士处死。 一天夜里，当下士离开一位妓女（还是＝比安卡）的房屋时，旗官用剑将他的右腿刺穿，随之逃窜。 旗官与摩尔人一起用装满沙子的长袜将苔丝狄蒙娜殴打致死，然后弄塌房顶以掩盖凶杀现场。 之后，摩尔人意识到妻子的死亡是旗官所为，便对他怀恨在心；旗官对下士说：是摩尔人刺伤了他的右腿并杀害了苔丝狄蒙娜。 下士向执政团告发。 摩尔人被带回威尼斯，遭受折磨但并不认罪；苔丝狄蒙娜的亲属出于报复，后来将其杀死。

人物述评
（Character Criticism）

对莎剧中的"人物"进行分析已不再时髦，而且还遭到了某些文学流派的批评。 无论我们是否赞同这一现代趋势，我们却不得不承认在过去的三个多世纪里，人们都将"我们的莎士比亚"（因为当时的人们都这样称谓）尊崇为人物塑造家。 "噢，莎士比亚与自然，"赫兹利特①曾叹道，改编一句著名的格言，"你们是谁抄袭了对方？"……本序言有别于赫兹利特等优秀批评家的观点，旨在强调奥赛罗与伊阿古的自身矛盾，主

① 赫兹利特（William Hazlitt）：英国作家、评论家（1778—1830），著有《莎剧人物》等。

张读者与演员可用不同的合理方式予以解读；而且，更想表明的是，奥赛罗与伊阿古本身会胜过对他们的所有评论。 我们可通过仔细观察莎氏的复杂人物获悉很多，但我们却无法探出他们内心的秘密。

奥赛罗
（Othello）

就奥赛罗的种族、服饰、年龄以及受损的视力而言，众说纷纭，难以确定。 我们不得不承认，就其人格与动机而言，我们同样也难以确定。他是充分自信，还是内心不安？ 他是爱苔丝狄蒙娜的灵魂，还是只想占有她的肉体？ 他是虔诚的基督徒，还是基督教信仰非常肤浅？ 考虑到这些问题，我们发现有两个难点。 首先，当伊阿古的毒药进入他的心灵时，他好像比别的悲剧人物变化更大：我们切勿将他的早期自我（earlier self）与他的后期自我（later self）混为一谈。 再者，当他谈及自身时，我们也不能信以为真，正如我们无法相信伊阿古的自我表露一样。 在《奥赛罗》剧中与在《哈姆雷特》剧中一样，有多种不确定性因素共存并相互作用。 某些不确定性因素可在剧院中自然消失（如，就他的视力是否受损而言，演员可自行裁决），但我们不应试图将所有不确定性因素都加以解决，因为它们在莎氏悲剧中不可或缺。

因详细介绍奥赛罗性格的篇幅有限，我想重点谈一谈几种相关的矛盾印象，因为正是这样的印象才使他好像成了一种矛盾的主体——换言之，使他成了一位血肉之躯。 他本人性格温和，也很爱"温柔的苔丝狄蒙娜"（1.2.25）；然而，当他认为自己遭到背叛时却言行野蛮。

他这种由前期自我到后期自我的发展并非径直向前，因为自 4.1.168以后我们看到他在两者之间反复摇摆，最初深信，后来却不由自主地满腹猜疑（4.2.1 及以下），但对伊阿古的信任却长此以往。 他易被说服，但对苔丝狄蒙娜绝望的恳求却无动于衷。 我们不禁会想，这些矛盾的印象或是旨在揭示奥赛罗的"另类性"（otherness），以及当时的旅行者所描述的非欧族裔（non-European races），尤其是巴巴里人①身上那种变化无常的性格。 实际上，莎士比亚对人们的反复无常倒是喜闻乐见，并在多个剧本中对此予以揭露。 然而，在奥赛罗身上，犹如在非欧族裔的卡利班②身上一样，莎士比亚以伦敦的文明优势为视角，将情绪的反复无常与其他"种族"特性（'racial' characteristics）连在一起：容易受骗、迷信、凶残、需要自我崇拜或自我贬低。 尽管人们不会将"来自殖民地的"卡利班与奥赛罗相提并论，但他们两人却可相互印证。 因此，奥赛罗不仅是一位代表人物，同时也是一位非同寻常的人物。

现在让我们看一看摩尔人的基督教信仰。 我们发现，伊阿古直接或间接地提及《圣经》的频率并不亚于奥赛罗——这是否可使他成为一位好的基督徒？ ……基督教可被用作一副面具——伊阿古有意将其戴上，奥赛罗也许无意而为，他采用一种富有战斗精神的基督徒语气，像是要阻止别人说他是外人，甚或是异教徒："看在上帝的份上，别再胡闹"（2.3.168）。 他能猜想别人如何在背后对他评头论足——"奴仆和异教徒将会掌管国事"（1.2.99）。 有些批评家将他视为一位基督教皈依者，并将他的语气归因为：他想要"比教皇更为神圣"。 别的批评家则表示反对，因为考虑到他将那位恶毒的裹头的土耳其人称为"受过割礼的贱狗"（5.2.351-3），即可证明他并非天生的穆斯林，而是天生的基督徒，因为裹头巾是穆斯林宗教的象征，割礼是其宗教仪式之一③。 然而，除了基督教之外，为什么却只有穆斯林信仰可供选择？ 为什么"奥赛罗之音（the Othello music）"就不能指向其他方向，指向一种更为原始的太阳崇拜、月亮崇拜或对自然力的崇拜，后来罩上一层基督教表象或态度？ 奥赛罗对那块手帕的首次描述（3.3.57-77）将其父母与一种莫名的异教紧密相连，可令人想起北非的巫医。

---

① 巴巴里人（Barbarians）：埃及以西的北非伊斯兰教地区居民。

② 非欧族裔的卡利班（non-European Caliban）：卡利班为莎剧《暴风雨》中丑陋而凶残的奴仆。

③ 应该指出的是，"摩尔人（a Moor）"通常被认为是伊斯兰教徒。 但就其宗教信仰而言，正像其他方面一样，奥赛罗是一个特例。

利维斯①曾围绕"真正的奥赛罗（the real Othello）"议题，向布拉德利②发起过一次有名的抨击。 利维斯指责布拉德利错误地将奥赛罗视为"非常高贵、刚强、慷慨和信赖，作为悲剧英雄……他只是一位受害者而已"。 "毫无疑问，实际上他是一位高贵的行动大汉（a nobly massive man of action），"利维斯争辩道，而"惯于自我赞许（self-approving）、自我表现（self-dramatization）是其性格的基本要素，这种自我理想化（self-idealization）变成了"一种对愚钝和野蛮的利己主义之掩饰"。 自负变成了愚蠢，残忍的愚蠢——"一种丧心病狂和自欺欺人的激情"。 布拉德利及其追随者将"真正的奥赛罗"置放在了该剧的前半部分，而利维斯则将其置放在了该剧的后半部分。 大部分批评家支持布拉德利的观点，另外的批评家则认为"真正的奥赛罗"介于两者之间。不过，假如我们抛开一种"固化的"人物观，我们也许能更接近于理解莎氏的匠心独运。 即，奥赛罗既不是什么"高贵的摩尔"，也不是什么"高贵的摩尔后来由残暴的利己主义者所取代"，任何类似的套话均忽略了其性格的复杂性。 ……简言之，我们应该将"真正的奥赛罗"视为一位过客（time traveler），跟每一位血肉之躯一样，背负着太多的心理包袱，因为谎言、误解、理想化、自欺欺人以及各种心计等我们不愿面对的事实，他对我们来说才变成了一位神秘莫测的人物。 然而，就我们对奥赛罗的理解而论，却没有多少"事实"可言，只不过是凭借印象、直觉或猜测，而随着剧情的展开，这些印象、直觉或猜测却大都会消散或者改变。 苔丝狄蒙娜，自认为了解"真正的奥赛罗"，尽管她见其面"如见其心一般"（1.3.253），也跟伊阿古一样，对他误解得一塌糊涂。 ……她从未充分地认识他；也许没人能准确地"认识"他。

奥赛罗与伊阿古两人最初都非常自信，但后来却变得愈发令人费解：奥赛罗怎么能意识不到苔丝狄蒙娜的真诚，反而相信伊阿古的谎言？ 我

---

① 利维斯（F. R. Leavis）：英国文学评论家（1895—1978），长期在英国剑桥大学教授英国文学，主要论著有《英国诗歌的新方向》等。

② 布拉德利（A. C. Bradley）：英国文学评论家（1851—1935），莎士比亚学者，著有《莎士比亚悲剧》。

们不禁自问。 总之，剧本如此设计，旨在使剧中的角色及剧院里的观众不能明了所发生的全部，因此"好奇之心"才会持续到终场。

伊阿古
（Iago）

多年来，批评家们都会在某种程度上将奥赛罗与伊阿古视为相互匹敌的对手（equal and opposite）。 …… 这种观点既值得称许，又容易产生误导。 在剧院里面，他们的角色也许会显得同样"高大"，有一位很有影响的评论家还曾将伊阿古赞誉为更加出色（布拉德利：208）。 尽管我非常欣赏伊阿古这位戏剧角色，但我认为奥赛罗这一角色的成就更大。首先，因为莎士比亚尽力告诉了我们更多关于他的故事。 其次，奥赛罗的情感变化幅度很大，而伊阿古就此而言则更为局限。 我们看到奥赛罗面临更大的压力，他摇摆不定、几近崩溃，而伊阿古始终都能保持自控；从奥赛罗的失败中，而不是从伊阿古的成功中，我们"知道"自己跟他更为熟悉。 而且，相比之下，奥赛罗与他人的关系也更为坦诚和多变；然而，尽管伊阿古与凯西奥（2.3.255 行至后）或罗德威克（4.1.264 行至后）的关系好像达到了无拘无束的程度，我们却发现其中存在着某种重复，即他需要占据上风。

奥赛罗与伊阿古在某种程度上可谓截然相反或互为补充，但伊丽莎白时代的人们也会好奇地认为他们二人很像。 根据中世纪的体液心理学（psychology of humours）可知：妒忌（jealousy）与羡慕（envy）密切相关，妒忌是"一种羡慕，而羡慕反过来就是一种嫉恨（hatred）"。 因此，奥赛罗与伊阿古所患的疾病相同，所以人们可将他们二人相提并论，因为他们均为职业军人，携带妻子外出服役，感到被妻子背叛，将他们杀害，并因此自我毁灭。 他们均为局外之人，奥赛罗为摩尔人，伊阿古对特权心怀不满；他们都与自己的同类保持距离，都想被他人接受。 上述某些相似之处为莎氏所增添，因为他喜欢情节对称（钦狄奥的旗官对凯西奥的阶层优越感并不怨恨，因为那位下士并非他的上司，他也没有杀害自己的妻子），然而，奥赛罗与伊阿古之间的差异定会远超他们的相同之处。

隐藏的动机或下意识的动机在莎氏的所有悲剧中都非常重要，这一点在《奥赛罗》剧中尤为明显。 早在弗洛伊德之前，莎氏便对睡梦和内心生活颇感兴趣，这一点也可帮助阐释奥赛罗与伊阿古两人的魅力之所在。伊阿古确实捏造了凯西奥的通奸之梦（3.3.416-30），因为他清楚奥赛罗会充分理解这种下意识的自我流露意味着什么。 而伊阿古本人的下意识动机同样也显而易见——他对社会特权的忿恨，他的轻蔑，他对权力的喜爱，以及他对操纵别人的自鸣得意——与其自视高明和怀才不遇的痛苦密切相连。

他对特权的忿恨显然体现于艺术高超的开场。 只会"纸上空谈的"凯西奥得以提拔，而他这位久经沙场的士兵，却被忽略——"而我，上帝宽恕，做黑阁下的旗官！"在一个主仆分明的世界里，尽管他不是"主人的驴子"，却是一位仆人。 勃拉班修说他"你是一个流氓"，他立刻回击道"您是……一个议员！"对特权的忿恨之情将类似的片段串连一起，并且往往是一触即发，这倒会让人感到他这种动机要比他对凯西奥与奥赛罗的痛恨更为强烈。 当凯西奥对苔丝狄蒙娜示以礼貌时，他的格外愤怒便会油然而生："对，对她笑，笑吧：我就用你的殷勤将你套住。 ……吻得好，多有礼貌！"当然，凯西奥也曾以居高临下的态度待他：

> 你可别恼羞成怒，好伊阿古，
> 我要向她致意；是我的教养
> 促使我如此大胆地示以礼貌。

（2.1.97-9）

——伊阿古对此无法忍受。 另一处体现"阶层意识（class feeling）"的事例可帮助阐释其未被提升为副官的怨恨之情：当他遇见葛莱西亚诺与罗德威克两位威尼斯贵族时，他们认出他是奥赛罗的旗官，"一位非常勇敢的男子"；但他们忘了他的名字，而他却知道他们的名字。

伊阿古　　　　罗德威克先生？

罗德威克　　　正是。（5.1.67-8）

随后，

伊阿古	葛莱西亚诺先生？我求您原谅：
	这些血腥的事故迫使我忽略了
	对您的礼节。
葛莱西亚诺	见到您我很高兴。（5.1.93-5）

现在是他首先提及自己的"礼节"，以此模仿他在独白中曾经嘲弄的"礼仪"。他想被人接纳为同类，因此他将凯西奥称为"兄弟"（本场71行）。此外，他想到罗德利哥的"身份"会被确认时，便将其呼为"我的朋友和亲爱的同胞"（5.1.89，102）。他多次以"绅士们"一词向威尼斯人邀宠（"掌灯，绅士们""诸位绅士，我怀疑这个贱货""先别走，绅士们""看见了，绅士们？""好绅士"……），希望他们能将他接纳为其中的一员，结果却事与愿违：一位绅士可不会这般举动。……胜过不幸的罗德利哥这位上层社会的成员，可以弥补这样的羞辱——特权阶层所拥有的那种优雅洒脱会"使我相形见绌"（5.1.20）。

伊阿古，作为艺术家，常被视为玩弄奥赛罗这头公牛的斗牛士，或作为剧作家，被视为许多剧情的创造者，他也从中得到满足。"愉快和忙碌的时光不会显长"（2.3.374）！他的演技乍一看也许并无过人之处：一开始他通过胡诌掌控了罗德利哥，随后躲在暗处激怒勃拉班修——一位特权阶层的代表。他对罗德利哥的盘剥及轻蔑之情在第一幕第三场已更为露骨（"把钱装进你的口袋"）；登上塞浦路斯岛之后，他作为谈话的主宰，其演技又得以充分地展示；采取冒险行动，在第二幕第三场挑起酗酒滋事，但全在其掌控之中。解释事故来龙去脉的大段台词（2.3.216-42），以及随后对凯西奥的"安慰"，使我们更为清晰地意识到了他的操纵技巧：他假装诚实和出于善意，说服别人接受他对事态的看法——按照他自己的观点——一种冒险的赌博。诱惑片段（the temptation scene）（3.3.92行及以下），也许是莎剧中最为惊心动魄的场景，由此开始逐渐展示伊阿古出众的戏剧天赋——莎士比亚式的天赋，也许我们可以说，莎氏作为伊阿古的创造者，将他本人的口才与心理洞察赋予了伊阿古。

"权力是我的情人，"拿破仑曾说，"但我是以一位艺术家的身份热爱权力。 我热爱权力犹如一位音乐家热爱他的小提琴一般。"罗德利哥、凯西奥与奥赛罗都是伊阿古的小提琴。 他发现要想"玩弄"苔丝狄蒙娜与爱米利娅却没那么容易，因为，尽管他聪明机敏，但他并不了解女人，正是这一点最终将他毁灭。

我想，最好以下列注脚向奥赛罗与伊阿古辞别：他们犹如音乐一般对我们娓娓道来，首尾呼应。 他们有各自的人格，富有局限但令人信服，只有莎士比亚才能对此心领神会。 我们只能感受，纵然想加以评判却无法言传。 "听罢阿波罗①的天籁之音，墨丘利②的话语便会显得刺耳"。

苔丝狄蒙娜
（Desdemona）

尽管该角色常由成年女性扮演，但有许多迹象表明苔丝狄蒙娜非常年轻，几乎像个孩子；比如，爱米利娅有关她与那块手帕的言论，"她时刻把手帕带在身边／跟它说话亲吻"（3.3.299-300），还有伊阿古的类似言论，"她那么年轻就这么会装样"（3.3.212；另见4.2.113行及以下，及4.3.82行）。 她与爱米利娅的关系很像朱丽叶与奶妈之间的关系，而她对爱米利娅的感情依赖更大。 我们也许该把她当成十五六岁的样子，而不是现代意义上的所谓"夫人（lady）"。 （人们确实把她称为"夫人"，但对朱丽叶也是这样称谓。）剧中的几乎每一个角色都误解了苔丝狄蒙娜。 勃拉班修把她称为"一位羞怯的姑娘"（1.3.95）；伊阿古认为"她定会变心"（1.3.352）；罗德利哥以为她可以用金钱收买。 有些女权主义批评家认为凯西奥同样弄错——"她真是完美无缺"（2.3.25）。 奥赛罗跟凯西奥一样，也将她理想化；我们可根据他的一次相当笼统的感叹：

---

① 阿波罗（Apollo）：即希腊神话与罗马神话中的太阳神，掌管音乐、诗歌等。
② 墨丘利（Mercury）：罗马神话中众神的信使。

> 噢，该死的婚姻！
>
> 我们能拥有这些尤物的躯体，
>
> 却不能拥有其情欲！

（3.3.272-4）

推断出她的性欲觉醒令他吃惊。 类似的误判表明问题大都出在说话者身上，而不是出在苔丝狄蒙娜身上。

有几位批评家觉得苔丝狄蒙娜"与伊阿古的低俗闲谈"（2.1.100 行及以下）令人反感——"莎剧中最令人失望的片段之一"（M. R. Ridley）。 维多利亚时代的舞台监管也会将其中的某些"粗俗"对话删节。美国第六任总统约翰·亚当斯的反应则更为强烈。 "谁会同情苔丝狄蒙娜？"他说，"她竟爱上一位黑摩尔并与他私奔……她不仅违背了自己对父亲、对家庭、对女性、对国家应尽的义务，而且她还采取了主动！"舞台监管及总统均为时代的产物。 至于该片段的目的，我们今天可以说，就是想表明苔丝狄蒙娜也懂得人情世故。 该片段还表明，随着伊阿古的戏谑越来越近乎淫秽而她也坚持攀谈，说明她不懂该何时住嘴——正如她要求奥赛罗将凯西奥召回时的情景一样（3.3.41-83，3.4.90 行及以下）。 她在剧中前半部分的过分自信可折射出她的天真无邪，她这种品质一直持续到终场。

她在该剧后半部分的表现有时会被指责为过分被动。 但我们应该记住，她的力量在一定程度上有赖于奥赛罗的恩爱：自从奥赛罗拒绝了她的手帕之后（3.4.51 行及以下），她的自信才开始受挫。 此后她好像显得有些被动；与其说她已从此败下阵来，倒不如说她是发自内心的迷惑不解。 没错，苔丝狄蒙娜是向奥赛罗的愤怒表示了屈服，尽管现代的妻子也许会拒绝如此，但我们仍不妨将她视为剧中最为坚强、最为崇高的人物。

爱米利娅

（Emilia）

爱米利娅，因为不如丈夫那么复杂，在演出时常被简化和歪曲。 她的装扮是否应该已到中年且相貌平平？ 若如此，人们不禁要问伊阿古为何会娶她，而且奥赛罗可能与她相爱（2 1.293 行至后）这种想法也会显得荒唐可笑。 伊阿古既"已在这个世界上观望了四七二十八年"（1.3.312-13），钦狄奥对旗官之妻的描述因此也适用于爱米利娅——"一位漂亮和诚实的年轻女子"（见故事来源）。 她的年龄定会比苔丝狄蒙娜更大，假定为二十五岁上下，显然楚楚动人。 因此伊阿古才会对她产生性占有欲望：他也许不爱她，但她有个情人这种可能却"像有毒的矿物腐蚀我肺腑"（2.1.295）。 尽管伊阿古与奥赛罗有别，但他们两人都在遭受相似的折磨——想象自己让人给戴了绿帽儿。

钦狄奥的叙述可帮我们阐释另一个相关的问题——爱米利娅对丈夫的感受。 钦狄奥的"爱米利娅"知道旗官想杀害苔丝狄蒙娜的阴谋，拒绝相助，但"因害怕丈夫，不敢据实相告。 她只是说：'注意别给您丈夫留下任何可怀疑的理由……'"。 出于对伊阿古的恐惧，尽管剧中没有明说，爱米利娅的这种态度随着悲剧的展开而得以彰显。 当他们二人首次单独出现时（3.3.304-23），他的嘲弄与她的怨恨表明他们并非亲密无间。 这种关系要比原作中的夫妻关系更为针锋相对，但他们这种关系却相当自然——考虑到他们在剧中的角色——直到后来发展为妻子蔑视丈夫以及丈夫残忍地报复妻子，这些内容均属莎氏所添加。

被卷入伊阿古阴谋中的爱米利娅，应该负有多少罪责？ 当苔丝狄蒙娜问她"我会在哪里丢了那手帕，爱米利娅？"而她却谎称，"我不知道，夫人"（3.4.23-4），人们的疑问此刻便会油然而生。 寥寥数语，但事关重大。 她若不是害怕伊阿古，可能会据实以告，伊阿古的阴谋便会由此败露。 莎氏还特意安排将谴责谎言的最为激愤的言论针对爱米利娅而发（"她像个跌入炽烈地狱的撒谎者"，5.2.127），爱米利娅随之便感到"报告真相"义不容辞。 她的"我不知道，夫人"也许不该被罚入炽烈的地狱，然而，当奥赛罗那么急切地盘问那块手帕时（3.4.52-99），她沉默不语又当何论？ 莎士比亚有意让爱米利娅耳闻目睹两人之间的激烈冲突，她不会不明白她撒谎的后果有多么严重。 但是，因为害怕，她只是警告苔丝狄蒙娜而未直接指责伊阿古（正如原作中旗官的妻子那

样）——"难道这人不妒忌？"（3.4.100）

我们现在须注意爱米利娅曾再三重复的一种声明：伊阿古"曾经上百次／求我把它偷走"；她称之为"您经常让我把它偷来的那块"；以及询问"您用它做啥，竟然这么迫切地／让我把它偷来？"（3.3.296-7，313，318-19）。 莎士比亚想让我们知道，伊阿古对那块手帕特别在意且爱米利娅也心知肚明——这一点在终场时再次得以重复，并直接导致了她的死亡。

> 因为他五次三番一本正经
> ——对这种物品本不该如此认真——
> 求我把它偷走。
>
> （5.2.225-7）

因此，爱米利娅在手帕片段里（the handkerchief scene）本该怀疑她那"古怪的丈夫"与奥赛罗的暴怒有某种牵连（3.4.51 行及以下）。 也许她确实怀疑。 这种怀疑也许体现在她对苔丝狄蒙娜的毁谤者的怒斥之中——

> 我以性命打赌,若非哪个恶棍……
> 编造了这种谗言,就把我绞死!
>
> （4.2.132-5）

——她尽可能直接地表达了她的怀疑。 然而，假如她的怀疑得以佐证，那么后果将会令人恐惧；因此，她便采取了一种权宜之计，认可了伊阿古对此的矢口否认，即"呸，哪有这种人呢！ 这不可能"。 后来当伊阿古的罪责变得确凿无疑时，爱米利娅重新提及了这次交锋。

> 罪恶,罪恶,罪恶!
> 我想起来啦,我有所察觉,罪恶啊!
> 果不出所料:我真是悲痛欲绝!
>
> （5.2.187-9）

"果不出所料"：她可能是指她想到了 4.2.132 行及以下的情况，即哪位流氓有意诽谤苔丝狄蒙娜；或者是她"当时"想到了伊阿古会对此负责。

这两种可能性表明莎士比亚或是想让我们觉得爱米利娅特别愚笨，或是将她描绘得太怕伊阿古（正如原作中旗官的妻子那样），不敢对他挑战，直到为时太晚。

爱米利娅值得人们关注：她与丈夫之间的关系变化，以及她在道义方面的升华均展现了莎士比亚对细节的驾驭能力不同凡响。

人际关系
（Relationships）

尽管评论界不会轻易予以认可，但莎士比亚注意到了人际关系的变化与人物性格的拓展同样动人心弦。 剧中的奥赛罗与伊阿古之间的关系已受到人们的广泛关注，然而奥赛罗与苔丝狄蒙娜两人心理上的关系同样值得关注。 我们也许可将该剧视为一位老作家所写的《罗密欧与朱丽叶》，只是《奥赛罗》剧中的两位理想主义者的婚姻涉及更多的情感因素。 从最初到第三幕第三场，可谓他们对浪漫爱情的欣喜若狂；随后夫妻关系遇到困扰，这时我们才意识到奥赛罗与苔丝狄蒙娜彼此之间几乎毫无了解。 他们年龄悬殊且种族不同，怎能一起体验生活？

莎士比亚将这种夫妻关系的破裂追溯到了它的本源，即苔丝狄蒙娜非常慷慨的感情冲动，这种因素在伊阿古的阴谋成形之前便已存在。 在求爱片段中（the wooing scene），如奥赛罗所说，她迈出了大胆的一步，然后又要求陪他前往塞浦路斯——两种不合习俗的举动。 当我们首次见他们两人独处时，她再次想对他发号施令，要求让凯西奥官复原职（3.3.41行及以下）。 她做得倒是颇为巧妙，将自己的干预归属于妻子般的关心；他对此有些不满，而她却不依不饶。 此处她首次选择了一种导致冲突的轨道，因为他已公开和明确地对凯西奥说过，"再也别做我的官员了"（2.3.245），而她恰好在此时入场，无疑会听到他的上述言辞。 甚至在此之前，当奥赛罗凯旋返回塞浦路斯时，她也纠正过奥赛罗。 针对他的"吉凶未卜的命运再也不会有／类似的慰藉"，她回答说"但愿上帝保佑／我们的爱情以及幸福能够／与日俱增"；以此回绝了他对爱情与

"命运"的悲观之念。

苔丝狄蒙娜为凯西奥求情的举动（3.3.41 行及以下）也很合乎常情，这一点可从她此前与奥赛罗之间的关系判定，尽管这在一定程度上属于伊阿古策划的家庭冲突。 接下来，当她叫他去午餐时（3.3.284），他因为无法温情地回答，便假装自己头疼。 她再次试图予以操控，开始为他包头：他拒绝那块手帕——以及嫌弃苔丝狄蒙娜的手势——应是该剧的重要转折点。 随后，她忽略了所有的危险信号并再次要求让凯西奥官复原职；甚至当他有些命令似的叫她去取回那块手帕时，她却依然为凯西奥求情。 在奥赛罗看来，尚不论伊阿古有关她的谎言是否真实，她的举动必定无法忍受，因为她再次试图对他发号施令。 她无意之间好像怀疑了他的男子气概；他因为在口才方面无法胜出，于是便像其他丈夫一样，退而求诸暴力。 而她，意识到自己的冲动竟会导致如此意外的后果，随之便抑制自己的感情，抛弃自己的天性，她在最后两幕几乎变成了另外一人。丈夫与妻子像这样拴在一起的事例也许相当独特，但夫妻关系的动态变化对我们来说却不会陌生：许多婚姻都属于类似的模式。 奥赛罗与苔丝狄蒙娜不仅是在为他们自己辩护，也是在为所有的丈夫与妻子代言。

剧中还有另外两种"家庭"关系，有迹象表明都是由莎氏创建，也都进展迅速。 伊阿古与爱米利娅和凯西奥与比安卡之间的关系，包括彼此的怀疑、突然的怨恨、控制权的争夺、相互蔑视，而且（其中一例）也犯下了杀妻之罪，以此对奥赛罗与苔丝狄蒙娜之间的关系予以衬托。 每一种关系都随着男女双方的发展而自然演变，同时也与其他各种发展中的关系同步进展。 值得注意的是，其他几种非家庭关系也是如此：比如伊阿古与凯西奥之间的关系，凯西奥与苔丝狄蒙娜之间的关系，苔丝狄蒙娜与爱米利娅之间的关系。

女权主义
（Feminism）

莎士比亚已在《罗密欧与朱丽叶》中将朱丽叶描绘得更为成熟——同

样热情，但在爱情的追求上却更富远见和坚定。 创作时间略早于《奥赛罗》的两部喜剧，即《皆大欢喜》与《第十二夜》，业已展示了这种"女权主义者"偏见——赋予女主角更多的感情与理智。 《奥赛罗》中的女人也被用以表明类似的观点。 苔丝狄蒙娜、爱米利娅与比安卡均被她们的男人甩在一边，前两位还被视为不忠，尽管我们知道她们都比丈夫更加忠诚；三位女人对爱情的付出均毫不吝啬，在这方面远超她们自私和抱有成见的丈夫。 人们确实不禁要问，男人是否会有无私的爱情？ 难道奥赛罗不是太容易变卦？ 比安卡对凯西奥的关心难道没超过凯西奥对她的关心？ 假如爱米利娅学会不去爱伊阿古，那么她对苔丝狄蒙娜的忠诚——这种忠诚迫使她谴责自己的丈夫——难道不是剧中最为有力和最为真挚的感情？

《杨柳歌》片段（*The Willow Song scene*）（4.3），尽管在演出时常遭大量删节，但对我们理解这种感情却必不可少，并使剧中的女权主义得以确证。 爱米利娅有关双重标准的慷慨陈词（4.3.85 行及以下）表明两位妻子均已遭受过丈夫的蔑视和情绪粗暴：她们彼此之间的默默同情激起了一种精神力量，这种力量后来挑战并战胜了奥赛罗与伊阿古所体现出的男人品性。 该歌曲本身引入了一种停顿——或者说，好让以苔丝狄蒙娜的"卸妆"为起点的慢动作得以持续。 这种卸妆，无论是指她的头发还是指她的套裙，都需要温存的身体接触并伴有沉默。 这种沉默，跟身体接触一样，表明两人情同手足，然而两人都在思虑各自的心事。 伴随着苔丝狄蒙娜的沉思，那首杨柳歌突然浮现，她从中想起了自己的困境，而且哼唱得如此动人，爱米利娅需用一种新的音调予以回答（此前她曾厉声劝道"喂，喂，别瞎说"，23 行）——

苔丝狄蒙娜 这是否预示着哭泣？

爱米利娅 那毫不相干。

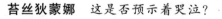

（4.3.58）

——她说话的口气不再像是一位仆人，而更像是一位呵护自己孩子的母亲。 该歌曲本身，以及两人在歌曲前后看似无足轻重的闲谈，是一种饱含女性温情与深情厚谊的高潮，唯有《李尔王》中的考迪丽娅向苏醒与困惑中的父亲讲话时的情景（4.7）可与此相提并论。

温情也许并非我们今天所理解的女权主义的特征。 然而，莎士比亚，曾帮助促成了包括女权主义在内的许多文化变革，实事求是地将女性的温情视为一种道德力量。 在《奥赛罗》剧中，这不仅包括在舞台上现身的那三位女人，同时也包括杨柳歌中的那位不幸的巴巴莉，以及需要那块手帕护身的奥赛罗的母亲：

> 可她一旦丢失，
>
> 或者赠送别人，我父亲就会
>
> 把她视为可厌，他的心思便会
>
> 另寻新欢。

（3.4.62-5）

《奥赛罗》剧中的女权主义，尽管不如《皆大欢喜》中那样明显，却已远远超过了《罗密欧与朱丽叶》。 在战火笼罩的塞浦路斯，女性的品质可谓"更加坚韧"。 这种传统的基督教观念并未将苔丝狄蒙娜的角色视为被动：她在剧中的道德征战中矢志不渝地维护并彰显了基督教美德（爱心、耐心、宽容）。 天使战胜了恶魔；她的道德力量可以分享"上帝的恩典"（2.1.85），尤其是她"撒谎"去保护自己的丈夫这一举动，可谓莎士比亚最为崇高的笔触之一。

> 没有谁。我自己。永别了。
>
> 向我亲爱的丈夫致意——噢，永别了！

（5.2.122-3）

[英]霍尼希曼

E. A. J. Honigmann

LIST OF ROLES

Othello *the Moor [a general in the service of Venice]*

Brabantio *father to Desdemona [a Venetian senator]*

Cassio *an honourable lieutenant [who serves under Othello]*

Iago *a villain [Othello's ancient or ensign]*

Roderigo *a gulled gentleman [of Venice]*

Duke *of Venice*

Senators *[of Venice]*

Montano *governor of Cyprus [replaced by Othello]*

Gentlemen *of Cyprus*

Lodovico *noble Venetian [Desdemona's cousin]*

Gratiano *noble Venetian [Desdemona's uncle]*

Sailor

Clown

Desdemona *wife to Othello [and Brabantio's daughter]*

Emilia *wife to Iago*

Bianca *a courtesan [and Cassio's mistress]*

[Messenger, Herald, Officers, Gentlemen, Musicians and Attendants

Scene: *Act I*, *Venice*; *Acts* Ⅱ - Ⅴ , *Cyprus*]

剧中人物

奥赛罗　　　摩尔人［威尼斯城邦的现任将军］

勃拉班修　　苔丝狄蒙娜的父亲［威尼斯元老院议员］

凯西奥　　　［奥赛罗部下］一正直的副官

伊阿古　　　恶棍［奥赛罗的旗手或掌旗官］

罗德利哥　　［威尼斯］一被哄骗的绅士

公爵　　　　威尼斯

元老院议员　［威尼斯］

蒙塔诺　　　塞浦路斯总督［由奥赛罗接替］

绅士　　　　塞浦路斯

罗德威克　　威尼斯贵族［苔丝狄蒙娜的堂兄］

葛莱西亚诺　威尼斯贵族［苔丝狄蒙娜的叔父］

水手

小丑

苔丝狄蒙娜　奥赛罗的妻子［勃拉班修的女儿］

爱米利娅　　伊阿古的妻子

比安卡　　　一妓女［凯西奥的情人］

［信差、传令官、军官、绅士、乐师及侍从。

地点：第一幕，威尼斯；第二幕至第五幕，塞浦路斯］

第一幕
ACT I

SCENE I

Enter Roderigo and Iago.

Roderigo Tush, never tell me, I take it much unkindly
That thou, Iago, who hast had my purse
As if the strings were thine, shouldst know of this.

Iago 'Sblood, but you'll not hear me. If ever I did dream
Of such a matter, abhor me.

5 **Roderigo**   Thou told'st me
Thou didst hold him in thy hate.

Iago   Despise me
If I do not. Three great ones of the city,
In personal suit to make me his lieutenant,
Off-capped to him, and by the faith of man,

10   I know my price, I am worth no worse a place.
But he, as loving his own pride and purposes,
Evades them, with a bombast circumstance
Horribly stuffed with epithets of war,
And in conclusion,

2

第一场

伊阿古与罗德利哥上。

罗德利哥　　呸！我不信，我对此非常不满，

你，伊阿古，随便使用我的钱袋，

好像拉绳由你掌控，竟知道此事。

伊阿古　　该死，您不听我说！我若曾梦到

会有此事，厌弃我。

罗德利哥　　　　　　　你对我说过　　　　　　　　　　5

你对他怀恨在心。

伊阿古　　　　　　　　我若不恨他，

您鄙视我。　城邦的三位贵人，

亲自求他让我做他的副官，

向他脱帽致敬；说句良心话，

我知道我的身价，能胜任该职。　　　　　　　　10

然而他，自命不凡、独断专行，

利用浮夸的言辞进行敷衍，

满口充斥着有关战争的辞令：

总而言之，

1.1. 地点：威尼斯，勃拉班修住宅外面的大街。　伊阿古与罗德利哥像是已争论了一番。　时间为夜晚（E. A. J. Honigmann；Arden Shakespeare, Third Series, 2008；即本译文的蓝本；下称"Honigmann"。　文中的所有脚注，若未标明出处，均出自该书。——译者附注）。3. 拉绳（strings）：用手一拉，即可将钱袋封住的绳子。　此事（this）：通常指奥赛罗与苔丝狄蒙娜的结婚（M. R. Ridley；Arden Shakespeare, Second Series, 1966；下称"Ridley"。——译者附注）。6. 他（him）：奥赛罗，直到本场第32行才指明其身份，在此遭到伊阿古的执意歪曲。

15   Nonsuits my mediators. For 'Certes,' says he,

'I have already chose my officer.'

And what was he?

Forsooth, a great arithmetician,

One Michael Cassio, a Florentine,

20   A fellow almost damned in a fair wife,

That never set a squadron in the field

Nor the division of a battle knows

More than a spinster—unless the bookish theoric,

Wherein the toged consuls can propose

25   As masterly as he. Mere prattle without practice

Is all his soldiership—but he, sir, had th'election

And I, of whom his eyes had seen the proof

At Rhodes, at Cyprus and on other grounds,

Christian and heathen, must be be-leed and calmed

30   By debitor and creditor. This counter-caster

回绝我的求情者。 "的确，"他说， 　　　　　15

"我已经选择好了我的副官。"

那是谁呢？

毫无疑问，一位伟大的数学家，

迈克尔·凯西奥，佛罗伦萨人，

因娶了娇妻而几乎遭殃的家伙，　　　　20

他从来没有带队上过战场，

至于摆兵布阵，不比娘儿们

懂得更多——不过是纸上空谈，

就此而言，犹如身穿官袍的

元老：只会空谈而毫无实践，　　　　25

是其军人本色——而他，居然当选，

可我，他曾目睹我在罗德岛、

塞浦路斯、基督教和异教徒的

国土上表现出色，却要对账房

先生甘拜下风。 这位数数的，　　　　30

---

16. 选择……副官（chose my officer）：指挥官可任命并解除自己的官员，因此也可谓是他们的"主人"（masters）（43 行）。 19. 佛罗伦萨人（a Florentine）：马基雅维利被视为典型的佛罗伦萨人，因此"一位狡猾的恶魔（a crafty devil）"。 20. 因……家伙（A…wife）：对此有多种解释，我觉得有一句意大利谚语对正确理解本句应有所帮助："你娶了一位娇妻？ 你就会遭殃（You have married a fair wife？ You are damned.）"。 若考虑到我们随后会发现凯西奥并不想与比安卡结婚，而是保持一定距离，伊阿古的言论可能与该谚语有关。 但我认为格兰维尔（Granville Barker, 1877—1946，英国演员、剧作家、评论家）的解释非常可取。 他指出原作故事中的凯西奥有一位妻子（曾帮他"描下"了手帕里的图案）。 因为"莎士比亚在写该句台词时，是想按照这种情节发展下去。 但后来，出于更好的理由，他改变了主意，而是让比安卡充当了凯西奥的情人，却忘了更改第一场中的这句台词"（Ridley）。 迎娶娇妻的男人因注定要做"乌龟"，所以他会遭殃（Jonathan Bate; Royal Shakespeare Company, 2008；下称"Bate"）。 ——译者附注）。 22. 娘儿们（spinster）：家庭妇女，以纺织为业（a housewife, one whose regular occupation is spinning）（David Bevington, Bantam Classic, 2005；下称"Bevington"）。 借鉴卞之琳先生的译文；下称"卞译"）。 ——译者附注）。 24. 身穿官袍（toged = togèd）：身穿托加袍（wearing a toga）——古罗马元老院议员及其他高官的典型服饰（Ridley）。 27. 罗德岛：地中海岛屿，位于塞浦路斯与希腊之间（Bate）。 28. 塞浦路斯：地中海岛屿，位于土耳其南部（Bate）。 30. 甘拜下风（be-leed）：可能指（一艘航行的船只）处在一艘敌船的背风面（下风），因无法扬帆而无能为力。

He, in good time, must his lieutenant be,

And I, God bless the mark, his Moorship's ancient!

Roderigo   By heaven, I rather would have been his hangman.

Iago   Why, there's no remedy, 'tis the curse of service:

35   Preferment goes by letter and affection,

And not by old gradation, where each second

Stood heir to th' first. Now sir, be judge yourself

Whether I in any just term am affined

To love the Moor.

Roderigo   I would not follow him then.

40 **Iago**   O sir, content you!

I follow him to serve my turn upon him.

We cannot all be masters, nor all masters

Cannot be truly followed. You shall mark

Many a duteous and knee-crooking knave

45   That, doting on his own obsequious bondage,

Wears out his time much like his master's ass,

For nought but provender, and, when he's old, cashiered.

Whip me such honest knaves! Others there are

Who, trimmed in forms and visages of duty,

50   Keep yet their hearts attending on themselves

And, throwing but shows of service on their lords,

Do well thrive by them, and, when they have lined their coats,

Do themselves homage: these fellows have some soul,

And such a one do I profess myself. For, sir,

　　　　　　　他,趁机,倒当上了他的副官,

　　　　　　　而我,上帝宽恕,做黑阁下的旗官!

罗德利哥　　向天发誓,我宁愿做他的刽子手。

伊阿古　　　唉,没办法,当兵的活该倒霉,

　　　　　　　晋升要靠他人的举荐和偏爱,　　　　　　　35

　　　　　　　而不是按照资历,从下往上

　　　　　　　依次提拔:先生,您自己想想,

　　　　　　　我是否要毕恭毕敬对这个摩尔

　　　　　　　忠心耿耿。

罗德利哥　　　　　　　　我可不愿跟随他了。

伊阿古　　　噢,先生,您放心。　　　　　　　　40

　　　　　　　我跟随他是为了自己的利益:

　　　　　　　大家不可能都当主人,也不是

　　　　　　　每个主人都值得跟随。　您注意,

　　　　　　　许多尽心尽职、卑躬屈膝的奴才,

　　　　　　　对自己的遭受奴役乐此不疲,　　　　　　45

　　　　　　　活像主人的驴子度过一生,

　　　　　　　只为一口草料,老了后,被抛弃。

　　　　　　　这么老实的家伙该抽! 有些人,

　　　　　　　他们,装模作样,虚情假意,

　　　　　　　一门心思关注自己的利益,　　　　　　　50

　　　　　　　摆出一副为主人效力的样子,

　　　　　　　却依靠他们发家,口袋鼓起,

　　　　　　　为自己谋利,这些人颇有心计,

　　　　　　　我承认自己属于这么一类……因为,先生

---

　　32. 旗官(ancient):旗手(standard-bearer, ensign)(Bate)。　47. 草料(provender):学徒和仆人的报酬往往就是在主人家里免费吃住。　54. 因为,先生(For, sir):格外音节(extra-metrical)。

55   It is as sure as you are Roderigo,

Were I the Moor, I would not be Iago.

In following him, I follow but myself:

Heaven is my judge, not I for love and duty,

But seeming so, for my peculiar end,

60   For when my outward action doth demonstrate

The native act and figure of my heart

In complement extern, 'tis not long after

But I will wear my heart upon my sleeve

For daws to peck at: I am not what I am.

65 **Roderigo**   What a full fortune does the thicklips owe

If he can carry't thus!

   Iago   Call up her father,

Rouse him, make after him, poison his delight,

Proclaim him in the streets, incense her kinsmen,

And, though he in a fertile climate dwell,

70   Plague him with flies! Though that his joy be joy,

Yet throw such changes of vexation on't

As it may lose some colour.

   Roderigo   Here is her father's house, I'll call aloud.

	正像您不是别人,而是罗德利哥,	55
	我若是那摩尔,就不会做伊阿古。	
	跟随他,不过是我跟随我自己。	
	上帝自会评判,我并非尽心尽职,	
	只是摆摆样子,为了个人目的。	
	因为我的外在行为若展示	60
	其本色,显露我的真心实意,	
	毫无遮掩,那就用不了多久,	
	我会把自己的心肺挂在袖口,	
	让乌鸦啄噬:我可是似是而非。	

罗德利哥 那厚嘴唇将有多大一笔财富,　　　　65
　　　　　假如他能成行!

伊阿古 　　　　　　　把她父亲叫醒,
　　　　惊扰他,追赶他,要令他扫兴,
　　　　将他公之于众,激怒她的亲族,
　　　　虽然他正沉浸在温柔乡里,
　　　　用苍蝇烦扰他;尽管他满心欢喜, 70
　　　　也要尽可能使他心烦意乱,
　　　　让他的喜乐黯然失色。

罗德利哥 她父亲就住在这里,我要大喊。

---

56. 我若是……伊阿古（Were I…Iago）：多数解读者均未对本句予以评注,但我觉得这句话并非那么直白易懂。 若将伊阿古这句话理解为"我若是主人,就不会做仆人",听起来未免有些奇怪和无力。 但大家可能会注意到,莎士比亚好像有意让伊阿古花言巧语,起初似乎非常动听且意味深长,但一经细查却言之无物。 请参考"人们应该表里如一,若并非如此,愿他们别装模作样。"（3. 3. 129-130）（Ridley）。 65. 那厚嘴唇（the thicklips）：该术语在伊丽莎白时代常指"黑人（negroes）"（Bevington）。 67. 惊扰他,追赶他,要令他扫兴（Rouse…his delight）：就文中的"him（他）"而言,存在着不同的理解：E. Honigmann 先生的注释为"i. e. Brabantio（指勃拉班修）"。 Barbara A. Mowat 女士（Folger Shakespeare Library,1993；下称"Mowat"）对"after him"的注释为"go after Othello（追赶奥赛罗）"。 译者更倾向于 Mowat 女士的观点,因为该句中的第三个短语"要令他扫兴（poison his delight）",若指向奥赛罗可能会更为合理,因为他此刻"正沉浸在温柔乡里"。 ——译者附注。

Iago	Do, with like timorous accent and dire yell	
75	As when, by night and negligence, the fire	
	Is spied in populous cities.	
Roderigo	What ho! Brabantio, Signior Brabantio, ho!	
Iago	Awake, What ho, Brabantio! Thieves, thieves, thieves!	
	Look to your house, your daughter, and your bags!	
80	Thieves, thieves!	

Brabantio [appears above] at a window.

Brabantio	What is the reason of this terrible summons?	
	What is the matter there?	
Roderigo	Signior, is all your family within?	
Iago	Are your doors locked?	
Brabantio	Why? Wherefore ask you this?	
85 **Iago**	Zounds, sir, you're robbed, for shame put on your gown!	
	Your heart is burst, you have lost half your soul,	
	Even now, now, very now, an old black ram	
	Is tupping your white ewe! Arise, arise,	
	Awake the snorting citizens with the bell,	
90	Or else the devil will make a grandsire of you,	
	Arise I say!	
Brabantio	What, have you lost your wits?	
Roderigo	Most reverend signior, do you know my voice?	
Brabantio	Not I. What are you?	

伊阿古	喊吧,要用骇人听闻的嚎叫,	
	就像发现人口稠密的城市	75
	夜间不慎失火一般。	
罗德利哥	嗬! 勃拉班修,勃拉班修先生,嗬!	
伊阿古	醒醒! 嗬,勃拉班修,有贼,有贼!	
	把家看好,您的女儿,您的钱包。	
	有贼,有贼!	80

勃拉班修[自上方]窗口出现。

勃拉班修	为啥这么吓人地大喊大叫?	
	到底出了啥事?	
罗德利哥	先生,您的家人都在吗?	
伊阿古	门锁好了吗?	
勃拉班修	为啥? 您为啥问这?	
伊阿古	哎,先生,您被盗了,呸,穿好衣服,	85
	您的心碎了,您已失去半个灵魂;	
	此时,此刻,一只老黑公羊	
	在跟您的白母羊交尾;起来,起来!	
	快用钟声将鼾睡的市民唤醒,	
	否则那魔鬼会让您做牲畜外公。	90
	起来,我说!	
勃拉班修	什么,难道你们疯了?	
罗德利哥	尊敬的先生,能听出我是谁吗?	
勃拉班修	听不出,您是谁?	

---

85. 呸（for shame）:伊阿古的秉性——自己说话不知廉耻,却责备勃拉班修丧风败俗!
87. 老黑公羊（old ram）:首次暗示了奥赛罗的年迈。 另外,公羊（ram）还有淫荡好色之义（rammish: lustful, lascivious）。 老夫少妻常为笑柄（An old husband and a young wife was a traditional butt of comedy）。 88. 白母羊（white ewe）:白（与黑相对）表示纯洁、无瑕（pure, unstained）;珍贵、可爱（precious, beloved）。

Roderigo		My name is Roderigo.
Brabantio	The worser welcome!	

95   I have charged thee not to haunt about my doors:

In honest plainness thou hast heard me say

My daughter is not for thee; and now in madness,

Being full of supper and distempering draughts,

Upon malicious bravery dost thou come

100   To start my quiet?

Roderigo   Sir, sir, sir—

Brabantio   But thou must needs be sure

My spirit and my place have in them power

To make this bitter to thee.

Roderigo   Patience, good sir!

Brabantio   What tell'st thou me of robbing? This is Venice:

My house is not a grange.

105 **Roderigo**   Most grave Brabantio,

In simple and pure soul I come to you—

Iago   Zounds, sir, you are one of those that will not

serve God, if the devil bid you. Because we come to

do you service and you think we are ruffians, you'll

110   have your daughter covered with a Barbary horse;

you'll have your nephews neigh to you; you'll have

coursers for cousins, and jennets for germans!

Brabantio   What profane wretch art thou?

罗德利哥	我是罗德利哥。	
勃拉班修	更不受欢迎！	
	我曾告诫你,不要上门搅扰：	95
	我已诚恳坦率地告诉过你,	
	我女儿不会嫁你；你丧心病狂,	
	饭饱酒足之后,头昏脑涨,	
	你小子胆大包天,竟敢前来	
	惊扰我的安宁？	100
罗德利哥	先生,先生,先生——	
勃拉班修	可你要明白	
	我的脾性和地位完全可以	
	让你为此叫苦。	
罗德利哥	耐心些,好先生！	
勃拉班修	你凭啥说我被盗？ 这是威尼斯：	
	我家不是农舍。	
罗德利哥	尊敬的勃拉班修,	105
	我可是真心诚意过来见您——	
伊阿古	哎,先生,像您这种人,假如魔鬼让您	
	侍奉上帝,您就会置之不理。我们过来	
	是想帮您,您却认为我们是流氓,您将	
	让您的女儿跟一匹巴巴里马交配；您的	110
	后代将会对您嘶鸣；您家里将会以战马	
	充当子孙,以西班牙矮马作为亲戚！	
勃拉班修	你是哪个无耻之徒？	

---

101. 先生,先生,先生（Sir, sir, sir）：格外音节（extra-metrical）。 勃拉班修的上下两个半句实际构成了一行五步抑扬格,只是罗德利哥试图将其打断而已。 110. 巴巴里马（Barbary horse）：阿拉伯马,即奥赛罗。 巴巴里：柏柏尔人（Berbers）或摩尔人的家乡,可指撒拉森人（Saracen）居住的北非沿海各国。 111. 后代（nephews）：子孙（grandsons, descendants）。

Iago		I am one, sir, that comes to tell you your daughter
115		and the Moor are now making the beast with two backs.
Brabantio		Thou art a villain!
Iago		You are a senator!
Brabantio		This thou shalt answer. I know thee, Roderigo!
Roderigo		Sir, I will answer anything. But I beseech you,
		If't be your pleasure and most wise consent,
120		As partly I find it is, that your fair daughter,
		At this odd-even and dull watch o'th' night,
		Transported with no worse nor better guard
		But with a knave of common hire, a gondolier,
		To the gross clasps of a lascivious Moor—
125		If this be known to you, and your allowance,
		We then have done you bold and saucy wrongs.
		But if you know not this, my manners tell me
		We have your wrong rebuke. Do not believe
		That from the sense of all civility
130		I thus would play and trifle with your reverence.
		Your daughter, if you have not given her leave,
		I say again, hath made a gross revolt,
		Tying her duty, beauty, wit and fortunes
		In an extravagant and wheeling stranger

伊阿古	我是，先生，来给您报信，您的女儿	
	跟那个摩尔，正在做双背兽游戏。	115
勃拉班修	你是个流氓！	
伊阿古	您是一个议员！	
勃拉班修	你要对此负责，罗德利哥，我认识你！	
罗德利哥	先生，我愿负责一切。　可我求您，	
	假如您高兴，而且心甘情愿，	
	我看大概如此，您的漂亮女儿	120
	在这半夜三更和死寂的时刻，	
	已由一位不好不坏的卫兵，	
	一位普通的男仆，凤尾船船夫，	
	送到好色淫荡的摩尔人怀中——	
	假如您对此知情，经过您允许，	125
	那说明我们粗鲁地将您冒犯。	
	但您若不知此事，礼仪告诉我，	
	您可错怪了我们。　您不要以为	
	我们对文明的举止麻木不仁，	
	我竟然会对您如此失敬。	130
	您的女儿，假如未经您允许，	
	我再说一遍，可是十足的叛逆，	
	将她的恭顺、美貌、才智和运气，	
	交给一位四处游荡的外国人，	

---

115. 做双背兽游戏（making…backs）：动物交配；交媾（copulating）。　116. 您是一个议员（You…senator）：表示轻蔑（此时也许会啐唾沫以表唾弃）。　在"您"，或"是"，或"一个"之后会稍有停顿。　注意其中的阶层意识（class feeling）。　若将自己的匹敌者（equals）称为"流氓（villain）"，可能会导致决斗。　119. 假如您高兴（If…pleasure）：挖苦（sarcastic）。　120. 我看大概如此（As…is）："因为，您不听我们好言相告，我多半相信您是心甘情愿（as, by your refusal to listen to us, I am half inclined to believe it is）。" 121. 半夜三更（odd-even）：莎氏新造词（a coinage），意为：既非此又非彼，既非黑夜又非白天（neither one thing nor the other, neither night nor day）。

135   Of here and everywhere. Straight satisfy yourself:

If she be in her chamber or your house,

Let loose on me the justice of the state

For thus deluding you.

Brabantio   Strike on the tinder, ho!

Give me a taper, call up all my people.

140   This accident is not unlike my dream,

Belief of it oppresses me already.

Light, I say, light!   *Exit above.*

Iago   Farewell, for I must leave you.

It seems not meet, nor wholesome to my place,

To be produced, as, if I stay, I shall,

145   Against the Moor. For I do know the state,

However this may gall him with some check,

Cannot with safety cast him, for he's embarked

With such loud reason to the Cyprus wars,

Which even now stands in act, that for their souls,

150   Another of his fathom they have none

To lead their business—in which regard,

Though I do hate him as I do hell-pains,

Yet for necessity of present life

I must show out a flag and sign of love,

155   Which is indeed but sign. That you shall surely find him,

他这人来历不明。　快去看看吧：　　　　　　　　　　　135

假如她在房间,或在您家里,

那就按照威尼斯国法惩罚

我的这种欺诈。

勃拉班修　　　　　　　　赶快点灯,嗬!

给我根蜡烛,把家人都叫起:

这种事情可真像是在做梦,　　　　　　　　　　　　　140

将信将疑已使我心情沉重。

点灯,快点灯!　　　　　　　　　　　　　自上方下。

伊阿古　　　　　　　　　再见,我必须告辞。

我若留下,就意味着出面作证,

与那摩尔人为敌,这不大合适,

也对我的职位不利,因为我知道,　　　　　　　　　145

虽然这会使他招致某些责难,

但不会被革职,因为他已受命,

众望所归,参加如火如荼的

塞浦路斯战争,哪怕他们用灵魂,

也换不来像他那样能干的将军　　　　　　　　　　150

为他们带兵出征——基于这种理由,

尽管我恨他就像恨地狱的惩罚,

然而,为了目前的生活所需,

我要打出一面彩旗,爱的幌子,

的确是幌子。　为确保能将他找到,　　　　　　　　155

---

135. 来历不明(Of…everywhere):其背景/来历无法断定(of uncertain background / origins)(Honigmann; Bevington)。 154. 幌子(sign):该词有两层含义:(1)标志,标记(token, sign);(2)军旗,队旗(military standard, banner)。 另外,伊阿古正好是奥赛罗的旗官或旗手。 (参考并借用梁实秋先生的译文;下称"梁译"。 ——译者附注)。

Lead to the Sagittary the raised search,

And there will I be with him. So farewell.   *Exit.*

Enter Brabantio in his night-gown and Servants with torches.

Brabantio   It is too true an evil, gone she is,

And what's to come of my despised time

160   Is nought but bitterness. Now Roderigo,

Where didst thou see her? —O unhappy girl!

With the Moor, say'st thou? —Who would be a father? —

How didst thou know 'twas she? —O, she deceives me

Past thought! —What said she to you? —Get more tapers,

165   Raise all my kindred. Are they married, think you?

Roderigo   Truly, I think they are.

Brabantio   O heaven, how got she out? O treason of the blood!

—Fathers, from hence trust not your daughters' minds

By what you see them act. —Is there not charms

170   By which the property of youth and maidhood

May be abused? Have you not read, Roderigo,

Of some such thing?

Roderigo   Yes sir, I have indeed.

Brabantio   Call up my brother. —O, would you had had her!

Some one way, some another. —Do you know

把唤起的搜索队带到人马旅店，

我将在那里与他汇合。　再见。　　　　　　　　　　　　　　　下。

勃拉班修着罩衣，与侍从持火把上。

勃拉班修　这可真是一种罪恶，她走了，

那后果呢，我丢人现眼的余生，

意味着只有辛酸。　喂，罗德利哥，　　　　　　　　　　160

在哪里看见她了？　——噢，可怜的姑娘！——

与摩尔人一起，你说？　——谁愿做父亲？——

你怎么知道是她？　——噢，她可真会

骗我！——她对您说些啥？　——再点些蜡烛，

把家人都叫起，他们结婚了，您看？　　　　　　　　　165

罗德利哥　我看他们确实结了。

勃拉班修　噢，天哪，她怎么出去的？　真是个孽种！

　　——父亲们从此，别以为女儿行动

温顺就信任她们。　——难道没有魔法

可以将青春少女们的童贞　　　　　　　　　　　170

骗取？　您没读过类似的事情吗，

罗德利哥？

罗德利哥　　　　　　我确实读过，先生。

勃拉班修　叫醒我弟弟。　——噢，但愿您娶了她！

一队走这边，一队走那边。　——您知道

---

156. 人马旅店（the Sagittary）：一家带有人马标志的旅馆或房舍（an inn or house with the sign of Sagittarius）。　人马（Sagittarius），即希腊神话中一种半人半马的怪兽（a Centaur: a mythological figure, with head, trunk, arms of a man and lower body and legs of a horse）。
159. 丢人现眼（despised）：女儿的私奔（就像妻子的不忠）会让做父亲的丢尽脸面。　167. 噢，天哪（O heaven）：格外音节（extra-metrical）。　167. 真是个孽种（treason of the blood）：有两层含义：（1）背叛了父亲和家人（betrayal of her father and family）；（2）情欲的反叛（rebellion of the passion）（Mowat）。

175   Where we may apprehend her and the Moor?

Roderigo   I think I can discover him, if you please

To get good guard and go along with me.

Brabantio   Pray you lead on. At every house I'll call,

I may command at most: get weapons, ho!

180   And raise some special officers of night.

On, good Roderigo, I'll deserve your pains.   *Exeunt.*

| | 能在哪里抓住她,和摩尔人吗? | 175 |

罗德利哥　我想我能搜到他。　假如您愿意
　　　　　　找些精兵强将,与我一同前往。

勃拉班修　求您给我带路,我要挨家去叫,
　　　　　　只要我能吩咐:拿上武器,嗬!
　　　　　　再去叫上几位巡夜的警官。　　　　　　　180
　　　　　　走,好罗德利哥,我会报答您的。　　　　　同下。

SCENE II

Enter Othello, Iago and Attendants with torches.

Iago   Though in the trade of war I have slain men,

Yet do I hold it very stuff o'th' conscience

To do no contrived murder: I lack iniquity

Sometimes to do me service. Nine or ten times

5   I had thought t'have yerked him here, under the ribs.

Othello   'Tis better as it is.

Iago   Nay, but he prated

And spoke such scurvy and provoking terms

Against your honour,

That with the little godliness I have

10   I did full hard forbear him. But I pray, sir,

Are you fast married? Be assured of this,

That the magnifico is much beloved,

And hath in his effect a voice potential

As double as the duke's: he will divorce you

第二场

奥赛罗、伊阿古与侍从持火把上。

伊阿古　　尽管打起仗来我将不少人杀害，

然而我觉得要是凭良心本身，

可不能预谋杀人；有时我为了

一己之利缺乏狠心：有八九次

我曾想从他的肋骨下面刺去。　　　　　　　　　　5

奥赛罗　　还是由它去吧。

伊阿古　　　　　　　　不行，他瞎说，

净说些下流和挑衅的话语

败坏您的声誉，

我这人本来就没有多少雅量，

对他简直忍无可忍：不过请问，　　　　　　　　10

您是否已完婚？　因为您要知道，

他这位要人可是德高望重，

他的权势和影响像公爵一样，

一人拥有两票：他可逼您离婚，

　　1.2. 地点：人马旅店外面的街上。　**4.** 八九次（Nine or ten times）：伊阿古假装模糊不清（with Iago's pretended indecisiveness）。　**5.** 他（him）：罗德利哥（见本场第58行）。　但也可能指勃拉班修。　**12.** 要人（magnifico）：威尼斯的首领有一种专称——权贵（要人）（The chief men of Venice are by a peculiar name called *Magnifici*, i. e. Magnificoes）（Ridley）。**13-4.** 像公爵……两票（as…duke's）：莎士比亚"（错误地）认为，在同等情况下，'公爵'在投票时一人可投两票"；伊阿古是说勃拉班修德高望重，"实际上可随心所欲，好像他一人也拥有两票似的"（Ridley；Honigmann）。

15 Or put upon you what restraint or grievance

The law, with all his might to enforce it on,

Will give him cable.

Othello   Let him do his spite;

My services, which I have done the signiory,

Shall out-tongue his complaints. 'Tis yet to know—

20 Which, when I know that boasting is an honour,

I shall promulgate—I fetch my life and being

From men of royal siege, and my demerits

May speak unbonneted to as proud a fortune

As this that I have reached. For know, Iago,

25 But that I love the gentle Desdemona,

I would not my unhoused free condition

Put into circumscription and confine

For the sea's worth. But look, What lights come yond?

Enter Cassio, with Officers and torches.

Iago   Those are the raised father and his friends,

You were best go in.

30 **Othello**   Not I, I must be found.

My parts, my title and my perfect soul

Shall manifest me rightly. Is it they?

Iago   By Janus, I think no.

或按法律所赋予他的权限， 　　　　　　　　　15

尽其所能地对您本人加以

限制或压迫。

奥赛罗　　　　　　　随他怨恨去吧；

我为执政团所立下的功劳，

会胜过他的控诉；尚无人知晓——

等我知道夸口是一种荣耀时， 　　　　　　　　20

我会公之于众——我本是皇室

贵族出身,而且我的功绩

与我得到的这一大笔财富

相比毫不逊色。　要知道,伊阿古,

若不是我爱温柔的苔丝狄蒙娜， 　　　　　　　25

纵将大海的宝藏全部给我,

也不会让我自由自在的生活

遭受限制与羁绊。　请看,那是啥光?

　　　　　　凯西奥及众军官持火把上。

伊阿古　　那是她被唤起的父亲和亲友，

您最好躲一躲。

奥赛罗　　　　　不躲,我不会躲的。 　　　　　　30

我的品性、身份和问心无愧

会证明我的清白:是他们吗?

伊阿古　　凭两面神起誓,我想不是。

---

18. 执政团(signiory):按照 1581 年的一位旅客记载,威尼斯的整个寡头统治集团约有 300 人,并由其中的约 40 人组成内阁(inner council)(Ridley)。 26. 大海的宝藏(sea's worth): 海洋被视为一座宝库,既有沉没的财宝,又有珍珠等(Ridley)。 27. 自由自在(unhoused):奥赛罗此前一直住在帐篷里面(1.3.86)。 33. 两面神(Janus):希腊神话中的两面神(杰纳斯)。 原本为"两面派"的伊阿古,也许是说"凭借那位能看清别人无法看清的神",因为当时是黑夜时分(Roman god with two faces, at front and back of the head. Iago, himself 'two-faced', may mean 'by the god who sees what others cannot see', because it is dark)。

Othello		The servants of the Duke? And my lieutenant?
35		The goodness of the night upon you, friends.
		What is the news?

Othello   The servants of the Duke? And my lieutenant?

35   The goodness of the night upon you, friends.

What is the news?

Cassio   The Duke does greet you, general,

And he requires your haste-post-haste appearance,

Even on the instant.

Othello   What's the matter, think you?

Cassio   Something from Cyprus, as I may divine;

40   It is a business of some heat. The galleys

Have sent a dozen sequent messengers

This very night, at one another's heels,

And many of the consuls, raised and met,

Are at the Duke's already. You have been hotly called for,

45   When, being not at your lodging to be found,

The Senate hath sent about three several quests

To search you out.

Othello   'Tis well I am found by you:

I will but spend a word here in the house

And go with you.   [*Exit.*]

Cassio   Ancient, what makes he here?

50 **Iago**   Faith, he tonight hath boarded a land carrack:

If it prove lawful prize, he's made for ever.

Cassio   I do not understand.

Iago   He's married.

奥赛罗	是公爵的奴仆,以及我的副官。	
	祝你们今夜平安无事,朋友!	35
	有啥消息?	
凯西奥	公爵向您致意,将军,	
	他还要您十万火急地前去,	
	决不能耽搁。	
奥赛罗	是啥事情,您想?	
凯西奥	有关塞浦路斯的情况,我猜;	
	这件事情可是非常紧迫,战舰	40
	已经连续派出了十几个信差,	
	就在今天夜晚,接二连三,	
	许多元老已经被叫起,已在	
	公爵府里聚集。　大家都在找您,	
	因为,发现您并不在房间里面,	45
	元老院又派出了三路人马	
	分头找您。	
奥赛罗	幸好您把我找到:	
	我先到屋里跟妻子道别一下,	
	再跟您同去。	〔下。〕
凯西奥	旗官,他在此做啥?	
伊阿古	天哪,他今晚登上一艘陆地宝船:	50
	若战利品合法,他会一劳永逸。	
凯西奥	我不明白。	
伊阿古	他已经结婚。	

---

　　50. 登上（boarded）：该词常含淫秽之义。　50. 宝船（carrack）：西班牙和葡萄的一种运宝船只（Ridley）；大型商船（large merchant ship）（Bevington）。　52. 我不明白……跟谁（I…To whom）：凯西奥,作为奥赛罗求婚时的亲信（3. 3. 70-3 行,与 94 行及以下）,此处竟然感到意外。　他也许是在假装吃惊,以免出卖朋友的信任（Ridley）。

Cassio   To whom?

Iago   Marry, to—

Enter Othello.

                  Come, captain, will you go?

Othello   Ha' with you.

Cassio   Here comes another troop to seek for you.

Enter Brabantio, Roderigo, with Officers and torches and weapons.

55 **Iago**   It is Brabantio: General, be advised,

                  He comes to bad intent.

Othello   Holla, stand there!

Roderigo   Signior, it is the Moor.

Brabantio   Down with him, thief!

                              [*They draw on both sides.*]

Iago   You, Roderigo! Come sir, I am for you.

Othello   Keep up your bright swords, for the dew will rust them.

60   Good signior, you shall more command with years

                  Than with your weapons.

Brabantio   O thou foul thief, where hast thou stowed my daughter?

                  Damned as thou art, thou hast enchanted her,

                  For I'll refer me to all things of sense,

65   If she in chains of magic were not bound,

                  Whether a maid so tender, fair and happy,

                  So opposite to marriage that she shunned

凯西奥	跟谁？
伊阿古	就是跟——

奥赛罗上。

快来,将军,走吗？

奥赛罗	走吧。
凯西奥	又有一队人马来此找您。

勃拉班修、罗德利哥、与众人持火把及武器上。

| 伊阿古 | 那是勃拉班修,将军,要小心, | 55 |
| | 他可是不怀好意。 | |

奥赛罗	站住,别动!
罗德利哥	先生,正是那摩尔。
勃拉班修	干掉他,盗贼!

[双方拔剑。]

伊阿古	罗德利哥,来吧,老兄,我跟您拼了!
奥赛罗	快收起亮剑,以免露水腐蚀;
	老先生,您的年纪要比您的	60
	武器更有威力。

勃拉班修	可恶的盗贼,把我女儿藏在何处？
	你这个魔鬼,你对她施了魔法,
	我要让大家对此做出评判,
	假如她没遭到巫术的困扰,	65
	这么年轻、美丽和欢快的姑娘,
	如此抵触婚姻,她曾经回绝了

---

58. 伊阿古专门挑战罗德利哥,似乎想证实他确实瞎说(prated)(第6行),并且是奥赛罗的祸根(Honigmann)。 伊阿古之所以主动要与罗德利哥打斗,是因为他不想让自己的财源葬送在乱战之中(Ridley)。 63. 你这个魔鬼(Damned as thou art):据信魔鬼为黑色,因此黑色意味着罪孽(Devils were thought to be black, so black implied damnation)。

The wealthy, curled darlings of our nation,

Would ever have, t'incur a general mock,

70 Run from her guardage to the sooty bosom

Of such a thing as thou? To fear, not to delight.

Judge me the world if 'tis not gross in sense

That thou hast practiced on her with foul charms,

Abused her delicate youth with drugs or minerals

75 That weaken motion: I'll have't disputed on,

'Tis probable, and palpable to thinking.

I therefore apprehend and do attach thee

For an abuser of the world, a practiser

Of arts inhibited and out of warrant.

80 Lay hold upon him; if he do resist,

Subdue him at his peril!

Othello   Hold your hands,

Both you of my inclining and the rest:

Were it my cue to fight, I should have known it

Without a prompter. Where will you that I go

To answer this your charge?

85 **Brabantio**   To prison, till fit time

Of law, and course of direct session

Call thee to answer.

Othello   What if I do obey?

How may the Duke be therewith satisfied,

Whose messengers are here about my side

90 Upon some present business of the state,

国内多少富有而英俊的青年，
居然会去招惹众人的讥笑，
抛弃亲人的保护而投向你这　　　　　　　　70
乌黑的怀抱？　去害怕，不是去喜欢。
让大家看看，是否显而易见，
是否对她偷施了邪恶的魔法，
使用麻木神经的药物或矿物
诱骗了她的芳华：我要申诉；　　　　　　75
这很有可能，也不难以想象。
因此我要逮捕你并扣留你，
罪名就是欺骗世人，明令
禁止和非法的巫术施行者。
把他抓起来，他若进行反抗，　　　　　　80
就用武力将他制服！

奥赛罗　　　　　　　　　都别动，
无论是支持我的，还是对方：
若是该我上阵，我自会清楚，
不用人提醒。　您想让我去何处
回应您的指控？

勃拉班修　　　　　　　　去监狱，直到　　　　85
正常或者专门的法律议程
唤你出庭。

奥赛罗　　　　　　我若遵命那又怎样？
我将如何对公爵进行交代，
他派来的信差就在我身边，
为了国家某些紧急的事情，　　　　　　　90

---

86. 正常……议程（course…session）：按照常规或专门为此履行的法律程序（regular or specially convened legal proceedings）（Bevington）。

To bring me to him?

Officer   'Tis true, most worthy signior,

The Duke's in council, and your noble self

I am sure is sent for.

Brabantio   How? The Duke in council?

In this time of the night? Bring him away:

95   Mine's not an idle cause, the Duke himself,

Or any of my brothers of the state,

Cannot but feel this wrong as 'twere their own.

For if such actions may have passage free,

Bond-slaves and pagans shall our statesmen be.   *Exeunt.*

要带我去见他？

军官　　　　　　　　　　真的,尊贵的先生,
公爵在开会,而且大人您本身
定在应召之列。

勃拉班修　　　　　　　　什么？　公爵在开会？
在这半夜三更？　把他带走！
我这案件并非等闲,公爵本人,　　　　　　　　　　95
或者是城邦的每一位弟兄,
都会对这种伤害感同身受。
因为若对这种行径听之任之,
奴仆和异教徒将会掌管国事。　　　　　　　　　　同下。

SCENE III

Enter Duke and Senators, set at a table, with lights and attendants.

Duke	There is no composition in these news
	That gives them credit.
1 Senator	Indeed, they are disproportioned.
	My letters say a hundred and seven galleys.
Duke	And mine a hundred and forty.
2 Senator	And mine, two hundred.

5 But though they jump not on a just account—

As in these cases, where the aim reports,

'Tis oft with difference—yet do they all confirm

A Turkish fleet, and bearing up to Cyprus.

Duke Nay, it is possible enough to judgement:

10 I do not so secure me in the error

But the main article I do approve

In fearful sense.

Sailor [*within*] What ho, what ho, what ho!

Enter Sailor.

Officer A messenger from the galleys.

Duke Now? What's the business?

第三场

公爵与众元老上,围桌而坐,侍从掌灯。

公爵　　　　这些消息彼此并不一致,
难以置信。

元老甲　　　　　　　　的确存在分歧;
我的信上说,战舰一百零七艘。

公爵　　　　我的说一百四十。

元老乙　　　　　　　　　我的说两百:
但尽管具体的数目并不相符——　　　　　　　　5
因为这种场合,报告多为猜测,
通常会有差异——可它们都证实
土耳其舰队正驶往塞浦路斯。

公爵　　　　是的,这一点当然容易判断:
我不会因为数目有别而心安,　　　　　　　　10
但我相信关键事情大致没错,
令人担忧。

水手　　　　[在内]　嗨嗨!嗨嗨!嗨嗨!

水手上。

军官　　　　来自战舰的信差。

公爵　　　　嗳,怎么回事?

1.3. 地点:会议室。　11. 关键事情(main articles):土耳其舰队正驶往塞浦路斯。

15	**Sailor**	The Turkish preparation makes for Rhodes,
		So was I bid report here to the state
		By Signior Angelo.
	Duke	How say you by this change?
	1 Senator	This cannot be,
		By no assay of reason: 'tis a pageant
20		To keep us in false gaze. When we consider
		Th'importancy of Cyprus to the Turk,
		And let ourselves again but understand
		That as it more concerns the Turk than Rhodes,
		So may he with more facile question bear it,
25		For that it stands not in such warlike brace,
		But altogether lacks th'abilities
		That Rhodes is dressed in. If we make thought of this,
		We must not think the Turk is so unskillful
		To leave that latest which concerns him first,
30		Neglecting an attempt of ease and gain
		To wake and wage a danger profitless.
	Duke	Nay, in all confidence, he's not for Rhodes.
	Officer	Here is more news.

Enter a Messenger.

	Messenger	The Ottomites, reverend and gracious,
35		Steering with due course toward the isle of Rhodes,
		Have there injointed them with an after fleet—

水手	土耳其舰队正驶往罗德岛，	15
	我受命前来，要向城邦报告，	
	由安杰洛先生指派。	
公爵	对此变化您意见如何？	
元老甲	这种说法，	
	不攻自破：这是在虚张声势，	
	让我们转移视线。　当我们想到	20
	塞浦路斯对土耳其的重要性时，	
	我们自己的心里可必须清楚，	
	它对土耳其要比罗德岛重要，	
	他可以更为轻易地将它攻取，	
	因为它的防御不怎么坚固，	25
	缺乏罗德岛所配备的那种	
	自卫能力。　我们若能想到这些，	
	千万别以为土耳其人如此愚蠢，	
	竟把最关切的事情留到最后，	
	忽略轻而易举的攻击和获取，	30
	甘愿去孤注一掷，徒劳无益。	
公爵	不会，毫无疑问，不是攻罗德岛。	
军官	又来了消息。	

　　　　　　一信差上。

信差	土耳其人，尊敬的元老殿下，	
	沿着预定的航线驶向罗德岛，	35
	然后与一支后卫舰队汇合——	

23. 它（it）：塞浦路斯（Mowat）。

1 Senator	Ay, so I thought; how many, as you guess?
Messenger	Of thirty sail; and now they do re-stem
	Their backward course, bearing with frank appearance
40	Their purposes toward Cyprus. Signior Montano,
	Your trusty and most valiant servitor,
	With his free duty recommends you thus
	And prays you to relieve him.
Duke	'Tis certain then for Cyprus.
45	Marcus Luccicos, is not he in town?
1 Senator	He's now in Florence.
Duke	Write from us to him; post-post-haste dispatch.
1 Senator	Here comes Brabantio and the valiant Moor.

Enter Brabantio, Othello, Cassio, Iago, Roderigo and Officers.

Duke	Valiant Othello, we must straight employ you
50	Against the general enemy Ottoman.
	[*to Brabantio*] I did not see you: welcome, gentle signior,
	We lacked your counsel and your help tonight.
Brabantio	So did I yours. Good your grace, pardon me,
	Neither my place nor aught I heard of business
55	Hath raised me from my bed, nor doth the general care
	Take hold on me, for my particular grief
	Is of so flood-gate and o'erbearing nature
	That it engluts and swallows other sorrows

元老甲	啊,如我所料;有多少,您推测?	
信差	有三十艘,它们现已调转船头	
	正在往回行驶,毫不掩饰地	
	驶向目标塞浦路斯。 蒙塔诺先生,	40
	您忠诚的和最为英勇的仆人,	
	恪尽职守地向您如实报告,	
	并求您派人去替他。	
公爵	定是奔塞浦路斯去了。	
	玛克斯·路齐科斯不在镇上吗?	45
元老甲	他现在佛罗伦萨。	
公爵	写信给他,望他火速赶到,赶快。	
元老甲	勃拉班修与勇猛的摩尔人来了。	

勃拉班修、奥赛罗、凯西奥、罗德利哥及众军官上。

公爵	英勇的奥赛罗,我们要立即派您,	
	去抗击大家的公敌土耳其人。	50
	[向勃拉班修]我没看见您;欢迎,尊贵的先生,	
	今夜可需要您的高见和帮助。	
勃拉班修	我也需要您的帮助,殿下,请原谅	
	不是我的职位,也不是听说有事,	
	将我从床上惊起,也不是众人的忧虑	55
	令我挂心,因为我个人的悲痛	
	像开闸倾泻的洪流势不可挡,	
	将其他悲伤吞并淹没之后	

---

37. 元老甲此处(也许还有25-31 行)的插话,看上去好像是莎士比亚后来添加的内容,以使该演员更富个性——一位过分殷勤、固执己见的老臣,与《哈姆雷特》剧中的波罗纽斯(Polonius)相差无几(Ridley)。 50. 公敌(the general enemy):所有基督徒的公敌(universal enemy to all Christians)(Bate)。 55. 从床上(from my bed):属后补内容,因此为格外音节(an after-thought, hence extra-metrical)。

And it is still itself.

Duke	Why? What's the matter?
Brabantio	My daughter! O my daughter!
All	Dead?

60   **Brabantio**   Ay, to me:

She is abused, stolen from me and corrupted

By spells and medicines bought of mountebanks,

For nature so preposterously to err,

Being not deficient, blind, or lame of sense,

65   Sans witchcraft could not.

     Duke   Whoe'er he be, that in this foul proceeding

Hath thus beguiled your daughter of herself,

And you of her, the bloody book of law

You shall yourself read, in the bitter letter,

70   After your own sense, yea, though our proper son

Stood in your action.

     Brabantio   Humbly I thank your grace.

Here is the man, this Moor, whom now it seems

Your special mandate for the state affairs

Hath hither brought.

     All   We are very sorry for't.

75   **Duke**   [*to Othello*]What in your own part can you say to this?

     Brabantio   Nothing, but this is so.

却依然如故。

公爵　　　　　　　　　　唉,是什么事情?

勃拉班修　　我女儿,噢,我女儿!

众人　　　　　　　　　死了?

勃拉班修　　　　　　　　　我看,是的:　　　　　　　60

她受骗了,被人盗走,用符咒

和从骗子那里买来的药物玷污,

因为本能不可能使她如此荒谬,

原本没有缺陷、既不瞎、也不傻,

除非用了巫术。　　　　　　　　65

公爵　　　无论谁,若干出这种罪恶行径,

将您的女儿骗得神魂颠倒,

从您身边把她劫走,您可根据

自己对那血腥法典的诠释,

严加惩处,哪怕被告是我的　　　　70

亲生儿子。

勃拉班修　　　　我谦恭地感谢殿下。

他就在这里,这个摩尔,好像您

为了国家大事已特地下令

让他来此。

众人　　　　　　我们感到非常遗憾。

公爵　　[向奥赛罗]您本人对此可有啥话要说?　　75

勃拉班修　　没有,情况属实。

63-5. 因为……巫术(For…could not):因本句的结构有所改变,容易费解:原文 65 行的"could not"后面需接原形动词"err",而不是 63 行的"to err"。正常的语序应为:"For, without witchcraft, nature—as long as it is not deficient, blind or defective in sense—could not err so preposterously." 68-70. 您可……惩处(the bloody…sense):原文结构颇为复杂,现引两处注释以助理解:"you shall be judge and pass sentence according to your own interpretation of the law, which provides for the death penalty (and therefore is called *the bloody book of law*)."(Mowat)另外,64 行所提及的巫术(witchcraft)本系死罪(Honigmann)。

	Othello	Most potent, grave, and reverend signiors,
		My very noble and approved good masters:
		That I have ta'en away this old man's daughter,
80		It is most true; true, I have married her.
		The very head and front of my offending
		Hath this extent, no more. Rude am I in my speech,
		And little blest with the soft phrase of peace,
		For since these arms of mine had seven years' pith,
85		Till now some nine moons wasted, they have used
		Their dearest action in the tented field,
		And little of this great world can I speak
		More than pertains to feats of broil and battle,
		And therefore little shall I grace my cause
90		In speaking for myself. Yet, by your gracious patience,
		I will a round unvarnished tale deliver
		Of my whole course of love, what drugs, what charms,
		What conjuration and what mighty magic
		For such proceeding I am charged withal
		I won his daughter.
95	**Brabantio**	A maiden never bold,
		Of spirit so still and quiet that her motion
		Blushed at herself; and she, in spite of nature,
		Of years, of country, credit, everything,
		To fall in love with what she feared to look on?
100		It is a judgement maimed and most imperfect

奥赛罗	最为威严、庄重和可敬的元老，	
	我非常尊贵和真正的好主人：	
	我已将这位老人的女儿带走，	
	的确如此；的确,我已跟她结婚。	80
	我对他所做出的最大冒犯	
	仅此而已。　尽管我说话粗鲁，	
	缺乏天赋使言辞文雅动听，	
	自从我七岁有力参战以来，	
	直到虚度的九个月以前,这双	85
	手臂的气力献给了野营的疆场，	
	除了有关混战与厮杀以外，	
	对这个伟大的世界知之甚少，	
	因此我不会粉饰我的理由	
	为自己辩护。　不过,您若能垂听，	90
	我将直言不讳地宣布我的	
	恋爱过程,用了啥药,什么符咒，	
	什么妖术,什么非凡的魔法——	
	因为我被控采取了这些举动——	
	得到了他女儿。	
勃拉班修	一位羞怯的姑娘，	95
	如此平和与娴静,稍一动心	
	即会脸红;而她,竟不顾性情、	
	年龄、种族、声誉,及各种差异，	
	去爱一个令她望而生畏的东西？	
	谁承认完美的姑娘会如此犯错、	100

---

84. 有力（pith）：pith = strength（力量）。 他从七岁就开始助战（He has helped in battles from the age of seven）：参考133 行的"从童年开始"。 85. 虚度的（wasted）：因为他将自己的人生奉献给了战争,故有浪费了时光之义（with a hint of squandered, as he devotes his life to war）。 88. 这个伟大的世界（this great world）：也许他此时会对元老们鞠躬致意。 威尼斯在 1600 年是一个独立的城邦及文化中心。

That will confess perfection so could err

Against all rules of nature, and must be driven

To find out practices of cunning hell

Why this should be. I therefore vouch again

105 That with some mixtures powerful o'er the blood,

Or with some dram conjured to this effect,

He wrought upon her.

Duke   To vouch this is no proof,

Without more certain and more overt test

Than these thin habits and poor likelihoods

110 Of modern seeming do prefer against him.

1 Senator   But, Othello, speak:

Did you by indirect and forced courses

Subdue and poison this young maid's affections?

Or came it by request and such fair question

As soul to soul affordeth?

115 **Othello**   I do beseech you,

Send for the lady to the Sagittary,

And let her speak of me before her father.

If you do find me foul in her report,

The trust, the office I do hold of you

120 Not only take away, but let your sentence

Even fall upon my life.

Duke   Fetch Desdemona hither.

Othello   Ancient, conduct them, you best know the place.

违背常情,谁就失去了理性,
荒谬至极；若有正常的判断,
定会去追根究底,查明其中的
邪恶阴险。　因此我再次保证,
他用某些可激起情欲的合剂, 105
或者专施以魔法的少许溶液,
令她着迷。

公爵　　　　　　　您这样指控无用,
缺乏更为确凿和明显的证据；
您对他的上述指控,不过是
浅显的寻常猜测,缺乏根据。 110

元老甲　不过,奥赛罗,您说：
您是通过欺诈和强迫的方式
慑服和玷污了这位少女的爱情？
还是通过请求,和心心相印的
坦诚交流博得其芳心？

奥赛罗　　　　　　　我求您, 115
派人到人马旅店请小姐前来,
让她在父亲面前予以说明；
您若听到她说我道德败坏,
您对我的信任,和我的官职,
不仅撤销,我还要让您将我 120
处以极刑。

公爵　把苔丝狄蒙娜叫来。

奥赛罗　旗官,给他们带路,那里您最熟。

---

105. 情欲（blood）：激情（的依托之处）（the supposed seat of "passion"）；性欲（sexual appetite）。　122. 苔丝狄蒙娜：公爵无须提醒便知其名。　威尼斯城邦的领导层是一个封闭的圈子（a closed circle）；奥赛罗显然是个局外人（outsider）。

And till she come, as truly as to heaven

Exeunt [*Iago and*] *two or three.*

125   I do confess the vices of my blood,

So justly to your grave ears I'll present

How I did thrive in this fair lady's love,

And she in mine.

Duke   Say it, Othello.

Othello   Her father loved me, oft invited me,

130   Still questioned me the story of my life

From year to year—the battles, sieges, fortunes

That I have passed.

I ran it through, even from my boyish days

To th' very moment that he bade me tell it,

135   Wherein I spake of most disastrous chances,

Of moving accidents by flood and field,

Of hair-breadth scapes i'th' imminent deadly breach,

Of being taken by the insolent foe

And sold to slavery; of my redemption thence

140   And portance in my travailous history;

Wherein of antres vast and deserts idle,

Rough quarries, rocks and hills whose heads touch heaven,

It was my hint to speak—such was the process—

And of the cannibals that each other eat,

145   The Anthropophagi, and men whose heads

Do grow beneath their shoulders. This to hear

在她到来之前,犹如对上帝

坦白我的堕落行为一般,　　　　　　　　　　　125

　　　　　　　　　[伊阿古与]两三名侍从下。

我将如实地向殿下您陈述

我们二人是如何彼此倾情,

相互爱慕。

公爵　　　　　　　　　　说吧,奥赛罗。

奥赛罗　她的父亲爱我,常邀我做客,

不断询问我个人的生活详情,　　　　　　　　130

起止年月——我所经历的战斗、

围攻和庆幸。

我讲述一遍,甚至从童年开始,

直到他让我陈说的时刻为止。

其中谈到我最为不幸的遭遇,　　　　　　　　135

谈到惊心动魄的海陆战争,

千钧一发时从城墙豁口逃生;

谈到被那傲慢的仇敌掳去

贩卖为奴;谈到随后的赎身

以及艰辛的旅程中如何行动;　　　　　　　　140

历经巨大的洞窟,荒芜的沙漠,

嶙峋的巨石,高耸入云的峻岭,

我趁机说起——这就是我的交代——

还说起彼此吞噬的食人生番,

吃人的民族,头颅长在肩膀　　　　　　　　　145

下方的怪物。　为了听到这些,

---

137. 千钧一发(i'th'…breach):从(被炮弹击破的)城墙豁口(逃脱),此情此景往往意味着死到临头(in the gap in a fortification [made by a battery], which presents an imminent danger of death)(Bate)。

Would Desdemona seriously incline,

But still the house affairs would draw her thence,

Which ever as she could with haste dispatch

150   She'd come again, and with a greedy ear

Devour up my discourse; which I, observing,

Took once a pliant hour and found good means

To draw from her a prayer of earnest heart

That I would all my pilgrimage dilate,

155   Whereof by parcels she had something heard

But not intentively. I did consent,

And often did beguile her of her tears

When I did speak of some distressful stroke

That my youth suffered. My story being done,

160   She gave me for my pains a world of sighs,

She swore in faith 'twas strange, 'twas passing strange,

'Twas pitiful, 'twas wondrous pitiful;

She wished she had not heard it, yet she wished

That heaven had made her such a man. She thanked me

165   And bade me, if I had a friend that loved her,

I should but teach him how to tell my story,

And that would woo her. Upon this hint I spake:

苔丝狄蒙娜会对我相当亲近；

但有些家务需要她过去处理，

只要她家务活一旦迅速办妥，

她就会回来，并用贪婪的耳朵　　　　　　　　　150

吞食我的话语；我见此情景，

便选了一个合适的时间，然后

巧妙地套取了她的一个心愿：

将我的人生历程详述一遍，

她原来只是听到了片言只语，　　　　　　　　155

未能专心听取。　我欣然同意，

当我谈到早年所遭受的某些

不幸打击时，往往就会骗得她

流下眼泪。　我的故事讲完以后，

她对我的苦难报以长吁短叹，　　　　　　　　160

并誓言这很奇怪，非常奇怪，

真是可怜，不可思议的可怜；

她希望没听到这些，但又希望

上帝将她造成这种男人。　她感谢

并吩咐我说，若有朋友爱她，　　　　　　　　165

只要我教会他讲述我的经历，

即可赢得其芳心。　我趁机说道：

---

148. 苔丝狄蒙娜像是个失去母亲的姑娘，要负责家务；部分原因在于剧中（除了 4. 3. 24 行以外）并未提及她的母亲。　151-4. 我见此……一遍（which…dilate）：奥赛罗迈出了第一步（Othello took the very first step）。　154. 人生历程（pilgrimage）：暗示自己的人生富有献身精神（implying that his was a dedicated life）。　160. 长吁短叹（a world of sighs）：借鉴梁译。——译者附注。　164. 将她造成（made her）：中世纪传奇故事中的女杰有时宁愿自己是男人（Romance heroines sometimes wish they were men），然而，该短语也可指"为她创造了这样一个男人（made such a man *for her*）"（Honigmann）。　有关"她（her）"是作宾格还是作与格，人们的意见分歧明显。　我认为显然是作宾格。　若作与格，那么她的希望不仅出人意料地"冒失（forward）"，也会让随后的"暗示（hint）"显得没有必要（Ridley）。

She loved me for the dangers I had passed,

And I loved her that she did pity them.

170   This only is the witchcraft I have used:

Enter Desdemona, Iago, Attendants.

Here comes the lady, let her witness it.

Duke   I think this tale would win my daughter too.

Good Brabantio, take up this mangled matter at the best:

Men do their broken weapons rather use

Than their bare hands.

175 **Brabantio**   I pray you, hear her speak.

If she confess that she was half the wooer,

Destruction on my head if my bad blame

Light on the man. Come hither, gentle mistress:

Do you perceive, in all this noble company,

Where most you owe obedience?

180 **Desdemona**   My noble father,

I do perceive here a divided duty.

To you I am bound for life and education:

My life and education both do learn me

How to respect you; you are the lord of duty,

185   I am hitherto your daughter. But here's my husband:

她因为我所经历的危难而爱我，

我是因为她同情它们而爱她。

这就是我所用过的唯一妖术：　　　　　　　　　　170

　　　　苔丝狄蒙娜、伊阿古、与侍从上。

小姐她来啦，让她自己见证吧。

公爵　　　这样的故事也会赢得我的女儿。

好勃拉班修，对这件事情您就勉为其难吧：

人们宁愿使用破损的刀剑，

而不愿赤手空拳。

勃拉班修　　　　　　　　求您听她说吧。　　　　175

她若承认自己有半点心意，

我将受灭顶之灾，要是我再

错怪于他！过来，温顺的小姐：

您看在座的这些贵人当中，

您最该顺从哪位？

苔丝狄蒙娜　　　　　　尊贵的父亲，　　　　180

我觉得我的义务该一分为二：

我应该感激您的养育之恩，

我的生命和教养让我懂得

该如何敬您，您是我的家长，

至此我是您女儿。　可这是我丈夫：　　　　185

---

173. 好勃拉班修（Good Brabantio）：格外音节（extra-metrical）。 勉为其难（take…the best）：在不利的情况下尽力而为，勉为其难（谚语）（make the best of this bad business / situation）（proverbial）（Mowat）。 178. 温顺的小姐（gentle mistress）：父亲一般不会这样称呼自己的女儿。 184. 家长（lord）：苔丝狄蒙娜在区分两种不同的主人和义务（见188行）：迄今为止您是我应该孝敬的主人（master），但现在我却对摩尔人——我的新主人，应尽一位妻子的本分（She distinguishes two kinds of *lord*［cf. 188］and duty: "You are the master of my duty hitherto, but now I owe a wife's duty to the Moor, my new lord."）。 185. 至此（hitherto）：暗示其作为妻子的新身份现已取代了此前作为女儿的身份（implying that her new identity as wife now supersedes the previous one as daughter）。

And so much duty as my mother showed

To you, preferring you before her father,

So much I challenge that I may profess

Due to the Moor my lord.

190 **Brabantio** God be with you, I have done.

Please it your grace, on to the state affairs;

I had rather to adopt a child than get it.

Come hither, Moor:

I here do give thee that with all my heart

195 Which, but thou hast already, with all my heart

I would keep from thee. For your sake, jewel,

I am glad at soul I have no other child,

For thy escape would teach me tyranny

To hang clogs on them. I have done, my lord.

200 **Duke** Let me speak like yourself, and lay a sentence

Which as a grise or step may help these lovers

Into your favour.

When remedies are past the griefs are ended

By seeing the worst which late on hopes depended.

205 To mourn a mischief that is past and gone

Is the next way to draw new mischief on.

What cannot be preserved when Fortune takes,

Patience her injury a mockery makes.

正如我母亲对您尽心尽职，

她爱您胜过了爱她的父亲，

我也有权，若能声明，对夫君

摩尔人尽职尽心。

勃拉班修　上帝保佑，我完了： 190

若殿下乐意，继续商谈国事吧；

我宁愿领养个孩子也不愿亲生；

你过来，摩尔：

我把女儿给你，我是死心塌地，

若非你已将她拥有，死心塌地， 195

不愿给你。　因为您的缘故，宝贝，

我打心里高兴再没别的孩子，

因为你的私奔会教我成暴君，

让他们戴上脚镣。　我完了，殿下。

公爵　让我替您说两句，用格言宣判， 200

作为阶梯或台阶帮助两位恋人

获得您好感。

事情无法补救便不再哀伤，

既已目睹本想规避的灾殃。

对已过去的不幸感到悲痛， 205

那就无异于招致更多不幸。

命运要夺走的不能够保全，

耐心使她的伤害丢人现眼。

---

200. 用格言宣判（lay a sentence）：原文"sentence"可指：见解（opinion）；（法庭的）判决（decision［of a court］）；格言、警句（pithy saying or maxim）。 203-4. 事情……灾殃（When…depended）：当事情已无可救药时，我们的忧伤就该到此为止，因为我们知道自己近期所希望不要发生的最坏事情业已发生（When all hope of remedy is past, our sorrows are ended by realizing that the worst has already happened which lately we hoped would not happen）（Bevington）。 207-8. 命运……现眼（What…makes）：当命运（女神）将我们无法保留的东西夺走时，耐心可使她的恶行成为笑柄（When fortune takes away what cannot be saved, patience makes a mockery of fortune's wrongdoing）（Bevington）。

		The robbed that smiles steals something from the thief,
210		He robs himself that spends a bootless grief.
	Brabantio	So let the Turk of Cyprus us beguile,
		We lose it not so long as we can smile;
		He bears the sentence well that nothing bears
		But the free comfort which from thence he hears:
215		But he bears both the sentence and the sorrow
		That, to pay grief, must of poor patience borrow.
		These sentences to sugar or to gall,
		Being strong on both sides, are equivocal.
		But words are words: I never yet did hear
220		That the bruised heart was pierced through the ear.
		I humbly beseech you, proceed to th'affairs of state.
	Duke	The Turk with a most mighty preparation makes
		for Cyprus. Othello, the fortitude of the place is best
		known to you, and, though we have there a substitute
225		of most allowed sufficiency, yet opinion, a sovereign
		mistress of effects, throws a more safer voice on you.
		You must therefore be content to slubber the gloss of
		your new fortunes with this more stubborn and
		boisterous expedition.
230	**Othello**	The tyrant custom, most grave senators,

	被盗者微笑可令盗贼被盗，	
	无益的悲伤等于自寻烦恼。	210
勃拉班修	就让土耳其骗取塞浦路斯，	
	咱未失去它若能一笑置之；	
	有谁只接受宣判中的抚慰，	
	即可表明他这人善于受罪：	
	若靠可怜的耐心减轻忧伤，	215
	他既忍受宣判又忍受惆怅。	
	这些宣判的疗效相当显著，	
	适用于幸福，也适用于痛苦。	
	但话总归是话：我从未听说	
	破碎的心灵可通过耳朵愈合。	220
	我现在求您，处理国家大事吧。	
公爵	土耳其人正在以强大无比的兵力驶向	
	塞浦路斯。奥赛罗，那座岛屿的防御	
	能力您最熟悉，尽管我们在那里驻有	
	一位很棒的替补，然而舆论，她这位	225
	至高的主宰，断言还是您去更为保险。	
	因此，您必须心甘情愿地用这种不近	
	人情以及突如其来的远征去冲淡您的	
	新婚喜庆。	
奥赛罗	习惯这位暴君，我崇敬的元老，	230

217-8. 这些……痛苦（These…equivocal）：这些优美的格言模棱两可，既可适用于幸福，又可适用于痛苦（These fine maxims are equivocal, being equally appropriate to happiness or bitterness）（Bevington）。　220. 破碎……愈合（That…ear）：一颗破碎的心灵仅靠通过耳朵传入的话语即可得到宽慰（That the crushed heart was relieved by mere words that reach it through the ear）。　224-6. 尽管……保险（though…you）：人们承认（塞浦路斯总督）蒙塔诺完全能胜任，但具有决定权的舆论却认为由您来指挥将更为安全（Montano is admitted to be thoroughly competent, but general opinion, which finally determines what ought to be done, will feel safer with you in command）（Ridley）。

Hath made the flinty and steel couch of war

My thrice-driven bed of down. I do agnize

A natural and prompt alacrity

I find in hardness, and do undertake

235   This present wars against the Ottomites.

Most humbly therefore, bending to your state,

I crave fit disposition for my wife,

Due reference of place, and exhibition,

With such accommodation and besort

240   As levels with her breeding.

Duke   Why, at her father's.

Brabantio   I'll not have it so.

Othello   Nor I.

Desdemona   Nor would I there reside

To put my father in impatient thoughts

By being in his eye. Most gracious duke,

245   To my unfolding lend your prosperous ear

And let me find a charter in your voice

T'assist my simpleness.

Duke   What would you, Desdemona?

Desdemona   That I did love the Moor to live with him

250   My downright violence and storm of fortunes

已将铁石般的战地眠床变成

我蓬松的羽绒卧榻。 我承认

自己对艰难困苦具有一种

天然的得心应手,我愿负责

这一场抵御土耳其人的战争。 235

因此我最为谦恭地,唯命是听,

请求我的妻子能有适当安置,

为她提供合适的住处,和费用,

安排与其身份相称的膳食

以及适当的随从。 240

公爵 嗨,住她父亲家里。

勃拉班修 我可不愿意。

奥赛罗 我也不。

苔丝狄蒙娜 我也不愿住在那里,

不愿让我父亲天天看见我,

心烦意乱。 最为仁慈的公爵,

敬请殿下听一听我的禀报, 245

并让我得到您的亲口恩准,

以弥补我的口拙。

公爵 您想做什么,苔丝狄蒙娜?

苔丝狄蒙娜 我爱摩尔人,与他一起生活,

我对习俗的违犯,对命运的轻蔑, 250

---

232. 蓬松的羽绒卧榻(thrice…down):特别柔软的床铺(羽绒经过三遍吹拂之后,只留用最为细小和轻柔的绒毛)(an exceedingly soft bed [The feathers, that is, have been winnowed (driven) three times so that only the smallest and softest remain])(Mowat)。 236. 唯命是听(bending to your state):听从公爵殿下的吩咐;也许会边说边鞠躬(submitting to your high office. He may bow respectfully as he speaks)。 246-7. 并让我……口拙(And…simpleness):授予我特别的恩准以弥补我的不善言辞(grant me the privilege of your voice to compensate for my lack of skill [simpleness] as a speaker)(Mowat)。

May trumpet to the world. My heart's subdued

Even to the very quality of my lord:

I saw Othello's visage in his mind,

And to his honours and his valiant parts

255 Did I my soul and fortunes consecrate,

So that, dear lords, if I be left behind,

A moth of peace, and he go to the war,

The rites for which I love him are bereft me,

And I a heavy interim shall support

260 By his dear absence. Let me go with him.

Othello Let her have your voices.

Vouch with me, heaven, I therefore beg it not

To please the palate of my appetite,

Nor to comply with heat, the young affects

265 In me defunct, and proper satisfaction,

But to be free and bounteous to her mind.

And heaven defend your good souls that you think

I will your serious and great business scant

可以向世界宣告：我的心灵

已经与他的秉性融为一体：

我见奥赛罗的面如见其心一般，

对他的荣誉，和他的英勇品质

我已将我的灵魂和命运奉献：　　　　　　　255

因此，亲爱的大人，若把我留下，

一只无用的飞蛾，而他去参战，

我爱他的权利被剥夺而去，

承受一段痛苦的过渡时间，

因他不在身边；让我跟他去吧。　　　　　　260

奥赛罗　　　请您准许她吧。

上天为我作证，我如此请求

并不是为了迎合我的情欲

也不是迎合激情——青春的欲火

已离我而去——以及正当的满足，　　　　　　265

只是想慷慨地成全她的心意。

但愿上天不会让您以为

她在我身边期间，我会忽略

251-2. 我的心灵……融为一体（My heart…lord）：原文"quality"意为：profession；nature, moral and mental identity（职业；天性，性情）；本句意为：她的身心已为奥赛罗的天性（和军职）所同化（her inmost being ［heart］ has been assimilated to Othello's nature ［and military profession］）。　253. 我一见到奥赛罗的面（色），就见到了他的心地；即：在她眼里，他的面色已由他的心灵改变。她并未直接提及他的肤色，但尽管如此，她好像还是略有歉意（I saw ［the colour of］ Othello's face in ［the quality of］ his mind, i. e. his face was transformed, in her eyes, by his mind. She does not refer to his colour directly but seems to be half apologizing for it）。　257. 一只无用的飞蛾（a moth of peace）：或指游手好闲者；或暗示飞蛾对光亮的向往：如果奥赛罗去参战，她因无法享受到他的荣誉和英勇品质，就会像黑暗中的飞蛾一般（*either* drone, idler; *or* alluding to the moth's attraction to light: if he goes away to war, she, deprived of his *honours* and *valiant parts*, will be like a moth in the dark）。　264-5. 也不是……满足（Nor to…satisfaction）：许多编辑觉得本段存有讹误。现引原注，以助理解："Nor to satisfy sexual passion—the youthful appetites that are extinct in me—and permissible gratification of desire."（Honigmann）——译者附注。

For she is with me. No, when light-winged toys

270   Of feathered Cupid seel with wanton dullness

My speculative and officed instrument,

That my disports corrupt and taint my business,

Let housewives make a skillet of my helm,

And all indign and base adversities

275   Make head against my estimation.

Duke   Be it as you shall privately determine,

Either for her stay or going: th'affair cries haste

And speed must answer it.

1 Senator   you must away tonight.

Desdemona   Tonight, my lord?

Duke   This night.

Othello   With all my heart.

280 **Duke**   At nine i'th' morning here we'll meet again.

Othello, leave some officer behind

And he shall our commission bring to you,

And such things else of quality and respect

As doth import you.

Othello   So please your grace, my ancient:

285   A man he is of honesty and trust.

To his conveyance I assign my wife,

With what else needful your good grace shall think

	您的重大事情。　不,若插翅的	
	丘比特用那令人嗜睡的嬉戏	270
	将我双眼的视觉功能关闭,	
	竟使我的欢娱损害我的勤勉,	
	就让主妇将我的头盔当烧锅,	
	让所有可耻与卑鄙的灾祸	
	云集一起去攻击我的声誉。	275
公爵	这件事情由你们私下决定,	
	无论她留还是去:情况紧急,	
	必须尽快。	
元老甲	您今晚就得出发。	
苔丝狄蒙娜	今晚,殿下?	
公爵	今晚。	
奥赛罗	我十分乐意。	
公爵	明天早上九点我们在此再见。	280
	奥赛罗,您要留下某位军官,	
	他将把我的委任状给您捎去,	
	以及其他与您的身份相关的	
	各种事宜。	
奥赛罗	若殿下乐意,我的旗官:	
	他是一位诚实可靠的人士。	285
	我也委派他护送我的妻子,	
	以及殿下您认为需要随后	

269-70. 插翅的丘比特(feathered Cupid):罗马神话中的爱神,通常被描绘成一位身长翅膀的小孩儿(因此被称为:轻飘的玩物 [light-winged toys])(Mowat)。　270. 令人嗜睡(wanton dullness):性生活过后的无精打采(post-coital lethargy)(Bate)。　279. 我十分乐意 (with all my heart):"奥赛罗充满渴望,甚至绝望地望着自己的新娘……然后不无感叹地说道……‘我十分乐意’"。　或是他想掩盖自己的失望,言不由衷;或想试图说服苔丝狄蒙娜。285. 诚实(honesty):剧中曾多次将该品质赋予伊阿古,此乃首次(Ridley)。

To be sent after me.

Duke   Let it be so.

Good-night to everyone. And, noble signior,

290   If virtue no delighted beauty lack,

Your son-in-law is far more fair than black.

1 Senator   Adieu, brave Moor, use Desdemona well.

Brabantio   Look to her, Moor, if thou hast eyes to see:

She has deceived her father, and may thee.

Exeunt [*Duke, Brabantio, Senators, Officers*].

295 **Othello**   My life upon her faith. Honest Iago,

My Desdemona must I leave to thee:

I prithee, let thy wife attend on her,

And bring them after in the best advantage.

Come, Desdemona, I have but an hour

300   Of love, of worldly matters and direction

To spend with thee. We must obey the time.

Exeunt Othello and Desdemona.

Roderigo   Iago!

Iago   What sayst thou, noble heart?

Roderigo   What will I do, think'st thou?

305 **Iago**   Why, go to bed and sleep.

Roderigo   I will incontinently drown myself.

Iago   If thou dost, I shall never love thee after. Why,

thou silly gentleman?

送达的各种物质。

公爵　　　　　　　　　　就这么办吧。

祝各位晚安。　还有，尊贵的先生，

假如美德不缺乏怡人之美，　　　　　　　　　　　290

您女婿可是白净而非黝黑。

元老甲　　再见，勇敢的摩尔，善待苔丝狄蒙娜。

勃拉班修　看好她，摩尔，你眼睛若有视力：

她已经骗了她父亲，也许会骗你。

　　　　　　　　　　　　［公爵、勃拉班修、众元老及军官］下。

奥赛罗　　我以性命保她忠诚。　诚实的伊阿古，　　　295

我要把苔丝狄蒙娜交托给你：

我求你，让你的妻子侍奉她吧，

并在最为便利时带她们前来。

快来，苔丝狄蒙娜，我只有一个

钟头与你亲热，并处理一些　　　　　　　　　　　300

琐碎事务。　我们要顺应时局。

　　　　　　　　　　　　　　　奥赛罗与苔丝狄蒙娜下。

罗德利哥　伊阿古！

伊阿古　　你想说啥，高贵的心肝？

罗德利哥　你觉得我该咋办？

伊阿古　　嗨，上床睡觉去呗。　　　　　　　　　　　305

罗德利哥　我宁愿立即淹死。

伊阿古　　若是那样的话，从此我绝不再爱你，唉，

你这个傻绅士？

---

295. 奥赛罗既对苔丝狄蒙娜的忠诚毫无疑心，又对伊阿古的诚实深信不疑，颇具反讽（Ridley）。　301. 顺应时局（obey the time）：我们必须服从紧急情况的需要（we must comply with the needs of this emergency）。　303. 你（thou）：伊阿古的支配地位自第一幕第一场起已逐步确立，此前他将罗德利哥称为"您（you）"和"先生（sir）"；"高贵的心肝（noble heart）"这一称谓几近无礼（close to insolence）。

Roderigo It is silliness to live when to live is torment;
310 and then have we a prescription to die, when death
is our physician.

Iago O villainous! I have looked upon the world for
four times seven years, and since I could distinguish
betwixt a benefit and an injury I never found a man
315 that knew how to love himself. Ere I would say I
would drown myself for the love of a guinea-hen, I
would change my humanity with a baboon.

Roderigo What should I do? I confess it is my shame
to be so fond, but it is not in my virtue to amend it.

320 **Iago** Virtue? A fig! 'Tis in ourselves that we are thus, or
thus. Our bodies are gardens, to the which our wills
are gardeners. So that if we will plant nettles or sow
lettuce, set hyssop and weed up thyme, supply it with
one gender of herbs or distract it with many, either to
325 have it sterile with idleness or manured with industry
—why, the power and corrigible authority of this lies
in our wills. If the balance of our lives had not one
scale of reason to poise another of sensuality, the
blood and baseness of our natures would conduct us

罗德利哥	假如活着只是受罪还要活着,那才叫傻;	
	当死亡变成了我们的医生时,那就按照	310
	医嘱去死吧。	

伊阿古	噢,真丢人!我已在这个世界上观望了	
	四七二十八年,自从我能在利与害之间	
	作出分辨以来,还从未见过曾经有哪位	
	懂得如何自爱。在我声言自己愿为一只	315
	珍珠母鸡殉情之前,我宁愿用我的人性	
	与一只狒狒交换。	

罗德利哥	那我该咋办?我承认自己如此痴迷非常	
	丢脸,但我又没有能力予以补救。	

伊阿古	能力?去你的!我们之所以这样,或者	320
	那样,全都在自己。我们的身体是花园,	
	意志是园丁。因此我们要栽荨麻或者种	
	莴苣,栽种海索草,拔除百里香,里面	
	只种植一种芳草,或分成小块多种几种,	
	或因游手好闲使它荒废,或者辛勤耕耘	325
	——嗨,这种能施以矫正的权威就在于	
	我们的意志。假如我们生命的天平之上	
	没有一盘理智与另一盘肉欲抗衡,我们	
	身上的那些七情六欲会把我们引向一种	

---

311. 医嘱(prescription):医生的指示(doctor's orders),而非具体的医药配方(not specific directions for compounding a medicine)(Ridley)。　316. 珍珠母鸡(a guinea-hen):伊阿古对苔丝狄蒙娜的蔑称(Mowat)。　317. 狒狒(a baboon):傻瓜(猴子也与淫荡相关)(Bate)。　320. 去你的(a fig):表示轻蔑的叹语;一种淫秽的手势,"包括将拇指插进两个并拢的手指之间,或插进嘴里(contemptuous exclamation; an obscene gesture 'which consisted in thrusting the thumb between two of the closed fingers or into the mouth)"。　321. 花园(gardens):暗指《圣经》"加拉太书"6章7节:"人种的是什么,收的也是什么(whatever a man soweth, that shall he also reap)"。　伊阿古在利用宗教的常谈进行虚假的布道。　323. 海索草(hyssop):一种香草(Bate)。

330		to most preposterous conclusions. But we have
		reason to cool our raging motions, our carnal stings,
		our unbitted lusts; whereof I take this, that you call
		love, to be a sect or scion.
	Roderigo	It cannot be.
335	**Iago**	It is merely a lust of the blood and a permission of

to most preposterous conclusions. But we have
reason to cool our raging motions, our carnal stings,
our unbitted lusts; whereof I take this, that you call
love, to be a sect or scion.

Roderigo It cannot be.

Iago It is merely a lust of the blood and a permission of
the will. Come, be a man! Drown thyself? Drown cats
and blind puppies. I have professed me thy friend,
and I confess me knit to thy deserving with cables
of perdurable toughness. I could never better stead
thee than now. Put money in thy purse, follow thou
the wars, defeat thy favour with an usurped beard;
I say, put money in thy purse. It cannot be that
Desdemona should long continue her love to the
Moor—put money in thy purse—nor he his to her. It
was a violent commencement in her, and thou shalt
see an answerable sequestration—put but money in
thy purse. These Moors are changeable in their wills
—fill thy purse with money. The food that to him
now is as luscious as locusts shall be to him shortly as
acerb as coloquintida. She must change for youth;
when she is sated with his body she will find the
error of her choice: she must have change, she must.

	最为荒谬的结局。然而我们却拥有理智	330
	使我们暴虐的情绪、冲动的性欲、放纵	
	的欲望得以平息；就您所谓的爱情而言，	
	我想只是一根插条或接穗。	

罗德利哥　那不可能。

伊阿古　这只不过是对色情的贪欲和意志的默许。　　335
喂，做个男子汉！淹死你自己？让小猫
和没睁眼的小狗淹死去。我已声明我是
你朋友，我也承认自己已与你紧密相连，
牢不可破。我从未像现在这样能够给你
提供帮助。把钱装进你的口袋，要跟着　　340
军队，戴上一副胡须去丑化自己的仪容；
我说，把钱装进你的口袋。苔丝狄蒙娜
不可能会长此以往地爱恋那个摩尔——
把钱装进口袋。——他也不会长久爱她。
她的爱是属于心血来潮，因此你会看到　　345
一种相应的戛然而止——把钱装进你的
口袋。这些摩尔人心中的念头容易改变
——把钱装进你的口袋。他现在的食物
像角豆荚一般甘美多汁，但不久就会像
药西瓜一样苦涩。她定会爱上一位青年；　　350
当她对他的肉体感到腻烦时，就会发现
自己把人选错：她定会变心，一定会的。

---

340. 把钱装进你的口袋（put…purse）：意为"卖掉你的资产以筹集现款"，罗德利哥也明白其意（第380行）。　341. 戴上……仪容（defeat…beard）：戴上假胡须就意味着损坏了原本俊秀的容貌（罗德利哥依然年轻，尚未长出胡须）。　349. 角豆荚（locusts）：可能暗指施洗者约翰在旷野中所吃的"角豆荚与蜂蜜（locusts and honey）"（"马太福音"3章4节）。　在马太与伊阿古的心目中，该词可能指角豆树的果子（the pods of the carob tree），之所以称为"蝗虫豆"（locust beans），因其形似蝗虫（Mowat）。　350. 药西瓜（coloquintida）：一种苦苹果（a bitter apple）；用作泻药。　青年（youth）：比奥赛罗年轻者。

Therefore, put money in thy purse. If thou wilt needs damn thyself, do it a more delicate way than
355 drowning—make all the money thou canst. If sanctimony, and a frail vow betwixt an erring barbarian and a super-subtle Venetian, be not too hard for my wits and all the tribe of hell, thou shalt enjoy her— therefore make money. A pox of drowning thyself, it
360 is clean out of the way: seek thou rather to be hanged in compassing thy joy than to be drowned and go without her.

Roderigo Wilt thou be fast to my hopes, if I depend on the issue?

365 **Iago** Thou art sure of me—go, make money. I have told thee often, and I re-tell thee again and again, I hate the Moor. My cause is hearted, thine hath no less reason: let us be conjunctive in our revenge against him. If thou canst cuckold him, thou dost
370 thyself a pleasure, me a sport. There are many events in the womb of time, which will be delivered. Traverse, go, provide thy money: we will have more of this tomorrow. Adieu!

Roderigo Where shall we meet i' th' morning?

375 **Iago** At my lodging.

Roderigo I'll be with thee betimes.

Iago Go to, farewell. —Do you hear, Roderigo?

Roderigo What say you?

因此,把钱装进你的口袋。假如你定要
糟蹋自己,也该用一种比淹死更为高雅
的方式——要尽可能地多筹钱款。假如　　　　　　355
流浪的蛮人与超优雅的威尼斯女子之间
的神圣婚礼与脆弱婚约,利用我的才智
与所有魔鬼不难攻破,你将会享受到她
——所以要筹款。你想淹死自己才该死!
那可是大错特错:你宁可因为饱尝性福　　　　　　360
而被绞死,也不要在你把她弄到手之前
自溺身亡。

罗德利哥　　要是我等待这样的结果,我真的能指望
你吗?

伊阿古　　　你只管放心——去吧,筹钱去。我已经　　　　　365
告诉过你多次,而且我要再三地告诉你,
我恨那个摩尔。我对他怀恨在心,你也
同样怨恨:我们俩要联合起来对他进行
报复。假如你能让他做成乌龟,你自己
可得到满足,我得到娱乐。时间的腹中　　　　　370
孕育着诸多事端,它们必将会一一分娩。
前进!去,快去筹钱:我们明天再对此
详加讨论。　再见!

罗德利哥　　我们上午在哪里会面?

伊阿古　　　在我的住处。　　　　　　　　　　　　　　375

罗德利哥　　我会一早去见你。

伊阿古　　　得了,再见。——听见没有,罗德利哥?

罗德利哥　　你说什么?

---

377. 得了(go to):伊阿古的常用语,用以哄逗别人(jolly others along),有时毫无意义
(等于 come on; well then)。

	Iago	No more of drowning, do you hear?	
380	**Roderigo**	I am changed. I'll sell all my land.	*Exit.*
	Iago	Go to, farewell, put money enough in your purse.	

Thus do I ever make my fool my purse:

For I mine own gained knowledge should profane

If I would time expend with such a snipe

385 But for my sport and profit. I hate the Moor

And it is thought abroad that 'twixt my sheets

He's done my office. I know not if't be true,

But I for mere suspicion in that kind

Will do as if for surety. He holds me well,

390 The better shall my purpose work on him.

Cassio's a proper man: let me see now,

To get his place, and to plume up my will

In double knavery. How? How? Let's see:

After some time to abuse Othello's ear

395 That he is too familiar with his wife.

He hath a person and a smooth dispose

To be suspected, framed to make women false.

The Moor is of a free and open nature

伊阿古	别再淹死了,听见没有?		
罗德利哥	我现已改变。　我要卖掉所有地产。	下。	380
伊阿古	得了,再见,要在你钱包里装够钱。		

　　　　　　　我总是这样用我的傻瓜做钱包:

　　　　　　　因为我若与这样的蠢货厮混,

　　　　　　　而不是为了我的消遣和利益,

　　　　　　　就是亵渎我的知识。　我恨那摩尔, 　　　　　　385

　　　　　　　并且外面在传他曾在我的

　　　　　　　被窝里替我尽职。　不知是否是真,

　　　　　　　但在那种事上尽管只是怀疑,

　　　　　　　也要把它当真。　他对我很好,

　　　　　　　我的图谋将在他身上更易实现。 　　　　　　390

　　　　　　　凯西奥是位美男:让我想想看,

　　　　　　　夺取他的职位,我用计如愿以偿

　　　　　　　一举两得:咋办?　咋办?　让我看看:

　　　　　　　过些时日我要向摩尔人造谣,

　　　　　　　说他与他的妻子过分亲热。 　　　　　　395

　　　　　　　他的俊美以及殷勤的性情

　　　　　　　可令人猜疑,造成女人失贞。

　　　　　　　这个摩尔人天生直爽坦率,

---

　　382. 总是(ever):表明伊阿古已是一位老练的骗子(hardened cheater)。　385. 亵渎(profane):对(神圣的东西)不敬。　此系伊阿古对该词颇为乖戾的滥用(cynically misuses the word),因为他的知识(knowledge)并非人们通常所理解的那样神圣(sacred),而是邪恶(evil)。　385-403. 注意其计策逐渐成形的各个阶段,他打算在每个阶段将走多远,以及每个阶段都有什么图谋,这一点对正确理解伊阿古这个人物非常重要。　他在这一首次独白中主要是想取代凯西奥的职位;报复奥赛罗尚属次要;他总结了凯西奥与奥赛罗两人身上对他有利的品质。　他也想到了诽谤凯西奥的最佳方式——促使奥赛罗对凯西奥与苔丝狄蒙娜之间的关系产生怀疑。然而,到目前为止,其计策只是刚刚"成形(engendered)"而已(Ridley)。　398. 直爽坦率(free and open):令人好奇的是,约翰逊在形容莎士比亚时曾重复了这些话语(echoed these words in describing Shakespeare)。

That thinks men honest that but seem to be so,

400   And will as tenderly be led by th' nose

As asses are.

I have't. It is engendered! Hell and night

Must bring this monstrous birth to the world's light.   *Exit*.

他认为诚实的人似是而非，

他会像一头蠢驴让人轻易　　　　　　　　　　　　　400

牵着鼻子。

我有了,计已成形！地狱和夜晚

必将这种怪胎带到世人面前。　　　　　　　　　　下。

第二幕
ACT 2

SCENE I

Enter Montano and two Gentlemen.

Montano   What from the cape can you discern at sea?

1 Gentleman Nothing at all, it is a high-wrought flood:

I cannot 'twixt the heaven and the main

Descry a sail.

5   **Montano**   Methinks the wind hath spoke aloud at land,

A fuller blast ne'er shook our battlements:

If it hath ruffianed so upon the sea,

What ribs of oak, when mountains melt on them,

Can hold the mortise? What shall we hear of this?

10   **2 Gentleman** A segregation of the Turkish fleet:

For do but stand upon the foaming shore,

The chidden billow seems to pelt the clouds,

The wind-shaked surge, with high and monstrous mane,

Seems to cast water on the burning bear

15

And quench the guards of th'ever-fired pole.

I never did like molestation view

On the enchafed flood.

第一场

蒙塔诺与两位绅士上。

蒙塔诺 您从海岬处能看清海上有啥？

绅士甲 没有什么,只是汹涌的大海:
在天空与水域之间我望不见
一艘帆船。

蒙塔诺 我想这大风也会在陆上呼啸,   5
这是城垛所遭受的最强风暴:
它若在海上如此穷凶极恶,
有哪一艘木船,面对排山巨浪,
尚能保全？ 其结果将会如何？

绅士乙 土耳其舰队定会被风吹散: 10
因为站在这泡沫飞溅的海岸,
咆哮的波涛像是在拍击云端,
风卷的怒涛,犹如怪兽的鬃毛,
好像要浇向闪耀的小熊星座,
将不息之北极星的卫星扑灭。   15
我从未见过暴怒的大海之上
曾有类似骚动。

    2.1. 地点:塞浦路斯一港口;码头边的空地(Bevington)。 **1.** 蒙塔诺:很可能是由奥赛罗取代的塞浦路斯总督。 **13.** 怪兽的鬃毛(monstrous mane):The surf is like the mane of a wild beast(怒涛犹如野兽的鬃毛一般)(Bevington)。 **15.** 卫星(guards):小熊星座中的两颗星星,其亮度仅次于北极星(Bate)。

Montano   If that the Turkish fleet

Be not ensheltered and embayed, they are drowned.

It is impossible to bear it out.

Enter a Third Gentleman.

20   **3 Gentleman**   News, lads: our wars are done!

The desperate tempest hath so banged the Turks

That their designment halts. A noble ship of Venice

Hath seen a grievous wrack and sufferance

On most part of their fleet.

Montano   How? Is this true?

25   **3 Gentleman**   The ship is here put in,

A Veronesa; Michael Cassio,

Lieutenant to the warlike Moor, Othello,

Is come on shore; the Moor himself at sea,

And is in full commission here for Cyprus.

30   **Montano**   I am glad on't; 'tis a worthy governor.

3 Gentleman   But this same Cassio, though he speak of comfort

Enter Cassio.

Touching the Turkish loss, yet he looks sadly

And prays the Moor be safe, for they were parted

With foul and violent tempest.

Montano   Pray heavens he be,

35   For I have served him, and the man commands

Like a full soldier. Let's to the seaside, ho!

蒙塔诺	若土耳其舰队
	没有进港躲避,他们会被淹死。
	不可能劫后余生。

绅士丙上。

绅士丙	好消息,伙计们:战争结束了!	20
	土耳其遭此可怕的风暴袭击,	
	其谋划已搁浅。　威尼斯一艘大船	
	目睹他们舰队中的多数船只	
	遭受了海难。	
蒙塔诺	什么?　这是真的?	
绅士丙	大船已在此进港,	25
	一艘维罗纳号;迈克尔·凯西奥,	
	英勇的摩尔人奥赛罗之副将,	
	已经靠岸;受命前来掌管	
	塞浦路斯的摩尔人仍在海上。	
蒙塔诺	我很高兴,他是位可敬的总督。	30
绅士丙	但这位凯西奥,尽管对土耳其的	

凯西奥上。

	损失感到欣慰,却面带愁容	
	并祈求摩尔人平安,因为他们	
	是被恶劣的风暴吹散。	
蒙塔诺	愿他安全,	
	我曾在他手下服役,他指挥起来	35
	像个完美的军人。　咱们去海边,嗬!	

---

26. 维罗纳号（Veronessa）：来自维罗纳（from Verona）。　莎氏此处可能是指"威尼斯海军中的一艘船只,隶属维罗纳市"。

As well to see the vessel that's come in

As to throw out our eyes for brave Othello,

Even till we make the main and th'aerial blue

An indistinct regard.

40 **3 Gentleman**   Come, let's do so,

For every minute is expectancy

Of more arrivance.

Cassio   Thanks, you the valiant of this warlike isle

That so approve the Moor. O, let the heavens

45   Give him defense against the elements,

For I have lost him on a dangerous sea.

Montano   Is he well shipped?

Cassio   His bark is stoutly timbered, and his pilot

Of very expert and approved allowance,

50   Therefore my hopes, not surfeited to death,

Stand in bold cure.

A Voice   [*within*]   A sail! A sail! A sail!

Cassio   What noise?

2 Gentleman   The town is empty: on the brow o'th 'sea

Stand ranks of people, and they cry 'A sail!'

55 **Cassio**   My hopes do shape him for the governor.   *A shot.*

2 Gentleman   They do discharge their shot of courtesy,

Our friends at least.

Cassio   I pray you sir, go forth

And give us truth who 'tis that is arrived.

去看看已经驶进港口的帆船，

同时也可遥望英勇的奥赛罗，

直到我们的眼睛无法分辨

大海与蓝天。

| 绅士丙 | 　　　　　快来，咱们去吧， | 40 |

因为每一分钟都有望看到

更多的船只进港。

| 凯西奥 | 谢谢，英勇海岛上的诸位勇士， |

这么称颂摩尔将军！噢，让上天

给他护佑以抵御恶劣的天气，　　　　　　45

因为我在凶险的海上与他失散。

| 蒙塔诺 | 他的船只好吗？ |

| 凯西奥 | 他的船只结构坚固，他的舵手 |

非常娴熟，以久经考验著称，

因此我的希望，并没有过度，　　　　　　50

依然乐观。

| 一声音 | ［内喊］　有船！有船！有船！ |

| 凯西奥 | 什么声音？ |

| 绅士乙 | 城里空无一人：海边的悬崖上 |

站着一排排民众，他们高呼"有船！"

| 凯西奥 | 我希望并想象那是总督返航。　　　鸣炮一声。55 |

| 绅士乙 | 他们所鸣放的是一门礼炮， |

至少是朋友。

| 凯西奥 | 　　　　　请求先生您，前去 |

给我们弄清究竟是谁到了。

50-1. 并没有过度，依然乐观（not…cure）：并非过度沉溺，依然有望实现（not indulged in excessively, persist in their optimism；bold = confident［确信的］）。　51. 舞台指示：［内喊］（within）：即后台（off stage）。　53. 悬崖（brow）：（可俯瞰大海的）峭壁的凸出边沿（projecting edge of a cliff［overlooking the sea］）。

	2 Gentleman	I shall.	*Exit.*
60	**Montano**	But, good lieutenant, is your general wived?	
	Cassio	Most fortunately: he hath achieved a maid	

That paragons description and wild fame;

One that excels the quirks of blazoning pens

And in th'essential vesture of creation

Does tire the inginer.

Enter Second Gentleman.

65   How now? Who has put in?

2 Gentleman   'Tis one Iago, ancient to the general.

Cassio   He's had most favourable and happy speed.

Tempests themselves, high seas, and howling winds,

The guttered rocks and congregated sands,

70   Traitors ensteeped to clog the guiltless keel,

As having sense of beauty, do omit

Their mortal natures, letting go safely by

The divine Desdemona.

Montano   What is she?

Cassio   She that I spoke of, our great captain's captain,

75   Left in the conduct of the bold Iago,

Whose footing here anticipates our thoughts

A se'nnight's speed. Great Jove, Othello guard,

And swell his sail with thine own powerful breath

绅士乙	我会的。	下。	
蒙塔诺	好副官,您的将军是否已婚配?		60
凯西奥	非常幸运:他赢得的这位姑娘		

胜过了言语描述和过分赞颂;

生花的妙笔也都无法形容,

上帝所赋予她的天生丽质

令人疲于言表。

绅士乙上。

怎么样? 是谁进港?   65

绅士乙	一位叫伊阿古的,将军的旗官。	
凯西奥	他倒是非常幸运,一帆风顺。	

风暴、巨浪以及怒吼的狂风,

凹凸的礁石以及淤积的沙洲——

使无辜船只搁浅的水下叛徒, 70

好像也有美感一般,竟忽略

置人于死地的本性,让圣洁的

苔丝狄蒙娜安然通过。

蒙塔诺	她是谁?	
凯西奥	我说的这位,是我们上尉的上尉,	

交给了勇敢的伊阿古护送, 75

他们要比我们的预期早到

一周。 伟大的朱庇特,保佑奥赛罗,

用强劲的气息吹胀他的船帆,

---

63. 生花的妙笔(blazoning pens):blazoning = describing(描述);boasting(夸示)。借鉴卞译。 ——译者附注。 64-5. 上帝……言表(And in…inginer):上帝所给予她的真善之美,(她)可挫败任何想赞美她的努力(and in her real, God-given, beauty,[she] defeats any attempt to praise her)。 其中,inginer 是指设计者,创造者;此处指诗人(An inginer is one who devises, here a poet)(Bevington)。

That he may bless this bay with his tall ship,

80   Make love's quick pants in Desdemona's arms,

Give renewed fire to our extincted spirits,

And bring all Cyprus comfort! —

Enter Desdemona, Iago, Roderigo and Emilia.

                    O, behold,

The riches of the ship is come on shore:

You men of Cyprus, let her have your knees!

85   Hail to thee, lady, and the grace of heaven,

Before, behind thee, and on every hand

Enwheel thee round!

Desdemona   I thank you, valiant Cassio.

What tidings can you tell me of my lord?

Cassio   He is not yet arrived, nor know I aught

90   But that he's well, and will be shortly here.

Desdemona   O, but I fear⋯how lost you company?

Cassio   The great contention of the sea and skies

Parted our fellowship. (*A Voice within*: ' *A sail*! *A sail*! ')

                But hark! A sail!

                        [*A shot is heard.*]

2 Gentleman They give their greeting to the citadel:

This likewise is a friend.

95 **Cassio**   See for the news.

                        [*Exit Gentleman.*]

好让他的大船保护这海湾，

心潮澎湃地投入苔丝狄蒙娜怀抱，　　　　　　　　　　80

使我们消沉的士气重新振作，

为塞浦路斯带来慰藉！——

　　　苔丝狄蒙娜、伊阿古、罗德利哥与爱米利娅上。

　　　　　　　　　　噢，看哪，

船上的瑰宝现在已经上岸：

你们塞浦路斯人，快给她跪下！

向你致意，夫人，愿上帝的恩典　　　　　　　　　　85

在你身前身后，和上下左右

将你环绕！

苔丝狄蒙娜　　　　　　谢谢您，勇敢的凯西奥。

我的丈夫他有什么消息？

凯西奥　　　他尚未到达，不过就我所知，

他一切安好，很快就会来到。　　　　　　　　　　90

苔丝狄蒙娜　唉，可我担心……你们怎么会失散？

凯西奥　　　大海与天空之间的一争高下

使我们彼此分离。　　　　　（内喊："有船！有船！"）

　　　　　　请听！有船！

　　　　　　　　　　　　　　　　　　　　［炮声。］

绅士乙　　　他们向城堡鸣放了一门礼炮：

这同样也是朋友。

凯西奥　　　　　　快去看看。　　　　　　　　　95

　　　　　　　　　　　　　　　　　　　［绅士下。］

---

80. 心潮澎湃（love's quick pants）："性高潮过后的气喘吁吁（The quick breathing that accompanies and ensues upon the orgasm）"。　然而，请注意凯西奥后来反对将性爱意象用于苔丝狄蒙娜（2. 3. 14 行及以下）。　"爱心的剧跳（panting of loving hearts）"倒颇为常见。 85. 你（thee）：凯西奥此处用了表示亲近的"你（thee）"，但后来（165 行）却用了"您（you）"。

Good ancient, you are welcome. [*To Emilia.*] Welcome, mistress.

Let it not gall your patience, good Iago,

That I extend my manners; 'tis my breeding

That gives me this bold show of courtesy. [*He kisses Emilia.*]

100 **Iago**   Sir, would she give you so much of her lips

As of her tongue she oft bestows on me,

You'd have enough.

Desdemona   Alas, she has no speech!

Iago   In faith, too much!

I find it still when I have list to sleep.

105   Marry, before your ladyship I grant,

She puts her tongue a little in her heart

And chides with thinking.

Emilia   You have little cause to say so.

Iago   Come on, come on, you are pictures out of doors,

110   Bells in your parlors, wild-cats in your kitchens,

Saints in your injuries, devils being offended,

Players in your housewifery, and housewives in⋯

好旗官,欢迎您。〔向爱米利娅〕欢迎,夫人。

您可别恼羞成怒,好伊阿古,

我要向她致意;是我的教养

促使我如此大胆地示以礼貌。　　　　　　　　　〔亲吻爱米利娅。〕

伊阿古　　先生,假如她向您献上的嘴唇　　　　　　　　　　100

就像她经常给我的舌剑一样,

您会叫苦不迭。

苔丝狄蒙娜　　　　　　哎,她沉默了!

伊阿古　　不,她话太多!

我想睡时她依然喋喋不休,

真是的,当着夫人的面,我承认,　　　　　　　　　　　　105

她现在一言不发,但心里却在

默默地责骂。

爱米利娅　　您这样胡说没有道理。

伊阿古　　得了,得了,你们在外像幅图画,

在客厅像闹钟,在厨房像野猫,　　　　　　　　　　　　110

伤人时像圣人,受伤时像魔鬼,

做家务时吊儿郎当,像个荡妇……

96-7. 好……好(good…good):注意其居高临下的色彩(note the touch of condescension in *good*)。 99. 舞台指示:也许是爱米利娅太愿意接受亲吻,才激怒了伊阿古。 101. 舌剑(tongue):伊阿古在粗俗地暗示用舌头亲吻,用舌头责骂。 102. 叫苦不迭(have enough):借鉴朱生豪先生译文。 ——译者附注。 109-166. 得了……赏识(You…scholar):这一段对许多读者来说,我也赞同,可谓莎剧中最为明显的败笔之一。 首先,它不合情理。 苔丝狄蒙娜的本能必定是亲自走向港口,而不是附带性地问一句是否有人去了港口(第120行)。 然后,观看她与伊阿古长时间的闲聊也令人不快,而且她对这种闲聊如此擅长,人们不禁要问她在途中会以这种方式度过多少时间。 ……也许,这一段只是对站票观众的献礼,因为对他们来说——丑角若被忽略——便无多少娱乐性可言(Ridley)。 另外,译者2015年秋在莎士比亚学院访学期间,曾观看过莎士比亚环球剧院于2007年录制的《奥赛罗》全剧(DVD),也注意到117-161行的内容全部删节。 ——译者附注。 109. 你们(you):他粗俗地也将苔丝狄蒙娜包括在内。 像幅图画(you are pictures):你们穿上最棒的衣服外出时美丽如画,"暗示她们的美丽有赖于涂脂抹粉"。 也可指"道貌岸然"(silent appearance [of virtue])。 112. 荡妇(housewives):可指"家庭主妇",也可指"轻佻的女子,贱妇(a 'light' woman, a hussy)"。

Your beds.

Desdemona   O, fie upon thee, slanderer!

Iago   Nay, it is true, or else I am a Turk:

115   You rise to play, and go to bed to work.

Emilia   You shall not write my praise.

Iago   No, let me not.

Desdemona What wouldst thou write of me, if thou shouldst praise me?

Iago   O, gentle lady, do not put me to't,

For I am nothing if not critical.

120 **Desdemona** Come on, assay. There's one gone to the harbour?

Iago   Ay, madam.

Desdemona I am not merry, but I do beguile

The thing I am by seeming otherwise.

Come, how wouldst thou praise me?

125 **Iago**   I am about it, but indeed my invention

Comes from my pate as birdlime does from frieze,

It plucks out brains and all; but my muse labours,

And thus she is delivered:

If she be fair and wise, fairness and wit,

130   The one's for use, the other useth it.

Desdemona Well praised. How if she be black and witty?

在你们床上！

苔丝狄蒙娜　　　　　　噢,去你的,诽谤家!

伊阿古　　不,是真的,否则我是变节者:

您起床就玩耍,上床就干活儿。　　　　　　　　　115

爱米利娅　　您不会赞美我的。

伊阿古　　　　　　　　对,别让我赞美。

苔丝狄蒙娜　　你若对我赞美,会说些啥呢?

伊阿古　　噢,温柔的夫人,可不要激我,

因为我除了挑剔啥都不会。

苔丝狄蒙娜　　快,试试看。　是否有人去了港口?　　　　120

伊阿古　　是的,夫人。

苔丝狄蒙娜　　我并不开心,不过是在掩饰

我的真实心情,强装笑颜。

快,你会如何赞美我呢?

伊阿古　　我在思索,我的灵感从头脑溢出,　　　　　　125

就像呢绒上的粘鸟胶难舍难分,

扯出脑浆;可我的缪斯在分娩,

她的胎儿现已降生:

假如她既漂亮来又明智,

一个被利用,一个利用之。　　　　　　　　　　130

苔丝狄蒙娜　　赞美得好。　假如她黑而明智呢?

---

115. 您(you):与109行的"你们"相比,此处更为直接地将矛头指向了苔丝狄蒙娜。 122-3. 也许是旁白。 123. 我的真实心情(The thing I am):我身为忧虑的妻子之真相(the fact that I am an anxious wife)。 125. 灵感(invention):可指"创造力(inventiveness)",也可指"创造物(the thing invented)"。 然而,125-128行可被视为散文。 126. 粘鸟胶(bird-lime):涂在树枝上用以捕鸟的黏胶(Bate)。 127-8. 可……降生(but…delivered):在玩弄两词的文字游戏,即:"labours(劳作,分娩)与"delivered(传送,分娩)";我的缪斯(my muse):我的灵感女神(my inspiring goddess)。 伊阿古假装自己具有绅士般的才能——可以作诗。 130. 即她的明智会利用她的美丽(her cleverness will make use of her beauty)(Beving-ton)。 131. 黑(black):黑头发(dark-haired)。 按照传统,苔丝狄蒙娜是金发,爱米利娅是黑发。

	Iago	If she be black, and thereto have a wit,
		She'll find a white that shall her blackness fit.
	Desdemona	Worse and worse.
135	**Emilia**	How if fair and foolish?
	Iago	She never yet was foolish that was fair,
		For even her folly helped her to an heir.

Desdemona These are old fond paradoxes to make fools laugh i'th' alehouse. What miserable praise hast 140 thou for her that's foul and foolish?

Iago There's none so foul, and foolish thereunto, But does foul pranks which fair and wise ones do.

Desdemona O heavy ignorance, thou praisest the worst best. But what praise couldst thou bestow on a 145 deserving woman indeed? One that in the authority of her merit did justly put on the vouch of very malice itself?

Iago She that was ever fair and never proud, Had tongue at will, and yet was never loud, 150 Never lacked gold, and yet went never gay,

伊阿古	她若黑脸蛋儿,并且有智慧,	
	就会找个白人匹配她的黝黑。	
苔丝狄蒙娜	越来越糟。	
爱米利娅	要是漂亮而愚蠢呢?	135
伊阿古	如果她很漂亮绝不会愚蠢,	
	因为愚蠢可帮她孕育儿孙。	
苔丝狄蒙娜	这些都是陈旧而愚蠢的谬论,让傻瓜	
	在酒馆里笑笑而已。假如她又丑又蠢,	
	你会怎样吝啬地称赞呢?	140
伊阿古	无论她多么丑陋,多么愚蠢,	
	也会像聪明人那样男女厮混。	
苔丝狄蒙娜	噢,极度的无知,你将最糟的说成了	
	最好。那你对一位实至名归的好女人	
	又将如何称颂?她是如此的德高望重,	145
	竟会迫使恶意本身出面作证对她表示	
	赞同?	
伊阿古	她长相俊美,然而从不骄傲,	
	谈吐随心所欲,但从不大叫。	
	不缺金钱,但衣着从不浮艳,	150

---

133. 配(fit):可指"适合(suit)",也可指"做爱时的插入(fit into during sex)"(Bate)。　133. 黝黑(blackness):可指女性的外阴。　137. 愚蠢(folly):"愚蠢(foolishness)",也可指"淫荡,下流(unchastity, lewdness)"。　137. 孕育儿孙(an heir):可指"嫁给一个继承人(to marry an heir)";也可指"生育杂种(to have a bastard child)"。142. 男女厮混(foul pranks):放荡不羁或淫荡行为(sexual pranks or acts)。　伊阿古的涉性韵句愈加露骨。　144. 实至名归的好女人(a…indeed):一位真正值得称颂的女人(a truly deserving woman)。　是指她本人?或是指向爱米利娅?　145-7. 她是……赞同(one…itself):她的美德是如此强大有力,竟可正当地迫使邪恶本身表示赞许(one whose virtue is so powerful that it rightfully compels the approving testimony of malice itself)(Bate)。　她对自己的美德深信不疑,不怕最为恶毒的攻击(one who, sure of her own merit, did not fear the worst that could be said against her)(Honigmann)。　148-60. 她长相俊美……鸡零狗碎(She…beer):参考《李尔王》3. 2. 81 行及以下由傻瓜道出的类似韵文,其实了无价值。　伊阿古在此扮傻以掩饰其本性,正如他在2. 3. 64 行及以下的表现一样;并以此炫耀自己的聪明。

Fled from her wish, and yet said 'now I may',

She that, being angered, her revenge being nigh,

Bade her wrong stay, and her displeasure fly,

She that in wisdom never was so frail

155 To change the cod's head for the salmon's tall,

She that could think, and ne'er disclose her mind,

See suitors following, and not look behind,

She was a wight, if ever such wights were

Desdemona To do what?

160 **Iago** To suckle fools, and chronicle small beer.

Desdemona O   most   lame   and   impotent   conclusion!
Do not learn of him, Emilia, though he be thy
husband. How say you, Cassio? Is he not a most
profane and liberal counselor?

165 **Cassio** He speaks home, madam, you may relish him
more in the soldier than in the scholar.

Iago [*aside*] He takes her by the palm; ay, well said,
whisper. With as little a web as this will I ensnare as
great a fly as Cassio. Ay, smile upon her, do: I will

节制欲念，尽管她可以实现。

她被人激怒，本可立即报复，

却忍受冤屈，指使怒气消除，

明白事理，面对诱惑不越轨，

不会让鳕鱼头更换鲑鱼尾， 155

她能思善想，但是声色不露，

知道追求者尾随，并不回头，

她是女的，若曾有过，就会——

苔丝狄蒙娜　　就会什么？

伊阿古　　给傻瓜哺乳，关注鸡零狗碎。 160

苔丝狄蒙娜　　噢，这种结尾可真是最为蹩脚和无力！

别听他的，爱米利娅，尽管他是你的

丈夫。您说呢，凯西奥，难道他不是

最会胡说八道的家伙？

凯西奥　　他说话中肯，夫人，您最好把他当成 165

军人而不是学者加以欣赏。

伊阿古　　[旁白]他牵着她的手；是的，干得好，

交头接耳。用这张小小罗网即可捕捉

凯西奥似的大傻。对，对她笑，笑吧：

---

151. 节制……实现（Fled…may）：节制自己的欲望，尽管她有能力予以实现（restrained from her desires though she had power to satisfy them）（Mowat）。　154. 越轨（frail）：脆弱（weak）；意志薄弱，经不住诱惑（morally weak, unable to resist temptation）。　155. 此处的"更换（change）"是一种"愚蠢的举动（to make a foolish exchange）"（Ridley）。莎士比亚肯定知道"（多种鱼类的）尾部很受欢迎，而鳕鱼头却毫无价值可言"。此处同时也在玩弄文字游戏，即：鳕鱼（cod）也可指阴茎（penis）；尾（tail）可指（女性的）外阴（pudenda）。158. 女的（wight）：指生灵（creature），人（person）。伊阿古在假装语塞。参考4. 1. 32行。　160. 关注（chronicle）：登记（register），记录（record）；即"挂念琐碎的事情（be concerned with trivialities）"。鸡零狗碎（small beer）：琐事（trivialities）。　167. 干得好（well said）：意为"well done（干得好）"，该短语常用以赞许行动，而不是称颂言语（as often, approving action, not speech）（Ridley）。　168. 罗网（web）：伊阿古站在一旁，犹如一只蜘蛛注视着一只苍蝇。如果奥赛罗到来时凯西奥依然握着苔丝狄蒙娜的手，这一幕将会使奥赛罗心生厌恶（this could be a poisonous image in Othello's mind later）。

170 gyve thee in thine own courtesies. You say true, 'tis
so indeed. If such tricks as these strip you out of
your lieutenantry, it had been better you had not
kissed your three fingers so oft, which now again you
are most apt to play the sir in. Very good, well kissed,
175 and excellent courtesy: 'tis so indeed! Yet again, your
fingers to your lips? Would they were clyster-pipes
for your sake! [*Trumpet within*]
The Moor! I know his trumpet!

Cassio   'Tis truly so.

Desdemona Let's meet him and receive him.

Enter Othello and Attendants.

Cassio   Lo, where he comes!

Othello O my fair warrior!

180 **Desdemona**   My dear Othello!

Othello It gives me wonder great as my content
To see you here before me! O my soul's joy,
If after every tempest come such calms,
May the winds blow till they have wakened death,

	我就用你的殷勤将你套住。说得没错，	170
	真是这样。这样的愚行若能剥夺你的	
	副官头衔，你最好还是不要如此频繁	
	地亲吻你的三个指头，你现在又乐此	
	不疲地假装风度翩翩。很好，吻得好，	
	多有礼貌：的确如此！又来啦，你的	175
	指头又放到了唇边？但愿它们是你的	
	灌肠管！〔内闻号角声〕	
	摩尔人！我知道他的号角！	
凯西奥	没错。	
苔丝狄蒙娜	咱们去迎接他吧。	

奥赛罗及随从上。

凯西奥	瞧，他来了！
奥赛罗	噢，我美丽的勇士！
苔丝狄蒙娜	我亲爱的奥赛罗！ 180
奥赛罗	看到您在我之前到了这里
	让我喜出望外！噢，我心旷神怡，
	若每次风暴过后有这种宁静，
	愿大风一直吹到将死人唤醒，

170-1. 说得没错，真是这样（You…indeed）：伊阿古在冷嘲热讽地假装对凯西奥说话（Bate）。 他并未听到凯西奥在说些什么，只是嘲笑他的肢体语言而已（Honigmann）。 171. 愚行（tricks）：可指任性或愚蠢的行为（capricious or foolish acts）；可指身敏手巧（feats of dexterity）；也可指伊阿古本人的诡计（Iago's own tricks）。 173. 亲吻你的三个指头（kissed…fingers）：一个接一个地亲吻（Honigmann）。 亲吻自己的手是绅士对淑女的常见礼仪（Ridley）。 177. 灌肠管（clyster-pipes）：（从肛门处）施用灌肠药剂的管子。 （手指、嘴唇、管子）这些意象与性有关（Honigmann）。 178. 我知道他的号角（I…trumpet）：著名的人物都有各自的号声，如《李尔王》2. 1. 77 行的舞台指示，"幕后鸣号"之后，到了 79 行的台词便是："听，公爵的号声；不知他为何来了"（Ridley）。 180. 美丽的勇士（fair warrior）：在爱情诗中女士常被称为勇士。

185	And let the labouring bark climb hills of seas,
	Olympus-high, and duck again as low
	As hell's from heaven. If it were now to die,
	'Twere now to be most happy, for I fear
	My soul hath her content so absolute
190	That not another comfort like to this
	Succeeds in unknown fate.

Desdemona   The heavens forbid

But that our loves and comforts should increase

Even as our days do grow.

Othello   Amen to that, sweet powers!

I cannot speak enough of this content,

195 It stops me here, it is too much of joy.

And this, and this the greatest discords be   *They kiss.*

That e'er our hearts shall make.

Iago   [*aside*]O, you are well tuned now: but I'll set down

The pegs that make this music, as honest

As I am.

200 **Othello**   Come, let us to the castle.

News, friends, our wars are done, the Turks are drowned.

How does my old acquaintance of this isle?

让颠簸的帆船爬上奥林帕斯　　　　　　　　　　　185

般的高山巨浪，再从天上跌入

地狱般的深渊。　若注定现在死去，

那可是最为幸福，因为我担心

我现在是如此彻底的心满意足，

吉凶未卜的命运再也不会有　　　　　　　　　　190

类似的慰藉。

苔丝狄蒙娜　　　　　　　但愿上帝保佑

我们的爱情以及幸福能够

与日俱增！

奥赛罗　　　　　　　但愿如此，可爱的神灵！

这种满足我简直无法形容，

已把我喉咙噎住，太令人喜悦。　　　　　　　　195

亲吻，亲吻将是我们两颗心　　　　　　　　他们亲吻。

发出的最大摩擦。

伊阿古　　[旁白]噢，你们现在音调和谐：可我要

让演奏这种音乐的琴弦降调，

我会说到做到。

奥赛罗　　　　　　　来，咱们去城堡。　　　　　200

好消息，战争结束，土耳其人已淹死。

岛上的老朋友你们一向可好？

---

185. 奥林帕斯（Olympus）：希腊神话中众神的居所。 193. 但愿……神灵（Amen…pow-ers）：原文"Amen（阿门、诚心所愿）"出自《圣经》；而"sweet powers（可爱的神灵）"则常指异教徒的神明。 195. 噎住（stops）：意为"窒息（chokes）"。 为其后来的语塞做了铺垫，尤其是 4. 1. 36 行。 196. 亲吻，亲吻（this, and this）：两个示意性的亲吻动作，也许没有身体接触，因为奥赛罗的化装用品会将苔丝狄蒙娜的脸庞弄黑（3. 3. 390）。 197. 摩擦（dis-cords）：可指音乐方面的"不协和、噪音（absence of harmony）"（伊阿古即取此意）；也可指"不和（disagreement）"、"冲突（strife）"。 199. 降调（set down）：可指将琴弦或（用以调节弦线松紧的）弦轴（pegs）调松，以使乐器发出噪音或完全失音；也许还可指将（人的）弦轴调低，因为弦轴也可指发出这种乐音的人——奥赛罗与苔丝狄蒙娜（Honigmann；Ridley）。

Honey, you shall be well desired in Cyprus,

I have found great love amongst them. O my sweet,

205 I prattle out of fashion, and I dote

In mine own comforts. I prithee, good Iago,

Go to the bay and disembark my coffers.

Bring thou the master to the citadel,

He is a good one, and his worthiness

210 Does challenge much respect. Come, Desdemona;

Once more, well met at Cyprus.

[*Exeunt all but Iago and Roderigo.*]

Iago Do thou meet me presently at the harbour. Come

hither: if thou be'st valiant—as, they say, base men

being in love have then a nobility in their natures,

215 more than is native to them—list me. The lieutenant

tonight watches on the court of guard. First I must

tell thee this: Desdemona is directly in love with him.

Roderigo With him? Why, 'tis not possible.

Iago Lay thy finger thus, and let thy soul be instructed.

220 Mark me with what violence she first loved the Moor,

but for bragging and telling her fantastical lies—and

will she love him still for prating? Let not thy discreet

heart think it. Her eye must be fed, and what delight

shall she have to look on the devil? When the blood is

　　　　　宝贝,您在塞浦路斯会倍受爱慕,

　　　　　他们待我很好。 噢,我的宝贝,

　　　　　我有些忘乎所以,只管沉溺在　　　　　　　　　205

　　　　　自己的幸福之中。 我求你,好伊阿古,

　　　　　前去港口将我的行李卸下,

　　　　　把那位船长带到城堡这里,

　　　　　他是一位好船长,他的才能

　　　　　真令人尊重。 来,苔丝狄蒙娜;　　　　　　　210

　　　　　再说一遍,很高兴在此相见!

　　　　　　　　　　　　　[除伊阿古与罗德利哥外,全下。]

伊阿古　　你立即到港口那边与我会面。这边来:

　　　　　假如你有胆量——据人们所说,恋爱

　　　　　中的懦夫所体现出的英雄气概要比他

　　　　　天生所具有的更多——听我说。副官　　　　　215

　　　　　今晚会在警卫处值班。首先,我必须

　　　　　告诉你:苔丝狄蒙娜显然是爱上他了。

罗德利哥　爱上他了? 嗨,那不可能!

伊阿古　　你要闭上嘴巴,让你的灵魂听我使唤。

　　　　　注意,她最初是多么疯狂地爱上摩尔,　　　　220

　　　　　只是为了他的吹嘘和异想天开的谎言——

　　　　　她会长久地爱他的空谈?你是明白人,

　　　　　可别这么想。她的眼睛定需满足,她

　　　　　看着那个魔鬼能有什么愉快?当欲火

---

　　203. 爱慕(desired):意为"追求(sought after)";颇具戏剧反讽,因为罗德利哥与伊阿古实际上均对她有意。 207. 在拉丁语喜剧中,一位奴隶或仆人有时要将其主人的行李从船上卸下(参考《错误的喜剧》5. 1. 410)。 奥赛罗几乎将伊阿古当成了自己的奴仆。 212. 你……会面(Do…harbour):也许是对一位士兵说的,因为伊阿古告诉罗德利哥去城堡与他会面(281行)。 另外,舞台指示"全下"并不意味着只剩下伊阿古与罗德利哥两人而已。 213-5. 据人们……更多(as…them):可能是旁白。 221. 伊阿古讨厌奥赛罗浮夸的言谈(1. 1. 12-3)。

225 made dull with the act of sport, there should be, again
to inflame it, and to give satiety a fresh appetite, love-
liness in favour, sympathy in years, manners and
beauties, all which the Moor is defective in. Now for
want of these required conveniences, her delicate
230 tenderness will find itself abused, begin to heave the
gorge, disrelish and abhor the Moor—very nature
will instruct her in it and compel her to some second
choice. Now sir, this granted—as it is a most pregnant
and unforced position—who stands so eminent in
235 the degree of this fortune as Cassio does? A knave
very voluble, no further conscionable than in putting
on the mere form of civil and humane seeming, for
the better compassing of his salt and most hidden
loose affection. Why none, why none: a slipper and
240 subtle knave, a finder out of occasions, that has an
eye, can stamp and counterfeit advantages, though
true advantage never present itself—a devilish knave;
besides, the knave is handsome, young, and hath all
those requisites in him that folly and green minds
245 look after. A pestilent complete knave, and the woman
hath found him already.

Roderigo I cannot believe that in her, she's full of most
blest condition.

Iago Blest fig's-end! The wine she drinks is made of

得到饱足而心生倦意时，便需要重新　　　　　　　　225
点燃，需给腻味一种新鲜，她就需要
找个相貌可爱，年龄接近，举止相当
的青年，而这些方面摩尔人都有缺陷。
由于缺乏这些必要的相像，她会觉得
自己的妙龄芳华受到伤害，开始恶心，　　　　　　　230
厌恶并且憎恨那个摩尔——她的本能
会就此加以开导并驱使她进行第二次
选择。先生，若这点没错——因为这
显而易见，顺理成章——又有谁能像
凯西奥那样占尽先机饱此艳福？一个　　　　　　　235
无常的恶棍，不过是一心一意地披上
知书达理的外衣装模作样而已，以便
更好地实现他那好色的和最为隐蔽的
淫念。无人能比，无人能比：圆滑而
狡诈的恶棍，投机取巧的家伙，目光　　　　　　　240
四处流盼，能够发明伪造机会，尽管
真实的机会从未出现——坏透的恶棍；
而且，这个恶棍年轻英俊，他身上也
具有那些必要的品质，令愚蠢和幼稚
的姑娘追寻。一个十足的恶棍，这个　　　　　　　245
女人已经看上他了。

罗德利哥　　我不信她是那种女人，她充满了最为
　　　　　　圣洁的品性。

伊阿古　　　圣洁的阴道！她喝的红酒也是用葡萄

---

244. 愚蠢（folly）：可指"愚蠢（foolishness）"，也可指"淫荡（wantonness）"。　249-50. 她喝的红酒也是用葡萄酿的（The wine…grapes）：伊阿古隐晦而笼统的断言之一，我们需要自己加以领会。　即："所有的葡萄酒都有渣滓，所有的女人都有缺点（No wine made of grapes but hath lees, no woman created of flesh but hath faults）（Honigmann）。""她跟别人没什么两样（也易受情欲影响）（she's as mortal［and open to desire］as the next person）"（Bate）。

250   grapes. If she had been blest, she would never have loved the Moor. Blest pudding! Didst thou not see her paddle with the palm of his hand? Didst not mark that?

Roderigo   Yes, that I did, but that was but courtesy.

255 **Iago**   Lechery, by this hand: an index and obscure prologue to the history of lust and foul thoughts. They met so near with their lips that their breaths embraced together. Villainous thoughts, Roderigo: when these mutualities so marshal the way, hard at

260   hand comes the master and main exercise, th'incorporate conclusion. Pish! But, sir, be you ruled by me. I have brought you from Venice: watch you tonight. For the command, I'll lay't upon you. Cassio knows you not, I'll not be far from you, do you find

265   some occasion to anger Cassio, either by speaking too loud or tainting his discipline, or from what other course you please, which the time shall more favourably minister.

Roderigo   Well.

270 **Iago**   Sir, he's rash and very sudden in choler, and

| | 酿的。她要是圣洁就绝不会爱上那个 | 250 |

酿的。她要是圣洁就绝不会爱上那个
摩尔。圣洁的阴茎！难道你没有看见
她用手指抚弄他的手心？你没有注意
到吗？

罗德利哥　我注意到了，不过那只是礼貌。

伊阿古　　是淫荡，我举手发誓：那不过是淫欲　　255
以及邪念历史中的索引和隐晦的开篇。
他们彼此的嘴唇是如此接近，他们的
呼吸彼此相拥。淫心邪念，罗德利哥：
当这些亲密无间将道路打通后，接着
就会出现那种主要的动作，即最终的　　260
融为一体。呸！不过，先生，您要听
我吩咐。我从威尼斯把您带来：今晚
要留意。我让您做领军人物。凯西奥
不认识您，我也会在您的附近，您要
找个时机激怒凯西奥，通过大喊大叫，　265
或诋毁他的军技，或通过其他您乐意
采取行动的理由，时机对您来说更为
有利。

罗德利哥　好吧。

伊阿古　　先生，他很鲁莽并且脾气暴躁，也许　　270

---

251. 阴茎（pudding）：可能指布丁（一种糊状甜食）。 但我推测应是委婉说法，即："圣洁的阴茎（blest penis）"，以及249行的"圣洁的阴道（Blest fig's end = vagina）"。 260. 动作（exercise）：可指"行为（action）"，也可指"性行为（sexual act）"（Bate）。 261. 融为一体（incorporate）：即"做双背兽游戏"（the"beast with two backs"）。 261. 呸（Pish）：表示轻蔑或厌烦的叹词，表明伊阿古对自己的窥淫癖（voyeurism）不屑一顾（或许是假装？）。 261. 先生（sir），您（you）：伊阿古换成了敬称：他要言归正传。 263. 我让您做领军人物（for…you）：至于（我们联合行动的）首要角色，我会留给您的（As for taking the lead [in our joint action], I'll leave it to you）（Honigmann）。 "我会安排您受到委派，接受命令（前去守夜）（I'll arrange for you to be appointed, given orders）"（Bevington）。

haply with his truncheon may strike at you: provoke him that he may, for even out of that will I cause these of Cyprus to mutiny, whose qualification shall come into no true trust again but by the displanting

275 of Cassio. So shall you have a shorter journey to your desires, by the means I shall then have to prefer them, and the impediment most profitably removed, without the which there were no expectation of our prosperity.

Roderigo I will do this, if I can bring it to any opportu-
280 nity.

Iago I warrant thee. Meet me by and by at the citadel: I must fetch his necessaries ashore. Farewell.

Roderigo Adieu. *Exit.*

Iago That Cassio loves her, I do well believe it,
285 That she loves him, 'tis apt and of great credit.

The Moor, howbeit that I endure him not,

Is of a constant, loving, noble nature,

And I dare think he'll prove to Desdemona

A most dear husband. Now, I do love her too,
290 Not out of absolute lust—though peradventure

I stand accountant for as great a sin—

But partly led to diet my revenge,

For that I do suspect the lusty Moor

会用他随身携带的警棍打您：要激怒
他来打您,因为仅这一点便足以让我
使塞浦路斯的人们掀起暴乱,他们的
怒气再也得不到平息,除非将凯西奥
革职。到时我将会采取措施加以促成,　　　　275
这样您就可以通过一条捷径如愿以偿,
这一障碍一旦被顺利地清除,做不到
这一点,我们的成功将毫无希望可言。

罗德利哥　　我会这样做的,假如你能为我提供些
机会。　　　　　　　　　　　　　　　280

伊阿古　　我向你保证。过一会儿到城堡去见我:
我必须把他的行李取上岸来。 再见。

罗德利哥　　再会。　　　　　　　　　　　　　　下。

伊阿古　　凯西奥爱她,我对此深信不疑,
她也爱他,很有可能也很可信。　　　　285
这个摩尔,尽管我无法容忍,
他可是本性忠诚、深情、高尚,
我敢说他会向苔丝狄蒙娜证明
他是个最棒的丈夫。 我也爱她,
不是出于纯粹的性欲——尽管偶尔　　　　290
我也会犯下如此严重的罪过——
部分原因是想满足报复之心,
因为我怀疑这个好色的摩尔

273-4. 他们的愤怒……平息（whose…trust）：鲁莽、火爆的塞浦路斯人只有通过（将凯西奥革职）才会变得心平气和（The heady, fiery Cypriots will be "allayed" into temperate mildness by…）（Ridley）。 278. 成功（prosperity）：此处意为"成功（success）"。 注意伊阿古如何以抽象概念混淆视听（Note how Iago befogs with abstractions）。 281. 你（thee）：伊阿古现已把罗德利哥说服,便回到原来的称谓。 282. 再见（farewell）：伊阿古以此把他打发走。 283 行的"再会（Adieu）"属于更为高雅的用语（is more "upper-class"）。

Hath leaped into my seat, the thought whereof

295 Doth like a poisonous mineral gnaw my inwards···

And nothing can or shall content my soul

Till I am evened with him, wife for wife···

Or, failing so, yet that I put the Moor

At least into a jealousy so strong

300 That judgement cannot cure; which thing to do,

If this poor trash of Venice, whom I trash

For his quick hunting, stand the putting on,

I'll have our Michael Cassio on the hip,

Abuse him to the Moor in the rank garb—

305 For I fear Cassio with my night-cap too—

Make the Moor thank me, love me, and reward me

For making him egregiously an ass,

And practicing upon his peace and quiet

Even to madness. 'Tis here, but yet confused:

310 Knavery's plain face is never seen, till used.   *Exit.*

曾跨上我的座椅,这种念头

就像有毒的矿物腐蚀我肺腑……　　　　　　　　295

什么都不会使我心满意足,

除非我跟他扯平,以妻还妻……

或者,假如失败,我至少也要

让那个摩尔心生强烈的妒忌,

理智都无法治愈;这件事办成,　　　　　　　　300

若威尼斯的这个废物,我要抑制

他那勤快的狗腿,听我使唤,

就会使我们的凯西奥由我摆布,

向摩尔人毁谤他行为放荡——

恐怕凯西奥也戴过我的夜帽——　　　　　　　　305

我让摩尔人谢我,爱我,报答我,

因为我使他成了非凡的蠢驴,

密谋让他失去平安与宁静,

直到发疯。　计上心头,仍然模糊:

狡诈的嘴脸只有行动才会显露。　　　　　下。　310

---

294. 跨上我的座椅(leaped into my seat):按照牛津英语词典(*OED*),对"*leap*"一词的第 9 项释义为:"of certain beasts: to spring upon (the female) in copulation." 指某些动物交媾时跳向(雌性动物)。 seat(座椅)= sexual seat(性座椅),his wife(他的妻子)。 297. 以妻还妻(wife for wife):参考《圣经》"出埃及记"21 章 23-4 节:但若受重伤,那就要以命偿命,以眼还眼,以牙还牙……。 301. 抑制(trash):抑制猎狗,因此意为:阻止,遏制(check a hound, hence, hold back, restrain)。 302. 听我使唤(stand putting on):继续对我的激励作出反应(暗示对猎狗的怂恿)(Bate)。 303. 摆布(on the hip):摔跤术语,意为"处于不利地位(at a disadvantage)"。 305. 夜帽(night-cap):睡眠时戴的一种帽子,情人(做爱时)不大可能戴着它:伊阿古有些想入非非。

SCENE Ⅱ

Enter Othello's Herald, with a proclamation.

Herald　[*Reads.*] *It is Othello's pleasure, our noble and valiant general, that, upon certain tidings now arrived, importing the mere perdition of the Turkish fleet, every man put himself into triumph*: *some to dance, some to* make bonfires, each man to what sport and revels his addiction leads him. For besides these beneficial news, it is the celebration of his nuptial. —So much was his pleasure should be proclaimed. All offices are open, and there is full liberty of feasting from this present hour of five till the bell have told eleven. Heaven bless the isle of Cyprus and our noble general Othello!　　　　　　　　　　　　　　　　*Exit.*

第二场

奥赛罗的传令官持布告上。

传令官　[宣读。]我们高贵勇敢的奥赛罗将军，
　　　　鉴于他现在已得到了确切消息，表明
　　　　土耳其舰队已经全军覆没，特邀大家
　　　　参加盛典：有些人可去跳舞，有些人
　　　　可燃篝火，每人均可根据自己的嗜好　　　　　　5
　　　　进行娱乐。因为除了上述利好消息外，
　　　　还有他的新婚庆典。——这就是他要
　　　　宣布的喜讯。所有厨房小灶一律开放，
　　　　从此刻下午五时开始直至十一点钟鸣，
　　　　大家可自由行动，尽情宴乐。愿上帝　　　　　10
　　　　保佑塞浦路斯岛屿和我们高贵的将军
　　　　奥赛罗！　　　　　　　　　　　　　　　　下。

2.2.　1. 传令官（herald）：传令官很可能是在对观众讲话，仿佛也包括塞浦路斯民众。 但不清楚有多少内容属于宣读，多少内容属于演说。 第一版四开本和第一版对折本全以罗马字体印刷。 我将1-7行印为斜体（断定为宣读的内容，其余为演说）。

SCENE Ⅲ

Enter Othello, Cassio and Desdemona.

Othello   Good Michael, look you to the guard tonight.
Let's teach ourselves that honourable stop
Not to outsport discretion.

Cassio   Iago hath direction what to do,
5   But notwithstanding with my personal eye
Will I look to't.

Othello   Iago is most honest.
Michael, good night. Tomorrow with your earliest
Let me have speech with you. Come, my dear love,
The purchase made, the fruits are to ensue:
10   That profit's yet to come 'tween me and you.
Good-night.   *Exeunt Othello and Desdemona.*

Enter Iago.

Cassio   Welcome, Iago, we must to the watch.
Iago   Not this hour, lieutenant, 'tis not yet ten o'th'

第三场

奥赛罗、凯西奥与苔丝狄蒙娜上。

奥赛罗	好迈克尔,今晚您要保持警惕。	
	我们自己要学会适可而止,	
	宴乐可不要过度。	
凯西奥	我已吩咐伊阿古负责此事,	
	但是尽管如此我自己也会	5
	多加留意。	
奥赛罗	伊阿古最最诚实。	
	迈克尔,晚安。　明天您要尽早	
	前来向我汇报。　来吧,亲爱的,	
	既然情已定,婚配接着要产生:	
	咱们之间的好事尚待进行。	10
	晚安。　　　　　　奥赛罗与苔丝狄蒙娜下。	

伊阿古上。

凯西奥	欢迎,伊阿古,我们要去巡夜。
伊阿古	还有一个多钟头,副官,还不到十点。

2.3.　9-10. 既然……进行(The purchase…you):尽管我们已结婚,但尚未同房示爱(奥赛罗也可能是指妊娠。　但无论如何,其性爱欲望显而易见)(Bevington)。　9. 婚配(fruits):果实,暗示"需要初次同房而完婚";也可指"婚姻由上帝设立'以结果实',即子女(marriage was instituted by God 'to bring forth fruit', i. e. children)"。　13-17: 伊阿古将对话换成了散文;凯西奥(勉强?)照办。　13. 还有一个多钟头(Not this hour):离宣布的十一点庆典结束还差一个多钟头(not for an hour yet; eleven has been announced as "closing time")(Ridley)。

clock. Our general cast us thus early for the love of
his Desdemona—whom let us not therefore blame;
he hath not yet made wanton the night with her, and
she is sport for Jove.

Cassio   She's a most exquisite lady.

Iago   And, I'll warrant her full of game.

Cassio   Indeed she's a most fresh and delicate creature.

Iago   What an eye she has! Methinks it sounds a parley
to provocation.

Cassio   An inviting eye; and yet methinks right modest.

Iago   And when she speaks, is it not an alarum to love?

Cassio   She is indeed perfection.

Iago   Well: happiness to their sheets! Come, lieutenant,
I have a stoup of wine, and here without are a brace
of Cyprus gallants that would fain have a measure to
the health of black Othello.

Cassio   Not tonight, good Iago, I have very poor and
unhappy brains for drinking. I could well wish
courtesy would invent some other custom of
entertainment.

Iago   O, they are our friends. But one cup, I'll drink for
you.

Cassio   I have drunk but one cup tonight, and that was
craftily qualified too, and behold what innovation it

我们的将军把我们这么早撺走是为了
与苔丝狄蒙娜寻欢——咱也不好怪他；　　　　　　15
他到目前为止还没有跟她过夜,而且
她可作朱庇特的玩物。

凯西奥　她是位精美绝伦的淑女。

伊阿古　我保证她会风情万种。

凯西奥　她的确是最鲜嫩可口的女人。　　　　　　20

伊阿古　多么迷人的眼神!我觉得它透出一种
挑逗意味。

凯西奥　是很诱人；但我觉得她非常端庄。

伊阿古　她的话语,难道不是爱情的号令?

凯西奥　她真是完美无缺。　　　　　　　　　　　25

伊阿古　好吧: 愿他们被窝里幸福!来,副官,
我这里还有一壶酒,外面还有两三个
塞浦路斯勇士,他们愿为黑奥赛罗的
健康干上一杯。

凯西奥　今晚不行,好伊阿古,我的体质很不　　　30
适合喝酒,一喝就头昏脑涨。我希望
礼仪能发明一些别的习俗,用来招待
客人。

伊阿古　噢,他们都是朋友。只喝一杯,我会
替您。　　　　　　　　　　　　　　　　　35

凯西奥　今天晚上我已喝了一杯,而且那还是
巧妙地兑过水的,看看我已经醉成了

---

17. 朱庇特（Jove）：即朱庇特（Jupiter）,罗马神话中的主神,以玩弄女性著称（a notorious womanizer）。 20. 凯西奥对伊阿古的观点半信半疑。 他可以此形容一位妓女。 他这是意志薄弱——还是头脑简单（Is he weak—or innocent?）。 27. 两三个（brace）：一对（couple）（伊阿古可能会故意少说,以便让凯西奥同意）。 35. 替您（for you）：代您（in your place）,即伊阿古会陪伴勇士们继续喝酒,而凯西奥只喝一杯即可（Bevington）。

makes here! I am unfortunate in the infirmity, and
dare not task my weakness with any more.

40 **Iago**   What, man, 'tis a night of revels, the gallants
desire it.

Cassio   Where are they?

Iago   Here, at the door, I pray you call them in.

Cassio   I'll do't, but it dislikes me.   *Exit.*

45 **Iago**   If I can fasten but one cup upon him,
With that which he hath drunk tonight already,
He'll be as full of quarrel and offense
As my young mistress' dog. Now my sick fool, Roderigo,
Whom love hath turned almost the wrong side out,

50   To Desdemona hath tonight caroused
Potations pottle-deep, and he's to watch.
Three else of Cyprus, noble swelling spirits
That hold their honours in a wary distance,
The very elements of this warlike isle,

55   Have I tonight flustered with flowing cups,
And they watch too. Now, 'mongst this flock of drunkards

什么样子!我不幸有这种缺陷,因此

实在不敢铤而走险。

伊阿古	哎呀,伙计!这是狂欢之夜,勇士们	40

都很想喝。

凯西奥　　他们在哪里?

伊阿古　　就在门口,请您叫他们进来。

凯西奥　　好吧,但我并不情愿。　　　　　　　　　　下。

伊阿古	假如我能够劝他喝上一杯,	45

加上他今晚已经喝下一杯,

他就会动辄争吵,乖张暴戾,

小姐的巴儿狗一样。　我的情痴,罗德利哥,

爱情几乎已使他行为反常,

今晚他为了苔丝狄蒙娜已经　　　　　　　　　　　50

干杯畅饮,他还要留心守候。

外加三位塞浦路斯青年,他们

自命不凡,避免让自己丢脸,

这是该尚武之岛的根本所在,

今晚我已将其灌得酩酊大醉,　　　　　　　　　　55

还有警卫。　在这群醉鬼之间

---

38. 样子(here):凯西奥是否已喝得头重脚轻(Is Cassio unsteady on his legs)? 40. 伙计(man):不怎么礼貌,想给凯西奥施压(less polite, putting pressure on Cassio)。 48. 小姐的巴儿狗一样(As…dog):就像年轻小姐的宠物小狗(有些小狗特别爱攻击)(as any young lady's lapdog [some small dogs are especially aggressive])。 48. 罗德利哥(Roderigo):格外音节。 49. 爱情……反常(Whom…out):爱情几乎已使他判若云泥(whom love has made almost the opposite of what he was)。 51. 干杯(pottle-deep):将容量为半加仑(约2.3升)一杯的酒一饮而尽(to the bottom of a half-gallon tankard)。 51. 留心守候(to watch):留神观察(激怒凯西奥的时机)(be on the lookout [for the chance to provoke Cassio])(Bate)。 53. 避免让自己丢脸(That…distance):尽量使自己的荣誉(与羞辱)保持距离,即:随时准备动武(that keep their honours cautiously at a distance [from disgrace], i.e. that are quick to take offence)。 54. 根本(elements):本质(essential constituents),即:生命力,命根子(life-blood)。

Am I to put our Cassio in some action

That may offend the isle.

Enter Cassio, Montano and Gentlemen.

But here they come.

If consequence do but approve my dream,

60   My boat sails freely, both with wind and stream.

Cassio   'Fore God, they have given me a rouse already.

Montano   Good faith, a little one, not past a pint, as I

am a soldier.

Iago   Some wine, ho!

[*Sings.*]

65   *And let me the cannikin clink, clink,*

And let me the cannikin clink.

A soldier's a man,

O, man's life's but a span,

Why then let a soldier drink!

70   Some wine, boys!

Cassio   'Fore God, an excellent song!

Iago   I learned it in England, where indeed they are

most potent in potting. Your Dane, your German,

and your swag-bellied Hollander—drink, ho! —are

75   nothing to your English.

Cassio   Is your Englishman so exquisite in his drinking?

Iago   Why, he drinks you with facility your Dane dead

drunk; he sweats not to overthrow your Almain; he

我要使我们的凯西奥采取行动

将全体岛民冒犯。

凯西奥、蒙塔诺与众绅士上。

他们来了。

假如结果证明正合我心意，

我就会一帆风顺，所向披靡。　　　　　　　　　60

凯西奥　　上帝作证，他们已让我干了一大杯了。

蒙塔诺　　说实话，一小杯，还不到一斤，我是

军人不骗您。

伊阿古　　上酒，嗬！

〔唱。〕

咱们一起来碰杯，来碰杯，　　　　　　　　65

咱们一起来碰杯。

军人是好汉，

噢，人生很短暂，

就让军人喝个醉！

上酒，伙计们！　　　　　　　　　　　70

凯西奥　　上帝作证，多棒的歌曲！

伊阿古　　我是在英格兰学的，那里的人们的确

都是饮酒高手。咱丹麦人，咱德国人，

咱大腹便便的荷兰人——喝酒，嗬！——

都比不上咱英国人。　　　　　　　　　75

凯西奥　　咱英国人在喝酒方面竟这么能干？

伊阿古　　嗨，他会轻而易举地将咱丹麦人喝得

烂醉如泥；将咱德国人喝倒毫不费力；

---

62. 一斤（pint）：一品脱 = 0.568 升。　——译者附注。　73-9. 咱（your）：请注意伊阿古
对该词的重复与强调。　他想激起一种志同道合（Iago wants to generate camaraderie）。

80 gives your Hollander a vomit ere the next pottle can be filled.

Cassio To the health of our general!

Montano I am for it, lieutenant, and I'll do you justice.

Iago O sweet England!

[*Sings.*]

85 *King Stephen was and-a worthy peer,*

His breeches cost him but a crown,

He held them sixpence all too dear,

With that he called the tailor lown.

He was a wight of high renown,

90 *And thou art but of low degree,*

'Tis pride that pulls the country down,

Then take thine auld cloak about thee.

Some wine, ho!

Cassio 'Fore God, this is a more exquisite song than

95 the other!

Iago Will you hear't again?

Cassio No, for I hold him to be unworthy of his place

	他在倒满下一杯之前将咱荷兰人喝得	
	呕吐。	80
凯西奥	为我们的将军干杯!	
蒙塔诺	我很赞成,副官,既然您喝干了我也	
	喝干。	
伊阿古	噢,可爱的英格兰!	
	[唱。]	

斯蒂芬国王值得称颂,　　　　　　　　　　85

　　他的裤子仅花一克朗,

他还嫌多付了半先令,

　　因此他骂裁缝是流氓。

他是一国之主有威望,

　　可是你的身份属下层,　　　　　　　　90

衣着铺张使国家遭殃,

　　还是披上你的旧斗篷。

	上酒,嗬!	
凯西奥	上帝作证,这一首歌谣比刚才的那首	
	更棒!	95
伊阿古	您还想听一遍吗?	
凯西奥	不想,因为我觉得他不配自己的职位,	

85-92. 斯蒂芬……旧斗篷（King…thee）：伊阿古所唱的这首歌曲改编自早期的歌谣,名为"我的贝尔夫人（Bell my wife）或"披上你的旧斗篷（Take thy old cloak about thee）"。 该歌谣共有8节,每节8行,由贝尔及其丈夫的歌词组成。 他们两人相伴已44年;时间为严寒的冬天,她告诉丈夫要披上他的旧斗篷,然后出去救救那头老奶牛。 她的诗节以"丈夫,披上你的旧斗篷"结尾;他的诗节则以"因为我要有件新斗篷"结尾。 他想抛弃自己的农民生活,前往宫廷寻求发展,而她却要他谨防骄傲。 毫无疑问,该歌谣的第6节与第7节是想表达对特权的厌烦（对伊阿古来说恰如其分）。 86. 克朗（crown）：等于5先令。 89-91. 伊阿古所唱的这三行歌词是否针对凯西奥,从而导致本场第105行及以下的反应? 91. 也许是说"衣着奢侈会使我们国家遭难（it is extravagance in dress that causes hard times in our country）"。 97. 不配（unworthy）：迷迷糊糊地意识到自己的失职,但他已喝得酩酊大醉,无法确切表达或完整表达自己的思想。

		that does ⋯ those things. Well, God's above all, and there be souls must be saved, and there be souls must
100		not be saved.
	Iago	It's true, good lieutenant.
	Cassio	For mine own part, no offense to the general nor any man of quality, I hope to be saved.
	Iago	And so do I too, lieutenant.
105	**Cassio**	Ay, but, by your leave, not before me. The lieutenant is to be saved before the ancient. Let's have no more of this, let's to our affairs. God forgive us our sins! Gentlemen, let's look to our business. Do not think, gentlemen, I am drunk: this is my ancient,
105		this is my right hand, and this is my left. I am not drunk now: I can stand well enough, and I speak well enough.
	All	Excellent well.
	Cassio	Why, very well then; you must not think then
115		that I am drunk. *Exit.*
	Montano	To the platform, masters, come, let's set the watch.
	Iago	You see this fellow that is gone before, He is a soldier fit to stand by Caesar And give direction. And do but see his vice,
120		'Tis to his virtue a just equinox, The one as long as th'other. 'Tis pity of him:

	竟然做……那种事情。上帝高于一切， 有些灵魂肯定会得救,有些灵魂肯定 不会得救。	100
伊阿古	一点没错,好副官。	
凯西奥	就我个人而言,无意冒犯我们的将军 或任何有身份的人士,我希望得救。	
伊阿古	我也希望得救,副官。	
凯西奥	没错,不过,对不起,不能在我之前。 副官是要比旗官先得救的。咱们别谈 这些了,该去值班了。上帝宽恕我们 的罪过!先生们,咱们都要留心。别 以为,先生们,我醉了:这是我旗官, 这是我右手,这是我左手。现在我还 没醉:我能够站得很稳,而且我吐字 清晰。	105 110
一绅士	太棒了。	
凯西奥	嗨,确实很棒;但是你们千万别以为 我已喝醉。	下。 115
蒙塔诺	去炮台,先生们,走,咱们去站岗。	
伊阿古	您看刚刚离开的那个家伙, 他适合充当恺撒的得力助手 发号施令。 但您看他的缺点, 与他的优点犹如昼夜平分, 彼此相等。 这一点令人遗憾:	120

---

99. 得救（be saved）:进入天堂（go to heaven）。 参考《圣经》"马太福音"10 章 22 节:唯有忍耐到底的必然得救（he that endureth to the end shall be saved）。 103. 有身份的（of quality）:出身高贵,社会地位优越（即,伊阿古除外）。 118. 恺撒的得力助手（stand by Caesar）:可指"与恺撒相提并论（as an equal）";也可指"做他的左膀右臂（as his right-hand man）"。

I fear the trust Othello puts him in

On some odd time of his infirmity

Will shake this island.

Montano   But is he often thus?

125 **Iago**   'Tis evermore the prologue to his sleep:

He'll watch the horologe a double set

If drink rock not his cradle.

Montano   It were well

The general were put in mind of it.

Perhaps he sees it not, or his good nature

130   Prizes the virtue that appears in Cassio

And looks not on his evils: is not this true?

Enter Roderigo.

Iago   [*aside*] How now, Roderigo?

I pray you, after the lieutenant, go!   *Exit Roderigo.*

Montano   And 'tis great pity that the noble Moor

135   Should hazard such a place as his own second

With one of an ingraft infirmity.

It were an honest action to say so

To the Moor.

Iago   Not I, for this fair island.

I do love Cassio well, and would do much

                                   A cry within: ' Help! Help!'

我担心奥赛罗对他的托付

会在他意志薄弱的非常时刻

将全岛震撼。

蒙塔诺　　　　　　他是否经常这样？

伊阿古　　这是他每晚入睡之前的序曲：　　　　　　　　　125

假如没有酒力为他摇篮，

他会昼夜不眠。

蒙塔诺　　　　　　最好是能够

有人将这件事情告知于将军。

或许他未注意，或天性善良，

只是看重凯西奥的非凡能力，　　　　　　　　　130

从而忽略他的缺陷：难道不是？

罗德利哥上。

伊阿古　　[旁白]怎么了，罗德利哥？

我求您，您要尾随副官，快去！　　　　　　罗德利哥下。

蒙塔诺　　真是非常遗憾，高贵的摩尔

竟然冒险将自己的副将职位　　　　　　　　　135

交给一位积习难改的人士。

将这一点告诉给摩尔是正直

之举。

伊阿古　　　　把这宝岛给我，我也不说。

我很爱凯西奥，也会尽力治愈

内呼："救命！救命！"

---

126. 摇篮（cradle）：意思含混；也许是说"他就像摇篮里的婴儿一般，需要借助酒力为他催眠。　127. 他会昼夜不眠（He…set）：时钟转上两圈（即 24 小时）他都不会有睡意（He'll stay awake twice round the clock or *horologe*）。　137-8. 正直之举（honest action）：伊阿古有机会做一件"正直"的事情时，却一口回绝（When Iago is offered a task which would be "honest", he declines it）（Ridley）。

140   To cure him of this evil. But hark, what noise?

Enter Cassio pursuing Roderigo.

Cassio	Zounds, You rogue! You rascal!
Montano	What's the matter, lieutenant?
Cassio	A knave teach me my duty? I'll beat the knave
	into a twiggen bottle!

145 **Roderigo**   Beat me?

Cassio	Dost thou prate, rogue?
Montano	Nay, good lieutenant! I pray you, sir, hold
	your hand.
Cassio	Let me go, sir, or I'll knock you o'er the

150   mazzard.

Montano	Come, come, you're drunk.
Cassio	Drunk? *They fight.*
Iago	[*aside to Roderigo*]Away, I say, go out and cry mutiny.

                                                   [*Exit Roderigo.*]

             Nay, good lieutenant! God's will, gentlemen—

155   Help ho! Lieutenant! Sir—Montano—sir—

             Help, masters, here's a goodly watch indeed.   *A bell rings.*

             Who's that which rings the bell? Diablo, ho!

             The town will rise, God's will, lieutenant, hold,

             You will be shamed for ever!

他这种恶习。 可您听,是啥声音? 　　　　　　　　　　140

凯西奥追赶罗德利哥上。

凯西奥	该死,你这无赖! 流氓!	
蒙塔诺	怎么了,副官?	
凯西奥	一个恶棍竟敢训我? 我要把这个恶棍 揍得遍体鳞伤!	
罗德利哥	想打我?	145
凯西奥	你还吹牛,无赖?	
蒙塔诺	别打,好副官!我求您,先生,请您 住手。	
凯西奥	放开我,先生,否则我就会敲打您的 脑壳。	150
蒙塔诺	得了,得了,您醉了。	
凯西奥	醉了?　　　　　　　　　　二人交手。	
伊阿古	[向罗德利哥旁白]快走,我说,出去呼喊有骚乱。	

　　　　　　　　　　　　　　　　　　[罗德利哥下。]

不行,好副官! 我的天哪,先生们——
快住手! 副官! 先生——蒙塔诺——先生——　　　　155
来人,先生们,这岗站得可真好!　　　　钟声响起。
是谁敲了警钟? 真是见鬼,嗬!
全城将大乱,天哪,副官,住手,
您从此再也没脸见人!

---

144. 揍(beat):对于比自己地位低下的人可以揍他,跟自己地位相等的人只能挑战他(Social inferiors were beaten, equals had to be challenged)。 144. 遍体鳞伤(twiggen bottle):意为"柳条篮子(wicker basket)"。 即,罗德利哥身上的伤痕将会(像枝编物一样)纵横交错(criss-crossed with wounds and bruises)(Bate)。 156. 可真好(goodly):反语(ironical)。

Enter Othello and Attendants.

Othello   What is the matter here?

160 **Montano**   Zounds, I bleed still;

I am hurt to th' death: he dies!   [*Lunges at Cassio.*]

Othello   Hold, for your lives!

Iago   Hold, ho! Lieutenant! Sir—Montano—gentlemen—

Have you forgot all sense of place and duty?

Hold, the general speaks to you: hold, for shame!

165 **Othello**   Why, how now, ho? From whence ariseth this?

Are we turned Turks? And to ourselves do that

Which heaven hath forbid the Ottomites?

For Christian shame, put by this barbarous brawl;

He that stirs next, to carve for his own rage,

170   Holds his soul light: he dies upon his motion.

Silence that dreadful bell, it frights the isle

From her propriety. What is the matter, masters?

Honest Iago, that look'st dead with grieving,

Speak: who began this? On thy love I charge thee.

175 **Iago**   I do not know, friends all, but now, even now,

In quarter and in terms like bride and groom

Devesting them for bed; and then, but now,

奥赛罗与侍从上。

奥赛罗　　这是怎么了？

蒙塔诺　　　　　　天哪，我还在流血；　　　　　　　　160

我伤得厉害：他死去！　　　　　　　　[扑向凯西奥。]

奥赛罗　　　　　　住手，若想活命！

伊阿古　　住手，嗬！副官！先生——蒙塔诺——绅士们——

你们忘了自己的身份和职责？

住手，将军要发话：住手，不像话！

奥赛罗　　唉，怎么了，嗬！为啥动起手来？　　　　　　165

我们成了叛徒？　去做上帝阻止

土耳其想做的事情——将我们毁灭？

看在上帝的份上，别再胡闹；

有谁敢再动，纵容他的怒气，

谁就是轻生：一动就让他毙命。　　　　　　170

停住那可怕的钟声，它惊扰了

全岛的宁静。　出了啥事，先生？

诚实的伊阿古，看上去悲痛欲绝，

说：是谁开的头？　你凭爱心，快说。

伊阿古　　我不知道，朋友们，刚才，就刚才，　　　　　　175

彼此之间就像宽衣解带准备

上床的新郎新娘；可随后，刚才，

166-7. 去做……毁灭（and…Ottomites）：难道我们，通过自我毁灭，去做土耳其人想做的事情，因为上帝已阻止他们亲自将其做成（Are we, in destroying ourselves, going to do the Turks' job for them, now that Heaven has prevented them doing it for themselves）？　（Ridley）。172. 先生（masters）：他意识到了他们的社会地位。　174. 你凭爱心（on thy love）：凭你对我的爱心（偏爱）（by your love［affection］for me）。　176. 彼此之间（in quarter and in term）：彼此之间的关系（in relation to each other）（Mowat）。　彼此之间的言谈举止。"quarter"意为"与另一位之间的相处（relation with, conduct towards, another）"；"terms"意为"言谈（language）"（Honigmann）。

As if some planet had unwitted men,

Swords out, and tilting one at other's breast

180　In opposition bloody. I cannot speak

Any beginning to this peevish odds,

And would in action glorious I had lost

Those legs that brought me to a part of it.

Othello　How comes it, Michael, you are thus forgot?

185 **Cassio**　I pray you pardon me, I cannot speak.

Othello　Worthy Montano, you were wont to be civil:

The gravity and stillness of your youth

The world hath noted, and your name is great

In mouths of wisest censure. What's the matter

190　That you unlace your reputation thus

And spend your rich opinion for the name

Of a night-brawler? Give me answer to it.

Montano　Worthy Othello, I am hurt to danger:

Your officer Iago can inform you—

195　While I spare speech, which something now offends me—

Of all that I do know; nor know I aught

By me that's said or done amiss this night,

Unless self-charity be sometimes a vice,

And to defend ourselves it be a sin

When violence assails us.

200 **Othello**　　　　　　　　　Now, by heaven,

My blood begins my safer guides to rule,

And passion, having my best judgement collied,

	好像有行星将人的理智剥夺，	
	他们拔出剑来，然后拼命地	
	刺向对方的心窝。 我不能说明	180
	这种无谓争执的具体起因，	
	但愿我在壮举之中将自己的	
	双腿失去，也不愿与此事牵连。	
奥赛罗	怎么回事，迈克尔，您如此忘形？	
凯西奥	求您原谅我吧，我无话可说。	185
奥赛罗	尊贵的蒙塔诺，您向来很有教养：	
	您年轻时的那种稳重与冷静	
	闻名遐迩，圣明贤达之士	
	都对您交口称颂。 是什么东西	
	竟使您解开装满名声的钱包，	190
	浪费自己的盛誉而换取一种	
	所谓的夜来闹？ 您要予以回答。	
蒙塔诺	尊贵的奥赛罗，我的伤势很重：	
	您的旗官伊阿古可向您汇报——	
	我不便多说，说话有些难受——	195
	我所知道的一切；我也不清楚	
	自己今晚说错或做错了什么，	
	除非自爱有时是一种邪恶，	
	当我们遭到暴力袭击时自我	
	防卫是一种罪过。	
奥赛罗	唉，天哪，	200
	我的血气已开始主宰理智，	
	而情绪，玷污了我的最佳判断，	

---

178. 将人的理智剥夺（had unwitted men）：人们相信如果行星太接近地球，就会使人发疯。

Assays to lead the way. Zounds, if I once stir,

Or do but lift this arm, the best of you

205　　Shall sink in my rebuke. Give me to know

How this foul rout began, who set it on,

And he that is approved in this offense,

Though he had twinned with me, both at a birth,

Shall lose me. What, in a town of war

210　　Yet wild, the people's hearts brimful of fear,

To manage private and domestic quarrel?

In night, and on the court and guard of safety?

'Tis monstrous. Iago, who began't?

Montano　If partially affined or leagued in office,

215　　Thou dost deliver more or less than truth,

Thou art no soldier.

Iago　　　　　　　　Touch me not so near.

I had rather have this tongue cut from my mouth

Than it should do offense to Michael Cassio,

Yet I persuade myself to speak the truth

215　　Shall nothing wrong him. Thus it is, general:

Montano and myself being in speech,

There comes a fellow crying out for help,

And Cassio following him with determined sword

To execute upon him. Sir, this gentleman

225　　Steps in to Cassio and entreats his pause,

Myself the crying fellow did pursue,

试图在前引路。　咄,我只要一动,

或举起这只胳膊,你们的精英

都会应声倒下。　快让我知道　　　　　　　　205

这场斗殴的起因,是谁开的头,

谁若是被证实对此负有罪责,

哪怕是我孪生兄弟,一母同胞,

也不留情。　怎么,在这戒备之城,

竟敢撒野,人们依然心有余悸,　　　　　　210

居然进行私下的争斗和内讧?

在夜间,且是站岗执勤的地点?

真是荒谬!伊阿古,是谁开的头?

蒙塔诺　你若出于偏心或因为是同事,

不将事情的真相据实以告,　　　　　　　　215

你就不是军人。

伊阿古　　　　　　　　别逼得太紧。

我宁愿将这根舌头从口中割掉,

也不愿让它伤害迈克尔·凯西奥,

然而我相信说出事情的真相

将不会害他。　是这样的,将军:　　　　　　220

蒙塔诺与我正在谈话之间,

跑过来一个呼喊救命的小子,

凯西奥尾随其后,决意使用

刀剑刺他。　先生,这位绅士,

出面制止凯西奥并求他住手,　　　　　　　225

我自己去追那个呼喊的小子,

---

212. 站岗执勤的地点（on…safety）：在警卫队总部而且还是在执勤期间（in the chief guardhouse and while on duty）（Mowat）。　216. 别逼得太紧（Touch me not so near）：没必要提及对我来说那么紧要的东西（我的军职）（there's need to allude to what concerns me so closely［my soldiership］）（Mowat）。

Lest by his clamour, as it so fell out,

The town might fall in fright. He, swift of foot,

Outran my purpose, and I returned the rather

230   For that I heard the clink and fall of swords

And Cassio high in oath, which till tonight

I ne'er might say before. When I came back,

For this was brief, I found them close together

At blow and thrust, even as again they were

235   When you yourself did part them.

More of this matter cannot I report.

But men are men, the best sometimes forget;

Though Cassio did some little wrong to him,

As men in rage strike those that wish them best,

240   Yet surely Cassio, I believe, received

From him that fled some strange indignity

Which patience could not pass.

Othello   I know, Iago,

Thy honesty and love doth mince this matter,

Making it light to Cassio. Cassio, I love thee,

Enter Desdemona, attended.

245   But never more be officer of mine.

Look if my gentle love be not raised up!

I'll make thee an example.

Desdemona   What's the matter, dear?

恐怕他的叫喊,果不其然,

将全城惊动。　他,腿脚麻利,

我望尘莫及,我便赶快返回,

因为我听见刀剑的撞击和劈杀,　　　　　　　　230

凯西奥高声咒骂,在今晚之前

可以说从未有过。　我回来之后,

因为很短暂,见他们扭作一团

相互厮杀,就像他们刚才那样,

您亲自将他们呵开。　　　　　　　　　　　　235

就此而言我只能汇报这些。

但人总是人,贤哲也会犯错;

尽管凯西奥对他稍有伤害,

正如人们发怒时会恩将仇报,

然而,凯西奥肯定,我相信,受到　　　　　　240

那个逃跑者某种格外的侮辱,

使他忍无可忍。

奥赛罗　　　　　　　　　我知道,伊阿古,

你的诚实和爱心对此轻描淡写,

想为凯西奥开脱。　凯西奥,我爱你,

苔丝狄蒙娜及侍从上。

但你再也别做我的官员了。　　　　　　　　　245

快看,我的爱妻是否被惊起!

我要让你做个警诫。

苔丝狄蒙娜　怎么了,亲爱的?

---

235. 该短行也许意味着此时稍有停顿(伊阿古擦拭自己的眉毛?)。　同时也意味着一种策略的改变:描述完事情的经过之后,他开始"保护"凯西奥。　244. 凯西奥(Cassio):奥赛罗此前都是对凯西奥直呼其名——"迈克尔(Michael)"(见2.1和本场184)(Ridley)。　245. 奥赛罗个人可任命或解雇自己的官员(参考1.1.8和1.1.16)。

	Othello	All's well now, sweeting,
		Come away to bed. —Sir, for your hurts,
250		Myself will be your surgeon. Lead him off. [*Montano is led off.*]
		Iago, look with care about the town
		And silence those whom this vile brawl distracted.
		Come, Desdemona: 'tis the soldier's life
		To have their balmy slumbers waked with strife.

Exeunt [*all but Iago and Cassio.*]

255	**Iago**	What, are you hurt, lieutenant?
	Cassio	Ay, past all surgery.
	Iago	Marry, God forbid!
	Cassio	Reputation, reputation, reputation! O, I have lost my reputation, I have lost the immortal part of
260		myself—and what remains is bestial. My reputation, Iago, my reputation!
	Iago	As I am an honest man, I thought you had received some bodily wound; there is more of sense in that than in reputation. Reputation is an idle and
265		most false imposition, oft got without merit and lost without deserving. You have lost no reputation at all, unless you repute yourself such a loser. What, man, there are ways to recover the general again. You are but now cast in his mood, a punishment more in
270		policy than in malice, even so as one would beat his

奥赛罗	现在好了,宝贝,	
	快去睡吧。 ——先生,至于您的伤口,	
	我确保能得到治疗。 扶他走吧。	［蒙塔诺被扶下。］ 250
	伊阿古,可要小心照看全城,	
	安抚被这场胡闹搅扰的民众。	
	来,苔丝狄蒙娜,这就是军旅营生,	
	他们的安眠常被吵闹惊醒。	

〔除伊阿古与凯西奥外〕全下。

伊阿古	怎么,您受伤了,副官?	255
凯西奥	是的,无药可救。	
伊阿古	真的,上帝保佑!	
凯西奥	名声,名声,名声!噢,我已经失去	
	我的名声,我已将本人不朽的那部分	
	失去——我成了一只走兽。我的名声,	260
	伊阿古,我的名声!	
伊阿古	既然我是个老实人,我觉得您不过是	
	受了些身体的创伤,与名声相比,它	
	更容易让人感受。名声这种身外之物	
	无用也最为虚伪,往往得到它而不配,	265
	失去它不应该。您没有失去半点名声,	
	除非您自命为一个失败者。唉,伙计,	
	有好多办法把将军争取过来。他只是	
	一怒之下将您解雇,这种惩罚更多的	
	是一种策略而非恶意,就像有人为了	270

---

250. 我……治疗（Myself…surgeon）：也许是通过将军的医生（参考5. 1. 100）。 也有人认为奥赛罗本人将为蒙塔诺包扎。 259. 不朽的那部分（the immortal part）：即"人生最好的财富就是留个清名（The purest treasure mortal times afford / Is spotless reputation）"。 人们的灵魂通常被称为"不朽的部分"。 267. 除非……失败者（unless…loser）：谚语，"幸福还是痛苦，在于个人的态度（A man is weal or woe as he thinks himself so）"。

offenceless dog to affright an imperious lion. Sue to him again, and he's yours.

Cassio I will rather sue to be despised, than to deceive so good a commander with so slight, so drunken, and so indiscreet an officer. Drunk? And speak parrot? And squabble? Swagger? Swear? And discourse fustian with one's own shadow? O thou invisible spirit of wine, if thou hast no name to be known by, let us call thee devil!

Iago What was he that you followed with your sword? What had he done to you?

Cassio I know not.

Iago Is't possible?

Cassio I remember a mass of things, but nothing distinctly; a quarrel , but nothing wherefore. O God, that men should put an enemy in their mouths, to steal away their brains! That we should with joy, pleasance, revel and applause, transform ourselves into beasts!

Iago Why, but you are now well enough: how came you thus recovered?

Cassio It hath pleased the devil drunkenness to give place to the devil wrath; one unperfectness shows me another, to make me frankly despise myself.

Iago Come, you are too severe a moraler. As the time, the place and the condition of this country stands, I could heartily wish this had not befallen; but since it

恐吓跛扈的狮子会击打他的无辜小狗。
求他原谅,他会答应。

凯西奥	我宁愿求他鄙视,也不愿求这样好的
	统帅原谅我这个如此无用、如此酗酒、
	如此轻率的军官。酗酒?还胡言乱语?
	争吵?吹牛?赌咒?而且对着自己的
	影子夸夸其谈?噢,你这无形的酒神,
	假如你还没有名字,那就让我们叫你
	魔鬼!

凯西奥 我宁愿求他鄙视,也不愿求这样好的 275

伊阿古 您拿着利剑在后面追赶的那个人是谁? 280
他怎么得罪您了?

凯西奥 我不知道。

伊阿古 那可能吗?

凯西奥 我记得有一堆事情,但没有一件能够
记清;吵了一架,但不知道为啥。噢, 285
上帝,人们竟把敌人放进他们的嘴巴,
让他将他们的脑筋盗走!我们竟会让
欣喜狂欢将自己变成了畜生!

伊阿古 嗨,您现在倒很清醒:您怎么恢复得
这么快呀? 290

凯西奥 这是醉鬼它一时高兴将自己的位置让
给了怒鬼;一种缺陷将我引向另一种
缺陷,使我毫无保留地鄙视自己。

伊阿古 好了,您这位道德家也太严。考虑到
事发的时间,地点和国家的局面,我 295
真心希望这件事情没有发生;但既然

---

292. 怒(wrath):可指生自己的气(273 行及以下),也可指尚未恢复平静,因为依然在生气;或指他对罗德利哥感到愤怒。

is as it is, mend it for your own good.

Cassio   I will ask him for my place again, he shall tell
me I am a drunkard: had I as many mouths as Hydra,
300   such an answer would stop them all. To be now a
sensible man, by and by a fool, and presently a beast!
O strange! —Every inordinate cup is unblest, and the
ingredient is a devil.

Iago   Come, come, good wine is a good familiar crea-
305   ture, if it be well used: exclaim no more against it.
And, good lieutenant, I think you think I love you.

Cassio   I have well approved it, sir. I drunk?

Iago   You, or any man living, may be drunk at some
time, man. I'll tell you what you shall do. Our
310   general's wife is now the general. I may say so in this
respect, for that he hath devoted and given up himself
to the contemplation, mark and denotement of her
parts and graces. Confess yourself freely to her,
importune her help to put you in your place again.
315   She is of so free, so kind, so apt, so blest a disposition
she holds it a vice in her goodness not to do
more than she is requested. This broken joint between
you and her husband entreat her to splinter—and my
fortunes against any lay worth naming, this crack of

事已至此，您就该设法补救。

凯西奥　　我要请求他给我官复原职，他会说我
　　　　　是酒鬼：我纵有九头蛇那样多的嘴巴，
　　　　　这一答复也会将其全部封住。我现在　　　　　　　　300
　　　　　正常，很快便成傻瓜，不久成为畜生！
　　　　　噢，奇怪！——每一次贪杯都是祸害，
　　　　　它的原料就是祸水！

伊阿古　　好了，好了，好酒是一种可亲的产物，
　　　　　假如能够好好利用：不要再咒骂它了。　　　　　　　305
　　　　　而且，好副官，我认为您认为我爱您。

凯西奥　　对此我已亲身验证，先生。　我醉了？

伊阿古　　您，或者任何活人，都会在某一时刻
　　　　　喝醉，伙计。我告诉您如何采取行动。
　　　　　将军的妻子现是将军。之所以这样说，　　　　　　　310
　　　　　是因为他现在正一门心思地使他自己
　　　　　致力于沉思、注意、和观察她身上的
　　　　　品质和风雅。要毫无保留地向她坦白，
　　　　　恳求她给以帮助以便能让您官复原职。
　　　　　她的性情如此慷慨、善良、乐于助人，　　　　　　　315
　　　　　要是她自己的所为没超过别人的所求，
　　　　　她会认为那是犯罪。您和她丈夫之间
　　　　　的这种裂痕，恳求她接合——用我的
　　　　　财富跟任何值得一提的东西打赌，您

---

299. 九头蛇（Hydra）：希腊神话中的多头怪蛇，大力神赫拉克勒斯的任务之一就是将其斩杀；每将它的一个头砍断，便会在原处长出两个头来（Ridley）。　304. 产物（creature）：参考《圣经》"提摩太前书"1-4 节，告诫人们谨防邪灵的诱导："让人们戒荤，可这都是神所造，让人们心怀感激予以领受……因为神造之物都是好的。"产物（creature）可等于任何创造出来的东西（包括食物和饮料）。　307. 先生（sir）：凯西奥感到伊阿古在向他施压。　318. 这种……接合（This…splinter）：源于谚语，"断裂的骨头一旦接好会更加牢固（A broken bone is the stronger when it is well set）"。

320		your love shall grow stronger than it was before.
	Cassio	You advise me well.
	Iago	I protest, in the sincerity of love and honest kindness.
	Cassio	I think it freely, and betimes in the morning I
325		will beseech the virtuous Desdemona to undertake for me. I am desperate of my fortunes if they check me here.
	Iago	You are in the right. Good-night, lieutenant, I must to the watch.
330	**Cassio**	Good-night, honest Iago. *Exit.*
	Iago	And what's he then that says I play the villain?
		When this advice is free I give and honest,
		Probal to thinking and indeed the course
		To win the Moor again? For 'tis most easy
335		Th'inclining Desdemona to subdue
		In any honest suit. She's framed as fruitful
		As the free elements: and then for her
		To win the Moor, were't to renounce his baptism,
		All seals and symbols of redeemed sin,
340		His soul is so enfettered to her love

	本次情义的裂痕会长得更加牢固。	320
凯西奥	您劝告得很好。	
伊阿古	我声明,是出于真诚的爱心和正直的 善意。	
凯西奥	这一点我完全相信,而且明天一早我 就去乞求那位高尚的苔丝狄蒙娜替我 说情。我的命运若就此受挫,便毫无 希望。	325
伊阿古	您说得很对。晚安吧,副官,我必须 去守夜了。	
凯西奥	晚安,诚实的伊阿古。　　下。	330
伊阿古	还有谁能说我在扮演恶棍? 我的劝告是如此坦率和真诚, 合乎情理也是重获摩尔人 好感的最佳途径? 因为使性情 随和的苔丝狄蒙娜有求必应 最为容易。 她生就慷慨大方, 像无私的阳光雨露:然后让她 说服那摩尔,即使让他放弃洗礼—— 得以救赎的各种保证和象征—— 他的灵魂被她的爱情如此操控,	335 340

331. 他接上了自己在 2.1.308 的话茬,但他的狡诈此刻已能清晰地看出下一步该如何行动。注意他对可能的回应是多么警觉(Honigmann)。 331-357,377-383. 由于伊阿古一直在费尽心机,阴谋终于成形。 饮酒插曲旨在使凯西奥采取某种行动以冒犯全岛——以此败坏凯西奥作为军人的声誉,并最终实现将其革职的图谋。 然而,凯西奥拒绝直接向奥赛罗恳求的心态(298-300)正中伊阿古的下怀,他便不失时机地建议他向苔丝狄蒙娜求情(309-320)。 在本次独白中他第一次看到自己的计谋不再"模糊"(2.1.309);而且,我们既能感到他对预期的报复颇为欣喜,也能感到他为自己能想出一种微妙而狡诈的计谋而沾沾自喜(Ridley)。 337. 无私的阳光雨露(free elements):她的天性就是专门利人,就像天然的要素(水、火、土、气)供人利用。339. 得以……象征(All…sin):按照基督教信仰,洗礼及其他圣礼是人类得以救赎,或罪得赦免的保证(seals)与外显(symbols)(Mowat)。

That she may make, unmake, do what she list,

Even as her appetite shall play the god

With his weak function. How am I then a villain

To counsel Cassio to this parallel course

345   Directly to his good? Divinity of hell!

When devils will the blackest sins put on,

They do suggest at first with heavenly shows,

As I do now. For whiles this honest fool

Plies Desdemona to repair his fortune,

350   And she for him pleads strongly to the Moor,

I'll pour this pestilence into his ear:

That she repeals him for her body's lust.

And by how much she strives to do him good,

She shall undo her credit with the Moor—

355   So will I turn her virtue into pitch,

And out of her own goodness make the net

That shall enmesh them all.

Enter Roderigo.

                         How now, Roderigo?

Roderigo   I do follow here in the chase, not like a hound

that hunts, but one that fills up the cry. My

她竟然可以对他为所欲为，

连她的癖好都会主宰他的

意志薄弱。　我怎么会是恶棍，

劝告凯西奥走这条并行之道

直接为了他好？　地狱的神学！ 　　　　　345

魔鬼唆使人去犯弥天大罪时，

首先用神圣的外表加以引诱，

如我现在这样。　因为这个傻子

恳求苔丝狄蒙娜帮他复职时，

她将尽力为他向摩尔人求情， 　　　　　350

我就会向他灌输这种谗言：

她将他召回是为了她的肉欲。

因此她越是力争为他做好事，

越会使摩尔人怀疑她的忠诚——

由此我将她的德行变成沥青， 　　　　　355

用她本人的善心织成罗网

将他们一网打尽。

罗德利哥上。

怎么样,罗德利哥？

罗德利哥　我跟着大军追逐到这里,不像是一只

追捕的猎狗,倒像是在群里瞎叫而已。

---

343. 意志薄弱（weak function）：他的行动能力因其对苔丝狄蒙娜的依恋而削弱（Mowat）。　其中,"weak"意为"受制于人（enslaved）"（Honigmann）。　344. 并行之道（parallel course）：貌似将他引向光明的正道,但实际上却适得其反,使他误入歧途（it seems to lead straight to his advantage but in fact takes him in the opposite direction, to his destruction）。 345. 地狱的神学（Divinity of hell）："噢,地狱里的宗教信仰（O, the theology of hell）"；或是针对撒旦（Satan）而言,"噢,地狱之神（O, god of hell）"。　355. 沥青（pitch）：沥青漆黑、难闻、胶黏；这种东西对伊阿古来说可谓完美无缺,使他幻想借此将他的牺牲品一网打尽（Mowat）。　359. 在群里瞎叫（fill up the cry）：在狗群里充数（make up one of the pack）（Bate）。　真正的猎狗在前面追寻动物的遗臭,而自己只是跟在后面汪汪大叫而已（the hounds who merely give tongue as they follow those who are really running the scent）（Ridley）。

360   money is almost spent, I have been tonight

exceedingly well cudgeled, and I think the issue will

be I shall have so much experience for my pains: and

so, with no money at all, and a little more wit, return

again to Venice.

365 **Iago**   How poor are they that have not patience!

What wound did ever heal but by degrees?

Thou know'st we work by wit and not by witchcraft,

And wit depends on dilatory time.

Does't not go well? Cassio hath beaten thee,

370   And thou by that small hurt hast cashiered Cassio.

Though other things grow fair against the sun,

Yet fruits that blossom first will first be ripe;

Content thyself awhile. By the mass, 'tis morning:

Pleasure and action make the hours seem short.

375   Retire thee, go where thou art billeted,

Away, I say, thou shalt know more hereafter:

Nay, get thee gone.   *Exit Roderigo.*

Two things are to be done:

My wife must move for Cassio to her mistress,

I'll set her on.

380   Myself the while to draw the Moor apart

	我的钱几乎已花光,今晚我还遭到了	360
	一顿毒打,我想这件事情的结果将是	
	我的痛苦经历就应该到此为止:因此,	
	既然钱已花光,多长了点见识,返回	
	威尼斯去吧。	

伊阿古　没有耐心的人们是多么可怜!　　　　　　　　365

　　　　　有什么创伤不是逐步愈合?

　　　　　你知道咱是靠智力不是靠魔法,

　　　　　然而智力要靠迟缓的时间。

　　　　　进展还不顺吗?　凯西奥打了你,

　　　　　你受点伤痛却将凯西奥革职。　　　　　　　370

　　　　　尽管万物都会在阳光下繁荣,

　　　　　然而先开花的果实毕竟先熟;

　　　　　你暂且知足。　天哪,已经拂晓:

　　　　　愉快和忙碌的时光不会显长。

　　　　　你走吧,回到你被委派的地方,　　　　　　375

　　　　　快走,我说,以后你会了解更多:

　　　　　哎,快离开。　　　　　　　　　　罗德利哥下。

　　　　　　　　尚有两件事要做:

　　　　　我妻子定会为凯西奥求她主人,

　　　　　我要敦促她。

　　　　　我本人同时将那个摩尔引开,　　　　　　　380

　　　371-2. 尽管……先熟(Though…ripe):这两行听起来像是谚语,会让罗德利哥相信伊阿古颇有智慧,但它们的意义却相当晦涩(Mowat)。　这两行意指:“尽管别人得到了苔丝狄蒙娜的青睐,我们也会成功地让自己的计策得以实现。”在这一牵强的类比中,“开花”就等于“凯西奥的毒打”(though others thrive in Desdemona's favour, we'll succeed in bringing our plots to fruition. In this false analogy blossom = Cassio's cudgeling!)(Honigmann)。　379. 伊阿古独白中的这一短行意味着有所停顿,比如他在思考一种新的计谋等(参考1. 3. 400, 3. 3. 323)。

And bring him jump when he may Cassio find

Soliciting his wife: ay, that's the way!

Dull not device by coldness and delay!   *Exit.*

然后让他回来正好碰见凯西奥
向他妻子求情：对,就这么办!
别让计策受到冷遇和拖延!　　　　　　　　　　　　下。

第三幕
ACT 3

SCENE I

Enter Cassio and some Musicians.

Cassio   Masters, play here, I will content your pains;
             Something that's brief, and bid 'Good morrow, general'.

They play. Enter Clown.

Clown   Why, masters, have your instruments been in
             Naples, that they speak i'th' nose thus?

5 **1 Musician** How, sir? How?

Clown   Are these, I pray you, wind instruments?

1 Musician Ay marry are they, sir.

Clown   O, thereby hangs a tail.

1 Musician Whereby hangs a tale, sir?

10 **Clown**   Marry, sir, by many a wind instrument that I
             know. But, masters, here's money for you, and the
             general so likes your music that he desires you, for

第一场

凯西奥与众乐师上。

凯西奥　　大师们,演奏吧,我会报答你们;
　　　　　乐曲需要简短,祝"将军,早安"。

奏乐。小丑上。

小丑　　嗨,大师们,难道您的乐器都曾去过
　　　　　那不勒斯,它们竟这样鼻音浓重?

乐师甲　怎么了,先生?　怎么了?　　　　　　　　　5

小丑　　我请问,您这是管乐器吗?

乐师甲　没错,是管乐器,先生。

小丑　　噢,原来挂着一条尾巴。

乐师甲　哪里挂着一条尾巴,先生?

小丑　　哎呀,先生,我知道好多胀气的乐器　　　　　10
　　　　　都是这样。大师们,这是给您的赏钱,
　　　　　将军如此喜欢您的音乐,他竟希望您,

3.1.　1-20. 小丑对乐师的戏弄属于"滑稽节目"(the Clown's baiting of the musicians was a "comic turn")。 2. 早安(Good morrow):一种传统的晨歌,旨在将新婚之夜过后的新娘与新郎唤醒(the traditional *aubade* to wake bride and groom after the wedding night)。 3-4. 去过……浓重(in…thus):是指能够侵蚀患者鼻子的花柳病(Neapolitan [veneral] disease),这种病在那不勒斯发生率很高。 他是说那些乐器呼哧呼哧作响(snuffle or scrape),而不能发出清脆的乐音(Honigmann; Bate)。 8. 尾巴(tail):可指阴茎(penis);也可指动物的尾巴(animal tail)(Honigmann)。 挂在管乐器的旁边,使人联想到阴茎(that hangs nearby the wind instrument suggests the penis)(Bevington)。 10. 胀气的乐器(wind instrument):在拿肠胃胀气开玩笑(A joke about flatulence)。

love's sake, to make no more noise with it.

1 Musician Well, sir, we will not.

15 **Clown** If you have any music that may not be heard to't,
again. But, as they say, to hear music the general
does not greatly care.

1 **Musician** We have none such, sir.

Clown Then put up your pipes in your bag, for I'll
20 away. Go, vanish into air, away! *Exeunt Musicians.*

Cassio Dost thou hear, mine honest friend?

Clown No, I hear not your honest friend, I hear you.

Cassio Prithee keep up thy quillets; there's a poor piece
of gold for thee—if the gentlewoman that attends the
25 general's wife be stirring, tell her there's one Cassio
entreats her a little favour of speech. Wilt thou do
this?

Clown She is stirring, sir; if she will stir hither, I shall
seem to notify unto her.

Enter Iago.

30 **Cassio** Do, good my friend. [*Exit Clown.*] In happy time, Iago.

Iago You have not been a-bed then?

Cassio Why no, the day had broke before we parted.
I have made bold, Iago, to send in
To your wife: my suit to her is that she will

看在爱的份上,别再制造噪音。

乐师甲	那好,先生,我们停止。	
小丑	假如您有无法让人听得见的音乐,可 继续演奏。不过,听人说,将军他对 音乐并不怎么喜欢。	15
乐师甲	我们没这样的音乐,先生。	
小丑	那就把您的乐器装进口袋,因为我要 走了。　去,赶快离开,滚吧!	众乐师下。　20
凯西奥	你是否听见了,我的好友?	
小丑	没有,我没听见您的好友,听见了您。	
凯西奥	求你别再吹毛求疵;这里有枚微薄的 金币给你——若侍奉将军夫人的那位 女士起身走动,就告诉她有位凯西奥 求她能赏光简短地谈上几句。你愿意 做吗?	25
小丑	她在骚动,先生;假如她能骚到这里, 我会设法通知她的。	

伊阿古上。

凯西奥	务必,我的好友。[小丑下。]来得正好,伊阿古。	30
伊阿古	难道您没回去睡觉?	
凯西奥	没有,咱们分手前天已破晓。 我已冒昧,伊阿古,传信进去 给您妻子:我是想求她设法	

---

13. 爱(love's):可指"你们对他的爱(the love you bear him)";也可指"奥赛罗与苔丝狄蒙娜的做爱(Othello's lovemaking with Desdemona)"(Bate)。　22. "故意误解"对小丑来说可谓司空见惯。　25. 女士(gentlewoman):本指一位出身高贵的女士;此外;也可指一位贵妇的女侍。　28. 骚动(stirring):他将该词曲解为"性骚动"(sexually exciting)。　32. 证明剧中的行动未曾间断(Ridley)。

35   To virtuous Desdemona procure me
               some access.

Iago   I'll send her to you presently,
And I'll devise a mean to draw the Moor
Out of the way, that your converse and business
May be more free.

Cassio   I humbly thank you for't.   *Exit* [*Iago.*]

40   I never knew
A Florentine more kind and honest.

Enter Emilia.

Emilia   Good morrow, good lieutenant. I am sorry
For your displeasure, but all will sure be well.
The general and his wife are talking of it,

45   And she speaks for you stoutly; the Moor replies
That he you hurt is of great fame in Cyprus
And great affinity,
And that in wholesome wisdom he might not but
Refuse you; but he protests he loves you

50   And needs no other suitor but his likings
To take the safest occasion by the front
To bring you in again.

Cassio   Yet I beseech you,
If you think fit, or that it may be done,
Give me advantage of some brief discourse

	能够让我见一见贞洁高尚的	35
	苔丝狄蒙娜。	
伊阿古	我叫她马上过来,	
	我还要想尽办法让那个摩尔	
	离开,好让你们的谈话和行事	
	更为随意一些。	
凯西奥	我对此非常感激。 　　　　　[伊阿古]下。	
	我从未见过	40
	佛罗伦萨人有谁更善良诚实。	

爱米利娅上。

爱米利娅	早上好,好副官。 对于您的失宠	
	我很抱歉,可一切都会好的。	
	将军和他的夫人正谈论此事,	
	她竭力为您开脱;摩尔人回答说	45
	您刺伤的人在塞浦路斯很有名望,	
	家族又有势力,	
	出于万全之策他只好将您	
	解职;不过他声言他很爱您,	
	不用别人说情,仅凭他的感情	50
	就会迎头抓住最佳的时机	
	让您官复原职。	
凯西奥	不过我求您,	
	您若认为合适,或能够做到,	
	就给我机会让我跟苔丝狄蒙	

---

41. 佛罗伦萨人(A Florentine):凯西奥是在评说伊阿古跟他(凯西奥)的同乡——佛罗伦萨市民一样诚实善良(Mowat)。 47. 此半行诗文可能本已删除,但后又误印入册。 54. 苔丝狄蒙(Desdemon):该称谓共出现过七次,主要由奥赛罗说出,以示更为亲近。

With Desdemon alone.

55 **Emilia**   Pray you come in,

I will bestow you where you shall have time

To speak your bosom freely.

Cassio   I am much bound to you.

Exeunt.

　　单独说句话吧。

爱米利娅　　　　　　　　　请您进来吧，　　　　　　　　　　55
我会给您安排一个地方,以便
让您畅所欲言。

凯西奥　　　　　　　　我非常感激。

　　　　　　　　　　　　　　　　　　同下。

SCENE Ⅱ

Enter Othello, Iago and Gentlemen.

Othello   These letters give, Iago, to the pilot,

And by him do my duties to the Senate;

That done, I will be walking on the works,

Repair there to me.

Iago   Well, my good lord, I'll do't.

5 **Othello**   This fortification, gentlemen, shall we see't?

1 Gentleman We'll wait upon your lordship.   *Exeunt.*

第二场

奥赛罗、伊阿古及众绅士上。

奥赛罗	伊阿古,把这些信件交给舵手,
	并让他代我向元老院致意;
	我要到防御工事上走走,办完后,
	请去那里见我。
伊阿古	是,将军,遵命。
奥赛罗	诸位,我们去看看防御工事吧? 5
绅士甲	我们愿意奉陪阁下。 同下。

3.2. 我们透过本场瞥见了奥赛罗的工作情况,他尚未因苔丝狄蒙娜的事情而分心(Honigmann)。该场同时也表明伊阿古"将那个摩尔引开"的计策就是:督促他去视察防御工事(Ridley)。

SCENE III

Enter Desdemona, Cassio and Emilia.

Desdemona Be thou assured, good Cassio, I will do
All my abilities in thy behalf.

Emilia Good madam, do, I warrant it grieves my husband
As if the cause were his.

5 **Desdemona** O, that's an honest fellow. Do not doubt, Cassio,
But I will have my lord and you again
As friendly as you were.

Cassio   Bounteous madam,
Whatever shall become of Michael Cassio,
He's never anything but your true servant.

10 **Desdemona** I know't, I thank you. You do love my lord,
You have known him long, and be you well assured
He shall in strangeness stand no farther off
Than in a politic distance.

Cassio   Ay, but, lady,
That policy may either last so long,

15 Or feed upon such nice and waterish diet,
Or breed itself so out of circumstance,

第三场

苔丝狄蒙娜、凯西奥与爱米利娅上。

苔丝狄蒙娜	你放心吧,好凯西奥,为了你
	我会竭尽自己的全部能力。
爱米利娅	好夫人,务请,我丈夫也为此难过,
	像是他的问题似的。
苔丝狄蒙娜	噢,那是个诚实人。 别担心,凯西奥,
	但我会确保让我的丈夫与您
	之间和好如初。
凯西奥	高尚的夫人,
	不管迈克尔·凯西奥将来会怎样,
	他永远都是您的忠诚奴仆。
苔丝狄蒙娜	我知道,谢谢您。 您爱我的丈夫,
	你们已相知很久,您尽管放心,
	他对您的疏远不是为了别的,
	只是权宜之计。
凯西奥	对,可是,夫人,
	这种计策也许会持续很久,
	或靠这么淡薄的饮食而消逝,
	或者使机会变得虚无缥缈,

5

10

15

That, I being absent and my place supplied,

My general will forget my love and service.

Desdemona Do not doubt that: before Emilia here

20   I give thee warrant of thy place. Assure thee,

If I do vow a friendship, I'll perform it

To the last article. My lord shall never rest,

I'll watch him tame and talk him out of patience;

His bed shall seem a school, his board a shrift,

25   I'll intermingle everything he does

With Cassio's suit: therefore be merry, Cassio,

For thy solicitor shall rather die

Than give thy cause away.

Enter Othello and Iago.

Emilia   Madam, here comes my lord.

30 **Cassio**   Madam, I'll take my leave.

Desdemona Why, stay and hear me speak.

Cassio   Madam, not now; I am very ill at ease,

Unfit for mine own purposes.

Desdemona Well, do your discretion.   *Exit Cassio.*

Iago   Ha, I like not that.

35 **Othello**   What dost thou say?

Iago   Nothing, my lord; or if—I know not what.

Othello   Was not that Cassio parted from my wife?

Iago   Cassio, my lord? No, sure, I cannot think it,

That he would steal away so guilty-like,

	或因我不在场职位被人取代，	
	将军会忘记我的友爱和效劳。	
苔丝狄蒙娜	别担心：当着爱米利娅的面，	
	我保证您会官复原职。　放心吧，	20
	我若发誓给人以帮助，我就会	
	一帮到底。　我丈夫将坐卧不安，	
	我要磨他，讲得他失去耐心，	
	他的床成学堂，餐桌变成忏悔所，	
	无论他做什么，我都用凯西奥的	25
	诉求去打岔：因此愉快些，凯西奥，	
	因为您的求情者宁可死去，	
	也不将您的诉求放弃。	

奥赛罗与伊阿古上。

爱米利娅	夫人，将军他来了。	
凯西奥	夫人，我这就告辞。	30
苔丝狄蒙娜	唉，别走，您听我说吗！	
凯西奥	夫人，不行，我现在很不舒服，	
	恐怕结果会对我不利。	
苔丝狄蒙娜	那好，您自己斟酌。　　　　　凯西奥下。	
伊阿古	哈！我不喜欢那样。	
奥赛罗	你说啥？	35
伊阿古	没啥，将军；若说了——也不知是啥。	
奥赛罗	刚离开我妻子的不是凯西奥吗？	
伊阿古	凯西奥，将军？　不会，肯定，我想	
	他不会一见您来就偷偷溜走，	

3.3.　23. 磨他（watch him tame）：使他无法入睡以便将其驯服（驯鹰术语）（Beving-ton）。　34. 您自己斟酌（do your discretion）：他的"斟酌"可谓导致灾难的祸首（Ridley）。

Seeing you coming.

40	**Othello**	I do believe 'twas he.
	Desdemona	How now, my lord?

I have been talking with a suitor here,

A man that languishes in your displeasure.

Othello Who is't you mean?

45 **Desdemona** Why, your lieutenant, Cassio. Good my lord,

If I have any grace or power to move you,

His present reconciliation take:

For if he be not one that truly loves you,

That errs in ignorance and not in cunning,

50 I have no judgement in an honest face.

I prithee, call him back.

Othello Went he hence now?

Desdemona Yes, faith, so humbled

That he hath left part of his grief with me

To suffer with him. Good love, call him back.

55 **Othello** Not now, sweet Desdemon, some other time.

Desdemona But shall't be shortly?

Othello The sooner, sweet, for you.

Desdemona Shall't be tonight, at supper?

Othello No, not tonight.

Desdemona Tomorrow dinner then?

Othello I shall not dine at home.

I meet the captains at the citadel.

60 **Desdemona** Why then, tomorrow night, or Tuesday morn;

看上去那么心虚。

奥赛罗　　　　　　　　　　我确信是他。　　　　　　　　　　40

苔丝狄蒙娜　什么事,将军?

我刚才正跟一位请愿者说话,

他因为您的不快在受折磨。

奥赛罗　您指的是谁?

苔丝狄蒙娜　嗨,您的副官,凯西奥。　好夫君,　　　　　45

我若有魅力或力量能将您打动,

那就立即与他言归于好:

因为假如他不是真的爱您,

出于无知并非蓄意而犯错,

表明我不会辨别,好歹不分。　　　　　　　　　50

求您,召回他吧。

奥赛罗　　　　　　　　　他是否刚走?

苔丝狄蒙娜　是的,他那么羞愧,

竟然将他的部分痛苦留下,

让我一起忍受。　亲爱的,召回他吧。

奥赛罗　现在不行,亲爱的苔丝狄蒙,得等等。　　　　55

苔丝狄蒙娜　是否能快些?

奥赛罗　　　　　　　　快些,宝贝儿,为了您。

苔丝狄蒙娜　今天晚餐时?

奥赛罗　　　　　　　　不行,不是今晚。

苔丝狄蒙娜　那明天午餐时?

奥赛罗　　　　　　　　我不在家午餐。

我要在城堡会见各位连长。

苔丝狄蒙娜　那就,明天晚上,或周二早上;　　　　　60

---

42. 伊阿古的第一枪因为苔丝狄蒙娜的率真而放空(Ridley)。

On Tuesday, noon or night; on Wednesday morn!

I prithee name the time, but let it not

Exceed three days: i'faith, he's penitent,

And yet his trespass, in our common reason

65 —Save that they say the wars must make examples

Out of their best—is not, almost, a fault

T'incur a private check. When shall he come?

Tell me, Othello. I wonder in my soul

What you would ask me that I should deny,

70 Or stand so mamm'ring on? What, Michael Cassio,

That came a-wooing with you, and so many a time

When I have spoke of you dispraisingly

Hath ta'en your part, to have so much to do

To bring him in? By'r lady, I could do much! —

75 **Othello** Prithee, no more. Let him come when he will,

I will deny thee nothing.

Desdemona   Why, this is not a boon,

'Tis as I should entreat you wear your gloves,

Or feed on nourishing dishes, or keep you warm,

Or sue to you to do a peculiar profit

80 To your own person. Nay, when I have a suit

Wherein I mean to touch your love indeed,

It shall be full of poise and difficult weight,

And fearful to be granted.

Othello   I will deny thee nothing.

Whereon I do beseech thee, grant me this,

85 To leave me but a little to myself.

Desdemona Shall I deny you? No. Farewell, my lord.

就周二,中午或晚上;周三早上!
我求您定个时间,但不要让它
超过三天:真的,他很懊悔,
然而他的过犯,就常理而言——
除非,据说战时才惩罚爱将   65
以作警诫——很难算得上过错,
不该受谴责。 他何时能回来?
告诉我,奥赛罗。 我无法想象
您求我某件事情我竟会拒绝,
或犹豫不决? 您来向我求婚时, 70
迈克尔·凯西奥是否陪着,多少次
每当我对您吹毛求疵的时候,
都替您说话,与他言归于好
竟如此艰难? 我发誓,不会罢休! ——

奥赛罗   求你,别说了。 他何时想来都行, 75
我全都依你。

苔丝狄蒙娜   嗨,这可不是恩惠!
这就像我求您戴上您的手套,
或者服用补品,或让您保暖,
或求您去做某件对您自己
格外有益的事情。 不,我的请求 80
意味着要考验您是不是真爱,
那将是举足轻重难以估量,
应允时会胆战心惊。

奥赛罗   我全都依你。
作为回报我求你,答应我一点,
让我自己能单独待上一会儿。 85

苔丝狄蒙娜 我会拒绝您吗? 不,再会,夫君。

	Othello	Farewell, my Desdemona, I'll come to thee straight.
	Desdemona	Emilia, come. —Be as your fancies teach you:
		Whate'er you be, I am obedient.

Exeunt Desdemona and Emilia.

90	**Othello**	Excellent wretch! Perdition catch my soul,
		But I do love thee! And when I love thee not,
		Chaos is come again.
	Iago	My noble lord—
	Othello	What dost thou say, Iago?
	Iago	Did Michael Cassio, when you wooed my lady,
		Know of your love?
95	**Othello**	He did, from first to last.
		Why dost thou ask?
	Iago	But for a satisfaction of my thought,
		No further harm.
	Othello	Why of thy thought, Iago?
	Iago	I did not think he had been acquainted with her.
100	**Othello**	O yes, and went between us very oft.
	Iago	Indeed?
	Othello	Indeed? Ay, indeed. Discern'st thou aught in that?
		Is he not honest?
	Iago	Honest, my lord?

奥赛罗	再会,我的苔丝狄蒙娜,一会儿再见。	
苔丝狄蒙娜	爱米利娅,过来。 ——您自己随意吧:	
	不管您怎样,我都会顺从。	

苔丝狄蒙娜与爱米利娅同下。

奥赛罗	多棒的淘气鬼! 假如我不爱你,	90
	灵魂就遭诅咒! 我永远爱你,	
	直到宇宙复归混沌。	
伊阿古	尊贵的将军——	
奥赛罗	你说什么,伊阿古?	
伊阿古	您向夫人求婚时,迈克尔·凯西奥,	
	可知道此事?	
奥赛罗	知道,从头到尾。	95
	你为啥问这?	
伊阿古	只是想满足我的好奇而已,	
	别无他意。	
奥赛罗	你为啥好奇,伊阿古?	
伊阿古	我本以为他并不认识夫人。	
奥赛罗	噢认识,在我们之间往来频繁。	100
伊阿古	真的?	
奥赛罗	真的? 对,真的。 你发现有啥异常?	
	他不诚实吗?	
伊阿古	诚实吗,将军?	

---

88. 您自己随意吧(as…you):结果却导致了他的妒忌和她的死亡(Ridley)。 89. 顺从(obedient):按照传统,妻子应顺从丈夫。 她是说,"您作为丈夫无论多好还是多糟,我都会做一位贤妻"。 91-2. 我永远……混沌(And…again):我爱你直到永远(My love for you will last forever, until the end of time when chaos will return)。 然而颇具反讽的是,本句也在无意中暗示:奥赛罗若因任何缘故不再爱苔丝狄蒙娜,结果将会乱成一团(if anything should induce Othello to cease loving Desdemona, the result would be chaos.)(Bevington)。 93. 著名的诱惑场景(the great temptation scene)由此拉开序幕。 伊阿古的伎俩显而易见……他首先简短地设问,随后便装出不情愿的样子,对问题的弦外之音予以阐释(Ridley)。

105	**Othello**	Honest? Ay, honest.
	Iago	My lord, for aught I know.
	Othello	What dost thou think?
	Iago	Think, my lord?
	Othello	Think, my lord! By heaven, thou echo'st me
110		As if there were some monster in thy thought
		Too hideous to be shown. Thou dost mean something.
		I heard thee say even now thou lik'st not that,
		When Cassio left my wife: what didst not like?
		And when I told thee he was of my counsel
115		In my whole course of wooing, thou criedst 'Indeed?'
		And didst contract and purse thy brow together
		As if thou then hadst shut up in thy brain
		Some horrible conceit. If thou dost love me,
		Show me thy thought.
	Iago	My lord, you know I love you.
120	**Othello**	I think thou dost.
		And for I know thou'rt full of love and honesty
		And weigh'st thy words before thou giv'st them breath,
		Therefore these stops of thine fright me the more.
		For such things in a false disloyal knave
125		Are tricks of custom, but in a man that's just
		They're close dilations, working from the heart,
		That passion cannot rule.
	Iago	For Michael Cassio,
		I dare be sworn, I think, that he is honest.

奥赛罗	诚实吗？　对，诚实。	105
伊阿古	将军，据我所知。	
奥赛罗	你在想什么？	
伊阿古	在想，将军？	
奥赛罗	在想，将军！天哪，你在重复我，	
	好像你心里怀有什么鬼胎，	110
	丑陋得难以表露。　你话里有话，	
	刚才凯西奥离开我的妻子时，	
	你说不喜欢那样：不喜欢什么？	
	当我告诉你他作为亲信参与	
	我的求爱全程时，你大喊"真的？"	115
	而且你表情严肃眉头紧皱，	
	好像在你的脑海里面藏着	
	某种可怕的念头。　假如你爱我，	
	就告诉我吧。	
伊阿古	将军，您知道我爱您。	
奥赛罗	我想是的。	120
	因为我知道你富有爱心也诚实，	
	话语出口之前你会掂量一番，	
	因此你吞吞吐吐更让我害怕。	
	因为这样的事情对小人来说	
	只是惯用伎俩，但对正人君子，	125
	那就是含蓄的揭发，出自内心，	
	情不自禁。	
伊阿古	至于迈克尔·凯西奥，	
	我敢发誓，我想，他是诚实的。	

---

110. 鬼胎（monster）：怪异（monstrosity）；怪物（monstrous creature）（Honigmann）。借鉴梁译。——译者附注。

	Othello	I think so too.
	Iago	Men should be what they seem,
130		Or those that be not, would they might seem none.
	Othello	Certain, men should be what they seem.
	Iago	Why then I think Cassio's an honest man.
	Othello	Nay, yet there's more in this:
		I prithee speak to me, as to thy thinkings,
135		As thou dost ruminate, and give thy worst of thoughts
		The worst of words.
	Iago	Good my lord, pardon me;
		Though I am bound to every act of duty,
		I am not bound to that all slaves are free to—
		Utter my thoughts? Why, say they are vile and false?
140		As where's that palace whereinto foul things
		Sometimes intrude not? Who has a breast so pure
		But some uncleanly apprehensions
		Keep leets and law-days and in session sit
		With meditations lawful?
145	**Othello**	Thou dost conspire against thy friend, Iago,
		If thou but think'st him wronged and mak'st his ear
		A stranger to thy thoughts.
	Iago	I do beseech you,
		Though I perchance am vicious in my guess
		—As I confess it is my nature's plague
150		To spy into abuses, and oft my jealousy
		Shapes faults that are not—that your wisdom
		From one that so imperfectly conceits

奥赛罗	我也这么想。	
伊阿古	人们该表里如一。	
	若并非如此,愿他们别装模作样。	130
奥赛罗	当然了,人们应该表里如一。	
伊阿古	那么我想凯西奥是个诚实人。	
奥赛罗	不,你还有言外之意:	
	我求你对我说说,你在想啥,	
	你要原汁原味,将最糟的想法	135
	用最坏字眼表达。	
伊阿古	好将军,请原谅;	
	尽管我有义务必须唯命是从,	
	却没义务放弃奴隶都有的自由——	
	说出心声?　我的思想若肮脏呢?	
	世上有哪座宫殿不曾侵入	140
	邪恶的东西?　谁的心胸如此纯净,	
	居然从未产生过龌蹉的念头,	
	不与正直的思想在开庭之日	
	彼此之间相互抗衡?	
奥赛罗	你就是陷害你的朋友,伊阿古,	145
	假如你认为他受到了冤屈,	
	却让他蒙在鼓里。	
伊阿古	我请求您,	
	我的揣测有时也许会邪恶——	
	因为我得承认天生有种恶习,	
	爱关注别人的毛病,我的警惕	150
	常会冤枉好人——您要有智慧	
	对这么一种如此残缺的想法	

---

138. 自由（free to）：源于谚语"Thought is free（思想自由）"。

Would take no notice, nor build yourself a trouble

Out of his scattering and unsure observance:

155   It were not for your quiet nor your good,

Nor for my manhood, honesty and wisdom,

To let you know my thoughts.

Othello   Zounds! What dost thou mean?

Iago   Good name in man and woman, dear my lord,

Is the immediate jewel of their souls:

160   Who steals my purse steals trash—'tis something, nothing,

'Twas mine, 'tis his, and has been slave to thousands—

But he that filches from me my good name

Robs me of that which not enriches him

And makes me poor indeed.

Othello   By heaven, I'll know thy thoughts!

165 **Iago**   You cannot, if my heart were in your hand,

Nor shall not whilst 'tis in my custody.

Othello   Ha!

Iago   O beware, my lord, of jealousy!

It is the green-eyed monster, which doth mock

The meat it feeds on. That cuckold lives in bliss

170   Who, certain of his fate, loves not his wronger,

But O, what damned minutes tells he o'er

不去在意,也不要从他那凌乱

和无稽的观察中自寻烦恼:

告诉您我的思想,既不利于　　　　　　　　　　　　　155

您的安康,也不利于我的

人格、诚实和才智。

奥赛罗　　　　　　　　　　天哪,你是何意?

伊阿古　　对男男女女来说,亲爱的将军,

好名声是他们心灵中的瑰宝:

谁偷我的钱,偷点臭钱——微不足道,　　　　　　160

我的变成他的,曾为万人服役——

但是他若盗走我的良好名声,

尽管这不能让他因此富有,

却使我贫穷。

奥赛罗　　　　　　　　天哪,我要知道你心思!

伊阿古　　不可能,哪怕我的心在您手里,　　　　　165

只要它由我看管您就休想。

奥赛罗　　哈!

伊阿古　　　　噢,要当心嫉妒,我的将军!

它是绿眼的怪物,它会玩弄

自己的食物。　戴绿帽的若不爱

妻子,知道她不忠,也能高兴,　　　　　　　170

可是噢,他将会怎样地度日如年,

---

165. 哪怕(if):伊阿古此处在进一步冒险——从心神不安的回避到直截了当的拒绝(Ridley)。　心在您手里(heart…hand):叛徒被处决之后,其心脏即刻被挖出(Honigmann)。
168-9. 玩弄自己的食物(mock…on):嘲弄使之存活的牺牲品(嫉妒者)(taunts the victim [the jealous man] that gives it life)(Bate)。　也许像猫与鼠一般(Honigmann)。　170. 妻子(wronger):可指妻子(wife);也可指妻子的情人(wife's lover)。　171. 意为"他将会遭受多么糟糕的煎熬(what accursed minutes does he suffer)"。　其中,minutes(分钟)= dragging minutes, slow time(拖延的时刻,缓慢的时间)(Honigmann)。　原文"tells he o'er"意为:"does he count"(数算)(Mowat)。

	Who dotes yet doubts, suspects yet strongly loves!
Othello	O misery!
Iago	Poor and content is rich, and rich enough,
175	But riches fineless is as poor as winter
	To him that ever fears he shall be poor.
	Good God, the souls of all my tribe defend
	From jealousy.
Othello	Why—why is this?
180	Think'st thou I'd make a life of jealousy,
	To follow still the changes of the moon
	With fresh suspicions? No: to be once in doubt
	Is once to be resolved. Exchange me for a goat
	When I shall turn the business of my soul
185	To such exsufflicate and blown surmises,
	Matching thy inference. 'Tis not to make me jealous
	To say my wife is fair, feeds well, loves company,
	Is free of speech, sings, plays and dances well:
	Where virtue is, these are more virtuous.
190	Nor from mine own weak merits will I draw
	The smallest fear or doubt of her revolt,
	For she had eyes and chose me. No, Iago,
	I'll see before I doubt, when I doubt, prove,
	And on the proof, there is no more but this:
195	Away at once with love or jealousy!
Iago	I am glad of this, for now I shall have reason

假如宠爱而怀疑,疑心却迷恋!

奥赛罗　噢可怜!

伊阿古　安贫就是富有,且足够富有,

谁若总害怕自己将来穷困,　　　　　　　　　　175

纵然财富无限犹如严冬贫寒。

救主啊,保佑我整个宗族的

灵魂免生嫉妒!

奥赛罗　为啥——为啥说这?

你觉得我会让嫉妒操控人生,　　　　　　　　180

心情总是随着月亮而亏盈,

猜疑不断翻新?　不:一旦生疑,

一次性消除。　你把我视为山羊,

假如我将自己心中的职责

变为这种可恶的捕风捉影,　　　　　　　　　185

去附和你说的情形。　我不会嫉妒,

你若说我妻子美丽、好吃、爱交际、

心直口快、能唱、能弹、会跳舞:

她若很贤惠,这可使她更贤惠。

我也不会因为自身的缺陷　　　　　　　　　　190

对她的不忠存有丝毫的疑虑,

因为是她看上了我。　不,伊阿古,

怀疑前我得看见,若怀疑,就证实,

一旦证据在握也不过如此:

或不再爱她,或不再猜疑!　　　　　　　　　195

伊阿古　我很高兴,现在我就有理由

---

174. 安贫(Poor and content):参考 1. 1. 40 行及以下:伊阿古并不安贫。　本句源于谚语:Contentment is great riches(知足便是大富)。　183. 山羊(goat):因为这种动物头上长角?　或因他们非常性骚(highly sexed),耽于淫荡(spend too much time in lustful activity)?

To show the love and duty that I bear you

With franker spirit: therefore, as I am bound,

Receive it from me. I speak not yet of proof:

200 Look to your wife, observe her well with Cassio.

Wear your eyes thus, not jealous nor secure;

I would not have your free and noble nature

Out of self-bounty be abused: look to't.

I know our country disposition well—

205 In Venice they do let God see the pranks

They dare not show their husbands; their best conscience

Is not to leave't undone, but keep't unknown.

Othello Dost thou say so?

Iago She did deceive her father, marrying you,

210 And when she seemed to shake, and fear your looks,

She loved them most.

Othello   And so she did.

Iago   Why, go to then:

She that so young could give out such a seeming,

To seel her father's eyes up, close as oak—

He thought 'twas witchcraft. But I am much to blame,

215 I humbly do beseech you of your pardon

For too much loving you.

Othello I am bound to thee for ever.

Iago I see this hath a little dashed your spirits.

Othello Not a jot, not a jot.

更为坦率地向您表达我的

爱心和忠诚：因此，我有义务，

您好好听着。 尚无证据可言：

注意您妻子，看她待凯西奥如何。 200

您睁开眼睛，既不怀疑也不确信；

我不愿让您直爽高尚的天性

因为宽厚而被人滥用：要当心！

我非常了解我们城邦的性格——

威尼斯女人宁愿上帝看见奸情， 205

也不敢向丈夫挑明；她们的良心

不是不做，而是不走漏风声。

奥赛罗 你这样认为？

伊阿古 她曾欺骗过父亲，与您结婚，

她假装对您的相貌胆战心惊时， 210

却爱得最深。

奥赛罗 她是这样。

伊阿古 嗨，得啦：

她那么年轻就这么会装样，

蒙住她父亲的眼睛，严丝合缝——

他认为那是妖术。 我太放肆了，

我谦恭地请求您能够原谅 215

我的过分爱您。

奥赛罗 我对你感激不尽。

伊阿古 我看这有点让您精神沮丧。

奥赛罗 没有，丝毫没有。

---

204. 这可谓伊阿古最为邪恶而奏效的王牌，他在利用奥赛罗的自感不谙社交。 这一招不仅增强了奥赛罗的疑心，而且——在伊阿古看来至关重要——他也不大可能就此直接挑战苔丝狄蒙娜，因为他害怕得到答案，他无法面对其中的可能（Ridley）。 218. 伊阿古以假装关心的样子表达了自己的幸灾乐祸。

Iago   I'faith, I fear it has.

220   I hope you will consider what is spoke

Comes from my love. But I do see you're moved;

I am to pray you not to strain my speech

To grosser issues nor to larger reach

Than to suspicion.

Othello   I will not.

225 **Iago**   Should you do so, my lord,

My speech should fall into such vile success

As my thoughts aim not at: Cassio's my worthy friend.

My lord, I see you're moved.

Othello   No, not much moved.

I do not think but Desdemona's honest.

230 **Iago**   Long live she so; and long live you to think so!

Othello   And yet how nature, erring from itself—

Iago   Ay, there's the point: as, to be bold with you,

Not to affect many proposed matches

Of her own clime, complexion and degree,

235   Whereto we see in all things nature tends—

Foh! One may smell in such a will most rank,

Foul disproportion, thoughts unnatural.

But pardon me, I do not in position

Distinctly speak of her, though I may fear

240   Her will, recoiling to her better judgement,

May fall to match you with her country forms,

And happily repent.

伊阿古	真的，我怕是的。

我希望您能认为刚才的话语　　　　　　　　　　220
是出于爱心。　可我看您有些动情；
我要恳求您别将我的言辞
曲解为下流结论，也不要超越
怀疑的范围。

奥赛罗　我不会的。

伊阿古　　　　　　万一您曲解，将军，　　　　　225
我的言辞会导致恶劣的后果，
那不是我本意：凯西奥是我好友。
将军，我看您已动情。

奥赛罗　　　　　　　　没，没咋动情。
我只是在想苔丝狄蒙娜忠诚。

伊阿古　愿她永远忠诚，愿您永远这么想！　　　　230
奥赛罗　可人们是多么容易违背天性——
伊阿古　对，关键在这里：对您直说吧，
多少同胞、同种、地位相同的
青年向她求婚，她都不为所动，
在我们看来，这都是理所当然——　　　　235
呸！人们可嗅到她的淫思邪念，
可恶的不伦不类，思想怪异。
请您原谅，我这种提议可不是
具体指她，尽管我也许会担心
她的意志恢复得更为清醒时，　　　　240
会将您与其同胞的风貌相比，
也许她会后悔。

225．与224行构成五步抑扬格，被"我不会的"给打断。

Othello		Farewell, farewell.
		If more thou dost perceive, let me know more:
		Set on thy wife to observe. Leave me, Iago.
	Iago	My lord, I take my leave.
245	**Othello**	Why did I marry?
		This honest creature doubtless
		Sees and knows more—much more—than he unfolds.
	Iago	My lord, I would I might entreat your honour
		To scan this thing no further. Leave it to time;
250		Although 'tis fit that Cassio have his place,
		For sure he fills it up with great ability,
		Yet if you please to hold him off a while,
		You shall by that perceive him, and his means:
		Note if your lady strain his entertainment
255		With any strong or vehement importunity,
		Much will be seen in that. In the meantime,
		Let me be thought too busy in my fears
		—As worthy cause I have to fear I am—
		And hold her free, I do beseech your honour.
260	**Othello**	Fear not my government.
	Iago	I once more take my leave. *Exit.*
	Othello	This fellow's of exceeding honesty,
		And knows all qualities, with a learned spirit,
		Of human dealings. If I do prove her haggard,
265		Though that her jesses were my dear heart-strings,

奥赛罗	再见，再见。
	若发现别的情况，要告诉我：
	也叫你妻子留心。　你走吧，伊阿古。
伊阿古	将军，我告辞了。
奥赛罗	我为啥结婚？ 245
	这个老实人的见闻
	无疑会更多——更多——尚未吐露。
伊阿古	将军，我很想恳求将军阁下
	别再想这件事了。　时间会证明；
	凯西奥官复原职尽管很合适， 250
	因为他非常能干肯定胜任，
	然而能否请您让他稍稍等待，
	您可由此观察他和他的手段：
	注意您夫人是否会为他的
	官复原职对您胡搅蛮缠， 255
	那将会说明很多。　然而同时，
	我觉得我的担心是爱管闲事——
	我有足够的理由这样担心——
	把她视为无辜，我请求将军。
奥赛罗	别担心我的自制。 260
伊阿古	我再次向您告辞。 下。
奥赛罗	这个家伙可是非常诚实，
	他见多识广，对各种人情世故
	了如指掌。　我若证实她桀骜不驯，
	哪怕她拴腿的皮绳是我心弦， 265

---

251. 反话正说（means the opposite of what he says）。 264. 桀骜不驯（haggard）：意为：未驯化的（wild, untamed）；本意为"羽毛长足后被捕捉的母野鹰（a wild female hawk caught in her adult plumage）"。

I'd whistle her off and let her down the wind
To prey at fortune. Haply, for I am black
And have not those soft parts of conversation
That chamberers have, or for I am declined

270 Into the vale of years—yet that's not much—
She's gone. I am abused, and my relief
Must be to loathe her. O curse of marriage,
That we can call these delicate creatures ours
And not their appetites! I had rather be a toad

275 And live upon the vapour of a dungeon
Than keep a corner in the thing I love
For others' uses. Yet 'tis the plague of great ones,
Prerogatived are they less than the base;
'Tis destiny unshunnable, like death—

280 Even then this forked plague is fated to us
When we do quicken.

Enter Desdemona and Emilia.

Look where she comes:
If she be false, O then heaven mocks itself,
I'll not believe't.

我也会吹哨把她顺风放飞，

让她四处飘荡。　也许因为我黑，

又没有宫廷风流男子具有的

那种文雅，或者因我已步入

年迈的幽谷——可这没多大关系——　　　　　　270

她毁了，我受了欺骗，我的补救，

只有憎恨她了。　噢，该死的婚姻！

我们能拥有这些尤物的躯体，

却不能拥有其情欲！我愿做蟾蜍，

我宁愿吸食地牢的潮气为生，　　　　　　　275

也不愿让心爱之物留下一角

供人享用。　可这是大人物的祸患，

他们要比贫贱之辈更难幸免；

这是命运，不可避免，就像死亡——

这种戴绿帽的折磨在我们降生　　　　　　　280

之前就已注定。

苔丝狄蒙娜与爱米利娅上。

你看她来了：

假如她不忠，噢，就是上天自嘲，

我不会相信。

---

266. 驯鹰者吹哨将猎鹰迎风放飞去捕捉猎物，顺风放飞则意味着将其放走（turn loose）。意为：苔丝狄蒙娜野性难驯；但奥赛罗此刻并不想伤害她。　270. 年迈的幽谷（vale of years）：暗指《圣经》"诗篇"23 篇 4 节："死亡的幽谷（alluding to 'the valley of the shadow of death' ［Psalm 23：4］）"？273. 拥有（ours）：英国上流社会的妻子原本被视为丈夫的财产，并称自己的丈夫为"主人"（lord = master）。见 1. 3. 184 注。274. 蟾蜍（toad）：令人痛恨和厌恶的东西。276. 一角（corner）：可指"角落"（nook）；也可指"阴道"（vagina）（Bate）。276. 物（thing）：参考 306 注。277. 享用（use）：参考 5. 2. 69-70 及注。277-8. 大人物……更难幸免（the plague…base）：莎士比亚可能是指，大人物做乌龟的风险会更大，因为他们公务缠身，需要外出（great ones are in greater danger because their duties keep them from home）。

Desdemona	How now, my dear Othello?
	Your dinner, and the generous islanders
285	By you invited, do attend your presence.
Othello	I am to blame.
Desdemona	Why do you speak so faintly?
	Are you not well?
Othello	I have a pain upon my forehead, here.
Desdemona	Faith, that's with watching, 'twill away again.
290	Let me but bind it hard, within this hour
	It will be well.
Othello	Your napkin is too little.

[*She drops her handkerchief.*]

Let it alone. Come, I'll go in with you.

Desdemona   I am very sorry that you are not well.

Exeunt Othello and Desdemona.

Emilia   I am glad I have found this napkin,

295   This was her first remembrance from the Moor.

My wayward husband hath a hundred times

Wooed me to steal it, but she so loves the token

—For he conjured her she should ever keep it—

That she reserves it evermore about her

300   To kiss and talk to. I'll have the work ta'en out

And give't Iago: what he will do with it

Heaven knows, not I,

I nothing, but to please his fantasy.

苔丝狄蒙娜	怎么了,亲爱的奥赛罗?
	您的午餐,以及您所邀请的
	岛上的贵宾,正在等您出席。

285

奥赛罗	是我不对。
苔丝狄蒙娜	您说话怎么有气无力?
	您不舒服吗?
奥赛罗	我感到额头这里有些疼痛。
苔丝狄蒙娜	没错,是没睡好,很快会好的。
	让我给您包紧,一小时之内

290

	它就会好的。
奥赛罗	您的手帕太小。

［她掉落手帕。］

	您别管了。　快,我跟您一同进去。
苔丝狄蒙娜	您不太舒服,我非常难过。

奥赛罗与苔丝狄蒙娜同下。

爱米利娅	我很高兴我捡到了这块手帕,
	这是摩尔人送她的首件礼物。

295

	我那古怪的丈夫曾经上百次
	求我把它偷走,可她太爱这信物
	——因为他告诫她要永远保存——
	所以她时刻把手帕带在身边,
	跟它说话亲吻。　我要把图样描下,

300

	再给伊阿古:他要用它做啥,
	上帝知道,我不清楚。
	我只想满足他的心血来潮。

---

288. 额头(forehead):在思考戴绿帽的折磨(forked plague)(Ridley)。 292. 进去(in):与客人会合;也许他们现在室外? 300. 跟它说话亲吻(To…to):由此看来,苔丝狄蒙娜仍是个孩子(scarcely older than a child)。 302. 她在暗示"我不想知道"(I don't want to know)。

Enter Iago.

Iago	How now! What do you here alone?
305 **Emilia**	Do not you chide, I have a thing for you—
Iago	You have a thing for me? It is a common thing—
Emilia	Ha?
Iago	To have a foolish wife.
Emilia	O, is that all? What will you give me now
	For that same handkerchief?
310 **Iago**	What handkerchief?
Emilia	What handkerchief?
	Why, that the Moor first gave to Desdemona,
	That which so often you did bid me steal.
Iago	Hast stolen it from her?
315 **Emilia**	No, faith, she let it drop by negligence,
	And, to th'advantage, I being here, took't up.
	Look, here it is.
Iago	A good wench, give it me.
Emilia	What will you do with't, that you have been so earnest
	To have me filch it?
Iago	[*Snatching it*] Why, what's that to you?
320 **Emilia**	If it be not for some purpose of import,
	Give't me again. Poor lady, she'll run mad
	When she shall lack it.
Iago	Be not acknown on't,

伊阿古上。

伊阿古	怎么！您独自在此干吗？	
爱米利娅	您别责怪，我有件东西给您——	305
伊阿古	有件东西给我？　那又没啥稀奇——	
爱米利娅	什么？	
伊阿古	娶来一位傻妻。	
爱米利娅	噢，是那样吗？　我若把那块手帕 给您，如何报答我呢？	
伊阿古	什么手帕？	310
爱米利娅	什么手帕？ 嗨，摩尔人最初送给苔丝狄蒙娜， 您经常让我把它偷来的那块。	
伊阿古	从她那里偷的？	
爱米利娅	没有，真的，她因疏忽把它掉落， 我当时在场，便趁机把它捡起。 看，就是这块。	315
伊阿古	好女郎，快给我。	
爱米利娅	您用它做啥，竟然这么迫切地 让我把它偷来？	
伊阿古	［夺取手帕］　嗨，那与您何干？	
爱米利娅	要是没有什么重要的用途， 就还给我。　可怜的夫人，她会疯的， 若发现它丢了。	320
伊阿古	别承认知道此事，	

306. 那又没啥稀奇（a common thing）：伊阿古假装将"东西"（a thing）误解为"女性外阴"（pudendum）；其中，common 可指"公用的"（free to be used by everyone），也可指"普通的，平凡的"（undistinguished, ordinary）。　322. 别承认知道此事（Be…on't）：别承认你与此有关（don't acknowledge that you have a part in it, keep out of it）（Honigmann）。　伊阿古的本意为：这件事情你了解得越少，对你越好（The less you know about it, the better for you）（Ridley）。

I have use for it. Go, leave me.   *Exit Emilia.*

I will in Cassio's lodging lose this napkin

325 And let him find it. Trifles light as air

Are to the jealous confirmations strong

As proofs of holy writ. This may do something.

The Moor already changes with my poison：

Dangerous conceits are in their natures poisons,

330 Which at the first are scarce found to distaste,

But with a little act upon the blood

Burn like the mines of sulphur.

Enter Othello.

                                   I did say so：

Look, where he comes! Not poppy nor mandragora

Nor all the drowsy syrups of the world

335 Shall ever medicine thee to that sweet sleep

Which thou owedst yesterday.

Othello   Ha! Ha! False to me?

Iago   Why, how now, general? No more of that.

Othello   Avaunt, be gone, thou hast set me on the rack!

I swear 'tis better to be much abused

Than but to know't a little.

340 **Iago**   How now, my lord?

我自会有用。　走吧,快走。　　　　　　　　爱米利娅下。

我要把它丢到凯西奥的住处,

并让他捡到。　轻如鸿毛的琐事　　　　　　　　　　325

对嫉妒者来说,就像圣经里的

证据一样确凿。　这会派上用场。

摩尔人已因我的毒药而改变:

危险的念头原本就是毒药,

最初很难发现有什么反感,　　　　　　　　　　　330

但略施小计即可使血液发作,

会像硫矿一般燃烧。

　　　　　　　奥赛罗上。

　　　　　我已说过:

快看他来了。　无论罂粟、曼陀罗,

还是世上所有令人昏睡的糖浆,

也都无法帮你继续去享用　　　　　　　　　　　335

你昨天的安眠。

奥赛罗　　　　　　哈!哈!对我不忠?

伊阿古　嗨,怎么了,将军?　别再想它了。

奥赛罗　你滚,走开,你已使我上了刑架!

我发誓宁愿暗中彻底受骗,

也不愿略闻风言。

伊阿古　　　　怎么了,将军?　　　　　　　　340

---

　　331. 小计（art）:技巧（skill）。　伊阿古对自己的"小计"颇为得意:另见"一举两得"
（double knavery）（1. 3. 393,与 400）;还有"咱是靠智力"（we work by wit）（2. 3.
367）（Honigmann）。在其他多个版本中,该词均为"act"。　——译者附注）。　331. 使血液
发作（upon the blood）:使他妒火中烧（to arouse passion）。　338. 刑架（rack）:一种分尸
的刑具（an instrument of torture that tore the body apart）（Mowat）。

Othello   What sense had I of her stolen hours of lust?

I saw't not, thought it not, it harmed not me,

I slept the next night well, fed well, was free and merry;

I found not Cassio's kisses on her lips;

345   He that is robbed, not wanting what is stolen,

Let him not know't and he's not robbed at all.

Iago   I am sorry to hear this.

Othello   I had been happy if the general camp,

Pioneers and all, had tasted her sweet body,

350   So I had nothing known. O now for ever

Farewell the tranquil mind, farewell content!

Farewell the plumed troops and the big wars

That make ambition virtue! O farewell,

Farewell the neighing steed and the shrill trump,

355   The spirit-stirring drum, th'ear-piercing fife,

The royal banner, and all quality,

Pride, pomp and circumstance of glorious war!

And, O you mortal engines whose rude throats

The immortal Jove's dread clamours counterfeit,

360   Farewell: Othello's occupation's gone.

Iago   Is't possible? My lord?

Othello   Villain, be sure thou prove my love a whore,

Be sure of it, give me the ocular proof,

[Catching hold of him]

奥赛罗	我对她的偷情有什么感觉？
	眼没见，不想它，对我没啥伤害，
	我晚上睡得好，吃得香，自在愉快；
	看不出凯西奥吻过她的嘴唇；
	被盗者若不缺少被盗的物品， 345
	别让他知道，他就没有被盗。
伊阿古	听到这话我很抱歉。
奥赛罗	我会很快乐，即便全体将士，
	包括工兵，品尝过她的玉体，
	只要我一无所知。 噢，从此开始， 350
	别了，宁静的心情，别了，满足！
	别了，头饰羽毛的大军，使野心
	化为美德的鏖战！噢，永别了，
	别了，嘶鸣的战马，尖厉的号角，
	令人振奋的战鼓，刺耳的横笛， 355
	光彩夺目的军旗，各种品性、
	自豪、壮观与光荣战争的盛典！
	还有噢，你这致命的大炮，以你
	粗鲁的喉咙模仿天神的雷鸣。
	别了：奥赛罗的生涯从此断送！ 360
伊阿古	怎么会这样，将军？
奥赛罗	恶棍，你必须证明我爱人是娼妇，
	必须证明，要给我目击的证据，

［揪住他］

---

341. 奥赛罗已对苔丝狄蒙娜的罪过深信不疑（伊阿古不在场时！）。 345-6. 源于谚语："He that is not sensible of his loss has lost nothing"（若不知道自己的损失就没有损失）。 361. 怎么会这样（Is't possible）：你居然会有这种感受，那可能吗（Is't possible that you should feel like this）？ 362：演员巴顿（Barton Booth）在表演本段时曾揪住伊阿古的脖子；其他演员则从本场 371 行开始如此——该举动可由 5. 2. 353 的台词得以证实。

Or by the worth of man's eternal soul,

365   Thou hadst been better have been born a dog

Than answer my waked wrath!

Iago   Is't come to this?

Othello   Make me to see't, or at the least so prove it

That the probation bear no hinge nor loop

To hang a doubt on, or woe upon thy life!

370 **Iago**   My noble lord—

Othello   If thou dost slander her and torture me,

Never pray more, abandon all remorse;

On horror's head horrors accumulate,

Do deeds to make heaven weep, all earth amazed,

375   For nothing canst thou to damnation add

Greater than that!

Iago   O grace! O heaven forgive me!

Are you a man? Have you a soul, or sense?

God buy you, take mine office. O wretched fool,

That lov'st to make thine honesty a vice!

380   O monstrous world! Take note, take note, O world,

	否则,我以人的不朽灵魂起誓,	
	你宁愿自己生来是一条狗,	365
	也不愿面对我的激怒!	
伊阿古	竟然如此?	
奥赛罗	让我眼见,或至少也要证明	
	你的证据将会是天衣无缝,	
	毋庸置疑,否则将遭受诅咒!	
伊阿古	尊贵的将军——	370
奥赛罗	你若是诽谤她旨在折磨我,	
	就别再祈祷,放弃所有悔罪,	
	你在惨状之上再堆积惨状,	
	让天使哭泣大地惊愕的勾当,	
	因为你那种行径遭到的诅咒	375
	将无以复加。	
伊阿古	噢天哪! 上天宽恕!	
	您是人吗? 您有灵魂和理性吗?	
	再见了,撤我职吧。 噢可怜的傻瓜,	
	竟爱把自己的诚实变为缺陷!	
	噢可怕的世界! 当心,当心噢,世人,	380

364. 人的（man's）：（与没有灵魂的狗相对而言）,意为：他将把伊阿古的灵魂罚入地狱（consign Iago's soul to eternal damnation）。 本句为一种含糊的誓言（a vague oath）。 另见《圣经》"马太福音" 26 章 24-5 节："但出卖人子的人有祸了! 那人不生在世上倒好。"出卖耶稣的犹大问他说："拉比,是我吗?"莎士比亚是否将伊阿古视为犹大? 371. 人们可以合情合理地认定奥赛罗要么从本行开始,要么从 366 行（激怒）开始,揪住伊阿古的脖子。 我认为,此时此刻,伊阿古意识到了自己的失算。 他本指望能使奥赛罗妒火中烧,以致丧失理智;但他却并未料到其中的部分危险会指向他本人。 而且,奥赛罗仍有足够的理智,以武力要求伊阿古拿出目击证据,伊阿古清楚自己对此无能为力。 从此刻开始,伊阿古明白,为了自身的安全,必须将凯西奥与苔丝狄蒙娜两人除掉,而且是越快越好,尽管他最初的计谋并不想让其中的任何一位死去（Ridley）。 372. 放弃所有悔罪（abandon all remorse）：因为你的所作所为无法得到宽恕。 375. 那种行径（that）：即诽谤苔丝狄蒙娜,折磨奥赛罗（Mowat）。 376. 宽恕（forgive）：即宽恕我的敢于"诚实（honest）"。 378-9. 噢……缺陷（O…vice）：他在自言自语。

To be direct and honest is not safe.

I thank you for this profit, and from hence

I'll love no friend, sith love breeds such offence.

Othello   Nay, stay, thou shouldst be honest.

385 **Iago**   I should be wise, for honesty's a fool

And loses that it works for.

Othello   By the world,

I think my wife be honest, and think she is not,

I think that thou art just, and think thou art not.

I'll have some proof. Her name, that was as fresh

390   As Dian's visage, is now begrimed and black

As mine own face. If there be cords or knives,

Poison, or fire, or suffocating streams,

I'll not endure it. Would I were satisfied!

Iago   I see, sir, you are eaten up with passion.

395   I do repent me that I put it to you.

You would be satisfied?

Othello   Would? Nay, and I will!

Iago   And may—but how? How satisfied, my lord?

Would you, the supervisor, grossly gape on?

Behold her topped?

Othello   Death and damnation! O!

400 **Iago**   It were a tedious difficulty, I think,

To bring them to that prospect. Damn them then

直率和诚实可会危及自身。

我谢谢您这种教训,从此以后,

不再爱朋友,因为爱竟带来伤害。

奥赛罗　别走,你好像很诚实。

伊阿古　我应该明智,因为诚实是傻子,　　　　　　　　　　385

并且费力不讨好。

奥赛罗　　　　　　　　　　向世界宣誓,

我想妻子很忠诚,又想她不是,

我想你很正直,又想你不是。

我须有证据。　她的名声,洁白

如戴安娜的脸庞,已跟我的一样　　　　　　　　　　390

又黑又脏。　只要有绳索、刀子、

毒药、火坑,或令人窒息的河流,

我不会忍受煎熬。　愿我能确信!

伊阿古　我看,先生,您现已情绪失控。

我很后悔曾对您提起此事。　　　　　　　　　　395

想要证据吗?

奥赛罗　　　　　　　想要?　不,我定要!

伊阿古　也许——但如何?　如何得到,将军?

您会,袖手旁观,呆呆地张望?

目睹他们交尾?

奥赛罗　　　　　　该死,罪孽!　噢!

伊阿古　我想,要让您目睹他们的那种　　　　　　　　　　400

场景会很难和无聊。　他们该死,

---

384. 好像(shouldst):可指"好像"(appear to be);也可指"应该"(ought to be)。
386. 费力不讨好(loses that it works for):其中,that = that which(Mowat);借鉴梁
译。——译者附注。 397. 伊阿古现已转向更为冷酷和令人疯狂的直白(Ridley)。 401. 他们
该死(Damn them then):他好像捡起了399行的话茬:"是的,他们的死亡和诅咒罪有应得
(Yes, their death and damnation is right)。"

If ever mortal eyes do see them bolster

More than their own. What then? How then?

What shall I say? Where's satisfaction?

405 It is impossible you should see this

Were they as prime as goats, as hot as monkeys,

As salt as wolves in pride, and fools as gross

As ignorance made drunk. But yet, I say,

If imputation and strong circumstances

410 Which lead directly to the door of truth

Will give you satisfaction, you may have't.

Othello Give me a living reason she's disloyal.

Iago I do not like the office.

But sith I am entered in this cause so far,

415 Pricked to't by foolish honesty and love,

I will go on. I lay with Cassio lately

And being troubled with a raging tooth

I could not sleep. There are a kind of men

So loose of soul that in their sleeps will mutter

420 Their affairs—one of this kind is Cassio.

In sleep I heard him say, 'Sweet Desdemona,

Let us be wary, let us hide our loves,'

And then, sir, would he gripe and wring my hand,

Cry, 'O sweet creature!' and then kiss me hard,

假如人们曾亲眼看见他们

彼此通奸。　那又怎样？　怎么办？

我有何可言？　会有什么证据？

您别想自己能看到这种场景，　　　　　　　　　　　　405

即便他们骚如山羊，猴子般淫荡，

狼一般发情，犹如烂醉如泥的

白痴一般愚蠢。　然而，我说，

假如能有证据确凿的归因

可以直接通往真相的大门，　　　　　　　　　　　　410

您将会如愿以偿，得到证据。

奥赛罗　　给我确凿的证据证明她不忠。

伊阿古　　我可不喜欢这种差使。

不过既然我已经深陷其中，

因为被愚忠及爱心所驱使，　　　　　　　　　　　　415

我会继续。　最近我与凯西奥同床，

由于要命的牙疼令我不安，

无法入眠。　世上有这么一种人，

他们满腹淫念，竟会在梦中

吐露心声——凯西奥就属于这种。　　　　　　　　420

我听见他说"亲爱的苔丝狄蒙娜，

咱们要小心，要隐瞒咱的恋情"，

然后，先生，他紧紧握住我的手，

喊道："噢，宝贝儿！"然后用力亲吻，

---

409. 证据确凿的归因（imputation…circumstances）：基于翔实证据的指控（a charge based on circumstantial evidence）（Mowat）。　其中：imputation = attribution（归因，归罪），circumstances = circumstantial evidence（确凿的证据）（Honigmann）。　410. 真相的大门（door of truth）：我认为在"大门（door）"一词之后稍作停顿；奥赛罗便会想象自己正站在紧闭的卧室门外（Ridley）。　416. 同床（I lay）：与人同床共眠在当时比较普遍。　色情梦（erotic dreams）在古典文学中已有描述，但凯西奥的梦纯属伊阿古捏造。　423-7. 然后（then）：注意该词的重复所带来的分量，依次将它们放置一起似可证明系列动作确实可信。

425　　　　　　　　As if he plucked up kisses by the roots

That grew upon my lips, lay his leg o'er my thigh,

And sigh, and kiss, and then cry 'Cursed fate

That gave thee to the Moor! '

Othello　　　　　　　　　　　　　　　　O monstrous! Monstrous!

Iago　　Nay, this was but his dream.

430 **Othello**　　But this denoted a foregone conclusion.

Iago　　'Tis a shrewd doubt, though it be but a dream,

And this may help to thicken other proofs

That do demonstrate thinly.

Othello　　I'll tear her all to pieces!

435 **Iago**　　Nay, yet be wise, yet we see nothing done,

She may be honest yet. Tell me but this,

Have you not sometimes seen a handkerchief

Spotted with strawberries, in your wife's hand?

Othello　　I gave her such a one, 'twas my first gift.

440 **Iago**　　I know not that, but such a handkerchief,

I am sure it was your wife's, did I today

See Cassio wipe his beard with.

Othello　　　　　　　　　　　　　　If it be that—

Iago　　If it be that, or any that was hers,

It speaks against her with the other proofs.

445 **Othello**　　O that the slave had forty thousand lives!

One is too poor, too weak for my revenge.

好像亲吻就长在我唇上,他要 425

连根拔起,他把腿放在我大腿上,

叹息、亲吻,然后喊:"该死的命运,

竟把你给了那摩尔!"

奥赛罗　　　　　　　　　噢可恶!可恶!

伊阿古　别急,这只是梦而已。

奥赛罗　但这表明他们以前有过体验。 430

伊阿古　敏锐的担心,尽管是梦而已,

这一点可以帮助证实其他

显得微薄的证据。

奥赛罗　我要把她碎尸万段。

伊阿古　不,要理智,我们尚未看到奸情, 435

她也许依然忠诚。请您告诉我,

您是否曾看见过一块手帕,

点缀着草莓,在您妻子手里?

奥赛罗　我给过她一块,是我的首件礼物。

伊阿古　这我不知道,但这么一块手帕, 440

肯定是您夫人的,我今天看见

凯西奥用它擦了胡子。

奥赛罗　　　　　　　　　若是那块——

伊阿古　若是那块,或她的任何一块,

连同其他证据可对她不利。

奥赛罗　噢,但愿那个杂种有四万条性命! 445

一条太少、太弱不够我复仇。

---

434. 碎尸万段(tear her all to pieces):借鉴梁译。 ——译者附注。 435. 看到(see):伊阿古在此前的 40 行诗文中旨在撩起奥赛罗的直观想象。此刻他要使出浑身解数,按照要求提供"目击的证据"(occular proof)(Ridley)。 438. 草莓(strawberries):可能暗示隐藏的罪恶,或圣母玛利亚的纯洁,或者滴滴鲜血? 440. 这我不知道(I know not that):他拒绝透露更多的情况,想以此证实自己的谎言。 444. 证据(proofs):有何证据(What proofs)?

Now do I see 'tis true. Look here, Iago,

All my fond love thus do I blow to heaven.

'Tis gone!

450 Arise, black vengeance, from the hollow hell,

Yield up, O love, thy crown and hearted throne

To tyrannous hate! Swell, bosom, with thy fraught,

For 'tis of aspics' tongues!

Iago   Yet be content!

Othello O blood, blood, blood!   *Othello kneels.*

455 **Iago** Patience, I say, your mind perhaps may change.

Othello Never, Iago. Like to the Pontic sea,

Whose icy current and compulsive course

Ne'er keeps retiring ebb but keeps due on

To the Propontic and the Hellespont:

460 Even so my bloody thoughts with violent pace

Shall ne'er look back, ne'er ebb to humble love,

Till that a capable and wide revenge

Swallow them up. Now by yond marble heaven,

In the due reverence of a sacred vow

I here engage my words.

465 **Iago**   Do not rise yet. *Iago kneels.*

Witness, you ever-burning lights above,

You elements that clip us round about,

Witness that here Iago doth give up

　　　　　现在看来都是真的。　噢,伊阿古,

　　　　　我要把所有痴情吹向空中:

　　　　　消失殆尽!

　　　　　邪恶的复仇,快从幽窟中升起,　　　　　　　　　　　　450

　　　　　爱情啊,将你的王冠和心中宝座

　　　　　让给残暴的仇恨! 肿胀吧,胸膛,

　　　　　因为它填满毒蛇的舌头!

伊阿古　　　　　　　　　　　　　冷静些!

奥赛罗　　噢,要杀,要杀,要杀!　　　　　　　　　奥赛罗跪下。

伊阿古　　耐心些,我说,您也许会改变主意。　　　　　　　455

奥赛罗　　决不会,伊阿古。　就像黑海里

　　　　　那种冰冷的激流被迫前涌,

　　　　　从不退潮而是勇往直前,

　　　　　注入马尔马拉海与赫勒斯滂:

　　　　　我嗜杀的思想同样汹涌澎湃,　　　　　　　　　　460

　　　　　决不回顾,向卑微的爱情低头,

　　　　　直到一种彻底和完全的复仇

　　　　　将他们吞没。　冷漠的苍天在上,

　　　　　以对神圣誓言的虔敬之心,

　　　　　我在此许下诺言。

伊阿古　　　　　　　　　　　先别起来。　　　　　伊阿古跪下。　465

　　　　　请见证,你们永远闪耀的天光,

　　　　　你们这环抱我们大地的辰星,

　　　　　见证伊阿古在此要将他的

　　456-9. 黑海……赫勒斯滂(the Pontic sea…Hellespont):黑海(The Black Sea = the Pontic sea)注入马尔马拉海(Marmora = the Propontic),然后经由达达尼尔海峡(Dardanelles = the Hellespont)注入地中海。　这种表面的潮流看上去从不倒退,或“退潮(retiring ebb)”,因为回流到黑海的海水是从海面以下很深的地方以潜流的方式进行(Mowat)。

The execution of his wit, hands, heart,

470   To wronged Othello's service. Let him command

And to obey shall be in me remorse,

What bloody business ever.

Othello   I greet thy love

Not with vain thanks but with acceptance bounteous,

And will upon the instant put thee to't.

475   Within these three days let me hear thee say

That Cassio's not alive.

Iago   My friend is dead,

'Tis done—at your request. But let her live.

Othello   Damn her, lewd minx: O damn her, damn her!

Come, go with me apart; I will withdraw

480   To furnish me with some swift means of death

For the fair devil. Now art thou my lieutenant.

Iago   I am your own for ever.   *Exeunt.*

全部身心交托,要为蒙受

冤屈的奥赛罗效劳。　由他掌控,　　　　　　　　　470

服从对我来说是一种天职,

无论行动多么血腥。

奥赛罗　　　　　　　　　谢谢你的爱,

不是空口致谢,而是全心接受,

我还要立刻让你经受考验。

三天之内要让我听你回话:　　　　　　　　　475

凯西奥已经毙命。

伊阿古　　　　　　　　我朋友死去,

按您要求——执行。　但要让她活着。

奥赛罗　诅咒她,娼妇:噢,诅咒她,诅咒她!

快,你跟我过来;我要离开这里,

想想办法让那个美丽的妖魔　　　　　　　　　480

尽快死去。　现在你是我的副官。

伊阿古　我永远属于将军。　　　　　　　　　同下。

---

　　470. 效劳(service):自1. 1. 41行起,伊阿古便将自己视为奥赛罗的仆人(servant);可现在,尽管他在保证效忠,但奥赛罗几乎已成了他这位口技大师的傀儡。　477. 但要让她活着(But let her live):伊阿古清楚,确保苔丝狄蒙娜死去的最佳方式就是建议她活着(Ridley)。

SCENE Ⅳ

Enter Desdemona, Emilia and Clown.

Desdemona	Do you know, sirrah, where Lieutenant Cassio lies?
Clown	I dare not say he lies anywhere.
Desdemona	Why, man?
5 **Clown**	He's a soldier, and for me to say a soldier lies, 'tis stabbing.
Desdemona	Go to, where lodges he?
Clown	To tell you where he lodges, is to tell you where I lie.
10 **Desdemona**	Can anything be made of this?
Clown	I know not where he lodges, and for me to devise a lodging and say he lies here, or he lies there, were to lie in mine own throat.
Desdemona	Can you enquire him out and be edified by
15	report?
Clown	I will catechize the world for him, that is, make questions and by them answer.
Desdemona	Seek him, bid him come hither. Tell him I

第四场

苔丝狄蒙娜、爱米利娅与小丑上。

苔丝狄蒙娜	您是否知道，老兄，凯西奥副官家在
	何处？
小丑	我不敢说他"假"在何处？
苔丝狄蒙娜	为啥，老兄？
小丑	他是一位士兵，要让我说士兵有"假"，
	就是找死。
苔丝狄蒙娜	得啦，他住在哪里？
小丑	要告诉您他住在哪里，就等于告诉您
	我在撒谎。
苔丝狄蒙娜	这究竟是什么意思？
小丑	我不知道他住在哪里，我若捏造一个
	住处，说他住在这里，或者住在那里，
	那就是彻头彻尾的谎言。
苔丝狄蒙娜	您是否能探出他的住处，通过向别人
	询问？
小丑	我要向全世界盘问他的下落，就是说，
	问到答案后我再转告。
苔丝狄蒙娜	去找他吧，叫他来这里，告诉他我已

5

10

15

　　3.4.　1-22. 这一段丑角插曲在演出时常被省略。　1. 老兄（sirrah）：用以称谓仆人或社会地位低下者。　3. "假（lies）"：该词系语义双关：即"躺卧"与"撒谎"之义。　译文借鉴朱译与卞译。　——译者附注。

		have moved my lord on his behalf, and hope all will
20		be well.
	Clown	To do this is within the compass of man's wit,
		and therefore I will attempt the doing it. *Exit.*
	Desdemona	Where should I lose that handkerchief, Emilia?
	Emilia	I know not, madam.
25	**Desdemona**	Believe me, I had rather have lost my purse
		Full of crusadoes; and but my noble Moor
		Is true of mind, and made of no such baseness
		As jealous creatures are, it were enough
		To put him to ill-thinking.
	Emilia	Is he not jealous?
30	**Desdemona**	Who, he? I think the sun where he was born
		Drew all such humours from him.
	Emilia	Look where he comes.

Enter Othello.

	Desdemona	I will not leave him now till Cassio
		Be called to him. How is't with you, my lord?
	Othello	Well, my good lady. [*aside*] O hardness to dissemble! —
		How do you, Desdemona?
35	**Desdemona**	Well, my good lord.

	为他向我丈夫求过情了,我希望一切	
	安好。	20
小丑	做这种事情是在人类的智力范围以内,	
	因此我倒愿意试上一试。	下。
苔丝狄蒙娜	我会在哪里丢了那块手帕,爱米利娅?	
爱米利娅	我不知道,夫人。	
苔丝狄蒙娜	相信我,我宁愿丢失我那装满	25
	金币的钱袋;除非我高贵的摩尔	
	真心诚意,不会像爱嫉妒之辈	
	那样心胸狭隘,恐怕这足以	
	使他心生怀疑。	
爱米利娅	难道他不妒忌?	
苔丝狄蒙娜	谁? 他吗? 我想他故乡的太阳	30
	已把他这种体液吸干。	
爱米利娅	瞧,他来了。	

奥赛罗上。

苔丝狄蒙娜	他若不马上将凯西奥召回,	
	我就不让他自在。 您好吗,夫君?	
奥赛罗	还好,我的好夫人。〔旁白〕噢,真难假装!——	
	您好吗,苔丝狄蒙娜?	
苔丝狄蒙娜	好,我的夫君。	35

---

26. 金币(crusadoes):葡萄牙硬币,印有十字架图形,当时在英格兰通用,币值约为三个先令(Ridley)。 29. 难道他不妒忌(Is he not jealous):也许意味着警告(参考本场 100 行)。 31. 体液(humour):据信可导致诸如嫉妒等性情的体液(bodily fluids)。 该词既可指人们的体液,也可指人们的性格,但就"太阳可将人的体液吸干"这一概念而言,此处则指可导致嫉妒的胆汁(black bile)(Mowat)。 另外三种体液分别为:血液(blood)、黏液(rheum)、忧郁液(melancholy)。 ——译者附注。 34. 我的好夫人(my good lady):对她的称谓从未如此正式(Ridley)。

	Othello	Give me your hand. This hand is moist, my lady.
	Desdemona	It yet has felt no age, nor known no sorrow.
	Othello	This argues fruitfulness and liberal heart:
		Hot, hot, and moist. This hand of yours requires
40		A sequester from liberty, fasting, and prayer,
		Much castigation, exercise devout,
		For here's a young and sweating devil, here,
		That commonly rebels. 'Tis a good hand,
		A frank one.
	Desdemona	You may indeed say so,
45		For 'twas that hand that gave away my heart.
	Othello	A liberal hand. The hearts of old gave hands
		But our new heraldry is hands, not hearts.
	Desdemona	I cannot speak of this. Come, now, your promise.
	Othello	What promise, chuck?
50	**Desdemona**	I have sent to bid Cassio come speak with you.
	Othello	I have a salt and sullen rheum offends me,
		Lend me thy handkerchief.
	Desdemona	Here, my lord.
	Othello	That which I gave you.
55	**Desdemona**	I have it not about me.
	Othello	Not?
	Desdemona	No, faith, my lord.

奥赛罗	您把手给我。　这手很湿润,夫人。	
苔丝狄蒙娜	是因为它还柔嫩,不知道烦恼。	
奥赛罗	这表明繁殖力强,心情奔放:	
	热情,热情,湿润。　您这手需要	
	与诱惑隔绝,斋戒以及祷告,	40
	需要多加惩戒,进行灵修,	
	因为里面有个年轻的情鬼,	
	往往会作乱。　它是一只好手,	
	自由大方。	
苔丝狄蒙娜	您的确可以这么说,	
	因为正是这只手将我的心献出。	45
奥赛罗	可真大方。　过去心诚才携手,	
	可现在却时兴只携手不诚心。	
苔丝狄蒙娜	这个我可不懂。　快,您的诺言。	
奥赛罗	什么诺言,宝贝儿?	
苔丝狄蒙娜	我已派人叫凯西奥来跟您说话。	50
奥赛罗	我有点难受,因为感冒流鼻涕,	
	你的手帕借我用用。	
苔丝狄蒙娜	给您,夫君。	
奥赛罗	我给您的那块。	
苔丝狄蒙娜	我没带在身边。	55
奥赛罗	没带?	
苔丝狄蒙娜	没带,夫君。	

---

36. 湿润(moist):手心如果湿热(hot and moist),即被视为欲望强烈的象征,如果干燥发凉(dry and cold),则正好相反(Ridley)。　45. 在订婚或结婚仪式上。　46-7. 过去……诚心(The hearts…hearts):过去人们对某件事情举手宣誓时会真心诚意,但在当今这个颓废的时代,携手不再具有那种神圣意义(in former times, people would give their hearts when they gave their hands to something, but in our decadent present age the joining of hands no longer has that spiritual sense)(Bevington)。

Othello   That's a fault. That handkerchief

Did an Egyptian to my mother give,

She was a charmer and could almost read

60   The thoughts of people. She told her, while she kept it,

'Twould make her amiable and subdue my father

Entirely to her love; but if she lost it

Or made a gift of it, my father's eye

Should hold her loathed and his spirits should hunt

65   After new fancies. She, dying gave it me,

And bid me, when my fate would have me wive,

To give it her. I did so, and—take heed on't!

Make it a darling, like your precious eye! —

To lose't or give't away were such perdition

As nothing else could match.

70 **Desdemona**   Is't possible?

Othello   'Tis true, there's magic in the web of it.

A sibyl that had numbered in the world

The sun to course two hundred compasses,

In her prophetic fury sewed the work;

75   The worms were hallowed that did breed the silk,

And it was dyed in mummy, which the skillful

Conserved of maidens' hearts.

Desdemona   I'faith, is't true?

奥赛罗	这可不对,那块手帕	
	是由一位埃及人送给我母亲,	
	她是一位女巫,几乎能看透	
	人们的心思。　对她说,她若带着,	60
	就会讨人喜欢,使我的父亲	
	全心宠爱。　可她一旦丢失,	
	或者赠送别人,我父亲就会	
	把她视为可厌,他的心思便会	
	另寻新欢。　母亲临终,把它给我,	65
	嘱咐我,如果将来有幸成婚,	
	就送给妻子。　我已照办,——要留心!	
	可要珍惜,就像您宝贵的眼睛!——	
	若丢失或者送人,这种损失	
	将会是无以能比。	
苔丝狄蒙娜	这可能吗?	70
奥赛罗	真的,这片织物里含有魔术。	
	世上的一位女预言家曾数算	
	太阳将继续环行两百周年,	
	她在神灵的感召中绣好图案;	
	吐出丝线的桑蚕被视为神圣,	75
	它用的染料是从精心保养的	
	处女心脏中提炼。	
苔丝狄蒙娜	真的,真的吗?	

62-5. 听起来像是迷信,不过(若非奥赛罗编造),就奥赛罗与苔丝狄蒙娜两人的关系而言,这种预言后来成真。　72-3. 女预言家……周年(A sibyl…compasses):其中,sibyl 是指古希腊与古罗马时代的女预言家。　意为:她已数算过太阳将继续环行两百圈,即世界末日将在两百年以后到来(故称"预言性的")。　数算世界的终结日期是文艺复兴时期的一种消遣(she had calculated that the sun would make two hundred [further] circuits, that the world would end in two hundred years [hence *prophetic*]. Calculating the date of the end of the world was a Renaissance pastime)。

	Othello	Most veritable, therefore look to't well.
	Desdemona	Then would to God that I had never seen't!
80	**Othello**	Ha! Wherefore?
	Desdemona	Why do you speak so startingly and rash?
	Othello	Is't lost? Is't gone? Speak, is't out o'th'way?
	Desdemona	Heaven bless us!
	Othello	Say you?
85	**Desdemona**	It is not lost, but what an if it were?
	Othello	How?
	Desdemona	I say it is not lost.
	Othello	Fetch't, let me see't.
	Desdemona	Why, so I can, sir; but I will not now.

This is a trick to put me from my suit.

90   Pray you, let Cassio be received again.

| | **Othello** | Fetch me the handkerchief, my mind misgives. |
| | **Desdemona** | Come, come, |

You'll never meet a more sufficient man.

	Othello	The handkerchief!
	Desdemona	I pray, talk me of Cassio.
	Othello	The handkerchief!
95	**Desdemona**	A man that all his time

Hath founded his good fortunes on your love,

Shared dangers with you—

奥赛罗	千真万确,因此要把它看好。	
苔丝狄蒙娜	那我但愿自己从未见过它!	
奥赛罗	哈! 为啥?	80
苔丝狄蒙娜	您说话为啥如此吓人和急迫?	
奥赛罗	手帕丢了? 不见了? 说,是否丢了?	
苔丝狄蒙娜	上帝保佑我们!	
奥赛罗	说呀?	
苔丝狄蒙娜	没丢,假如丢了那又怎样?	85
奥赛罗	什么?	
苔丝狄蒙娜	我说没丢。	
奥赛罗	拿出来,让我看看。	
苔丝狄蒙娜	嗨,我能拿,先生; 但不是现在。	
	这是推托我请求的一种计策。	
	求您,让凯西奥官复原职。	90
奥赛罗	快把手帕拿来,我满心疑虑。	
苔丝狄蒙娜	快,快,	
	您再也找不到比他能干的男人。	
奥赛罗	那块手帕!	
苔丝狄蒙娜	求您,跟我说凯西奥。	
奥赛罗	那块手帕!	
苔丝狄蒙娜	他这人向来都将	95
	自己的前程寄托于您的厚爱,	
	与您患难与共——	

84. 说呀(Say you): What do you have to say for yourself? (Sparknotes)。 85. 这好像是谎言,因为我们知道她把手帕丢了(23行); 不过,她有可能相信: 尽管丢了,还会找到。 原文中的 an if = if。 88. 先生(sir): 该词令两人的感情疏远(creates distance between them)。 91-9. 就《奥赛罗》而言,喜剧色彩遍布其中,因为莎士比通常会在悲剧之中穿插一些喜剧情节。伊阿古安排其傀儡——奥赛罗,旁听他想让他听到的内容,以便对他加以误导。 ……奥赛罗三次追问"那块手帕",以及苔丝狄蒙娜持续为凯西奥求情的情节(3. 4. 87-99),可谓一种惯用的戏剧性"目标冲突"(a comic "cross-purposes" routine)。

Othello	The handkerchief!
Desdemona	I'faith, you are to blame.
Othello	Zounds! *Exit.*
100 **Emilia**	Is not this man jealous?
Desdemona	I ne'er saw this before,

Sure there's some wonder in this handkerchief;

I am most unhappy in the loss of it.

Emilia   'Tis not a year or two shows us a man.

105   They are all but stomachs, and we all but food:

They eat us hungerly, and when they are full

They belch us.

Enter Iago and Cassio.

Look you, Cassio and my husband.

Iago   There is no other way, 'tis she must do't,

And lo, the happiness! Go and importune her.

110 **Desdemona**   How now, good Cassio! What's the news with you?

Cassio   Madam, my former suit. I do beseech you

That by your virtuous means I may again

Exist, and be a member of his love

Whom I, with all the office of my heart

115   Entirely honour. I would not be delayed:

If my offence be of such mortal kind

That nor my service past nor present sorrows

Nor purposed merit in futurity

Can ransom me into his love again,

奥赛罗	那块手帕！	
苔丝狄蒙娜	真的，是您不对。	
奥赛罗	该死！	下。
爱米利娅	难道这人不妒忌？	100

苔丝狄蒙娜　我从未见他这样，

这块手帕里面定有些奇妙；

我可真是不幸竟把它丢掉。

爱米利娅　一两年不足于认清男人的本相。

他们是胃口，我们不过食物：　　　　　　　105

贪婪地把我们吞下，饱足之后

把我们吐出。

伊阿古与凯西奥上。

您看，凯西奥和我丈夫。

伊阿古　没有别的办法，必须靠她，

快看，真幸运！快去祈求她吧。

苔丝狄蒙娜　怎么样，好凯西奥，有啥消息？　　　　110

凯西奥　夫人，还是原来的请求，我求您，

通过您的得力相助我能再次

复原，并能得到他的厚爱，

我对他全心效忠，并充满了

敬重之情。　我不想再耽搁下去：　　　　115

我的过犯若如此罪大恶极，

我过去的军功或现在的懊悔，

或者将来要尽心尽职的许诺，

均不能让我重拾他的恩宠，

---

113. 复原（Exist）：恢复正常（凯西奥作为副将）（be myself ［as Lieuenant Cassio］）。

120 But to know so must be my benefit;

So shall I clothe me in a forced content

And shut myself up in some other course

To Fortune's alms.

Desdemona   Alas, thrice-gentle Cassio,

My advocation is not now in tune;

125 My lord is not my lord, nor should I know him

Were he in favour as in humour altered.

So help me every spirit sanctified

As I have spoken for you all my best

And stood within the blank of his displeasure

130 For my free speech. You must awhile be patient:

What I can do I will, and more I will

Than for myself I dare. Let that suffice you.

Iago   Is my lord angry?

Emilia   He went hence but now,

And certainly in strange unquietness.

135 **Iago**   Can he be angry? I have seen the cannon

When it hath blown his ranks into the air

And like the devil, from his very arm,

Puffed his own brother—and can he be angry?

Something of moment then. I will go meet him,

140 There's matter in't indeed, if he be angry.

Desdemona   I prithee, do so. [*Exit*(*Iago*).] Something sure of state,

只要实情相告定对我有益；　　　　　　　　　　120

因此我会让自己强装满意，

我只好另觅出路，期盼命运

女神之眷顾。

苔丝狄蒙娜　　　　　　　　哎呀，文雅的凯西奥，

我的辩护现在已不合时宜；

我丈夫已不是我丈夫，很难认出，　　　　　　125

假如他的外表和心绪改变。

各位圣洁的神灵帮帮我吧，

因为我已经尽力为您说话，

我因为直言不讳变成了他

发泄怒气的靶子。　您必须耐心：　　　　　　130

我会尽力而为，比为我自己的

事情还敢冒险。　您要就此满足。

伊阿古　　将军发怒了？

爱米利娅　　　　　　他刚离开这里，

确实异乎寻常地焦躁不安。

伊阿古　　他竟会发怒？　我曾看到大炮　　　　135

将他的士兵轰到了空中，

而他魔鬼般平静，目睹身边的

兄弟血肉横飞——他竟会发怒？

那说明事关重大。　我前去见他，

一定是问题严重，他才会发怒。　　　　　　140

苔丝狄蒙娜　　求您快去。　［（伊阿古）下。］或是来自威尼斯的

---

135. 他竟会发怒（Can he be angry）：伊阿古明知故问（参考 3. 3. 434 及以下）。　本段台词因省略而变得晦涩：意为："我曾看到他的士兵被轰到空中……同时我也看到他从容镇定。他现在竟会发怒？"（"I have seen his ranks blown into the air…and meanwhile have seen him cool and unruffled. And can he now be angry?"）138. 兄弟（brother）：我们从本场得知了奥赛罗的父亲、母亲、兄弟、埃及人、女预言家——他的背景。

Either from Venice, or some unhatched practice

Made demonstrable here in Cyprus to him,

Hath puddled his clear spirit, and in such cases

145 Men's natures wrangle with inferior things,

Though great ones are their object. 'Tis even so,

For let our finger ache, and it indues

Our other healthful members even to that sense

Of pain. Nay, we must think men are not gods,

150 Nor of them look for such observancy

As fits the bridal. Beshrew me much, Emilia,

I was, unhandsome warrior as I am,

Arraigning his unkindness with my soul,

But now I find I had suborned the witness,

And he's indicted falsely.

155 **Emilia**   Pray heaven it be

State matters, as you think, and no conception

Nor no jealous toy, concerning you.

Desdemona Alas the day, I never gave him cause.

Emilia But jealous souls will not be answered so:

160 They are not ever jealous for the cause,

But jealous for they're jealous. 'Tis a monster

Begot upon itself, born on itself.

Desdemona Heaven keep that monster from Othello's mind!

Emilia Lady, amen.

165 **Desdemona** I will go seek him. Cassio, walk here about,

国家大事,或塞浦路斯某件

筹划中的阴谋已向他显明,

搅得他神志不清,在此情况下,

人们倾向于为次要事情吵闹,　　　　　　　　　　　145

尽管他们关切的是大事。　是这样,

因为我们的手指疼痛时,会使

我们肢体的其他部位同样

难受。　不,可不能将男人当天神,

也不能指望他们会像新婚时　　　　　　　　　　　150

礼貌殷勤。　我该死,爱米利娅,

我是在,我这不合礼仪的勇士,

用心灵的法庭控告他的无情,

可现在我发现自己买通了证人,

他受到了诬陷。

爱米利娅　　　　　　　　　　但愿是因为　　　　　155

国家大事,如您所想,并非猜测,

也不是对您产生了妒忌之念。

苔丝狄蒙娜　多么不幸,我从未做错什么。

爱米利娅　但妒忌之辈可不这样认为:

他们的妒忌并非有理有据,　　　　　　　　　　　160

而是因妒忌而妒忌。　它是个怪物,

它可以自我怀胎,自我降生。

苔丝狄蒙娜　愿上帝让那怪物与奥赛罗无缘!

爱米利娅　阿门,夫人!

苔丝狄蒙娜　我去找他。　凯西奥,您别走远,　　　　165

---

152. 勇士(warrior):见2. 1. 180("噢,我美丽的勇士!")。　154. 证人(witness):她本人。　165. 别走远(here about):奥赛罗与苔丝狄蒙娜是在一私密之处谈话(花园内?):凯西奥到外面走动时,正好让比安卡碰见。

If I do find him fit, I'll move your suit

And seek to effect it to my uttermost.

Cassio   I humbly thank your ladyship.

Exeunt Desdemona and Emilia.

Enter Bianca.

Bianca   Save you, friend Cassio!

Cassio   What make you from home?

170   How is't with you, my most fair Bianca?

I'faith, sweet love, I was coming to your house.

Bianca   And I was going to your lodging, Cassio.

What, keep a week away? Seven days and nights?

Eight score eight hours? And lovers' absent hours

175   More tedious than the dial, eight score times!

O weary reckoning!

Cassio   Pardon me, Bianca,

I have this while with leaden thoughts been pressed,

But I shall in a more continuate time

Strike off this score of absence. Sweet Bianca,

[*Giving her Desdemona's handkerchief*]

Take me this work out.

180 **Bianca**   O Cassio, whence came this?

This is some token from a newer friend!

To the felt absence now I feel a cause:

Is't come to this? Well, well.

Cassio   Go to, woman,

Throw your vile guesses in the devil's teeth,

185   From whence you have them! You are jealous now

That this is from some mistress, some remembrance:

	我见他心情好时再为您求情，	
	我会竭尽全力将此事促成。	
凯西奥	我敬谢夫人阁下。	

苍丝狄蒙娜与爱米利娅下。

比安卡上。

比安卡	保佑您,凯西奥朋友!	
凯西奥	怎么离开家了?	
	您好吗,我最为漂亮的比安卡?	170
	说实话,亲爱的,我正要去您家呢。	
比安卡	我也正要去您的住处,凯西奥。	
	怎么,一星期不见?　七天七夜?	
	一百六十八个钟头?　情人的别离	
	要超过时钟一百六十倍的枯燥!	175
	噢,令人厌倦的数算!	
凯西奥	原谅我,比安卡,	
	此时此刻我心情有些沉重,	
	不过等我的时间更为空闲时,	
	会将这笔离别债勾销。　好比安卡,	

[将苍丝狄蒙娜的手帕给她]

	把图案描下。	
比安卡	噢,凯西奥,这是哪来的?	180
	这是一位新情人赠送的信物!	
	我已觉察避而不见的原因:	
	竟会这样?　好啊,好啊!	
凯西奥	走开,女人,	
	把您从魔鬼嘴里得来的恶意	
	猜测扔回去吧!　您现在疑心	185
	这是哪位情人送的纪念物品:	

No, by my faith, Bianca.

Bianca   Why, whose is it?

Cassio   I know not neither, I found it in my chamber.

I like the work well: ere it be demanded,

190   As like enough it will, I'd have it copied.

Take it, and do't, and leave me for this time.

Bianca   Leave you? Wherefore?

Cassio   I do attend here on the general,

And think it no addition, nor my wish,

To have him see me womaned.

195 **Bianca**   Why, I pray you?

Cassio   Not that I love you not.

Bianca   But that you do not love me.

I pray you, bring me on the way a little,

And say if I shall see you soon at night.

200 **Cassio**   'Tis but a little way that I can bring you,

For I attend here, but I'll see you soon.

Bianca   'Tis very good: I must be circumstanced.   *Exeunt.*

不,我发誓,比安卡。

比安卡　　　　　　　　　唉,那是谁的?

凯西奥　我也不知道,我在我房间里捡的。

我喜欢这图案:有人索要之前,

因为大概会的,我想把图案描下。　　　　　　　190

拿去,描一描,暂且离开我片刻。

比安卡　离开您?　为什么?

凯西奥　我现在正在此处等候着将军,

认为这没有好处,也有违心愿,

让他看见有女人相伴。

比安卡　　　　　　　　　求您,为啥?　　　　　　195

凯西奥　不是因为我不爱您。

比安卡　而是因为您不爱我。

我求您,请陪我走一段路程,

告诉我今晚能否与您见面。

凯西奥　我能陪您的路程不过很短,　　　　　　200

因为我在等候,但很快会去见您。

比安卡　这样很好:我必须随遇而安。　　　　　　同下。

第四幕
ACT 4

SCENE I

Enter Othello and Iago.

Iago   Will you think so?

Othello   Think so, Iago?

Iago   What,

To kiss in private?

Othello   An unauthorized kiss!

Iago   Or to be naked with her friend in bed

An hour or more, not meaning any harm?

5   **Othello**   Naked in bed, Iago, and not mean harm?

It is hypocrisy against the devil:

They that mean virtuously, and yet do so,

The devil their virtue tempts, and they tempt heaven.

Iago   So they do nothing, 'tis a venial slip;

第一场

奥赛罗与伊阿古上。

伊阿古	您真这么想？
奥赛罗	这么想，伊阿古？
伊阿古	什么，
	偷偷地亲吻？
奥赛罗	伤风败俗的亲吻！
伊阿古	或者赤身裸体与朋友同床，
	一小时或者更长，毫无邪念？
奥赛罗	裸体同床，伊阿古，没有邪念？
	这是用以欺骗魔鬼的伪善：
	他们貌似邪恶却没有邪念，
	让魔鬼试探他们，他们试探上帝。
伊阿古	只要他们不做，就是可恕的罪过；

5

4.1. 1. 如1.1.1一样，此处的开场白表明说话者已谈论了片刻。 现在是奥赛罗重复伊阿古，他们之间转换了角色（3.3.103及以下）；伊阿古在尽力唤起奥赛罗的直观想象。 6. 欺骗魔鬼的伪善（hypocracy…devil）：若貌似善良而作恶多端，就是欺骗上帝的伪善；若貌似作恶却"毫无邪念"，就是欺骗魔鬼的伪善（if to seem good while doing evil is hypocracy against God, then to seem evil while "meaning no harm" is hypocracy against the devil）（Mowat）。 该句意为：欺骗魔鬼的伪善。 因为普通的伪君子是通过貌似善良而实际作恶而骗人；而这些人将会欺骗魔鬼，通过给他一些讨其喜欢的希望，最终却未犯他认为他们就要犯下的罪过（"This means, hypocracy to cheat the devil. As common hypocrites cheat men by seeming good, and yet living wickedly, these men would cheat the devil, by giving him flattering hopes, and at last avoiding the crime which he thinks them ready to commit"）（Ridley）。 8. 试探（tempts）：可指"试探"（puts to the test）；"引诱"（incites to evil）。 见《圣经》"马太福音"4章1-7节：耶稣走到旷野"遭受魔鬼的试探"，并对他说"不可试探主你的神"（Honigmann）。 将上帝赋予他们避免犯罪的恩典进行试探（put to the test God's grace to keep them from sin）（Mowat）。

10		But if I give my wife a handkerchief—
	Othello	What then?
	Iago	Why, then, 'tis hers, my lord, and being hers,
		She may, I think, bestow't on any man.
	Othello	She is protectress of her honour too:
15		May she give that?
	Iago	Her honour is an essence that's not seen,
		They have it very oft that have it not.
		But for the handkerchief—
	Othello	By heaven, I would most gladly have forgot it!
20		Thou said'st—O, it comes o'er my memory
		As doth the raven o'er the infected house,
		Boding to all—he had my handkerchief.
	Iago	Ay, what of that?
	Othello	That's not so good now.
	Iago	What if I had said I had seen him do you wrong?
25		Or heard him say—as knaves be such abroad
		Who, having by their own importunate suit
		Or voluntary dotage of some mistress,
		Convinced or supplied them, cannot choose
		But they must blab—
	Othello	Hath he said anything?
30	**Iago**	He hath, my lord, but be you well assured,

	但假如我给我妻子一块手帕——	10
奥赛罗	那又怎样？	
伊阿古	嗨，那就是她的，将军，若是她的，	
	她可以，我想，赠予任何男人。	
奥赛罗	她的名声也是属于她自己：	
	那也能给人？	15
伊阿古	她的名声是一种无形的东西，	
	好多人不配拥有反而拥有。	
	不过那块手帕——	
奥赛罗	天哪，但愿我能把它给忘掉！	
	你说过——噢，现在我想起来了，	20
	犹如乌鸦盘旋于感染瘟疫之家	
	预示着凶兆——他拥有我的手帕。	
伊阿古	是的，那又怎样？	
奥赛罗	那可不好。	
伊阿古	我若说见他伤害过您怎么办？	
	或听他说过——因为放肆的无赖，	25
	他们，将某位女人引诱上钩，	
	要么通过自己的胡搅蛮缠，	
	要么通过女人的自甘迷恋，	
	定会大肆吹嘘——	
奥赛罗	他说过什么吗？	
伊阿古	他说过，将军，但您必须明白，	30

---

17. 伊阿古的神秘言谈之一，意为：许多人被错误地赋予了这种无形的东西（Ridley）。
21. 犹如……之家（As…house）：人们相信乌鸦不仅是一种不祥之鸟和死亡的信使，而且也是传染病的携带者（Ridley）。　23. 那可不好（That's…now）：典型的轻描淡写。只有9个音节的诗行：也许"That's"应为"That is"。　25-9. 因为……吹嘘（as…blab）：本句结构复杂，现引一英文注释以助理解："since there are rascals enough who, having seduced a women either through their own importunity or through the woman's willing infatuation, cannot keep quiet about it."（Bevington）

No more than he'll unswear.

Othello   What hath he said?

Iago   Faith, that he did—I know not what. He did—

Othello   What? What?

Iago   Lie.

Othello   With her?

Iago   With her, on her, what you will.

35 **Othello**   Lie with her? Lie on her! We say lie on her
when they belie her! Lie with her, zounds, that's
fulsome! —Handkerchief! Confessions! Handkerchief!
To confess, and be hanged for his labour ! First to be
hanged, and then to confess: I tremble at it. Nature

40   would not invest herself in such shadowing passion
without some instruction. It is not words that shakes
me thus. Pish! Noses, ears, and lips. Is't possible?
Confess! Handkerchief! O devil!

                                                    [*He*]*Falls in a trance.*

Iago   Work on,

45   My medicine, work! Thus credulous fools are caught,
And many worthy and chaste dames even thus,
All guiltless, meet reproach. —What, ho! My lord!
My lord, I say! Othello!

　　　　　　他会予以否认。

| 奥赛罗 | 　　　　　　　他说过什么？ |

| 伊阿古 | 他说,他曾——我不清楚什么。　他曾—— |

| 奥赛罗 | 什么？　什么？ |

| 伊阿古 | 睡觉。 |

| 奥赛罗 | 　　　跟她？ |

| 伊阿古 | 　　　　　　跟她,骑她,任您想吧。 |

奥赛罗　　跟她睡觉？欺她？人们在对她诽谤时,　　　　　　　35
　　　　　我们可说欺她!跟她睡觉,该死,真
　　　　　令人作呕!——手帕!认罪吧!手帕!
　　　　　先认罪,后绞死,这是他的回报!先
　　　　　绞死,后认罪:我气得发抖。天性她
　　　　　不会如此怒不可遏,若不是她获悉了　　　　　　40
　　　　　事情的真相。只是言辞不会使我如此
　　　　　战栗。呸!磨鼻子,咬耳朵,亲嘴唇。
　　　　　这可能吗?　认罪!手帕!噢,魔鬼!

　　　　　　　　　　　　　　　　　　[他]昏厥倒地。

伊阿古　　发作吧,
　　　　　毒药,发作!轻信的傻瓜就这样上当,　　　　　　45
　　　　　有多少体面贞洁的女士就这样,
　　　　　毫无过错,遭受羞辱。　——嗬!将军!
　　　　　将军,我说!奥赛罗!

---

　　34. 骑她（on her）：正是这一点最终将奥赛罗压垮（Ridley）。　35-6. 他在思虑"跟她睡觉"（lie with her）与"欺她"（on her）两个短语的意义。　Lie on 除了可指"骑在她身上"（on top of her）之外,还可指"造谣中伤"（tell lies about）,所以"当人们对她造谣中伤时"（belie her）,我们可以说"欺她"（lies on her）。　但短语"跟她睡觉"（lie with her = copulate with her ［与她交媾］）却使他无法自圆其说。　38-9. 先绞死,后认罪（first…to confess）：奥赛罗颠倒了众所周知的"先认罪,后绞死",不许凯西奥死前有忏悔的时间（Bevington）。47. 嗬!将军（What…lord）：他听到有人接近时便呼喊起来。　48. 奥赛罗:直呼其名,也许因为奥赛罗仍在昏迷之中。

Enter Cassio.

How now, Cassio?

Cassio   What's the matter?

50 **Iago**   My lord is fallen into an epilepsy;

This is his second fit, he had one yesterday.

Cassio   Rub him about the temples.

Iago   No, forbear:

The lethargy must have his quiet course,

If not, he foams at mouth, and by and by

55   Breaks out to savage madness. Look, he stirs;

Do you withdraw yourself a little while,

He will recover straight. When he is gone,

I would on great occasion speak with you.   [*Exit Cassio.*]

How is it, general? Have you not hurt your head?

Othello   Dost thou mock me?

60 **Iago**   I mock you? No, by heaven!

Would you would bear your fortune like a man!

Othello   A horned man's a monster, and a beast.

Iago   There's many a beast then in a populous city,

And many a civil monster.

Othello   Did he confess it?

65 **Iago**   Good sir, be a man,

凯西奥上。

怎么了,凯西奥?

凯西奥	出了啥事?	
伊阿古	将军陷入了一种癫痫状态;	50
	这是第二次了,昨天犯过一次。	
凯西奥	按摩他的太阳穴。	
伊阿古	不行,别动:	
	他这种昏睡必须顺其自然,	
	否则,他口吐白沫,立刻之间	
	就会暴怒发疯,快看,他在动;	55
	请您暂时离开这里一会儿,	
	他会马上康复。　他离开之后,	
	我会就一件要事与您商谈。	[凯西奥下。]
	怎么样了,将军?　您没伤到头吧?	
奥赛罗	你嘲笑我吗?	
伊阿古	嘲笑您?　没有,我发誓!	60
	愿您男人般经受命运的考验!	
奥赛罗	头上长角的男人是怪物,是野兽。	
伊阿古	那拥挤的市区会有许多野兽,	
	许多文雅的野兽。	
奥赛罗	他是否已供认?	
伊阿古	好先生,做个男人,	65

---

51. 昨天(yesterday):何时?　在海上,或与苔丝狄蒙娜一起退场之后,被斗殴惊醒之前?旨在表示"较长的时间"(long time)(Ridley)。　56-8. 伊阿古反应灵敏,如此安排既可躲避因奥赛罗清醒之后与凯西奥对质而带来的危险,也可确保他准备就绪之后再让凯西奥返回(Ridley)。　59. 伤到头(hurt your head):即跌倒时。　奥赛罗以为头上长出了兽角。　65. 做个男人(be a man):正如伊阿古对罗德利哥的控制一样,他已取得了对奥赛罗的支配地位。　该短语反而会使奥赛罗失去男子汉气概(unman Othello)。

Think every bearded fellow that's but yoked

May draw with you. There's millions now alive

That nightly lie in those unproper beds

Which they dare swear peculiar: your case is better.

70 O, 'tis the spite of hell, the fiend's arch-mock,

To lip a wanton in a secure couch

And to suppose her chaste. No, let me know,

And, knowing what I am, I know what she shall be.

Othello   O, thou art wise, 'tis certain.

75 **Iago**   Stand you a while apart,

Confine yourself but in a patient list.

Whilst you were here o'erwhelmed with your grief

—A passion most unsuiting such a man—

Cassio came hither. I shifted him away

80 And laid good 'scuse upon your ecstasy,

Bade him anon return and here speak with me,

The which he promised. Do but encave yourself

And mark the fleers, the gibes and notable scorns

That dwell in every region of his face;

85 For I will make him tell the tale anew,

Where, how, how oft, how long ago, and when

He hath and is again to cope your wife.

I say, but mark his gesture; marry, patience,

　　　　　每个有家室之累的须眉男子

　　　　　会与您并驾齐驱。　现有上百万人

　　　　　晚间躺在那些并非专属的床上，

　　　　　却敢发誓专用：您的情况好些。

　　　　　噢，那是邪恶的诅咒，魔鬼的讥讽，　　　　　　70

　　　　　在床上自由地亲吻一个妓女，

　　　　　却以为她贞洁。　不，我想知道真相，

　　　　　知道我是啥人，就知道她会怎样。

奥赛罗　　噢，你真聪明，肯定是的。

伊阿古　　请您暂时走开，　　　　　　　　　　　　75

　　　　　您可要控制好自己的耐心。

　　　　　您刚才因为痛苦在此昏睡时

　　　　　——您这样的人本不该如此动情——

　　　　　凯西奥来过。　我已打发他走开，

　　　　　我对您的昏厥做了一番解释，　　　　　　　80

　　　　　并叫他马上回来与我会话，

　　　　　他就此应允。　您暂且躲避起来，

　　　　　看他那嘲弄、讥讽和明显的轻蔑

　　　　　定会布满他面部的每个角落；

　　　　　因为我要让他把故事重讲一遍：　　　　　　85

　　　　　地点、方式、频率、多久以前，

　　　　　何时与夫人交媾及下次的时间。

　　　　　我说，注意他的举止；但要耐心，

---

　　66. 须眉男子（bearded fellow）：凯西奥留有胡须（3. 3. 442）。　这可能意味着奥赛罗也留有胡须。　68. 并非专属的（unproper）：并非自己独享（因为妻子的情人也在使用）（Mowat）。　69. 您的情况好些（your…better）：因为您知道真相。　74. 肯定是的（'tis certain）：既可指伊阿古的聪明，也可指苔丝狄蒙娜的不忠。　75. 暂时走开（Stand…apart）：喜剧中的惯用手法：受害者被骗——去旁听别人想让他听到的内容（A victim is tricked into overhearing what others want him to hear）。　80. 一番解释（'scuse = explanation）：暗示奥赛罗的昏厥有些丢人。

Or I shall say you're all in all in spleen,

And nothing of a man.

90 **Othello**   Dost thou hear, Iago?

I will be found most cunning in my patience;

But—dost thou hear? —most bloody.

Iago   That's not amiss,

But yet keep time in all. Will you withdraw?

[*Othello withdraws.*]

Now will I question Cassio of Bianca,

95   A housewife that by selling her desires

Buys herself bread and clothes: it is a creature

That dotes on Cassio—as 'tis the strumpet's plague

To beguile many and be beguiled by one.

He, when he hears of her, cannot refrain

100   From the excess of laughter. Here he comes.

Enter Cassio.

As he shall smile, Othello shall go mad.

And his unbookish jealousy must construe

Poor Cassio's smiles, gestures and light behaviour

Quite in the wrong. How do you now, lieutenant?

105 **Cassio**   The worser, that you give me the addition

Whose want even kills me.

Iago   Ply Desdemona well, and you are sure on't.

[*Speaking lower*] Now if this suit lay in Bianca's power,

不然，我就会说您脾气暴躁，

毫无男子气概。

奥赛罗　　　　　　　　　　　听好了，伊阿古？　　　　　　　90

你会发现我这人最善于忍耐。

但——你听好了？　——最为残忍。

伊阿古　　　　　　　　　　　　　没啥不妥，

但要自我克制。　您躲起来好吗？

　　　　　　　　　　　　　　　　〔奥赛罗退至一侧。〕

现在我要向凯西奥问起比安卡，

一位贱妇，通过出卖她的魅力　　　　　95

为自己换些衣食：这个女人

对凯西奥痴情——这是淫妇的祸根：

迷惑多人并被一人迷惑。

他，听人说起她时，一定会

情不自禁地放声大笑。　他来了。　　　100

　　　　　　　　凯西奥上。

他发笑时，奥赛罗就会发疯。

他那无知的妒忌必将可怜的

凯西奥的微笑、手势和轻浮举动

阐释得大错特错。　您好吗，副官？

凯西奥　您用这头衔相称，那就更糟，　　　105

没有它真是要命。

伊阿古　好好抓住苔丝狄蒙娜，肯定能行。

〔压低声音〕这种请求若由比安卡决定，

----

91. 喜剧的一种惯例：没有耐心的人誓要耐心。　100. 他来了（Here he comes）：凯西奥的适时到来表明一切尽在伊阿古的掌控之中。　102. 无知的（unbookish）：莎氏新造词。　参考1. 1. 23：伊阿古对爱读书的（bookish）和不爱读书的（unbookish）均表示轻蔑。

How quickly should you speed!

Cassio   Alas, poor caitiff!

110 **Othello**   Look how he laughs already!

Iago   I never knew a woman love man so.

Cassio   Alas, poor rogue! I think i'faith she loves me.

Othello   Now he denies it faintly, and laughs it out.

Iago   Do you hear, Cassio?

Othello   Now he importunes him

115   To tell it o'er; go to; well said, well said.

Iago   She gives it out that you shall marry her;

Do you intend it?

Cassio   Ha, ha, ha!

Othello   Do you triumph, Roman, do you triumph?

120 **Cassio**   I marry! What, a customer! Prithee, bear some

charity to my wit, do not think it so unwholesome.

Ha, ha, ha!

Othello   So, so, so, so: they laugh that win.

Iago   Faith, the cry goes that you shall marry her.

125 **Cassio**   Prithee say true!

Iago   I am a very villain else.

Othello   Have you stored me? Well.

Cassio   This is the monkey's own giving out. She is

persuaded I will marry her , out of her own love and

您将会何等顺利！

凯西奥　　　　　　　　　　　唉,可怜的人哪!

奥赛罗　　你看他已经在笑! 　　　　　　　　　　　　　　　110

伊阿古　　我从未见过女人这么爱男人。

凯西奥　　唉,可怜的宝贝儿,我确信她爱我。

奥赛罗　　他并未完全否认,一笑了之。

伊阿古　　您是否听说,凯西奥?

奥赛罗　　　　　　　　　　　他正要求他

重讲一遍;说吧,做得好,做得好。 　　　　　　　　　115

伊阿古　　她对人宣称您要跟她结婚;

您真有此意?

凯西奥　　哈,哈,哈!

奥赛罗　　您凯旋了,罗马人,您凯旋了?

凯西奥　　我要结婚,跟一个娼妓!求您对我的 　　　　　120

判断力高看一点,别以为它如此缺陷。

哈,哈,哈!

奥赛罗　　好,好,好,好,胜者才笑。

伊阿古　　真的,大家在传说您要娶她。

凯西奥　　您别开玩笑了! 　　　　　　　　　　　　　　　125

伊阿古　　我要说谎,就真是恶棍。

奥赛罗　　您已为我播种?　那好。

凯西奥　　这都是猴子自己散布的流言。她以为

我会娶她,这是出自她本人的爱意和

---

119. 罗马人（Roman）：奥赛罗对凯西奥的冷嘲热讽。 因为凯旋（triumph）本是一种罗马
仪式,这使他联想到了罗马人。 123. 胜者才笑（they…win）：参考谚语：they that laugh last
laugh best（谁笑在最后,谁笑得最好）。 127. 播种（stored）：可指"维持某一品种的繁衍
（provide for the continuance of a stock or breed）",也可指"生儿育女（to produce off-
spring）"。 128. 猴子（monkey's）：表示戏谑性的轻蔑（playful contempt）,主要用于年轻
人,多指男孩儿。

130   flattery, not out of my promise.

Othello   Iago beckons me: now he begins the story.

Cassio   She was here even now, she haunts me in every place. I was the other day talking on the sea-bank with certain Venetians, and thither comes the bauble

135   and, by this hand, falls me thus about my neck—

Othello   Crying 'O dear Cassio!' as it were: his gesture imports it.

Cassio   So hangs and lolls and weeps upon me, so shakes and pulls me! Ha, ha, ha!

140 **Othello**   Now he tells how she plucked him to my chamber. O, I see that nose of yours, but not that dog I shall throw it to.

Cassio   Well, I must leave her company.

Iago   Before me! Look where she comes!

Enter Bianca.

145 **Cassio**   'Tis such another fitchew; marry, a perfumed one. What do you mean by this haunting of me?

Bianca   Let the devil and his dam haunt you! What did you mean by that same handkerchief you gave me even now? I was a fine fool to take it—I must

150   take out the work! A likely piece of work, that you should find it in your chamber and not know who left it there! This is some minx's token, and I must

	自诩，不是出自我的应许。	130
奥赛罗	伊阿古在向我示意：他正要讲述经过。	
凯西奥	她刚才还在这里，她对我真可谓紧追 不舍。几天前我在岸边与一位威尼斯 人交谈的时候，这个小东西到了那里， 然后，我发誓，就这样搂住我的脖子——	135
奥赛罗	好像喊道"噢，亲爱的凯西奥！"他的 手势已经表明。	
凯西奥	她吊着我，靠着我，还对我哭哭啼啼， 她对我又扯又摇！哈，哈，哈！	
奥赛罗	现在他要讲述她是如何将他拉到我的 卧室。噢，我能看见您那只鼻子，但 看不见要喂的那条狗。	140
凯西奥	我要跟她断绝往来。	
伊阿古	天哪！您看她来了！	

比安卡上。

凯西奥	这真是一只鸡貂；哎呀，涂过香水的 鸡貂。您为何对我纠缠不休？	145
比安卡	愿魔鬼与他的老娘去纠缠您吧！刚才 您把那一块绣花的手帕送给我是什么 意思？我接过来可是真傻——我必须 把图案给描下！一则多棒的故事，您 居然在自己的房间里捡到它，却不知 它是谁的！这是哪位娼妇的信物，我	150

141-2. 参考《圣经》"出埃及记"22 章 31 节："田间被野兽撕裂牲畜的肉，你们不可吃，要丢给狗吃。"143. 来往（company）：可能指"性关系"（sexual connection）。 145. 鸡貂（fitchew）：以其体味难闻和生性淫荡而著称。 147. 老娘（dam）：源于谚语"魔鬼的母亲要比魔鬼邪恶（the 'devil's dam" was more evil than the devil)"（Mowat）。

take out the work? There, give it your hobby-horse;
wheresoever you had it, I'll take out no work on't!

155 **Cassio**   How now, my sweet Bianca, how now, how now?

Othello   By heaven, that should be my handkerchief!

Bianca   If you'll come to supper tonight, you may; if
you will not, come when you are next prepared for.   *Exit.*

Iago   After her, after her!

160 **Cassio**   Faith, I must, she'll rail in the street else.

Iago   Will you sup there?

Cassio   Faith, I intend so.

Iago   Well, I may chance to see you, for I would very
fain speak with you.

165 **Cassio**   Prithee come, will you?

Iago   Go to, say no more.   *Exit Cassio.*

Othello   How shall I murder him, Iago?

Iago   Did you perceive how he laughed at his vice?

Othello   O Iago!

170 **Iago**   And did you see the handkerchief?

Othello   Was that mine?

Iago   Yours, by this hand: and to see how he prizes the
foolish woman your wife! She gave it him, and he
hath given it his whore.

175 **Othello**   I would have him nine years a-killing.   A fine
woman, a fair woman, a sweet woman!

要把图案描下？拿去，还给您的淫妇；

无论您从哪里弄到，我都不会描它！

| 凯西奥 | 咋了，我亲爱的比安卡，咋了，咋了？ | 155 |

| 奥赛罗 | 天哪，那一定是我的手帕！ | |

比安卡　今晚您若想过来一起晚饭，那就来吧；

您若不想，那就再也没有下一次了。　　　　　　下。

| 伊阿古 | 去追她，去追她！ | |

| 凯西奥 | 没错，去追她，不然她会在街上叫喊。 | 160 |

| 伊阿古 | 您在她那里晚饭？ | |

| 凯西奥 | 没错，我有此意。 | |

伊阿古　好吧，也许我去见您，因为我很乐意

跟您说话。

| 凯西奥 | 求您过来，好吗？ | 165 |

| 伊阿古 | 好了，别说了。　　　　　　　　　　凯西奥下。 | |

| 奥赛罗 | 我将如何处死他，伊阿古？ | |

| 伊阿古 | 您是否看到他对自己的邪恶怎样大笑？ | |

| 奥赛罗 | 噢，伊阿古！ | |

| 伊阿古 | 您是否看到那块手帕？ | 170 |

| 奥赛罗 | 那是我的吗？ | |

伊阿古　是您的，我发誓：您看见他如何珍惜

您那痴心的夫人！她把手帕给他，他

又把它给了他的妓女。

奥赛罗　但愿我能把他连杀九年。一个雅致的　175

女人，漂亮的女人，可爱的女人！

153. 淫妇（hobby-horse）：因为任何人都可骑她（because anyone can "mount" her）？（Ridley）。 167. 伊阿古与奥赛罗两人从本行开始首次使用散文。 175. 连杀（a-killing）：屠宰（in the killing），即让他死得非常缓慢。 175-6. 此处及随后的台词中，由恨到爱的突然转变几乎使悲剧成了闹剧（with their sudden flipover from hate to love, tragedy comes close to farce）。

Iago		Nay, you must forget that.
Othello		Ay, let her rot and perish and be damned tonight, for she shall not live. No, my heart is turned to stone: I strike it, and it hurts my hand. O, the world hath not a sweeter creature: she might lie by an emperor's side and command him tasks.
Iago		Nay, that's not your way.
Othello		Hang her, I do but say what she is: so delicate with her needle, an admirable musician. O, she will sing the savageness out of a bear ! Of so high and plenteous wit and invention!
Iago		She's the worse for all this.
Othello		O, a thousand, a thousand times: and then of so gentle a condition!
Iago		Ay, too gentle.
Othello		Nay, that's certain. But yet the pity of it, Iago —O, Iago, the pity of it, Iago!
Iago		If you are so fond over her iniquity, give her patent to offend, for if it touch not you , it comes near nobody.
Othello		I will chop her into messes! Cuckold me!
Iago		O, 'tis foul in her.
Othello		With mine officer!
Iago		That's fouler.
Othello		Get me some poison, Iago, this night. I'll not expostulate with her, lest her body and beauty unprovide my mind again. This night, Iago.

180 185 190 195 200

伊阿古	不,您要把它忘掉。	
奥赛罗	唉,今夜就让她腐烂、死去、并下到 地狱,因为她不能存活。 不,我的心 已变成石头,我捶它,它会伤手。 噢, 世上再没有这么可爱的人了:她可以 躺在国王身边吩咐他听从差遣。	180
伊阿古	不,那不是您的本色。	
奥赛罗	她该死,我只想对她如实评说:她的 针线如此精巧,令人钦佩的乐师。噢, 她会将一只野熊唱得俯首帖耳!她是 如此聪颖和富于想象!	185
伊阿古	这些优点使她更糟。	
奥赛罗	噢,一千倍更糟,一千倍更糟:她有 如此温柔的性情。	190
伊阿古	唉,太过温柔。	
奥赛罗	是的,没错。 不过真是遗憾,伊阿古 ——噢,伊阿古,真遗憾,伊阿古!	
伊阿古	既然您如此溺爱她的罪过,就授权她 去犯罪好了,因为若对您无妨,没人 会受影响。	195
奥赛罗	我要把她剁成肉末! 让我做乌龟!	
伊阿古	噢,她真是糟糕。	
奥赛罗	私通我的部下!	
伊阿古	那就更糟。	200
奥赛罗	你给我弄些毒药,伊阿古,今晚。 我 不会跟她争辩,我怕她的肉体和美丽 将我的决心动摇。 今晚,伊阿古。	

Iago		Do it not with poison, strangle her in her bed—
205		even the bed she hath contaminated.
Othello		Good, good, the justice of it pleases; very good!
Iago		And for Cassio, let me be his undertaker. You shall hear more by midnight.
210 **Othello**		Excellent good. [*A trumpet within.*] What trumpet is that same?
Iago		I warrant something from Venice.

Enter Lodovico, Desdemona and Attendants.

'Tis Lodovico, this, comes from the duke.

See, your wife's with him.

215 **Lodovico** God save you, worthy general.

Othello With all my heart, sir.

Lodovico The Duke and senators of Venice greet you.

[*Gives him a letter.*]

Othello I kiss the instrument of their pleasures.

[*Opens the letter and reads.*]

Desdemona And what's the news, good cousin Lodovico?

220 **Iago** I am very glad to see you, signior.

Welcome to Cyprus.

Lodovico I thank you. How does Lieutenant Cassio?

Iago Lives, sir.

Desdemona Cousin, there's fallen between him and my lord

225 An unkind breech, but you shall make all well—

| 伊阿古 | 您别用毒药，就在床上勒死她吧——
就在她玷污过的那张床上。 | 205 |

| 奥赛罗 | 很好，很好，这样做可真是公道；很
好！ | |

| 伊阿古 | 至于凯西奥，交给我去办好了。半夜
之前您会听到报告。 | |

| 奥赛罗 | 真是棒极了。〔内有号角声。〕怎么会
传来号角？ | 210 |

| 伊阿古 | 我想是有人从威尼斯来到。 | |

　　　　　　　罗德威克、苔丝狄蒙娜与侍从上。

是罗德威克，他，由公爵派来。

您看，夫人跟他一起。

罗德威克	上帝保佑您，尊贵的将军。	215
奥赛罗	我衷心感谢，先生。	
罗德威克	公爵与威尼斯元老向您致意。	

　　　　　　　　　　　　　　　　〔给他一信函。〕

| 奥赛罗 | 我会按他们信中的旨意奉行。 | |

　　　　　　　　　　　　　　　　〔拆信而读。〕

苔丝狄蒙娜	是什么消息，罗德威克好堂兄？	
伊阿古	见到您我非常高兴，先生。 欢迎来到塞浦路斯。	220
罗德威克	谢谢您。副官凯西奥他还好吗？	
伊阿古	还活着，先生。	
苔丝狄蒙娜	堂兄，他与我丈夫之间发生了 不幸的裂痕，可您能把它补好——	225

　　204．购买毒药会给伊阿古带来危险（Ridley）。　206-7．很好……很好（Good…good）：本场的某些重复表明奥赛罗此时的神情恍惚不定。　216．人们期望奥赛罗会回敬同样的祝愿，但他只是受之而已。

Othello	Are you sure of that?
Desdemona	My lord?
Othello	[*Reads.*] *This fail you not to do, as you will—*
Lodovico	He did not call, he's busy in the paper.

230 Is there division 'twixt my lord and Cassio?

Desdemona	A most unhappy one: I would do much
	To atone them, for the love I bear to Cassio.
Othello	Fire and brimstone!
Desdemona	My lord?
Othello	Are you wise?
Desdemona	What, is he angry?
Lodovico	May be the letter moved him.

235 For, as I think, they do command him home,

Deputing Cassio in his government.

Desdemona	By my troth, I am glad on't.
Othello	Indeed!
Desdemona	My lord?
Othello	I am glad⋯to see you mad.
Desdemona	Why, sweet Othello?
Othello	Devil!　　　　　　　　　　[*Striking her*]

240 **Desdemona** I have not deserved this.

Lodovico	My lord, this would not be believed in Venice,
	Though I should swear I saw't. 'Tis very much;
	Make her amends, she weeps.

奥赛罗	您能够保证？	
苔丝狄蒙娜	夫君？	
奥赛罗	［读信。］务请遵照执行，因为您——	
罗德威克	他没有回应，他正忙于读信。	
	将军与凯西奥之间有些分歧？	230
苔丝狄蒙娜	最为不幸的分歧：我愿尽力	
	使他们和好，因为我爱凯西奥。	
奥赛罗	火湖与硫黄！	
苔丝狄蒙娜	夫君？	
奥赛罗	您明智吗？	
苔丝狄蒙娜	怎么，他发怒了？	
罗德威克	也许信函让他心烦。	
	因为，我想，他们已命令他返回，	235
	任命凯西奥代他行使职权。	
苔丝狄蒙娜	说真的，我对此高兴。	
奥赛罗	真的吗！	
苔丝狄蒙娜	夫君？	
奥赛罗	我高兴……见您发疯。	
苔丝狄蒙娜	怎么了，好奥赛罗？	
奥赛罗	魔鬼！　　　　　　　　　　［打她］	
苔丝狄蒙娜	我不该受这种待遇。	240
罗德威克	将军，这在威尼斯难以置信，	
	尽管我发誓已目睹。非常过分；	
	向她道歉，她在哭。	

232. 爱（love）：喜爱，慈爱（affection）；善意（goodwill）；但奥赛罗以为是性爱（sexual love）。　233. 火湖与硫黄（Fire and brimstone）：通常跟地狱相关。参考《圣经》"创世纪"19章24节和"启示录"19章20节。　238. 他在重复或模仿苔丝狄蒙娜的"我高兴"（I am glad），意为：见您如此愚蠢（疯狂）（竟承认自己对凯西奥的爱意）（i. e. to see you so foolish [mad] [as to admit your love for Cassio]）。

Othello   O devil, devil!

If that the earth could teem with woman's tears,

245   Each drop she falls would prove a crocodile:

Out of my sight!

Desdemona   I will not stay to offend you.

Lodovico   Truly, an obedient lady.

I do beseech your lordship, call her back.

Othello   Mistress!

250 **Desdemona**   My lord?

Othello   What would you with her, sir?

Lodovico   Who, I, my lord?

Othello   Ay, you did wish that I would make her turn.

Sir, she can turn, and turn, and yet go on

And turn again. And she can weep, sir, weep.

255   And she's obedient: as you say, obedient,

Very obedient. —Proceed you in your tears. —

Concerning this, sir—O well-painted passion! —

I am commanded home. —Get you away.

I'll send for you anon. —Sir, I obey the mandate

260   And will return to Venice. —Hence, avaunt! —

[*Exit Desdemona.*]

Cassio shall have my place. And, sir, tonight

I do entreat that we may sup together.

You are welcome, sir, to Cyprus. Goats and monkeys!

Exit.

奥赛罗	噢,魔鬼,魔鬼!

若大地能因女人的眼泪而受孕,

她的每滴眼泪会成一条鳄鱼:　　　　　　　　　　　　245

给我滚开!

苔丝狄蒙娜	我不会待着让您生气。
罗德威克	真的,一位温顺的女士。

我请求将军阁下,叫她回来。

奥赛罗	夫人!
苔丝狄蒙娜	夫君?　　　　　　　　　　　　250
奥赛罗	您要跟她做啥,先生?
罗德威克	谁,我吗,将军?
奥赛罗	是的,是您希望我叫她转身。

先生,她可以转身,转身,转身,

再转身。 她可以哭泣,先生,哭泣。

她也很温顺:如您所说,温顺,　　　　　　　　　255

非常温顺。 ——继续流您的泪吧。 ——

关于此事,先生——噢,虚情假意! ——

我被命令回家。 ——您给我滚开。

我很快派人叫您。 ——先生,我遵命,

将会返回威尼斯。 ——快滚,滚开! ——　　　260

　　　　　　　　　　　　　　　[苔丝狄蒙娜下。]

凯西奥将接替我的位置。 先生,今晚

我请求大家能够共进晚餐。

欢迎,先生,到塞浦路斯。 山羊和猴子!　　　　　下。

252-3. 转身(turn):可指"往回走(turn back)";也可指"变心(be fickle[turn = change])";也可指"床上的最佳翻转(the best turn i'th' bed)"。 258. 回家(home):可指威尼斯或毛里塔尼亚(4. 2. 226);但260行表明,他将其理解为威尼斯。 263. 山羊和猴子(Goats and monkeys):参考"骚如山羊,猴子般淫荡"(3. 3. 406)。 "这些词语仍在奥赛罗的耳中回荡"。

	Lodovico	Is this the noble Moor whom our full senate
265		Call all in all sufficient? This the nature

Lodovico Is this the noble Moor whom our full senate
265 Call all in all sufficient? This the nature
Whom passion could not shake? Whose solid virtue
The shot of accident nor dart of chance
Could neither graze nor pierce?

Iago   He is much changed.

Lodovico Are his wits safe? Is he not light of brain?

270 **Iago** He's that he is: I may not breathe my censure
What he might be; if what he might, he is not,
I would to heaven he were!

Lodovico   What! Strike his wife!

Iago Faith, that was not so well; yet would I knew
That stroke would prove the worst.

Lodovico   Is it his use?

275 Or did the letters work upon his blood
And new-create this fault?

Iago   Alas, alas!
It is not honesty in me to speak
What I have seen and known. You shall observe him,
And his own courses will denote him so
280 That I may save my speech. Do but go after
And mark how he continues.

Lodovico I am sorry that I am deceived in him.   *Exeunt.*

罗德威克	这就是我们全体元老称之为	
	全能的摩尔？　他那高尚的本性	265
	不为感情所动？　他气概顽强，	
	偶然的射击或者意外的飞镖	
	都不能将他刺伤？	

伊阿古　　　　　　　　　　　　他已经大变。

罗德威克　他清醒吗？　他的神志没失常吗？

伊阿古	他就是这样：我可不敢评判	270
	他的情况；他若不是应该的那样，	
	愿上帝保他是原样！	

罗德威克　　　　　　　　　怎么！打他妻子！

伊阿古　真的,这种情况不妙；但愿我能说
　　　　这会证明糟糕透顶。

罗德威克	他习惯如此？	
	还是因为信函把他给激怒，	275
	才初次这样犯错？	

伊阿古	哎呀,哎呀！	
	我要是说出我的所见所知，	
	那就是不忠。　您去观察他吧，	
	他自己的行动会表明实情，	
	因此我保持沉默。　您只消跟随	280
	并留意他接着会怎样。	

罗德威克　很遗憾我竟把他这人给看错。　　　　同下。

---

267. 本行的原文注解为：（neither） accidental shot nor a chance spear （thrust）, i. e. no unforeseen misfortune （［无论］偶然的射击还是意外的长矛［刺杀］,即意外的不幸）。
271-2. 也许是伊阿古类似台词中最为神秘的一处（Ridley）。 *Might* 一词似乎可导致歧义：首先,奥赛罗也许有错（所以要受到评判）；再者,他也许未变（因此"愿上帝保他是原样"）（*Might* seems to change its meaning: first, Othello might be at fault ［therefore to be censured］; second, he might be unchanged ［hence "would to heaven he were"］）。

SCENE II

Enter Othello and Emila.

Othello		You have seen nothing, then?
Emilia		Nor ever heard, nor ever did suspect.
Othello		Yes, you have seen Cassio and⋯she together.
Emilia		But then I saw no harm, and then I heard
5		Each syllable that breath made up between them.
Othello		What, did they never whisper?
Emilia		Never, my lord.
Othello		Nor send you out o'the way?
Emilia		Never.
Othello		To fetch her fan, her gloves, her mask, nor nothing?
10	**Emilia**	Never, my lord.
Othello		That's strange.
Emilia		I durst, my lord, to wager she is honest,
		Lay down my soul at stake: if you think other,
		Remove your thought, it doth abuse your bosom.
15		If any wretch have put this in your head,
		Let heaven requite it with the serpent's curse,

第二场

奥赛罗与爱米利娅上。

奥赛罗	那您什么都没有看见？
爱米利娅	也从没有听见，也从没有怀疑。
奥赛罗	但，您见过凯西奥和……她在一起。
爱米利娅	但没看见有啥不对，我也听见
	他们之间发出的每一个音节。 5
奥赛罗	怎么，他们从未耳语？
爱米利娅	没有，将军。
奥赛罗	也从未把您支开？
爱米利娅	没有。
奥赛罗	比如为她取扇子、手套、面具等？
爱米利娅	没有，将军。 10
奥赛罗	这就怪了。
爱米利娅	将军，我敢打赌她这人贞洁，
	以我的灵魂为注：您若有疑心，
	就赶快消除，它伤害您的心胸。
	若哪个恶棍将它灌进您头脑， 15
	愿上帝用对毒蛇的诅咒回报，

4.2.　9. 面具（mask）：威尼斯女士在狂欢节期间会戴上面具。　15. 跟她原先的观点自相矛盾，即"嫉妒可以自我怀胎"（3．4．159-62）。　本句台词也为132行及以下的内容做好了铺垫。　16. 对毒蛇的诅咒（the serpent's curse）：上帝对诱骗夏娃的毒蛇之诅咒。　（参考《圣经》"创世纪"3章14节：神对蛇说："你既做了这事，就必受诅咒，比一切的牲畜野兽更甚。你必须用肚子行走，终身吃土。"）（Bevington）

For if she be not honest, chaste and true,

There's no man happy: the purest of their wives

Is foul as slander.

Othello   Bid her come hither; go.   *Exit Emilia.*

20   She says enough; yet she's a simple bawd

That cannot say as much. This is a subtle whore,

A closet, lock and key, of villainous secrets;

And yet she'll kneel and pray, I have seen her do't.

Enter Desdemona and Emilia.

Desdemona My lord, what is your will?

Othello   Pray, chuck, come hither.

Desdemona What is your pleasure?

25 **Othello**   Let me see your eyes.

Look in my face.

Desdemona   What horrible fancy's this?

Othello [*to Emilia*] Some of your function, mistress,

Leave procreants alone and shut the door;

Cough, or cry hem, if anybody come.

30   Your mystery, your mystery: nay, dispatch!   *Exit Emilia.*

Desdemona Upon my knees, what doth your speech import?

I understand a fury in your words,

But not the words.

Othello Why, what art thou?

35 **Desdemona** Your wife, my lord: your true and loyal wife.

假如她不忠诚,不贞洁,不可靠,

就没有幸福男人:最贞洁的妻子

也该受诽谤。

奥赛罗　　　　　　　叫她过来,去吧。　　　　　　爱米利娅下。

她花言巧语;但唯有愚钝的老鸨　　　　　　　　　　　　　20

才不会自圆其说。　这个狡猾的娼妓,

私房里隐藏着邪恶的秘密;

她也会下跪祷告,我亲眼所见。

苔丝狄蒙娜与爱米利娅上。

苔丝狄蒙娜　夫君,您有何吩咐?

奥赛罗　　　　　　　宝贝儿,请过来。

苔丝狄蒙娜　您要我做啥?

奥赛罗　　　　　　我看看您的眼睛。　　　　　　　　　　　25

看着我的脸。

苔丝狄蒙娜　　　　多么可怕的念头?

奥赛罗　[向爱米利娅]去尽您的职责,夫人,

让交媾者单独留下,把门关上;

咳一下,或哼一声,若有人前来。

您的职业,您的职业,快,赶快!　　　　爱米利娅下。　30

苔丝狄蒙娜　我下跪请求,告诉我您是何意?

我能懂您的话语里有些怒气,

但不懂您的话语。

奥赛罗　唉,你是啥人?

苔丝狄蒙娜　您的妻子,夫君:您真诚的妻子。　　　　　　　35

20-1. 唯有……自圆其说(she's…much):若有哪位老鸨或掮客不能像爱米利娅那样编造一则貌似真实的故事,就说明她非常笨拙(any procuress or go-between who couldn't make up as plausible a story as Emilia's would have to be pretty stupid)(Bevington)。　21. 娼妓(whore):也许指爱米利娅,也许指苔丝狄蒙娜(Mowat)。　27. 职责(function):将爱米利娅视为妓院的老鸨。

Othello   Come, swear it, damn thyself,

Lest, being like one of heaven, the devils themselves

Should fear to seize thee: therefore be double-damned,

Swear thou art honest!

Desdemona   Heaven doth truly know it.

40 **Othello**   Heaven truly knows that thou art false as hell.

Desdemona   To whom, my lord? With whom? How am I false?

Othello   Ah, Desdemon! Away, away, away!

Desdemona   Alas the heavy day, why do you weep?

Am I the motive of these tears, my lord?

45   If haply you my father do suspect

An instrument of this your calling back,

Lay not your blame on me: if you have lost him,

Why, I have lost him too.

Othello   Had it pleased heaven

To try me with affliction, had they rained

50   All kinds of sores and shames on my bare head,

Steeped me in poverty to the very lips,

Given to captivity me and my utmost hopes,

I should have found in some place of my soul

A drop of patience; but, alas, to make me

奥赛罗	快,就此发誓,遭受诅咒,
	恐怕,你貌似天使,魔鬼自身
	竟害怕抓你:发誓你很忠诚,
	为此遭双倍诅咒!
苔丝狄蒙娜	上帝明了一切。
奥赛罗	上帝明了你这人地狱般不忠。
苔丝狄蒙娜	对谁,夫君？　跟谁？　怎么不忠？
奥赛罗	啊,苔丝狄蒙,走开,走开,走开!
苔丝狄蒙娜	唉,真令人伤心,您为啥哭泣？
	难道我是您落泪的诱因,夫君？
	也许您会怀疑我的父亲
	就您的本次召回起了作用,
	请不要怪我:您若失去了他,
	唉,我也失去了他。
奥赛罗	若上帝愿意
	用折磨对我试炼,即使他向我
	光秃的头顶降下各种痛苦与羞辱,
	使我沉浸在绝望的贫困之中,
	让我沦为奴隶,夙愿成泡影,
	我都会在我心灵的某处找到
	一丝耐心;然而,唉,让我成为

40

45

50

37-8. 魔鬼……抓你（the devils…thee）：魔鬼也许只负责将那些在心灵上属于他们的罪人送往地狱。　38. 双倍诅咒（double-damned）：（1）因为通奸（for adultery），（2）因为假誓（for perjury）。　42. 走开（away）：或是她抱住了他,他将她推开；或是他想走开；或是他在说"咱们放弃这种胡扯"。　47. 失去了他（lost him）：苔丝狄蒙娜在回想过去,那时她父亲很"爱"奥赛罗,且"常邀他作客"；此处意为"失去了"一位朋友（Ridley）。　48-54. 参考"约伯的折磨"：上帝将这些（痛苦、贫穷等）降到约伯身上（"约伯记"2章7节,20章23节）。49. 他（they）：是否该将文中的"they"读作"he（他）",将"heaven"读作"God"？50. 降下（rained）：注意与"水"（water）相关的意象：降下（rained）、沉浸（Steeped）、一滴（drop）、源头（fountain）、血脉（current）、枯竭（dries up）、污池（cistern）。

55 The fixed figure for the time of scorn

To point his slow and moving finger at!

Yet could I bear that too, well, very well:

But there where I have garnered up my heart,

Where either I must live or bear no life,

60 The fountain from the which my current runs

Or else dries up—to be discarded thence!

Or keep it as a cistern for foul toads

To knot and gender in! Turn thy complexion there,

Patience, thou young and rose-lipped cherubin,

65 Ay, here look, grim as hell!

Desdemona I hope my noble lord esteems me honest.

Othello O, ay, as summer flies are in the shambles,

That quicken even with blowing. O thou weed,

Who art so lovely fair and smell'st so sweet

70 That the sense aches at thee, would thou hadst ne'er been born!

Desdemona Alas, what ignorant sin have I committed?

Othello Was this fair paper, this most goodly book,

Made to write 'whore' upon? What committed!

Committed? O thou public commoner!

75 I should make very forges of my cheeks

那种千秋万代所轻蔑的笑柄，　　　　　　　　　　55

犹如被缓慢的时针指着不动！

可这些我也都能忍受，忍受：

可我所有情感的依托之处，

我赖以生存或者死亡之所，

使我的血脉得以畅通或者　　　　　　　　　　　　60

枯竭的源头——从此将我抛弃！

或成一座污池供丑陋的蟾蜍

在其中繁衍生息！快改变神情，

耐心，你这妙龄朱唇的天使，

唉，一看这里，面目狰狞！　　　　　　　　　　　65

苔丝狄蒙娜　希望我高贵的夫君认为我贞洁。

奥赛罗　噢，对，就像夏季屠场里的苍蝇，

任凭风吹照孕不误。　噢，你这杂草，

冒充鲜花如此可爱，如此芳香，

看见你就心痛，愿你从未降生！　　　　　　　　　70

苔丝狄蒙娜　唉，我竟犯下何种无知的罪过？

奥赛罗　这张白纸，这本最精美的书册

是用以书写"娼妇"？　犯下什么！

犯下什么？　噢，你这公用的娼妇！

我的双颊将成为鼓风铁炉，　　　　　　　　　　　75

55-6. 那种……不动（A fixed…at）：该意象也许是说，奥赛罗，犹如表盘上的一个数字，被时针指定，但该时针运行得如此缓慢，好像原地不动。　他仿佛成了全世界嘲笑的对象（The image may be that of Othello as like a number on the dial of a clock, with the hand that points to him moving so slowly that it does not seem to move at all. He seems forever to be an object of scorn to the world）（Mowat）。　63-5. 快改变……狰狞（Turn…hell）：请关注这里，耐心，你那年轻红润和天使般的神情，一看到这种地狱般的场景，随之会变为狰狞！（Direct your gaze there, Patience, and your youthful and rosy cherubic countenance will turn grim and pale at this hellish spectacle!）（Bevington）。　65. 一看这里（here look）：最初他并未直接指向苔丝狄蒙娜（58-64），但现在他将矛头直接指向了她（Honigmann）。　其中，原文里的"here"在某些版本里为"there"，如上文所引贝文顿版。　——译者附注。

That would to cinders burn up modesty,

Did I but speak thy deeds. What committed!

Heaven stops the nose at it, and the moon winks,

The bawdy wind that kisses all it meets

80 Is hushed within the hollow mine of earth

And will not hear't. What committed!

Impudent strumpet!

Desdemona   By heaven, you do me wrong.

Othello   Are not you a strumpet?

Desdemona   No, as I am a Christian.

85 If to preserve this vessel for my lord

From any hated foul unlawful touch

Be not to be a strumpet, I am none.

Othello   What, not a whore?

Desdemona   No, as I shall be saved.

Othello   Is't possible?

Desdemona   O heaven forgive us!

90 **Othello**   I cry you mercy then,

I took you for that cunning whore of Venice

That married with Othello. You! Mistress!

Enter Emilia.

That have the office opposite to Saint Peter

And keep the gates of hell—you, you, ay you!

95 We have done our course, there's money for your pains,

会把羞怯之心化为灰烬,

我若说出你的行为。　犯下什么!

上帝会就此掩鼻,月神会闭目,

所到之处无不亲吻的淫荡之风,

静息在自己地下的洞窟之内, 80

也都会拒绝倾听。　犯下什么!

无耻的淫妇!

苔丝狄蒙娜　　　　　　天哪,您冤枉我了!

奥赛罗　　难道您不是淫妇?

苔丝狄蒙娜　不是,因为我是基督徒。

假如为我夫君保全这副躯体 85

免受任何污秽和非法的接触

不算是淫妇,那我肯定不是。

奥赛罗　　怎么,不是娼妇?

苔丝狄蒙娜　　　　不是,我想得救。

奥赛罗　　这可能吗?

苔丝狄蒙娜　上帝啊,宽恕我们!

奥赛罗　　　　　　那我求您原谅, 90

把您当成了威尼斯狡猾的娼妓,

嫁给了奥赛罗为妻。　您! 夫人!

爱米利娅上。

您的职责与圣彼得恰恰相反,

把守地狱之门——您,您,唉您!

我们的好事已办,这是您的酬劳, 95

---

80. 洞窟(mine):地下通道(根据神话,风会隐退到地洞之中)(Mowat)。 90. 求您原谅(cry you mercy):讥讽(sarcastic)。 93-4. 参考《圣经》"马太福音"16章18-19节:……你是彼得(Peter),……我要把天国的钥匙给你……。 94. 把守地狱之门(keep…hell):参考《圣经》"箴言"7章27节:她(淫妇)的家是在阴间之路,下到死亡之宫(Mowat)。

	I pray you turn the key and keep our counsel.	*Exit.*
Emilia	Alas, what does this gentleman conceive?	
	How do you, madam? How do you, my good lady?	
Desdemona	Faith, half asleep.	
100 **Emilia**	Good madam, what's the matter with my lord?	
Desdemona	With whom?	
Emilia	Why, with my lord, madam.	
Desdemona	Who is thy lord?	
Emilia	He that is yours, sweet lady.	
Desdemona	I have none. Do not talk to me, Emilia;	
105	I cannot weep, nor answer have I none	
	But what should go by water. Prithee, tonight	
	Lay on my bed my wedding sheets; remember,	
	And call thy husband hither.	
Emilia	Here's a change indeed! *Exit.*	
Desdemona	'Tis meet I should be used so, very meet.	
110	How have I been behaved that he might stick	
	The small'st opinion on my greatest misuse?	

Enter Iago and Emilia.

Iago	What is your pleasure, madam? How is't with you?
Desdemona	I cannot tell. Those that do teach young babes
	Do it with gentle means and easy tasks.
115	He might have chide me so, for, in good faith,

	求您把门锁上并给我们保密。		下。
爱米利娅	唉,他这位绅士在想些什么?		
	您好吗,夫人? 您好吗,我的好夫人?		
苔丝狄蒙娜	真的,半睡半醒。		
爱米利娅	好夫人,我的主人是怎么回事?		100
苔丝狄蒙娜	你说谁?		
爱米利娅	嗨,我的主人,夫人。		
苔丝狄蒙娜	谁是你主人?		
爱米利娅	您夫君啊,好夫人。		
苔丝狄蒙娜	我没夫君。 别跟我说话,爱米利娅;		
	我无法哭泣,也没什么回答,		105
	除了以泪传递。 我求你,今晚		
	你把我的新婚床单铺上;记住,		
	要把你丈夫叫来。		
爱米利娅	可真是变了!		下。
苔丝狄蒙娜	我活该受这种对待,非常公道。		
	我会犯下怎样的大错特错,		110
	竟会使他对我如此敌视?		

伊阿古与爱米利娅上。

伊阿古	您有何吩咐,夫人? 您还好吗?
苔丝狄蒙娜	我不知道。 大人教训小孩时,
	都以委婉的方式轻微地处罚。
	他本可这样骂我,因为,说真的, 115

---

107. 新婚床单（wedding sheets）：可使奥赛罗想起他们从前的爱情；也有不祥之兆,因为妻子死后有时会以新婚床单裹尸下葬。 109. 活该……公道（meet…well）：苔丝狄蒙娜对这两个词的使用带有讥讽意味（Ridley）。 110. 大错特错（greatest misuse / abuse）：她的最大过错是如此微小,因此也不该受到责备（even her greatest fault is so small that it does not merit censure）（Ridley）。

I am a child to chiding.

Iago   What's the matter, lady?

Emilia   Alas, Iago, my lord hath so bewhored her,

Thrown such despite and heavy terms upon her

That true hearts cannot bear it.

Desdemona   Am I that name, Iago?

120 **Iago**   What name, fair lady?

Desdemona   Such as she says my lord did say I was.

Emilia   He called her whore. A beggar in his drink

Could not have laid such terms upon his callat.

Iago   Why did he so?

125 **Desdemona**   I do not know; I am sure I am none such.

Iago   Do not weep, do not weep: alas the day!

Emilia   Hath she forsook so many noble matches,

Her father, and her country, and her friends,

To be called whore? Would it not make one weep?

Desdemona   It is my wretched fortune.

130 **Iago**   Beshrew him for't!

How comes this trick upon him?

Desdemona   Nay, heaven doth know.

Emilia   I will be hanged if some eternal villain,

Some busy and insinuating rogue,

Some cogging, cozening slave, to get some office,

135   Have not devised this slander, I'll be hanged else!

Iago   Fie, there is no such man, it is impossible.

Desdemona   If any such there be, heaven pardon him.

我还不习惯挨骂。

伊阿古	怎么了,夫人?

爱米利娅　唉,伊阿古,我主人骂她是娼妇,

用这样的污言秽语羞辱她,

真诚的人无法忍受。

苔丝狄蒙娜　我是那种人吗,伊阿古?

伊阿古　　　　　　　　　哪种人,夫人?　　　　　　　　　　120

苔丝狄蒙娜　就是她说我夫君所说的那种。

爱米利娅　他叫她娼妇。 一个醉酒的乞丐

也不会对他的妓女如此称谓。

伊阿古　他为何这样?

苔丝狄蒙娜　我不知道;只知道我不是那种人。　　　　　　125

伊阿古　别哭了,别哭了,唉,多么不幸!

爱米利娅　她拒绝了那么多贵人的求婚,

抛弃了父亲、国家,以及朋友,

为了娼妇之名? 这不令人伤心?

苔丝狄蒙娜　我命该不幸。

伊阿古　　　　　　　　他为此该受诅咒,　　　　　　　　130

他怎么会有这种念头?

苔丝狄蒙娜　　　　　　　　　天才知道。

爱米利娅　我以性命打赌,若非哪个恶棍,

哪个爱管闲事和谄媚的流氓,

坑蒙拐骗的奴才,想要某一官职,

编造了这种谗言,就把我绞死!　　　　　　　　　　135

伊阿古　呸,哪有这种人呢! 这不可能。

苔丝狄蒙娜　若是真有,愿上帝宽恕他吧!

---

134. 想要某一官职（to get some office）:爱米利娅感到某个像伊阿古似的家伙会对此负责,也许还会怀疑是他（见 147-9）。

Emilia		A halter pardon him, and hell gnaw his bones!
		Why should he call her whore? Who keeps her company?
140		What place, what time, what form, what likelihood?
		The Moor's abused by some most villainous knave,
		Some base notorious knave, some scurvy fellow.
		O heaven, that such companions thou'dst unfold,
		And put in every honest hand a whip
145		To lash the rascals naked through the world
		Even from the east to th' west!
	Iago	Speak within doors.
	Emilia	O fie upon them! Some such squire he was
		That turned your wit the seamy side without
		And made you to suspect me with the Moor.
	Iago	You are a fool, go to.
150	**Desdemona**	O God, Iago,
		What shall I do to win my lord again?
		Good friend, go to him, for, by this light of heaven,
		I know not how I lost him. Here I kneel:
		If e'er my will did trespass 'gainst his love
155		Either in discourse of thought or actual deed,
		Or that mine eyes, mine ears or any sense
		Delighted them in any other form,
		Or that I do not yet, and ever did,
		And ever will—though he do shake me off
160		To beggarly divorcement—love him dearly,
		Comfort forswear me! Unkindness may do much,

爱米利娅	绞索宽恕他,地狱啃他的骨头!	
	他为何要叫她娼妇?　跟谁一起?	
	何地,何时,何种方式,怎么可能?	140
	摩尔人被某个极坏的恶棍欺骗,	
	某个卑鄙的小人,无耻之徒。	
	上帝啊,你要揭露这样的家伙,	
	要让每位诚实之人手拿鞭子,	
	抽打这些无赖的赤身裸体,	145
	从东方抽到西方!	
伊阿古	你小声点儿。	
爱米利娅	噢,他们该死!　哪位类似的乡绅,	
	曾使您失去理智,丢人现眼,	
	竟使您怀疑我与那摩尔有染。	
伊阿古	你是个傻瓜,闭嘴。	
苔丝狄蒙娜	上帝啊,伊阿古,	150
	我怎样才能挽回丈夫的欢心?	
	好朋友,去找他,因为,我对天发誓,	
	不知道他为何不再爱我。　我跪下:	
	我若曾有意背叛他的爱情,	
	无论心思意念还是实际行动,	155
	若我的眼睛、耳朵或其他器官	
	曾从别人身上获得过快感,	
	若我不再爱他,或不曾爱他,	
	或有朝一日——纵然他将我抛弃,	
	让我沦为乞丐——不深深爱他,	160
	愿我不得安生!　无情会伤人,	

---

147. 乡绅(squire):表示轻蔑。　159. 将我抛弃(shake me off):参考3. 3. 266,"吹哨把她顺风放飞(I'd whistle her off)"。

And his unkindness may defeat my life,

But never taint my love. I cannot say whore:

It doth abhor me now I speak the word;

165 To do the act that might the addition earn

Not the world's mass of vanity could make me.

Iago I pray you, be content, 'tis but his humour;

The business of the state does him offence,

And he does chide with you.

Desdemona If 'twere no other—

170 **Iago** 'Tis but so, I warrant. [*Trumpets.*]

Hark how these instruments summon to supper:

The messengers of Venice stay the meat,

Go in, and weep not; all things shall be well.

Exeunt Desdemona and Emilia.

Enter Roderigo.

How now, Roderigo?

175 **Roderigo** I do not find that thou deal'st justly with me.

Iago What in the contrary?

Roderigo Every   day   thou   doff'st   me   with   some   device,

Iago, and rather, as it seems to me now, keep'st from

me all conveniency than suppliest me with the least

180 advantage of hope. I will indeed no longer endure it;

nor am I yet persuaded to put up in peace what

already I have foolishly suffered.

Iago Will you hear me, Roderigo?

Roderigo Faith,   I   have   heard   too   much;   and   your—

185 words and performances are no kin together.

他的无情会毁灭我的人生，

却不能玷污我爱情。　我不能提娼妓：

一提该词语就会不寒而栗；

世间的富贵荣华也不能使我　　　　　　　　　　165

做那种事情去获取这一名称。

伊阿古　　我求您,别担心,他只是在闹情绪；

是因为国家的大事让他心烦,

他才跟您争吵。

苔丝狄蒙娜　若只是这样——

伊阿古　　　　　　　　　就是这样,我保证。　　　　［号角声。］170

请听,号角正召唤我们吃晚饭：

威尼斯的使者正在等候用餐,

进去吧,别哭了；一切都会好的。

　　　　　　　　　　　　苔丝狄蒙娜与爱米利娅同下。

　　　　　　　　　罗德利哥上。

你好吗,罗德利哥？

罗德利哥　我觉得你可没有公正地待我。　　　　　　175

伊阿古　为何这么说呢？

罗德利哥　每天你都会耍一些花招对我进行推托,

伊阿古,在我看来,你并不是在为我

寻找什么有利时机,倒是在想方设法

避免为我提供便利。我已是忍无可忍；　　　180

而且,我对自己原先愚蠢的忍气吞声

再也不会善罢甘休。

伊阿古　您愿听我说吗,罗德利哥？

罗德利哥　说真的,我已经听得太多；而且,您

这个人的言行并不一致。　　　　　　　　185

Iago	You charge me most unjustly.
Roderigo	With nought but truth. I have wasted myself out of my means. The jewels you have had from me to deliver to Desdemona would half have corrupted a votarist. You have told me she hath received them, and returned me expectations and comforts of sudden respect and acquaintance, but I find none.
Iago	Well, go to; very well.
Roderigo	'Very well,' 'go to' ! I cannot go to, man, nor 'tis not very well. By this hand, I think it is scurvy, and begin to find myself fopped in it.
Iago	Very well.
Roderigo	I tell you, 'tis not very well! I will make myself known to Desdemona: if she will return me my jewels, I will give over my suit and repent my unlawful solicitation; if not, assure yourself I will seek satisfaction of you.
Iago	You have said now.
Roderigo	Ay, and said nothing but what I protest intendment of doing.
Iago	Why, now I see there's mettle in thee, and even from this instant do build on thee a better opinion than ever before. Give me thy hand, Roderigo. Thou hast taken against me a most just exception—but yet I protest I have dealt most directly in thy affair.
Roderigo	It hath not appeared.
Iago	I grant indeed it hath not appeared, and your suspicion is not without wit and judgement. But,

190

195

200

205

210

伊阿古	您真是太冤枉我了。	
罗德利哥	一点都不冤枉。我的钱财现在几乎已 全部花光。您已从我这里拿去要送给 苔丝狄蒙娜的珠宝可使一位修女半推 半就。您告诉我说她已收下这些珠宝, 回报我有利的许诺和鼓励,暗示即刻 就会考虑和报偿,可我一无所获。	190
伊阿古	好吧,算了,很好。	
罗德利哥	"很好","算了"!我不能算了,伙计, 也不是很好。我举手发誓,我认为这 很卑鄙,并开始发现自己受骗。	195
伊阿古	很好。	
罗德利哥	我告诉您,这可不是很好!我将会向 苔丝狄蒙娜自我介绍:如果她愿归还 我的珠宝,我会放弃我的追求并忏悔 我不道德的求爱;不然,您放心好了, 我会找您算账。	200
伊阿古	您说得很好。	
罗德利哥	是的,不只是说了,我还会发誓自己 有意付诸行动。	205
伊阿古	嗨,现在我发现你倒是有些骨气,从 此刻开始,我对你比以往任何时候都 更加器重。把你的手给我,罗德利哥。 你对我表示异议也非常合理——不过 我声明我对你这件事情非常坦诚。	210
罗德利哥	好像并非这样。	
伊阿古	我承认它看上去并非那样,而且你的 疑心多少也会有一些合情合理。但是,	

200. 忏悔(repent):一种奇特的忏悔——要有先决条件!

215 Roderigo, if thou hast that in thee indeed which I have greater reason to believe now than ever—I mean purpose, courage, and valour—this night show it. If thou the next night following enjoy not Desdemona, take me from this world with treachery and devise engines for my life.

220 **Roderigo** Well—what is it? Is it within reason and compass?

Iago Sir, there is especial commission come from Venice to depute Cassio in Othello's place.

Roderigo Is that true? Why, then Othello and
225 Desdemona return again to Venice.

Iago O no, he goes into Mauritania and taketh away with him the fair Desdemona, unless his abode be lingered here by some accident—wherein none can be so determinate as the removing of Cassio.

230 **Roderigo** How do you mean, removing of him?

Iago Why, by making him uncapable of Othello's place: knocking out his brains.

Roderigo And that you would have me to do!

Iago Ay, if you dare do yourself a profit and a right.
235 He sups tonight with a harlotry, and thither will I go to him. He knows not yet of his honourable fortune: if you will watch his going thence—which I will

	罗德利哥，假如你能像我有充足理由	215
	信赖的那样，确有那种品质——我指	
	决心、勇气和魄力——今晚就该展现。	
	假如你明天晚上不能享用苔丝狄蒙娜，	
	请你用计让我从世上消失，设法将我	
	的性命除掉。	
罗德利哥	那好——是什么计策？它是否合理与	220
	可行？	
伊阿古	先生，从威尼斯传来了专门的委任状，	
	任命凯西奥接替奥赛罗的职位。	
罗德利哥	这是真的？嗨，这样的话，奥赛罗与	
	苔丝狄蒙娜就要返回威尼斯了。	225
伊阿古	噢，不，他要去毛里塔尼亚，并随身	
	携带美丽的苔丝狄蒙娜，除非有什么	
	意外事故能够让他延期——其中再也	
	没有比将凯西奥除掉更为保险。	
罗德利哥	将他除掉，您是何意？	230
伊阿古	嗨，就是让他无法接替奥赛罗的职位：	
	将他的脑袋敲破。	
罗德利哥	这件事您想让我去做！	
伊阿古	是的，假如您敢为自己谋取一些权益。	
	他今晚要跟一位妓女晚餐，我会前去	235
	见他。他还不知道自己已经交上好运：	
	假如您能守候他从那里走过——我会	

---

226. 毛里塔尼亚（Mauretania）：北非摩尔人的故乡。 假如这是谎言（参考4.1.235），伊阿古又能从中得到什么？ 苔丝狄蒙娜若在毛里塔尼亚，将会使罗德利哥鞭长莫及，因此他必须马上行动。 236. 他……好运（He…fortune）：伊阿古不可能确知此事。 他是在暗示，凯西奥还不会像新任总督那样也许会有侍卫，因此更容易受到袭击。

240 fashion to fall out between twelve and one—you may take him at your pleasure. I will be near to second your attempt, and he shall fall between us. Come, stand not amazed at it, but go along with me: I will show you such a necessity in his death that you shall think yourself bound to put it on him. It is now high supper time, and the night grows to waste: about it.

245 **Roderigo**   I will hear further reason for this.

Iago   And you shall be satisfied.   *Exeunt.*

将这安排在十二点与一点之间——您
可随意将他干掉。我也会在附近助您
一臂之力,他会因咱的联合行动倒下。 240
快,别站着发呆,快跟我走吧:我会
向您解释为什么他非死不可,您就会
觉得自己有义务将他除掉。现在已是
晚饭时间,夜晚已快耗尽:赶快行动。

罗德利哥 　我还要听听这样做的缘由。 245
伊阿古 　我将会让您信服。 　　　　　　　　　　同下。

241-3. 我会……除掉(I will…him):伊阿古(或莎士比亚)有时会不属于任何解释(3. 3.
322-3,5. 3. 320),就此例而言,相应的解释出现在随后的台词中(5. 1. 8-10)。

SCENE III

Enter Othello, Lodovico, Desdemona, Emilia and Attendants.

Lodovico   I do beseech you, sir, trouble yourself no further.

Othello   O, pardon me, 'twill do me good to walk.

Lodovico   Madam, good night: I humbly thank your ladyship.

Desdemona   Your honour is most welcome.

Othello   Will you walk, sir?

O, Desdemona—

Desdemona   My lord?

5   **Othello**   Get you to bed

On th'instant; I will be returned forthwith.

Dismiss your attendant there: look't be done.

Desdemona   I will, my lord.

                        Exeunt Othello, Lodovico and Attendants.

Emilia   How goes it now? He looks gentler than he did.

10   **Desdemona**   He says he will return incontinent,

And hath commanded me to go to bed

And bid me to dismiss you.

Emilia   Dismiss me?

Desdemona   It was his bidding; therefore, good Emilia,

Give me my nightly wearing, and adieu.

第三场

奥赛罗、罗德威克、苔丝狄蒙娜、爱米利娅与侍从上。

罗德威克	我求您,先生,请您就此留步。
奥赛罗	噢,请原谅,走走对我倒很好。
罗德威克	夫人,晚安:我敬谢夫人阁下。
苔丝狄蒙娜	欢迎阁下光临。
奥赛罗	一起走走吧,先生?
	噢,苔丝狄蒙娜——
苔丝狄蒙娜	夫君?
奥赛罗	您现在

就去睡吧,我马上就会回来。

您把侍从打发走开:务请照办。

苔丝狄蒙娜	遵命,夫君。

奥赛罗、罗德威克与侍从下。

爱米利娅	现在怎么样了? 他显得温和多了。
苔丝狄蒙娜	他说他立刻之间就会回来,
	并且还吩咐我去上床歇息,
	还叫我让您走开。
爱米利娅	让我走开?
苔丝狄蒙娜	他这样吩咐;因此,好爱米利娅,
	把我的晚装拿来,然后道别。

5

10

4.3.　1-8. 散文还是诗文? 因对话短促,不易分辨。

15		We must not now displease him.
	Emilia	Ay. —Would you had never seen him!
	Desdemona	So would not I; my love doth so approve him
		That even his stubbornness, his checks, his frowns
		—Prithee unpin me—have grace and favour.
20	**Emilia**	I have laid those sheets you bade me on the bed.
	Desdemona	All's one. Good faith, how foolish are our minds!
		If I do die before thee, prithee shroud me
		In one of these same sheets.
	Emilia	Come, come, you talk.
	Desdemona	My mother had a maid called Barbary,
25		She was in love, and he she loved proved mad
		And did forsake her. She had a song of 'willow',
		An old thing 'twas, but it expressed her fortune,
		And she died singing it. That song tonight
		Will not go from my mind; I have much to do
30		But to go hang my head all at one side
		And sing it like poor Barbary. Prithee dispatch.
	Emilia	Shall I go fetch your night-gown?
	Desdemona	No, unpin me here.
	Emilia	This Lodovico is a proper man. A very hand-
35		some man.
	Desdemona	He speaks well.
	Emilia	I know a lady in Venice would have walked barefoot
		to Palestine for a touch of his nether lip.

	我们现在可别惹他生气。	15
爱米利娅	好吧。 ——但愿您从未见过他!	
苔丝狄蒙娜	我可不这么希望:我如此爱他,	
	甚至连他的粗鲁、责怪、皱眉	
	——求您给我卸妆——也很优雅可爱。	
爱米利娅	我已按您吩咐把那些床单铺好。	20
苔丝狄蒙娜	都一样。 真的,我们的念头有多傻!	
	假如我比你先死,求你用其中的	
	一张为我裹尸。	
爱米利娅	喂,喂,别瞎说!	
苔丝狄蒙娜	我母亲曾有个叫巴巴莉的女仆,	
	她有个恋人,恋人后来发疯	25
	并将她抛弃。 她有一首"杨柳",	
	是一首老歌,却表达了她的命运,	
	她唱着这首歌死去。 那首歌今晚	
	萦绕在我的心头。 我必须尽力	
	避免让自己把头倒向一侧,	30
	像可怜的巴巴莉唱歌。 求你快点。	
爱米利娅	要我去给您取睡衣吗?	
苔丝狄蒙娜	不用,只为我卸妆。	
爱米利娅	这位罗德威克是位英俊的男子。 非常	
	潇洒的男士。	35
苔丝狄蒙娜	他谈吐优雅。	
爱米利娅	我知道威尼斯有位女士宁愿赤脚走到	
	巴勒斯坦,为了吻一吻他的下唇。	

21. 都一样(All's one):没什么区别(It's all the same);没关系(It doesn't matter)。
21. 傻(foolish):因为想到了死亡(略表歉意)。 23. 别瞎说(you talk):看你说的!(how you talk)她的口吻几乎是在对一个孩子说话。

Desdemona   [*Sings.*]

   The poor soul sat sighing by a sycamore tree,

40

    Sing all a green willow:

   Her hand on her bosom, her head on her knee,

    Sing willow, willow, willow.

   The fresh streams ran by her and murmured her moans,

    Sing willow, willow, willow:

45

   Her salt tears fell from her and softened the stones,

    Sing willow, willow, willow.

[*Speaks.*] Lay by these.

   Willow, willow—

[*Speaks.*] Prithee hie thee: he'll come anon.

50

   Sing all a green willow must be my garland.

   Let nobody blame him, his scorn I approve—

[*Speaks.*] Nay, that's not next. Hark, who is't that knocks?

Emilia   It's the wind.

Desdemona   [*Sings.*]

   I called my love false love; but what said he then?

55

    Sing willow, willow, willow:

   If I court more women, you'll couch with more men.

[*Speaks.*] So, get thee gone; good night. Mine eyes do itch,

Doth that bode weeping?

Emilia   'Tis neither here nor there.

Desdemona   I have heard it said so. O, these men, these men!

60

Dost thou in conscience think—tell me, Emilia—

That there be women do abuse their husbands

苔丝狄蒙娜　〔唱。〕

　　　　可怜的人儿坐在枫树旁哀伤，

　　　　　　歌唱青青的杨柳：　　　　　　　　　　　40

　　　　她手扶胸口，把头贴到膝上，

　　　　　　歌唱杨柳，杨柳，杨柳。

　　　　清溪在身旁流淌，哭诉她的凄惨，

　　　　　　歌唱杨柳，杨柳，杨柳：

　　　　她流的辛酸泪水，让石头松软，　　　　　　45

　　　　　　歌唱杨柳，杨柳，杨柳。

　　〔说。〕把这些放在一边。

　　　　　　杨柳，杨柳——

　　〔说。〕求你快点：他很快就到。

　　　　歌唱青青的杨柳必作我的花环。　　　　　　50

　　　　大家别怪他，他的轻蔑我赞同——

　　〔说。〕不对，没唱对。　你听，谁在敲门？

爱米利娅　　那是风。

苔丝狄蒙娜　〔唱。〕

　　　　我称恋人负心汉，你猜他说啥？

　　　　　　歌唱杨柳，杨柳，杨柳：　　　　　　　55

　　　　我若寻花问柳，你就水性杨花。

　　〔说。〕好了，你走吧；晚安。　我的眼发痒，

　　这是否预示着哭泣？

爱米利娅　　　　　　　　那毫不相干。

苔丝狄蒙娜　听说是的。　噢，这些男人，这些男人！

　　你是否真以为——告诉我，爱米利娅——　　　60

　　有女人会用这么不像话的方式

　　51-2. 大家……没唱对（Let…next）：口误（a Freudian slip）（她潜意识地想保护奥赛罗免受责备）。

In such gross kind?

Emilia   There be some such, no question.

Desdemona   Wouldst thou do such a deed for all the world?

Emilia   Why, would not you?

Desdemona   No, by this heavenly light!

65 **Emilia**   Nor I neither, by this heavenly light:

I might do't as well i'th' dark.

Desdemona   Wouldst thou do such a deed for all the world?

Emilia   The world's a huge thing: it is a great price

For a small vice.

Desdemona   Good troth, I think thou wouldst not.

70 **Emilia**   By my troth, I think I should, and undo't when I

had done. Marry, I would not do such a thing for

a joint-ring, nor for measures of lawn, nor for gowns,

petticoats, nor caps, nor any petty exhibition. But for

the whole world? ud's pity, who would not make

75   her husband a cuckold to make him a monarch? I

should venture purgatory for't.

Desdemona   Beshrew me, if I would do such a wrong

For the whole world!

Emilia   Why, the wrong is but a wrong i'th' world; and

80   having the world for your labour, 'tis a wrong in your

own world, and you might quickly make it right.

Desdemona   I do not think there is any such woman.

欺骗丈夫？

爱米利娅　　　　　　　　有这种女人，肯定。

苔丝狄蒙娜　把世界给你，你会做这种事吗？

爱米利娅　嗨，您不会吗？

苔丝狄蒙娜　　　　　　　不会，对上天发誓！

爱米利娅　我也不会，在这光天化日之下：　　　　　　　　65

夜间倒可能会做。

苔丝狄蒙娜　把世界给你，你会做这种事情？

爱米利娅　世界可很庞大：这是大奖赏

小罪过。

苔丝狄蒙娜　　　　　说真的，我想你不会做的。

爱米利娅　说真的，我想我会做的，做完之后再　　　　　70

予以挽回。真的，若只为了一枚订婚

戒指、几尺麻纱，或几套睡衣、裙子、

帽子，或其他小小礼物，我不会做的。

但要换取全世界？上帝怜悯，谁不愿

让她的丈夫做个乌龟好让他做个国王？　　　　75

我愿为此冒炼狱的折磨。

苔丝狄蒙娜　我该死，假如我为了换取世界

会干这种坏事！

爱米利娅　嗨，这种坏事不过是世上的一桩小错；

拥有世界作为你的酬劳，这就是自己　　　　　80

世界里的过错，您可以很快纠正。

苔丝狄蒙娜　我想世上不会有这种女人。

64-6. 嗨……会做（Why…dark）：我认为莎士比亚删除了这几行台词，因为爱米利娅知道，自第四幕第二场之后，苔丝狄蒙娜的贞洁并非笑料（not a joking matter）。 68. 奖赏（price）：可指"要付出的代价"（price to be paid）；也可指"奖赏"（prize）。 74. 上帝（ud's = God's）。 76. 炼狱（purgatory）：说明该剧的背景为天主教世界。

Emilia	Yes, a dozen, and as many to th' vantage as would
	store the world they played for.
85	But I do think it is their husbands' faults
	If wives do fall. Say that they slack their duties
	And pour our treasures into foreign laps;
	Or else break out in peevish jealousies,
	Throwing restraint upon us; or say they strike us,
90	Or scant our former having in despite,
	Why, we have galls: and though we have some grace,
	Yet have we some revenge. Let husbands know
	Their wives have sense like them: they see, and smell,
	And have their palates both for sweet and sour,
95	As husbands have. What is it that they do
	When they change us for others? Is it sport?
	I think it is. And doth affection breed it?
	I think it doth. Is't frailty that thus errs?
	It is so too. And have not we affections?
100	Desires for sport? And frailty, as men have?
	Then let them use us well: else let them know,
	The ills we do, their ills instruct us so.
Desdemona	Good night, good night. God me such usage send
	Not to pick bad from bad, but by bad mend! *Exeunt.*

爱米利娅	有，会有一打，而且会多到能将她们	
	赢得的世界给填满。	
	不过我想那是当丈夫的过错，	85
	若妻子堕落。　比如说他们失职，	
	将我们的种子送给别的女人；	
	或者莫名其妙地妒火中烧，	
	限制我们的自由；或殴打我们，	
	或出于恶意缩减我们的开销，	90
	嗨，我们也会怨恨：尽管仁厚，	
	但也会报复。　要让丈夫们知道：	
	妻子同样是人：也能看，也能闻，	
	跟丈夫一样也有味觉，尝得出	
	酸与甜。　他们究竟为了什么，	95
	抛弃我们另寻她人？　为了游戏？	
	我想是的。　他们的情欲使然？	
	我想是的。　是脆弱使他们犯错？	
	也会是的。　难道我们没有情欲？	
	不想游戏？　不像男人一样脆弱？	100
	让他们善待我们：否则让他们知道，	
	我们的恶行，是对他们的仿效。	
苔丝狄蒙娜	晚安，晚安。　愿上帝这样恩待：	
	不要以坏学坏，而要引以为戒！	同下。

83-4. 以散文开头、诗文接续的台词并不多见。　85-102. 继续 3. 4. 104-7 的话题。　尽管她最初会想到奥赛罗，但很快便指向了自己的婚姻。　这种对"双重标准"的抗议并非罕见。87. 将……女人（And…laps）：意为"不忠，将本该属于我们的东西（精子）给了别的女人"（i. e. are unfaithful, give what is rightfully ours［semen］to other women）（Bevington）。102. 参考《威尼斯商人》3. 1. 71-2 行夏洛克的言论："你们教给我的凶恶，我就要实行（The villainy you teah me, I will execute）"。　他那段台词（犹太人没有眼吗？）跟爱米利娅此处的台词颇为相似。　104. 不要……为戒（Not…mend）：不要学习别人身上的坏处（像爱米利娅建议的那样，女人要向男人学坏），而要通过认识何为坏处去改进我的行为方式，并从邪恶与逆境之中使心灵受益（not to learn bad conduct from other's badness［as Emilia has suggested women learn from men］, but to mend my ways by perceiving what badness is, making spiritual benefit out of evil and adversity）（Bevington）。　译文借鉴梁译。　——译者附注。

第五幕
ACT 5

SCENE I

Enter Iago and Roderigo.

Iago	Here, stand behind this bulk, straight will he come.
	Wear thy good rapier bare, and put it home;
	Quick, quick, fear nothing, I'll be at thy elbow.
	It makes us or it mars us, think on that
5	And fix most firm thy resolution.
Roderigo	Be near at hand, I may miscarry in't.
Iago	Here, at thy hand: be bold, and take thy stand. [*Retires.*]
Roderigo	I have no great devotion to the deed;
	And yet he hath given me satisfying reasons:
10	'Tis but a man gone. Forth, my sword: he dies.
Iago	I have rubbed this young quat almost to the sense,
	And he grows angry. Now, whether he kill Cassio
	Or Cassio him, or each do kill the other,
	Every way makes my gain. Live Roderigo,
15	He calls me to a restitution large
	Of gold and jewels that I bobbed from him
	As gifts to Desdemona:
	It must not be. If Cassio do remain,

第一场

伊阿古与罗德利哥上。

伊阿古	这里,站棚子后面,他立刻就到。
	拔出你的利剑,要奋力刺去;
	快,快,别怕,我会伴你左右。
	我们的成败在此一举,要记住,
	还要使你的决心坚定不移。

5

罗德利哥　你别走远,也许我会失手。

伊阿古　　就在你身后:勇敢些,赶快就位。　　　　［后退。］

罗德利哥　对这种举动我没多大热情,

　　　　　　然而他却给了我充足的理由:

　　　　　　一人离去而已。　剑,出鞘:他死去! 　　10

伊阿古　　我几乎把这个小脓包给擦破,

　　　　　　他有些生气。　无论他杀死凯西奥,

　　　　　　还是凯西奥杀死他,或两败俱伤,

　　　　　　都会对我有利。　罗德利哥若活着,

　　　　　　他就会叫我归还我从他那里　　　　　15

　　　　　　骗取、说是送给苔丝狄蒙娜的

　　　　　　大量金银珠宝:

　　　　　　这绝对不行。　假如凯西奥活着,

5.1.　10. 出鞘(forth):此刻他才勉强拔出剑来。

He hath a daily beauty in his life

20   That makes me ugly; and besides, the Moor

May unfold me to him—there stand I in much peril.

No, he must die. Be't so. I hear him coming.

Enter Cassio.

Roderigo   I know his gait, 'tis he. Villain, thou diest!

[*Makes a thrust at Cassio.*]

Cassio   That thrust had been mine enemy indeed

25   But that my coat is better than thou know'st:

I will make proof of thine.

[*Draws, and wounds Roderigo.*]

Roderigo   O, I am slain!

[*Iago from behind wounds Cassio in the leg, and exit.*]

Cassio   I am maimed for ever! Help, ho! Murder! Murder!

Enter Othello.

Othello   The voice of Cassio. Iago keeps his word.

Roderigo   O, villain that I am!

Othello   It is even so.

30   **Cassio**   O, help ho! Light! A surgeon!

Othello   'Tis he. O brave Iago, honest and just,

That hast such noble sense of thy friend's wrong!

Thou teachest me. Minion, your dear lies dead,

And your unblest fate hies; strumpet, I come.

在日常生活中如此优雅洒脱，

会使我相形见绌；而且，那摩尔　　　　　　　　　　　　20

也许会同他对质——我会非常危险。

他非死不可。　就这样！我听见他来了。

凯西奥上。

罗德利哥　　我了解他的步态，是他。　恶棍，死去！

［向凯西奥刺去。］

凯西奥　　这可真是对我致命的一击，

但我结实的内衣出乎你意料：　　　　　　　　　　25

我要试试你的。

［拔剑，刺伤罗德利哥。］

罗德利哥　　　　　　噢，我已遇害！

［伊阿古从身后刺伤凯西奥的腿部，然后退下。］

凯西奥　　我将终生残废！救命，嗬！凶杀！凶杀！

奥赛罗上。

奥赛罗　　凯西奥的声音。　伊阿古说话算数。

罗德利哥　　噢，我这个恶棍！

奥赛罗　　　　　　一点不错。

凯西奥　　噢，救命，嗬！点灯！外科医生！　　　　　30

奥赛罗　　是他。　勇敢的伊阿古啊，诚实正直，

竟为朋友的冤屈伸张正义！

我向你学习。　荡妇，你的情人已死，

你的诅咒即将来临；婊子，我来了。

---

25. 内衣（coat）：铠甲（undercoat［of proof armour］）。　26. 舞台指示：伊阿古之所以刺伤凯西奥的腿部，因为他听见凯西奥说他的内衣可保护其上身。　29. 一点不错（It is even so）：因为奥赛罗并不了解罗德利哥的情况，也看不见他，因此他认为那是凯西奥在说话。

35   Forth of my heart those charms, thine eyes, are blotted,

Thy bed, lust-stained, shall with lust's blood be spotted.

Exit.

Enter Lodovico and Gratiano.

Cassio	What ho, no watch, no passage? Murder, murder!
Gratiano	'Tis some mischance, the voice is very direful.
Cassio	O help!
40 **Lodovico**	Hark!
Roderigo	O wretched villain!
Lodovico	Two or three groan. It is a heavy night;
	These may be counterfeits, let's think't unsafe
	To come in to the cry without more help.
45 **Roderigo**	Nobody come? Then shall I bleed to death.

Enter Iago, with a light.

Lodovico	Hark!
Gratiano	Here's one comes in his shirt, with light and weapons.
Iago	Who's there? Whose noise is this that cries on murder?
Lodovico	We do not know.
Iago	Did not you hear a cry?
Cassio	Here, here! For heaven's sake help me!
50 **Iago**	What's the matter?
Gratiano	This is Othello's ancient, as I take it.
Lodovico	The same indeed, a very valiant fellow.
Iago	What are you here that cry so grievously?
Cassio	Iago? O, I am spoiled, undone by villains!
55	Give me some help.
Iago	O me, lieutenant! What villains have done this?

你双眼的魅力从我心中消除，　　　　　　　　　　　　35

你沾满淫迹的床铺,将布满血污。

　　　　　　　　　　　　　　　　　　　　　　　下。

　　　　　　　罗德威克与葛莱西亚诺上。

凯西奥	怎么,巡警呢,没人路过？ 凶杀,凶杀!
葛莱西亚诺	是一件不幸事故,叫声很凄惨。
凯西奥	救命啊!
罗德威克	您听!

　　　　　　　　　　　　　　　　　　　　　　　40

罗德利哥　噢,可怜的恶棍!

罗德威克　两三个人在呻吟。 阴沉的夜晚;

　　　　　这也许是假象,若不多叫些帮手

　　　　　就接近吼声,恐怕很不安全。

罗德利哥　没人来吗？ 我就会流血而死了。　　　　　45

　　　　　　　　伊阿古持火把上。

罗德威克　注意!

葛莱西亚诺　来者穿着睡衣,拿着火把和武器。

伊阿古　　那边是谁？ 是谁在呼喊凶杀?

罗德威克　我们不知道。

伊阿古　　　　　　　没听到有人喊吗?

凯西奥　　这里,这里! 天哪,救我!

伊阿古　　　　　　　　　怎么了？　　　　　　　50

葛莱西亚诺　我想,那个人是奥赛罗的旗官。

罗德威克　正是他,一位非常勇敢的男子。

伊阿古　　是谁在这里,叫声如此凄惨?

凯西奥　　伊阿古？ 噢,我毁了,遭恶棍暗算!

　　　　　快救救我吧。　　　　　　　　　　　　55

伊阿古　　天哪,是副官! 这是哪个恶棍干的?

	Cassio	I think that one of them is here about
		And cannot make away.
	Iago	O treacherous villains!
		What are you there? Come in, and give some help.
60	**Roderigo**	O, help me here!
	Cassio	That's one of them.
	Iago	O murderous slave! O villain!

[Stabs Roderigo.]

	Roderigo	O damned Iago! O inhuman dog!
	Iago	Kill men i'th' dark? Where be these bloody thieves?
		How silent is this town! Ho, murder! murder!
65		What may you be? Are you of good or evil?
	Lodovico	As you shall prove us, praise us.
	Iago	Signior Lodovico?
	Lodovico	He, sir.
	Iago	I cry you mercy: here's Cassio hurt by villains.
70	**Gratiano**	Cassio?
	Iago	How is't, brother?
	Cassio	My leg is cut in two.
	Iago	Marry, heaven forbid!
		Light, gentlemen, I'll bind it with my shirt.

Enter Bianca.

	Bianca	What is the matter, ho? Who is't that cried?
	Iago	Who is't that cried?
75	**Bianca**	O my dear Cassio!

凯西奥	我想其中的一个还在附近,	
	他无法逃脱。	
伊阿古	噢,奸诈的恶棍!	
	你们是什么人?　进来,帮帮忙吧。	
罗德利哥	噢,快来救我!	60
凯西奥	那是个同伙。	
伊阿古	噢,残忍的奴才! 恶棍!	

　　　　　　　　　　　　　　　　　　　　　　[刺杀罗德利哥。]

罗德利哥	噢,该死的伊阿古! 噢,没人性的狗!	
伊阿古	暗中伤人?　这帮血腥的盗贼呢?	
	全城多么寂静! 嗬,凶杀,凶杀!	
	你们是谁?　是好人还是坏人?	65
罗德威克	先考验我们,再做评价。	
伊阿古	罗德威克先生?	
罗德威克	正是。	
伊阿古	我求您原谅:凯西奥被恶棍刺伤。	
葛莱西亚诺	凯西奥?	70
伊阿古	怎么样,兄弟?	
凯西奥	我的腿被砍成两截。	
伊阿古	哎呀,上帝保佑!	
	掌灯,绅士们,我用睡衣包扎。	

　　　　　　　　　　　比安卡上。

比安卡	这是怎么回事,嗬?　谁在喊叫?	
伊阿古	谁在喊叫?	
比安卡	噢,我亲爱的凯西奥!	75

---

　　59. 进来（Come in）:伊阿古已进入棚内,去救助凯西奥。　64. 伊阿古喜欢喧嚣:见 1.1.66 及以下,2.3.153。　73. 掌灯（Light）:他熄灭自己的火把,好腾出手来给凯西奥包扎伤口。

		My sweet Cassio! O Cassio, Cassio, Cassio!
	Iago	O notable strumpet! Cassio, may you suspect
		Who they should be that have thus mangled you?
	Cassio	No.
80	**Gratiano**	I am sorry to find you thus;
		I have been to seek you.
	Iago	Lend me a garter. So. —O for a chair
		To bear him easily hence!
	Bianca	Alas, he faints! O Cassio, Cassio, Cassio!
85	**Iago**	Gentlemen all, I do suspect this trash
		To be a party in this injury.
		Patience awhile, good Cassio. Come, come,
		Lend me a light. Know we this face, or no?
		Alas, my friend and my dear countryman,
90		Roderigo? No—yes sure! —O heaven, Roderigo!
	Gratiano	What, of Venice?
	Iago	Even he, sir. Did you know him?
	Gratiano	Know him? Ay.
	Iago	Signior Gratiano? I cry you gentle pardon:
		These bloody accidents must excuse my manners
		That so neglected you.
95	**Gratiano**	I am glad to see you.
	Iago	How do you, Cassio? O, a chair, a chair!
	Gratiano	Roderigo?
	Iago	He, he, 'tis he. [*A chair is brought in.*] O, that's well said,
		the chair.
		Some good man bear him carefully from hence,

	我可爱的凯西奥！噢,凯西奥,凯西奥!	
伊阿古	噢,著名的娼妇！凯西奥,您是否	
	清楚会是谁竟把您伤成这样?	
凯西奥	不清楚。	
葛莱西亚诺	我很难过看到您这样;	80
	我一直在到处找您。	
伊阿古	给我个袜带。 对。 ——噢,但愿有副	
	担架把他轻轻抬走!	
比安卡	哎呀,他晕了！噢,凯西奥,凯西奥!	
伊阿古	诸位绅士,我怀疑这个贱货	85
	与这次伤亡事故有所牵连。	
	且忍耐一下,好凯西奥。 快,快,	
	拿灯来。 我们是否认识这副面孔?	
	哎呀,我的朋友和亲爱的同胞,	
	罗德利哥? 不——没错! ——噢天哪,罗德利哥!	90
葛莱西亚诺	什么,威尼斯的?	
伊阿古	是他,先生。 您认识?	
葛莱西亚诺	认识? 是的。	
伊阿古	葛莱西亚诺先生? 我求您原谅:	
	这些血腥的事故迫使我忽略了	
	对您的礼节。	
葛莱西亚诺	见到您我很高兴。	95
伊阿古	您怎么样了,凯西奥? 噢,担架,担架!	
葛莱西亚诺	罗德利哥?	
伊阿古	是他,是他。 [担架抬上。]噢,做得好,	
	担架来了。	
	来几个壮汉把他小心地抬走,	

82. 袜带(garter):作绷带或吊带。

| 100 | | I'll fetch the general's surgeon. [*To Bianca.*]For you, mistress, |

100   I'll fetch the general's surgeon. [*To Bianca.*]For you, mistress,

                      Save you your labour. —He that lies slain here, Cassio,

                      Was my dear friend. What malice was between you?

Cassio   None in the world, nor do I know the man.

Iago   [*to Bianca.*]What, look you pale? —O, bear him out o'th' air.

105   —Stay you, good gentlemen. —Look you pale, mistress?

                      —Do you perceive the gastness of her eye?

                      —Nay, if you stare, we shall hear more anon.

                      —Behold her well, I pray you, look upon her:

                      Do you see, gentlemen? Nay, guiltiness will speak,

                      Though tongues were out of use.

Enter Emilia.

110 **Emilia**   'Las, what's the matter?

                      What's the matter, husband?

Iago   Cassio hath here been set on in the dark

                      By Roderigo and fellows that are 'scaped:

                      He's almost slain, and Roderigo dead.

115 **Emilia**   Alas, good gentleman! Alas, good Cassio!

Iago   This is the fruits of whoring. Prithee, Emilia,

                      Go know of Cassio where he supped tonight.

                      What, do you shake at that?

Bianca   He supped at my house, but I therefore shake not.

120 **Iago**   O, did he so? I charge you, go with me.

Emilia   O fie upon thee, strumpet!

Bianca   I am no strumpet

	我去叫将军的医生。〔向比安卡。〕至于您,小姐,	100
	不用您管了。 ——死去的这位,凯西奥,	
	是我亲爱的朋友。 你们有啥冤仇?	
凯西奥	毫无冤仇,我也不认识这人。	
伊阿古	〔向比安卡〕怎么,脸色苍白? ——噢,抬他进屋。	
	——先别走,绅士们。 ——脸色苍白,小姐?	105
	——你们是否看出她眼神有些惧怕?	
	——不,您若注视我们,很快就会明了。	
	——好好看看她,我求你们,看看她:	
	看出了,绅士们? 不,罪人自会露馅,	
	尽管舌头不作发言。	

爱米利娅上。

爱米利娅	唉,怎么了?	110
	怎么回事,丈夫?	
伊阿古	凯西奥在黑暗中被罗德利哥	
	以及几个在逃的家伙暗算:	
	他几乎遇害,罗德利哥已死。	
爱米利娅	哎呀,好绅士们! 哎呀,好凯西奥!	115
伊阿古	这是嫖娼的后果。 求您,爱米利娅,	
	去问问凯西奥今晚在何处用餐。	
	怎么,您为此心虚?	
比安卡	他在我家晚餐,可我并不心虚。	
伊阿古	啊,是真的? 我命令您,快跟我走。	120
爱米利娅	噢,你该死,婊子!	
比安卡	我不是婊子。	

---

101. 不用您管了(save…labour):比安卡在照护凯西奥(Ridley)。 104. 抬他进屋(bear…air):据信新鲜空气对伤口有害(Bevington)。 107. 注视(stare):伊阿古在假装对比安卡的惊慌失措进行阐释,即不打自招(an involuntary confession of guilt)(Bevington)。

But of life as honest as you, that thus

Abuse me.

Emilia   As I? Foh, fie upon thee!

Iago   Kind gentlemen, let's go see poor Cassio dressed.

125   Come, mistress, you must tell's another tale.

Emilia, run you to the citadel

And tell my lord and lady what hath happed.

—Will you go on afore? —This is the night

That either makes me or fordoes me quite.   *Exeunt.*

我这人跟您一样忠诚，竟然

这样骂我。

爱米利娅　　　　　跟我一样？　呸，你该死！

伊阿古　　好绅士，咱们去给凯西奥包扎。

来，小姐，您要给我们另换说词。　　　　　　　　125

爱米利娅，您跑步前去城堡，

告诉将军和夫人所发生的事情。

——你们能否先走一步？　——这个黑夜

要么将我成全，要么将我毁灭。

　　　　　　　　　　　　同下。

---

122. 忠诚（honest）：贞洁（sexually honest）。　若泛泛而论，她的确要比爱米利娅更为诚实，因为爱米利娅曾就手帕一事撒谎（3. 4. 24）。

SCENE II

Enter Othello, with a light. Desdemona in her bed [asleep].

Othello   It is the cause, it is the cause, my soul!

Let me not name it to you, you chaste stars!

It is the cause. Yet I'll not shed her blood,

Nor scar that whiter skin of hers than snow

5   And smooth as monumental alabaster:

Yet she must die, else she'll betray more men.

Put out the light, and then put out the light!

If I quench thee, thou flaming minister,

I can again thy former light restore

10   Should I repent me. But once put out thy light,

Thou cunning'st pattern of excelling nature,

I know not where is that Promethean heat

That can thy light relume: when I have plucked the rose,

I cannot give it vital growth again,

15   It needs must wither: I'll smell thee on the tree;

O balmy breath, that dost almost persuade

第二场

奥赛罗持火把上。苔丝狄蒙娜在床上［熟睡］。

奥赛罗　　理由正当,理由正当,我的灵魂!

别让我对你们明说,贞洁的星辰,

理由正当。　可我不会让她流血,

也不会让她那比雪还要白皙、

石碑般平滑的皮肤留下疤痕:　　　　　　　　5

但她必死,不然会骗更多男人。

先熄灭烛光,再熄灭生命之光!

若将你熄灭,你这光明的使者,

我可以将你的亮光重新点燃,

假如反悔。　可一旦熄灭你的光亮,　　　　10

你这超越自然的精美典范,

不知哪里有普罗米修斯火种

能让你光亮复燃:若掐断玫瑰,

我就不可能再让它继续生长,

它必然枯萎。　我要在枝上吻你;　　　　15

噢,芳香的气息,几乎说服正义

5.2.　1. 理由正当（It is the cause）:从下一行可以看出,所谓的理由（cause）是指苔丝狄蒙娜的不忠（unchastity）。　值得注意的是,正如第 6 行所示,第 17-19 行所证实的那样,他认为自己将要采取的行动是一种不可避免的正义之举,而不再是一种报复行为（Ridley）。　灵魂（my soul）:在《圣经》和古典文学作品里,对自己的灵魂讲话颇为常见,如"创世纪"49 章 6 节等。2. 星辰（stars）:各种天体,包括代表贞洁的月亮。　按希腊神话,宙斯所追求的女子若不顺从,则被变为星辰。　12. 普罗米修斯（Promethean）:莎氏似将两则有关普罗米修斯的希腊神话合而为一:（1）他把火从天上带给人类;（2）他是人类的创造者（Mowat）。　16-7. 正义女神（Justice）:利剑与天平是正义之神（传统上为女性）的象征。　天平用以衡量证据,利剑用以惩罚。

Justice to break her sword! Once more, once more:

Be thus when thou art dead and I will kill thee

And love thee after. Once more, and that's the last.

He [*smells, then*] *kisses her.*

20 So sweet was ne'er so fatal. I must weep,

But they are cruel tears. This sorrow's heavenly,

It strikes where it doth love. She wakes.

Desdemona Who's there? Othello?

Othello   Ay, Desdemona.

Desdemona Will you come to bed, my lord?

Othello Have you prayed tonight, Desdemon?

25 **Desdemona**   Ay, my lord.

Othello If you bethink yourself of any crime

Unreconciled as yet to heaven and grace,

Solicit for it straight.

Desdemona Alack, my lord, what may you mean by that?

30 **Othello** Well, do it, and be brief; I will walk by.

I would not kill thy unprepared spirit,

No, heaven forfend, I would not kill thy soul.

Desdemona Talk you of killing?

Othello   Ay, I do.

Desdemona   Then, heaven,

Have mercy on me!

Othello   Amen, with all my heart.

35 **Desdemona** If you say so, I hope you will not kill me.

女神将利剑折断！ 再闻闻,再闻闻:

你死后若这样美丽,我就要杀你

然后再爱你。　再闻闻,最后一次。

他[闻,随后]吻她。

如此甜美不该如此致命。　我要落泪,　　　　　　　　　20

却是无情的泪水。　这是上帝的悲伤,

因为爱心才会责罚。　她醒了。

苔丝狄蒙娜	是谁？　奥赛罗？
奥赛罗	没错,苔丝狄蒙娜。
苔丝狄蒙娜	您要歇息吗,夫君？
奥赛罗	今晚祷告了,苔丝狄蒙？
苔丝狄蒙娜	是的,夫君。

25

奥赛罗	您若想起自己犯下什么罪过

尚未向上帝坦白并得到宽恕,

赶快就此祈祷。

苔丝狄蒙娜	哎呀,夫君,您这是什么意思？
奥赛罗	好了,祈祷,要简短:我在附近走走。

30

我不想杀害你未做准备的心灵,

不,上帝保佑,不想诅咒你灵魂。

苔丝狄蒙娜	您在说杀害？
奥赛罗	是的,在说。
苔丝狄蒙娜	愿上帝,

怜悯我吧！

奥赛罗	阿门,我衷心祝愿！
苔丝狄蒙娜	您若这么说,希望您不会杀我。

35

21-2. 这是……责罚（This…love）:参考《圣经》"箴言"3章12节:因为耶和华所爱的,他必责备。　正如父亲责备所喜爱的儿子。　31-2. 他若将她未做准备的心灵杀害,就意味着"杀害"了她的灵魂,从而将其送往地狱。

	Othello	Hum!
	Desdemona	And yet I fear you, for you're fatal then

Othello   Hum!

Desdemona   And yet I fear you, for you're fatal then

When your eyes roll so. Why I should fear I know not,

Since guiltiness I know not. But yet I feel I fear.

Othello   Think on thy sins.

40 **Desdemona**   They are loves I bear to you.

Othello   Ay, and for that thou diest.

Desdemona   That death's unnatural that kills for loving.

Alas, why gnaw you so your nether lip?

Some bloody passion shakes your very frame,

45   These are portents: but yet I hope, I hope

They are not point on me.

Othello   Peace, and be still.

Desdemona   I will. So: what's the matter?

Othello   That handkerchief

Which I so loved and gave thee, thou gavest

To Cassio.

Desdemona   No, by my life and soul:

Send for the man and ask him.

50 **Othello**   Sweet soul, take heed,

Take heed of perjury. Thou art on thy death-bed.

Desdemona   I? —But not yet to die!

Othello   Yes, presently.

Therefore confess thee freely of thy sin,

For to deny each article with oath

55   Cannot remove nor choke the strong conception

奥赛罗	哼!
苔丝狄蒙娜	但我怕您,您这样瞪着眼睛
	表明可以致命。 不清楚为何会怕,
	因为我问心无愧。 可我觉得害怕。
奥赛罗	想想你的罪过。
苔丝狄蒙娜	只因我太爱您。
奥赛罗	没错,你要为此而死。
苔丝狄蒙娜	因为爱您而被杀这不近人情。
	唉,您为何那样咬您的下唇?
	嗜杀的怒气使您躯体颤动,
	这都是凶兆:但我希望,希望
	它们不是冲我而来。
奥赛罗	安静,别动。
苔丝狄蒙娜	好吧。 究竟是怎么回事?
奥赛罗	那块手帕,
	我如此喜爱并赠送与你,你却
	给了凯西奥。
苔丝狄蒙娜	没有,凭生命和灵魂起誓:
	派人叫他来问问。
奥赛罗	亲爱的,要当心,
	当心伪证。 你已躺在临终床上。
苔丝狄蒙娜	我? ——我可不想死去!
奥赛罗	是的,立刻。
	因此你要毫无保留地认罪,
	因为你发誓否认每一项指控,
	也无法消除或窒息我为这种

40

45

50

55

---

40. 太爱您(loves…you):暗指爱人胜过爱上帝这种罪过(An allusion to the sin of loving a human being more than God)。

That I do groan withal. Thou art to die.

Desdemona   Then Lord have mercy on me!

Othello   I say, amen.

Desdemona   And have you mercy too. I never did

Offend you in my life, never loved Cassio

60   But with such general warranty of heaven

As I might love: I never gave him token.

Othello   By heaven, I saw my handkerchief in's hand!

O perjured woman, thou dost stone my heart

And makest me call what I intend to do

65   A murder, which I thought a sacrifice!

I saw the handkerchief.

Desdemona   He found it then,

I never gave it him. Send for him hither,

Let him confess the truth.

Othello   He hath confessed.

Desdemona   What, my lord?

Othello   That he hath—ud's death! —used thee.

Desdemona   How? Unlawfully?

Othello   Ay.

70 **Desdemona**   He will not say so.

Othello   No, his mouth is stopped. Honest Iago

Hath ta'en order for't.

Desdemona   O, my fear interprets!

What, is he dead?

Othello   Had all his hair been lives,

	念头所受的折磨。　你要死去。	
苔丝狄蒙娜	愿上帝怜悯我吧！	
奥赛罗	我说阿门！	
苔丝狄蒙娜	您也怜悯我吧。　我一生从未	
	冒犯过您，从未爱过凯西奥，	
	除了上帝准许我怀有的那种	60
	纯洁之情：我从未给过他信物。	
奥赛罗	天哪，我看见他拿着我的手帕！	
	噢，作伪证的女人，你逼我心硬，	
	我本想把你当作赎罪的献祭，	
	你却迫使我将它叫作凶杀！	65
	我看见那块手帕。	
苔丝狄蒙娜	那是他捡的，	
	我从未给他。　您派人叫他前来，	
	让他供认真相吧。	
奥赛罗	他已供认。	
苔丝狄蒙娜	什么，夫君？	
奥赛罗	他说——该死！——用过你。	
苔丝狄蒙娜	什么？　用过我？	
奥赛罗	没错。	
苔丝狄蒙娜	他不会这么说。	70
奥赛罗	不会，他已闭嘴。　诚实的伊阿古	
	为此采取了措施。	
苔丝狄蒙娜	噢，我担心不妙！	
	怎么，他死了？	
奥赛罗	哪怕他生命多如毛发，	

---

56. 念头（conception）：（1）相信你不忠（belief in your guilt），（2）我心中的计划（plan in my mind）（Bevington）。　70. 用过我（unlawfully）：通奸（In adultery）（Gayle Holste; Shakespare Made Easy, 2002; 下称"Holste"）。　——译者附注。

My great revenge had stomach for them all.

75 **Desdemona**   Alas, he is betrayed, and I undone.

Othello   Out, strumpet, weep'st thou for him to my face?

Desdemona   O, banish me, my lord, but kill me not!

Othello   Down, strumpet!

Desdemona   Kill me tomorrow, let me live tonight!

80 **Othello**   Nay, if you strive—

Desdemona   But half an hour!

Othello   Being done, there is no pause—

Desdemona   But while I say one prayer!

Othello   It is too late.

Desdemona   O Lord! Lord! Lord!   [*He*] *smothers her.*

Emilia   [*within*] My lord, my lord! What, ho, my lord, my lord!

85 **Othello**   What noise is this? Not dead? Not yet quite dead?

I that am cruel am yet merciful,

I would not have thee linger in thy pain.

So, so.

Emilia   [*within*] What ho! My lord! My lord!

Othello   Who's there?

Emilia   [*within*] O good my lord, I'd speak a word with you.

90 **Othello**   Yes. 'Tis Emilia. —[*to Emilia.*] By and by. —She's dead.

'Tis like she comes to speak of Cassio's death.

The noise was high. Ha, no more moving?

Still as the grave. Shall she come in? Were't good?

I think she stirs again. No—what's best to do?

	我的复仇心也能将其全部吞下。	
苔丝狄蒙娜	哎呀,他遭人陷害,我就此被毁!	75
奥赛罗	呸,婊子,当着我的面为他哭泣?	
苔丝狄蒙娜	噢,流放我吧,夫君,您别杀我!	
奥赛罗	躺下,婊子!	
苔丝狄蒙娜	明天再杀我吧,让我活过今夜!	
奥赛罗	不行,您若反抗——	80
苔丝狄蒙娜	只活半小时!	
奥赛罗	一旦执行,不会暂停——	
苔丝狄蒙娜	让我再祷告一下!	
奥赛罗	为时已晚。	
苔丝狄蒙娜	噢,主啊! 主啊! 主啊!　　　　　　[他]将她闷死。	
爱米利娅	[在内]将军,将军! 怎么了,嗬,将军,将军!	
奥赛罗	是什么声音? 没死? 还没死去?	85
	我很残忍但也有怜悯之心,	
	我不愿让你在痛苦之中拖延。	
	好,好。	
爱米利娅	[在内]怎么了! 将军! 将军!	
奥赛罗	是谁呀?	
爱米利娅	[在内]噢,好将军,我要跟您说话。	
奥赛罗	对,是爱米利娅。 ——[向爱米利娅。]马上。 ——她死了。	90
	可能是她来报告凯西奥的死讯,	
	噪音很大。 哈,你不再动了?	
	死一般寂静。 让她进来? 那好吗?	
	我想她又在动。 不行——咋办才好?	

---

75. 陷害(betrayed):遭到仇人的陷害;奥赛罗以为是"(奸情)败露"(revealed [as her lover])。 76. 当着……哭泣(weep'st…him):他再次误解。 92. 很大(high):室内可以听到外面的吵闹声(所以罗德威克与葛莱西亚诺会在第五幕第一场中前往事发现场)。

95		If she come in, she'll sure speak to my wife.
		My wife, my wife! What wife? I have no wife.
		O insupportable, O heavy hour!
		Methinks it should be now a huge eclipse
		Of sun and moon, and that th'affrighted globe
		Should yawn at alteration.
100	**Emilia**	[*within*] I do beseech you
		That I may speak with you! O good my lord!
	Othello	I had forgot thee: O come in, Emilia.
		Soft, by and by. Let me the curtains draw.
		Where art thou? What's the matter with thee now?

[He unlocks the door.]

Enter Emila.

105	**Emilia**	O my good lord, yonder's foul murders done!
	Othello	What, now?
	Emilia	But now, my lord.
	Othello	It is the very error of the moon,
		She comes more nearer earth than she was wont
		And makes men mad.
110	**Emilia**	Cassio, my lord, hath killed
		A young Venetian, called Roderigo.
	Othello	Roderigo killed? And Cassio killed?
	Emilia	No, Cassio is not killed.
	Othello	Not Cassio killed?

	她若进来,肯定要跟我妻子说话。	95
	我妻子,我妻子! 啥妻子? 我没妻子。	
	噢,难以承受,噢,沉痛的时刻!	
	我想太阳和月亮现在也会	
	变得黯然失色,惊恐的大地	
	为此变故而裂开大口。	

爱米利娅　［在内］　　　　　我求您, 　　　　100
我有话要对您说! 噢,好将军!

奥赛罗　我把你忘了:噢,进来,爱米利娅。
稍等,很快。 让我把床幔拉上。
你在哪里? 你此刻想做什么?

　　　　　　　　　　　　　　［他把门打开。］

　　　　　　　　爱米利娅上。

爱米利娅　噢,好将军,那边发生了凶杀! 　　　105
奥赛罗　什么? 现在?
爱米利娅　刚才,将军。
奥赛罗　这是月亮离开了她的轨道,
她与地球的距离比往常更近,
使人们发疯。
爱米利娅　　　　　凯西奥,将军,杀死了 　　　110
一名叫罗德利哥的威尼斯青年。
奥赛罗　罗德利哥被杀? 凯西奥被杀?
爱米利娅　不,凯西奥没被杀。
奥赛罗　　　　　凯西奥没被杀?

---

100. 变故(alteration):（因苔丝狄蒙娜之死而导致的）改变。 裂开大口(yawn):作为对日食与月食的回应而出现裂口（因地震所致）。 110. 使人们发疯(makes men mad):"精神错乱"(lunacy)这个词本身说明:长期以来人们深信月亮与发疯之间的关联(Ridley)。

Then murder's out of tune, and sweet revenge

Grows harsh.

115 **Desdemona**　　　　　　　O falsely, falsely murdered!

Emilia　　　O lord, what cry is that?

Othello　　　That? What?

Emilia　　　Out and alas, that was my lady's voice:

　　　　　　　　　　　　　　　[*She draws the bed-curtains.*]

Help, help, ho, help! O lady, speak again,

120　　　　　　Sweet Desdemona, O sweet mistress, speak!

Desdemona　　　A guiltless death I die.

Emilia　　　　　　　　　　O, who hath done

This deed?

Desdemona　　　　　　　Nobody. I myself. Farewell.

Commend me to my kind lord—O, farewell!　　*She dies.*

Othello　　　Why, how should she be murdered?

Emilia　　　　　　　　　　　　　Alas, who knows?

125 **Othello**　　　You heard her say herself it was not I.

Emilia　　　She said so; I must needs report the truth.

Othello　　　She's like a liar gone to burning hell:

'Twas I that killed her.

Emilia　　　　　　　　　O, the more angel she,

And you the blacker devil!

130 **Othello**　　　She turned to folly, and she was a whore.

Emilia　　　Thou dost belie her, and thou art a devil.

Othello　　　She was false as water.

Emilia　　　　　　　　　Thou art rash as fire to say

That she was false. O, she was heavenly true!

Othello　　　Cassio did top her: ask thy husband else.

说明凶杀跑了调,动听的复仇

变得刺耳。

苔丝狄蒙娜　　　　　　噢,冤枉,死得冤枉!　　　　　　115

爱米利娅　噢主啊,是谁在喊?

奥赛罗　在喊?　什么?

爱米利娅　哎呀,天哪,那是夫人的声音:

　　　　　　　　　　　　　　　　[她拉开床幔。]

救命,救命,嗬,救命! 噢夫人,说话呀,

可爱的苔丝狄蒙娜,噢,好夫人,说话!　　　　　　120

苔丝狄蒙娜　我是无辜而死。

爱米利娅　　　　　　　　噢,是谁干的

这种行径?

苔丝狄蒙娜　　　　　没有谁。 我自己。 永别了。

向我亲爱的丈夫致意——噢,永别了!　　　　　死去。

奥赛罗　唉,她怎么会被杀害?

爱米利娅　　　　　　　　谁知道呢?

奥赛罗　您听见她亲口说出可不是我。　　　　　　125

爱米利娅　她这样说过;我必须报告真相。

奥赛罗　她像个跌入炽烈地狱的撒谎者。

是我杀了她。

爱米利娅　　　　　噢,她更是个天使,

您更是个恶魔!

奥赛罗　她放荡不羁,她是一个娼妓。　　　　　　130

爱米利娅　你造谣中伤,你是一个魔鬼。

奥赛罗　她水一般轻浮。

爱米利娅　　　　　　你火一样暴躁,

竟说她轻浮。 噢,她可是情真意切!

奥赛罗　凯西奥与她通奸:不信问你丈夫。

135   O, I were damned beneath all depth in hell

But that I did proceed upon just grounds

To this extremity. Thy husband knew it all.

Emilia   My husband?

Othello   Thy husband.

Emilia   That she was false?

To wedlock?

Othello   Ay, with Cassio. Had she been true,

140   If heaven would make me such another world

Of one entire and perfect chrysolite,

I'd not have sold her for it.

Emilia   My husband?

Othello   Ay, 'twas he that told me on her first;

An honest man he is, and hates the slime

That sticks on filthy deeds.

Emilia   My husband?

145 **Othello**   What needs

This iterance, woman? I say thy husband.

Emilia   O mistress, villainy hath made mocks with love!

My husband say she was false!

Othello   He, woman;

I say thy husband: dost understand the word?

150   My friend thy husband, honest, honest Iago.

Emilia   If he say so, may his pernicious soul

Rot half a grain a day! He lies to th' heart:

She was too fond of her most filthy bargain!

噢,把我罚入地狱的万丈深渊,　　　　　　　　　　135

我采取这种极端行为若不是

有理有据。　你丈夫知道一切。

爱米利娅　　我的丈夫?

奥赛罗　　　　　　　　你的丈夫。

爱米利娅　　　　　　　　　　　说她不忠?

与人通奸?

奥赛罗　　　　　　　　　对,与凯西奥。　她若贞洁,

即使上帝给我另造一个世界,　　　　　　　　140

全由完美无缺的黄宝石组成,

我也不会拿她兑换。

爱米利娅　　　　　　　　　　我的丈夫?

奥赛罗　　对,是他首先告诉我她的不忠:

他是个诚实人,痛恨那些污秽

邪恶的行径。

爱米利娅　　　　　　　　我的丈夫?

奥赛罗　　　　　　　　　　干吗要　　　　　　　　145

这样重复,女人?　我说是你丈夫。

爱米利娅　　噢,夫人,是邪恶将爱情给嘲弄!

我丈夫说她不忠?

奥赛罗　　　　　　　　　是他,女人;

我说是你丈夫:你懂这个词吗?

我朋友你丈夫,诚诚实实的伊阿古。　　　　　150

爱米利娅　　他若这么说,愿他那邪恶的灵魂

每天烂掉一点儿!他胡说八道:

她太痴情于她的污秽丈夫!

---

152. 一点儿(grain):苟延残喘最为悲惨(A slow death is the worst):参考 4. 1. 175 "连杀九年"。

	Othello	Ha!
155	Emilia	Do thy worst:
		This deed of thine is no more worthy heaven
		Than thou wast worthy her.
	Othello	Peace, you were best!
	Emilia	Thou hast not half that power to do me harm
		As I have to be hurt. O gull, O dolt,
160		As ignorant as dirt! Thou hast done a deed

[*He threatens her with his sword.*]

—I care not for thy sword, I'll make thee known,

Though I lost twenty lives. Help, help, ho, help!

The Moor hath killed my mistress! Murder, murder!

Enter Montano, Gratiano and Iago.

	Montano	What is the matter? How now, general?
165	Emilia	O, are you come, Iago? You have done well,
		That men must lay their murders on your neck.
	Gratiano	What is the matter?
	Emilia	Disprove this villain, if thou be'st a man;
		He says thou told'st him that his wife was false,
170		I know thou didst not, thou'rt not such a villain.
		Speak, for my heart is full.
	Iago	I told him what I thought, and told no more
		Than what he found himself was apt and true.
	Emilia	But did you ever tell him she was false?
175	Iago	I did.
	Emilia	You told a lie, an odious, damned lie!
		Upon my soul, a lie, a wicked lie!

奥赛罗	哈！	
爱米利娅	随你的便吧：	155
	你这种行径既不配进入天堂，	
	也不配她的爱情。	
奥赛罗	您最好住口！	
爱米利娅	即使你竭尽全力加害于我，	
	也不够我忍受。　噢傻子，噢，呆子，	
	粪便一般无知！你干了件蠢事	160

[他挥剑威胁她。]

	——我不怕你的剑，我要把你揭露，	
	哪怕死去二十次。　救命，嗬，救命！	
	摩尔人杀害了夫人！凶杀，凶杀！	

蒙塔诺、葛莱西亚诺与伊阿古上。

蒙塔诺	这是怎么回事？　怎么了，将军？	
爱米利娅	噢，您来了，伊阿古？　您干的好事，	165
	别人能把凶杀栽到您的头上！	
葛莱西亚诺	这是怎么回事？	
爱米利娅	反驳这个恶棍，你若是个男人；	
	他说你告诉他他妻子不忠，	
	我知道你不会，你不是这种恶棍。	170
	快说，因为我心里发堵。	
伊阿古	我告诉过他我的想法，那都是	
	他自己觉得可能并且真实。	
爱米利娅	您是否对他说过他妻子不忠？	
伊阿古	说过。	175
爱米利娅	那是谎言，可恶、该死的谎言！	
	以灵魂起誓，谎言，邪恶的谎言！	

	She false with Cassio? Did you say with Cassio?
Iago	With Cassio, mistress. Go to, charm your tongue.
180 **Emilia**	I will not charm my tongue, I am bound to speak:
	My mistress here lies murdered in her bed.
All	O heavens forfend!
Emilia	And your reports have set the murder on.
Othello	Nay, stare not, masters, it is true indeed.
185 **Gratiano**	'Tis a strange truth.
Montano	O monstrous act!
Emilia	Villainy, villainy, villainy!
	I think upon't, I think I smell't, O villainy!
	I thought so then: I'll kill myself for grief!
190	O villainy, villainy!
Iago	What, are you mad? I charge you, get you home.
Emilia	Good gentlemen, let me have leave to speak.
	'Tis proper I obey him—but not now.
	Perchance, Iago, I will ne'er go home.
195 **Othello**	O! O! O! *Othello falls on the bed.*
Emilia	Nay, lay thee down and roar,
	For thou hast killed the sweetest innocent
	That e'er did lift up eye.
Othello	O, she was foul.
	I scarce did know you, uncle: there lies your niece
200	Whose breath, indeed, these hands have newly stopped;
	I know this act shows horrible and grim.

　　　　　　　　　她与凯西奥通奸？　您说与凯西奥？

伊阿古　　　　与凯西奥,夫人。　得啦,你闭嘴吧。

爱米利娅　　　我不会闭嘴,我有义务诉说:　　　　　　　　180

　　　　　　　　　夫人已被杀害,现躺在床上。

众人　　　　　噢,上帝保佑!

爱米利娅　　　是你的谎言导致了这场凶杀。

奥赛罗　　　　不用惊讶,先生们,千真万确。

葛莱西亚诺　　真难以置信。　　　　　　　　　　　　　　185

蒙塔诺　　　　噢,骇人听闻!

爱米利娅　　　罪恶,罪恶,罪恶!

　　　　　　　　　我想起来啦,我有所察觉,罪恶啊!

　　　　　　　　　果不出所料:我真是悲痛欲绝!

　　　　　　　　　噢,罪恶,罪恶!　　　　　　　　　　　190

伊阿古　　　　什么,你疯了?　我命令你,快回家。

爱米利娅　　　诸位先生,请让我把话说完。

　　　　　　　　　我本该顺服于他——但不是现在。

　　　　　　　　　也许,伊阿古,我从此不再回家。

奥赛罗　　　　噢!噢!噢!　　　　　　　奥赛罗倒在床上。195

爱米利娅　　　好,你倒下怒吼吧,

　　　　　　　　　因为你杀害了世上曾有过的

　　　　　　　　　最可爱天真的女士!

奥赛罗　　　　　　　　　　噢,她不贞洁!

　　　　　　　　　我几乎没认出您,叔父:您的侄女,

　　　　　　　　　正是被这双手刚断送了气息;　　　　　200

　　　　　　　　　我知道该举动显得残忍可怕。

---

　　189. 果不出所料(I thought so then):可指"她想到了4. 2. 132行及以下的情况,即:哪位流氓有意诽谤苔丝狄蒙娜";也可指"她'当时'(then)想到了伊阿古会对此负责"(详见《序言》"爱米利娅"一节)。　　193. 参考《圣经》"以弗所书"5章24节:教会怎么顺服基督,妻子也要怎样凡事顺服丈夫(as the Church is subject unto Christ, likewise the wives to their own husbands in all things)。

Gratiano	Poor Desdemona, I am glad thy father's dead;
	Thy match was mortal to him, and pure grief
	Shore his old thread in twain. Did he live now,
205	This sight would make him do a desperate turn,
	Yea, curse his better angel from his side,
	And fall to reprobance.
Othello	'Tis pitiful; but yet Iago knows
	That she with Cassio hath the act of shame
210	A thousand times committed. Cassio confessed it,
	And she did gratify his amorous works
	With that recognizance and pledge of love
	Which I first gave her: I saw it in his hand,
	It was a handkerchief, an antique token
215	My father gave my mother.
Emilia	O God! O heavenly God!
Iago	Zounds, hold your peace!
Emilia	'Twill out, 'twill out! I peace?
	No, I will speak as liberal as the north.
	Let heaven and men and devils, let them all,
220	All, all cry shame against me, yet I'll speak.
Iago	Be wise, and get you home.
Emilia	I will not. [*Iago tries to stab Emilia.*]
Gratiano	Fie! Your sword upon a woman?
Emilia	O thou dull Moor, that handkerchief thou speak'st of

葛莱西亚诺	可怜的苔丝狄蒙,幸亏你父亲死了;
	你的婚姻使他伤命,极度的悲痛
	将其生命线一刀两断。　他若在世,
	这种场景会使他孤注一掷, 205
	是的,将护卫天使从身旁骂走,
	从而遭受诅咒。
奥赛罗	这非常可悲;但伊阿古知道,
	她与凯西奥做过的无耻勾当
	有上千次之多。　凯西奥已承认, 210
	她为了报答他的爱抚行动,
	竟将我最初给她的象征爱情的
	信物给他:我见他手里拿着,
	是一块手帕,一件古代的礼物,
	由我父亲送给母亲。 215
爱米利娅	上帝啊,神圣的上帝!
伊阿古	该死,闭嘴!
爱米利娅	会揭穿,会揭穿,我闭嘴?
	不,我要像北风那样自由发言。
	哪怕上天、人类和魔鬼,他们全都,
	全都,全都骂我羞耻,我也要说。 220
伊阿古	明智点儿,快回家。
爱米利娅	我不回。　　　　　　[伊阿古欲刺杀爱米利娅。]
葛莱西亚诺	呸!竟用剑对付女人?
爱米利娅	噢愚钝的摩尔,你说的那块手帕

204. 生命线(thread):在希腊神话中,生命由一根丝线表示,该丝线由克洛索(Clotho)纺织,由拉基西斯(Lachesis)丈量,由阿特洛波斯(Atropos)剪断。　她们被称为命运三女神(the Fates)(Mowat)。　215. 这与3. 4. 57及以下的内容自相矛盾。　有人认为他当时是想吓唬苔丝狄蒙娜;不过,该矛盾也许是一个疏忽(an oversight)。　220. 羞耻(shame):因为她蔑视自己的丈夫?

225

I found by fortune and did give my husband,

For often, with a solemn earnestness

—More than indeed belonged to such a trifle—

He begged of me to steal't.

Iago   Villainous whore!

Emilia   She give it Cassio? No, alas, I found it,

And I did give't my husband.

Iago   Filth, thou liest!

230 **Emilia**   By heaven I do not, I do not, gentlemen!

O murderous coxcomb, what should such a fool

Do with so good a wife?

[*Othello runs at Iago. Iago stabs his wife.*]

Othello   Are there not stones in heaven

But what serves for the thunder? Precious villain!

Gratiano   The woman falls, sure he hath killed his wife.

235 **Emilia**   Ay, ay; O lay me by my mistress' side.   *Exit Iago.*

Gratiano   He's gone, but his wife's killed.

Montano   'Tis a notorious villain. Take you this weapon

Which I have here recovered from the Moor;

Come, guard the door without, let him not pass,

240

But kill him rather. I'll after that same villain,

For 'tis a damned slave.   *Exeunt Montano and Gratiano.*

Othello   I am not valiant neither,

But every puny whipster gets my sword.

是我碰巧捡到并给了我丈夫，

因为他五次三番一本正经　　　　　　　　　　　225

——对这种物品本不该如此认真——

求我把它偷走。

伊阿古　　　　　　　　邪恶的娼妇！

爱米利娅　她给了凯西奥？　不，唉，是我捡到

并把它给了我丈夫。

伊阿古　　　　　　　　贱货，你撒谎！

爱米利娅　发誓我没撒谎，没撒谎，先生们！　　　230

噢残忍的蠢货，你这傻瓜怎配

这样的贤妻？

　　　　　　　　[奥赛罗冲向伊阿古。伊阿古刺杀妻子。]

奥赛罗　　　　　　难道雷神只有

雷鸣没有霹雳？　十足的恶棍！

葛莱西亚诺　这女人倒了，定是他刺杀了妻子。

爱米利娅　是，是；噢，把我放在夫人身旁！　　　　　伊阿古下。235

葛莱西亚诺　他跑了，可他妻子已死。

蒙塔诺　歹毒的恶棍。　您拿上这件武器，

是我从摩儿身上取下来的；

快，从外面把住门，宁可杀死他，

也别让他通过。　我去追这个恶棍，　　　　　　　240

这个该死的小人。　　　　　　蒙塔诺与葛莱西亚诺下。

奥赛罗　　　　　　　我不再勇猛，

每一个毛孩子都可使我缴械。

---

241. 不再勇猛（not valiant neither）：他好像是在表达自己的思绪：我是个"愚钝的摩尔"，我未能杀死伊阿古，我是个失败者——而且"我也不再勇猛"。　他已不再是1. 3. 48-9所说的那位"英勇的奥赛罗"。　一种自我评估的进程业已开始。

But why should honour outlive honesty?

Let it go all.

Emilia   What did thy song bode, lady?

245 Hark, canst thou hear me? I will play the swan

And die in music. [*Sings.*] *Willow, willow, willow.*

—Moor, she was chaste, she loved thee, cruel Moor,

So come my soul to bliss as I speak true!

So speaking as I think, alas, I die.   *She dies.*

250 **Othello** I have another weapon in this chamber,

It is a sword of Spain, the ice-brook's temper;

O, here it is. Uncle, I must come forth.

Gratiano [*within*] If thou attempt it, it will cost thee dear;

Thou hast no weapon, and perforce must suffer.

255 **Othello** Look in upon me then, and speak with me,

Or, naked as I am, I will assault thee.

Enter Gratiano.

Gratiano What is the matter?

Othello   Behold, I have a weapon,

A better never did itself sustain

Upon a soldier's thigh. I have seen the day

体面已失,何必在乎身后之名?

由它去吧。

爱米利娅　　　　　您的歌预示什么,夫人?

听,您能听见我吗? 我要学天鹅, 245

临终时唱歌。 〔唱。〕杨柳,杨柳,杨柳。

——摩尔,她贞洁,她爱你,残忍的摩尔,

我灵魂升天,因为我说真话!

我是心口如一,哎呀,我死了! 死去。

奥赛罗　　我的房间里还有一件武器, 250

一把西班牙利剑,用冰水锻炼;

噢,就是它。 叔父,我这就出去。

葛莱西亚诺　〔在内〕你若想尝试,会付出高昂代价;

你没有武器,因此你定会受伤。

奥赛罗　　那你进来看看,跟我说说话, 255

尽管我手无寸铁,依然会攻击。

葛莱西亚诺上。

葛莱西亚诺　怎么回事?

奥赛罗　　　　　　请看,我有件武器,

再也没有更好的利剑曾挂在

一位兵士的腰间。 当年我曾

---

243. 体面……之名(why…honesty):体面人生中真正意义上的体面既已丧失,何必还在乎名声(why should any concern for reputation remain active when honour in the true sense of an honourable life has been lost?)(Ridley)。 光彩的名声为何会比光彩本身更为持久(why should the reputation of being honorable outlast honor itself)(Mowat)。 245. 听……我吗(Hark…me):是指一种信念,即:死者的灵魂会在其尸体附近逗留片刻。 245-6. 学天鹅……唱歌(play…music):像是谚语,据说天鹅会在临终时歌唱(Mowat)。 251. 西班牙以铸造利剑而著称(即托莱多剑[Toledo blades])。 冰水(ice-brook's):可能指铸剑过程中的淬火用水。"诸如塔霍河(Tagus)之类的西班牙河流,因为源于融化的雪水,据信可对西班牙利剑的品质有所裨益"。

260   That with this little arm and this good sword

I have made my way through more impediments

Than twenty times your stop: but, O vain boast,

Who can control his fate? 'Tis not so now.

Be not afraid, though you do see me weaponed:

265   Here is my journey's end, here is my butt

And very sea-mark of my utmost sail.

Do you go back dismayed? 'Tis a lost fear:

Man but a rush against Othello's breast

And he retires. Where should Othello go?

270   Now: how dost thou look now? O ill-starred wench,

Pale as thy smock. When we shall meet at compt,

This look of thine will hurl my soul from heaven,

And fiends will snatch at it. Cold, cold, my girl,

Even like thy chastity. O cursed, cursed slave!

275   Whip me, ye devils,

From the possession of this heavenly sight!

Blow me about in winds, roast me in sulphur,

Wash me in steep-down gulfs of liquid fire!

O Desdemon! Dead, Desdemon. Dead! O, O!

凭借这只手臂和这把利剑，　　　　　　　　　260

冲破了远超您所能设置的

二十倍的阻拦：噢，自我吹嘘！

谁能掌控命运？　现已今非昔比。

别怕，尽管您见我佩有武器：

这是我旅程的终点，我的归宿，　　　　　　265

这是我最远航程的终极边缘。

您因恐慌而后退？　虚惊而已：

用一根灯草刺向奥赛罗的胸脯，

他都会退去。　奥赛罗该去何方？

唉：看看你的脸色，不幸的女子，　　　　　　270

布一般苍白！审判日我们相见时，

你这面容会将我灵魂从天堂抛下，

让魔鬼捉住。　冰冷，冰冷，我的女人，

犹如你的贞洁。　噢，该死的小人！

抽我，魔鬼们，　　　　　　　　　　　　275

别让我享有这种神圣的场景！

让我随风飘荡，硫黄中炙烤，

万丈深渊的火海里将我浸泡！

噢，苔丝狄蒙！死了，苔丝狄蒙。　死了！噢，噢！

---

　　265. 这（here）：是指"苔丝狄蒙娜"？　还是指"此处（here in this place）？"。
271. 审判日（compt = account）：文艺复兴时期的画家喜爱这一主题，他们常在画中展示遭受诅咒者被从天堂抛下，在半空中让魔鬼给捉住。　273-4. 冰冷……贞洁（Cold…chastity）：莎士比亚常将贞洁（chastity）与冰冷（coldness）相连，有时将其与炽热的性欲（the heat of lust）形成对立，有时还会将其与戴安娜这位贞洁女神连在一起（Mowat）。　276. 享有（possession）：他不配享有这种神圣的场景：地狱才是他该去的地方。　神圣（heavenly）：该词与"圣洁的苔丝狄蒙娜"相连。　278. 万丈……火海（steep…fire）：也许与《圣经》"路加福音"16章9节及以下有关：有一位在地狱的火焰中遭受折磨的富人，抬头望见拉撒路在亚伯拉罕的怀里。　在他们之间有一道"深渊"（great gulf）。

Enter Lodovico, Montano, Officers with Iago,
prisoner, and Cassio in a chair.

280 **Lodovico**	Where is this rash and most unfortunate man?
Othello	That's he that was Othello? Here I am.
Lodovico	Where is that viper? Bring the villain forth.
Othello	I look down towards his feet, but that's a fable.
	If that thou be'st a devil, I cannot kill thee. [*Wounds Iago.*]
Lodovico	Wrench his sword from him.
285 **Iago**	I bleed, sir, but not killed.
Othello	I am not sorry neither, I'd have thee live:
	For in my sense 'tis happiness to die.
Lodovico	O thou Othello, that wert once so good,
	Fallen in the practice of a cursed slave,
	What shall be said to thee?
290 **Othello**	Why, anything;
	An honorable murderer, if you will,
	For nought I did in hate, but all in honour.
Lodovico	This wretch hath part confessed his villainy.
	Did you and he consent in Cassio's death?
295 **Othello**	Ay.
Cassio	Dear general, I never gave you cause.
Othello	I do believe it, and I ask your pardon.
	Will you, I pray, demand that demi-devil
	Why he hath thus ensnared my soul and body?
300 **Iago**	Demand me nothing. What you know, you know.

罗德威克、蒙塔诺、警官押着伊阿古，

与凯西奥坐担架上。

罗德威克	那位鲁莽的可怜虫现在何处？	280
奥赛罗	是指曾经的奥赛罗？　我在这里。	
罗德威克	那条毒蛇呢？　把那个恶棍带上来。	
奥赛罗	我看一下他的脚,那是偶蹄。	
	你若是个魔鬼,我无法杀你。　　　　　　[刺伤伊阿古。]	
罗德威克	把他的剑夺走。	
伊阿古	我在流血,但没死。	285
奥赛罗	我并不觉得遗憾,我宁愿你活着:	
	因为我感到死去是一种幸福。	
罗德威克	你这个奥赛罗呀,曾如此出色,	
	竟落入一个邪恶小人的陷阱,	
	该对你说些啥呢？	
奥赛罗	唉,说啥都行;	290
	一位正直的凶手,您若愿意,	
	我做的是出于善意,而非仇恨。	
罗德威克	这恶棍已将其部分罪行供认。	
	您是否与他一起谋害凯西奥？	
奥赛罗	是的。	295
凯西奥	亲爱的将军,我从未做错什么。	
奥赛罗	我确实相信,我也求您原谅。	
	我求您,能否问问这个人魔,	
	为何要这样陷害我的灵魂肉体？	
伊阿古	不要问我,您自己心知肚明。	300

283. 偶蹄（fable）：魔鬼的脚为分趾蹄（the devil had cloven hoofs for feet）（Ridley）。
285. 我……没死（I…killed）：讽刺（sarcastic）：我在流血（跟常人一样）,但并未被杀死（因此我也许是魔鬼）。　292. 善意（in honour）：自欺欺人？　298. 人魔（demi-devil）：奥赛罗承认伊阿古在流血,因此他不是真正的魔鬼。

From this time forth I never will speak word.

Lodovico What, not to pray?

Gratiano Torments will ope your lips.

Othello Well, thou dost best.

Lodovico Sir, you shall understand what hath befallen,

305 Which, as I think, you know not. Here is a letter

Found in the pocket of the slain Roderigo,

And here another: the one of them imports

The death of Cassio, to be undertook

By Roderigo.

Othello O villain!

310 **Cassio** Most heathenish and most gross!

Lodovico Now here's another discontented paper

Found in his pocket too, and this, it seems,

Roderigo meant t'have sent this damned villain,

But that, belike, Iago in the nick

315 Came in, and satisfied him.

Othello O thou pernicious caitiff!

How came you, Cassio, by that handkerchief

That was my wife's?

Cassio I found it in my chamber,

And he himself confessed but even now

320 That there he dropped it for a special purpose

Which wrought to his desire.

Othello O fool, fool, fool!

从此以后我将一句话不说。

罗德威克　　怎么,不祷告?

葛莱西亚诺　　　　　　折磨会使你开口。

奥赛罗　　好,你最好别说。

罗德威克　　先生,您会明白所发生的事情,

　　　　　　我想,您还不知。　这封信是从　　　　　　　　305

　　　　　　遇害的罗德利哥口袋中找到,

　　　　　　这里还有一封:这一封谈及

　　　　　　凯西奥的死亡,罗德利哥应该

　　　　　　如何执行。

奥赛罗　　噢,恶棍!

凯西奥　　　　　　最为野蛮最为丑恶。　　　　　　　　310

罗德威克　　这里还有一封充满了怨声,

　　　　　　也是从他口袋中找到,好像是,

　　　　　　罗德利哥本想送给这个恶棍,

　　　　　　然而,也许,就在此刻伊阿古

　　　　　　前来,并使他息怒。　　　　　　　　　　　315

奥赛罗　　噢,你这险恶的无赖!

　　　　　　您是如何,凯西奥,得到我妻子的

　　　　　　那块手帕?

凯西奥　　　　　　在我房间里捡的,

　　　　　　就在刚才他本人曾经供认:

　　　　　　为某种特殊目的将它丢在那里,　　　　　320

　　　　　　那使他如愿以偿。

奥赛罗　　　　　　　　噢傻,傻,傻!

---

320. 特殊目的（special purpose）:参考 4. 2. 241-3 注。　321. 噢……傻（O…fool）:他对自己的过错认识肤浅（He sees only the least of his errors）:与罗德利哥形成鲜明对比,"噢,我这个恶棍!"（5. 1. 29）。

Cassio	There is besides in Roderigo's letter
	How he upbraids Iago, that he made him
	Brave me upon the watch, whereon it came
325	That I was cast; and even but now he spake,
	After long seeming dead, Iago hurt him,
	Iago set him on.
Lodovico	[*to Othello*] You must forsake this room and go with us.
	Your power and your command is taken off,
330	And Cassio rules in Cyprus. For this slave,
	If there be any cunning cruelty
	That can torment him much and hold him long,
	It shall be his. You shall close prisoner rest
	Till that the nature of your fault be known
335	To the Venetian state. Come, bring him away.
Othello	Soft you, a word or two before you go.
	I have done the state some service, and they know't:
	No more of that. I pray you, in your letters,
	When you shall these unlucky deeds relate,
340	Speak of me as I am. Nothing extenuate,
	Nor set down aught in malice. Then must you speak
	Of one that loved not wisely, but too well;
	Of one not easily jealous, but, being wrought,
	Perplexed in the extreme; of one whose hand,
345	Like the base Indian, threw a pearl away
	Richer than all his tribe; of one whose subdued eyes,
	Albeit unused to the melting mood,
	Drop tears as fast as the Arabian trees
	Their medicinable gum. Set you down this,

凯西奥	此外罗德利哥还在信中提及	
	他如何责骂伊阿古,因为叫他	
	挑衅我的执勤,并由此导致	
	我的解职;就在刚才他还说话,	325
	好像已死去很久,伊阿古害了他,	
	伊阿古唆使他。	

罗德威克	[向奥赛罗]您必须离开这里与我们同去。	
	您的职位和兵权已被解除,	
	凯西奥统治塞浦路斯。 至于这小人,	330
	假如会有什么严酷的刑罚	
	能使他苦不堪言并苟延残喘,	
	他罪有应得。 您将被囚禁起来,	
	直到我们将您的犯罪行为	
	呈报威尼斯政府。 快,把他带走。	335

奥赛罗	且慢,请您听我说句话再走。	
	我对国家做过贡献,他们也知道:	
	不提它了。 我求您,在您的信中,	
	当您讲述这些不幸的事件时,	
	要实话实说,不要轻描淡写,	340
	也不要恶意夸张。 那么您要说	
	此人对爱情无知,又过于痴情;	
	此人不容易妒忌,可一旦着魔,	
	便会极度困惑;此人的双手,	
	像那愚昧的印度人,将珍珠丢弃,	345
	不知其价值连城:他低沉的眼睛,	
	尽管对情绪的感化并不习惯,	
	也会像那流注药脂的阿拉伯	
	树木泪水涟涟。 把这些记下,	

350		And say besides, that in Aleppo once,
		Where a malignant and a Turbanned Turk
		Beat a Venetian and traduced the state,
		I took by th' throat the circumcised dog
		And smote him—thus! *He stabs himself.*
	Lodovico	O bloody period!
355	**Gratiano**	All that's spoke is marred.
	Othello	I kissed thee ere I killed thee: no way but this,
		Killing myself, to die upon a kiss.
		[Kisses Desdemona, and] dies.
	Cassio	This did I fear, but thought he had no weapon,
		For he was great of heart.
	Lodovico	*[to Iago]* O Spartan dog,
360		More fell than anguish, hunger, or the sea,
		Look on the tragic loading of this bed:
		This is thy work. The object poisons sight,
		Let it be hid. Gratiano, keep the house,
		And seize upon the fortunes of the Moor,
365		For they succeed on you. To you, lord governor,

　　　　　　另外请您添上,阿勒颇曾有,　　　　　　　　　　　350

　　　　　　一个恶毒、裹头巾的土耳其人,

　　　　　　殴打一威尼斯人并诋毁城邦,

　　　　　　我掐住那受过割礼的贱狗脖子,

　　　　　　就这样——将他刺死。　　　　　　　　　　　自杀。

罗德威克　　噢,血腥的结局!

葛莱西亚诺　　　　　　　所有决定白费。　　　　　　　　355

奥赛罗　　　我杀你之前曾吻你:只有这样,

　　　　　　我现在自杀,在亲吻之中死亡。

　　　　　　　　　　[亲吻苔丝狄蒙娜,然后]死去。

凯西奥　　　我就怕这样,本想他没有武器,

　　　　　　因为他心性豪爽。

罗德威克　　[向伊阿古]　　噢,斯巴达狗,

　　　　　　比剧痛、饥饿,或大海还要残忍!　　　　　　360

　　　　　　你看看这张床上凄惨的尸首:

　　　　　　这是你的杰作。　真是惨不忍睹,

　　　　　　盖上它吧。　葛莱西亚诺,看好房屋

　　　　　　并接收摩尔人的所有财物,

　　　　　　因为该您继承。　由您,总督阁下,　　　　　　365

---

　　353. 受过割礼的(circumcised):割礼是伊斯兰教信徒的一种宗教仪式;因此,奥赛罗此处的轻蔑口吻表明他“向来都不是伊斯兰教信徒”。 不过,这也许只是一种辱骂,就像《圣经》中所说的“未受割礼的(uncircumcised)”那样。 参考《圣经》“撒母耳记上”17 章 26 节及以下。 355. 所有决定白费(All…marred):本句的现代英语译文为:All that has been decided is ruined [*that is, concerning Othello's trial and punishment*](即:有关奥赛罗的审判和惩罚])(Gayle)。 另外,译者曾两次就此请教过英国导演巴特(Nicholas Barter)先生,他的解释是:Everything he said about himself is spoiled(他关于自己的言论全部被毁)。 因为他(奥赛罗)想让人们报道他高尚的一面,解释他如何被人误入歧途。 他也知道自己犯下了罪过,但相信自己的无辜。 他此番表示歉意的话语因其自杀身亡而白费(By killing himself Othello has spoiled all the noble reports that he would want connected with him to explain how he has been misled. He knows he has done wrong but believes himself to be innocent and his speech of apology has been spoiled by his act of suicide)。 ——译者附注。 359. 斯巴达狗(Spartan dog):斯巴达狗以其残暴和安静著称(noted for their savagery and silence)(Bevington)。 365. 总督阁下(lord governor):提醒平时优柔寡断的凯西奥:作为总督,他要严加管制;因此,也要“执行”(367 行)。 (He reminds Cassio, who is mildly ineffective when sober, to take charge firmly as governor; hence, too, *enforce it*, 367。)

Remains the censure of this hellish villain,

The time, the place, the torture: O, enforce it!

Myself will straight aboard, and to the state

This heavy act with heavy heart relate.   *Exeunt.*

FINIS.

对这个阴险的恶魔进行审判，
确定时间、地点,酷刑。　噢,要执行!
我本人要立即上船,赶往城邦,
以沉痛的心情将悲剧细说端详。　　　　　　　　　同下。

剧 终

参考文献

1. M. R. Ridley, *Othello*, The Arden Shakespeare, Second Series; Methuen & Co Ltd. 1966.

2. Barbara A. Mowat, *Othello*, Folger Shakespeare Library, 1993.

3. Gayle Holste, *Othello*, Shakespeare Made Easy, Barroris, 2002.

4. David Bevington, *Othello*, The New Bantam Shakespeare, 2005.

5. E. A. J. Honigmann, *Othello*, The Arden Shakespeare, Third Series, 中国人民大学出版社,2008.

6. Jonathan Bate, *Othello*, Royal Shakespeare Company, 外语教学与研究出版社,2008.

7. *Othello*, http://nfs. sparknotes. com/othello/.

8. *The Holy Bible*, New International Version, Zondervan, Michigan,1990.

9. 卞之琳,《奥赛罗》(莎士比亚悲剧四种),人民文学出版社,1988。

10. 梁实秋,《奥赛罗》(莎士比亚四大悲剧),中国广播电视出版社,2002。

11. 朱生豪,《奥赛罗》(莎士比亚喜剧悲剧集),译林出版社,2002。

12. 孙大雨,《奥赛罗》(莎士比亚四大悲剧),上海译文出版社,2002。

13.《圣经》,和合本,中国基督教协会,2008。

译 后 记

译者在翻译《奥赛罗》的整个过程中,曾得到了许多朋友和同事的大力帮助和不吝指教。 对此,译者感到非常荣幸,也不胜感激!

首先,要感谢良师、益友和同事——杨成虎老师。 杨老师指导并帮助译者确立了该研究课题的申请、立项以及翻译准则,使译者受益匪浅。

再者,要感谢另一位良师和益友——浙江大学宁波理工学院的魏健老师。 魏老师受托对全剧译文进行了非常认真细致的检查,对译文中的错字、别字、拗口的句子以及不符合汉语表达习惯的标点符号等,都提出了具体而富有见地的修改意见,使译者受益无穷。

另外,还要感谢英国皇家戏剧艺术学院的前院长巴特先生(Nicolas Batter),译者曾有幸于 2016 年秋在上海戏剧学院与其相识,并当面向他请教了有关正确理解该剧的许多疑难问题,得了他非常详细、耐心和清晰的回答,使译者感到非常荣幸和庆幸。

李其金
2017 年 3 月

图书在版编目(CIP)数据

奥赛罗：英汉对照／(英)威廉·莎士比亚著；
李其金译. —杭州：浙江大学出版社，2020.4
（莎士比亚四大悲剧合集）
ISBN 978-7-308-19749-6

Ⅰ.①奥… Ⅱ.①威… ②李… Ⅲ.①悲剧—剧本—
英国—中世纪—英、汉 Ⅳ.①I561.33

中国版本图书馆 CIP 数据核字(2019)第 271129 号

莎士比亚四大悲剧合集（英汉对照）

[英]威廉·莎士比亚 著　李其金 译

责任编辑	余健波	
责任校对	刘序雯	
封面设计	周　灵	
出版发行	浙江大学出版社	
	（杭州市天目山路 148 号　邮政编码 310007）	
	（网址：http://www.zjupress.com）	
排　　版	杭州好友排版工作室	
印　　刷	杭州高腾印务有限公司	
开　　本	710mm×1000mm　1/16	
印　　张	92	
字　　数	1668 千	
版 印 次	2020 年 4 月第 1 版　2020 年 4 月第 1 次印刷	
书　　号	ISBN 978-7-308-19749-6	
定　　价	298.00 元（全四册）	

版权所有　翻印必究　印装差错　负责调换

浙江大学出版社市场运营中心联系方式：(0571) 88925591；http://zjdxcbs.tmall.com